THE RODERICK ALLEYN MYSTERIES

The Nursing Home Murder
Death in a White Tie
Final Curtain

Ngaio Marsh

Diamond Books
an imprint of HarperCollins*Publishers*,
77–85 Fulham Palace Road,
Hammersmith, London W6 8JB

This Diamond Books Omnibus edition first published 1993
9 8 7 6 5 4 3 2 1

Published in the UK by Grange Books
An imprint of Grange Books plc,
The Grange, Grange Yard, London SE1 3AG

ISBN 1 85627 428 4 (UK)
ISBN Diamond Books 0 261 66155 8 (international edition)

Printed in France by Maury-Eurolivres

Contents

The Nursing Home Murder

Contents

CHAPTER I

10 Downing Street

Friday, the fifth. Afternoon.
The Home Secretary, with an air of finality, laid down the papers
from which he had been reading and glanced round the table. He
was struck, not for the first time, by the owlish solemnity of the
other members of the Cabinet. "Really," he thought, "we look for
all the world like a Cabinet Meeting in a cinema. We are too good to
be true." As if to confirm this impression, the Prime Minister flung
himself back in his chair, laid the palms of his hands on the table,
and cleared his throat.

"Well, gentlemen," he said portentously, "there we have it."

"Strong!" said the Foreign Secretary. He folded his arms and
stared at the ceiling.

"Drastic!" added the Lord Chancellor. "I venture to think—
drastic."

"But in my opinion," the Postmaster-General said, "neither too
strong nor too drastic." He fidgeted with his tie and became almost
human. "Damn it all," he said irritably, "we've got to do something."

There was a pause. The Home Secretary drew in his breath
sharply.

"Well," repeated the Prime Minister, "we have talked a great
deal, gentlemen, and now we've heard the proposed Bill. We have
all the facts. To put it briefly, we are perfectly well aware of the
activities of these anarchistic personages. We know what they are
about and we know they mean to take definite action. We are
agreed that the importance of the matter can hardly be overstated.
The reports from the F.O., the Secret Service and the C.I.D. are

sufficiently conclusive. We have to deal with a definite menace and a growing menace. It's a bad business. This Bill"—he made a gesture towards the Home Secretary—"may be drastic. Does anyone think it too drastic? Should it be modified?"

"No," said the Postmaster-General. "No."

"I agree," said the Attorney-General.

"Has it occurred to you," asked the Lord Chancellor, looking across the table to the Home Secretary, "that you yourself, Sir Derek, have most cause to hesitate?"

The others looked at him. The Home Secretary smiled faintly.

"As sponsor for this Bill," continued the Lord Chancellor, "you will get a lot of limelight. We know what these people are capable of doing. Assassination is a word that occurs rather frequently in the reports." The Home Secretary's smile broadened a little. "I think I do not exaggerate if I say their attention will be focused on yourself. Have you considered this possibility, my dear fellow?"

"I quite appreciate your point," answered the Home Secretary. "The Bill is my child—I'll not disclaim parentship and I'll look after myself."

"I think the Home Secretary should be given proper protection," said the Chancellor of the Exchequer.

"Certainly," agreed the Prime Minister warmly. "We owe it to the country. Her valuable assets must be guarded. The Home Secretary is an extremely valuable asset."

Sir Derek made a curious grimace.

"I can assure you," he said, "that I'm in no hurry to play the hero's part in a theatrical assassination. On the other hand, I really don't feel there is any necessity for me to walk down to the House surrounded by policemen dressed up as private secretaries and journalists."

"I met Roderick Alleyn of the C.I.D. yesterday," said the Prime Minister ponderously, "and discussed this business quite unofficially with him. He's had these gentry under his eye for some time. He's the last man on earth to exaggerate a position of this sort. He considers that the Minister who introduces a Bill to deal with them will be in real danger from the organisation. I strongly urge you to let the Yard take any measures it thinks necessary for your protection."

"Very well," said Sir Derek. He moved uneasily in his chair and passed his hand over his face. "I take it," he added wearily, "that the Cabinet approves the introduction of the Bill?"

They fell to discussing again the suggested measures. Their behaviour was weirdly solemn. They used parliamentary phrases and politicians' gestures. It was as though they had so saturated themselves with professional behaviourism that they had lost the knack of being natural. The Home Secretary sat with his eyes fixed on the papers before him, as though sunk in a profound and unwilling meditation.

At last the Prime Minister put the matter to the vote—did the Cabinet consider the introduction of the Home Secretary's Bill advisable? It did.

"Well," said the Prime Minister, "that is as far as we need go."

The Home Secretary groaned slightly.

They all turned to him. His face was extremely white and he was leaning forward over the table.

"O'Callaghan!" exclaimed the Postmaster-General. "What's the matter? You're ill?"

"It's all right. Pain. Pass off in a moment."

"Brandy," said the Prime Minister and stretched out his hand to a bell.

"Water," whispered Sir Derek. "Just water." When it came he drank it greedily and then mopped his face.

"Better," he told them presently, "I'm sorry."

They looked uncomfortable and concerned. The Lord Chancellor hovered uncertainly over him. The others eyed him with that horrified ineptitude with which we observe sudden illness in our fellow men.

"I must apologise," said Sir Derek. "I've had one or two bouts like this lately. Appendix, I imagine. I'll have to get vetted. It's an infernal bore for myself and everyone else. I want to stave it off until after this business if I can." He drew himself up in his chair, paused a moment, and then got slowly to his feet.

"Everything settled?" he asked.

"Yes, yes. Won't you lie down for a little?" suggested the Prime Minister.

"Thank you so much, P.M.—no, I'll go home, I think. If someone could tell my chauffeur——" A secretary was summoned. O'Callaghan turned to the door. The Postmaster-General made as if to take his arm. Sir Derek nodded his thanks, but walked out independently. In the hall the secretary took his coat from the butler and helped him into it.

".Shall I come out to the car, Sir Derek?"

"No, thank you, my boy. I'm my own man again." With a word of farewell to the Prime Minister he went out alone.

"He looks devilish ill," said the Prime Minister irritably. "I hope to heaven it's not serious."

"It'll be damned awkward if it is," said the Postmaster-General. "Poor old O'Callaghan," he added hurriedly.

In his car the Home Secretary looked out of the window drearily. They turned out of Downing Street into Whitehall. It was a cold, gusty evening. The faces of the people in the streets looked pinched and their clothes drab and uneventful. Their heads were bent to the wind. A thin rain was driving fitfully across the window-pane. He wondered if he was going to be very ill. He was overwhelmed with melancholy. Perhaps he would die of this thing that seized him with such devastating agony. That would save the anarchists and the C.I.D. a lot of trouble. It would also save him a lot of trouble. Did he really care tuppence about his Bill or about the machinations of people who wanted to revolutionise the system of British government? Did he care about anything or anybody? He was conscious only of a pallid indifference and an overwhelming inertia. He was going to be ill.

At the top of Constitution Hill his car was held up by a traffic jam. A taxi drew up close beside it. He could see that there was a fare inside, but no more than that. The driver looked several times at O'Callaghan's chauffeur and called out something which his man answered gruffly. O'Callaghan had the feeling that the person inside the taxi stared in at his window. He was being watched. He had experienced this sensation many times lately. He thought, with a sort of amusement, of the Prime Minister's anxiety. He pulled a cord and the inside of the car was flooded with light.

"Give them a good view while I'm about it," he thought grimly.

To his surprise the windows of the taxi were lit up as if in answer. He peered across, shading the pane with his hand. The taxi's fare was a solitary man in a dinner-jacket. He sat with his hands resting on the knob of a stick. His silk hat was worn at a slight angle, revealing a clear-cut and singularly handsome profile. It was an intelligent and well-bred face, with a straight nose, firm mouth and dark eyes. The man did not turn his head, and while Sir Derek O'Callaghan still watched him, the ranks of cars moved on and the taxi was left behind.

"That's someone I know," thought O'Callaghan with a kind of languid surprise. He tried for a moment to place this individual, but it was too much bother. He gave it up. In a few minutes his chauffeur pulled up outside his own house in Catherine Street and opened the door of the car.

The Home Secretary got out slowly and toiled up the steps. His butler let him in. While he was still in the hall his wife came downstairs. He stood and contemplated her without speaking.

"Well, Derek," she said.

"Hallo, Cicely."

She stood at the foot of the stairs and watched him composedly.

"You're late," she observed after a moment.

"Am I? I suppose I am. Those fellows jawed and jawed. Do you mind if I don't change? I'm tired."

"Of course not. There's only Ruth dining."

He grimaced.

"I really can't help it if your sister likes to see you occasionally," remarked Lady O'Callaghan tranquilly.

"All right," said her husband wearily. "All right."

He glanced at her inimically and thought how tiresomely good-looking she was. Always so perfectly groomed, so admirably gowned, so maddeningly remote. Their very embraces were masked in a chilly patina of good form. Occasionally he had the feeling that she rather disliked him, but as a rule he had no feeling about her at all. He supposed he had married her in a brief wave of enthusiasm for polar exploration. There had been no children. Just as well since there was a taint of insanity in his own family. He supposed he was all right himself. His wife would have brought out any traces of it, he reflected sardonically. Cicely was an acid test for normality.

She walked away from him towards the drawing-room. At the door she paused for a moment to ask:

"Have you been worried at all by that pain to-day?"

"Oh, yes," said O'Callaghan.

"What a bore it is," she murmured vaguely, and went into the drawing-room.

He looked after her for a moment and then crossed the little hall and entered his own study, a companionable room with a good fireplace, a practical desk and deep square-angled chairs. Cedar logs blazed in the grate and a tray with glasses and a decanter of his particular sherry waited near his particular chair.

13

She certainly saw to it that he was adequately looked after.

He poured himself out a glass of sherry and opened his afternoon post. It was abysmally dull. His secretary had dealt with the bulk of his letters and evidently considered that these were all personal. Most of them were so marked. One writer begged for money, another for preferment, a third for information. A typewritten envelope had already been opened by his secretary. It contained an anonymous and threatening message and was merely the latest of a long series of such communications. He picked up the last letter, glanced at the envelope, raised his eyebrows and then frowned. He finished his sherry and poured out another glass before he opened the letter and read it.

It was from Jane Harden.

From Jane. He might have known he wouldn't hear the end of that business in a hurry. He might have known he was a fool to suppose she would let him go without making difficulties. That week-end in Cornwall—it had been pleasant enough but before it was over he'd known he was in for trouble. Damn it all, women were never fair—never. They talked about leading their own lives, said they wanted to get their experience like men, and then broke all the rules of the game. He glanced again over the letter. She reminded him that she had "given herself" to him (what nonsense that was. She'd wanted it as much as he had!), that their families had been neighbours in Dorset for generations before her father went bankrupt. He flinched away from the imputation of disloyalty which, since he was a tolerably honest and conservative man, made him profoundly uncomfortable. She said he'd treated her as though she was a suburban pick-up. He wished fretfully that she had been. She wrote that she was going to a post in a private nursing-home. Would he write to her at the Nurses' Club? Up to this point the letter had apparently been written with a certain amount of self-control, but from then onwards O'Callaghan saw, with something like horror, that Jane's emotions had run away with her pen. She loved him but what had she left to offer him? she asked. Must they both forget? She was fighting for her soul and nothing was too desperate. There was a devil tearing at her soul and if she lost him it would get her. She added again that she loved him and that if he persisted in ignoring her she would do something terrible. With a sudden petulant gesture he crumpled up the sheet of paper and threw it on the fire.

"Blast!" he said. "Blast! Blast! Blast!"

There was a light tap on the door, which opened far enough to disclose a large nose, a vague mouth, a receding chin, and a gigantic earring.

"Affairs of state, Derry?" asked a coy voice. "Affairs of state?"

"Oh, come in, Ruth," said Sir Derek O'Callaghan.

CHAPTER II

Introduces a Patent Medicine

Friday, the fifth. Evening.

During the following week the Home Secretary followed his usual routine. He had become more or less accustomed to the attacks of pain. If anything they occurred more often and with increasing severity. He told himself that the day after he had introduced his Bill, he would consult a doctor. Meanwhile he took three tablets of aspirin whenever the pain threatened to become unendurable, and grew more and more dispirited and wretched. The memory of Jane Harden's letter lurked at the back of his thoughts, like a bad taste in the conscience.

His sister Ruth, an advanced hypochondriac, with the persistence of a missionary, continually pressed upon him strange boluses, pills and draughts. She made a practice of calling on him after dinner armed with chemists' parcels and a store of maddening condolences and counsels. On Friday night he retreated to his study, begging his wife to tell Ruth, if she appeared, that he was extremely busy, and not to be interrupted. His wife looked at him for a moment.

"I shall ask Nash," she said, "to say we are both out."

He paused and then said uncomfortably:

"I don't think I quite like——"

"I too," said his wife, "find myself bored by Ruth."

"Still, Cicely—after all she is exceedingly kind. Perhaps it would be better——"

"You will see her then?"

"No, damn it, I won't."

"Very well, Derek. I'll tell Nash. Has your pain been worrying

16

you lately?"

"Quite a lot, thank you."

"That, of course, is why you are irritable. I think you are foolish not to see a doctor."

"I think I told you I would call in John Phillips as soon as this Bill was through."

"It's for you to decide, of course. Shall I ask Nash to take your coffee into the study?"

"If you please."

"Yes." She had a curiously remote way of saying "Yes," as though it was a sort of bored comment on everything he uttered.

"Good night, Derek. I am going up early and won't disturb you."

"Good night, Cicely."

She stepped towards him and waited. By some mischance his kiss fell upon her lips instead of her cheek. He almost felt he ought to apologise. However, she merely repeated "Good night" and he went off to his study.

Here his secretary Ronald Jameson awaited him. Jameson, just down from Oxford, was an eager but not too tiresomely earnest young man. He did his work well, and was intelligent. Normally, O'Callaghan found him tolerable and even likeable. To-night, the sight of his secretary irritated and depressed him.

"Well, Ronald?"

He sank down into his chair, and reached for a cigar.

"Sir John Phillips has rung up, sir, and would like to come and see you this evening if you are free."

"Phillips? Has anyone been talking about me to Phillips? What does he want? Is it a professional visit?"

"I don't think so, sir. Sir John didn't mention your—indisposition."

"Ring him up and say I'll be delighted. Anything else?"

"These letters. There's another of the threatening variety. I do wish, sir, that you'd let me talk to Scotland Yard."

"No. Anything else?"

"Only one, marked personal. It's on your desk."

"Give it to me, will you?"

Jameson brought the letter and handed it to him. He looked at it and experienced the sensation of going down in a lift. It was from Jane Harden. O'Callaghan let his arm swing down by the side of his chair. The letter hung from his fingers. He remained

17

staring at the fire, the unlighted cigar between his lips.

Ronald Jameson waited uncomfortably. At last he produced his lighter and advanced it towards O'Callaghan's cigar.

"Thank you," said O'Callaghan absently.

"Is there anything I can do, sir?"

"No, thank you."

Jameson hesitated, looked uneasily at his employer's white face, reflected that Sir John Phillips still awaited his message, and left the room.

For some time after the door had shut behind his secretary O'Callaghan sat and stared at the fire. At last, with an enormous effort, he forced himself to read through the letter. Jane Harden had written a frantic, bitter arraignment, rather than an appeal. She said she felt like killing herself. A little further on, she added that if an opportunity presented itself she would not hesitate to kill him: "Don't cross my path. I'm warning you for my own sake, not for yours. I mean it, Derek, for you and all men like you are better out of the way. This is my final word.—Jane Harden."

O'Callaghan had a swift mental picture of the letter as it would appear in the columns of the penny Press. Rather to his surprise O'Callaghan heard his wife speak to the secretary in the hall outside. Something in the quality of her voice arrested his attention. He listened.

"—something seems to be worrying him."

"I think so too, Lady O'Callaghan," Jameson murmured.

"—any idea—any letters?" The voice faded away.

"To-night—seemed to upset—of course this Bill——"

O'Callaghan got up and strode across the room. He flung open the door.

His wife and Ronald Jameson stood facing each other with something of the air of conspirators. As he opened the door they turned their faces towards him. Jameson's became very red and he looked swiftly from husband to wife. Lady O'Callaghan merely regarded Sir Derek placidly. He felt himself trembling with anger.

"Hitherto," he said to Jameson, "I have seen no reason to suppose you did not understand the essentially confidential nature of your job. Apparently I have been mistaken."

"I'm—I'm terribly sorry, Sir Derek—it was only because——"

"You have no business to discuss my letters with anyone. With *anyone*. You understand?"

18

"Yes, sir."

"Please don't be absurd, Derek," said his wife. "I asked Mr. Jameson a question that he could not avoid answering. We are both very worried about you."

O'Callaghan jerked his head. Jameson made a miserable little bow and turned away. At the door of his own room he paused, murmured "I'm extremely sorry, sir," and disappeared.

"Really, Derek," said Lady O'Callaghan, "I think you are unreasonable. I merely asked that unfortunate youth if you had received any letter that might account for your otherwise rather unaccountable behaviour. He said a letter in this evening's mail seemed to upset you. What was this letter, Derek? Was it another threat from these people—these anarchists or whatever they are?"

He was not so angry that he did not hear an unusual note in her voice.

"Such threats are an intolerable impertinence," she said hastily. "I cannot understand why you do not deal with these people."

"The letter had nothing whatever to do with them, and my "unaccountable behaviour," as you call it, has nothing to do with the letter. I am unwell and I'm worried. It may satisfy you to hear that John Phillips is coming in this evening."

"I'm delighted to hear it."

The front-door bell sounded. They looked at each other questioningly.

"Ruth?" murmured Lady O'Callaghan.

"I'm off," he said quickly. Suddenly he felt more friendly towards her. "You'd better bolt, Cicely," he said.

She moved swiftly into his study and he followed her. They heard Nash come out and open the door. They listened, almost in sympathy with each other.

"Sir Derek and my lady are not at home, madam."

"But there's a light in the study!"

They exchanged horrified glances.

"Perhaps Mr. Jameson——" said Nash.

"Just the man I want to see."

They heard Nash bleating in dismay and the sound of Miss Ruth O'Callaghan's umbrella being rammed home in the ship's bucket. With one accord they walked over to the fireplace. Lady O'Callaghan lit a cigarette.

The door opened, and Ruth came in. They had a brief glimpse

19

of Nash's agonised countenance and then were overwhelmed in embraces.

"*There* you are, darlings. Nash said you were out."

"We're only 'not at home,' Ruth darling," said Lady O'Callaghan, very tranquilly. "Derek expects his doctor. It was too stupid of Nash not to realise you were different."

"Ah-ha," said Ruth, with really terrifying gaiety, "you don't defeat your old sister like that. Now, Derry darling, I've come especially to see you, and I shall be very cross and dreadfully hurt if you don't do exactly what I tell you."

She rummaged in an enormous handbag, and fetched up out of its depths the familiar sealed white parcel.

"Really, Ruth, I can *not* swallow every patent medicine that commends itself to your attention."

"I don't want you to do that, darling. I know you think your old sister's a silly-billy"—she squinted playfully at him—"but she knows what's good for her big, famous brother. Cicely, he'll listen to you. Please, please, persuade him to take just one of these teeny little powders. They're too marvellous. You've only to read the letters——"

With eager, clumsy fingers she undid the wrapping and disclosed a round green box decorated with the picture of a naked gentleman, standing in front of something that looked like an electric shock.

"There are six powders altogether," she told them excitedly, "but after the first, you feel a *marked* improvement. 'Fulvita-volts'. Hundreds of letters, Derry, from physicians, surgeons, politicians—*lots* of politicians, Derry. They all swear by it. Their symptoms were precisely the same as yours. Honestly."

She looked pathetically eager. She was so awkward and vehement with her thick hands, her watery eyes, and her enormous nose.

"You don't know what my symptoms are, Ruth."

"Indeed I do. Violent abdominal seizures. Cicely—do read it all."

Lady O'Callaghan took the box and looked at one of the folded cachets.

"I'll give him one to-night, Ruth," she promised, exactly as though she was humouring an excitable child.

"That's topping!" Ruth had a peculiar trick of using unreal slang. "I'm most awfully bucked. And in the morning all those

20

horrid pains will have *flown* away." She made a sort of blundering, ineffectual gesture. She beamed at them.

"And now, old girl, I'm afraid you'll have to fly away yourself," said O'Callaghan with a desperate effort to answer roguishness with brotherly playfulness. "I think I hear Phillips arriving."

"Come along, Ruth," said his wife. "We must make ourselves scarce. Good night again, Derek."

Ruth laid a gnarled finger on her lips and tiptoed elaborately to the door. There she turned and blew him a kiss.

He heard them greet Sir John Phillips briefly and go upstairs. In his relief at being rid of his sister, O'Callaghan felt a wave of good-fellowship for John Phillips. Phillips was an old friend. It would be a relief to tell him how ill he felt—to learn how ill he really was. Perhaps Phillips would give him something that would help him along for the time being. He already felt a little better. Very likely it was a trifling thing after all. Phillips would know. He turned to the door with an air of pleased expectancy. Nash opened the door and came in.

"Sir John Phillips, sir."

Phillips entered the room.

He was an extremely tall man with an habitual stoop. His eyes, full-lidded and of a peculiarly light grey, were piercingly bright. No one ever saw him without his single eye-glass and there was a rumour that he wore it ribbonless while he operated. His nose was a beak and his under lip jutted out aggressively. He was unmarried, and unmoved, so it was said, by the general tendency among his women patients to fall extravagantly in love with him. Perhaps next to actors medical men profit most by the possession of that curious quality that people call "personality". Sir John Phillips was, very definitely, a personage. His rudeness was more glamorously famous than his brilliant ability.

O'Callaghan moved towards him, his hand extended.

"Phillips!" he said, "I'm delighted to see you."

Phillips ignored the hand and stood stockstill until the door had closed behind Nash. Then he spoke.

"You will be less delighted when you hear my business," he said.

"Why—what on earth's the matter with you?"

"I can scarcely trust myself to speak to you."

"What the devil do you mean?"

"Precisely what I say. I've discovered your are a blackguard and

21

I've come to tell you so."

O'Callaghan stared at him in silence.

"Apparently you are serious," he said at last. "May I ask if you intend merely to call me names and then walk out? Or am I to be given an explanation?"

"I'll give you your explanation. In two words. Jane Harden."

There was a long silence. The two men stared at each other. At last O'Callaghan turned away. A kind of mulish huffiness in his expression made him look ridiculous and unlikeable.

"What about Jane Harden?" he said at last.

"Only this. She's a nurse at my hospital. For a very long time her happiness has been an important thing for me. I have asked her to marry me. She has refused, over and over again. To-day she told me why. It seems you made capital out of a friendship with her father and out of her present poverty. You played the 'old family friend' combined with the distinguished philanderer."

"I don't know what you're talking about."

"Don't lie, O'Callaghan!"

"Look here——"

"I know the facts."

"What sort of tale have you listened to?"

"One that brought me here to-night angrier than I ever remember myself before. I know the precise history of your—your friendship with her. You amused yourself, evidently. I dislike overstatement but I believe it would be no overstatement if I said, as I do say, that you've ruined Jane's life for her."

"Damn' sentimental twaddle!" said O'Callaghan breathlessly. "She's a modern young woman and she knows how to enjoy herself."

"That's a complete misrepresentation." Phillips had turned exceedingly white, but he spoke evenly. "If, by the phrase 'a modern young woman', you mean a 'loose woman' you must know yourself it's a lie. This is the only episode of the sort in her life. She loved you and you let her suppose she was loved in return."

"Nothing of the sort. She gave me no reason to suppose she attached more importance to the thing than I did myself. You say she's in love with me. If it's true I'm sorry. I don't think it's true. What does she want? It's not——" O'Callaghan stopped short and looked frightened. "It's not that she's going to have a child?"

"Oh, no. She has no actual claim on you. No legal claim.

22

Evidently you don't recognise moral obligations."

"I've sent her £300. What more will she want?"

"I'm so near hitting you, O'Callaghan, I think I'd better go."

"You can go to hell if you like. What's the matter with you? If you don't want to marry her there's an alternative. It ought to be quite simple—I had no difficulty."

"You swine!" shouted Phillips. "My God——" He stopped short. His lips moved tremblingly. When he spoke again it was more quietly. "You'd do well to keep clear of me," he said. "I assure you that if the opportunity presented itself I should have no hesitation—none—in putting you out of the way."

Something in O'Callaghan's face made him pause. The Home Secretary was looking beyond him, towards the door.

"Excuse me, sir," said Nash quietly. He crossed the room with a tray holding glasses and a decanter. He put the tray down noiselessly and returned to the door.

"Is there anything further, sir?" asked Nash.

"Sir John Phillips is leaving. Will you show him out?"

"Certainly, sir."

Without another word Phillips turned on his heel and left the room.

"Good night, Nash," said O'Callaghan.

"Good night, sir," said Nash softly. He followed Sir John Phillips out and closed the door.

O'Callaghan gave a sharp cry of pain. He stumbled towards his chair and bent over it, leaning on the arm. For a minute or two he hung on, doubled up with pain. Then he managed to get into the chair, and in a little while poured out half a tumbler of whisky. He noticed Ruth's patent medicine lying on the table beside him. With a tremulous hand he shook one of the powders into the glass and gulped it down with the whisky.

CHAPTER III

Sequel to a Scene in the House

Thursday, the eleventh. Afternoon.
The Home Secretary paused and looked round the House. The sea of faces was blurred and nightmarish. They were playing that trick on him that he had noticed before. They would swim together like cells under a microscope and then one face would come out clearly and stare at him. He thought: "I may just manage it—only one more paragraph", and raised the paper. The type swirled and eddied, and then settled down. He heard his own voice. He must speak up.

"In view of the extraordinary propaganda——"

They were making too much noise.

"Mr. Speaker——"

A disgusting feeling of nausea, a kind of vapourish tightness behind his nose.

"Mr. Speaker——"

He looked up again. A mistake. The sea of faces jerked up and revolved very quickly. A tiny voice, somewhere up in the attic, was calling: "He's fainted."

He did not feel himself pitch forward across the desk. Nor did he hear a voice from the back benches that called out: "You'll be worse than that before you've finished with your bloody Bill."

"Who's his doctor—anyone know?"

"Yes—I do. It's bound to be Sir John Phillips—they're old friends."

"Phillips? He runs that nursing-home in Brook Street, doesn't he?"

"I've no idea."

24

"Somebody must ring Lady O'Callaghan."

"I will if you like. I know her."

"Is he coming round?"

"Doesn't look like it. Tillotley went to see about the ambulance."

"Here he is. Did you fix up for an ambulance, Tillotley?"

"It's coming. Where are you sending him?"

"Cuthbert's gone to ring up his wife."

"God, he looks bad!"

"Did you hear that fellow yell out from the back benches?"

"Yes. Who was it?"

"I don't know. I say, do you think there's anything fishy about this?"

"Oh, rot!"

"Here's Dr. Wendover—I didn't know he was in the House."

They stood back from O'Callaghan. A little tubby man, Communist member for a North Country constituency, came through the group of men and knelt down.

"Open those windows, will you?" he said.

He loosened O'Callaghan's clothes. The others eyed him respectfully. After a minute or two he looked round.

"Who's his medical man?" he asked.

"Cuthbert thinks it's Sir John Phillips. He's ringing his wife now."

"Phillips is a surgeon. It's a surgical case."

"What's the trouble, Dr. Wendover?"

"Looks like an acute appendix. There's no time to be lost. You'd better ring the Brook Street Private Hospital. Is the ambulance there? Can't wait for his wife."

From the doorway somebody said: "The men from the ambulance."

"Good. Here's your patient."

Two men came in carrying a stretcher. O'Callaghan was got on to it, covered up, and carried out. Cuthbert hurried in.

"Yes," he said, "it's Phillips. She wants him taken to Phillips's nursing-home."

"He's going there," said little Dr. Wendover, and walked out after the ambulance men.

O'Callaghan climbed up, sickeningly, from nowhere into semi-consciousness. Grandiloquent images slid rapidly downwards.

His wife's face came near and then receded. Somebody groaned close to him. Somebody was in bed beside him, groaning.

"Is the pain very bad?" said a voice.

He himself was in pain.

"Bad," he said solemnly.

"The doctor will be here soon. He'll give you something to take it away."

He now knew it was he who had groaned.

Cicely's face came close.

"The doctor's coming, Derek."

He closed his eyes to show he had understood.

"Poor old Derry, poor old boy."

"I'll just leave you with him for a minute, Lady O'Callaghan. If you want me, will you ring? I think I hear Sir John." A door closed.

"This pain's very bad," said O'Callaghan clearly.

The two women exchanged glances. Lady O'Callaghan drew up a chair to the bed and sat down.

"It won't be for long, Derek," she said quietly. "It's your appendix, you know."

"Oh."

Ruth had begun to whisper.

"What's Ruth say?"

"Never mind me, Derry-boy. It's just silly old Ruthie."

He muttered something, shut his eyes, and seemed to fall asleep.

"Cicely darling, I know you laugh at my ideas, but listen. As soon as I heard about Derry I went and saw Harold Sage. He's the *brilliant* young chemist I told you about. I explained *exactly* what was the matter and he gave me something that he says will relieve the pain *at once* and can do no harm at all. It's an invention of his own. In a few months all the hospitals will use it."

She began a search in her handbag.

"Suggest it to Sir John if you like, Ruth. Of course nothing can be done without his knowledge."

"Doctors are so bigoted. I *know*, my dear. The things Harold has told me——!"

"You seem to be very friendly with this young man."

"He interests me enormously, Cicely."

"Really?"

The nurse came back.

"Sir John would like to see you for a moment, Lady O'Callaghan."

"Thank you. I'll come."

Left alone with her brother, Ruth dabbed at his hand. He opened his eyes.

"Oh, God, Ruth," he said, "I'm in such pain."

"Just hold on for one moment, Derry. I'll make it better."

She had found the little package. There was a tumbler of water by the bedside.

In a few minutes Phillips came back with the nurse.

"Sir John is going to make an examination," said Nurse Graham quietly to Ruth. "If you wouldn't mind joining Lady O'Callaghan for a moment."

"I shan't keep you long," said Phillips and opened the door.

Ruth, with a distracted and guilty look at her brother, gathered herself up and blundered out of the room.

O'Callaghan had relapsed into unconsciousness. Nurse Graham uncovered the abdomen and Phillips with his long inquisitive fingers pressed it there—and there—and there. His eyes were closed and his brain seemed to be in his hands.

"That will do," he said suddenly. "It looks like peritonitis. He's in a bad way. I've warned them we may need the theatre." The nurse covered the patient and in answer to a nod from Phillips fetched the two women. As soon as they came in, Phillips turned to Lady O'Callaghan but did not look at her. "The operation should be performed immediately," he said. "Will you allow me to try to get hold of Somerset Black?"

"But you, Sir John, won't you do it yourself?"

Phillips walked over to the window and stared out.

"You wish me to operate?" he said at last.

"Of course I do. I know that sometimes surgeons dislike operating on their friends, but unless you feel—I do hope—I beg you to do it."

"Very well."

He returned to the patient.

"Nurse," he said, "tell them to get Dr. Thoms. He's in the hospital and has been warned that an operation may be necessary. Ring up Dr. Grey and arrange for the anæsthetic—I'll speak to him myself. Tell the theatre sister I'll operate as soon as they are ready. Now, Lady O'Callaghan, if you don't mind leaving the patient, Nurse will show you where you can wait."

The nurse opened the door and the others moved away from the bed. At the threshold they were arrested by a kind of stifled cry. They turned and looked back to the bed. Derek O'Callaghan had opened his eyes and was staring as if hypnotised at Phillips.

"Don't——" he said. "Don't—let——"

His lips moved convulsively. A curious whining sound came from them. For a moment or two he struggled for speech and then suddenly his head fell back.

"Come along, Lady O'Callaghan," said the nurse gently. "He doesn't know what he is saying, you know."

In the anteroom of the theatre two nurses and a sister prepared for the operation.

"Now you mustn't forget," said Sister Marigold, who was also the matron of the hospital, "that Sir John likes his instruments left on the tray. He does *not* like them handed to him."

She covered a tray of instruments and Jane Harden carried it into the theatre.

"It's a big responsibility," said the sister chattily, "for a surgeon, in a case of this sort. It would be a terrible catastrophe for the country if anything happened to Sir Derek O'Callaghan. The only strong man in the Government, in my opinion."

Nurse Banks, an older woman than her superior, looked up from the sterilising apparatus.

"The biggest tyrant of the lot," she remarked surprisingly.

"Nurse! What did you say?"

"My politics are not Sir Derek O'Callaghan's, Matron, and I don't care who knows it."

Jane Harden returned from the theatre. Sister Marigold cast an indignant glance at Nurse Banks and said briefly:

"Did you look at the hyoscine solution, Nurse, and the anti-gas ampoule?"

"Yes, Matron."

"Gracious, child, you look very white. Are you all right?"

"Quite, thank you," answered Jane. She busied herself with tins of sterilised dressings. After another glance at her, the matron returned to the attack on Nurse Banks.

"Of course, Nurse, we all know you are a Bolshie. Still, you can't deny greatness when you see it. Now Sir Derek is my idea of a big—a *really* big man."

"And for that reason he's the more devilish," announced Banks

28

with remarkable venom. "He's done murderous things since he's been in office. Look at his Casual Labour Bill of last year. He's directly responsible for every death from under-nourishment that has occurred during the last ten months. He's the enemy of the proletariat. If I had my way he'd be treated as a common murderer or else as a homicidal maniac. He ought to be certified. There is insanity in his blood. Everybody knows his father was dotty. That's what I think of your Derek O'Callaghan with a title bought with blood-money," said Banks, making a great clatter with sterilised bowls.

"Then perhaps"—Sister Marigold's voice was ominously quiet—"perhaps you'll explain what you're doing working for Sir John Phillips. Perhaps his title was bought with blood-money too."

"As long as this rotten system stands, we've got to live," declared Banks ambiguously, "but it won't be for ever and I'll be the first to declare myself when the time comes. O'Callaghan will have to go and all his blood-sucking bourgeois party with him. It would be a fine thing for the people if he went now. There, Matron!"

"It would be a better thing if you went yourself, Nurse Banks, and if I had another theatre nurse free, go you would. I'm ashamed of you. You talk about a patient like that—what are you thinking of?"

"I can't help it if my blood boils."

"There's a great deal too much blood, boiling or not, in your conversation."

With the air of one silenced but not defeated, Banks set out a table with hypodermic appliances and wheeled it into the theatre.

"Really, Nurse Harden," said Sister Marigold, "I'm ashamed of that woman. The vindictiveness! She ought not to be here. One might almost think she would——" Matron paused, unable to articulate the enormity of her thought.

"No such—thing," said Jane. "I'd be more likely to do him harm than she."

"And that's an outside chance," declared matron more genially. "I must say, Nurse Harden, you're the best theatre nurse I've had for a long time. A real compliment, my dear, because I'm very particular. Are we ready? Yes. And here come the doctors."

Jane put her hands behind her back and stood to attention.

Sister Marigold assumed an air of efficient repose. Nurse Banks appeared for a moment in the doorway, seemed to recollect something, and returned to the theatre.

Sir John Phillips came in followed by Thoms, his assistant, and the anæsthetist. Thoms was fat, scarlet-faced and industriously facetious. Dr. Roberts was a thin, sandy-haired man, with a deprecating manner. He took off his spectacles and polished them.

"Ready, Matron?" asked Phillips.

"Quite ready, Sir John."

"Dr. Roberts will give the anæsthetic. Dr. Grey is engaged. We were lucky to get you, Roberts, at such short notice."

"I'm delighted to come," said Roberts. "I've been doing a good deal of Grey's work lately. It is always an honour, and an interesting experience, to work under you, Sir John."

He spoke with a curious formality as if he considered each sentence and then offered it to the person he addressed.

"If I may I'll just take a look at the anæsthetising-room before we begin."

"Certainly."

The truculent Banks reappeared.

"Nurse Banks," said the matron, "go with Dr. Roberts to the anæsthetising-room, please."

Dr. Roberts blinked at Banks, and followed her out.

Sir John went into the theatre and crossed to a small table, enamelled white, on which were various appliances concerned with the business of giving hypodermic injections. There were three syringes, each in a little dish of sterile water. Two were of the usual size known to the layman. The third was so large as to suggest it was intended for veterinary rather than human needs. The small syringes held twenty-five minims each, the larger at least six times as much. An ampoule, a bottle, a small bowl and a measure-glass also stood on the table. The bottle was marked: '*Hyoscine solution 0.25 per cent. Five minims contains $^1/_{100}$ a grain.*' The ampoule was marked: '*Gas-Gangrene Antitoxin (concentrated).*' The bowl contained sterile water.

Phillips produced from his pocket a small hypodermic case from which he took a tiny tube labelled: '*Hyoscine gr. $^1/_{100}$.*' The tube being completely covered by its label, it was difficult to see the contents. He removed the cork, examined the inside closely, laid down the tube and took another, similarly labelled, from his

30

case. His fingers worked uncertainly, as though his mind was on something else. At last he took one of the smaller syringes, filled it with sterile water, and squirted its contents into the measure-glass. Then he dropped in the hyoscine, stirred it with the needle of the syringe, and finally, pulling back the piston, sucked the solution into the syringe.

Thoms came into the theatre.

"We ought to get washed up, sir," he said.

He glanced at the table.

"Hallo!" he shouted. "*Two* tubes! You're doing him proud."

"One was empty." Phillips picked them up automatically and put them back in his case.

Thoms looked at the syringe.

"You use a lot of water, don't you?" he observed.

"I do," said Phillips shortly. Taking the syringe with him, he walked out of the theatre into the anæsthetic-room. Thoms, wearing that air of brisk abstraction which people assume when they are determined to ignore a snub, remained staring at the table. He joined the others a few minutes later in the anteroom. Phillips returned from the anæsthetic-room.

Jane Harden and Sister Marigold helped the two surgeons to turn themselves into pieces of sterilized machinery. In a little while the anteroom was an austere arrangement in white, steel, and rubber-brown. There is something slightly repellent as well as something beautiful in absolute white. It is the negation of colour, the expression of coldness, the emblem of death. There is less sensuous pleasure in white than in any of the colours, and more suggestion of the macabre. A surgeon in his white robe, the warmth of his hands hidden by sleek chilly rubber, the animal vigour of his hair covered by a white cap, is more like a symbol in modern sculpture than a human being. To the layman he is translated, a priest in sacramental robes, a terrifying and subtly fascinating figure.

"Seen this new show at the Palladium?" asked Thoms. "Blast this glove! Give me another, Matron."

"No," said Sir John Phillips.

"There's a one-act play. Anteroom to a theatre in a private hospital. Famous surgeon has to operate on a man who ruined him and seduced his wife. Problem—does he stick a knife into the patient? Grand Guignol stuff. Awful rot, I thought it."

Phillips turned slowly and stared at him. Jane Harden uttered a little stifled cry.

"What's that, Nurse?" asked Thoms. "Have you seen it? Here, give me the glove."

"No, sir," murmured Jane, "I haven't seen it."

"Jolly well acted it was, and someone had put them right about technical matters, but, of course, the situation was altogether too far-fetched. I'll just go and see——" He walked out, still talking, into the theatre, and after a minute or two called to the matron, who followed him.

"Jane," said Phillips.

"Yes?"

"This—this is a queer business."

"Nemesis, perhaps," said Jane Harden.

"What do you mean?"

"Oh, nothing," she said drearily. "Only it is rather like a Greek play, don't you think? 'Fate delivers our enemy into our hands.' Mr. Thoms would think the situation very far-fetched."

Phillips washed his hands slowly in a basin of sterilised water. "I knew nothing of this illness," he said. "It's the merest chance that I was here at this hour. I'd only just got in from St. Jude's. I tried to get out of it, but his wife insisted. Evidently she has no idea we—quarrelled."

"She could hardly know *why* you quarrelled, could she?"

"I'd give anything to be out of it—anything."

"And I. How do you think I feel?"

He squeezed the water off his gloves and turned towards her, holding his hands out in front of him. He looked a grotesque and somehow pathetic figure.

"Jane," he whispered, "won't you change your mind? I love you so much."

"No," she said. "No. I loathe him. I never want to see him again, but as long as he's alive I can't marry you."

"I don't understand you," he said heavily.

"I don't understand myself," answered Jane, "so how should you?"

"I shall go on—I shall ask you again and again."

"It's no good. I suppose I'm queer, but as long as he's there I—I'm in pawn."

"It's insane—after his treatment of you. He's—he's discarded you, Jane."

She laughed harshly.

"Oh, yes. It's quite according to Victorian tradition. I'm a 'ruined girl', you know!"

"Well, stick to the Victorian tradition and let me make an honest woman of you."

"Look here," said Jane suddenly. "I'll try and be an honest woman *with* you. I mean I'll try and explain what's inexplicable and pretty humiliating. I told him I wanted to live my own life, experience everything, all that sort of chat. I deceived myself as well as him. In the back of my mind I knew I was simply a fool who had lost her head as well as her heart. Then, when it happened, I realised just how little it meant to him and just how much it meant to me. I knew I ought to keep up the game, shake hands and part friends, and all that. Well—I couldn't. My pride wanted to, but—I couldn't. It's all too grimly commonplace. I 'loved and hated' him at the same time. I wanted to keep him, knew I hadn't a chance, and longed to hurt him. I wrote to him and told him so. It's a nightmare and it's still going on. There! Don't ask me to talk about it again. Leave me alone to get over it as best I may."

"Couldn't I help?"

"No. Someone's coming—be careful."

Thoms and Roberts returned and washed up. Roberts went away to give the anæsthetic. Phillips stood and watched his assistant.

"How did your play end?" he asked suddenly.

"What? Oh. Back to the conversation we first thought of. It ended in doubt. You were left to wonder if the patient died under the anæsthetic, or if the surgeon did him in. As a matter of fact, under the circumstances, no one could have found out. Are you thinking of trying it out on the Home Secretary, sir? I thought you were a pal of his?"

The mask over Phillips's face creased as though he were smiling. "Given the circumstances," he said, "I suppose it might be a temptation."

He heard a movement behind him and turned to see Nurse Banks regarding him fixedly from the door into the theatre. Sister Marigold appeared behind her, said: "If you please, Nurse," in a frigid voice, and came through the door.

"Oh, Matron," said Phillips abruptly, "I have given an injection of hyoscine, as usual. If we find peritonitis, as I think we shall, I shall also inject serum."

"I remembered the hyoscine, of course, Sir John. The stock solution had been put out, but I saw you had prepared your own injection."

"Yes, we won't need the stock solution. Always use my own tablets—like to be sure of the correct dosage. Are we all ready?"

He went into the theatre.

"Well," said Sister Marigold, "I'm sure the stock solution is good enough for most people."

"You can't be too careful, Matron," Thoms assured her genially. "Hyoscine's a ticklish drug, you know."

The sickly reek of ether began to drift into the room.

"I must say I don't quite understand why Sir John is so keen on giving hyoscine.'

"It saves anæsthetic and it has a soothing effect after the operation. I give it myself," added Thoms importantly.

"What is the usual dose, sir?" asked Nurse Banks abruptly.

"From a hundredth to a two-hundredth of a grain, Nurse."

"As little as that!"

"Oh, yes. I can't tell you the minimum lethal dose—varies with different cases. A quarter-grain would do anyone in."

"A quarter of a grain," said Nurse Banks thoughtfully. "Fancy!"

CHAPTER IV

Post-operative

Thursday, the eleventh. Late afternoon.
Sir John waited in the theatre for his patient.

The matron, Jane and Nurse Banks came in with Thoms. They stood near the table, a group of robed and expressionless automata. They were silent. The sound of wheels. A trolley appeared with Dr. Roberts and the special nurse walking behind it. Dr. Roberts held the anæsthetic mask over the patient's face. On the trolley lay the figure of the Home Secretary. As they lifted it on the table the head spoke suddenly and inconsequently.

"Not to-day, not to-day, not to-day, damn' the bloody thing," it said very rapidly.

The special nurse went away.

The reek of ether rose up like incense round the table. Dr. Roberts wheeled forward his anæsthetising apparatus, an object that, with its cylinders of compressed gases carried in an iron framework, resembled a gigantic cruet. A low screen was fixed across the patient's chest to shut off the anæsthetist. Thoms looked at the patient curiously.

"He's a striking-looking chap, isn't he?" he remarked lightly. "Curious head. What do you make of it, Roberts? You're a bit of a dog at that sort of thing, aren't you? Read your book the other day. There's insanity somewhere in the racial make-up here, isn't there? Wasn't his old man bats?"

Roberts looked scandalised.

"That is so," he said stiffly, "but one would hardly expect to find evidence of racial insanity clearly defined in the facial structure, Mr. Thoms."

The sister arranged the sterile coverings over the abdomen. With the head screened, the patient was no longer an individual. A subject for operation lay on the table—that was all.

Sir John took up a scalpel and made the first incision.

"Peritonitis, all right," said Thoms presently.

"Hal-lo!" he added a little later. "Ruptured abscess. He's made a job of it."

"Accounts for the attacks of pain," Phillips grunted.

"Of course, sir. Wonder he kept going so long—look there."

"Nasty mess," said Phillips. "Good God, Matron, are you deaf? I said forceps."

Sister Marigold bridled slightly and gave a genteel cough. There was silence for some time. Sir John's fingers worked, nervously, inquisitively, and with a kind of delicate assurance.

"The pulse is weak, Sir John," said Roberts suddenly.

"Oh? Look at this, Thoms."

"I don't like this pulse."

"What's the matter, Roberts? Pulse?"

"Yes. It's rather weak. I don't like his looks. Get me an injection of camphor, will you, Nurse?"

Nurse Banks filled the second small hypodermic syringe and brought it to him.

"Give it, Nurse, at once, please."

She did so.

"Serum," grunted Phillips.

"Serum, Nurse Harden," murmured the sister.

Jane crossed to the table of apparatus. There was a little delay.

"Well—well, where is it?" asked Phillips impatiently.

"Nurse!" called Thoms angrily. "What are you doing?"

"I'm sorry—but——"

"It's the large syringe," said Nurse Banks.

"Very well," said Jane faintly.

She bent over the table.

Phillips finished sewing up the incision.

"Nurse," repeated Thoms, "*will* you bring me that syringe? What's the matter with you?"

An agitated drop appeared on the end of his nose. Sister Marigold cast an expert glance at it and wiped it off with a piece of gauze.

Jane came back uncertainly, holding the tray. Phillips straightened his back and stood looking at the wound. Thoms put on the dressing and then gave the injection.

"Well," he said, "that's that. Very nasty case. I suppose he's neglected it."

"I believe so," answered Phillips slowly, "I saw him the other evening and I had no idea he was ill—no idea of it."

"How's the condition now, Roberts?" asked Thoms.

"Not too brilliant."

"Well—take him to bed," said Phillips.

"And take that tray away," added Thoms irritably to Jane who still stood at his elbow.

She turned her head and looked into Phillips's eyes. He seemed to avoid her gaze and moved away. She turned towards the other table. Her steps grew more uncertain. She stopped, swayed a little, and fell forward on the tiled floor.

"Good God, what's the girl up to now?" shouted Thoms.

Phillips strode across the theatre and stood staring down at her.

"Fainted," he said behind his mask. He looked at his blood-stained gloves, pulled them off and knelt beside her. Sister Marigold "Tut-tut-tutted" like a scandalised hen and rang a bell. Nurse Banks glanced across and then stolidly helped Thoms to cover the patient and lift him back on the trolley. Dr. Roberts did not even look up. He had bent over the patient in an attitude of the most intense concentration. Two nurses came in.

"Nurse Harden's fainted," said the matron briefly.

They managed to get Jane to her feet. She opened her eyes and looked vaguely at them. Between them they half carried her out of the theatre.

The patient was wheeled away.

Phillips walked off into the anteroom followed by Thoms.

"Well, sir," remarked Thoms cheerfully, "I think the usual state of things has been reversed. You are the fierce member of the party as a rule, but to-day you're a perfect sucking-dove and I damned that poor girl to heaps. I'm sorry about it. Suppose she was feeling groggy all through the op."

"I suppose so," said Phillips, turning on a tap.

"I'm sorry about it. She's a nice girl and a good nurse. Attractive. Wonder if she's engaged."

"No."

"Not?"

"No."

Thoms paused, towel in hand, and stared curiously at his

senior. Sir John washed up sedately and methodically.

"Unpleasant game, operating on your friends, isn't it?" ventured Thoms, after a pause. "And such a distinguished friend, too. Jove, there are lots of Bolshie-minded gentlemen that wouldn't be overwhelmed with grief if O'Callaghan faded out! I can see it's hit you up a bit, sir. I've never before seen the faintest tremor in your hands."

"My dear Thoms, there's nothing the matter with my hands."

"Oh—I'm sorry."

"Nothing to be sorry about." He took off his gown and cap and brushed his hair. "You're quite right," he said suddenly, "I didn't enjoy the operation."

Thoms grinned good-naturedly and then looked sympathetic. The door opened and Dr. Roberts came in.

"I just looked in to report, Sir John," he began. "The patient's condition is rather disquieting. The camphor injection helped matters at the time but the pulse is still unsatisfactory." He glanced nervously from one surgeon to the other and polished his glasses. "I must confess I feel rather anxious," he said. "It's—it's such an important case."

"All cases are important," said Phillips.

"Of course, Sir John. What I meant to convey was my possible over-anxiety, occasioned by the illustriousness of the patient."

"You speak like your books, Roberts," said Thoms facetiously.

"However," continued Roberts with a doubtful glance at the fat little man. "However, I *am* anxious."

"I'll come and look at him," answered Phillips. "I can understand your concern. Thoms, you'd better come along with us."

"I won't be a minute, sir."

"There's something about his condition that one doesn't quite expect," Roberts said. He went into details. Phillips listened attentively. Thoms darted a complacent glance at the mirror.

"I'm ready," he told them.

He turned to Roberts.

"That's a rum-looking old stethoscope you sport, Roberts," he said jovially.

Roberts looked at it rather proudly. It was an old-fashioned straight instrument of wood with a thick stem, decorated by a row of notches cut down each quadrant.

"I wouldn't part with that for the latest and best thing on the

38

market, Mr. Thoms," said Roberts.

"It looks like a tally-stick. What are the notches in aid of?"

Roberts looked self-conscious. He glanced deprecatingly at Phillips.

"I'm afraid you'll set me down as a very vain individual," he said shyly.

"Come on," said Thoms. "Spill the beans! Are they all the people you've killed or are they your millionaire patients?"

"Not that—no. As a matter of fact, it is a sort of tally. They represent cases of severe heart disease to whom I have given anæsthetic successfully."

Thoms roared with laughter and Roberts blushed like a schoolboy.

"Are you ready?" asked Phillips coldly.

They all went out together.

In the theatre Sister Marigold, Nurse Banks, and a nurse who had appeared to "scally", cleaned up and prepared for another operation, an urgent bronchoscopy, to be performed by a throat specialist. Jane had been taken off to the nurses' quarters.

"Two urgent ops. in one evening!" exclaimed the matron importantly; "we *are* busy. What's the time, Nurse?"

"Six thirty-five," said Banks.

"Whatever was the matter with Harden, Matron?" asked the scally.

"I'm sure I don't know, Nurse," rejoined Sister Marigold.

"I do," said Nurse Banks grimly.

Sister Marigold cast upon her a glance in which curiosity struggled with dignity. Dignity triumphed. Fortunately the scally was not so handicapped.

"Well, Banks," she said, "come clean. Why *did* she faint?"

"She knew the patient."

"What! Knew Sir Derek O'Callaghan? Harden?"

"Oh, yes! Their people were neighbours down in Dorset, don't you know," aped Banks with what she imagined to be the accent of landed proprietorship.

Sister Marigold's starch seemed to crackle disapproval.

"Nurse Harden comes of a very nice family," she said pointedly to the scally.

"Oh, most fraytefully nayce," jeered Banks. "Yes, she knew O'Callaghan all right. I happened to say, about a month ago it was, that he was probably the most completely unscrupulous of the Tories and she didn't half flare up. Then she told me."

"Thank you, Nurse Banks, that will do," said Matron icily. "The theatre is not the place for politics. I think we are ready now. I want a word with the doctor about this case."

She rustled out of the theatre.

"You've got a nerve, Banks," said the scally. "Fancy talking like that about Sir Derek. I think he looks lovely in his photos."

"You think because he's got a face like Conrad Veidt he's a suitable leader of the people—a man to make laws. Typical bourgeois ignorance and stupidity! However, he's probably the last of his species and he'll be the first to go when the Dawn breaks."

"Whatever are you talking about?"

"I know what I'm talking about."

"Well, I'm sure I don't. What Dawn?"

"The Dawn of the Proletariat Day."

"What's that? No, don't lose your hair, Banks. I'd like to know."

"You will know," said Banks. "Very shortly."

Upon which the throat specialist appeared and inquired if they were all ready for him. In ten minutes' time the figure of a child was wheeled into the theatre and once again the fumes of the anæsthetic rose like incense about the table. In another ten minutes the child was taken away. Nurse Banks and the scally began to clear up again. The throat specialist whistled as he washed up in the anteroom. He thrust his head in at the door, remarked: "No rest for the wicked, Nurse," and took himself off.

The two women worked in silence for a little while. Nurse Banks seemed preoccupied and rather morose.

"Hallo," said the scally, "there's Pips growling on the stairs." ('Pips' was hospital slang for Sir John Phillips.) "*And* Thomcat. Wonder how he is now. Sir Derek, I mean."

Nurse Banks did not answer.

"I don't believe you care."

"Oh, I'm quite interested."

The voices grew louder but neither of the two nurses could hear what was said. They stood very still, listening intently.

Presently there seemed to be some kind of movement. A woman's voice joined in the conversation.

"Who's that?" asked the scally.

"Sounds like Marigold," said Banks. "God, that woman

40

infuriates me!"

"Ssh! What's it all about, I wonder?"

Sir John Phillips's voice sounded clearly above the others. "I'd better attend to that," it said.

"Pip sounds absolutely *rampant*," breathed the scally.

"Yes," said Thoms clearly. "Yes."

A sound of footsteps. Then suddenly the door into the theatre opened and O'Callaghan's special nurse burst into the room.

"Isn't it frightful!" she said. "Oh, isn't it frightful!"

"What? What's the matter with you?"

"He's dead—Sir Derek O'Callaghan's dead!"

"Nurse!" The scally gazed at her speechless.

"It really is awful," said Nurse Graham. "Lady O'Callaghan is there now—she wanted to be left alone with him. I felt I simply must tell somebody."

There was a dead silence, and then, prompted perhaps by some kind of mental telepathy, they both turned and stared at Banks.

The older woman's head was tipped back. She held her arms stiffly at her sides. Her eyes shone and her lips worked convulsively.

"Banks!" said the scally, "Banks! How can you behave like that? I believe you're glad he's gone!"

"If I hadn't cast off the worn-out shackles of religion," said Banks, "I should say 'Praise the Lord for He hath cast down our Enemy'."

"You disgusting old horror," said the special, and went out of the theatre.

CHAPTER V

Lady O'Callaghan Insists

Friday, the twelfth. Afternoon.

"Lady O'Callaghan, I'm terribly sorry to bother, but may I speak to you for a moment?"

Ronald Jameson paused and looked apologetically at the widow of his late employer. She was very handsome in black. Her hair—he could never make up his mind whether it was a warm white or a white blonde—looked as though it had been ironed into place. Her hands, thin and elegant, hung relaxed against the matt surface of her dress. Her pale blue eyes under their heavy lids regarded him with a kind of polite detachment.

"Yes," she said vaguely. "Come into my room, Mr. Jameson."

He followed her into that place of frozen elegance. She sat down leisurely, her back to the light.

"Yes," she repeated. "Sit down, Mr. Jameson."

Ronald said: "Thank you so much," nervously, and sat on the most uncomfortable chair.

"I've just come back from the House," he began. "The Prime Minister saw me in his room. He is terribly distressed about—about yesterday. He wished me to tell you that—that he is entirely at your service should there be anything——"

"So kind of him," she said.

"Of course, he is also very much troubled about the Bill—Sir Derek's Anarchy Bill, you know. The business arising from it has to go forward, you see, and this tragedy has complicated matters." He paused again.

"I see—yes."

"It's a question of Sir Derek's private notes. They can do

42

nothing without them. I said that the matter would have to wait until after the—until after tomorrow; but the Prime Minister thinks the whole business is so urgent that he ought to see them immediately. I believe they are in the desk in the study, but of course, before I could do anything about it, I felt I must have your permission."

She took so long to answer that he felt quite alarmed. At last, looking at her hands which lay delicately clasped on her lap, she said: "This Bill. Will it deal with the persons who killed him?"

He was so completely dumbfounded by this amazing inquiry that he could think of nothing to say. He was a young man with a good deal of *savoir-faire*, but evidently her extraordinary assumption took him unawares.

"I'm afraid I don't—do you mean—surely, Lady O'Callaghan, you can't believe——" He could get no further with it.

"Oh, yes," she said tranquilly, "I'm iuite sure they killed him."

"But—who?"

"These people. Anarchists, aren't they? They threatened to kill my husband. I believe they have done so. I understand his Bill was designed to suppress such persons. Please do anything you can to help it to go forward."

"Thank you," said Ronald idiotically.

"Yes. Is that all, Mr. Jameson?"

"But, Lady O'Callaghan—please—have you thought—honestly, you have simply amazed me. It's a terrible idea. Surely the doctors' report is clear! Sir Derek had acute peritonitis."

"Sir John Phillips said the operation was successful. He was poisoned."

"By peritonitis and a ruptured abscess. Really, I can't think anything else. How could he be deliberately poisoned?"

"One of the letters threatened poison. The one he had last Monday, it was."

"But many leading politicians get letters of that sort. Nothing ever happens. Forgive me, Lady O'Callaghan, but I'm sure you are utterly wrong. How *could* they have poisoned him? It's—it's impossible. I do beg you not to distress yourself." He glanced uncomfortably at her placid face. "I'm sure you are quite mistaken," ended Ronald wildly.

"Let us go into his room," she murmured and, without another word, led the way into O'Callaghan's study.

43

They unlocked the desk and she sat and watched, while Ronald went through the papers in the top pigeon-holes.

"The drawers on the left," he explained to her, "were used for private correspondence—I did not have anything to do with them."

"They will have to be opened. I will do that."

"Of course. Here is one of the threatening letters—several—I think all of them. I wanted to show them to Chief Detective-Inspector Alleyn at the Yard. Sir Derek wouldn't allow me to do so."

"Let me see them."

He gave her the bundle of letters and returned to the pigeon-holes.

"Here are his notes," he said presently. She did not answer, and he glanced up and was astonished to surprise in her face an expression of some sort of an emotion. She looked venomous.

"Here is the letter I spoke of," she said. "You will see that they threaten to poison him."

"Yes. I see."

"You still do not believe me, Mr. Jameson?"

"I'm sorry. I'm afraid I don't."

"I shall insist upon an inquiry."

"An inquiry? Oh Lord!" said Ronald involuntarily. "I mean—I wouldn't, really, Lady O'Callaghan. It's—we've no grounds for it."

"Are you taking these notes to the Prime Minister to-day?"

"Yes."

"Will you tell him, if you please, what I propose to do? You may discuss it with him. In the meantime I shall go through the private letters. Have you the keys of those drawers?"

Ronald took a bunch of keys from the desk, and with an air of reluctance put them in her hand.

"When is your appointment?"

"For three o'clock."

"It is now only half-past two. Please come and see me before you leave."

As he left her she was fitting a key to the bottom drawer.

To anybody who had the curiosity to watch him—Nash, the butler, for instance—Ronald Jameson would have appeared to be very much upset. He went up to his bedroom, wandered aimlessly about, smoked three cigarettes, and finally sat on the

44

bed, staring in a sort of trance at a wood-engraving that hung above his dressing-table. At last he looked at his watch, went downstairs, got his hat and umbrella and returned to the study.

He found Lady O'Callaghan seated at the desk with a neatly arranged pile of letters in front of her. She did not turn her head when he came in. She simply stared very fixedly at a paper she held in her hand. It struck him that she had sat like that for some time—while he himself had done much the same thing upstairs in his room. Her face was always pale—she did not use rouge—but he thought now that it was deadly white. There was a thin ridge, like a taut thread, linking her nostrils with the corners of her mouth.

"Come here," she said quietly.

He went and stood by the desk.

"You told me that night, a week ago, I think, that my husband had received a letter that seemed to upset him. Was this the letter?"

He glanced at it and then looked away.

"I did not see the letter," he stammered. "Only the envelope."

"Is that the envelope?"

"I—I think so. I can't be sure."

"Read it."

With an expression of extreme distaste he read the letter. It was Jane Harden's.

"If an opportunity presented itself," Jane had written, "I would not hesitate to kill you."

Ronald put it down on the desk.

"Now read this."

The second letter was from Sir John Phillips. Phillips had written it at fever-heat on the night he got home from his interview with O'Callaghan, and had posted it before he had time to cool down.

I gather you're going to cut your losses and evade what, to any decent man, would be a responsibility. You talked of sending Jane a cheque. She will, of course, either tear it up or return it. I cannot force your hand, for that would do still more harm to a lady who is already deeply wronged. I warn you, however, to keep clear of me. I've a certain devil in me that I thought was scotched, but you have brought it to life again, and I think I could very easily kill you. This may sound like hyperbole; as a

45

matter of fact it is meiosis.

"Have you seen that before?" asked Lady O'Callaghan.

"Never," said Ronald.

"You notice the signature? It was written by the man who operated on my husband."

"Yes."

"Who is this woman—Jane Harden?"

"Honestly, I have no idea, Lady O'Callaghan."

"No? A nurse, evidently. Look at the address, Mr. Jameson."

"Good God," said Ronald. "It's—it's the nursing-home."

"Yes. We sent him to a strange place for his operation."

"But——"

"Will you please take these letters with you?"

"But, Lady O'Callaghan, I can't possibly show them to the P.M.—the Prime Minister—really!"

"Then I shall have to do so myself. Of course, there must be an inquest."

"Forgive me, but in the shock of reading these letters and—and realising their inferences, have you considered the effect any publicity would have on yourself?"

"What do you mean? What shock? Do you suppose I did not know he had mistresses?"

"I've no idea, I'm sure," said poor Ronald unhappily.

"Of course I knew," she said composedly. "That seems to me to have nothing to do with the point we are discussing. I knew he had been murdered. I thought at first that these other people——" She made a slight gesture towards the neat little pile on the desk. "Now I find he had bitter enemies nearer to him than that." Her hand closed over the letters on her knee. "He has been murdered. Probably by this nurse or by Sir John Phillips; possibly by both of them in collaboration. I shall demand an inquest."

"An inquest! You know, I doubt very much if you would be given permission."

"To whom does one apply?"

"One can't just order an inquest," Ronald said evasively.

"Who can do so, Mr. Jameson?"

"The—well, the coroner for the district, I imagine."

"Or the police?"

Ronald winced.

46

"I suppose so—yes."

"Yes. Thank you, Mr. Jameson."

Ronald, in a panic, took himself off to the House.

Lady O'Callaghan put a jade paper-weight on the little heap of letters and opened the telephone directory. The number she wanted was printed in large letters on a front page. She dialled it, and was answered immediately.

"Is that New Scotland Yard?" she asked, pitching her voice in a sort of serene falsetto. "It is Lady O'Callaghan speaking. My husband was Sir Derek O'Callaghan, the late Home Secretary. I want to speak to someone in authority, in reference to the death of my husband. No, not on the telephone. Perhaps someone would call? Immediately, if possible. Thank you."

She hung up the receiver and leant back in her chair. Then she rang for Nash, who came in looking like a Stilton in mourning.

"Nash," she said, "an officer from Scotland Yard is calling in ten minutes. It is in reference to the funeral. I wish to speak to him myself. If Miss O'Callaghan calls, will you tell her I am unable to see her? Show the officer in here when he comes."

"Very good, m'lady," breathed Nash and withdrew.

Cicely O'Callaghan then went to the room where her husband lay, awaiting his last journey down Whitehall. She was an Anglo-Catholic, so candles burned, small golden plumes, at the head and foot of the coffin. The room, a large one, was massed heavily with flowers. It smelt like a tropical island, but was very cold. A nun from the church that the O'Callaghans attended knelt at a little distance from the coffin. She did not look up when Lady O'Callaghan came in.

The wife knelt beside her for a moment, crossed herself with a thin vague movement of her hand, and then rose and contemplated her husband.

Derek O'Callaghan looked impressive. The heavy eyebrows, black hair, jutting nose and thin wide mouth were striking accents in the absolute pallor of his face. His hands, stiffly crossed, obediently fixed a crucifix to the hard curve of his breast. His wife, only a little less pale than he, stared at him. It would have been impossible to guess her thoughts. She simply looked in the direction of the dead face. In the distance a door opened and shut. She turned away from the bier, and walked out of the room.

In the hall Nash waited gloomily, while a tall, thickly built man handed him hat and umbrella.

47

"Inspector Fox, my lady."

"Will you come in here?"

She took the inspector into the study. Nash had lit the fire, and she held her thin hands towards it.

"Please sit down," she murmured. They sat facing each other. Inspector Fox regarded her with respectful attention.

"I asked you to come and see me," she began very quietly, "because I believe my husband to have been murdered."

Fox did not speak for a moment. He sat stockily, very still, looking gravely before him.

"I'm sorry to hear that, Lady O'Callaghan," he said at last. "It sounds rather serious."

Apparently she had met her match in understatement.

"Of course, I should not have called you in unless I had material evidence to put before you. I believe the police are aware of the activities of those persons against whom my husband's Anarchy Bill was directed?"

"We know a good deal about them."

"Yes. My husband had received many threatening letters which were believed to come from these people. I wished him to let the police see the letters, but he refused."

"We were informed of the matter from another source," said Fox.

"The Prime Minister, perhaps?"

Fox regarded her placidly, but did not reply.

"I have the letters here," she continued, after a moment, "and would like you to read them." She took them from the desk and gave them to him.

Fox took a spectacle case from an inner pocket and put on a pair of gold-rimmed glasses. He looked extremely respectable.

He read the letters through stolidly, laying them down neatly one on top of the other. When the last was finished, he clasped his enormous hands together and said:

"Yes. That's the sort of things these people write."

"Now, will you read these?"

She gave him the letters from Sir John Phillips and Jane Harden. He read them carefully, in exactly the same way.

"Sir John Phillips is the surgeon who operated upon my husband. I understand the other letter is from a nurse in the hospital."

"Is that so, Lady O'Callaghan?" said Fox politely.

"My husband had peritonitis but I believe he died of poisoning. I believe he was poisoned."

"In view of these letters? These two, or the others?"

"I do not know. I am inclined to regard the personal ones as being more important. They definitely threaten his life."

"Yes. Very vindictive, they seem to be."

"I wish to have an inquest."

"I see," said Fox. "Now that's quite a serious matter, Lady O'Callaghan."

A faint redness appeared in her cheeks. Another woman would possibly have screamed in his face.

"Of course it is serious," she said.

"I mean, if you understand me, that before an order is made for an inquest, the coroner who makes it has to be certain of one or two points. What about the death certificate, for instance?"

"What do you mean?"

"Well, was one signed?"

"Yes."

"By Sir John Phillips?"

"I don't know. Possibly. Mr. Thoms, the assistant surgeon, may have signed it."

"Yes. Well, now, Mr. Thoms is a well-known surgeon. Sir Derek was a distinguished patient. He would take every care before he signed. I think that would be considered sufficiently conclusive by the coroner."

"But these threats! I am convinced he was murdered. I shall demand an inquest."

Fox stared gravely into the fire.

"Perhaps," he said, rather ponderously, "perhaps you would like me to ring up the coroner and put the case before him."

"Certainly, if you will."

"It would be better if you could tell him, definitely, who signed the certificate."

"Mr. Jameson, my husband's secretary, may know. He had an appointment with the Prime Minister at three."

"It's fifteen minutes to four."

"I shall ring up the House," she said, and did.

She got Ronald at last and asked her question.

"It was Mr. Thoms?" she said into the telephone. Ronald's voice quacked audibly in the room. "Yes. Thank you. Have you discussed the matter? I see. No, I think not, Mr. Jameson; I am communicating directly with the police."

She hung up the receiver and informed Fox that Thoms had signed the certificate.

Inspector Fox then rang up the coroner. He held a long and muffled conversation. The coroner talked a great deal and appeared to be agitated. Lady O'Callaghan listened. Her fingers drummed bonily on the arm of her chair. For her, it was a terrific gesture. At last Fox rang off.

"It's as I thought," he said. "He says he cannot interfere."

"Then I shall go direct to the Prime Minister."

He got rather ponderously to his feet.

"I don't think I'd do that, Lady O'Callaghan—at least not yet. If you'll allow me to I'd like to talk it over with my superior, Chief Detective-Inspector Alleyn."

"Alleyn? I think I've heard of him. Isn't he—" She paused. Cicely O'Callaghan had nearly dropped a brick. She had been about to say "Isn't he a gentleman?" She must have been really very much perturbed to come within hail of such a *gaffe*. Inspector Fox answered her very simply.

"Yes," he said, "he's rather well known. He's a very highly educated man. Quite a different type from me, you might say."

Again a faint pink tinged her cheeks.

"I'm grateful to you for the trouble you are taking," she told him.

"It's all in the day's work," said Fox. "If you'll excuse me, Lady O'Callaghan, I'll get along. I'll speak to the chief at once. If you're agreeable, I'll show him the correspondence."

"Yes."

"Thank you very much. I'll wish you good afternoon."

"Will you have something to drink before you go?"

"No, thank you. Very kind of you, I'm sure." He tramped to the door, turned and made a little bow.

"I hope you'll allow me to offer my sympathy," he said. "It's a great loss to the nation."

"Thank you."

"Good afternoon, Lady O'Callaghan."

"Good afternoon, Inspector."

So Inspector Fox went to the Yard to see Alleyn.

CHAPTER VI

Chief Detective-Inspector Alleyn

Friday, the twelfth. Afternoon and evening.
"Hallo, Brer Fox," said Alleyn, looking up from his desk.
"Where've you been in your new bowler?"

"Paying a call on the Snow Queen," replied Fox with unexpected imaginativeness. "And when I say 'Snow Queen' I don't mean cocaine, either."

"No? Then what do you mean? Sit down and have a smoke. You look perturbed."

"Well, I am," said Fox heavily. He produced a pipe and blew down it, staring solemnly at his superior. "I've been to see the wife of the late Home Secretary," he said.

"What? You *are* coming on."

"Look here, chief. She says it's murder."

"She says what's murder?"

"Him. Sir Derek O'Callaghan."

Alleyn put his pipe down and swung round slowly in his chair.

"Oh!" he said. He raised one eyebrow to an excruciating height and twisted his mouth sideways. This trick invested his handsome face with a kind of impish fastidiousness.

"What sort of woman is she?" he asked.

"A very cold fishy sort of lady," answered Fox. "A Snow Queen, in fact. Not the hysterical sort, if that's what you mean."

"She was a Rattisbon. All the Rattisbons are a bit frosty. I was at school with her brother—who was, of course, called 'Ratsbane'. I speak like Mr. Gossip, don't I? A very churlish fellow, he was. Well, let's have the whole story."

Fox told him the whole story, dwelling a little on the letters.

51

"I see," said Alleyn. "And she's hell-bent on an inquest?"

"That she is. If we won't do anything, she's going to the Prime Minister. He's a friend of yours, isn't he, sir?"

"I know the old creature, yes. As a matter of fact, he summoned me to the presence on another matter about a fortnight ago and we had an Oppenheimian conversation about anarchists. He was very perturbed and asked me if I didn't consider O'Callaghan would be in personal danger if he pushed the Bill. Well, one never knows, and I said so. Some bright young Communist might bowl a bomb. As a matter of cold fact, I greatly doubt it. They do a certain amount of mischief, they're an almighty nuisance, but as murderers I've no real faith in the British anarchist. Anarchist! The word is *vieux jeu*."

"I suppose that's French?"

"Quite right, Fox. I always said you had a flair for languages."

"I'm teaching myself with the gramophone. All the same, sir, these anarchists are no joke."

"Of course they're not. The P.M., as I believe the member for Little Squidgemere calls him, thought O'Callaghan ought to have police protection. I quite agreed. I couldn't very well do anything else. O'Callaghan pooh-poohed the idea. As you know, we were looking after him in our unassuming way. On the afternoon of the Cabinet Meeting, when they decided to introduce the Bill, I went along to Downing Street myself. I'd got wind of that insufferable nuisance Nicholas Kakaroff, and found him standing about in the street, dressed up as something rather ridiculous—a photographer, I think. He made off, with all his infra-red rays and what not, as soon as he saw me. I took a taxi and followed O'Callaghan home. We were alongside each other at one moment. He turned up the lights in his car and I returned the compliment."

"His servants are all right, aren't they?" asked Fox.

"Oh, yes; we went as far as that. But, of course, we couldn't do much without O'Callaghan's permission or knowledge."

"No. I think her ladyship suspects the surgeon or the girl."

" 'The Surgeon or the Girl'—it sounds like a talkie. Sir John Phillips is a very able man and handy, so I understand, with the knife. She thinks he dug it into an unlawful spot, because O'Callaghan had been interfering with his girl—is that it?"

"She thinks Sir Derek was poisoned, otherwise that seems to be the general idea, but of course his letter isn't very explicit."

"Have you got the letters?"

"Yes. Here they are."

Alleyn read them carefully.

"You know, Fox, hundreds of people write letters like these without planning murder."

"Isn't that what I tried to tell her!"

"My poor Foxkin! See if you can find the Press report of his death."

Fox produced a paper.

"I brought it with me," he said.

"You think of everything. Here we are. He died an hour after the operation was over. The anæsthetist was worried—peritonitis—ruptured abscess—'unwilling to run aside from the gigantic task'—he'd neglected his tummy, evidently. It sounds straightforward enough, and yet—"

Alleyn took the tip of his straight nose between his thumb and finger and pulled it thoughtfully.

"Oh, lord!" he said sadly. "I'll have to go and see the lady."

Fox looked relieved.

"If there's anything in it," he reflected, "it'll be a hell of a big case. What you call"—he paused self-consciously—"a *cause célèbre*."

"It will indeed," said Alleyn, who never made too much fun of anybody. "I wonder if she would see me this evening?"

"I'm certain she would, sir."

"I'll ask."

Alleyn rang up the house in Catherine Street. "Is that Lady O'Callaghan's house? Is it her butler speaking? Chief Inspector Alleyn, Scotland Yard, here. Will you ask her ladyship if I may call on her to-night at any time that would suit her? Inspector Alleyn, yes. Thank you."

He stared absent-mindedly at Fox while he waited for the reply.

"At nine o'clock. Thank you so much."

He hung up the receiver.

"I'm for it," he said.

After Fox had gone Alleyn sat and gazed at the opposite wall for twenty minutes. Then he rang up the divisional surgeon and talked to him about the human appendix, peritonitis and anæsthetics. Then he went to his flat near Coventry Street, bathed, changed into a dinner-jacket, dined, and read the first scene in *Hamlet*, to which he was partial. By that time it was twenty to nine. He decided to walk to Catherine Street. His servant, Vassily [see *A Man Lay Dead*], helped him into his overcoat.

"Vassily," said Alleyn, "do you ever see anything of your disreputable pals—The Pan-Soviet Brotherhood, or whatever they were—nowadays?"

"No, sir. Not now am I such a foolish old rascal. I am one bite too shy."

"So I should hope, you old donkey. You don't happen to remember hearing any gossip about Nicholas Kakaroff?"

Vassily crossed himself lavishly from right to left.

"*Hospodi bozhe moy!* He is one of the most worst of them," he said energetically. "A bad fellow. Before the Soviet he was young and anysing but conserff-a-tiff. After the Soviet he was older and always up to no-goods. The Soviet pleased him no better than the Romanoffs. So sometimes he was killing officials, and at last he has heated up Russia for himself too much, so has come to England."

"Where he seems to have been given the usual hearty welcome. Yes, I knew all that, Vassily. Thank you. Don't wait up. Good night."

"Good night, sir," Vassily laid his hand on Alleyn's sleeve. "Please, sir," he said, "have no business with Nikolai Alexaivich—he is a very bad rascal."

"Well, you ought to know," Alleyn remarked lightly, and went out smiling to himself.

At Catherine Street he was received by Nash, who stared like a boiled owl at the inspector. Nash, who carried in his head a sort of social ladder, had quietly decided that police officers of all ranks were to be graded with piano-tuners. Chief Detective-Inspector Alleyn did not conform, in appearance or in manner, to this classification. Nash performed a reluctant mental somersault.

"Lady O'Callaghan?" asked Alleyn.

"Her ladyship is expecting you, sir." Alleyn gave him his hat and overcoat. Nash said: "Thank you, sir," and waddled off towards the study. Alleyn followed him. Nash opened the door.

"Mr. Alleyn, m'lady," he said. Obviously the degrading titles were better omitted.

Alleyn walked in.

Cicely O'Callaghan sat before the fire in her husband's armchair. As Alleyn came in she rose to her feet and looked serenely at him.

"How do you do?" she said.

"How do you do? I am extremely sorry to bother you, Lady

54

O'Callaghan."

He thought: "Golly, she *is* like Ratsbane!"

"But I wished to see you. It is good of you to come so promptly."

"Not a bit." This was an exceedingly polite introduction to a murder story.

"Do sit down. I suppose the man who came here this afternoon has told you my reason for communicating with the police?"

"I believe Inspector Fox gave me a full account of your conversation."

"Yes. I am convinced that my husband was murdered—probably poisoned."

"I am sorry that in addition to your grief you should suffer the pain occasioned by such a suspicion," said Alleyn, and wondered how long they were to make speeches at each other.

"Thank you. Do you agree with me that the circumstances warrant an inquest?"

"I think I should like to hear a little more about them. I have read the letters."

"Surely they in themselves are enough to arouse anybody's suspicion?"

"Lady O'Callaghan, it is extremely unusual for a person contemplating homicide to write such letters. I do not say it is unknown, but it *is* very unusual. I expect Fox told you that."

"I believe he said something of the sort. My point is this: I do not think the murderer contemplated homicide when writing the letter. I do think that a person capable of writing such a letter would also be capable of seizing the opportunity when it presented itself."

"So it *is* Phillips and the girl she's after," thought Alleyn.

"I see your point, of course," he said slowly.

"There is another incident which I did not go into with—Inspector Fox. Before my husband's operation I was in his room with him. He did not realise where he was or what had happened to him. I tried to explain about the appendix. Then Sir John Phillips came into the room. When my husband saw him he exclaimed: "Don't—don't let——" and then he collapsed. He seemed terrified by the presence of Sir John Phillips and I am certain that he tried to say: 'Don't let him touch me'. I must tell you that a week before this Sir John called on my husband. I hoped that it was for a consultation about his pain, which was then very severe. Next morning I asked my husband if Sir John had examined him. He evaded my question, and seemed very much upset. I had met Sir John in the hall and had thought his manner most unusual. His letter was written that same night, evidently as a result of the interview."

"You definitely connect Sir John's letter with the other, signed Jane Harden?"

"Yes. She is a nurse in the hospital where my husband was a patient. After your man left, this afternoon, I rang up the hospital and under pretext of wishing to thank the nurses concerned in the case, I found out their names. She was actually present in the operating theatre and I dare say assisted Sir John."

She drawled all this out in her serene, high-pitched voice, exactly as though she was reading aloud.

"Forgive me," said Alleyn, "but did you know anything about this business? I hope you will understand that I only ask because——"

"Because you wonder if I am prejudiced?"

"Exactly."

"I knew my husband was unfaithful to me from time to time. I also believed these incidents to be more or less casual encounters."

"You were unaware of this Miss Harden's existence?"

"Quite."

Alleyn was silent for a little while. Then he rose to his feet.

"I think, with you, that there should be an inquest," he told her.

She made a slight movement and the heavy folds of her dress stirred. It was as though she had suddenly gone tense all over. When she spoke, however, it was with her customary equanimity.

"You have, I am sure, made a very wise decision."

"I'm afraid we shall have difficulty with the coroner. Naturally he is rather chary about starting such an alarming hare. It will be impossible to keep the thing even moderately quiet. The papers already have wind of these threatening letters from Sir Derek's political enemies."

He watched her closely, but beyond a faint expression of distaste, could find no evidence of any sort of emotion.

"That will be rather disagreeable," she murmured.

"I am afraid so. Is there anything else that you would like to discuss?"

"I was going to suggest that you speak to Mr. Ronald Jameson, my husband's secretary. He will, I think, confirm what I have said about Sir Derek's reaction to these letters."

"If you wish it, I will see him. Of course, if the post-mortem shows that poison has been given, it will then be my duty to make very exhaustive inquiries."

"Of course," she agreed.

Evidently she had made up her mind Alleyn should see Jameson, because she sent for him then and there. Ronald came in looking very perturbed and uneasy.

"This is my husband's secretary—Mr. Jameson, Mr. Alleyn."

"How do you do, sir?" said Ronald. "You won't have the foggiest recollection of me, I'm afraid, but we have met before."

"I've a filthy memory," declared Chief Inspector Alleyn.

"It was at Nigel Bathgate's."

"Oh, yes." Alleyn was polite, but non-committal.

"Really?" murmured Lady O'Callaghan. "Yes, I thought too that perhaps I had seen you—that your face——" She seemed uncertain how to go on.

"People often find they are familiar with the faces of the police," said Alleyn gravely.

"It's not that, sir," Ronald turned to Lady O'Callaghan. "Mr. Alleyn is in some of Mr. Rattisbon's photos in the study at Karnelly."

"Ratsbane's cricketing groups," thought Alleyn. "Oh, Lord!"

"Oh," said Lady O'Callaghan. "Yes." She stared rather blankly at him.

"Mr. Jameson," Alleyn began, "I believe Lady O'Callaghan wants me to speak to you about an incident that took place here a week before Sir Derek's operation."

Ronald jumped and glanced nervously at the lady.

"I have spoken to Mr. Alleyn about my suspicions. He agrees that there should be an inquest."

"Really, sir? Look here—I mean, of course, you know best, but, well—it's—it's a pretty ghastly thought, isn't it?"

"You remember the evening my husband had the letter signed Jane Harden?"

"Yes," said Ronald very reluctantly.

"You remember that you told me the letter seemed to upset him very much?"

"Yes—but——"

"And when he overheard you speaking of it he was quite unreasonably angry?"

"I don't think *unreasonably*, Lady O'Callaghan," Ronald protested. "Sir Derek was quite right. I should not have mentioned his correspondence. I had never done so before."

"Why did you do so then?" she asked him.

"Really," thought Alleyn, "she might be an Attorney-General."

"Because—well, because it seemed to upset him so much." Ronald saw the fence too late and crashed into it.

"Yes," said Lady O'Callaghan.

"Would you describe him as being alarmed?" Alleyn asked.

"Well—more sort of disturbed and distressed. After all, sir, it *was* an unpleasant letter to get."

Ronald seemed to be in a perfect agony of embarrassment.

"Certainly," Alleyn agreed. "You were not present, were you, at any time during the interview between Sir Derek and Sir John Phillips?"

"No. I—no, I wasn't."

"What were you going to say? Was anyone else there?"

"Nash, the butler, took in the tray."

"Has he spoken to you on the subject?" asked Alleyn casually.

"Er—yes. Servants' gossip. I rather snubbed him, sir."

"What did he say before you'd snubbed him?"

"He's an awful old woman—Nash. He seemed to think Sir John had used some sort of threatening expression. Honestly, sir, he's a fearful ass."

"I see. I think that's all, Lady O'Callaghan. Perhaps the apprehensive Nash will make an appearance when I go."

She rang the bell.

"He should have come in with the tray by this time," she said vaguely.

When Nash appeared it was with the tray, which he set down delicately.

"Mr. Alleyn, will you——?"

"No thank you so much. I must be off. Good-bye, Lady O'Callaghan. I'll ring you up if I may."

"Yes. Thank you. Good-bye."

Nash opened the door and followed Alleyn into the hall. Jameson made as if to see the inspector out.

"Oh—Mr. Jameson," said Lady O'Callaghan. He hesitated and then returned to the study, closing the door.

As he took his hat and coat from the butler Alleyn paused and looked directly at him.

"Perhaps you realise why I am here?" he said.

"Not altogether, sir," murmured Nash composedly.

"It is in connection with Sir Derek's death." Nash bowed very slightly.

"If I ask you a question," Alleyn continued, "you must understand there is no obligation to answer if you don't want to. I particularly do not wish the matter mentioned in or out of the servants' hall. You understand?"

"Certainly, sir," said Nash quietly.

"I believe I can depend on you. How long have you been with Sir Derek?"

"Twenty years, sir. I was footman to his father."

"Yes. Did you hear Sir John Phillips say anything to your master the last time he came here?"

"Yes, sir."

"What was it?"

" 'If the opportunity presented itself, I should have no hesitation in putting you out of the way'. Those were the exact words, sir."

"I see. Have you told anyone about this?"

"Mr. Jameson, sir. I considered it my duty. No one in the hall has any idea of the incident, sir."

"What did Mr. Jameson think about it?"

"He appeared to attach no importance to it, sir."

"No? Thank you, Nash."

"Thank you very much, sir. Shall I get you a taxi, sir?"

"No, I'll walk. Good night."

"Good evening, sir."

Nash opened the door and Alleyn went out into the street. He paused for a moment to light a cigarette. He had taken a few steps along the pavement when he heard something that made him pause and turn.

Ronald Jameson had come out of the house and hurried after him, bareheaded.

"Please, forgive me, sir," he said hurriedly, "but I felt I must have another word with you. It was rather difficult with Lady O'Callaghan present. About these ideas of hers. I'm certain there's nothing in it. Sir Derek was a man of the world and—and, of course, he had his relaxations. She seems very cold and all that, but I believe she was frightfully jealous and she wants to punish this girl. I'm sure that's all it is."

"Oh. Why should she want to punish Sir John Phillips as well as Miss Harden?"

"Oh, Lord knows. You can't tell with women, sir, can you?"

"I haven't tried," said Alleyn.

"I expect you think it frightful cheek, my butting in like this, but, you see, I—well, Sir Derek was rather a marvellous person to me, and I simply loathe the idea of everything being dragged out and made public. It's a ghastly thought."

Something of Ronald's semi-diplomatic air of winning tactfulness still appeared in his rather dishevelled manner. He gazed with anxious deference into Alleyn's sardonic face. The inspector cocked an eyebrow.

"And yet," he said, "I imagine, if Sir Derek was actually killed, you would rather the murderer didn't get off scot-free?"

"Yes, but, you know, I'm sure he wasn't. Those two letters didn't mean anything—I thought so at—" Ronald stopped short.

"Were you about to say 'at the time'?" inquired Alleyn.

"I meant at the time Lady O'Callaghan found them."

"Where were the letters kept, Mr. Jameson?"

"In his private drawer," said Ronald with a very red face.

"And the keys?"

"Er—oh, usually in the desk."

"I see. Well, we must pursue the subject no more until we discover whether Sir Derek was murdered."

"I'm absolutely certain there's nothing in it, sir."

"I hope you are right. Good night."

"Thank you so much, sir," said Ronald, all eager and charming. "Good night."

Alleyn swung his stick up, turned on his heel, and walked away. Ronald gazed after the long, elegant figure for some seconds. His fingers fidgeted with his tie. Then he looked up at the windows of the house, slightly shrugged his shoulders, and ran up the steps and through the door.

Alleyn heard the door slam. As he turned out of Catherine Street towards Buckingham Gate he began to whistle Ophelia's song:

He is dead and gone, lady,
He is dead and gone;
At his head a grass-green turf.
At his heels a stone.

CHAPTER VII

Post-Mortem

Monday, the fifteenth. Afternoon.

"Everybody talks to me about "P.M's'," complained Chief Detective-Inspector Alleyn to Inspector Fox on Monday afternoon, "and I never know whether they mean post-mortem or Prime Minister. Really, it's very difficult when you happen to be involved with both."

"It must be," said Fox dryly. "How's the case going?"

"It's too young to be called a case. So far it's only a naughty thought. As you know, Lady O'Callaghan urged the inquest and threatened to appeal to the P.M. However, the coroner ordered the inquest, which opened on Saturday a.m. and was adjourned for a P.M. which has been going on during the week-end p.m. and a.m. You see how tricky it all is?"

"I can see you're worried, chief."

"When you call me "chief", Fox, I feel like a cross between an Indian brave and one of those men with jaws and cigars in gangster films."

"Okay, chief," said Fox imperturbably. "It's a big job, this," he added sombrely.

"It is," said Alleyn. "I don't mind admitting I was nervous over the inquest. I should have looked remarkably silly if it had gone the other way and no P.M. had been ordered."

"It might very easily have happened. Phillips did his best to put the kybosh on a post-mortem."

"You thought so?"

"Well—didn't you?"

"Yes, I suppose so. Oh, yes."

"Of course," said Fox slowly, "an innocent man in his position would have been anxious for a P.M."

"Not if he thought someone else had done the trick."

"Oh," Fox ruminated. "That's the big idea, is it, sir?"

"It's only one idea—possibly a silly one. What did you think of the matron's contribution to the evidence? Sister Marigold?"

"Couldn't make her out at all and that's a fact. She seemed to welcome the inquest. She obviously resented any hint of criticism against Sir John Phillips."

"She made one or two very acid remarks about the other nurse—Nurse Banks."

"Yes. Now, that struck me as rum, too, sir. No suggestion of anything as regards the Harden girl, but when Nurse Banks was mentioned——"

"She bridled like a Persian," said Alleyn. "I know—'rum's' the word, Fox."

"The medical witnesses are always a bit trying in a case like this," reflected Inspector Fox. "On the defensive, as you might say. They all pull together."

"Now that's exactly what I thought they did *not* do. I've just read over the shorthand report of the inquest and the thing that struck me all of a heap was that the hospital gang seemed to be playing a sort of tig-in-the-dark game. Or rather tug-of-war in the dark. They wanted to pull together, but didn't know which way to pull. Here's the report. Let us go over it, shall we? Where's your pipe?"

They lit up. Alleyn shoved a carbon copy of the verbatim report on the inquest across to his subordinate.

"First you get straight-out evidence on the operation. Phillips said Sir Derek O'Callaghan, suffering from a ruptured abscess of the appendix, was admitted to the Brook Street hospital. He examined the patient, advised an immediate operation, which, at Lady O'Callaghan's request, he undertook to perform himself. Peritonitis was found. The anæsthetist was Dr. Roberts, engaged for the job because the usual man was unavailable. Phillips says Roberts used all possible care and he can find no fault in that department. Thoms, the assistant, agrees. So do Sister Marigold and the two nurses. Before he began, Phillips injected hyoscine, his usual procedure for all operations. For this injection he used tablets he brought with him, saying that he preferred them to the solution in the theatre, as hyoscine is an extremely tricky drug.

"All care taken, no responsibility accepted." one feels moved to remark. He prepared the syringe himself. At the end of the operation a concoction prettily named *"Concentrated Gas-Gangrene Antitoxin"*, used in cases of peritonitis, was injected. The serum, together with a large syringe, was laid out by Nurse Banks before the operation. It was a commercial preparation kept in an ampoule from which she simply filled the syringe. Nurse Harden fetched the syringe and gave it to Thoms, who injected the stuff. Meanwhile Roberts, the anæesthetist, had got all hot and hectic about the patient's heart and had asked for an injection of camphor, which was prepared and given by the elder nurse. They then tacked up the tear in the tummy and away went the patient. He died an hour later, presumably, one longs to say, of heart-failure, but my medical friends tell me that's as good as saying 'he died of dying'. So we can only murmur humbly 'he died as the result of an operation which, apart from this little incident, was a howling success.' "

"Well," said Fox, "so far they all agree."

"Yes, but did you notice that where it came to the bit about Jane Harden fetching the syringe with the anti-gas, as they call it for short, they all went rather warily. She herself looked pretty sick when the coroner asked her about it. Here it is:

" 'The Coroner: I understand you brought the syringe containing the anti-gas, to Dr. Thoms?

" 'Nurse Harden (after a pause): Yes.

" 'The Coroner: There was no unusual delay, or anything of that sort?

" 'Nurse Harden: I—I did hesitate a moment. The syringe was already full and I paused to make sure it was the right one.

" 'The Coroner: Did you not expect to find it prepared?

" 'Nurse Harden: I was not sure. I—I wasn't well, and for a moment I hesitated and then Nurse Banks said it was the large syringe and I brought it to Dr. Thoms."

" 'Sir John Phillips, recalled, said that the delay was of no significance. Nurse Harden was unwell and had subsequently fainted.

" 'The Coroner: I understand you were personally acquainted with the deceased?

" 'Nurse Harden: Yes.' "

Alleyn laid down the report.

"That's the incident," he said. "It's all perfectly natural, but I smelt high tension among the expert witnesses, whenever it was mentioned."

He waited for a moment and then said slowly:

"That incident would never have come out if it hadn't been for Thoms."

"I noticed that, sir. Mr. Thoms let it out during his evidence and then looked as if he wished he hadn't."

"Yes," said Alleyn dryly.

Fox eyed him cautiously and then went on:

"That girl must have been in a pretty good fatigue—in the light of what we know, I mean. There was this man to whom she'd been writing—the man she'd gone off with, as far as we can tell. She'd reckoned on some sort of permanent understanding, anyway, according to her letter, and when there was nothing doing she'd said she'd like to kill him and—there he was."

"Very dramatic," said Alleyn. "The same line of chat, with a difference, may be applied to Sir John Phillips."

"That's so," admitted Fox. "They may have been in collusion."

"I'm entirely against any sort of speculation until we get the analyst's report, Fox. I have not interviewed any of these people. As you know, I thought it best to start no hares before the inquest. I wanted the inquest to be as colourless as possible. The post-mortem may be a wash-out, in which case we'll want to fade away with the minimum amount of publicity."

"That's right," said Fox heavily.

"We're only noting any points of interest in the evidence that may come in handy for future reference. Exhibit A—Nurse Harden and the anti-gas. Exhibit B—curious behaviour of Nurse Banks while giving evidence. The woman closely resembled a chestnut on the hob. She might have spontaneously combusted at any moment. However, she didn't, more's the pity perhaps, but I think she managed to fill the minds of the jury with strange surmises. It struck me that she hadn't exactly hero-worshipped the late Home Secretary. There was more than a suspicion of a snort in her references to him."

"Bolshie-minded, perhaps," ruminated Fox.

"Dare say. She looks like that."

"He may have carried on with her too."

"Oh, Fox! She does *not* look like that."

"People take very strange fancies sometimes, sir."

"How true that is. No speculations, Foxkin."

"All right, sir, all right. What about Exhibit C?"

"Exhibit C, *In re* above. Heavy restraint of the matron, Sister Marigold, when Banks was mentioned. Marigold seemed to me to seethe with suppressed information. 'Wild horses wouldn't get me to tell, but, my oath, if wild horses could——?' "

"And Sir John himself?"

"*Agitato ma non troppo*, and unnaturally *ppp*. This abbreviation business is insidious. Sir John was so anxious to let everybody know he had prepared the hyoscine injection, wasn't he?"

"Very straightforward of him, I thought," remarked Fox doubtfully.

"Oh," said Alleyn vaguely, "so did I. As honest as the day." Fox regarded him suspiciously.

"Lady O'Callaghan gave her evidence well," he said.

"Admirably. But, oh, lummie, how we did hover on the brink of those letters. I'd warned the coroner, who had, of course, read them and thought they were sufficient grounds for a post-mortem. However, he agreed it was better they should not come out. He was very coy about the whole thing anyway, and would have repressed pints of hyoscine——"

"Hyoscine!" shouted Fox. "Aha—you are thinking of hyoscine!"

"Don't shriek at me like that; I nearly bit my pipe stem in half. I'm not thinking particularly of hyoscine. I was about to remark that I was in deadly fear Lady O'Callaghan would drag in the letters. I'd warned her, advised her, implored her not to, but she's not a Ratsbane for nothing, and you never know."

"And Thoms?"

"Thoms took the line that the whole show was unnecessary, but he gave his evidence well, appeared to have nothing to conceal apart from his regret over divulging the fainting episode, an seemed to resent the slightest criticism of Phillips."

"Yes," Fox agreed, "I noticed that. Roberts took much the same line. That's what I mean about the experts sticking together."

"Oh quite. They wanted to pull together but I'm pretty certain they were not all agreed. I did rather feel that they were uneasy about Nurse Harden's delay over the anti-gas syringe, and that there was something about Nurse Banks that both Sister Marigold and Jane Harden shied away from."

"There were three injections altogether," said Fox thoughtfully. He held up as many short fingers. "The hyoscine, prepared and injected by Phillips; the camphor, prepared and injected by Nurse Banks; and the anti-gas, prepared by Nurse Banks and injected by Mr. Thoms."

"Sounds like a petrol station. Well, there it is. If his tummy turns up a natural, we can forget all about it. If dirty weather sets in, it'll be with a vengeance. Do you like cocktail metaphors?"

"I've been talking to Inspector Boys about the political side," said Fox. "He's got all the Kakaroff crowd taped out and he doesn't think there's much in it."

"Nor do I. Since the Krasinky lot were roped in they've piped down considerably [see *A Man Lay Dead*]. Still, you never know with these people. They may mean business. If that Bill goes through next week, it'll larn 'em. I hope there's no nonsense at the funeral to-morrow. We're making elaborate enough arrangements for burying the poor chap—shutting the stable door with a gold padlock. They might possibly choose the moment to celebrate at the funeral, but, no, I don't think they were in on the murder. I'm inclined to think they would have staged something more spectacular—a suitable echo to the Yugoslavia affair. Hyoscine doesn't sound their cup of tea at all."

"Why hyoscine?" asked Fox with massive innocence.

"You old devil," said Alleyn, "I refuse to discuss the case with you. Go and catch pickpockets."

"Sorry, sir."

"And if anything comes of this P.M. business, you can jolly well deal with Lady O'Callaghan yourself. That makes you blanch. What's the time?"

"Three o'clock, sir. The results of the post-mortem ought to come in fairly soon."

"I suppose so. Our famous pathologist is going to ring me up himself as soon as he has informed the coroner."

Alleyn got up and walked about the room hunching up one shoulder and whistling under his breath. The desk telephone rang. Fox answered it.

"It's a Miss O'Callaghan asking for you," he said stolidly.

"Miss——? Who the devil——? Oh, all right. *Now* what's in the wind, do you suppose?"

"Send her up," said Fox to the telephone. "I'd better push off, sir," he added.

"I suppose you had. This is all very rum—very rum indeed."

Fox departed. Alleyn knocked out his pipe, opened the window, and sat behind the desk. A woman's voice sounded in the passage outside. The door was opened by a police-constable, who said: "Miss O'Callaghan, sir," and withdrew.

Ruth O'Callaghan walked into the room. She appeared to be dressed in a series of unrelated lengths of material. Her eye-glasses were canted over the top angle of her enormous nose. Her handbag and umbrella, wedded by an unhappy confusion of cords and leather thongs, dangled from a gaunt wrist. Her face, exclusive of the nose, was pale. She seemed to be grievously agitated.

Alleyn rose and waited politely.

"Oh!" said Ruth, catching sight of him. "Oh!" She came towards him at a kind of gallop and held out the hand that was encumbered with the umbrella and handbag. Alleyn shook it.

"How do you do?" he murmured.

"So good of you to see me," Ruth began. "I know how busy you must be. The statistics of crime are so appalling. Too kind."

"I am making no arrests this afternoon," said Alleyn gravely.

She gazed at him dubiously and then broke into a sort of whooping laugh.

"Oh, no, no, no," said Ruth. "That's very funny—no, of course, I didn't suppose——" She stopped laughing abruptly and looked disconcertingly lugubrious.

"No," she repeated. "But it *is* kind, all the same, when I expect you think I'm a jolly old nuisance of an interfering woman."

"Do sit down," said Alleyn gently, and pulled forward a chair. Ruth shut up rather like a two-foot rule. He pushed the chair under her and returned to his own. She leant forward, resting her elbows on his desk and gazed earnestly at him.

"Mr. Alleyn," Ruth began, "what is this dreadful, dreadful suspicion about my brother's death?"

"At the moment, Miss O'Callaghan, it can scarcely be called a suspicion."

"I don't understand. I've been talking to my sister-in-law. She said some dreadful things to me—terrible—appalling. She says my brother was——" Ruth drew in her breath noisily and on the crest of the intake uttered the word "murdered."

"Lady O'Callaghan attaches a certain amount of importance to threatening letters which were sent to Sir Derek. You have heard of these letters, I expect."

"You mean from those horrible anarchist people? Of course, I know they behaved very badly, but Derry—my brother, you know—always said they wouldn't do anything, and I'm quite certain he was right. Nobody else could have any reason for wishing him harm." ("She hasn't heard about the other letters, then," thought Alleyn.) "Everybody adored him, simply adored him, dear old boy. Mr. Alleyn, I've come to *beg* you not to go on with the case. The inquest was bad enough, but the other—the—you know what I mean. I can't endure the thought of it. Please—please, Mr. Alleyn——" She fumbled desperately in the bag and produced a colossal handkerchief.

"I'm so sorry," said Alleyn. "I know it's a beastly idea, but just think a little. Does it matter so much what they do to our bodies when we've finished with them? I can't think so. It seems to me that the impulse to shrink from such things is based on a fallacy. Perhaps it is impertinent of me to speak so frankly." Ruth gurgled and shook her head dolefully. "Well then, suppose there was no post-mortem, what about your feelings then? There would always be an unscotched suspicion whenever you thought of your brother."

"He was ill. It was his illness. If only he had followed my advice! Mr. Alleyn, I have a friend, a brilliant young chemist, a rising man. I consulted him about my brother and he—generously and nobly—gave me a wonderful remedy, "Fulvita-volts", that would have cured my brother. I *begged* him to take it. It *would* have cured him; I know it would. My friend assured me of it and he *knows*. He said—" She broke off abruptly and darted a curiously frightened glance at Alleyn. "My brother always laughed at me," she added quickly.

"And he refused to try this 'Fulvitavolts'?"

"Yes—at least—yes, he did. I left the tablets there but, of course—he just laughed. My sister-in-law is not very——" Here Ruth floundered unhappily. "I'm sure he didn't take them."

"I see. People are generally very conservative about medicine."

"Yes, *aren't* they?" agreed Ruth eagerly and then stopped again and blew her nose.

"The lack of interest shown in chemical research must be very discouraging to a young man like your friend," Alleyn went on. "I know a brilliant fellow—only twenty-five—who has already——" He stopped and bent towards her. "I suppose we can't possibly be speaking of the same person?"

68

Ruth beamed at him through her tears.

"Oh, no," she assured him.

"Now, how do you know, Miss O'Callaghan?" said Alleyn gaily. "I'm a very great believer in coincidence. My man is James Graham."

"No, no." She hesitated again, oddly, and then in another burst of confidence: "I'm talking about Harold Sage. Perhaps you've heard of him too? He's getting quite famous. He's—he's practically thirty."

"The name seems to strike a chord," lied Alleyn thoughtfully. The desk telephone rang.

"Will you excuse me?" he asked her, and took off the receiver.

"Hallo? Yes, speaking. Yes. Yes. I see. Thank very much. I'm engaged at the moment, but if I may I'll come round and see you to-morrow? Right." He hung up the receiver. Ruth had just got to her feet.

"I mustn't keep you, Mr. Alleyn. Only before I go—please, please let me beg you to go no further with these investigations. I've—I've got a reason—I mean I'm so sure Derry died naturally. It is all so dreadful. If I could be sure you were satisfied——" She made an ineffectual movement with her hands, a clumsy gesture of entreaty. "Tell me you'll go no further!" begged Ruth.

"I am extremely sorry," said Alleyn formally, "but that would be impossible. The post-mortem has already been held. That message gave me the result."

She stood gaping at him, her mouth half open, her big hands clutching at her bag.

"But what—what is it? What do they say?"

"Your brother died of an overdose of a dangerous drug," said Alleyn.

She stared at him in utter dismay and then, without another word, turned and blundered out of the room.

Alleyn wrote the name 'Harold Sage' in a minute notebook that he carried. Having done so, he stared at it with an air of incredulity, sighed, shut up his book and went to find Fox.

CHAPTER VIII

Hyoscine

Tuesday, the sixteenth. Afternoon.

On the following afternoon, five days after his death, Derek O'Callaghan was buried with a great deal of pomp and ceremony. Alleyn was right about the funeral—there was no demonstration from the late Home Secretary's obscure opponents, and the long procession streamed slowly down Whitehall without disturbance. Meanwhile the inquest had been resumed and concluded. After hearing the pathologist's and the analyst's reports, the jury returned a verdict of murder against "a person or persons unknown". Alleyn had had a few words in private with the pathologist before the inquest opened.

"Well," said the great man, "there wasn't much doubt about the hyoscine. The usual dose is a hundredth to a two-hundredth of a grain. My calculations, based on traces of hyoscine found in the organs, show that more than a quarter of a grain had been given. The minimum lethal dose would be something very much less."

"I see," said Alleyn slowly.

"Did you expect hyoscine, Alleyn?"

"It was on the *tapis*. I wish to heaven you hadn't found it."

"Yes. Unpleasant business."

"Do they ever put hyoscine in patent medicines?"

"Oh, yes. Had Sir Derek taken patent medicines?"

"I don't know. It's possible."

"The dosage would be too small to enter into the picture."

"If he swallowed an entire packet?"

The pathologist shrugged his shoulders. "Would he take an entire packet?" Alleyn did not answer. "I can see you've got

70

something in mind," said the pathologist, who knew him.

"Sir John Phillips injected hyoscine. Suppose O'Callaghan had taken a patent medicine containing the drug?" Alleyn suggested.

"The average injection, as I have said, is about, say, a hundredth of a grain. The amount in patent medicines would be very much less. The two together, even if he had taken quantities of his rot-gut, could scarcely constitute a lethal dose—unless, of course, O'Callaghan had an idiosyncrasy for hyoscine, and even if there was an idiosyncrasy for hyoscine, it wouldn't account for the amount we found. If you want my private opinion, for what it is worth, I consider the man was murdered."

"Thank you for all the trouble you have taken," said Alleyn glumly. "I shan't wait to hear the verdict; it's a foregone conclusion. Fox can grace the court for me. There's one other point. Were you able to find the marks of the injections?"

"Yes."

"How many were there?"

"Three."

"Three. That tallies. Damn!"

"It's not conclusive, Alleyn. There might be a fourth injected where we couldn't see it. Inside the ear, under the hair, or even into the exact spot where one of the others was given."

"I see. Oh, well, I must bustle away and solve the murder."

"Let me know if there's anything further I can do."

"Thank you, I will. Good-bye."

Alleyn went out, changed his mind and stuck his head round the door.

"If I send you a pill or two, will you have them dissected for me?"

"Analysed?"

"If you'd rather. Good-bye."

Alleyn took a taxi to the Brook Street home. He asked a lugubrious individual in a chastened sort of uniform if Sir John Phillips was in the hospital. Sir John had not yet come in. When would he be in? The lugubrious individual was afraid he "reely couldn't say."

"Please find someone who can say," said Alleyn. "And when he's free give Sir John this card."

He was invited to wait in one of those extraordinary drawing-rooms that can only be found in expensive private hospitals in the West End of London. Thick carpet, subfusc curtains of pseudo-empire pattern and gilt-legged chairs combined to disseminate the atmosphere of a mausoleum. Chief Inspector Alleyn and a marble woman whose salient features were picked out embarrassingly in gilt stared coldly at each other. A nurse came in starchily, glanced in doubt at Alleyn, and went out again. A clock, flaunted aloft by a defiant bronze-nude, swung its pendulum industriously to and fro for twenty minutes. A man's voice sounded somewhere and in a moment the door opened and Phillips came in.

He was, as usual, immaculate, a very model for a fashionable surgeon, with his effective ugliness, his eye-glass, his air of professional cleanliness, pointed by the faint reek of ether. Alleyn wondered if the extreme pallor of his face was habitual.

"Inspector Alleyn?" he said. "I am sorry to have kept you waiting."

"Not a bit, sir," said Alleyn. "I must apologise for bothering you, but I felt you would like to know the report of the post-mortem as soon as it came through."

Phillips went back to the door and shut it quietly. His face was turned away from his visitor as he spoke.

"Thank you. I shall be relieved to hear it."

"I'm afraid 'relieved' is scarcely the word."

"No?"

Phillips faced round slowly.

"No," said Alleyn. "They have found strongly marked traces of hyoscine in the organs. He must have had at least a quarter of a grain."

"*A quarter of a grain!*" He moved his eyebrows and his glass fell to the floor. He looked extraordinarily shocked and astonished. "Impossible!" he said sharply. He stooped and picked up his monocle.

"There has been no mistake," said Alleyn quietly.

Phillips glanced at him in silence.

"I beg your pardon, Inspector," he said at last. "Of course, you have made certain of your facts, but—hyoscine—it's incredible."

"You understand that I shall be forced to make exhaustive inquiries."

"I—I suppose so."

"In a case of this sort the police feel more than usually helpless. We must delve into highly technical matters. I will be quite frank with you, Sir John. Sir Derek died of the effects of a lethal dose of hyoscine. Unless it can be proved that he took the drug himself, we are faced with a very serious situation. Naturally I shall have to go into the history of his operation. There are many questions which I should like to put to you. I need not remind you that you are under no compulsion to answer them."

Phillips took his time in replying to this. Then he said courteously:

"Of course, I quite understand. I shall be glad to tell you anything that will help—anxious to do so. I owe it to myself. O'Callaghan came here as my patient. I operated on him. Naturally I shall be one of the possible suspects."

"I hope we shall dispose of your claims to that position very early in the game. Now, first of all—Sir Derek O'Callaghan, as you told us at the inquest, had been given hyoscine."

"Certainly. One-hundredth of a grain was injected prior to the operation."

"Exactly. You approved of this injection, of course?"

"I gave it," said Phillips evenly.

"So you did. I'm afraid I know absolutely nothing about the properties of this drug. Is it always used in cases of peritonitis?"

"It had nothing to do with peritonitis. It is always my practice to give an injection of hyoscine before operating. It reduces the amount of anæsthetic necessary and the patient is more comfortable afterwards."

"It is much more generally used nowadays than, say, twenty years ago?"

"Oh, yes."

"Do you mind telling me just how, and at what stage of the proceedings, it is given? This was not stated specifically at the inquest I think."

"It was given in the anæsthetising-room immediately before the operation and after the patient was under the anæsthetic. A hypodermic syringe was used."

"Prepared, I imagine, by the nurse in charge of the theatre?"

"In this instance, no. I thought this was all perfectly clear, Inspector. I prepared the injection myself."

"Yes, of course—how stupid I am!" Alleyn exclaimed. "That makes it much simpler for me. What exactly did you do? Dip the syringe in a blue bottle and suck up a dram?"

"Not quite." Phillips smiled for the first time and produced a cigarette-case. "Shall we sit down?" he said. "And will you smoke?"

"Do you mind if I have one of my own? Good cigarettes are wasted on me."

They sat on two incredibly uncomfortable chairs under the right elbow of the marble woman.

"As regards the actual solution," said Phillips, "I used a tablet of a hundredth of a grain. This I dissolved in twenty-five minims of distilled water. There was a stock solution of hyoscine in the theatre which I did not use."

"Less reliable or something?"

"It's no doubt perfectly reliable, but hyoscine is a drug that should be used with extreme care. By preparing it myself I am sure of the correct dosage. In most theatres nowadays, it's put out in ampoules. I shall see," added Phillips grimly, "that this procedure is followed here in future."

"In this instance you went through the customary routine?"

"I did."

"Were you alone when you prepared the syringe?"

"There may have been a nurse in the theatre—I don't remember." He paused and then added: "Thoms came in just as I finished."

"Did he go out with you?"

"I really don't know. I rather think he returned to the ante-room a few moments later. I left him in the theatre. I went to the anæsthetic-room and gave the injection."

"Of course, you have no doubt in your own mind about the dosage?"

"I know quite well what you are thinking, Inspector Alleyn. It is a perfectly reasonable suspicion. I am absolutely assured that I dissolved one tablet and one tablet only. I filled the syringe with distilled water, squirted it into a measuring-glass, shook one tablet into my hand, saw that it *was* a single tablet, and dropped it into the glass."

Phillips leant back, looked steadily into Alleyn's eyes, and thrust his hands into his pockets. "I am prepared to swear to that," he said.

"It's perfectly clear, sir," said Alleyn, "and although I had to consider the possibility of a mistake, I realise that even if you had dropped two tablets into the water it would have only meant a dosage of a fiftieth of a grain. Probably the entire contents of the tube would not be a quarter of a grain—the amount estimated."

For the first time Phillips hesitated. "They are packed in tubes

74

of twenty," he said at last, "so an entire tube would contain a fifth of a grain of hyoscine." He felt in his coat pocket and produced a hypodermic case which he handed to Alleyn.

"The actual tube is still in there. I have since used one tablet."

Alleyn opened the case and took out a glass tube completely covered by its paper label. He pulled out the tiny cork and looked in.

"May I?" he asked, and shook out the contents into his hand. There were eighteen tablets.

"That settles it," he said cheerfully. "Do you mind if I take these for analysis? Purely a matter of routine, as one says in crime fiction."

"Do," said Phillips, looking rather bored.

Alleyn took an envelope from his pocket, put the tablets back into the tube, the tube into the envelope, and the envelope into his pocket.

"Thank you so much," he said. "You've been extremely courteous. You've no idea how scared we are of experts at the Yard."

"Indeed?"

"Yes, indeed. This must have been a distressing business for you."

"Very."

"I believe Sir Derek was a personal friend."

"I knew him personally—yes."

"Had you seen much of him recently?"

Phillips did not answer immediately. Then, looking straight in front of him, he said: "What do you call recently?"

"Well—a fortnight or so."

"I called at his house on the Friday evening before the operation."

"A professional call?"

"No."

"Did you think he was heading for a serious illness then?"

"I did not know there was anything the matter with him."

"He did not mention a patent medicine?"

"No," said Phillips sharply. "What is this about patent medicines?"

"Merely a point that arises."

"If there is any question of his taking a drug," said Phillips more cordially, "it should be gone into most thoroughly."

"That is my view," Alleyn answered coolly.

"He may," Phillips went on, "have had an idiosyncrasy for hyoscine and if he had been taking it——"

75

"Exactly."

The two men seemed to have changed positions. It was the surgeon who now made the advances. Alleyn was polite and withdrawn.

"Is there any evidence that O'Callaghan had taken a patent medicine?"

"It's possible."

"Damn fool!" ejaculated Phillips.

"Strange he didn't tell you he was ill on the Friday."

"He—I—we discussed another matter altogether."

"Would you care to tell me what it was?"

"It was purely personal."

"Sir John," said Alleyn mildly, "I think I should let you know at once that I have seen your letter to Sir Derek."

Phillips's head jerked up as though he had come suddenly face to face with a threatening obstacle. He did not speak for perhaps half a minute and then he said very softly:

"Do you enjoy reading other people's private correspondence?"

"About as much as you enjoy glaring into a septic abdomen, I should think," rejoined Alleyn. "It has a technical interest."

"I suppose you've spoken to the butler?"

"Would you like to give me your own explanation of the business?"

"No," said Phillips. "No."

"Speaking unofficially—a thing I am far too prone to do—I am extremely sorry for you, Sir John."

Phillips looked at him.

"Do you know, I think I believe you," he said. "Is there anything else?"

"No, I've kept you quite long enough. Would it be an awful bore for everyone if I had a word with the nurses who attended the case?"

"I don't think they can tell you very much further."

"Probably not, but I think I ought to see them unless they are all heavily engaged in operations."

"The theatre is not in use at the moment. The matron and the nurse who assists her—Nurse Banks—will be free."

"Splendid. What about Sir Derek's personal nurse and the other one from the theatre—Nurse Harden, wasn't it?"

"I will find out," said Phillips. "Do you mind waiting?"

"Not at all," murmured Alleyn with an involuntary glance at

the marble woman. "May I see them one by one—it will be less violently embarrassing for all of us?"

"You do not impress me," rejoined Phillips, "as a person who suffers from shyness, but no doubt you would rather sleuth in secret. You shall see them one by one."

"Thank you."

Alleyn waited only a few minutes after Sir John left him and then the door reopened to admit Sister Marigold in whose countenance gentility, curiosity and resentment were exquisitely reflected.

"How do you do, Matron?" said Alleyn.

"Good afternoon," said Sister Marigold.

"Won't you sit down? Here? Or under the statue?"

"Thank you very much, I'm sure." She sat with a rustle, and eyed the inspector guardedly.

"Perhaps Sir John has told you the report on the post-mortem?" Alleyn suggested.

"It's terrible. Such a loss, as I say, to the country."

"Unthinkable. One of the really strong men in the right party," said Alleyn with low cunning.

"Just what I said when it happened."

"Now look here, Matron, will you take mercy on a wretched ignorant policeman and help me out of the awful fog I'm wallowing in? Here's this man, perhaps the foremost statesman of his time, lying dead with a quarter of a grain of hyoscine inside him, and here am I, an abysmally incompetent layman, with the terrific task before me of finding out how it got there. What the devil am I to do about it, Matron?"

He smiled very charmingly into her competent spectacles. Her very veil seemed to lose starch.

"Well, really," said Sister Marigold, "I'm sure it's all very trying for everybody."

"Exactly. You yourself must have had a great shock."

"Well, I did. Of course, in the ordinary way we nurses become accustomed to the sad side of things. People think us dreadfully hard-hearted sometimes."

"You won't get me to believe that. Of course, this discovery—"

"That's what makes it so dreadful, Mr.—er—I never could have believed it, never. Such a thing has never happened in the whole of my experience. And for it to be after an operation in my own theatre! Nobody could have taken more care. Nothing went

77

wrong."

"Now you've hit the nail right on the head!" exclaimed Alleyn, gazing at her as if she was a sort of sibyl. "I felt assured of that. You know as well as I do, Matron, that Sir Derek was a man with many bitter enemies. I may tell you in confidence that at the Yard we know where to look. We are in close touch with the Secret Service"—he noted with satisfaction the glint of intrigue in her eye—"and we are pretty sure how the land lies. In our midst—in our very midst, Matron—are secret agents, secret societies, powers of evil known to the Yard but unsuspected by the general public. Mercifully so." He stopped short, folded his arms, and wondered how much of this the woman would swallow. Apparently the whole dose.

"Fancy!" breathed Sister Marigold. "Just fancy!"

"Well—that's the position," said Alleyn grandly, throwing himself back in his chair. "But here's my difficulty. Before we can fire point-blank we've got to clear away the other possibilities. Suppose we made an arrest now—what would be the defence? An attempt would be made to throw suspicion on innocent persons, on the very people who fought to save Sir Derek's life, on the surgeon who operated, and on his assistants."

"But that's terrible!"

"Nevertheless it is what would happen. Now to meet that position I must have the actual history of Sir Derek's operation, in all its details, at my fingers' ends. That is why I have laid my cards on the table, Matron, and that is why I have come to you."

Sister Marigold stared at him so long that he wondered nervously if he had been inartistic. However, when she did speak, it was with the greatest air of earnestness.

"I shall consider it my duty," she said, "to give you what help I can."

Alleyn thought it better not to shake hands with her. He merely said with quiet reverence:

"Thank you, Matron, you have made a wise decision. Now to come down to tin tacks. I understand Sir John performed the operation assisted by Mr. Thoms and with Dr. Roberts as anæsthetist. Sir John gave the hyoscine injection and prepared it himself."

"Yes. Sir John always does that. As I always say, he's so conscientious."

"Splendid, isn't it? And Mr Thoms gave the anti-gas injection.

78

Nurse Harden brought it to him, didn't she?"

"Yes, she did. Poor Harden, she was dreadfully upset. Sir Derek was a great friend of her own family, a very old Dorsetshire family, Mr.—er——"

"Really? Strange coincidence. She fainted afterwards, didn't she, poor girl?"

"Yes. But I assure you she did her work all through the op., quite as usual—really." Sister Marigold's voice trailed away doubtfully.

"Someone said something about a delay over the anti-gas injection."

"It was only for a moment. She told me afterwards she was so faint she had to pause before she brought it across."

"Yes, I see. Frightfully bad luck. Nurse Banks gave the camphor injection, didn't she?"

"She did." Sister Marigold's thin lips closed in a whippy line.

"And prepared the serum?"

"That is so."

"I suppose I'll have to see her. Between you and me and the Marble Lady, Matron, she rather alarms me."

"H'm!" said Sister Marigold. "Really? Fancy!"

"Still, it *is* my duty and I *must*. Is she on the premises?"

"Nurse Banks is leaving us to-morrow. I believe she is in the hospital this afternoon."

"Leaving you, is she? Does she frighten you too, Matron?" Sister Marigold pursed her lips.

"She is not a type I care to have nursing for me," she said. "As I say, personal feelings should not interfere with a nurse's work, much less political opinions."

"I *thought* she looked as if she was suffering from High Ideals," Alleyn remarked.

"Call them high ideals! Beastly Bolshevik nonsense," said Sister Marigold vigorously. "She had the impertinence to tell me, in my own theatre, that she would be glad if the patient—" She stopped short and looked extremely uncomfortable. "Not, of course, that she meant anything. Still, as I say——"

"Yes, quite. They'd say anything, some of these people. Of course with those views she'd loathe the very sight of O'Callaghan."

"How she dared!" fumed Sister Marigold.

"Tell me about it," said Alleyn winningly.

After a little hesitation she did.

79

CHAPTER IX

Three Nurses

Tuesday, the sixteenth. Afternoon.

The unbosoming of Sister Marigold was almost an epic. Once the floodgates of her wrath were opened the spate of disclosure flowed turbulently. Alleyn decided that in the Marigold's eye Banks was a murderess. Derek O'Callaghan's nurse had told Sister Marigold of Banks's triumph at the news of his death. The theatre scally had lost her head and told everybody. At first, prompted no doubt by her anxiety to stifle the breath of scandal in her hospital, Sister Marigold had determined to say as little as possible about the unspeakable Banks. Alleyn's hints that Phillips, his assistants, even she herself, would come under suspicion had evidently decided her to speak. She now said that Banks was obviously an agent of Sir Derek's political enemies. Alleyn let her talk and talk, and contrived to remain brilliantly non-committal. He discovered that she had an excellent memory, and, by dint of careful questioning, he arrived at the procession of events during, and immediately before, the operation. It appeared that the only members of the party who had been alone in the theatre were Phillips, herself, Thoms, and possibly one of the nurses. Mr. Thoms, she thought, had come out of the theatre into the anteroom a few moments after Sir John had prepared his syringe. When she had told him everything two or three times over, Alleyn said that he was a brute to keep her so long and could he see the private nurse and the scally. He asked her not to mention the result of the post-mortem. The scally came first. She was alarmed and inclined to shy off his questions, but quietened down presently and stuck to her story of Banks's indecent rejoicing. She said Banks was always dinning

80

Soviet teaching into the other nurses. She added nervously that Banks was a good nurse and would never forget her duty to a patient. She described the impedimenta that were put out on a side table before the operation—a full bottle of hyoscine solution, an ampoule of anti-gas serum, syringes, a bowl of distilled water. She was quite sure the bottle of hyoscine solution had been full. She believed that a small amount had since been used. She hadn't looked at it immediately after the operation. This tallied with information already given by the matron. The scally herself had put all the things away and had cleaned the outsides of all the jars carefully. Matron was so particular. "No use looking for prints on this job," thought Alleyn with a sigh. He thanked her and let her go.

Nurse Graham, O'Callaghan's special, was then sent into the room. She came in quietly, smiled at Alleyn and stood with her hands behind her back waiting. She had blue eyes, set far apart, a wide humorous mouth, slightly prominent teeth and a neat figure. She had an air of repose and efficiency which pleased the inspector.

"Do sit down, won't you?" Alleyn invited her. She sat down comfortably and didn't fidget.

"You nursed Sir Derek, didn't you?" he began.

"Yes."

"How long was it from the time he was admitted until the operation?"

"Nearly an hour, I think. He came in soon after I went on duty at five o'clock. The operation was at a quarter to six."

"Yes. Look here, Nurse Graham, will you tell me the whole story of that hour as though you were writing it down in detail?"

She looked gravely at him for a moment or two.

"I'll try," she said at last. Alleyn took out a notebook and with an uneasy glance at it she began: "Soon after I came on duty a message came up that he was on his way and I was to 'special' him. I met the stretcher, put him to bed, and prepared him for the operation."

"Did you give him an injection of any sort?"

"No. The usual injection of morphia and atropine was not given. Sir John's injection of hyoscine took its place."

"I see. Well, nurse?"

"While that was being done Lady O'Callaghan and Sir Derek's sister arrived and when the preparation was over they went into his room. He was semi-conscious. Am I doing this properly?"

"Admirably. Please go on."

"Well, let me think. I was in the room with them at first. Lady O'Callaghan was very good—quiet, and didn't upset the patient. Miss O'Callaghan was rather distressed. They sat down by the bed. I went out to speak to Sir John. When I came back they were talking together. Sir Derek was lying with his eyes closed, but he opened them for a moment and groaned. I think he was conscious just then and he seemed very uncomfortable. Lady O'Callaghan came out and spoke for a minute to Sir John. Then we all returned and Sir John made an examination. The patient seemed much easier, but I thought that now he was quite unconscious, more deeply so than he had been since he came in. Sir John diagnosed ruptured appendix abscess and offered to get Mr. Somerset Black to operate immediately. Lady O'Callaghan begged him to do it himself and he finally said he would. I took Lady O'Callaghan and Miss O'Callaghan out."

Nurse Graham paused and looked very earnestly at the inspector.

"Was there any further incident before they left the room?" Alleyn asked.

"You mean—? There was something else, but please, Inspector Alleyn, do not attach too much importance to it. The patient, I am sure, did not realise in the least what he said."

"What did he say?"

"He opened his eyes and said "Don't—don't let——" and then relapsed again."

"Did you get any idea of what he was trying to say?"

"It might have been anything."

"At what was he looking?"

"He looked at Sir John, who was nearest the bed."

"How would you describe his look? Appealing? Entreating? What?"

"N-no. He—he seemed frightened. It might have been anything. He looked rather like a patient who had been given a drug—morphia, for instance. It's a kind of frowning stare—I have often noticed it appear when the drug is beginning to take effect."

"And yet you tell me he had not had anything of the sort."

"I gave him nothing," Nurse Graham said.

"There's a curious inflexion in your voice, Nurse. *You* gave him nothing? Now of what are you thinking?"

She moved uneasily and her face became rather pink.

"I have said nothing about this to anybody," she told him. "It seemed to me a dangerous thing to speak of what was—was—not absolute fact."

"Quite right. Don't you think, though, that you should tell me? Nurse Graham, Sir Derek O'Callaghan was murdered." He watched her closely. She seemed both startled and shocked. She gave a quick look as if she hoped she had mistaken what he'd said. After a moment he went on:

"He was given a lethal dose of hyoscine. At least four people come under the possibility of suspicion. The very incident you are shying away from might be the one to save an innocent person. I am too old a hand to jump at asinine conclusions. Do you really think you can do any good by keeping me in the dark?"

"Perhaps not."

"Let me help you. You think, don't you, that someone had given O'Callaghan something—a drug of some sort?"

"It looked like it, and yet it was too soon for a drug to act."

"What happened when you returned to your patient? What did you find?"

"You are—very acute," she said. "When I went back I tidied the room. The patient seemed to be asleep. I lifted his eyelid and he was quite unconscious. The pupil was not contracted. I knew then that he could not have had morphia. Then I saw under a chair by the bed a small piece of white paper. I picked it up and noticed that it had broken pieces of sealing-wax on it. It was certainly not there when Sir Derek was admitted."

"Have you kept it?"

"I—yes, I have. I wondered then if he had been given anything, and when the room was done out I put the paper into a drawer in his dressing-table. It will still be there."

"I'll look at it later on if I may. Who had sat in the chair?"

"Miss O'Callaghan," she said uneasily.

"And Miss O'Callaghan was alone with the patient for—how long? Three minutes? Five minutes?"

"Quite five, I should think."

"Notice anything else? Had he had a drink of water, do you think?"

"The glass on the bedside table had been used."

"You are a model witness. I suppose this glass has also been

83

cleaned? Yes. A hospital is a poor hunting-ground for the likes of me. Now don't worry too much about this. It may be quite beside the point. In any case it would have been criminal to withhold it. Consciousness of having done the right thing brings, I understand, solace to the troubled breast."

"I can't say it does to mine."

"Nonsense. Now will you be very kind and get your scrap of paper for me? Bring Nurse Banks back with you, and don't mention homicide. By the way, what did you think about her reception of the glad tidings—I gather she looked upon them as glad?"

"She's an ass," answered Nurse Graham unexpectedly, "but she's no murderer."

"What did she say exactly?"

"Oh, something out of the Bible about praising the Lord for He hath cast down our enemies."

"Good lack!" apostrophised Alleyn. "What an old—I beg your pardon, Nurse. Ask the lady to come here, will you? And if you hear me scream come in and rescue me. I've no desire to die at the feet of that marble goddess there—who is she, by the way—Anæsthesia?"

"I've no idea, Inspector," said Nurse Graham with a sudden broad smile. She went out briskly and returned in a few minutes to give him a small square of white paper such as chemists use in wrapping up prescriptions. Fragments of red sealing-wax remained on the margins and the creases suggested that it had contained a round box. Alleyn put it in his pocket-book.

"Nurse Banks is waiting," remarked Nurse Graham.

"Loose her," said Alleyn. "Good-bye, Nurse."

"Good-bye, Inspector."

Miss Banks made a somewhat truculent entrance. She refused a chair and stood uncomfortably erect, just inside the door. Alleyn remained politely on his feet.

"Perhaps Nurse Graham has told you of my business here?" he suggested.

"She said something about Scotland Yard," sniffed Banks. "I didn't know what she was talking about."

"I am investigating the circumstances of Sir Derek O'Callaghan's death."

"I said all there was to say about it at that inquest."

Alleyn decided that finesse was not indicated.

"You didn't mention it was murder," he remarked.

For a moment he thought she looked frightened. Then she said woodenly:

"Is it?"

"Yes. What do you think of that?"

"How do you know?"

"The post-mortem revealed indications of at least a quarter of a grain of hyoscine."

"A quarter of a grain!" exclaimed Banks. He was reminded of Phillips. Neither of these two had ejaculated 'Hyoscine!' as one might have expected, but had exclaimed at the amount.

"Wouldn't you have expected that to kill him?" he asked.

"Oh, yes. Mr. Thoms said——" She stopped short.

"What did Mr. Thoms say?"

"Heard him say before the op. that a quarter-grain would be a fatal dose."

"How did the subject arise?"

"Don't remember."

"I understand you prepared and gave the camphor injection and prepared the anti-gas injection."

"Yes. I didn't put hyoscine in either if that's what you're thinking."

"No doubt there will be some means of proving that," said Alleyn smoothly. "I shall have the matter investigated, of course."

"You'd better," snorted Banks.

"Sir John prepared and gave the hyoscine."

"Well, what if he did? Sir John Phillips wouldn't poison his worst enemy in the theatre. Too much the little surgeon."

"I'm glad you think so," said Alleyn mildly.

Banks was silent.

"I hear you look upon the affair as a dispensation of Providence," he added.

"I am an agnostic. I said 'if'."

" 'If?' "

"If I wasn't, I would."

"Oh," said Alleyn. "It's cryptic, but I get you. Can you tell me which members of the party were alone in the theatre before the operation?"

"No, I can't."

"Do try. Do you remember if you were?"

85

"No. Phillips was. Thoms was."

"When?"

"Just before they washed up. We were in the anteroom. Phillips came in first and that little fool followed him."

"Meaning Mr. Thoms?"

"I said so, didn't I?"

"Are you going to hear Nicholas Kakaroff speak to-night?"

This was a shot in the dark. Kakaroff was to address a large meeting of Soviet sympathisers. The Yard would think it worth while to put in an amiable appearance. Nurse Banks threw up her chin and glared at him.

"I shall be proud to be there," she said loudly.

"That's the spirit!" cried Alleyn.

Inspired perhaps by fiery recollections of former meetings, Nurse Banks suddenly came out strong with a speech.

"You may stand there with a smile on your lips," she stormed, "but you won't smile for long. I know your type—the gentleman policeman—the latest development of the capitalist system. You've got where you are by influence while better men do bigger work for a slave's pittance. You'll go, and all others like you, when the Dawn breaks. You think I killed Derek O'Callaghan. I didn't, but I'll tell you this much—I should be proud—proud, do you hear, if I had."

She reeled all this out with remarkable fluency, as though it was a preposterous recitation. Alleyn had a swift picture of her covering her friends' suburban tea-parties with exquisite confusion. Small wonder the other nurses fought shy of her.

"Do you know, Nurse," he said, "until the Dawn does break I rather think I'd pipe down a bit if I were you. Unless you really fancy the martyr's crown, you're talking like a remarkably silly woman. You had as good a chance as anyone else of pumping hyoscine into the deceased. You're now shrieking your motive into my capitalist face. I'm not threatening you. No, you'd better not say anything more at the moment, but when the mantle of Mr. Kakaroff is laid aside you may think it advisable to make a statement. Until then, Nurse Banks, if you'll forgive me the suggestion, I should really pipe down. Will you tell Nurse Harden I'm ready?"

He opened the door for her. She stood for a moment staring above his head. Then she walked to the door, paused, and looked directly at him.

"I'll tell you this much," she said. "Neither Phillips nor Harden did it. Phillips is a conscientious surgeon and Harden is a conscientious nurse. They are hidebound by their professional code, both of them."

With this emphatic assertion she left him. Alleyn screwed his face sideways and opened his notebook. Here, in an incredibly fine and upright hand he wrote "Thoms—conversation about hyoscine," and after a moment's hesitation "P and H—hidebound by their professional code, says the B."

He wrote busily, shut his little book, glanced up and gave a start of surprise. Jane Harden had come in so quietly that he had not heard her. There she stood, her fingers twisted together, staring at the inspector. He had thought at the inquest that she was very good-looking. Now, with the white veil behind it, the extreme pallor of her face was less emphatic. She was beautiful, with that peculiar beauty that covers delicate bone. The contour of the forehead and cheek-bones, the little hollows of the temples, and the fine-drawn arches of the eyes had the quality of a Holbein drawing. The eyes themselves were a very dark grey, the nose absolutely straight, and the mouth, rather too small, with drooping corners, was at once sensuous and obstinate.

"I beg your pardon," said Alleyn; "I did not hear you come in. Please sit down."

He pulled forward the nearest of the preposterous chairs, turning it towards the window. The afternoon had darkened and a chilly sort of gloom masked the ceiling and corners of the room. Jane Harden sat down and clasped the knobs of the chair-arms with long fingers that even the exigencies of nursing had not reddened.

"I expect you know why I'm here?" said Alleyn.

"What was the—is the post-mortem finished?" She spoke quite evenly, but with a kind of breathlessness.

"Yes. He was murdered. Hyoscine."

She seemed to stiffen and become uncannily still.

"So the hunt is up," added Alleyn calmly.

"Hyoscine," she whispered. "Hyoscine. How much?"

"At least a quarter of a grain. Sir John injected a hundredth, he tells me. Therefore someone else gave the patient a little more than a fifth of a grain—six twenty-fifths, to be exact. It may have been more, of course. I don't know if the post-mortem can be relied upon to account for every particle."

"I don't know either," said Jane.

"There are one or two questions I must ask you."

"Yes?"

"I'm afraid this is all very distressing for you. You knew Sir Derek personally, I believe?"

"Yes."

"I'm terribly sorry to have to bother you. Let's get it over as soon as possible. As regards the anti-gas injection. At the close of the operation Sir John or Mr. Thoms asked for it. Sister Marigold told you to get it. You went to a side table, where you found the syringe. Was it ready—prepared for use?"

"Yes."

"At the inquest it appeared that you delayed a little while. Why was this?"

"There were two syringes. I felt faint and could not think, for a moment, which was the right one. Then Banks said: "The large syringe", and I brought it."

"You did not hesitate because you thought there might be something wrong with the large syringe?"

This suggestion seemed to startle her very much. She moved her hands nervously and gave a soft exclamation.

"Oh! No. No—Why should I think that?"

"Nurse Banks prepared this syringe, didn't she?"

"Yes," said Jane.

Alleyn was silent for a minute. He got up and walked across to the window. From where she sat his profile looked black, like a silhouette with blurred edges. He stared out at the darkening roofs. Something about a movement of his shoulders suggested a kind of distaste. He shoved his hands down into his trouser pockets and swung round, facing the room. He looked shadowy, but larger than life against the yellowish window-pane.

"How well did you know Sir Derek?" he asked suddenly. His voice sounded oddly flat in the thickly furnished room.

"Quite well," she said after another pause.

"Intimately?"

"I don't know what you mean."

"Well—did you meet often—as friends, shall I say?"

She stared at his darkened face. Her own, lit by the sallow light from the window, looked thin and secret.

"Sometimes."

"Recently?"

88

"No. I can't see what my acquaintanceship with him has to do with the matter."

"Why did you faint?"

"I was—I wasn't well; I'm run down."

"It had nothing to do with the identity of the patient? It wasn't because Sir Derek was so ill?"

"Naturally that distressed me."

"Have you ever written to him?"

She seemed to shrink back into the chair as though he had actually hurt her.

"You need not answer any of these questions if you think it better not to," he announced. "Still, I shall, of course, go to other people for the information."

"*I* have done nothing to hurt *him*," she said loudly.

"No. But have you ever written to him? That was my question, you know."

She took a long time to answer this. At last she murmured: "Oh yes."

"How often?"

"I don't know——

"Recently?"

"Fairly recently."

"Threatening letters?"

"She moved her head from side to side as though the increasing dusk held a menace.

"No," said Jane.

He saw now that she looked at him with terror in her eyes. It was a glance to which he had become accustomed, but since in his way he was a sensitive man, never quite reconciled.

"I think it would be better," he pronounced slowly, "if you told me the whole story. There is no need, is there, for me to tell you that you are one of the people whom I must take into consideration? Your presence in the operating theatre brings you into the picture. Naturally I want an explanation."

"I should have thought my—distress—would have given you that," she whispered, and in that half-light he saw her pallor change to a painful red. "You see, I loved him," added Jane.

"I think I understand that part of it," he said abruptly. "I am extremely sorry that these beastly circumstances oblige me to pry into such very painful matters. Try to think of me as a sort of automaton, unpleasant but quite impersonal. Can you do that, do you think?"

"I suppose I must try."

"Thank you. First of all—was there anything beyond ordinary friendship between you and O'Callaghan?"

She made a slight movement.

"Not—" She paused and then said: "Not really."

"Were you going to say 'Not now'? I think there had been. You say you wrote to him. Perhaps your letters terminated a phase of your friendship?"

She seemed to consider this and then answered uneasily: "The second did."

He thought: "Two letters. I wonder what happened to the other?"

Aloud, he said: "Now, as I understand it, you had known Sir Derek for some time—an old family friendship. Recently this friendship changed to a more intimate association. When was this?"

"Last June—three months ago."

"And it went on—for how long?"

Her hands moved to her face. As if ashamed of this pitiful gesture she snatched them away, and raising her voice, said clearly: "Three days."

"I see," said Alleyn gently. "Was that the last time you saw him?"

"Yes—until the operation."

"Had there been any quarrel?"

"No."

"None?"

"No." She tilted her head back and began to speak rapidly. "It was a mutual agreement. People make such a fuss about sex. It's only a normal physical experience, like hunger or thirst. The sensible thing is to satisfy it in a perfectly reasonable and natural way. That's what we did. There was no need to meet again. We had had our experience."

"My poor child!" Alleyn ejaculated.

"What do you mean?"

"You reel it all off as if you'd learnt it out of a textbook. 'First Steps in Sex'. 'O Brave New World', as Miranda and Mr. Huxley would say! And it didn't work out according to the receipt?"

"Yes, it did."

"Then why did you write those letters?"

90

Her mouth opened. She looked pitifully ludicrous and, for a moment, not at all pretty.

"You've seen them—you've—"

"I'm afraid so," said Alleyn.

She gave a curious dry sob and put her hands up to the neck of her uniform as though it choked her.

"You see," Alleyn continued, "it would be better to tell me the truth, really it would."

She began to weep very bitterly.

"I can't help it. I'm sorry. It's been so awful—I can't help it."

Alleyn swung round to the light again.

"It's all right," he said to the window-pane. "Don't mind about me—only an automaton, remember."

She seemed to pull herself together quickly. He heard a stifled sob or two and a rustle as if she had made a violent movement of some sort.

"Better," she murmured presently. When he turned back to the room she was sitting there, staring at him, as though there had been no break in their conversation.

"There's not much more," he began—very businesslike and pleasant. "Nobody accuses you of anything. I simply want to check up on the operation. You did not see Sir Derek from June until he was brought into the theatre. Very well. Beyond these two letters you did not communicate with him in any way whatever? All right. Now the only place where you step into the picture is where you fetched the syringe containing the anti-gas concoction. You delayed. You were faint. You are positive you brought the right syringe?"

"Oh, yes. It was much bigger than the others."

"Good enough. I'll look at it presently if I may. Now I understand that the jar, bottle, or pot containing the serum——"

"It was an ampoule," said Jane.

"So it was—and the pipkin, cruse, or pottle containing hyoscine were on the table. Could you, feeling all faint and bothered, have possibly sucked up hyoscine by mistake?"

"But, don't you understand, it was ready!" she said impatiently.

"So I am told, but I've got to make sure, you know. You are positive, for instance, that you didn't squirt out the contents and refill the syringe?"

"Of course—positive." She spoke with more assurance and less agitation than he had expected.

"You remember getting the syringe? You were not so groggy that you did it more or less blindly?"

That seemed to get home. She looked frightened again.

"I—I was very faint, but I *know*, I *know* I made no mistake."

"Right. Anyone watch you?"

He watched her himself, closely. The light was now very dim, but her face was still lit from the window behind him.

"They—may—have. I didn't notice."

"I understand Mr. Thoms complained of the delay. Perhaps he turned to see what you were doing?"

"He's always watching—I beg your pardon; that's got nothing to do with it."

"What were you going to say?"

"Only that Mr. Thoms has rather an offensive trick of staring."

"Did you happen to notice, before the operation, how much of the hyoscine solution there was in the bottle?"

She thought for some time.

"I think it was full," she said.

"Has it been used since?"

"Once, I believe."

"Good."

He moved away from the window briskly, found the light switch and snapped it down. Jane rose to her feet. Her hands shook and her face was a little marked with tears.

"That's all," said Alleyn brightly. "Cheer up, Nurse Harden."

"I'll try."

She hesitated a moment after he had opened the door, looked as if she wanted to say something further, but finally, without another word, left the room.

After she had gone Alleyn stood stock-still and stared at the opposite wall.

At last, catching sight of himself in an ornate mirror, he made a wry face at his own reflection.

"Oh, damn the doings," said Alleyn.

CHAPTER X

Thoms in the Theatre

Tuesday, the sixteenth. Afternoon.

It was Mr. Thoms who took Alleyn into the theatre. After Jane left
him the inspector had wandered into the hall and run into the
plump little surgeon. Alleyn had explained who he was, and
Thoms instantly assumed an expression of intense seriousness that
made him look rather like a clown pulling a mock-tragic face.

"I say!" he exclaimed. "You're not here about Sir Derek
O'Callaghan's business, are you?"

"That's it, Mr. Thoms," Alleyn rejoined wearily. "The man was
murdered."

Thoms began to babble excitedly. Alleyn held up a long hand.

"Hyoscine. At least a quarter of a grain. Wilful murder," he said
briefly.

"Lor'!" ejaculated Thoms.

"Lor' it is. I've been badgering nurses and now I want to see the
theatre of operations. It never struck me till just then what a
localised implication that phrase has."

"See the theatre?" said Thoms. "Yes. Of course. Look here. It's
not in use now. Sir John's gone out. I'll show you round if you
like."

"Thank you so much," said Alleyn.

Thoms talked excitedly as he led the way. "It's the most amazing
thing I ever heard. Damn' nasty business, too. I hope to God you
don't think I pumped hyoscine into the man. Thought you police
chaps must have something up your sleeves when you pushed the
inquest. Yes. Well, here we are. This is an anteroom to the theatre,
where we wash and dress ourselves up for the business. Along

93

there's the anæsthetising-room. Here's the theatre."

He butted open the swing-doors.

"Wait a bit," said Alleyn. "Let's get a sort of picture of the proceedings, may we? Before the operation you and the other medical men foregathered in here."

"That's it. Sir John and I came in here together. Dr Roberts came in for a moment and then went off to the anæsthetising-room, where the patient was brought to him."

"Anyone else in here during that time?"

"With Phillips and me, you mean? Oh, yes—the matron, Sister Marigold, you know. She does theatre sister. It's only a small hospital, and she rather fancies herself at the job, does old Marigold. Then, let me see, the other two nurses were dodging about. Thingummy, the Bolshie one, and that pretty girl that did a faint—Harden."

"What did you all talk about?"

"*Talk* about?" echoed Thoms. He had a curious trick of gaping at the simplest question as though much taken aback. His eyes popped and his mouth fell open. He then gave a short and, to Alleyn, tiresome guffaw. "What did we *talk* about?" he repeated. "Well, let's see. Oh, I asked Sir John if he had seen the show at the Palladium this week and——" He stopped short and again his eyes bolted.

"Well—what about it?" asked Alleyn patiently.

"He said he hadn't," said Thoms. He looked ridiculously uncomfortable, as though he had nearly said something frightfully improper.

"I missed the Palladium this week," Alleyn remarked. "It's particularly good, I hear."

"Oh," Thoms mumbled, "not bad. Rather rot really."

He seemed extraordinarily embarrassed.

"And had Sir John seen the show?" asked Alleyn lightly.

"Er—no, no, he hadn't."

"Did you discuss any particular part of it?"

"No. Only mentioned the show—nothing particular."

There was a long pause during which Thoms whistled under his breath.

"During this time," said Alleyn at last, "was any one member of the theatre party alone?"

"In here?"

"In here."

94

"Let me think," begged Thoms. Alleyn let him think. "No—
no. As far as I remember, we were all here. Then one of the
nurses showed Roberts to the anæsthetising-room. That left Sir
John and the other two nurses and myself. I went with Marigold
into the theatre to look round. That left Sir John and the other
nurse—the pretty one—in this room. They were here when I got
back. Then Roberts and I washed up while Sir John went into the
theatre to fix his hyoscine injection. He always does that and gives
it himself. Rum idea. We usually leave all that game to the
anæsthetist. Of course, in this instance everything had been very
hurried. The patient had not been given the usual morphia and
atropine injection. Well, let's see. The females were dodging
about, I suppose. I remember the—what's-her-name—the Banks
woman asked me why Sir John didn't use the stock solution."

"Why didn't he?"

"Oh—well, because he wanted to be sure of the dosage, I
suppose."

"And then?"

"I went into the theatre."

"Where you joined Phillips?"

"Yes. He'd just put the hyoscine tablet into the water, I think."

"Did you notice the little bottle—how many tablets were left? I
simply want to check up, you understand."

"Of course. Well, it's a tube; you can't see the number of
tablets unless you peer into it, and then you can only guess, but,
of course, there would be nineteen, because it was a new lot."

"How do you know that, Mr Thoms?"

"Well, as a matter of fact, I saw he had two tubes and said
something about it, and he said one of them was empty, so he'd
opened another."

"What happened to the empty one?"

"Eh? Search me. Chucked it away, I suppose. I say—er—look
here, what *is* your name?"

"Alleyn."

"Oh. Well, look here, Alleyn, you're not attaching any
importance to the second tube, are you? Because you jolly well
needn't. It's all perfectly simple. Phillips uses a hypodermic case
which holds two of these little phials. He'd obviously used the last
tablet on a previous case without realising it was the last. Very
easy thing to do."

"I see that. All this business is merely by way of checking up."

"Yes, but——"

"For my own sake I've got to account for every movement of the game, Mr. Thoms. It's all frightfully muddling and I've got to try to learn it like a lesson. Do you remember anything that was said just then?"

"Well,—well, I chaffed him about the two tubes—said he was doing Sir Derek proud, and then I—I remarked that he used a lot of water."

"Did this seem to upset him at all?"

"Oh, Lord—no. I mean, Sir John always stands a bit on his dignity. I mean, he rather shut me up. He hasn't got what I call a sense of humour."

"Really? Did you go out together?"

"Yes. I went into the anteroom and Sir John into the anæsthetic-room to give the injection. I went first."

"Sure, Mr. Thoms?"

"Oh, yes," said Thoms, opening his eyes very wide. "Why?"

"I only want to get the order of events. Now let's look at the theatre, shall we?"

Once again Thoms butted the swing-doors with his compact little stern, and this time Inspector Alleyn followed him through.

The theatre was scrupulously, monstrously immaculate—a place of tiles and chromium and white enamel. Thoms turned on a switch and for a moment an enormous high-powered cluster of lights poured down its truncated conical glare on the blank surface of the table. The theatre instantly became alive and expectant. He snapped it off and in its stead an insignificant wall bracket came to life over a side table on rubber castors.

"Is this how it was for the operation?" asked Alleyn. "Everything in its right place?"

"Er—yes, I think so. Yes."

"Which way did the patient lie?"

"Head here. Eastward position, eh? Ha ha!"

"I see. There would be a trolley alongside the table, perhaps?"

"It would be wheeled away as soon as the patient was taken off it."

"That's the side table, over by the windows, where the syringes were set out?"

"That's it."

"Can you show me just where you all stood at the time each of the injections was given? Wait a bit—I'll make a sort of plan. My

96

memory's hopeless. Damn, where's my pencil?"

Alleyn opened his notebook and produced a small rule from his pocket. He measured the floor space, made a tiny plan and marked the positions of the two tables, and, as Thoms instructed him, those of the surgeons and nurses.

"Sir John would be here, about half-way along the table, isn't it? I stood opposite there. Marigold hovered round here, and the other two moved about a bit."

"Yes. Well, where, as near as you can give it, would they all be for the operation?"

"The surgeons and anæsthetist where I have shown you. Marigold on Sir John's right and the other two somewhere in the background."

"And for the camphor injection?"

"As before, except for the Bolshie, who gave it. She would be here, by the patient's arm, you see."

"Did you watch Nurse Banks give this injection?"

"Don't think so. I wouldn't notice. Probably wouldn't see her hands—they'd be hidden by the little screen across the patient's chest."

"Oh. I'll take a look at that afterwards if I may. Now the anti-gas injection."

"That was after Sir John had sewed him up. I dressed the wound and asked for the serum. I damned that girl to heaps for keeping me waiting—felt rather a brute when she hit the floor two minutes later—what? I stood here, on the inside of the table; Sir John was opposite; Marigold had moved round to my side. Roberts and Banks, if that's her name, were fussing round over the patient, and Roberts kept bleating about the pulse and so on. They were both at the patient's head."

"Wait a bit. I'll fix those positions. Perhaps I'll get you to help me to reconstruct the operation later on. You have no doubts, I suppose, about it being the correct syringe—the one you used, I mean?"

"None. It seemed to be perfectly in order."

"Was there any marked change in the patient's condition after this injection?"

"Roberts is the man to ask about that. My own idea is that he was worried about the patient for some time before I gave the injection. He asked for camphor, remember. Naturally, you'll think, I want to stress that point. Well, Inspector, so I do. I suppose the serum injection is the dangerous corner as far as I'm concerned. Still, I did *not* prepare the syringe and I could hardly palm it and produce another from behind my left ear. Could I? What? Ha ha ha!"

"Let's have a look at it," said Alleyn imperturbably, "and we'll see."

Thoms went to one of the shelves and returned with a syringe at the sight of which the inspector gave a little shout of horror.

"Good God, Mr. Thoms, are you a horse-coper? You don't mean to tell me you jabbed that horror into the poor man? It's the size of a fire extinguisher!"

Thoms stared at him and then roared with laughter. "He didn't feel it. Oh, yes, we plugged it into him. Well, now, I could hardly produce a thing like that by sleight of hand, could I?"

"Heavens, no! Put it away, do; it makes me feel quite sick. A disgusting, an indecent, a revolting implement."

Thoms made a playful pass at the inspector, who seized the syringe and bore it away. He examined it, uttering little noises of disgust.

"This is the type used for the other two injections," explained Thoms, who had been peering into the array of instruments. He showed Alleyn a hypodermic syringe of the sort familiar to the layman.

"Sufficiently alarming, but not so preposterous. This would be the kind of thing Dr. Roberts handled?"

"Yes—or rather, no. Roberts didn't give the camphor injection. The nurse gave it."

"Oh, yes. Is that usual?"

"It's quite in order. Generally speaking, that injection is given by the anæsthetist, but there's nothing in his asking the nurse to give it."

"This needle's a delicate-looking thing. I suppose you never carry a syringe about ready for use?"

"Lord, no! In the theatre, of course, they are laid out all complete."

"Would you mind filling this one for me?"

He gave Thoms a small syringe. The surgeon poured some water into a measuring-glass, inserted the needle and pulled back the piston.

"There you are. If a tablet's used, the usual procedure is to squirt the syringe half full into the glass, dissolve the tablet, and then draw it up again."

"The whole business only takes a few seconds?"

"Well—the tablet has to dissolve. In the case of the serum and the camphor the stuff was there ready."

"Yes, I've got that. May I see the bottle the serum is kept in?"

"It's not kept in a bottle, but in ampoules which hold the exact amount and are then thrown away. There aren't any kicking about in the theatre. I'll beat some up for you to see if you like."

"Very good of you, Mr. Thoms. I'm being a crashing bore, I'm afraid."

Thoms protested his freedom from boredom and fussed away. Alleyn prowled meditatively round the theatre until the fat man returned.

"Here we are," said Thoms cheerfully. "Here are ampoules of oil and camphor. Here's the anti-gas serum and here's the hyoscine solution. All labelled, as you see. Tell you what I'll do: I'll set out the table as it would have been for the op. How will that do you?"

"Splendid!"

"Let's see now—ampoules here, serum there. Here's the bottle of hyoscine solution; thought you'd want to see that too. Old-fashioned idea—it should be in ampoules, but matron's a bit of a dug-out."

"The bottle's nearly full, I see."

"Yes. I believe one injection had been given." Alleyn noted mentally that this tallied with Nurse Harden's and the scally's impression that the bottle had been full before the operation and had since been used once.

"Can anyone have access to this bottle?" asked Alleyn suddenly.

"What? Oh, yes—any of the theatre staff."

"May I have a small amount—I may have to get it tested?"

He produced a tiny bottle from his pocket and Thoms, looking rather intrigued, filled it with the solution.

"There you are. Now—where were we? Oh! Along here, small syringe for the camphor, another small syringe for the hyoscine—they hold twenty-five minims each. That would be the one Sir John would use for his tablet. Now the whopper for the serum. It holds ten c.c.'s."

"Ten c.c.'s?

"That's about a hundred and sixty minims," explained Thoms.

"What's that in gallons?"

Thoms looked at the inspector as if he had uttered something in Chinese and then burst out laughing.

"Not quite as solid as that," he said. "One hundred and sixty minims is equal to two and two-thirds drachms. That any better?"

"Not much," grumbled Alleyn. "The dawn may break later on. I'm talking like Nurse Banks. What's the strength of this hyoscine?"

"Quarter per cent."

"But—what does that mean? They'll have to get someone cleverer than me for this game."

"Cheer up. It's one grain in one point one ounces of water."

"That sounds as though it means something. I must look up those horrid little things at the end of an arithmetic-book. Wait a moment, now. Don't say a word, Mr. Thoms, if you please," begged Alleyn. "I'm doing sums."

He screwed up his face and did complicated things with his fingers. "Twenty-fives into ones, you can't. No, anyway you don't want to. Drat. Wait a bit." He opened his eyes suddenly and began to speak rapidly. "The twenty-five-minim syringe could hold a twentieth of a grain of hyoscine, and the vet's pump could hold eleven thirty-seconds of a grain. There!" he added proudly.

"Quite correct—good for you!" shouted Thoms, clapping the inspector on the back.

"There's more to come. I can do better than that. Eleven thirty-seconds is three thirty-seconds more than a quarter, which is only eight thirty-seconds. How's that?"

"Brilliant, but I don't see the application?"

"Don't you?" asked Alleyn anxiously. "And yet I know I thought it rather important a moment ago. Ah, well—it's gone now. I'll just write the others down."

Mr. Thoms moved to his elbow and looked curiously at his tiny hieroglyphics.

"I can't see," complained Alleyn and walked over to the light.

Mr. Thoms didn't follow and so did not see the last of his minute entries, which read:

"The large syringe could hold a little over the amount found at the P.M."

He shut his little book tenderly and put it in his pocket.

"Thank you a thousand times, Mr. Thoms," he said. "You've made it very easy for me. Now there's only one more person I've got to see to-day and that's Dr. Roberts. Can you tell me where I'll find him?"

"Well, he's not the usual anæsthetist here, you know. He does a lot of Dr. Grey's work for him. Hasn't been in since this affair. I should think at this time you'd find him at his private address. I'll ring up his house if you like."

"That's very good of you. Where does he live?"

"Not sure. His name's Theodore. I know that because I heard Grey calling him Dora. Dora!" Mr. Thoms laughed extensively and led the way to a black hole with a telephone inside it.

He switched on a light and consulted the directory.

"Here we are. Roberts, Roberts, Roberts. Dr. Theodore. Wigmore Street. That's your man."

He dialled the number. Alleyn leant patiently against the door.

"Hallo. Dr. Roberts's house? Is he in? Ask him if he can see Inspector——" He paused and put his hand over the receiver. "Alleyn, isn't it? Yes—ask him if he can see Inspector Alleyn if he comes along now."

Thoms turned towards Alleyn. "He's in—that'll be all right, I expect. Hallo, is that you, Roberts? It's Thoms here. Inspector Alleyn has just been over the O'Callaghan business with me. They've found hyoscine—quarter of a grain. That makes you sit up. What? I don't know. Yes of course it is. Well, don't get all agitated. They're not going to arrest you. Ha ha ha! What! All right—in about twenty minutes, I should think. Look out, my boy—don't give yourself away—what!"

He hung up, and taking Alleyn by the elbow, walked with him to the front door.

"Poor old Roberts is in an awful hum about it, spluttering away down the telephone like I don't know what. Well, let me know if there's anything more I can do."

"I will indeed. Thank you so much. Good night."

"Good night. Got a pair of handcuffs for Roberts? Ha ha ha!"

"Ha ha ha!" said Alleyn. "Good night."

CHAPTER XI

The Anæsthetist

Tuesday, the sixteenth. Afternoon and evening.
Dr. Roberts lived in a nice little house in Wigmore Street. It was a narrow house with two windows on the first floor, and on the street level was a large vermilion front door that occupied a fair proportion of the wall.

A man-servant, small and cheerful to suit the house, showed Alleyn into a pleasant drawing-room-study with apple-green walls and bookshelves, glazed chintz curtains, and comfortable chairs. Above the fireplace hung an excellent painting of lots of little people skating on a lake surrounded by Christmas trees. A wood fire crackled on the hearth. On a table near the bookcase was a sheaf of manuscript weighted down by the old wooden stethoscope that Mr. Thoms had found so funny.

After an appreciative glance at the picture, Alleyn walked over to the bookcase, where he found a beguiling collection of modern novels, a Variorum Shakespeare that aroused his envy, and a number of works on heredity, eugenics and psycho-analysis. Among these was a respectable-looking volume entitled *Debased Currency*, by Theodore Roberts. Alleyn took it out and looked at the contents. They proved to be a series of papers on hereditary taints. Roberts evidently had read them at meetings of the International Congress on Eugenics and Sex Reform.

Alleyn was still absorbed in this evidence of Roberts's industry when the author himself came in.

"Inspector Alleyn, I believe," said Roberts.

With a slight effort Alleyn refrained from answerlng "Dr. Roberts, I presume." He closed the book over his thumb and came forward to meet the anæsthetist. Roberts blinked apprehensively and then glanced at the volume in the inspector's hand.

"Yes, Dr. Roberts," said Alleyn, "you've caught me red-handed. I never can resist plucking from bookshelves and I was so interested to see that you yourself wrote."

"Oh," answered Roberts vaguely, "the subject interests me. Will you sit down, Inspector?"

"Thank you. Yes, the problems of heredity have an extraordinary fascination, even for a layman like myself. However, I haven't come here to air my ignorance of your country, but to try and fill out some of the blanks in my own. About this O'Callaghan business——"

"I am extremely sorry to hear of the result of the autopsy," said Roberts formally. "It is terribly distressing, shocking, an irreplaceable loss." He moved his hands nervously, gulped, and then added hurriedly: "I am also exceedingly distressed for more personal reasons. As anæsthetist for the operation I feel that I may be held responsible, that perhaps I should have noticed earlier that all was not well. I *was* worried, almost from the start, about his condition. I said so to Sir John and to Thoms."

"What did they answer?"

"Sir John was very properly concerned with his own work. He simply left me to deal with mine, after, I think, commenting in some way on my report. I do not remember that Thoms replied at all. Inspector Alleyn, I sincerely hope you are able to free Sir John from any possibility of the slightest breath of suspicion. Any doubt in that direction is quite unthinkable."

"I hope to be able to clear up his part in the business as soon as the usual inquiries have been made. Perhaps you can help me there, Dr. Roberts?"

"I should be glad to do so. I will not attempt to deny that I am also very selfishly nervous on my own account."

"You gave no injection, did you?"

"No. I am thankful to say, no."

"How was that? I should have imagined the anæsthetist would have given the camphor and the hyoscine injections."

Roberts did not speak for a moment, but sat gazing at Alleyn with a curiously helpless expression on his sensitive face. Alleyn noticed that whenever he spoke to Roberts the doctor seemed to suppress a sort of wince. He did this now, tightening his lips and drawing himself rigidly upright in his chair.

"I—I never give injections," he said. "I have a personal and very painful reason for not doing so."

"Would you care to tell me what it is? You see, the fact that you did not give an injection is very important from your point of view. You did not see the patient while he was conscious and so—to be frank—could hardly have poured hyoscine down his throat without someone noticing what you were up to."

"Yes. I see. I will tell you. Many years ago I gave an overdose of morphia and the patient died as the result of my carelessness. I—I have never been able to bring myself to give an injection since. Psychologically my behaviour has been weak and unsound. I should have overcome this repulsion, but I have been unable to do so. For some time I even lost my nerve as an anæsthetist. Then I was called in for an urgent case with heart disease and the operation was successful." He showed Alleyn his stethoscope and told him its history. "This instrument represents an interesting experiment in psychology. I began to mark on it all my successful cases of heart disease. It helped enormously but I have never been able to face an injection. Perhaps some day I may. Sir John is aware of this—peculiarity. I told him of it the first time I gave an anæsthetic for him. It was some time ago in a private house. He very thoughtfully remembered. I believe that in any case he prefers to give the hyoscine injection himself."

He turned very white as he made his unhappy confession, and it was curious to see how, in spite of his obvious distress, he did not lose his trick of formal phraseology.

"Thank you so much, Dr. Roberts," said Alleyn gently. "We need not trouble any more about that. Now, you say you were worried almost from the start about Sir Derek's condition. Would you describe this condition as consistent with hyoscine poisoning?"

"Ever since Thoms rang up I have been considering that point. Yes, I think I should. In the light of the autopsy, of course, one is tempted to correlate the two without further consideration."

"Did you notice any definite change in the patient's condition, or did the same symptoms simply get more and more acute, if that's the right way of putting it?"

"The pulse was remarkably slow when I first examined him in the anæsthetising-room. The condition grew steadily more disquieting throughout the operation."

"But, to stress my point, there was no decided change at any time, only a more or less gradual progression?"

"Yes. There was perhaps a rather marked increase in the symptoms after Sir John made the first incision."

"That would be after he had given the hyoscine injection, wouldn't it?"

Roberts glanced at him sharply.

"Yes, that is true," he said quickly, "but do you not see, the small amount Sir John injected—a hundredth of a grain, I think it was—would naturally aggravate the condition if hyoscine had already been given?"

"That's perfectly true," agreed Alleyn. "It's an important point, too. Look here, Dr. Roberts, may I take it that it's your opinion that hyoscine—a fatal amount—was somehow or other got into the man before the operation?"

"I think so," Roberts blinked nervously. He had that trick of blinking hard, twice—it reminded Alleyn of a highly strung boy. "Of course," he added uneasily, "I realise, Inspector, that it would probably be to my advantage if I said that I thought the lethal dose was given when the patient was on the table. That, however, is, in my opinion, most improbable."

"I must here trot out my customary cliché that it is always to an innocent person's advantage to tell the truth," Alleyn assured him. "Do you know, it's my opinion that at least two-thirds of the difficulties in homicidal cases are caused by innocent asses lying for all they're worth."

"Indeed? I suppose there is no possibility of suicide in this instance?"

"It seems very unlikely so far. Why? How? Where's the motive?"

"There need not necessarily be any usual motive." Roberts hesitated and then spoke with more assurance than he had shown so far. "In suggesting this," he said, "I may be accused of mounting my special hobby-horse. As you have seen I am greatly interested in hereditary taints. In Sir Derek O'Callaghan's family there is such a taint. In his father, Sir Blake O'Callaghan, it appeared. I believe he suffered at times from suicidal mania. There has been a great deal of injudicious inbreeding. Mark you, I am perfectly well aware that the usual whole-hearted condemnation of inbreeding is to be revised in the light——"

He had lost all his nervousness. He lectured Alleyn roundly for ten minutes, getting highly excited. He quoted his own works and other authorities. He scolded the British public in the person of one of their most distinguished policemen for their criminal neglect of racial problems. Alleyn listened, meek and greatly interested. He asked questions. Roberts got books from his shelves, read long passages in a high-pitched voice, and left the volumes on the hearthrug. He told Alleyn he should pay more attention to such things, and finally, to the inspector's secret amusement, asked him flatly if he knew, if he had taken the trouble to find out, whether he himself was free from all traces of hereditary insanity.

"I had a great-aunt who left all her money to a muffin-man with coloured blood," said Alleyn. "She was undoubtedly bats. Otherwise I have nothing to tell you, Dr. Roberts."

Roberts listened to this gravely and continued his harangue. By the time it was over Alleyn felt that he had heard most of the theories propounded at the International Congress on Sex Reform and then some more. They were interrupted by the man-servant, who came in to announce dinner.

"Inspector Alleyn will dine," said Roberts impatiently.

"No—really," said Alleyn. "Thank you so much, but I must go. I'd love to, but I can't." The man went out.

"Why not?" asked Roberts rather huffily.

"Because I've got a murder to solve."

"Oh," he said, rather nonplussed and vexed. Then as this remark sank in, his former manner returned to him. He eyed Alleyn nervously, blinked, and got to his feet.

"I am sorry. I become somewhat absorbed when my pet subject is under discussion."

"I too have been absorbed," Alleyn told him. You must forgive me for staying so long. I may have to reconstruct the operation—perhaps if I do you will be very kind and help me by coming along?"

"I—yes, if it is necessary. It will be very distasteful."

"I know. It may not be necessary, but if it is——"

"I shall do my part, certainly."

"Right, I must bolt. This has been an unpropitious sort of introduction, Dr. Roberts, but I hope I may be allowed to renew our talk without prejudice some time. The average bloke's ignorance of racial problems is deplorable."

"It's worse than that," said Roberts crisply. "It's lamentable—criminal. I should have thought in your profession it was essential to understand at least the rudiments of the hereditary problem. How can you expect——" He scolded on for some time. The servant looked in, cast up his eyes in pious resignation and waited. Roberts gave Alleyn his book. "It's the soundest popular work on the subject, though I do not pretend to cover a fraction of the ground. You'd better come back here when you've read it."

"I will. Thank you a thousand times," murmured the inspector and made for the door. He waited until the servant had gone into the hall and then turned back.

"Look here," he said quietly. "Can I take it you think the man committed suicide?"

Again Roberts turned into a rather frightened little man.

"I can't say—I—sincerely hope so. In view of his history, I think it's quite possible—but, of course, the drug—hyoscine— it's very unusual." He stopped and seemed to think deeply for a moment. Then he gave Alleyn a very earnest and somewhat pathetic look. "I hope very much indeed that it may be found to be suicide," he said quietly. "The alternative is quite unthinkable. It would cast the most terrible slur conceivable upon a profession of which I am an insignificant unit, but which I deeply revere. I would hold myself in part responsible. Self-interest is at the bottom of most motives, they say, but something more than self-interest, I think, prompts me to beg most earnestly that you explore the possibility of suicide to its utmost limit. I have kept you too long. Good night, Inspector Alleyn."

"Good night, Dr. Roberts."

Alleyn walked slowly down Wigmore Street. He reflected that in some ways his last interview had been one of the oddest in his experience. What a curious little man! There had been no affectation in that scientific outburst. The inspector could recognise genuine enthusiasm when he met it. Roberts was in a blue funk over the O'Callaghan business, yet the mere mention of his pet subject could drive any feeling of personal danger clean out of his head. "He's very worried about something, though," thought Alleyn, "and it rather looks as though it's Phillips. Phillips! Damn. I want my Boswell. Also, I want my dinner."

He walked to Frascati's and dined alone, staring so fixedly at the tablecloth that his waiter grew quite nervous about it. Then he rang up Fox and gave him certain instructions, after which he took a taxi to Chester Terrace to call on his Boswell.

"And I suppose the young ass will be out," thought Alleyn bitterly.

But Nigel Bathgate was at home. When the front door opened Alleyn heard the brisk patter of a typewriter. He walked sedately upstairs, pushed open the sitting-room door and looked in. There was Nigel, seated gloomily at his machine, with a pile of copy-paper in a basket beside it.

"Hello, Bathgate," said Alleyn. "Busy?"

Nigel jumped, turned in his chair, and then grinned.

"You!" he said happily. "I'm glad to see you, Inspector. Take a pew."

He pushed forward a comfortable chair and clapped down a cigarette-box on the broad arm. The telephone rang. Nigel cursed and answered it. "Hallo!" A beatific change came over him. "Good evening, darling." Alleyn smiled. "Who do you imagine I've got here? An old friend of yours. Inspector Alleyn. Yes. Why not hop into a taxi and pay us a visit? You will? Splendid. He's probably in difficulties and wants our help. Yes. Right." He hung up the receiver and turned, beaming, to Alleyn.

"It's Angela," he said. Miss Angela North was Nigel's betrothed.

"So I imagined," remarked the inspector. "I shall be delighted to see the minx again."

"She's thrilled at the prospect herself," Nigel declared. He made up the fire, glanced anxiously at his desk and made an effort to tidy it.

"I've just been writing you up," he informed Alleyn.

"What the devil do you mean? What have I got to do with your perverted rag?"

"We're hard up for a story and you've got a certain news value, you know. 'The case is in the hands of Chief Detective-Inspector Roderick Alleyn, the most famous crime expert of the C.I.D. Inspector Alleyn is confident——' Are you confident, by the way?"

"Change it to 'inscrutable'. When I'm boxed I fall back on inscrutability."

"Are you boxed?" asked Nigel. "That, of course, is why you've come to me. What can I do for you, Inspector?"

"You can take that inordinately conceited look off your face and compose it into its customary mould of startled incredulity. I want to talk and I can think of no one who would really like to listen to me. Possibly you yourself are too busy?"

"I've finished, but wait until Angela comes."

"Is she to be trusted? All right, all right."

Nigel spent the next ten minutes telling Alleyn how deeply Miss Angela North was to be trusted. He was still in full swing when the young woman herself arrived. She greeted Alleyn as an old friend, lit a cigarette, sat on the hearth, and said:

"Now—what have you both been talking about?"

"Bathgate has talked about you, Miss Angela. I have not talked."

"But you will. You were going to, and I can guess what about. Pretend I'm not here."

"Can Bathgate manage that?"

"He'll have to."

"I won't look at her," said Nigel.

"You'd better not," said Angela. "Please begin, Inspector Alleyn."

"Speak!" said Nigel.

"I will. List, list, oh list."

"I will."

"Don't keep interrupting. I am engaged on a murder case in which the victim is not a relation of yours, nor yet, as far as I know, is the murderer your friend. In view of our past experiences, this is very striking [see *Enter a Murderer* and *A Man Lay Dead*] and remarkable."

"Come off the rocks. I suppose you mean the O'Callaghan business?"

"I do. The man was murdered. At least three persons assisting at his operation had sufficient motive. Two of them had actually threatened him. No, that is not for publication. No, don't argue. I'll let you know when it is. I have reached that stage in the proceedings when, like heroines in French dramas, I must have my confidante. You are she. You may occasionally roll up your eyes and exclaim "*Hélas, quelle horreur!*" or, if you prefer it, "Merciful Heaven, can I believe my ears?" Otherwise, beyond making sympathetic noises, don't interrupt."

"Right ho."

Alleyn smiled amiably at him.

"You're a patient cove, Bathgate, and I get much too facetious. It's an infirmity—a disease. I do it when I'm bothered and this is a bothering case. Here's the cast of characters, and, look here, the whole conversation is confidential."

"Oh murder!" said Nigel. This was a favourite ejaculation of his. "It hurts, but again—Right you are."

"Thank you. As you know, O'Callaghan either took or was given an overdose of hyoscine. At least a quarter of a grain. He never recovered consciousness after his operation. As far as the experts can tell us, the stuff must have been given within the four hours preceding his death, but I'm not fully informed on that point. Now—*dramatis personae*. You'll know most of them from the inquest. Wife—the ice-maiden type. Knew her husband occasionally kicked over the traces. Too proud to fight. Urged inquest. Sister—rum to a degree and I think has gone goofy on a chemist who supplied her with patent medicines. Urged patent medicines on brother Derek on bedder-sickness in hospital prior to operation. Now very jumpy and nervous. Private secretary—one of the new young men. Semi-diplomatic aroma. All charm and engaging manners. Friend of Mr. Bathgate, so may be murderer. Name, Ronald Jameson. Any comment?"

"Young Ronald? Gosh, yes. I'd forgotten he'd nailed that job. You've described him. He's all right, really."

"I can't bear the little creature," said Angela vigorously. "Sorry!" she added hurriedly.

"Surgeon—Sir John Phillips. Distinguished gent. Friend of victim till victim took his girl away for a week-end and then dropped her. Severed friendship. Visited victim and scolded him. In hearing of butler expressed burning desire to kill victim, who then died. That makes you blanch, I see. Injected hyoscine which he prepared himself. Very unusual in surgeons, but he always does it. No real proof he didn't give overdose. No proof he did. Assistant surgeon—Thoms. Comedian. Solemn warning to Inspector Alleyn not to be facetious. Injected serum with thing like a pump. Was in the theatre alone before operation, but said he wasn't. This may be forgetfulness. Could have doctored serum-pump, but no known reason why he should. Anæsthetist—Dr. Roberts. Funny little man. Writes books about heredity and will talk on same for hours. Good taste in books, pictures and house decoration. Nervous. Very scared when murder is mentioned. In past killed patient with overdose of morphia, so won't give any injections now. Matron of hospital—Sister Marigold. Genteel. Horrified. Could have doctored serum, but imagination boggles at thought. First theatre nurse—Banks, a Bolshie. Expressed delight at death of O'Callaghan, whom she considered enemy of proletariat. Attends meetings held by militant Communists who had threatened O'Callaghan. Gave camphor injection. Second theatre nurse—Jane Harden. Girl friend mentioned above. Spent week-end with deceased and cut up rough when he ended affair. Very good-looking. Threatened deceased in letter. Brought anti-gas syringe to Thoms. Delayed over it. Subsequently fainted. You may well look startled. It's a rich field, isn't it?"

"Is that all—not that it isn't enough?"

"There's his special nurse. A nice sensible girl who could easily have given him poison. She found out about Miss O'Callaghan handing out the patent medicine."

"Perhaps she lied."

"Oh, do you think so? Surely not."

"Don't be facetious," said Nigel.

"Thank you, Bathgate. No, but I don't think Nurse Graham lied. Jane Harden did over her letters. Well, there they all are. Have one of your celebrated lucky dips and see if you can spot the winner."

"For a win," Nigel pronounced at last, "the special nurse. For a place the funny little man."

"Why?"

"Oh, the crime-fiction line of reasoning. The two outsiders. The nurse looks very fishy. And funny little men are rather a favourite line in villains nowadays. He might turn out to be Sir Derek's illegitimate brother and that's why he's so interested in heredity. I'm thinking of writing detective fiction."

"You should do well at it."

"Of course," said Nigel slowly, "there's the other school in which the obvious man is always the murderer. That's the one you favour at the Yard, isn't it?"

"Yes, I suppose it is," agreed Alleyn.

"Do you read crime fiction?"

"I dote on it. It's such a relief to escape from one's work into an entirely different atmosphere."

"It's not as bad as that," Nigel protested.

"Perhaps not quite as bad as that. Any faithful account of police investigations, in even the most spectacular homicide case, would be abysmally dull. I should have thought you'd seen enough of the game to realise that. The files are a plethora of drab details, most of them entirely irrelevant. Your crime novelist gets

111

over all that by writing grandly about routine work and then selecting the essentials. Quite rightly. He'd be the world's worst bore if he did otherwise."

"May I speak?" inquired Angela.

"Do," said Alleyn.

"I'm afraid I guess it's Sir John Phillips."

"I've heard you say yourself that the obvious man is usually the ace," ruminated Nigel after a pause.

"Yes. Usually," said Alleyn.

"I suppose, in this case, the obvious man *is* Phillips."

"That's what old Fox will say," conceded Alleyn with a curious reluctance.

"I suppose it's hopeless to ask, but have you made up your mind yet, Inspector?"

Alleyn got up, walked to the fireplace, and then swung round and stared at his friend.

"I regret to say," he said, "that I haven't the foggiest notion who killed Cock Robin."

CHAPTER XII

The Lenin Hall Lot

Tuesday, the sixteenth. Night.

"Of course," said Angela suddenly, "it may be the matron. I always suspect gentility. Or, of course——" She stopped.

"Yes?" asked Alleyn. "There's still some of the field left."

"I knew you'd say that. But I *do* mistrust people who laugh too much."

Alleyn glanced at her sharply.

"Do you? I must moderate my mirth. Well, there's the case, and I'm glad to have taken it out and aired it. Shall we go to the Palladium?"

"Why!" asked Nigel, astonished.

"There's a sketch on the programme that I am anxious to see. Will you both come? We'll only miss the first two numbers."

"We'd love to," said Angela. "Are you up to one of your tricks?" she added suspiciously.

"I don't know what you mean, Miss Angela. Bathgate, will you ring up for seats?"

They went to the Palladium and enjoyed themselves. Thoms's sketch was the third number in the second half. It had not run three minutes before Nigel and Angela turned and stared owlishly at the inspector. The sketch was well cast and the actor who played the surgeon was particularly clever. Alleyn sensed a strange feeling of alertness in the audience. Here and there people murmured together. Behind them a man's voice asked: "Wonder if Sir John Phillips goes to the Palladium?" "Ssh," whispered a woman.

"The great British public twitching its nose," thought Alleyn

113

distastefully. The sketch drew to a close. The surgeon came back from the operating theatre, realistically bloody. A long-drawn "Ooooo" from the audience. He pulled off his mask, stood and stared at his gloved hands. He shuddered. A nurse entered up-stage. He turned to face her: "Well, Nurse?"

"He's gone." The surgeon walked across to a practical basin and began to wash his hands as a drop curtain, emblazoned with an enormous question-mark, was drawn down like a blind over the scene.

"So that's why we came?" said Angela, and remained very quiet until the end of the show.

They had supper at Alleyn's flat, where Angela was made a fuss of by Vassily.

"Curious coincidence, that little play, didn't you think?" asked Alleyn.

"Very rum," agreed Nigel. "When did you hear about it?"

"Thoms told me that he and Phillips discussed it before the operation. Thoms seemed so anxious not to talk about it I thought it might be worth seeing. I can't help wondering if he meant to convey precisely that suggestion."

"Had Sir John seen it?" inquired Angela.

"No. Thoms told him about it."

"I say," said Nigel. "Do you think that could have given Phillips the big idea?"

"It might be that."

"Or it might be—something quite different," added Angela, watching him.

"I congratulate you, Miss Angela," said Alleyn.

"Did Mr. Thoms tell you quite frankly about their conversation?"

"No, child, he didn't. He flustered like an old hen."

"And what did you deduce from that?" asked Angela innocently.

"Perhaps he was afraid of incriminating his distinguished colleague and senior."

"Oh," she said flatly. "What's he like in other ways?"

"Besides being a bit of a buffoon? Well, I should say either rather forgetful or a bit of a liar. He says he came out of the theatre with Phillips after the latter had prepared the hyoscine injection. Phillips, Matron and Banks say he didn't."

"Oh," said Angela, "they do, do they?"

114

"I haven't the least idea what you're driving at, Angela," complained Nigel. "I should like to hear more about the funny little man. Didn't he behave at all queerly?"

"He behaved very queerly indeed," said Alleyn. "He was as scary as a rabbit whenever the murder was mentioned. He's obviously very frightened whenever he thinks of it. And yet I don't think his alarm is purely selfish. He said it was, I believe. Thoms, in that asinine way of his, made very merry over Roberts's alarm when he rang up."

Alleyn looked steadily at Angela.

"Roberts is the man, depend upon it," pronounced Nigel. "I'll back him with you for a quid."

"I won't," said Angela. "I'll back——"

"I'm afraid the official conscience won't allow me to join in this cold-blooded gamble," said Alleyn. He looked at them both curiously. "The attitude of the intelligent layman is very rum," he observed.

"I lay you two to one the field, bar Roberts, Angela," said Nigel.

"Done," said Angela. "In guineas," she added grandly. "And what were you saying, Inspector?"

"I was only reflecting. Does the decision rest with the judge?"

"What do you mean?"

"Well—if it does, you are betting on a man or woman who, if you're right, will presumably be hanged. I can't imagine you doing this over any other form of death. That's what I mean about the attitude of the layman."

Angela turned red.

"That's the second time in our acquaintanceship you've made me feel a pig," she said. "The first was because I was too sensitive. The bet's off, Nigel."

"You can be pretty cold-blooded yourself, Alleyn," said Nigel indignantly.

"Oh, yes," said Alleyn, "but I'm an official."

"Anyway," argued Angela, "I was betting on Dr. Roberts's innocence."

"So you were."

"And, anyway," said Nigel, "I think he did it."

"How?"

"Er—well—somehow. With an injection."

"He gave no injections."

"Who *could* have done it?" asked Angela. "I mean who had the opportunity?"

"Phillips, who prepared and gave an injection. The special, who was alone with the patient. Ruth, ditto. Banks, who prepared and gave an injection. Thoms gave an injection, but did not prepare it. He was alone in the theatre for a few minutes if Phillips and the matron are telling the truth. He used the big syringe, and as he quite frankly pointed out, he could hardly have palmed another. Jane Harden had time to empty and refill with hyoscine."

"Which of them do you say were alone in the theatre before the operation?"

"All the nurses. Thoms and Phillips had the chance to be there, I suppose."

"Not Roberts?" asked Nigel.

"I think not. He went straight to the anæsthetic-room, where he was joined by the special with the patient."

"Bad luck, darling," said Angela. "It really looks as though he's the only man who couldn't have murdered Sir Derek."

"Then he's a certainty," declared Nigel. "Isn't it true that when there's a cast-iron alibi the police always prick up their ears?"

"Personally, I let mine flop with a thankful purr," said Alleyn. "But you may be right. This is scarcely an alibi. Roberts was there; he merely had no hypodermic to give and no syringe to use."

"And no motive," added Angela.

"Look for the motive," said Nigel.

"I will," said Alleyn. "There's precious little else to look for. Has it occurred to you, if the lethal injection *was* given during the operation, how extraordinarily favourable the *mise en scène* was for the murderer? As soon as a patient is wheeled away they set to work, and as far as I can see, they literally scour out the theatre. Nothing is left—everything is washed, sterilised, polished. The syringes—the dishes—the instruments—the floor—the tables. Even the ampoules that held the injections are cast into outer darkness. If you wanted to think of a perfect place to get rid of your tracks, you couldn't choose a likelier spot." He got up and looked at his watch.

"He wants us to go," remarked Angela calmly.

"It's only eleven o'clock," murmured Alleyn. "I wondered if

you'd both care to do a job of work for me?"

"What sort of job?" they asked.

"Attend a Bolshevik meeting at midnight."

"To-night?"

"I'd adore to," said Angela quickly. "Where is it? What's the time? What do we do?"

"It'll be a bit of copy for you, Bathgate," said Alleyn. "Mr. Nicholas Kakaroff, agent of a certain advanced section of Soviet propagandists, is holding a meeting at Lenin Hall, Saltarrow Street, Blackfriars. Lenin Hall is a converted warehouse. Mr. Kakaroff is a converted minor official, originally from Krakov. I feel sure Kakaroff is a made-up name. 'Kakaroff of Krakov'—it's too good to be really true, don't you feel? There's an air of unreality about his whole gang. As far as we know, they are not officially recognised by Russia or any other self-respecting country. Your genuine Soviet citizen is an honest-to-God sort of chap in his own way, once you get past his prejudices. But these fellows are grotesques—illegitimate offsprings of the I.W.W. You'll see. Nurse Banks attends the meeting. So do we. Myself disguised and feeling silly. Banks might penetrate my disguise, which would not be in the great tradition, so you sit next to her and get her confidence. You have been given your tickets by one Mr. Marcus Barker, who will not be there. He's an English sympathiser at present in custody for selling prohibited literature. He has a bookshop in Long Acre. Don't talk about him; you'd get into a mess if you did. I want you to pump the lady. You are enthusiastic converts. Let her hear that from your conversation together and leave it to her to make friends. If you can do it artistically, rejoice over O'Callaghan's death. Now wait a moment—I want to ring Fox up. Here, read this pamphlet and see if you can get down some of the line of chat."

He looked in his desk, produced a pamphlet bound in a vermilion folder, entitled "The Soviet Movement in Britain, by Marcus Barker." Angela and Nigel sat side by side and began to read it.

Alleyn rang up Fox, who was at the Yard.

"Hallo, Brer Fox. Any news?"

"Hallo, sir. Well, I don't know that I've got anything much for you. Inspector Boys checked up on that heredity business. It seems to be quite O.K. Sir Derek's father was what you might call a bit wanting, very queer old gentleman he seems to have been. There's a great-uncle who fancied he was related to the Royal Family and did himself in in a very peculiar manner with a hedger's knife, and a great-aunt who started some religious affair and had to be shut up over it. She was always undressing herself, it seems."

"Really? What about Ruth?"

"Well, as soon as you rang off I called at Miss O'Callaghan's house to inspect the hot-water cistern and I had a cup of tea with the cook and the housemaid. They were both rather talkative ladies and full of *l'affaire O'Callaghan*," said Fox with one of his excursions into French. "They like Miss O'Callaghan all right, but they think she's a bit eccentric. It seems she was very much attached to her brother and it seems she's very thick with this chemist affair—Mr. Harold Sage. It seems he visits her a great deal. The housemaid gave it as her opinion that they were courting. Miss O'Callaghan takes a lot of his medicines."

"Say it with soda-mints? Anything more?"

"One useful bit of information, sir. Mr. Sage is a Communist."

"The devil he is! Bless me, Fox, that's a plum. Sure?"

"Oh, yes—quite certain, I should say. He's always leaving his literature about. Cook showed me a pamphlet. One of the Marcus Barker lot, it was.

Alleyn glanced through the study door at Nigel and Angela sitting very close together, their heads bent over the vermilion leaflet.

"Did you gather if Miss O'Callaghan sympathised with these views?" he asked.

At the other end of the telephone Fox blew his nose thoughtfully.

"Well, no; it seems not. Nina, that's the housemaid, said she thought the lady was trying to influence him the other way. She gave it as her opinion that Sir Derek would have had a fit if he'd known what was going on."

"Highly probable. You've done a good bit of work there, Fox. What a success you are with the ladies!"

"I'm more at home below-stairs," said Fox simply, "and the cook was a very nice sort of woman, Is that all, sir?"

"Unless you've any more gossip. See you later."

"That's right, sir. *Au revoir*."

"Bung-oh, you old devil."

Alleyn returned to the study and repeated the gist of Fox's

information. "See if you can hear anything of this Sage who is Miss O'Callaghan's soul-mate," he said. "He may be there tonight. Bathgate, I'm just going to change. Won't be five minutes. Ask Vassily to call a taxi and give yourself a drink."

He vanished into his tiny dressing-room, where they heard him whistling very sweetly in a high key.

"Darling," said Nigel, "this is like old times. You and I on the warpath."

"I won't have you getting into trouble," said Angela. "You did last time, you know."

"That was because I was so much in love I couldn't think."

"Indeed? And I suppose that no longer applies?"

"Do you? Do you?"

"Nigel—darling, this is no moment for dalliance."

"Yes, it is."

Alleyn's whistling drifted into the silent room. "Hey, Robin, jolly Robin, tell me how thy lady does," whistled the inspector. In a very short time he was back again, incredibly changed by a dirty chin, a very ill-cut shoddy suit, a cheap-smart overcoat, a cap, a dreadful scarf, and pointed shoes. His hair was combed forward under the cap.

"Oh!" exclaimed Angela, "I can't bear it—you always look so frightfully well turned out and handsome."

To Nigel's amusement Inspector Alleyn turned red in the face, and for the first time in their acquaintance seemed at a loss for an answer.

"Has no one ever told you you are handsome, Inspector?" pursued Angela innocently.

"Fox raves over me," said Alleyn. "What are you standing there for, Bathgate, with that silly grin on your face? Have you ordered the taxi? Have you had a drink?"

Nigel had done neither of these things. However, this was soon remedied and a couple of minutes later they were in a taxi, heading for the Embankment.

"We'll walk the last part of the way," said Alleyn. "Here are your tickets. We got these three with a good deal of difficulty. The brethren are becoming rather exclusive. Now do be careful. Remember *The Times* criticised me for employing Bright Young People in the Frantock case. Repeat your lesson."

They did this, interrupting each other a good deal, but giving the gist of his instructions.

"Right. Now it's only eleven-twenty. We're early, but there will be plenty of people there already. With any luck I'll spot Banks and you may get near her. If not, drift in her direction afterwards. I'll be near the door. As you come out brush up against me, and if you've been shown the Sage, point him out to each other so that I can hear you. See? Good. Here's where we get out, for fear of seeming proud."

He stopped the taxi. They were still down by the river. The air felt chilly and dank, but exciting. The river, busy with its night traffic, had an air of being apart and profoundly absorbed. There were the wet black shadows, broken lights, and the dark, hurried flow of the Thames towards the sea. London's water-world was about its nightly business. The roar of the streets became unimportant and remote down here, within sound of shipping sirens and the cold lap of deep water against stone.

Alleyn hurried them along the Embankment for a short way and then turned off somewhere near Blackfriars Underground Station. They went up a little dark street that resembled a perspective in a woodcut. A single street lamp, haloed in mist, gave accent to shadows as black as printer's ink. Beyond the lamp a flight of stone steps led dramatically downwards. They followed these steps, came out in a narrow alley, took several more turns and fetched up at last by an iron stairway.

"Up you go," said Alleyn. "We've arrived."

The stairs ended in an iron landing which rang coldly under their feet. Here, by a closed door, stood a solitary man, who struck his hands together and blew on his fingers. Alleyn showed him his ticket, which he inspected by the light of an electric torch. Nigel and Angela followed. The man flashed his torch on their faces, a disconcerting business.

"New, aren't you?" he said to Nigel.

"Yes," said Angela quickly, "and terribly excited. Will it be a good meeting?"

"Should be," he answered, and opened the door behind him. They went through and found themselves in a narrow passage lit by a solitary globe at the far end. Under this lamp stood another man, who watched them steadily as they came towards him. Angela took Nigel's arm.

" 'Evening," said Alleyn.

" 'Evening, comrade," said the man self-consciously. "You're early to-night."

"That's right. Many here?"

"Not many yet. Show your tickets, please." He turned to the others. "You newcomers?"

"Yes," said Nigel.

"I'll have to take your names, comrades."

"That's new," remarked Alleyn.

"Instructions from headquarters. We've got to be more careful."

"Just as well. I'm bringing Miss Northgate and Mr. Batherston. Friends of Comrade Marcus Barker." He spelt the names while the man wrote them down. "They come from Clearminster-Storton, Dorset, and are both right-minded."

"Anything doing in your part of the world?" asked the man.

"Gosh, no!" said Nigel. "All landed gentry, bourgeoisie and wage-slaves."

"Bone from the eyes up," added Angela perkily.

The man laughed loudly.

"You've said it! Just sign these cards, will you?"

With an effort they remembered their new names and wrote them at the foot of two pieces of pasteboard that seemed to be inscribed with some sort of profession of secrecy. Angela felt rather guilty. While they did this someone came in at the outside door and walked along the passage. The man took their cards, pulled open the door and turned to the newcomer. Led by Alleyn, they all walked through the door, which immediately was shut behind them.

They found themselves in a large room that still looked like a warehouse. Six office lamps with china shades hung from the ceiling. The walls were unpapered plaster in bad condition. A few Soviet propagandist posters, excellent in design, had been pasted on the walls. The Russian characters looked strange and out of place. At the far end a rough platform had been run up. On the wall behind it was an enlarged photograph of Lenin draped in a grubby festoon of scarlet muslin. There were some thirty people in the room. They stood about in small groups, talking quietly together. One or two had seated themselves among the chairs and benches that faced the platform. Nigel, who prided himself on this sort of thing, tried to place some of them. He thought he detected a possible newsagent, two undergraduates, three Government school teachers, compositors, shopkeepers, a writing bloke or two, and several nondescripts who might be anything from artists to itinerant hawkers. There were one or two women of the student type, but as Alleyn made no sign, Nigel concluded that none of these was Nurse Banks. Evidently the inspector had been to former meetings. He went up to a middle-aged, vehement-looking man with no teeth, who greeted him gloomily and in a little while began to talk very excitedly about the shortcomings of someone called Sage. "He's got no guts," he repeated angrily, "no guts at all."

More people came in at intervals; a few looked like manual labourers, but the majority seemed to belong to that class abhorred of Communists, the bourgeoisie. Nigel and Angela saw Alleyn point them both out to his gloomy friend, who stared morosely at them for a moment and then burst into an offensive guffaw. Presently Alleyn rejoined them.

"My friend has just come in," he said quietly. "She's that tall woman in a red hat."

They looked towards the door and saw the tall woman. Her face, as well as her hat, was red, and was garnished with pince nez and an expression of general truculence. Banks was as formidable out of uniform as she was in it, Alleyn reflected. She glanced round the room and then marched firmly towards the second row of chairs.

"Off you go," murmured Alleyn. "Remember, you come from O'Callaghan's county, but are not of it."

They walked down the centre aisle and seated themselves alongside Nurse Banks.

She produced an uncompromising mass of wool, grey in colour, and began to knit.

"Don't you feel ever so excited, Claude?" asked Angela loudly in a very second-rate voice.

Nigel suppressed a slight start and checked an indignant glance.

"It's a wonderful experience, Pippin," he replied.

He felt Angela quiver.

"I wish I knew who everyone was," she said. "We're so out of touch. These are the people who are really getting things done and we don't know their names. If only Mr. Barker had been here."

"Ye gods, it makes me wild!" apostrophised Nigel. "And they call this a free country. Free!"

Angela, who was next to Banks, dared not look at her. Banks's needles clicked resolutely.

"Do you think," ventured Angela after a pause, "do you think we could ever make any headway down in the dear old village?"

"The dear old village, so quaint and old-world," gibed Nigel. "So typically English, don't you know. No, I don't. The only headway you could make there would be with a charge of dynamite. God, I'd like to see it done!"

"They'll all be in heavy mourning now, of course."

"Yes—for Sir Derek Bloody O'Callaghan."

They both laughed uproariously and then Angela said: "Ssh— be careful," and glanced apprehensively at Banks. She was smiling.

"I wonder if he's here yet?" whispered Angela.

"Who?"

"Kakaroff."

"There's someone going on to the platform now."

"Claude! Can it be he?"

This exclamation sounded so incredible that she instantly regretted it and was infinitely relieved to hear Miss Banks remark in a firm baritone:

"Comrade Kakaroff isn't here yet. That's Comrade Robinson."

"Thanks ever so," said Angela brightly. "We're strangers ourselves and don't know anybody, but we're terribly keen."

Banks smiled.

"You see," continued Angela, "we come from the backwoods of Dorset, where everything died about the time Anne did."

"The counties," said Banks, "are moribund, but in the North there are signs of rebirth."

"That's right!" ejaculated Nigel fervently. "I believe it will come from the North."

"I hope you were not very shocked at what my gentleman-friend said just now about O'Callaghan?" Angela ventured.

"Shocked!" said Banks. "Scarcely!" She laughed shortly.

"Because, you see, we come from the same place as his family and we're about fed to the back teeth with the mere name. It's absolutely feudal—you can't imagine."

"And every election time," said Nigel, "they all trot along like good little kids and vote for dear Sir Derek once again."

"They won't do that any more."

The other seats in their row filled up with a party of people engaged in an earnest and rather bloodthirsty conversation. They paid no attention to anyone but themselves. Nigel continued the

123

approach of Banks.

"What did you think about the inquest?" he asked blandly.

She turned her head slowly and looked at him. "I don't know," she said. "What did you?"

"I thought it rather peculiar myself. Looks as if the police know something. Whoever had the guts to fix O'Callaghan I reckon was a national hero. I don't care who knows it either," said Nigel defiantly.

"You're right," cried Banks, "you're right. You can't heal a dog-bite without a cautery." She produced this professional analogy so slickly that Nigel guessed it was a standardised argument. "All the same," added Banks with a slight change of voice, "I don't believe anyone could, if they would, claim the honour of striking this blow for freedom. It was an accident—a glorious accident."

Her hands trembled and the knitting-needles chattered together. Her eyes were wide open and the pupils dilated.

"Why, she's demented," thought Angela in alarm.

"Hyoscine," murmured Nigel. "Wasn't that the drug Crippen used?"

"I believe it was," said Angela. "Isn't that the same as Twilight Sleep?"

She paused hopefully. Banks made no answer. A young man came and sat in front of them. He looked intelligent and would have been rather a handsome fellow if his blond curls had been shorter and his teeth less aggressively false.

"I don't know," said Nigel; "I'm no chemist. Oh! Talking of chemists, we must see if we can find that chap Harold Sage here. I'd like to meet him."

"Well, it's so difficult. They never said what he was like. Perhaps—er——" Angela turned towards Miss Banks. "Perhaps you could help us. There's a gentleman here who knows a friend of ours." She wondered if this was risky. "His name's Harold Sage. He's a chemist, and we thought if we could see him——"

The young man with the blond curls turned round and flashed a golden smile at her.

"Pardon," he fluted throatily. "That won't be very difficult. May neem's Hawrold Seege."

124

CHAPTER XIII

Surprising Antics of a Chemist

Tuesday to Wednesday. The small hours

To say that Nigel and Angela were flabbergasted by this announcement is to give not the slightest indication of their derangement. Their mouths fell open and their eyes protruded. Their stomachs, as the saying is, turned over. Mr. Sage continued the while to smile falsely upon them. It seemed as if they took at least three minutes to recover. Actually about five seconds elapsed before Angela, in a small voice that she did not recognise, said:

"Oh—fancy! What fun!"

"Oh," echoed Nigel, "fancy! What luck! Yes."

"Yes," said Angela.

"I thought I heard someone taking my name in vain," continued Mr. Sage playfully. It would be tedious to attempt a phonetic reproduction of Mr. Sage's utterances. Enough to say that they were genteel to a fantastic degree.

"Aye thot Aye heeard somewon teeking may neem in veen," may give some idea of his rendering of the above sentence. Let it go at that.

"I was just going to make you known to each other," said Nurse Banks. So great was their dilemma they had actually forgotten Nurse Banks.

Mr. Sage cast a peculiarly reluctant glance upon her and then turned to his quarry. "And who," he asked gaily, "is the mutual friend?"

Frantic alternatives chased each other through Angela's and Nigel's brains. Suppose they risked naming Marcus Barker

125

again—he of the vermilion pamphlet. He had a shop. He was in prison. That was all they knew of Comrade Barker. Suppose——

Nigel drew a deep breath and leant forward.

"It is——" he began.

"Comrades!" shouted a terrific voice. "We will commence by singing the Internationale."

They turned, startled, to the platform. A gigantic bearded man, wearing a Russian blouse, confronted the audience. Comrade Kakaroff had arrived.

The comrades, led by the platform, instantly burst into a deafening rumpus. Nigel and Angela, pink with relief, made grimaces indicative of thwarted communication at Mr. Sage, who made a suitable face in return and then stood to attention and, with a piercing headnote, cut into the Internationale.

When they talked the affair over afterwards with Inspector Alleyn they could not remember one utterance of Comrade Kakaroff during the first half of his speech. He was a large Slav with a beautiful voice and upright hair. That was all they took in. When the beautiful voice rose to an emotional bellow they managed to exchange a panicky whisper.

"Shall we slip away?"

"We *can't*. Not now."

"Afterwards?"

"Yes—perhaps too fishy."

"What do you mean?"

"Ssh! I'm going to——"

"Ssh!"

They glared at each other. To his horror, Nigel saw that Angela was about to get the giggles. He frowned at her majestically and then folded his arms and stared, with an air of interest, at Comrade Kakaroff. This unfortunately struck Angela, who was no doubt hysterical, as being intolerably funny. Her blood ran cold, her heart sank, she was panic-stricken, but she felt she must laugh.

"Shut up," breathed Nigel out of the corner of his mouth. He was foolish enough to kick her. Her chair quivered. She looked round wildly to the four corners of the room. In the fourth corner, between a diagonal vista of rapt faces, she saw someone who watched her. It was the man to whom Alleyn had spoken when they first arrived. Her throat quivered no longer. It went dry. Suddenly nothing seemed funny. Perhaps no one had noticed her. Banks, uttering an occasional "Hear! hear! in a tone of magisterial approval, gazed only at Nicholas Kakaroff. Mr. Sage's back was towards them. Angela was herself again and greatly ashamed. She began to think coherently and presently she formed a plan. Alleyn had talked at some length about Ruth O'Callaghan. He had a vivid trick of description and Angela felt she knew exactly what Miss O'Callaghan was like. Suppose——? She stared like an attentive angel at Comrade Kakaroff and as she stared she made up her mind. As if in echo of her thoughts, she suddenly became aware of his utterances.

"The death of the late Home Secretary—Derek O'Callaghan," boomed Comrade Kakaroff. Jerked out of their unhappy meditation, they began to listen with a will.

"——not for us the sickly sentiment of an effete and decadent civilisation. Not for us the disgusting tears of the wage-slave hypocrite. It was in a good hour that man died. Had he lived he would have worked us great evil. He was struck down with the words of tyranny on his lips. I say it was in a good hour he died. We know it. Let us boldly declare it. He was the enemy of the people, a festering sore that drained the vitality of the proletariat. Listen to me, all of you. If he was deliberately exterminated and I knew the man who had done it, I would greet that man with the outstretched hand of brotherhood. I would hail that man as—Comrade."

He sat down amidst loud noises of encouragement. Mr. Sage had sprung excitedly to his feet.

"Comrade!" he shouted excitedly. It was as if he had touched a spring. The age-old yeast of mob-hysteria was at work. Half of them were on their feet yelling. Miss Banks cast down her knitting and made curious staccato gestures with her hands. "Up the anarchists!" someone screamed behind them. The uproar lasted for some minutes while Kakaroff gazed intently at his work. Then Comrade Robinson walked to the edge of the platform and held up his hands. It was not until the Russian, half contemptuously, had joined him that the din died away.

"Friends," said Kakaroff, "have patience. It will not be for long. In the meantime—be patient. It is with difficulty we manage to hold these meetings. Let us not arouse too much suspicion in the brilliant brains of those uniformed automatons who guard the interests of the capitalist—our wonderful police."

The comrades made merry. Angela distinctly heard the rare

laugh of Inspector Alleyn. The meeting broke up after a brief word from Comrade Robinson about outstanding subscriptions. Mr. Sage, a winning smile upon his face, turned eagerly towards them.

"Magnificent, wasn't it?" he cried.

"Marvellous!"

"Wonderful!"

"And now," continued Mr. Sage, looking admiringly upon Angela, "please tell me—who is our mutual friend?"

"Well, she's not exactly a *close* friend," said Angela, "although we both like her ever so much." She glanced round her and leant forward. Mr. Sage gallantly inclined his curls towards her.

"Miss Ruth O'Callaghan," said Angela, just loud enough for Nigel to hear. He instantly supposed she had gone crazy.

Mr. Sage must have tilted his chair too far backwards, for he suddenly clutched at the air in a very singular manner. His feet shot upwards and the next instant he was decanted over their feet.

"Murder!" ejaculated Nigel, and hurriedly bent over him. Mr. Sage fought him off with great violence, and after a galvanic struggle, regained his feet. "I say," said Angela, remembering her new voice, "I do hope you haven't hurt yourself. I'm ever so sorry."

Mr. Sage gazed at Nigel in silence for some moments. At last he drew in his breath and said: "No, thanks. Aye'm quate O.K."

"But you've gone pale. It was an awful bump you came. Sit down for a moment."

"Thanks," he said, and sank into a chair. "Dear me, that was a very silly thing to do."

"Very painful, I should say," remarked Nigel solemnly.

Suddenly Angela began to laugh.

"Oh," she said, "I'm awfully sorry. It's just horrid of me, but I can't help it."

"Really, An—Pippin!" scolded Nigel.

"The instinct to laugh at bodily injury," said Mr. Sage, who had recovered his colour, "is a very old one. Possibly it goes back to the snarl of the animal about to engage an adversary. You can't help yourself."

"It's nice of you to take it like that," said Angela through her tears. "It was rather a funny introduction."

"Yes."

"I'd better explain," continued Angela. Nigel, who had

128

regarded the upsetting of Mr. Sage as a dispensation of Providence, listened in horror. "We come from Clearminster-Storton in Dorset, near the holy ancestral home of the O'Callaghans. We've no time for the others and let it be known frankly. But she's different, isn't she, Claude?"

"Quite different."

"Yes. We've seen her in London and tried to make her look at things in the enlightened way, and although she's hide-bound by the tradition of her class, she doesn't refuse to listen. She told us about you, Mr. Sage. She thinks you're awfully clever, doesn't she, Claude?"

"That's right," said poor Nigel.

"So that is the way of it?" said Mr. Sage. "I have too attempted to make Miss O'Callaghan think, to open her eyes. She is a customer of mine and is interested in my work. I accept patronage from nobody, mind. She has not offered patronage, but comradeship. I don't really know her well, and——" He paused and then, looking straight at Nigel, he added: "To be frank with you, I have not seen much of her since O'Callaghan introduced his infamous Bill. I felt the situation would be too severe a strain on our friendship. We have never discussed her brother. She knows my views and would understand. Er—quite."

"Oh, quite," murmured Angela.

"Just so," said Nigel.

"As a matter of fact," continued Mr. Sage, "I must own I don't go as far as Comrade Kakaroff in the matter of O'Callaghan's death. Undoubtedly it is well he is gone. I realise that theoretically there is such a thing as justifiable extermination, but murder—as this may have been—no."

"This *was* justifiable extermination," said Nigel fiercely.

"Then it should have been done openly for the Cause."

"No one fancies the rope."

"Claude, you are awful. I agree with Mr. Sage."

"Thank you Miss—er. Pardon, I'm afraid I don't know——"

"Pippin!" exclaimed Nigel suddenly. "We're keeping our pal waiting. He's hanging round outside the door there. Murder! It's half-past one and we swore we'd meet those other chaps before then."

"Ow, gracious, how awful!" said Angela. They grasped Mr. Sage's hand, said hurriedly they hoped they'd meet again, and scuttled away.

The comrades had broken up into groups. Many of them had gone. Nigel and Angela saw Alleyn at the door with his gloomy friend. A short, well-dressed man followed them out, passed them, walked quickly to the outer door, and ran noisily down the iron stairs. Alleyn stood and stared after him. He and the truculent man exchanged a glance.

"Come on," said Alleyn.

As they all walked out Nigel and Angela kept up a rather feverish conversation in their assumed voices. Alleyn was completely silent and so was his friend. Angela felt rather frightened. Did this man suspect them?

"I thought it was a perfectly marvellous meeting," she said loudly as they walked down the empty street.

"Stimulating—that's what it was, stimulating," gushed Nigel.

The man grunted. Alleyn was silent.

"I was so pleased to meet Comrade Sage," continued Angela with an air of the greatest enthusiasm.

"He's all right," conceded Nigel, "but I wouldn't say he was quite sound."

"You mean about O'Callaghan? Oh, I don't know. What did you think about O'Callaghan, comrade?" Angela turned desperately to Alleyn.

"Oh, I'm all for bloodshed," said Alleyn dryly. "Aren't you, comrade?" He turned to his friend.

The man uttered a short sinister laugh. Angela took Nigel's hand. "He was an ulcer," she said confusedly, but with energy. "When we find an ulcer we——we——"

"Poultice it?" suggested Alleyn.

"*Paw onzcorager les autres*," said the man in diabolical French.

"Oh," said Nigel, "not exactly that, comrade——er——?"

"Fox," said Alleyn. "You've met before."

"?!!"

"It's all right, sir," said Inspector Fox soothingly. "It's the removal of my dentures that did it. Rather confusing. You were getting on very nicely. It was quite a treat to listen to you."

"Stimulating—that's what it was, stimulating," added Alleyn.

"Inspector Alleyn," said Angela furiously, "I'll never forgive you for this—never."

"Hist!" said Alleyn. "The very walls have ears."

"Oh!" stormed Angela. "Oh! Oooo! Oh!"

"Murder!" said Nigel very quietly.

130

They walked on in silence until they came out by the river. A taxi drew up alongside them and they got in. Inspector Fox took a cardboard box from his pocket, turned delicately aside, and inserted his plates.

"Begging your pardon, miss," he said, "but it's pleasanter to have them."

"And now," said Alleyn, "just exactly what have you been up to?"

"I won't tell you."

"Won't you, Miss Angela? That's going to make it rather difficult."

"Oh, come on, Angela," said Nigel resignedly. "He'll have to know. Let's come clean."

They came clean. The two policeman listened in silence.

"Yes," said Alleyn when they had finished. "That's all very interesting. It's informative too. Let me get it straight. You say that when you quoted Miss O'Callaghan as your friend—a very dangerous trick, Miss Angela—Sage fell over backwards. Do you think he did this accidentally or deliberately? Do you think he got such a shock he over-balanced and crashed, or did you feel he used this painful ruse to distract your attention? Or were you both acting your socks off so enthusiastically that you did not notice?"

"Certainly not. At least——"

"I think he got a shock," said Nigel.

"Well, yes," agreed Angela, "so do I. But he seemed more upset, oddly enough, afterwards, when he was lying there. His face went pea-green. Oh dear, he *did* look dreadfully funny."

"No doubt. What did you say—did you say anything that would account for this diverting phenomenon?"

"I—no. Nigel said something. We both exclaimed, you know."

"I grabbed hold of him and he fairly fought me off."

"And then, you know, he got up and we asked if he was hurt and he said he was 'quate O.K.' and seemed to get better."

"What was it you said, Bathgate?"

"I dunno. 'Gosh!' or 'Help!' or 'Oh fie!' Something."

"Subsequently he said that he did not altogether respond to Comrade Kakaroff's wave of brotherly love for O'Callaghan's murderer—that it?"

"He seemed to think that was going a bit far."

"And yet"—Alleyn went on—"and yet I seem to remember that at the conclusion of Kakaroff's jolly little talk, Comrade Sage

131

leapt to his feet and yelled 'Comrade'."

"Yes—he did," Nigel agreed, "but he may have been all carried away. He's not a bad little tick, really, I should say, once you've got past his frightful refinement."

"He spoke quite decently about Miss O'Callaghan," added Angela.

"So it appears. Did he and my girl-friend Banks have anything to say to each other?"

"Not a word."

"Well, Fox?"

"Well, sir?"

"I suppose I visit Mr. Sage at his shop to-morrow—oh, Lord, it's to-day, isn't it? What's the time?"

Inspector Fox drew his watch from the inside pocket of the threadbare coat he was wearing. He held it up in a large and filthy paw. "Just on two, I make it," he said. "Listen."

He lowered the window of the taxi. The lost, woe-begone voice of a siren sounded out on the river. Then Big Ben, up in the cold night air, tolled two.

Inspector Fox regarded his watch with grave approval, put it away, and laid his hands on his knees.

"Longing for your bed, Fox?" asked Alleyn.

"I am for mine," said Angela.

"Suppose we let Bathgate take the taxi on, and turn into the office for half an hour?"

"Right ho, sir."

"Here we are."

He tapped on the window and the taxi stopped. The two detectives got out. Their breath hung mistily on the frosty air. Alleyn spoke for a moment to the driver and then looked inside.

"Thank you so much for your help, both of you," he said.

"I say, Alleyn, I hope you don't think we've made awful mugs of ourselves?" said Nigel lugubriously.

Alleyn thought for a moment.

"It was a very spirited effort, I consider," he said at last.

"We shall have to get you both in the Force, sir," added Fox. His matter-of-fact voice sounded oddly remote out there in the cold.

"Ah, Inspector Fox," said Nigel suspiciously, "I've heard you say that before."

"Good night, Comrade Angela," said Alleyn, "sleep well."

"Good night, Inspector; I don't grudge you your joke."

"Bless you," answered Alleyn gently and slammed the door.

The taxi drove off. Farther along the Embankment men were hosing down the street surface. A great fan of water curved out and made all the sound there was except for the siren and the distant toot of the taxi. The two men stared at one another.

"I wonder just how much harm they've done," said Alleyn.

"None at all, sir, I should say."

"I hope you're right. My fault if they have. Come on, let's have a smoke."

In Alleyn's room they lit their pipes. Alleyn wrote at his desk for some time. Fox stared gravely at the opposite wall. They looked a queer couple with their dreadful clothes, grimy faces and blackened hands.

"She seems a very nice young lady," Fox said presently. "Is she Mr Bathgate's fiancée, sir, if I may ask?"

"She is."

"A very pleasant young couple."

Alleyn looked at him affectionately.

"You're a quaint old bag of nonsense." He laid down his pen. "I don't think, really, I took too big a risk with them. The little man was nowhere near them. You recognised him, of course?"

"Oh, yes—from the inquest. I didn't see who it was till he passed us in the doorway, but I'd noticed him earlier in the evening. He had his back towards us."

"Yes, I saw him, too. His clothes were good enough to shine out in that assembly. No attempt made to dress down to comrade level."

"No," said Fox. "Funny—that."

"It's altogether very rum. Passing strange. He walked straight past Sage and Nurse Banks. None of them batted an eyelash."

"That's so. If they are in collusion, it might be deliberate."

"You know, Fox, I can't think this Communist stuff is at the root of it. They're a bogus lot, holding their little meetings, printing little pamphlets, making their spot of trouble. A nuisance from our point of view, but not the stuff that assassins are made of. Of course, given one fanatic——" He stopped and shook his head.

"Well," said Fox, "that's so. They don't amount to much. Perhaps he's different, though. Perhaps he's the fanatic."

"Not that sort, I'd have thought. I'll go and see him again. Tomorrow. To-day. I rather like the bloke. We'll have to get hold of the expert who's doing the Kakaroff bunch and find out if he's deep in. It's been a field day, this. It seems an age since we sat here and waited for the report on the post-mortem. Damn. I feel we are as one about to be had. I feel we are about to give tongue and run off on a false scent. I feel we are about to put two and two together and make a mess."

"That's a pity," said Fox.

"What's the time? Half-past two. Perhaps Bathgate will be back in his own flat by now, having dropped Miss Angela, who looked tired, at her uncle's house. I think I shall send him to bed happy."

He dialled a number on his telephone and waited.

"Hallo, Bathgate. How much are you betting on your funny little man?"

"Roberts?" quacked Nigel's voice clearly.

"Yes, Roberts."

"Two to one, wasn't it? Why? What's up?"

"Did you notice he was at the meeting to-night?"

"Robets!"

"Yes, Roberts. Good night."

He hung up the receiver.

"Come on," he said wearily. "Let's put two and two together and make a mess."

CHAPTER XIV

"Fulvitavolts"

Wednesday, the seventeenth. Morning and afternoon.
The following morning Chief Inspector Alleyn and Inspector Fox
reviewed their discussion.

"The Lenin Hall theory looks even shoddier by the light of
day," said Alleyn.

"Well, sir," said Fox, "I won't say it isn't weak in places, but
we can't ignore the thing, can we?"

"No. I suppose not. No."

"If there's nothing in it, it's a peculiar coincidence. Here's this
lady, deceased's sister——"

"Oh yes, Fox, and by the way, I'm expecting the family
solicitor. Mr. Rattisbon, of Knightley, Knightley and Rattisbon,
an uncle of Lady O'Callaghan's, I believe. Unusually come-toish
advance—rang up and suggested the visit himself. He mentioned
Miss O'Callaghan so guardedly that I can't help feeling she plays a
star part in the will. You were saying?"

"I was going to say here's this lady, deceased's sister, giving
him patent medicines. Here's the Sage affair, the chemist, a
member of the advanced party that threatened deceased, supplying them. Here's the doctor that gave the anæsthetic turning
up at the same meeting as the chemist and the nurse that gave the
injection. The nurse knows the chemist; the chemist, so Mr.
Bathgate says, isn't so keen to know the nurse. The doctor,
seemingly, knows neither of them. Well now, that may be bluff
on the doctor's part. Suppose they were all working in collusion?
Sage wouldn't be very keen on associating himself with Nurse
Banks. Dr. Roberts might think it better to know neither of

them. Suppose Sage had supplied Miss O'Callaghan with a drug containing a certain amount of hyoscine, Nurse Banks had injected a bit more, and Dr. Roberts had made a job of it by injecting the rest?"

"All of them instructed by Comrade Kakaroff?"

"Well—yes."

"But why? Why involve three people when one might do the trick? And anyway, none of them knew O'Callaghan was going to throw a fit and lie-for-dead in the House of Commons and then be taken to Sir John Phillips's nursing-home."

"That's so, certainly, but Sage would know, through Miss O'Callaghan, that her brother intended having Sir John to look at him as soon as the Bill was read. It seems they knew it was appendix. Mightn't they even have said he'd better go to the hospital and have it out? The lady tells Mr. Sage about this. He reports. He and Nurse Banks and Dr. Roberts think they'll form a plan of action."

"And, lo and behold, it all comes to pass even as they had said. I don't like it, Fox. And anyway, my old one, how did Dr. Roberts give the injection with no syringe? Why didn't he take the golden opportunity of exercising his obvious right of giving the hypodermic? To establish his innocence, you will say. He gave it on the sly, all unbeknown. But how? You can't carry a syringe all ready for use, complete with lethal dose, in your trouser pocket. And anyway, his trousers, like all the rest of him, were covered with a white nightie. And he was never alone with the patient."

"That's so, and I admit it's a bit of a facer. Well—perhaps he simply arranged the matter with Miss Banks and she gave the injection, using hyoscine instead of camphor."

"Subsequently letting everyone know how delighted she was at the death. Do you think that was subtlety or stupidity?"

Fox shook his head solemnly.

"I don't say I support the theory, chief, but it *is* a theory."

"Oh, yes. There's another point about the hyoscine. It's kept in a bottle, which Thoms tells me is very out of date—it should be in an ampoule. Phillips, I suppose, doesn't object, as he always uses his own tablets. Now Jane Harden says that the bottle was full and that one injection has since been used. I've checked that. When I saw the bottle it was almost full. Thoms brought it to me."

"Thoms did?" repeated Fox in his slow way.

"Yes. I got a sample and am having it analysed. If anyone has added water, the solution will be below strength."

"Yes—but they might have managed to add more solution."

"I don't see how. Where would they get it from? It would have to be done there and then."

Alleyn got up and walked about the room. "You've never told me your views on intuition," he said.

"I can't say I've got any. No views, I mean—and no intuition either, for a matter of that. Very unimaginitive I've always been. I recollect at school I was a poor hand at writing compositions, as they called them. Still I wouldn't say," said Fox cautiously, "that there is no such thing as intuition. I've known you come out rather strong in that line yourself."

"Thank you, Fox. Well, the weird is upon me now, if that's the expression. By the pricking of my thumbs, something wicked this way comes. I've got a hunch that the Bolshie lot is not one of the principal factors. It's a secondary theme on the bloody cantata. And, yet, blast it, we'll have to follow it up."

"Oh well," Fox rose to his feet. "What's my job of work for to-day, sir?"

"Get hold of Boys or whoever has been watching the comrades and see if Roberts's connection with them can be traced. If there's anything in this we'll have to try and get evidence of collusion. Since the Krasinky-Tokareff affair Sumiloff has had to fade out, but there's Comrade Robinson. He seems to have wormed his way into the foreground. You'd better call him in. We pay the brute enough; let him earn it. Call him in, Fox, and tell him to ferret. He might tell the comrades we've been asking questions and see how they respond. And, talking about ferreting, I've been going through the reports on the medical gentlemen. It's the devil's own game beating it all up and there's a lot more to be done. So far there's nothing very much to excite us." He pulled forward a sheaf of papers. "Here you are. Phillips—Educated at Winchester and Cambridge. Medical training at Thomas's. Brilliant record. Distinguished war service. You can read it. Inspector Allison has spent days on this stuff. Thomas's was full of enthusiasm for one of its brightest boys. No bad marks anywhere. Here's Detective-Sergeant Bailey on Roberts. Educated at home. Delicate child. Medical training at Edinburgh and abroad, in Vienna. After qualifying went to Canada, Australia, and New Zealand, returning to England after war. Red Cross work, during war, in Belgium. Books on heredity—he lent me one and it seems damn' good. I suppose we'll have to go into the history abroad. I'll ring up Toronto to-night. We'll have to check up on that story about the overdose. Talk about routine! How long, O Lord, how long! Thoms—Educated St Bardolph's, Essex, and Guy's. I rang up a friend of mine at Guy's who was his contemporary. Very good assistant surgeon and never likely to get much farther than that. Undistinguished but blameless career, punctuated by mild scandals about women. Little devil! My friend was rather uncomplimentary about Thoms. He called him a 'lecherous little blight.' That's as far as we've got."

The telephone rang and Alleyn answered it.

"It's Mr. Rattisbon. Go down and make much of him, Fox. Bring him up tenderly, treat him with care. If he's anything like the rest of his family, he'll need warming. Use your celebrated charm."

"O.K." said Fox. "*Toojoor la politesse*. I'm on to the third record now, chief, but their peculiar ways of pronunciation give me a lot of trouble. Still, it's a sort of hobby, as you might say."

He sighed and went, returning to usher in Mr. James Rattisbon, of Knightley, Knightley and Rattisbon, uncle to Lady O'Callaghan and solicitor to the deceased 'and his family. Mr. Rattisbon was one of those elderly solicitors whose appearance explains why the expression 'dried-up' is so inevitably applied by novelists to men of law. He was desiccated. He was dressed in clothes of a dated type that looked rather shabby, but were actually in good repair. He wore a winged collar, rather high, and a dark tie, rather narrow. He was discreetly bald, somewhat blind, and a little tremulous. He had a kind of quick shuttering utterance, and a curious trick of thrusting out his pointed tongue and rattling it exceedingly rapidly between his thin lips. This may have served as an antidote to the stutter or it may have signified a kind of professional relish. His hands were bird-like claws with very large purplish veins. It was impossible to picture him in any sort of domestic surroundings.

As soon as the door had been closed behind him he came forward very nimbly and said with incredible speed:

"Chief Detective-Inspector Alleyn?"

"Good morning, sir," said Alleyn. He advanced a chair towards Mr. Rattisbon and offered to take his hat.

"Good morning, good morning," said Mr. Rattisbon.

"Thank—yer, thank—yer. No, thank—yer. Thank—yer."

He clung to his hat and took the chair.

"It's good of you to call. I would have been delighted to save you the trouble by coming to your office. I believe you want to see me about the O'Callaghan business?"

"That is the business—that is the reason—it is in connection with that matter that I have waited upon you, yes," rattled Mr. Rattisbon. He stopped short, darted a glance at Alleyn, and beat a finicky tattoo on the crown of his hat.

"Oh yes," said Alleyn.

"As no doubt you are aware, Inspector Alleyn, I was the late Sir Derek O'Callaghan's solicitor. I am also his sister's, Miss Catherine Ruth O'Callaghan's, solicitor, and of course his wife's—his wife's—ah, solicitor."

Alleyn waited.

"I understand from my clients that certain representations made by Lady O'Callaghan were instrumental in prompting you to take the course you have subsequently adopted."

"Yes."

"Yes. I understand that is the case. Inspector Alleyn, this is not, strictly speaking, a professional call. Lady O'Callaghan is my niece. Naturally I have a personal as well as a professional interest in the matter."

He looked, thought Alleyn, as though he was incapable of any interest that was not professional.

"Of course, sir," said Alleyn.

"My niece did not consult me before she took this step. I must confess that had she done so I should—I should have entertained grave doubts as to the advisability of her action. However, as matters have turned out, she was fully justified. I was of course present at the inquest. Since then I have had several interviews with both these ladies. The last took place yesterday afternoon and was—was of a somewhat disquieting nature."

"Really, sir?"

"Yes. It is a matter of some delicacy. I have hesitated—I have hesitated for some time before making this appointment. I learn that since the inquest Miss O'Callaghan has visited you and has—has suggested that you go no farther with your investigation."

"Miss O'Callaghan," said Alleyn, "was extremely distressed at the idea of the post-mortem."

139

"Quite. Quite so. It is at her request that I have come to see you myself."

"Is it, by Jove!" thought Alleyn.

"Miss O'Callaghan," continued Mr Rattisbon, "fears that in her distress she spoke foolishly. I found it difficult to get from her the actual gist of her conversation, but it seems that she mentioned a young protégé of hers, a Mr. Harold Sage, a promising chemist, she tells me."

"She did speak of a Mr. Sage."

"Yes." Mr. Rattisbon suddenly rubbed his nose very hard and then agitated his tongue. "She appears to think she used somewhat ambiguous phrasing as regards the young man, and she—in short, Inspector, the lady has got it into her head that she may have presented him in a doubtful light. Now I assured her that the police are not to be misled by casual words spoken at a time of emotional stress, but she implored me to come and see you, and though I was disinclined to do so, I could scarcely refuse."

"You were in a difficult position, Mr. Rattisbon."

"I *am* in a difficult position. Inspector Alleyn, I feel it my duty to warn you that Miss Ruth O'Callaghan, though by no means *non compos mentis*, is at the same time subject to what I can only call periods of hysterical enthusiasm and equally hysterical depression. She is a person of singularly naive intelligence. This is not the first occasion on which she has raised an alarm about a matter which subsequently proved to be of no importance whatever. Her imagination is apt to run riot. I think it would not be improper to attribute this idiosyncrasy to an unfortunate strain in her heredity."

"I quite appreciate that," Alleyn assured him. "I know something of this family trait. I believe her father——"

"Quite so. Quite," said Mr. Rattisbon, shooting a shrewd glance at him. "I see you take my point. Now, Inspector Alleyn, the only aspect of the matter that causes me disquietude is the possibility of her calling upon you again, actuated by further rather wild and, I'm afraid, foolish motives. I did think that perhaps it would be well to——"

"To put me wise, sir? I'm grateful to you for having done so. I should in any case have called on you, as I shall be obliged to make certain inquiries as regards the deceased's affairs."

Mr. Rattisbon appeared to tighten all over. He darted another glance at the inspector, took off his glasses, polished them, and in an exceedingly dry voice said:

"Oh, yes."

"We may as well get it over now. We have not yet got the terms of Sir Derek's will. Of course, sir, we shall have to know them."

"Oh, yes."

"Perhaps you will give me this information now. Just the round terms, you know."

It is perfectly true that people more often conform to type than depart from it. Mr. Rattisbon now completed his incredibly classical portrait of the family lawyer by placing together the tips of his fingers. He did this over the top of his bowler. He then regarded Alleyn steadily for about six seconds and said:

"There are four legacies of one thousand pounds each and two of five hundred. The residue is divided between his wife and his sister in the proportion of two-thirds to Lady O'Callaghan and one-third to Miss Catherine Ruth O'Callaghan."

"And the amount of the entire estate? Again in round terms?"

"Eighty-five thousand pounds."

"Thank you so much, Mr. Rattisbon. Perhaps later on I may see the will, but at the moment that is all we want. To whom do the legacies go?"

"To the funds of the Conservative Party, to the London Hospital, to his godchild, Henry Derek Samond, and to the Dorset Benevolent Fund, one thousand in each instance. To Mr. Ronald Jameson, his secretary, five hundred pounds. To be divided among his servants in equal portions of one hundred each, the sum of five hundred pounds."

Alleyn produced his notebook and took this down. Mr. Rattisbon got up.

"I must keep you no longer, Inspector Alleyn. This is an extremely distressing affair. I trust that the police may ultimately—um——"

"I trust so, sir," said Alleyn. He rose and opened the door.

"Oh, thank-yer, thank-yer," ejaculated Mr. Rattisbon. He shot across the room, paused, and darted a final look at Alleyn.

"My nephew tells me you were at school together," he said. "Henry Rattisbon, Lady O'Callaghan's brother."

"I believe we were," answered Alleyn politely.

"Yes. Interesting work here? Like it?"

"It's not a bad job."

"Um? Oh, quite. Well, wish you success," said Mr. Rattisbon, who had suddenly become startlingly human. "And don't let poor Miss Ruth mislead you."

"I'll try not to. Thank you so much, sir."

"Um? Not at all, not at all. Quite the reverse. Good morning. Good morning."

Alleyn closed the door and stood in a sort of trance for some minutes. Then he screwed his face up sideways, as though in doubt, appeared to come to a decision, consulted the telephone directory, and went to call upon Mr. Harold Sage.

Mr. Sage had a chemist's shop in Knightsbridge. Inspector Alleyn walked to Hyde Park Corner and then took a bus. Mr. Sage, behind his counter, served an elderly lady with dog powders designed, no doubt, for a dyspeptic pug which sat and groaned after the manner of his kind at her feet.

"These are our own, madam," said Mr. Sage. "I think you will find they give the little fellow immediate relief."

"I *hope* so," breathed the elderly lady. "And you *really* think there's no need to worry?"

The pug uttered a lamentable groan. Mr. Sage made reassuring noises and tenderly watched them out.

"Yes, sir?" he said briskly, turning to Alleyn.

"Mr. Harold Sage?" asked the inspector.

"Yes," agreed Mr. Sage, a little surprised.

"I'm from Scotland Yard. Inspector Alleyn."

Mr. Sage opened his eyes very wide, but said nothing. He was naturally a pale young man.

"There are one or two questions I should like to ask you, Mr. Sage," continued Alleyn. "Perhaps we could go somewhere a little more private? I shan't keep you more than a minute or two."

"Mr. Brayght," said Mr. Sage loudly.

A sleek youth darted out from behind a pharmaceutical display.

"Serve, please," said Mr. Sage. "Will you just walk this way?" he asked Alleyn and led him down a flight of dark steps into a storeroom which smelt of chemicals. He moved some packages off the only two chairs and stacked them up, very methodically, in a dark corner of the room. Then he turned to Alleyn.

"Will you take a chair?" he asked.

"Thank you. I've called to check up one or two points that have arisen in my department. I think you may be able to help us."

"In what connection?"

"Oh, minor details," said Alleyn vaguely. "Nothing very exciting, I'm afraid. I don't want to take up too much of your time. It's in connection with certain medicines at present on the market. I believe you sell a number of remedies made up from your own prescriptions—such as the pug's powders, for instance?" He smiled genially.

"Oh—quayte," said Mr. Sage.

"You do? Right. Now with reference to a certain prescription which you have made up for a Miss Ruth O'Callaghan."

"Pardon?"

"With reference to a certain prescription you made up for a Miss Ruth O'Callaghan."

"I know the lady you mean. She has been a customer for quite a while."

"Yes. This was one of your own prescriptions?"

"Speaking from memory, I think she has had several of my little lines—from tayme to tayme."

"Yes. Do you remember a drug you supplied three weeks ago?"

"I'm afraid I don't remember off-hand——"

"This is the one that contained hyoscine," said Alleyn. In the long silence that followed Alleyn heard the shop door buzzer go, heard footsteps and voices above his head, heard the sound of the Brompton Road train down beneath them and felt its vibration. He watched Harold Sage. If there was no hyoscine in any of the drugs, the chemist would say so, would protest, would be bewildered. If there was hyoscine, an innocuous amount, he might or might not be flustered. If there was hyoscine, a fatal amount—what would he say?

"Yes," said Mr. Sage.

"What was the name of this medicine?"

" 'Fulvitavolts.' "

"Ah, yes. Do you know if she used it herself or bought it for anyone else?"

"I reely can't say. For herself, I think."

"She did not tell you if she wanted it for her brother?"

"I reely don't remember, not for certain. I think she said something about her brother."

"May I see a packet of this medicine?"

Mr Sage turned to his shelves, ferreted for some time and finally produced an oblong package. Alleyn looked at the spirited picture of a nude gentleman against an electric shock.

"Oh, this is not the one, Mr. Sage," he said brightly. "I mean the stuff in the round box—so big—that you supplied afterwards. This has hyoscine in it as well, has it? What was the other?"

"It was simply a prescription. I—I made it up for Miss O'Callaghan."

"From a doctor's prescription, do you mean?"

"Yes."

"Who was the doctor?"

"I reely forget. The prescription was returned with the powder."

"Have you kept a record?"

"No."

"But surely you have a prescription-book or whatever it is called?"

"I—yes—but—er—an oversight—it should have been entered."

"How much hyoscine was there in this prescription?"

"May I ask," said Mr. Sage, "why you think it contained hyoscine at all?"

"You have made that quite clear yourself. How much?"

"I—think—about one two-hundreth—something very small."

"And in 'Fulvitavolts'?"

"Less. One two-hundred-and-fiftieth."

"Do you know that Sir Derek O'Callaghan was probably murdered?"

"My Gawd, yes."

"Yes ... With hyoscine."

"My Gawd, yes."

"Yes. So you see we want to be sure of our facts."

"He 'ad no hoverdose of 'yoscine from 'ere," said Mr. Sage, incontinently casting his aitches all over the place.

"So it seems. But, you see, if he had taken hyoscine in the minutest quantity before the operation we want to trace it as closely as possible. If Miss O'Callaghan gave him 'Fulvitavolts' and this other medicine, that would account for some of the hyoscine found at the post-mortem. Hyoscine was also injected at the operation. That would account for more."

"You passed the remark that he was murdered," said Mr. Sage more collectedly.

"The coroner did," corrected Alleyn. "Still, we've got to explore the possibility of accident. If you could give me the name

144

of the doctor who prescribed the powder, it would be a great help."

"I can't remember. I make up hundreds of prescriptions every week."

"Do you often forget to enter them?"

Mr. Sage was silent.

Alleyn took out a pencil and an envelope. On the envelope he wrote three names.

"Was it any of those?" he asked.

"No."

"Will you swear to that?"

"Yes. Yes, I would."

"Look here, Mr. Sage, are you sure it wasn't your own prescription that you gave Miss O'Callaghan?"

" 'Fulvitavolts' is my own invention. I told you that."

"But the other?"

"No, I tell you—no."

"Very well. Are you in sympathy with Comrade Kakaroff over the death of Sir Derek O'Callaghan?"

Mr. Sage opened his mouth and shut it again. He put his hands behind him and leant against a shelf.

"To what do you refer?" he said.

"You were at the meeting last night."

"I don't hold with the remarks passed at the meeting. I never 'ave. I've said so. I said so last night."

"Right. I don't think there's anything else."

Alleyn put the packet of 'Fulvitavolts' in his pocket.

"How much are these?"

"Three and nine."

Alleyn produced two half-crowns and handed them to Mr. Sage, who, without another word, walked out of the room and upstairs to the shop. Alleyn followed. Mr. Sage punched the cash register and conjured up the change. The sleek young man leant with an encouraging smile towards an incoming customer.

"Thank you very much, sir," said Mr. Sage, handing Alleyn one and threepence.

"Thank you. Good morning."

"Good morning, sir."

Alleyn went to the nearest telephone-booth and rang up the Yard.

"Anything come in for me?"

"Just a moment, sir ... Yes. Sir John Phillips is here and wants to see you."

"Oh. Is he in my room?"

"Yes."

"Ask him to speak to me, will you?"

A pause.

"Hallo."

"Hallo. Is that Sir John Phillips?"

"Yes. Inspector Alleyn—I want to see you. I want to make a clean breast of it."

"I'll be there in ten minutes," said Alleyn.

CHAPTER XV

The "Clean Breast" of Sir John Phillips

Wednesday to Thursday.

Phillips stared at Chief Inspector Alleyn's locked desk, at his chair, at the pattern of thick yellow sunlight on the floor of his room. He looked again at his watch. Ten minutes since Alleyn had rung up. He said he would be there in ten minutes. Phillips knew what he was going to say. There was no need to go over that again. He went over it again. A light footstep in the passage outside. The door handle turned. Alleyn came in.

"Good morning, sir," he said. "I'm afraid I've kept you waiting." He hung up his hat, pulled off his gloves and sat down at his desk. Phillips watched him without speaking. Alleyn unlocked the desk and then turned towards his visitor.

"What is it you want to tell me, Sir John?"

"I've come to make a statement. I'll write it down afterwards if you like. Sign it. That's what you have to do, isn't it?"

"Suppose I hear what it's all about first," suggested Alleyn.

"Ever since you went away yesterday I've been thinking about this case. It seems to me I must be suspected of the murder. It seems to me things look very black for me. You know what I wrote to O'Callaghan. You know I injected a lethal drug. I showed you the tablets—analysis will prove they only contain the normal dosage, but I can't prove the one I gave was the same as the ones you analysed. I can't prove I only gave one tablet. Can I?"

"So far as I know, you can't."

"I've thought of all that. I didn't kill O'Callaghan. I threatened to kill him. You've seen Thoms. Thoms is a decent little ass, but I can see he thinks you suspect me. He's probably told you I used a lot of water for the injection and then bit his head off because he said so. So I did. He drove me nearly crazy with his bloody facetiousness. Jane—Nurse Harden—told me what you'd said to her. You know a hell of a lot—I can see that. You possibly know what I'm going to tell you. I want her to marry me. She won't, because of the other business with O'Callaghan. I think she believes I killed him. I think she was afraid at the time. That's why she was so upset, why she hesitated over the serum, why she fainted. She was afraid I'd kill O'Callaghan. She heard Thoms tell me about that play. D'you know about the play?"

"Thoms mentioned that you discussed it."

"Silly ass. He's an intelligent surgeon, but in other matters he's got as much *savoir-faire* as a child. He'd swear his soul away I didn't do it and then blurt out something like that. What I want to make clear to you is this. Jane Harden's distress in the theatre was on my account. She thinks I murdered O'Callaghan. I know she does, because she won't ask me. Don't, for God's sake, put any other interpretation on it. She's got a preposterous idea that she's ruined my life. Her nerves are all to blazes. She's anaemic and she's hysterical. If you arrest me, she may come forward with some damn' statement calculated to drag a red herring across my trail. She's an idealist. It's a type I don't pretend to understand. She did nothing to the syringe containing the serum. When Thoms cursed her for delaying, I turned and looked at her. She simply stood there dazed and half fainting. She's as innocent as— I was going to say as I am, but that may not carry much weight. She's completely innocent."

He stopped abruptly. To Alleyn it had seemed a most remarkable little scene. The change in Phillips's manner alone was extraordinary. The smooth, guarded courtesy which had characterised it during their former interview had vanished completely. He had spoken rapidly, as if urged by some appalling necessity. He now sat glaring at Alleyn with a hint of resigned ferociousness.

"Is that all you came to tell me, Sir John?" asked Alleyn in his most non-committal voice.

"All? What do you mean?"

"Well, you see, you prepared me for a bombshell, I wondered what on earth was coming. You talked of making a clean breast of it, but, forgive me, you've told me little that we did not already know."

148

Phillips took his time over answering this. At last he said:
"I suppose that's true. Look here, Alleyn. Can you give me
your assurance that you entertain no suspicions as regards Jane
Harden?"

"I'm afraid I can't. I shall consider everything you have told me
very carefully, but I cannot, at this stage, make a definite
announcement of that sort. Miss Harden is in a very equivocal
position. I hope she may be cleared, but I cannot put her aside
simply because, to put it baldly, you tell me she is innocent."

Phillips was silent. After a moment he clasped his well-shaped,
well-kept hands together, and looking at them attentively, began
to speak again.

"There's something more. Has Thoms told you that I opened a
new tube of tablets for the hyoscine injection?"

Alleyn did not move, but he seemed to come to attention.
"Oh yes," he said quietly.

"He has! Lord, what an ingenuous little creature it is! Did you
attach any significance to this second tube?"

"I remembered it."

"Then listen. During the week before the operation I'd been
pretty well at the end of my tether. I suppose when a man of my
age gets it, he gets it badly—the psychologists say so—and—well,
I could think of nothing but the ghastly position we were in—
Jane and I. That Friday when I went to see O'Callaghan I was
nearly driven crazy by his damned insufferable complacence. I
could have murdered him then. I wasn't sleeping. I tried alcohol
and I tried hypnotics. I was in a bad way, Alleyn. Then on top of
it he came in, a sick man, and I had to operate. Thoms rubbed it
in with his damn-fool story of some play or other. I scarcely knew
what I did. I seemed to behave like an automaton." He stopped
short and raised his eyes from the contemplation of his hands.
"It's possible," he said, "that I may have made a mistake over the
first tube. It may not have been empty."

"Even if the tube had been full," suggested Alleyn, "would that
explain how the tablets got into the measure-glass?"

"I ... what do you say?"

"You say that the first tube may not have been empty, and you
wish me to infer from this that you are responsible for Sir Derek's
death?"

"I ... I ... That is my suggestion," stammered Phillips.

"Deliberately responsible or accidentally?"

149

"I am not a murderer," said Phillips angrily.

"Then how did the tablets get into the measure-glass?"

Phillips was silent.

The inspector waited for a moment and then, with an unusual inflexion in his deep voice, he said:

"So you don't understand the idealistic type?"

"What! No!"

"I don't believe you."

Phillips stared at him, flushed painfully and then shrugged his shoulders. "Do you want a written statement of all this?" he asked.

"I don't think so. Later, if it's necessary. You have been very frank. I appreciate both the honesty and the motive. Look here— what can you tell me to help yourself? It's an unusual question from a police officer, but—there it is."

"I don't know. I suppose the case against me, apart from the suggestion I have just made, is that I gave him an overdose of hyoscine. It looks fishy, my giving the injection at all, but it is my usual practice, especially when Roberts is the anæsthetist, as he dislikes the business. It looks still more suspicious using a lot of water. That, again, is my usual practice. I can prove it. I can prove that I suggested another surgeon to Lady O'Callaghan and that she urged me to operate. That's all. Except that I don't think—No, that's all."

"Have you any theories about other people?"

"Who did it, you mean? None. I imagine it was political. How it was done, I've no idea. I can't possibly suspect any of the people who worked with me. It's unthinkable. Besides—why? You said something about patent medicines. Is there anything there?"

"We're on that tack now. I don't know if there's anything in it. By the way, why does Dr. Roberts object to giving injections?"

"A private reason. Nothing that can have any bearing on the case."

"Is it because he once gave an overdose?"

"If you knew that, why did you ask me? Testing my veracity?"

"Put it like that. He was never alone with the patient?"

"No. No, never."

"Was any one of the nurses alone in the theatre before the operation?"

"The nurses? I don't know. I wouldn't notice what they did.

150

They'd been preparing for some time before we came on the scene."

"We?"

"Thoms, Roberts and myself."

"What about Mr. Thoms?"

"I can't remember. He may have dodged in to have a look round."

"Yes. I think I must have a reconstruction. Can you spare the time to-day or to-morrow?"

"You mean you want to go through the whole business in pantomime?"

"If I may. We can hardly do it actually, unless I discover a P.C. suffering from an acute abscess of the appendix."

Phillips smiled sardonically.

"I might give him too much hyoscine if you did," he said. "Do you want the whole pack of them?"

"If it's possible."

"Unless there's an urgent case, nothing happens in the afternoon. I hardly think there will be an urgent case. Business," added Phillips grimly, "will probably fall off. My last major operation is enjoying somewhat unfavourable publicity."

"Well—will you get the others for me for to-morrow afternoon?"

"I'll try. It'll be very unpleasant. Nurse Banks has left us, but she can be found."

"She's at the Nurses' Club in Chelsea."

Phillips glanced quickly at him.

"Is she?" he said shortly. "Very well. Will five o'clock suit you?"

"Admirably. Can we have it all as closely reproduced as possible—same impedimenta and so on?"

"I think it can be arranged. I'll let you know." Phillips went to the door.

"Good-bye for the moment," he said. "I've no idea whether or not you think I killed O'Callaghan, but you've been very polite."

"We are taught manners at the same time as point-duty," said Alleyn. Phillips went away and Alleyn sought out Detective-Inspector Fox, to whom he related the events of the morning. When he came to Phillips's visit Fox thrust out his under lip and looked at his boots.

"That's your disillusioned expression, Fox," said Alleyn.

"What's it in aid of?"

"Well, sir, I must say I have my doubts about this self-sacrifice business. It sounds very nice, but it isn't the stuff people hand out when they think it may be returned to them tied up with rope."

"I can't believe you were no good at composition. Do you mean you mistrust Phillips's motive in coming here, or Nurse Harden's hypothetical attempt to decoy my attention?"

"Both, but more particularly number one. To my way of thinking, we've got a better case against Sir John Phillips than any of the others. I believe you're right about the political side—it's not worth a great deal. Now Sir John knows how black it looks against him. What's he do? He comes here, says he wants to make a clean breast of it, and tells you nothing you don't know already. When you point this out to him he says he may have made a slip over the two tubes. Do you believe that, chief?"

"No—to do the job he'd have had to dissolve the contents of a full tube. However dopey he felt he couldn't do that by mistake."

"Just so. And he knows you'll think of that. You ask me, sir," said Fox oratorically: " 'What's the man's motive?' "

"What's the man's motive?" repeated Alleyn obediently.

"Spoof's his motive. He knows it's going to be a tricky business bringing it home to him and he wants to create a good impression. The young lady may or may not have been in collusion with him. She may or may not come forward with the same kind of tale. 'Oh, please don't arrest him; arrest me. I never did it, but spare the boy-friend,' " said Fox in a very singular falsetto and with dreadful scorn.

Alleyn's mouth twitched. Rather hurriedly he lit a cigarette.

"You seem very determined all of a sudden," he observed mildly. "This morning you seduced me with tales of Sage, Banks, and Roberts."

"So I did, sir. It was an avenue that had to be explored. Boys is exploring, and as far as he's got it's a wash-out."

"Alack, what news are these! Discover them."

"Boys got hold of Robinson, and Robinson says it's all my eye. He says he's dead certain the Bolshie push hasn't an idea who killed O'Callaghan. He says if they'd had anything to do with it he'd have heard something. It was Kakaroff who told him about it and Kakaroff was knocked sideways at the news. Robinson says if there had been any organisation from that quarter they'd have kept quiet and we'd have had no rejoicing. They're as pleased as punch and as innocent as angels."

"Charming! All clapping their hands in childish glee. How about Dr. Roberts?"

"I asked him about the doctor. It seems they don't know anything much about him and look upon him as a bit of an outsider. They've even suspected him of being what they call 'unsound'. Robinson wondered if he was one of our men. You recollect Marcus Barker sent out a lot of pamphlets on the Sterilisation Bill. They took it up for a time. Well, the doctor is interested in the Bill."

"Yes, of course," agreed Alleyn thoughtfully. "It's in his territory."

"From the look of some of the sons of the Soviet," said Fox, "I'd say they'd be the first to suffer. The doctor saw one of these pamphlets and went to a meeting. He joined the Lenin Hall lot because he thought they'd push it. Robinson says he's always nagging at them to take it up again."

"So that's that. It sounds reasonable enough, Fox, and certainly consistent with Roberts's character. With his views on eugenics he'd be sure to support sterilisation. You don't need to be a Bolshie to see the sense of it, either. It looks as though Roberts had merely been thrown in to make it more difficult."

Fox looked profound.

"What about Miss Banks and little Harold?" asked Alleyn.

"Nothing much. The Banks party has been chucking her weight about ever since the operation, but she doesn't say anything useful. You might call it reflected glory."

"How like Banks. And Sage?"

"Robinson hasn't heard anything. Sage is not a prominent member."

"He was lying about the second dose Miss O'Callaghan gave O'Callaghan. He admitted he had provided it, that it was from a doctor's prescription, and that he had not noted it in his book. All my eye. We can sift that out easily enough by finding out her doctor, but of course Sage may simply be scared and as innocent as a babe. Well, there we are. Back again face to face with the clean breast of Sir John Phillips."

"Not so clean, if you ask me."

"I wonder. I'm doing a reconstruction to-morrow afternoon. Phillips is arranging it for me. Would you say he was a great loss to the stage?"

153

"How do you mean, chief?"

"If he's our man, he's one of the best actors I've ever met. You come along to-morrow to the hospital, Fox, and see what you shall see. Five o'clock. And now I'm going to lunch. I want to see Lady O'Callaghan before the show, and Roberts too, if possible. I may as well get his version of the Lenin Hall lot. *Au revoir*, Fox."

"Do you mind repeating that, sir?"

"*Au revoir.*"

"*Au revoir*, monsieur," said Fox carefully.

"I'm coming to hear those records of yours one of these nights, if I may."

Fox became plum-coloured with suppressed pleasure.

"I'd take it very kindly," he said stiffly and went out.

Alleyn rang up the house in Catherine Street and learnt that Lady O'Callaghan would be pleased to receive him at ten to three the following afternoon. He spent half an hour on his file of the case. The analyst's report on Phillips's tablets and the hyoscine solution had come in. Both contained the usual dosage. He sent off the 'Fulvitavolts' and the scrap of paper that had enclosed Ruth O'Callaghan's second remedy. It was possible, but extremely unlikely, that there might be a trace of the drug spilt on the wrapper. At one o'clock he went home and lunched. At two o'clock he rang up the Yard and found there was a message from Sir John Phillips to the effect that the reconstruction could be held the following afternoon at the time suggested. He asked them to tell Fox and then rang Phillips up and thanked him.

Alleyn spent the rest of the day adding to the file on the case and in writing a sort of résumé for his own instruction. He sat over it until ten o'clock and then deliberately put it aside, read the second act of *Hamlet*, and wondered, not for the first time, what sort of a hash the Prince of Denmark would have made of a job at the Yard. Then, being very weary, he went to bed.

The next morning he reviewed his notes, particularly that part of them which referred to hyoscine.

"Possible sources of hyoscine," he had written:

"1. *The bottle of stock solution.*

"Probably Banks, Marigold, Harden, Thoms, Phillips, all had opportunity to get at this. All in theatre before operation. Each could have filled anti-gas syringe with hyoscine. If this was done, someone had since filled up bottle with 10 c.c.'s of the correct solution. No one could have done this during the operation.

154

Could it have been done later? No good looking for prints.

"2. *The tablets.*

"Phillips could have given an overdose when he prepared the syringe. May have to trace his purchases of h.

"3. *The patent medicines.*

"(a) *'Fulvitavolts.'* Negligible quantity unless Sage had doctored packet supplied to Ruth. Check up.

"(b) *The second p.m.* (more p.m.'s!) supplied to Ruth. May have been lethal dose concocted by Sage, hoping to do in O'Callaghan, marry Ruth and the money, and strike a blow for Lenin, Love and Liberty."

After contemplating these remarks with some disgust Alleyn went to the hospital, made further arrangements for the reconstruction at five and after a good deal of trouble succeeded in getting no farther with the matter of the stock solution. He then visited the firm that supplied Sir John Phillips with drugs and learnt nothing that was of the remotest help. He then lunched and went to call on Lady O'Callaghan. Nash received him with that particular nuance of condescension that hitherto he had reserved for politicians. He was shown into the drawing-room, an apartment of great elegance and no character. Above the mantelpiece hung a portrait in pastel of Cicely O'Callaghan. The artist had dealt competently with the shining texture of the dress and hair, and had made a conscientious map of the face. Alleyn felt he would get about as much change from the original as he would from the picture. She came in, gave him a colourless greeting, and asked him to sit down.

"I'm so sorry to worry you again," Alleyn began. 'It's a small matter, one of those loose ends that probably mean nothing, but have to be tidied up."

"Yes. I shall be pleased to give you any help. I hope everything is quite satisfactory?" she said. She might have been talking about a new hot-water system.

"I hope it will be," rejoined Alleyn. "At the moment we are investigating any possible sources of hyoscine. Lady O'Callaghan, can you tell me if Sir Derek had taken any drugs of any sort at all before the operation?" As she did not answer immediately, he added quickly: "You see, if he had taken any medicine containing hyoscine, it would be necesary to try and arrive at the amount in order to allow for it."

"Yes," she said, "I see."

"Had he, do you know, taken any medicine? Perhaps when the pain was very bad?"

"My husband disliked drugs of all kinds."

"Then Miss Ruth O'Callaghan's suggestion about a remedy she was interested in would not appeal to him?"

"No. He thought it rather a foolish suggestion."

"I'm sorry to hammer away at it like this, but do you think there'a a remote possibility that he did take a dose? I believe Miss O'Callaghan did actually leave some medicine here—something called 'Fulvitavolts,' I think she said it was?"

"Yes. She left a packet here."

"Was it lying about where he might see it?"

"I'm afraid I don't remember. The servants, perhaps——" Her voice trailed away. "If it's at all important——" she said vaguely.

"It is rather."

"I am afraid I don't quite understand why. Obviously my husband was killed at the hospital."

"That," said Alleyn, "is one of the theories. The 'Fulvitavolts' are of some importance because they contain a small amount of hyoscine. You will understand that we must account for any hyoscine—even the smallest amount—that was given?"

"Yes," said Lady O'Callaghan. She looked serenely over his head for a few seconds and then added: "I'm afraid I cannot help you. I hope my sister-in-law, who is already upset by what has happened, will not be unnecessarily distressed by suggestions that she was responsible in any way."

"I hope not," echoed Alleyn blandly. "Probably, as you say, he did not touch the 'Fulvitavolts'. When did Miss O'Callaghan bring them?"

"I believe one night before the operation."

"Was it the night Sir John Phillips called?"

"That was on the Friday."

"Yes—was it then, do you remember?"

"I think perhaps it was."

"Can you tell me exactly what happened?"

"No, about Miss O'Callaghan."

She took a cigarette from a box by her chair. Alleyn jumped up and lit it for her. It rather surprised him to find that she smoked. It gave her an uncanny resemblance to something human.

"Can you remember at all?" he said.

"My sister-in-law often came in after dinner. At times my

156

husband found these visits a little trying. He liked to be quiet in the evenings. I believe on that night he suggested that she should be told he was out. However, she came in. We were in the study."

"You both saw her, then?"

"Yes."

"What happened?"

"She urged him to try this medicine. He put her off. I told her he expected Sir John Phillips and that we ought to leave them alone. I remember she and I met Sir John in the hall. I thought his manner very odd, as I believe I told you."

"So you went out, leaving the medicine in the study?"

"I suppose so—yes."

"Did you come across it again?"

"I don't think so."

"May I speak to your butler—Nash, isn't it?"

"If you think it is any help." She rang the bell.

Nash came in and waited.

"Mr. Alleyn wants to speak to you, Nash," said Lady O"Callaghan. Nash turned a respectful eye towards him.

"I want you to think back to the Friday evening before Sir Derek's operation," Alleyn began. "Do you remember that evening?"

"Yes, sir."

"There were visitors?"

"Yes, sir. Miss O'Callaghan and Sir John Phillips."

"Exactly. Do you remember noticing a chemist's parcel anywhere in the study?"

"Yes, sir. Miss O'Callaghan brought it with her, I believe."

"That's the one. What happened to it?"

"I had it removed to a cupboard in Sir Derek's bathroom the following morning, sir."

"I see. Had it been opened?"

"Oh, yes, sir."

"Can you find it now, Nash, do you think?"

"I will ascertain, sir."

"Do you mind, Lady O'Callaghan?" asked Alleyn apologetically.

"Of course not."

Nash inclined his head solemnly and left the room. While he was away there was a rather uncomfortable silence. Alleyn, looking very remote and polite, made no effort to break it. Nash returned after a few minutes with the now familiar carton, on a silver salver. Alleyn took it and thanked him. Nash departed.

"Here it is," said the inspector cheerfully. "Oh, yes, Nash was quite right; it has been opened and—let me see—one powder has been taken. That doesn't amount to much." He put the carton in his pocket and turned to Lady O'Callaghan. "It seems ridiculous, I know, to worry about so small a matter, but it's part of our job to pick up every thread, however unimportant. This, I suppose, was the last effort Miss O'Callaghan made to interest Sir Derek in any remedy?"

Again she waited for a few seconds.

"Yes," she murmured at last. "I believe so."

"She did not mention another remedy to you after he had been taken to the hospital?"

"Really, Inspector Alleyn, I cannot possibly remember. My sister-in-law talks a great deal about patent medicines. She tries to persuade everyone she knows to take them. I believe my uncle, Mr. James Rattisbon, has already explained this to you. He tells me that he made it quite clear that we did not wish the matter to be pursued."

"I am afraid I cannot help pursuing it."

"But Mr. Rattisbon definitely instructed you."

"Please forgive me," said Alleyn very quietly, "if I seem to be unduly officious." He paused. She looked at him with a kind of cold huffiness. After a moment he went on. "I wonder if you have ever seen or read a play called *Justice*, by Galsworthy? It is no doubt very dated, but there is an idea in it that I think explains far better than I can the position of people who become involved, whether voluntarily or involuntarily, with the law. Galsworthy made one of his characters—a lawyer, I think—say that once you have set in motion the chariot wheels of Justice, you can do nothing at all to arrest or deflect their progress. Lady O'Callaghan, that is the exact truth. You, very properly, decided to place this tragic case in the hands of the police. In doing so you switched on a piece of complicated and automatic machinery which, once started, you cannot switch off. As the police officer in charge of this case I am simply a wheel in the machine. I must complete my revolutions. Please do not think I am impertinent if I say that neither you nor any other lay person, however much involved, has the power to stop the machine of justice or indeed to influence it in any way whatever." He stopped abruptly. "I am afraid you *will* think me impertinent—I have no business to talk like this. If you will excuse me——"

He bowed and turned away.

"Yes," said Lady O'Callaghan, "I quite understand. Good afternoon."

"There's one other thing." said Alleyn. "I had nearly forgotten it. It's something that you can do, if you will, to help us as regards the hospital side of the problem."

She listened, apparently without any particular surprise or agitation, to his request, and agreed at once to do as he suggested.

"Thank you very much indeed, Lady O'Callaghan. You understand that we should like Miss O'Callaghan to be with you?"

"Yes," she said after a long pause.

"Shall I see her, or—perhaps you would rather ask her yourself?"

"Perhaps that would be better. I would much prefer her to be spared this unnecessary ordeal."

"I assure you," said Alleyn dryly, "that it may save her a more unpleasant one."

"I'm afraid I do not understand you. However, I shall ask her."

In the hall he walked straight into Miss Ruth O'Callaghan. When she saw him she uttered a noise that was something between a whoop of alarm and a cry of supplication, and bolted incontinently into the drawing-room. Nash, who had evidently just admitted her, looked scandalised.

"Is Mr. Jameson in, Nash?" asked Alleyn.

"Mr. Jameson has left us, sir."

"Really?"

"Yes, sir. His duties, as you might say, have drawn to a close."

"Yes," said Alleyn, unconsciously echoing Lady O'Callaghan. "I quite understand. Good afternoon."

CHAPTER XVI

Reconstruction Begun

Thursday, the eighteenth. Afternoon.

Alleyn found he still had over an hour to wait before the reconstruction. He had tea and then rang up Dr. Roberts, found he was at home, and made his way once more to the little house in Wigmore Street. He wanted, if possible, to surprise Roberts with an unexpected reference to the Lenin Hall meeting. The diminutive man-servant admitted him and showed him into the pleasant sitting-room, where he found Roberts awaiting him.

"I hope I'm not a great nuisance," said Alleyn. "You did ask me to come back some time, you know."

"Certainly," said Roberts, shaking hands. "I am delighted to see you. Have you read my book?" He swept a sheaf of papers off a chair and pulled it forward. Alleyn sat down.

"I've dipped into it—no time really to tackle it yet, but I'm enormously interested. At Lord knows what hour this morning I read the chapter in which you refer to the Sterilisation Bill. You put the case for sterilisation better than any other sponsor I have heard."

"You think so?" said Roberts acidly. "Then you will be surprised to hear that although I have urged that matter with all the force and determination I could command, I have made not one inch of headway—not an inch! I am forced to the conclusion that most of the people who attempt to administer the government of this country are themselves certifiable." He gave a short falsetto laugh and glared indignantly at Alleyn, who contented himself with making an incredulous and sympathetic noise.

"I have done everything—everything," continued Roberts. "I

160

joined a group of people professing enlightened views on the matter. They assured me they would stick at nothing to force this Bill through Parliament. They professed the greatest enthusiasm. *Have* they done anything?" He paused oratorically and then in a voice of indescribable disgust he said: "They merely asked me to wait in patience till the Dawn of the Proletariat Day in Britain."

Chief Inspector Alleyn felt himself to be in the foolish position of one who sets a match to the dead stick of a rocket. Dr. Roberts had most effectively stolen his fireworks. He had a private laugh at himself. Roberts continued angrily:

"They call themselves Communists. They have no interest in the welfare of the community—none. Last night I attended one of their meetings, and I was disgusted. All they did was to rejoice for no constructive or intelligent reason over the death of the late Home Secretary."

He stopped abruptly, glanced at Alleyn, and then with that curious return to nervousness which the inspector had noticed before he said: "But, of course, I had forgotten. That is very much your business. Thoms rang me up just now to ask me if I could attend at the hospital this afternoon."

"*Thoms* rang you up?"

"Yes. Sir John had asked him to, I believe. I don't know why," said Dr. Roberts, suddenly looking surprised and rather bewildered, "but I sometimes find Thoms's manner rather aggravating."

"Do you?" murmured Alleyn, smiling. "He is rather facetious."

"Facetious! Exactly. And this afternoon I found his facetiousness in bad taste."

"What did he say?"

"He said something to the effect that if I wished to make my get-away he would be pleased to lend me a pair of ginger-coloured whiskers and a false nose. I thought it in bad taste."

"Certainly," said Alleyn, hurriedly blowing his own nose.

"Of course," continued Dr. Roberts, "Mr. Thoms knows himself to be in an impregnable position, since he could not have given any injection without being observed, and had no hand in preparing the injection which he did give. I felt inclined to point out to him that I myself am somewhat similarly situated, but do not feel, on that account, free to indulge in buffoonery."

"I suppose Mr. Thoms was in the anteroom all the time until you went into the theatre?"

161

"I've no idea," said Roberts stiffly. "I myself merely went to the anteroom with Sir John, said what was necessary, and joined my patient in the anæsthetic-room."

"Ah, well—we shall get a better idea of all your movements from the reconstruction."

"I suppose so," agreed Roberts, looking perturbed. "It will be a distressing experience for all of us. Except, no doubt, Mr. Thoms."

He waited a moment and then said nervously:

"Perhaps this is a question that I should not ask, Inspector Alleyn, but I cannot help wondering if the police have a definite theory as regards this crime?"

Alleyn was used to this question.

"We've got several theories, Dr. Roberts, and all of them more or less fit. That's the devil of it."

"Have you explored the possibility of suicide?" asked Roberts wistfully.

"I have considered it."

"Remember his heredity."

"I have remembered it. After he had the attack in the House his physical condition would have rendered suicide impossible, and he could hardly have taken hyoscine while making his speech."

"Again remember his heredity. He might have carried hyoscine tablets with him for some time and under the emotional stimulus of the occasion suffered a sudden ungovernable impulse. In the study of suicidal psychology one comes across many such cases. Did his hand go to his mouth while he was speaking? I see you look incredulous, Inspector Alleyn. Perhaps you even think it suspicious that I should urge the point. I—I—*have* a reason for hoping you find that O'Callaghan killed himself, but it does not spring from a sense of guilt."

A strangely exalted look came into the little doctor's eyes as he spoke. Alleyn regarded him intently.

"Dr. Roberts," he said at last, "why not tell me what is in your mind?"

"No," said Robert's emphatically, "no—not unless—unless the worst happens."

"Well," said Alleyn, "as you know, I can't force you to give me your theory, but it's a dangerous business, withholding information in a capital charge."

"It may not be a capital charge," cried Roberts in a hurry.

"Even suppose your suicide theory is possible, it seems to me that a man of Sir Derek's stamp would not have done it in such a way as to cast suspicion upon other people."

"No," agreed Roberts. "No. That is undoubtedly a strong argument—and yet inherited suicidal mania sometimes manifests itself very abruptly and strangely. I have known instances——"

He went to his bookcase and took down several volumes, from which he read in a rapid, dry and didactic manner, rather as though Alleyn was a collection of students. This went on for some time. The servant brought in tea, and with an air of patient benevolence, poured it out himself. He placed Roberts's cup on a table under his nose, waited until the doctor closed the book with which he was at the moment engaged, took it firmly from him and directed his attention to the tea. He then moved the table between the two men and left the room.

"Thank you," said Roberts vaguely some time after he had gone.

Roberts, still delivering himself of his learning, completely forgot to drink his tea or to offer some to Alleyn, but occasionally stretched out a hand towards the toast. The time passed rapidly. Alleyn looked at his watch.

"Good Lord!" he exclaimed, "it's half-past four. We'll have to collect ourselves, I'm afraid."

"Tch!" said Roberts crossly.

"I'll call a taxi."

"No, no. I'll drive you there, Inspector. Wait a moment." He darted out into the hall and gave flurried orders to the little servant who silently insinuated him into his coat and gave him his hat. Roberts shot back into the sitting-room and fetched his stethoscope.

"What about your anæsthetising apparatus?" ventured Alleyn.

"Eh?" asked Roberts squinting round at him.

"Your anæsthetising apparatus."

"D'you want that?"

"Please—if it's not a great bore. Didn't Sir John tell you?"

"I'll get it," said Roberts. He darted off across the little hall.

"Can I assist you, sir?" asked the servant.

"No, no. Bring out the car."

He reappeared presently, wheeling the cruet-like apparatus with its enormous cylinders.

"You can't carry that down the steps by yourself," said Alleyn.

163

"Let me help."

"Thank you, thank you," said Roberts. He bent down and examined the nuts that fastened the frame at the bottom. "Wouldn't do for these nuts to come loose," he said. "You take the top, will you? Gently. Ease it down the steps."

With a good deal of bother they got the thing into Roberts's car and drove off to Brook Street, the little doctor talking most of the time.

As they drew near the hospital, however, he grew quieter, seemed to get nervous, and kept catching Alleyn's eye and hurriedly looking away again. After this had happened some three or four times Roberts laughed uncomfortably.

"I—I'm not looking forward to this experiment," he said. "One gets moderately case-hardened in our profession, I suppose, but there's something about this affair"—he blinked hard twice—"something profoundly disquieting. Perhaps it is the element of uncertainty."

"But you have got a theory, Dr. Roberts?"

"I? No. I did hope it might be suicide. No—I've no specific theory."

"Oh, well. If you won't tell me, you won't," rejoined Alleyn.

Roberts looked at him in alarm, but said no more.

At Brook Street they found Fox placidly contemplating the marble woman in the waiting-room. He was accompanied by Inspector Boys, a large red-faced officer with a fruity voice and hands like hams. Boys kept a benevolent but shrewd eye on the activities of communistic societies, on near-treasonable propagandists, and on Soviet-minded booksellers. He was in the habit of alluding to such persons who came into these categories as though they were tiresome but harmless children.

"Hallo," said Alleyn. "Where are the star turns?"

"The nurses are getting the operating theatre ready," Fox told him. "Sir John Phillips asked me to let him know when we are ready. The other ladies are upstairs."

"Right. Mr. Thoms here?"

"Is that the funny gentleman, sir?" asked Boys.

"It is."

"He's here."

"Then in that case we're complete. Dr. Roberts has gone up to the theatre. Let us follow him. Fox, let Sir John know, will you?"

Fox went away and Alleyn and Boys took the lift up to the

164

theatre landing, where they found the rest of the *dramatis personae* awaiting them. Mr. Thoms broke off in the middle of some anecdote with which he was apparently regaling the company.

"Hallo, 'allo, 'allo!" he shouted. "Here's the Big Noise itself. Now we shan't be long."

"Good evening, Mr. Thoms," said Alleyn. "Good evening, Matron. I hope I haven't kept you all waiting."

"Not at all," said Sister Marigold.

Fox appeared with Sir John Phillips. Alleyn spoke a word to him and then turned and surveyed the group. They eyed him uneasily and perhaps inimically. It was a little as though they drew together, moved by a common impulse of self-preservation. He thought they looked rather like sheep, bunched together, their heads turned watchfully towards their protective enemy, the sheep-dog.

"I'd better give a warning bark or two," thought Alleyn and addressed them collectively.

"I'm quite sure," he began, "that you all realise why we have asked you to meet us here. It is, of course, in order to enlist your help. We are faced with a difficult problem in this case and feel that a reconstruction of the operation may go far towards clearing any suspicion of guilt from innocent individuals. As you know, Sir Derek O'Callaghan died from hyoscine poisoning. He was a man with many political enemies, and from the outset the affair has been a complicated and bewildering problem. The fact that he, in the course of the operation, was given a legitimate injection of hyoscine has added to the complications. I am sure you are all as anxious as we are to clear up this aspect of the case. I ask you to look upon the reconstruction as an opportunity to free yourselves of any imputation of guilt. As a medium in detection the reconstruction has much to commend it. The chief argument against it is that sometimes innocent persons are moved, through nervousness or other motives, to defeat the whole object of the thing by changing the original circumstances. Under the shadow of tragedy it is not unusual for innocent individuals to imagine that the police suspect them. I am sure that you are not likely to do anything so foolish as this. I am sure you realise that this is an opportunity, not a trap. Let me beg you to repeat as closely as you can your actions during the operation on the deceased. If you do this, there is not the faintest cause for alarm." He looked at his watch.

"Now then," he said. "You are to imagine that time has gone back seven days. It is twenty-five minutes to four on the afternoon of Thursday February 4th. Sir Derek O'Callaghan is upstairs in his room, awaiting his operation. Matron, when you get word will you and the nurses who are to help you begin your preparations in the anteroom and the theatre? Any dialogue you remember you will please repeat. Inspector Fox will be in the anteroom and Inspector Boys in the theatre. Please treat them as pieces of sterile machinery." He allowed himself a faint smile and turned to Phillips and Nurse Graham, the special.

"We'll go upstairs."

They went up to the next landing. Outside the door of the first room Alleyn turned to the others. Phillips was very white, but quite composed. Little Nurse Graham looked unhappy, but sensibly determined.

"Now, Nurse, we'll go in. If you'll just wait a moment, sir. Actually you are just coming upstairs."

"I see," said Phillips.

Alleyn swung open the door and followed Nurse Graham into the bedroom.

Cicely and Ruth O'Callaghan were at the window. He got the impression that Ruth had been sitting there, perhaps crouched in that arm-chair, and had sprung up when the door opened. Cicely O'Callaghan stood erect, very *grande dame* and statuesque, a gloved hand resting lightly on the window-sill.

"Good evening, Inspector Alleyn," she said. Ruth gave a loud sob and gasped "Good evening."

Alleyn felt that his only hope of avoiding a scene was to hurry things along at a business-like canter.

"It was extremely kind of you both to come," he said briskly. "I shan't keep you more than a few minutes. As you know, we are to go over the events of the operation, and I thought it better to start from here." He glanced cheerfully at Ruth.

"Certainly," said Lady O'Callaghan.

"Now." Alleyn turned towards the bed, immaculate with its smooth linen and tower of rounded pillows. "Now, Nurse Graham has brought you here. When you come in you sit— where? On each side of the bed? Is that how it was, Nurse?"

"Yes. Lady O'Callaghan was here," answered the special quietly.

"Then if you wouldn't mind taking up those positions——"

166

With an air of stooping to the level of a rather vulgar farce, Lady O'Callaghan sat in the chair on the right-hand side of the bed.

"Come along, Ruth," she said tranquilly.

"But why? Inspector Alleyn—it's so dreadful—so horribly cold-blooded—unnecessary. I don't understand … You were so kind …" She boggled over her words, turned her head towards him with a gesture of complete wretchedness. Alleyn walked quickly towards her.

"I'm so sorry," he said. "I know it's beastly. Take courage—your brother would understand, I think."

She gazed miserably at him. With her large unlovely face blotched with tears, and her pale eyes staring doubtfully up into his, she seemed dreadfully vulnerable. Something in his manner may have given her a little help. Like an obedient and unwieldy animal she got up and blundered across to the other chair.

"What now, Nurse?"

"The patient half regained consciousness soon after we came in. I heard Sir John and went out."

"Will you do that, please?"

She went away quietly.

"And now," Alleyn went on, "what happened? Did the patient speak?"

"I believe he said the pain was severe. Nothing else," murmured Lady O'Callaghan.

"What did you say to each other?"

"I—I told him it was his appendix and that the doctor would soon be here—something of that sort. He seemed to lose consciousness again, I thought."

"Did you speak to each other?"

"I don't remember."

Alleyn made a shot in the dark.

"Did you discuss his pain?"

"I do not think so," she said composedly.

Ruth turned her head and gazed with a sort of damp surprise at her sister-in-law.

"You remember doing so, do you, Miss O'Callaghan?" said Alleyn.

"I think—yes—oh, Cicely!"

"What is it?" asked Alleyn gently.

"I said something—about—how I wished—oh, Cicely!"

The door opened and Nurse Graham came in again.

"I think I came back about now to say Sir John would like to see Lady O'Callaghan," she said with a troubled glance at Ruth.

"Very well. Will you go out with her, please, Lady O'Callaghan?" They went out and Ruth and the inspector looked at each other across the smug little bed. Suddenly Ruth uttered a veritable howl and flung herself face-down among the appliqué-work on the counterpane.

"Listen," said Alleyn, "and tell me if I'm wrong. Mr. Sage had given you a little box of powders that he said would relieve the pain. Now the others have left the room, you feel you must give your brother one of these powders. There is the water and the glass on the table by your side. You unwrap the box, drop the paper on the floor, shake out one of the powders and give it to him in a glass of water. It seems to relieve the pain and when they return he's easier? Am I right?"

"Oh," wailed Ruth, raising her head. "Oh, how did you know? Cicely said I'd better not say. I told her. Oh, what shall I do?"

"Have you kept the box with the other powders?"

"Yes. He—they told me not to, but—but I thought if they were poison and I'd killed him——" Her voice rose with a shrill note of horror. "I thought I'd take them—myself. Kill myself. Lots of us do, you know. Great-Uncle Eustace did, and Cousin Olive Casebeck, and——"

"You're not going to do anything so cowardly. What would he have thought of you? You're going to do the brave thing and help us to find the truth. Come along," said Alleyn, for all the world as if she were a child, "come along. Where are these terrible powders? In that bag still, I don't mind betting."

"Yes," whispered Ruth, opening her eyes very wide. "They are in that bag. You're quite right. You're quite right. You're very clever to think of that. I thought if you arrested me——" She made a very strange gesture with her clenched hand, jerking it up across her mouth.

"Give them to me," said Alleyn.

She began obediently to scuffle in the vast bag. All sorts of things came shooting out. He was in a fever of impatience lest the others should return, and moved to the door. At last the round cardboard box appeared. He gathered up the rest of Ruth's junk and bundled it back as the door opened. Nurse Graham stood aside to let Phillips in.

"I think it was about now," she said.

"Right," said Alleyn. "Now, Sir John, I believe Miss O'Callaghan left the room while you examined the patient, diagnosed the trouble, and decided on an immediate operation."

"Yes. When Lady O'Callaghan returned I suggested that Somerset Black should operate."

"Quite so. Lady O'Callaghan urged you to do it yourself. Everyone agree to that?"

"Yes," said Nurse Graham quietly. Ruth merely sat and gaped. Lady O'Callaghan turned with an unusual abruptness and walked to the window.

"Then you, Sir John, went away to prepare for the operation?"

"Yes."

"That finishes this part of the business, then."

"No!"

Cicely O'Callaghan's voice rang out so fiercely that they all jumped. She had faced round and stood with her eyes fixed on Phillips. She looked magnificent. It was as if a colourless façade had been flood-lit.

"No! Why do you deliberately ignore what we all heard, what I myself have told you? Ask Sir John what my husband said when he saw who it was we had brought here to help him." She turned deliberately to Phillips. "What did Derek say to you—what did he say?"

Phillips looked at her as though he saw her for the first time. His face expressed nothing but a profound astonishment. When he answered it was with a kind of reasonableness and with no suggestion of heroics.

"He was frightened," he said.

"He cried out to us: 'Don't let——' You remember"—she appealed with assurance to Nurse Graham—"you remember what he looked like—you understood what he meant?"

"I said then," said Nurse Graham with spirit, "and I say now, that Sir Derek did not know what he was saying."

"Well," remarked Alleyn mildly, "as we all know about it I think you and I, Sir John, will go downstairs." He turned to the O'Callaghans.

"Actually, I believe you both stayed on in the hospital during the operation, but, of course, there is no need for you to do so now. Lady O'Callaghan, shall I ask for your car to take you back to Catherine Street? If you will forgive me, I must go to the theatre."

Suddenly he realised that she was in such a fury that she could not answer. He took Phillips by the elbow and propelled him through the door.

"We will leave Nurse Graham," he said, "alone with her patient."

CHAPTER XVII

Reconstruction Concluded

Thursday, the eighteenth. Late afternoon.

The "theatre party" appeared to have entered heartily into the spirit of the thing. A most convincing activity was displayed in the anteroom, where Sister Marigold, Jane Harden and a very glum-faced Banks washed and clattered while Inspector Fox, his massive form wedged into a corner, looked on with an expressionless countenance and a general air of benignity. A faint bass drone from beyond the swing-door informed Alleyn of the presence in the theatre of Inspector Boys.

"All ready, Matron?" asked Alleyn.

"Quite ready, Inspector."

"Well, here we all are." He stood aside and Phillips, Thoms and Roberts walked in.

"Are you at about the same stage as you were when the doctors came in?"

"At exactly the same stage."

"Good. What happens now?" He turned to the men. No one spoke for a moment. Roberts turned deferentially towards Phillips, who had moved across to Jane Harden. Jane and Phillips did not look at each other. Phillips appeared not to have heard Alleyn's question. Thoms cleared his throat importantly.

"Well now, let's see. If I'm not speaking out of my turn, I should say we got down to the job straight away. Roberts said he'd go along to the anæsthetic-room and Sir John, I believe, went into the theatre? That correct, sir?"

"Did you go into the theatre immediately, Sir John?" asked Alleyn.

171

"What? I? Yes, I believe so."

"Before you washed?"

"Naturally."

"Well, let's start, shall we? Dr. Roberts, did you go alone to the anæsthetic-room?"

"No. Nurse—er——?" Roberts blinked at Banks. "Nurse Banks went with me. I looked at the anæsthetising apparatus and asked Nurse Banks to let Sir Derek's nurse know when we were ready."

"Will you go along, then? Fox, you take over with Dr. Roberts. Now, please, Sir John."

Phillips at once went through into the theatre, followed by Alleyn. Boys broke off his subterranean humming and at a word from Alleyn took his place in the anteroom. Phillips, without speaking, crossed to the side table, which was set out as before with the three syringes in dishes of water. The surgeon took his hypodermic case from his pocket, looked at the first tube, appeared to find it empty, took out the second, and having squirted a syringeful of water into a measure-glass, dropped in a single tablet.

"That is what—what I believe I did," he said.

"And then? You returned to the anteroom? No. What about Mr. Thoms?"

"Yes. Thoms should be here now."

"Mr. Thoms, please!" shouted Alleyn.

The doors swung open and Thoms came in.

"Hallo, hallo. Want me?"

"I understood you watched Sir John take up the hyoscine solution into the syringe."

"Oh! Yes, b'lieve I did," said Thoms, rather less boisterously.

"You commented on the amount of water."

"Yes, I know, but—look here, you don't want me to go thinking——"

"I simply want a reconstruction without comment, Mr. Thoms."

"Oh, quite, quite."

Phillips stood with the syringe in his hand. He looked gravely and rather abstractedly at his assistant. At a nod from Alleyn he filled the syringe.

"It is now that Thoms remarks on the quantity of water," he said quietly. "I snub him and go back into the anæsthetic-room,

172

where I give the injection. The patient is there with the special nurse."

He took up the syringe and walked away. Thoms moved away with a grimace at Alleyn, who said abruptly:

"Just a moment, Mr. Thoms. I think you stayed behind in the theatre for a minute or two."

"No, I didn't—beg your pardon, Inspector. I thought I went out to the anteroom before Sir John moved."

"Sir John thought not, and the nurses had the impression you came in a little later."

"Maybe," said Thoms. "I really can't remember."

"Have you no idea what you did during the two or three minutes?"

"None."

"Oh. In that case I'll leave you. Boys!"

Inspector Boys returned to the theatre and Alleyn went out. In about a minute Thoms joined him.

Sir John appeared in the anteroom and washed up, assisted by Jane Harden and the matron, who afterwards helped the surgeons to dress up.

"I feel rather an ass," said Thoms brightly. Nobody answered him.

"It is now," said Phillips in the same grave, detached manner, "that Mr. Thoms tells me about the play at the Palladium."

"All agreed?" Alleyn asked the others. The women murmured an assent.

"Now what happens?"

"Pardon me, but I remember Mr. Thoms went into the theatre and then called me in to him," murmured Sister Marigold.

"Thank you, Matron. Away you go, then," Alleyn waited until the doors had swung to and then turned to where Phillips, now wearing his gown and mask, stood silently beside Jane Harden.

"So you were left alone together at this juncture?" he said, without stressing it.

"Yes," said Phillips.

"Do you mind telling me what was said?"

"Oh, please," whispered Jane. "Please, please!" It was the first time she had spoken.

"Can't you let her off this?" said Phillips. There was a sort of urgency in his voice now.

"I'm sorry—I would if I could."

173

"I'll tell him, Jane. We said it was a strange situation. I again asked her to marry me. She said no—that she felt she belonged to O'Callaghan. Something to that effect. She tried to explain her point of view."

"You've left something out—you're not thinking of yourself." She stood in front of him, for all the world as though she was prepared to keep Alleyn off. "He said then that he didn't want to operate and that he'd give anything to be out of it. His very words. He told me he'd tried to persuade—her—*his* wife—to get another surgeon. He hated the idea of operating. Does that look as though he meant any harm? Does it? He never thinks of himself—he only wants to help me, and I'm not worth it. I've told him so a hundred times——"

"Jane, my dear, don't."

There was a tap on the outer door and Roberts looked in. "I think it's time I came and washed up," he said.

"Come in, Dr. Roberts."

Roberts glanced at the others.

"Forgive me, Sir John," he began with the deference that he always used when he spoke to Phillips, "but as I remember it, Mr. Thoms came in with me at this juncture."

"You're quite right, Roberts," agreed Phillips courteously.

"Mr. Thoms, please," called Alleyn again.

Thoms shot back into the room.

"Late again, am I?" he remarked. "Truth of the matter is I can't for the life of me remember all the ins and outs of it. I suppose I wash up now? What?

"If you please," said Alleyn sedately.

At last they were ready and Roberts returned to Inspector Fox and the anæsthetic-room. The others, accompanied by Alleyn, went to the theatre.

The cluster of lights above the table had been turned up and Alleyn again felt that sense of expectancy in the theatre. Phillips went immediately to the window end of the table and waited with his gloved hands held out in front of him. Thoms stood at the foot of the table. Sister Marigold and Jane were farther away.

There was a slight vibratory, rattling noise. The door into the anæsthetic-room opened and a trolley appeared, propelled by Banks. Dr. Roberts and Nurse Graham walked behind it. His hands were stretched out over the head of the trolley. On it was a sort of elongated bundle made of pillows and blankets. He and

174

Banks lifted this on the table and Banks put a screen, about two feet high, across the place that represented the patient's chest. The others drew nearer. Banks pushed the trolley away.

Now that they had all closed round the table the illusion was complete. The conical glare poured itself down between the white figures, bathing their masked faces and the fronts of their gowns in a violence of light, and leaving their backs in sharp shadow, so that between shadow and light there was a kind of shimmering border that ran round their outlines. Boys and Fox had come in from their posts and stood impassive in the doorways. Alleyn walked round the theatre to a position about two yards behind the head of the table.

Roberts wheeled forward the anæsthetising apparatus. Suddenly, entirely without warning, one of the white figures gave a sharp exclamation, something between a cry and a protest.

"It's too horrible—really—I can't——!"

It was the matron, the impeccable Sister Marigold. She had raised her hands in front of her face as if shutting off some shocking spectacle. Now she backed away from the table and collided with the anæsthetising apparatus. She stumbled, kicked it so that it moved, and half fell, clutching at it as she did so.

There was a moment's silence and then a portly little figure in white suddenly screamed out an oath.

"What the bloody hell are you doing? Do you want to kill——"

"What's the matter?" said Alleyn sharply. His voice had an incisive edge that made all the white heads turn. "What is it, Mr Thoms?"

Thoms was down on his knees, an absurd figure, frantically reaching out to the apparatus. Roberts, who had stooped down to the lower framework of the cruet-like stand and had rapidly inspected it, thrust the little fat man aside. He tested the nuts that held the frame together. His hands shook a little and his face, the only one unmasked, was very pale.

"It's perfectly secure, Thoms," he said. "None of the nuts are loose. Matron, please stand away."

"I didn't mean—I'm sorry," began Sister Marigold.

"Do you realise——" said Thoms in a voice that was scarcely recognisable——"do you realise that if one of those cylinders had fallen out and burst, we'd none of us be alive. Do you know that?"

"Nonsense, Thoms," said Roberts in an unsteady voice. "It's

175

most unlikely that anything of the sort could occur. It would take more than that to burst a cylinder, I assure you."

"I'm sure I'm very sorry, Mr. Thoms," said Matron sulkily. "Accidents will happen."

"Accidents mustn't happen," barked Thoms. He squatted down and tested the nuts.

"Please leave it alone, Mr. Thoms," said Roberts crisply. "I assure you it's perfectly safe."

Thoms did not answer. He got to his feet and turned back to the table.

"And now what happens?" asked Alleyn. His deep voice sounded like a tonic note. Phillips spoke quietly.

"I made the incision and carried on with the operation. I found peritonitis and a ruptured abscess of the appendix. I proceeded in the usual way. At this stage, I think, Dr. Roberts began to be uneasy about the pulse and the general condition. Am I right, Roberts?"

"Quite right, sir. I asked for an injection of camphor."

Without waiting to be told, Nurse Banks went to the side table, took up the ampoule of camphor, went through the pantomime of filling a syringe and returned to the patient.

"I injected it," she said concisely.

Through Alleyn's head ran the old jingle: "A made an apple pie, B bit it, C cut it—I injected it," he added mentally.

"And then?" he asked.

"After completing the operation I asked for the anti-gas serum."

"I got it," said Jane bravely.

She walked to the table.

"I stood, hesitating. I felt faint. I—I couldn't focus things properly."

"Did anybody notice this?"

"I looked round and saw something was wrong," said Phillips. "She simply stood there swaying a little."

"You notice this, Mr. Thoms?"

"Well, I'm afraid, Inspector, I rather disgraced myself by kicking up a rumpus. What, nurse? Bit hard on you, what? Didn't know how the land lay. Too bad, wasn't it?"

"When you had finished, Nurse Harden brought the large syringe?"

"Yes."

Jane came back with the syringe on a tray. "Thoms took it," went the jingle in Alleyn's head.

"I injected it," said Thoms.

"Mr. Thoms then asked about the condition," added Roberts. "I said it was disquieting. I remember Sir John remarked that although he knew the patient personally he had had no idea he was ill. Nurse Banks and I lifted the patient on to the trolley and he was taken away."

They did this with the dummy.

"Then I fainted," said Jane.

"A dramatic finish—what?" shouted Thoms, who seemed to have quite recovered his equilibrium.

"The end," said Alleyn, "came later. The patient was then taken back to his room, where you attended him, Dr. Roberts. Was anyone with you?"

"Nurse Graham was there throughout. I left her in the room when I returned here to report on the general condition, which I considered markedly worse."

"And in the meantime Sir John and Mr. Thoms washed up in the anteroom?"

"Yes," said Phillips.

"What did you talk about?"

"I don't remember."

"Oh yes, sir, you do, surely," said Thoms. "We talked about Nurse Harden doing a faint, and I said I could see the operation had upset you, and you—" he grinned—"you first said it hadn't, you know, and then said it had. Very natural, really," he explained to Alleyn, who raised one eyebrow and turned to the nurses.

"And you cleaned up the theatre, and Miss Banks gave one of her well-known talks on the Dawn of the Proletariat Day?"

"I did," said Banks with a snap.

"Meanwhile Dr. Roberts came down and reported, and you and Mr. Thoms, Sir John, went up to the patient?"

"Yes. The matron, Sister Marigold, joined us. We found the patient's condition markedly worse. As you know, he died about half an hour later, without regaining consciousness."

"Thank you. That covers the ground. I am extremely grateful to all of you for helping us with this rather unpleasant business. I won't keep you any longer." He turned to Phillips. "You would like to get out of your uniforms, I'm sure."

177

"If you're finished," agreed Phillips. Fox opened the swing-door and he went through, followed by Thoms, Sister Marigold, Jane Harden, and Banks. Dr. Roberts crossed to the anæsthetising apparatus.

"I'll get this out of the way," he said.

"Oh—do you mind leaving it while you change?" said Alleyn. "I just want to make a plan of the floor."

"Certainly," said Roberts.

"Would you be very kind and see if you can beat me up a sheet of paper and a pencil, Dr. Roberts? Sorry to bother you, but I hardly like to send one of my own people hunting for it."

"Shall I ask?" suggested Roberts.

He put his head round the door into the anteroom and spoke to someone on the other side.

"Inspector Alleyn would like——"

Fox walked heavily across from the other end of the theatre.

"I can hear a telephone ringing its head off out there, sir," he said, looking fixedly at Alleyn.

"Really? I wonder if it's that call from the Yard? Go and see, will you, Fox? Sister Marigold won't mind, I'm sure."

Fox went out.

"Inspector Alleyn," ventured Roberts, "I do hope that the reconstruction has been satisfactory——" He broke off. Phillips's resonant voice could be heard in the anteroom. With a glance towards it Roberts ended wistfully:—"from every point of view."

Alleyn smiled at him, following his glance.

"From *that* point of view, Dr. Roberts, most satisfactory."

"I'm extremely glad."

Jane Harden came in with a sheet of paper and pencil which she gave Alleyn. She went out. Roberts watched Alleyn lay the paper on the side table and take out his steel tape measure. Fox returned.

"Telephone for Dr. Roberts, I believe, sir," he announced.

"Oh—for you, is it?" said Alleyn.

Roberts went out through the anæsthetic-room.

"Shut that door, quick," said Alleyn urgently.

Evidently he had changed his mind about making a plan. He darted like a cat across the room and bent over the frame of the anæsthetic apparatus. His fingers were busy with the nuts.

Boys stood in front of one door, Fox by the other.

"Hell's teeth, it's stiff," muttered Alleyn.

178

The double doors from the anteroom opened suddenly, banging Inspector Boys in the broad of his extensive back.

"Just a minute, sir, just a minute," he rumbled.

Under his extended arm appeared the face of Mr. Thoms. His eyes were fixed on Alleyn.

"What are you doing?" he said. "What are you doing?"

"Just a minute, if you please, sir," repeated Boys, and with an enormous but moderate paw he thrust Thoms back and closed the doors.

"Look at this!" whispered Alleyn.

Fox and Boys, for a split second, glimpsed what he held in his hand. Then he bent down again and worked feverishly.

"What'll we do?" asked Fox quietly. "Go right into it—now?"

For an instant Alleyn hesitated. Then he said:

"No—not here. Wait! Work it this way."

He had given his instructions when Roberts returned from the telephone.

"Nobody there," he told them. "I rang up my house, but there's no message. Whoever it was must have been cut off."

"Bore for you," said Alleyn.

Sister Marigold came in, followed by Thoms. Marigold saw the Yard men still in possession, and hesitated.

"Hallo, 'allo," shouted Thoms, "what's all this? Caught Roberts in the act?"

"Really, Mr. Thoms," said Roberts in a rage and went over to his apparatus. "All right, matron," said Alleyn, "I've done. You want to clear up, I expect."

"Oh, well—yes."

"Go ahead. We'll make ourselves scarce. Fox, you and Boys give Dr. Roberts a hand out with that cruet-stand."

"Thank you," said Roberts, "I'll manage."

"No trouble at all, sir," Fox assured him.

Alleyn left them there. He ran downstairs and out into Brook Street, where he hailed a taxi.

In forty minutes the same taxi put him down in Wigmore Street. This time he had two plain-clothes sergeants with him. Dr. Roberts's little butler opened the door. His face was terribly white. He looked at Alleyn without speaking and then stood aside. Alleyn, followed by his men, walked into the drawing-room. Roberts stood in front of the fireplace. Above him the picture of the little lake and the Christmas trees shone cheerfully

179

in the lamplight. Fox stood inside the door and Boys near the window. The anæsthetic apparatus had been wheeled over by the desk.

When Roberts saw Alleyn he tried to speak, but at first could not. His lips moved as though he was speaking, but there were no words. Then at last they came.

"Inspector Alleyn—why—have you sent these men—after me?"

For a moment they looked at each other.

"I had to," said Alleyn. "Dr. Roberts, I have a warrant here for your arrest. I must warn you——"

"What do you mean!" screamed Roberts. "You've no grounds—no proof—you fool—what are you doing?"

Alleyn walked over to the thing like a cruet. He stooped down, unscrewed something that looked like a nut and drew it out. With it came a hypodermic syringe. The 'nut' was the top of the piston.

"Grounds enough," said Alleyn.

It took the four men to hold Roberts and they had to put handcuffs on him. The insane are sometimes physically very strong.

CHAPTER XVIII

Retrospective

Saturday, the twentieth. Evening.

Two evenings after the arrest Alleyn dined with Nigel and
Angela. The inspector had already been badgered by Nigel for
copy and had thrown him a few bones to gnaw. Angela, however,
pined for first-hand information. During dinner the inspector was
rather silent and withdrawn. Something prompted Angela to kick
Nigel smartly on the shin when he broached the subject of the
arrest. Nigel suppresed a cry of pain and glared at her. She shook
her head slightly.

"Was it very painful, Bathgate?" asked Alleyn. "Er—oh—
yes," said Nigel sheepishly.

"How did you know I kicked him?" Angela inquired. "You
must be a detective."

"Not so that you would notice it, but perhaps I am about to
strike form again."

"Hallo—all bitter, are you? Aren't you pleased with yourself
over this case, Mr. Alleyn?" Angela ventured.

"One never gets a great deal of gratification from a fluke."

"A fluke!" exclaimed Nigel.

"Just that——"

He held his glass of port under his nose, glanced significantly at
Nigel and sipped it.

"Go on," he said resignedly. "Go on. Ask me. I know perfectly
well why I'm here and you don't produce a wine like this every
evening. Bribery. Subtle corruption. Isn't it, now?"

"Yes," said Nigel simply.

"I won't have Mr. Alleyn bullied," said Angela.

"You would if *he* could," rejoined Alleyn cryptically. "I know your tricks and your manners."

The others were silent.

"As a matter of fact," Alleyn continued, "I have every intention of talking for hours."

They beamed.

"What an angel you are, to be sure," said Angela. "Bring that decanter next door. Don't dare sit over it in here. The ladies are about to leave the dining-room."

She got up; Alleyn opened the door for her, and she went through into Nigel's little sitting-room, where she hastily cast four logs on the fire, pulled up a low table between two armchairs, and sat down on the hearthrug.

"Come on!" she called sternly.

They came in. Alleyn put the decanter down reverently on the table, and in a moment they were all settled.

"Now," said Angela, "I do call this fun."

She looked from Nigel to Alleyn. Each had the contented air of the well-fed male. The fire blazed up with a roar and a crackle, lighting the inspector's dark head and his admirable hands. He settled himself back and, easing his chin, turned and smiled at her.

"You may begin," said Angela.

"But—where from?"

"From the beginning—well, from the operating theatre."

"Oh. The remark I invariably make about the theatre is that it afforded the ideal setting for a murder. The whole place was cleaned up scientifically—hygienically—completely—as soon as the body of the victim was removed. No chance of a fingerprint, so significant bits and pieces left on the floor. Nothing. As a matter of fact, of course, had it been exactly as it was, we should have found nothing that pointed to Roberts." Alleyn fell silent again.

"Begin from where you first suspected Roberts," suggested Nigel.

"From where *you* suspected him, rather. The funny little man, you know."

"By gum, yes. So I did."

"Did *you*?" Angela asked.

"I had no definite theory about him," said Alleyn. "That's why I talked about a fluke. I was uneasy about him. I had a hunch, and I hate hunches. The first day I saw him in his house I began to feel jumpy about him, and fantastic ideas kept dodging about at the back of my mind. He was, it seemed, a fanatic. That long, hectic harangue about hereditary taints—somehow it was too vehement. He was obviously nervous about the case and yet he couldn't keep off it. He very delicately urged the suicide theory and backed it up with a lecture on eugenics. He was certainly sincere, too sincere, terribly earnest. The whole atmosphere was unbalanced. I recognised the man with an *idée fixe*. Then he told me a long story about how he'd once given an overdose, and that was why he never gave injections. That made me uncomfortable, because it was such a handy proof of innocence. '*He* can't have done the job, because he never gives an injection.' Then I saw his stethoscope with rows of notches on the stem and again there was a perfect explanation. He said it was a sort of tally for every anæsthetic he gave successfully to patients with heart disease. I was reminded of Indian tomahawks and Edward S. Ellis, and more particularly of a catapult I had as a boy and the notches I cut in the handle for every bird I killed. The fantastic notion that the stethoscope was *that* sort of tally-stick nagged and nagged at me. When we found he was one of the Lenin Hall lot I wondered if he could possibly be their agent, and yet I didn't somehow think there was anything in the Lenin Hall lot. When we discovered he had hoped to egg them on over the Sterilisation Bill I felt that accounted perfectly for his association with them. Next time I saw him I meant to surprise him with a sudden question about them. He completely defeated me by talking about them of his own accord. That might have been a subtle move, but I didn't think so. He lent me his book and here again I found the fanatic. I don't know why it is that pursuit of any branch of scientific thought which is greatly concerned with sex so often leads to morbid obsession. Not always, by any means—but very often. I've met it over and over again. It's an interesting point and I'd like to know the explanation. Roberts's book is a sound, a well-written plea for rational breeding. It is not in the least hysterical, and yet, behind it, in the personality of the writer, I smelt hysteria. There was one chapter where he said that a future civilisation might avoid the expense and trouble of supporting its a-ments and de-ments by eliminating them altogether. 'Sterilisation,' he wrote, 'might in time be replaced by extermination.' After reading that I forced myself to face up to that uneasy idea that had worried me ever since I first spoke to him. O'Callaghan came of what Roberts would regard as tainted stock. Suppose—suppose, thought I, blushing at my own credulity, suppose Roberts had got the bright idea of starting the good work by destroying such people every time he got the opportunity? Suppose he had brought if off several times before, and that every time he'd had a success he ticked it up on his stethoscope?"

"Oh, murder!" Nigel apostrophised.

"You may say so."

"Have some port."

"Thank you. It sounded so incredibly far-fetched that I simply hadn't the nerve to confide in Fox. I carried on with all the others—Mr. Sage and his remedies, Phillips and his girl, Banks and the Bolshies. Well, the patent medicine Sage provided through Miss O'Callaghan—'Fulvitavolts,' he calls it—has an infinitesimal amount of hyoscine. The second lot that Miss O'Callaghan administered in the hospital was an unknown quantity until I got the remnant from her. Of course, the fact that he had been responsible for O'Callaghan taking any hyoscine at all threw our Harold into a fearful terror, especially as he was one of the Lenin Hall lot. He tried to get me to believe the second concoction was a doctor's prescription, and very nearly led himself into real trouble. We have since found that this drug, too, only contained a very small amount of hyoscine. Exit Mr. Sage. Banks might have substituted hyoscine for camphor when she prepared the syringe, but I found that the stock solution of hyoscine contained the full amount minus one dose that was accounted for. She might have smuggled in another somehow, or she might have filled up the jar afterwards, but it didn't seem likely. Phillips remained and Phillips worried me terribly. He loomed so large with his threats, his opportunity, his motive. Roberts paled beside him. I caught myself continually opposing these two men. After all, as far as one could see, Roberts had had no chance of giving a hypodermic injection, whereas Phillips, poor devil, had had every opportunity. I staged the reconstruction partly to see if there *was* any way in which Roberts could have done it. I called for him at his house. Now, although I had asked Phillips specifically to have the anæsthetic appliance, Roberts was coming away without it. When I reminded him, he went and got it. I noticed that he wasn't keen on my handling it, and that several times he touched the nuts. It was perfectly reasonable, but it made me look at them and kept them in my mind. Remember I was by no means wedded to my fantastic idea—rather the reverse. I was ashamed of it and I still reasoned, though I did not feel, that Phillips was the principal suspect. We watched them all closely. Then came the fluke—the amazing, the incredible fluke. Old Marigold lost her nerve and did a trip over the cruet-thing that holds the gasometers. Thoms helped Roberts, in a way, by a spirited rendering of the jack-in-office. Thoms is a bit of a funk and he was scared. He made a rumpus. If it hadn't been for my 'idea,' I shouldn't have watched Roberts. As it was, he gave a magnificent performance. But he went green round the gills and he was most careful to let no one touch the nuts. As a matter of fact, I believe Thoms's funk was entirely superfluous—it is most unlikely that the cylinder would blow up. Think what a shock it must have been to Roberts. Suppose the syringe had fallen out! Practically an impossibility—but in the panic of the moment his imagination, his 'guilty knowledge' if you like, would play tricks with his reason. I rather felt I had allowed mine to do the same. My dears, my head was in a whirl, I promise you."

"But when," asked Angela, "did Dr. Roberts inject the hyoscine?"

"I think soon after the patient was put on the table. The screen over the chest would hide his hands."

"I see."

"After the reconstruction Roberts wouldn't leave us alone. He hung about in the theatre, intent, of course, on keeping me away from the cruet. Fox, bless his heart, rumbled this ruse and staged a bogus telephone call. He saw I wanted to be rid of Roberts. As soon as we were alone I fell on the cruet, and, after a nerve-racking fumble, unearthed the syringe. Eureka! Dénouement! Fox nearly had a fit of the vapours."

"So you arrested him there and then!" cried Angela.

"No. No, I didn't. For one thing I hadn't a warrant and for another—oh, well——"

Alleyn rested his nose on his clasped hands.

"Now what's coming?" asked Angela.

"I rather liked the little creature. It would have been an unpleasant business pulling him in there. Anyway, I went off and got a warrant and Fox and Boys accompanied him home. They watched him carefully in case he tried to give himself the *coup de*

185

grâce, but he didn't. When I arrested him he had, I believe, a sudden and an appalling shock, a kind of dreadful moment of lucidity. He fought us so violently that he seemed like a sane man gone mad, but I believe he was a madman gone sane. It only lasted a few minutes. Now I don't think he cares at all. He has made a complete confession. He's batty. He'll have to stand his trial, but I think they'll find that the nut in the cruet-stand is not the only one loose. It may even be that Roberts, recognising the taint of madness in himself, felt the eugenic urge the more strongly and the need for eliminating the unfit. In that point of view there is precisely the kind of mad logic one would expect to find in such a case."

"If it hadn't been for the matron's trip, would you never have got him?" asked Nigel.

"I think we should—in the end. We should have got his history from Canada and Australasia. It's coming through now. When it's complete I am pretty certain we shall find a series of deaths after anæsthetics given by Roberts. They will all prove to be cases where there were signs of hereditary insanity. I shouldn't mind betting they correspond with the notches on the stethoscope—minus one."

"Minus one?" asked Nigel.

"He added a fresh notch, no doubt, on Thursday, the eleventh. The last one does look more recent, although he'd rubbed a bit of dirt into it. You may think, as judges say when they mean you ought to think, that it was an extremely rum thing for him to leave the syringe in the cruet after the job was done. Not so rum. It was really the safest place imaginable. Away from there it would have been a suspicious-looking object, with a nut, instead of the ordinary top, to the piston. I believe that extraordinary little man filled it up with hyoscine whenever he was called out to give an anæsthetic to someone he did not know, just on the off-chance the patient should turn out to be what I understand sheep-farmers call a 'cull'. It's a striking example of the logic of the lunatic."

"Oh," cried Angela, "I do hope they find him insane."

"Do you?"

"Don't you?"

"I hardly know. That means a criminal lunatic asylum. It's a pity we are not allowed to hand him one of his own hypodermics."

There was a short silence.

186

"Have some port?" said Nigel.

"Thank you," said Alleyn. He did not pour it out, however, but sat looking abstractedly into the fire.

"You see," he murmured at last, "he's done his job. From his point of view it's all a howling success. He does nothing but tell us how clever he's been. His one anxiety is lest he may not be appreciated. He's busy writing a monograph for which all your gods of Fleet Street, Bathgate, will offer fabulous prices. At least he is assured of competent defence."

"What about Sir John Phillips and Jane Harden?" asked Angela.

"What about them, Miss Angela?"

"Is she going to marry him now?"

"How should I know?"

"She'll be a fool if she doesn't," said Angela emphatically.

"I'm afraid you've got the movie-mind. You want a final close-up. 'John—I want you to know that—that—' Ecstatic glare at short distance into each other's faces. Sir John utters an amorous growl: 'You damned little fool,' and snatches her to his bosom. Slow fade-out."

"That's the stuff," said Angela. "I like a happy ending."

"We don't often see it in the Force," said Alleyn. "Have some port?"

"Thank you."

Death in a White Tie

Contents

THE CHARACTERS IN THE TALE

Chief Detective-Inspector Roderick Alleyn, CID	
Lady Alleyn	*His mother*
Sarah Alleyn	*His débutante niece*
Miss Violet Harris	*Secretary to Lady Carrados*
Lady Evelyn Carrados	*A London hostess*
Bridget O'Brien	*Her daughter*
Sir Herbert Carrados	*Her husband*
Lord Robert Gospell ('Bunchy')	*A relic of Victorian days*
Sir Daniel Davidson	*A fashionable London physician*
Agatha Troy, RA	*A painter*
Lady Mildred Potter	*Lord Robert's widowed sister*
Donald Potter	*Her son – a medical student*
Mrs Halcut-Hackett	*A social climber*
General Halcut-Hackett	*Her husband*
Miss Rose Birnbaum	*Her protégée*
Captain Maurice Withers ('Wits')	*A man about town*
Colombo Dimitri	*A fashionable caterer*
Lucy, Dowager Marchioness of Lorrimer	*An eccentric old lady*
A Taxi-driver	
Miss Smith	*A friend of Miss Harris*

Detective-Inspector Fox,
  CID
Percy Percival   *A young man about town*
Mr Trelawney-Caper   *His friend*
James d'Arcy Carewe   *A detective-constable*
François Dupont   *Dimitri's servant*
Mr Cuthbert   *Manager of the Matador*
Vassily   *Alleyn's servant*
The Reverend Walter Harris   *A retired clergyman*
Mrs Walter Harris   *His wife*
The Assistant Commissioner

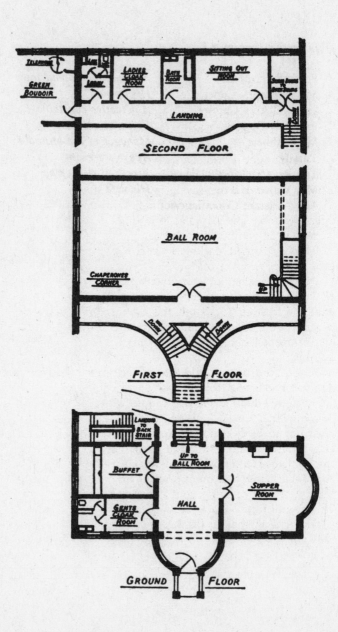

CHAPTER ONE

The Protagonists

'Roderick,' said Lady Alleyn, looking at her son over the top of her spectacles, 'I am coming out.'

'Out?' repeated Chief Detective-Inspector Alleyn vaguely. 'Out where, mama? Out of what?'

'Out into the world. Out of retirement. Out into the season. Out. Dear me,' she added confusedly, 'how absurd a word becomes if one says it repeatedly. Out.'

Alleyn laid an official-looking document on the breakfast-table and stared at his mother.

'What can you be talking about?' he said.

'Don't be stupid, darling. I am going to do the London season.'

'Have you taken leave of your senses?'

'I think perhaps I have. I have told George and Grace that I will bring Sarah out this coming season. Here is a letter from George and here is another from Grace. Government House, Suva. They think it charming of me to offer.'

'Good Lord, mama,' said Alleyn, 'you must be demented. Do you know what this means?'

'I believe I do. It means that I must take a flat in London. It means that I must look up all sorts of people who will turn out to be dead or divorced or remarried. It means that I must give little luncheon-parties and cocktail-parties and exchange cutlets with hard-working mothers. It means that I must sit in ballrooms praising other women's grand-daughters and securing young men for my own. I shall be up until four o'clock five nights out of seven and I'm afraid, darling, that my black lace and my silver charmeuse will not be quite equal to the strain. So that in addition

195

to buying clothes for Sarah I shall have to buy some for myself. And I should like to know what you think about that, Roderick?'

'I think it is all utterly preposterous. Why the devil can't George and Grace bring Sarah out themselves?'

'Because they are in Fiji, darling.'

'Well, why can't she stay in until they return?'

'George's appointment is for four years. In four years your niece will be twenty-two. An elderly sort of débutante.'

'*Why* has Sarah got to come out? Why can't she simply emerge?'

'That I cannot tell you, but George and Grace certainly could. I rather see it, I must say, Roderick. A girl has such fun doing her first season. There is nothing like it, ever again. And now we have gone back to chaperones and all the rest of it, it really does seem to have some of the old glamour.'

'You mean débutantes have gone back to being treated like hothouse flowers for three months and taking their chance as hardy perennials for the rest of their lives?'

'If you choose to put it like that. The system is not without merit, my dear.'

'It may be quite admirable, but isn't it going to be a bit too exhausting for you? Where is Sarah, by the way?'

'She is always rather late for breakfast. How wonderfully these children sleep, don't they? But we were talking about the season, weren't we? I think I shall enjoy it, Rory. And really and truly it won't be such hard work. I've heard this morning from Evelyn Carrados. She was Evelyn O'Brien, you know. Evelyn Curtis, of course, in the *first* instance, but that's so long ago nobody bothers about it. Not that she's as old as that, poor girl. She can't be forty yet. Quite a chicken, in fact. Her mother was my greatest friend. We did the season together when we came out. And now here's Evelyn bringing her own girl out and

196

offering to help with Sarah. Could anything be more fortunate?'

'Nothing,' responded Alleyn dryly. 'I remember Evelyn O'Brien.'

'I should hope you do. I did my best to persuade you to fall in love with her.'

'Did I fall in love with her?'

'No. I could never imagine why, as she was quite lovely and very charming. Now I come to think of it, you hadn't much chance as she herself fell madly in love with Paddy O'Brien who returned suddenly from Australia.'

'I remember. A romantic sort of bloke, wasn't he?'

'Yes. They were married after a short engagement. Five months later he was killed in a motor accident. Wasn't it awful?'

'Awful.'

'And then in six months or so along came this girl, Bridget. Evelyn called her Bridget because Paddy was Irish. And then, poor Evelyn, she married Herbert Carrados. Nobody ever knew why.'

'I'm not surprised. He's a frightful bore. He must be a great deal older than Evelyn.'

'A thousand years and so pompous you can't believe he's true. You know him evidently.'

'Vaguely. He's something pretty grand in the City.'

Alleyn lit his mother's cigarette and his own. He walked over to the french window and looked across the lawn.

'Your garden is getting ready to come out, too,' he said. 'I wish I hadn't to go back to the Yard.'

'Now, darling? This minute?'

'Afraid so. It's this case.' He waved some papers in his hand. 'Fox rang up late last night. Something's cropped up.'

'What sort of case is it?'

'Blackmail, but you're not allowed to ask questions.'

'Rory, how exciting. Who's being blackmailed? Somebody frightfully important, I hope?'

'Do you remember Lord Robert Gospell?'

'*Bunchy* Gospell, do you mean? Surely he's not being blackmailed. A more innocent creature – '

'No, mama, he isn't. Nor is he a blackmailer.'

'He's a dear little man,' said Lady Alleyn emphatically. 'The nicest possible little man.'

'Not so little nowadays. He's very plump and wears a cloak and a sombrero like G.K.C.'

'Really?'

'You must have seen photographs of him in your horrible illustrated papers. They catch him when they can. "Lord Robert ('Bunchy') Gospell tells one of his famous stories." That sort of thing.'

'Yes, but what's he got to do with blackmail?'

'Nothing. He is, as you say, an extremely nice little man.'

'Roderick, don't be infuriating. Has Bunchy Gospell got anything to do with Scotland Yard?'

Alleyn was staring out into the garden.

'You might say,' he said at last, 'that we have a very great respect for him at the Yard. Not only is he charming – he is also, in his own way, a rather remarkable personage.'

Lady Alleyn looked at her son meditatively for some seconds.

'Are you meeting him today?' she asked.

'I think so.'

'Why?'

'Why, darling, to listen to one of his famous stories, I suppose.'

It was Miss Harris's first day in her new job. She was secretary to Lady Carrados and had been engaged for the London season. Miss Harris knew quite well what this meant. It was not, in a secretarial sense, by any means her first season. She was a competent young woman, almost

198

frighteningly unimaginative, with a brain that was divided into neat pigeon-holes, and a mind that might be said to label all questions 'answered' or 'unanswered'. If a speculative or unconventional idea came Miss Harris's way, it was promptly dealt with or promptly shut up in a dark pigeon-hole and never taken out again. If Miss Harris had not been able to answer it immediately, it was unanswerable and therefore of no importance. Owing perhaps to her intensive training as a member of the large family of a Buckinghamshire clergyman she never for a moment asked herself why she should go through life organising fun for other people and having comparatively little herself. That would have seemed to Miss Harris an irrelevant and rather stupid speculation. One's job was a collection of neatly filed duties, suitable to one's station in life, and therefore respectable. It had no wider ethical interest of any sort at all. This is not to say Miss Harris was insensitive. On the contrary, she was rather touchy on all sorts of points of etiquette relating to her position in the houses in which she was employed. Where she had her lunch, with whom she had it, and who served it, were matters of great importance to her and she was painfully aware of the subtlest nuances in her employers' attitude towards herself. About her new job she was neatly optimistic. Lady Carrados had impressed her favourably, had treated her, in her own phrase, like a perfect lady. Miss Harris walked briskly along an upstairs passage and tapped twice, not too loud and not too timidly, on a white door.

'Come in,' cried a far-away voice.

Miss Harris obeyed and found herself in a large white bedroom. The carpet, the walls and the chairs were all white. A cedar-wood fire crackled beneath the white Adam mantelpiece, a white bearskin rug nearly tripped Miss Harris up as she crossed the floor to the large white bed where her employer sat propped up with pillows. The bed was strewn about with sheets of notepaper.

199

'Oh, good morning, Miss Harris,' said Lady Carrados. 'You can't think how glad I am to see you. *Do* you mind waiting a moment while I finish this note? Please sit down.'

Miss Harris sat discreetly on a small chair. Lady Carrados gave her a vague, brilliant smile, and turned again to her writing. Miss Harris with a single inoffensive glance had taken in every detail of her employer's appearance.

Evelyn Carrados was thirty-seven years old, and on her good days looked rather less. She was a dark, tall woman with little colour but a beautiful pallor. Paddy O'Brien had once shown her a copy of the Madonna di San Sisto and had told her that she was looking at herself. This was not quite true. Her face was longer and had more edge and character than Raphael's complacent virgin, but the large dark eyes were like and the sleek hair parted down the centre. Paddy had taken to calling her 'Donna' after that and she still had his letters beginning: 'Darling Donna.' Oddly enough, Bridget, his daughter, who had never seen him, called her mother 'Donna' too. She had come into the room on the day Miss Harris was interviewed and had sat on the arm of her mother's chair. A still girl with a lovely voice. Miss Harris looking straight in front of her remembered this interview now while she waited. '*He* hasn't appeared yet,' thought Miss Harris, meaning Sir Herbert Carrados, whose photograph faced her in a silver frame on his wife's dressing-table.

Lady Carrados signed her name and hunted about the counterpane for blotting-paper. Miss Harris instantly placed her own pad on the bed.

'Oh,' said her employer with an air of pleased astonishment, 'you've got some! Thank you so much. There, that's settled *her*, hasn't it?'

Miss Harris smiled brightly. Lady Carrados licked the flap of an envelope and stared at her secretary over the top.

'I see you've brought up my mail,' she said.

'Yes, Lady Carrados. I did not know if you would prefer me to open all – '

'No, no. No, please not.'

Miss Harris did not visibly bridle, she was much too competent to do anything of the sort, but she was at once hurt in her feelings. A miserable, a hateful, little needle of mortification jabbed her thin skin. She had overstepped her mark.

'Very well, Lady Carrados,' said Miss Harris politely.

Lady Carrados bent forward.

'I know I'm all wrong,' she said quickly. 'I know I'm not behaving a bit as one should when one is lucky enough to have a secretary but, you see, I'm not used to such luxuries, and I still like to pretend I'm doing everything myself. So I shall have all the fun of opening my letters and all the joy of handing them over to you. Which is very unfair, but you'll have to put up with it, poor Miss Harris.'

She watched her secretary smile and replied with a charming look of understanding.

'And now,' she said, 'we may as well get it done, mayn't we?'

Miss Harris laid the letters in three neat heaps on the writing-pad and soon began to make shorthand notes of the answers she was to write for her employer. Lady Carrados kept up a sort of running commentary.

'Lucy Lorrimer. Who is Lucy Lorrimer, Miss Harris? *I* know, she's that old Lady Lorrimer who talks as if everybody was deaf. What does she want? "Hear you are bringing out your girl and would be so glad – " Well, we'll have to see about that, won't we? If it's a free afternoon we'd be delighted. There you are. Now, this one. Oh, *yes*, Miss Harris, now this is *most* important. It's from Lady Alleyn, who is a *great* friend of mine. Do you know who I mean? One of her sons is a deadly baronet and the other is a detective. Do you know?'

'Is it Chief Inspector Alleyn, Lady Carrados? The famous one?'

'That's it. Terribly good-looking and remote. He was in the Foreign Office when the war broke out and then after the war he suddenly became a detective. I can't tell you why. Not that it matters,' continued Lady Carrados, glancing at the attentive face of her secretary, 'because this letter is nothing to do with him. It's about his brother George's girl whom his mother is bringing out and I said I'd help. So you must remember, Miss Harris, that Sarah Alleyn is to be asked to *everything*. And Lady Alleyn to the mothers' lunches and all those games. Have you got that? There's her address. And remind me to write personally. Now away we go again and – '

She stopped so suddenly that Miss Harris glanced up in surprise. Lady Carrados was staring at a letter which she held in her long white fingers. The fingers trembled slightly. Miss Harris with a sort of fascination looked at them and at the square envelope. There was a silence in the white room – a silence broken only by the hurried inconsequent ticking of a little china clock on the mantelpiece. With a sharp click the envelope fell on the heap of letters.

'Excuse me, Lady Carrados,' said Miss Harris, 'but are you feeling unwell?'

'What? No. No, thank you.'

She put the letter aside and picked up another. Soon Miss Harris's pen was travelling busily over her pad. She made notes for the acceptance, refusal and issuing of invitations. She made lists of names with notes beside them and she entered into a long discussion about Lady Carrados's ball.

'I'm getting Dimitri – the Shepherd Market caterer, you know – to do the whole thing,' explained Lady Carrados. 'It seems to be the – ' she paused oddly ' – safest way.'

'Well, he *is* the best,' agreed Miss Harris. 'You were

202

speaking of expense, Lady Carrados. Dimitri works out at about twenty-five shillings a head. But that's *everything*. You do know where you are and he is good.'

'Twenty-five? Four hundred, there'll be, I think. How much is that?'

'Five hundred pounds,' said Miss Harris calmly.

'Oh, dear, it is a lot, isn't it? And then there's the band. I do think we must have champagne at the buffet. It saves that endless procession to the supper-room which I always think is such a bore.'

'Champagne at the buffet,' said Miss Harris crisply. 'That will mean thirty shillings a head, I'm afraid.'

'*Oh*, how awful!'

'That makes Dimitri's bill six hundred. But, of course, as I say, Lady Carrados, that will be every penny you pay.'

Lady Carrados stared at her secretary without replying. For some reason Miss Harris felt as if she had made another *faux pas*. There was, she thought, such a very singular expression in her employer's eyes.

'I should think a thousand pounds would cover the whole of the expenses, band and everything,' she added hurriedly.

'Yes, I see,' said Lady Carrados. 'A thousand.'

There was a tap at the door and a voice called: 'Donna!'

'Come in, darling!'

A tall, dark girl carrying a pile of letters came into the room. Bridget was very like her mother but nobody would have thought of comparing her to the Sistine Madonna. She had inherited too much of Paddy O'Brien's brilliance for that. There was a fine-drawn look about her mouth. Her eyes, set wide apart, were deep under strongly marked brows. She had the quality of repose but when she smiled all the corners of her face tipped up and then she looked more like her father than her mother. 'Sensitive,' thought Miss Harris, with a mild flash of illumination. 'I hope she stands up to it all right. Nuisance when they get nerves.'

She returned Bridget's punctilious 'Good morning' and watched her kiss her mother.

'Darling Donna,' said Bridget, 'you are so sweet.'

'Hullo, my darling,' said Lady Carrados, 'here we are plotting away for all we're worth. Miss Harris and I have decided on the eighth for your dance. Uncle Arthur writes that we may have his house on that date. That's General Marsdon, Miss Harris. I explained, didn't I, that he is lending us Marsdon House in Belgrave Square? Or did I?'

'Yes, thank you, Lady Carrados. I've got all that.'

'Of course you have.'

'It's a mausoleum,' said Bridget, 'but it'll do. I've got a letter from Sarah Alleyn, Donna. Her grandmother, your Lady Alleyn, you know, is taking a flat for the season. Donna, please, I want Sarah asked for *everything*. Does Miss Harris know?'

'Yes, thank you, Miss Carrados. I beg pardon,' said Miss Harris in some confusion, 'I should have said, Miss O'Brien, shouldn't I?'

'Help, yes! Don't fall into that trap whatever you do,' cried Bridget. 'Sorry, Donna darling, but really!'

'Ssh!' said Lady Carrados mildly. 'Are those your letters?'

'Yes. All the invitations. I've put a black mark against the ones I really do jib at and all the rest will just have to be sorted out. Oh, and I've put a big Y on the ones I want specially not to miss. And – '

The door opened again and the photograph on the dressing-table limped into the room.

Sir Herbert Carrados was just a little too good to be true. He was tall and soldierly and good-looking. He had thin sandy hair, a large guardsman's moustache, heavy eyebrows and rather foolish light eyes. You did not notice they were foolish because his eyebrows gave them a spurious fierceness. He was not, however, a stupid man but only a rather vain and pompous one. It was his pride that he looked like a soldier and not like a successful financier. During the Great War he had held down a staff appointment of bewildering unimportance which had kept him in Tunbridge Wells for the duration and which had not hampered his sound and at times brilliant activities in the City. He limped a little and used a stick. Most people took it as a matter of course that he had been wounded in the leg, and so he had – by a careless gamekeeper. He attended military reunions with the greatest assiduity and was about to stand for Parliament.

Bridget called him Bart, which he rather liked, but he occasionally surprised a look of irony in her eyes and that he did not at all enjoy.

This morning he had *The Times* under his arm and an expression of forbearance on his face. He kissed his wife, greeted Miss Harris with precisely the correct shade of cordiality, and raised his eyebrows at his stepdaughter.

'Good morning, Bridget. I thought you were still in bed.'

'Good morning, Bart,' said Bridget. 'Why?'

'You were not at breakfast. Don't you think perhaps it would be more considerate to the servants if you breakfasted before you started making plans?'

'I expect it would,' agreed Bridget and went as far as the door.

'What are your plans for today, darling?' continued Sir Herbert, smiling at his wife.

'Oh – everything. Bridget's dance. Miss Harris and I are – are going into expense, Herbert.'

'Ah, yes?' murmured Sir Herbert. 'I'm sure Miss Harris is a perfect dragon with figures. What's the total, Miss Harris?'

'For the ball, Sir Herbert?' Miss Harris glanced at Lady Carrados who nodded a little nervously. 'It's about a thousand pounds.'

'Good God!' exclaimed Sir Herbert and let his eyeglass fall.

205

'You see, darling,' began his wife in a hurry, 'it just *won't* come down to less. Even with Arthur's house. And if we have champagne at the buffet – '

'I cannot see the smallest necessity for champagne at the buffet, Evelyn. If these young cubs can't get enough to drink in the supper-room all I can say is, they drink a great deal too much. I must say,' continued Sir Herbert with an air of discovery, 'that I do not understand the mentality of modern youths. Gambling too much, drinking too much, no object in life – look at that young Potter.'

'If you mean Donald Potter,' said Bridget dangerously, ' I must – '

'Bridgie!' said her mother.

'You're wandering from the point, Bridget,' said her step-father.

'Me!'

'My point is,' said Sir Herbert with a martyred glance at his wife, 'that the young people expect a great deal too much nowadays. Champagne at every table – '

'It's not that – ' began Bridget from the door.

'It's only that it saves – ' interrupted her mother.

'However,' continued Sir Herbert with an air of patient courtesy, 'if you feel that you can afford to spend a thousand pounds on an evening, my dear – '

'But it isn't all Donna's money,' objected Bridget. 'It's half mine. Daddy left – '

'Bridget, darling,' said Lady Carrados, 'breakfast.'

'Sorry, Donna,' said Bridget. 'All right.' She went out.

Miss Harris wondered if she too had better go, but nobody seemed to remember she was in the room and she did not quite like to remind them of her presence by making a move. Lady Carrados with an odd mixture of nervousness and determination was talking rapidly.

'I know Paddy would have meant some of Bridgie's money to be used for her coming out, Herbert. It isn't as if – '

206

'My dear,' said Sir Herbert with an ineffable air of tactful reproach, and a glance at Miss Harris. 'Of course. It's entirely for you and Bridget to decide. Naturally. I wouldn't dream of interfering. I'm just rather an old fool and like to give any help I can. Don't pay any attention.'

Lady Carrados was saved the necessity of making any reply to this embarrassing speech by the entrance of the maid.

'Lord Robert Gospell has called, m'lady, and wonders if – '

''Morning, Evelyn,' said an extraordinarily high-pitched voice outside the door. 'I've come up. Do let me in.'

'Bunchy!' cried Lady Carrados in delight. 'How lovely! Come in!'

And Lord Robert Gospell, panting a little under the burden of an enormous bunch of daffodils, toddled into the room.

On the same day that Lord Robert Gospell called on Lady Carrados, Lady Carrados herself called on Sir Daniel Davidson in his consulting-rooms in Harley Street. She talked to him for a long time and at the end of half an hour sat staring rather desperately across the desk into his large black eyes.

'I'm frightfully anxious, naturally, that Bridgie shouldn't get the idea that there's anything the matter with me,' she said.

'There is nothing *specifically* wrong with you,' said Davidson, spreading out his long hands. 'Nothing, I mean, in the sense of your heart being overworked or your lungs at all unsound or any nonsense of that sort. I don't think you are anaemic. The blood test will clear all that up. But' – and he leant forward and pointed a finger at her – '*but* you are very tired. You're altogether too tired. If I was an honest physician I'd tell you to go into a nursing-home and lead the life of a placid cow for three weeks.'

'I can't do that.'

'Can't your daughter come out next year? What about the little season?'

'Oh, no, it's impossible. Really. My uncle has lent us his house for the dance. She's planned everything. It would be almost as much trouble to put things off as it is to go on with them. I'll be all right, only I do rather feel as if I've got a jellyfish instead of a brain. A wobbly jellyfish. I get these curious giddy attacks. And I simply *can't* stop bothering about things.'

'I know. What about this ball? I suppose you're hard at it over that?'

'I'm handing it all over to my secretary and Dimitri. I hope you're coming. You'll get a card.'

'I shall be delighted, but I wish you'd give it up.'

'Truly I can't.'

'Have you got any particular worry?'

There was a long pause.

'Yes,' said Evelyn Carrados, 'but I can't tell you about that.'

'Ah, well,' said Sir Daniel, shrugging his shoulders. '*Les maladies suspendent nos vertus et nos vices.*'

She rose and he at once leapt to his feet as if she was royalty.

'You will get that prescription made up at once,' he said, glaring down at her. 'And, if you please, I should like to see you again. I suppose I had better not call?'

'No, please. I'll come here.'

'*C'est entendu.*'

Lady Carrados left him, wishing vaguely that he was a little less florid and longing devoutly for her bed.

Agatha Troy hunched up her shoulders, pulled her smart new cap over one eye and walked into her one-man show at the Wiltshire Galleries in Bond Street. It always embarrassed her intensely to put in these duty appearances

208

at her own exhibitions. People felt they had to say something to her about her pictures and they never knew what to say and she never knew how to reply. She became gruff with shyness and her incoherence was mistaken for intellectual snobbishness. Like most painters she was singularly inarticulate on the subject of her work. The careful phrases of literary appreciation showered upon her by highbrow critics threw Troy into an agony of embarrassment. She minded less the bland commonplaces of the philistines though for these also she had great difficulty in finding suitable replies.

She slipped in at the door, winked at the young man who sat at the reception desk and shied away as a large American woman bore down upon him with a white-gloved finger firmly planted on a price in her catalogue.

Troy hurriedly looked away and in a corner of the crowded room, sitting on a chair that was not big enough for him, she saw a smallish round gentleman whose head was aslant, his eyes closed and his mouth peacefully open. Troy made for him.

'Bunchy!' she said.

Lord Robert Gospell opened his eyes very wide and moved his lips like a rabbit.

'Hullo!' he said. 'What a scrimmage, ain't it? Pretty good.'

'You were asleep.'

'May have been having a nap.'

'That's a pretty compliment,' said Troy without rancour.

'I had a good prowl first. Just thought I'd pop in,' explained Lord Robert. 'Enjoyed myself.' He balanced his glasses across his nose, flung his head back and with an air of placid approval contemplated a large landscape. Without any of her usual embarrassment Troy looked with him.

'Pretty good,' repeated Bunchy. 'Ain't it?'

He had an odd trick of using Victorian colloquialisms;

legacies, he would explain, from his distinguished father. 'Lor'!' was his favourite ejaculation. He kept up little Victorian politenesses, always leaving cards after a ball and often sending flowers to the hostesses who dined him. His clothes were famous – a rather high, close-buttoned jacket and narrowish trousers by day, a soft wide hat and a cloak in the evening. Troy turned from her picture to her companion. He twinkled through his glasses and pointed a fat finger at the landscape.

'Nice and clean,' he said. 'I like 'em clean. Come and have tea.'

'I've only just arrived,' said Troy, 'but I'd love to.'

'I've got the Potters,' said Bunchy. 'My sister and her boy. Wait a bit. I'll fetch 'em.'

'Mildred and Donald?' asked Troy.

'Mildred and Donald. They live with me, you know, since poor Potter died. Donald's just been sent down for some gambling scrape or other. Nice young scamp. No harm in him. Only don't mention Oxford.'

'I'll remember.'

'He'll probably save you the trouble by talking about it himself. I like having young people about. Gay. Keeps one up to scratch. Can you see 'em anywhere? Mildred's wearing a puce toque.'

'Not a *toque*, Bunchy,' said Troy. 'There she is. It's a very smart purple beret. She's seen us. She's coming.'

Lord Robert's widowed sister came billowing through the crowd followed by her extremely good-looking son. She greeted Troy breathlessly but affectionately. Donald bowed, grinned and said: 'We *have* been enjoying ourselves. Frightfully good!'

'Fat lot you know about it,' said Troy good-humouredly. 'Mildred, Bunchy suggests tea.'

'I must say I should be glad of it,' said Lady Mildred Potter. 'Looking at pictures is the most exhausting pastime, even when they are your pictures, dear.'

210

'There's a restaurant down below,' squeaked Lord Robert. 'Follow me.'

They worked their way through the crowd and downstairs. Donald who was separated from them by several strangers, shouted: 'I say, Troy, did you hear I was sent down?' This had the effect of drawing everyone's attention first to himself and then to Troy.

'Yes, I did,' said Troy severely.

'Wasn't it awful?' continued Donald, coming alongside and speaking more quietly. 'Uncle Bunch is *furious* and says I'm no longer The Heir. It's not true, of course. He's leaving me a princely fortune, aren't you, Uncle Bunch, my dear?'

'Here we are,' said Lord Robert thankfully as they reached the door of the restaurant. 'Will you all sit down. I'm afraid I must be rather quick.' He pulled out his watch and blinked at it. 'I've an appointment in twenty minutes.'

'Where?' said Troy. 'I'll drive you.'

'Matter of fact,' said Lord Robert, 'it's at Scotland Yard. Meeting an old friend of mine called Alleyn.'

CHAPTER TWO

Bunchy

'Lord Robert Gospell to see you, Mr Alleyn,' said a voice in Alleyn's desk telephone.

'Bring him up, please,' said Alleyn.

He pulled a file out of the top drawer and laid it open before him. Then he rang through to his particular Assistant Commissioner.

'Lord Robert has just arrived, sir. You asked me to let you know.'

'All right, Rory, I'll leave him to you, on second thoughts. Fox is here with the report on the Temple case and it's urgent. Make my apologies. Say I'll call on him any time that suits him if he thinks it would be any good. You know him, don't you? Personally, I mean?'

'Yes. He's asked for me.'

'That's all right, then. Bring him along here if it's advisable, of course, but I'm snowed under.'

'Very good, sir,' said Alleyn.

A police sergeant tapped, and opened the door.

'Lord Robert Gospell, sir.'

Lord Robert entered twinkling and a little breathless.

'Hullo, Roderick. How-de-do,' he said.

'Hullo, Bunchy. This is extraordinarily good of you.'

'Not a bit. Like to keep in touch. Enjoy having a finger in the pie, you know. Always did.' He sat down and clasped his little hands over his stomach. 'How's your mother?' he asked.

'She's very well. She knows we are meeting today and sent you her love.'

'Thank yer. Delightful woman, your mother. Afraid I'm a bit late. Took tea with another delightful woman.'

'Did you indeed?'

'Yes. Agatha Troy. Know her?'

There was a short silence.

'Yes,' said Alleyn.

'Lor', yes. Of course you do. Didn't you look after that case where her model was knifed?'

'Yes, I did.'

'Charming,' said Lord Robert. 'Ain't she?'

'Yes,' said Alleyn, 'she is.'

'I like her awfully. M'sister Mildred and her boy Donald and I had been to Troy's show. You know m'sister Mildred, don't you?'

'Yes,' said Alleyn, smiling.

'Yes. No end of a donkey in many ways but a good woman. The boy's a young dog.'

'Bunchy,' said Alleyn, 'you're better than Victorian, you're Regency.'

'Think so? Tell you what, Roderick, I've got to come out of my shell and do the season a bit.'

'You always do the season, don't you?'

'I get about a bit. Enjoy myself. Young Donald's paying his addresses to a gel called Bridget O'Brien. Know her?'

'That's funny,' said Alleyn. 'My mama is bringing out brother George's girl and it appears she's the bosom friend of Bridget O'Brien. She's Evelyn and Paddy O'Brien's daughter, you know.'

'I know. Called on Evelyn this morning. She married that ass Carrados. Pompous. Clever in the City, I'm told. I had a look at the gel. Nice gel, but there's something wrong somewhere in that family. Carrados, I suppose. D'you like the gel?'

'I don't know her. My niece Sarah likes her.'

'Look here,' said Lord Robert, spreading out his hands and staring at them in mild surprise. 'Look here. Dine with us for Lady C.'s dance. Will you? Do.'

'My dear Bunchy, I'm not asked.'

213

'Isn't your niece goin'?'

'Yes, I expect she is.'

'Get you a card. Easy as winking. Do come. Troy's dining too. Donald and I persuaded her.'

'Troy,' said Alleyn. 'Troy.'

Lord Robert looked sharply at him for about two seconds.

'Never mind if you'd rather not,' he said.

'I can't tell you how much I should like to come,' said Alleyn slowly, 'but you see I'm afraid I might remind Miss Troy of – of that very unpleasant case.'

'Oh. 'm. Well, leave it open. Think it over. You're sure to get a card. Now – what about business?'

He made a funny eager grimace, pursed his lips, and with a deft movement of his hand slung his glasses over his nose. 'What's up?' he asked.

'We rather think blackmail,' said Alleyn.

'Lor',' said Lord Robert. 'Where?'

'Here, there and everywhere in high society.'

'How d'yer know?'

'Well.' Alleyn laid a thin hand on the file. 'This is rather more than usually confidential, Bunchy.'

'Yes, yes, yes. All right. I'll be as silent,' said Lord Robert, 'as the grave. Mum's the word. Let's have the names and all the rest of it. None of your Mr and Mrs Xes.'

'All right. You know Mrs Halcut-Hackett? Old General Halcut-Hackett's wife?'

'Yes. American actress. Twenty years younger than H-H. Gorgeous creature.'

'That's the one. She came to us last week with a story of blackmail. Here it is in this file. I'll tell you briefly what she said, but I'm afraid you'll have to put up with one Madame X.'

'Phoo!' said Lord Robert.

'She told us that a very great woman-friend of hers had

confided in her that she was being blackmailed. Mrs H-H wouldn't give this lady's name so there's your Mrs X.'

'Um,' said Lord Robert doubtfully. 'Otherwise Mrs 'Arris?'

'Possibly,' said Alleyn, 'but that's the story and I give it to you as Mrs H-H gave it to me. Mrs X, who has an important and imperious husband, received a blackmailing letter on the first of this month. It was written on Woolworth paper. The writer said he or she had possession of an extremely compromising letter written to Mrs X by a man-friend. The writer was willing to sell it for £500. Mrs X's account is gone into very thoroughly every month by her husband and she was afraid to stump up. In her distress (so the story went) she flew to Mrs Halcut-Hackett who couldn't provide £500 but persuaded Mrs X to let her come to us with the whole affair. She gave us the letter. Here it is.'

Alleyn laid the file on Lord Robert's plump little knees. Lord Robert touched his glasses and stared for quite thirty seconds at the first page in the file. He opened his mouth, shut it again, darted a glance at Alleyn, touched his glasses again and finally read under his breath:

' "If you would care to buy a letter dated April 20th, written from the Bucks Club addressed to Darling Dodo and signed M., you may do so by leaving £500 in notes of small denomination in your purse behind the picture of the Dutch funeral above the fireplace in the ballroom of Comstock House on the evening of next Monday fortnight." '

Lord Robert looked up.

'That was the night the Comstocks ran their charity bridge-party,' he said. 'Big show. Thirty tables. Let's see, it was last Monday.'

'It was. On the strength of this letter we saw the Comstocks, told them a fairy-story and asked them to let

215

us send in a man dressed as a waiter. We asked Mrs H-H to get her distressed friend to put the purse full of notes, which we dusted with the usual powder, behind the Dutch funeral. Mrs H-H said she would save her friend much agony and humiliation by doing this office for her.' Alleyn raised one eyebrow and bestowed a very slow wink upon Lord Robert.

'Poor thing,' said Lord Robert.

'Did she suppose she'd taken you in?'

'I don't know. I kept up a polite pretence. Our man, who I may say is a good man, attended the party, saw Mrs H-H tuck away the bag, and waited to see what would happen.'

'What did happen?'

'Nothing. Our man was there all night and saw a maid discover the bag next morning, put it unopened on the mantelpiece and call Mrs Comstock's attention to it. Mrs Comstock, in the presence of our man and the maid, opened it, saw the paper, was surprised, could find nothing to indicate the owner and told the maid to put it aside in case it was asked for.'

'And what,' asked Lord Robert, suddenly hugging himself with his short arms, 'what do you deduce from that, my dear Roderick?'

'They rumbled our man.'

'Is it one of the Comstocks' servants?'

'The whole show was done by Dimitri, the Shepherd Market caterer. You know who I mean, of course. He does most of the big parties nowadays. Supplies service, food and everything.'

'One of Dimitri's men?'

'We've made extremely careful enquiries. They've all got splendid references. I've actually spoken to Dimitri himself. I told him that there had been one or two thefts lately at large functions and we were bound to make enquiries. He got in no end of a tig, of course, and showed me a mass of references for all his people. We followed them up. They're genuine enough. He employs the best that can be found in the world. There's a strict rule that all objects left lying about at these shows should be brought at once to him. He then, himself, looks to see if he can find the owner and in the case of a lost purse or bag returns it in person or else, having seen the contents, sends it by one of his men. He explained that he did this to protect both his men and himself. He always asks the owner to examine a bag the moment it is handed to her.'

'Still – '

'I know it's by no means watertight but we've taken a lot of trouble over the Dimitri staff and in my opinion there's not a likely man among 'em.'

'Dimitri himself?'

Alleyn grimaced.

'Wonders will never cease, my dear Bunchy, but – '

'Yes, yes, of course, I quite see. He's a bit too damn grand for those capers, you'd imagine. Anything else?'

'We've been troubled by rumours of blackmail from other sources. You can see the file if you like. Briefly they all point to someone who works in the way suggested by Mrs Halcut-Hackett alias Mrs X. There's one anonymous letter sent to the Yard, presumably by a victim. It simply says that a blackmailer is at work among society people. Nothing more. We haven't been able to trace it. Then young Kremorn shot himself the other day and we found out that he had been drawing very large sums in bank-notes for no known reason. His servant said he'd suspected blackmail for some time.' Alleyn rubbed his nose. 'It's the devil. And of all the filthy crimes this to my mind is the filthiest. I don't mind telling you we're in a great tig over it.'

'Bad!' said Lord Robert, opening his eyes very wide. 'Disgusting! Where do I come in?'

'Everywhere, if you will. You've helped us before and

we'll be damn glad if you help us again. You go everywhere, Bunchy,' said Alleyn with a smile at his little friend. 'You toddle in and out of all the smart houses. Lovely ladies confide in you. Heavy colonels weep on your bosom. See what you can see.'

'Can't break confidences, you know, can I! Supposing I get 'em.'

'Of course you can't, but you can do a little quiet investigation on your own account and tell us as much as – ' Alleyn paused and added quickly: 'As much as a man of integrity may. Will you?'

'Love to!' said Lord Robert with a great deal of energy. 'Matter of fact, but it'd be a rum go if it was – coincidence.'

'What?'

'Well. Well, see here, Roderick, this is between ourselves. Thing is, as I told you, I called on Evelyn Carrados this morning. Passing that way and saw a feller selling daffodils so thought I'd take her some. Damn pretty woman, Evelyn, but – ' He screwed up his face. 'Saddish. Never got over Paddy's death, if you ask me. Devoted to the gel and the gel to her, but if you ask me Carrados comes the high horse a bit. Great pompous exacting touchy sort of feller, ain't he? Evelyn was in bed. Snowed under with letters. Secretary. Carrados on the hearth-rug looking injured. Bridget came in later on. Well now. Carrados said he'd be off to the City. Came over to the bed and gave her the sort of kiss a woman doesn't thank you for. Hand each side of her. Right hand under the pillow.'

Lord Robert's voice suddenly skipped an octave and became high-pitched. He leant forward with his hands on his knees, looking very earnestly at Alleyn. He moved his lips rather in the manner of a rabbit and then said explosively:

'It was singular. It was damned odd. He must have touched a letter under her pillow because when he straightened up it was in his right hand – a common-looking

218

envelope addressed in a sort of script – letters like they print 'em only done by hand.'

Alleyn glanced quickly at the file but said nothing.

'Carrados said: "Oh, one of your letters, m'dear," squinting at it through his glass and then putting it down on the counterpane. "Beg pardon," or something. Thing is, she turned as white as the sheet. I promise you as white as anything, on my honour. And she said: "It's from one of my lame ducks. I must deal with it," and slid it under the others. Off he went, and that was that. I talked about their ball and so on and paid my respects and pretended I'd noticed nothing, of course, and, in short, I came away.'

Still Alleyn did not speak. Suddenly Lord Robert jabbed at the letter in the file with his fat finger.

'Thing is,' he said most emphatically. 'Same sort of script.'

'Exactly the same? I mean, would you swear to the same writer?'

'No, no! 'Course not. Only got a glimpse of the other, but I rather fancy myself on handwriting, you know.'

'We rather fancy you, too.'

'It was very similar,' said Lord Robert. 'It was exceedingly similar. On my honour.'

'Good Lord,' said Alleyn mildly. 'That's what the Americans call a break. Coincidence stretches out a long arm. So does the law. "Shake," says Coincidence. Not such a very long arm, after all, if this pretty fellow is working among one class only and it looks as if he is.' He shoved a box of cigarettes in Lord Robert's direction. 'We had an expert at that letter – the Mrs H-H one you've got there. Woolworth paper. She didn't show us the envelope, of course. Woolworth ink and the sort of nib they use for script writing. It's square with a feeder. You notice the letters are all neatly fitted between the ruled lines. That and the script nib and the fact that the letters are careful copies of ordinary print completely knocks out any sort

of individuality. There were no finger-prints and Mrs
Halcut-Hackett hadn't noticed the postmark. Come in!'

A police constable marched in with a packet of letters,
laid them on the desk and marched out again.

'Half a moment while I have a look at my mail, Bunchy;
there may just be – yes, by gum, there is!'

He opened an envelope, glanced at a short note, unfolded
an enclosure, raised his eyebrows and handed it to Lord
Robert.

'Wheeoo!' whistled Lord Robert.

It was a sheet of common ruled paper. Three or four
rows of script were fitted neatly between the lines. Lord
Robert read aloud:

' "Unforeseen circumstances prevented collection
on Monday night. Please leave bag with same sum
down between seat and left-hand arm of blue sofa
in concert-room, 57 Constance Street, next Thursday
afternoon." '

'Mrs Halcut-Hackett,' said Alleyn, holding out the note,
'explains that her unfortunate friend received this letter
by yesterday evening's post. What's happening on Thursday
at 57 Constance Street? Do you know?'

'Those new concert-rooms. Very smart. It's another
charity show. Tickets on sale everywhere. Three guineas
each. Chamber music. Bach. Sirmione Quartette. I'm
going.'

'Bunchy,' said Alleyn, 'let nothing wean you from the
blue sofa. Talk to Mrs Halcut-Hackett. Share the blue sofa
with her and when the austere delights of Bach knock at
your heart pay no attention but with the very comment
of your soul – '

'Yes, yes, yes. Don't quote now, Roderick, or somebody
may think you're a detective.'

'Blast you!' said Alleyn.

Lord Robert gave a little crowing laugh and rose from his chair.

'I'm off,' he said. Alleyn walked with him into the corridor. They shook hands. Alleyn stood looking after him as he walked away with small steps, a quaint out-of-date figure, black against a window at the end of the long passage. The figure grew smaller and smaller, paused for a second at the end of the passage, turned the corner and was gone.

CHAPTER THREE

Sequence to a Cocktail-party

A few days after his visit to the Yard, Lord Robert Gospell attended a cocktail-party given by Mrs Halcut-Hackett for her plain protégée. Who this plain protégée was, nobody seemed to know, but it was generally supposed that Mrs Halcut-Hackett's object in bringing her out was not entirely philanthropic. At the moment nobody ever remembered the girl's name but merely recognized her as a kind of coda to Mrs Halcut-Hackett's social activities.

This was one of the first large cocktail-parties of the season and there were as many as two hundred and fifty guests there. Lord Robert adored parties of all kinds and was, as Alleyn had pointed out, asked everywhere. He knew intimately that section of people to whom the London season is a sort of colossal hurdle to be taken in an exhilarating leap or floundered over as well as may be. He was in tremendous demand as a chaperone's partner, could be depended on to help with those unfortunate children of seventeen who, in spite of all the efforts of finishing schools, dressmakers, hairdressers, face-specialists and their unflagging mothers, were apt to be seen standing alone nervously smiling on the outskirts of groups. With these unhappy débutantes Lord Robert took infinite trouble. He would tell them harmless little stories and when they laughed would respond as if they themselves had said something amusing. His sharp little eyes would search about for younger men than himself and he would draw them into a group round himself and the girl. Because of his reputation as a gentle wit, the wariest and most conceited young men were always glad to be seen talking to Lord Robert, and soon the débutante would find herself the only girl in a group of men who seemed to be enjoying themselves. Her nervous smile would vanish and a delicious feeling of confidence would inspire her. And when Lord Robert saw her eyes grow bright and her hands relax, he would slip away and join the cluster of chaperones where he told stories a little less harmless and equally diverting.

But in the plain protégée of General and Mrs Halcut-Hackett he met his Waterloo. She was not so very plain but only rather disastrously uneventful. Every inch of this unhappy child had been prepared for the cocktail-party with passionate care and at great expense by her chaperone – one of those important American women with lovely faces and cast-iron figures. Lord Robert was greeted by Mrs Halcut-Hackett, who looked a little older than usual, and by her husband the General, a notable fire-eater who bawled 'What!' two or three times and burst into loud surprising laughter which was his method of circulating massed gaiety. Lord Robert twinkled at him and passed on into the thick of the party. A servant whom he recognized as the Halcut-Hackett's butler gave him a drink. 'Then they're not having Dimitri or anybody like that,' thought Lord Robert. He looked about him. On the right-hand side of the enormous room were collected the débutantes, and the young men who, in the last analysis, could make the antics of the best dance-bands in London, all the efforts of all the Dimitris, Miss Harrises, and Mrs Halcut-Hacketts to the tune of a thousand pounds, look like a single impotent gesture. Among them were the young men who were spoken of, in varying degrees of irony, as 'The Debs' Delight.' Lord Robert half suspected his nephew Donald of being a Debs' Delight. There he was in the middle of it all with Bridget O'Brien, making himself agreeable. Very popular, evidently. 'He'll have to settle down,' thought Lord Robert. 'He's altogether too irresponsible and he's beginning to look dissipated. Don't like it.'

Then he saw the plain protégée of Mrs Halcut-Hackett.

She had just met a trio of incoming débutantes and had taken them to their right side of the room. He saw how they all spoke politely and pleasantly to her but without any air of intimacy. He saw her linger a moment while they were drawn into the whirlpool of high-pitched conversation. Then she turned away and stood looking towards the door where her chaperone dealt faithfully with the arrivals. She seemed utterly lost. Lord Robert crossed the room and greeted her with his old-fashioned bow.

'How-de-do. This *is* a good party,' he said, with a beaming smile.

'Oh! Oh – I'm so glad.'

'I'm an old hand, y'know,' continued Lord Robert, 'and I always judge a cocktail-party by the time that elapses between one's paying one's respects and getting a drink. Now this evening I was given this excellent drink within two minutes of shaking hands with the General. Being a thirsty, greedy old customer, I said to myself: "Good party." '

'I'm so glad,' repeated the child.

She was staring, he noticed, at her chaperone, and he saw that Mrs Halcut-Hackett was talking to a tall smooth man with a heavy face, lack-lustre eyes and a proprietary manner. Lord Robert looked fixedly at this individual.

'Do tell me,' he said, 'who is that man with our hostess?'

The girl started violently and without taking her gaze off Mrs Halcut-Hackett, said woodenly: 'It's Captain Withers.'

'Ah,' thought Lord Robert, 'I fancied it was.' Aloud he said: 'Withers? Then it's not the same feller. I rather thought I knew him.'

'Oh,' said the protégée. She had turned her head slightly and he saw that she now looked at the General. 'Like a frightened rabbit,' thought Lord Robert. 'For all the world like a frightened rabbit.' The General had borne down upon his wife and Captain Withers. Lord Robert now

224

witnessed a curious little scene. General Halcut-Hackett glared for three seconds at Captain Withers who smiled, bowed, and moved away. The General then spoke to his wife and immediately, for a fraction of a second, the terror – Lord Robert decided that terror was not too strong a word – that shone in the protégée's eyes was reflected in the chaperone's. Only for a second, and then with her husband she turned to greet a new arrival who Lord Robert saw with pleasure was Lady Alleyn. She was followed by a thin girl with copper-coloured hair and slanting eyebrows that at once reminded him of his friend Roderick. 'Must be the niece,' he decided. The girl at his side suddenly murmured an excuse and hurried away to greet Sarah Alleyn. Lord Robert finished his drink and was given another. In a few minutes he was surrounded by acquaintances and was embarked upon one of his new stories. He made his point very neatly, drifted away on the wave of laughter that greeted it, and found Lady Alleyn.

'My dear Bunchy,' she said, 'you are the very person I hoped to see. Come and gossip with me. I feel like a phoenix.'

'You look like a princess,' he said. 'Why do we meet so seldom? Where shall we go?'

'If there is a corner reserved for grandmothers I ought to be in it. Good heavens, how everybody screams. How old are you, Bunchy?'

'Fifty-five, m'dear.'

'I'm sixty-five. Do you find people very noisy nowadays or are you still too much of a chicken?'

'I enjoy parties, awfully, but I agree that there ain't much repose in modern intercourse.'

'That's it,' said Lady Alleyn, settling herself in a chair. 'No repose. All the same I like the moderns, especially the fledgelings. As Roderick says, they finish their thoughts. *We* only did that in the privacy of our bedrooms and very often asked forgiveness of our Creator for doing it. What do you think of Sarah?'

'She looks a darling,' said Lord Robert emphatically.

'She's a pleasant creature. Amazingly casual but she's got character and, I think, looks,' said her grandmother. 'Who are those young things she's talking to?'

'Bridget O'Brien and my young scapegrace of a nephew.'

'So that's Evelyn Carrados's girl. She's like Paddy, isn't she?'

'She's very like both of 'em. Have you seen Evelyn lately?'

'We dined there last night for the play. What's the matter with Evelyn?'

'Eh?' exclaimed Lord Robert. 'You've spotted it, have you? You're a wise woman, m'dear.'

'She's all over the place. Does Carrados bully her?'

'Bully ain't quite the word. He's devilish grand and patient, though. But – '

'But there's something more. What was the reason for your meeting with Roderick the other day?'

'Hi!' expostulated Lord Robert in a hurry. 'What are you up to?'

'I shouldn't let you tell me if you tried. I trust,' said Lady Alleyn untruthfully but with great dignity, 'that I am not a curious woman.'

'That's pretty rich.'

'I don't know what you mean,' said Lady Alleyn grandly. 'But I tell you what, Bunchy. I've got neurotic women on the brain. Nervous women. Women that are on their guard. It's a most extraordinary thing,' she continued, rubbing her nose with a gesture that reminded Lord Robert of her son, 'but there's precisely the same look in our hostess's mascaraed eyes as Evelyn Carrados had in her naturally beautiful ones. Or has this extraordinary drink gone to my head?'

'The drink,' said Lord Robert firmly, 'has gone to your head.'

'Dear Bunchy,' murmured Lady Alleyn. Their eyes met and they exchanged smiles. The cocktail-party surged politely about them. The noise, the smoke, the festive smell of flowers and alcohol, seemed to increase every moment. Wandering parents eddied round Lady Alleyn's chair. Lord Robert remained beside her listening with pleasure to her cool light voice and looking out of the corner of his eye at Mrs Halcut-Hackett. Apparently all the guests had arrived. She was moving into the room. This was his chance. He turned round and suddenly found himself face to face with Captain Withers. For a moment they stood and looked at each other. Withers was a tall man and Lord Robert was obliged to tilt his head back a little. Withers was a fine arrogant figure, Lord Robert a plump and comical one. But oddly enough it was Lord Robert who seemed the more dominant and more dignified of these two men and before his mild glare the other suddenly looked furtive. His coarse, handsome face became quite white. Some seconds elapsed before he spoke.

'Oh – ah – how do you do?' said Captain Withers very heartily.

'Good evening,' said Lord Robert and turned back to Lady Alleyn. Captain Withers walked quickly away.

'Why, Bunchy,' said Lady Alleyn softly, 'I've never seen you snub anybody before.'

'D'you know who that was?'

'No.'

'Feller called Maurice Withers. He's a throw-back to my Foreign Office days.'

'He's frightened of you.'

'I hope so,' said Lord Robert. 'I'll trot along and pay my respects to my hostess. It's been charming seeing you. Will you dine with me one evening? Bring Roderick. Can you give me an evening? Now?'

'I'm so busy with Sarah. May we ring you up? If it can be managed – '

227

'It must be. *Au 'voir,* m'dear.'

'Good-bye, Bunchy.'

He made his little bow and picked his way through the crowd to Mrs Halcut-Hackett.

'I'm on my way out,' he said, 'but I hoped to get a word with you. Perfectly splendid party.'

She turned all the headlights of her social manner full on him. It was, he decided compassionately, a bogus manner. An imitation, but what a good imitation. She called him 'dear Lord Robert' like a grande dame in a slightly dated comedy. Her American voice, which he remembered thinking charming in her theatrical days, was now much disciplined and none the better for it. She asked him if he was doing the season very thoroughly and he replied with his usual twinkle that he got about a bit.

'Are you going to the show at the Constance Street Rooms on Thursday afternoon?' he asked. 'I'm looking forward to that awfully.'

Her eyes went blank but she scarcely paused before answering yes, she believed she was.

'It's the Sirmione Quartette,' said Lord Robert. 'Awfully good, ain't they? Real top-notchers.'

Mrs Halcut-Hackett said she adored music, especially classical music.

'Well,' said Lord Robert, 'I'll give myself the pleasure of looking out for you there if it wouldn't bore you. Not so many people nowadays enjoy Bach.'

Mrs Halcut-Hackett said she thought Bach was marvellous.

'Do tell me,' said Lord Robert with his engaging air of enjoying a gossip. 'I've just run into a feller whose face looked as familiar as anything, but I can't place him. Feller over there talking to the girl in red.'

He saw patches of rouge on her cheeks suddenly start up in hard isolation and he thought: 'That's shaken her, poor thing.'

228

She said: 'Do you mean Captain Maurice Withers?'

'Maybe. The name don't strike a chord, though. I've got a shocking memory. Better be getting along. May I look out for you on Thursday? Thank you so much. Good-bye.'

'Good-bye, dear Lord Robert,' said Mrs Halcut-Hackett.

He edged his way out and was waiting patiently for his hat and umbrella when someone at his elbow said:

'Hullo, Uncle Bunch, are you going home?'

Lord Robert turned slowly and saw his nephew.

'What? Oh, it's you, Donald! Yes, I am! Taking a cab. Want a lift?'

'Yes, please,' said Donald.

Lord Robert looked over his glasses at his nephew and remarked that he seemed rather agitated. He thought: 'What the deuce is the matter with everybody?' but he only said: 'Come along, then,' and together they went out into the street. Lord Robert held up his umbrella and a taxi drew in to the kerb.

''Evening, m'lord,' said the driver.

'Oh, it's you, is it?' said Lord Robert. ''Evening. We're going home.'

'Two hundred Cheyne Walk. Very good, m'lord,' wheezed the driver. He was a goggle-eyed, grey-haired, mottle-faced taximan with an air of good-humoured truculence about him. He slammed the door on them, jerked down the lever of his meter, and started up his engine.

'Everybody knows you, Uncle Bunch,' said Donald in a voice that was not quite natural. 'Even the casual taxi-driver.'

'This feller cruises about in our part of the world,' said Lord Robert. He twisted himself round in his seat and again looked at his nephew over the top of his glasses. 'What's up?' he asked.

'I – well – nothing. I mean, why do you think anything's up?'

'Now then,' said Lord Robert. 'No jiggery-pokery. What's up?'

'Well, as a matter of fact,' answered Donald, kicking the turned-up seat in front of him, 'I did rather want a word with you. I – I'm in a bit of a tight corner, Uncle Bunch.'

'Money?' asked his uncle.

'How did you guess?'

'Don't be an ass, my boy. What is it?'

'I – well, I was wondering if you would mind – I mean, I know I've been a bit extravagant. I'm damn sorry it's happened. I suppose I've been a fool but I'm simply draped in sackcloth and steeped in ashes. Never again!'

'Come, come, come,' said Lord Robert crisply. 'What is it? Gambling?'

'Well – yes. With a slight hint of riotous living. Gambling mostly.'

'Racing? Cards?'

'A bit, but actually I dropped the worst packet at roulette.'

'Good Gad!' exclaimed Lord Robert with surprising violence. 'Where the devil do you play roulette?'

'Well, actually it was at a house out at Leatherhead. It belongs to a man who was at that party. Some people I know took me there. It turned out to be a rather enterprising sort of gamble with a roulette-table and six fellows doing croupier. All in order, you know. I mean it's not run for anything but fun naturally, and Captain Withers simply takes on the bank – '

'*Who?*'

'The person's name is Withers.'

'When was this party?'

'Oh, a week or so ago. They have them fairly regularly. I paid all right, but – but it just about cleaned me up. I had the most amazing bad luck, actually. Would you believe it, there was a run of seventeen against me on the

230

even chances? Bad. Very bad,' said Donald with an unconvincing return to his lighter manner. 'Disastrous, in fact.'

'You're shying about,' said Lord Robert. 'What's the real trouble?'

'One of my cheques has been returned R/D. I'm bust.'

'I paid your Oxford debts and started you off with five hundred as a yearly allowance. Are you telling me you've gone through five hundred since you came down?'

'I'm sorry,' said Donald. 'Yes.'

'Your mother gives you four pounds a week, don't she?'

'Yes.'

Lord Robert suddenly whisked out a notebook.

'How much was this returned cheque?'

'Fifty quid. Awful, isn't it?' He glanced at his uncle's profile and saw that his lips were pursed in a soundless whistle. Donald decided that it was not as bad as he had feared and said more hopefully: 'Isn't it a bore?'

Lord Robert, his pencil poised, said: 'Who was it made out to?'

'To Wits – Withers – everyone calls him Wits. You see, I had a side bet with him.'

Lord Robert wrote, turned, and looked over his spectacles at his nephew.

'I'll send Withers a cheque tonight,' he said.

'Thank you so much, Uncle Bunch.'

'What's the address?'

'Shackleton House, Leatherhead. He's got a flat in town but the Leatherhead address is all right.'

'Any other debts?'

'One or two shops. They seem to be getting rather testy about it. And a restaurant or two.'

'Here we are,' said Lord Robert abruptly.

The taxi drew up outside the house he shared with his sister. They got out. Lord Robert paid and tipped the driver.

'How's the lumbago?' he asked.

231

'Not too bad, m'lord, thank you, m'lord.'

'Good. 'Evening to you.'

'Good evening, m'lord.'

They entered the house in silence. Lord Robert said over his shoulder: 'Come to my room.'

He led the way, a small, comic, but somehow a rather resolute figure. Donald followed him into an old-fashioned study. Lord Robert sat at his desk and wrote a cheque with finicky movements of his fat hands. He blotted it meticulously and swung round in his chair to face his nephew.

'You still of the same mind about this doctoring?' he asked.

'Well, that's the big idea,' said Donald.

'Passed some examinations for it, didn't you?'

'Medical prelim,' said Donald easily. 'Yes, I've got that.'

'Before you were sent down for losing your mother's money. And mine.'

Donald was silent.

'I'll get you out of this mess on one condition. I don't know the way you set about working for a medical degree. Our family's been in the diplomatic for a good many generations. High time we did something else, I dare say. You'll start work at Edinburgh as soon as they'll have you. If that's not at once I'll get a coach and you'll go to Archery and work there. I'll show you as much as the usual medical student gets and I'll advise your mother to give you no more. That's all.'

'Edinburgh! Archery!' Donald's voice was shrill with dismay. 'But I don't want to go to Edinburgh for my training. I want to go to Thomas's.'

'You're better away from London. There's one other thing I must absolutely insist upon, Donald. You are to drop this feller Withers.'

'Why should I?'

'Because the feller's a bad 'un. I know something about

him. I have never interfered in the matter of your friendships before, but I'd be neglectin' my duty like anything if I didn't step in here.'

'I won't give up a friend simply because you choose to say he's no good.'

'I give you my word of honour this man's a rotter – a criminal rotter. I was amazed when I recognized Withers this afternoon. My information dates from my Foreign Office days. It's unimpeachable. Very bad record. Come now, be sensible. Make a clean break and forget all about him. Archery's a nice old house. Your mother can use it as a *pied-à-terre* and see you sometimes. It's only ten miles out of Edinburgh.'

'But – '

'Afraid it's definite.'

'But – I don't want to leave London. I don't want to muck about with a lot of earnest Scots from God knows where. I mean the sort of people who go there are just simply The End!'

'Why?' asked Lord Robert.

'Well, because, I mean, you know what I mean. They'll be the most unspeakable curiosities. No doubt perfectly splendid but – '

'But not in the same class with young men who contract debts of honour which they cannot meet and do the London season on their mother's money?'

'That's not fair,' cried Donald hotly.

'Why?' repeated Lord Robert.

'I'll bet you got into the same sort of jams when you were my age.'

'You're wrong,' said Lord Robert mildly. 'I did as many silly things as most young men of my day. But I did not contract debts that I was unable to settle. It seemed to me that sort of thing amounted to theft. I didn't steal clothes from my tailor, drink from my hotel, or money from my friends.'

233

'But I knew it would be all right in the end.'

'You mean, you knew I'd pay?'

'I'm not ungrateful,' said Donald angrily.

'My dear fellow, I don't want you to be grateful.'

'But I won't go and stay in a deserted mausoleum of a Scotch house in the middle of the season. There's – there's Bridget.'

'Lady Carrados's gel? Is she fond of you?'

'Yes.'

'She seems a nice creature. You're fortunate. Not one of these screeching rattles. She'll wait for you.'

'I won't go.'

'M'dear boy, I'm sorry, but you've no alternative.'

Donald's face was white but two scarlet patches burned on his cheek-bones. His lips trembled. Suddenly he burst out violently.

'You can keep your filthy money,' he shouted. 'By God, I'll look after myself. I'll borrow from someone who's not a bloody complacent Edwardian relic and I'll get a job and pay them back as I can.'

'Jobs aren't to be had for the asking. Come now – '

'Oh, shut up!' bawled Donald and flung out of the room.

Lord Robert stared at the door which his nephew had not neglected to slam. The room was very quiet. The fire settled down with a small whisper of ashes and Lord Robert's clock ticked on the mantelpiece. It ticked very loudly. The plump figure, only half-lit by the lamp on the desk, was quite still, the head resting on the hand. Lord Robert sighed, a slight mournful sound. At last he pulled an envelope towards him and in his finicky writing addressed it to Captain Withers, Shackleton House, Leatherhead. Then he wrote a short note, folded a cheque into it and put them both in the envelope. He rang for his butler.

'Has Mr Donald gone out?'

'Yes, m'lord. He said he would not be returning.'

'I see,' said Lord Robert. 'Thank you. Will you see that this letter is posted immediately?'

CHAPTER FOUR

Blackmail to Music

Lord Robert had sat on the blue sofa since two-fifteen but he was not tired of it. He enjoyed watching the patrons of music arriving and he amused himself with idle speculations on the subject of intellectual snobbishness. He also explored the blue sofa, sliding his hands cautiously over the surface of the seat and down between the seat and the arms. He had taken the precaution of leaving his gloves on a chair on the left of the sofa and a little behind it. A number of people came and spoke to him, among them Lady Carrados, who was looking tired.

'You're overdoing it, Evelyn,' he told her. 'You look charming – that's a delightful gown, ain't it? – but you're too fragile, m'dear.'

'I'm all right, Bunchy,' she said. 'You've got a nice way of telling a woman she's getting older.'

'No, I say! It wasn't that. Matter of fact it rather suits you bein' so fine-drawn, but you are too thin, you know. Where's Bridgie?'

'At a matinée.'

'Evelyn, do you know if she sees anything of my nephew?'

'Donald Potter? Yes. We've heard all about it, Bunchy.'

'He's written to his mother who no doubt is giving him money. I suppose you know he's sharing rooms with some other feller?'

'Yes. Bridgie sees him.'

'Does Bridgie know where he is?'

'I think so. She hasn't told me.'

'Is she fond of the boy, Evelyn?'

'Yes.'

'What do you think of him?'

'I don't know. He's got a lot of charm, but I wish he'd settle down.'

'Is it botherin' you much?'

'That?' She caught her breath. 'A little, naturally. Oh, *there's* Lady Alleyn! We're supposed to be together.'

'Delightful woman, ain't she? I'm waiting for Mrs Halcut-Hackett.'

'I shouldn't have thought her quite your cup of tea,' said Lady Carrados vaguely.

Lord Robert made his rabbit-face and winked.

'We go into mutual raptures over Bach,' he said.

'I must join Lady Alleyn. Good-bye, Bunchy.'

'Good-bye, Evelyn. Don't worry too much – over anything.'

She gave him a startled look and went away. Lord Robert sat down again. The room was nearly full and in ten minutes the Sirmione Quartette would appear on the modern dais.

'Is she waiting for the lights to go down?' wondered Lord Robert. He saw Agatha Troy come in, tried to catch her eye, and failed. People were beginning to settle down in the rows of gilt chairs and in the odd armchairs and sofas round the walls. Lord Robert looked restlessly towards the door and saw Sir Daniel Davidson. Davidson made straight for him. Sir Daniel had once cured Lord Robert's sister of indigestion and Mildred, who was an emotional woman, had asked him to dinner. Lord Robert had been amused and interested by Davidson. His technique as a fashionable doctor was superb. 'If Disraeli had taken to medicine instead of primroses,' Lord Robert had said, 'he would have been just such another.' And he had encouraged Davidson to launch out on his favourite subject, The Arts, with rather emphatic capitals. He had capped Davidson's Latin tags, quoted Congreve against him, and listened with amusement to a preposterous parallel drawn between Rubens and Dürer. 'The extrovert and the introvert of Art,' Davidson had cried, waving his beautiful hands,

237

and Lord Robert had twinkled and said: 'You are talking above my head.' 'I'm talking nonsense,' Davidson had replied abruptly, 'and you know it.' But in a minute or two he had been off again as flamboyantly as ever and had left at one o'clock in the morning, very pleased with himself and overflowing with phrases.

'Ah!' he said now as he shook hands. 'I might have guessed I should find you here. Doing the fashionable thing for the unfashionable reason. Music! My God!'

'What's wrong?' asked Lord Robert.

'My dear Lord Robert, how many of these people will know what they are listening to, or even listen? Not one in fifty.'

'Oh, come now!'

'Not one in fifty! There goes that fellow Withers whose aesthetic appreciation is less than that of a monkey on a barrel-organ. What's he here for? I repeat, not one in fifty of these humbugs knows what he's listening to. And how many of the forty-nine have the courage to confess themselves honest philistines?'

'Quite a number, I should have thought,' said Lord Robert cheerfully. 'Myself for one. I'm inclined to go to sleep.'

'Now, why say that? You know perfectly well – What's the matter?'

'Sorry. I was looking at Evelyn Carrados. She looks damn seedy,' said Lord Robert. Davidson followed his glance to where Lady Carrados sat beside Lady Alleyn. Davidson watched her for a moment and then said quietly:

'Yes. She's overdoing it. I shall have to scold her. My seat is somewhere over there, I believe.' He made an impatient gesture. 'They all overdo it, these mothers, and the girls overdo it, and the husbands get rattled and the young men neglect their work and then there are half a dozen smart weddings, as many nervous breakdowns and there's your London season.'

238

'Lor'!' said Lord Robert mildly.

'It's the truth. In my job one sees it over and over again. Yes, yes, yes, I know! I am a smart West End doctor and I encourage all these women to fancy themselves ill. That's what you may very well think, but I assure you, my dear Lord Robert, that one sees cases of nervous exhaustion that are enough to make a cynic of the youngest ingénue. And they are so charming, these mamas. I mean really charming. Women like Lady Carrados. They help each other so much. It is not all a cutlet for a cutlet. But' – he spread out his hands – 'what is it for? What is it all about? The same people meeting each other over and over again at great expense to the accompaniment of loud negroid noises of jazz bands. For what?'

'Damned if I know,' said Lord Robert cheerfully. 'Who's that feller who came in behind Withers? Tall, dark feller with the extraordinary hands. I seem to know him.'

'Where? Ah.' Davidson picked up his glasses which he wore on a wide black ribbon. 'Who is it, now! I'll tell you who it is. It's the catering fellow, Dimitri. He's having his three guineas' worth of Bach with the *haute monde* and, by God, I'll wager you anything you like that he's got more appreciation in his extraordinary little finger – you are very observant, it *is* an odd hand – than most of them have in the whole of their pampered carcasses. How do you do, Mrs Halcut-Hackett?'

She had come up so quietly that Lord Robert had actually missed her. She looked magnificent. Davidson, to Lord Robert's amusement, kissed her hand.

'Have you come to worship?' he asked.

'Why, certainly,' she said and turned to Lord Robert. 'I see you have not forgotten.'

'How could I?'

'Now isn't that nice?' asked Mrs Halcut-Hackett, looking slantways at the blue sofa. Lord Robert moved aside and she at once sat down, spreading her furs.

239

'I must find my seat,' said Davidson. 'They are going to begin.'

He went to a chair beside Lady Carrados on the far side of the room. Mrs Halcut-Hackett asked Lord Robert if he did not think Sir Daniel a delightful personality. He noticed that her American accent was not quite so strictly repressed as usual and that her hands moved restlessly. She motioned him to sit on her right.

'If you don't mind,' he said, 'I'll stick to my chair. I like straight backs.'

He saw her glance nervously at his chair which was a little behind the left arm of the sofa. Her bag was on her lap. It was a large bag and looked well filled. She settled her furs again so that they fell across it. Lord Robert perched on his hideously uncomfortable chair. He noticed that Dimitri had sat down at the end of a row of seats close by. He found himself idly watching Dimitri. 'Wonder what he thinks of us. Always arranging food for our parties and he could buy most of us up and not notice it, I shouldn't mind betting. They *are* rum hands and no mistake. The little finger's the same length as the third.'

A flutter of polite clapping broke out and the Sirmione String Quartette walked on to the dais. The concealed lights of the concert chamber were dimmed into darkness, leaving the performers brilliantly lit. Lord Robert experienced that familiar thrill that follows the glorious scrape of tuning strings. But he told himself he had not come to listen to music and he was careful not to look towards the dais lest his eyes should be blinded by the light. Instead he looked towards the left-hand arm of the blue sofa. The darkness gradually thinned and presently he could make out the dim sheen of brocade and the thick depth of blackness that was Mrs Halcut-Hackett's furs. The shape of this blackness shifted. Something glinted. He bent forward. Closer than the exquisite pattern of the music he caught the sound made by one fabric rubbed against

240

another, a sliding rustle. The outline of the mass that was Mrs Halcut-Hackett went tense and then relaxed. 'She's stowed it away,' thought Lord Robert.

Nobody came near them until the lights went up for the interval and then Lord Robert realized how very well the blackmailer had chosen when he lit upon the blue sofa as a post-box, for the side door beyond it was thrown open during the interval and instead of going out into the lounge by the main entrance many people passed behind the blue sofa and out by this side door. And as the interval drew to a close people came in and stood behind the sofa gossiping. Lord Robert felt sure that his man had gone into the lounge. He would wait until the lights were lowered and come in with the rest of the stragglers, pass behind the sofa and slip his hand over the arm. Most of the men and many of the women had gone out to smoke, but Lord Robert remained uncomfortably wedded to his chair. He knew very well that Mrs Halcut-Hackett writhed under the pressure of conflicting desires. She wished to be alone when the bag was taken and she dearly loved a title. She was to have the title. Suddenly she murmured something about powdering her nose. She got up and left by the side door.

Lord Robert rested his head on his hand and devoted the last few minutes of the interval to a neat imitation of an elderly gentleman dropping off to sleep. The lights were lowered again. The stragglers, with mumbled apologies, came back. There was a little group of people still standing in the darkness behind the sofa. The performers returned to the dais.

Someone had advanced from behind Lord Robert and stood beside the sofa.

Lord Robert felt his heart jump. He had placed his chair carefully, leaving a space between himself and the left-hand arm of the sofa. Into this space the shadowy figure now moved. It was a man. He stood with his back to the lighted

241

dais and he seemed to lean forward a little as though he searched the darkness for something. Lord Robert also leant forward. He emitted the most delicate hint of a snore. His right hand propped his head. Through the cracks of his fat fingers he watched the left arm of the sofa. Into this small realm of twilight came the shape of a hand. It was a curiously thin hand and he could see quite clearly that the little finger was as long as the third.

Lord Robert snored.

The hand slid over into the darkness and when it came back it held Mrs Halcut-Hackett's bag.

As if in ironic appreciation the music on the dais swept up a sharp crescendo into a triumphant blare. Mrs Halcut-Hackett returned from powdering her nose.

CHAPTER FIVE

Unqualified Success

The ball given by Lady Carrados for her daughter Bridget
O'Brien was an unqualified success. That is to say that
from half-past ten when Sir Herbert and Lady Carrados
took up their stand at the head of the double staircase
and shook hands with the first guests until half-past three
the next morning when the band, white about the gills
and faintly glistening, played the National Anthem, there
was not a moment when it was not difficult for a young
man to find the débutantes with whom he wished to dance
and easy for him to avoid those by whom he was not
attracted. There was no ominous aftermath when the guests
began to slide away to other parties, to slip through the
doors with the uncontrollable heartlessness of the un-
amused. The elaborate structure, built to pattern by Lady
Carrados, Miss Harris and Dimitri, did not slide away like
a sand-castle before a wave of unpopularity, but held up
bravely till the end. It was, therefore, an unqualified success.

In the matter of champagne Lady Carrados and Miss
Harris had triumphed. It flowed not only in the supper-
room but also at the buffet. In spite of the undoubted
fact that débutantes did not drink, Dimitri's men opened
two hundred bottles of Heidsieck '28 that night, and Sir
Herbert afterwards took a sort of well-bred pride in the
rows of empty bottles he happened to see in a glimpse
behind the scenes.

Outside the house it was unseasonably chilly. The mist
made by the breathing of the watchers mingled with drifts
of light fog. As the guests walked up the strip of red carpet
from their cars to the great door they passed between two
wavering masses of dim faces. And while the warmth and

festive smell of flowers and expensive scents reached the noses of the watchers, through the great doors was driven the smell of mist so that footmen in the hall told each other from time to time that for June it was an uncommonly thickish night outside.

By midnight everybody knew the ball was a success and was able when an opportunity presented itself to say so to Lady Carrados. Leaving her post at the stairhead she came into the ballroom looking very beautiful and made her way towards the far end where most of the chaperones were assembled. On her way she passed her daughter dancing with Donald Potter. Bridget smiled brilliantly at her mother, and raised her left hand in gay salute. Her right hand was crushed against Donald's chest and round the misty white nonsense of her dress was his black arm and his hard masculine hand was pressed against her ribs. 'She's in love with him,' thought Lady Carrados. And up through the maze of troubled thoughts that kept her company came the remembrance of her conversation with Donald's uncle. She wondered suddenly if women ever fainted from worry alone and as she smiled and bowed her way along the ballroom she saw herself suddenly crumpling down among the dancers. She would lie there while the band played on and presently she would open her eyes and see people's legs and then someone would help her to her feet and she would beg them to get her away quickly before anything was noticed. Her fingers tightened on her bag. Five hundred pounds! She had told the man at the bank that she wanted to pay some of the expenses of the ball in cash. That had been a mistake. She should have sent Miss Harris with the cheque and made no explanation to anybody. It was twelve o'clock. She would do it on her way to supper. There was that plain Halcut-Hackett protégée without a partner again. Lady Carrados looked round desperately and to her relief saw her husband making his way towards the girl. She

244

felt a sudden wave of affection for her husband. Should she go to him tonight and tell him everything? And just sit back and take the blow? She must be very ill indeed to dream of such a thing. Here she was in the chaperones' corner and there, thank God, was Lady Alleyn with an empty chair beside her.

'Evelyn!' cried Lady Alleyn. 'Come and sit down, my dear, in all your triumph. My granddaughter has just told me this is the very pinnacle of all balls. Everybody is saying so.'

'I'm so thankful. It's such a toss-up nowadays. One never knows.'

'Of course one doesn't. Last Tuesday at the Gainscotts' by one o'clock there were only the three Gainscott girls, a few desperate couples who hadn't the heart to escape, and my Sarah and her partner whom I had kept there by sheer terrorism. Of course, they didn't have Dimitri, and I must say I think he *is* a perfect magician. Dear me,' said Lady Alleyn, 'I *am* enjoying myself.'

'I'm so glad.'

'I hope you are enjoying yourself, too, Evelyn. They say the secret of being a good hostess is to enjoy yourself at your own parties. I have never believed it. Mine always were a nightmare to me and I refuse to admit they were failures. But they are so exhausting. I suppose you wouldn't come down to Danes Court with me and turn yourself into an amiable cow for the week-end?'

'Oh,' said Lady Carrados, 'I wish I could.'

'Do.'

'That's what Sir Daniel Davidson said I should do – lead the life of a placid cow for a bit.'

'It's settled, then.'

'But – '

'Nonsense. There is Davidson, isn't it? That dark flamboyant-looking man talking to Lucy Lorrimer. On my left.'

'Yes.'

'Is he clever? Everyone seems to go to him. I might show him my leg one of these days. If you don't promise to come, Evelyn, I shall call him over here and make a scene. Here comes Bunchy Gospell,' continued Lady Alleyn with a quick glance at her hostess's trembling fingers, 'and I feel sure he's going to ask you to sup with him. Why, if that isn't Agatha Troy with him!'

'The painter?' said Lady Carrados faintly. 'Yes. Bridgie knows her. She's going to paint Bridgie.'

'She did a sketch portrait of my son Roderick. It's amazingly good.'

Lord Robert, looking, with so large an expanse of white under his chin, rather like Mr Pickwick, came beaming towards them with Troy at his side. Lady Alleyn held out her hand and drew Troy down to a stool beside her. She looked at the short dark hair, the long neck and the spare grace that was Troy's and wished, not for the first time, that it was her daughter-in-law that sat at her feet. Troy was the very wife she would have chosen for her son, and, so she believed, the wife that he would have chosen for himself. She rubbed her nose vexedly. 'If it hadn't been for that wretched case!' she thought. And she said:

'I'm so pleased to see you, my dear. I hear the exhibition is the greatest success.'

Troy gave her a sideways smile.

'I wonder,' continued Lady Alleyn, 'which of us is the most surprised at seeing the other. I have bounced out of retirement to launch my granddaughter.'

'I was brought by Bunchy Gospell,' said Troy. 'I'm so seldom smart and gay that I'm rather enjoying it.'

'Roderick had actually consented to come but he's got a tricky case on his hands and has to go away again tomorrow at the crack of dawn.'

'Oh,' said Troy.

Lord Robert began to talk excitedly to Lady Carrados.

'Gorgeous!' he cried, pitching his voice very high in order to top the band which had suddenly begun to make a terrific din. 'Gorgeous, Evelyn! Haven't enjoyed anything – ages – superb!' He bent his knees and placed his face rather close to Lady Carrados's. 'Supper!' he squeaked. 'Do say you will! In half an hour or so. Will you?'

She smiled and nodded. He sat down between Lady Carrados and Lady Alleyn and gave them each a little pat. His hand alighted on Lady Carrados's bag. She moved it quickly. He was beaming out into the ballroom and seemed lost in a mild ecstasy.

'Champagne!' he said. 'Can't beat it! I'm not inebriated, my dears, but I am, I proudly confess, a little exalted. What I believe is nowadays called nicely thank you. How-de-do? Gorgeous, ain't it?'

General and Mrs Halcut-Hackett bowed. Their smiling lips moved in a soundless assent. They sat down between Lady Alleyn and Sir Daniel Davidson and his partner, Lady Lorrimer.

Lucy, Dowager Marchioness of Lorrimer, was a woman of eighty. She dressed almost entirely in veils and untidy jewellery. She was enormously rich and not a little eccentric. Sir Daniel attended to her lumbago. She was now talking to him earnestly and confusedly and he listened with an air of enraptured attention. Lord Robert turned with a small bounce and made two bobs in their direction.

'There's Davidson,' he said delightedly, 'and Lucy Lorrimer. How are you, Lucy?'

'What?' shouted Lucy Lorrimer.

'How are yer?'

'Busy. I thought you were in Australia.'

'Why?'

'What?'

'Why?'

'Don't interrupt,' shouted Lucy Lorrimer. 'I'm talking.'

'Never been there,' said Lord Robert; 'the woman's mad.'

The Halcut-Hacketts smiled uncomfortably. Lucy Lorrimer leant across Davidson and bawled: 'Don't forget tomorrow night!'

'Who? Me?' asked Lord Robert. 'Of course not.'

'Eight-thirty sharp.'

'I know. Though how you could think I was in Australia – '

'I didn't see it was you,' screamed Lucy Lorrimer. 'Don't forget now.' The band stopped as abruptly as it had begun and her voice rang out piercingly. 'It wouldn't be the first night you had disappointed me.'

She leant back chuckling and fanning herself. Lord Robert took the rest of the party in with a comical glance.

'Honestly, Lucy!' said Lady Alleyn.

'He's the most absent-minded creature in the world,' added Lucy Lorrimer.

'Now to that,' said Lord Robert, 'I do take exception. I am above all things a creature of habit, upon my honour. I could tell you, if it wasn't a very boring sort of story, exactly to the minute what I shall do with myself tomorrow evening and how I shall ensure my punctual arrival at Lucy Lorrimer's party.'

'Suddenly remember it at a quarter to nine and take a cab,' said Lucy Lorrimer.

'Not a bit of it.'

Mrs Halcut-Hackett suddenly joined in the conversation.

'I can vouch for Lord Robert's punctuality,' she said loudly. 'He always keeps his appointments.' She laughed a little too shrilly and for some unaccountable reason created an uncomfortable atmosphere. Lady Alleyn glanced sharply at her. Lucy Lorrimer stopped short in the middle of a hopelessly involved sentence; Davidson put up his glass and stared. General Halcut-Hackett said, 'What!' loudly and uneasily. Lord Robert examined his fat little hands with an air of complacent astonishment. The inexplicable tension was relieved by the arrival of Sir

248

Herbert Carrados with the plain protégée of the Halcut-Hacketts. She held her long chiffon handkerchief to her face and she looked a little desperately at her chaperone. Carrados who had her by the elbow was the very picture of British chivalry.

'A casualty!' he said archly. 'Mrs Halcut-Hackett, I'm afraid you are going to be very angry with me!'

'Why, Sir Herbert!' said Mrs Halcut-Hackett; 'that's surely an impossibility.'

The General said 'What!'

'This young lady,' continued Carrados, squeezing her elbow, 'no sooner began to dance with me than she developed toothache. Frightfully bad luck – for both of us.'

Mrs Halcut-Hackett eyed her charge with something very like angry despair.

'What's the matter,' she said, 'darling?'

'I'm afraid I'd better go home.'

Lady Carrados took her hand.

'That *is* bad luck,' she said. 'Shall we see if we can find something to – '

'No, no, please,' said the child. 'I think really, I'd better go home. I – I'm sure I'd better. Really.'

The General suddenly became human. He stood up, took the girl by the shoulders, and addressed Lady Carrados.

'Better at home,' he said. 'What? Brandy and oil of cloves. Damn bad show. Will you excuse us?' He addressed his wife. 'I'll take her home. You stay on. Come back for you.' He addressed his charge: 'Come on, child. Get your wrap.'

'You need not come back for me, dear,' said Mrs Halcut-Hackett. 'I shall be quite all right. Stay with Rose.'

'If I may,' squeaked Lord Robert, 'I'll give myself the pleasure of driving your wife home, Halcut-Hackett.'

'No, no,' began Mrs Halcut-Hackett, 'I – please – '

'Well,' said the General. 'Suit splendidly. What? Say good

249

night. What?' They bowed and shook hands. Sir Herbert walked away with both of them. Mrs Halcut-Hackett embarked on a long polite explanation and apology to Lady Carrados.

'Poor child!' whispered Lady Alleyn.

'Poor child, indeed,' murmured Troy.

Mrs Halcut-Hackett had made no further reply to Lord Robert's offer. Now, as he turned to her, she hurriedly addressed herself to Davidson.

'I must take the poor lamb to a dentist,' she said. 'Too awful if her face should swell half-way through the season. Her mother is my dearest friend but she'd never forgive me. A major tragedy.'

'Quite,' said Sir Daniel rather dryly.

'Well,' said Lucy Lorrimer beginning to collect her scarves, 'I shall expect you at eight twenty-seven. It's only me and my brother, you know. The one that got into difficulties. I want some supper. Where is Mrs Halcut-Hackett? I suppose I must congratulate her on her ball, though I must say I always think it's the greatest mistake – '

Sir Daniel Davidson hurriedly shouted her down.

'Let me take you down and give you some supper,' he suggested loudly with an agonized glance at Mrs Halcut-Hackett and Lady Carrados. He carried Lucy Lorrimer away.

'Poor Lucy!' said Lady Alleyn. 'She never has the remotest idea where she is. I wish, Evelyn, that he hadn't stopped her. What fault do you suppose she was about to find in your hospitality?'

'Let's follow them, Evelyn,' said Lord Robert, 'and no doubt we shall find out. Troy, m'dear, there's a young man making for you. May we dance again?'

'Yes, of course, Bunchy dear,' said Troy, and went off with her partner.

Lady Carrados said she would meet Lord Robert in the

supper-room in ten minutes. She left them, threading her way down the ballroom, her fingers clutching her bag. At the far end she overtook Sir Daniel and Lucy Lorrimer.

Lady Alleyn, looking anxiously after her, saw her sway a little. Davidson stepped up to her quickly and took her arm, steadying her. Lady Alleyn saw him speak to her with a quick look of concern. She saw Evelyn Carrados shake her head, smiling at him. He spoke again with emphasis and then Lucy Lorrimer shouted at him and he shrugged his shoulders and moved away. After a moment Lady Carrados, too, left the ballroom.

Lord Robert asked Mrs Halcut-Hackett if she would 'take a turn' with him once round the room. She excused herself, making rather an awkward business of it:

'I fancy I said that I would keep this one for – I'm so sorry – Oh, yes – here he comes right now.'

Captain Withers had come from the farther side of the ballroom. Mrs Halcut-Hackett hurriedly got up and went to meet him. Without a word he placed his arm round her and they moved off together, Withers looking straight in front of him.

'Where's Rory?' Lord Robert asked Lady Alleyn. 'I expected to find him here tonight. He refused to dine with us.'

'Working at the Yard. He's going north early tomorrow. Bunchy, that was your Captain Withers, wasn't it? The man we saw at the Halcut-Hacketts' cocktail-party?'

'Yes.'

'Is she having an affair with him, do you suppose? They've got that sort of look.'

Lord Robert pursed his lips and contemplated his hands.

'It's *not* malicious curiosity,' said Lady Alleyn. 'I'm worried about those women. Especially Evelyn.'

'You don't suggest Evelyn –?'

'Of course not. But they've both got the same haunted look. And if I'm not mistaken Evelyn nearly fainted just

251

then. Your friend Davidson noticed it and I think he gave her the scolding she needs. She's at the end of her tether, Bunchy.'

'I'll get hold of her and take her into the supper-room.'

'Do. Go after her now, like a dear man. There comes my Sarah.'

Lord Robert hurried away. It took him some time to get round the ballroom and as he edged past dancing couples and over the feet of sitting chaperones he suddenly felt as if an intruder had thrust open all the windows of this neat little world and let in a flood of uncompromising light. In this cruel light he saw the people he liked best and they were changed and belittled. He saw his nephew Donald, who had turned aside when they met in the hall, as a spoilt, selfish boy with no honesty or ambition. He saw Evelyn Carrados as a woman haunted by some memory that was discreditable, and hag-ridden by a blackmailer. His imagination leapt into extravagance, and in many of the men he fancied he saw something of the unscrupulousness of Withers, the pomposity of Carrados, and the stupidity of old General Halcut-Hackett. He was plunged into a violent depression that had a sort of nightmarish quality. How many of these women were what he still thought of as 'virtuous'? And the débutantes? They had gone back to chaperones and were guided and guarded by women, many of whose own private lives would look ugly in this flood of hard light that had been let in on Lord Robert's world. The girls were sheltered by a convention for three months but at the same time they heard all sorts of things that would have horrified and bewildered his sister Mildred at their age. And he wondered if the Victorian and Edwardian eras had been no more than freakish incidents in the history of society and if their proprieties had been as artificial as the paint on a modern woman's lips. This idea seemed abominable to Lord Robert and he felt old and lonely for the first time in his life.

252

'It's the business with Donald and this blackmailing game,' he thought as he twisted aside to avoid a couple who were dancing the rumba. He had reached the door. He went into the lounge which opened off the ballroom, saw that Evelyn Carrados was not there, and made for the staircase. The stairs were covered with couples sitting out. He picked his way down and passed his nephew Donald who looked at him as if they were strangers.

'No good trying to break that down,' thought Lord Robert. 'Not here. He'd only cut me and someone would notice.' He felt wretchedly depressed and tired, and was filled with a premonition of disaster that quite astonished himself. 'Good God,' he thought suddenly, 'I must be going to be ill.' And oddly enough this comforted him a little. In the lower hall he found Bridget O'Brien with a neat, competent-looking young woman whose face he dimly remembered.

'Now, Miss Harris,' Bridgie was saying, 'are you sure you're getting on all right? Have you had supper?'

'Well, thank you so much, Miss O'Brien, but really it doesn't matter – '

Of course, it was Evelyn's secretary. Nice of Evelyn to ask her. Nice of Bridgie to take trouble. He said:

'Hullo, m'dear. What a grand ball. Has your mother come this way?'

'She's in the supper-room,' said Bridget without looking at him, and he realized that of course she had heard Donald's side of their quarrel. He said:

'Thank you, Bridgie, I'll find her.' He saw Miss Harris was looking a little like a lost child so he said: 'Wonder if you'd be very nice and give me a dance later on? Would you?'

Miss Harris turned scarlet and said she would be very pleased thank you, Lord – Lord Gospell.

'Got it wrong,' thought Lord Robert. 'Poor things, they

253

don't get much fun. Wonder what *they* think of it all. Not much, you may depend upon it.'

He found Lady Carrados in the supper-room. He took her to a corner table, made her drink champagne and tried to persuade her to eat.

'I know what you're all like,' he told her. 'Nothing all day in your tummies and then get through the night on your nerves. I remember mama used to have the vapours whenever she gave a big party. She always came round in time to receive the guests.'

He chattered away, eating a good deal himself and getting over his own unaccountable fit of depression in his effort to help Lady Carrados. He looked round and saw that the supper-room was inhabited by only a few chaperones and their partners. Poor Davidson was still in Lucy Lorrimer's toils. Withers and Mrs Halcut-Hackett were tucked away in a corner. She was talking to him earnestly and apparently with great emphasis. He glowered at the table and laughed unpleasantly.

'Lor'!' thought Lord Robert, 'she's giving him his marching orders. Now why's that? Afraid of the General or of – what? Of the blackmailer? I wonder if Withers is the subject of those letters. I wonder if Dimitri has seen her with him some time. I'll swear it was Dimitri's hand. But what does he know about Evelyn? The least likely woman in the world to have a guilty secret. And, damme, there is the fellow as large as you please, running the whole show.'

Dimitri had come into the supper-room. He gave a professional look round, spoke to one of his waiters, came across to Lady Carrados and bowed tentatively and then went out again.

'Dimitri is a great blessing to all of us,' said Lady Carrados. She said it so simply that he knew at once that if Dimitri was blackmailing her she had no idea of it. He

254

was hunting in his mind for something to reply when Bridget came into the supper-room.

She was carrying her mother's bag.

Everything seemed to happen at the same moment. Bridget calling gaily: 'Really, Donna darling, you're *hopeless*. There was your bag, simply preggy with bank-notes, lying on the writing-table in the green boudoir. And I *bet* you didn't know where you'd left it.' Then Bridget, seeing her mother's face and crying out: 'Darling, what's the matter?' Lord Robert himself getting up and interposing his bulk between Lady Carrados and the other tables. Lady Carrados half-laughing, half-crying and reaching out frantically for the bag. Himself saying: 'Run away, Bridget, I'll look after your mother.' And Lady Carrados, in a whisper: 'I'm all right. Run upstairs, darling, and get my smelling-salts.'

Somehow they persuaded Bridget to go. The next thing that happened was Sir Daniel Davidson, who stood over Evelyn Carrados like an elegant dragon.

'You're all right,' he said. 'Lord Robert, see if you can open that window.'

Lord Robert succeeded in opening the window. A damp hand seemed to be laid on his face. He caught sight of street lamps blurred by impalpable mist.

Davidson held Lady Carrados's wrist in his long fingers and looked at her with a sort of compassionate exasperation.

'You women,' he said. 'You impossible women.'

'I'm all right. I simply felt giddy.'

'You ought to lie down. You'll faint and make an exhibition of yourself.'

'No I won't. Has anybody – ? '

'Nobody's noticed anything. Will you go up to your room for half an hour?'

'I haven't got a room. It's not my house.'

'Of course it's not. The cloakroom, then.'

'I – yes. Yes, I'll do that.'

'Sir Daniel!' shouted Lucy Lorrimer in the corner.

'For Heaven's sake go back to her,' implored Lady Carrados, 'or she'll be here.'

'*Sir Daniel!*'

'Damn!' whispered Davidson. 'Very well, I'll go back to her. I expect your maid's here, isn't she? Good. Lord Robert, will you take Lady Carrados?'

'I'd rather go alone. Please!'

'Very well. But *please* go.'

He made a grimace and returned to Lucy Lorrimer.

Lady Carrados stood up, holding her bag.

'Come on,' said Lord Robert. 'Nobody's paying any attention.'

He took her elbow and they went out into the hall. It was deserted. Two men stood just in the entrance to the cloakroom. They were Captain Withers and Donald Potter. Donald glanced round, saw his uncle, and at once began to move upstairs. Withers followed him. Dimitri came out of the buffet and also went upstairs. The hall was filled with the sound of the band and with the thick confusion of voices and sliding feet.

'Bunchy,' whispered Lady Carrados. 'You must do as I ask you. Leave me for three minutes. I – '

'I know what's up, m'dear. Don't do it. Don't leave your bag. Face it and let him go to the devil.'

She pressed her hand against her mouth and looked wildly at him.

'You *know*?'

'Yes, and I'll help. I know who it is. You don't, do you? See here – there's a man at the Yard – whatever it is – '

A look of something like relief came into her eyes.

'But you don't know what it's about. Let me go. I've *got* to do it. Just this once more.'

256

She pulled her arm away and he watched her cross the hall and slowly climb the stairs.

After a moment's hesitation he followed her.

CHAPTER SIX

Bunchy Goes Back to the Yard

Alleyn closed his file and looked at his watch. Two minutes to one. Time for him to pack up and go home. He yawned, stretched his cramped fingers, walked over to the window and pulled aside the blind. The row of lamps hung like a necklace of misty globes along the margin of the Embankment.

'Fog in June,' muttered Alleyn. 'This England!'

Out there in the cold, Big Ben tolled one. At that moment three miles away at Lady Carrados's ball, Lord Robert Gospell was slowly climbing the stairs to the top landing and the little drawing-room.

Alleyn filled his pipe slowly and lit it. An early start tomorrow, a long journey, and a piece of dull routine at the end of it. He held his fingers to the heater and fell into a long meditation. Sarah had told him Troy was going to the ball. She was there now, no doubt.

'Oh, well!' he thought and turned off his heater.

The desk telephone rang. He answered it.

'Hullo?'

'Mr Alleyn? I thought you were still there, sir. Lord Robert Gospell.'

'Right.'

A pause and then a squeaky voice:

'Rory?'

'Bunchy?'

'You said you'd be at it till late. I'm in a room by myself at the Carrados's show. Thing is, I think I've got him. Are you working for much longer?'

'I can.'

'May I come round to the Yard?'

258

'Do!'

'I'll go home first, get out of this boiled shirt and pick up my notes.'

'Right. I'll wait.'

'It's the cakes-and-ale feller.'

'Good Lord! No names, Bunchy.'

"Course not. I'll come round to the Yard. Upon my soul it's worse than murder. Might as well mix his damn' brews with poison. And he's working with – Hullo! Didn't hear you come in.'

'Is someone there?' asked Alleyn sharply.

'Yes.'

'Good-bye,' said Alleyn, 'I'll wait for you.'

'Thank you so much,' squeaked the voice. 'Much obliged. Wouldn't have lost it for anything. Very smart work, officer. See you get the reward.'

Alleyn smiled and hung up his receiver.

Up in the ballroom Hughie Bronx's Band packed up. Their faces were the colour of raw cod and shone with a fishy glitter, but the hair on their heads remained as smooth as patent leather. The four experts who only ten minutes ago had jigged together with linked arms in a hot rhythm argued wearily about the way to go home. Hughie Bronx himself wiped his celebrated face with a beautiful handkerchief and lit a cigarette.

'OK, boys,' he sighed. 'Eighty-thirty tomorrow and if any — calls for "My Girl's Cutie" more than six times running we'll quit and learn anthems.'

Dimitri crossed the ballroom.

'Her ladyship particularly asked me to tell you,' he said, 'that there is something for you gentlemen at the buffet.'

'Thanks a lot, Dim,' said Mr Bronx. 'We'll be there.'

Dimitri glanced round the ballroom, walked out and descended the stairs.

Down in the entrance hall the last of the guests were

collected. They looked wan and a little raffish but they shouted cheerfully, telling each other what a good party it had been. Among them, blinking sleepily through his glasses, was Lord Robert. His celebrated cape hung from his shoulders and in his hands he clasped his broad-brimmed black hat. Through the open doors came wreaths of mist. The sound of people coughing as they went into the raw air was mingled with the noise of taxi engines in low gear and the voices of departing guests.

Lord Robert was among the last to go.

He asked several people, rather plaintively, if they had seen Mrs Halcut-Hackett. 'I'm supposed to be taking her home.'

Dimitri came up to him.

'Excuse me, my lord, I think Mrs Halcut-Hackett has just left. She asked me if I had seen you, my lord.'

Lord Robert blinked up at him. For a moment their eyes met.

'Oh. Thank you,' said Lord Robert. 'I'll see if I can find her.'

Dimitri bowed.

Lord Robert walked out into the mist.

His figure, looking a little like a plump antic from one of Verlaine's poems, moved down the broad steps. He passed a crowd of stragglers who were entering their taxis. He peered at them, watched them go off, and looked up and down the street. Lord Robert walked slowly down the street, seemed to turn into an insubstantial wraith, was hidden for a moment by a drift of mist, reappeared much farther away, walking steadily into nothingness, and was gone.

In his room at the Yard Alleyn woke with a start, rushing up on a wave of clamour from the darkness of profound sleep. The desk telephone was pealing. He reached out

for it, caught sight of his watch and exclaimed aloud. Four
o'clock! He spoke into the receiver.

'Hullo?'

'Mr Alleyn?'

'Yes.'

He thought: 'It's Bunchy. What the devil – ! '

But the voice in the receiver said:

'There's a case come in, sir. I thought I'd better report
to you at once. Taxi with a fare. Says the fare's been
murdered and has driven straight here with the body.'

'I'll come down,' said Alleyn.

He went down thinking with dismay that another case
would be most unwelcome and hoping that it would be
handed on to someone else. His mind was full of the
blackmail business. Bunchy Gospell wouldn't have said
he'd found his man unless he was damn certain of him.
The cakes-and-ale fellow. Dimitri. Well, he'd have
opportunities, but what sort of evidence had Bunchy got?
And where the devil was Bunchy? A uniformed sergeant
waited for Alleyn in the entrance hall.

'Funny sort of business, Mr Alleyn. The gentleman's
dead all right. Looks to me as if he'd had a heart attack
or something, but the cabby insists it was murder and won't
say a word till he sees you. Didn't want me to open the
door. I did, though, just to make sure. Held my watch-
glass to the mouth and listened to the heart. Nothing! The
old cabby didn't half go off pop. He's a character.'

'Where's the taxi?'

'In the yard, sir. I told him to drive through.'

They went out to the yard.

'Dampish,' said the sergeant and coughed.

It was very misty down there near the river. Wreaths
of mist that were almost rain drifted round them and
changed on their faces into cold spangles of moisture. A
corpse-like pallor had crept into the darkness and the vague
shapes of roofs and chimneys waited for the dawn. Far

261

down the river a steamer hooted. The air smelt dank and unwholesome.

A vague huge melancholy possessed Alleyn. He felt at once nerveless and over-sensitized. His spirit seemed to rise thinly and separate itself from his body. He saw himself as a stranger. It was a familiar experience and he had grown to regard it as a precursor of evil. 'I must get back,' cried his mind and with the thought the return was accomplished. He was in the yard. The stones rang under his feet. A taxi loomed up vaguely with the overcoated figure of its driver standing motionless by the door as if on guard.

'Cold,' said the sergeant.

'It's the dead hour of the night,' said Alleyn.

The taxi-driver did not move until they came right up to him.

'Hullo,' said Alleyn, 'what's it all about?'

''Morning, governor.' It was the traditional hoarse voice. He sounded like a cabby in a play. 'Are you one of the inspectors?'

'I am.'

'I won't make no report to any copper. I got to look after meself, see? What's more, the little gent was a friend of mine, see?'

'This is Chief Detective-Inspector Alleyn, daddy,' said the sergeant.

'All right. That's the stuff. I got to protect meself, ain't I? Wiv a blinking stiff for a fare.'

He suddenly reached out a gloved hand and with a quick turn flung open the door.

'I ain't disturbed 'im,' he said. 'Will you switch on the glim?'

Alleyn's hand reached out into the darkness of the cab. He smelt leather, cigars and petrol. His fingers touched a button and a dim light came to life in the roof of the taxi.

262

He was motionless and silent for so long that at last the sergeant said loudly:

'Mr Alleyn?'

But Alleyn did not answer. He was alone with his friend. The small fat hands were limp. The feet were turned in pathetically, like the feet of a child. The head leant sideways, languidly, as a sick child will lean its head. He could see the bare patch on the crown and the thin ruffled hair.

'If you look froo the other winder,' said the driver, 'you'll see 'is face. 'E's dead all right. Murdered!'

Alleyn said: 'I can see his face.'

He had leant forward and for a minute or two he was busy. Then he drew back. He stretched out his hand as if to close the lids over the congested eyes. His fingers trembled.

He said: 'I mustn't touch him any more.' He drew his hand away and backed out of the taxi. The sergeant was staring in astonishment at his face.

'Dead,' said the taxi-driver. 'Ain't he?'

' — you!' said Alleyn with a violent oath. 'Can't I see he's dead without – '

He broke off and took three or four uncertain steps away from them. He passed his hand over his face and then stared at his fingers with an air of bewilderment.

'Wait a moment, will you?' he said.

'I'm sorry,' said Alleyn at last. 'Give me a moment.'

'Shall I get someone else, sir?' asked the sergeant. 'It's a friend of yours, isn't it?'

'Yes,' said Alleyn. 'It's a friend of mine.'

He turned on the taxi-driver and took him fiercely by the arm.

'Come here,' he said and marched him to the front of the car.

'Switch on the headlights,' he said.

The sergeant reached inside the taxi and in a moment the driver stood blinking in a white flood of light.

263

'Now,' said Alleyn. 'Why are you so certain it was murder?'

'Gorblimy, governor,' said the driver, 'ain't I seen wiv me own eyes 'ow the ovver bloke gets in wiv 'im, and ain't I seen wiv me own eyes 'ow the ovver bloke gets out at 'is lordship's 'ouse dressed up in 'is lordship's cloak and 'at and squeaks at me in a rum little voice same as 'is lordship: 'Sixty-three Jobbers Row, Queens Gate'? Ain't I driven 'is corpse all the way there, not knowing? 'Ere! You say 'is lordship was a friend of yours. So 'e was o' mine. This is bloody murder, this is, and I want to see this Mr Clever, what's diddled me and done in as nice a little gent as ever I see, swing for it. That's me.'

'I see,' said Alleyn. 'All right. I'll get a statement from you. We must get to work. Call up the usual lot. Get them all here. Get Dr Curtis. Photograph the body from every angle. Note the position of the head. Look for signs of violence. Routine. Case of homicide. Take the name, will you? Lord Robert Gospell, two hundred Cheyne Walk – '

CHAPTER SEVEN

Stop Press News

LORD ROBERT GOSPELL DIES IN TAXI
Society Shocked. Foul Play Suspected
Full Story of Ball on Page 5

Evelyn Carrados let the paper fall on the counterpane and
stared at her husband.

'The papers are full of it,' she said woodenly.

'Good God, my dear Evelyn, of course they are! And
this is only the ten o'clock racing edition brought in by
a damn pup of a footman with my breakfast. Wait till
we see the evening papers! Isn't it enough, my God, that
I should be rung up by some jack-in-office from Scotland
Yard at five o'clock in the morning and cross-examined
about my own guests without having the whole thing thrust
under my nose in some insulting bloody broadsheet!'

He limped angrily about the room.

'It's perfectly obvious that the man has been murdered.
Do you realize that at any moment we'll have some damned
fellow from Scotland Yard cross-questioning us and that
all the scavengers in Fleet Street will be hanging about
our door for days together? Do you realize – '

'I think he was perhaps my greatest friend,' said Evelyn
Carrados.

'If you look at their damned impertinent drivel on page
five you will see the friendship well advertised. My God,
it's intolerable. Do you realize that the police rang up
Marsdon House at quarter-past four – five minutes after
we'd gone, thank God! – and asked when Robert Gospell
left? Some fellow of Dimitri's answered them and now a

265

blasted snivelling journalist has got hold of it. Do you realize – '

'I only realize,' said Evelyn Carrados, 'that Bunchy Gospell is dead.'

Bridget burst into the room, a paper in her hands.

'Donna! Oh, Donna – it's our funny little Bunchy. Our funny little Bunchy's dead! Donna!'

'Darling – I know.'

'But, Donna – *Bunchy*!'

'Bridget,' said her stepfather, 'please don't be hysterical. The point we have to consider is – '

Bridget's arm went round her mother's shoulders.

'But we *mind*,' she said. 'Can't you see – Donna minds *awfully*.'

Her mother said: 'Of course we mind, darling, but Bart's thinking about something else. You see, Bart thinks there will be dreadful trouble – '

'About what?'

Bridget's eyes blazed in her white face as she turned on Carrados.

'Do you mean Donald? *Do you*? Do you dare to suggest that Donald would – would – '

'Bridgie!' cried her mother, 'what are you saying!'

'Wait a moment, Evelyn,' said Carrados. 'What is all this about young Potter?'

Bridget pressed the back of her hand against her mouth, looked distractedly from her mother to her stepfather, burst into tears and ran out of the room.

'BUNCHY' GOSPELL DEAD
Mysterious death in Taxi
Sequel to the Carrados Ball

Mrs Halcut-Hackett's beautifully manicured hands closed like claws on the newspaper. Her lips were stretched in a smile that emphasised the carefully suppressed lines from her nostrils to the corners of her mouth. She stared at nothing.

General Halcut-Hackett's dressing-room door was flung open and the General, wearing a dressing-gown but few teeth, marched into the room. He carried a copy of a ten o'clock sporting edition.

'What!' he shouted indistinctly. 'See here! By God!'

'I know,' said Mrs Halcut-Hackett. 'Sad, isn't it?'

'Sad! Bloody outrage! What!'

'Shocking,' said Mrs Halcut-Hackett.

'Shocking!' echoed the General. 'Preposterous!' and the explosive consonants pronounced through the gap in his teeth blew his moustache out like a banner. His bloodshot eyes goggled at his wife. He pointed a stubby forefinger at her.

'He said he'd bring you home,' he spluttered.

'He didn't do so.'

'When did you come home?'

'I didn't notice. Late.'

'Alone?'

Her face was white but she looked steadily at him.

'Yes,' she said. 'Don't be a fool.'

STRANGE FATALITY
Lord Robert Gospell dies
after Ball
Full Story

Donald Potter read the four headlines over and over again. From the centre of the page his uncle's face twinkled at him. Donald's cigarette-butt burnt his lips. He spat it into his empty cup, and lit another. He was shivering as if he had a rigor. He read the four lines again. In the next room somebody yawned horribly.

Donald's head jerked back.

'Wits!' he said. 'Wits! Come here!'

'What's wrong?'

'*Come here!*'

Captain Withers, clad in an orange silk dressing-gown, appeared in the doorway.

'What the hell's the matter with you?' he enquired.

'Look here.'

Captain Withers, whistling between his teeth, strolled up and looked over Donald's shoulder. His whistling stopped. He reached out his hand, took the newspaper, and began to read. Donald watched him.

'Dead!' said Donald. 'Uncle Bunch! Dead!'

Withers glanced at him and returned to the paper. Presently he began again to whistle through his teeth.

DEATH OF LORD ROBERT GOSPELL
Tragic end to a distinguished career
Suspicious Circumstances

Lady Mildred Potter beat her plump hands on the proofs of the *Evening Chronicle* obituary notice and turned upon Alleyn a face streaming with tears.

'But who could have *wanted* to hurt Bunchy, Roderick? Everyone adored him. He hadn't an enemy in the world. Look what the *Chronicle* says – and I must say I think it charming of them to let me see the things they propose to say about him – but look what it says. "Beloved by all his friends!" And so he was. So he was. By all his friends.'

'He must have had one enemy, Mildred,' said Alleyn.

'I can't believe it. I'll never believe it. It must be an escaped lunatic.' She pressed her handkerchief to her eyes and sobbed violently. 'I shall never be able to face all this dreadful publicity. The police! I don't mean you, Roderick, naturally. But everything – the papers, everyone poking and prying. Bunchy would have detested it. I can't face it. I can't.'

'Where's Donald?'

'He rang up. He's coming.'

'From where?'

'From this friend's flat, wherever it is.'

'He's away from home?'

'Didn't Bunchy tell you? Ever since that awful afternoon when he was so cross with Donald. Bunchy didn't understand.'

'Why was Bunchy cross with him?'

'He had run into debt rather. And now, poor boy, he is no doubt feeling too dreadfully remorseful.'

Alleyn did not answer immediately. He walked over to the window and looked out.

'It will be easier for you,' he said at last, 'when Donald gets here. I suppose the rest of the family will come too?'

'Yes. All our old cousins and aunts. They have already rung up. Broomfield – Bunchy's eldest nephew, you know – I mean my eldest brother's son is away on the Continent. He's the head of the family, of course. I suppose I shall have to make all the arrangements and – and I'm so dreadfully shaken.'

'I'll do as much as I can. There are some things that I must do. I'm afraid, Mildred, I shall have to ask you to let me look at Bunchy's things. His papers and so on.'

'I'm sure,' said Lady Mildred, 'he would have preferred you to anyone else, Roderick.'

'You make it very easy for me. Shall I get it done now?'

Lady Mildred looked helplessly about her.

'Yes. Yes, please. You'll want his keys, won't you?'

'I've got the keys, Mildred,' said Alleyn gently.

'But – where – ?' She gave a little cry. 'Oh, poor darling. He always took them with him everywhere.' She broke down completely. Alleyn waited for a moment and then he said:

'I shan't attempt the impertinence of condoling phrases. There is small comfort in scavenging in this mess for crumbs

269

of consolation. But I tell you this, Mildred, if it takes me the rest of my life, and if it costs me my job, by God! if I have to do the killing myself, I'll get this murderer and see him suffer for it.' He paused and made a grimace. 'Good Lord, what a speech! Bunchy *would* have laughed at it. It's a curious thing that when one speaks from the heart it is invariably in the worst of taste.'

He looked at her grey hair arranged neatly and unfashionably and enclosed in a net. She peered at him over the top of her drenched handkerchief and he saw that she had not listened to him.

'I'll get on with it,' said Alleyn, and made his way alone to Lord Robert's study.

LORD ROBERT GOSPELL
DIES IN TAXI
Last night's shocking Fatality
Who was the Second Passenger?

Sir Daniel Davidson arrived at his consulting-rooms at half-past ten. At his front door he caught sight of the news placard and, for the first time in his life, bought a sporting edition. He now folded the paper carefully and laid it on top of his desk. He lit a cigarette, and glanced at his servant.

'I shan't see any patients,' he said. 'If anybody rings up – I'm out. Thank you.'

'Thank you, sir,' said the servant and removed himself.

Sir Daniel sat thinking. He had trained himself to think methodically and he hated slipshod ideas as much as he despised a vague diagnosis. He was, he liked to tell his friends, above all things, a creature of method and routine. He prided himself upon his memory. His memory was busy now with events only seven hours old. He closed his eyes and saw himself in the entrance-hall of Marsdon House at four o'clock that morning. The last guests, wrapped in coats and furs, shouted cheerfully to each other and

270

passed through the great doors in groups of twos and threes. Dimitri stood at the foot of the stairs. He himself was near the entrance to the men's cloakroom. He was bent on avoiding Lucy Lorrimer, who had stayed to the bitter end, and would offer to drive him home if she saw him. There she was, just going through the double doors. He hung back. Drifts of fog were blown in from the street. He remembered that he had wrapped his scarf over his mouth when he noticed the fog. It was at that precise moment he had seen Mrs Halcut-Hackett, embedded in furs, slip through the entrance alone. He had thought there was something a little odd about this. The collar of her fur wrap turned up, no doubt against the fog, and the manner in which she slipped, if so majestic a woman could be said to slip, round the outside of the group! There was something furtive about it. And then he himself had been jostled by that fellow Withers, coming out of the cloakroom. Withers had scarcely apologized, but had looked quickly round the melting group in the hall and up the stairs.

It was at that moment that Lord Robert Gospell had come downstairs. Sir Daniel twisted the heavy signet ring on his little finger and still with closed eyes he peered back into his memory. Withers had seen Lord Robert. There was no doubt of that. Sir Daniel heard again that swift intake of breath and noticed the quick glance before the fellow unceremoniously shoved his way through the crowd and disappeared into the fog. Then Lord Robert's nephew, young Donald Potter, came out of the buffet near the stairs. Bridget O'Brien was with him. They almost ran into Lord Robert, but when Donald saw his uncle he sheered off, said something to Bridget, and then went out by the front entrance. One more picture remained.

Bunchy Gospell speaking to Dimitri at the foot of the stairs. This was the last thing Sir Daniel saw before he, too, went out into the fog.

He supposed that those moments in the hall would be

271

regarded by the police as highly significant. The papers said that the police wished to establish the identity of the second fare. Naturally, since he was obviously the murderer! The taxi-driver had described him as a well-dressed gentleman who, with Lord Robert, had entered the cab about two hundred yards up the street from Marsdon House. 'Was it one of the guests?' asked the paper. That meant the police would get statements from everyone who left the house about the same time as Lord Robert. The last thing in the world that Sir Daniel wanted was to appear as a principal witness at the inquest. That sort of publicity did a fashionable physician no good. His name in block capitals, as likely as not, across the front sheets of the penny press and before you knew where you were some fool would say: 'Davidson? Wasn't he mixed up in that murder case?' He might even have to say he saw the Halcut-Hackett woman go out, with Withers in hot pursuit. Mrs Halcut-Hackett was one of his most lucrative patients. On the other hand, he would look extremely undignified if they found out that he was one of the last to leave and had not come forward to say so. It might even look suspicious. Sir Daniel swore picturesquely in French, reached for his telephone and dialled WHI1212.

MYSTERY IN MAYFAIR
Lord Robert Gospell suffocated in Taxi
Who was the second fare?

Colombo Dimitri in his smart flat in the Cromwell Road drew the attention of his confidential servant to the headlines.

'What a tragedy,' he said. 'It may be bad for us at the beginning of the season. Nobody feels very gay after a murder. He was so popular, too. It is most unfortunate.'

'Yes, monsieur,' said the confidential servant.

'I must have been almost the last person to speak with

272

him,' continued Dimitri, 'unless, of course, this dastardly assassin addressed him. Lord Robert came to me in the hall and asked me if I had seen Mrs Halcut-Hackett. I told him I had just seen her go away. He thanked me and left. I, of course, remained in the hall. Several of the guests spoke to me after that, I recollect. And then, an hour later, when I had left, but my men were still busy, the police rang up. He was a charming personality. I am very, very sorry.'

'Yes, monsieur.'

'It would be a pleasant gesture for us to send flowers. Remind me of it. In the meantime, if you please, no gossip. I must instruct the staff on this point. I absolutely insist upon it. The affair must not be discussed.'

'C'est entendu, monsieur.'

'In respect of malicious tittle-tattle,' said Dimitri virtuously, 'our firm is in the well-known position of Caesar's wife.' He glanced at his servant's face. It wore a puzzled expression. 'She did not appear in gossip columns,' explained Dimitri.

MYSTERY OF UNKNOWN FARE
'Bunchy' Gospell dead
Who was the Man in Dress Clothes?

Miss Harris finished her cup of tea but her bread and butter remained untasted on her plate. She told herself she did not fancy it. Miss Harris was gravely upset. She had encountered a question to which she did not know the answer and she found herself unable to stuff it away in one of her pigeon-holes. The truth was Miss Harris's heart was touched. She had seen Lord Robert several times in Lady Carrados's house and last night Lord Robert had danced with her. When Lady Carrados asked Miss Harris if she would like to come to the ball she had never for a moment expected to dance at it. She had expected to

273

spend a gratifying but exceedingly lonely night watching the fruits of her own labours. Her expectations had been realized until the moment when Lord Robert asked her to dance, and from then onwards Miss Harris had known a sort of respectable rapture. He had found her on the upper landing where she was sitting by herself outside the little green boudoir. She had just come out of the 'Ladies' and had had an embarrassing experience practically in the doorway. So she had sat on a chair on the landing to recover her poise and because there did not seem to be anywhere else much to go. Then she had pulled herself together and gone down to the ballroom. She was trying to look happy and not lost when Lord Robert came up and remembered his request that they should dance. And dance they did, round and round in the fast Viennese waltz, and Lord Robert had said he hadn't enjoyed himself so much for ages. They had joined a group of dizzily 'right' people and one of them, Miss Agatha Troy the famous painter it was, had talked to her as if they had been introduced. And then, when the band played another fast Viennese waltz because they were fashionable, Miss Harris and Lord Robert had danced again and had afterwards taken champagne at the buffet. That had been quite late – not long before the ball ended. How charming he had been, making her laugh a great deal and feel like a human young woman of thirty and not a dependent young lady of no age at all.

And now, here he was, murdered.

Miss Harris was so upset that she could not eat her breakfast. She glanced automatically at her watch. Twelve o'clock. She was to be at Lady Carrados's house by two in case she was needed. If she was quick she would have time to write an exciting letter home to the Buckinghamshire vicarage. The girl-friend with whom she shared the flatlet was still asleep. She was a night operator in a telephone exchange. But Miss Harris's bosom could contain this

274

dreadful news no longer. She rose, opened the bedroom door and said:

'Smithy!'

'Uh!'

'Smithy, something awful has happened. Listen!'

'Uh?'

'The girl has just brought in a paper. It's about Lord Gospell. I mean Lord Robert Gospell. You know. I told you about him last night – '

'For God's sake!' said Miss Smith. 'Did you have to wake me up again to hear all about your social successes?'

'No, but Smithy, *listen*! It's simply frightful! He's murdered.'

Miss Smith sat up in bed looking like a sort of fabulous goddess in her mass of tin curling-pins.

'My dear, he isn't,' said Miss Smith.

'My dear, he is!' said Miss Harris.

CHAPTER EIGHT

Troy and Alleyn

When Alleyn had finished his examination of the study he sat at Lord Robert's desk and telephoned to Marsdon House. He was answered by one of his own men.

'Is Mr Fox there, Bailey?'

'Yes, sir. He's upstairs. I'll just tell him.'

Alleyn waited. Before him on the desk was a small, fat notebook and upon the opened page he read again in Lord Robert's finicky writing the notes he had made on his case:

> '*Saturday, May 8th.* Cocktail-party at Mrs H-H's house in Halkin Street. Arrived 6.15. Mrs H-H *distraite.* Arranged to meet her June 3rd, Constance Street Hall. Saw Maurice Withers, ref. drug affair 1924. Bad lot. Seems thick with Mrs H-H. Shied off me. *Mem.* Tell Alleyn about W's gambling hell at L.

> '*Thursday, June 3rd.* Constance Street Hall. Recital by Sirmione Quartette. Arrived 2.15. Met Mrs H-H 2.30. Mrs H-H sat on left-hand end of blue sofa (occupant's left). Sofa about 7 feet inside main entrance and 8 feet to right as you enter. Sofa placed at right angles to right-hand corner of room. Side entrance on right-hand wall about ten feet behind sofa. My position in chair behind left arm of sofa. At 3.35 immediately after interval observed Mrs H-H's bag taken from left end of sofa where previously I watched her place it. She had left the room during interval and returned after bag had gone. Will swear that hand taking the bag was that of Dimitri of Shepherd Market Catering Company. Saw him there.

Seat nearby. Little finger same length as next and markedly crooked. Withers was there. *N.B.* Think Mrs H-H suspects me of blackmail. R.G.'

Fox's voice came through the receiver.

'Hullo, sir?'

'Hullo, Fox. Have you seen the room where he telephoned to me?'

'Yes. It's a room on the top landing. One of Dimitri's waiters saw him go in. The room hasn't been touched.'

'Right. Anything else?'

'Nothing much. The house is pretty well as it was when the guests left. You saw to that, sir.'

'Is Dimitri there?'

'No.'

'Get him, Fox. I'll see him at the Yard at twelve o'clock. That'll do him for the moment. Tell Bailey to go all over the telephone room for prints. We've got to find out who interrupted that call to the Yard. And, Fox – '

'Sir?'

'Can you come round here? I'd like a word with you.'

'I'll be there.'

'Thank you,' said Alleyn, and hung up the receiver.

He looked again at the document he had found in the central drawer of Lord Robert's desk. It was his will. A very simple little will. After one or two legacies he left all his possessions and the life interest on £40,000 to his sister, Lady Mildred Potter, to revert to her son on her death and the remainder of his estate, £20,000, to that same son, his nephew, Donald Potter. The will was dated January 1st of that year.

'His good deed for the New Year,' thought Alleyn.

He looked at the two photographs in leather frames that stood on Lord Robert's desk. One was of Lady Mildred Potter in the presentation dress of her girlhood. Mildred had been rather pretty in those days. The other was of a young man of about twenty. Alleyn noted the short Gospell nose and wide-set eyes. The mouth was pleasant and weak, the chin one of those jutting affairs that look determined and are too often merely obstinate. It was rather an attractive face. Donald had written his name across the corner with the date, January 1st.

'I hope to God,' thought Alleyn, 'that he can give a good account of himself.'

'Good morning,' said a voice from the doorway.

He swung round in his chair and saw Agatha Troy. She was dressed in green and had a little velvet cap on her dark head and green gloves on her hands.

'Troy!'

'I came in to see if there was anything I could do for Mildred.'

'You didn't know I was here?'

'Not till she told me. She asked me to see if you had everything you wanted.'

'Everything I wanted,' repeated Alleyn.

'If you have,' said Troy, 'that's all right. I won't interrupt.'

'Please,' said Alleyn, 'could you *not* go just for a second?'

'What is it?'

'Nothing. I mean, I've no excuse for asking you to stay, unless, if you will forgive me, the excuse of wanting to look at you and listen for a moment to your voice.' He held up his hand. 'No more than that. You liked Bunchy and so did I. He talked about you the last time I saw him.'

'A few hours ago,' said Troy. 'I was dancing with him.'

Alleyn moved to the tall windows . . . They looked out over the charming little garden to the Chelsea reaches of the Thames.

'A few hours ago' – he repeated her words slowly – 'the river was breathing mist. The air was threaded with mist and as cold as the grave. That was before dawn broke.

It was beginning to get light when I saw him. And look at it now. Not a cloud. The damned river's positively sparkling in the sunlight. Come here, Troy.'

She stood beside him.

'Look down there into the street. Through the side window. At half-past three this morning the river mist lay like a pall along Cheyne Walk. If anybody was awake at that mongrel hour or abroad in the deserted streets they would have heard a taxi come along Cheyne Walk and stop outside this gate. If anybody in this house had had the curiosity to look out of one of the top windows they would have seen the door of the taxi open and a quaint figure in a cloak and wide-brimmed hat get out.'

'What do you mean? *He got out?*'

'The watcher would have seen this figure wave a gloved hand and heard him call to the driver in a shrill voice: 'Sixty-three Jobbers Row, Queens Gate.' He would have seen the taxi drive away into the mist – and then – what? What did the figure do? Did it run like a grotesque with flapping cloak towards the river to be swallowed up in vapour? Or did it walk off sedately into Chelsea? Did it wait for a moment, staring after the taxi? Did Bunchy's murderer pull off his cloak, fold it and walk away with it over his arm? Did he hide his own tall hat under the cloak before he got out of the taxi, and afterwards change back into it? And where are Bunchy's cloak and hat, Troy? Where are they?'

'What did the taxi-driver say?' asked Troy. 'There's nothing coherent in the papers. I don't understand.'

'I'll tell you. Fox will be here soon. Before he comes I can allow myself a few minutes to unload my mind, if you'll let me. I've done that before – once – haven't I?'

'Yes,' murmured Troy. 'Once.'

'There is nobody in the world who can listen as you can. I wish I had something better to tell you. Well, here it is. The taxi-driver brought Bunchy to the Yard at four

279

o'clock this morning, saying he was murdered. This was his story. He picked Bunchy up at three-thirty some two hundred yards from the doors of Marsdon House. There was a shortage of taxis and we suppose Bunchy had walked so far, hoping to pick one up in a side street, when this fellow came along. The unnatural mist that hung over London last night was thick in Belgrave Square. As the taximan drove towards Bunchy he saw another figure in an overcoat and top-hat loom through the mist and stand beside him. They appeared to speak together. Bunchy held up his stick. The cabby knew him by sight and addressed him:

' "'Morning, m'lord. Two hundred Cheyne Walk?"

' "Please," said Bunchy.

'The two men got into the taxi. The cabby never had a clear view of the second man. He had his back turned as the taxi approached and when it stopped he stood towards the rear in shadow. Before the door was slammed the cabby heard Bunchy say: "You can take him on." The cabby drove to Cheyne Walk by way of Chesham Place, Cliveden Place, Lower Sloane Street and Chelsea Hospital and across Tite Street. He says it took about twelve minutes. He stopped here at Bunchy's gate and in a few moments Lord Robert, as he supposed him to be, got out and slammed the door. A voice squeaked through a muffler: "Sixty-three Jobbers Row, Queens Gate," and the cabby drove away. He arrived at Jobbers Row ten minutes later, waited for his fare to get out and at last got out himself and opened the door. He found Bunchy.'

Alleyn waited for a moment, looked gravely at Troy's white face. She said:

'There was no doubt – '

'None. The cabby is an obstinate, opinionated, cantankerous old oddity, but he's no fool. He satisfied himself. He explained that he once drove an ambulance and knew certain things. He headed as far as he could

for the Yard. A sergeant saw him; saw everything; made
sure it was – what it was, and got me. I made sure, too.'

'What had been done to Bunchy?'

'You want to know? Yes, of course you do. You're too
intelligent to nurse your sensibilities.'

'Mildred will ask me about it. What happened?'

'We think he was struck on the temple, stunned and
then suffocated,' said Alleyn, without emphasis. 'We shall
know more when the doctors have finished.'

'Struck?'

'Yes. With something that had a pretty sharp edge. About
as sharp as the back of a thick knife-blade.'

'Did he suffer?'

'Not very much. Hardly at all. He wouldn't know what
happened.'

'His heart was weak,' said Troy suddenly.

'His heart? Are you sure of that?'

'Mildred told me the other day. She tried to persuade
him to see a specialist.'

'I wonder,' said Alleyn, 'if that made it easier – for both
of them.'

Troy said:

'I haven't seen you look like that before.'

'What do you mean, Troy?'

He turned to her a face so suddenly translated into
gentleness that she could not answer him.

'I – it's gone now.'

'When I look at you I suppose all other expression is
lost in an effect of general besottedness.'

'How can I answer that?' said Troy.

'Don't. I'm sorry. What *did* you mean?'

'You looked savage.'

'I feel it when I think of Bunchy.'

'I can understand that.'

'The hunt is up,' said Alleyn. 'Have you ever read in
the crime books about the relentless detective who swears

281

he'll get his man if it takes him the rest of his life? That's me, Troy, and I always thought it rather a bogus idea. It is bogus in a way, too. The real heroes of criminal investigation are Detective-Constables X, Y and Z – the men in the ranks who follow up all the dreary threads of routine without any personal feeling or interest, who swear no full round oaths, but who, nevertheless, *do* get their men in the end; and with a bit of luck and the infinite capacity for taking pains. Detective-Constables X, Y and Z are going to be kept damned busy until this gentleman is laid by the heels. I can promise them that.'

'I don't feel like that,' said Troy. 'I mean, I don't feel anything in particular about this murderer except that I think he must be mad. I know he should be found but I can't feel savage about him. It's simply Bunchy who did no harm in this world; no harm at all, lying dead and lonely. I must go now, and see what I can do for Mildred. Has Donald come in?'

'Not yet. Do you know where he is staying?'

'He wouldn't tell Mildred because he thought she would tell Bunchy, and he wanted to be independent. She's got the telephone number. I've seen it written on the memorandum in her room. I suppose you heard about the difference?'

'Yes, from Mildred. It was his debts, wasn't it?'

'Yes. Mildred has always spoilt Donald. He's not a bad child really. He will be terribly upset.'

Alleyn looked at the photograph.

'Did you see him at the dance?'

'Yes. He danced a lot with Bridgie O'Brien.'

'Did he stay until the end, do you know?'

'I didn't stay till the end myself. Mildred and I left at half-past one. She dropped me at my club. Bunchy – Bunchy – was seeing us home, but he came and asked us if we'd mind going without him. He said he was feeling gay.'

'Did you see much of him, please?'

'I danced three times with him. He *was* very gay.'

'Troy, did you notice anything? Anything at all?'

'What sort of things?'

'Did there seem to be any hint of something behind his gaiety? As if, do you know, he was thinking in the back of his head?'

Troy sat on the edge of the desk and pulled off her cap. The morning sun came through the window and dappled her short dark hair with blue lights. It caught the fine angle of her jaw and her cheek-bone. It shone into her eyes, making her screw them up as she did when she painted. She drew off her green gloves and Alleyn watched her thin intelligent hands slide out of their sheaths and lie delicately in the fur of her green jacket. He wondered if he would ever recover from the love of her.

He said: 'Tell me everything that happened last night while you were with Bunchy. Look back into your memory before it loses its edge and see if there is anything there that seemed a little out of the ordinary. Anything, no matter how insignificant.'

'I'll try,' said Troy. 'There was nothing when we danced except – yes. We collided once with another couple. It was a Mrs Halcut-Hackett. Do you know her?'

'Yes. Well?'

'It's a tiny thing, but you say that doesn't matter. She was dancing with a tall coarse-looking man. Bunchy apologized before he saw who they were. He danced very bouncily, you know, and always apologized when there were collisions. Then we swung round and he saw them. I felt his hand tighten suddenly and I looked over his shoulder at them. The man's red face had gone quite pale and Mrs Halcut-Hackett looked very odd. Frightened. I asked Bunchy who the man was and he said: "Feller called Withers," in a queer frozen little voice. I said: "Don't you like him?" and he said: "Not much, m'dear," and then began to talk about something else.'

'Yes,' said Alleyn. 'That's interesting. Anything more?'

'Later on, Bunchy and I went to chaperones' corner. You know, the end of the ballroom where they all sit. Your mother was there. Mrs Halcut-Hackett came up with her husband and then the girl she's bringing out arrived with that old ass Carrados. The girl had toothache, she said, but I'm afraid the wretched child was really not having a great success. There's something so blasted cruel and barbaric about this season game,' said Troy vigorously.

'I know.'

'Your mother noticed it. We said something to each other. Well, General Halcut-Hackett said he'd take the girl home and Bunchy offered to take Mrs Halcut-Hackett home later on. The General thanked him but *she* looked extraordinarily put out and seemed to me to avoid answering. I got the impression that she hated the idea. There was one other thing just about then. Wait a second! Bunchy started a conversation about punctuality with old Lucy Lorrimer. You know?'

'Lord, yes. She's a friend of my mama's. Dotty.'

'That's her. She twitted Bunchy about being late or something and Mrs Halcut-Hackett suddenly said in a loud, high voice that she knew all about Bunchy's punctual habits and could vouch for them. It sounds nothing, but for some extraordinary reason it made everybody feel uncomfortable.'

'Can you remember exactly what she said?'

Troy ran her fingers through her hair and scowled thoughtfully.

'No, not exactly. It was just that she knew he always kept appointments. Your mother might remember. I went away to dance soon after that. Evelyn Carrados was there but – '

'But what?'

'You'll think I'm inventing vague mysteries but I thought she seemed very upset, too. Nothing to do with Bunchy.

284

She looked ill. I heard someone say afterwards that she nearly fainted in the supper-room. She looked rather as if she might when I saw her. I noticed her hands were tense. I've often thought I'd like to paint Evelyn's hands. They're beautiful. I watched them last night. She kept clutching a great fat bag in her lap. Bunchy sat between her and your mother and he gave each of them a little pat – you know Bunchy's way. His hand touched Evelyn's bag and she started as if he'd hurt her and her fingers tightened. I can see them now, white, with highlights on the knuckles, dug into the gold stuff of the bag. I thought again I'd like to paint them and call the thing: "Hands of a frightened woman." And then later on – but look here,' said Troy, 'I'm simply maundering.'

'God bless your good painter's eyes, you're not. Go on.'

'Well, some time after supper when I'd danced again with Bunchy, I sat out with him in the ballroom. We were talking away and he was telling me one of his little stories, a ridiculous one about Lucy Lorrimer sending a wreath to a wedding and a toasting-fork to a funeral, when he suddenly stopped dead and stared over my shoulder. I turned and saw he was looking at Evelyn Carrados. There was nothing much to stare at. She still looked shaken, but that was all. Dimitri, the catering man you know, was giving her back that bag. I suppose she'd left it somewhere. What's the matter?'

Alleyn had made a little exclamation.

He said: 'That great fat bag you had noticed earlier in the evening?'

'Yes. But it wasn't so fat this time,' said Troy quickly. 'Now I think of it, it was quite limp and flat. You see, I was looking at her hands again. I remember thinking subconsciously that it seemed such a large bag for a ball-dress. Mildred came up and we left soon after that. I'm afraid that's all.'

285

'Afraid? Troy, you don't know what an important person you are.'

'Don't I?'

She looked at him with an air of bewildered friendliness and at once his whole face was lit by his fierce awareness of her. Troy's eyes suddenly filled with tears. She reached out her hand and touched him.

'I'll go,' she said. 'I'm so sorry.'

Alleyn drew back. He struck one hand against the palm of the other and said violently:

'For God's sake, don't be kind! What is this intolerable love that forces me to do the very things I wish with all my soul to avoid? Yes, Troy, please go now.'

Troy went without another word.

CHAPTER NINE

Report from Mr Fox

Alleyn walked about the room swearing under his breath. He was found at this employment by Detective-Inspector Fox, who arrived looking solid and respectable.

'Good morning, sir,' said Fox.

'Hullo, Fox. Sit down. I've found the will. Everything goes to his sister and her son. The boy's in debt and has quarrelled with his uncle. He's living away from home but will be in any moment. I've found Lord Robert's notes on the blackmail case. He told me when he rang up at one o'clock this morning that he'd call here first to get out of his boiled shirt and collect the notes. There they are. Look at 'em.'

Fox put on his spectacles and took the little notebook in his enormous fist. He read solemnly with his head thrown back a little and his eyebrows raised.

'Yes,' he said when he had finished. 'Well now, Mr Alleyn, that's quite an interesting little bit of evidence, isn't it? It puts this Mr Dimitri in what you might call a very unfavourable light. We can get him for blackmail on this information if the lady doesn't let us down. This Mrs Halcut-Hackett, I mean.'

'You notice Lord Robert thought she suspected him himself of taking the bag at the concert.'

'Yes. That's awkward. You might say it gives her a motive for the murder.'

'If you can conceive of Mrs Halcut-Hackett, who is what the drapers call a queenly woman, dressing up as a man during the ball, accosting Lord Robert in the street, getting him to give her a lift, knocking him out, smothering him, and striding home in the light of dawn in somebody's trousers.'

'That's right,' said Fox. 'I can't. She might have an accomplice.'

'So she might.'

'Still, I must say Dimitri looks likelier,' Fox plodded on thoughtfully. 'If he found out Lord Robert had a line on him. But how would he find out?'

'See here,' said Alleyn. 'I want you to listen while I go over that telephone call. I was working late at the Yard on the Temple case. I would have gone north today, as you know, if this hadn't happened. At one o'clock Lord Robert rang me up from a room at Marsdon House. He told me he had proof positive that Dimitri was our man. Then he said he'd come round to the Yard. And then – ' Alleyn shut his eyes and screwed his face sideways. 'I want to get his exact words,' he said. 'I'm my own witness here. Wait, now, wait. Yes. He said: "I'll come round to the Yard. Upon my soul, it's worse than murder. Might as well mix his damn brews with poison," and then, Fox, he added this phrase: "And he's working with – " He never finished it. He broke off and said: "Hallo, I didn't hear you come in." I asked if anyone was there and he said yes and pretended he'd rung up about lost property. He must have done that because he realized this new arrival had overheard him mention the Yard. See here, Fox, we've got to get the man or woman who overheard that call.'

'If it was Dimitri,' began Fox.

'Yes, I know. If it was Dimitri! And yet, somehow, he sounded as if he was speaking to a friend. "Hallo, I didn't hear you come in." Might well have been. But we've got to get at it, Fox.'

' "And he's working with – " ' quoted Fox. 'What do you reckon he was going to say? Name an accomplice?'

'No. He was too old a hand to use names on the telephone. It might have been "with somebody else", or it might have

288

been "with devilish ingenuity". I wish to God we knew. And now what have you done?'

Fox unhooked his glasses.

'Following your instructions,' he said, 'I went to Marsdon House. I got there at eight o'clock. I found two of our chaps in charge, and got a report from them. They arrived there at four-twenty, a quarter of an hour after the taxi got to the Yard and five minutes after you rang up. Dimitri had left the house, but our chaps, having the office from you, sir, telephoned him at his flat to make sure he was there and sent a plain-clothes man round to watch it. He's being relieved at ten o'clock by that new chap, Carewe. I thought he might take it on. He's a bit too fanciful for my liking. Well, to go back to Marsdon House. They took statements from the men Dimitri had left to clear up the house, sent them away, and remained in charge until I got there at eight. We've located the room where Lord Robert rang you up. The telephone was left switched through there for the whole evening. We've sealed it up. I've got a guest list. Bit of luck, that. We found it in the buffet. Names and addresses all typed out, very methodical. It's a carbon copy. I suppose Lady Carrados's secretary must have done it. I found out from Dimitri's men some of the people who had left early. The men's cloakroom attendant was still there and could remember about twenty of them. He managed to recollect most of the men who were the last to go. I started off on them. Rang them up and asked if they noticed Lord Robert Gospell. Several of them remembered him standing in the hall at the very end. Most of the people left in parties and we were able to check up on these at once. We found that Dimitri was in the hall at this time. I called in at his flat just now before I came here. You'll notice he's a witness of some importance as well as, on the strength of what you've told me, a prime suspect. I've got a list, very likely incomplete, of the guests who left alone about the same time as Lord

289

Robert. Here it is. A bit rough. I've put it together from notes on my way here.'

Fox took out a fat notebook, opened it and handed it to Alleyn, who read:

'*Mrs Halcut-Hackett.* Seen leaving alone by footman at door, Dimitri, and linkman, who offered to call a taxi for her. She refused and walked away. Lord Robert had not left. Dimitri says he thinks Lord Robert came downstairs about this time.

'*Captain Maurice Withers.* Seen leaving alone by Dimitri, footman and by several members of a party whom he passed on the steps outside the house. Refused a lift. Footman thinks Capt. W. left after Mrs H-H. Impression confirmed by Dimitri. Lord Robert at foot of stairs.

'*Mr Donald Potter.* Seen saying good-bye to Miss O'Brien by Dimitri and by two servants near door into buffet at foot of stairs. Dimitri noticed him meet Lord Robert, appear to avoid him, and go away hurriedly.

'*Sir Daniel Davidson.* Seen leaving alone immediately after this by Dimitri and two of the servants.

'*Miss Violet Harris.* Secretary to Lady Carrados, seen leaving alone by cloakroom attendant standing at door, to whom she said good night. Unnoticed by anyone else.

'*Mr Trelawney-Caper.* Young gentleman who had lost Mr Percy Percival. Asked repeatedly for him. Handed a ten-shilling note to footman who remembers him. Described by footman as being "nicely decorated but not drunk."

'*Lord Robert Gospell.* Both footmen and a linkman saw him go. One footman places his departure immediately after Sir Daniel Davidson's. The other says it was some minutes later. The cloakroom attendant says it was about two minutes after Miss Harris and five after Sir D.D.'

Alleyn looked up.

'Where was Dimitri, then?' he asked. 'He seems to have faded out.'

'I asked him,' said Fox. 'He said he went into the buffet about the time Sir Daniel left and was kept there for some time. The buffet's at the foot of the stairs.'

'Any confirmation of that?'

'One of his men remembers him there but can't say exactly when or for how long. He was talking to Sir Herbert Carrados.'

'To Carrados? I see. How did Dimitri shape when you saw him?'

'Well,' said Fox slowly, 'he's a pretty cool customer, isn't he? Foreign, half-Italian, half-Greek, but that's hardly noticeable in his speech. He answered everything very smoothly and kept saying it was all very regrettable.'

'I trust he'll find it even more so,' said Alleyn and returned to the notebook.

'The rest,' said Fox, 'left after Lord Robert and as far as we can make out, some time after. There are only three names and I don't fancy they'll amount to much, but I thought we'd better have them.'

'When did the Carrados party go? Last of all, of course?'

'Yes. Sir Herbert and Lady Carrados were at the head of the stairs on the ballroom landing saying good-bye most of this time, but Sir Herbert must have come down to the buffet if it's right that Dimitri talked to him there. I've left Sir Herbert to you, Mr Alleyn. From what I hear of him he'll need handling.'

'Extraordinarily kind of you,' said Alleyn grimly. 'Is there any exit from the buffet other than the one into the hall?'

291

'Yes, there is. A door that gives on to the back stairs down to the basement.'

'So it's conceivable that Dimitri might have gone out into the street that way?'

'Yes,' agreed Fox. 'It's possible, all right. And come back.'

'He would have been away at least forty minutes,' said Alleyn, 'if he's our man. If, if, if! Would he be able to get hold of a topper? The murderer wore one. What would he say to Bunchy to persuade him to give him a lift? "I want to talk to you about blackmail?" Well – that might work.'

'For all we know,' said Fox, 'it may not have been any of the guests or Dimitri.'

'True enough. For all we know. All the same, Fox, it looks as if it was. It's not easy to fit an outsider into what facts we've got. Try. An unknown in full evening dress wearing an overcoat and a top-hat stands outside Marsdon House waiting for Lord Robert to come out and on the off-chance of getting a lift. He doesn't know when Lord Robert will leave, so he has to hang about for three hours. He doesn't know if he'll get a chance to speak to Lord Robert, whether Lord Robert will leave in a party or alone, in a private car or a taxi. He doesn't know a heavy mist is going to crawl over London at one o'clock.'

'He might have just happened to come up,' said Fox and added immediately: 'All right, all right, sir. I won't press it. We've got plenty to go on from inside and it's a bit far-fetched, I will allow.'

'The whole thing's too damn far-fetched, in my opinion,' said Alleyn. 'We're up against a murder that was very nearly unpremeditated.'

'How do you make that out?'

'Why, Fox, for the reasons we've just ticked off. Lord Robert's movements could not be anticipated. I have just

292

learned that he had intended to leave much earlier with his sister, Lady Mildred Potter, and Miss Troy.'

'Miss Agatha Troy?'

'Yes, Fox.' Alleyn turned aside and looked out of the window. 'She's a friend of the family. I've spoken to her. She's here.'

'Fancy that, now,' said Fox comfortably.

'I think,' continued Alleyn after a pause, 'that when the murderer went out from the lighted house into that unwholesome air he perhaps knew that Bunchy – Lord Robert – was returning alone. He may have seen him alone in the hall. That's why your little list is important. If the man was Dimitri he went out with the deliberate intention of accomplishing his crime. If it was one of the guests he may have made up his mind only when he caught a glimpse of Bunchy standing alone in the mist, waiting for a taxi. He may have meant to threaten, or reason, or plead. He may have found Bunchy obdurate, and on an impulse killed him.'

'How do you reckon he brought it off? With what?'

'Back to the jurists' maxim,' said Alleyn with a slight smile: *'Quis, quid, ubi, quibus auxiliis, cur, quomodo, quando?'*

'I never can remember it that way,' said Fox, 'knowing no Latin. But I've got old Gross's rhyme all right:

    'What was the crime, who did it, when was it done, and where?

    How done, and with what motive, who in the deed did share?'

'Yes,' said Alleyn. 'We've got *quid, quomodo* and *ubi,* but we're not so sure of *quibus auxiliis.* Dr Curtis says the abrasion on the temple is two and a half inches long and one-twelfth of an inch across. The blow, he thinks, was not necessarily very heavy, but sharp and extremely

293

accurate. What sort of implement does that suggest to you, Fox?'

'I've been thinking that – '

The desk telephone rang. Alleyn answered it.

'Hullo?'

'Mr Alleyn? The Yard here. Sir Daniel Davidson has rung up and says he may have something to tell you. He'll be in all day.'

'Where is he?'

'In his rooms, number fifty St. Luke's Chambers, Harley Street.'

'Say I'll call at two o'clock. Thank him.' Alleyn put the receiver down.

'Davidson,' he said, 'thinks he may have something to relate. I bet he had a heart-to-heart talk with himself before he decided to ring up.'

'Why?' asked Fox. 'Do you mean he feels shaky?'

'I mean he's a fashionable doctor and they don't care for the kind of publicity you get from criminal investigations. If he's a clever fellow, and I imagine he must be to have got where he is, he's realized he was one of the last people to see Lord Robert. He's decided to come to us before we go to him. According to your notes, Fox, Sir Daniel was the first of the last three people to leave before Lord Robert. The other two were a tight young gentleman and a female secretary. Sir Daniel would have seen Lord Robert was alone and about to leave. He could have waited outside in the mist and asked for a lift in the taxi as easily as anybody. I wonder if he realizes that.'

'No motive,' said Fox.

'None, I should imagine. I mustn't get fantastic, must I? Damn young Potter, why doesn't he come?'

'Have you finished here, sir?'

'Yes. I got here at five o'clock this morning, broke the news to Lady Mildred, and settled down to Lord Robert's dressing-room, bedroom and this study. There's nothing

294

at all to be found except his notes and the will. From seven until ten I looked in their garden, the neighbouring gardens and up and down the Embankment for a cloak and a soft hat. With no success. I've got a squad of men at it now.'

'He may not have got rid of them.'

'No. He may have been afraid of leaving some trace of himself. If that's the case he'll want to destroy or lose them. It was low tide at three o'clock this morning. To drop them in the driver he'd have to get to a bridge. What sort of house is Dimitri's?'

'It's a small two-roomed flat in the Cromwell Road. He keeps a servant. French, I should say.'

'We'll go round there at noon when he's due at the Yard, and see if we can find anything. You've seen the flat. Where's his telephone?'

'On the landing.'

'Right. You'd better ring from the nearest call-box as soon as I've gone in. Keep the servant on the telephone as long as possible. You can put a string of questions about the time Dimitri got in, ask for the names of some of the men, anything. I'll have a quick look round for a possible spot to hide a largish parcel. We must get the dust-bins watched, though he's not likely to risk that. Blast this nephew. Fox, go and do your stuff with the maids. Don't disturb Lady Mildred, but ask for Mr Donald's telephone number. It's written on a memorandum in her room, but they may have it, too.'

Fox went out and returned in a few minutes.

'Sloane 8405.'

Alleyn reached for the telephone and dialled a number. 'Chief Detective-Inspector Alleyn, Scotland Yard. I want you to trace Sloane 8405 at once, please. I'll hang on.'

He waited, staring absently at Fox, who was reading his own notes with an air of complacent detachment.

'What?' said Alleyn suddenly. 'Yes. Will you repeat that. Thank you very much. Good-bye.'

He put back the receiver.

'Mr Donald Potter's telephone number,' he said, 'is that of Captain Maurice Withers, one hundred and ten Grandison Mansions, Sling Street, Chelsea. Captain Maurice Withers, as you will have noticed, appears in Lord Robert's notes. He was at the cocktail-party at Mrs Halcut-Hackett's and "seemed thick with her". He was at the concert when Dimitri took her bag. Now look at this – '

Alleyn took a cheque book from a drawer in the desk and handed it to Fox.

'Look at the heel of the book. Turn up June 8th, last Saturday.'

Fox thumbed over the leaves of the heel until he found it.

'Fifty pounds. M. Withers. (D) Shackleton House, Leatherhead.'

'That's the day of the cocktail-party at Mrs Halcut-Hackett's. This case is beginning to make a pattern.'

Fox, who had returned to Lord Robert's notes, asked:

'What's this he says about Captain Withers being mixed up in a drug affair in 1924?'

'It was rather in my salad days at the Yard, Fox, but I remember, and so will you. The Bouchier-Watson lot. They had their headquarters at Marseilles and Port Said, but they operated all over the shop. Heroin mostly. The FO took a hand. Bunchy was there in those days and helped us enormously. Captain Withers was undoubtedly up to his nasty neck in it, but we never quite got enough to pull him in. A very dubious person. And young Donald's flown to him for sanctuary. Besotted young ninny! Oh, blast! Fox, blast!'

'Do you know the young gentleman, sir?'

'What? Yes. Oh, yes, I know him vaguely. What's going to come of this? I'll have to probe. A filthy crime-dentist!

And quite possibly I'll haul up young Potter wriggling like a nerve on the end of a wire. These people are supposed to be my friends! Fun, isn't it? All right, Fox, don't look perturbed. But if Donald Potter doesn't show up here before – '

The door was suddenly flung open and Donald walked into the room.

He took half a dozen steps, pulled up short, and glared at Alleyn and Fox. He looked awful. His eyes were bloodshot and his face pallid.

He said: 'Where's my mother?'

Alleyn said: 'Agatha Troy's looking after her. I want to speak to you.'

'I want to see my mother.'

'You'll have to wait,' said Alleyn.

CHAPTER TEN

Donald

Donald Potter sat on a chair facing the window. Alleyn was at Lord Robert's desk. Fox sat in the window, his notebook on his knee, his pencil in his hand. Donald lit one cigarette from the butt of another. His fingers shook.

'Before we begin,' said Alleyn, 'I should like to make one point quite clear to you. Your uncle has been murdered. The circumstances under which he was murdered oblige us to go most thoroughly into the movements of every person who was near to him within an hour of his death. We shall also find it necessary to make exhaustive enquiries into his private affairs, his relationship with members of his own family, and his movements, conversation and interests during the last weeks or perhaps months of his life. Nothing will be sacred. You, of course, are most anxious that his murderer should be arrested?'

Alleyn paused. Donald wetted his lips and said:

'Naturally.'

'Naturally. You will therefore give us all the help you can at no matter what cost to yourself?'

'Of course.'

'You will understand, I am sure, that everything the police do is done with one purpose only. If some of our enquiries seem impertinent or irrelevant that cannot be helped. We must do our job.'

'Need we go into all this?' said Donald.

'I hope it has been quite unnecessary. When did you last speak to your uncle?'

'About ten days ago.'

'When did you leave this house?'

'On the same day,' said Donald breathlessly.

298

'You left as the result of a misunderstanding with your uncle?'

'Yes.'

'I'm afraid I shall have to ask you to tell me about it.'

'I – it's got nothing to do with this – this awful business. It's not too pleasant to remember. I'd rather not – '

'You see,' said Alleyn, 'there was some point in my solemn opening speech.' He got up and reached out a long hand, and touched Donald's shoulder. 'Come,' he said. 'I know it's not easy.'

'It wasn't that I didn't like him.'

'I can't believe anyone could dislike him. What was the trouble? Your debts?'

'Yes.'

'Then why did you quarrel?'

'He wanted me to go to Edinburgh to take my medical.'

'And you didn't want to go?'

'No.'

'Why?'

'I thought it would be so damned dull. I wanted to go to Thomas's. He had agreed to that.'

Alleyn returned to his seat at the desk. 'What made him change his mind?' he asked.

'This business about my debts.'

'Nothing else?'

Donald ground out his cigarette with a trembling hand and shook his head.

'Did he object to any of your friends, for instance?' Alleyn asked.

'I – well, he may have thought – I mean, it wasn't that.'

'Did he know you were acquainted with Captain Maurice Withers?'

Donald darted a glance of profound astonishment at Alleyn, opened his mouth, shut it again, and finally said:

'I think so.'

'Aren't you certain?'

299

'He knew I was friendly with Withers. Yes.'

'Did he object to this friendship?'

'He did say something, now I come to think about it.'

'It didn't leave any particular impression on you?'

'Oh, no,' said Donald.

Alleyn brought his hand down sharply on Lord Robert's cheque book.

'Then, I take it,' he said, 'you have forgotten a certain cheque for fifty pounds.'

Donald stared at the long thin hand lying across the blue cover. A dull flush mounted to the roots of his hair.

'No,' he said, 'I remember.'

'Did he pay this amount to Withers on your behalf?'

'Yes.'

'And yet it left no particular impression on you?'

'There were,' said Donald, 'so many debts.'

'Your uncle knew you were friendly with this man. He had certain information about him. I know that. I ask you whether, in fact, he did not object most strongly to your connection with Withers?'

'If you like to put it that way.'

'For God's sake,' said Alleyn, 'don't hedge with me. I want to give you every chance.'

'*You – don't – think – I*'

'You're his heir. You quarrelled with him. You've been in debt. You are sharing rooms with a man against whom he warned you. You're in no position to try and save your face over smaller matters. You want to spare your mother as much as possible, don't you? Of course you do, and so do I. I ask you most earnestly as a friend, which I should not do, to tell me the whole truth.'

'Very well,' said Donald.

'You're living in the same flat as Captain Withers. What have you been doing there?'

'I – we – I was waiting to see if I couldn't perhaps go to Thomas's, after all.'

300

'How could you afford to do that?'

'My mother would have helped me. I've got my prelim, and I thought if I read a bit and tried to earn a bit, later on I could start.'

'How did you propose to earn a bit?'

'Wits was helping me – Captain Withers, I mean. He's been perfectly splendid. I don't care what anybody says about him, he's not a crook.'

'What suggestions did he make?'

Donald fidgeted.

'Oh, nothing definite. We were going to talk it over.'

'I see. Is Captain Withers doing a job of work himself?'

'Well, not exactly. He's got a pretty decent income, but he's thinking of doing something one of these days. He hates being idle, really.'

'Will you tell me, please, why you were in debt to him for fifty pounds?'

'I – simply owed it to him.'

'Evidently. For what? Was it a bet?'

'Yes. Well, one or two side bets, actually.'

'On what – horses?'

'Yes,' said Donald quickly.

'Anything else?'

Silence.

'Anything else?'

'No. I mean . . . I can't remember exactly.'

'You must remember. Was it at poker? Cards of any sort?'

'Yes, poker.'

'There's something else,' said Alleyn. 'Donald, I can't exaggerate the harm you may do if you insist on hedging with us. Don't you see that with every fresh evasion you put your friend in an even more dubious light than the one in which he already appears? For God's sake think of your uncle's death and your mother's sensibilities and your own foolish skin. How else did you lose money to Captain Withers?'

Alleyn watched Donald raise his head, knit his brows, and put his fingers to his lips. His eyes were blank but they were fixed on Alleyn's and presently an expression of doubtful astonishment crept into them.

'I don't know what to do,' he said naïvely.

'You mean you owe something to Withers. You have made some promise, I suppose. Is that it?'

'Yes.'

'To me the young men of your generation are rather bewildering. You seem to be a great deal more knowing then we were and yet I swear I would never have been taken in by a flashy gentleman with persuasive manners and no occupation, unless running an illicit hole-and-corner casino may be called an occupation.'

'I never mentioned roulette,' said Donald in a hurry.

'It is indeed a shame to take your money,' rejoined Alleyn.

Fox gave a curious little cough and turned a page of his notebook.

Alleyn said: 'Has Captain Withers, by any chance, suggested that you should earn an honest penny by assisting him?'

'I can't answer any more questions about him,' said Donald in a high voice. He looked as if he would either fly into a violent rage or burst into tears.

'Very well,' said Alleyn. 'When did you hear of this tragedy?'

'This morning when the sporting edition came in.'

'About an hour and a half ago?'

'Yes.'

'How long does it take to get here from Captain Withers's flat? It's in Sling Street, Chelsea, isn't it? About five minutes' walk. Why were you so long coming here?'

'I wasn't dressed, and though you may not believe it, I got a shock when I heard of my uncle's death.'

302

'No doubt. So did your mother. I wonder she didn't ring you up.'

'The telephone's disconnected,' said Donald.

'Indeed? Why is that?'

'I forgot to pay the bloody bill. Wits left it to me. I rang her from a call-box.'

'I see. Fox, one of our men is out there. Ask him to go to one hundred and ten Grandison Mansions, Sling Street, and tell Captain Withers I shall call on him in a few minutes and will be obliged if he remains indoors.'

'Very good, Mr Alleyn,' said Fox, and went out.

'Now then,' Alleyn continued. 'I understand you were among the last to leave Marsdon House this morning. Correct?'

'Yes.'

'I want you to tell me exactly what happened just before you left. Come now, will you try to give me a clear account?'

Donald looked slightly more at his ease. Fox came back and resumed his seat.

'I'll try, certainly,' said Donald. 'Where do you want me to begin?'

'From the moment when you came into the hall to go out.'

'I was with Bridget O'Brien. I had the last dance with her and then we went into the buffet downstairs for soup.'

'Anybody else there?'

'Her stepfather. I said good night to him and then Bridgie and I went into the hall.'

'Who was in the hall?'

'I don't remember except – '

'Yes?'

'Uncle Bunch was there.'

'Did you speak to him?'

'No, I wish to God I had.'

'What was he doing?'

'He had his cloak on. You know that extraordinary

garment he wears? I think I heard him asking people if they'd seen Mrs Halcut-Hackett.'

'Had you seen her?'

'Not for some time, I think.'

'So you remember nobody in the hall except your uncle and Miss O'Brien?'

'That's right. I said good night to Bridgie and went away.'

'Alone?'

'Yes.'

'Captain Withers was not at the ball?'

'Yes, but he'd gone.'

'Why did you not go away together?'

'Wits was going on somewhere. He had a date.'

'Do you know where he went and with whom?'

'No.'

'When you left Marsdon House what did you do?'

'Some people waiting outside for a taxi asked me to go on with them to the Sauce Boat, but I didn't want to. To get rid of them I walked to the corner to look for a taxi.'

'Which corner?'

'First on the left as you come out of Marsdon House. Belgrave Road, I think it is.'

'Anyone see you?'

'I don't know. Shouldn't think so. There was a damned heavy mist lying like a blanket over everything.'

'We'll have to find your taxi.'

'But I didn't get a taxi.'

'What!'

Donald began to speak rapidly, his words tumbling over each other, as though he had suddenly opened all the doors of his thoughts.

'There wasn't a taxi at the corner, so I walked. I walked on and on through Eaton Square. It was late – after three o'clock. Lots of taxis passed me, of course, but they were all engaged. I was thinking about things. About Bridget.

I meant to keep her out of this but I suppose you'll hear everything now. Everything will be dragged out and – and made to look awful. Bridgie, and – and Uncle Bunch – and taking my medical – and everything. I hardly noticed where I was going. It's queer walking through mist. Your footsteps sound odd. Everything seemed thin and simple. I can't describe it. I went on and on and presently there weren't any more taxis and I was in the Kings Road so I just walked home. Past the Chelsea Palace and then off to the right into Sling Street. That's all.'

'Did you meet anyone?'

'I suppose I must have met a few people. I didn't notice.'

'What time did you get home?'

'I didn't notice.'

Alleyn looked gravely at him.

'I want you, please, to try very hard to remember if you met anybody on that walk, particularly in the early stages, just after you left Marsdon House. I see no reason why I should not point out the importance of this. As far as we can make out your uncle left the house a few minutes after you did. He, too, walked a short way round the square. He hailed a taxi and was joined at the last minute by a man in evening dress who got into the taxi with him. It is the identity of this man that we are anxious to establish.'

'You can't think I would do it!' Donald said. 'You can't! You've been our friend. You can't treat me like this, as though I was just anybody under suspicion. You *know* us! Surely to God – ! '

Alleyn's voice cut coldly across his protestations.

'I am an investigating officer employed by the police. I must behave as if I had no friends while I am working on this case. If you think for a little you will see that this must be so. At the risk of sounding pompous I must go a bit further and tell you that if I found my friendship with your uncle, your mother, or yourself, was in any way

305

influencing my conduct of this case I should be obliged
to give up. Ask to be relieved of the job. Already I have
spoken to you as a friend – I should not have done this.
If you are innocent, you are in no danger unless you
prevaricate or shift ground, particularly in matters relating
to your acquaintance with Captain Withers.'

'You can't suspect Withers! Why should he want to kill
Uncle Bunch? It's got nothing to do with him.'

'In that case he has nothing to fear.'

'On that account, of course, he hasn't. I mean – oh,
hell!'

'Where were you when you lost this money to him?'

'In a private house.'

'Where was it?'

'Somewhere near Leatherhead. Shackleton House, I
think it's called.'

'Was it his house?'

'Ask him. *Ask him.* Why do you badger me with all
this! My God, isn't it enough that I should be faced with
the other business! I can't stand any more. Let me out
of this.'

'You may go, certainly. There will be a statement for
you to sign later on.'

Donald got up and walked to the door. He turned and
faced Alleyn.

'I'm as anxious as you,' he said, 'that the man should
be caught. Naturally, I'm as anxious as anybody.'

'Good,' said Alleyn.

Donald's face was puckered into the sort of grimace
a small boy makes when he is trying not to cry. For some
reason this gave him a strong look of his uncle. Alleyn
felt his heart turn over. He got up, crossed the room in
six long strides, and took Donald roughly by the arm.

'There!' he said, 'if you're innocent you're safe. As for
this other mess you've got yourself into, stick to the truth

306

and we'll do what we can for you. Tell your mama the house is rid of us for the time being. Now, march!'

He turned Donald round, shoved him through the door, and slammed it behind him.

'Come on, Fox,' he said. 'Pack up those things – the will and the notes. Ring up the Yard and see if the post-mortem report is through, tell them to look Withers up in the record, and if one of my men is free, send him straight off to Shackleton House, Leatherhead. He'd better take a search-warrant, but he's not to use it without ringing me up first. If the place is locked up he's to stay there and report to me by telephone. Tell him we want evidence of a gambling hell. Fix that while I see the men outside and then we'll be off.'

'To see Withers?'

'Yes. To see Captain Maurice Withers who, unless I'm much mistaken, has added a gambling hell to his list of iniquitous sources of livelihood. My God, Fox, as someone was out for blood, why the hell couldn't they widen their field to include Captain Maurice Withers? Come on.'

CHAPTER ELEVEN

Captain Withers at Home

The report on the post-mortem was ready. Fox took it down over the telephone and he and Alleyn discussed it on their way to Sling Street.

'Dr Curtis,' said Fox, 'says there's no doubt that he was suffocated. They've found' – and here Fox consulted his book – 'Tardieu's ecchymosis on the congested lungs and on the heart. There were signs of fatty degeneration in the heart. The blood was dark-coloured and very liquid – '

'All right,' said Alleyn violently. 'Never mind that. Sorry, Fox. On you go.'

'Well, sir, they seem to think that the condition of the heart would make everything much more rapid. That's what you might call a merciful thing, isn't it?'

'Yes.'

'Yes. Barring the scar on the temple, Dr Curtis says there are no marks on the face. The mucous membrane in the fore-part of the palate is slightly congested. Posteriorly it is rather bleached. But there are no marks of violence.'

'I noticed that. There was no struggle. He was unconscious after the blow on the temple,' said Alleyn.

'That's what Dr Curtis thinks.'

'This murderer knew what he was about,' said Alleyn. 'Usually your asphyxiating homicide merchant goes in for a lot of unnecessary violence. You get marks round the mouth. Has Curtis any idea what was used?'

'He says possibly a plug of soft material introduced into the mouth and held over the nostrils.'

308

'Yes. Not Bunchy's handkerchief. That was quite uncreased.'

'Perhaps his own handkerchief.'

'I don't think so, Fox. I found a trace of fine black woollen fluff in the mouth.'

'The cloak?'

'Looks like it. It might be. One of the reasons why the cloak was got out of the way. By the way, Fox, did you get a report from that PC in Belgrave Square last night?'

'Yes. Nothing suspicious.'

They plodded on, working out lines to take in the endless interviews. They correlated, sorted and discussed each fragment of information. 'Finding the pattern of the case,' Alleyn called it. A five minutes' walk brought them to Sling Street and to a large block of rather pretentious service flats. They took the lift up to 110 and rang the bell.

'I'm going to take some risks here,' said Alleyn.

The door was opened by Captain Withers himself.

He said: 'Good morning. Want to see me?'

'Good morning, sir,' said Alleyn. 'Yes. You had our message just now, I hope. May we come in?'

'Certainly,' said Withers and walked away from the door with his hands in his pockets.

Alleyn and Fox went in. They found themselves in a mass-production furnished sitting-room with a divan bed against one wall, three uniform armchairs, a desk, a table and built-in cupboards. It had started off by being an almost exact replica of all the other 'bachelor flats' in Grandison Mansions, but since it is impossible to live in any place without leaving some print of yourself upon it, this room bore the impress of Captain Maurice Withers. It smelt of hairwash, cigars and whisky. On one wall hung a framed photograph of the sort advertised in magazines as 'artistic studio studies from the nude'. On the bookshelves guides to the Turf stood between shabby copies of novels Captain Withers had bought on the Riviera and, for some reason, troubled to smuggle into England. On a table by the divan bed were three or four medical text-books. 'Donald Potter's,' thought Alleyn. Through a half-open door Alleyn caught a glimpse of a small bedroom and a second masterpiece that may have been a studio study but appeared to be an exercise in pornographic photography.

Captain Withers caught Fox's bland gaze directed at this picture and shut the bedroom door.

'Have a drink?' he said.

'No, thank you,' said Alleyn.

'Well, sit down then.'

Alleyn and Fox sat down, Fox with extreme propriety, Alleyn with an air of leisurely fastidiousness. He crossed one long leg over the other, hung his hat on his knee, pulled off his gloves, and contemplated Captain Withers. They made a curious contrast. Withers was the sort of man who breathes vulgarity into good clothes. His neck was too thick, his fingers too flat and pale and his hair shone too much; his eyes were baggy and his eyelashes were white. Yet in spite of these defects he was a powerful dominant animal with a certain coarse arrogance that was effective. Alleyn, by contrast, looked fine-drawn, a cross between a monk and a grandee. The planes of Alleyn's face and head were emphatically defined, the bony structure showed clearly. There was a certain austerity in the chilly blue of his eyes and in the sharp blackness of his hair. Albrecht Dürer would have made a magnificent drawing of him, and Agatha Troy's sketch portrait of Alleyn is one of the best things she has ever done.

Withers lit a cigarette, blew the smoke down his nose and said:

'What's it all about?'

Fox produced his official notebook. Captain Withers eyed the letters M.P. on the cover and then looked at the carpet.

'First, if I may,' said Alleyn, 'I should like your full name and address.'

'Maurice Withers and this address.'

'May we have the address of your Leatherhead house as well, please?'

'What the hell d'you mean?' asked Withers quite pleasantly. He looked quickly at the table by the divan and then full in Alleyn's face.

'My information,' lied Alleyn, 'does not come from the source you suppose, Captain Withers. The address, please.'

'If you mean Shackleton House, it is not mine. It was lent to me.'

'By whom?'

'For personal reasons, I'm afraid I can't tell you that.'

'I see. Do you use it much?'

'Borrow it for week-ends sometimes.'

'Thank you,' said Alleyn, 'Now, if you please, I want to ask you one or two questions about this morning. The early hours of this morning.'

'Oh, yes,' said Withers, 'I suppose you're thinking of the murder.'

'Whose murder?'

'Why, Bunchy Gospell's.'

'Was Lord Robert Gospell a personal friend of yours, Captain Withers?'

'I didn't know him.'

'I see. Why do you think he was murdered?'

'Well, wasn't he?'

'I think so. Evidently you think so. Why?'

'Judging from the papers it looks like it.'

'Yes, doesn't it?' said Alleyn. 'Won't you sit down, Captain Withers?'

'No, thanks. What about this morning?'

'When did you leave Marsdon House?'

'After the ball was over.'

'Did you leave alone?'

Withers threw his cigarette with great accuracy into a tin waste-paper bin.

'Yes,' he said.

'Can you remember who was in the hall when you went away?'

'What? I don't know that I can. Oh, yes. I bumped into Dan Davidson. You know. The fashionable quack.'

'Is Sir Daniel Davidson a friend of yours?'

'Not really. I just know him.'

'Did you notice Lord Robert in the hall as you left?'

'Can't say I did.'

'You went out alone. Did you take a taxi?'

'No. I had my own car. It was parked in Belgrave Road.'

'So you turned to the left when you went away from Marsdon House. That,' said Alleyn, 'is what the murderer, if there is, as you say, a murderer, must have done.'

'Better choose your words a bit more carefully, hadn't you?' enquired Captain Withers.

'I don't think so. As far as I can see my remark was well within the rules. Did you see any solitary man in evening dress as you walked from Marsdon House to Belgrave Road? Did you overtake or pass any such person?'

Withers sat on the edge of the table and swung his foot. The fat on his thighs bulged through his plaid trouser leg.

'I might have. I don't remember. It was misty.'

'Where did you go in your car?'

'To the Matador.'

'The night club in Sampler Street?'

'That's right.'

'Did you meet anybody there?'

'About a hundred and fifty people.'

'I mean,' said Alleyn with perfect courtesy, 'did you meet a partner there by arrangement?'

'Yes.'

'May I have her name?'

'No.'

312

'I shall have to find out by the usual routine,' murmured Alleyn. 'Make a note of it will you, Fox?'

'Very good, Mr Alleyn,' said Fox.

'You can produce no witness to support your statement that you drove to the Matador from Marsdon House?'

The swinging foot was suddenly motionless. Withers waited a moment and then said: 'No.'

'Perhaps your partner was waiting in your car, Captain Withers. Are you sure you did not drive her there? Remember there is a commissionaire at the Matador.'

'Is there?'

'Well?'

'All right,' said Withers. 'I did drive my partner to the Matador but I shan't give you her name.'

'Why not?'

'You seem to be a gentleman. One of the new breed at the Yard, aren't you? I should have thought you'd have understood.'

'You are very good,' said Alleyn, 'but I am afraid you are mistaken. We shall have to use other methods, but we shall find out the name of your partner. Have you ever studied wrestling, Captain Withers?'

'What? What the hell has that got to do with it?'

'I should be obliged if you would answer.'

'I've never taken it up. Seen a bit out East.'

'Ju-jitsu?'

'Yes.'

'Do they ever use the side of the hand to knock a man out? On one of the vulnerable points or whatever you call them? Such as the temple?'

'I've no idea.'

'Have you any medical knowledge?'

'No.'

'I see some text-books over there by the bed.'

'They don't belong to me.'

'To Mr Donald Potter?'

313

'That's right.'

'He is living here?'

'You've been talking to him, haven't you? You must be a bloody bad detective if you haven't nosed that out.'

'Do you consider that you have a strong influence over Mr Potter?'

'I'm not a bear leader!'

'You prefer fleecing lambs, perhaps?'

'Is that where we laugh?' asked Withers.

'Only, I am afraid, on the wrong side of our faces. Captain Withers, do you recollect the Bouchier-Watson drug-running affair of 1924?'

'No.'

'You are fortunate. We have longer memories at the Yard. I am reminded of it this morning by certain notes left in his private papers by Lord Robert Gospell. He mentions the case in connection with recent information he gleaned about an illicit gambling club at Leatherhead.'

The coarse white hands made a convulsive movement which was immediately checked. Alleyn rose to his feet.

'There is only one other point,' he said. 'I believe your telephone is disconnected. Inspector Fox will fix that. Fox, will you go out to the post office at the corner? Wait a second.'

Alleyn took out his notebook, scribbled: 'Get Thompson to tail W at once,' and showed it to Fox. 'Give that message, will you, and see that Captain Withers's telephone is reconnected immediately. As soon as it's through, ring me here. What's the number?'

'Sloane 8405,' said Withers.

'Right. I'll join you, Fox.'

'Very good, sir,' said Fox. 'Good morning, sir.'

Withers did not answer. Fox departed.

'When your telephone is working again,' Alleyn said, 'I would be glad if you'd ring up Mr Donald Potter to suggest that as his mother is in great distress, you think

314

it would be well if he stayed with her for the time being. You will send his property to Cheyne Walk in a taxi.'

'Are you threatening me?'

'No. I am warning you. You are in rather uncertain country at the moment, you know.'

Alleyn walked over to the divan bed and looked at the books.

'Taylor's *Medical Jurisprudence,'* he murmured. 'Is Mr Potter thinking of becoming a medical jurist?'

'I haven't the slightest idea.'

Alleyn ruffled the pages of a large blue volume.

'Here we have the fullest information on asphyxia. Very interesting. May I borrow this book? I'll return it to Mr Potter.'

'I've no objection. Nothing to do with me.'

'Splendid. Have you any objection to my looking at your dress clothes?'

'None,' said Withers.

'Thank you so much. If you wouldn't mind showing them to me.'

Withers walked into the bedroom and Alleyn followed him. While Withers opened his wardrobe and pulled open drawers Alleyn had a quick look round the room. Apart from the photograph, which was frankly infamous, the only item of interest was a row of paper-bound banned novels of peculiar indecency and no literary merit whatsoever.

Withers threw a tail coat, a white waistcoat and a pair of trousers on the bed. Alleyn examined them with great care, smelt the coat and turned out the pockets, which were empty.

'Had you a cigarette-case?' he asked.

'Yes.'

'May I see it?'

'It's in the next room.'

Withers went into the sitting-room. Alleyn, with a cat-

315

like swiftness, looked under the bed and in at a cupboard door.

Withers produced a small, flat silver case.

'Is this the only case you possess?'

'It is.'

Alleyn opened it. The inside lid was inscribed: 'Maurice from Estelle.' He returned it and took another from his pocket.

'Will you look at this case carefully, please, and tell me if you have seen it before?'

Withers took it. It was a thin, smooth, gold case, uninscribed, but with a small crest in one corner.

'Open it, will you, please?'

Withers opened it.

'Do you know it?'

'No.'

'You don't by any chance recognise the crest?'

'No.'

'It is not Mr Donald Potter's crest, for instance?'

Withers made a quick movement, opened his mouth, shut it again and said:

'It isn't his. I've seen his. It's on his links. They're here somewhere.'

'May I see them?' said Alleyn, taking the case.

Withers crossed to the dressing-table. Alleyn rapidly wrapped his silk handkerchief round the case and put it in his pocket.

'Here they are,' said Withers.

Alleyn solemnly inspected Donald's links and returned them.

The telephone rang in the next room.

'Will you answer it, please?' said Alleyn.

Withers went into the sitting-room. Alleyn whipped off the dust jacket from one of the banned novels and coolly slipped it in his overcoat pocket. He then followed Withers.

'It's for you,' Withers said, 'if you're Alleyn.'

'Thank you.'

It was Fox; to say in an extremely low voice that Thompson was well on his way.

'Splendid,' said Alleyn. 'Captain Withers wanted to use it at once.'

He hung up the receiver and turned to Withers.

'Now, please,' he said. 'Will you telephone Mr Potter? I'd be glad if you would not mention that it was my suggestion. It would come more gracefully from you.'

Withers dialled the number with as bad a grace as well might be. He got Donald, whose voice came over in an audible quack.

'Hullo.'

'Hullo, Don, it's Wits.'

'Oh, God, Wits, I'm most frightfully worried, I – '

'You'd better not talk about your worries on the telephone. I rang up to say I thought it might be as well if you stayed with your mother for a bit. She'll want you there with all this trouble. I'll send your things round.'

'Yes, but listen, Wits. About the house at – '

Captain Withers said: 'You stay where you are,' and rang off.

'Thank you,' said Alleyn. 'That will do nicely. How tall are you, Captain Withers?'

'Five foot eight and a half in my socks.'

'Just about Lord Robert's height,' said Alleyn, watching him.

Withers stared blankly at him.

'I suppose there must be some sense in a few of the things you say,' he said.

'I hope so. Can you remember what Lord Robert was saying on the telephone when you walked into the room at one o'clock this morning?'

'What room?'

'At Marsdon House.'

'You're talking through your hat. I never heard him on any telephone.'

'That's all right then,' said Alleyn. 'Were you on the top landing near the telephone-room round about one o'clock?'

'How the devil should I know? I was up there quite a bit.'

'Alone?'

'No. I was there with Don sometime during the supper dances. We were in the first sitting-out room. Old Carrados was up there then.'

'Did you hear anyone using a telephone?'

'Fancy I did, now you mention it.'

'Ah well, that's the best we can do at the moment, I suppose,' said Alleyn, collecting Taylor's *Medical Jurisprudence.* 'By the way, would you object to my searching these rooms? Just to clear your good name, you know.'

'You can crawl over them with a microscope, if you like.'

'I see. Thank you very much. Some other time, perhaps. Good morning.'

He'd got as far as the door when Withers said:

'Here! Stop!'

'Yes?'

Alleyn turned and saw a flat white finger pointed at his face.

'If you think,' said Captain Withers, 'that I had anything to do with the death of this buffoon you're wasting your time. I didn't. I'm not a murderer and if I was I'd go for big game – not domestic pigs.'

Alleyn said: 'You are fortunate. In my job we often have to hunt the most unpleasant quarry. A matter of routine. Good morning.'

CHAPTER TWELVE

Report from a Waiter

In the street outside Alleyn met Detective-Sergeant
Thompson, who did not look like a detective-sergeant. As
Captain Withers's windows enjoyed an uninterrupted view
of Sling Street Alleyn did not pause to speak to Thompson,
but he remarked to the air as they passed:

'Don't lose him.'

Fox was waiting outside the post office.

'He's a nasty customer, I should say,' he remarked as
they fell into step.

'Who? Withers? I believe you, my old – '

'You were pretty well down on him, Mr Alleyn.'

'I was in a fix,' said Alleyn. 'I'd have liked to raid this
place at Leatherhead without giving him any warning, but
the wretched Donald is sure to let him know what he told
us and Withers will close down his gambling activities.
The best we can hope for in that direction is that our
man will find something conclusive if he gets into the house.
We'd better take a taxi to Dimitri's. What time was he
to be at the Yard?'

'Midday.'

'It's a quarter to twelve. He ought to have left. Come
on.'

They got a taxi.

'How about Withers?' asked Fox, staring solemnly at
the driver's back.

'For a likely suspect? He's the right height to within
an inch. Good enough in the cloak and hat to diddle the
taxi-man. By the way, there's nowhere in the bedroom
where he could have stowed them. I saw inside the wardrobe
and had a quick look under the bed and in the cupboard

while he was on the telephone. Anyway, he said I could crawl over the flat with a microscope if I liked and he wasn't calling my bluff either. If he's got anything to hide it's at the house at Leatherhead.'

'The motive's not so hot,' said Fox.

'What is the motive?'

'He knew Lord Robert had recognized him and thought he was on his trail. He wants to get hold of the money and knows young Potter is the heir.'

'That's two of his motives. But well? Damn,' said Alleyn, 'nearly a quotation! Bunchy warned me against 'em. Associating with the peerage, that's what it is. There's a further complication. Mrs Halcut-Hackett may think Bunchy was a blackmailer. From his notes Bunchy seems to have got that impression. He was close to her when her bag was taken and had stuck to her persistently. If Withers is having an affair with the woman, she probably confided the blackmail stunt to him. Withers is possibly the subject of the Halcut-Hackett blackmail. The letter the blackmailer has got hold of may be one from Mrs H-H to Withers or t'other way round. If she told him she thought Lord Robert was the blackmailer – '

'That's three of his motives,' said Fox.

'You may say so. On the other hand Withers may be the blackmailer. It's quite in his line.'

'Best motive of all,' said Fox, 'if he thought Lord Robert was on to him.'

'How you do drone on, you old devil. Well, if we want to, we can pull him in for having dirty novels in his beastly flat. Look at this.'

Alleyn pulled the book jacket out of his pocket. It displayed in primary colours a picture of a terrible young woman with no clothes on, a florid gentleman and a lurking harridan. It was entitled: *The Confessions of a Procuress*.

'Lor'!' said Fox. 'You oughtn't to have taken it.'

'What a stickler you are to be sure.' Alleyn pulled a

fastidious grimace. 'Can't you see him goggling over it in some bolt-hole on the Côte d'Azur! I've got his nasty flat prints on my own cigarette-case. We'll see if he's handled Donald Potter's "Taylor". Particularly the sections that deal with suffocation and asphyxia. I fancy, Fox, that a Captain Withers who was uninstructed in the art of smothering would have made the customary mistake of using too much violence. We'll have to see if he's left any prints in this telephone room at Marsdon House.'

'The interruption,' said Fox thoughtfully. 'As I see it, we've got to get at the identity of the individual who came in while Lord Robert was talking to you on the telephone. If the party's innocent, well, there'll be no difficulty.'

'And contrariwise. I tried to bounce Withers into an admission. Took it for granted he was the man.'

'Any good?'

'Complete wash-out. He never batted an eyelid. Seemed genuinely astonished.'

'It may have been Dimitri. At least,' said Fox, 'we know Dimitri collects the boodle. What we want to find out is whether he's on his own or working for someone else.'

'Time enough. Which brings us back to Bunchy's broken sentence. "And he's working with – " With whom? Or is it with what? Hullo, one arrives.'

The taxi pulled up at a respectable old apartment house in the Cromwell Road. On the opposite pavement sat a young man mending the seat of a wicker chair.

'That's Master James D'Arcy Carewe, detective-constable,' said Alleyn.

'What him!' cried Fox in a scandalized voice. 'So it is. What's he want to go dolling himself up in that rig for?'

'He's being a detective,' Alleyn explained. 'His father's a parson and he learnt wicker-work with the Women's Institute or something. He's been pining to disguise himself ever since he took the oath.'

'Silly young chap,' said Fox.

321

'He's quite a bright boy really, you know.'

'Why's he still there, anyway?'

'Dimitri hasn't left yet, evidently. Wait a moment.'

Alleyn slid back the glass partition of the taxi and addressed the driver:

'We're police officers. In a minute or two a man will come out of this house and want a cab. Hang about for him. He will probably ask you to drive him to Scotland Yard. If he gives any other address I want you to write it quickly on this card while he is getting into the cab. Drop the card through the gear lever slit in the floor. Here's a pencil. Can you do this?'

'Right you are, governor,' said the taximan.

'I want you to turn your car and pass that fellow mending a chair seat. Go as slow as you can, drive two hundred yards up the road and let us out. Then wait for your man. Here's your fare and all the rest of it.'

'Thank you sir. OK, sir,' said the taximan.

He turned, Alleyn lowered the window and, as they passed the wicker expert, leant out and said:

'Carewe! Pick us up.'

The expert paid no attention.

'I told you he's not as silly as he looks,' said Alleyn. 'There we are.'

They got out. The taxi turned once more. They heard the driver's hoarse: 'Taxi, sir?' heard him pull up, heard the door slam, heard the cab drive away. 'He hasn't dropped his card,' said Alleyn staring after the taxi. They continued to walk up the Cromwell Road. Presently a cry broke out behind them.

'*Chairs to mend! Chairs to mend!*'

'There!' said Fox in exasperation. 'Listen to him making an exhibition of himself! It's disgraceful. That's what it is. Disgraceful.'

They turned and found the wicker-worker hard at their heels, followed by long trails of withy.

'Sir!' said the wicker-worker in consternation.

'Tell me,' Alleyn went on, 'why are you presenting the Cries of London to an astonished world?'

'Well, sir,' said the chair-mender, 'following your instructions, I proceeded – '

'Quite. But you should understand by this time that the art of disguise is very often unnecessary and is to be attained by simpler means than those which embrace a great outlay in willow wands, envious slivers, and cabriole legs. What, may I ask, would you have done with all this gear when the hunt was up?'

'There's a taxi rank round the corner, sir. If I whistled – '

'And a pretty sight you'd have looked,' said Fox indignantly, 'whistling cabs in that rig-out. By the time you'd wound yourself in and out of that muck and got yourself aboard, your man would have been half-way to Lord knows where. If that's the sort of stuff they teach you at – '

'Yes, all right, Fox,' said Alleyn hastily. 'Very true. Now, look here, Carewe, you go away and undress and report to me at the Yard. You can go back by Underground. Don't look so miserable or the old ladies will start giving you coppers.'

Carewe departed.

'Now then, Fox,' Alleyn continued, 'give me a few minutes in that flat and then ring up as if from the Yard and keep Dimitri's servant on the telephone as long as possible. You'd better have a list of names and places. Say Dimitri has given them to you and say you will be able to confirm them. All right?'

'Right oh, Mr Alleyn.'

'You can use the call-box at the taxi rank. Then away with you to the Yard and keep Dimitri going until I come. Arrange to have him tailed when he leaves.'

Alleyn returned to Dimitri's flat which was on the ground

floor. The door was opened by a thin dark man who exuded quintessence of waiter.

'Is Mr Dimitri in?' asked Alleyn.

'Monsieur has just left, sir. May I take a message?'

'He's gone, has he?' said Alleyn very pleasantly. 'What a bore, I've just missed him. Do you know if he was going to Scotland Yard?'

The man hesitated.

'I'm not sure, sir. I think – '

'Look here,' said Alleyn, 'I'm Chief Inspector Alleyn. Here's my card. I was in this part of the world and I thought I'd save Mr Dimitri the trouble of moving if I called. As I am here I may as well get you to clear up one or two points for me. Do you mind?'

'Please, sir! Not at all, but it is a little difficult – '

'It is rather, out here. May I come in?' asked Alleyn, and walked in without waiting for the answer.

He found himself in a sitting-room that had an air of wearing a touch of black satin at the neck and wrists but was otherwise unremarkable. The servant followed him and stood looking uneasily at his own hands.

'You will have guessed,' Alleyn began, 'that I am here on business connected with the death of Lord Robert Gospell.'

'Yes, sir.'

'The first thing I have to say is that we would be glad if you'd use great discretion in discussing this affair. Indeed it would be better if you did not discuss it at all, with anybody. Except of course, Mr Dimitri himself.'

The man looked relieved.

'But it is understood perfectly, sir. Monsieur has already warned me of this himself. I shall be most discreet.'

'Splendid. We feel it our duty to protect Mr Dimitri and any other person of position from the unpleasant notoriety that unfortunately accompanies such accidents as these.'

'Yes, certainly, sir. Monsier himself was most emphatic.'

'I'm sure he was. You will understand,' Alleyn went on, 'that it is also necessary to have before us a clear account of the movements of many persons. What is your name?'

'François, sir, François Dupont.'

'Were you at Marsdon House last night?'

'Yes, sir. By an unusual chance I was there.'

'How did that happen?'

'An important member of our staff failed M. Dimitri yesterday afternoon. It seems that he was afflicted suddenly with appendicitis. M. Dimitri was unable to replace him satisfactorily at so short notice and I took his place.'

'This was unusual?'

'Yes, sir. I am M. Dimitri's personal servant.'

'Where were you stationed at Marsdon House?'

A telephone rang in the entrance passage.

'Excuse me, sir,' said the servant. 'The telephone.'

'That's all right,' said Alleyn.

The man went out closing the door softly behind him.

Alleyn darted into an adjoining bedroom, leaving the door ajar. He opened built-in cupboards, ran his hands between hanging suits, amongst neatly stacked shirts and under-garments, disturbing nothing, exploring everywhere. Thanking his stars that the drawers ran easily he moved with economy, swiftness and extreme precision. The adjoining bedroom was innocently naked. Dimitri's servant looked after him well. There was no hiding-place anywhere for a bulky cloth cloak. Everything was decently ordered. Alleyn returned silently to the sitting-room. He could hear the servant's voice:

'Hullo? Hullo? Yes, sir. I am still here. Yes, sir, that is quite correct. It is as Monsieur Dimitri says, sir. We returned together at three-thirty in a taxi. At three-thirty. No, sir, no. At three-thirty. I am sorry, sir, I will repeat. At three-thirty we return – '

The sideboard contained only bottles and glasses, the

bookcases only books. The desk was locked but it was a small one. Dimitri and his servant were tidy men with few possessions. Alleyn opened the last cupboard. It contained two suitcases. He tipped them gingerly. No sound of anything. He opened them. They were empty. Alleyn shut the cupboard door tenderly and returned to the middle of the sitting-room where he stood with his head slanted, listening to Dimitri's servant whose voice had risen to a painful falsetto.

'But I am telling you. Permit me to speak. Your colleague is here. He is about to ask me all these questions himself. He has given me his card. It is the Chief Inspector Alleyne. Ah, *mon Dieu! Mon Dieu!*'

Alleyn went into the passage. He found François with his shoulders up to his ears and his unoccupied hand sketching desperation to the air.

'What is it?' asked Alleyn. 'Is it for me?'

'Here is M. l'Inspecteur!' screamed François into the receiver. 'Will you have the goodness – '

Alleyn addressed the telephone.

'Hullo!'

'Hullo there!' Fox's voice in accents of exasperation.

'Is that you, Fox? What's the matter?'

'Nothing, I hope, Mr Alleyn,' said Fox, falling back on an indistinct mumble.

'It's Alleyn, here. There's been a slight misunderstanding. I have missed Mr Dimitri but will come along as soon as possible. Will you ask him to wait? Apologise for me.'

'I hope there *was* time. I'll get along to the Yard now.'

'Very well. That's perfectly all right,' said Alleyn and rang off.

He returned to the sitting-room followed by François.

'A slight misunderstanding,' explained Alleyn blandly. 'My colleague did not quite follow you. He is unfortunately rather deaf and is about to retire.'

François muttered.

326

'To resume,' said Alleyn. 'You were going to tell me where you were stationed last night.'

'By the top landing, sir. The gallery above the ballroom. My duties were to keep the ash-trays emptied and to attend to the wishes of the guests who sat out dances on this floor.'

'What are the rooms on this gallery?'

'At the stairhead, sir, one finds a green baize door leading to the servants' quarters, the back stairs and so on. Next to this door is a room which last night was employed as a sitting-room. One finds next a bathroom, bedroom and toilet used last night for ladies. Last at the end of the gallery, a green boudoir also used as a sitting-room for the ball.'

'Was there a telephone in any of these rooms?'

'In the green boudoir, sir. It was used several times during the evening.'

'You are an excellent witness, François. I compliment you. Now tell me. You were stationed on this landing. Do you remember the names of the persons who used the telephone?'

François pinched his lower lip.

'It was used by Lady Jennifer Trueman to enquire for her little girl who is ill. Her ladyship requested me to get the number for her. It was used by a young gentleman who called a toll number to say that he would not be returning to the country. Early in the evening it was answered by Sir Daniel Davidson, who, I think, is a doctor. He spoke about a patient who had had an operation. It was also used, sir, by Lord Robert Gospell.'

Alleyn waited a moment. With a sort of astonishment he realized his heart had quickened.

'Could you hear what Lord Robert said?'

'No, sir.'

'Did you notice if anyone went into the room while Lord Robert was at the telephone?'

327

'No, sir. Immediately after Lord Robert entered this room I was summoned by Sir Herbert Carrados who came out of the other sitting-room and spoke to me about the lack of matches. Sir Herbert was annoyed. He sent me into this room to see for myself and ordered me to go at once and fetch more matches. There did not appear to me to be any lack of matches but I did not, of course, say so. I fetched more matches from downstairs. When I returned I went to the telephone-room and found it empty. I attended to the ash-tray and the matches in the telephone-room, also.'

Alleyn sighed.

'Yes, I see. I've no doubt you made a good job of it. Any cigar-stumps in the telephone-room? You wouldn't remember, of course.'

'No, sir.'

'No. François – who was in the other sitting-room and who was on the landing before Lord Robert telephoned? Before Sir Herbert Carrados sent you away. Can you remember?'

'I will try, sir. There were two gentlemen who also sent me away.'

'What?'

'I mean, sir, that one of them asked me to fetch two whiskies-and-sodas. That is not at all a usual request under the circumstances. It is not even *comme il faut* at a ball of this sort, where there is champagne at the buffet and also whisky, to order drinks as if it were an hotel. I received the impression that these two gentlemen wished to be alone on the landing. I obtained their drinks, using the back stairs. When I returned I gave them the drinks. At that time, sir, Lord Robert Gospell had just come up the stairs and when they saw him these two gentlemen moved into the first sitting-room which was unoccupied.'

'Do you mean that they seemed to avoid him?'

'I received the impression, sir, that these gentlemen wished to be alone. That is why I remember them.'

'Their names?'

'I do not know their names.'

'Can you describe them?'

'One, sir, was a man perhaps forty-five or fifty years of age. He was a big man with a red face and thick neck. His voice was an unsympathetic voice. The other was a young gentleman, dark, rather nervous. I observed that he danced repeatedly with Miss Bridget O'Brien.'

'Thank you,' said Alleyn. 'That is excellent. Any others?'

'I cannot recall any others, sir. Wait! There *was* someone who was there for some time.'

François put his first finger to his chin like a sort of male dairymaid and cast his eyes to the ceiling.

'*Tiens!*' he exclaimed, 'who could it have been? *Alors*, I have it. It is of no importance at all, sir. It was the little mademoiselle, the secretary, who was known to few and therefore retired often to the gallery. I have remembered too that Sir Daniel Davidson, the physician, came upstairs. That was earlier. Before Lord Robert appeared. I think Sir Daniel looked for a partner because he went quickly in and out of both rooms and looked about the landing. I have remembered now that it was for Lady Carrados he enquired but she had gone downstairs a few minutes earlier. I told Sir Daniel this and he returned downstairs.'

Alleyn looked over his notes.

'See now,' he said. 'I am right in saying this? The persons who, as far as you know, could have gone into the telephone-room while Lord Robert was using the telephone were Sir Herbert Carrados and the two gentlemen who sent you for whisky.'

'Yes, sir. And the mademoiselle. Miss Harris is her name. I believe she entered the ladies' toilet just as Lord Robert went into the telephone-room. I have remarked that when ladies are much disengaged at balls they frequently enter

329

the dressing-room. It is,' added François with an unexpected flash of humanity, 'a circumstance that I find rather pathetic.'

'Yes,' said Alleyn. 'Very pathetic. I am right, then, in saying that before Lord Robert went to telephone, you fetched drinks for these two men and immediately after that he began to telephone. You were sent away by Sir Herbert Carrados, leaving him, Miss Harris and possibly others, whom you have forgotten, on the landing, and the two gentlemen in the other sitting-out room. Sir Daniel Davidson had gone downstairs some minutes previously. Lady Carrados before Sir Daniel, who was looking for her. You're sure of that?'

'Yes, sir. It is in my memory because after her ladyship had gone I entered the telephone-room and saw she had left her bag there. Monsieur – Mr Dimitri – came up at that time, saw it, and said he would return it to her ladyship. I told him she had gone downstairs and he returned, I think, by the back stairs.'

'He fits in between Lady Carrados and Sir Daniel. Did he return?'

'No, sir. I believe, sir, that I have mentioned everyone who was on the landing. At that time nearly all the guests were at supper. Later, of course, many ladies used the cloakroom toilet.'

'I see. Now for the rest of the evening. Did you see Lord Robert again?'

'No, sir. I remained on the top landing until the guests had gone, I then took a tray to Monsieur in the butler's pantry.'

'Was this long after the last guest had left?'

'No, sir. To be correct, sir, I fancy there may still have been one or two left in the hall. Monsieur was in the buffet when I came down.'

'Was Sir Herbert Carrados in the buffet?'

330

'He left as I entered. It was after he left that Monsieur ordered his little supper.'

'When did you go home?'

'As I have explained to your colleague, at three-thirty, with Monsieur. The police rang up this flat before Monsieur had gone to bed.'

'You carried Monsieur Dimitri's luggage for him, no doubt?'

'His luggage, sir? He had no luggage.'

'Right. I think that is all. You have been very helpful and obliging.'

François took his tip with a waiter's grace and showed Alleyn out.

Alleyn got a taxi. He looked at his watch. Twenty past twelve. He hoped Fox was keeping Dimitri for him. Dimitri! Unless François lied, it looked as if the odds against Dimitri being the murderer were lengthening.

'And the worst of it is,' muttered Alleyn, rubbing his nose, 'that I think François, blast his virtue, spoke nothing but the truth.'

CHAPTER THIRTEEN

Dimitri Cuts His Fingers

In his room at the Yard Alleyn found Dimitri closeted with Fox. Fox introduced them solemnly.

'This is Mr Dimitri; Chief Detective-Inspector Alleyn, who is in charge of this case.'

'Ah, yes?' said Dimitri bowing. 'I believe we have met before.'

Alleyn said: 'I have just come from your flat, Mr Dimitri. I was up that way and hoped to save you a journey. I was, however, too late. I saw your servant and ventured to ask him one or two questions. He was most obliging.'

He smiled pleasantly at Dimitri and thought: 'He's looking sulky. Not a good head. Everything's a bit too narrow. He's got a mean look. No fool, though. Expensive clothes, fishy hands, uses a lot of hair oil. Honey and flowers. Ears set very low. No lobes to them. Less than an eye's width between the two eyes. I fancy the monocle is a dummy. Dents by the nostrils. False teeth. A smooth gentleman.'

Dimitri said: 'Your colleague has already rung my servant, Mr Alleyn.'

'Yes,' said Fox. 'I just checked up the time Mr Dimitri left. I've been explaining, sir, that we realize Mr Dimitri doesn't want to appear more than can be avoided.'

'In my position, Chief Inspector,' said Dimitri, 'it is most undesirable. I have been seven years building up my business and it is a specialized business. You understand that I have an extremely good clientèle. I may say the very best. It is essential to my business that my clients should have complete faith in my discretion. But essential! In my position one sees and hears many things.'

'I have no doubt of that,' said Alleyn, looking steadily at him. 'Things that with a less discreet, less scrupulous person, might be turned to advantage.'

'That is a dreadful thought, Mr Alleyn. One cannot with equanimity contemplate such a base idea. But I must tell you that in my business the finest shades of discretion must be observed.'

'As in ours. I shall not ask you to repeat any scandals, Mr Dimitri. We will confine ourselves to the simplest facts. Your own movements, for instance.'

'Mine?' asked Dimitri, raising his eyebrows.

'If you please. We are anxious to get a little information about a small green boudoir on the top gallery at Marsdon House. It has a telephone in it. Do you know the room I mean?'

'Certainly,' The sharp eyes were veiled, the mouth set in a thin line.

'Did you at any time visit this room?'

'Repeatedly. I make it my business to inspect all the rooms continually.'

'The time in which we are interested is about one o'clock this morning. Most of Lady Carrados's guests were at supper. Captain Maurice Withers and Mr Donald Potter were on this top landing. So was your servant, François. Do you remember going upstairs at this time?'

Dimitri spread out his hands.

'It is impossible for me to remember, I am so very sorry.' He removed his rimless eyeglass and began to turn it between the fingers and thumb of his left hand.

'Let me try to help you. I learnt that at about this time you returned Lady Carrados's bag to her. One of the guests noticed you. Where did you find this bag, Mr Dimitri? Perhaps that will help.'

Dimitri suddenly put his hands in his pockets and Alleyn knew that it was an unfamiliar gesture. He could see that the left hand was still secretly busy with the eyeglass.

333

'That is correct. I seem to think the bag was in the room you mention. I am very particular about such things. My servants may not touch any bags that are left lying about the rooms. It is incredible how careless many ladies are with their bags, Mr Alleyn. I make it a rule that only I myself return them. Thus,' said Dimitri virtuously, 'am I solely responsible.'

'It might be quite a grave responsibility. So the bag was in the green room. Anybody there?'

'My servant François. I trust there was nothing missing from this bag?' asked Dimitri with an air of alarm. 'I asked her ladyship to be good enough to look at it.'

'Her ladyship,' said Alleyn, 'has made no complaint.'

'I am extremely relieved. For a moment I wondered – however.'

'The point is this,' said Alleyn, 'At one o'clock Lord Robert telephoned from this little green room. My informant is not your servant, Mr Dimitri. I must make that clear. At this time I think he was downstairs. My informant tells me that you were on the landing. Perhaps it was shortly after you collected Lady Carrados's bag.'

'If it was I did not hear anything of it,' said Dimitri instantly. 'Your informant is himself misinformed. I did not see Lord Robert on this gallery. I did not notice him at all until he was leaving.'

'You saw him then?'

'Yes. He enquired if I had seen Mrs Halcut-Hackett. I informed his lordship that she had left.'

'This was in the hall?'

'Yes.'

'Did you see Lord Robert leave?'

There was a marked pause and then Dimitri said:

'I have already explained all this to your colleague. After speaking to his lordship I went to the buffet on the ground floor. I remained there for a time speaking to Sir Herbert Carrados.'

Alleyn took a piece of paper from his pocket-book and handed it to Dimitri.

'This is the order of departure amongst the last guests. We have got our information from several sources. Mr Fox was greatly helped in compiling it by his interview with you earlier this morning. Would you mind glancing at it?'

Dimitri surveyed the list.

'It is correct, as far as I can remember, up to the time I left the hall.'

'I believe you saw the encounter at the foot of the stairs between Lord Robert and his nephew, Mr Donald Potter?'

'It was scarcely an encounter. They did not speak.'

'Did you get the impression that they avoided each other?'

'Mr Alleyn, we have already spoken of the need for discretion. Of course, one understands this is a serious matter. Yes. I did receive this impression.'

'Right. Then before you went to the buffet you noticed Mrs Halcut-Hackett, Captain Withers, Mr Potter and Sir Daniel Davidson leave separately, and in that order?'

'Yes.'

'Do you know Captain Withers?'

'Professionally? No. He does not entertain, I imagine.'

'Who left the buffet first, you or Sir Herbert?'

'I really do not remember. I did not remain very long in the buffet.'

'Where did you go?'

'I was fatigued. I made certain that my staff was working smoothly and then my servant brought me a light supper to the butler's pantry which I had reserved for my office.'

'How long was this after Lord Robert left?'

'I really do not know. Not long.'

'Did François remain in the butler's pantry?'

'Certainly not.'

'Did anyone come in while you were there?'

'I do not remember.'

335

'If, on reflection, you do recall any witness to your solitary supper-party it would help us in our work and free you from further embarrassment.'

'I do not understand you. Do you attempt to establish my alibi in this most regrettable and distressing fatality? Surely it is obvious that I could not have been in a taxi-cab with Lord Robert Gospell and in the buffet at Marsdon House at the same moment.'

'What makes you think that this crime was committed during the short time you spent in the buffet, Mr Dimitri?'

'Then or later, it is all the same. Still I am ready to help you, Chief Inspector. I will try to remember if I was seen in the pantry.'

'Thank you. I believe you attended the Bach recital by the Sirmione Quartette in the Constance Street Hall on June 3rd?'

The silence that followed Alleyn's question was so complete that the rapid tick of his desk clock came out of obscurity to break it. Alleyn was visited by a fantastic idea. There were four clocks in the room: Fox, Dimitri, himself and that small mechanical pulse on the writing desk.

Dimitri said: 'I attended the concert, yes. I am greatly attached to the music of Bach.'

'Did you happen to notice Lord Robert at this concert?'

It was as if the clock that was Dimitri was opened, and the feverish little pulse of the brain revealed. Should he say yes; should he say no?

'I am trying to remember. I think I do remember that his lordship was present.'

'You are quite correct, Mr Dimitri. He was not far away from you.'

'I pay little attention to externals when I listen to beautiful music.'

'Did you return her bag to Mrs Halcut-Hackett?'

Dimitri gave a sharp cry. Fox's pencil skidded across

336

the page of his notebook. Dimitri drew his left hand out of his pocket and stared at his fingers. Three drops of blood fell from them to his striped trouser leg.

'Blood on your hand, Mr Dimitri,' said Alleyn.

Dimitri said: 'I have broken my glass.'

'Is the cut deep? Fox, my bag is in the cupboard there. I think there is some lint and strapping in it.'

'No,' said Dimitri, 'it is nothing.' He wrapped his fine silk handkerchief round his fingers and nursed them in his right hand. He was white to the lips.

'The sight of blood,' he said, 'affects me unpleasantly.'

'I insist that you allow me to bandage your hand,' said Alleyn. Dimitri did not answer. Fox produced iodine, lint and strapping. Alleyn unwrapped the hand. Two of the fingers were cut and bled freely. Dimitri shut his eyes while Alleyn dressed them. The hand was icy cold and clammy.

'There,' said Alleyn. 'And your handkerchief to hide the blood-stains which upset you so much. You are quite pale, Mr Dimitri. Would you like some brandy?'

'No. No, thank you.'

'You are recovered?'

'I do not feel well. I must ask you to excuse me.'

'Certainly. When you have answered my last question. Did you ever return Mrs Halcut-Hackett's bag?'

'I do not understand you. We spoke of Lady Carrados's bag.'

'We speak now of Mrs Halcut-Hackett's bag which you took from the sofa at the Sirmione Concert. Do you deny that you took it?'

'I refuse to prolong this interview. I shall answer no more questions without the advice of my solicitor. That is final.'

He rose to his feet. So did Alleyn and Fox.

'Very well,' said Alleyn. 'I shall have to see you again, Mr Dimitri; and again, and I daresay again. Fox, will you show Mr Dimitri down?'

337

When the door had closed Alleyn spoke into his telephone.

'My man is leaving. He'll probably take a taxi. Who's tailing him?'

'Anderson relieving Carewe, sir.'

'Ask him to report when he gets a chance, but not to take too big a chance. It's important.'

'Right, Mr Alleyn.'

Alleyn waited for Fox's return. Fox came in grinning.

'He's shaken up a fair treat to see, Mr Alleyn. Doesn't know if he's Mayfair, Soho, or Wandsworth.'

'We've a long way to go before he's Wandsworth. How are we ever going to persuade women like Mrs Halcut-Hackett to charge their blackmailers? Not in a lifetime, unless – '

'Unless what?'

'Unless the alternative is even more terrifying. Fox, do you think it within the bounds of possibility that Dimitri ordered his trifle of caviare and champagne at Sir Herbert's expense, that François departed and Dimitri, hurriedly acquiring a silk hat and overcoat, darted out by the back door just in time to catch Lord Robert in the mist, ask him preposterously for a lift and drive away? Can you swallow this camel of unlikelihood and if so, can you open your ponderous and massy jaws still farther and engulf the idea of Dimitri performing his murder and subsequent masquerade, returning to Marsdon House, and settling down to his supper without anybody noticing anything out of the ordinary?'

'When you put it that way, sir, it does sound funny. But we don't know it's impossible.'

'No, we don't. He's about the right height. I've a strong feeling, Fox, that Dimitri is not working this blackmail game on his own. We're not allowed strong feelings, so ignore it. If there is another scoundrel in the game they'll try to get into touch. We'll have to do something about

338

that. What's the time? One o'clock, I'm due at Sir Daniel's at two and I'll have to see the AC before then. Coming?'

'I'll do a bit of work on the file first. We ought to hear from the fellow at Leatherhead any time now. You go to lunch, Mr Alleyn. When did you last eat anything?'

'I don't know. Look here – '

'Did you have any breakfast?' asked Fox, putting on his spectacles and opening the file.

'Good Lord, Fox, I'm not a hothouse lily.'

'This isn't a usual case, sir, for you. It's a personal matter, say what you like, and you'll do no good if you try and work it on your nerves.'

Fox glanced at Alleyn over the top of his spectacles, wetted his thumb, and turned a page.

'Oh God,' said Alleyn, 'once the wheels begin to turn, it's easier to forget the other side. If only I didn't see him so often. He looked like a child, Fox. Just like a child.'

'Yes,' said Fox. 'It's a nasty case, personal feelings aside. If you see the Assistant Commissioner now, Mr Alleyn, I'll be ready to join you for a bite of lunch before we go to Sir Daniel Davidson's.'

'All right, blast you. Meet me downstairs in a quarter of an hour.'

'Thank you, sir,' said Fox. 'I'll be pleased.'

About twenty minutes later he presided over Alleyn's lunch with all the tranquil superiority of a nannie. They arrived at St. Luke's Chambers, Harley Street, at two o'clock precisely. They sat in a waiting-room lavishly strewn with new periodicals. Fox solemnly read *Punch*, while Alleyn, with every appearance of the politest attention, looked at a brochure appealing for clothes and money for the Central Chinese Medical Mission. In a minute or two a secretary told them that Sir Daniel would see them and showed them into his consulting-room.

'The gentlemen from Scotland Yard, Sir Daniel. Mr Alleyn and Mr Fox.'

Davidson, who had apparently been staring out of the window, came forward and shook hands.

'It's very good of you to come to me,' he said. 'I said on the telephone that I was quite ready to report at Scotland Yard whenever it suited you. Do sit down.'

They sat down. Alleyn glanced round the room and what he saw pleased him. It was a charming room with apple-green walls, an Adam fireplace and silver-starred curtains. Above the mantelpiece hung a sunny landscape by a famous painter. A silk praying-mat that would not have disgraced a collector's walls did workaday service before the fireplace. Sir Daniel's desk was an adapted spinet, his inkwell recalled the days when sanded paper was inscribed with high-sounding phrases in quill-scratched calligraphy. As he sat at his desk Sir Daniel saw before him in Chinese ceramic, a little rose-red horse. A beautiful and expensive room, crying in devious tones of the gratitude of wealthy patients. The most exalted, if not the richest, of these stared with blank magnificence from a silver frame.

Sir Daniel himself, neat, exquisite in London clothes and a slightly flamboyant tie, with something a little exotic about his fine dark head, looked as though he could have no other setting than this. He seated himself at his desk, joined his hands and contemplated Alleyn with frank curiosity.

'Surely you are Roderick Alleyn?' he said.

'Yes.'

'I have read your book.'

'Are you interested in criminology?' asked Alleyn with a smile.

'Enormously! I hardly dare to tell you this because you must so often fall a victim to the enthusiasm of fools. I, too! "Oh, Sir Daniel, it must be *too* marvellous to be able to look into the minds of people as you do." Their minds! My God! Their stomachs are enough. But I often think

340

quite seriously that I should have liked to follow medical jurisprudence.'

'We have lost a great figure then,' said Alleyn.

'That's very graceful. But it's untrue, I'm afraid. I am too impatient and altogether too much of a partisan. As in this case. Lord Robert was a friend of mine. It would be impossible for me to look at this case with an equal eye.'

'If you mean,' said Alleyn, 'that you do not feel kindly disposed towards his murderer, no more do we. Do we, Fox?'

'No, sir, that we do not,' said Fox.

Davidson's brilliant eyes rested for a moment on Fox. With a single glance he seemed to draw him into the warm circle of his confidence and regard. 'All the same,' thought Alleyn, 'he's uneasy. He doesn't quite know where to begin.' And he said:

'You very kindly rang up to say you might be able to help us.'

'Yes,' said Davidson, 'yes, I did.' He lifted a very beautiful jade paperweight and put it down. 'I don't know how to begin.' He darted a shrewd and somehow impish glance at Alleyn. 'I find myself in the unenviable position of being one of the last people to see Lord Robert.'

Fox took out his notebook. Davidson looked distastefully at it.

'When did you see him?' Alleyn asked.

'In the hall. Just before I left.'

'You left, I understand, after Mrs Halcut-Hackett, Captain Withers and Mr Donald Potter, who went away severally about three-thirty.'

Davidson's jaw dropped. He flung up his beautiful hands.

'Believe it or not,' he said, 'I had a definite struggle with my conscience before I made up my mind to admit it.'

'Why was that?' asked Alleyn.

341

Again that sideways impish glance.

'I didn't want to come forward at all. Not a bit. It's very bad for us parasites to appear in murder trials. In the long run, it is very bad indeed. By the way, I suppose it *is* a case of homicide. No doubt about it? Or shouldn't I ask?'

'Of course you can ask. There seems to be no doubt at all. He was smothered.'

'Smothered!' Davidson leant forward, his hands clasped on the desk. Alleyn read in his face the subtle change that comes upon all men when they embark on their own subject. 'Good God!' he said, 'he wasn't a Desdemona! Why didn't he make a rumpus? Is he marked?'

'There are no marks of violence.'

'None? Who did the autopsy?'

'Curtis. He's our expert.'

'Curtis, Curtis? – yes, of course. How does he account for the absence of violence? Heart? His heart was in a poor condition.'

'How do you know that, Sir Daniel?'

'My dear fellow, I examined him most thoroughly three weeks ago.'

'Did you!' exclaimed Alleyn. 'That's very interesting. What did you find?'

'I found a very unpleasant condition. Evidence of fatty degeneration. I ordered him to avoid cigars like the plague, to deny himself his port and to rest for two hours every day. I am firmly persuaded that he paid no attention whatsoever. Nevertheless, my dear Mr Alleyn, it was not a condition under which I would expect an unprovoked heart attack. A struggle certainly might induce it and you tell me there is no evidence of a struggle.'

'He was knocked out.'

'Knocked out! Why didn't you say so before? Because I gave you no opportunity, of course. I see. And quietly asphyxiated? How very horrible and how ingenious.'

342

'Would the condition of the heart make it quicker?'

'I should say so, undoubtedly.'

Davidson suddenly ran his fingers through his picturesque hair.

'I am more distressed by this abominable, this unspeakable crime than I would have thought possible. Mr Alleyn, I had the deepest regard for Lord Robert. It would be impossible to exaggerate my regard for him. He seemed a comic figure, an aristocratic droll with an unusual amount of charm. He was much more than that. He had a keen brain. In conversation, he understood everything that one left unsaid, his mind was both subtle and firm. I am a man of the people. I adore all my smart friends and I understand – *Cristo Mio,* do I not understand! – my smart patients! But I am not, deep in my heart, at ease with them. With Lord Robert I was at ease. I showed off and was not ashamed afterwards that I had done so.'

'You pay him a great compliment when you confess as much,' said Alleyn.

'Do I not? Listen. If it had been anyone else, do you know what I should have done? I should have kept quiet and I should have said to myself *il ne faut pas réveiller le chat qui dort,* and hoped nobody would remember that I stood in the hall this morning at Marsdon House and watched Lord Robert at the foot of the stairs. But as it is I have screwed myself up to making the superb gesture of coming to you with information you have already received. *Gros-Jean en remontre à son curé!*'

'Not altogether,' said Alleyn. 'It is not entirely *une vieille histoire.* You may yet glow with conscious virtue. I am longing for a precise account of those last minutes in the hall. We have the order of the going but not the nature of it. If you don't mind giving us a microscopically exact version?'

'Ah!' Davidson frowned. 'You must give me a moment to arrange my facts. A microscopically exact version! Wait

343

now.' He closed his eyes and his right hand explored the surface of the carved jade paperweight. The deliberate movement of the fingers arrested Alleyn's attention. The piece of jade might have been warm and living, so sensitively did the fingertips caress it. Alleyn thought: 'He loves his beautiful possessions.' He determined to learn more of this *poseur* who called himself a man of the people and spattered his conversation with French and Italian tags, who was at once so frankly theatrical and so theatrically frank.

Davidson opened his eyes. The effect was quite startling. They were such remarkable eyes. The light grey iris, unusually large, was ringed with black, the pupil a sharp black accent. 'I bet he uses that trick on his patients to some effect,' thought Alleyn, and then realized that Davidson was smiling. 'Blast him, he's read my thoughts.' And he found himself returning the smile as if he and Davidson shared an amusing secret.

'Take this down, Fox,' said Alleyn.

'Very good, sir,' said Fox.

'As you have noticed,' Davidson began, 'I have a taste for the theatrical. Let me present this little scene to you as if we watched it take place behind the footlights. I have shaken hands with my host and hostess where the double flight of stairs meet in a gallery outside the ballroom. I come down the left-hand flight of stairs, thinking of my advancing years and longing for my bed. In the hall are scattered groups of people; coated, cloaked, ready for departure. Already the great house seems exhausted and a little raffish. One feels the presence of drooping flowers, one seems to smell the dregs of champagne. It is indeed time to be gone. Among the departing guests I notice an old lady whom I wish to avoid. She's rich, one of my best patients, but her chief complaint is a condition of chronic, complicated and acute verbal diarrhoea. I have ministered to this complaint already this evening and as I have no wish to be offered a lift in her car I dart into

344

the men's cloakroom. I spend some minutes there, marking time. It is a little awkward as the only other men in the cloakroom are obviously engaged in an extremely private conversation.'

'Who are they?' asked Alleyn.

'A certain Captain Withers who is newly come upon the town and that pleasant youth, Donald Potter. They both pause and stare at me. I make a great business of getting my coat and hat. I chat with the cloakroom attendant after I have tipped him. I speak to Donald Potter, but am so poorly received that in sheer decency I am forced to leave. Lucy Lorrimer – *tiens,* there I go!'

'It's all right,' said Alleyn, 'I know all about Lucy Lorrimer.'

'What a woman! She is still screaming out there. I pull up my scarf and lurk in the doorway, waiting for her to go. Having nothing else to do I watch the other people in the hall. The *grand seigneur* of the stomach stands at the foot of the stairs.'

'Who?'

'The man who presides over all these affairs. What is his name?'

'Dimitri?'

'Yes, Dimitri. He stand there like an imitation host. A group of young people go out. Then an older woman, alone, comes down the stairs and slips through the doors into the misty street. It was very strange, all that mist.'

'Was this older woman Mrs Halcut-Hackett?'

'Yes. That is who it was,' said Davidson a little too casually.

'Is Mrs Halcut-Hackett a patient of yours, Sir Daniel?'

'It so happens that she is.'

'Why did she leave alone? What about her husband and – hasn't she got a débutante attached to her?'

'The protégée, who is unfortunately *une jeune fille un peu farouche,* fell a prey to toothache earlier in the evening and was removed by the General. I heard Lord Robert offer to escort Mrs Halcut-Hackett home.

'Why did he not do so?'

'Perhaps because they missed each other.'

'Come now, Sir Daniel, that's not your real opinion.'

'Of course it's not, but I don't gossip about my patients.'

'I needn't assure you that we shall be very discreet. Remember what you said about your attitude towards this case.'

'I do remember. Very well. Only please, if you can avoid my name in subsequent interviews, I shall be more than grateful. I'll go on with my recital. Mrs Halcut-Hackett, embedded in ermine, gives a swift look round the hall and slips out through the doors into the night. My attention is arrested by something in her manner, and while I stare after her somebody jostles me so violently that I actually stumble forward and only just save myself from falling. It is Captain Withers, who has come out of the cloakroom behind me. I turn to receive his apologies and find him with his mouth set and his unpleasant eyes – I mistrust people with white lashes – goggling at the stairhead. He does not even realize his own incivility, his attention is fixed on Lord Robert Gospell, who has begun to descend the stairs. This Captain Withers's expression is so singular that I, too, forget our encounter. I hear him draw in his breath. There is a second's pause and then he, too, thrusts his way through a party of chattering youngsters and goes out.'

'Do you think Withers was following Mrs Halcut-Hackett?'

'I have no reason to think so, but I do think so.'

'Next?'

'Next? Why, Mr Alleyn, I pull myself together and start for the door. Before I have taken three steps young Donald Potter comes out of the buffet with Bridget O'Brien. They meet Lord Robert at the foot of the stairs.'

346

'Yes?' said Alleyn, as Davidson paused.

'Donald Potter,' he said at last, 'says what is no doubt a word of farewell to Bridget, and then he too goes out by the front entrance.'

'Without speaking to his uncle?'

'Yes.'

'And Lord Robert?'

'Lord Robert is asking in that very penetrating high-pitched voice of his if Dimitri has seen Mrs Halcut-Hackett. I see him now and hear him – the last thing I do see or hear before the double doors close behind me.'

CHAPTER FOURTEEN

Davidson Digresses

'That was a very vivid little scene,' said Alleyn.

'Well, it was not so long ago, after all,' said Davidson.

'When you got outside the house, did you see any of the others, or had they all gone?'

'The party of young people came out as I did. There was the usual bustle for taxis with linkmen and porters. Those linkmen! They are indeed a link with past glories. When one sees the lights from their torches flicker on the pale, almost wanton faces of guests half-dazed with dancing, one expects Millamant herself to come down the steps and all the taxis to turn into sedan chairs. However, I must not indulge my passion for elaboration. The party of young people surged into the three taxis that had been summoned by the porter. He was about to call one for me when, to my horror, I saw a Rolls-Royce on the other side of the road. The window was down and there, like some Sybil, mopping and mowing, was Lucy Lorrimer. "Sir Daniel! Sir Daniel." I shrank further into my scarf, but all in vain. An officious flunkey cries out: "The lady is calling you, sir." Nothing for it but to cross the road. "Sir Daniel! Sir Daniel! I have waited for you. Something most important! I shall drive you home and on the way I can tell you – " An impossible woman. I know what it means. She is suffering from a curious internal pain that has just seized her and now is the moment for me to make an examination. I must come in. She is in agony. I think furiously and by the time I reach her window I am prepared. "Lady Lorrimer – forgive me – not a moment to spare – the Prime Minister – a sudden indisposition – !" and while she still gapes I turn and bolt like a rabbit into the mist!'

For the first time since the tragedy of last night Alleyn laughed. Davidson gave him a droll look and went on with his story.

'I ran as I have not done since I was a boy in Grenoble, pursued by that voice offering, no doubt, to drive me like the wind to Downing Street. Mercifully the mist thickened. On I went, looking in vain for a taxi. I heard a car and shrank into the shadows. The Rolls-Royce passed. I crept out. At last a taxi! It was coming behind me. I could just see the two misted headlights. Then voices, but indistinguishable. The taxi stopped, came on towards me. Engaged! *Mon Dieu,* what a night! I walked on, telling myself that sooner or later I must find a cab. Not a bit of it! By this time, I suppose, the last guest had gone. It was God knows what time of the morning and the few cabs I did meet were all engaged. I walked from Belgrave Square to Cadogan Gardens, and I assure you, my dear Mr Alleyn, I have never enjoyed a walk more. I felt like a middle-aged harlequin in search of adventure. That I found none made not the smallest matter.'

'Unless I'm much mistaken,' said Alleyn, 'you missed it by a very narrow margin. Adventure is perhaps not the right word. I fancy tragedy passed you by, Sir Daniel, and you did not recognise it.'

'Yes,' said Davidson, and his voice was suddenly sombre. 'Yes, I believe you may be right. It is not so amusing, after all.'

'That taxi-cab. Which way did you turn when you fled from Lady Lorrimer?'

'To my right.'

'How far had you run when you heard the taxi?'

'I don't know. It is almost impossible to judge. Perhaps four hundred yards. Not far, because I had stopped and hidden from Lucy Lorrimer.'

349

'You tell us you heard voices. Did you recognise them?'

Davidson waited, staring thoughtfully at Alleyn.

'I realize how important this is,' he said at last. 'I am almost afraid to answer. Mr Alleyn, I can only tell you that when those voices – I could hear no words, remember – reached me through the mist, I thought at first that one was a woman's voice and then I changed my mind and thought it was a man's. It was a high-pitched voice.'

'And the other?'

'Definitely a man's.'

'Can you remember anything else, anything at all, about this incident?'

'Nothing. Except that when the taxi passed me I thought the occupants were men.'

'Yes. Will you give us a signed statement?'

'About the taxi incident? Certainly.'

'Can you tell me who was left behind at Marsdon House when you went away?'

'After the noisy party that went when I did, very few remained. Let me think. There was a very drunk young man. I think his name is Percival and he came out of the buffet just before I left and went into the cloakroom. There was somebody else. Who was it? Ah, yes, it was a curious little lady who seemed to be rather a fish out of water. I had noticed her before. She was quite unremarkable and one would never have seen her if she had not almost always been alone. She wore glasses. That is all I can tell you about her except – yes – I saw her dancing with Lord Robert. I remember now that she was looking at him as he came downstairs. Perhaps she felt some sort of gratitude towards him. She would have been pathetic if she had not looked so composed. I shouldn't be surprised if she was a dependant of the house. Perhaps Bridget's ex-governess, or Lady Carrados's companion. I fancy I encountered her myself somewhere during the evening. Where was it? I forget!'

'The ball was a great success, I believe?'

'Yes. Lady Carrados was born under a star of hospitality. It is always a source of wonderment to me why one ball should be a great success and another offering the same band, caterer and guests an equally great failure. Lady Carrados, one would have said, was at a disadvantage last night.'

'You mean she was unwell?'

'So you've heard about that. We tried to keep it quiet. Yes, like all these mothers, she's overdone herself.'

'Worrying about something, do you imagine?' asked Alleyn, and then in reply to Davidson's raised brows, he said: 'I wouldn't ask if it was not relevant.'

'I can't imagine, I must confess, how Lady Carrados's indisposition can have any possible connection with Lord Robert Gospell's death. She is nervously exhausted and felt the strain of her duties.' Davidson added as if to himself: 'This business will do her no good, either.'

'You see,' said Alleyn, 'in a case of this sort we have to look for any departure from the ordinary or the expected. I agree that this particular departure seems quite irrelevant. So, alas, will many of the other facts we bring to light. If they cannot be correlated they will be discarded. That is routine.'

'No doubt. Well, all I can tell you is that I noticed Lady Carrados was unwell, told her to go and lie down in the ladies' cloakroom, which I understand was on the top landing, and to send her maid for me if she needed me. Getting no message, I tried to find her, but couldn't. She reappeared later on and told me she felt a little better and not to worry about her.'

'Sir Daniel, did you happen to see the caterer, Dimitri, return her bag to Lady Carrados?'

'I don't think so. Why?'

'I've heard that for a time last night she thought she had lost it and was very distressed.'

351

'She said nothing to me about it. It might account for her upset. I noticed that bag. It has a very lovely emerald and ruby clasp – an old Italian setting and much too choice a piece to bedizen a bit of tinsel nonsense. But nowadays people have no sense of congruity in ornament. None.'

'I have been looking at your horse. You, at least, have an appreciation of the beautiful. Forgive me for forgetting my job for a moment but – a ray of sunshine has caught that little horse. Rose red and ochre! I've a passion for ceramics.'

Davidson's face was lit from within. He embarked eagerly on the story of how he acquired his little horse. His hands touched it as delicately as if it was a rose. He and Alleyn stepped back three thousand centuries into the golden age of pottery and Inspector Fox sat as silent as stout Cortez with his official notebook open on his knees and an expression of patient tolerance on his large solemn face.

' – and speaking of Benvenuto,' said Davidson who had talked himself into the Italian Renaissance, 'I saw in a room at Marsdon House last night, unless I am a complete nincompoop, an authentic Cellini medallion. And where, my dear Alleyn, do you suppose it was? To what base use do you imagine it had been put?'

'I've no idea,' said Alleyn, smiling.

'It had been sunk; sunk, mark you, in a machine-turned gold case with a devilish diamond clasp and it was surrounded with brilliants. Doubtless this sacrilegious abortion was intended as a receptacle for cigarettes.'

'Where was this horror?' asked Alleyn.

'In an otherwise charming green sitting-room.'

'On the top landing?'

'That's the one. Look for this case yourself. It's worth seeing in a horrible sort of way.'

'When did you visit this room?'

'When? Let me see. It must have been about half-past

eleven. I had an urgent case yesterday and the assistant surgeon rang me up to report.'

'You didn't go there again?'

'No. I don't think so. No, I didn't.'

'You didn't,' persisted Alleyn, 'happen to hear Lord Robert telephone from that room?'

'No. No, I didn't return to it at all. But it was a charming room. A Greuze above the mantelpiece and three or four really nice little pieces on a pie-crust table and with them this hell-inspired crime. I could not imagine a person with enough taste to choose the other pieces, allowing such a horror as a Benvenuto medallion – and a very lovely one – sunk, no doubt cemented, by its perfect reverse, to this filthy cigarette-case.'

'Awful,' agreed Alleyn. 'Speaking of cigarettes, what sort of case did you carry last night?'

'Hullo!' Davidson's extraordinary eyes bored into his. 'What sort of – ' He stopped and then muttered to himself: 'Knocked out, you said. Yes, I see. On the temple.'

'That's it,' said Alleyn.

Davidson pulled a flat silver case from his pocket. It was beautifully made with a sliding action and bevelled edges. Its smooth surface shone like a mirror between the delicately tooled margins. He handed it to Alleyn.

'I don't despise frank modernity, you see.'

Alleyn examined the case, rubbing his fingers over the tooling. Davidson said abruptly:

'One could strike a sharp blow with it.'

'One could,' said Alleyn, 'but it's got traces of plate-powder in the tooling and it's not the right kind, I fancy.'

'I wouldn't have believed it possible that I could have been so profoundly relieved,' said Davidson. He waited for a moment and then with a nervous glance at Fox, he added: 'I suppose I've no alibi?'

'Well, no,' said Alleyn, 'I suppose you haven't, but I

shouldn't let it worry you. The taximan may remember passing you.'

'It was filthily misty,' said Davidson peevishly. 'He may not have noticed.'

'Come,' said Alleyn, 'you mustn't get investigation nerves. There's always Lucy Lorrimer.'

'There is indeed always Lucy Lorrimer. She has rung up three times this morning.'

'There you are. I'll have to see her myself. Don't worry; you've given us some very useful information, hasn't he, Fox?'

'Yes, sir. It's kind of solidified what we had already.'

'Anything you'd like to ask Sir Daniel, Fox?'

'No, Mr Alleyn, thank you. I think you've covered the ground very thoroughly. Unless – '

'Yes?' asked Davidson. 'Come on, Mr Fox.'

'Well, Sir Daniel, I was wondering if you could give us an opinion on how long it would take a man in Lord Robert Gospell's condition to die under these circumstances.'

'Yes,' said Davidson, and again that professional note sounded in his voice. 'Yes. It's not easy to give you the sort of answer you want. A healthy man would go in about four minutes if the murderer completely stopped all access of air to the lungs. A man with a condition of the heart which I believe to have obtained in this instance would be most unlikely to live for four minutes. Life might become extinct within less than two. He might die almost immediately.'

'Yes. Thank you, sir.'

Alleyn said: 'Suppose the murderer had some slight knowledge of medicine and was aware of Lord Robert's condition, would he be likely to realize how little time he needed?'

'That is rather a difficult question to answer. His slight knowledge might not embrace asphyxia. I should say that

354

any first-year student would probably realize that a diseased heart would give out very rapidly under these conditions. A nurse would know. Indeed, I should have thought most laymen would think it probable. The actual time to within two or three minutes might not be appreciated.'

'Yes. Thank you.'

Alleyn got up.

'I think that really is everything. We'll get out a statement for you to sign, if you will. Believe me, we do realize that it has been very difficult for you to speak of your patients under these extremely disagreeable circumstances. We'll word the beastly document as discreetly as may be.'

'I'm sure you will. Mr Alleyn, I think I remember Lord Robert telling me he had a great friend at Scotland Yard. Are you this friend? I see you are. Please don't think my question impertinent. I am sure that you have suffered, with all his friends, a great loss. You should not draw too much upon your nervous energy, you know, in investigating this case. It is quite useless for me to tell you this, but I *am* a physician and I do know something about nerves. You are subjecting yourself to a very severe discipline at the moment. Don't overdo it.'

'Just what I'd like to tell him, sir,' said Fox unexpectedly.

Davidson turned on him a face cordial with appreciation. 'I see we understand each other, Mr Fox.'

'It's very kind of you both,' said Alleyn with a grin, 'but I'm not altogether a hothouse flower. Good-bye, Sir Daniel. Thank you so much.'

They shook hands and Fox and Alleyn went out.

'Where do we go now?' asked Fox.

'I think we'd better take a look at Marsdon House. Bailey ought to have finished by now. I'll ring up from there and see if I can get an appointment with the Carrados family *en masse.* It's going to be difficult, that. There seems to be no doubt that Lady Carrados is one of the blackmailing victims. Carrados himself is a difficult type,

355

a frightful old snob he is, and as vain as a peacock. Police investigation will undoubtedly stimulate all his worst qualities. He's the sort of man who'd go to any lengths to avoid the wrong kind of publicity. We'll have go to warily if we don't want him to make fools of us and a confounded nuisance of himself.'

On the way to Marsdon House they went over Davidson's evidence.

'It's a rum thing, when you come to think of it,' ruminated Fox. 'There was Sir Daniel looking at that taxi and wishing it wasn't booked and there inside it were Lord Robert and the man who had made up his mind to kill him. He must have started in to do it almost at once. He hadn't got much time, after all.'

'No,' said Alleyn, 'the time factor is important.'

'How exactly d'you reckon he set about it, sir?'

'I imagine them sitting side by side. The murderer takes out his cigarette-case, if indeed it was a cigarette-case. Perhaps he says something to make Lord Robert lean forward and look through the window. He draws back his hand and hits Lord Robert sharply on the temple with the edge and point of the case – the wound seems to indicate that. Lord Robert slumps back. The murderer presses his muffled hand over the nose and mouth, not too hard but carefully. As the mouth opens he pushes the material he is using between the teeth and further and further back towards the throat. With his other hand he keeps the nostrils closed. And so he sits until they are nearly at Cheyne Walk. When he removes his hands the pulse is still, there is no attempt at respiration. The head falls sideways and he knows it is all over.' Alleyn clenched his hands. 'He might have been saved even then, Fox. Artificial respiration might have saved him. But there was the rest of the drive to Queens Gate and then on to the Yard. Hopeless!'

'The interview with Sir Herbert Carrados ought to clear

up this business of Dimitri,' Fox said. 'If Sir Herbert was any length of time in the buffet with Dimitri.'

'We'll have to go delicately with Carrados. I wonder if the obscure lady will be there. The lady that nobody noticed but who, since she did not dance very much, may have fulfilled the traditional office of the onlooker. Then there's the Halcut-Hackett game. We'll have to get on with that as soon as possible. It links up with Withers.'

'What sort of a lady is Mrs Halcut-Hackett? She came and saw you at the Yard, didn't she, about the blackmail business?'

'Yes, Fox, she did. She played the old, old game of pretending to be the friend of the victim. Still she had the pluck to come. That visit of hers marked the beginning of the whole miserable affair. You may be sure that I do not forget this. I asked Bunchy to help us find the blackmailer. If I hadn't done that he'd be alive now, I suppose, unless . . . unless, my God! Donald killed his uncle for what he'd get out of it. If blackmail's at the bottom of the murder, I'm directly responsible.'

'Well, sir, if you'll excuse me, I don't think that's a remark to get you or anyone else much further. Lord Robert wouldn't have thanked you for it and that's a fact. We don't feel obliged to warn everybody who helps in a blackmail case that it's liable to turn to murder. And why?' continued Fox with the nearest approach to animation that Alleyn had ever seen in him. 'Because up to now it never has.'

'All right, Brer Fox,' said Alleyn. 'I'll pipe down.'

And for the rest of the way to Marsdon House they were both silent.

CHAPTER FIFTEEN

Simple Soldier-man

Marsdon House had been put into a sort of cold-storage by the police. Dimitri's men had done a certain amount of clearing up before Alleyn's men arrived, but for the most part the great house seemed to be suffering from a severe form of carry-over. It smelt of stale cigarette butts. They were everywhere, bent double, stained red, stained brown, in ash-trays, fireplaces and waste-paper boxes; ground into the ballroom floor, dropped behind chairs, lurking in dirty cups and floating in a miserable state of disintegration among the stalks of dying flowers. Upstairs in the ladies' dressing-room they lay in drifts of spilt powder, and in the green boudoir someone had allowed a cigarette to eat a charred track across the margin of a pie-crust table.

Alleyn and Fox stood in the green boudoir and looked at the telephone.

'There he sat,' said Alleyn, and once more he quoted: ' "The cakes-and-ale feller. Might as well mix his damn brews with poison. And he's working with – " Look, Fox, he must have sat in this chair, facing the door. He wouldn't see anybody coming because of that very charming screen. Imagine our interloper sneaking through the door. He catches a word that arrests his attention, stops for a second and then, realising what Lord Robert is doing, comes round the screen. Lord Robert looks up: "Hullo, I didn't see you," and knowing he has just mentioned the Yard, pitches his lost property story and rings off. I've left word at the Yard that every name on that guest list is to be traced and each guest asked as soon as possible if he or she butted in on that conversation. I'm using a lot of men on this

358

case, but the AC's behaving very prettily, thank the Lord. Get that PC, will you?'

The constable who had been left in charge reported that Detective-Sergeant Bailey had been all over the room for prints and had gone to the Yard before lunch.

'Is the telephone still switched through to this room?'

'I believe so, sir. Nothing's been touched.'

'Fox, ring up the Yard and see if there's anything new.'

While Fox was at the telephone Alleyn prowled about the room looking with something like despair at the evidence of so many visitors. It was useless to hope that anything conclusive would be deduced from Bailey's efforts. They might find Lord Robert's prints on the telephone but what was the good of that? If they could separate and classify every print that had been left in the room it would lead them exactly nowhere.

Fox turned away from the telephone.

'They've got through the list of guests, sir. Very smart work. Five men on five telephones. None of the guests admit to having overheard Lord Robert, and none of the servants.'

'That's our line, then. Find the interloper. Somehow I thought it would come to that.' Alleyn wandered about the room. 'Davidson was right; it's a pleasant room.'

'The house belongs to an uncle of Lady Carrados, doesn't it?'

'Yes, General Marsdon. He would appear to be a fellow of taste. The Greuze is charming. And these enamels. Where's the offensive Cellini conversion, I wonder.' He bent over the pie-crust table. 'Nothing like it here. That's funny. Davidson said it was on this table, didn't he? It's neither here nor anywhere else in the room. Rum! Must have belonged to one of the guests. Nothing much in it. Still, we'd better check it. What a hellish bore! All through the guests again, unless we strike it lucky! François might have noticed it sometime when he was doing the ash-trays. Better ask him.'

He rang up François, who said he knew nothing of any stray cigarette-case. Alleyn sighed and took out his notes. Fox cruised solemnly about the top landing.

'Hi!' called Alleyn after ten minutes. 'Hi! Fox!'

'Hullo, sir?'

'I've been trying to piece these people's movements together. As far as I can see, it goes something like this. Now pay attention, because it's very muddly and half the time I won't know what I'm talking about. Some time during the supper interlude Lady Carrados left her bag in this room. François saw Dimitri collect it and go downstairs. Miss Troy, who was dancing with Bunchy, saw him return the bag to Lady Carrados in the ballroom. Miss Troy noticed it looked much emptier than before. We don't know if there were any witnesses to the actual moment when she left the bag, but it doesn't matter. Bunchy saw her receive it from Dimitri. At one o'clock he rang me up to say he had a strong line on the blackmailer and the crucial conversation took place. Now, according to François, there were four people who might have overheard this conversation. Withers, Donald Potter, Sir Herbert Carrados, and the colourless Miss Harris, who may or may not have been in the lavatory, but was certainly on this landing. Someone else may have come and gone while François was getting matches for the enraged Carrados. On François's return he went into the telephone-room and found it empty. Sounds easier when you condense it. All right. Our job is to find out if anyone else could have come upstairs, listened to the telephone, and gone down again while François was in the servants' quarters. Withers says he heard the telephone when he was in the other sitting-room. He also says Carrados was up here at that time so, liar though no doubt he is, it looks as if he spoke the truth about that. Come on, Fox, let's prowl.'

360

The gallery was typical of most large, old-fashioned London houses. The room with the telephone was at the far end, next it was a lavatory. This turned out to be a Victorian affair with a small ante-room and a general air of varnish and gloom. The inner door was half-panelled with thick clouded glass which let through a little murky daylight. Beyond it was a bedroom that had been used as a ladies' cloakroom and last, at the top of the stairs, the second sitting-out room. Beside the door of this room was another green baize door leading to servants' quarters and back stairs. The other side of the gallery was open and looked over the great well of the house. Alleyn leant on the balustrade and stared down the steep perspective of twisting stairs into the hall two storeys below.

'A good vantage spot this,' he said. 'We'll go down, now.'

On the next landing was the ballroom. Nothing could have looked more desolate than the great empty floor, the chairs that wore that disconcerting air of talking to each other, the musicians' platform, littered with cigarette butts and programmes. A fine dust lay over everything and the great room echoed to their footsteps. The walls sighed a little as though the air imprisoned behind them sought endlessly for escape. Alleyn and Fox hunted about but found nothing to help them and went down the great stairs to the hall.

'Here he stood,' said Alleyn, 'at the foot of the left-hand flight of stairs. Dimitri is not far off. Sir Daniel came out of the cloakroom over there on the left. The group of noisy young people was nearer the front entrance. And through this door, next the men's cloakroom, was the buffet. Let's have a look at it. You've seen all this before, Brer Fox, but you must allow me to maunder on.'

They went into the buffet.

'It stinks like a pot-house, doesn't it? Look at Dimitri's neat boxes of empty champagne bottles under the tables.

361

Gaiety at ten pounds a dozen. This is where Donald and Bridget came from in the penultimate scene and where Dimitri and Carrados spoke together just before Lord Robert left. And for how long afterwards? Look, Fox, here's a Sherlock Holmes touch. A cigar stump lying by a long trace of its own ash. A damn good cigar and has been carefully smoked. Here's the gentleman's glass beside it and here, on the floor, is the broken band. A Corona-Corona.' Alleyn sniffed at the glass. 'Brandy. Here's the bottle, Courvoisier '87. I'll wager that wasn't broadcast among the guests. More likely to have been kept for old Carrados. Fox, ring up Dimitri and find out if Sir Herbert drank brandy and smoked a cigar when he came in here after the party. And at the same time you might ask if we can see the Carrados family in about half an hour. Then we'll have to go on to the Halcut-Hackett group. Their house is close by here, Halkin Street. We'll have to come back. I want to see Carrados first. See if General and Mrs Halcut-Hackett will see us in about two hours, will you, Fox?'

Fox padded off to the telephone and Alleyn went through the second door of the buffet into a back passage. Here he found the butler's pantry. Dimitri's supper tray was still there. 'He did himself very well,' thought Alleyn, noticing three or four little green-black pellets on a smeared plate. 'Caviare. And here's the wing of a bird picked clean. Champagne, too. Sleek Mr Dimitri, eating away like a well-fed cat behind the scenes.'

He rejoined Fox in the hall. 'Mr Dimitri,' said Fox, 'remembered giving Sir Herbert Carrados brandy from a special bottle reserved for him. He thought that Sir Herbert smoked a cigar while he took his brandy, but would not swear to it.'

'We'd better print the brandy-glass,' said Alleyn. 'I'll get Bailey to attend to it and then, I think, they can clean up here. How did you get on?'

'All right, sir. The Halcut-Hacketts will see us any time later on this afternoon.'

'What about Carrados?'

'He came to the telephone,' said Fox. 'He'll see us if we go round now.'

'How did he sound? Bloody-minded?'

'If you like to put it that way, sir. He seemed to be sort of long-suffering, more than angry, I thought, and said something about hoping he knew his duty. He mentioned that he is a great personal friend of the chief commissioner.'

'Oh, Lord, Lord! Huff and grandeur! Uncertain, coy, and hard to please. Don't I know it. Fox, we must continue to combine deference with a suggestion of high office. Out with the best butter and lay it on in slabs. Miserable old article, he is. Straighten your tie, harden your heart, and away we go.'

Sir Herbert and Lady Carrados lived in Green Street. A footman opened the door to Alleyn.

'Sir Herbert is not at home, sir. Would you care to leave a message?'

'He has an appointment with me,' said Alleyn pleasantly, 'so I expect he is at home really. Here's my card.'

'I beg pardon, sir,' said the footman, looking at Alleyn's clothes, which were admirable. 'I understood it was the police who were calling.'

'We are the police,' said Alleyn.

Fox, who had been dealing with their taxi, advanced. The footman's eye lit on his bowler and boots.

'I beg pardon, sir,' he said, 'will you come this way, please?'

He showed them into a library. Three past Carradoses, full length, in oils, stared coldly into space from the walls. The firelight wavered on a multitude of books uniformly bound, behind glass doors. Sir Herbert, in staff-officer's uniform with shiny boots and wonderful breeches, appeared

363

in a group taken at Tunbridge Wells, the centre of his wartime activities. Alleyn looked at it closely, but the handsome face was as expressionless as the tightly-breeched knees which were separated by gloved hands resting with embarrassing importance on the inside of the thighs. A dumb photograph. It was flanked by two illuminated addresses of which Sir Herbert was the subject. A magnificent cigar box stood on a side table. Alleyn opened it and noted that the cigars were the brothers of the one that had been smoked in the buffet. He gently closed the lid and turned to inspect a miniature French writing-cabinet.

Fox, completely at his ease, stood like a rock in the middle of the room. He appeared to be lost in a mild abstraction, but he could have gone away and described the library with the accuracy of an expert far-gone in Pelmanism.

The door opened and Carrados came in. Alleyn found himself unaccountably reminded of bereaved royalty. Sir Herbert limped rather more perceptibly than usual and employed a black stick. He paused, screwed his glass in his eye, and said:

'Mr Alleyn?'

Alleyn stepped forward and bowed.

'It is extremely kind of you to see us, sir,' he said.

'No, no,' said Carrados, 'one must do one's duty however hard one is hit. One has to keep a stiff upper lip. I was talking to your chief commissioner just now, Mr Alleyn. He happens to be a very old friend of mine – er – won't you sit down both of you? Mr – er – ?'

'This is Inspector Fox, sir.'

'Oh, yes,' said Carrados, extending his hand. 'Do sit down, Fox. Yes – ' he turned again to Alleyn when they were all seated. 'Your CO tells me you are a son of another old friend. I knew your mother very well years ago and she sees quite a lot of my wife, I believe. She was at Marsdon

House last night.' He placed his hand over his eyes and repeated in an irritating whisper: 'At Marsdon House. Ah, well!'

Alleyn said: 'We are very sorry indeed, sir, to bother you after what has happened. This tragedy has been a great shock to you, I'm afraid.'

Carrados gave him an injured smile.

'Yes,' he said, 'I cannot pretend that it has not. Lord Robert was one of our dearest friends. Not only have we a great sense of personal bereavement but I cannot help thinking that my hospitality has been cruelly abused.'

This reduction of homicide to terms of the social amenities left Alleyn speechless. Sir Herbert appeared to regard murder as a sort of inexcusable *faux pas*.

'I suppose,' he continued, 'that you have come here armed with a list of questions. If that is so I am afraid you are doomed to disappointment. I am a simple soldier-man, Mr Alleyn, and this sort of thing is quite beyond my understanding. I may say that ever since this morning we have been pestered by a crew of insolent young pups from Fleet Street. I have been forced to ask Scotland Yard, where I believe my name is not unknown, if we had no redress from this sort of damnable persecution. I talked about it to your chief who, as I think I told you, is a personal friend of mine. He agrees with me that the behaviour of journalists nowadays is intolerable.'

'I am sorry you have been badgered,' said Alleyn. 'I will be as quick as I can with our business. There *are* one or two questions, I'm afraid, but only one or two and none of them at all formidable.'

'I can assure you I am not in the least afraid of police investigation,' said Carrados with an injured laugh. His hand still covered his eyes.

'Of course not, sir. I wanted first of all to ask you if you spoke to Lord Robert last night. I mean something more than hail and farewell. I thought that if there was

365

anything at all unusual in his manner it would not escape your notice as it would the notice of, I am afraid, the majority of people.'

Carrados looked slightly less huffy.

'I don't pretend to be any more observant than the next fellow,' he said, 'but as a soldier-man I've had to use my eyes a bit and I think if there's anything wrong anywhere I'm not likely to miss it. Yes, I spoke to Lord Robert Gospell once or twice last night and I can assure you he was perfectly normal in every possible way. He was nice enough to tell me he thought our ball the most successful of the season. Perfectly normal.'

Alleyn leant forward and fixed Carrados with a reverent glare.

'Sir Herbert,' he said, 'I'm going to do a very unconventional thing and I hope you won't get me my dismissal as I'm sure you very easily could. I'm going to take you wholly into our confidence.'

It was pleasant to see the trappings of sorrow fall softly away from Carrados, and to watch his posture change from that of a stricken soldier-man to an exact replica of the Tunbridge Wells photograph. Up came his head. The knees were spread apart, the hands went involuntarily to the inside of the thighs. Only the gloves and breeches were lacking. A wise son of Empire sat confessed.

'It would not be the first time,' said Carrados modestly, 'that confidence has been reposed in me.'

'I'm sure it wouldn't. This is our difficulty. We have reason to believe that the key to this mystery lies in a single sentence spoken by Lord Robert on the telephone from Marsdon House. If we could get a true report of the conversation that Lord Robert held with an unknown person at one o'clock this morning I believe we would have gone a long way towards making an arrest.'

'Ah!' Carrados positively beamed. 'This bears out my own theory, Mr Alleyn. It was an outside job. You see

366

I am conversant with your phraseology. From the moment we heard of this tragedy I said to my wife that I was perfectly satisfied that none of our guests could be in any way implicated. A telephone message from outside! There you are!'

'I had half-hoped,' said Alleyn modestly, 'that you might have heard about this call. I suppose it was stupid of me.'

'When was it?'

'At one o'clock. We've got so far.'

'At one o'clock. One o'clock. Let me see!' Carrados drew his heavy brows down over his foolish eyes and scowled importantly. 'At the moment I must confess I cannot quite recall – '

'Most of your guests were still at supper, I think,' said Alleyn. 'I've spoken to the servant on duty on the top landing and he fancies he can remember that you came upstairs round about that time.'

The purple veins in Sir Herbert's red cheeks suddenly started up.

'By God, I should think the fellow did remember, confound his impudence. Certainly, I went on to the top landing and it *was* one o'clock. You are perfectly right, Mr Alleyn. I pay these damn caterers a fortune to organize the whole affair and I expect, not unreasonably I hope, a certain standard of efficiency. And what do I find? No matches! No matches in the sitting-out room at the head of the stairs and the damn place smothered in ash. A lighted cigarette burning the mantelpiece! It was underneath the clock. That's how I remember the time. Just on one o'clock, as you say. I trust I'm a reasonable sort of fellow, Alleyn, but I don't mind telling you I saw red. I went out on to the landing and I gave that fellow a dressing-down he won't forget in a hurry. Sent him haring off downstairs with a flea in his ear. Damn, spoon-fed dago!'

'Were you on the landing all this time, sir?'

'Of course I wasn't on the landing all the time! I was

367

in and out of the blasted sitting-room, damn it. I went upstairs at, I suppose, about five to one, walked into this room and found it in the condition I've described. I would have looked at the other room, the one with the telephone, but I saw there was a couple sitting out in there. Behaving, I may say, more like a footman and a housemaid than the sort of people one is accustomed to receive as one's guests. However! The man came sneaking out just as I was blasting this damned waiter-fellow. He hung about the landing. This fellow Withers, I mean. Don't know if I gave you his name before. Then the lady came out and scuttled into the cloakroom. Yes, by God, sir, and Robert Gospell came upstairs and went into the telephone room.'

Carrados blew out his moustache triumphantly. 'There you are!' he said. 'Into the room to telephone.'

'Splendid, sir. Now may I just go over this to make sure I've got it right? You came out of the first sitting-room and spoke to the waiter. Captain Withers came out of the second room (the telephone-room) followed in a moment by Mrs Halcut-Hackett, who went into the cloakroom.'

'Here!' ejaculated Carrados, 'I didn't mention the lady's name, Alleyn. By God, I hope I know my manners better than to use a lady's name out of turn.'

Alleyn achieved an expression of gentlemanly cunning.

'I'm afraid, sir, I rather jumped to conclusions.'

'Really? D'you mean it's common talk? An American, wasn't she? Well, well, well, I'm sorry to hear that. Halcut-Hackett's a very old friend of mine. I'm very sorry to hear that.'

Alleyn reflected acidly that Sir Herbert was enjoying himself thoroughly and hurried on.

'At this moment, just as you return to the sitting-room, having sent the waiter downstairs, and Mrs Halcut-Hackett dives into the cloakroom, Lord Robert comes upstairs. What does Withers do?'

'Sheers off and comes sloping into the sitting-room after me. I had to make conversation with the fellow. Young Potter was sulking about in there too. I hope I've got as much tolerance for the youngsters as any other old fogey, Alleyn, but I must confess I – '

He stopped and looked uncomfortable.

'Yes?' murmured Alleyn.

'I – it doesn't matter. Stick to the point, eh? Withers, eh? Yes. Well now, I flatter myself, Alleyn, that I can get along with most people, but I freely confess I did not enjoy Withers's company. Calls himself Captain. What was his regiment?'

'I don't know at all. Could you, by any chance, hear Lord Robert from the other room?'

'No. No, I couldn't. Now you mention it, I believe I heard the extension bell doing that damned dialling tinkle. The fact is I couldn't stand any more of that confounded outsider's conversation. I made my excuses and went downstairs.'

'Did you meet anybody coming up?'

'I don't think so. Mrs Halcut-Hackett was going down ahead of me.'

'So while you were still in the sitting-room, sir, anybody might have come upstairs and gone into the room where Lord Robert sat telephoning?'

'I suppose so.'

'Mrs Halcut-Hackett might have gone in before you went downstairs. Captain Withers or Donald Potter might have done it afterwards?'

'Yes, by Gad, they might. If you want to get an account of this telephone conversation you might ask 'em. I don't like to make the suggestion about one of my guests, but upon my soul I wouldn't put it past Withers to listen to a private conversation. What's young Potter doing, cottoning on to a cad twenty years his senior, I'd like to know? However! Anything more?'

'Yes, sir. Did you by any chance notice a Miss Harris while you were upstairs? The man said something – '

'Harris? D'you mean m'wife's secretary? Yes, of course I saw her. She bolted into the lavatory when I came up. I didn't see her come out.'

'I see. Perhaps I might have a word with her before I go.'

'Certainly, but you'll find her a bit difficult. She's a shy little thing – pity there aren't more like her. Nowadays they don't give a damn who sees them coming out of any door.'

Sir Herbert suddenly made up his mind he had said something amusing and broke into loud baying laughter in which Alleyn was careful to join.

'Poor little Harris,' Carrados said. 'Well, well, well!'

'Now,' continued Alleyn when the laughter had died away, 'about the end of the ball. We would like to trace Lord Robert's movements, of course. I don't know, sir, if you can give us any help at all.'

'Ah! Yes. Well, let me see. My wife and I stood on the ballroom gallery at the head of the stairs saying good-bye to our guests – those of them who were old-fashioned enough to think it necessary to thank their hosts. Some of the young cubs didn't take the trouble, I may tell you. Lord Robert came, of course, and was perfectly charming. Let me see, now. He went downstairs, into the cloakroom and out again wearing that extraordinary cloak of his. I remember this because I came down and passed him. I went into the buffet.'

'Did you come out again before Lord Robert left?'

'No.' Carrados returned for a moment to the stricken soldier-man. 'No. That was the last I shall ever see of Robert Gospell. Ah, well! I don't mind admitting, Alleyn, that this thing has hit me pretty hard. Pretty hard! Still, we've got to bite on the bullet, haven't we? What were we saying?

370

Oh yes. I stayed in the buffet for some time. I don't mind admitting I was about all in. I smoked a cigar and had a peg of brandy. I had a word with that fellow Dimitri and then I went home.'

'With Lady Carrados and Miss O'Brien?'

'What? No. No, I packed them off earlier in the other car. My wife was absolutely fagged out. I wanted to have a look round. Make sure everything was all right. I wouldn't trust anybody else. These people are so damned careless, leaving lighted cigarettes all over the place. I satisfied myself everything was all right and then I went home. The chauffeur came back for me. Daresay you'd like to see him.'

'No, sir, thank you. I think we may take that as read.'

'I've no wish to be treated differently from anyone else, but that's as you please, of course. Anything else?'

'If I might have a word with Lady Carrados, sir?'

'I don't think my wife can give you any information, Alleyn. She's absolutely prostrated by this business. Robert Gospell was a very great friend of hers and she's taken it damn hard. Matter of fact, she's not up.'

Alleyn paused.

'I am so sorry,' he said at last. 'That's most unfortunate. I wanted if possible to save her appearing at the inquest.'

'When is the inquest?'

'Tomorrow morning, sir.'

Carrados glared at him.

'She will certainly be too unwell for any such thing. I shall see that her doctor forbids it. And it is equally impossible for her to see you this afternoon. I know that if I were to disturb her, which I have no intention of doing as she is asleep in bed, she would refuse. That's definite.'

The door opened and the footman came in.

'Her ladyship, sir, wishes me to say that if Mr Alleyn

has a few minutes to spare she would be very pleased to see him.'

He waited, gently closing the door on an extremely uncomfortable silence.

CHAPTER SIXTEEN

Lady Carrados Looks Back

Alleyn followed the footman upstairs, leaving Fox in the library to make the best of a sticky situation.

The footman handed Alleyn over to a maid who took him to Lady Carrados. She was not in bed. She was in her boudoir erect in a tall blue chair and wearing the look that had prompted Paddy O'Brien to compare her with a Madonna. She held out her hands when she saw Alleyn and as he took them a phrase came into his mind. He thought: 'She is an English lady and these are an English lady's hands, thin, unsensual, on the end of delicate thin arms.'

She said: 'Roderick! I do call you Roderick, don't I?'

Alleyn said: 'I hope so. It's a long time since we met, Evelyn.'

'Too long. Your mother tells me about you sometimes. We spoke to each other today on the telephone. She was so very kind and understanding, Roderick, and she told me that you would be too. Do sit down and smoke. I should like to feel that you are not a great detective but an old friend.'

'I should like to feel that too,' said Alleyn. 'I must tell you, Evelyn, that I was on the point of asking to see you when I got your message.'

'An official call?'

'Yes, bad luck to it. You've made everything much pleasanter by asking for me.'

She pressed the thin hands together and Alleyn, noticing the bluish lights on the knuckles, remembered how Troy had wanted to paint them.

Lady Carrados said, 'I suppose Herbert didn't want you to see me?'

'He wasn't very pleased with the idea. He thought you were too tired and distressed.'

She smiled faintly: 'Yes,' she said, and it was impossible to be sure that she spoke ironically. 'Yes, he is very thoughtful. What do you want to ask me, Roderick?'

'All sorts of dreary questions, I'm afraid. I'm sorry about it. I know you were one of Bunchy's friends.'

'So were you.'

'Yes.'

'What is your first question?'

Alleyn went over the final scene in the hall and found she had nothing new to tell him. She answered him quickly and concisely. He could see that his questions held no particular significance for her and that her thoughts were lying in wait, anxiously, for what was yet to come. As soon as he began to speak of the green room on the top landing he knew that he touched her more nearly. He felt a profound distaste for his task. He went on steadily, without emphasis.

'The green sitting-room with the telephone. We know that he used the telephone and are anxious to find out if he was overheard. Someone says you left your bag there, Evelyn. Did you?'

'Yes.'

'Dimitri returned it to you?'

'Yes.'

'When was this?'

'Soon after I had come up from supper – about half-past twelve or a quarter to one.'

'Not as late as one o'clock?'

'No.'

'Why are you so certain of this, please?'

'Because,' said Lady Carrados, 'I was watching the time rather carefully.'

'Were you? Does the peak of a successful ball come at a specific moment?'

'Well, one rather watches the time. If they don't begin to drift away after supper it looks as if it will be a success.'

'Where were you when Dimitri returned your bag?'

'In the ballroom.'

'Did you notice Bunchy at about this time?'

'I – don't think – I remember.'

The hands were pressed closer together as if she held her secret between them; as if it might escape. Her lips were quite white.

The door opened and Bridget came in. She looked as if she had been crying.

'Oh, Donna,' she said, 'I'm sorry, I didn't know – '

'This is my girl, Roderick. Bridget, this is Sarah's uncle.'

'How do you do,' said Bridget. 'The detective one?'

'The detective one.'

'Sarah says you're quite human really.'

'That's very kind of Sarah,' said her uncle drily.

'I hope you're not heckling my mother,' said Bridget, sitting on the arm of the chair. She had an air of determined sprightliness.

'I'm trying not to. Perhaps you could help us both. We are talking about last night.'

'Well, I might be able to tell you something frightfully important without knowing it myself, sort of, mightn't I?'

'It's happened before now,' said Alleyn with a smile. 'We were talking about your mother's bag.'

'The one she left upstairs and that I found?'

'Bridgie!' whispered Lady Carrados. 'Oh, Bridgie!'

'It's all right, Donna, my sweet. That had nothing to do with Bunchy. Oh – he was there, wasn't he? In the supper-room when I brought it to you?'

Bridget, perched on the arm of the wing chair, could not see her mother's face and Alleyn thought: 'Now we're in for it.'

375

He said: '*You* returned the bag in the *supper-room*, did you?'

Lady Carrados suddenly leant back and closed her eyes.

'Yes,' Bridget said, 'and it was simply squashed full of money. But why the bag? Does it fit somewhere frightfully subtle? I mean was the motive really money and did the murderer think Donna gave Bunchy the money, sort of? Or something?'

Lady Carrados said: 'Bridgie, darling. I'm by way of talking privately to Mr Alleyn.'

'Oh, are you, darling? I'm sorry. I'll whizz off. Shall I see you again before you go, Mr Alleyn?'

'Please, Miss Bridget.'

'Well, come along to the old nursery. I'll be there.'

Bridget looked round the corner of the chair at her mother, who actually managed to give her a smile. She went out and Lady Carrados covered her face with her hands.

'Don't try to tell me, Evelyn,' said Alleyn gently. 'I'll see if I can tell you. Come now, it may not be so dreadful, after all. Listen. Someone has been blackmailing you. You have had letters written in script on Woolworth paper. One of them came on the morning Bunchy brought you spring flowers. You put it under your pillow. Last night you left your bag in the green room, because you had been told to leave it there. It contained the money the blackmailer demanded. It now appears that Bridget returned your bag, still full of notes, while you were in the supper-room with Bunchy. Did you replace it in the green sitting-room? You did . . . and later it was returned to you, empty – while you were in the ballroom?'

'But – you *know* all this! Roderick, do you also know what they have found out?'

'No. I have no idea what they found out. Had Bunchy?'

'That is what horrifies me. Bunchy knew, at least, that I was being persecuted. When Bridgie brought back that

376

hideous bag last night I nearly collapsed. I can't tell you what a shock it was to me. You are quite right, a letter, like the one you described, came a few days ago. There had been others. I didn't answer them. I destroyed them all and tried to put them out of my mind. I thought perhaps they wouldn't go on with it if I paid no attention. But this one threatened dreadful things, things that would hurt Bridgie so much – so much. It said that if I didn't do as I was ordered Herbert and Bridgie would be told about – everything. I couldn't face that. I did what they said. I put five hundred pounds in green notes in the bag and left it on the little table in the green sitting-room before one o'clock. And then Bridgie must have seen it. I shall never forget her coming into the supper-room, laughing and holding out that bag. I suppose I must have looked frightful. It's all muddled in my mind now, like the memory of a terrible dream. Somehow we got rid of Bridgie. Bunchy must have been splendid. Sir Daniel Davidson was there. I've been to see him lately about my health and he had said something to me before that evening. I got rid of him, too, and then Bunchy and I went out into the hall and Bunchy said he knew what I wanted to do with my bag and begged me not to do it. I was frantic. I broke away from him and went back again to the green sitting-room. Nobody was there. I put the bag back on the table. It was then twenty to one. I put it behind a big ormolu and enamel box on the table. Then I went down to the ballroom. I don't know how much later it was when I saw Dimitri coming through the room with the bag. At first I thought the same thing had happened again, but when I took it in my hand I knew the money had gone. Dimitri had found the bag, he said, and recognized it as mine. That's all.'

'That's all,' repeated Alleyn. 'It's a good deal. Look here, Evelyn, I'm going to ask you point-blank, is it possible that Dimitri is the man who is blackmailing you?'

'Dimitri!' Her eyes opened wide. 'Good heavens, no! No, no, it's out of the question. He couldn't possibly have any idea, any means of knowing. Not possibly.'

'Are you sure of that? He is in and out of people's houses and has free access to their rooms. He has opportunities of overhearing conversations, of watching people when they are off their guard.'

'How long has he been doing this work?'

'He told me seven years.'

'My secret is more than twice as old as that. "Lady Audley's Secret"! But it's not so amusing, Roderick, when you carry it about with you. And yet, do you know, there have been times when I have almost forgotten my secret. It all happened so very long ago. The years have sifted past and mounted like sand into smooth unremarkable shapes and they have gradually hidden the old times. I thought I should never be able to speak of this to anyone in the world, but, oddly enough, it is rather a relief to talk about it.'

'You realize, don't you, that I am here to investigate a murder? It's my job to work out the circumstances surrounding it. I must have no consideration for anybody's feelings if they come between me and the end of the job. Bunchy knew you were the victim of a blackmailer. You are not the only victim. He was actually working with us on information we had from another source but which points directly to the same individual. It's quite possible, and to us it seems probable, that the blackmailing may be linked with the murder. So we have a double incentive to get at the blackmailer's identity.'

'I know what you are going to ask me. I have no idea who it is. None. I've asked myself over and over again who it could be.'

'Yes. Now see here, Evelyn, I could get up to all the old tricks, and with any luck I'd probably get a line on this secret of yours. I'd trap you into little admissions and

378

when I got away from here I'd write them all down, add them up, and see what I could make of the answer. Probably there wouldn't be an answer so we'd begin to dig and dig. Back through those years that have sifted over your trouble and hidden it. And sooner or later we would find something. It would all be very disagreeable and I should hate it and the final result would be exactly the same as if you told me your whole story now.'

'I can't. I can't tell you.'

'You are thinking of the consequences. Newspaper publicity. Court proceedings. You know it wouldn't be nearly as bad as you imagine. Your name would probably never appear.'

'Madame X,' said Lady Carrados with a faint smile, 'and everybody in court knowing perfectly well who I was. Oh, it's not for myself I mind. It's Bridgie. And Herbert. You've met Herbert and you must realize how he'd take a blow of this sort. I can think of nobody who would mind more.'

'And how is he going to take it if we find out for ourselves? Evelyn, think! You're one of Bunchy's friends.'

'I'm not a revengeful woman.'

'Good God, it's not a question of revenge. It's a question of leaving a blackmailing murderer at large.'

'You needn't go on, Roderick. I know quite well what I ought to do.'

'And I know quite well that you're going to do it.'

They looked squarely at each other. Her hands made a gesture of surrender.

'Very well,' said Lady Carrados. 'I give in. How much more dignified it would have been, wouldn't it, if I had accepted my duty at first?'

'I had no doubt about what you'd do. It's quite possible, you know, that your side of the business need never come out. Of course, I can't promise this, but it is possible we'll work on your information without putting it in as evidence.'

'That's very kind of you,' she said faintly.

'You're being ironical,' said Alleyn with a grin, 'and that shows you're not going to mind as much as you feared, or I hope it does. Now then. It's something about Bridget, isn't it, and it happened more than fourteen years ago. Bridget's how old? Seventeen?'

Lady Carrados nodded.

'I don't believe I ever met your first husband, Evelyn. Is Bridget very like him?'

'Yes. She's got all Paddy's gaiety.'

'My mother told me that. Bridget doesn't remember him, of course. Ought we to begin with him?'

'Yes. You needn't go on being delicate, Roderick. I think you've guessed, haven't you? Paddy and I were not married.'

'Bless my soul,' said Alleyn, 'how very courageous of you, Evelyn.'

'I think it was now but it didn't seem so then. Nobody knew. It's the *Jane Eyre* theme but I hadn't Miss Eyre's moral integrity. Paddy left a wife in an Australian lunatic asylum, came home, and fell in love with me. As you would say in your report, we went through a form of marriage and lived happily and bigamously together. Then Paddy died.'

'Weren't you afraid it would come out?'

'No. Paddy's wife had no relations.' Lady Carrados waited for a moment. She seemed to be gravely contemplating the story she had decided to relate. When she spoke again it was with composure and even, or so Alleyn fancied, an air of relaxation. He wondered if she had often marshalled the facts in her own mind and rehearsed her story to an imaginary listener. The quiet voice went on sedately: 'She was a music-hall comedienne who had been left stranded in a little town in New South Wales. He married her there and took her to Sydney. Six weeks later she became hopelessly insane. He found out that her mother was in a lunatic asylum somewhere in America.

380

Paddy had not told anybody of his marriage and he had not looked up any of his acquaintances in Sydney. When he arranged to have her put away it was under her maiden name. He invested a sum of money, the interest on which was enough to pay the fees and expenses. He left the whole thing in the hands of the only man who knew the truth. He was Anthony Banks, Paddy's greatest friend, and was absolutely above suspicion, I am sure. He lived in Sydney and helped Paddy all through that time. He held Paddy's power of attorney. Even he did not know Paddy had remarried. Nobody knew that.'

'What about the parson who married them?'

'I remember that Paddy said he was a very old man. The witnesses were his wife and sister. You see, we talked it all over very carefully and Paddy was quite certain there was no possibility of discovery.'

'There is something more, isn't there?'

'Yes. Something that I find much more difficult.' The even voice faltered for a moment. Alleyn saw that she mustered up all her fortitude before she went on. 'Five months after we were married he was killed. I had started Bridgie and came up to London to stay with my mother and to see my doctor. Paddy was to motor up from our house at Ripplecote and drive me back. In the morning I had a telegram from him. It said: 'The best possible news from Anthony Banks.' On the way the car skidded and crashed into the wall of a bridge. It was in a little village. He was taken into the vicarage and then to the cottage hospital. When I got there he was unconscious and he didn't know that I was with him when he died.'

'And the news?'

'I felt certain that it could only be one thing. His wife must have died. But we could find no letters or cables at all, so he must have destroyed whatever message he had been sent by Anthony Banks. The next thing that happened was that Paddy's solicitors received five thousand pounds from Australia and a letter from Anthony Banks to say it was forwarded in accordance with Paddy's instructions. In the meantime I had written to Anthony Banks. I told him of Paddy's death but wrote as a cousin of Paddy's. He replied with the usual sort of letter. He didn't, of course, say anything about Paddy's wife, but he did say that a letter from him must have reached Paddy just before he died and that if it had been found he would like it to be destroyed unopened. You see, Roderick, Anthony Banks must have been honest because he could have kept that five thousand pounds himself quite easily, when she died. And he didn't know Paddy had remarried.'

'Yes, that's quite true. Are you certain from what you knew of Paddy that he would have destroyed Banks's letter?'

'No. I've always thought he would have kept it to show me.'

'Do you think he asked the people in the vicarage or at the hospital to destroy his letters?'

'They had found his name and address on other letters in his wallet, so it wasn't that.' For the first time the quiet voice faltered a little. 'He only spoke once, they said. He asked for me.'

'Do you remember the name of the people at the vicarage?'

'I don't. I wrote and thanked them for what they had done. It was some very ordinary sort of name.'

'And the cottage hospital?'

'It was at Falconbridge in Buckinghamshire. Quite a big hospital. I saw the superintendent doctor. He was an elderly man with a face like a sheep. I think his name was Bletherley. I'm perfectly certain that he was not a blackmailer, Roderick. And the nurses were charming.'

'Do you think that he could possibly have left the letter in the case, or that it could have dropped out of his pocket?'

'I simply cannot believe that if he kept it at all it would be anywhere but in his wallet. And I was given the wallet.

382

It was in the breast pocket of his coat. You see, Roderick, it's not as if I didn't try to trace the letter. I was desperately anxious to see the message from Anthony Banks. I asked again and again if anything could have been overlooked at the hospital and endless enquiries were made.'

She stopped for a moment and looked steadily at Alleyn.

'You can see now,' she said, 'why I would go almost to any length to keep this from Bridget.'

'Yes,' said Alleyn, 'I can see.'

CHAPTER SEVENTEEN

The Element of Youth

Alleyn saw Bridget in her old nursery which had been converted into a very human sitting-room. She made him take a large armchair and jiggled a box of cigarettes under his nose.

'It's no good being official and pretending you don't. I can see you do.'

'Really!' exclaimed Alleyn with a look at his fingers which were not stained with nicotine. 'How?'

'The outline of your case shows through your coat. You should take up detection, Mr Alleyn, it's *too* interesting.'

Alleyn took a cigarette.

'Got me there,' he said. 'Have you yourself any ideas about being a policewoman?' He fingered the outline that showed through his breast-pocket.

'I suppose one has to begin at the bottom,' said Bridget. 'What's the first duty of a policewoman?'

'I don't know. We are not allowed to hang around the girls in the force.'

'What a shame!' said Bridget. 'I won't join. I should like you to hang round me, Mr Alleyn.'

Alleyn thought: 'She's being just a bit too deliberately the audacious young charmer. What's up with her? Young Donald, damn his eyes!'

He said: 'Well, so I must for the moment. I want to talk to you about last night, if I may.'

'I'm afraid I won't be much good,' said Bridget. 'I hope you find whoever it was. It's worrying Donna to death, and Bart's being absolutely lethal over it. Bart's my stepfather. You've met him, haven't you? All pukka sahib

384

and horsewhips. Is a horsewhip any worse than an ordinary one, do you know?'

'You knew Lord Robert pretty well, didn't you?' asked Alleyn.

'Yes. He was a great friend of Donna's. I suppose you think I'm being hard and modern about him. I'd have been sorrier if it had happened longer ago.'

'That's rather cryptic,' said Alleyn. 'What does it mean?'

'It doesn't mean I'm not sorry now. I am. We all loved him and I mind most dreadfully. But I found out I didn't really know him well. He was harder than you'd ever believe. In a way that makes it worse; having been out of friends with him. I feel I'd give anything to be able to tell him I – I – I – I'm sorry.'

'Sorry for what?'

'For not being nice to him last night. I snubbed him.'

'Why did you snub poor Bunchy?'

'Because he was beastly to his nephew who happens to be rather a particular friend of mine.'

'Donald Potter? Yes, I know about that. Don't you think it's possible that Donald was rather hard on his uncle?'

'No, I don't. Donald's a man now. He's got to stand on his own feet and decide things for himself. Bunchy simply wouldn't understand that. He wanted to choose Donald's friends, settle his career, and treat him exactly as if he was a schoolboy. Bunchy was just hopelessly Victorian and conventional.'

'Do you like Captain Withers?' asked Alleyn suddenly.

'What?' Bridget became rather pink. 'I can't say he's exactly my cup of tea. I suppose he is rather ghastly in a way, but he's a marvellous dancer and he can be quite fun. I can forgive anybody almost anything if they're amusing, can't you?'

'What sort of amusement does Captain Withers provide?'

'Well, I mean he's gay. Not exactly gay but he goes everywhere and everybody knows him, so he's always quite good value. Donald says Wits is a terribly good business man. He's been frightfully nice about advising Donald and he knows all sorts of people who could be useful.'

'Useful in what way? Donald is going in for medicine, isn't he?'

'Well – ' Bridget hesitated. 'Yes. That was the original idea, but Wits rather advises him not to. Donald says there's not much in medicine nowadays and, anyway, a doctor is rather a dreary sort of thing to be.'

'Is he?' asked Alleyn. 'You mean not very smart?'

'No, of course I don't mean that,' said Bridget. She glared at Alleyn. 'You *are* a pig,' she said. 'I suppose I do. I hate drab, worthy sort of things and, anyway, it's got nothing to with the case.'

'I should like to know what career Captain Withers has suggested for Donald.'

'There's nothing definite yet. They've thought of starting a new night club. Wits has got wonderfully original ideas.'

'Yes,' agreed Alleyn. 'I can quite imagine it. He's doing quite well with the place at Leatherhead, isn't he? Why doesn't he take Donald in there?'

Bridget looked surprised.

'How did you know about that?' she asked.

'You must never say that to policemen,' said Alleyn. 'It steals their thunder. As a matter of fact, I have been talking to Withers and the Leatherhead venture cropped up.'

'Well, I dare say you know more about it than I do,' said Bridget. 'Donald says it's just a small men's club. More for fun than to make money. They play bridge and things. I don't think there's any opening there.'

'Have you spoken to Donald since his uncle died?'

Bridget clenched her hands and thumped them angrily on her knees.

'Of course, he rang me up. I'd just got to the telephone when Bart came in looking like a beastly old Cochin China

386

rooster and took the receiver from me. I could have killed him, he was so infuriating! He was all sort of patient and old-world. He sympathized with Donald and then he said: 'If you don't mind old fellow speaking frankly, I think it would be better if you didn't communicate with my step-daughter for the time being!' I said: 'No! Give it to me,' but he simply turned his back on me and went on: 'You understand. I'm afraid I must forbid it,' and put the receiver down. I stormed at him but we were in Donna's room and she was so upset I had to give in and promise I wouldn't write or anything. It's so beastly, *beastly* unfair. And it's all because Bart's such a filthy old snob and is afraid of all the reporters and scandal and everything. Horrid bogus old man. And he's absolutely *filthy* to darling Donna. How she ever married him! After daddy, who must have been so gay, and charming, and who loved her so much. How she could! And if Bart thinks I'm going to give Donald up he's jolly well got another think coming.'

'Are you engaged?'

'No. We're waiting till Donald begins to earn.'

'And how much must Donald earn before he is marriageable?'

'You don't put it very nicely, do you? I suppose you think I'm hard and modern and beastly. I dare say I am, but I can't bear the idea of everything getting squalid and drab because we have to worry about money. A horrid little flat, second-rate restaurants, whitewood furniture painted to look fresh and nice. Ugh! I've seen these sorts of marriages,' said Bridget looking worldly-wise, 'and I *know*.'

'Donald is his uncle's heir, you know.'

Bridget was on her feet, her eyes flashing.

'Don't you dare,' she said, 'don't you dare to say that because Donald gets the money he had anything to do with this. Don't you dare.'

'And don't you go putting ideas into people's heads by

387

getting on the defensive before you've been given cause,' said Alleyn very firmly indeed. He put his hand inside his breast-pocket. The slight bulge disappeared and out came Alleyn's notebook. In the midst of her fury Bridget's glance fell on it. She looked from the notebook to Alleyn. He raised one eyebrow and screwed his face into an apologetic grimace.

'The idea was perfectly magnificent,' he said. 'It did look like a cigarette-case. The edges of the bulge weren't quite sharp enough.'

'Pig!' said Bridget.

'Sorry,' said Alleyn. 'Now then. Three or four offical questions, if you please. And look here, Miss Bridget, will you let me offer you a very dreary piece of advice? It's our set-piece for innocent witnesses. Don't prevaricate. Don't lose your temper. And don't try any downright thumping lies, because if you do, as sure as eggs is eggs, you'll be caught out and it'll look very nasty indeed for anyone whom you thought you were going to protect. You think Donald is innocent, don't you?'

'I *know* he is innocent.'

'Right. Then you have nothing in the wide world to fear. Away we go. Did you sit out in the green sitting-room on the top gallery?'

'Yes. Lots of times.'

'During the supper hour? Between twelve and one?'

Bridget pondered. As he watched her Alleyn looked back at youth and marvelled at its buoyancy. Bridget's mind bounced from thoughts of death to thoughts of love. She was sorry Bunchy was murdered, but as long as Donald was not suspected she was also rather thrilled at the idea of police investigation. She was sincerely concerned at her mother's distress and ready to make sacrifices on Lady Carrados's behalf. But ready to meet all sorrow, anger or fright was her youth, like a sort of pneumatic armour that received momentary impressions of these things but

388

instantly filled out again. Now, when she came to her
mother's indisposition she spoke soberly, but it was
impossible to escape the impression that on the whole she
was stimulated rather than unnerved by tragedy.

'I was up there with Donald until after most people had
gone into the supper-room. We both came down together.
That was when I returned her bag to Donna. Donna wasn't
well. She's awfully tired. She nearly fainted when I found
her in the supper-room. She said afterwards it was the
stuffiness.'

'Yes?'

'It was a queer sort of night, hot indoors, but when
any of the windows were opened the mist came in and
it brought a kind of dank chilliness. Donna asked me to
fetch her smelling-salts. I ran upstairs to the ladies'
cloakroom. Donna's maid Sophie was there. I got the
smelling-salts from Sophie and ran downstairs. I couldn't
find Donna but I ran into Bunchy who said she was all
right again. I had booked that dance with Percy Percival.
He was a bit drunk and was making a scene about my
having cut him out. So I danced with him to keep him
quiet.'

'Did you go up to the green sitting-room again?'

'Not for some time. Donald and I went up there towards
the end of the party.'

'Did you at any stage of the proceedings leave your
cigarette-case on the pie-crust table in that room?'

Bridget stared at him.

'I haven't got a cigarette-case; I don't smoke. Is there
something about a cigarette-case in the green sitting-room?'

'There may be. Do you know if anybody overheard
Bunchy telephone from that room at about one o'clock?'

'I haven't heard of it,' said Bridget. He saw that her
curiosity was aroused. 'Have you asked Miss Harris?' she
said. 'She was on the top landing a good deal last night.
She's somewhere in the house now.'

'I'll have a word with her. There's just one other point. Lord Robert was with your mother when you returned her bag, wasn't he? He was there when she felt faint?'

'Yes. Why?'

'Did he seem upset in any way?'

'He seemed very concerned about Donna but that was all. Sir Daniel – Donna's doctor – came up. Bunchy opened a window. They all seemed to want me out of the way. Donna asked for her smelling-salts, so I went and got them. That's all. What about a cigarette-case? Do tell me.'

'It's gold with a medallion sunk in the lid and surrounded by brilliants. Do you know it?'

'It sounds horribly grand. No, I don't think I do.'

Alleyn got up.

'That's all, then,' he said. 'Thank you so much, Miss Bridget. Good-bye.' He had got as far as the door before she stopped him.

'Mr Alleyn!'

'Yes?'

She was standing very erect in the middle of the room, her chin up and a lock of hair falling across her forehead.

'You seem to be very interested in the fact that my mother was not well last night. Why?'

'Lord Robert was with her at the time – ' Alleyn began.

'You seem equally interested in the fact that I returned my mother's bag to her. Why? Neither of these incidents had anything to do with Bunchy Gospell. My mother's not well and I won't have her worried.'

'Quite right,' said Alleyn. 'I won't either if I can help it.'

She seemed to accept that, but he could see that she had something else to say. Her young, beautifully made-up face in its frame of careful curls had a frightened look.

'I want you to tell me,' said Bridget, 'if you suspect Donald of anything.'

'It is much too soon for us to form any definite suspicion

390

of anybody,' Alleyn said. 'You shouldn't attach too much significance to any one question in police interrogations. Many of our questions are nothing but routine. As Lord Robert's heir – no, don't storm at me again, you asked me and I tell you – as Lord Robert's heir Donald is bound to come in for his share of questions. If you are worrying about him, and I see you are, may I give you a tip? Encourage him to return to medicine. If he starts running night clubs the chances are that sooner or later he will fall into our clutches. And then what?'

'Of course,' said Bridget thoughtfully, 'it'll be different now. We could get married quite soon, even if he was at a hospital or something all day. He will have *some* money.'

'Yes,' agreed Alleyn, 'yes.'

'I mean I don't want to be heartless,' continued Bridget looking at him quite frankly, 'but naturally one can't help thinking of that. We're terribly, terribly sorry about Bunchy. We couldn't be sorrier. But he wasn't young like us.'

Into Alleyn's mind came suddenly the memory of a thinning head, leant sideways, of fat hands, of small feet turned inwards.

'No,' he said, 'he wasn't young like you.'

'I think he was stupid and tiresome over Donald,' Bridget went on in a high voice, 'and I'm not going to pretend I don't, although I am sorry I wasn't friends with him last night. But all the same I don't believe he'd have minded us thinking about the difference the money would make. I believe he would have understood that.'

'I'm sure he would have understood.'

'Well then, don't look as if you're thinking I'm hard and beastly.'

'I don't think you're beastly and I don't believe you are really very hard.'

'Thank you for nothing,' said Bridget and added immediately: 'Oh, damn, I'm sorry.'

'That's all right,' said Alleyn. 'Good-bye.'

'Yes, but – '

'Well?'

'Nothing. Only, you make me feel shabby and it's not fair. If there was anything I could do for Bunchy I'd do it. So would Donald, of course. But he's dead. You can't do anything for dead people.'

'If they have been murdered you can try to catch the man that killed them.'

' "An eye for an eye." It doesn't do them any good. It's only savagery.'

'Let the murderer asphyxiate someone else if it's going to suit his book,' said Alleyn. 'Is that the idea?'

'If there was any real thing we could do – '

'How about Donald doing what his uncle wanted so much? Taking his medical? That is,' said Alleyn quickly, 'unless he really has got a genuine ambition in another direction. Not by way of Captain Withers's night clubs.'

'I've just said he might be a doctor, now, haven't I?'

'Yes,' said Alleyn, 'you have. So we're talking in circles.' His hand was on the door-knob.

'I should have thought,' said Bridget, 'that as a detective you would have wanted to make me talk.'

Alleyn laughed outright.

'You little egoist,' he said, 'I've listened to you for the last ten minutes and all you want to talk about is yourself and your young man. Quite right too, but not the policeman's cup of tea. You take care of your mother who needs you rather badly just now, encourage your young man to renew his studies and, if you can, wean him from Withers. Good-bye, now, I'm off.'

CHAPTER EIGHTEEN

Predicament of a Secretary

When he had closed the nursery door behind him, Alleyn made for the stairs. If Fox was still closeted in the library with Carrados conversation must be getting a bit strained. He passed Lady Carrados's room and heard a distant noise.

'It's insufferable, my dear Evelyn, that – '

Alleyn grimaced and went on downstairs.

He found Fox alone in the library.

'Hullo, Brer Fox,' said Alleyn. 'Lost the simple soldier-man?'

'Gone upstairs,' said Fox. 'I can't say I'm sorry. I had a job to keep him here at all after you went.'

'How did you manage it?'

'Asked him if he had any experience of police investigation. That did it. We went from there to how he helped the police catch a footman that stole somebody's pearls in Tunbridge and how if he just hadn't happened to notice the man watching the vase on the piano nobody would ever have thought of looking in the Duchess's pot-pourri. Funny how vain some of these old gentlemen get, isn't it?'

'Screamingly. As we seem to have this important room all to ourselves we'd better see if we can get hold of Miss Harris. You might go and ask – '

But before Fox got as far as the door it opened and Miss Harris herself walked in.

'Good afternoon,' she said crisply, 'I believe you wished to see me. Lady Carrados's secretary.'

'We were on the point of asking for you, Miss Harris,' said Alleyn. 'Won't you sit down? My name is Alleyn and this is Inspector Fox.'

393

'Good afternoon,' repeated Miss Harris and sat down.

She was neither plain nor beautiful, short nor tall, dark nor fair. It crossed his mind that she might have won a newspaper competition for the average woman, that she represented the dead norm of femininity. Her clothes were perfectly adequate and completely without character. She was steeped in nonentity. No wonder that few people had noticed her at Marsdon House. She might have gone everywhere, heard everything like a sort of upper middle-class Oberon at Theseus's party. Unless, indeed, nonentity itself was conspicuous at Marsdon House last night.

He noticed that she was not in the least nervous. Her hands rested quietly in her lap. She had laid a pad and pencil on the arm of her chair exactly as if she was about to take notes at his dictation. Fox took his own notebook out and waited.

'May we have your name and address?' asked Alleyn.

'Certainly, Mr Alleyn,' said Miss Harris crisply. 'Dorothea Violet Harris. Address – town or country?'

'Both, please.'

'Town: fifty-seven Ebury Mews, S.W. Country: The Rectory, Barbicon-Bramley, Bucks.' She glanced at Fox. 'B-a-r-b-i – '

'Thank you, miss, I think I've got it,' said Fox.

'Now, Miss Harris,' Alleyn began, 'I wonder if you can give me any help at all in this business.'

To his tense astonishment Miss Harris at once opened her pad on which he could see a column of shorthand hieroglyphics. She drew out from her bosom on a spring extension a pair of rimless pince-nez. She placed them on her nose and waited with composure for Alleyn's next remark.

He said: 'Have you some notes there, Miss Harris?'

'Yes, Mr Alleyn. I saw Miss O'Brien just now and she told me you would be requiring any information I could give about Lord Gospell's movements last night and this

394

morning. I thought it better to prepare what I have to say. So I just jotted down one or two little memos.'

'Admirable! Let's have 'em.'

Miss Harris cleared her throat.

'At about twelve-thirty,' she began in an incisive monotone, 'I met Lord Robert Gospell in the hall. I was speaking to Miss O'Brien. He asked me to dance with him later in the evening. I remained in the hall until a quarter to one. I happened to glance at my watch. I then went downstairs to top landing. Remained there. Period of time unknown but I went down to the ballroom landing before one-thirty. Lord Gospell – I mean Lord Robert Gospell – then asked me to dance.'

Miss Harris's voice stopped for a moment. She moved her writing-pad on the arm of her chair.

'We danced,' she continued. 'Three successive dances with repeats. Lord Robert introduced me to several of his friends and then he took me into the buffet on the street-level. We drank champagne. He then remembered that he had promised to dance with the Duchess of Dorminster – ' Here Miss Harris appeared to lose her place for a moment. She repeated: 'Had promised to dance with the Duchess of Dorminster,' and cleared her throat again. 'He took me to the ballroom and asked me for the next Viennese waltz. I remained in the ballroom. Lord Robert danced with the Duchess and then with Miss Agatha Troy, the portrait painter, and then with two ladies whose names I do not know. Not at once, of course,' said Miss Harris in parenthesis. 'That would be ridiculous. I still remained in the ballroom. The band played the 'Blue Danube'. Lord Robert was standing in a group of his friends close to where I sat. He saw me. We danced the 'Blue Danube' together and revisited the buffet. I noticed the time. I had intended leaving much earlier and was surprised to find that it was nearly three o'clock. So I stayed till the end.'

She glanced up at Alleyn with the impersonal attentive

air proper to her position. He felt so precisely that she was indeed his secretary that there was no need for him to repress a smile. But he did glance at Fox, who for the first time in Alleyn's memory, looked really at a loss. His large hand hovered uncertainly over his own notebook. Alleyn realized that Fox did not know whether to take down Miss Harris's shorthand in his own shorthand.

Alleyn said: 'Thank you, Miss Harris. Anything else?'

Miss Harris turned a page.

'Details of conversation,' she began. 'I have not made memos of *all* the remarks I have remembered. Many of them were merely light comments on suitable subjects. For instance, Lord Robert spoke of Lady Carrados and expressed regret that she seemed to be tired. That sort of thing.'

'Let us have his remarks under this heading,' said Alleyn with perfect gravity.

'Certainly, Mr Alleyn. Lord Robert asked me if I had noticed that Lady Carrados had been tired for some time. I said yes I had, and that I was sorry because she was so nice to everybody. He asked if I thought it was entirely due to the season. I said I expected it was, because many ladies I have had posts with have found the season very exhausting, although in a way Lady Carrados took the entertaining side very lightly. Lord Robert asked me if I liked being with Lady Carrados. I replied that I did, very much. Lord Robert asked me several questions about myself. He was very easy to talk to. I told him about the old days at the rectory and how we ought to have been much better off, and he was very nice, and I told about my father's people in Bucks and he seemed quite interested in so many of them being parsons and what an old Buckinghamshire family we really are.'

'Oh, God,' thought Alleyn on a sudden wave of painful compassion. 'And so they probably are and because for the last two or three generations they've had to haul down

the social flag inch by inch their children are all going
to talk like this and nobody's going to feel anything but
uncomfortably incredulous.'

He said: 'You come from Barbicon-Bramley? That's not
far from Bassicote, is it? I know that part of Bucks fairly
well. Is your father's rectory anywhere near Falconbridge?'

'Oh, no. Falconbridge is thirty miles away. My uncle
Walter was rector at Falconbridge.'

Alleyn said: 'Really? Long ago?'

'When I was a small girl. He's retired now and lives
in Barbicon-Bramley. All the Harrises live to ripe old ages.
Lord Robert remarked that many of the clergy do. He
said longevity was one of the more dubious rewards of
virtue,' said Miss Harris with a glance at her notes.

Alleyn could hear the squeaky voice uttering this gentle
epigram.

'He *was* amusing,' added Miss Harris.

'Yes. Now look here, Miss Harris, we're coming to
something rather important. You tell me you went up to
the top landing between, say, a quarter to one and one-
fifteen. Do you think you were up there all that time?'

'Yes, Mr Alleyn, I think I was.'

'Whereabouts were you?'

Miss Harris turned purple with the rapidity of a
pantomime fairy under a coloured spotlight.

'Well, I mean to say, I sat on the gallery, I went into
the ladies' cloakroom on the landing to tidy and see if
everything was quite nice, and then I sat on the gallery
again and – I mean I was just about.'

'You were on the gallery at one o'clock, you think?'

'I – really I'm not sure if I – '

'Let's see if we can get at it this way. Did you go into
the cloakroom immediately after you got to the landing?'

'Yes. Yes, I did.'

'How long were you in the cloakroom?'

'Only a few minutes.'

'So you were back on the gallery again well before one.'

'Yes,' said Miss Harris without enthusiasm, 'but – '

'At about the time I am trying to get at, Captain Withers and Mr Donald Potter were on the gallery, from where they moved into the sitting-room on that landing. Sir Herbert Carrados was in and out of the sitting-room and you may have heard him order the servant on duty up there to attend to the ash-trays and matches. Do you remember this?'

'No. Not exactly. I think I remember seeing Captain Withers and Mr Potter through the sitting-room door as I passed to go downstairs. The larger sitting-room – not the one with the telephone. Lord Robert was in the telephone-room.'

'How do you know that?'

'I – heard him.'

'From the cloakroom?'

'The – I mean – '

'The room between the cloakroom and the telephone-room, perhaps,' said Alleyn, mentally cursing the extreme modesty of Miss Harris.

'Yes,' said Miss Harris looking straight in front of her. Her discomfiture was so evident that Alleyn himself almost began to feel shy.

'Please don't mind if I ask for very exact information,' he said. 'Policemen are rather like doctors in these instances. Things don't count. When did you go into this ladies' room?'

'As soon as I got upstairs,' said Miss Harris. 'Hem!'

'Right. Now let's see if we can get things straight, shall we? You came upstairs at, say, about ten or fifteen minutes to one. You went straight to this door next the green sitting-room with the telephone. Did you see anyone?'

'Captain Withers was just coming out of the green sitting-room. I think there was a lady in there. I saw her through the open door as I – as I opened the other.'

398

'Yes. Anyone else?'

'I think I noticed Sir Herbert in the other sitting-room, the first one, as I passed the door. That's all.'

'And then you went into the ladies' room?'

'Yes,' admitted Miss Harris, shutting her eyes for a moment and opening them again to stare with something like horror at Fox's pencil and notebook. Alleyn felt that already she saw herself being forced to answer these and worse questions shouted at her by celebrated counsel at the Old Bailey.

'How long did you remain in this room?' he asked.

White to the lips Miss Harris gave a rather mad little laugh. 'Oh,' she said, 'oh, quayte a tayme. You know.'

'And while you were there you heard Lord Robert telephoning in the next room?'

'Yes, I did,' said Miss Harris loudly with an air of defiance.

'She's looking at me,' thought Alleyn, 'exactly like a trapped rabbit.'

'So Lord Robert probably came upstairs after you. Do you suppose the lady you had noticed was still in the green room when he began telephoning?'

'No. I heard her come out and – and she – I mean she tried to – tried to – '

'Yes, yes,' said Alleyn, 'quite. And went away?'

'Definitely.'

'And then Lord Robert began to telephone? I see. Could you hear what he said?'

'Oh, no. He spoke in a low tone, of course. I made no attempt to listen.'

'Of course not.'

'I could not have heard if I had tried,' continued Miss Harris. 'I could only hear the tone of the voice and that was quite unmistakable.'

'Yes?' said Alleyn encouragingly. 'Now,' he thought, 'now at last are we getting to it?' Miss Harris did not go

399

on, however, but sat with her mouth done up in a maddening button of conscious rectitude.

'Did you hear the end of the conversation?' he said at last.

'Oh, yes! The end. Yes. At least someone came into the room. I heard Lord Robert say: "Oh, hello!" Those were the only words I did distinguish, and almost immediately I heard the telephone tinkle, so I knew he had rung off.'

'And the other person? Was it a man?'

'Yes. Yes, a man.'

'Could you,' said Alleyn in a level voice, 'could you recognise this man?'

'Oh, *no*,' cried Miss Harris with an air of relief. 'No *indeed*, Mr Alleyn, I haven't the faintest idea. You see, after that I didn't really hear anything at all in the next room. Nothing at all. Really.'

'You returned to the landing?'

'Not immediately. No.'

'Oh!' said Alleyn. He could think of nothing else to say. Even Fox seemed to have caught the infection of extreme embarrassment. He cleared his throat loudly. Miss Harris, astonishingly, broke into a high-pitched prattle, keeping her eyes fixed on the opposite wall and clenching and unclenching her hands.

'No. Not for some minutes and then, of course, when I did return they had both gone. I mean when I finally returned. Of course Lord Robert went before then and – and – so that was perfectly all right. Perfectly.'

'And the other man?'

'He – it was most unfortunate. A little mistake. I assure you I did not see who it was. I mean as soon as he realized it was the wrong door he went out again. Naturally. The inner door being half-glass made it even more unfortunate though of course there being two rooms was – was better for all concerned than if it was the usual arrangement.

400

And I mean that he didn't see me so that in a way it didn't matter. It didn't really matter a scrap. Not a scrap.'

Alleyn, listening to this rigmarole, sent his memory back to the top gallery of Marsdon House. He remembered the Victorian ante-room that opened off the landing, the inner gloomy sanctum beyond. The chaotic fragments of Miss Harris's remarks joggled together in his brain and then clicked into a definite pattern.

'Not a scrap, really,' Miss Harris still repeated.

'Of course not,' agreed Alleyn cheerfully. 'I think I understand what happened. Tell me if I go wrong. While you were still in the inner room the man who had interrupted Lord Robert's telephone conversation came out of the green sitting-room and blundered through the wrong door into the ante-room of the ladies' lavatory. That it?'

Miss Harris blanched at the unfortunate word but nodded her head.

'Why are you so sure it was this same man, Miss Harris?'

'Well, because, because I heard their voices as they came to the door of the next room and then Lord Robert's voice on the landing and then – then it happened. I just knew that was who it was.'

Alleyn leant forward.

'The inner door,' he said, 'is half-glass. Could you see this intruder?'

'Dimly, dimly,' cried Miss Harris. 'Greatly obscured, I assure you. I'm sorry to say I forgot for some seconds to switch off my light. The other was on.'

'So you actually could see the shape of this person, however shadowy, through the clouded glass?'

'Yes. For a second or two. Before he went away. I think perhaps he was feeling unwell.'

'Drunk?'

'No, no. Certainly not. It was not a bit like that. He looked more as if he'd had a shock.'

'Why?'

'He – the shape of him put its hands to its face and it swayed towards the glass partition and for a moment leant against it. Thank God,' said Miss Harris with real fervour, 'I had locked the door.'

'The silhouette would be clearer, more sharply defined, as it came closer to the door?'

'I suppose so. Yes, it was.'

'Still you did not recognise it?'

'No. Never for an instant.'

'Suppose – for the sake of argument, I were to say this man was either Sir Herbert Carrados, Captain Withers, the waiter on the landing, Mr Donald Potter, or Dimitri the caterer. Which would you think most likely?'

'I don't know. Perhaps Dimitri. I don't know.'

'What height?'

'Medium.'

'Well,' said Alleyn, 'what happened next?'

'He took his hands from his face. He had turned away with his back against the door. I – I got the impression he suddenly realized where he was. Then the shape moved away and turned misty and then disappeared. I heard the outer door shut.'

'And at last you were able to escape?'

'I waited for a moment.' Miss Harris looked carefully at Alleyn. Perhaps she saw something in his eye that made her feel, after all, her recital had not been such a terrible affair.

'It *was* awkward,' she said, 'wasn't it? Honestly?'

'Honestly,' said Alleyn, 'it was.'

CHAPTER NINETEEN

The General

'Then your idea is,' said Fox as they headed again for Belgrave Square, 'that this chap in the WC was the murderer.'

'Yes, Fox, that *is* my idea. There's no earthly reason why an innocent person should not admit to interrupting the telephone call and nobody has admitted to it. I'm afraid we'll have to go again through the whole damn boiling, guests, servants and all, to make sure of our ground. *And* we'll have to ask every man jack of 'em if they burst across the threshold of Miss Harris's outer sanctuary. Every *man* jack. Thank the Lord there's no need for the women, though from what I know of my niece Sarah we wouldn't meet with many mantling cheeks and conscious looks among the débutantes. If nobody admits to the telephone incident, or to the sequel in the usual offices, then we can plot another joint in our pattern. We can say there is a strong probability that our man overheard Bunchy telephone to me, interrupted the sentence: "and he's working with – " waited in the green sitting-room until Bunchy had gone and then blundered into the ante-room.'

'But why would he do that?' said Fox. 'Did he think it was a man's, or was he trying to avoid somebody? Or what?'

'It's a curious picture, isn't it? That dim figure seen through the thick glass. Even in her mortal shame Miss Harris noticed that he seemed to be agitated. The hands over the face, the body leaning for a moment against the door. And then suddenly he pulls himself together and goes out. He looked, said Miss Harris, as though he'd had a shock. He'd just intercepted a telephone call to the Yard from a man who apparently knew all there was to know about his blackmailing activities. He might well feel he must blunder through the first door he came to and have a moment alone to pull himself together.'

'Yes,' agreed Fox, 'so he might. I'd like something a bit more definite to hinge it on, though.'

'And so, I promise you, would I. The detestable realms of conjecture! How I hate them.'

'Miss Harris didn't get us any further with the business down in the hall.'

'The final departures? No, she didn't. She simply bore out everything we'd already been told.'

'She's an observant little lady, isn't she?' said Fox.

'Yes, Fox, she's no fool, for all her tender qualms. And now we have a delightful job ahead of us. We've got to try to bamboozle, cajole, or bully Mrs Halcut-Hackett into giving away her best young man. A charming occupation.'

'Will we be seeing the General, too? I suppose we'll have to. I don't think the other chaps will have tackled him. I told them not to touch any of our lot.'

'Quite right,' said Alleyn, with a sigh. 'We shall be seeing the General. And here we are at Halkin Street. The Halcut-Hacketts of Halkin Street! An important collection of aspirates and rending consonants. The General first, I suppose.'

The General was expecting them. They walked through a hall which, though it had no tongue, yet it did speak of the most expensive and most fashionable house decorator in London. They were shown into a study smelling of leather and cigars and decorated with that pleasant sequence of prints of the Nightcap Steeplechase. Alleyn wondered if the General had stood with his cavalry sabre on the threshold of this room, daring the fashionable decorator to come on and see what he would get. Or possibly Mrs Halcut-Hackett, being an American, caused her husband's study to be aggressively British. Alleyn and Fox waited

404

for five minutes before they heard a very firm step and a loud cough. General Halcut-Hackett walked into the room.

'Hullo! Afternoon! What!' he shouted.

His face was terra-cotta, his moustache formidable, his eyes china blue. He was the original ramrod brass-hat, the subject of all army jokes kindly or malicious. It was impossible to believe his mind was as blank as his face would seem to confess. So true to type was he that he would have seemed unreal, a two-dimensional figure that had stepped from a coloured cartoon of a regimental dinner, had it not been for a certain air of solidity and a kind of childlike constancy that was rather appealing. Alleyn thought: 'Now, *he* really *is* a simple soldier-man.

'Sit down,' said General Halcut-Hackett. 'Bad business! Damn blackguardly killer. Place is getting no better than Chicago. What are you fellows doing about it? What? Going to get the feller? What?'

'I hope so, sir,' said Alleyn.

'Hope so! By Gad, I should hope you hope so. Well, what can I do for you?'

'Answer one or two questions, if you will, sir.'

"Course I will. Bloody outrage. The country's going to pieces in my opinion and this is only another proof of it. Men like Robert Gospell can't take a cab without gettin' the life choked out of them. What it amounts to. Well?'

'Well, sir, the first point is this. Did you walk into the green sitting-room on the top landing at one o'clock this morning while Lord Robert Gospell was using the telephone?'

'No. Never went near the place. Next!'

'What time did you leave Marsdon House?'

'Between twelve and one.'

'Early,' remarked Alleyn.

'My wife's charge had toothache. Brought her home.

405

Whole damn business had been too much for her. Poodle-faking and racketing! All people think of nowadays. Goin' through her paces from morning till night. Enough to kill a horse.'

'Yes,' said Alleyn. 'One wonders how they get through it.'

'Is your name Alleyn?'

'Yes, sir.'

'George Alleyn's son, are you? You're like him. He was in my regiment. I'm sixty-seven,' added General Halcut-Hackett with considerable force. 'Sixty-seven. Why didn't you go into your father's regiment? Because you preferred this? What?'

'That's it, sir. The next point is – '

'What? Get on with the job, eh? Quite right.'

'Did you return to Marsdon House?'

'Why the devil should I do that?'

'I thought perhaps your wife was – '

The General glared at the second print in the Nightcap series and said:

'M'wife preferred to stay on. Matter of fact, Robert Gospell offered to see her home.'

'He didn't do so, however?'

'Damn it, sir, my wife is not a murderess.'

'Lord Robert might have crossed the square as escort to your wife, sir, and returned.'

'Well, he didn't. She tells me they missed each other.'

'And you, sir. You saw your daughter in and then –'

'She's not my daughter!' said the General with a good deal of emphasis. 'She's the daughter of some friend of my wife's.' He glowered and then muttered half to himself: 'Unheard of in my day, that sort of thing. Makes a woman look like a damn trainer. Girl's no more than a miserable scared filly. Pah!'

Alleyn said: 'Yes, sir. Well, then, you saw Miss – '

406

'Birnbaum. Rose Birnbaum, poor little devil. Call her Poppet.'

' – Miss Birnbaum in and then – '

'Well?'

'Did you stay up?'

To Alleyn's astonishment the General's face turned from terra-cotta to purple, not, it seemed, with anger, but with embarrassment. He blew out his moustache several times, pouted like a baby, and blinked. At last he said:

'Upon my soul, I can't see what the devil it matters whether I went to bed at twelve or one.'

'The question may sound impertinent,' said Alleyn. 'If it does I'm sorry. But, as a matter of police routine, we want to establish alibis – '

'*Alibis!*' roared the General. '*Alibis!* Good God, sir, are you going to sit there and tell me I'm in need of an alibi? Hell blast it, sir – '

'But, General Halcut-Hackett,' said Alleyn quickly, while the empurpled General sucked in his breath, 'every guest at Marsdon House is in need of an alibi.'

'Every guest! Every guest! But, damn it, sir, the man was murdered in a bloody cab, not a bloody ballroom. Some filthy bolshevistic fascist,' shouted the General, having a good deal of difficulty with this strange collection of sibilants. He slightly dislodged his upper plate but impatiently champed it back into position. 'They're all alike!' he added confusedly. 'The whole damn boiling.'

Alleyn hunted for a suitable phrase in a language that General Halcut-Hackett would understand. He glanced at Fox who was staring solemnly at the General over the top of his spectacles.

'I'm sure you'll realize, sir,' said Alleyn, 'that we are simply obeying orders.'

'*What!*'

'That's done it,' thought Alleyn.

'Orders! I can toe the line as well as the next fellow,'

407

said the General, and Alleyn, remembering Carrados had used the same phrase, reflected that in this instance it was probably true. The General, he saw, *was* preparing to toe the line.

'I apologize,' said the General. 'Lost me temper. Always doing it nowadays. Indigestion.'

'It's enough to make anybody lose their temper, sir.'

'Well,' said the General, 'you've kept yours. Come on, then.'

'It's just a statement, sir, that you didn't go out again after you got back here and, if possible, someone to support the statement.'

Once again the General looked strangely embarrassed.

'I can't give you a witness,' he said. 'Nobody saw me go to bed.'

'I see. Well then, sir, if you'll just give me your word that you didn't go out again.'

'But, damme, I did take a – take a – take a turn round the Square before I went to bed. Always do.'

'What time was this?'

'I don't know.'

'You can't give me an idea? Was it long after you got home?'

'Some time. I saw the child to her room and stirred up my wife's maid to look after her. Then I came down here and got myself a drink. I read for a bit. I dare say I dozed for a bit. Couldn't make up my mind to turn in.'

'You didn't glance at the clock on the mantelpiece there?'

Again the General became acutely self-conscious.

'I may have done so. I fancy I did. Matter of fact, I remember now I did doze off and woke with a bit of a start. The fire had gone out. It was devilish chilly.' He glared at Alleyn and then said abruptly: 'I felt wretchedly down in the mouth. I'm getting an old fellow nowadays and I don't enjoy the small hours. As you say, I looked

408

at the clock. It was half-past two. I sat there in this chair
trying to make up my mind to go to bed. Couldn't. So
I took a walk round the Square.'

'Now that's excellent, sir. You may be able to give us
the very piece of information we're after. Did you by chance
notice anybody hanging about in the Square?'

'No.'

'Did you meet anybody at all?'

'Constable.'

Alleyn glanced at Fox.

'PC Titheridge,' said Fox. 'We've got his report, sir.'

'All right,' said Alleyn. 'Were people beginning to leave
Marsdon House when you passed, sir?'

The General muttered something about 'might have
been,' paused for a moment and then said: 'It was devilish
murky. Couldn't see anything.'

'A misty night; yes,' said Alleyn. 'Did you happen to
notice Captain Maurice Withers in the mist?'

'No!' yelled the General with extraordinary vehemence.
'No, I did not. I don't know the feller. No!'

There was an uncomfortable pause and then the General
said: 'Afraid that's all I can tell you. When I got in again
I went straight to bed.'

'Your wife had not returned?'

'No,' said the General very loudly. 'She had not.'

Alleyn waited for a moment and then he said:

'Thank you very much, sir. Now, we'll prepare a
statement from the notes Inspector Fox has taken, and
if you've no objection, we'll get you to sign it.'

'I – um – um – um – I'll have a look at it.'

'Yes. And now, if I may, I'd like to have a word with
Mrs Halcut-Hackett.'

Up went the General's chin again. For a moment Alleyn
wondered if they were in for another outburst. But the
General said: 'Very good. I'll tell her,' and marched out
of the room.

'Crikey!' said Fox.

'That's Halcut-Hackett, that was,' said Alleyn. 'Why the devil,' he added rubbing his nose, 'why the devil is the funny old article in such a stew over his walk round the Square?'

'Seems a natural thing for a gentleman of his kind to do,' Fox ruminated. 'I'm sure I don't know. I should have thought he's the sort that breaks the ice on the Serpentine every morning as well as walking round the Square every night.'

'He's a damn bad liar, poor old boy. Or is he a poor old boy? Is he not perhaps a naughty old boy? Blast! Why the devil couldn't he give us a nice straight cast-iron alibi? Poking his nose into Belgrave Square; can't tell us exactly when or exactly why or for exactly how long. What did the PC say?'

'Said he'd noticed nothing at all suspicious. Never mentioned the General. I'll have a word with Mr PC Titheridge about this.'

'The General is probably a stock piece if he walks round Belgrave Square every night,' said Alleyn.

'Yes, but not at half-past two in the morning,' objected Fox.

'Quite right, Fox, quite right. Titheridge must be blasted. What the devil was old Halcut-Hackett up to last night! We can't let it go, you know, because, after all, if he suspects – '

Alleyn broke off. He and Fox stood up as Mrs Halcut-Hackett made her entrance.

Alleyn, of course, had met her before, on the day she came to his office with the story of Mrs X and the blackmailing letters. He reflected now that in a sense she had started the whole miserable business. 'If it hadn't been for this hard, wary, stupid woman's visit,' he thought, 'I shouldn't have asked Bunchy to poke his head into a death-trap. Oh, God!' Mrs Halcut-Hackett said:

410

'Why, Inspector, they didn't tell me it was you. Now, do you know I never realized, that day I called about my poor friend's troubles, that I was speaking to Lady Alleyn's famous son.'

Inwardly writhing under this blatant recognition of his snob-value Alleyn shook hands and instantly introduced Fox to whom Mrs Halcut-Hackett was insufferably cordial. They all sat down. Alleyn deliberately waited for a moment or two before he spoke. He looked at Mrs Halcut-Hackett. He saw that under its thick patina of cream and rouge her face was sagging from the bones of her skull. He saw that her eyes and her hands were frightened.

He said: 'I think we may as well begin with that same visit to the Yard. The business we talked about on that occasion seems to be linked with the death of Lord Robert Gospell.'

She sat there, bolt upright in her expensive stays and he knew she was terrified.

'But,' she said, 'that's absurd. No, honestly, Mr Alleyn, I just can't believe there could be any possible connection. Why, my friend – '

'Mrs Halcut-Hackett,' said Alleyn, 'I am afraid we must abandon your friend.'

She shot a horrified glance at Fox, and Alleyn answered it.

'Mr Fox is fully acquainted with the whole story,' he said. 'He agrees with me that your friend had better dissolve. We realize that beyond all doubt you yourself were the victim of these blackmailing letters. There is no need for you to feel particularly distressed over this. It is much better to tackle this sort of thing without the aid of an imaginary Mrs X. She makes for unnecessary confusion. We now have the facts – '

'But – how do you – ?'

Alleyn decided to take a risk. It was a grave risk.

'I have already spoken to Captain Withers,' he said.

411

'*My God, has Maurice confessed?*'

Fox's notebook dropped to the floor.

Alleyn, still watching the gaping mouth with its wet red margin, said: 'Captain Withers has confessed nothing.' And he thought: 'Does she realize the damage she's done?'

'But I don't mean that,' Mrs Halcut-Hackett gabbled. 'I don't mean that. It's not that. You must be crazy. He couldn't have done it.' She clenched her hands and drummed with her fists on the arms of the chair. 'What did he tell you?'

'Very little I'm afraid. Still we learned at least that it was not impossible – '

'You must be crazy to think he did it. I tell you he couldn't do it.'

'He couldn't do what, Mrs Halcut-Hackett?' asked Alleyn.

'The thing – Lord Robert . . .' She gaped horridly and then with a quick and vulgar gesture, covered her mouth with her ringed hand. Horrified intelligence looked out of her eyes.

'What did you think Captain Withers had confessed?'

'Nothing to do with this. Nothing that matters to anyone but me. I didn't mean a thing by it. You've trapped me. It's not fair.'

'For your own sake,' said Alleyn, 'you would be wise to try to answer me. You say you did not mean to ask if Captain Withers had confessed to murder. Very well, I accept that for the moment. What might he have confessed? That he was the author of the letter your blackmailer had threatened to use. Is that it?'

'I won't answer. I won't say anything more. You're trying to trap me.'

'What conclusion am I likely to draw from your refusal to answer? Believe me, you take a very grave risk if you refuse.'

'Have you told my husband about the letter?'

412

'No. Nor shall I do so if it can be avoided. Come now.'
Alleyn deliberately drew all his power of concentration
to a fine point. He saw his dominance drill like a sort
of mental gimlet through her flabby resistance. 'Come now.
Captain Withers is the author of this letter. Isn't he?'

'Yes, but – '

'Did you think he had confessed as much?'

'Why, yes, but – '

'And you suppose Lord Robert Gospell to have been
the blackmailer? Ever since that afternoon when he sat
behind you at the concert?'

'Then it was Robert Gospell!' Her head jerked back.
She looked venomously triumphant.

'No,' said Alleyn. 'That was a mistake. Lord Robert
was not a blackmailer.'

'He was. I know he was. Do you think I didn't see him
last night, watching us. Why did he ask me about Maurice?
Why did Maurice warn me against him?'

'Did Captain Withers suggest that Lord Robert was a
blackmailer?' In spite of himself a kind of cold disgust
deadened Alleyn's voice. She must have heard it because
she cried out:

'Why do you speak of him like that? Of Captain Withers,
I mean. You've no right to insult him.'

'My God, this is a stupid woman,' thought Alleyn. Aloud
he said: 'Have I insulted him? If so I have gone very far
beyond my duty. Mrs Halcut-Hackett, when did you first
miss this letter?'

'About six months ago. After my charade party in the
little season.'

'Where did you keep it?'

'In a trinket-box on my dressing-table.'

'A locked box?'

'Yes. But the key was sometimes left with others in the
drawer of the dressing-table.'

'Did you suspect your maid?'

413

'No. I can't suspect her. She has been with me for fifteen years. She's my old dresser. I know she wouldn't do it.'

'Have you any idea who could have taken it?'

'I can't think, except that for my charade party I turned my room into a buffet, and the men moved everything round.'

'What men?'

'The caterer's men. Dimitri. But Dimitri superintended them the whole time. I don't believe they had an opportunity.'

'I see,' said Alleyn.

He saw she now watched him with a different kind of awareness. Alleyn had interviewed a great number of Mrs Halcut-Hacketts in his day. He knew very well that with such women he carried a weapon that he was loath to use, but which nevertheless fought for him. This was the weapon of his sex. He saw with violent distaste that some taint of pleasure threaded her fear of him. And the inexorable logic of thought presented him to himself, side by side with her lover.

He said: 'Suppose we get the position clear. In your own interest I may tell you that we have already gathered a great deal of information. Lord Robert was helping us on the blackmail case, and he has left us his notes. From them and from our subsequent enquiries we have pieced this much together. In your own case Captain Withers was the subject of the blackmailing letters. Following our advice you carried out the blackmailer's instruction and left your bag in the corner of the sofa at the Constance Street Hall. It was taken. Because Lord Robert deliberately sat next to you and because Captain Withers had, as you put it, warned you against him, you came to the conclusion that Lord Robert took the bag and was therefore your blackmailer. Why did you not report to the police the circumstances of the affair at the concert? You had agreed

414

to do so. Were you advised to let the case drop as far as the Yard was concerned?'

'Yes.'

'By Captain Withers? I see. That brings us to last night. You say you noticed that Lord Robert watched you both during the ball. I must ask you again if Captain Withers agrees with your theory that Lord Robert was a blackmailer.'

'He – he simply warned me against Lord Robert.'

'In view of these letters and the sums of money the blackmailer demanded, did you think it advisable to keep up your friendship with Captain Withers?'

'We – there was nothing anybody could – I mean – '

'What do you mean?' asked Alleyn sternly.

She wetted her lips. Again he saw that look of subservience and thought that of all traits in an ageing woman this was the unloveliest and most pitiable.

She said: 'Our friendship is partly a business relationship.'

'A business relationship?' Alleyn repeated the words blankly.

'Yes. You see Maurice – Captain Withers – has very kindly offered to advise me and – I mean right now Captain Withers has in mind a little business venture in which I am interested, and I naturally require to talk things over so – you see – ?'

'Yes,' said Alleyn gently, 'I do see. This venture of Captain Withers is of course the club at Leatherhead, isn't it?'

'Why, yes, but – '

'Now then,' said Alleyn quickly, 'about last night. Lord Robert offered to see you home, didn't he? You refused or avoided giving an answer. Did you go home alone?'

She might as well have asked him how much he knew, so clearly did he read the question in her eyes. He thanked his stars that he had made such a fuss over Withers's telephone. Evidently Withers had not rung her up to warn

415

her what to say. Frightened his call would be tapped, thought Alleyn with satisfaction, and decided to risk a further assumption. He said:

'You saw Captain Withers again after the ball, didn't you?'

'What makes you think that?'

'I have every reason to believe it. Captain Withers's car was parked in a side street off Belgrave Square. How long did you sit there waiting for him?'

'I don't admit I sat there.'

'Then if Captain Withers tells me he took a partner to the Matador last night after the ball I am to conclude that it was not you?'

'Captain Withers would want to protect me. He's very, very thoughtful.'

'Can you not understand,' said Alleyn, 'that it is greatly to your advantage and his, if you can prove that you both got into his car and drove to the Matador last night?'

'Why? I don't want it said that – '

'Mrs Halcut-Hackett,' said Alleyn: 'Do you want an alibi for yourself and Captain Withers or don't you?'

She opened her mouth once or twice like a gaping fish, looked wildly at Fox and burst into tears.

Fox got up, walked to the far end of the room, and stared with heavy tact at the second print in the Nightcap series. Alleyn waited while scarlet claws scuffled in an elaborate handbag. Out came a long piece of monogrammed tulle. She jerked at it violently.

Something clattered to the floor. Alleyn darted forward and picked it up.

It was a gold cigarette-case with a medallion set in the lid and surrounded by brilliants.

CHAPTER TWENTY

Rose Birnbaum

Mrs Halcut-Hackett dabbed at the pouches under her eyes as if her handkerchief was made of blotting-paper.

'You frighten me,' she said. 'You frighten me so. I'm just terrified.'

Alleyn turned the cigarette-case over in his long hands.

'But there is no need to be terrified, none at all. Don't you see that if you can give me proof that you and Captain Withers motored straight from Marsdon House to the Matador, it clears you at once from any hint of complicity in Lord Robert's death?'

He waited. She began to rock backwards and forwards, beating her hands together and moving her head from side to side like a well-preserved automaton.

'I can't. I just can't. I won't say anything more. I just won't say another thing. It's no good. I won't say another thing.'

'Very well,' said Alleyn, not too unkindly. 'Don't try. I'll get at it another way. This is a very magnificent case. The medallion is an old one. Italian Renaissance, I should think. It's most exquisitely worked. It might almost be Benvenuto himself who formed those minute scrolls. Do you know its history?'

'No. Maurice picked it up somewhere and had it put on the case. I'm crazy about old things,' said Mrs Halcut-Hackett with a dry sob. 'Crazy about them.'

Alleyn opened the lid. An inscription read 'E. from M.W.' He shut the case but did not return it to her.

'Don't lose it, Mrs Halcut-Hackett. The medal is a collector's piece. Aren't you afraid to carry it about with you?'

417

She seemed to take heart of grace at his interest. She dabbed again at her eyes and said: 'I'm just terribly careless with my things. Perhaps I ought not to use it. Only last night I left it lying about.'

'Did you? Where?'

She looked terrified again the moment he asked her a question.

'Some place at the ball,' she said.

'Was it in the green sitting-room on the top landing?'

'I – yes – I think maybe it was.'

'At what time?'

'I don't know.'

'During the supper hour didn't you sit in that room with Captain Withers?'

'Yes. Why not? Why shouldn't I?' She twisted the handkerchief round her hands and said: 'How do you know that? My husband – I'm not – *he's not having me watched?*'

'I don't for a moment suppose so. I simply happened to know that you sat in this room some time just before one o'clock. You tell me you left your cigarette-case there. Now when you came out of that room what did you do?'

'I went into the cloakroom to tidy. I missed the case when I opened my bag in the cloakroom.'

'Right. Now as you went from the green sitting-room to the cloakroom two doors away, did you happen to notice Lord Robert on the landing? Please don't think I am trying to entrap you. I simply want to know if you saw him.'

'He was coming upstairs,' she said. Her voice and manner were more controlled now.

'Good. Did you hear the dialling sound on the telephone extension while you were in the cloakroom?'

'Yes. Now you remind me I did hear it.'

'When you came out of the cloakroom did you go back for your case?'

'No. No, I didn't.'

'Why not?'

418

'Why? Because I forgot.'

'You forgot it again!'

'I didn't just forget but I went to the head of the stairs and Maurice was in the other sitting-out room at the stairhead, waiting for me. I went in there, and then I remembered my case and he got it for me.'

'Had the telephone rung off?' asked Alleyn.

'I don't know.'

'Was anyone else on the landing?'

'I guess not.'

'Not, by any chance, a short rather inconspicuous lady sitting alone?'

'No. There wasn't anybody on the landing. Donald Potter was in the sitting-room.'

'Was Captain Withers long fetching your case?'

'I don't think so,' she said nervously. 'I don't remember. I talked to Donald. Then we all went downstairs.'

'Captain Withers did not say whether there was anyone else in the telephone-room when he got the cigarette-case?'

'No, he didn't say anything about it.'

'Will you be very kind and let me keep this case for twenty-four hours?'

'Why? Why do you want it?'

Alleyn hesitated and at last he said: 'I want to see if anybody else recognises it. Will you trust me with it?'

'Very well,' she said. 'I can't refuse, can I?'

'I'll take great care of it,' said Alleyn. He dropped it in his pocket and turned to Fox who had remained at the far end of the room. Fox's notebook was open in his hand.

'I think that's all, isn't it?' asked Alleyn. 'Have I missed anything, Fox?'

'I don't fancy so, sir.'

'Then we'll bother you no longer, Mrs Halcut-Hackett,' said Alleyn, standing before her. She rose from her chair. He saw that there was a sort of question in her eyes. 'Is there anything you would like to add to what you have said?' he asked.

'No. No. But you said a little while ago that you would find out about what you asked me before. You said you'd trace it another way.'

'Oh,' said Alleyn cheerfully, 'you mean whether you went from Marsdon House to the Matador in Captain Withers's car, and if so, how long it took. Yes, we'll ask the commissionaire and the man in the office at the Matador. They may be able to help.'

'My God, you mustn't do that!'

'Why not?'

'You can't do that. For God's sake say you won't. For God's sake . . .'

Her voice rose to a stifled, hysterical scream, ending in a sort of gasp. Fox sighed heavily and gave Alleyn a look of patient endurance. Mrs Halcut-Hackett drew breath. The door opened.

A plain girl, dressed to go out, walked into the room.

'Oh, I'm sorry,' she said, 'I didn't know – '

Mrs Halcut-Hackett stared round her with the air of a trapped mastodon and finally blundered from the room as fast as her French heels would carry her.

The door slammed behind her.

The plain girl, who was most beautifully curled, painted and dressed, looked from Alleyn to Fox.

'I'm so sorry,' she repeated nervously. 'I'm afraid I shouldn't have come in. Ought I to go and see if there's anything I can do?'

'If I were you,' said Alleyn, 'I don't think I should. Mrs Halcut-Hackett is very much distressed over last night's tragedy and I expect she would rather be alone. Are you Miss Birnbaum?'

'Yes, I am. You're detectives, aren't you?'

'That's us. My name is Alleyn and this is Mr Fox.'

'Oh, how d'you do?' said Miss Birnbaum hurriedly. She

420

hesitated and then gave them her hand. She looked doubtfully into Alleyn's face. He felt the chilly little fingers tighten their grip like those of a frightened child.

'I expect you've found it rather upsetting too, haven't you?'

'Yes,' she said dutifully. 'It's dreadful, isn't it?' She twisted her fingers together. 'Lord Robert was very kind, wasn't he? He was very kind to me.'

'I hope your toothache's better,' said Alleyn.

She looked at her hands and then up into his face.

'I didn't have toothache,' she said.

'No?'

'No. I just wanted to go home. I *hate* coming out,' added Miss Birnbaum with extraordinary vigour. 'I knew I would and I do.'

'That's bad luck. Why do you do it?'

'Because,' said Miss Birnbaum with devastating frankness, 'my mother paid Mrs Hackett, I mean Mrs Halcut-Hackett, five hundred pounds to bring me out.'

'Hi!' said Alleyn, 'aren't you talking out of school?'

'You won't tell anybody I said that, will you? I've never breathed a word about it before. Not to a single soul. But you look my kind of person. And I'm absolutely fed up. I'm simply not the social kind. Golly, what a relief to get that off my chest!'

'What would you like to do?'

'I want to be an art student. My grandfather was a painter, Joseph Birnbaum. Have you ever heard of him?'

'I think I have. Didn't he paint a thing called "Jewish Sabbath"?'

'That's right. He was a Jew, of course. I'm a Jewess. My mother isn't, but I am. That's another thing I'm not supposed to say. I'm only sixteen. Would you have thought I was older?'

'I think I should.'

'That,' said Miss Birnbaum, 'is because I'm a Jewess.

They mature very quickly, you know. Well, I suppose I mustn't keep you.'

'I should like to keep *you* for a minute, if I may.'

'That's all right then,' said Miss Birnbaum and sat down. 'I suppose Mrs Halcut-Hackett won't come back, will she?'

'I don't think so.'

'I don't mind so much about the General. He's stupid, of course, but he's quite kind. But I'm *terrified* of Mrs Halcut-Hackett. I'm such a failure and she hates it.'

'Are you sure you're such a failure?'

'Oh, yes. Last night only four people asked me to dance. Lord Robert, when I first got there, and a fat man, and the General, and Sir Herbert Carrados.'

She looked away for a moment and her lips trembled.

'I tried to pretend I had a soul above social success,' she said, 'but I haven't at all. I minded awfully. If I could paint and get out of it all it wouldn't matter, but when you're in a thing it's beastly to be a failure. So I got toothache. I must say it *is* queer me saying all this to you.'

'The General took you home, didn't he?'

'Yes. He *was* very kind. He got Mrs Halcut-Hackett's maid, whom I hate worse than poison, to give me oil of cloves and Ovaltine. *She* knew all right.'

'Did you go to sleep?'

'No. I tried to think of a way to write to mother so that she would let me give it up. And then everything began to go through and through my head. I tried to think of other things but all the failure-parties kept coming up.'

'Did you hear the others return?'

'I heard Mrs Halcut-Hackett come in. It was frightfully late. She goes past my door to her room and she's got diamanté shoe buckles that make a clicking noise with every step. I had heard the clock strike four. Did the General go back to the dance?'

'He went out again, I think.'

'Well, then it must have been the General I heard come

along the passage at a quarter-past three. Just after. I heard every clock chime from one till six. Then I fell asleep. It was quite light then.'

'Yes.'

Alleyn took a turn up and down the room.

'Have you met Agatha Troy?' he asked.

'The painter? She was there last night. I wanted awfully for someone to introduce us but I didn't like to ask. I think she's the best living English painter, don't you?'

'Yes, I believe I do. She teaches, you know.'

'Does she? Only geniuses, I suppose.'

'I think only students who have gone a certain distance.'

'If I were allowed to go a certain distance first, I wonder if she would ever have me.'

'Do you think you would be good?' asked Alleyn.

'I'm sure I would be able to draw. I'm not so sure of paint. I see everything in line. I say.'

'Hallo?'

'D'you think this will make any difference to the coming-out game? Is she going to be ill? I've thought so lots of times lately. She's so bloody-minded.'

'Don't say "she" and don't say "bloody-minded". The one's common and you're too young for the other.'

Miss Birnbaum grinned delightedly.

'Well,' she said, 'it's what I think anyway. And she's not even virtuous. Do you know the Withers person?'

'Yes.'

'He's her boy-friend. Don't pretend to be shocked. I wrote and told mother about it. I hoped it'd shake her a bit. My father wrote and asked me if he was called Maurice and was like a red pig – that's a frightful insult, you know – because if he was I wasn't to stay. I like my father. But mother said if he was a friend of Mrs Halcut-Hackett he must be all right. I thought that frightfully funny. It's about the only thing that is at all funny in the whole business. I don't think it can be very amusing to be frightened of your boy-friend and your husband, do you?'

Alleyn rubbed his head and stared at Miss Birnbaum.

'Look here,' he said, 'you're giving us a good deal of information, you know. There's Mr Fox with his notebook. What about that?'

The dark face was lit with an inward smouldering fire. Two sharp lines appeared at the corners of the thick lips.

'Do you mean she may get into trouble? I hope she does. I hate her. She's a wicked woman. She'd murder anyone if she wanted them out of the way. She's felt like murdering me pretty often. She says things to me that twist me up inside, they hurt so. "My dear child, how can you expect me to do anything with you if you stare like a fish and never utter?" "My God, what have I done to be saddled with a burden like this?" "My dear child, I suppose you can't help looking what you are, but at least you might make some effort to sound a little less like Soho." And then she imitates my voice. Yesterday she told me there was a good deal to be said for the German point of view, and asked me if I had any relations among the refugees because she heard quite a number of English people were taking them as maids. I hope she is a murderess. I hope you catch her. I hope they hang her by her beastly old neck until she's dead.'

The thick soft voice stopped. Miss Birnbaum was trembling very slightly. A thin line of damp appeared above her upper lip.

Alleyn grimaced, rubbed his nose and said:

'Do you feel any better for that?'

'Yes.'

'Vindictive little devil! Can't you get on top of it all and see it as something intensely disagreeable that won't last for ever? Have you tried drawing as a counter-irritant?'

'I've done a caricature of Her. When I get away from here I'll send it to her if she's not in gaol by that time.'

424

'Do you know Sarah Alleyn?'

'She's one of the successes. Yes, I know her.'

'Do you like her?'

'She's not bad. She actually remembers who I am when she sees me.'

Alleyn decided to abandon his niece for the moment.

'Well,' he said, 'I dare say you're nearer to escape than you imagine. I'll be off now. I hope we meet again.'

'So do I. I suppose you think I'm pretty ghastly.'

'That's all right. Make up your mind everybody hates you and you'll always be happy.'

Miss Birnbaum grinned.

'You think you're clever,' she said, 'don't you? Good-bye.'

They shook hands in a friendly manner, and she saw them out into the hall. Alleyn had a last glimpse of her standing stocky, dark and truculent against a background of restrained and decorous half-tones and beautiful pseudo-Empire curtains.

CHAPTER TWENTY-ONE

Statement by Lucy Lorrimer

It was nearly six o'clock in the evening when Alleyn and Fox returned to Scotland Yard. They went to Alleyn's room. Fox got to work on his notes, Alleyn tackled the reports that had come in while they were away. They both lit pipes and between them was established that pleasant feeling of unexpressed intimacy that comes to two people working in silence at the same job.

Presently Alleyn put down the reports and looked across at his friend. He thought: 'How often we have sat like this, Fox and I, working like a couple of obscure clerks in the offices of the Last Judgment concern, filing and correlating the misdeeds of men. Fox is getting quite grizzled and there are elderly purple veins in his cheeks. I shall go home later on, a solitary fellow, to my own hole.' And into his thoughts came the image of a woman who sat in a tall blue chair by his fire, but that was too domestic a picture. Rather, she would sit on the hearth-rug. Her hands would be stained with charcoal and they would sweep beautiful lines across a white surface. When he came in she would look up from her drawing and Troy's eyes would smile or scowl. He jerked the image away and found that Fox was looking at him with his usual air of bland expectancy.

'Finished?' said Alleyn.

'Yes, sir. I've been trying to sort things out. There's the report on the silver cleaning. Young Carewe took that on and he seems to have made a fair job of it. Got himself up as a Rat and Mice Destruction Officer and went round all the houses and palled up with the servants. All the Carrados silver was cleaned this morning including Sir

Herbert's cigar-case which isn't the right shape anyway, because he saw it in the butler's pantry. Sir Daniel's man does his silver cleaning on Mondays and Fridays, so it was all cleaned up yesterday. François does Dimitri's stuff every day or says he does. Young Potter and Withers are looked after by the flat service and only their table silver is kept polished. The Halcut-Hacketts' cases are cleaned once a week – Fridays – and rubbed up every morning. That's that. How's the report from Bailey?'

'Bailey hasn't much. There's nothing in the taxi. He got Withers's prints from my cigarette-case but, as we expected, the green sitting-room was simply a mess. He *has* found Withers's and young Potter's prints on the pages of Taylor's *Medical Jurisprudence*. The pages that refer to asphyxiation.'

'By gum, that's something.'

'Not such a great deal, Fox. They will tell us that when the newspaper report came out they were interested and turned up Taylor on suffocation; and who is to call them liars? The man who went to Leatherhead had a success. Apparently Withers keeps a married couple there. Our man pitched a yarn that he had been sent by the borough to inspect the electrical wiring in the house, and got in. What's more he seems to have had a good look round. He found a roulette wheel and had the intelligence to examine it pretty closely. The middle dozen slots had been very slightly opened. I expect the idea is that Master Donald or some other satellite of Withers should back the middle dozen. The wheel seems brand new. There was an older one that showed no signs of irregularity. There were also several packs of cards which had been lightly treated with the favourite pumice-stone. Luckily for us the married couple had a violent row with the gallant Captain and were prepared to talk. I think we've got enough to pull him in on a gambling-hell charge. Thompson reports that Withers has stayed in all day. The telephone was

427

disconnected as soon as we left. Donald Potter's clothes were returned to him by taxi. Nobody has visited Withers. Dimitri comes next. Dimitri went home after he left here, visiting a chemist on the way to get his hand bandaged. He, too, has remained indoors, and has made no telephone calls. Most exemplary behaviour. How the blazes are we going to get any of these victims to charge Dimitri?'

'You're asking me!' said Fox.

'Yes. Not a hope in a hundred. Well now, Fox, I've been over this damnable, dreary, involved, addling business of the green sitting-room. It boils down to this. The people who could have overheard Lord Robert's telephone conversation were Withers, Sir Herbert Carrados, Miss Harris, Mrs Halcut-Hackett and Donald. They were all on or about the top landing and wouldn't have to lie particularly freely in avoiding any reference to a brief dart in and out of the telephone-room. But, but, but, and a blasted but it is, it is quite possible that while Lord Robert telephoned, someone came upstairs and walked into the telephone-room. Mrs Halcut-Hackett was in the cloakroom; Withers, Donald and Carrados in the other sitting-room, Miss Harris in the lavatory. Dimitri says he was downstairs but who the devil's to prove it? If the others are speaking the truth, anybody might have come up and gone down again unseen.'

'The gentleman who burst into the lavatory?'

'Precisely. He may even have hidden in there till the coast was clear, though I can't see why. There's nothing particularly fishy in coming out of a sitting-room.'

'Ugh,' said Fox.

'As I see the case now, Fox, it presents one or two highlights. Most of them seem to be concentrated on cigarette-cases. Two cigarette-cases. The murderer's and Mrs Halcut-Hackett's.'

'Yes,' said Fox.

'After the cigarette-cases comes the lost letter. The letter

428

written by Paddy O'Brien's friend in Australia. The letter that somebody seems to have stolen eighteen years ago in Buckinghamshire. It's odd, isn't it, that Miss Harris's uncle was sometime rector of Falconbridge, the village where Paddy O'Brien met with his accident? I wonder if either Miss Harris or Lady Carrados realizes there is this vague connection. I think our next move after the inquest is to go down to Barbicon-Bramley where we may disturb the retirement of Miss Harris's uncle. Then we'll have to dive into the past history of the hospital in Falconbridge. But what a cold trail! A chance in a thousand.'

'It's a bit of a coincidence Miss Harris linking up in this way, isn't it?' ruminated Fox.

'Are you building up a picture with Miss Harris as the agent of an infamous old parson who had treasured a compromising letter for eighteen years, and now uses it? Well, I suppose it's not so impossible. But I don't regard it as a *very* great coincidence that Miss Harris has drifted into Lady Carrados's household. Coincidences become increasingly surprising as they gain in importance. One can imagine someone telling Miss Harris about Paddy O'Brien's accident and Miss Harris saying the parson at Falconbridge was her uncle. Everybody exclaims tiresomely at the smallness of the world and nobody thinks much more of it. Mix a missing letter up in the story and we instantly incline to regard Miss Harris's remote connection with Falconbridge as a perfectly astonishing coincidence.'

'She'd hardly have mentioned it so freely,' admitted Fox, 'if she'd had anything to do with the letter.'

'Exactly. Still, we'll have to follow it up. And, talking of following things up, Fox, there's Lady Lorrimer. We'll have to check Sir Daniel Davidson's account of himself.'

'That's right, sir.'

Fox unhooked his spectacles and put them in their case.

'On what we've got,' he asked, 'have you any particular leaning to anyone?'

429

'Yes. I've left it until we had a moment's respite to discuss it with you. I wanted to see if you'd arrived independently at the same conclusion yourself.'

'The cigarette-case and the telephone call.'

'Yes. Very well, Fox: "in a contemplative fashion and a tranquil frame of mind," let us discuss the cigarette-cases. Point one.'

They discussed the cigarette-cases.

At seven o'clock Fox said:

'We're not within sight of making an arrest. Not on that evidence.'

Alleyn said: 'And don't forget we haven't found the cloak and hat.'

Fox said: 'It seems to me, Mr Alleyn, we'll have to ask every blasted soul that hasn't got an alibi if we can search their house. Clumsy.'

'Carrados,' began Alleyn, 'Halcut-Hackett, Davidson, Miss Harris. Withers and Potter go together. I swear the hat and cloak aren't in that flat. Same goes for Dimitri.'

'The garbage-tins,' said Fox gloomily. 'I've told the chaps about the garbage-tins. They're so unlikely they're enough to make you cry. What would anybody do with a cloak and hat, Mr Alleyn, if they wanted to get rid of 'em? We know all the old dodges. You couldn't burn 'em in any of these London flats. It was low tide, as you've pointed out, and they'd have had to be dropped off the bridge which would have been a pretty risky thing to do. D'you reckon they'll try leaving 'em at a railway office?'

'We'll have to watch for it. We'll have to keep a good man to tail our fancy. I don't somehow feel it'll be a left-luggage affair, Brer Fox. They've been given a little too much publicity of late years. Limbs and torsos have bobbed up in corded boxes with dreary insistence, not only up and down the LNER and kindred offices, but throughout the pages of detective fiction. I rather fancy the parcels post myself. I've sent out the usual request. If they were

430

posted it was probably during the rush hour at one of the big central offices, and how the suffering cats we're to catch up with that is more than I can tell. Still, we'll hope for a lucky break, whatever that may be.'

The desk telephone rang. Alleyn, suddenly and painfully reminded of Lord Robert's call, answered it.

His mother's voice asked if he would dine with her.

'I don't suppose you can get away, my dear, but as this flat is only five minutes in a taxi it might suit you to come in.'

'I'd like to,' said Alleyn. 'When?'

'Eight, but we can have it earlier if you like. I'm all alone.'

'I'll come now, mama, and we'll have it at eight. All right?'

'Quite all right,' said the clear little voice. 'So glad, darling.'

Alleyn left his mother's telephone number in case anybody should want him, and went by taxi to the flat she had taken in Catherine Street for the London season. He found Lady Alleyn surrounded by newspapers and wearing horn-rimmed glasses.

'Hullo, darling,' she said. 'I shan't pretend I'm not reading about poor Bunchy, but we won't discuss it if you don't want to.'

'To tell you the truth,' said Alleyn, 'I rather feel I want to sit in an armchair, stare at nothing, and scarcely speak. Charming company for you, mama.'

'Why not have a bath?' suggested Lady Alleyn without looking up from her paper.

'Do I smell?' asked her son.

'No. But I always think a bath is rather a good idea when you've got to the staring stage. What time did you get up this morning?'

'*Yesterday* morning. But I have bathed and shaved since then.'

431

'No bed at all last night? I should have a bath. I'll run it for you. Use my room. I've sent for a change of clothes.'

'Good Lord!' said Alleyn, and then: 'You're something rather special in the maternal line, aren't you?'

He bathed. The solace of steaming water wrapped him in a sort of luxurious trance. His thoughts, that for sixteen hours had been so sharply concentrated, became blurred and nebulous. Was it only 'this morning' that he had crossed the courtyard to a taxi, half-hidden by wreaths of mist? This morning! Their footsteps had sounded hollow on the stone pavement. 'I got to look after meself, see?' A door opened with a huge slow movement that was full of horror. 'Dead, ain't 'e? *Dead, ain't 'e?* DEAD, AIN'T 'E? 'Suffocated!' gasped Alleyn and woke with his nose full of bath-water.

His man had sent clean linen and a dinner-suit. He dressed slowly, feeling rarefied, and rejoined his mother in the sitting-room.

'Help yourself to a drink,' she said from behind her newspaper.

He got his drink and sat down. He wondered vaguely why he should feel so dog-tired. He was used to missing a night's sleep and working straight through the twenty-four hours. It must be because it was Bunchy. And the thought came into his mind that there must be a great many people at this hour who with him remembered that comic figure and regretted it.

'He had a great deal of charm,' said Alleyn aloud and his mother's voice answered him tranquilly.

'Yes, a great deal of charm. The most unfair of all the attributes.'

'You don't add: "I sometimes think," ' said Alleyn.

'Why should I?'

'People so often use that phrase to water down their ideas. You are too positive to use it.'

'In Bunchy's case the charm was one of character and

432

then it is not unfair,' said Lady Alleyn. 'Shall we dine? It's been announced.'

'Good Lord,' said Alleyn, 'I never noticed.'

Over their coffee he asked: 'Where's Sarah?'

'She's dining and going to a play with a suitably chaperoned party.'

'Does she see anything of Rose Birnbaum?'

'My dear Roderick, who on earth is Rose Birnbaum?'

'She's Mrs Halcut-Hackett's burden for the season. Her professional burden.'

'Oh, that gel! Poor little thing, yes. I've noticed her. I don't know if Sarah pays much attention. Why?'

'I wish you'd ask her here some time. Not a seasonable party. She's got an inferiority complex about them. She's one of the more unfortunate by-products of the season.'

'I see. I wonder why that singularly hard woman has involved herself with a paying protégée. Are the Halcut-Hacketts short of money?'

'I don't know. I should think she might be at the moment.'

'Withers,' said Lady Alleyn.

'Hullo. You know all about Withers, do you?'

'My dear Rory, you forget I sit in chaperones' corner.'

'Gossip,' said Alleyn.

'The gossip is not as malicious as you may think. I always maintain that men are just as avid scandalmongers as women.'

'I know you do.'

'Mrs Halcut-Hackett is not very popular, so they don't mind talking about her in chaperones' corner. She's an opportunist. She never gives an invitation that will not bring its reward and she never accepts one that is likely to lower her prestige. She is not a kind woman. She's extremely common, but that doesn't matter. Lots of common people are charming. Like bounders. I believe no woman ever falls passionately in love with a man unless he has just the least touch of the bounder somewhere in his composition.'

'Really, mama!'

'I mean in a very rarified sense. A touch of arrogance. There's nothing like it, my dear. If you're too delicately considerate of a woman's feelings she may begin by being grateful, but the chances are she'll end by despising you.'

Alleyn made a wry face. 'Treat 'em rough?'

'Not actually, but let them think you *might*. It's humiliating but true that ninety-nine women out of a hundred like to feel their lover is capable of bullying them. Eighty of them would deny it. How often does one not hear a married woman say with a sort of satisfaction that her husband won't let her do this or that? Why do abominably written books with strong silent heroes still find a large female public? What do you suppose attracts thousands of women to a cinema actor with the brains of a mosquito?'

'His ability as a cinema actor.'

'That, yes. Don't be tiresome, Roderick. Above all, his arrogant masculinity. That's what attracts ninety-nine out of a hundred, you may depend upon it.'

'There is, perhaps fortunately, always the hundredth woman.'

'And don't be too sure of her. I am *not*, I hope, one of those abominable women who cries down her own sex. I'm by way of being a feminist, but I refuse to allow the ninety-nine (dear me, this begins to sound like a hymn) to pull the wool over the elderly eyes.'

'You're an opinionated little party, mama, and you know it. But don't suppose you can pull the wool over my eyes either. Do you suggest that I go to Miss Agatha Troy, haul her about her studio by her hair, tuck her under my arrogant masculine arm, and lug her off to the nearest registry office?'

'Church, if you please. The Church knows what I'm

434

talking about. Look at the marriage service. A direct and
embarrassing expression of the savagery inherent in our
ideas of mating.'

'Would you say the season came under the same heading?'

'In a way I would say so. And why not? As long as
one recognizes the more savage aspects of the season, one
keeps one's sense of proportion and enjoys it. As I do.
Thoroughly. And as Bunchy Gospell did. When I think
of him,' said Lady Alleyn, her eyes shining with tears, 'when
I think of him this morning, gossiping away to all of us,
so pleased with Evelyn's ball, so gay and – and *real*, I
simply cannot realize – '

'I know.'

'I suppose Mrs Halcut-Hackett comes into the picture,
doesn't she? And Withers?'

'What makes you think so?'

'He had his eye on them. Both there and at the Halcut-
Hacketts' cocktail-party. Bunchy knew something about
Captain Withers, Roderick. I saw that and I remarked on
it to him. He told me not to be inquisitive, bless him,
but he admitted I was right. Is there anything more in
it than that?'

'A good deal. Withers has a bad record and Bunchy
knew it.'

'Is that a motive for murder?' asked Lady Alleyn.

'It might be. There are several discrepancies. I've got
to try to settle one of them tonight.'

'Tonight? My dear, you'll fall asleep with the customary
warning on your lips.'

'Not I. And I'm afraid there's no occasion as yet for
the customary warning.'

'Does Evelyn Carrados come into the picture at all?'

Alleyn sat up.

'Why do you ask that?'

'Because I could see that Bunchy had his eye on her
too.'

435

'We'd better change jobs, darling. You can go into the Yard and watch people having their eyes on each other and I'll sit in chaperones' corner, pounce at young men for Sarah, and make conversation with Lady Lorrimer. I've got to see her some time soon, by the way.'

'Lucy Lorrimer! You don't mean to tell me she's in this business. I can well understand somebody murdering *her*, but I don't see her on the other side of the picture. Of course she *is* mad.'

'She's got to supply half an alibi for Sir Daniel Davidson.'

'Good heavens, who next! Why Davidson?'

'Because he was the last man to leave before Bunchy.'

'Well, I hope it's not Sir Daniel. I was thinking of showing him my leg. Roderick, I suppose I can't help you with Lucy Lorrimer. I can easily ring her up and ask her to tea. She must be seething with excitement and longing to talk to everybody. Bunchy was to dine with her tonight.'

'Why?'

'For no particular reason. But she kept saying she knew he wouldn't come, that he'd forget. I can easily ring her up and she shouts so loudly you need only sit beside me to hear every word.'

'All right,' said Alleyn, 'let's try. Ask her if she saw anything of Bunchy as she was leaving. You sit in the chair here, darling, and I'll perch on the arm. We can have the receiver between us.'

Lady Lorrimer's telephone was persistently engaged but at last they got through. Her ladyship, said a voice, was at home.

'Will you say it's Lady Alleyn? Thank you.'

During the pause that followed Lady Alleyn eyed her son with a conspiratorial air and asked him to give her a cigarette. He did so and provided himself with pencil and paper.

'We'll be *ages*,' she whispered, waving the receiver to and fro rather as if it were a fan. Suddenly it emitted a loud crackling sound and Lady Alleyn raised it gingerly to within four inches of her right ear.

'Is that you, Lucy?'

'My *dear*:' shouted the receiver, 'I'm *so* glad. I've been *longing* to speak to you for, of course, you can tell us *everything*. I've always thought it was *such* a pity that good-looking son of yours turning himself into a policeman because, say what you will, it must be frightfully bad for them so long in the one position only moving their arms and the internal organs taking *all* the strain which Sir Daniel tells me is the cause of half the diseases of women, though I must own I think his practice is getting rather beyond him. Of course in the case of the Prime Minister everything must be excused.'

Lady Alleyn looked an inquiry at her son who nodded his comprehension of this amazing tarradiddle.

'Yes, Lucy?' murmured Lady Alleyn.

'Which brings me to this *frightful* calamity,' continued the telephone in a series of cracks and splutters. '*Too* awful! And you know he was to dine with me tonight. I put my brother off because I felt I could never accustom myself to the idea that there but for the Grace of God sat Bunchy Gospell. Not perhaps the Grace of God but His ways are inscrutable indeed and when I saw him come down the staircase humming to himself I little thought that he was going to his grave. I shall *never* forgive myself, of course, that I did not offer to drive him and as it turned out with the Prime Minister being so ill I might have done so.'

'Why do you keep introducing the Prime Minister into this story, Lucy?' asked Lady Alleyn. She clapped her hand over the mouthpiece and said crossly: 'But *I* want to know, Roderick.'

'It's all right,' said Alleyn. 'Davidson pretended – do listen, darling, she's telling you.'

' – I can't describe the agony, Helena,' quacked the telephone, 'I really thought I should *swoon* with it. I felt

437

Sir Daniel must examine me without losing a moment, so I told my chauffeur to look out for him because I promise you *I* was too ill to distinguish one man from another. Then I saw him coming out of the door. "Sir Daniel, Sir Daniel!" He did not hear me and all would have been lost if one of the linkmen had not seen my distress and drawn Sir Daniel's attention to me. He crossed the street and as a very old patient I don't mind admitting to you, Helena, I *was* rather *disappointed* but of course with the country in the state it is one must make sacrifices. He was extremely agitated. The Prime Minister had developed some terrible complaint. Please tell nobody of this, Helena. I know you are as silent as the grave but Sir Daniel would no doubt be gravely compromised if it were ever to leak out. Under those conditions I could do nothing but bear my cross in silence and it was not until he had positively *run* away that I thought of driving him to Downing Street. By the time my fool of a chauffeur had started the car, of course, it was too late. No doubt Sir Daniel had raced to the nearest taxi-cab and, although I have rung up to inquire tactfully, he is continually engaged, so that one fears the worst.'

'Mad!' said Lady Alleyn to her son.

' – I can't tell you how much it has upset me but I hope I know my duty, Helena, and having just recollected that your boy was a constable I said to myself that he should learn of this extraordinary man whom I am firmly persuaded is an assassin. What other explanation can there be?'

'Sir Daniel Davidson!' exclaimed Lady Alleyn.

'Good heavens, Helena, are you mad! For pity's sake tell your son to come and see me himself in order that there may be no mistake. How could it be my poor Sir Daniel, who was already on his way to Downing Street? I attribute my appalling condition at this moment to the shock I received. Do you remember a play called *The Face*

438

at the Window? I was reminded of it. I assure you I screamed aloud – my chauffeur will bear witness. The nose was flat and white and the moustache quite frightful, like some hairy monster gummed to the window-pane. The eyes rolled, I could do nothing but clutch my pearls. 'Go away!' I screamed. My chauffeur, fool that he is, had seen nothing and by the time he roused himself it had disappeared.'

Alleyn held a sheet of paper before his mother's nose. On it he had written: 'Ask her who it was.'

'Have you any idea who it was, Lucy?' asked Lady Alleyn.

'There is no doubt whatsoever in my mind, Helena, and I should have thought little in yours. These appalling cases that have occurred! The papers are full of them. The Peeping Tom of Peckham, though how he has managed to go there every night from Halkin Street – '

Alleyn gave a stifled exclamation.

'From Halkin Street?' repeated Lady Alleyn.

'There is no doubt that his wife's appalling behaviour has turned his head. He suspected poor Robert Gospell. You must have heard, as I did, how he asked her to let him take her home. No doubt he was searching for them. The jury will bring in a strong recommendation for mercy or perhaps they will find him guilty but insane, as no doubt he is.'

'But, Lucy! Lucy, listen. *Whom are you talking about?*'

'Don't be a fool, Helena, who should it be but George Halcut-Hackett?'

CHAPTER TWENTY-TWO

Night Club

'Well Roderick,' said Lady Alleyn when she had at last got rid of Lucy Lorrimer, 'you may be able to make something of this but it seems to me that Lucy has at last gone completely insane. Do you for an instant suppose that poor old General Halcut-Hackett is the Peeping Tom of Peckham?'

'Some case the Press had made into a front-page story – no, of course, it's completely irrelevant. But all the same it does look as though old Halcut-Hackett flattened his face against the window of Lucy Lorrimer's car.'

'But Lucy stayed till the end, she says, and I know he took that unfortunate child away soon after midnight. What was the poor creature doing in Belgrave Square at half-past three?'

'He told me he went for a constitutional,' murmured Alleyn.

'Rubbish. One doesn't peer into old ladies' cars when one takes constitutionals at half-past three in the morning. The whole thing's preposterous.'

'It's so preposterous that I'm afraid it must be included in my dreary programme. Would you care to come to a night club with me, mama?'

'No thank you, Rory.'

'I thought not. I must go alone to the Matador. I imagine they open at about eleven.'

'Nobody goes until after midnight or later,' said Lady Alleyn.

'How do you know?'

'Sarah is forever pestering me to allow her to "go on to the Matador". She now hopes to produce a chaperone, but I imagine it is scarcely the haunt of chaperones. I have no intention of letting her go.'

'It's one of those places that offer the attractions of a tiny dancing-floor, a superlative band and a crowd so dense that you spend the night dancing cheek-to-cheek with somebody else's partner. It is so dimly lit that the most innocent visitor takes on an air of intrigue and the guiltiest has at least a sporting chance of going unrecognized.'

'You seem to be remarkably familiar with its amenities,' said his mother dryly.

'We've had our eye on the Matador for some time. It will meet with one of three fates. The smartest people will get tired of it and it will try to hold them by relaxing its vigilance in the matter of drink; or the smartest people will get tired of it and it will gradually lose its prestige and continue to make money out of the less exclusive but equally rich; or the smartest people will get tired of it and it will go bust. We are interested in the first contingency and they know it. They are extremely polite to me at the Matador.'

'Shall you be long there?'

'No. I only want to see the commissionaire and the secretary. Then I'll go home and to bed. May I use your telephone?'

Alleyn rang up Fox and asked him if he had seen the constable on night duty in Belgrave Square.

'Yes,' said Fox. 'I've talked to him. He says he didn't report having seen the General, you know who – double aitch – because he didn't think anything of it, knowing him so well. He says he thought the General had been at the ball and was on his way home.'

'When was this?'

'About three-twenty when most of the guests were leaving Marsdon House. Our chap says he didn't notice the General earlier in the evening when he took the young lady home. He says he still had his eye on the crowd outside the front door at that time and might easily have missed him. He says it's right enough that the old gentleman generally takes a turn round the Square of an evening but he's never noticed him as late as this before. I've told him a few things about what's expected of him and why sergeants lose their stripes,' added Fox. 'The fact of the matter is he spent most of his time round about the front door of Marsdon House. Now there's one other thing, sir. One of these linkmen has reported he noticed a man in a black overcoat with a white scarf pulled up to his mouth, and a black trilby hat, standing for a long time in the shadow on the outskirts of the crowd. The linkman says he was tall and looked like a gentleman. Thinks he wore evening clothes under his overcoat. Thinks he had a white moustache. He says this man seemed anxious to avoid notice and hung about in the shadows, but he looked at him several times and wondered what he was up to. The linkman reckons this man was hanging about on the other side of the street in the shadow of the trees, when the last guests went away. Now, sir, I reckon that's important.'

'Yes, Fox. Are you suggesting that this lurker was the General?'

'The description tallies, sir. I thought I'd arrange for this chap, who's still here at the Yard, to get a look at the General and see if he can swear to him.'

'You do. Better take your linkman off to the Square. See if you can catch the General doing his evening march. He'll be able to see him in the same light under the same conditions as last night's.'

'That's right.'

'I'm going to the Matador and then home. Ring me up if there's anything.'

'Very good, Mr Alleyn. Good night.'

'Good night, Brer Fox.'

Alleyn turned from the telephone and stared at his mother.

'It looks as if Lucy Lorrimer isn't altogether dotty,' he said. 'Old Halcut-Hackett seems to have behaved in a very curious manner last night. If, indeed, it was the General, and I fancy it must have been. He was so remarkably evasive about his own movements. Do you know him at all well?'

'Not very, darling. He was a brother-officer of your father's. I rather think he was one of those large men whom regimental humour decrees shall be called "Tiny". I can't remember ever hearing that he had a violent temper or took drugs or seduced his colonel's wife or indeed did anything at all remarkable. He didn't marry this rather dreadful lady of his until he was about fifty.'

'Was he rich?'

'I rather think he was fairly rich. Still is, I should have thought from that house. He's got a country place too, I believe, somewhere in Kent.'

'Then why on earth does she bother with paying débutantes?'

'Well, you know, Rory, if she's anxious to be asked everywhere and do everything she's more likely to succeed with something young behind her. Far more invitations would come rolling in.'

'Yes. I rather think there's more to it than that. Good night, darling. You are the best sort of mama. Too astringent to be sweet, thank God, but nevertheless comfortable.'

'Thank you, my dear. Come in again if you want to. Good night.'

She saw him out with an air of jauntiness, but when she returned to her drawing-room she sat still for a long time thinking of the past of her son, of Troy, and of her own fixed determination never to meddle.

Alleyn took a taxi to the Matador in Soho. The Matador commissionaire was a disillusioned giant in a plum-coloured uniform. He wore beautiful gloves, a row of medals, and an expression of worldly wisdom. He stood

443

under a representation in red neon lights of a capering bull-fighter, and he paid the management twenty pounds a year for his job. Alleyn gave him good evening and walked into the entrance-hall of the Matador. The pulsation of saxophones and percussion instruments hung on the air, deadened in this ante-room by draperies of plum-coloured silk caught up into classic folds by rows of silvered tin sunflowers. A lounge porter came forward and directed Alleyn to the cloakroom.

'I wonder if you know Captain Maurice Withers by sight,' asked Alleyn. 'I'm supposed to join his party and I'm not sure if I've come to the right place. He's a member here.'

'I'm sorry, sir. I've only just taken this job myself and I don't know the members by sight. If you ask at the office, sir, they'll tell you.'

With a silent anathema on this ill-chance Alleyn thanked the man and looked for the box-office. He found it beneath a large sunflower and surrounded by richer folds of silk. Alleyn peered into it and saw a young man in a beautiful dinner-jacket, morosely picking his teeth.

'Good evening,' said Alleyn.

The young man abandoned the toothpick with lightning sleight-of-hand.

'Good evening, sir,' he said brightly in a cultured voice.

'May I speak to you for a moment – Mr – ?'

The young man instantly looked very wary.

'Well – ah – I am the manager. My name is Cuthbert.'

Alleyn slid his card through the peep-hole. The young man looked at it, turned even more wary, and said:

'Perhaps if you wouldn't mind walking round to the side door, Mr – Oh! – Inspector – ah! – Alleyn. Simmons!'

A cloakroom attendant appeared. On the way to the side door Alleyn tried his story again but neither the cloakroom attendant nor the commissionaire, who was recalled, knew Withers by sight. The attendant conducted

444

Alleyn by devious ways into a little dim room behind the box-office. Here he found the manager.

'It's nothing very momentous,' said Alleyn. 'I want you to tell me, if you can, about what time Captain Maurice Withers arrived at this club last night – or rather this morning?'

He saw Mr Cuthbert glance quickly at an evening paper on which appeared a quarter-page photograph of Robert Gospell. During the second or two that elapsed before he replied, Alleyn heard again that heavy insistent thudding of the band.

'I'm afraid I have no idea at all,' said Mr Cuthbert at last.

'That's a pity,' said Alleyn. 'If you can't tell me I suppose I'll have to make rather a business of it. I'll have to ask all your guests if they saw him and when and so on. I'm afraid I shall have to insist on seeing the book. I'm sorry. What a bore for you!'

Mr Cuthbert looked at him with the liveliest distaste.

'You can understand,' he began, 'that in our position we have to be extremely tactful. Our guests expect it of us.'

'Oh, rather,' agreed Alleyn. 'But there's not going to be nearly such a fluster if you give me the information I want quietly, as there will be if I have to start asking all sorts of people all sorts of questions.'

Mr Cuthbert stared at his first finger-nail and then bit it savagely.

'But if I don't know,' he said peevishly.

'Then we're just out of luck. I'll try your commissionaire and – Simmons, is it? If that fails we'll have to start on the guests.'

'Oh, damn!' ejaculated Mr Cuthbert. 'Well, he came in late. I do remember that.'

'How do you remember that, please?'

'Because we had a crowd of people who came from –

445

from the Marsdon House Ball at about half-past three or a quarter to four. And then there was a bit of a lull.'

'Yes?'

'Yes, well, and then a good deal later Captain Withers signed in. He ordered a fresh bottle of gin.'

'Mrs Halcut-Hackett arrived with him, didn't she?'

'I don't know the name of his partner.'

'A tall, big, blonde woman of about forty to forty-five, with an American accent. Perhaps you wouldn't mind calling – '

'All right, then, all right. She did.'

'Was it as late as half-past four when they arrived?'

'I don't – look here, I mean – '

'It's quite possible you may hear no more of this. The more exact your information, you know, the less troublesome our subsequent enquiries.'

'Yes, I know, but we owe a DUTY to our guests.'

'Do you know actually to within say ten minutes when this couple arrived? I think you do. If so, I most strongly advise you to tell me.'

'Oh, all right. As a matter of fact it was a quarter-past four. There'd been such a long gap with nobody coming in – we were practically full anyway of course – that I *did* happen to notice the time.'

'That's perfectly splendid. Now if you'll sign a statement to this effect I don't think I need bother you any more.'

Mr Cuthbert fell into a profound meditation. Alleyn lit a cigarette and waited with an air of amiability. At last Mr Cuthbert said:

'Am I likely to be called as a witness to anything?'

'Not very. We'll spare you if we can.'

'I could refuse.'

'And I,' said Alleyn, 'could become a member of your club. You couldn't refuse that.'

'Delighted, I'm sure,' said Mr Cuthbert unhappily. 'All right. I'll sign.'

Alleyn wrote out a short statement and Mr Cuthbert signed it. Mr Cuthbert became more friendly and offered Alleyn a drink, which he refused with the greatest amiability. Mr Cuthbert embarked on a long eulogistic account of the Matador and the way it was run and the foolishness of night-club proprietors who attempted to elude the lawful restriction imposed on the sale of alcoholic beverages.

'It never pays,' cried Mr Cuthbert. 'Sooner or later they get caught. It's just damn silly.'

A waiter burst into the room, observed something in Mr Cuthbert's eye, and flew out again. Mr Cuthbert cordially invited Alleyn to accompany him into the dance-room. He was so insistent that Alleyn allowed himself to be ushered through the entrance-hall and down a plum-coloured tunnel. The sound of the band swelled into a rhythmic all-pervading rumpus. Alleyn was aware of more silver sunflowers; of closely ranked tables and faces dimly lit from below, of a more distant huddle of people ululating and sliding in time to the band. He stood just inside the entrance, trying to accustom his eyes to this scene, while Mr Cuthbert prattled innocently 'Ruddigore' – 'We only cut respectable capers.' He was about to turn away when he knew abruptly that someone was watching him. His eyes followed this intangible summons. He turned slowly to the left and there at a corner table sat Bridget O'Brien and Donald Potter.

They were both staring at him and with such intensity that he could not escape the feeling that they had wished to attract his attention. He deliberately met their gaze and returned it. For a second or two they looked at each other and then Bridget made a quick gesture, inviting him to join them.

He said: 'I see some friends. Do you mind if I speak to them for a moment?'

Mr Cuthbert was delighted and melted away on a wave

447

of tactfulness. Alleyn walked over to the table and bowed.

'Good evening.'

'Will you sit down for a minute?' said Bridget. 'We want to speak to you.'

One of Mr Cuthbert's waiters instantly produced a chair.

'What is it?' asked Alleyn.

'It's Bridgie's idea,' said Donald. 'I can't stand it any longer. I've said I'll do whatever Bridgie says. I suppose I'm a fool but I give in. In a way I want to.'

'He's got nothing to fear,' said Bridget. 'I've told him – '

'Look here,' said Alleyn, 'this doesn't seem a particularly well-chosen spot for the kind of conversation that's indicated.'

'I know,' said Bridget. 'If Donna or Bart ever finds out I've been here there'll be a row of absolutely horrific proportions. The Matador! Unchaperoned! With Donald! But we were desperate – we *had* to see each other. Bart has driven me stark ravers, he's been so awful. I managed to ring Donald up from an outside telephone and we arranged to meet here. Donald's a member. We've talked it all over and we were coming to see you.'

'Suppose you do so now. The manager here knows I'm a policeman so we'd better not leave together. Here's my address. Come along in about fifteen minutes. That do?'

'Yes, thank you,' said Bridget, 'won't it, Donald?'

'All right, all right,' said Donald. 'It's your idea, darling. If it lands me in – '

'It won't land you anywhere but in my flat,' said Alleyn. 'You've both come to a very sensible decision.'

He rose and looked down at them. 'Good Lord,' he thought, 'they *are* young.' He said: 'Don't weaken. *Au revoir,*' and walked out of the Matador.

On the way to his flat he wondered if the loss of the best part of another night's sleep was going to get him any nearer a solution.

CHAPTER TWENTY-THREE

Donald on Wits

Alleyn walked restlessly about his sitting-room. He had
sent Vassily, his old servant, off to bed. The flat, at the
end of a cul-de-sac behind Coventry Street, was very silent.
He was fond of this room. It had a contradictory air of
monastic comfort that was, if he had realized it, a direct
expression of himself. Dürer's praying hands were raised
above his mantelpiece. At the other end of the room Troy's
painting of the wharf at Suva uttered, in sharp cool colours,
a simple phrase of beauty. He had bought this picture
secretly from one of her exhibitions and Troy did not know
that it hung there in his room. Three comfortable elderly
chairs from his mother's house at Bossicote, his father's
desk and, waist-high all round the walls, a company of
friendly books. But this June night his room seemed chilly.
He put a match to the wood fire and drew three armchairs
into the circle of its radiance. Time those two arrived. A
taxi came up the cul-de-sac and stopped. The door banged.
He heard Bridget's voice and went to let them in.

He was reminded vividly of two small children entering
a dentist's waiting-room. Donald was the victim, Bridget
the not very confident escort. Alleyn tried to dispel this
atmosphere, settled them in front of the fire, produced
ciagrettes, and remembering they were grown-up offered
them drinks. Bridget refused. Donald with an air of
grandeur accepted a whisky and soda.

'Now then,' said Alleyn, 'What's it all about?' He felt
he ought to add: 'Open wide!' and as he handed Donald
his drink: 'Rinse, please.'

'It's about Donald,' said Bridget in a high determined
voice. 'He's promised to let me tell you. He doesn't like

it but I say I won't marry him unless he does, so he's
going to. And besides, he really thinks he ought to do
it.'

'It's a damn fool thing to do,' said Donald. 'There's
no reason actually why I should come into it at all. I've
made up my mind but all the same I don't see – '

'All the same, you are in it, darling, so it doesn't much
matter if you see why or not, as the case may be.'

'All right. That's settled anyway, isn't it? We needn't
go on arguing. Let's tell Mr Alleyn and get it over.'

'Yes, Let's. Shall I?'

'If you like.'

Bridget turned to Alleyn.

'When we met tonight,' she began, 'I asked Donald about
Captain Withers, because the way you talked about him
this afternoon made me think perhaps he's not a good
idea. I made Donald tell me *exactly* what he knows about
Wits.'

'Yes?'

'Yes. Well, Wits is a crook. Isn't he Donald?'

'I suppose so.'

'He's a crook because he runs a gambling hell at
Leatherhead. Don says you know that or anyway you
suspect it. Well, he does. And Donald said he'd go in with
him only he didn't know then how crooked Wits was. And
then Donald lost money to Wits and couldn't pay him
back and Wits said he'd better stand in with him because
he'd make it pretty hot for Donald if he didn't. What with
Bunchy and everything.'

'But Bunchy paid your debts to Withers,' said Alleyn.

'Not all,' said Donald with a scarlet face but a look
of desperate determination ('First extraction,' thought
Alleyn.) 'I didn't tell him about all of it.'

'I see.'

'So Donald said he'd go in with Wits. And then when
he quarrelled with Bunchy and went to live with Wits he

451

found out that Wits was worse of a crook than ever. Don found out that Wits was getting money from a woman. Do I have to tell you who she was?'

'Was it Mrs Halcut-Hackett?'

'Yes.'

'Was it much?' Alleyn asked Donald.

'Yes, sir,' said Donald. 'I don't know how much. But she – he told me she had an interest in the Leatherhead club. I thought at first it was all right. Really I did. It's hard to explain. I just got sort of used to the way Wits talked. Everything is a ramp nowadays – a racket – that's what Wits said and I began rather to think the same way. I suppose I lost my eye. Bridget says I did.'

'I expect she's right, isn't she?'

'I suppose so. But – I don't know. It was all rather fun in a way until – well, until today.'

'You mean since Bunchy was murdered?'

'Yes. I do. But – you see – '

'Let me,' said Bridget. 'You see, Mr Alleyn, Donald got rather desperate. Wits rang up and told him to keep away. That was this morning.'

'I know. It was at my instigation,' said Alleyn. 'I was there.'

'Oh,' said Donald.

'Well, anyway,' said Bridget, 'Donald got a bit of a shock. What with your questions and Wits always rubbing it in that Donald was going to be quite well off when his uncle died.'

'Did Captain Withers make a lot of that?'

Bridget took Donald's hand.

'Yes,' she said, 'he did. Didn't he, Donald?'

'Anyone would think, Bridget, that you wanted to hang one of us, Wits or me,' said Donald and raised her hand to his cheek.

Bridget said: 'I'm going to tell *everything*. You're

452

innocent, and if you're innocent you're safe. My mother would say that. You say it, don't you, Mr Alleyn?'

'Yes,' said Alleyn.

'Well, this afternoon,' Bridget went on, 'Donald's things came back from Wits' flat. His clothes and his books. When he unpacked them he saw one book was missing.

'The first volume of Taylor's *Medical Jurisprudence?*'

Donald wetted his lips and nodded.

'That upset Donald awfully,' Bridget continued, growing rather white in the face, 'because of one chapter in the book. After they read the papers this morning Donald and Wits had an argument about how long it took to – to – '

'Oh God!' said Donald suddenly.

'To asphyxiate anybody?' asked Alleyn.

'Yes. And Donald looked it up in this book.'

'Did Captain Withers handle the book?'

Donald looked quickly at Bridget and said: 'Yes, he did. He read a bit of it and then lost interest. He thought it would have taken longer, he said.'

'Donald was puzzled about the book not arriving, and about Wits telling him not to come to the flat,' said Bridget. 'He thought about it all the afternoon, and the more he thought the less he liked it. So he rang up. Wits answered but when he heard Donald's voice he simply cut him off without another word. Didn't he, darling?'

'Yes,' said Donald. 'I rang again and he didn't answer. I – I couldn't think clearly at all. I felt stone cold in the pit of my stomach. It was simply ghastly to find myself cut dead like that. *Why* shouldn't he answer me, *why*? Why hadn't he sent the book? Only this morning we'd been together in his flat, perfectly friendly. Until the news came – after that I didn't listen to anything Wits said. As soon as I knew Uncle Bunch had been murdered I couldn't think of anything else. I wasn't dressed when the papers came. Mother had known for hours but, the telephone being

453

disconnected then, she couldn't get hold of me. I hadn't told her my address. Wits kept talking. I didn't listen. And then, when I did get home, you were there, getting at me, getting at me. And then my mother crying, and the flowers, and everything. And on top of it all this business of Wits not wanting to speak to me. I couldn't think. I just *had* to see Bridget.'

'Yes,' said Bridget, 'he had to see me. But you're muddling things, Donald. We ought to keep them in their right order. Mr Alleyn, we've got as far as this afternoon. Well, Donald got so rattled about the telephone and the missing book that in spite of what Wits had said, he felt he *had* to see him. So after dinner he took a taxi to Wits's flat and he could see a light under the blind, so he knew Wits was in. Donald still had his own latch-key so he went straight in and up to the flat. Now you go on, Donald.'

Donald finished his whisky and soda and with unsteady fingers lit a fresh cigarette. 'All right,' he said. 'I'll tell you. When I walked into the sitting-room he was lying on the divan bed. I stood in the middle of the room looking at him. He didn't move, and he didn't speak at all loudly. He called me a foul name and told me to get out. I said I wanted to know why he'd behaved as he did. He just lay there and looked at me. I said something about you, sir – I don't know what – and in a split second he was on his feet. I thought he was going to start a fight. He asked me what the bloody hell I'd said to you about him. I said I'd avoided speaking about him as much as possible. But he began to ask all sorts of questions. God, he did look ugly. You often read about the veins swelling with rage in people's faces. They did in his. He sat on the edge of the table swinging one foot and his face got sort of dark.'

'Yes,' said Alleyn. 'I can see Captain Withers. Go on.'

'He said – ' Donald caught his breath. Alleyn saw his fingers tighten round Bridget's. 'He said that unless I kept

454

my head and held my tongue he'd begin to talk himself.
He said that after all I had quarrelled with Uncle Bunch
and I had been in debt and I was Uncle Bunch's heir.
He said if he was in this thing up to his knees I was in
it up to my neck. He pulled his hand out of his pocket
and pointed his flat finger at my neck. Then he told me
to remember, if I didn't want to commit suicide, that when
he left Marsdon House he went to his car and drove to
the Matador. I was to say that I'd seen him drive off with
his partner.'

'Did you see this?'

'No. I left after him. I did think I saw him walking
ahead of me towards his car. It was parked in Belgrave
Road.'

'Why, do you suppose, did Withers take this
extraordinary attitude when you saw him tonight?'

'He thought I'd given him away to you. He told me
so.'

'About Leatherhead?'

'Yes. You said something about – about – '

'Fleecing lambs,' said Bridget.

'Yes. So I did,' admitted Alleyn cheerfully.

'He thought I'd lost my nerve and talked too much.'

'And now you are prepared to talk?'

'Yes.'

'Why?'

'We've told you – ' Bridget began.

'Yes, I know. You've told me that you persuaded Donald
to come to me because you thought it better for him to
explain his association with Withers. But I rather think
there's something more behind it than that. Would I be
wrong, Donald, if I said that you were at least encouraged
to take this decision by the fear that Withers himself might
get in first and suggest that you had killed your uncle?'

Bridget cried out: 'No! *No!* How can you be so cruel?
How can you think that of Donald! Donald!'

455

But Donald looked steadily at Alleyn and when he spoke again it was gravely and with a certain dignity that became him very well.

He said: 'Don't, Bridget. It's perfectly natural Mr Alleyn should think that I'm afraid of Wits accusing me. I *am* afraid of it. I didn't kill Uncle Bunch. I think I was fonder of him than anyone else in the world except you, Bridgie. But I had quarrelled with him. I wish to God I hadn't. I didn't kill him. The reason I'm quite ready now to answer any questions about Wits, even if it means implicating myself – ' He stopped and took a deep breath.

'Yes?' asked Alleyn.

' – is that after seeing Wits this evening I believe he murdered my uncle.'

There was a long silence.

'Motive?' asked Alleyn at last.

'He thought he had a big enough hold over me to get control of the money.'

'Proof?'

'I've none. Only the way he spoke tonight. He's afraid I believe he'd murder anyone if he'd enough incentive.'

'That's not proof, nor anything like it.'

'No. It seemed good enough,' said Donald, 'to bring me here when I might have kept quiet.'

The telephone rang. Alleyn went over to the desk and answered it.

'Hullo?'

'Roderick, is that you?'

'Yes. Who is it, please?'

'Evelyn Carrados.'

Alleyn looked across to the fireplace. He saw Bridget bend forward swiftly and kiss Donald.

'Hullo!' he said. 'Anything the matter?'

'Roderick, I'm so worried. I don't know what to do. Bridgie has gone out without saying a word to anyone. I've rung up as many people as I dared and I haven't an inkling where she is. I'm so terrified she's done something wild and foolish. I thought she might be with Donald Potter and I wondered if you could tell me his telephone number. Thank Heaven Herbert is out at a regimental dinner, at Tunbridge. I'm distraught with anxiety.'

'It's all right, Evelyn,' said Alleyn. 'Bridget's here with me.'

'*With you?*'

'Yes. She wanted to talk to me. She's quite all right. I'll bring her back – '

'Is Donald Potter there?'

'Yes.'

'*But why?* What have they *done* it for? Roderick, I want to see you. I'll come and get Bridget, may I?'

'Yes, do,' said Alleyn and gave her his address.

He hung up the receiver and turned to find Bridget and Donald looking very startled.

'*Donna!*' whispered Bridget. 'Oh, golly!'

'Had I better go?' asked Donald.

'I think perhaps you'd better,' said Alleyn.

'If Bridgie's going to be hauled over the coals I'd rather stay.'

'No, darling,' said Bridget, 'it will be better not, honestly. As long as Bart doesn't find out I'll be all right.'

'Your mother won't be here for ten minutes,' said Alleyn. 'Look here, Donald, I want a full account of this gambling business at Leatherhead. If I put you in another room will you write one for me? It will save us a great deal of time and trouble. It must be as clear as possible with no trimmings and as many dates as you can conjure up. It will, I hope, lead to Captain Withers's conviction.'

Donald looked uncomfortable.

'It seems rather a ghastly sort of thing to do. I mean – '

'Good heavens, you have just told me you think the man's a murderer and you apparently know he's a

457

blackguard. He's used you as a cat's-paw and I understand his idea has been to swindle you out of your money!'

'All right,' said Donald. 'I'll do it.'

Alleyn took him into the dining-room and settled him there with pen and paper.

'I'll come in later on and see what sort of fist you've made of it. There will have to be witnesses to your signature.'

'Shall I be had up as an accomplice?'

'I hardly think so. How old are you?'

'Twenty-one in August. It's not that I mind for myself. At least it would be pretty bloody, wouldn't it? But I've said I'll go through with it.'

'So you have. Don't make too big a sainted martyr of yourself,' said Alleyn good-naturedly. Donald looked up at him and suddenly the ghost of Lord Robert's twinkle came into his eyes.

'All right,' he said. 'I won't.'

Alleyn returned to Bridget and found her sitting on the hearth-rug. She looked very frightened.

'Does Bart know?'

'No, but your mother's been very worried.'

'Well, that's not all me. Bart's nearly driving her dotty. I can't tell you what he's like. Honestly it would never astonish me if Bart had an apoplectic fit and went crazy.'

'Dear me,' said Alleyn.

'No, honestly. I don't know what he told you when you interviewed him but I suppose you saw through the famous Carrados pose, didn't you? Of course you did. But you may not have realized what a temper he's got. I didn't for a long time. I mean not until I was about fifteen.'

'Two years ago?' asked Alleyn with a smile. 'Tell me about it.'

'It was simply frightful. Donna had been ill and she was sleeping very badly. Bart was asked if he'd mind going into his dressing-room. I didn't realize then, but I do now,

458

that that was what annoyed him. He always gets the huff when Donna's ill. He takes it as a sort of personal insult and being a beastly old Victorian Turk the dressing-room idea absolutely put the tin cupola on it. Are you shocked?'

'I suppose not,' said Alleyn cautiously. 'Anyway, go on.'

'Well, you're not. And so he went into his dressing-room. And then Donna got really ill and I said we must have Sir Daniel because she *was* so ill and he's an angel. And Bart rang him up. Well, I wanted to get hold of Sir Daniel first to tell him about Donna before Bart did. So I went downstairs into Bart's study because I told the butler to show Sir Daniel in there. Bart was up with Donna telling her how "seedy" he felt, and it didn't matter, she wasn't to notice. And then Sir Dan came in and was angelic and I told him about Donna. Did you notice in the study there's a French escritoire thing on a table?'

'Yes.'

'Well, Sir Dan adores old things and he saw it and raved about it and said it was a beautiful piece and told me when it was made and how they used sometimes to put little secret drawers in them and you just touch a screw and they fly out. He said it was a museum piece and asked me if I didn't think some of the vanished ladies might come back and open the secret drawer with ghostly fingers. So I thought I'd like to see, and when Sir Dan had gone up to Donna I tried prodding the screws with a pencil and at last a little drawer did fly out triangularly, sort of. There was a letter in it. I didn't touch it, naturally, but while I was looking at the drawer, Bart must have come in. What did you say?'

'Nothing,' said Alleyn. 'Go on.'

'I can't *tell* you what he was like. He went absolutely stark *ravers,* honestly. He took hold of my arm and twisted it so much I screamed before I could stop myself. And then he turned as white as the washing and called me a little bastard. I believed he'd have actually hit me if Sir

459

Dan hadn't come down. I think Sir Dan had heard me yell and he must have guessed what had happened because he had one glance at my arm – I had short sleeves – and then he said in a lovely *dangerous* sort of voice: "Are you producing *another* patient for me, Carrados?" Bart banged the little drawer shut, began to splutter and try to get up some sort of explanation. Sir Daniel just looked at him through his glasses – the ones with the black ribbon. Bart tried to pretend I'd slipped on the polished floor and he'd caught me by the arm. Sir Daniel said: "Very curious indeed," and went on looking at my arm. He gave me a prescription for some stuff to put on it and was frightfully nice to me, and didn't ask questions, but just ignored Bart. It made me absolutely *crawl* with shame to hear Bart trying to do his simple-soldier stuff and sort of ingratiate himself with Sir Dan. And when he'd gone Bart apologized to me and said he was really terribly nervy and ill and had never recovered from the war, which was pretty good as he spent it in Tunbridge Wells. That was the worst of all, having to hear him apologize. He said there was a letter from his mother in the drawer and it was very sacred. Of course I felt simply *lousy*. He's never forgiven me and I've never forgotten. My private belief is there was something about his miserable past in that drawer.'

Bridget's voice at last stopped. Alleyn, who had sat in his chair, was silent for so long that at last she turned from the fire and looked into his face.

'It's a queer story, isn't it?' she said.

'Very queer, indeed,' said Alleyn. 'Have you ever told anyone else about it?'

'No. Well, only Donald.' She wriggled across the hearth-rug. 'It's funny,' she said. 'I suppose I ought to be frightened of you, but I'm not. Why's Donna coming?'

'She wants to collect you, and see me,' said Alleyn absently.

'Everybody wants to see you.' She clasped her hands over her knees. 'Don't they?' insisted Bridget.

'For no very flattering reason, I'm afraid.'

'Well, I think you're really rather a lamb,' said Bridget.

'Tell me,' said Alleyn, 'do you think anyone else knows the secret of that French writing-case?'

'I shouldn't think so. You'd never know unless somebody showed you.'

'None of the servants?'

'I'm not sure. Bart slammed the drawer shut as soon as Sir Daniel came in.'

'Has Sir Daniel ever been alone in that room?'

'Sir Dan? Good heavens, you don't think my angelic Sir Dan had anything to do with Bart's beastly letter?'

'I simply want to clear things up.'

'Well, as a matter of fact I don't think he's been in the study before or since and he was never alone there that day. When Sir Dan comes, the servants always show him straight upstairs. Bart hates his room to be used for visitors.'

'Has Dimitri, the catering man, ever been alone in that room?'

'Why – I don't know. Yes, now you come to mention it he *did* interview Donna there, about a month before our ball-dance. I went down first and he was alone in the room.'

'When was this? Can you remember the date?'

'Let me see. I'll try. Yes. Yes, I can. It was on the tenth of May. We were going to Newmarket and Dimitri came early in the morning because of that.'

'Would you swear he was alone in the room?'

'Yes, yes, I would. But, please, what does it mean?'

'See here,' said Alleyn. 'I want you to forget all about this. Don't speak of it to anyone, not even to Donald. Understood?'

'Yes, but – '

461

'I want your promise.'
'All right, I promise.'
'Solemnly?'
'Solemnly.'
The front-door bell rang.
'Here's your mother,' said Alleyn.

CHAPTER TWENTY-FOUR

The Dance is Wound Up

When Alleyn opened the door to Evelyn Carrados, he saw her as a dark still figure against the lighted street. Her face was completely shadowed and it was impossible for him to glean anything from it. So that when she walked into the sitting-room he was not prepared for her extraordinary pallor, her haunted eyes and the drawn nervousness of her mouth. He remembered that she had gone to her room before she missed Bridget, and he realized with compassion that she had removed her complexion and neglected to replace it. Perhaps Bridget felt something of the same compassion, for she uttered a little cry and ran to her mother. Lady Carrados, using that painful gesture of all distracted mothers, held Bridget in her arms. Her thin hands were extraordinarily expressive.

'Darling,' she murmured. With a sort of hurried intensity she kissed Bridget's hair. 'How could you frighten me like this, Bridgie, how *could* you?'

'I thought you wouldn't know. Donna, *don't*. It's all right, really it is. It was only about Donald. I didn't want to worry you. I'm so sorry, *dear* Donna.' Lady Carrados gently disengaged herself and turned to Alleyn.

'Come and sit down, Evelyn,' he said. 'There's nothing to worry about. I would have brought your daughter home, but she had some interesting news and I thought you would trust her with me for half an hour.'

'Yes, Roderick, of course. If only I had known. Where's Donald? I thought he was here.'

'He's in the next room. Shall we send Bridget to join him for a minute or two?'

'Please.'

463

'Don't interrupt him,' said Alleyn as Bridget went out.

'All right.'

The door closed behind her.

Alleyn said: 'Do you ever drink brandy, Evelyn?'

'Never, why?'

'You're going to do so now. You're quite done up. Warm your hands at my fire while I get it for you.'

He actually persuaded her to drink a little brandy, and laughed at her convulsive shudder.

'Now then,' he said, 'there's no need for you to fuss about Bridget. She's been, on the whole, a very sensible young person and her only fault is in giving a commonplace visit the air of a secret elopement.'

'My nerves have gone, I think. I began to imagine all sorts of horrible things. I even wondered if she suspected Donald of this crime.'

'She is, on the contrary, absolutely assured of Donald's innocence.'

'Then why did she do this?'

'I'd better tell you the whole story. The truth is, Evelyn, they were longing for each other's bright eyes. Bridget wanted to convince me of Donald's innocence. She also wanted him to tell me this and that about a third person who doesn't matter at the moment. They met, most reprehensibly, at the Matador.'

'The Matador! Roderick, how naughty of them! It just simply isn't done by débutantes. No, really that was *very* naughty.'

Alleyn was both relieved and surprised to find that this departure from débutantes' etiquette took momentary precedence over Lady Carrados's other troubles.

'They had only just arrived, I imagine, when I ran into them there. The place was only half-full, Evelyn. It was too early for the smart people. I shouldn't think anyone else saw them. I brought them on here.'

'I'm very glad you did,' she said doubtfully.

'Was that all that worried you?'

'No. It's Herbert. He's been so extraordinary, Roderick, since this tragedy. He's stayed indoors all day and he never takes his eyes off me. I was afraid he would give up this dinner tonight, but, thank Heaven, he didn't. It is followed by the annual regimental dance and he has to present trophies or something so it will keep him quite late. I should have gone too, but I couldn't face it. I couldn't face another hour with him. He keeps making curious hints as if he – Roderick, almost as if he suspected me of something.'

'Tell me what he says.'

She leant back in her chair and relaxed. He saw that, not for the first time, he was to play the part of confidant. 'An odd rôle for a CID man,' he thought, 'and a damn useful one.' He settled himself to listen.

'It began soon after you left. While we were at tea. We had tea in my boudoir. I asked my secretary, Miss Harris, to join us, because I thought if she was there it might be a little easier. Naturally enough, but most unfortunately, poor Miss Harris began to speak to Bridget about Bunchy. She said she'd been reading a book on famous trials and somehow or other the word "blackmail" cropped up. I – I'm afraid I was startled and showed it. The very word was enough as you may imagine. I looked up to find Herbert's eyes fixed on me with an expression of – how can I describe it? – of knowing terror. He didn't go with the others after tea but hung about the room watching me. Suddenly he said: "You were very friendly with Robert Gospell, weren't you?" I said: "Of course I was." Then he asked me to show him my bank-book. It sounded perfectly insane, right on top of his other question. Almost funny – as if he suspected I'd been keeping poor Bunchy. But it wasn't very funny. It terrified me. He never worries about my money as a rule. He generally makes rather a point of not doing so, because, apart from the allowance he gives me, I've got my own, and what Paddy left me.

465

I knew if he saw my bank-book it would show that I had been drawing large sums – five hundred pounds, to meet the demands of – to – '

'The five hundred that went into that big bag of yours last night. How did you draw it out, Evelyn?'

'I drew some myself. I cashed a cheque for five hundred. I can't think that Herbert knew, or that he could have suspected the truth, if he did know. It's all so terribly disturbing. I put him off by saying I couldn't find the book, that I thought I had sent it back to the bank. He hardly seemed to listen. Suddenly he asked me if Bunchy had ever called when I was out? It seemed a perfectly inane question. I said I didn't know. He sat glaring at me till I could have screamed, and then he said: "Did he know anything about old furniture?" '

Alleyn glanced up quickly: 'Old furniture?'

'I know! It sounds demented, doesn't it? I repeated it like you, and Herbert said: "Well antiques. Pieces like the escritoire in my study." And then he leaned forward and said: "Do you think he knew anything about that?" I said: "Herbert, what *are* you talking about?" and he said: "I suppose I'm going to pieces. I feel I have been surrounded by treachery all my life!" It sounds just silly, but it frightened me. I rather lost my head, and asked him how he could talk like that. I began to say that Bridget was always loyal, when he burst out laughing. "Your daughter," he said, "loyal! How far do you suppose her loyalty would take her? Would you care to put it to the test?" '

Lady Carrados pressed her hands together.

'He's always disliked Bridgie. He's always been jealous of her. I remember once, it must be two years ago now, they had some sort of quarrel, and Herbert actually hurt her. He hurt her arm. I should never have found out if I hadn't gone to her room and seen the marks. I think he sees some reflection of Paddy in her. Roderick, do you think Herbert can know about Paddy and me? Is there the smallest possibility that the blackmailer has written to him?'

'It is possible, of course,' said Alleyn slowly, 'but I don't think it quite fits in. You say this extraordinary change in Carrados began after Miss Harris and Bridget talked of blackmail, and you showed you were startled?'

'Yes.'

'Do you think your obvious dismay could have suggested to him that you yourself were the victim of blackmail?'

'I don't know. It certainly suggested something pretty ominous,' said Lady Carrados, with the ghost of a smile. 'He's in the most extraordinary state of mind, it terrifies me.'

'When did you marry him, Evelyn?'

'When? Two years after Paddy died. He had wanted me to marry him before. Herbert was a very old friend of my family's. He had always been rather attached to me.'

'He's never given any sign of this sort of behaviour before?'

'Not *this* sort. Of course, he's rather difficult sometimes. He's very touchy. He's eighteen years older than I am, and he hates to be reminded of it. One has to be rather tactful. I suppose he's vain. Bridgie thinks so, I know.'

The gentle voice, with its tranquil, level note, faltered for a moment, and then went on steadily. 'I suppose you wonder why I married him, don't you?'

'A little, yes. Perhaps you felt that you needed security. You had had your great adventure.'

'It was exactly that. But it wasn't right, I see that now. It wasn't fair. Although Herbert knew quite well that he was not my great love, and was very chivalrous and humble about it, he couldn't really resign himself to the knowledge, and he grew more and more inclined to be rather a martyr. It's pathetically childish sometimes. He tries to draw my attention to his little ailments. He gets a sort of patient

467

look. It irritates Bridgie dreadfully, which is such a pity. And yet, although Herbert seems simple, he's not. He's a mass of repressions, and queer twisted thoughts. Do you know, I think he is still intensely jealous of Paddy's memory.'

'Did you see much of him before Paddy died?'

'Yes. I'm afraid, poor Herbert, that he rather saw himself as the faithful, chivalrous friend who continued to adore me quite honourably after I was – married. You see, I still think of myself as Paddy's wife. We used to ask Herbert to dine quite often. He bored Paddy dreadfully but – well, I'm afraid Paddy rather gloried in some of Herbert's peculiarities. He almost dined out on them. It was very naughty of him, but he was so gay always and so charming that he was forgiven everything. Everything.'

'I know.'

'Herbert rather emphasized the sacrificial note in his friendship, and of course Paddy saw that, and used to tease me about him. But I was very attached to him. No, he wasn't quite so touchy in those days, poor fellow. He was always very kind indeed. I'm afraid both Paddy and I rather got into the way of making use of him.'

'You are sure he suspected nothing?'

'Absolutely. In a way he was our greatest friend. I told you that I was staying with my mother when Paddy was hurt. She rang Herbert up when the news came through. Almost instinctively we turned to him. He was with us in a few minutes. Why, I suppose in a way I owe it to Herbert that I was in time to see Paddy before he died.'

Alleyn opened his mouth, and shut it again. Lady Carrados was staring into the fire, and gave no sign that she realized the significance of this last statement. At last Alleyn said: 'How did that come about?'

'Didn't I tell you this afternoon? It was Herbert who drove me down to the Vicarage at Falconbridge on the day Paddy died.'

It was one o'clock in the morning when Alleyn saw Lady Carrados, Bridget and Donald into a taxi, thankfully shut his door and went to bed. Less than twenty-four hours had passed since Robert Gospell met with his death, yet in that short time all the threads but one of the most complicated homicide cases he had ever dealt with had been put into his hands. As he waited for sleep, so long delayed, he saw the protagonists as a company of dancers moving in a figure so elaborate that the pattern of their message was almost lost in the confusion of individual gestures. Now it was Donald and Bridget who met and advanced through the centre of the maze; now Withers, marching on the outskirts of the dance, who turned to encounter Mrs Halcut-Hackett. Evelyn Carrados and her husband danced back to back into the very heart of the measure. Sir Daniel Davidson, like a sort of village master of ceremonies, with a gigantic rosette streaming from his buttonhole, gyrated slowly across and across. Dimitri slipped like a thief into the dance, offering a glass of champagne to each protagonist. Miss Harris skipped in a decorous fashion round the inner figure, but old General Halcut-Hackett, peering anxiously into every face, seemed to search for his partner. To and fro the figures swam more and more dizzily, faster and faster, until the confusion was intolerable. And then, with terrifying abruptness, they were stricken into immobility, and before he sank into oblivion, Alleyn, in a single flash, saw the pattern of the dance.

CHAPTER TWENTY-FIVE

Benefit of Clergy

The inquest on Lord Robert Gospell was held at eleven o'clock the next morning. It was chiefly remarkable for the circumstance that more people were turned away from it than had ever been turned away from any previous inquest in the same building. The coroner was a cross-grained man with the poorest possible opinion of society with a small 's' and a perfectly venomous hatred of Society with a large one. He suffered from chronic dyspepsia and an indeterminate but savage conviction that somebody was trying to get the better of him. The proceedings were coloured by his efforts to belittle the whole affair when he thought of the fashionable spectators, and to make the very most of it when he reflected that this sort of thing was the direct outcome of the behaviour of those sorts of people. However, apart from this personal idiosyncrasy, he was a good coroner. He called Donald, who, very white-faced, gave formal evidence of identification. He then heard the evidence of the taxi-driver, was particular about time, place and route, and called Alleyn.

Alleyn described his first view and examination of the body. In formal phrases he gave a precise account of the injuries he had found on the body of his friend. Dr Curtis followed with his report on the post-mortem. One of Dimitri's men gave evidence on the time Lord Robert left Marsdon House. The coroner with a vindictive glance at the audience said he saw no reason to call further evidence, addressed the jury in words that left them in no possible doubt as to the verdict they should return and when they had duly returned it, ordered an adjournment. He then fixed a baleful blue eye on the farthest wall and pronounced an expression of sympathy with the relatives. The whole proceedings had lasted twenty minutes.

'Swish!' said Fox when he met Alleyn in the street outside. 'That's old "Slap-Bang, Here-we-are-again." You can't beat him for speed, can you, sir?'

'Mercifully, you can't. Fox, we're off to Barbicon-Bramley. I've borrowed my mother's car and I've a hell of a lot to tell you, and I rather think the spell is wound up.'

'Sir?'

'You are quite right, Fox. Never quote, and if you do certainly not from Macbeth.'

Lady Alleyn's car was parked in a side street. Fox and Alleyn got into it and headed for the Uxbridge Road. On the way Alleyn related Bridget's and Donald's and Lady Carrados's stories. When he had finished Fox grunted and they were both silent for ten minutes.

'Well,' said Fox at last, 'it all points to the same thing doesn't it, Mr Alleyn?'

'Yes, Fox. In a dubious sort of way it does.'

'Still, I don't see how we can exclude the others.'

'Nor do I unless we get something definite from these people. If necessary we'll have to go on to Falconbridge and visit the hospital, but I'm in hopes that Miss Harris's uncle will come out of his retirement and go back to his gay young rectorish days seventeen years ago.'

'What a hope!' said Fox.

'As you indicate, the chances are thin.'

'If they couldn't find this chap O'Brien's letter on the premises then how can we expect to trace it now, seventeen years later?'

'Well urged, Brer Fox, well urged. But I fancy we know something now that they didn't know then.'

'Oh, well,' conceded Fox. 'Maybe. But all the same I

471

wouldn't give you a tuppenny damn for our chances and that's flat.'

'I'm a little more sanguine than that. Well, if we fail here we'll have to peg away somewhere else.'

'There's the missing cloak and hat.'

'Yes. Any report come in this morning from the postal people?'

'No. I've followed your suggestion and asked them to try to check yesterday's overseas parcels post. Our chaps have gone into the rubbish-bin game and there's nothing there. The Chelsea and Belgrave bins were emptied this morning and there's no cloaks or hats in any of them. Of course something may come in from farther afield.'

'I don't fancy the rubbish-bins, Fox. Too risky. For some reason he wanted those things to be lost completely. Hair oil, perhaps. Yes, it might be hair oil. I'm afraid, you know, that we *shall* have to ask all these people if we may search their houses.'

'Carrados is sure to object, sir, and you don't want to have to get search warrants yet, do you?'

'I think we can scare him by saying that Dimitri, Withers, Davidson, Halcut-Hackett and Lady Potter are all going to be asked to allow a search of their houses. He'll look a bit silly if he refuses on top of that.'

'Do you think the cloak and hat may still be hidden away in – well, in the guilty party's house?'

'No, blast it. I think he got rid of them yesterday before we had covered the first phase of investigation.'

'By post?'

'Well, can you think of a better method? In London? We've decided the river's barred because of the tide. We've advertised the damn thing well enough – they haven't been shoved down anyone's area. We've searched all the way along the Embankment. The men are still at it but I don't think they'll find them. The murderer wouldn't have time to do anything very elaborate in the way of hiding them and anyway, if we're right, it's off his beat.'

'Where would he send them?' ruminated Fox.

'Put yourself in his place. What address would you put on an incriminating parcel?'

'Care of Private Hoo Flung Dung, forty-second battalion, Chop Suey, Mah Jongg, Manchuria, to wait till called for,' suggested Fox irritably.

'Something like that,' said Alleyn. 'Something very like that, Brer Fox.'

They drove in silence for the rest of the way to Barbicon-Bramley.

Miss Harris's natal village proved to be small and rather self-consciously picturesque. There was a preponderance of ye olde-ness about the few shops and a good deal of pseudo-Tudor half-timbering on the outlying houses. They stopped at the post office and Alleyn asked to be directed to the Reverend Mr Walter Harris's house.

'I understand he is not the rector but his brother.'

'Oo, yes,' agreed the post office lady rattling her basket cuffs and flashing a smile. 'That will be the old gentleman. Quayte an aydentity in the district. First to the left into Oakapple Lane and straight on to the end. "The Thatch." It's ever so unmistakable. The last residence on the left, standing back in its own grounds.'

'Thank you so much,' said Alleyn.

They found 'The Thatch' as she had predicted, without any difficulty. The grounds of its own in which it stood back were an eighth of an acre of charming cottage garden. Alleyn and Fox had only got half-way up the cobbled path when they came upon two rumps up-ended behind a tall border of rosemary and lavender. The first was clad in patched trousers of clerical grey, the second in the navy blue decency of a serge skirt. Fragrant herbs hid the rest of these two gardeners from view.

473

'Good afternoon, sir,' said Alleyn, removing his hat.

With a slow upheaving movement, the Reverend and Mrs Walter Harris became wholly vertical and turned about.

'Oh!' they said gently. 'Good afternoon.'

They were very old indeed and had the strange marital likeness that so often comes upon a man and woman who have worked together all their lives. Their faces, though they differed in conformation, echoed each other in expression. They both had mild grey eyes surrounded by a network of kindly lines; they were both weather-beaten, and each of their mouths in repose, curved into a doubtful smile. Upon Mrs Harris's hair rather than her head was a wide garden hat with quite a large rent in the crown through which straggled a straight grey lock or two. Her husband also wore well over his nose a garden hat, an ancient panama with a faded green ribbon. His long crêpey neck was encircled by a low clerical collar, but instead of the usual grey jacket an incredibly faded All Souls blazer hung from his sharp shoulder-blades. He now tilted his head backwards in order to look at Alleyn under his hat-brim and through his glasses which were clipped half-way down his nose.

Alleyn said: 'I'm so sorry to bother you, sir.'

'No matter,' said Mr Harris, 'no matter.' His voice had the authentic parsonic ring.

'There's nothing more maddening than to be interrupted when you've settled down to a good afternoon's gardening,' Alleyn added.

'Twitch!' said Mr Harris violently.

'I beg your pardon?'

'Twitch! It's the bane of my existence. It springs up like veritable dragon's teeth and I assure you it's a great deal more difficult to extract. Three wheelbarrow loads since last Thursday forenoon.'

474

'Walter,' said his wife, 'these gentlemen want to speak to you.'

'We won't keep you more than a few minutes, sir,' said Alleyn.

'Yes, dear. Where shall I take them?'

'Into your den,' said Mrs Harris, as if her husband was a carnivorous ravager.

'Certainly, certainly. Come along. Come along,' said Mr Harris in the patient voice of vicarage hospitality. 'Come along.'

He took them through a french window into a little faded red room where old dim photographs of young men in cassocks hung beside old dim photographs of famous cathedrals. The shelves were full of dusty volumes of sermons and the works of Mrs Humphry Ward, Charles Kingsley, Charlotte M. Yonge, Dickens and Sir Walter Scott. Between a commentary and an *Imitation of Christ* was a copy of *The Martyrdom of Man,* truculently solid. For Mr Harris had once been an earnest undergraduate and had faced things. It was a shabby, friendly old room.

'Sit down, sit down,' said Mr Harris.

He hurriedly gathered up from the chairs, parish magazines, *Church Times* and seed catalogues. With his arms full of these papers, he wandered vaguely about his den.

Alleyn and Fox sat down on the horsehair chairs.

'That's right,' said Mr Harris. He incontinently dropped all his papers on the floor and sat down.

'Now, what can I have the pleasure – ? Um?'

'First, sir, I must tell you we are police officers.'

'Dear me,' said Mr Harris, 'not young Hockley again, I hope. Are you sure it's not my brother you want? The rector of Barbicon-Bramley? He's been very interested in the case and he told me that if the poor lad was not charged he could find a post for him with some kind souls who are prepared to overlook – '

'No, sir,' interrupted Alleyn gently, 'it's you we want to see.'

'But I'm retired,' said Mr Harris opening his eyes very wide. 'I'm quite retired, you know.'

'I am going to ask you to go back to the days when you were rector of Falconbridge.'

'Of Falconbridge!' Mr Harris beamed at them. 'Now this is really the greatest pleasure. You come from dear old Falconbridge! Let me see, I don't recollect either of your faces though, of course, I have been retired now for fifteen years and I'm afraid my memory is not what it used to be. Now tell me your names.'

'Mr Harris, we don't come from Falconbridge, we are from Scotland Yard. My name is Alleyn and this is Inspector Fox.'

'How do you do? I hope nothing has gone wrong in the dear old village,' ejaculated Mr Harris anxiously. He suddenly remembered his panama hat and snatched it from his head revealing a shining pink pate with an aura of astonished white fluff.

'No, no,' said Alleyn hastily. 'At least, not recently.' He darted a venomous glance at Fox who was grinning broadly. 'We are investigating a case, sir, and are anxious to trace a letter which we believe to have been lost in Falconbridge between seventeen and eighteen years ago.'

'A letter! Dear me, I'm afraid if it was addressed to me there is very little hope of recovery. Only this morning I found I had mislaid a most important letter from a very dear old friend, Canon Worsley of All Saints, Chipton. It's a most *extraordinary* thing where that letter has gone. I distinctly remember that I put it in the pocket of this jacket and – '

He thrust his hands in the side pockets of his blazer

and pulled out a collection of string, seed-packets, pencils and pieces of paper.

'Why, there it is!' he exclaimed, staring at an envelope that had fallen to the floor. 'There, after all, it is! I am ASTOUNDED.'

'Mr Harris,' said Alleyn loudly. Mr Harris instantly threw his head back and looked at Alleyn through his glasses.

'Eighteen years ago,' continued Alleyn very rapidly, 'there was a motor accident on the bridge outside the rectory at Falconbridge. The driver, Captain O'Brien, was severely injured and was taken into the rectory. Do you remember?'

Mr Harris had opened his mouth in astonishment but he said nothing. He merely continued to gape at Alleyn.

'You were very kind to him,' Alleyn went on; 'you kept him at the rectory and sent for help. He was taken to the hospital and died there a few hours later.'

He paused, but Mr Harris's expression had not changed. There was something intensely embarrassing in his posture and his unexpected silence.

'Do you remember?' asked Alleyn.

Without closing his mouth Mr Harris slowly shook his head from side to side.

'But it was such a serious accident. His young wife motored down from London. She went to the hospital but he died without regaining consciousness.'

'Poor fellow!' said Mr Harris in his deepest voice. 'Poor fell-oh!'

'Can't you remember, now?'

Mr Harris made no reply but got to his feet, went to the french window, and called into the garden.

'Edith! Edith!'

'Hoo-ee?' replied a wavering voice close at hand.

'Can you spare-ah a moment?'

'Coming.'

He turned away from the window and beamed at them.

'Now we shan't be long,' he announced.

But when Alleyn saw Mrs Harris amiably blunder up the garden path he scarcely shared in this optimistic view. They all stood up. She accepted Alleyn's chair and drew her gardening gloves from her old hands. Mr Harris contemplated her as if she was some rare achievement of his own.

'Edith, my dear,' he said loudly, 'would you tell these gentlemen about an accident?'

'Which accident?'

'That, I'm afraid, I don't know, dear. Indeed we are depending upon you to inform us.'

'I don't understand you, Walter.'

'I don't understand myself very well, I must admit, Edith. I find it all very puzzling.'

'What?' said his wife. Alleyn now realized that she was slightly deaf.

'Puzzling,' shouted Mr Harris.

'My husband's memory is not very good,' explained Mrs Harris smiling gently at Alleyn and Fox. 'He was greatly shaken by his cycling accident some months ago. I suppose you have called about the insurance.'

Raising his voice Alleyn embarked once more on his recital. This time he was not interrupted, but as neither of the Harrises gave any sign of understanding, it was impossible to tell whether or not he spoke in vain. By the time he had finished, Mr Harris had adopted his former disconcerting glare. Mrs Harris, however, turned to her husband and said:

'You remember the blood on the carpet, Walter? At dear old Falconbridge?'

'Dear me, yes. Now *that's* what I was trying to recollect. Of course it was. Poor fellow. Poor fell-oh!'

'Then you *do* remember?' Alleyn cried.

'Indeed I do,' said Mrs Harris reproachfully. 'The poor

young wife wrote us such a charming letter, thanking us for the little we had been able to do for him. I would have liked to answer it but unfortunately my husband lost it.'

'Edith, I have discovered dear old Worsley's letter. It was in my pocket. Fancy!'

'Fancy, dear, yes.'

'Talking of letters,' said Alleyn to Mrs Harris. 'Can you by any chance remember anything about a letter that was lost on the occasion of Captain O'Brien's accident? I think you were asked if it had been found in the vicarage.'

'I'm afraid I didn't catch – '

Alleyn repeated it.

'To be sure I do,' said Mrs Harris. 'Perfectly.'

'You were unable to give any information about this letter?'

'On the contrary.'

'What!'

'On the contrary,' repeated Mrs Harris firmly. 'I sent it after him.'

'*After who?*' roared Fox so loudly that even Mrs Harris gave a little jump. 'I'm sure I beg pardon, sir,' said Fox hastily, 'I don't know what came over me.' He opened his notebook in some confusion.

'Mrs Harris,' said Alleyn, 'will you please tell us everything you can remember about this letter?'

'Yes, please do, Edith,' said her husband unexpectedly. 'She'll find it for you,' he added in an aside. 'Don't distress yourselves.'

'Well,' began Mrs Harris. 'It's a long time ago now and I'm afraid I'm rather hazy. It was after they had taken him away, I fancy, that we found it under the couch in the study. That was when we noticed the stain on the carpet you remember, Walter. At first, of course, I thought it was one of my husband's letters – it was not in an envelope.

479

But when I glanced at it I realized at once that it was not, as it began "Dear Daddy" and we have no children.'

' "Dear Daddy," ' repeated Alleyn.

'I decided afterwards that it was perhaps "Dear Paddy" but as my husband's name is Walter Bernard it didn't signify. "Why," I said, or something of that sort. "Why, it must have dropped out of that poor fellow's coat when the ambulance man examined him." And – of course, I remember it now as clearly as if it was yesterday – and I said to little Violet: "Pop on your bicycle and take it to the hospital as quickly as you can, dear, because they may be looking for it." So little Violet – '

'Who was she, please?' asked Alleyn rather breathlessly.

'I beg your pardon?'

'*Who was little Violet?*' shouted Alleyn.

'My small niece. My husband's brother's third daughter. She was spending her holidays with us. She is grown up now and has a delightful post in London with a Lady Carrados.'

'Thank you,' said Alleyn. 'Please go on.'

CHAPTER TWENTY-SIX

Alleyn Plots a Dénouement

But there was not much more to tell. Apparently Violet
Harris had bicycled off with Paddy O'Brien's letter and
had returned to say she had given it to the gentleman who
had brought the lady in the motor-car. The gentleman had
been sitting in the motor-car outside the hospital. As far
as Mrs Harris could state, and she and her husband went
into a mazed avuncular family history to prove their point,
little Violet had been fifteen years old at the time. Alleyn
wrote out her statement, shorn of its interminable
parentheses, and she signed it. Throughout the interview
neither she nor her husband gave the faintest sign of any
form of curiosity. Apparently it did not strike either of
them as singular that the interest in a letter lost eighteen
years ago should suddenly be excited to such a pitch that
CID officers thought it necessary to seek for signed
statements in the heart of Buckinghamshire.

They insisted on taking Alleyn and Fox round their
garden. Alleyn hadn't the heart to refuse and besides he
had a liking for gardens. Mrs Harris gave them each a
bunch of lavender and rosemary, which flowers, she said,
were less conspicuous for gentlemen to carry than the gayer
blossoms of summer. The sight of Fox solemnly grasping
a posy in his enormous fist and examining a border of
transplanted pansies was almost too much for his superior
officer. It was two o'clock when the tour of the garden
was completed.

'You must come in whenever you are passing,' said Mrs
Harris, blinking cordially at Alleyn, 'and I shall remember
what you say about your mother's herb garden.'

481

'Yes, yes,' agreed Mr Harris. 'Whenever you are passing. Of course. Anybody from dear old Falconbridge is doubly welcome.'

They stood side by side at the gate and waved, rather in the manner of children, as Alleyn turned the car and drove away down Oakapple Lane.

'Well!' ejaculated Fox. 'Well!'

'Not another word,' said Alleyn, 'until we get to that pub outside Barbicon-Bramley. Do you realize we've had no lunch? I refuse to utter another word until I've drunk a pint of bitter.'

'And some bread and cheese and pickles,' said Fox. 'Pickles with plenty of onions in them.'

'Lord! Lord! Fox, what a choice! Now I come to think of it, though, it sounds damn good. "Bread and cheese and pickles," Fox, it's what we need. New white bread, mouse-trap cheese, home-made pickles and bitter.'

'That's the idea, Mr Alleyn. You're a great gourmet,' said Fox who had taught himself French, 'and don't think I haven't enjoyed some of those dinners you've given me when everything seemed to sort of slide into something else. I have. But when you're famished and in the English countryside you can't beat bread and cheese and pickles.'

The pub provided them with these delicacies. They took about a quarter of an hour over their meal and then set out again.

'Now then,' said Alleyn.

'The thing that beats me,' said Fox, wiping his short moustache with his handkerchief, 'is little Violet. We knew she was a niece of this old gentleman's but, by gum, we didn't know she was staying there at the time, now, did we?'

'No, Brer Fox, we didn't.'

'I suppose she may not know it herself,' continued Fox. 'I mean to say, Miss Violet Harris may not realize that

Lady Carrados was this Mrs O'Brien whose husband was brought into her uncle's vicarage when she was a kid of fifteen.'

'Quite possible. I hope she remembers the bicycle ride. We'll have to jog her memory, I dare say.'

'Yes. Now I reckon, on what we've heard, that it was Carrados who took that letter from little Violet. Carrados, sitting in the car outside the hospital, while the poor chap who'd got the letter from Australia was dying inside. And then, later on, when there's all the fuss about a missing letter, what does he do?'

Alleyn knew this question was purely rhetorical and didn't interrupt.

'He tells the widow,' said Fox; 'he tells the widow that he's made every inquiry and there isn't a letter to be found.'

'Yes,' agreed Alleyn. 'No doubt he tells her that.'

'Right. Now, why does he do that? I reckon it's because Sir Herbert Carrados is what you might call a bit of a moral coward with a kind of mental twist. What these psycho-johnnies call a repression or some such thing. As I see it he didn't want to admit to having seen the letter because he'd actually read it. This Australian bloke knew Captain O'Brien had married a loony and wrote to tell him he was now a widower. If what Lady Carrados told you was correct and he'd fancied her for a long time, that letter must have shaken him up a bit. Now perhaps he says to himself, being a proud, snobbish sort of chap and yet having set his heart on her, that he'll let sleeping dogs lie.'

'Cut the whole thing dead? Yes. That's sound enough. It's in character.'

'That's what I mean,' said Fox in a gratified voice. 'But all the same he doesn't destroy the letter. Or does he?'

'That,' said Alleyn, 'is exactly what we've got to find out.'

483

'Well, sir, we've got our suspicions, haven't we?'

'Yes. Before this evening, Fox, I want to make certainties of our suspicions.'

'By gum, Mr Alleyn, if we can do that we'll have made a tidy job of this case. Don't count your chickens, as well I know, but if we can get an arrest within two days after the crime, in a complicated case like this, we're not doing too badly, now are we?'

'I suppose not, you old warrior, I suppose not.' Alleyn gave a short sigh. 'I wish – ' he said. 'Oh God, Fox, I do wish he hadn't died. No good maundering. I also wish very much that we'd been able to find some trace of something, just *something* in the taxi. But not a thing.'

'The funeral's at three o'clock tomorrow, isn't it?' asked Fox.

'Yes. Lady Mildred has asked me to be one of the bearers. It's pretty strange under the circumstances, but I'd like to do it. And I'd like to think we had our killer locked up before then. When we get back, Fox, we'll have to arrange for these people to come round to the Yard. We'll want Miss Harris, Bridget O'Brien, her mother, Carrados himself, Davidson, Withers, Dimitri and Mrs Halcut-Hackett. I'll see Lady Carrados alone first. I want to soften the shock a little if it's possible.'

'When shall we get them to come, sir?'

'It'll be four o'clock by the time we're back to the Yard. I think we'll make it this evening. Say nine o'clock. It's going to be devilish tricky. I'm counting on Dimitri losing his head. It's a cool head, blast it, and he may keep his wits about him. Talking of wits, there's the gallant Captain to be reckoned with. Unless I'm a Dutchman, Donald Potter's given me enough in his statement to lock the gallant Captain up for a nice long stretch. That's some comfort.'

They were silent until they got as far as the Cromwell Road and then Fox said: 'I suppose we are right, Mr Alleyn.

I know that seems a pretty funny thing to say at this stage, but it's a worrying business and that's a fact. It's the trickiest line of evidence I've *ever* come across. We seem to be hanging our case on the sort of things you usually treat with a good deal of suspicion.'

'Don't I know it. No, Fox, I think it'll hold firm. It depends on what these people say in their second interviews tonight, of course. If we can establish the facts about the two cigarette-cases, the secret drawer, the telephone conversation and the stolen letter, we're right. Good Lord, that sounds like a list of titles from the old Sherlock Holmes stories. I think part of the charm of those excellent tales lies in Watson's casual but enthralling references to cases we never hear of again.'

'The two cigarette-cases,' repeated Fox slowly, 'the secret drawer, the telephone conversation, and the stolen letter. Yes. Yes, that's right. You may say we hang our case on those four hooks.'

'The word "hang," ' said Alleyn grimly, 'is exceedingly apposite. You may.'

He drove Fox to the Yard.

'I'll come up with you and see if anything fresh has come in,' he said.

They found reports from officers who were out on the job. Dimitri's men reported that François had gone to the local stationers and bought a copy of this morning's *Times*. The stationer had told the Yard man that Dimitri as a rule took the *Daily Express*.

Alleyn laid the report down.

'Beat up a *Times*, Brer Fox.'

Fox went out. He was away for some time. Alleyn brought his file up to date and lit his pipe. Then he rang up Lady Carrados.

'Evelyn? I've rung you up to ask if you and your husband and Bridget will come to my office at the Yard tonight.

485

It's some more tidying up of this affair. If possible I'd like to have a word with you first. Would you rather it was here or in your house?'

'In your office, *please,* Roderick. It would be easier. Shall I come now?'

'If you will. Don't be fussed. I'm so sorry to bother you.'

'I'll come at once,' said the faint voice.

Fox returned with a *Times* which he laid on Alleyn's desk. He pointed a stubby finger at the personal column.

'What about the third from the top?' he said.

Alleyn read it aloud.

' "Childie Darling. Living in exile. Longing. Only want Daughter. Daddy." '

'Um,' said Alleyn. 'Has daddy had anything else to say to Childie during the last week or so?'

'Not during the last fortnight, anyway. I've looked up the files.'

'There's nothing else in the agony column. The others are old friends, aren't they?'

'That's right.'

'We'd better ask Father *Times* about Daddy.'

'I'll do that,' said Fox, 'and I'll get going on these people for tonight.'

'Thank you, Fox. I've tackled Lady Carrados who is coming to see me now. If you've time I'd be glad if you'd fix the others. I ought to go and see Lady Mildred about the arrangements for tomorrow.'

'You'll have time for that later on.'

'Yes. I must report to the AC before this evening. I'll go along now, I think, and see if he's free. Ask them to show Lady Carrados up here, Fox, and ring through when she arrives.'

'Very good, Mr Alleyn.'

486

Alleyn saw the Assistant Commissioner's secretary, who sent him in to the great man. Alleyn laid the file on the desk. The AC disregarded it.

'Well, Rory, how goes it? I hear you've got half the Yard mudlarking on Chelsea Embankment and the other half tailing the aristocracy. What's it all about?' asked the AC, who had been kept perfectly *au fait* with the case but whose favourite pose was one of ignorance. 'I suppose you want me to read this damn nonsense?' he added, laying his hand on the file.

'If you will, sir. I've summed-up at the end. With your approval I'm collecting the relevant people here tonight and if the interviews go the right way I hope to be able to make an arrest. If you agree, I'd like a blank warrant.'

'You're a pretty cool customer, aren't you?' grunted the AC. 'And if the interviews go all wrong you return the warrant and think of something else? That it?'

'Yes, sir. That's it.'

'See here, Rory, our position in this affair is that we've got to have a conviction. If your customer gets off on this sort of evidence, opposing counsel is going to make us look like so many Aunt Sallies. It's so damn shaky. Can't you hear what old Harrington-Barr will do with you if he's briefed? Make you look a boiled egg, my good man, unless you've got a damning admission or two to shove at the jury. *And* all this blackmail stuff. How are you going to get any of these people to charge their blackmailer? You know what people are over blackmail.'

'Yes, sir. I do rather hope for a damning admission.'

'Do you, by Gad! All right, all right. See them in here. In my room. I'd better know the worst at once, I suppose.' He scowled at Alleyn. 'This goes a bit close to you, doesn't it? Lord Robert was a friend of yours, wasn't he?'

'He was, sir, yes.'

'Ugh! He was a nice little chap. I understand the FO

487

is making tender enquiries. In case a foreign power remembers him pottering about twenty years ago and has decided to assassinate him. Silly asses. Well, I'm sorry you've had this knock, Rory. It doesn't seem to have cramped your style. Quick work, if it's accurate.'

'If!' said Alleyn. 'I hope to Heaven we haven't gone wrong.'

'What time's the dénouement tonight?'

'Nine o'clock, sir.'

'All right. Trot 'em along here. Thank you, Rory.'

'Thank you, sir.'

On his return to his own room he found Fox was waiting for him.

'Lady Carrados is downstairs, sir.'

'Go and bring her up, Fox, will you?'

Fox turned in the doorway.

'I've got on to *The Times*,' he said. 'They were a bit dignified about it but I know one of the chaps who deals with the agony-column notices and got hold of him. He told me the Childie Darling thing came by mail with a postal order for double rates and a request that it should appear, very particular, in this morning's edition. The note said the advertiser would call to collect the change, if any, and was signed W.A.K. Smith, address GPO, Erith.'

'Postmark?'

'They'd lost the envelope but he'll look for it. The writing,' said Fox, 'was in script on common notepaper.'

'Was it indeed?' murmured Alleyn.

'There's one other thing,' said Fox. 'The reports have come through from the post offices. A clerk at the Main Western District says that during the rush hour yesterday someone left a parcel on the counter. He found it later on in the day. It was soft, about the right weight and had five bob in tuppenny stamps on it, one and fivepence more than was necessary. He remembers the address was to somewhere in China and it was written in script. So my Private Hoo Flung Dung may have been a fair guess. We've got on to Mount Pleasant and it's too late. A parcels post went out to China this afternoon.'

'Blast!' said Alleyn.

'I'll be off,' said Fox, 'and get her ladyship.'

While he waited for Lady Carrados, Alleyn cut the little notice out of *The Times*. After a moment's consideration he unlocked a drawer in his desk and took out Mrs Halcut-Hackett's gold cigarette-case. He opened it and neatly gummed the notice inside the lid.

Fox showed Lady Carrados in and went away.

'I'm so sorry, Evelyn,' said Alleyn. 'I've been closeted with my superior. Have you been here long?'

'No. What is it now, please, Roderick?'

'It's this. I want you to allow what may seem a rather drastic step. I want you to give me permission to talk to your husband, in front of you, about Paddy O'Brien.'

'You mean – tell him that we were not married?'

'If it seems necessary.'

'I can't.'

'I shouldn't do it if it wasn't vitally necessary. I do not believe, Evelyn, that he would' – Alleyn hesitated – 'that he would be as shocked as you imagine.'

'But I *know* he would be terribly shocked. Of course he would.'

'I think I can promise you that you have nothing to fear from this decision. I mean that Carrados's attitude to yourself and Bridget will not be materially affected by it.'

'I cannot believe that. I cannot believe that he will not be dreadfully wounded. Even violent.'

'I promise you that I honestly believe that it may help you both to a better understanding.'

'If only I could think that!'

489

'It will certainly help us to see justice done on your blackmailer. Evelyn, I don't want to be intolerably priggish, but I do believe it is your duty to do this.'

'I had almost made up my mind to tell him.'

'All the better. Come now. Look at me! Will you let me deal with it?'

She looked at him. Quite deliberately he used the whole force of that thing people call personality and of which he knew – how could he not know? – he had his share. He imposed his will on hers as surely as if it was a tangible instrument. And he saw her give way.

She raised her hands and let them fall limply back on her lap.

'Very well, I'm so bemused and puzzled, I don't know, I give up. My house is falling about my ears. I'll do whatever you think best, Roderick.'

'You need say very little.' He went into details. She listened attentively and repeated his instructions. When that was over he rose and looked down at her. 'I'm sorry,' he said. 'It's no good my trying to make light of this. It *is* a very upsetting business for you. But take heart of grace. Bridget need not know, although I think if I were you I should tell her. She's got plenty of courage and the moderns don't make nearly such heavy weather of that sort of thing as we did. My niece Sarah prattles away about people born in and out of wedlock as if it was a fifty-fifty chance. Upon my word, Evelyn, I wouldn't be surprised if your daughter found a certain amount of romantic satisfaction in the story you have been at such pains to hide from her.'

'That would be almost funny, wouldn't it?' Lady Carrados looked into Alleyn's compassionate eyes. She reached out her hand and he took it firmly between both of his.

'Roderick,' she said, 'how old are you?'

490

'Forty-three, my dear.'

'I'm nearly forty,' and absent-mindedly she added, as women do: 'Isn't it awful?'

'Dreadful,' agreed Alleyn, smiling at her.

'Why haven't you married?'

'My mother says she tried to make a match of it between you and me. But Paddy O'Brien came along and I hadn't a chance.'

'That seems odd, now, doesn't it? If it's true. I don't remember that you ever paid me any particular attention.'

He saw that she had reached the lull in the sensibilities that sometimes follows extreme emotional tension. She spoke idly with an echo of her customary gentle gaiety. She sounded as if her mind had gone as limp as the thin hand he still held.

'You ought to marry,' she said vaguely and added: 'I must go.'

'I'm coming down. I'll see you to your car.'

As she drove away he stood looking after her for a second or two, and then shook his head doubtfully and set out for Cheyne Walk.

CHAPTER TWENTY-SEVEN

Interlude for Love

Alleyn wondered if it was only because he knew the body of his friend had come home that he felt its presence. Perhaps the house was not more quiet than it had been that morning. Perhaps the dead did not in truth cast about them so deep a spell. And then he smelt lilies and all the hushed chill of ceremonial death closed about his heart. He turned to Bunchy's old butler who was in the condition so often found in the faithful retainers of Victorian melodrama. He had been weeping. His eyes were red and his face blotted with tears, and his lips trembled. He showed Alleyn into Mildred's sitting-room. When she came forward in her lustreless black clothes, he found in her face the same unlovely reflection of sorrow. Mildred wore the customary expression of bereavement, and though he knew it to be the stamp of sincere grief, he felt a kind of impatience. He felt a profound loathing of the formalities of death. A dead body was nothing, nothing but an intolerable caricature of something someone had loved. It was a reminder of unspeakable indignities, and yet people surrounded their dead with owlish circumstances, asked you, as Mildred was asking him now, in a special muted voice, to look at them.

'I know you'd like to see him, Roderick.'

He followed her into a room on the ground floor. The merciless scent of flowers was so heavy here that it hung like mist on the cold air. The room was crowded with flowers. In the centre, on three shrouded trestles, Robert Gospell's body lay in its coffin.

It was the face of an elderly baby, dignified by the

possession of some terrific secret. Alleyn was not troubled by the face. All dead faces looked like that. But the small fat hands, which in life had moved with staccato emphasis, were obediently folded, and when he saw these his eyes were blinded by tears. He groped in his overcoat pocket for a handkerchief and his fingers found the bunch of rosemary from Mr Harris's garden. The grey-green spikes were crisp and unsentimental and they smelt of the sun. When Mildred turned aside, he gave them to the dead.

He followed her back to her drawing-room and she began to tell him about the arrangements for the funeral.

'Broomfield, who as you know is the head of the family, is only sixteen. He's abroad with his tutor and can't get back in time. We are not going to alter his plans. So that Donald and I are the nearest. Donald is perfectly splendid. He has been such a comfort all day. Quite different. And then dear Troy has come to stay with me and has answered all the letters and done everything.'

Her voice, still with that special muted note, droned on, but Alleyn's thoughts had been arrested by this news of Troy and he had to force himself to listen to Mildred. When she had finished he asked her if she wished to know anything about his side of the picture and discovered that she was putting all the circumstances of her brother's death away from her. Mildred had adopted an ostrich attitude towards the murder and he got the impression that she rather hoped the murderer would never be caught. She wished to cut the whole thing dead and he thought it was rather clever and rather nice of her to be able to welcome him so cordially as a friend and pay no attention to him as a policeman.

After a minute or two there seemed to be nothing more to say to Mildred. Alleyn said good-bye to her, promised to attend the memorial service at eleven and to do his part at the funeral. He went out into the hall.

In the doorway he met Troy.

He heard his own voice saying: 'Hullo, you're just in time. You're going to save my life.'

'Whatever do you mean?'

'It's nearly five. I've had six hours' sleep in the last fifty-eight hours. That's nothing for us hardy coppers but for some reason I'm feeling sorry for myself. Will you take tea or a drink or possibly both with me? For God's sake say you will.'

'Very well, where shall we go?'

'I thought,' said Alleyn, who up to that moment had thought nothing of the sort, 'that we might have tea at my flat. Unless you object to my flat.'

'I'm not a débutante,' said Troy. 'I don't think I need coddle my reputation. Your flat let it be.'

'Good,' said Alleyn. 'I've got mother's car. I'll just warn my servant and tell the Yard where to find me. Do you think I may use the telephone.'

'I'm sure you may.'

He darted to telephone and was back in a minute.

'Vassily is tremendously excited,' he said. 'A lady to tea! Come on.'

On the way Alleyn was so filled with astonishment at finding himself agreeably alone with Troy that he fell into a trance from which he only woke when he pulled the car up outside his own flat. He did not apologize for his silence: he felt a tranquillity in Troy that had accepted it, and when they were indoors he was delighted to hear her say: 'This is peaceful,' and to see her pull off her cap and sit on a low stool before the fireplace.

'Shall we have a fire?' asked Alleyn. 'Do say yes. It's not a warm day, really.'

'Yes, let's,' agreed Troy.

'Will you light it while I see about tea?'

He went out of the room to give Vassily a series of

494

rather confused orders, and when he returned there was Troy before the fire, bareheaded, strangely familiar.

'So you're still here,' said Alleyn.

'It's a nice room, this.'

He put a box of cigarettes on the floor beside her and took out his pipe. Troy turned and saw her own picture of Suva at the far end of the room.

'Oh, yes,' said Alleyn, 'there's that.'

'How did you get hold of it?'

'I got someone to buy it for me.'

'But why – '

'I don't know why I was so disingenuous about it except that I wanted it so very badly for reasons that were not purely aesthetic and I thought you would see through them if I made a personal business of it.'

'I should have been rather embarrassed, I suppose.'

'Yes.' Alleyn waited for a moment and then said: 'Do you remember how I found you that day, painting and cursing? It was just as the ship moved out of Suva. Those sulky hills and that ominous sky were behind you.'

'We had a row, didn't we?'

'We did.'

Troy's face became rather pink.

'In fact,' said Alleyn, 'there is scarcely an occasion on which we have met when we have not had a row. Why is that, do you suppose?'

'I've always been on the defensive.'

'Have you? For a long time I thought you merely disliked me.'

'No. You got under my guard.'

'If it hadn't been for that damned case, things might have gone better,' said Alleyn. 'What a pity it is that we cannot sometimes react to situations like characters in the less honest form of novel. The setting should have been ideal, you know. A murder in your house. You with just

495

enough motive to make a "strong situation" and not enough seriously to implicate you. Me, as the grim detective finding time for a bit of Rochester stuff. You should have found yourself drawn unwillingly into love, Troy. Instead of which I merely acquired a sort of post-mortem disagreeableness. If you painted a surrealist picture of me I would be made of Metropolitan Police notebooks, one eye would be set in a keyhole, my hands would be occupied with somebody else's private correspondence. The background would be a morgue and the whole pretty conceit wreathed with festoons of blue tape and hangman's rope. What?'

'Nonsense,' said Troy.

'I suppose so. Yes. The vanity of the male trying to find extraordinary reasons for a perfectly natural phenomenon. You don't happen to love me. And why the devil should you?'

'You don't happen to understand,' said Troy shortly, 'and why the devil should you.'

She took a cigarette and tilted her face up for him to give her a light. A lock of her short dark hair had fallen across her forehead. Alleyn lit the cigarette, threw the match into the fire and tweaked the lock of hair.

'Abominable woman,' he said abruptly. 'I'm so glad you've come to see me.'

'I tell you what,' said Troy more amiably. 'I've always been frightened of the whole business. Love and so on.'

'The physical side?'

'Yes, that, but much more than that. The whole business. The breaking down of all one's reserves. The mental as well as the physical intimacy.'

'My mind to me a kingdom is.'

'I feel it wouldn't be,' said Troy.

'I feel it rather terrifyingly still would be. Don't you think that in the closest possible union there must always be moments when one feels oneself completely separate,

496

completely alone? Surely it must be so, otherwise we would not be so astonished on the rare occasions when we read each other's thoughts.'

Troy looked at him with a sort of shy determination that made his heart turn over.

'Do you read my thoughts?' she asked.

'Not very clearly, Troy. I dare not wish I could.'

'I do yours, sometimes. That is one of the things that sends my defences up.'

'If you could read them now,' said Alleyn, 'you might well be frightened.'

Vassily came in with tea. He had, Alleyn saw at a glance, excitedly rushed out to his favourite delicatessen shop round the corner and purchased caviare. He had made a stack of buttered toast, he had cut up many lemons, and he had made tea in an enormous Stuart pot of Lady Alleyn's which her son had merely borrowed to show to a collector. Vassily had also found time to put on his best coat. His face was wreathed in smiles of embarrassing significance. He whispered to himself as he set this extraordinary feast out on a low table in front of Troy.

'Please, please,' said Vassily. 'If there is anysink more, sir. Should I not perhaps – ?'

'No, no,' said Alleyn hastily, 'that will do admirably.'

'Caviare!' said Troy. 'Oh, how glad I am – a heavenly tea.'

Vassily broke into a loud laugh, excused and bowed himself out, and shut the doors behind him with the stealth of a soubrette in a French comedy.

'You've transported the old fool,' said Alleyn.

'What is he?'

'A Russian carry-over from a former case of mine. He very nearly got himself arrested. Can you really eat caviare and drink Russian tea? He's put some milk there.'

'I don't want milk and I shall eat any quantity of caviare,' said Troy.

When they had finished and Vassily had taken away the tea things, Troy said: 'I must go.'

'Not yet.'

'Oughtn't you to be at Scotland Yard?'

'They'll ring me up if I'm wanted. I'm due there later on.'

'We've never once mentioned Bunchy,' said Troy.

'No.'

'Shall you get an early night tonight?'

'I don't know, Troy.'

Alleyn sat on the footstool by her chair. Troy looked down on his head propped between his long thin hands.

'Don't talk about the case if you'd rather not. I only wanted to let you know that if you'd like to, I'm here.'

'You're here. I'm trying to get used to it. Shall you ever come again, do you think? Do you know I swore to myself I would not utter one word of love this blessed afternoon? Well, perhaps we'd better talk about the case. I shall commit a heinous impropriety and tell you I may make an arrest this evening.'

'You *know* who killed Bunchy?'

'We believe we do. If tonight's show goes the right way we shall be in a position to make the arrest.'

He turned and looked into her face.

'Ah,' he said, 'my job again! Why does it revolt you so much?'

Troy said: 'It's nothing reasonable – nothing I can attempt to justify. It's simply that I've got an absolute horror of capital punishment. I don't even know that I agree with the stock arguments against it. It's just one of those nightmare things. Like claustrophobia. I used to adore the Ingoldsby Legends when I was a child. One day I came across the one about my Lord Tomnoddy and the

498

hanging. It made the most extraordinary impression on me. I dreamt about it. I couldn't get it out of my head. I used to turn the pages of the book, knowing that I would come to it, dreading it, and yet – I had to read it. I even made a drawing of it.'

'That should have helped.'

'I don't think it did. I suppose most people, even the least imaginative, have got a bogey man in the back of their minds. That has always been mine. I've never spoken of it before. And so you see when you and I met in that other business and it ended in your arrest of someone I knew – ' Her voice wavered. 'And then there was the trial and – the end – '

With a nervous movement she touched his head.

'It's not you. And yet I mind so much that it is you.'

Alleyn pulled her hand down against his lips.

There was complete silence. Everything he had ever felt; every *frisson,* the most profound sorrow, the least annoyance, the greatest joy and the smallest pleasure had been but preparation for this moment when her hand melted against his lips. Presently he found himself leaning over her. He still held her hand like a talisman and he spoke against the palm.

'This must be right. I swear it must be right. I can't be feeling this alone. Troy?'

'Not now,' Troy whispered. 'No more, now. Please.'

'Yes.'

'Please.'

He stooped, took her face between his hands, and kissed her hard on the mouth. He felt her come to life beneath his lips. Then he let her go.

'And don't think I shall ask you to forgive me,' he said. 'You've no right to let this go by. You're too damn particular by half, my girl. I'm your man and you know it.'

They stared at each other.

'That's the stuff to give the troops,' Alleyn added. 'The arrogant male.'

'The arrogant turkey-cock,' said Troy shakily.

'I know, I know. But at least you didn't find it unendurable. Troy, for God's sake can't we be honest with each other? When I kissed you just then you seemed to meet me like a flame. Could I have imagined that?'

'No.'

'It was as if you shouted with your whole body that you loved me. How can I not be arrogant?'

'How can I not be shaken?'

When he saw that she was indeed greatly shaken an intolerable wave of compassion drowned his thoughts. He stammered. 'I'm sorry, I'm sorry.'

Troy began to speak slowly.

'Let me go away now. I want to think. I will try to be honest. I promise you I did not believe I loved you. It seemed to me that I couldn't love you when I resented so much the feeling that you made some sort of demand whenever we met. I don't understand physical love. I don't know how much it means. I'm just plain frightened, and that's a fact.'

'You shall go. I'll get a taxi. Wait a moment.'

He ran out and got a taxi. When he returned she was standing in front of the fire holding her cap in her hand and looked rather small and lost. He brought her coat and dropped it lightly across her shoulders.

'I've been very weak,' said Troy. 'When I said I'd come I thought I would keep it all very peaceful and impersonal. You looked so worn and troubled and it was so easy just to do this. And now see what's happened?'

'The skies have opened and the stars have fallen. I feel

as if I'd run the world in the last hour. And now you must leave me.'

He took her to the taxi. Before he shut the door he said: 'Your most devoted turkey-cock.'

CHAPTER TWENTY-EIGHT

Alleyn Marshals the Protagonists

The assistant Commissioner's clock struck a quarter to nine as Alleyn walked into the room.

'Hello, Rory.'

'Good evening, sir.'

'As you have no doubt observed with your trained eye, my secretary is not present. So you may come off the official rocks. Sit down and light your pipe.'

'Thank you,' said Alleyn.

'Feeling a bit shaky?'

'A bit. I shall look such an egregious ass if they don't come up to scratch.'

'No doubt. It's a big case, Chief Inspector.'

'Don't I know it, sir!'

'Who comes first?'

'Sir Herbert and Lady Carrados.'

'Any of 'em arrived yet?'

'All except Dimitri. Fox has dotted them about the place. His room, mine, the waiting-room and the charge-room. As soon as Dimitri arrives, Fox'll come and report.'

'Right. In the meantime, we'll go over the plan of action again.'

They went over the plan of action.

'Well,' said the Assistant Commissioner, 'it's ticklish, but it may work. As I see it, everything depends on the way you handle them.'

'Thank you, sir,' said Alleyn grimly, 'for those few reassuring words.'

The Assistant Commissioner's clock struck nine. Alleyn

knocked out his pipe. There was a tap on the door and Fox came in.

'We are all ready, sir,' he said.

'All right, Mr Fox. Show them in.'

Fox went out. Alleyn glanced at the two chairs under the central lamp, and then at the Assistant Commissioner sitting motionless in the green-shaded light from his desk. Alleyn himself stood before the mantelpiece.

'Stage set,' said the quiet voice beyond the green lamp. 'And now the curtain rises.'

There was a brief silence, and then once more the door opened.

'Sir Herbert and Lady Carrados, sir.'

They came in. Alleyn moved forward, greeted them formally, and then introduced them to the Assistant Commissioner. Carrados's manner as he shook hands was a remarkable mixture of the condescension of a viceroy and the fortitude of an early Christian martyr.

The Assistant Commissioner was crisp with them.

'Good evening, Lady Carrados. Good evening, Sir Herbert. In view of certain information he has received, Chief Detective-Inspector Alleyn and I decided to invite you to come and see us. As the case is in Mr Alleyn's hands, I shall leave it to him to conduct the conversation. Will you both sit down?'

They sat. The light from the overhead lamp beat down on their faces, throwing strong shadows under the eyes and cheek-bones. The two heads turned in unison to Alleyn.

Alleyn said: 'Most of what I have to say is addressed to you, Sir Herbert.'

'Indeed?' said Carrados. 'Well, Alleyn, as I fancy I told you yesterday afternoon, I am only too anxious to help you to clear up the wretched business. As Lord Robert's host on that fatal night – '

'Yes, we quite realize that, sir. Your attitude encourages

503

one to hope that you will understand, or at any rate excuse, my going over old ground, and also breaking into new. I am in a position to tell you that we have followed a very strange trail since yesterday – a trail that has led us to some remarkable conclusions.'

Carrados turned his eyes, but not his head, towards his wife. He did not speak.

'We have reason to believe,' Alleyn went on, 'that the murder of Lord Robert Gospell is the outcome of blackmail. Did you speak, sir?'

'No. No! I cannot see, I fail to understand – '

'I'll make myself clearer in a moment, I hope. Now, for reasons into which I need not go at the moment, the connection between this crime and blackmail leads us to one of two conclusions. Either Lord Robert was a blackmailer, and was killed by one of his victims, or possibly someone wishing to protect his victim – '

'What makes you say that?' asked Carrados hoarsely. 'It's impossible!'

'Impossible? Why, please?'

'Because, Lord Robert, Lord Robert was not – it's impossible to imagine – have you any proof that he was a blackmailer?'

'The alternative is that Lord Robert had discovered the identity of the blackmailer, and was murdered before he could reveal it.'

'You say this,' said Carrados, breathlessly, 'but you give no proof.'

'I ask you, sir, simply to accept my statement that rightly or wrongly we believe our case to rest on one or the other of those alternatives.'

'I don't pretend to be a detective, Alleyn, but – '

'Just a minute, sir, if you don't mind. I want you now to go back with me to a day nearly eighteen years ago, when you motored Lady Carrados down to a village called

504

Falconbridge in Buckinghamshire. You were not married then.'

'I frequently motored her into the country in those days.'

'You will have no difficulty in remembering this occasion. It was the day on which Captain Paddy O'Brien met with his accident.'

Alleyn waited. He saw the sweat round Carrados's eyes shine in the strong lamplight.

'Well?' said Carrados.

'You do remember that day?' Alleyn asked.

'But Herbert,' said Lady Carrados, 'of course you do.'

'I remember, yes. But I fail to see – '

'Please, sir! I shall fire point-blank in a moment. You remember?'

'Naturally.'

'You remember that Captain O'Brien was taken first to the vicarage and from there, in an ambulance, to the hospital, where he died a few hours later?'

'Yes.'

'You remember that, after he died, your wife, as she is now, was very distressed because she believed that a certain letter which Captain O'Brien carried had been lost?'

'I have no recollection of this.'

'Let me help you. She said that he had probably carried it in his pocket, that it must have fallen out, that she was most anxious to recover it. Am I right, Lady Carrados?'

'Yes – quite right.'

Her voice was low, but perfectly steady. She was looking at Alleyn with an air of shocked bewilderment.

'Did you ask Sir Herbert if he had enquired everywhere for this missing letter?'

'Yes.'

'Do you remember now, Sir Herbert?'

'I think – I remember – something. It was all very

distressing. I tried to be of some use; I think I may have been of some use.'

'Did you succeed in finding the letter?'

'I – don't think so.'

'Are you sure?'

A little runnel of sweat trickled down each side of his nose into that fine moustache.

'I am tolerably certain.'

'Do you remember sitting in your car outside the hospital while Lady Carrados was with Captain O'Brien?'

Carrados did not speak for a long time. Then he swung round in his chair, and addressed that silent figure in the green lamplight.

'I can see no possible reason for this extraordinary procedure. It is most distressing for my wife, and I may say, sir, it strikes me as being damnably offensive and outside the duties of your office.'

'I don't think it is, Sir Herbert,' said the Assistant Commissioner. 'I advise you to answer Mr Alleyn, you know.'

'I may tell you,' Carrados began, 'that I am an intimate friend of your chief's. He shall hear about this.'

'I expect so,' said the Assistant Commissioner. 'Go on, Mr Alleyn.'

'Lady Carrados,' said Alleyn, 'did you, in point of fact, leave Sir Herbert in the car when you went into the hospital?'

'Yes.'

'Yes. Now, Sir Herbert, while you waited there, do you remember a schoolgirl of fifteen or so coming up on her bicycle?'

'How the devil can I remember a schoolgirl on a bicycle eighteen years ago?'

'Only because she gave you the letter that we have been discussing.'

Evelyn Carrados uttered a stifled cry. She turned and looked at her husband, as though she saw him for the first time. He met her with what Alleyn thought one of the most extraordinary glances he had ever seen – accusation, abasement, even a sort of triumphant misery, were all expressed in it; it was the face of a mean martyr. 'The mask of jealousy,' thought Alleyn. 'There's nothing more pitiable or more degrading. My God, if ever I – ' He thrust the thought from him, and began again.

'Sir Herbert, did you take that letter from the schoolgirl on the bicycle?'

Still with a sort of smile on his mouth, Carrados turned to Alleyn.

'I have no recollection of it,' he said.

Alleyn nodded to Fox, who went out. He was away for perhaps two minutes. Nobody spoke. Lady Carrados had bent her head, and seemed to look with profound attention at her gloved hands, clasped tightly together in her lap. Carrados suddenly wiped his face with his palm, and then drew out his handkerchief. Fox came back.

He ushered in Miss Harris.

'Good evening, Miss Harris,' said Alleyn.

'Good evening, Mr Alleyn. Good evening, Lady Carrados. Good evening, Sir Herbert. Good evening,' concluded Miss Harris with a collected glance at the Assistant Commissioner.

'Miss Harris,' said Alleyn, 'do you remember staying with your uncle, Mr Walter Harris, when he was vicar at Falconbridge? You were fifteen at the time I mean.'

'Yes Mr Alleyn, certainly,' said Miss Harris.

Carrados uttered some sort of oath. Lady Carrados said: ' But – what do you mean, Miss Harris?'

'Certainly, Lady Carrados,' said Miss Harris brightly.

'At that time,' said Alleyn, 'there was a fatal motor accident.'

507

'To Captain O'Brien. Pardon me, Lady Carrados. Yes, Mr Alleyn.'

'Good Lord!' ejaculated Alleyn, involuntarily. 'Do you mean to say that you have realized that – '

'I knew Captain "Paddy" O'Brien was Lady Carrados's first husband, naturally.'

'But,' said Alleyn, 'did you never think of telling Lady Carrados that there was this, well, this link, between you?'

'Oh, no,' said Miss Harris, 'naturally not, Mr Alleyn. It would not have been at all my place to bring it up. When I was given the list of vacant posts at the Friendly Cousins Registry Office I thought this seemed the most suitable, and I – please excuse me, Lady Carrados – I made enquiries, as one does, you know. And I said to my friend Miss Smith: "What an extraordinary coincidence," because when I learned of Lady Carrados's former name I realized it must be the same, and I said to Smithy: "I think that must be an omen," so I applied for the post.'

'I see,' said Alleyn, 'and do you remember Sir Herbert, too?'

'Oh, yes. At least, I wasn't quite sure at first, but afterwards I was. Sir Herbert was the gentleman in the car. Perhaps I should explain?'

'Please do.'

'I had actually spoken to him.' She looked apologetically at Carrados. 'I'm quite sure Sir Herbert has quite forgotten, because I was just a gawky schoolgirl at the time.'

'That will do, Miss Harris,' said Carrados violently. 'You will please not answer any further questions.'

Miss Harris looked extremely startled, turned bright pink, and opened her eyes very wide indeed. She closed her lips in a prudent button.

'Go on, Miss Harris,' said Alleyn.

'Which do you wish me to do, Lady Carrados?' asked her secretary.

508

'I think you had better go on,' said the faint voice.

'Very well, Lady Carrados. You see, I had the pleasure of returning a letter that had been left behind at the vicarage.'

'That is an absolute lie,' said Carrados, loudly.

'Pardon me,' said Miss Harris, 'but I cannot let that pass. I am speaking the truth.'

'Thank you, Miss Harris,' said Alleyn quickly. 'Would you mind waiting outside for a moment? Fox.'

Fox shepherded her out.

'By God!' began Carrados. 'If you take the word of a – '

'Wait a moment,' said Alleyn, 'I think I shall go on with my story. Our case, Sir Herbert, is that you did, in fact, take this letter, and for some reason never gave it to the lady who afterwards married you. Our case is that, having read the letter, you kept it for eighteen years, in the drawer of a miniature writing-desk in your study.'

'I protest. I absolutely deny – '

'You deny this, too?'

'It is outrageous! I tell you this, sir, if I have any influence – '

'Just a moment,' said Alleyn, 'Lady Carrados is speaking.'

The focus of attention shifted to the woman. She sat there as if she attended a meeting of some society in which she was interested. Her furs, her expensive, unnoticeable clothes, her gloves, her discreet make-up, might have been taken as symbols of controlled good breeding. It was the fierce rigidity of her figure that gave expression to her emotion. Her voice scarcely wavered. Alleyn realized that she was oblivious to her surroundings, and to the presence of other people in the room, and that seemed to him to be the most significant indication of her distress. She spoke directly to her husband.

509

'You knew! All these years you have watched me, and known how much I suffered. Why did you hide the letter? Why did you marry me, knowing my past history? It seems to me you must be mad. I understand now why you have watched me, why, since this awful business, you have never taken your eyes off me. You knew. You knew I was being blackmailed.' She caught her breath, and moved round stiffly until she faced her husband. 'You've done it,' she whispered. 'It's you. You're mad, and you've done it to torture me. You've always been jealous of Paddy. Ever since I told you it could never be the same with anyone else. You were jealous of dead Paddy.'

'Evelyn,' said Alleyn gently. She made a slight impatient gesture, but she spoke only to Carrados.

'You wrote those letters. It's you.'

Carrados stared at her like an idiot. His mouth was open. His eyebrows were raised in a sort of imbecile astonishment. He shook his head from side to side.

'No,' he said. 'No, Evelyn, no.'

'Make him tell you, Roderick,' she said, without turning her head.

'Sir Herbert,' said Alleyn. 'Do you deny you kept this letter in the secret drawer of that desk?'

'Yes.'

Fox glanced at Alleyn, went out, and returned, after another deadly silence, with Bridget.

Lady Carrados gave a little moaning cry, and caught at her daughter's hand.

'Miss O'Brien,' said Alleyn, 'I've asked you to come here in order that the Assistant Commissioner may hear of an incident you related to me yesterday. You told me that on one occasion, when you were alone in the study of your stepfather's house, you examined the miniature writing-cabinet in that room. You told me that when you

510

pressed a tiny screw a triangular drawer opened out of the cabinet, and that there was a letter in it. Is this true?'

'Donna?' Bridget looked anxiously at her mother.

'Yes, yes, darling. Tell them. Whatever it is, tell them.'

'It's quite true,' said Bridget.

'Your stepfather came into the study at this juncture?'

'Yes.'

'What was his attitude when he saw what you had done?'

'He was very angry indeed.'

'What did he do?'

'He twisted my arm, and bruised it.'

'A lie. The child has always hated me. Everything I have tried to do for her – a lie, a wicked spiteful lie!'

'Fox,' said Alleyn, 'will you ask Sir Daniel to come in?'

Sir Daniel had evidently been sitting in the secretary's office, as he came in almost immediately. When he saw the two Carradoses and Bridget, he greeted them exactly as if they were fellow guests at a party. He then shook hands with the Assistant Commissioner, and turned to Alleyn.

'Sir Daniel,' said Alleyn. 'I've asked you to come in as I understand you were witness to a scene which Miss O'Brien has just described to us. It took place about two years ago. Do you remember that Miss O'Brien rang you up and asked you to come and see her mother who was unwell?'

'That has happened more than once,' said Davidson.

'On this particular visit you went into the study and talked to Miss O'Brien about a small French writing-cabinet.'

Davidson moved his eyebrows.

'Oh, yes?'

'Do you remember it?'

'I do. Very well.'

511

'You told her that there was probably a secret drawer in the box. Then you went upstairs to see Lady Carrados.'

'Yes. That's how it was, I think.'

'When you returned, were Miss O'Brien and Sir Herbert together in the study?'

'Yes,' said Davidson, and set his lips in an extremely firm line.

'Will you describe the scene that followed?'

'I am afraid not, Mr Alleyn.'

'Why not?'

'Let us say, for reasons of professional etiquette.'

Lady Carrados said: 'Sir Daniel, if you are thinking of me, I implore you to tell them what they want to know. I want the truth as much as anyone here. If I don't know the truth now, I shall go to pieces.'

Davidson looked at her in astonishment.

'*You* want me to tell them about that afternoon?'

'Yes, yes, I do.'

'And you, Carrados?' Davidson stared at Carrados, as if he were a sort of curiosity.

'Davidson, I implore you to keep your head. I am sure you saw nothing that could be construed – that could be regarded as evidence – that – Davidson, you know me. You know that I'm not a vindictive man. You know.'

'Come,' said Alleyn, 'we can cut this short. Sir Daniel, did you examine Miss O'Brien's arm when you returned to the study?'

'I did,' said Davidson, turning his back on Carrados.

'What did you find?'

'A certain amount of contusion, for which I prescribed a lotion.'

'To what cause did you attribute these bruises?'

'They suggested that the arm had been tightly held, and twisted.'

512

'What were the relative positions of Sir Herbert and his stepdaughter when you came into the study?'

'He held her by the arm.'

'Would it be correct to say he was storming at her?'

Davidson looked thoughtfully at Bridget. They exchanged half-smiles. 'He was shouting a good deal, certainly,' said Davidson dryly.

'Did you notice the writing-desk?'

'I don't think I noticed it the second time I went into the room. I realized that Sir Herbert Carrados was talking about it when I came in.'

'Yes. Thank you, Sir Daniel. Will you and Miss O'Brien wait outside? We'll see Mr Dimitri, if you please, Fox.'

Davidson and Bridget both went out. Dimitri was ushered in by Fox. He was very sleek, with a clean bandage round his cut finger, oil on his hair, scent on his person. He looked out of the corners of his eyes, and bowed extensively.

'Good evening, my lady. Good evening, gentlemen.'

'Mr Dimitri,' Alleyn began, 'I have – '

'Stop.'

Carrados had got to his feet. He stood with his hand raised before his face in a curious gesture, half-defensive, half-declamatory. Then he slowly extended his arm, and pointed to Dimitri. The action was both ridiculous and alarming.

'What's the matter, Sir Herbert?' asked Alleyn.

'What's he doing here? My God, now I know – I know – '

'Well, Sir Herbert? What do you know?'

'Stop! I'll tell you. I did it! I did it! I confess. I confess everything. I did it!'

513

CHAPTER TWENTY-NINE

Climax

'You did what, Sir Herbert?'

It was the AC's voice, very quiet and matter-of-fact.

'I kept the letter.' Carrados looked directly at his wife. 'You know why. If ever you had spoken of him, if ever you had compared me to that fellow, if I had found you – You know why.'

'Yes,' said Lady Carrados. 'I know why.'

'For God's sake,' Carrados said, 'for God's sake, gentlemen, let this go no further. It's a private matter between my wife and myself.'

'It has gone much further than that,' said Alleyn. 'Did you not in fact write blackmailing letters to your wife purely in order to torture her mind? Did you not do this?'

'You fool,' shouted Carrados. 'You fool! It's I who have suffered. It's I who have dreaded what might happen. The letter was stolen. It was stolen. It was stolen.'

'Now,' said Alleyn, 'it seems we are going to get the truth. When did you miss the letter?'

Carrados looked from one face to the other. For a frightful moment Alleyn thought he was going to burst into tears. His lips were shaking. He seemed an old man. He began to speak.

'It was when we came back from Newmarket. That evening I was alone in my study. Bridget had been very inconsiderate all day, leaving us and going off with a young man of whom I could not approve. My wife had taken her part against me. I was alone in my study. I found myself looking at the French writing-cabinet. There was something different in the arrangement of the pieces in front of it. I went to re-arrange them, and being there I tried the hidden drawer. It was empty! I tell you the letter was there the day before. I saw it there. The day before I had been very angry with my wife. She had been cruel to me. I am very sensitive and my nerves are shattered. I am alone. Terribly lonely. Nobody cares what becomes of me. She was so thoughtless and cruel. So I looked at the letter because the letter gave me comfort. It was there the night before. And do you know who was alone in my room on May the ninth?'

'Yes,' said Alleyn. 'I am glad you, too, remember. It was Mr Colombo Dimitri.'

'Ah,' said Carrados shakily. 'Ah, now we're getting at it. Now, we're getting at it.'

'I am afraid I do not understand,' said Dimitri. 'Is Sir Herbert perhaps ill?'

Carrados slewed round and again he pointed at Dimitri.

'You stole it, you filthy dago. I know you stole it. I have suspected it from the first. I could do nothing – nothing.'

'Excuse me, Mr Alleyn,' said Dimitri, 'but I believe that I may charge Sir Herbert Carrados with libel on this statement. Is it not so?'

'I don't think I advise you to do so, Mr Dimitri. On the other hand I shall very strongly advise Lady Carrados to charge you with blackmail. Lady Carrados, is it a fact that on the morning of May twenty-fifth, when Lord Robert Gospell paid you a visit, you received a blackmailing letter?'

'Yes.'

'Do you believe that the only source from which the blackmailer could have got his information was the letter lost on the day of Captain O'Brien's accident?'

'Yes.'

Alleyn took an envelope from his pocket, handed it to her.

515

'Was the blackmailing letter written in a similar style to this?'

She glanced at it and turned her head away.

'It was exactly like that.'

'If I tell you that the lady to whom this letter is addressed had been blackmailed as you have been blackmailed and that we have positive evidence that the man who wrote this address was Colombo Dimitri, are you prepared to charge him with blackmail?'

'Yes.'

'It is completely false,' said Dimitri. 'I shall certainly sue for libel.'

His face was ashen. He put his bandaged hand to his lips and pressed it against them.

'Before we go any further,' said Alleyn, 'I think I should explain that Lord Robert Gospell was in the confidence of Scotland Yard as regards these blackmailing letters. He was working for us on the case. We've got his signed statement that leaves no doubt at all that Mr Dimitri collected a sum of money at a concert held at the Constance Street Hall on Thursday, June the third. Lord Robert actually watched Mr Dimitri collect his money.'

'He – ' Dimitri caught his breath, his lips were drawn back from his teeth in a sort of grin. 'I deny everything,' he said. 'Everything. I wish to send for my lawyer.'

'You shall do so, Mr Dimitri, when I have finished. On June the eighth, two nights ago, Lady Carrados gave a ball at Marsdon House. Lord Robert was there. As he knew so much about Mr Dimitri already, he thought he would find out a little more. He watched Mr Dimitri. He now knew the method employed. He also knew that Lady Carrados was the victim of blackmail. Is that right, Lady Carrados?'

'Yes. I had a conversation with him about it. He knew what I was going to do.'

'What were you going to do?'

'Put my bag containing five hundred pounds in a certain place in the green sitting-room upstairs.'

'Yes,' said Alleyn. 'Now, Lord Robert saw Mr Dimitri return her empty bag to Lady Carrados shortly before one o'clock. At one o'clock he rang me up and told me he now had enough evidence. The conversation was interrupted by someone who must have overheard at least one very significant phrase. Two and a half hours later Lord Robert was murdered.'

The quiet of the room was blown into piercing clamour. Dimitri had screamed like a woman, his mouth wide open. This shocking rumpus lasted for a second and stopped. Alleyn had a picture of an engine-driver pulling a string and then letting it go. Dimitri stood, still with a gaping mouth, wagging his finger at Alleyn.

'Now then, now then,' said Fox and stepped up to him.

'False!' said Dimitri, frantically snapping his fingers in Fox's face and then shaking them as if they were scorched. 'False! You accuse me of murder. I am not an assassin. I am innocent. *Cristo mio,* I am innocent, innocent, innocent!'

For a moment it looked as if he'd try to bolt from the room. He might have been a tenor giving an excruciatingly bad performance in a second-rate Italian opera. He mouthed at Alleyn, tore his hair, crumpled on to a chair, and burst into tears. Upon the five English people in the office there descended a heavy aura of embarrassment.

'I am innocent,' sobbed Dimitri. 'As innocent as a child. The blessed saints bear witness to my innocence. The blessed saints bear witness – '

'Unfortunately,' said Alleyn, 'their evidence is not acceptable in a court of law. If you will keep quiet for a moment, Mr Dimitri, we can get on with our business. Will you ask Mrs Halcut-Hackett to come in, please, Fox?'

The interval was enlivened by the sound of Dimitri biting his nails and sobbing.

Mrs Halcut-Hackett, dressed as if she was going to a Continental restaurant and looking like a beauty specialist's mistake, came into the office. Fox followed with an extra chair which he placed for her. She sat down and drew up her bust until it seemed to perch like some super-structure on a rigid foundation. Then she saw Lady Carrados. An extraordinary look passed between the two women. It was as if they had said to each other: 'You, too?'

'Mrs Halcut-Hackett,' said Alleyn. 'You have told me that after a charade party you gave in December you found that a document which you valued was missing from a box on your dressing-table. Had this man, Colombo Dimitri, an opportunity of being alone in this room?'

She turned her head and looked at Dimitri who flapped his hands at her.

'Why, yes,' she said. 'He certainly had.'

'Did Lord Robert sit near you at the Sirmione Quartette's concert on June the third?'

'You know he did.'

'Do you remember that this man, Colombo Dimitri, sat not very far away from you?'

'Why – yes.'

'Your bag was stolen that afternoon?'

'Yes.' She looked again at Lady Carrados who suddenly leant forward and touched her hand.

'I'm so sorry,' she said. 'I, too. Indeed you have nothing to fear from us. We have suffered, too. I have made up my mind to hide nothing now. Will you help by also hiding – nothing?'

'Oh, my dear!' said Mrs Halcut-Hackett in a whisper.

'We need not ask for very much more,' said Alleyn.

518

'Would it have been possible for Dimitri to have taken your bag while you were out of the concert-room?'

'Lord Robert might have seen,' said Mrs Halcut-Hackett.

'Lord Robert did see,' said Alleyn.

'The dead!' cried Dimitri. 'I cannot be accused by the dead.'

'If that was true,' said Alleyn, 'as it often is, what a motive for murder! I tell you we have a statement, written and signed by the dead.'

Dimitri uttered a sort of moan and shrank back in his chair.

Alleyn took from his pocket the cigarette-case with the medallion.

'This is yours, isn't it?' he asked Mrs Halcut-Hackett.

'Yes. I've told you so.'

'You left it in the green sitting-room at Marsdon House?'

'Yes – only a few minutes.'

'A minute or two, not more, after you came out of that room you heard the dialling tinkle of the telephone?'

'Yes.'

'You had seen Lord Robert coming upstairs?'

'Yes.'

Alleyn nodded to Fox who again left the room.

'After you had joined your partner in the other sitting-out room, you discovered the loss of your case?'

'Yes, I did.'

'Your partner fetched it.'

She wetted her lips. Dimitri was listening avidly. Carrados had slumped down in his chair with his chin on his chest. Alleyn felt he was giving, for anybody that had time to notice it, a quiet performance of a broken man. Lady Carrados sat upright, her hands folded in her lap, her face looked exhausted. The AC was motionless behind the green lamp.

'Well, Mrs Halcut-Hackett? Your partner fetched your case from the green sitting-room, didn't he?'

'Yes.'

The door opened and Withers walked in after Fox. He stood with his hands in his pockets and blinked his white eyelashes.

'Hallo,' he said. 'What's the idea?'

'I have invited you to come here, Captain Withers, in order that the Assistant Commissioner may hear your statement about your movements on the night of the ball at Marsdon House. I have discovered that although you left Marsdon House at three-thirty you did not arrive at the Matador Night Club until four-fifteen. You therefore have no alibi for the murder of Lord Robert Gospell.'

Withers looked at Mrs Halcut-Hackett with a sort of sneer.

'She can give me one,' he said.

She looked at him and spoke to Alleyn. Her voice was quite expressionless.

'I'd made up my mind it would have to come out. Between the time we left the ball and the time we got to the Matador, Captain Withers drove me about in his car. I was afraid of my husband. I had seen him watching me. I wanted to talk to Captain Withers. I was afraid to say this before.'

'I see,' said Alleyn. 'You accept that, Captain Withers?'

'It's true enough.'

'Very well. Now, to return to Marsdon House. You told me that at one o'clock you were in the sitting-room at the head of the stairs.'

'So I was.'

'You did not tell me you were also in the telephone-room.'

Withers stared at Mrs Halcut-Hackett. She had been watching him like a frightened animal but as soon as his eyes turned towards her she looked away from him.

520

'Why should I?' said Withers

'You were in the telephone room with Mrs Halcut-Hackett before you went to the other room. You returned to it from the other room to fetch this.'

Alleyn's long arm shot up. Seven heads followed the movement. Seven pairs of eyes were concentrated on the gold cigarette-case with the jewelled medallion.

'And what if I did?'

'Where did you find this case?'

'On a table in the room with the telephone.'

'When I asked you yesterday if you overheard Lord Robert telephoning in this room, as we know he did at one o'clock, you denied it.'

'There wasn't anybody in the room when I fetched the case. I told you I heard the dialling tinkle on the extension a bit before then. If it was Gospell I suppose he'd gone when I got there.'

'Is there any reason why anybody, say Mr Dimitri in the corner there, should not have gone into the telephone-room after you left it with Mrs Halcut-Hackett, and before you returned for the case?'

'No reason at all as far as I'm concerned.'

'Dimitri,' said Alleyn, 'have you seen this case before? Look at it. Have you seen it before?'

'Never. I have never seen it. I do not know why you ask. I have never seen it.'

'Take it in your hands. Look at it.'

Dimitri took the case.

'Open it.'

Dimitri opened it. From where Alleyn stood he could see the little cutting taken from *The Times*. Dimitri saw it too. His eyes dilated. The case dropped through his hands to the floor. He pointed a shaking finger at Alleyn.

'I think you must be the devil himself,' he whispered.

'Fox,' said Alleyn, 'will you pass the case round?'

It passed from hand to hand. Withers, Evelyn Carrados and Carrados all looked at it. Withers handled it as if he had done so before, but seemed quite unmoved by the cutting. The Carradoses both looked blankly at it and passed it on. Mrs Halcut-Hackett opened the case and stared at the scrap of paper.

'This wasn't here before,' she said. 'What is it? Who put it here?'

'I'm sorry,' said Alleyn. 'It's done no damage. It will come off quite easily.'

He took the case from her.

Dimitri suddenly leapt to his feet. Fox who had never taken his eyes off him moved in front of the door.

'Sit down, Mr Dimitri,' said Alleyn.

'I am going. You can keep me here no longer against my will. You accuse, you threaten, you lie! I say I can endure it no longer. I am an innocent man, a man of standing with a clientèle of great excellence. I will see a lawyer. My God, let me pass!'

He plunged forward. Alleyn caught him by one arm. Fox by the other. He struggled violently. The AC pressed a bell on his desk, the door was opened from the outside and two plain-clothes men walked into the room. Beyond, in the brightly lit secretary's room three startled faces, Bridget's, Davidson's and Miss Harris's, peered over the shoulders of more Yard men, and through the doorway.

Dimitri, mouthing and panting, was taken over by the two officers.

'Now then,' they said. 'Now then.'

'Lady Carrados,' said Alleyn, 'will you formally charge this man?'

'I do charge him.'

'In a moment,' said Alleyn to Dimitri, 'you will be taken to the charge-room, but before we talk about the exact nature of the charge – ' He looked through the door: 'Sir

Daniel? I see you're still there. May I trouble you again for a moment?'

Davidson, looking very startled, came through.

'Good God, Alleyn!' he said, staring at Dimitri. 'What's this?'

Alleyn said: 'You can, I believe, give me the final piece of evidence in an extremely involved affair. You see this cigarette-case?'

Davidson took it.

'My dear fellow,' he said, 'that's the abortion. I told you about it. It's part of the collection at Marsdon House. You remember?'

He moved to the light and after another startled glance at Dimitri, who had gone perfectly still and stared at him like a lost soul, Davidson put up his glasses and examined the case.

'You know, I believe it *is* Benvenuto,' he said, looking over his glasses at Alleyn.

'Yes, yes, I dare say. Will you tell us where you saw it?'

'Among a collection of *objets d'art* on a pie-crust table in an upstairs room at Marsdon House.'

'At what time, Sir Daniel?'

'My dear Alleyn, I told you. About eleven-thirty or so. Perhaps earlier.'

'Would you swear you noticed it no later than eleven-thirty?' insisted Alleyn.

'But of course I would,' said Davidson. 'I did not return to that room. I am quite ready to swear it.'

He held the cigarette-case up in his beautifully shaped hand.

'I swear I saw this case on the table in the green sitting-room not later than eleven-thirty. That do?'

The silence was broken only by Dimitri's laboured breathing.

And then, surprisingly clear and firm, Mrs Halcut-Hackett's voice:

'But that can't be true.'

Alleyn said: 'Will you open the case?'

Davidson, who was gazing in amazement at Mrs Halcut-Hackett, opened the cigarette-case and saw the notice.

'Will you read that press cutting?' said Alleyn. 'Aloud, please.'

The deep expressive voice read the absurd message.

' "Childie Darling. Living in exile. Longing. Only want Daughter. Daddy." '

'What in the name of all wonders is this?'

'We believe it to be a murderer's message,' said Alleyn. 'We think this man, Dimitri, can translate it.'

Davidson shut the case with a snap.

Something had gone wrong with his hands. They shook so violently that the diamonds on the gold case seemed to have a separate flashing life of their own.

'So Dimitri is a murderer,' he said.

'Look out!' said Alleyn loudly.

Dimitri flung himself forward with such extreme and sudden violence that the men who held him were taken off their guard and his hands were at Davidson's throat before they had regained their hold on him. In a moment the room was full of struggling men. Chairs crashed to the floor, a woman screamed. Fox's voice shouted urgently: 'Get to it. What are you *doing*?' There was a concerted upheaval against the edge of the desk. The green-shaded lamp smashed into oblivion.

'That's better,' said Alleyn's voice. 'Now then. Hands together.'

A sharp click, a cry from Dimitri, and then the figures resolved themselves into a sort of tableau: Dimitri, hand-

524

cuffed and held by three men, against the desk; Davidson in the centre of the room with Alleyn, Fox and a plain-clothes man grasping his arms behind his back; the Assistant Commissioner, between the two groups, like a distinguished sort of referee.

'Murderer!' screamed Dimitri. 'Treacherous, filthy assassin! I confess! Gentlemen, I confess! I have worked for him for seven years and now, now, *now* he will stand aside and let me go to the gallows for the crime he has himself committed. I will tell you everything. *Everything*.'

'Speak up, Rory,' said the AC.

'Daniel Davidson,' said Alleyn, 'I arrest you for the murder of Lord Robert Gospell, and I warn you . . .'

CHAPTER THIRTY

Confessions from Troy

'I thought,' said Alleyn, 'that you would like to know at once, Mildred.'

Lady Mildred Potter shook her head, not so much in disagreement as from a sort of general hopelessness.

'It was nice of you to come, Roderick. But I'm afraid I simply cannot take it in. Sir Daniel has always been perfectly charming to both of us. Bunchy liked him very much. He told me so. And there's no doubt Sir Daniel did wonders with my indigestion. Quite cured it. Are you sure you are not mistaken?'

'Quite sure, I am afraid, Mildred. You see, Dimitri has confessed that Davidson has been in a sort of infamous partnership with him for seven years. Davidson knew something about Dimitri in the first instance, I think. That's probably how he managed to get his hold over Dimitri. Davidson has been extremely careful. He has found the data but he has left Dimitri to carry out the practical work. Davidson saw the open drawer and the letter in Carrados's writing-cabinet. Davidson came in on the scene between Carrados and Bridget. He was careful never to be left alone in the room himself, but he told Dimitri about the secret drawer and instructed Dimitri how to steal the letter. He told Dimitri that there might be something interesting there. Dimitri did all the dirty work. He collected the handbags of the blackmailed ladies. He wrote the letters. Sometimes he got the ideas. Mrs Halcut-Hackett's trinket-box was one of Dimitri's brightest ideas, I imagine.'

'I'm lost in it, Roderick. Troy, darling, do *you* understand?'

526

Alleyn looked at Troy, sitting on the floor at Mildred's feet.

'I think I'm beginning to understand,' said Troy.

'Well, go on, Roderick,' said Mildred drearily.

'There were three things that I could not fit into the pattern,' said Alleyn, and he spoke more to Troy than to Mildred. 'It seemed at first that if Dimitri overheard the telephone call he had an overwhelming motive. We knew he was a blackmailer, and we knew Bunchy was on his track. But we found that Dimitri literally could not have done the murder. His alibi stood up to the time factor and came out on top.

'Withers is a bad lot, and Bunchy knew that too, but somehow I could not see Withers as the killer. He's hard, wary and completely unscrupulous. If he did ever murder it would be deliberately, and with forethought. The whole thing would be worked out to the last second. This job was, we believed, unpremeditated until within two and a half hours of its execution. Still Withers had to be considered. There was a gap in his alibi. I now know that he spent that gap driving his woman-dupe about in his car in order to discuss a situation which had become acute. Into this department, and again I implore your silence because I certainly shouldn't tell you about it, came old General Halcut-Hackett like an elderly harlequin dodging about in the fog of Belgrave Square at the crucial time when the guests left Marsdon House. He, of course, was looking for his wife. Next came Carrados. Old Carrados was an infernal bore. His alibi, which overlapped Dimitri's, held good, but his behaviour was rum in the extreme. It was not until I heard of an incident eighteen years old that I managed to fit him into the pattern. And all the time there were three things about Davidson for which I could find only one explanation. He told me he saw a certain cigarette-case in the green sitting-room at about

527

eleven-thirty. Certainly not later. We found that the cigarette-case in question was only in this room for about four minutes round about one o'clock during which the telephone conversation took place. Why should Davidson lie? He had thought the case was a set-piece – one of the Marsdon House possessions; he had *not* realized that it was the personal property of one of the guests. He stated most emphatically that he did not overhear the conversation and indeed did not return to the room after eleven-thirty. But there is a curious point about the telephone conversation. Bunchy said to me: "He might as well mix his damn brews with poison." Davidson must have overheard that sentence because it came just before Bunchy broke off. Bunchy was talking about Dimitri, of course, but I believe Davidson thought he was talking about him. The broken sentence: "with such filthy ingenuity," or something of that sort. Davidson probably thought the next word Bunchy spoke would be his (Davidson's) name. That's odd, isn't it?

'As for the figure Miss Harris saw beyond the glass panel, undoubtedly it was Davidson's. At his wits' end he must have dived through the nearest door and there, I suppose, pulled himself together and decided to murder Bunchy.'

'Then there is the other cigarette-case.'

Alleyn looked at Lady Mildred. Her head nodded like a mandarin's. He turned back to Troy and spoke softly.

'I mean the weapon. On the morning after the murder I asked to see Davidson's case. He showed me a cigarette-case that was certainly too small for the job and said it was the one he had carried last night. I noticed how immaculate it was, looked closely at it, and found traces of plate-powder in the tooling. We learnt that Davidson's cases were cleaned the morning before the ball and had not been touched after the ball. It seemed to me that this case had certainly not been out all night. It shone like

528

a mirror and I would have sworn had not been used since it was put in his pocket. It was a thin bit of evidence but it did look as if he had lied when he said it was the case he took to Marsdon House. And then there was the condition – is Mildred asleep?'

'Yes,' said Lady Mildred. 'Do you mind very much, dear Roderick, if I go to bed? I'm afraid I shall never understand, you see, and I am really so very tired. I think sorrow is one of the most tiring things, don't you? Troy, my dear, you will look after poor Roderick, won't you? Donald will be in late and I don't know where he is just now.'

'I think he took Bridget Carrados home,' said Alleyn, opening the door for Mildred. 'Evelyn and her husband wanted to be alone and Donald was in the waiting-room looking hopeful.'

'He seems to be very attached to her,' said Mildred, pausing at the door and looking at Alleyn with tear-stained eyes. 'Is she a nice girl, Roderick?'

'Very nice. I think she'll look after him. Good night, Mildred.'

'Good night.'

Alleyn shut the door after her and returned to Troy.

'May I stay for a little longer?'

'Yes, please. I want to hear the end of it all.' Troy looked sideways at him. 'How extraordinarily well-trained your eye must be! To notice the grains of plate-powder in the tooling of a cigarette-case; could anything be more admirable? What else did you notice?'

'I notice that although your eyes are grey there are little flecks of green in them and that the iris is ringed with black. I notice that when you smile your face goes crooked. I notice that the third finger of your left hand has a little spot of vermillion on the inside where a ring should hide it; and from that, Miss Troy, I deduce that you are a painter

529

in oils and are not so proud as you should be of your lovely fingers.'

'Please tell me the end of the case.'

'I would rather tell you that since this afternoon in the few spare moments I have had to spend upon it I have considered your case and that I have decided to take out a warrant for your arrest. The charge is impeding an officer of the law in the execution of his duty.'

'Don't be so damned facetious,' said Troy.

'All right. Where was I?'

'You had got to the third point against Davidson.'

'Yes. The third point was in the method used in committing the crime. I don't think Bunchy would mind if he knew that even while I described his poor little body I was thinking of the woman to whom I spoke. Do you? He was such an understanding person, wasn't he, with just the right salty flavour of irony? I'm sure he knew how short-lived the first pang of sorrow really is if only people would confess as much. Well, Troy, the man who killed him knew how easy it was to asphyxiate people and I didn't think many killers would know that. The only real mark of violence was the scar made by the cigarette-case. A doctor would realize how little force was needed and Bunchy's doctor would know how great an ally that weak heart would be. Davidson told me about the condition of the heart because he knew I would discover he had examined Bunchy. He kept his head marvellously when I interviewed him, did Sir Daniel. He's as clever as paint. We're searching his house tonight. Fox is there now. I don't think we'll find anything except perhaps the lethal cigarette-case, but I've more hopes of Dimitri's desk. I couldn't get into that yesterday.'

'What about the cloak and hat?'

'That brings us to a very curious episode. We have searched for the cloak and hat ever since four o'clock

530

yesterday morning and we have not found them. We did our usual routine stuff, going round all the dust-bin experts and so on and we also notified the parcels-post offices. This afternoon we heard of a parcel that had been dumped at the Main Western office during the rush hour yesterday. It was over-stamped with tuppenny stamps and addressed to somewhere in China. The writing was script which was our blackmailer's favourite medium of expression. It's gone, alas, but I think there's just a chance we may trace it. It's a very long chance. Now who is likely to have an unlimited supply of tuppenny stamps, my girl?'

'Somebody who gives receipts?'

'Bless me, if you're not a clever old thing. Right as usual,' said the Duchess. 'And who should give receipts but Sir Daniel, the fashionable physician? Who but he?'

'Dimitri for one.'

'I'm sorry to say that is perfectly true, darling. But when I was in Davidson's waiting-room, I saw several of those things that I think are called illustrated brochures. They appealed for old clothes for the Central Chinese Medical Mission at God knows where. It is our purpose, my dear Troy, to get one of those brochures and write to the Central Chinese Mission asking for further information.'

'I wonder,' murmured Troy.

'And so, you may depend upon it, do I. There's one other point which has been kindly elucidated by the gibbering Dimitri. This morning he sent his servant out for a *Times*. When we heard of this we had a look at *The Times,* too. We found the agony-column notice that I talked about when poor Mildred was trying not to go to sleep, and before I could tell you how much I approve of the solemn way you knit your brows when you listen to me. Now, this notice read like this: "Childie Darling. Living in exile. Longing. Only want Daughter. Daddy." A rum affair, we thought, and we noticed in our brilliant

531

way that the initial letters read "C.D. Lie low. D.D." which might not be too fancifully elaborated into "Colombo Dimitri, lie low, Daniel Davidson." And, in fact, Mr Dimitri confessed to this artless device. It was arranged, he says, that if anything unprecedented, untoward, unanticipated, ever occurred, Davidson would communicate with Dimitri in precisely this manner. It was a poor effort, but Sir Daniel hadn't much time. He must have composed it as soon as he got home after his night's work. Anything more?'

'What about Dimitri and Withers?'

'They were taken to the charge-room, and duly charged. The one with blackmail, the other with running a gaming-house. I'll explain the gaming-house some other time. They are extremely nasty fellows, but if Dimitri hadn't been quite such a nasty fellow, we wouldn't have stood as good a chance of scaring him into fits and getting the whole story about Davidson. I gambled on that, and by jingo, Troy, it *was* a gamble.'

'What would have happened if Dimitri had kept quiet even though he did think you were going to arrest him for murder?'

'We would still have arrested him for blackmail, and would have had to plug away at Davidson on what we'd got. But Dimitri saw we had a clear case on the blackmail charge. He'd nothing to gain in protecting Davidson.'

'Do you think he really *knows* Davidson did the murder?'

'I think we shall find that Davidson tried to warn him against collecting Evelyn Carrados's bag at the ball. Davidson saw Bunchy was with Evelyn, when Bridget returned her bag the first time.'

'You didn't tell me about that.'

Alleyn told her about it.

'And isn't that really all?' he asked.

'Yes. That's all.'

'Troy, I love you more than anything in life. I've tried

532

humility; God knows, I am humble. And I've tried effrontery. If you can't love me, tell me so, and please let us not meet again because I can't manage meeting you unless it is to love you.'

Troy raised a white face and looked solemnly at him.

'I know my mind at last,' she said. 'I couldn't be parked.'

'Darling, darling Troy.'

'I do love you. Very much indeed.'

'Wonder of the world!' cried Alleyn, and took her in his arms.

Epilogue

Down a sun-baked mud track that ran through the middle of the most remote of all the Chinese Medical Mission's settlements in Northern Manchuria walked a short, plump celestial. He was followed by six yellow urchins upon each of whose faces was an expression of rapt devotion, and liveliest envy. If his face and legs had been visible, it would have been seen that sweat poured down them in runnels. But his face was hidden by a black hat, and his legs by the voluminous folds of a swashbuckling cloak. There was glory in his gait.

In the receiving office of the mission, a jaded young Englishman gazed in perplexity at a telegram a month old. It had been forwarded from the head depot and had done the rounds of most of the settlements. It was from New Scotland Yard, London.

The young Englishman gazed blankly through the open door at the little procession in the sun-baked track outside.

Final Curtain

For Joan and Cecil
with my love

Contents

CHAPTER I

Siege of Troy

I

"Considered severally," said Troy, coming angrily into the studio, "a carbuncle, a month's furlough and a husband returning from the antipodes don't sound like the ingredients of a hell-brew. Collectively they amount to precisely that."

Katti Bostock stepped heavily back from her easel, screwed up her eyes, and squinting dispassionately at her work said: "Why?"

"They've telephoned from C.1. Rory's on his way. He'll probably get here in about three weeks. By which time I shall have returned, cured of my carbuncle, to the girls in the back room."

"At least," said Miss Bostock, scowling hideously at her work, "he won't have to face the carbuncle. There is that."

"It's on my hip."

"I know that, you owl."

"Well—but, Katti," Troy argued, standing beside her friend, "you will allow and must admit, it's a stinker. You *are* going it," she added, squinting at Miss Bostock's canvas.

"You'll have to move into the London flat a bit earlier, that's all."

"But if only the carbuncle, and Rory and my leave had come together—well, the carbuncle a bit earlier, certainly—we'd have had a fortnight down here together. The A.C. promised us that. Rory's letters have been full of it. It *is* tough, Katti, you can't deny it. And if you so much as look like saying there are worse things in Europe——"

"All right, all right," said Miss Bostock, pacifically. "I was only going to point out that it's reasonably lucky your particular back

539

room and Roderick's job both happen to be in London. Look for the silver lining, dear," she added unkindly. "What's that letter you keep taking in and out of your pocket?"

Troy opened her thin hand and disclosed a crushed sheet of notepaper. "That?" she murmured. "Oh, yes, there's that. You never heard anything so dotty. Read it."

"It's got cadmium red all over it."

"I know. I dropped it on my palette. It's on the back, luckily."

Miss Bostock spread out the letter on her painting-table, adding several cobalt finger-prints in the process. It was a single sheet of pre-war notepaper, thick, white, with an engraved heading surmounted by a crest—a cross with fluted extremities.

"Crickey!" said Miss Bostock. "Ancreton Manor. That's the—Crickey!" Being one of those people who invariably read letters aloud she began to mutter:

> Miss Agatha Troy (Mrs. Roderick Alleyn)
> Tatlers End House
> Bossicot, Bucks.
> Dear Madam,
> My father-in-law, Sir Henry Ancred, asks me to write to you in reference to a portrait of himself in the character of Macbeth, for which he would be pleased to engage your services. The picture is to hang in the entrance hall at Ancreton Manor, and will occupy a space six by four feet in dimension. As he is in poor health, he wishes the painting to be done here, and will be pleased if you can arrange to stay with us from Saturday, November 17th, until such time as the portrait is completed. He presumes this will be in about a week. He will be glad to know, by telegram, whether this arrangement will suit you, and also your fee for such a commission.
> I am,
> Yours faithfully,
> MILLAMANT ANCRED.

"Well," said Miss Bostock, "of all the cheek!"

Troy grinned. "You'll notice I'm to dodge up a canvas six by four in seven days. I wonder if he expects me to throw in the three witches and the Bloody Child."

"Have you answered it?"

"Not yet," Troy mumbled.

"It was written six days ago," scolded Miss Bostock.

"I know. I must. How shall I word the telegram: "Deeply regret am not house painter"?

Katti Bostock paused, her square fingers still planted under the crest. "I thought only peers had those things peppered about on their notepaper," she said.

"You'll notice it's a cross, with ends like an anchor. Hence Ancred, one supposes."

"Oh! I say!" said Katti, rubbing her nose with her blue finger. "That's funny."

"What is?"

"Didn't you do a set of designs for that production of *Macbeth*?"

"I did. That may have given them the idea."

"Good Lord! Do you remember," said Miss Bostock, "we saw him in the play. You and Roderick, and I? The Bathgates took us. Before the war."

"Of course I do," said Troy. "He was magnificent, wasn't he?"

"What's more, he looked magnificent. *What* a head. Troy, do you remember, we said——"

"So we did. Katti," said Troy, "you're *not* by any chance going to suggest——"

"No, no, of course not. Good Lord, no! But it's rum that we did say it would be fun to have a go at him in the grand manner. Against the backcloth they did from your design; lolloping clouds and a black simplified castle form. The figure cloaked and dim."

"He wouldn't thank you for that, I dare say. The old gentleman probably wishes to appear in a flash of lightning, making faces. Well, I'd better send the telegram. Oh, damn!" Troy sighed. "I wish I could settle down to something."

Miss Bostock glowered thoughtfully at Troy. Four years of intensive work at pictorial surveys for the army, followed by similar and even more exacting work for U.N.R.R.A., had, she thought, tried her friend rather high. She was thin and a bit jumpy. She'd be better if she could do more painting, thought Katti, who did not regard the making of pictorial maps, however exquisite, as full compensation for the loss of pure art. Four years' work with little painting and no husband. "Thank God," Katti thought, "I'm different. I get along nicely."

"If he gets here in three weeks," Troy was saying, "where do you suppose he is now? He might be in New York. But he'd cable

541

if he was in New York. The last letter was still from New Zealand, of course. And the cable."

"Why don't you get on with your work?"

"Work?" said Troy vaguely. "Oh, well. I'll send off that telegram." She wandered to the door and came back for the letter. "Six by four," she said. "Imagine it!"

II

"Mr. Thomas Ancred?" said Troy, looking at the card in her hand. "My dear Katti, he's actually *here* on the spot."

Katti, who had almost completed her vigorous canvas, laid down her brushes and said: "This is in answer to your telegram. He's come to badger you. Who is he?"

"A son of Sir Henry Ancred's, I fancy. Isn't he a theatrical producer? I seem to remember seeing: 'Produced by Thomas Ancred' under casts of characters? Yes, of course he is. That production of *Macbeth* we were talking about at the Unicorn. He was in the picture somewhere then. Look, there's Unicorn Theatre scribbled on the card. We'll have to ask him to dinner, Katti. There's not a train before nine. That'll mean opening another tin. *What* a bore."

"I don't see why he need stay. There's a pub in the village. If he chooses to come on a fool's errand!"

"I'll see what he's like."

"Aren't you going to take off that painting smock?"

"I don't suppose so," Troy said vaguely, and walked up the path from her studio to her house. It was a cold afternoon. Naked trees rattled in a north wind and leaden clouds hurried across the sky. "Suppose," Troy pretended, "I was to walk in and find it was Rory. Suppose he'd kept it a secret and there he was waiting in the library. He'd have lit the fire so that it should be there for us to meet by. His face would be looking like it did the first time he stood there, a bit white with excitement. Suppose——" She had a lively imagination and she built up her fantasy quickly, warming her thoughts at it. So clear was her picture that it brought a physical reaction; her head knocked, her hand, even, trembled a little as she opened the library door.

The man who stood before the unkindled hearth was tall and stooped a little. His hair, which had the appearance of floss, stood up thinly like a child's. He wore glasses and blinked behind them

542

at Troy.

"Good afternoon," he said. "I'm Thomas Ancred, but of course you know that because of the card. I hope you don't mind my coming. I didn't really want to, but the family insisted."

He held out his hand, but didn't do anything with it when Troy took it, so that she was obliged to give it a slight squeeze and let it go. "The whole thing's silly," he said. "About Papa's portrait, I mean, of course. We call him 'Papa,' you know. Some people think it sounds affected, but there it is. About Papa's portrait. I must tell you they all got a great shock when your telegram came. They rang me up. They said you couldn't have understood and I was to come and explain."

Troy lit the fire. "Do sit down," she said, "you must be frozen. What did they think I hadn't understood?"

"Well, first of all, that it was an honour to paint Papa. I told them that it would have been the other way round, if anything, supposing you'd consented. Thank you, I will sit down. It's quite a long walk from the station and I think I've blistered my heel. Do you mind if I have a look? I can feel through my sock, you know."

"Look away," said Troy.

"Yes," said Thomas after a pause, "it is a blister. I'll just keep my toe in my shoe for manners and I dare say the blister will go down. About my father. Of course you know he's the Grand Old Man of the British stage so I needn't go into all that. Do you admire his acting at all?"

"A great deal," said Troy. She was glad that the statement was truthful. This curious man, she felt, would have recognized a polite evasion.

"*Do* you?" he said. "That's nice. He is quite good, of course, though a little creaky at times, don't you feel? And then, all those mannerisms! He can't play an emotional bit, you know, without sucking in his breath rather loudly. But he really is good in a magnificent Mrs. Beeton sort of way. A recipe for everything and only the best ingredients used."

"Mr Ancred," Troy said, "what is all this about?"

"Well, it's part of the build-up. It's supposed to make you see things in a different light. The great British actor painted by the great British artist, don't you know? And although I don't suppose you'd *like* Ancreton much it might amuse you to see it. It's very baronial. The portrait would hang under the minstrels' gallery with special lighting. He doesn't mind what he pays. It's to commemorate his seventy-fifth birthday. His own idea is that the nation ought to have given it to him, but as the nation doesn't seem to have thought of that he's giving it to himself. And to posterity, of course," Thomas added as an afterthought, cautiously slipping his finger inside his loosened shoe.

"If you'd like me to suggest one or two painters who might——"

"Some people prick blisters," said Thomas, "but I don't. No, thank you, they've made a second-best list. I was telling you about Ancreton. You know those steel engravings of castles and halls in Victorian books? All turrets and an owl flying across the moon? That's Ancreton. It was built by my great-grandfather. He pulled down a nice Queen Anne house and erected Ancreton. There was a moat but people got diphtheria so it was let go and they're growing vegetables in it. The food is quite good, because there are lots of vegetables, and Papa cut down the Great East Spinney during the war and stored the wood, so there are still fires."

Thomas smiled at his hostess. He had a tentative sidelong smile. "Yes," he said, "that's Ancreton. I expect you'd hate it, but you couldn't help laughing."

"As I'm not going, however——" Troy began with a rising sense of panic.

But Thomas continued unmoved. "And then, of course, there's the family. Well! Papa and Millamant and Pauline and Panty to begin with. Are you at all keen on the emotions?"

"I haven't an idea what you mean."

"My family is very emotional. They feel everything most deeply. The funny thing about *that*," said Thomas, "is that they really do feel deeply. They really are sensitive, only people are inclined to think nobody could really be as sensitive as they seem to be, so that's hard luck on the family." Thomas took off his spectacles and gazed at Troy with short-sighted innocence. "Except," he added, "that they have the satisfaction of knowing that they are so much more sensitive than any one else. That's a point that might interest you."

"Mr Ancred," Troy said patiently, "I am on leave because I've not been well——"

"Indeed! You look all right. What's the matter with you?"

"A carbuncle," said Troy angrily.

"Really?" said Thomas, clucking his tongue. "How sickening

for you."

"——and in consequence I'm not at the top of my form. A commission of the sort mentioned in your sister-in-law's letter would take at least three weeks' intensive work. The letter gives me a week."

"How long is your leave?"

Troy bit her lips. "That's not the point," she said. "The point is——"

"I had a carbuncle once. You feel better if you keep on with your job. Less depressed. Mine," said Thomas proudly, "was on my bottom. Now that *is* awkward." He looked inquiringly at Troy, who by this time, according to her custom, was sitting on the hearth-rug. "Obviously," Thomas continued, "yours——"

"It's on my hip. It's very much better——"

"Well, then——"

"——but that's not the point. Mr. Ancred, I can't accept this commission. My husband is coming home after three years' absence——"

"When?" Thomas asked instantly.

"As far as we know in three weeks," said Troy, wishing she could bring herself to lie freely to her visitor. "But one can never tell. It might be sooner."

"Well, of course Scotland Yard will let you know about that, won't they? Because, I mean, he's pretty high up, isn't he? Supposing you did go to Ancreton, they could ring you up there just as well as here."

"The point is," Troy almost shouted, "I don't want to paint your father as Macbeth. I'm sorry to put it so bluntly, but I just don't."

"I told them you wouldn't," said Thomas complacently. "The Bathgates thought they knew better."

"The Bathgates? Do you mean Nigel and Angela Bathgate?"

"Who else? Nigel and I are old friends. When the family started all this business I went to see him and asked if he thought you'd do it. Nigel said he knew you were on leave, and he thought it would be nice for you."

"He knows nothing whatever about it."

"He said you liked meeting queer people. He said you'd revel in Papa as a subject and gloat over his conversation. It only shows you how little we understand our friends, doesn't it?"

"Yes," said Troy, "it does."

"But I can't help wondering what you'd make of Panty."

Troy had by this time determined to ask Thomas Ancred no questions whatever, and it was with a sense of impotent fury that she heard her own voice: "Did you say 'Panty'?"

"She's my niece, you know. My sister Pauline's youngest. We call her Panty because her bloomers are always coming down. She's a Difficult Child. Her school, which is a school for Difficult Children, was evacuated to Ancreton. They are quartered in the west wing under a *very* nice person called Caroline Able. Panty is frightful."

"Oh," said Troy, as he seemed to expect some comment.

"Yes, indeed. She's so awful that I rather like her. She's a little girl with two pigtails and a devilish face. This sort of thing."

Thomas put his long forefingers at right angles to his head, scowled abominably and blew out his cheeks. His eyes glittered. Much against her will, Troy was suddenly confronted with the face of a bad child. She laughed shortly. Thomas rubbed his hands. "If I were to tell you," he said, "of the things that little girl does, you would open your eyes. Well, a cactus, for instance, in Sonia's bed! Unfortunately she's Papa's favourite, which makes control almost impossible. And, of course, one mustn't beat her except in anger, because that's not proper child psychology."

He stared thoughtfully into the fire. "Then there's Pauline, my eldest sister; she's the important type. And Milly, my sister-in-law, who perpetually laughs at nothing and housekeeps for Papa, since her husband, my eldest brother, Henry Irving, died."

"*Henry Irving!*" Troy ejaculated, thinking with alarm: "Evidently he's mad."

"Henry Irving Ancred, of course. Papa had a great admiration for Irving, and regards himself as his spiritual successor, so he called Hal after him. And then there's Sonia. Sonia is Papa's mistress." Thomas cleared his throat old-maidishly. "Rather a Biblical situation really. You remember David and Abishag the Shunammite? They all dislike Sonia. I must say she's a *very* bad actress. Am I boring you?"

Troy, though not bored, was extremely reluctant to say so. She muttered: "Not at all," and offered Thomas a drink. He replied: "Yes, thank you, if you've got plenty." She went off to fetch it, hoping in the interim to sort out her reactions to her visitor. She found Katti Bostock in the dining-room.

"For pity's sake, Katti," said Troy, "come back with me. I've got a sort of monster in there."

"Is it staying to dinner?"

"I haven't asked it, but I should think so. So we shall have to open one of Rory's tins."

"Hadn't you better go back to this bloke?"

"Do come too. I'm afraid of him. He tells me about his family, presenting each member of it in a repellent light, and yet expecting me to desire nothing more than their acquaintance. And the alarming thing is, Katti, that the narrative has its horrid fascination. Important Pauline, acquisitive Sonia; dreadful little Panty, and Milly, who laughs perpetually at nothing; that's Millamant, of course, who wrote the letter. And Papa, larger than life, and presenting himself with his own portrait because the Nation hasn't come up to scratch——"

"You aren't going to tell me you've accepted!"

"Not I. Good Lord, no! I'd be demented. But—keep an eye on me, Katti," said Troy.

III

Thomas accepted the invitation to dinner, expressing himself as delighted with his share of tinned New Zealand crayfish. "We've got friends in New Zealand and America too," he said, "but unfortunately tinned fish brings on an attack of Papa's gastro-enteritis. If we have it he can't resist it, and so Milly doesn't let us have it. Next time I go to Ancreton she's giving me several tins to take back to my flat."

"You don't live at Ancreton?" Troy asked.

"How could I when my job's in London? I go there sometimes for week-ends to give them all an opportunity of confiding in me. Papa likes us to go. He's having quite a party for his birthday. Pauline's son, Paul, who has a wounded leg, will be there, and Millamant's son, Cedric, who is a dress-designer. I don't think you'd care for Cedric. And my sister Desdemona, who is at liberty just now, though she hopes to be cast for a part in a new play at the Crescent. My other sister-in-law, Jenetta, will be there too, I hope, with her daughter, Fenella. Her husband, my eldest brother Claude, is a Colonel in the occupation forces and hasn't come home yet."

"Rather a large party," said Katti. "Fun for you."

"There'll be a good many rows, of course," Thomas replied.

"When you get two or three Ancreds gathered together they are certain to hurt each other's feelings. That's where I come in handy, because I'm the insensitive one and they talk to me about each other. And about Sonia, I needn't say. We shall all talk about Sonia. We'd hoped to unveil your portrait of Papa on this occasion," he said, looking wistfully at Troy. "Indeed, that's really what the party's for."

Troy mumbled something indistinguishable.

"Papa had a lovely time last week looking out the Macbeth clothes," Thomas continued. "I wonder if you remember his costume. Motley did it for us. It's red, a Paul Veroneseish red, dark but clear, with a smoky overcloak. We've got a miniature theatre at Ancreton, you know. I brought down the original backdrop for one of the inset scenes and hung it. It's quite a coincidence, isn't it," Thomas went on innocently, "that you did the original designs for that production? Of course, you remember the one I mean. It's very simple. A boldly distorted castle form seen in silhouette. He dressed himself and stood in front of it, resting on his claymore with his head stooped, as if listening. 'Good things of day begin to droop and drowse,' do you remember?"

Troy remembered that line very well. It was strange that she should have recalled it; for Alleyn was fond of telling her how, in the small hours of a stormy morning, a constable on night duty had once quoted it to him. Thomas, speaking the line, with an actor's sense of its value, sounded like an echo of her husband, and her thoughts were filled with memories of his voice.

"——He's been ill off and on for some time," Thomas was saying, "and gets very depressed. But the idea of the portrait bucked him up no end, and he's set his heart on you to paint it. You see, you did his hated rival."

"Sir Benjamin Corporal?" Troy muttered, eyeing Katti.

"Yes. And old Ben makes a great story about how you only paint subjects that you take a fancy to—pictorially, I mean. He told us you took a great fancy to him pictorially. He said he was the only actor you'd ever wanted to paint."

"On the contrary," Troy said angrily. "It was a commission from his native town—Huddersfield. Old popinjay!"

"He told Papa he'd only be snubbed if he approached you. Actually, Papa was dressed as Macbeth when your telegram arrived. He said: "Ah! This is propitious. Do you think, my dear,

548

that Miss Troy—should he have said "Mrs. Alleyn?"—will care for this pose?" He was quite young-looking when he said it. And then he opened your telegram. He took it rather well, really. He just gave it to Milly, and said: "I shouldn't have put on these garments. It was always an unlucky piece. I'm a vain old fool." And he went away and changed and had an attack of gastro-enteritis, poor thing. It must almost be time, I thought of walking back to the station mustn't it?"

"I'll drive you," Troy said.

Thomas protested mildly, but Troy overruled him brusquely when the time came, and went off to start her car. Thomas said good-bye politely to Katti Bostock.

"You're a clever chap, Mr. Ancred," said Katti grimly.

"Oh, do you think so?" asked Thomas, blinking modestly. "Oh, no! Clever? Me? Goodness, no. Good night. It's been nice to meet you."

Katti waited for half an hour before she heard the sound of the returning car. Presently the door opened and Troy came in. She wore a white overcoat. A lock of her short dark hair hung over her forehead. Her hands were jammed in her pockets. She walked self-consciously down the room looking at Katti out of the corners of her eyes.

"Got rid of your rum friend?" asked Miss Bostock.

Troy cleared her throat. "Yes. He's talked himself off."

"Well," said Miss Bostock, after a long silence, "when do you leave for Ancreton?"

"To-morrow," said Troy shortly.

CHAPTER II

Departure

I

Troy wished that Thomas Ancred would say good-bye and leave her to savour the moment of departure. She enjoyed train journeys enormously, and, in these days, not a second of the precious discomfort should be left unrelished. But there stood Thomas on the Euston platform with nothing to say, and filled, no doubt, with the sense of tediousness that is inseparable from these occasions. "Why doesn't he take off his hat and walk away?" Troy thought fretfully. But when she caught his eye, he gave her such an anxious smile that she instantly felt obliged to reassure him.

"I have been wondering," Thomas said, "if, after all, you will merely loathe my family."

"In any case I shall be working."

"Yes," he agreed, looking immensely relieved, "there *is* that. I can't tell you how much I dislike many actors, and yet, when I begin to work with them, sometimes I quite love them. If they do what I tell them, of course."

"Are you working this morning?" And she thought: how unreal the activities seem of people one leaves behind on railway stations.

"Yes," said Thomas, "a first rehearsal."

"Please don't wait," she said for the fourth time, and for the fourth time he replied: "I'll just see you off," and looked at his watch. Doors were slammed farther down the train. Troy leant out of the window. At last she was off. A man in uniform, peering frenziedly into carriage after carriage, was working his way towards her. "Nigel!" Troy shouted. "Nigel!"

"Oh, God, there you are!" cried Nigel Bathgate. "Hallo, Thomas! Here! Troy! I knew I wouldn't have time to talk so I've written." He thrust a fat envelope at her. A whistle blew. The train clunked, and Thomas said: "Well, good-bye; they *will* be pleased"; raised his hat and slid out of view. Nigel walked rapidly along beside the window. "What a go! You will laugh," he said. "Is this a novel?" Troy asked, holding up the envelope. "Almost! You'll see." Nigel broke into a run. "I've always wanted to—you'll see—when's Roderick—?" "Soon!" Troy cried. "In three weeks!" "Good-bye! I can't run any more." He had gone.

Troy settled down. A young man appeared in the corridor. He peered in at the door and finally entered the already crowded carriage. With a slight twittering noise he settled himself on his upturned suitcase, with his back to the door, and opened an illustrated paper. Troy noticed that he wore a jade ring on his first finger, a particularly bright green hat and suede shoes. The other passengers looked dull and were also preoccupied with their papers. Rows of backyards and occasional heaps of rubble would continue for some time in the world outside the window pane. She sighed luxuriously, thought how much easier it would be to wait for her husband now that she was forced to paint, fell into a brief day-dream, and finally opened Nigel's letter.

Three sheets of closely typed reporter's paper fell out, together with a note written in green ink.

"13 hours, G.M.T.," Nigel had written. "Troy, my dear, two hours ago Thomas Ancred, back from his visit to you, rang me up in a triumph. You're in for a party but the G.O.M. will be grand to paint. I've always died to write up the Ancreds but can't afford the inevitable libel action. So I've amused myself by dodging up the enclosed *jeu d'esprit*. It may serve to fill in your journey. N.B."

The typescript was headed: "Note on Sir Henry Ancred, Bart., and his Immediate Circle." "Do I want to read it?" Troy wondered. "It was charming of Nigel to write it, but I'm in for two weeks of the Ancreds and Thomas's commentary was exhaustive." And she let the pages fall in her lap. At the same time the young man on the suitcase lowered his modish periodical, and stared fixedly at her. He impressed her disagreeably. His eyes suggested a kind of dull impertinence. Under the line of hair on his lip his mouth was too fresh, and projected too far above a small white chin. Everything about him was over-elegant, Troy thought, and dismissed him as an all-too-clearly-defined type. He continued to stare at her. "If he was opposite," she thought, "he would begin to ask questions about the windows. What does he want?" She lifted the sheets of Nigel's typescript and began to read.

II

"Collectively and severally," Nigel had written, "the Ancreds, all but one, are over-emotionalised. Anyone attempting to describe or explain their behaviour must keep this characteristic firmly in mind, for without it they would scarcely exist. Sir Henry Ancred is perhaps the worst of the lot, but, because he is an actor, his friends accept his behaviour as part of his stock-in-trade, and apart from an occasional feeling of shyness in his presence, seldom make the mistake of worrying about him. Whether he was drawn to his wife (now deceased) by the discovery of a similar trait in her character, or whether, by the phenomenon of marital acclimatisation, Lady Ancred learnt to exhibit emotion with a virtuosity equal to that of her husband, cannot be discovered. It can only be recorded that she did so; and died.

"Their elder daughters, Pauline (Ancred played in *The Lady of Lyons* in '96) and Desdemona (*Othello*, 1909), and their sons, Henry Irving (Ancred played a bit-part in *The Bells*) and Claude (Pauline's twin) in their several modes, have inherited or acquired the emotional habit. Only Thomas (Ancred was resting in 1904 when Thomas was born) is free of it. Thomas, indeed, is uncommonly placid. Perhaps for this reason his parent, sisters, and brothers appeal to him when they hurt each other's feelings, which they do punctually, two or three times a week, and always with an air of tragic astonishment.

"Pauline, Claude, and Desdemona, in turn, followed their father's profession. Pauline joined a northern repertory company, married John Kentish, a local man of property, retired upon provincial glories more enduring than those she was likely to enjoy as an actress, and gave birth to Paul and, twelve years later, Patricia (born 1936 and known as Panty). Like all Ancred's children, except Thomas, Pauline was extremely handsome, and has retained her looks.

"Claude, her twin, drifted from Oriel into the O.U.D.S., and thence, on his father's back, into romantic juveniles. He married the Hon. Miss Jenetta Cairnes, who had a fortune, but never, he is fond of saying, has understood him. She is an intelligent woman. They have one daughter, Fenella.

"Desdemona, Sir Henry's fourth child (aged thirty-six at the time of this narrative), has become a good emotional actress, difficult to place, as she has a knack of cracking the seams of the brittle, slickly drawn rôles for which West-End managements, addled by her beauty, occasionally cast her. She has become attached to a Group, and appears in pieces written by two surrealists, uttering her lines in such a heartrending manner that they seem, even to Desdemona herself, to be fraught with significance. She is unmarried and has suffered a great deal from two unhappy love affairs.

"The eldest son, Henry Irving Ancred, became a small-part actor and married Mildred Cooper, whom his father promptly rechristened Millamant, as at that time he was engaged upon a revival of *The Way of the World*. Millamant she has remained, and, before her husband died, gave birth to a son, Cedric, about whom the less said the better.

"Your friend, Thomas, is unmarried. Having discovered, after two or three colourless ventures, that he was a bad actor, he set about teaching himself to become a good producer. In this, after a struggle, he succeeded, and is now established as director for Incorporated Playhouses, Limited, Unicorn Theatre. He has never been known to lose his temper at rehearsals, but may sometimes be observed, alone in the stalls, rocking to and fro with his head in his hands. He lives in a bachelor's flat in Westminster.

"All these offspring, Pauline, Claude, Desdemona and Thomas, their sister-in-law, Millamant, and their children, are like details in a design, the central motive of which is Sir Henry himself. Sir Henry, known to his associates as the G.O.M. of the Stage, is believed to be deeply attached to his family. That is part of his légend, and the belief may be founded in fact. He sees a great deal of his family, and perhaps it would be accurate to say that he loves best those particular members of it of whom, at any given moment, he sees least. His wife he presumably loved. They never quarrelled and always sided together against whichever of their young had wounded the feelings of one or the other of them. Thomas was the exception to this, as he is to most other generalities one might apply to the Ancreds.

" 'Old Tommy!' Sir Henry will say. 'Funny chap! Never quite know where you are with him. T'uh!' This scarcely articulated noise, 'T'uh,' is used by all the Ancreds (except, of course, Thomas) to express a kind of disillusioned resignation. It's

553

uttered on a high note and is particularly characteristic.

"Sir Henry is not a theatrical knight but a baronet, having inherited his title, late in life, from an enormously wealthy second cousin. It's a completely obscure baronetcy, and, although perfectly genuine, difficult to believe in. Perhaps this is because he himself is so obviously impressed by it and likes to talk about Norman ancestors with names that sound as if they'd been chosen from the dramatis personæ in a Lyceum programme, the Sieur D'Ancred, and so on. His crest is on everything. He looks, as his dresser is fond of saying, every inch the aristocrat—silver hair, hook nose, blue eyes. Up to a few years ago he still appeared in drawing-room comedies, giving exquisite performances of charming or irascible buffers. Sometimes he forgot his lines, but, by the use of a number of famous mannerisms, diddled his audiences into believing it was a lesser actor who had slipped. His last Shakespearian appearance was as Macbeth on the Bard's birthday, at the age of sixty-eight. He then developed a chronic gastric disorder and retired from the stage to his family seat, Ancreton, which in its architectural extravagances may possibly remind him of Dunsinane.

"There he remains, guarded by Millamant, who, since the death of her husband, has house-kept for her father-in-law, and who is supposed by the rest of her family to be feathering a nest for her son, the egregious Cedric, who is delicate. The family (excepting Thomas) is inclined to laugh with bitter emphasis when Cedric is mentioned, and to criticise poor Milly's treatment of the G.O.M. Milly is a jolly woman and laughs at them. She once told Thomas that if either of his sisters cared to take on her job she'd be delighted to relinquish it. She had them there, for though they all visit Ancreton a great deal, they invariably leave after a few days in a tempest of wounded feelings.

"Occasionally they close their ranks. They have done so at the moment, being at war, as a family, with Miss Sonia Orrincourt, with whom, at the age of seventy-five, their father is having a fling. This astounding old man has brought the lady to Ancreton, and there, it appears, she intends to remain. She is an erstwhile member of the chorus and was selected as a type to understudy a small part in a piece at the Unicorn. This was a shattering innovation. The Unicorn, in the theatre world, is as Boodles in clubland. No musical comedy artist, before Miss Orrincourt, had enlivened its stage-door. Sir Henry watched a rehearsal. In three

554

weeks Miss Orrincourt, having proved a complete washout as an understudy, was given the sack by Thomas. She then sought out his father, wept on his waistcoat, and reappeared in her present unmistakable rôle at Ancreton. She is a blonde. Pauline and Desdemona say that she is holding out on the Old Man with a view to matrimony, Thomas believes her to have taken the more complaisant attitude. Claude, in the Middle East, has sent a cable so guarded in its phrases that the only thing it makes clear is his rage. Claude's wife, Jenetta, a shrewd and amusing woman, who maintains a detached attitude to her relations-by-marriage, has been summoned, in Claude's absence, to a conclave. It is possible that her only child, Fenella, hitherto a second favourite with Sir Henry after Pauline's child Panty, might lose ground if he married. Even jolly Millamant is shaken. Her appalling Cedric is the senior grandson, and Sir Henry has of late begun to drop disconcerting hints that there is life in the old dog yet.

"This, then, is the set-up at Ancreton. My information has come by way of occasional visits and Thomas, who, as you will have discovered, is a talkative chap and doesn't know the meaning of the word reticence.

"In some such fashion as this, dear Troy, would I begin the novel that I dare not attempt. One word more. I understand you are to paint Sir Henry in the character of Macbeth. May I assure you that with Pauline's child Panty on the premises you will find yourself also furnished with a Bloody Child."

III

Troy folded the typescript, and replaced it in its envelope across which Nigel had written her name in bo.d cha·acters. The young man on the suitcase stared fixedly at the envelope. She turned it face downwards on her lap. His illustrated paper hung open across his knee. She saw, with annoyance, her own photograph.

So that was what he was up to. He'd recognized her. Probably, she thought, he potters about doing fancy little drawings. He looks like it. If the other people get out before we reach Ancreton Halt, he'll introduce himself and my lovely train journey will be ruined. Damn!

The country outside the window changed to a hurrying tapestry of hedgerows, curving downs and naked trees. Troy watched it contentedly. Having allowed herself to be bamboozled into taking this commission, she had entered into a state of emotional suspension. It was deeply satisfactory to know that her husband would soon return. She no longer experienced moments of something like terror lest his three years absence should drop like a curtain between their understanding of each other. The Commissioner had promised she should know two days before-hand of Alleyn's arrival, and in the meantime the train carried her to a job among strangers who at least would not be commonplace. But I hope, Troy thought, that their family upheaval won't interfere with the old boy's sittings. That *would* be a bore.

The train drew into a junction, and the other passengers, with the exception of the young man on the suitcase, began to collect themselves. Just what she'd feared, thought Troy. She opened her lunch-basket and a book. If I eat and read at him, she thought, that may keep him off; and she remembered Guy de Maupassant's strictures upon people who eat in the train.

Now they were off again. Troy munched her sandwiches and read the opening scene of *Macbeth*. She had decided to revisit that terrible country whose only counterpart, she thought, was to be found in Emily Brontë. This fancy pleased her, and she paused to transport the wraiths of Heathcliff and Cathy to the blasted heath or to follow Fleance over the moors to Wuthering Heights. But, if I am to paint Macbeth, she thought, I must read. And as the first inflexions in the voice of a friend who is re-met after a long absence instantly prepare us for tones that we are yet to hear, so with its opening phrases, the play, which she thought she had forgotten, returned wholly to her memory.

"*Do* forgive me for interrupting," said a high-pitched voice, "but I've been madly anxious to talk to you, and this is such a *magical* opportunity."

The young man had slid along the seat and was now opposite. His head was tilted ingratiatingly to one side and he smiled at Troy. "*Please* don't think I'm seething with sinister intentions," he said. "Honestly, there's *no* need to pull the communication cord."

"I didn't for a moment suppose there was," said Troy.

"You are Agatha Troy, aren't you?" he continued anxiously. "I couldn't be mistaken. I mean, it's too shatteringly coincidental, isn't it? Here I am, reading my little journal, and what should I see but a perfectly blissful photograph of you. *So* exciting and so miraculously *you*. And if I'd had the weeniest doubt left, that alarming affair you're reading would have settled it."

Troy looked from her book to the young man. "*Macbeth*?" she said. "I'm afraid I don't understand."

"Oh, but it was too conclusive," he said. "But, of course, I haven't introduced myself, have I? I'm Cedric Ancred."

"Oh," said Troy after a pause. "Oh, yes. I see."

"And then to clinch it, there was your name on that envelope. I'm afraid I peered shamelessly. But it's too exciting that you're actually going to make a picture of the Old Person in all his tatts and bobs. You can't imagine what that costume is like! And the toque! Some terrifically powerful man beat it out of solid steel for him. He's my Grandpa, you know. My mother is Millamant Ancred. My father, only promise you won't tell anyone, was Henry Irving Ancred. Imagine!"

Troy could think of nothing to say in reply to this recital and took another bite out of her sandwich.

"So, you see, I had to make myself known," he continued with an air that Troy thought of as 'winsome'. "I'm so burnt up always about your work, and the prospect of meeting you was absolutely tonic."

"But how did you know," Troy asked, "that I was going to paint Sir Henry?"

"I rang up Uncle Thomas last night and he told me. I'd been commanded to the presence, and had decided that I couldn't face it, but immediately changed my plans. You see," said Cedric with a boyish frankness which Troy found intolerable, "you see, I actually try to paint. I'm with Pont et Cie. and I do the designs. Of course everything's too austerity and grim nowadays, but we keep toddling."

His suit was silver grey. His shirt was pale green, his pullover was dark green, and his tie was orange. He had rather small eyes, and in the middle of his soft round chin there was a dimple.

"If I may talk about your work," he was saying, "there's a quality in it that appeals to me enormously. It—how can I describe it?—its design is always consistent with its subject matter. I mean, the actual *pattern* is not something arbitrarily imposed on the subject but an inevitable consequence of it. Such integrity, always. Or am I talking nonsense?"

He was not talking complete nonsense and Troy grudgingly admitted it. There were few people with whom she cared to discuss her work. Cedric Ancred watched her for a few seconds. She had the unpleasant feeling that he sensed her distaste for him.

557

His next move was unexpected. He ran his fingers through his hair, which was damply blond and wavy. "God!" he said. "People! The things they say! If only one could break through, as you have. God! Why is life so perpetually bloody?"

"Oh, *dear*!" Troy thought and shut her luncheon basket. Cedric was gazing at her fixedly. Evidently she was expected to reply.

"I'm not much good," she said, "at generalities about life."

"No!" he muttered and nodded his head profoundly. "Of course not. I so agree. You are perfectly right, of course."

Troy looked furtively at her watch. A full half-hour, she thought, before we get to Ancreton Halt and then, he's coming too.

"I'm boring you," Cedric said loudly. "No, don't deny it. God! I'm boring you. T'uh!"

"I just don't know how to carry on this sort of conversation, that's all."

Cedric began to nod again.

"You were reading," he said. "I stopped you. One should never do that. It's an offence against the Holy Ghost."

"I never heard such nonsense," said Troy with spirit.

Cedric laughed gloomily. "Go on!" he said. "Please go on. Return to your 'Blasted Heath'. It's an atrociously bad play, in my opinion, but go on reading it."

But it was not easy to read, knowing that a few inches away he was glaring at her over his folded arms. She turned a page. In a minute or two he began to sigh. "He sighs," thought Troy, "like the Mock Turtle, and I think he must be mad." Presently he laughed shortly, and, in spite of herself, Troy looked up. He was still glaring at her. He had a jade cigarette case open in his hand.

"You smoke?" he asked.

She felt certain that if she refused he would make some further peculiar scene, so she took one of his cigarettes. He lit it in silence and flung himself back in his corner.

After all, Troy thought, I've got to get on with him, somehow, and she said: "Don't you find it extraordinarily tricky hitting on exactly the right note in fashion drawings? When one thinks of what they used to be like! There's no doubt that commercial art—"

"Prostitution!" Cedric interrupted. "Just that. If you don't mind the initial sin it's quite amusing."

"Do you work at all for the theatre?"

558

"So sweet of you to take an interest," Cedric answered rather acidly. "Oh, yes. My Uncle Thomas occasionally uses me. Actually I'm madly keen on it. One would have thought that with the Old Person behind one there would have been an opening. Unfortunately he is not behind me, which is so sickening. I've been cut out by the Infant Monstrosity." He brightened a little. "It's some comfort to know I'm the eldest grandson, of course. In my more optimistic moments I tell myself he can't leave me *completely* out of his will. My worst nightmare is the one when I dream I've inherited Ancreton. I always wake screaming. Of course, with Sonia on the tapis, almost anything may happen. You've heard about Sonia?"

Troy hesitated and he went on: "She's the Old Person's little bit of nonsense. Immensely decorative. I can't make up my mind whether she's incredibly stupid or not, but I fear not. The others are all for fighting her, tooth and claw, but I rather think of ingratiating myself in case he does marry her. What do you think?"

Troy was wondering if it was a characteristic of all male Ancreds to take utter strangers into their confidence. But they couldn't all be as bad as Cedric. After all, Nigel Bathgate had said Cedric was frightful, and even Thomas—she thought suddenly how nice Thomas seemed in retrospect when one compared him with his nephew.

"But *do* tell me," Cedric was saying, "how do you mean to paint him? All beetling and black? But whatever you decide it will be marvellous. You will let me creep in and see, or are you dreadfully fierce about that?"

"Rather fierce, I'm afraid," said Troy.

"I suspected so." Cedric looked out of the window and immediately clasped his forehead. "It's coming," he said. "Every time I brace myself for the encounter and every time, if there was a train to take me, I would rush screaming back to London. In a moment we shall see it. I can't bear it. God! That one should have to face such horrors."

"What in the world's the matter?"

"Look!" cried Cedric, covering his eyes. "Look! Katzenjammer Castle!"

Troy looked through the window. Some two miles away, on the crest of a hill, fully displayed, stood Ancreton.

CHAPTER III

Ancreton

I

It was an astonishing building. A Victorian architect, fortified and encouraged by the Ancred of his day, had pulled down a Queen Anne house and, from its rubble, caused to rise up a sublimation of his most exotic day-dreams. To no one style or period did Ancreton adhere. Its façade bulged impartially with Norman, Gothic, Baroque and Rococo excrescences. Turrets sprouted like wens from every corner. Towers rose up from a multiplicity of battlements. Arrow slits peered furtively at exopthalmic bay-windows, and out of a kaleidoscope field of tiles rose a forest of variegated chimney-stacks. The whole was presented, not against the sky, but against a dense forest of evergreen trees, for behind Ancreton crest rose another and steeper hillside, richly planted in conifers. Perhaps the imagination of this earlier Ancred was exhausted by the begetting of his monster, for he was content to leave, almost unmolested, the terraced gardens and well-planted spinneys that had been laid out in the tradition of John Evelyn. These, maintaining their integrity, still gently led the eye of the observer towards the site of the house and had an air of blind acquiescence in its iniquities.

Intervening trees soon obliterated Troy's first view of Ancreton. In a minute or two the train paused magnanimously at the tiny station of Ancreton Halt.

"One must face these moments, of course," Cedric muttered, and they stepped out into a flood of wintry sunshine.

There were only two people on the platform—a young man in second lieutenant's uniform and a tall girl. They were a good-looking pair and somewhat alike—blue-eyed, dark and thin.

560

They came forward, the young man limping and using his stick.

"Oh, lud!" Cedric complained. "Ancreds by the shoal. Greetings, you two."

"Hallo, Cedric," they said without much show of enthusiasm, and the girl turned quickly and cordially towards Troy.

"This is my cousin, Fenella Ancred," Cedric explained languidly. "And the warrior is another cousin, Paul Kentish. Miss Agatha Troy, or should it be Mrs. Alleyn? So difficult."

"It's splendid that you've come," said Fenella Ancred. "Grandfather's terribly excited and easily ten years younger. Have you got lots of luggage? If so, we'll either make two journeys or would you mind walking up the hill? We've only brought the governess-cart and Rosinante's a bit elderly."

"Walk!" Cedric screamed faintly. "My dear Fenella, you must be demented! Me? Rosinante (and may I say in parentheses I consider the naming of this animal an insufferable piece of whimsy), Rosinante shall bear me up the hill though it be its last conscious act."

"I've got two suitcases and my painting gear," said Troy, "which is pretty heavy."

"We'll see what can be done about it," said Paul Kentish, eyeing Cedric with distaste. "Come on, Fen."

Troy's studio easel and heavy luggage had to be left at a cottage, to be sent up later in the evening by carrier, but they packed her worn hand luggage and Cedric's green shade suitcases into the governess-cart and got on top of them. The fat white pony strolled away with them down a narrow lane.

"It's a mile to the gates," Paul Kentish said, "and another mile up to the house. We'll get out at the gates, Fen."

"I should like to walk," said Troy.

"Then Cedric," said Fenella with satisfaction, "can drive."

"But I'm not a horsy boy," Cedric protested. "The creature might sit down or turn round and bite me. Don't you think you're being rather beastly?"

"Don't be an ass," said Fenella. "He'll just go on walking home."

"Who's in residence?" Cedric demanded.

"The usual," she said. "Mummy's coming for the weekend after this. I'm on leave for a fortnight. Otherwise, Aunt Milly and Aunt Pauline. That's Cedric's mother and Paul's mother," Fenella explained to Troy. "I expect you'll find us rather

561

muddling to begin with. Aunt Pauline's Mrs. Kentish and Mummy's Mrs. Claude Ancred, and Aunt Millamant's Mrs. Henry Ancred."

"Henry *Irving* Ancred, don't forget," Cedric cut in, "deceased. My papa, you know."

"That's all," said Fenella, "in our part. Of course there's Panty" (Cedric moaned), "Caroline Able and the school in the West Wing. Aunt Pauline's helping them, you know. They're terribly short staffed. That's all."

"All?" cried Cedric. "You don't mean to tell me Sonia's gone?"

"No, she's there. I'd forgotten her," said Fenella shortly.

"Well, Fenella, all I can say is you've an enviable faculty for forgetting. You'll be saying next that everyone's reconciled to Sonia."

"Is there any point in discussing it?" said Paul Kentish very coldly.

"It's the only topic of any interest at Ancreton," Cedric rejoined. "Personally I find it vastly intriguing. I've been telling Mrs. Alleyn all about it in the train."

"Honestly, Cedric," said Paul and Fenella together, "you *are*!"

Cedric gave a crowing laugh and they drove on in an uncomfortable silence. Feeling a little desperate, Troy at last began to talk to Paul Kentish. He was a pleasant fellow, she thought, serious-minded, but friendly and ready to speak about his war service. He had been wounded in the leg during the Italian campaign and was still having treatment. Troy asked him what he was going to do when he was discharged, and was surprised to see him turn rather pink.

"As a matter of fact I rather thought—well, actually I had wondered about the police," said Paul.

"My dear, how terrifying," Cedric interposed.

"Paul's the only one of us," Fenella explained, "who really doesn't want to have anything to do with the theatre."

"I would have liked to go on in the army," Paul added, "only now I'm no good for that. Perhaps, I don't know, but perhaps I'd be no good for the police either."

"You'd better talk to my husband when he comes back," Troy said, wondering if Alleyn would mind very much if he did.

"I say!" said Paul. "That would be perfectly marvellous if you really mean it."

"Well, I mean he could just tell you whether your limp would

562

make any difference."

"How glad I am," Cedric remarked, "about my duodenal ulcer! I mean I needn't even pretend I want to be brave or strenuous. No doubt I've inherited the Old Person's guts."

"Are you going on the stage?" Troy asked Fenella.

"I expect so now the war's over. I've been a chauffeur for the duration."

"You will play exotic rôles, Fenella, and I shall design wonderful clothes for you. It would be rather fun," Cedric went on, "when and if I inherit Ancreton, to turn it into a frightfully exclusive theatre. The only catch in that is that Sonia might be there as the dowager baronetess, in which case she would insist on playing all the leading rôles. Oh, dear, I *do* want some money so badly. What do you suppose is the best technique, Fenella? Shall I woo the Old Person or suck up to Sonia? Paul, you know all about the strategy of indirect approach. Advise me, my dear."

"Considering you're supposed to earn about twice as much as any of the rest of us!"

"Pure legend. A pittance, I assure you."

The white pony had sauntered into a lane that ran directly up to the gates of Ancreton, which was now displayed to its greatest advantage. A broad walk ran straight from the gates across a series of terraces, and by way of flights of steps up to a platform before the house. The carriage-drive swept away to the left and was hidden by woods. They must be an extremely rich family, Troy decided, to have kept all this going, and as if in answer to her thoughts, Fenella said: "You wouldn't guess from here how much the flower gardens have gone back, would you?"

"Are the problem children still digging for a Freudian victory?" asked Cedric.

"They're doing a jolly good job of work," Paul rejoined. "All the second terrace was down in potatoes this year. You can see them up there now." Troy had already noticed a swarm of minute figures on the second terrace.

"The potato!" Cedric murmured. "A pregnant sublimation, I feel sure."

"You enjoy eating them, anyway," Fenella said bluntly.

"Here we are, Mrs. Alleyn. Do you honestly feel like walking? If so, we'll go up the Middle Walk and Cedric can drive."

They climbed out. Paul opened the elaborate and becrested iron gates, explaining that the lodge was now used as a storehouse for vegetables. Cedric, holding the reins with a great show of distaste, was borne slowly off to the left. The other three began the ascent of the terraces.

The curiously metallic sound of children's singing quavered threadily in the autumn air.

> "Then sing a yeo-heave ho,
> Across the seas we'll go;
> There's many a girl that I know well
> On the banks of the Sacramento."

As they climbed the second flight of steps a woman's crisp voice could be heard, dominating the rest.

> "And *Down*, and *Kick*, and *Hee-ee-eeve*. Back.
> And *Down*, and *Kick* and *Hee-ee-ve*."

On the second terrace some thirty little girls and boys were digging in time to their own singing. A red-haired young woman, clad in breeches and sweater, shouted the rhythmic orders. Troy was just in time to see a little boy in the back row deliberately heave a spadeful of soil down the neck of a near-by little girl. Singing shrilly, she retaliated by catching him a swinging smack across the rump with the flat of her spade.

"And *Down* and *Kick* and *Heave*. Back," shouted the young woman, waving cheerfully to Paul and Fenella.

"Come over here!" Fenella screamed. The young woman left her charges and strode towards them. The singing continued, but with less vigour. She was extremely pretty. Fenella introduced her: Miss Caroline Able. She shook hands firmly with Troy, who noticed that the little girl, having downed the little boy, now sat on his face and had begun methodically to plaster his head with soil. In order to do this she had been obliged first to remove a curious white cap. Several of the other children, Troy noticed, wore similar caps.

"You're keeping them hard at it, aren't you, Carol?" said Fenella.

"We stop in five minutes. It's extraordinarily helpful, you know. They feel they're doing something constructive. Something socially worth while," said Miss Able glowingly. "And once you can get these children, especially the introverted types, to do

564

that, you've gone quite a bit of the way."

Fenella and Paul, who had their backs to the children, nodded gravely. The little boy, having unseated the little girl, was making a brave attempt to bite the calf of her left leg.

"How are their heads?" Paul asked solemnly. Miss Able shrugged her shoulders. "Taking its course," she said. "The doctor's coming again tomorrow."

Troy gave an involuntary exclamation, and at the same moment the little girl screamed so piercingly that her voice rang out above the singing, which instantly stopped.

"It's—perhaps you ought to look," said Troy, and Miss Able turned in time to see the little girl attempting strenuously to kick her opponent, who nevertheless maintained his hold on her leg. "Let go, you cow," screamed the little girl.

"*Patricia! David!*" cried Miss Able firmly and strode towards them. The other children stopped work and listened in silence. The two principals, maintaining their hold on each other, broke into mutual accusations.

"Now, I wonder," said Miss Able brightly, and with an air of interest, "just what made you two feel you'd like to have a fight." Confused recriminations followed immediately. Miss Able seemed to understand them, and, to Troy's astonishment, actually jotted down one or two notes in a little book, glancing at her watch as she did so.

"And now," she said, still more brightly, "you feel ever so much better. You were just angry, and you had to work it off, didn't you? But you know I can think of something that would be much better fun than fighting."

"No, you can't," said the little girl instantly, and turned savagely on her opponent. "I'll kill you," she said, and fell upon him.

"Suppose," shouted Miss Able with determined gaiety above the shrieks of the contestants, "we all shoulder spades and have a jolly good marching song."

The little girl rolled clear of her opponent, scooped up a handful of earth, and flung it madly and accurately at Miss Able. The little boy and several of the other children laughed very loudly at this exploit. Miss Able, after a second's pause, joined in their laughter.

"Little devil," said Paul. "Honestly, Fenella, I really do think a damn good hiding——"

"No, no," said Fenella, "it's the method. Listen."

The ever-jolly Miss Able was saying: "Well, I expect I do look pretty funny, don't I? Now, come on, let's all have a good rowdy game. Twos and threes. Choose your partners."

The children split up into pairs, and Miss Able, wiping the earth off her face, joined the three onlookers.

"How you can put up with Panty," Paul began.

"Oh, but she really is responding, splendidly," Miss Able interrupted. "That's the first fight in seven and a half hours, and David began it. He's rather a bad case of maladjustment, I'm afraid. Now, Patricia," she shouted. "Into the middle with you. And David, you see if you can catch her. One tries as far as possible," she explained, "to divert the anger impulse into less emotional channels."

They left her, briskly conducting the game, and continued their ascent. On the fourth terrace they encountered a tall and extremely good-looking woman dressed in tweeds and a felt hat, and wearing heavy gauntleted gloves.

"This is my mother," said Paul Kentish.

Mrs Kentish greeted Troy rather uncertainly: "You've come to paint Father, haven't you?" she said, inclining her head in the manner of a stage dowager. "Very nice. I do hope you'll be comfortable. In these days—one can't quite"—she brightened a little—"but perhaps as an artist you won't mind rather a Bohemian——" Her voice trailed away and she turned to her son: "Paul, *darling*," she said richly, "you shouldn't have walked up all those steps. Your poor leg. Fenella, dear, you shouldn't have let him."

"It's good for my leg, Mother."

Mrs Kentish shook her head and gazed mistily at her glowering son. "Such a brave old boy," she said. Her voice, which was a warm one, shook a little, and Troy saw with embarrassment that her eyes had filled with tears. "Such an old Trojan," she murmured. "Isn't he, Fenella?"

Fenella laughed uncomfortably and Paul hastily backed away. "Where are you off to?" he asked loudly.

"To remind Miss Able it's time to come in. Those poor children work so hard. I can't feel—however. I'm afraid I'm rather old-fashioned, Mrs. Alleyn. I still feel a mother knows best."

"Well, but Mother," Paul objected, "something had to be done about Panty, didn't it? I mean, she really was pretty frightful."

"Poor old Panty!" said Mrs. Kentish bitterly.

"We'd better move on, Aunt Pauline," Fenella said. "Cedric is driving up. He won't do anything about unloading if I know him."

"Cedric!" Mrs. Kentish repeated. "T'uh!"

She smiled rather grandly at Troy and left them.

"My mother," Paul said uncomfortably, "gets in a bit of a flap about things. Doesn't she, Fen?"

"Actually," said Fenella, "they all do. That generation, I mean. Daddy rather wallows in emotion and Aunt Dessy's a snorter at it. They get it from Grandfather, don't you think?"

"All except Thomas."

"Yes, all except Thomas. Don't you think," Fenella asked Troy, "that if one generation comes in rather hot and strong emotionally, the next generation swings very much the other way? Paul and I are as hard as nails, aren't we, Paul?"

Troy turned to the young man. He was staring fixedly at his cousin. His dark brows were knitted and his lips were pressed together. He looked preternaturally solemn and did not answer Fenella. "Why," thought Troy, "he's in love with her."

II

The interior of Ancreton amply sustained the promise of its monstrous façade. Troy was to learn that "great" was the stock adjective at Ancreton. There was the Great West Spinney, the Great Gallery and the Great Tower. Having crossed the Great Drawbridge over the now dry and cultivated moat, Troy, Fenella, and Paul entered the Great Hall.

Here the tireless ingenuity of the architect had flirted with a number of Elizabethan conceits. There was a plethora of fancy carving, a display of stained-glass windows bearing the Ancred arms, and a number of presumably collateral quarterings. Between these romped occasional mythical animals, and, when mythology and heraldry had run short, the Church had not been forgotten, for crosslets-ancred stood cheek-by-jowl in mild confusion with the keys of St. Peter and the Cross of St. John of Jerusalem.

Across the back of the hall, facing the entrance, ran a minstrels' gallery, energetically chiselled and hung at intervals with banners. Beneath this, on a wall whose surface was a mass of scrolls and bosses, the portrait, Fenella explained, was to hang. By day, as Troy at once noticed, it would be chequered all over with the reflected colours of a stained-glass heraldry and would take on the aspect of a jig-saw puzzle. By night, according to Paul, it would be floodlit by four lamps specially installed under the gallery.

There were a good many portraits already in the hall, and Troy's attention was caught by an enormous canvas above the fireplace depicting a nautical Ancred of the eighteenth century, who pointed his cutlass at a streak of forked lightning with an air of having made it himself. Underneath this work, in a huge armchair, warming himself at the fire, was Cedric.

"People are seeing about the luggage," he said, struggling to his feet, "and one of the minor ancients has led away the horse. Someone has carried dearest Mrs. Alleyn's paints up to her inaccessible eyrie. *Do* sit down, Mrs. Alleyn. You must be madly exhausted. My Mama is on her way. The Old Person's entrance is timed for eight-thirty. We have a nice long time in which to relax. The Ancient of Days, at my suggestion, is about to serve drinks. In the name of my ridiculous family, in fact, welcome to Katzenjammer Castle."

"Would you like to see your room first?" asked Fenella.

"Let me warn you," Cedric added, "that the visit will entail another arduous climb and a long tramp. Where have they put her, Fenella?"

"The *Siddons* room."

"I couldn't sympathise more deeply, but of course the choice is appropriate. A steel engraving of that abnormally muscular actress in the rôle of Lady Macbeth hangs over the washhand-stand, doesn't it, Fenella? I'm in the *Garrick*, which is comparatively lively, especially in the rat season. Here comes the Ancient of Days. *Do* have a stirrup-cup before you set out on your polar expedition."

An extremely old man-servant was coming across the hall with a tray of drinks. "Barker," said Cedric faintly. "You are welcome as flowers in spring."

"Thank you, Mr Cedric," said the old man. "Sir Henry's compliments, Miss Fenella, and he hopes to have the pleasure of joining you at dinner. Sir Henry hopes Mrs. Alleyn has had a pleasant journey."

Troy said that she had, and wondered if she should return a

formal message. Cedric, with the nearest approach to energy that he had yet displayed, began to mix drinks. "There is one department of Katzenjammer Castle to which one can find no objection, and that is the cellar," he said. "Thank you, Barker, from my heart. Ganymede himself couldn't foot it more featly."

"I must say, Cedric," Paul muttered when the old butler had gone, "that I don't think your line of comedy with Barker is screamingly funny."

"Dear Paul! Don't you? I'm completely shattered."

"Well, he's old," said Fenella quickly, "and he's a great friend."

Cedric darted an extraordinarily malicious glance at his cousins. "How very feudal," he said. "*Noblesse oblige*. Dear me!"

At this juncture, rather to Troy's relief, a stout smiling woman came in from one of the side doors. Behind her, Troy caught a glimpse of a vast formal drawing-room.

"This is my Mama," Cedric explained, faintly waving his hand.

Mrs. Henry Ancred was a firmly built, white-skinned woman. Her faded hair was scrupulously groomed into a rather wig-like coiffure. She looked, Troy thought, a little as if she managed some quiet but extremely expensive boarding-house or perhaps a school. Her voice was unusually deep, and her hands and feet unusually large. Unlike her son, she had a wide mouth, but there was a resemblance to Cedric about the eyes and chin. She wore a sensible blouse, a cardigan, and a dark skirt, and she shook hands heartily with Troy. A capable woman.

"So glad you've decided to come," she said. "My father-in-law's quite excited. It will take him out of himself and fill in his day nicely."

Cedric gave a little shriek: "Milly, *darling*!" he cried. "How— you can!" He made an agonised face at Troy.

"Have I said something I shouldn't?" asked his mother. "So like me!" And she laughed heartily.

"Of course you haven't," Troy said hurriedly, ignoring Cedric. "I only hope the sittings won't tire Sir Henry."

"Oh, he'll tell you at once if he's tired," Millamant Ancred assured her, and Troy had an unpleasant picture of a canvas six by four feet, to be completed in a fortnight, with a sitter who had no hesitation in telling her when he felt tired.

"Well, anyway," Cedric cried shrilly. "Drinks!"

They sat round the fire, Paul and Fenella on a sofa, Troy

opposite them, and Millamant Ancred, squarely, on a high chair. Cedric pulled a humpty up to his mother, curled himself on it, and rested an arm on her knees. Paul and Fenella glanced at him with ill-concealed distaste.

"What have you been doing, dear?" Millamant asked her son, and put her square white hand on his shoulder.

"Such a lot of tiresome jobs," he sighed, rubbing his cheek on the hand. "Tell us what's going to happen here. I want something gay and exciting. A party for Mrs. Alleyn. Please! You'd like a party, wouldn't you?" he persisted, appealing to Troy. "Say you would."

"But I've come to work," said Troy, and because he made her feel uncomfortable she spoke abruptly. "Damn!" she thought. "Even that sounds as if I expected her to take him seriously."

But Millamant laughed indulgently. "Mrs. Alleyn will be with us for The Birthday," she said, "and so will you, dear, if you really can stay for ten days. Can you?"

"Oh, yes," he said fretfully. "The office-place is being tatted up. I've brought my dreary work with me. But The Birthday! How abysmally depressing! Darling Milly, I don't think, really, that I can face another Birthday."

"Don't be naughty," said Millamant in her gruff voice.

"Let's have another drink," said Paul loudly.

"Is somebody talking about drink?" cried a disembodied voice in the minstrels' gallery "Goody! Goody! Goody!"

"Oh, God!" Cedric whispered. "Sonia!"

III

It had grown dark in the hall, and Troy's first impression of Miss Sonia Orrincourt was of a whitish apparition that fluttered down the stairs from the far side of the gallery. Her progress was accompanied by a number of chirruping noises. As she reached the hall and crossed it, Troy saw that she wore a garment which even in the second act of a musical extravaganza would still have been remarkable. Troy supposed it was a négligée.

"Well, for heaven's sake," squeaked Miss Orrincourt, "look who's here! Ceddie!" She held out both her hands and Cedric took them.

"You look too marvellous, Sonia," he cried. "Where did it come from?"

"Darling, it's a million years old. Oh, pardon me," said Miss Orrincourt, inclining towards Troy, "I didn't see——"

Millamant stonily introduced her. Fenella and Paul having moved away from the sofa, Miss Orrincourt sank into it. She extended her arms and wriggled her fingers. "Quick! Quick! Quick!" she cried babyishly. "Sonia wants a d'ink."

Her hair was almost white. It fell in a fringe across her forehead and in a silk curtain to her shoulders, and reminded Troy vaguely of the inside of an aquarium. Her eyes were as round as saucers, with curving black lashes. When she smiled, her short upper lip flattened, the corners of her mouth turned down, and the shadow of grooves-to-come ran away to her chin. Her skin was white and thick like the petals of a camellia. She was a startling young woman to look at, and she made Troy feel exceedingly dumb.

"But she'd probably be pretty good to paint in the nude," she reflected. "I wonder if she's ever been a model. She looks like it."

Miss Orrincourt and Cedric were conducting an extraordinarily unreal little conversation. Fenella and Paul had moved away, and Troy was left with Millamant Ancred, who began to talk about the difficulties of housekeeping. As she talked, she stitched at an enormous piece of embroidery, which hypnotised Troy by its monstrous colour scheme and tortuous design. Intricate worms and scrolls strangled each other in Millamant's fancy work. No area was left undecorated, no motive was uninterrupted. At times she would pause and eye it with complacency. Her voice was monotonous.

"I suppose I'm lucky," she said. "I've got a cook and five maids and Barker, but they're all very old and have been collected from different branches of the family. My sister-in-law, Pauline, Mrs. Claude Ancred, you know, gave up her own house in the evacuation time and has recently joined us with two of her maids. Desdemona did the same thing, and she makes Ancreton her headquarters now. She brought her old Nanny. Barker and the others have always been with us. But even with the West Wing turned into a school it's difficult. In the old days of course," said Millamant with a certain air of complacency, "there was a swarm."

"Do they get on together?" Troy asked vaguely. She was watching Cedric and Miss Orrincourt. Evidently he had decided to adopt ingratiating tactics, and a lively but completely synthetic flirtation had developed. They whispered together.

571

"Oh, no," Millamant was saying. "They fight." And most unexpectedly she added: "Like master like man, they say, don't they?" Troy looked at her. She was smiling broadly and blankly. It is a characteristic of these people, Troy reflected, that they constantly make remarks to which there is no answer.

Pauline Ancred came in and joined her son and Fenella. She did this with a certain air of determination, and the smile she gave Fenella was a dismissal. "Darling," she said to Paul, "I've been looking for you." Fenella at once moved away. Pauline, using a gesture that was Congrevian in its accomplishment, raised a pair of lorgnettes and stared through them at Miss Orrincourt, who now reclined at full length on the sofa. Cedric was perched on the arm at her feet.

"I'll get you a chair, Mother," said Paul hastily.

"Thank you, dear," she said, exchanging a glance with her sister-in-law. "I should like to sit down. No, *please*, Mrs. Alleyn, don't move. So sweet of you. Thank you, Paul."

"Noddy and I," said Miss Orrincourt brightly, "have been having such fun. We've been looking at some of that old jewellery." She stretched her arms above her head and yawned delicately.

"Noddy!" Troy wondered. "But who is Noddy?" Miss Orrincourt's remark was followed by a rather deadly little pause. "He's all burnt up about having his picture taken," Miss Orrincourt added. "Isn't it killing?"

Pauline Ancred, with a dignified shifting of her torso, brought her sister-in-law into her field of vision. "Have you seen Papa this afternoon, Millamant?" she asked, not quite cordially, but with an air of joining forces against a common enemy.

"I went up as usual at four o'clock," Millamant rejoined, "to see if there was anything I could do for him." She glanced at Miss Orrincourt. "He was engaged, however."

"T'uh!" said Pauline lightly, and she began to revolve her thumbs one around the other. Millamant gave the merest sketch of a significant laugh and turned to Troy.

"We don't quite know," she said cheerfully, "if Thomas explained about my father-in-law's portrait. He wishes to be painted in his own little theatre here. The backcloth has been hung and Paul knows about the lights. Papa would like to begin at eleven tomorrow morning, and if he is feeling up to it he will sit for an hour every morning and afternoon."

"I thought," said Miss Orrincourt, "it would be ever so thrilling if Noddy was on a horse in the picture."

"Sir Henry," said Millamant, without looking at her, "will, of course, have decided on the pose."

"But Aunt Milly," said Paul, very red in the face, "Mrs. Alleyn might like—I mean—don't you think——"

"Yes, Aunt Milly," said Fenella.

"Yes, indeed, Milly," said Cedric. "I *so* agree. Please, *please* Milly and Aunt Pauline, and please Sonia, angel, *do* consider that Mrs. Alleyn is the one to—oh, my goodness," Cedric implored them, "pray *do* consider."

"I shall be very interested," said Troy, "to hear about Sir Henry's plans."

"That," said Pauline, "will be very nice. I forgot to tell you, Millamant, that I heard from Dessy. She's coming for The Birthday."

"I'm glad you let me know," said Millamant, looking rather put out.

"And so's Mummy, Aunt Milly," said Fenella. "I forgot to say."

"Well," said Millamant, with a short laugh, "I *am* learning about things, aren't I?"

"Jenetta coming? Fancy!" said Pauline. "It must be two years since Jenetta was at Ancreton. I hope she'll be able to put up with our rough and ready ways."

"Considering she's been living in a two-roomed flat," Fenella began rather hotly and checked herself. "She asked me to say she hoped it wouldn't be too many."

"I'll move out of *Bernhardt* into *Bracegirdle*," Pauline offered. "Of course."

"You'll do nothing of the sort, Pauline," said Millamant. "*Bracegirdle* is piercingly cold, the ceiling leaks, and there are rats. Desdemona complained bitterly about the rats last time she was here. I asked Barker to lay poison for them, but he's lost the poison. Until he finds it, *Bracegirdle* is uninhabitable."

"Mummy could share *Duse* with me," said Fenella quickly. "We'd love it and it'd save fires."

"Oh, we couldn't dream of *that*," said Pauline and Millamant together.

"Mrs. Alleyn," said Fenella loudly, "I'm going up to change. Would you like to see your room?"

"Thank you," said Troy, trying not to sound too eager. "Thank you, I would."

IV

Having climbed the stairs and walked with a completely silent Fenella down an interminable picture gallery and two long passages, followed by a break-neck ascent up a winding stair, Troy found herself at a door upon which hung a wooden plaque bearing the word '*Siddons*'. Fenella opened the door, and Troy was pleasantly welcomed by the reflection of leaping flames on white painted walls. White damask curtains with small garlands, a sheepskin rug, a low bed, and there, above a Victorian washstand, sure enough, hung Mrs. Siddons. Troy's painting gear was stacked in a corner.

"What a nice room," said Troy.

"I'm glad you like it," said Fenella in a suppressed voice. Troy saw with astonishment that she was in a rage.

"I apologise," said Fenella shakily, "for my beastly family."

"Hallo," said Troy, "what's all this?"

"As if they weren't damned lucky to get you! As if they wouldn't still be damned lucky if you decided to paint Grandpa standing on his head with garlic growing out of the soles of his boots. It's *such cheek*. Even that frightful twirp Cedric was ashamed."

"Good Lord!" said Troy. "That's nothing unusual. You've no conception how funny people can be about portraits."

"I hate them! And you heard how catty they were about Mummy coming. I do think old women are *foul*. And that bitch Sonia lying there lapping it all up. How they can, in front of her! Paul and I were so ashamed."

Fenella stamped, dropped on her knees in front of the fire and burst into tears. "I'm sorry," she stammered. "I'm worse than they are, but I'm so sick of it all. I wish I hadn't come to Ancreton. I loathe Ancreton. If you only knew what it's like."

"Look here," Troy said gently, "are you sure you want to talk to me like this?"

"I know it's frightful, but I can't help it. How would you feel if *your* grandfather brought a loathsome blonde into the house? How would you feel?"

Troy had a momentary vision of her grandfather, now

574

deceased. He had been an austere and somewhat finicky don.

"Everybody's laughing at him," Fenella sobbed. "And I used to like him so much. Now he's just *silly*. A silly amorous old man. He behaves like that himself and then when I—when I went to— it doesn't matter. I'm terribly sorry. It's awful, boring you like this."

Troy sat on a low chair by the fire and looked thoughtfully at Fenella. The child really is upset, she thought, and realised that already she had begun to question the authenticity of the Ancreds' emotions. She said: "You needn't think it's awful, and you're not boring me. Only don't say things you'll feel inclined to kick yourself for when you've got under way again."

"All right." Fenella got to her feet. She had the fortunate knack, Troy noticed, of looking charming when she cried. She now tossed her head, bit her lips, and gained mastery of herself. "She'll make a good actress," Troy thought, and instantly checked herself. "Because," she thought, "the child manages to be so prettily distressed, why should I jump to the conclusion that she's not as distressed as she seems? I'm not sympathetic enough." She touched Fenella's arm, and although it was quite foreign to her habit, returned the squeeze Fenella instantly gave to her hand.

"Come," said Troy, "I thought you said this afternoon that your generation of Ancreds was as hard as nails."

"Well, we try," Fenella said. "It's only because you're so nice that I let go. I won't again."

"Help!" Troy thought, and said aloud: "I'm not much use really, I'm afraid. My husband says I shy away from emotion like a nervous mare. But let off steam if you want to."

Fenella said soberly: "This'll do for a bit, I expect. You're an angel. Dinner's at half-past eight. You'll hear a warning gong." She turned at the door. "All the same," she said, "there's something pretty ghastly going on at Ancreton just now. You'll see."

With an inherited instinct for a good exit line, Fenella stepped backwards and gracefully closed the door.

CHAPTER IV

Sir Henry

I

In her agitation Fenella had neglected to give Troy the usual host-esses' tips on internal topography. Troy wondered if the nearest bathroom was at the top of another tower or at the end of some interminable corridor. Impossible to tug the embroidered bell-pull and cause one of those aged maids to climb the stairs! She decided to give up her bath in favour of Mrs. Siddons, the wash-stand and a Victorian can of warm water which had been left beside it.

She had an hour before dinner. It was pleasant, after the severely rationed fires of Tatler's End, to dress leisurely before this sump-tuous blaze. She made the most of it, turning over in her mind the events of the day and sorting out her impressions of the Ancreds. Queer Thomas, she decided, was, so far, the best of the bunch, though the two young things were pleasant enough. Was there an understanding between them and had Sir Henry objected? Was that the reason for Fenella's outburst? For the rest: Pauline appeared to be suffering from a general sense of personal affront, Millamant was an unknown quantity, while her Cedric was frankly awful. And then, Sonia! Troy giggled. Sonia really was a bit thick.

Somewhere outside in the cold, a deep-toned clock struck eight. The fire had died down. She might as well begin her journey to the hall. Down the winding stair she went, wondering whose room lay beyond a door on the landing. Troy had no sense of direction. When she reached the first long corridor she couldn't for the life of her remember whether she should turn left or right. A perspective of dark crimson carpet stretched away on each hand, and at intervals the corridor was lit by pseudo-antique candelabra. "Oh, well," thought Troy and turned to the right.

She passed four doors and read their legends: *'Duse'* (that was Fenella's room), *'Bernhardt'* (Pauline's), *'Terry,'* *'Lady Bancroft,'* and, near the end of the passage, the despised *'Bracegirdle'*. Troy did not remember seeing any of these names on her way up to her tower. "Blast!" she thought, "I've gone wrong." But she went on uncertainly. The corridor led at right-angles into another, at the far end of which she saw the foot of a flight of stairs like those of her own tower. Poor Troy was certain that she had looked down just such a vista on her way up. "But I suppose," she thought, "it must have been its opposite number. From outside, the damn place looked as if it was built round a sort of quadrangle, with a tower at the middle and ends of each wing. In that case, if I keep on turning left, oughtn't I to come back to the picture gallery?"

As she hesitated, a door near the foot of the stairs opened slightly, and a magnificent cat walked out into the passage.

He was white, with a tabby saddle on his back, long haired and amber eyed. He paused and stared at Troy. Then, wafting his tail slightly, he paced slowly towards her. She stooped and waited for him. After some deliberation he approached, examined her hand, bestowed upon it a brief cold thrust of his nose, and continued on his way, walking in the centre of the crimson carpet and still elegantly wafting his tail.

"And one other thing," said a shrill voice beyond the open door, "if you think I'm going to hang round here like a bloody extra with the family handing me out the bird in fourteen different positions you've got another think coming."

A deep voice rumbled unintelligibly.

"I know all about that, and it makes no difference. Nobody's going to tell me I lack refinement and get away with it. They treat me as if I had one of those things in the strip ads. I kept my temper down there because I wasn't going to let them see I minded. What do they think they are? My God, do they think it's any catch living in a mausoleum with a couple of old tats and a kid that ought to be labelled 'Crazy Gang'?"

Again the expostulatory rumble.

"I know, I know, I know. It's so merry and bright in this dump it's a wonder we don't all die of laughing. If you're as crazy as all that about me, you ought to put me in a position where I'd keep my self-respect ... You owe it to me ... After all I've done for you. I'm just miserable ... And when I get like this, I'm warning you, Noddy, look out." The door opened a little further.

Troy, who had stood transfixed, picked up her skirts, turned back on her tracks, and fairly ran away down the long corridor.

II

This time she reached the gallery and went downstairs. In the hall she encountered Barker, who showed her into an enormous drawing-room which looked, she thought, as if it was the setting for a scene in '*Victoria Regina*'. Crimson, white, and gold were the predominant colours, damask and velvet the prevailing textures. Vast canvases by Leader and MacWhirter occupied the walls. On each occasional table or cabinet stood a silver-framed photograph of Royalty or Drama. There were three of Sir Henry at different stages of his career, and there was one of Sir Henry in Court dress. In this last portrait, the customary air of a man who can't help feeling he looks a bit of an ass was completely absent, and for a moment Troy thought Sir Henry had been taken in yet another of his professional rôles. The unmistakable authenticity of his Windsor coat undeceived her. "Golly," she thought, staring at the photograph, "it's a good head and no mistake."

She began a tour of the room and found much to entertain her. Under the glass lid of a curio table were set out a number of orders, miniatures and decorations, several *objets d'art*, a signed programme from a command performance, and, surprisingly, a small book of antique style, bound in half-calf and heavily tooled. Troy was one of those people who, when they see a book lying apart, must handle it. The lid was unlocked. She raised it and opened the little book. The title was much faded, and Troy stooped to make it out.

"The Antient Arte of the Embalming of Corpſes," she read. "To which is added a Diſcourſe on the Concoction of Fluids for the Purpoſe of Preſerving Dead Bodies.

By William Hurſte, Profeſſor of Phyſic, London.

Printed by Robert White for John Crampe at the Sign of the Three Bibles in St. Paul's Churchyard. 1678."

It was horribly explicit. Here, in the first chapter, were various recipes "For the Conſumation of the Arte of Preſerving the Dead in perfect Veriſimilitude of Life. It will be remarked," the author continued, "that in ſpite of their diverſity the chimical of Arſenic is Common to All." There was a particularly macabre passage on

"The uſe of Coſmeticſ to Diſguiſe the ghaſtly Pallor of Death."

"But what sort of mind," Troy wondered, "could picture with equanimity, even with pleasure, these manipulations upon the body from which it must some day, perhaps soon, be parted?" And she wondered if Sir Henry Ancred had read this book and if he had no imagination or too much. "And why," she thought, "do I go on reading this horrid little book?"

She heard a voice in the hall, and with an illogical feeling of guilt hurriedly closed the book and the glass lid. Millamant came in, wearing a tidy but nondescript evening dress.

"I've been exploring," Troy said.

"Exploring?" Millamant repeated with her vague laugh.

"That grisly little book in the case. I can't resist a book and I'm afraid I opened the case. I do hope it's allowed."

"Oh," said Millamant. "Yes, of course." She glanced at the case. "What book is it?"

"It's about embalming, of all things. It's very old. I should think it might be rather valuable."

"Perhaps," said Millamant, "that's why Miss Orrincourt was so interested in it."

She moved to the fireplace, looking smugly resentful.

"Miss Orrincourt?" Troy repeated.

"I found her reading a small book when I came in the other day. She put it in the case and dropped the lid. Such a bang! It's a wonder it didn't break, really. I suppose it must have been that book, mustn't it?"

"Yes," said Troy, hurriedly rearranging her already chaotic ideas of Miss Sonia Orrincourt. "I suppose it must."

"Papa," said Millamant, "is not quite at his best this evening but he's coming down. On his bad days he dines in his own rooms."

"I hope," said Troy, "that the sittings won't tire him too much."

"Well, he's so looking forward to them that I'm sure he'll try to keep them up. He's really been much better lately, only sometimes," said Millamant ambiguously, "he gets a little upset. He's very highly strung and sensitive, you know. I always think that all the Ancreds are like that. Except Thomas. My poor Cedric, unfortunately, has inherited their temperament."

Troy had nothing to say to this, and was relieved when Paul Kentish and his mother came in, followed in a moment by

579

Fenella. Barker brought a tray with sherry. Presently an extraordinarily ominous gong sounded in the hall.

"Did anyone see Cedric?" asked his mother. "I do hope he's not going to be late."

"He was still in his bath when I tried to get in ten minutes ago," said Paul.

"Oh, dear," said Millamant.

Miss Orrincourt, amazingly dressed, and looking at once sulky, triumphant and defiant, drifted into the room. Troy heard a stifled exclamation behind her, and turned to see the assembled Ancreds with their gaze riveted to Miss Orrincourt's bosom.

It was adorned with a large diamond star.

"Milly," Pauline muttered.

"Do you see what I see?" Millamant replied with a faint hiss.

Miss Orrincourt moved to the fire and laid one arm along the mantelpiece. "I hope Noddy's not going to be late," she said. "I'm starving." She looked critically at her crimson nails and touched the diamond star. "I'd like a drink," she said.

Nobody made any response to this statement, though Paul uncomfortably cleared his throat. The tap of a stick sounded in the hall.

"Here is Papa," said Pauline nervously, and they all moved slightly. Really, thought Troy, they might be waiting to dine with some minor royalty. There was precisely the same air of wary expectation.

Barker opened the door, and the original of all the photographs walked slowly into the room, followed by the white cat.

III

The first thing to be said about Sir Henry Ancred was that he filled his rôle with almost embarrassing virtuosity. He was unbelievably handsome. His hair was silver, his eyes, under heavy brows, were fiercely blue. His nose was ducal in its prominence. Beneath it sprouted a fine snowy moustache, brushed up to lend accent to his actor's mouth. His chin jutted out squarely and was adorned with an ambassadorial tuft. He looked as if he had been specially designed for exhibition. He wore a velvet dinner-jacket, an old-fashioned collar, a wide cravat and a monocle on a broad ribbon. You could hardly believe, Troy thought, that he was true. He came in slowly, using a black and

580

silver stick, but not leaning on it overmuch. It was, Troy felt, more of an adjunct than an aid. He was exceeding tall and still upright.

"Mrs Alleyn, Papa," said Pauline.

"Ah," said Sir Henry.

Troy went to meet him. "Restraining myself," as she afterwards told Alleyn, "from curtsying, but with difficulty."

"So this is our distinguished painter?" said Sir Henry, taking her hand. "I am delighted."

He kept her hand in his and looked down at her. Behind him, Troy saw in fancy a young Henry Ancred bending his gaze upon the women in his heyday and imagined how pleasurably they must have melted before it. "Delighted," he repeated, and his voice underlined adroitly his pleasure not only in her arrival but in her looks. "Hold your horses, chaps," thought Troy and removed her hand, "I hope you continue of that mind," she said politely.

Sir Henry bowed. "I believe I shall," he said. "I believe I shall." She was to learn that he had a habit of repeating himself.

Paul had moved a chair forward. Sir Henry sat in it facing the fire, with the guest and family disposed in arcs on either side of him.

He crossed his knees and rested his left forearm along the arm of his chair, letting his beautifully kept hand dangle elegantly. It was a sort of Charles II pose, and, in lieu of the traditional spaniel, the white cat leapt gracefully on his lap, kneaded it briefly and reclined there.

"Ah, Carabbas!" said Sir Henry, and stroked it, looking graciously awhile upon his family and guest. "This is pleasant," he said, including them in a beautiful gesture. For a moment his gaze rested on Miss Orrincourt's bosom. "Charming," he said. "A conversation piece. Ah! A glass of sherry."

Paul and Fenella dispensed the sherry, which was extremely good. Rather elaborate conversation was made, Sir Henry conducting it with the air of giving an audition. "But I thought," he said, "that Cedric was to join us. Didn't you tell me, Millamant——"

"I'm so sorry he's late, Papa," said Millamant. "He had an important letter to write, I know. I think perhaps he didn't hear the gong."

"Indeed! Where have you put him?"

"In Garrick, Papa."

"Then he certainly must have heard the gong."

Barker came in and announced dinner.

"We shall not, I think, wait for Cedric," Sir Henry continued. He removed the cat, Carabbas, from his knees and rose. His family rose with him. "Mrs. Alleyn, may I have the pleasure of taking you in?" he said.

"It's a pity," Troy thought as she took the arm he curved for her, "that there isn't an orchestra." And as if she had recaptured the lines from some drawing-room comedy of her childhood, she made processional conversation as they moved towards the door. Before they reached it, however, there was a sound of running footsteps in the hall. Cedric, flushed with exertion and wearing a white flower in his dinner-jacket, darted into the room.

"Dearest Grandpapa," he cried, waving his hands, "I creep, I grovel. So sorry, truly. Couldn't be more contrite. Find me some sackcloth and ashes somebody, quickly."

"Good evening, Cedric," said Sir Henry icily. "You must make your apologies to Mrs. Alleyn, who will perhaps be very kind and forgive you."

Troy smiled like a duchess at Cedric and inwardly grinned like a Cheshire cat at herself.

"Too heavenly of you," said Cedric quickly. He slipped in behind them. The procession had splayed out a little on his entrance. He came face to face with Miss Orrincourt. Troy heard him give a curious, half-articulate exclamation. It sounded involuntary and unaffected. This was so unusual from Cedric that Troy turned to look at him. His small mouth was open. His pale eyes stared blankly at the diamond star on Miss Orrincourt's bosom, and then turned incredulously from one member of his family to another.

"But"—he stammered—"but, I say—I say."

"Cedric," whispered his mother.

"Cedric," said his grandfather imperatively.

But Cedric, still speaking in that strangely natural voice, pointed a white finger at the diamond star and said loudly: "But, my God, it's Great-Great-Grandmama Ancred's sunburst!"

"Nice, isn't it?" said Miss Orrincourt equally loudly. "I'm ever so thrilled."

"In these unhappy times, alas," said Sir Henry blandly, arming Troy through the door, "one may not make those gestures with

582

which one would wish to honour a distinguished visitor! 'A poor small banquet,' as old Capulet had it. Shall we go in?"

IV

The poor small banquet was, if nothing else, a tribute to the zeal of Sir Henry's admirers in the Dominions and the United States of America. Troy had not seen its like for years. He himself, she noticed, ate a mess of something that had been put through a sieve. Conversation was general, innocuous, and sounded a little as if it had been carefully memorised beforehand. It was difficult not to look at Miss Orrincourt's diamonds. They were a sort of visual *faux pas* which no amount of blameless small-talk could shout down. Troy observed that the Ancreds themselves constantly darted furtive glances at them. Sir Henry continued bland, urbane, and, to Troy, excessively gracious. She found his compliments, which were adroit, rather hard to counter. He spoke of her work and asked if she had done a self-portrait. "Only in my student days when I couldn't afford a model," said Troy. "But that's very naughty of you," he said. "It is now that you should give us the perfect painting of the perfect subject."

"Crikey!" thought Troy.

They drank Rüdesheimer. When Barker hovered beside him, Sir Henry, announcing that it was a special occasion, said he would take half a glass. Millamant and Pauline looked anxiously at him.

"Papa, darling," said Pauline. "*Do* you think——?" And Millamant murmured: "Yes, Papa. *Do* you think——?"

"Do I think what?" he replied, glaring at them.

"Wine," they murmured disjointedly. "Dr. Withers ... not really advisable ... however."

"Fill it up, Barker," Sir Henry commanded loudly, "fill it up." Troy heard Pauline and Millamant sigh windily.

Dinner proceeded with circumspection but uneasily. Paul and Fenella were silent. Cedric, on Troy's right hand, conversed in feverish spasms with anybody who would listen to him. Sir Henry's flow of compliments continued unabated through three courses, and to Troy's dismay, Miss Orrincourt began to show signs of marked hostility. She was on Sir Henry's left, with Paul on her other side. She began an extremely grand conversation with Paul, and though he responded with every sign of discomfort

583

she lowered her voice, cast significant glances at him, and laughed immoderately at his monosyllabic replies. Troy, who was beginning to find her host very heavy weather indeed, seized an opportunity to speak to Cedric.

"Noddy," said Miss Orrincourt at once, "what are we going to do tomorrow?"

"Do?" he repeated, and after a moment's hesitation became playful. "What does a litt!e girl want to do?"

Miss Orrincourt stretched her arms above her head. "She wants things to *happen*!" she cried ecstatically. "Lovely things."

"Well, if she's very, very good perhaps we'll let her have a tiny peep at a great big picture."

Troy heard this with dismay.

"What else?" Miss Orricourt persisted babyishly but with an extremely unenthusiastic glance at Troy.

"We'll see," said Sir Henry uneasily.

"But Noddy——"

"Mrs. Alleyn," said Millamant from the foot of the table, "shall we——?"

And she marshalled her ladies out of the dining-room.

The rest of the evening passed uneventfully. Sir Henry led Troy through the pages of three albums of theatrical photographs. This she rather enjoyed. It was strange, she thought, to see how the fashion in Elizabethan garments changed in the world of theatre. Here was a young Victorian Henry Ancred very much be-pointed, be-ruffed, encased and furbished, in a perfect welter of velvet, ribbon and leather; here a modern elderly Henry Ancred in a stylised and simplified costume that had apparently been made of painted scenic canvas. Yet both were the Duke of Buckingham.

Miss Orrincourt joined a litt!e fretfully in this pastime. Perched on the arm of Sir Henry's chair and disseminating an aura of black market scent, she giggled tactlessly over the earlier photographs and yawned over the later ones. "My dear," she ejaculated, "look at you! You've got everything on but the kitchen sink!" This was in reference to a picture of Sir Henry as Richard II. Cedric tittered and immediately looked frightened. Pauline said: "I must say, Papa, I don't think anyone else has ever approached your flair for exactly the right costume."

"My dear," her father rejoined, "it's the way you wear 'em." He patted Miss Orrincourt's hand. "You do very well, my child,"

584

he said, "in your easy modern dresses. How would you manage if, like Ellen Terry, you had two feet of heavy velvet in front of you on the stage and were asked to move like a queen down a flight of stairs? You'd fall on your nice little nose."

He was obviously a vain man. It was extraordinary, Troy thought, that he remained unmoved by Miss Orrincourt's lack of reverence, and remembering Thomas's remark about David and Abishag the Shunammite, Troy was forced to the disagreeable conclusion that Sir Henry was in his dotage about Miss Orrincourt.

At ten o'clock a grog-tray was brought in. Sir Henry drank barley water, suffered the women of his family to kiss him goodnight, nodded to Paul and Cedric, and, to her intense embarrassment, kissed Troy's hand. "*A demain*," he said in his deepest voice. "We meet at eleven. I am fortunate."

He made a magnificent exit, and ten minutes later, Miss Orrincourt, yawning extensively, also retired.

Her disappearance was the signal for an outbreak among the Ancreds.

"Honestly, Milly! Honestly, Aunt Pauline. Can we believe our *eyes*!" cried Cedric. "The Sunburst! I mean *actually*!"

"Well, Millamant," said Pauline, "I now see for myself how things stand at Ancreton."

"You wouldn't believe me when I told you, Pauline," Millamant rejoined. "You've been here a month, but you wouldn't——"

"Has he *given* it to her, will somebody tell me?" Cedric demanded.

"He can't," said Pauline. "He can't. And what's more, I don't believe he would. Unless——" She stopped short and turned to Paul. "If he's given it to her," she said, "he's going to marry her. That's all."

Poor Troy, who had been making completely ineffectual efforts to go, seized upon the silence that followed Pauline's announcement to murmur: "If I may, I think I shall——"

"*Dear* Mrs. Alleyn," said Cedric, "I implore you not to be tactful. Do stay and listen."

"I don't see," Paul began, "why poor Mrs. Alleyn should be inflicted——"

"She knows," said Fenella. "I'm afraid I've already told her, Paul."

585

Pauline suddenly made a gracious dive at Troy. "Isn't it disturbing?" she said with an air of drawing Troy into her confidence. "You see how things are? Really, it's too naughty of Papa. We're all so dreadfully worried. It's not what's happening so much as what might happen that terrifies one. And now the Sunburst. A little too much. In its way it's a historic jewel."

"It was a little *cadeau d'estime* from the Regent to Great-Great-Grandmama Honoria Ancred," Cedric cut in. "Not only historical, but history repeating itself. And *may* I point out, Aunt Pauline, that I personally am rocked to the foundations. I've always understood that the Sunburst was to come to me."

"To your daughter," said Paul. "The point is academic."

"I'm sure I don't know why you think so," said Cedric, bridling. "Anything might happen."

Paul raised his eyebrows.

"Really, Pauline," said Millamant. "Really, Paul!"

"Paul, darling," said Pauline offensively, "don't tease poor Cedric."

"Anyway," said Fenella, "I think Aunt Pauline's right. I think he means to marry, and if he does, I'm never coming to Ancreton again. Never!"

"What shall you call her, Aunt Pauline?" Cedric asked impertinently. "Mummy, or a pet name?"

"There's only one thing to be done," said Pauline. "We must tackle him. I've told Jenetta and I've told Dessy. They're both coming. Thomas will have to come too. In Claude's absence he should take the lead. It's his duty."

"Do you mean, dearest Aunt Pauline, that we are to lie in ambush for the Old Person and make an altogether-boys bounce at him?"

"I propose, Cedric, that we ask him to meet us all and that we simply—we simply——"

"And a fat lot of good, if you'll forgive me for saying so, Pauline, that is likely to do," said Millamant, with a chuckle.

"Not being an Ancred, Millamant, you can't be expected to feel this terrible thing as painfully as we do. How Papa, with his deep sense of pride in an old name—we go back to the Conquest, Mrs. Alleyn—how Papa can have allowed himself to be entangled! It's too humiliating."

"No being an Ancred, as you point out, Pauline, I realise Papa, as well as being blue-blooded, is extremely hot-blooded.

586

Moreover, he's as obstinate and vain as a peacock. He likes the idea of himself with a dashing young wife."

"Comparatively young," said Cedric.

Pauline clasped her hands, and turning from one member of her family to another, said, "I've thought of something! Now listen all of you. I'm going to be perfectly frank and impersonal about this. I know I'm the child's mother, but that needn't prevent me. Panty!"

"What about Panty, Mother?" asked Paul nervously.

"Your grandfather adores the child. Now, suppose Panty were just to drop a childish hint."

"If you suggest," said Cedric, "that Panty should wind her little arms round his neck and whisper: 'Grandpapa, when will the howwid lady wun away?' I can only say I don't think she'd get into the skin of the part."

"He adores her," Pauline repeated angrily. "He's like a great big boy with her. It brings the tears into my eyes to see them together. You can't deny it, Millamant."

"I dare say it does, Pauline."

"Well, but Mother, Panty plays up to Grandpapa," said Paul bluntly.

"And in any case," Cedric pointed out, "isn't Panty as thick as thieves with Sonia?"

"I happen to know," said Millamant, "that Miss Orrincourt encouraged Panty to play a very silly trick on me last Sunday."

"What did she do?" asked Cedric.

Fenella giggled.

"She pinned a very silly notice on the back of my coat when I was going to church," said Millamant stuffily.

"What did it say, Milly, darling?" Cedric asked greedily.

"Roll out the Barrel," said Fenella.

"This is getting us nowhere," said Millamant.

"And now," said Troy hurriedly, "I really think if you'll excuse me——"

This time she was able to ger away. The Ancreds distractedly bade her good night. She refused an escort to her room, and left them barely waiting, she felt, for her to shut the door before they fell to again.

Only a solitary lamp burned in the hall, which was completely silent, and since the fire had died out, very cold. While Troy climbed the stairs she felt as she had not felt before in this enormous house, that it had its own individuality. It stretched out on all sides of her, an undiscovered territory. It housed, as well as the eccentricities of the Ancreds, their deeper thoughts and the thoughts of their predecessors. When she reached the gallery, which was also dim, she felt that the drawing-room was now profoundly distant, a subterranean island. The rows of mediocre portraits and murky landscapes that she now passed had a life of their own in this half-light and seemed to be indifferently aware of her progress. Here, at last, was her own passage with the tower steps at the end. She halted for a moment before climbing them. Was it imagination, or had the door, out of sight on the half-landing above her, been softly closed? "Perhaps," she thought, "somebody lives in the room below me," and for some reason the notion affected her unpleasantly. "Ridiculous!" thought Troy, and turned on a switch at the foot of the stairs. A lamp, out of sight beyond the first spiral, brought the curved wall rather stealthily to life.

Troy mounted briskly, hoping there would still be a fire in her white room. As she turned the spiral, she gathered up her long dress with her right hand and with her left reached out for the narrow rail.

The rail was sticky.

She snatched her hand away with some violence and looked at it. The palm and the under-surface were dark. Troy stood in the shadow of the inner wall, but she now moved up into light. By the single lamps she saw that the stain on her hand was red.

Five seconds must have gone by before she realised that the stuff on her hand was paint.

CHAPTER V

The Bloody Child

I

At half past ten the following morning Troy, hung with paint boxes and carrying a roll of canvas and stretchers, made her way to the little theatre. Guided by Paul and Cedric, who carried her studio easel between them, she went down a long passage that led out of the hall, turned right at a green baize door, "beyond which," Cedric panted, "the Difficult Children ravage at will," and continued towards the rear of that tortuous house. Their journey was not without incident, for as they passed the door of what, as Troy later discovered, was a small sitting-room, it was flung open and a short plumpish man appeared, his back towards them, shouting angrily: "If you've no faith in my treatment, Sir Henry, you have an obvious remedy. I shall be glad to be relieved of the thankless task of prescribing for a damned obstinate patient and his granddaughter." Troy made a valiant effort to forge ahead, but was blocked by Cedric, who stopped short, holding the easel diagonally across the passage and listening with an air of the liveliest interest. "Now, now, keep your temper," rumbled the invisible Sir Henry. "I wash my hands of you," the other proclaimed. "No, you don't. You keep a civil tongue in your head, Withers. You'd much better look after me and take a bit of honest criticism in the way it's intended." "This is outrageous," the visitor said, but with a note of something like despair in his voice. "I formally relinquish the case. You will take this as final." There was a pause, during which Paul attempted, without success, to drag Cedric away. "I won't accept it," Sir Henry said at last, "Come, now, Withers, keep your temper. You ought to understand. I've a great deal to try me. A great deal. Bear with an

589

old fellow's tantrums, won't you? You shan't regret it. See here, now. Shut that door and listen to me." Without turning, the visitor slowly shut the door.

"And *now*," Cedric whispered, "he'll tell poor Dr. Withers he's going to be remembered in the Will."

"Come on, for God's sake," said Paul, and they made their way to the little theatre.

Half an hour later Troy had set up her easel, stretched her canvas, and prepared paper and boards for preliminary studies. The theatre was a complete little affair with a deepish stage. The *Macbeth* backcloth was simple and brilliantly conceived. The scenic painter had carried out Troy's original sketch very well indeed. Before it stood three-dimensional monolithic forms that composed well and broke across the cloth in the right places. She saw where she would place her figure. There would be no attempt to present the background in terms of actuality. It would be frankly a stage set. "A dangling rope would come rather nicely," she thought, "but I suppose they wouldn't like that. If only he'll stand!"

Cedric and Paul now began to show her what could be done with the lights. Troy was enjoying herself. She liked the smell of canvas and glue and the feeling that this was a place where people worked. In the little theatre even Cedric improved. He was knowledgeable and quickly responsive to her suggestions, checking Paul's desire to flood the set with a startling display of lighting and getting him to stand in position while he himself focussed a single spot. "We must find the backcloth discreetly," he cried. "Try the ground row." And presently a luminous glow appeared, delighting Troy.

"But how are you going to *see*?" cried Cedric distractedly. "Oh, lawks! How *are* you going to see?"

"I can bring down a standard spot on an extension," Paul offered. "Or we could uncover a window."

Cedric gazed in an agony of inquiry at Troy. "But the window light would infiltrate," he said. "Or wouldn't it?"

"We could try."

At last by an ingenious arrangement of screens Troy was able to get daylight on her canvas and a fair view of the stage.

The clock—it was, of course, known as the Great Clock—in the central tower struck eleven. A door somewhere backstage opened and shut, and dead on his cue Sir Henry, in the character of

Macbeth, walked onto the lighted set.

"Golly!" Troy whispered. "Oh, Golly!"

"Devastatingly fancy dress," said Cedric in her ear, "but in its ridiculous way rather exciting. Or not? Too fancy?"

"It's not too fancy for me," Troy said roundly, and walked down the aisle to greet her sitter.

II

At midday Troy drove her fingers through her hair, propped a large charcoal drawing against the front of the stage and backed away from it down the aisle. Sir Henry took off his helmet, groaned a little, and moved cautiously to a chair in the wings.

"I suppose you want to stop," said Troy absently, biting her thumb and peering at her drawing.

"One grows a trifle stiff," he replied. She then noticed that he was looking more than a trifle tired. He had made up for her sitting, painting heavy shadows round his eyes and staining his moustache and the tuft on his chin with water-dye. To this he had added long strands of crepe hair. But beneath the greasepaint and hair his face sagged a little and his head drooped.

"I must let you go," said Troy. "I hope I haven't been too exacting. One forgets."

"One also remembers," said Sir Henry. "I have been remembering my lines. I played the part first in 1904."

Troy looked up quickly, suddenly liking him.

"It's a wonderful rôle," he said. "Wonderful."

"I was very much moved by it when I saw you five years ago."

"I've played it six times and always to enormous business. It hasn't been an unlucky piece for me."

"I've heard about the Macbeth superstition. One mustn't quote from the play, must one?" Troy made a sudden pounce at her drawing and wiped her thumb down a too dominant line. "Do you believe it's unlucky!" she asked vaguely.

"It has been for other actors," he said, quite seriously. "There's always a heavy feeling offstage during performance. People are nervy."

"Isn't that perhaps because they remember the superstition?"

"It's there," he said. "You can't escape the feeling. But the piece has never been unlucky for me." His voice, which had sounded tired, lifted again. "If it were otherwise, should I have

591

chosen this rôle for my portrait? Assuredly not. And now," he
said with a return of his arch and over-gallant manner, "am I to be
allowed a peep before I go?"

Troy was not very keen for him to have his peep, but she took
the drawing a little way down the aisle and turned it towards him.
"I'm afraid it won't explain itself," she said, "It's merely a sort of
plot of what I hope to do."

"Ah, yes!" He put his hand in his tunic and drew out a pair of
gold-rimmed pince-nez and there, in a moment, was Macbeth,
with glasses perched on his nose, staring solemnly at his own
portrait. "Such a clever lady," he said. "Very clever!" Troy put
the drawing away and he got up slowly. "Off, ye lendings!" he
said. "I must change." He adjusted his cloak with a practised
hand, drew himself up, and, moving into the spot-light, pointed
his dirk at the great naked canvas. His voice, as though
husbanded for this one flourish, boomed through the empty
theatre.

> " 'Well, may you see things well done there: adieu!
> Lest our old robes sit easier than our new!' "

"God's benison go with you!" said Troy, luckily remembering
the line. He crossed himself, chuckled and strode off between the
monoliths to the door behind the stage. It slammed and Troy was
alone.

She had made up her mind to start at once with the laying out
of her subject on the big canvas. There would be no more
preliminary studies. Time pressed and she knew now what she
wanted. There is no other moment, she thought, to compare with
this, when you face the tautly stretched surface and raise your
hand to make the first touch upon it. And, drawing in her breath,
she swept her charcoal across the canvas. It gave a faint drum-like
note of response. "We're off," thought Troy.

Fifty minutes went by and a rhythm of line and mass grew
under her hand. Back and forward she walked, making sharp
accents with the end of her charcoal or sweeping it flat across the
grain of the canvas. All that was Troy was now poured into her
thin blackened hand. At last she stood motionless, ten paces back
from her work, and, after an interval, lit a cigarette, took up her
duster and began to flick her drawing. Showers of charcoal fell
down the surface.

592

"Don't you like it?" asked a sharp voice.

Troy jumped galvanically and turned. The little girl she had seen fighting on the terrace stood in the aisle, her hands jammed in the pockets of her pinafore and her feet planted apart.

"Where did you come from?" Troy demanded.

"Through the end door. I came quietly because I'm not allowed. Why are you rubbing it out? Don't you like it?"

"I'm not rubbing it out. It's still there." And indeed the ghost of her drawing remained. "You take the surplus charcoal off," she said curtly. "Otherwise it messes the paints."

"Is it going to be Noddy dressed up funny?"

Troy started at this use of a name she had imagined to be Miss Orrincourt's prerogative and invention.

"I call him Noddy," said the child, as if guessing at her thought, "and so does Sonia. She got it from me. I'm going to be like Sonia when I'm grown up."

"Oh," said Troy, opening her paint box and rummaging in it.

"Are those your paints?"

"Yes," said Troy, looking fixedly at her. "They are. Mine."

"I'm Patricia Claudia Ellen Ancred Kentish."

"So I'd gathered."

"You couldn't have gathered all of that, because nobody except Miss Able ever calls me anything but Panty. Not that I care," added Panty, suddenly climbing onto the back of one of the stools and locking her feet in the arms. "I'm double jointed," she said, throwing herself back and hanging head downwards.

"That won't help you if you break your neck," said Troy.

Panty made an offensive gargling noise.

"As you're not allowed here," Troy continued, "hadn't you better run off?"

"No," said Panty.

Troy squeezed a fat serpent of Flake White out on her palette. "If I ignore this child," she thought, "perhaps she will get bored and go."

Now the yellows, next the reds. How beautiful was her palette!

"I'm going to paint with those paints," said Panty at her elbow.

"You haven't a hope," said Troy.

"I'm going to." She made a sudden grab at the tray of long brushes. Troy anticipated this move by a split second.

"Now, see here, Panty," she said, shutting the box and facing the child, "if you don't pipe down I shall pick you up by the slack of your breeches and carry you straight back to where you belong. You don't like people butting in on your games, do you? Well, this is my game, and I can't get on with it if you butt in."

"I'll kill you," said Panty.

"Don't be an ass," said Troy mildly.

Panty scooped up a dollop of vermilion on three of her fingers and flung it wildly at Troy's face. She then burst into peals of shrill laughter.

"You can't whack me," she shrieked. "I'm being brought up on a system."

"Can't I?" Troy rejoined. "System or no system——" And indeed there was nothing she desired more at the moment than to beat Panty. The child confronted her with an expression of concentrated malevolence. Her cheeks were blown out with such determination that her nose wrinkled and turned up. Her mouth was so tightly shut that lines resembling a cat's whiskers radiated from it. She scowled hideously. Her pigtails stuck out at right angles to her head. Altogether she looked like an infuriated infant Boreas.

Troy sat down and reached for a piece of rag to clean her face. "Oh, Panty," she said, "you do look so exactly like your Uncle Thomas."

Panty drew back her arm again. "No, don't," said Troy. "Don't do any more damage with red paint, I implore you. Look here, I'll strike a bargain with you. If you'll promise not to take any more paint without asking, I'll give you a board and some brushes and let you make a proper picture."

Panty glared at her. "When?" she said warily.

"When we've asked your mother or Miss Able. I'll ask. But no more nonsense. And especially," Troy added, taking a shot in the dark, "no more going to my room and squeezing paint on the stair rail."

Panty stared blankly at her. "I don't know what you're talking about," she said flatly. "When can I paint? I want to. Now."

"Yes, but let's get this cleared up. What did you do before dinner last night?"

"I don't know. Yes, I do. Dr. Withers came. He weighed us

all. He's going to make me bald because I've got ringworm. That's why I've got this cap on. Would you like to see my ringworm?"

"No."

"I got it first. I've given it to sixteen of the others."

"Did you go up to my room and mess about with my paints?"

"No."

"Honestly, Panty?"

"Honestly what? I don't know where your room is. When can I paint?"

"Do you promise you didn't put paint ..."

"You are *silly*!" said Panty furiously. "Can't you see a person's telling the truth?"

And Troy, greatly bewildered, thought that she could.

While she was still digesting this queer little scene, the door at the back of the stalls opened and Cedric peered round it.

"So humble and timid," he lisped. "Just a mouse-like squeak to tell you luncheon is almost on the table. *Panty!*" he cried shrilly, catching sight of his cousin. "You gross child! Back to the West Wing, miss! How dare you muscle your hideous way in here?"

Panty grinned savagely at him. "Hallo, Sissy," she said.

"Wait," said Cedric, "just wait till the Old Person catches you. What he won't do to you!"

"Why?" Panty demanded.

"Why! You ask me why. Infamy! With the grease-paint fresh on your fingers."

Both Panty and Troy gaped at this. Panty glanced at her hand. "That's her paint," she said, jerking her head at Troy. "That's not grease-paint."

"Do you deny," Cedric pursued, shaking his finger at her, "do you deny, you toxic child, that you went into your grandfather's dressing-room while he was sitting for Mrs. Alleyn, and scrawled some pothouse insult in lake-liner on his looking-glass? Do you deny, moreover, that you painted a red moustache on the cat, Carabbas?"

With an air of bewilderment that Troy could have sworn was genuine, Panty repeated her former statement. "I don't know what you're talking about. I didn't."

"Tell that," said Cedric with relish, "to your grandpapa and see if he believes you."

"Noddy likes me," said Panty, rallying. "He likes me best in the family. He thinks you're awful. He said you're a simpering popinjay."

"See here," said Troy hastily. "Let's get this straight. You say Panty's written something in grease-paint on Sir Henry's looking-glass. What's she supposed to have written?"

Cedric coughed. "Dearest Mrs. Alleyn, we mustn't allow you for a second to be disturbed ..."

"I'm not disturbed," said Troy. "What was written on the glass?"

"My mama would have wiped it off. She was in his room tidying, and saw it. She hunted madly for a rag but the Old Person, at that moment, walked in and saw it. He's roaring about the house like a major prophet."

"But what was it, for pity's sake?"

" 'Grandfather's a bloody old fool,' " said Cedric. Panty giggled. "There!" said Cedric. "You see! Obviously she wrote it. Obviously she made up the cat."

"I didn't. *I didn't.*" And with one of those emotional *volte-faces* by which children bewilder us, Panty wrinkled up her face, kicked Cedric suddenly but half-heartedly on the shin, and burst into a storm of tears.

"You odious child!" he ejaculated, skipping out of her way.

Panty flung herself on her face, screamed industriously and beat the floor with her fists. "You all hate me," she sobbed. "Wicked beasts! I wish I was dead."

"Oh, la," said Cedric, "how tedious! Now, she'll have a fit or something."

Upon this scene came Paul Kentish. He limped rapidly down the aisle, seized his sister by the slack of her garments and, picking her up very much as if she was a kitten, attempted to stand her on her feet. Panty drew up her legs and hung from his grasp, in some danger, Troy felt, of suffocation. "Stop it at once, Panty," he said. "You've been a very naughty girl."

"Wait a minute," said Troy. "I don't think she has, honestly. I mean, not in the way you think. There's a muddle, I'm certain of it."

Paul relinquished his hold. Panty sat on the floor, sobbing harshly, a most desolate child.

"It's all right," said Troy, "I'll explain. You didn't do it, Panty, and you shall paint if you still want to."

"She's not allowed to come out of school," said Paul. "Caroline

596

Able will be here in a minute."

"Thank God for that," said Cedric.

Miss Able arrived almost immediately, cast a professionally breezy glance at her charge and said it was dinner-time. Panty, with a look at Troy which she was unable to interpret, got to her feet.

"Look here ..." said Troy.

"Yes?" said Miss Able cheerfully.

"About this looking-glass business. I don't think that Panty ..."

"Next time she feels like that we'll think of something much more sensible to do, won't we, Patricia?"

"Yes, but I don't think she did it."

"We're getting very good at just facing up to these funny old things we do when we're silly, aren't we, Patricia? It's best just to find out why and then forget about them."

"But ..."

"Dinner!" cried Miss Able brightly and firmly. She removed the child without any great ado.

"Dearest Mrs. Alleyn," said Cedric, waving his hands. "Why are you so sure Panty is not the author of the insult on the Old Person's mirror?"

"Has she ever called him 'Grandfather'?"

"Well, no," said Paul. "No, actually she hasn't."

"And what's more ..." Troy stopped short. Cedric had moved to her painting table. He had taken up a piece of rag and was using it to clean a finger-nail. Only then did Troy realize that the first finger of the right hand he had waved at her had been stained dark crimson under the nail.

He caught her eye and dropped the rag.

"Such a Paul Pry!" he said. "Dipping my fingers in your paint." But there had been no dark crimson laid out on her palette. "Well," said Cedric shrilly, "shall we lunch?"

III

By the light of her flash-lamp Troy was examining the stair rail in her tower. The paint had not been cleaned away and was now in the condition known as tacky. She could see clearly the mark left by her own hand. Above this, the paint was untouched. It had not been squeezed out and left, but brushed over the surface. At one point only, on the stone wall above the rail, someone had left the faint red print of two fingers. "How Rory would laugh at me," she thought, peering at them. They were small, but not small enough, she thought, to have been made by a child. Could one of the maids have touched the rail and then the wall? But beyond the mark left by her own grip there were no other prints on the rail. "Rory," she thought, "would take photographs, but how could one ever get anything from these things? They're all broken up by the rough surface. I couldn't even make a drawing of them." She was about to move away when the light from her torch fell on an object that seemed to be wedged in the gap between a step and the stone wall. Looking more closely she discovered it to be one of her own brushes. She worked it out, and found that the bristles were thick with half-dry Rose Madder.

She went down to the half-landing. There was the door that she had fancied she heard closing last night when she went to bed. It was not quite shut now and she gave it a tentative shove. It swung inwards, and Troy was confronted with a Victorian bathroom.

"Well," she thought crossly, remembering her long tramp that morning in search of a bath, "Fenella might have told me I'd got one of my own."

She had dirtied her fingers on the brush and went in to wash them. The soap in the marble hand-basin was already stained with Rose Madder. "This is a mad-house," thought Troy.

IV

Sir Henry posed for an hour that afternoon. The next morning, Sunday, was marked by a massive attendance of the entire family (with Troy) at Ancreton church. In the afternoon, however, he gave her an hour. Troy had decided to go straight for the head. She had laid in a general scheme for her work, an exciting affair of wet shadows and sharp accents. This could be completed without him. She was painting well. The touch of flamboyancy that she had dreaded was absent. She had returned often to the play. Its threat of horror was now a factor in her approach to her work. She was strongly aware of that sense of a directive power which comes only when all is well with painters. With any luck, she thought, I'll be able to say: "Did the fool that is me, make this?"

At the fourth sitting, Sir Henry returning perhaps to some bygone performance, broke the silence by speaking without warning the lines she had many times read:

"Light thickens, and the crow
Makes wing to the rooky wood ..."

He startled Troy so much that her hand jerked and she waited
motionless until he had finished the speech, resenting the genuine
twist of apprehension that had shaken her. She could find nothing
to say in response to this unexpected and oddly impersonal
performance, but she had the feeling that the old man knew very
well how much it had moved her.

After a moment she returned to her work and still it went well.
Troy was a deliberate painter, but the head grew with almost
frightening rapidity. In an hour she knew that she must not touch
it again. She was suddenly exhausted. "I think we'll stop for
today," she said, and again felt that he was not surprised.

Instead of going away, he came down into the front of the
theatre and looked at what she had done. She had that feeling of
gratitude to her subject that sometimes follows a sitting that has
gone well, but she did not want him to speak of the portrait and
began hurriedly to talk of Panty.

"She's doing a most spirited painting of red cows and a green
aeroplane."

"T'uh!" said Sir Henry on a melancholy note.

"She wants to show it to you herself."

"I have been deeply hurt," said Sir Henry, "by Patricia.
Deeply hurt."

"Do you mean," said Troy uncomfortably, "because of
something she's supposed to have written on—on your looking-
glass?"

"Supposed! The thing was flagrant. Not only that, but she
opened the drawers of my dressing-table and pulled out my
papers. I may tell you, that if she were capable of reading the two
documents that she found there, she would perhaps feel some
misgivings. I may tell you that they closely concerned herself, and
that if there are any more of these damnable tricks——" He
paused and scowled portentously. "Well, we shall see. We shall
see. Let her mother realize that I cannot endure for ever. And my
cat!" he exclaimed. "She has made a fool of my cat. There are still
marks of grease-paint in his whiskers," said Sir Henry angrily.
"Butter has not altogether removed them. As for the insult to
me——"

"But I'm sure she didn't. I was here when they scolded her

599

about it. Honestly, I'm sure she knew nothing whatever about it."

"T'uh!"

"No, but really——" Should she say anything about the dark red stain under Cedric's finger-nail? No, she'd meddled enough. She went on quickly: "Panty brags about her naughtiness. She's told me about all her practical jokes. She never calls you grandfather and I happen to know she spells it 'farther,' because she showed me a story she had written, and the word occurs frequently. I'm sure Panty's too fond of you," Troy continued, wondering if she spoke the truth, "to do anything so silly and unkind."

"I've loved that child," said Sir Henry with the appallingly rich display of sentiment so readily commanded by the Ancreds, "as if she was my own. My little Best-Beloved, I've always called her. I've never made any secret of my preference. After I'm Gone," he went on to Troy's embarrassment, "she would have known—however." He sighed windily. Troy could think of nothing to say and cleaned her palette. The light from the single uncovered window had faded. Sir Henry had switched off the stage lamps and the little theatre was now filled with shadows. A draught somewhere in the borders caused them to move uneasily and a rope-end tapped against the canvas backcloth.

"Do you know anything about embalming?" Sir Henry asked in his deepest voice. Troy jumped.

"No, indeed," she said.

"I have studied the subject," said Sir Henry, "deeply."

"Oddly enough," said Troy after a pause, "I did look at that queer little book in the drawing-room. The one in the glass case."

"Ah, yes. It belonged to my ancestor who rebuilt Ancreton. He himself was embalmed and his fathers before him. It has been the custom with the Ancreds. The family vault," he rambled on depressingly, "is remarkable for that reason. If I lie there—the Nation may have other wishes: it is not for me to speculate—but if I lie there, it will be after their fashion. I have given explicit directions."

"I *do* wish," Troy thought, "*how* I do wish he wouldn't go on like this." She made a small ambiguous murmuring.

"Ah, well!" said Sir Henry heavily and began to move away. He paused before mounting the steps up to the stage. Troy thought that he was on the edge of some further confidence, and hoped that it would be of a more cheerful character.

"What," said Sir Henry, "is your view on the matter of

600

marriage between first cousins?"

"I—really, I don't know," Troy replied, furiously collecting her wits. "I fancy I've heard that modern medical opinion doesn't condemn it. But I really haven't the smallest knowledge——"

"I am against it," he said loudly. "I cannot approve. Look at the Hapsburgs! The House of Spain! The Romanoffs!" His voice died away in an inarticulate rumble.

Hoping to divert his attention Troy began: "Panty——"

"Hah!" said Sir Henry. "These doctors don't know anything. Patricia's scalp! A common childish ailment, and Withers, having pottered about with it for weeks without doing any good, is now going to dose the child with a depilatory. Disgusting! I have spoken to the child's mother, but I'd have done better to hold my tongue. Who," Sir Henry demanded, "pays any attention to the old man? Nobody. Ours is an Ancient House, Mrs. Alleyn. We have borne arms since my ancestor, the Sieur d'Ancred, fought beside the Conqueror. And before that. Before that. A proud house. Perhaps in my own humble way I have not disgraced it. But what will happen when I am Gone? I look for my Heir and what do I find? A Thing! An emasculated Popinjay!"

He evidently expected some reply to this pronouncement on Cedric, but Troy was quite unable to think of one.

"The last of the Ancreds!" he said, glaring at her. "A family that came in with the Conqueror to go out with a——"

"But," said Troy, "he may marry and ..."

"And have kittens! P'shaw!"

"Perhaps Mr. Thomas Ancred ..."

"Old Tommy! No! I've talked to old Tommy. He doesn't see it. He'll die a bachelor. And Claude's wife is past it. Well, it was my hope to know the line was secure before I went. I shan't."

"But, bless my soul," said Troy, "you're taking far too gloomy a view of all this. There's not much wrong with a man who can pose for an hour with a helmet weighing half a hundredweight on his head. You may see all sorts of exciting things happen."

It was astonishing, it was almost alarming, to see how promptly he squared his shoulders, how quickly gallantry made its reappearance. "Do you think so?" he said, and Troy noticed how his hand went to his cloak, giving it an adroit hitch. "Well, perhaps, after all, you're right. Clever lady! Yes, yes. I *may* see something exciting and what's more—" he paused and gave a very queer little giggle—"what's more, my dear, so may other people."

Troy was never to know if Sir Henry would have elaborated on this strange prophecy, as at that moment a side door in the auditorium was flung open and Miss Orrincourt burst into the little theatre.

"Noddy!" she shouted angrily. "You've got to come. Get out of that funny costume and protect me. I've had as much of your bloody family as I can stand. It's them or me. Now!"

She strode down the aisle and confronted him, her hands on her hips, a virago.

Sir Henry eyed her with more apprehension, Troy thought, than astonishment, and began a placatory rumbling.

"No you don't," she said. "Come off it and *do* something. They're in the library, sitting round a table. Plotting against me. I walked in, and there was Pauline giving an imitation of a cat-fight and telling them how I'd have to be got rid of."

"My dear, please, I can't allow ... Surely you're mistaken."

"Am I dopey? I tell you I *heard* her. They're all against me. I warned you before and I'm warning you again and it's the last time. They're going to frame me. I know what I'm talking about. It's a frame-up. I tell you they've got me all jittery, Noddy. I can't stand it. You can either come and tell them where they get off or it's thanks for the buggy-ride and me for Town in the morning."

He looked at her disconsolately, hesitated, and took her by the elbow. Her mouth drooped, she gazed at him dolorously. "It's lonely here, Noddy," she said. "Noddy, I'm scared."

It was strange to watch the expression of extreme tenderness that this instantly evoked; strange, and to Troy, painfully touching.

"Come," Sir Henry said, stooping over her in his terrifying costume. "Come along. I'll speak to these children."

V

The little theatre was on the northern corner of the East Wing. When Troy had tidied up she looked out of doors and found a wintry sun still glinting feebly on Ancreton. She felt stuffed-up with ther work. The carriage drive, sweeping downhill through stiffly naked trees, invited her. She fetched a coat and set out bareheaded. The frosty air stung her eyes with tears, the ground rang hard under her feet. Suddenly exhilarated, she began to run. Her hair lifted, cold air ran over her scalp and her ears burned icily. "How ridiculous to run and feel happy," thought Troy, breathless.

And slowing down, she began to make plans. She would leave the head. In two days, perhaps, it would be dry. Tomorrow, the hands and their surrounding drape, and, when he had gone, another hour or so through the background. Touch after touch and for each one the mustering of thought and muscle and the inward remembrance of the schme.

The drive curved down between banks of dead leaves, and, overhead, frozen branches rattled in a brief visitation of wind, and she thought: "I'm walking under the scaffolding of summer." There, beneath her, were the gates. The sun had gone, and already fields of mist had begun to rise from the hollows. "As far as the gates," thought Troy, "and then back up the terraces." She heard the sound of hooves behind her in the woods and the faint rumbling of wheels. Out of the trees came the governess-cart and Rosinante, and there, gloved and furred and apparently recovered from her fury, sat Miss Orrincourt, flapping the reins.

Troy waited for her and she pulled up. "I'm going to the village," she said. "Do you want to come? Do, like a sweet, because I've got to go to the chemist, and this brute might walk away if nobody watched it."

Troy got in. "Can you drive?" said Miss Orrincourt. "Do, like a ducks. I hate it." She handed the reins to Troy and at once groped among her magnificent furs for her cigarette case. "I got the willies up there," she continued. "They've all gone out to dinner at the next-door morgue. Well, next door! It's God knows how far away. Cedric and Paul and old Pauline. What a bunch! With their tails *well* down, dear. Well, I mean to say, you saw how upset I was, didn't you? So did Noddy." She giggled. "Look, dear, you should have seen him. With that tin toque on his head and everything. Made the big entrance into the library and called them for everything: 'This lady,' he says, 'is my guest and you'll be good enough to remember it.' And quite a lot more. Was I tickled! Pauline and Milly looking blue murder and poor little Cedric bleating and waving his hands. He made them apologise. Oh, well," she said, with a sigh, "it was something happening anyway. That's the worst of life in this dump. Nothing ever happens. Nothing to do and all day to do it in. God, what a flop! If anybody'd told me a month ago I'd be that fed up I'd get round to crawling about the place in a prehistoric prop this I'd have thought they'd gone hay-wire. Oh, well, I suppose it'd have been worse in the army."

"Were you ever in the army?"

"I'm delicate," said Miss Orrincourt with an air of satisfaction. "Bronchial asthma. I was fixed up with E.N.S.A. but my chest began a rival show. The boys in the orchestra said they couldn't hear themselves play. So I got out. I got an understudy at the Unicorn. It was that West End you barked your shins on the ice. Then," said Miss Orrincourt simply, "Noddy noticed me."

"Was that an improvement?" asked Troy.

"Wouldn't you have thought so? I mean, ask yourself. Well, you know. A man in his position. Top of the tree. Mind, I think he's sweet. I'm crazy about him, in a way. But I've got to look after myself, haven't I? If you don't look after yourself in this old world nobody's going to look after you. Well, between you and I, Mrs. Alleyn, things were a bit tricky. Till yesterday. Look, a girl doesn't stick it out in an atmosphere like this, unless there's a future in it, does she? Not if she's still conscious, she doesn't."

Miss Orrincourt inhaled deeply and then made a petulant little sound. "Well, I *am* fed up," she said as if Troy had offered some word of criticism. "I don't say he hasn't given me things. This coat's rather nice, don't you think? It belonged to a lady who was in the Wrens. I saw it advertised. She'd never worn it. Two hundred and dirt cheap, really."

They jogged on in a silence broken only by the clop of Rosinante's hooves. There was the little railway Halt and there, beyond a curve in the low hills, the roofs of Ancreton village.

"Well, I mean to say," said Miss Orrincourt, "when I fixed up with Noddy to come here I didn't know what I was letting myself in for. I'll say I didn't! Well, *you* know. On the surface it looked like a win. It's high up, and my doctor says my chest ought to be high up, and there wasn't much doing in the business. My voice isn't so hot, and I haven't got the wind for dancing like I had, and the 'legitimate' gives me a pain in the neck. So what have you?"

Stumped for an answer, as she had so often been since her arrival at Ancreton, Troy said: "I suppose the country does feel a bit queer when you're used to bricks and mortar."

"It feels, to be frank, like death warmed up. Not that I don't say you could do something with that Jack's-come-home up there. You know. Week-end parties, with the old bunch coming down and all the fun and games. And no Ancreds. Well, I wouldn't mind Ceddie. He's one-of-those, of course, but I always think they're good mixers in their own way. I've got it all worked out. Something to do, isn't it, making plans? It may come up in

604

the lift one of these days; you never know. But no Ancreds when I throw a party in the Baronial Hall. You bet, no Ancreds."

"Sir Henry?" Troy ventured.

"Well," said Miss Orrincourt, "I was thinking of later on, if you know what I mean."

"Good Lord!" Troy ejaculated involuntarily.

"Mind, as I say, I'm fond of Noddy. But it's a funny old world, and there you have it. I must say it's nice having someone to talk to. Someone who isn't an Ancred. I can't exactly *confide* in Ceddie, because he's the heir, and he mightn't quite see things my way."

"Possibly not."

"No. Although he's quite nice to me." The thin voice hardened. "And, don't you worry, I know why," Miss Orrincourt added. "He's stuck for cash, silly kid, and he wants me to use my influence. He'd got the burns on his doorstep when the jitterbugs cleaned up his place, and then he went to the Jews and now he doesn't know where to go. He's scared to turn up at the flat. He'll have to wait till I'm fixed up myself. Then we'll see. I don't mind much," she said, moving restlessly, "which way it goes, so long as I'm fixed up."

They faced each other across the bucket-cart. Troy looked at her companion's beautifully painted face. Behind it stood wraithlike trees, motionless, threaded with mist. It might have been a sharp mask, by a surrealist, hung on that darkling background, thought Troy.

A tiny rhythmic sound grew out of the freezing air. "I can hear a cat mewing somewhere," said Troy, pulling Rosinante up.

"That's a good one!" said Miss Orrincourt, laughing and coughing. "A cat mewing! It's my chest, dear. This damn night air's catching me. Can you hurry that brute up?"

Troy stirred him up, and presently they clopped sedately down the one street of Ancreton village and pulled up outside a small chemist's shop, that seemed also to be a sort of general store.

"Shall I get whatever it is?" Troy offered.

"All right. I don't suppose there's anything worth looking at in the shop. No perfume. Thanks, dear. It's the stuff for the kid's ringworm. The doctor's ordered it. It's meant to be ready."

The elderly rubicund chemist handed Troy two bottles tied together. One had an envelope attached. "For the children up at the Manor? he said. "Quite so. And the small bottle is for Sir Henry." When she had climbed back into the governess-cart, she

605

found that he had followed her and stood blinking on the pavement. "They're labelled," he said fussily. "If you'd be good enough to point out the enclosed instructions. The dosage varies, you know. It's determined by the patient's weight. Dr. Withers particularly asked me to draw Miss Able's attention. Quite an unusual prescription, actually. Thallium acetate. Yes. Both labelled. Thank you. One should exercise care ... So sorry we're out of wrapping paper. Good evening." He gave a little whooping chuckle and darted back into his shop. Troy was about to turn Rosinante when Miss Orrincourt, asking her to wait, scrambled out and went into the shop, returning in a few minutes with a bulge in her pocket.

"Just something that caught my eye," she said. "Righty ho, dear! Home John and don't spare the horses." On their return journey she exclaimed repeatedly on the subject of the children's ringworm. She held the collar of her fur coat across her mouth and her voice sounded unreal behind it. "Is it tough, or is it tough? That poor kid Panty. All over her head, and her hair's her one beauty, you might say."

"You and Panty are rather by way of being friends, aren't you?" said Troy.

"She's a terrible kiddy, really. You know. The things she does! Well! Scribbling across Noddy's mirror with a lake-liner and such a common way to put it, whatever she thought. A few more little cracks like that and she'll cook her goose if she only knew it. The mother's wild about it, naturally. Did you know the kid's favourite in the Will? She won't hold that rôle down much longer if she lets her sense of comedy run away with her. And then the way she put that paint on your banister! I call it the limit."

Troy stared at her. "How did you know about that?"

A spasm of coughing shook her companion. "I was crazy," gasped the muffled voice, "to come out in this lousy fog. Might have known. Pardon me, like a ducks, if I don't talk."

"Did Panty tell you?" Troy persisted. "*I* haven't told anyone. Did she actually tell you she did it?"

A violent paroxysm prevented Miss Orrincourt from speaking, but with her lovely and enormous eyes fixed on Troy and still clasping her fur collar over the lower part of her face, she nodded three times.

"I'd never have believed it," said Troy slowly. "Never."

Miss Orrincourt's shoulders quivered and shook. "For all the world," Troy thought suddenly, "as if she was laughing."

CHAPTER VI

Paint

I

It was on that same night that there was an open flaring row between Paul and Fenella on the one hand and Sir Henry Ancred on the other. It occurred at the climax of a game of backgammon between Troy and Sir Henry. He had insisted upon teaching her this complicated and maddening game. She would have enjoyed it more if she hadn't discovered very early in the contest that her opponent disliked losing so intensely that her own run of beginner's luck had plunged him into the profoundest melancholy. He had attempted to explain to her the chances of the possible com binations of a pair of dice, adding, with some complacency, that he himself had completely mastered this problem. Troy had found his explanation utterly incomprehensible, and began by happily moving her pieces with more regard for the pattern they made on the board than for her chances of winning the game. She met with uncanny success. Sir Henry, who had entered the game with an air of gallantry, finding pretty frequent occasions to pat Troy's fingers, became thoughtful, then pained, and at last gloomy. The members of his family, aware of his mortification, watched in nervous silence. Troy moved with reckless abandon. Sir Henry savagely rattled his dice. Greatly to her relief the tide turned. She gave herself a "blot" and looked up, to find Fenella and Paul watching her with an extraordinary expression of anxiety. Sir Henry prospered and soon began to "bear", Paul and Fenella exchanged a glance. Fenella nodded and turned pale.

"Aha!" cried Sir Henry in triumph. "The winning throw, I think! The winning throw!"

He cast himself back in his chair, gazed about him and laughed

607

delightedly. It was at this juncture that Paul, who was standing on the hearthrug with Fenella, put his arm round her and kissed her with extreme heartiness and unmistakable intention. "Fenella and I," he said loudly, "are going to be married."

There followed an electrified silence, lasting perhaps for ten seconds.

Sir Henry then picked up the backgammon board and threw it a surprising distance across the drawing-room.

"And temper," Paul added, turning rather pale, "never got anybody anywhere."

Miss Orrincourt gave a long whistle. Millamant dropped on her knees and began to pick up backgammon pieces.

Pauline Kentish, gazing with something like terror at her son, gabbled incoherently: "No, darling! No, please! No, Paul, don't be naughty. No! Fenella!"

Cedric, his mouth open, his eyes glistening, rubbed his hands and made his crowing noise. But he, too, looked frightened.

And all the Ancreds, out of the corners of their eyes, watched Sir Henry.

He was the first man Troy had ever seen completely given over to rage. She found the exhibition formidable. If he had not been an old man his passion would have been less disquieting because less pitiable. Old lips, shaking with rage; old eyes, whose fierceness was glazed by rheum; old hands, that jerked in unco-ordinated fury; these were intolerable manifestations of emotion.

Troy got up and attempted an inconspicuous retreat to the door.

"*Come back*," said her host violently. Troy returned. "Hear how these people conspire to humiliate me. Come back, I say." Troy sat on the nearest chair.

"Papa!" whispered Pauline, weaving her hands together, and "Papa!" Millamant echoed, fumbling with the dice. "Please! So bad for you. Upsetting yourself! Please!"

He silenced them with a gesture and struggled to his feet. Paul, holding Fenella by the arm, waited until his grandfather stood before him and then said rapidly: "We're sorry to make a scene. I persuaded Fen that this was the only way to handle the business. We've discussed it with you in private, Grandfather, and you've told us what you feel about it. We don't agree. It's our show, after all, and we've made up our minds. We could have gone off and got married without saying anything about it, but neither of us

608

wanted to do that. So we thought——"

"We thought," said Fenella rather breathlessly, "we'd just make a general announcement."

"Because," Paul added, "I've sent one already to the papers and we wanted to tell you before you read it."

"But, Paul darling——" his mother faintly began.

"You damned young puppy," Sir Henry roared out, "what do you mean by standing up with that god-damned conceited look on your face and talking poppycock to ME?"

"Aunt Pauline," said Fenella, "I'm sorry if you're not pleased, but——"

"Ssh!" said Pauline.

"Mother is pleased," said Paul. "Aren't you, Mother?"

"Ssh!" Pauline repeated distractedly.

"Be silent!" Sir Henry shouted. He was now in the centre of the hearth-rug. It seemed to Troy that his first violence was being rapidly transmuted into something more histrionic and much less disturbing. He rested an elbow on the mantelpiece. He pressed two fingers and a thumb against his eyelids, removed his hand slowly, kept his eyes closed, frowned as if in pain, and finally sighed deeply and opened his eyes very wide indeed.

"I'm an old fellow," he said in a broken voice. "An old fellow. It's easy to hurt me. Very easy. You have dealt me a shrewd blow. Never mind. Let me suffer. Why not? It won't be for long. Not for long, now."

"Papa, *dearest*," cried Pauline, sweeping up to him and clasping her hands. "You make us utterly miserable. Don't speak like that, don't. Not for the world would my boy cause you a moment's unhappiness. Let me talk quietly to these children. Papa, I implore you."

"This," a voice whispered in Troy's ear, "is perfect Pinero." She jumped violently. Cedric had slipped round behind his agitated relations and now leant over the back of her chair, "She played the name part, you know, in a revival of *The Second Mrs. Tanqueray*."

"It's no use, Pauline. Let them go. They knew my wishes. They have chosen the cruellest way. Let them," said Sir Henry with relish, "dree their weird."

"Thank you, Grandfather," said Fenella brightly, but with a shake in her voice. "It's our weird and we shall be delighted to dree it."

Sir Henry's face turned an uneven crimson. "This is insufferable," he shouted, and his teeth, unable to cope with the violence of his diction, leapt precariously from their anchorage and were clamped angrily home. Fenella giggled nervously. "You are under age," Sir Henry pronounced suddenly. "Under age, both of you. Pauline, if you have the smallest regard for your old father's wishes, you will forbid this lunacy. I shall speak to your mother, miss. I shall cable to your father."

"Mother won't mind," said Fenella.

"You know well, you know perfectly well, why I cannot countenance this nonsense."

"You think, don't you, Grandfather," said Fenella, "that because we're cousins we'll have loopy young. Well, we've asked about that and it's most unlikely. Modern medical opinion——"

"Be silent! At least let some semblance of decency——"

"I *won't* be silent," said Fenella, performing with dexterity the feat known by actors as topping the other man's lines. "And if we're to talk about decency, Grandfather, I should have thought it was a damn sight more decent for two people who are young and in love to say they're going to marry each other than for an old man to make an exhibition of himself——"

"*Fenella!*" shouted Pauline and Millamant in unison.

"——doting on a peroxide blonde fifty years younger than himself, and a brazen gold-digger into the bargain."

Fenella then burst into tears and ran out of the room, followed rigidly by Paul.

Troy, who had once more determined to make her escape, heard Fenella weeping stormily outside the door and stayed where she was. The remaining Ancreds were all talking at once. Sir Henry beat his fist on the mantelpiece until the ornaments danced again, and roared out: "My God, I'll not have her under my roof another hour! My God——!" Millamant and Pauline, on either side of him like a distracted chorus, wrung their hands and uttered plaintive cries. Cedric chattered noisily behind the sofa, where Miss Orrincourt still lay. It was she who put a stop to this ensemble by rising and confronting them with her hands on her hips.

"I am not remaining here," said Miss Orrincourt piercingly, "to be insulted. Remarks have been passed in this room that no self-respecting girl in my delicate position can be expected to endure. Noddy!"

Sir Henry, who had continued his beating of the mantelpiece during this speech, stopped short and looked at her with a kind of nervousness.

"Since announcements," said Miss Orrincourt, "are in the air, Noddy, haven't we got something to say ourselves in that line? Or," she added ominously, "have we?"

She looked lovely standing there. It was an entirely plastic loveliness, an affair of colour and shape, of line and texture. It was so complete in its kind, Troy thought, that to bring a consideration of character or vulgarity to bear upon it would be to labour at an irrelevant synthesis. In her kind she was perfect. "What about it, Noddy?" she said.

Sir Henry stared at her, pulled down his waistcoat, straightened his back and took her hand. "Whenever you wish, my dear," he said, "whenever you wish."

Pauline and Millamant fell back from them, Cedric drew in his breath and touched his moustache. Troy saw, with astonishment, that his hand was shaking.

"I had intended," Sir Henry said, "to make this announcement at The Birthday. Now, however, when I realize only too bitterly that my family cares little, cares nothing for my happiness" ("*Papa!*" Pauline wailed), "I turn, in my hour of sorrow, to One who does Care."

"Uh-huh!" Miss Orrincourt assented. "But keep it sunny-side-up, Petty-pie."

Sir Henry, less disconcerted than one would have thought possible by this interjection, gathered himself together.

"This lady," he said loudly, "has graciously consented to become my wife."

Considering the intensity of their emotions, Troy felt that the Ancreds really behaved with great aplomb. It was true that Pauline and Millamant were, for a moment, blankly silent, but Cedric almost immediately ran out from cover and seized his grandfather by the hand.

"Dearest Grandpapa—couldn't be more delighted—too marvellous. Sonia, *darling*," he babbled, "*such* fun," and he kissed her.

"Well, Papa," said Millamant, following her son's lead but not kissing Miss Orrincourt, "we can't say that it's altogether a surprise, can we? I'm sure we all hope you'll be very happy."

Pauline was more emotional. "Dearest," she said, taking her

611

father's hands and gazing with wet eyes into his face, "dearest, dearest Papa. Please, please believe my only desire is for your happiness."

Sir Henry inclined his head. Pauline made an upward pounce at his moustache. "Oh, Pauline," he said with an air of tragic resignation, "I have been wounded, Pauline! Deeply wounded!"

"No," cried Pauline. "No!"

"Yes," sighed Sir Henry. "Yes."

Pauline turned blindly from him and offered her hand to Miss Orrincourt. "Be good to him," she said brokenly. "It's all we ask. Be good to him."

With an eloquent gesture, Sir Henry turned aside, crossed the room, and flung himself into a hitherto unoccupied armchair.

It made a loud and extremely vulgar noise.

Sir Henry, scarlet in the face, leapt to his feet and snatched up the loose cushioned seat. He exposed a still partially inflated bladder-like object, across which was printed a legend, "The Raspberry. Makes your Party go off with a Bang." He seized it, and again, through some concealed orifice, it emitted its dreadful sound. He hurled it accurately into the fire and the stench of burning rubber filled the room.

"Well, I mean to say," said Miss Orrincourt, "fun's fun, but I think that kid's getting common in her ways."

Sir Henry walked in silence to the door, where, inevitably, he turned to deliver an exit line. "Millamant," he said, "in the morning you will be good enough to send for my solicitor."

The door banged. After a minute's complete silence Troy was at last able to escape from the drawing-room.

II

Troy was not much surprised in the morning to learn that Sir Henry was too unwell to appear, though he hoped in the afternoon to resume the usual sitting. A note on her early tea-tray informed her that Cedric would be delighted to pose in the costume if this would be of any service. She thought it might. There was the scarlet cloak to be attended to. She had half-expected a disintegration of the family forces, at least the disappearance, possibly in opposite directions, of Fenella and Paul. She had yet to learn of the Ancreds' resilience in inter-tribal warfare. At breakfast they both appeared—Fenella, white and

612

silent; Paul, red and silent. Pauline arrived a little later. Her attitude to her son suggested that he was ill of some not entirely respectable disease. With Fenella she adopted an air of pained antipathy and would scarcely speak to her. Millamant presided. She was less jolly than usual, but behind her anxiety, if she was indeed anxious, Troy detected a hint of complacency. There was more than a touch of condolence in her manner towards her sister-in-law, and this, Troy felt, Pauline deeply resented.

"Well, Milly," said Pauline after a long silence, "do you propose to continue your rôle under new management?"

"I'm always rather lost, Pauline, when you adopt theatrical figures of speech."

"Are you going to house-keep, then, for the new châtelaine?"

"I hardly expect to do so."

"Poor Milly," said Pauline. "It's going to be difficult for you, I'm afraid."

"I don't think so. Cedric and I have always thought we'd like to have a little *pied-à-terre* together in London."

"Yes," Pauline agreed much too readily, "Cedric will have to draw in his horns a bit too, one supposes."

"Perhaps Paul and Fenella would consider allowing me to house-keep for them," said Millamant, with her first laugh that morning. And with an air of genuine interest she turned to them. "How *are* you going to manage, both of you?" she asked.

"Like any other husband and wife without money," said Fenella. "Paul's got his pension and I've got my profession. We'll both get jobs."

"Oh, well," said Millamant comfortably, "perhaps after all, your grandfather——"

"We don't want Grandfather to do anything, Aunt Milly," said Paul quickly. "He wouldn't anyway, of course, but we don't want him to."

"Dearest!" said his mother. "So hard! So bitter! I don't know you, Paul, when you talk like that. Something"—she glanced with extraordinary distaste at Fenella—"has changed you so dreadfully."

"Where," asked Millamant brightly, "is Panty?"

"Where should she be if not in school?" Pauline countered with dignity. "She is not in the habit of breakfasting with us, Milly."

"Well, you never know," said Millamant. "She seems to get about quite a lot, doesn't she? And, by the way, Pauline, I've a bone to pick with Panty myself. Someone has interfered with My Work. A large section of embroidery has been deliberately unpicked. I'd left it in the drawing-room and——"

"Panty never goes there," cried Pauline.

"Well, I don't know about that. She must, for instance, have been in the drawing-room last evening during dinner."

"Why?"

"Because Sonia, as I suppose we must call her, says she sat in that chair before dinner, Pauline. She says it was perfectly normal."

"I can't help that, Milly. Panty did not come into the drawing-room last night at dinner-time for the very good reason that she and the other children were given their medicine then and sent early to bed. You told me yourself, Milly, that Miss Able found the medicine in the flower-room and took it straight in for Dr. Withers to give the children."

"Oh, yes," said Millamant. "Would you believe it, the extraordinary Sonia didn't trouble to take it in to Miss Able, or to give Papa's bottle to me. She merely went to the flower-room, where it seems," said Millamant with a sniff, "orchids had been brought in for her; and dumped the lot. Miss Able hunted everywhere before she found it, and so did I."

"T'uh," said Pauline.

"All the same," said Paul. "I don't mind betting that Panty——"

"It has yet to be proved," Pauline interrupted with spirit rather than conviction, "that Panty had anything to do with—with——"

"With the Raspberry!" said Paul, grinning. "Mother, of course she did."

"I have reason to believe——" Pauline began.

"No, really, Mother. It's Panty all over. Look at her record."

"Where did she get it? I've never given her such a thing."

"Another kid, I suppose, if she didn't buy it. I've seen them in one of the village shops; haven't you, Fen? I remember thinking to myself that they ought to have been sent to a rubber dump."

"I've had a little talk with Panty," said Panty's mother obstinately, "and she promised me on her word of honour she didn't know anything about it. I know when that child is speaking the truth, Milly. A mother always knows."

"*Honestly*, Mother!" said Paul.

"I don't care what anyone says——" Pauline began, but was interrupted by the entrance of Cedric, very smooth and elegant, and with more than a touch of smugness in his general aspect.

"Good morning, dearest Mrs. Alleyn. Good morning, my sweets," he said. "Planning how to lay out the proverbial shilling to advantage, Paul dear? I've been so excited thinking up a scheme for a double wedding. It's a teeny bit involved. The Old Person, you see, in Uncle Claude's absence, must give Fenella away and then whisk over to the other side as First Bridegroom. I thought I might be joint Best Man and Paul could double Second Bridegroom and Sonia's papa. It's like a rather intricate ballet. Uncle Thomas is to be a page and Panty a flower-girl, which will give her wonderful opportunities for throwing things. And you, dearest Mama, and all the aunts shall be Dowagers-in-Waiting. I've invented such marvellously intimidating gowns for you."

"Don't be naughty," said Millamant.

"No, but truly," Cedric went on, bringing his plate to the table.

"I *do* feel, you two, that you've managed your affairs the least bit clumsily."

"It's not given to all of us," said Paul dryly, "to be quite as nimble after the main chance as you."

"Well, I do rather flatter myself I've exhibited a pretty turn of low cunning," Cedric agreed readily. "Sonia's going to let me do her trousseau, and the Old Person said that I at least showed some family feeling. But I'm afraid, dearest Auntie Pauline, that Panty has lost ground almost irretrievably. Such a very robust sense of comedy."

"I have already told your mother, Cedric, that I have reason to believe that Panty was not responsible for that incident."

"Oh, Gracious!" said Cedric. "*So* touching. Such faith."

"Or for the writing on your grandfather's looking-glass."

Cedric made one of his ingratiating wriggles at Troy. "Panty has another champion," he said.

Pauline turned quickly to Troy, who, with a sense of stepping from the stalls up to the stage, murmured: "I didn't think Panty wrote on the glass. I thought her protests rang true."

"There!" cried Pauline emotionally, and stretched out her hand to Troy. "There, all of you! *Thank* you, Mrs. Alleyn. *Someone* has faith in *my poor old Panty*."

But Troy's faith in Panty Kentish, already slightly undermined, was to suffer a further jolt.

She went from the dining-room to the little theatre. Her canvas was leaning, face to the wall, where she had left it. She dragged it out, tipped it up on one corner, set it on the lowered tray of her easel and stepped back to look at it.

Across the nose and eyes of the completed head somebody had drawn in black paint an enormous pair of spectacles.

III

For perhaps five seconds alternate lumps of ice and red-hot coal chased each other down her spine and round her stomach. She then touched the face. It was hard dry. The black spectacles were still wet. With a sense of relief that was so violent that it came upon her like an attack of nausea, Troy dipped a rag in oil and gingerly wiped off the addition. She then sat down and pressed her shaking hands together. Not a stain, not a blur on the bluish shadows that she had twisted under the eyes, not a trace of dirt across the strange pink veil that was the flesh under his frontal bone. "Oh, Golly!" Troy whispered. "Oh, Golly! Thank God! Oh, Golly!"

"Good morning," said Panty, coming in by the side door. "I'm allowed to do another picture. I want some more board and lots more paint. Look, I've finished the cows and the aeroplane. Aren't they good?"

She dumped her board on the floor against the foot of the easel, and, with a stocky imitation of Troy, fell back a pace and looked at it, her hands clasped behind her back. Her picture was of three vermilion cows in an emerald meadow. Above them, against a sky for which Panty had used neat New Blue, flew an emerald aeroplane in the act of secreting a black bomb.

"Damn good," said Panty, "isn't it?" She tore her gaze away from her picture and allowed it to rest on Troy's.

"That's good too," she said. "It's nice. It gives me a nice feeling inside. I think you paint good pictures."

"Somebody," said Troy, watching her, "thought it would be better if I put in a pair of spectacles."

"Well, they must have been pretty silly," said Panty. "Kings don't wear spectacles. That's a king."

"Whoever it was, painted them on the face."

"If anybody puts spectacles on my cows," Panty said, "I'll kill them."

616

"Who do you think could have done it?"

"I dunno," said Panty without interest. "Did Noddy?"

"I hardly think so."

"I suppose it was whoever put whatever it was on Noddy's glass. Not me, anyway. Now can I have another board and more paint? Miss Able likes me to paint."

"You may go up to my room and get yourself one of the small boards in the cupboard."

"I don't know where your room is."

Troy explained as best she could. "Oh, well," said Panty, "if I can't find it I'll just yell till somebody comes."

She stumped away to the side door. "By the way," Troy called after her, "would you know a Raspberry if you saw one?"

"You bet," said Panty with interest.

"I mean a rubber thing that makes a noise if you sit on it."

"What sort of noise?"

"Never mind," said Troy wearily. "Forget about it."

"You're mad," said Panty flatly and went out.

"If I'm not," Troy muttered, "there's somebody in this house who is."

IV

All that morning she painted solidly through the background. In the afternoon Sir Henry posed for an hour and a half with two rests. He said nothing, but sighed a great deal. Troy worked at the hands, but he was restless, and kept making small nervous movements so that she did little more than lay down the general tone and shape of them. Millamant came in just before the end of the sitting, and, with a word of apology, went to him and murmured something indistinguishable. "No, no," he said angrily. "It must be to-morrow. Ring up again and tell them so."

"He says it's very inconvenient."

"That be damned. Ring up again."

"Very well, Papa," said the obedient Millamant.

She went away, and Troy, seeing that he was growing still more restless, called an end to the sitting, telling him that Cedric had offered to pose for the cloak. He left with evident relief. Troy grunted disconsolately, scraped down the hands, and turned again to the background. It was a formalised picture of a picture. The rooky wood, a wet mass, rimmed with boldly stated strokes of her brush, struck sharply across a coldly luminous night sky. The monolithic forms in the middle distance were broadly set down as interlocking masses. Troy had dragged a giant brush down the canvas, each stroke the summing-up of painful thinking that suddenly resolved itself in form. The background was right, and the Ancreds, she reflected, would think it very queer and unfinished. All of them, except, perhaps, Cedric and Panty. She had arrived at this conclusion when on to the stage pranced Cedric himself, heavily and most unnecessarily made-up, moving with a sort of bouncing stride, and making much of his grandfather's red cloak.

"Here I am," he cried, "feeling *so* keyed up with the mantle of high tragedy across my puny shoulders. Now, what *precisely* is the pose?"

There was no need to show him, however. He swept up his drape, placed himself, and, with an expert wriggle, flung it into precisely the right sweep. Troy eyed it, and, with a sense of rising excitement, spread unctuous bands of brilliant colour across her palette.

Cedric was an admirable model. The drape was frozen in its sculptured folds. Troy worked in silence for an hour, holding her breath so often that she became quite stuffy in the nose.

"Dearest Mrs. Alleyn," said a faint voice, "I have a tiny cramp in my leg."

"Lord, I'm sorry!" said Troy.

"You've been wonderful. Do have a rest."

He came down into the auditorium, limping a little but still with an air, and stood before her canvas.

"It's so piercingly *right*," he said. "Too exciting! I mean, it really *is* theatre, and the Old Person and that devastating Bard all synthesised and made eloquent and everything. It terrifies me."

He sank into a near-by stall, first spreading his cloak over the back, and fanned himself. "I can't tell you how I've died to prattle," he went on, "all the time I was up there. This house is simply *seething* with intrigue."

Troy, who was herself rather exhausted, lit a cigarette, sat down, and eyed her work. She also listened with considerable interest to Cedric.

"First I must tell you," he began, "the Old Person has positively sent for his solicitor. Imagine! Such lobbyings and whisperings! One is reminded of Papal elections in the seventeenth century. First the marriage settlement, of course. What do you suppose darling Sonia will have laid down as the minimum? I've tried *piteously* hard to wheedle it out of her, but she's turned rather secretive and *grande dame*. But, of course, however much it is it's got to come from *somewhere*. Panty was known to be first favourite. He's left her some fabulous sum to make her a *parti* when she grows up. But we all feel her little pranks will have swept her right out of the running. So perhaps darling Sonia will have that lot. Then there's Paul and Fenella, who have undoubtedly polished themselves off. I rather *hope*," said Cedric with a modest titter and a very sharp look in his eye, "that I *may* reap something there. I *think* I'm all right, but you never know. He simply detests me, really, and the entail is quite ridiculous. Somebody broke it up or something ages ago, and I *may* only get this awful house and nothing whatever to keep it up with. Still, I really have got Sonia on my side."

He touched his moustache and pulled a small pellet of cosmetic off his eyelashes. "I made up," he explained in parentheses, "because I felt it was so essential to get the feeling of the Macsoforth *seeping* through into every fold of the mantle. And partly because it's such fun painting one's face."

He hummed a little air for a moment or two and then continued: "Thomas and Dessy and the Honourable Mrs. A. are all pouring in on Friday night. The Birthday is on Saturday, did you realize? The Old Person and the Ancient of Days will spend Sunday in bed, the one suffering from gastronomic excess, the other from his exertions as Ganymede. The family will no doubt pass the day in mutual recrimination. The general feeling is that the *pièce-de-résistance* for the Birthday will be an announcement of the new Will."

"But, good Lord——!" Troy ejaculated. Cedric talked her down.

"Almost certain, I assure you. He has always made public each new draft. He can't resist the dramatic *mise-en-scène*."

"But how often does he change his Will?"

"I've never kept count," Cedric confessed after a pause, "but on an average I should say once every two years, though for the last three years Panty has held firm as first favourite. While she was still doing baby-talk and only came here occasionally he adored her, and she, most unfortunately, was crazy about him.

619

Pauline must curse the day when she manœuvred the school to Ancreton. Last time I was *grossly* unpopular and down to the bare bones of the entail. Uncle Thomas was second to Panty with the general hope that he would marry and have a son, and I remain a celibate with Ancreton as a millstone round my poor little neck. "*Isn't* it all too tricky?"

There was scarcely a thing that Cedric did or said of which Troy did not wholeheartedly disapprove, but it was impossible to be altogether bored by him. She found herself listening quite attentively to his recital, though after a time his gloating delight in Panty's fall from grace began to irritate her.

"I still think," she said, "that Panty didn't play these tricks on her grandfather." Cedric, with extraordinary vehemence, began to protest, but Troy insisted. "I've talked to her about it. Her manner, to my mind, was conclusive. Obviously she didn't know anything about last night's affair. She'd never heard of the squeaking cushion."

"That child," Cedric announced malevolently, "is incredibly, terrifyingly subtle. She is not an Ancred for nothing. She was acting. Depend upon it, she was acting."

"I don't believe it. And what's more, she didn't know her way to my room."

Cedric, who was biting his nails, paused and stared at her. After a long pause he said: "Didn't know her way to your room? But, dearest Mrs. Alleyn, what has that got to do with it?"

It was on the tip of her tongue to relate the incident of the painted banister. She had even begun: "Well, if you promise——" And then, catching sight of his face with its full pouting mouth and pale eyes, she suddenly changed her mind. "It doesn't matter," Troy said, "it wouldn't convince you. Never mind."

"Dearest Mrs. Alleyn," Cedric tittered, pulling at his cloak, "you are mysterious. Anyone would suppose you didn't trust me."

CHAPTER VII

Fiesta

I

On Friday, a week after her arrival at Ancreton, Troy dragged her canvas out of the property room, where she now kept it locked up, and stared at it with mixed sensations of which the predominant was one of astonishment. How in the world had she managed it? Another two days would see its completion. Tomorrow night Sir Henry would lead his warring celebrants into the little theatre and she would stand awkwardly in the background while they talked about it. Would they be very disappointed? Would they see at once that the background was not the waste before Forres Castle but a theatrical cloth presenting this; that Troy had painted, not Macbeth himself, but an old actor looking backwards into his realization of the part? Would they see that the mood was one of relinquishment?

Well, the figure was completed. There were some further places she must attend to—a careful balancing stroke here and here. She was filled with a great desire that her husband should see it. It was satisfactory, Troy thought, that of the few people to whom she wished to show her work her husband came first. Perhaps this was because he said so little yet was not embarrassed by his own silence.

As the end of her work drew near her restlessness increased and her fears for their reunion. She remembered phrases spoken by other women: "The first relationship is never repeated." "We were strangers again when we met." "It wasn't the same." "It feels extraordinary. We were shy and had nothing to say to each other." Would her reunion also be inarticulate? "I've no technique," Troy thought, "to see me through. I've no marital

621

technique at all. Any native adroitness I possess has gone into my painting. But perhaps Roderick will know what to say. Shall I tell him at once about the Ancreds?"

She was cleaning her palette when Fenella ran in to say a call had come through for her from London.

It was the Assistant Commissioner at the Yard. Troy listened to him with a hammer knocking at her throat. He thought, he said with arch obscurity, that she might enjoy a run up to London on Monday. If she stayed the night, the Yard might have something of interest to show her on Tuesday morning. A police car would be coming in by way of Ancreton Halt early on Monday and would be delighted to give her a lift. "Thank you," said Troy in an unrecognisable voice. "Yes, I see. Yes, of course. Yes, very exciting. Thank you."

She fled to her room, realising as she sat breathless on her bed that she had run like a madwoman up three flights of stairs. "It's as well," she thought, "that the portrait's finished. In this frame of mind I'd be lucky if I reached Panty's form."

She began distractedly to imagine their meeting. "But I can't see his face," she thought in a panic. "I can't remember his voice. I've forgotten my husband."

She felt by turns an unreasonable urge for activity and a sense of helpless inertia. Ridiculous incidents from the Ancred repertoire flashed up in her mind. "I must remember to tell him that," she would think, and then wonder if, after all, the Ancreds in retrospect would sound funny. She remembered with a jolt that she must let Katti Bostock know about Tuesday. They had arranged for Alleyn's old servant to go to London and open the flat.

"I should have done it at once," she cried, and returned downstairs. While she waited, fuming, in a little telephone-room near the front doors, for her call to go through, she heard wheels on the drive, the sound of voices, and finally the unmistakable rumpus of arrival in the hall. A charming voice called gaily: "Milly, where are you? Come down. It's Dessy and Thomas and me. Dessy found a Colonel, and the Colonel had a car, and we've all arrived together."

"Jenetta!" Millamant's disembodied voice floated down from the gallery. Still more distantly Pauline's echoed her: "Jenetta!"

Was there an overtone of disapproval, not quite of dismay, in this greeting, Troy wondered, as she quietly shut the door?

Jenetta, the Hon. Mrs. Claude Ancred, unlike Millamant, had caught none of the overtones of her relations-in-law. She was a nice-looking woman, with a gay voice, good clothes, an intelligent face, and an air of quietly enjoying herself. Her conversation was unstressed and crisp. If she sensed internecine warfare she gave no hint of doing so, and seemed to be equally pleased with, and equally remote from, each member of that unlikely clan.

Desdemona, on the other hand, was, of all the Ancreds after Sir Henry, most obviously of the theatre. She was startlingly good-looking, of voluptuous build, and had a warm ringing voice that seemed to be perpetually uttering important lines of climax from a West-End success. She ought really, Troy thought, to be surrounded by attendant figures: a secretary, an author, an agent, perhaps a doting producer. She had an aura of richness and warmth, and a knack of causing everybody else to subscribe to the larger-than-life atmosphere in which she herself moved so easily. Her Colonel, after a drink, drove away to his lawful destination, with Dessy's magnificent thanks no doubt ringing in his ears. Troy, emerging from the telephone-room, found herself confronted by the new arrivals. She was glad to see Thomas: already she thought of him as "old Thomas", with his crest of faded hair and his bland smile. "Oh, hallo," he said, blinking at her, "so here you are! I hope your carbuncle is better."

"It's gone," said Troy.

"We're all talking about Papa's engagement," said Thomas. "This is my sister-in-law, Mrs. Claude Ancred, and this is my sister, Desdemona. Milly and Pauline are seeing about rooms. Have you painted a nice picture?"

"Not bad. Are you producing a nice play?"

"It's quite good, thank you," said Thomas primly.

"Darling Tommy," said Desdemona, "how *can* it be quite good with that woman? What were you thinking about when you cast it?"

"Well, Dessy, I told the management you wanted the part."

"I didn't want it. I could play it, but I didn't want it, thank you."

"Then everybody ought to be pleased," said Thomas mildly. "I suppose, Jenetta," he continued, "you are anxious to see Fenella and Paul. Papa's engagement has rather swamped theirs, you may feel. Are you as angry as he is about them?"

"I'm not a bit angry," she said, catching Troy's eye and smiling at her. "I'm fond of Paul and want to talk to him."

"That's all very nice," said Dessy restlessly, "but Milly says it was Paul and Fenella who exploded the bomb."

"Oh, well," said Thomas comfortably, "I expect it would have gone off anyway. Did you know Mr. Rattisbon has been sent for to make a new Will? I suppose Papa'll tell us all about it at the Birthday Dinner to-morrow. Do you expect to be cut out this time, Dessy?"

"My dear," cried his sister, sinking magnificently into the sofa and laying her arms along the back of it, "I've said so often exactly what I think of the Orrincourt that he can't possibly do anything else. I don't give a damn, Tommy. If Papa expects me to purr round congratulating them, he's never been more mistaken. I can't do it. It's been a hideous shock to me. It hurts me, *here*," she added, beating a white fist on her striking bosom. "All my respect, my love, my *ideal*—shattered." She flashed her eyes at her sister-in-law. "You think I exaggerate, Jen. You're lucky. You're not easily upset."

"Well," said Jenetta lightly, "I've yet to meet Miss Orrincourt."

"He's not your father," Dessy pointed out with emotion.

"No more he is," she agreed.

"T'uh!" said Dessy bitterly.

This conversation was interrupted by Fenella, who ran downstairs, flew across the hall, and, with an inarticulate cry, flung herself into her mother's arms.

"Now, then," said Jenetta softly, holding her daughter for a moment, "no high strikes."

"Mummy, you're not furious! Say you're not furious?"

"Do I look furious, you goat? Where's Paul?"

"In the library. Will you come? Mummy, you're Heaven. You're an angel."

"Do pipe down, darling. And what about Aunt Dessy and Uncle Thomas?"

Fenella turned to greet them. Thomas kissed her carefully. "I hope you'll be happy," he said. "It ought to be all right, really. I looked up genetics in a medical encyclopedia after I read the announcement. The chap said the issue of first cousins was generally quite normal, unless there was any marked insanity in the family which was common to both."

624

"Tommy!" said his sister. "Honestly, you *are*!"

"Well," said Jenetta Ancred, "with that assurance to fortify us, Fen, suppose you take me to see Paul."

They went off together. Millamant and Pauline came downstairs. "Such a nuisance," Millamant was saying, "I really don't quite know how to arrange it."

"If you're talking about rooms, Milly," said Desdemona, "I tell you flatly that unless something has been done about the rats I won't go into *Bracegirdle*."

"Well, but Dessy——" Pauline began.

"Has something been done about the rats?"

"Barker," said Millamant unhappily, "has lost the arsenic. I think he did Miss Orrincourt's rooms some time ago, and after that the tin disappeared."

"Good God!" said Thomas quietly.

"Pity he didn't put some in her tooth-glass," said Desdemona vindictively.

"What about *Ellen Terry*?"

"I was putting Jenetta into *Terry*."

"Come into *Bernhardt* with me, Dess," Pauline suggested richly. "I'd love to have you. We can talk. Let's."

"The only thing against that," said Millamant, knitting her brows, "is that since Papa had all those large Jacobean pieces put in *Bernhardt*, there really isn't anywhere for a second bed. I can put one in my room, Desdemona. I wondered if you'd mind ... *Lady Bancroft*, you know. Quite spacious and plenty of hanging room."

"Well, Milly, if it isn't turning you upside down."

"Not at all," said Millamant coldly.

"And you can still talk to me," said Pauline. "I'll be next door."

III

On Friday night the weather broke and a deluge of rain beat down on the tortuous roofs of Ancreton. On Saturday morning Troy was awakened by a regular sequence of sharp percussionlike notes: Ping, ping, ping.

On going to her bath she nearly fell into a basin that had been placed on the landing. Into it fell a continuous progression of water-drops from a spreading patch in the roof. All day it rained. At three o'clock it had grown too dark to paint in the little theatre, but she had worked through the morning, and, having laid her last touch against the canvas, walked away from it and sat down. She felt that curious blankness which follows the completion of a painting. It was over. Her house was untenanted. It did not long remain so, for now, unchecked by the discipline of her work, Troy's thoughts were filled with the anticipation of reunion. "The day after to-morrow I shall be saying: 'Tomorrow.' " The Ancreds and their machinations now seemed unreal. They were two-dimensional figures gesticulating on a ridiculously magnificent stage. This reaction was to colour all memories of her last two days at Ancreton, blurring their edges, lending a tinge of fantasy to commonplace events, and causing her to doubt the integrity of her recollections when, in a little while, it would be imperative for her to recount them accurately.

She was to remember that Sir Henry was invisible all day, resting in preparation for his Birthday Dinner; that there was an air of anticipation in his enormous house, that his presents were set out in the library, a dark no-man's-land in the east wing, and that the members of his family visited this Mecca frequently, eyeing each other's gifts with intense partiality. Troy herself, in readiness for The Birthday, had made a lively and diverting sketch of Panty, which she had mounted and placed among the other gifts, wondering if, in view of Panty's fall from grace, it was too preposterously inept. The sketch was viewed with wholehearted favour by Panty herself and her mother, and by nobody else except Cedric, who chose to regard it as an acid comment on the child's character, which it was not.

Troy remembered afterwards how she had looked at the long dresses she had brought with her and decided that they were nothing like grand enough for the occasion. She remembered how the air of festivity had deepened as evening came, and how Barker and his retinue of elderly maids were in a continuous state of controlled bustle. Most often, though still with a feeling of incredulity, would it seem to her that there had been a sense of impending climax in the house, an impression of something drawing to its close. At the time Troy said to herself: "It's because Rory's coming. It's because I've finished an intensive bit of work done at concert pitch." But in retrospect these answers sounded unconvincing, and she wondered if the thoughts of one malevolent creature could have sent out a thin mist of apprehension.

Troy had cleaned her palette, shut her paint-box on ranks of depleted tubes, and washed her brushes for the last time at Ancreton. The portrait had been set up on the stage and framed in crimson velvet curtains that did their best to kill it. "If it was spring-time," Troy thought, "I believe they'd have festooned it in garlands." The act-drop had been lowered in front of the portrait and there it waited on a dark stage for the evening's ceremony. She couldn't glower at it. She couldn't walk in that deluge. She was unendurably restless. The dinner itself was at nine; she had three hours to fill in. Taking a book with her, she wandered uncertainly from one vast room to another, and wherever she went there seemed to be two Ancreds in private conversation. Having disclosed Paul and Fenella tightly embraced in the study, disturbed Desdemona and Pauline hissing together in the drawing-room, and interrupted Millamant in what appeared to be angry parley with Barker under the stairs, she made her way to a room next the library, known as the Great Boudoir (the Little Boudoir was upstairs). Unnerved by her previous encounters, Troy paused outside the door and listened. All was still. She pushed open the door, and was confronted by Cedric and Miss Orrincourt side by side on a sofa, doubled up in an ecstasy of silent laughter.

She was well into the room before they saw her. Their behaviour was extraordinary. They stared at her with their mouths open, the laughter drying out on their faces as if she had scorched it. Cedric turned an ugly red, Miss Orrincourt's eyes were as hard as blue glass marbles. She was the first to speak.

"Well, for crying out loud," she said in a flat voice, "look who's here."

"Dearest Mrs. Alleyn," said Cedric breathlessly, "do come in. We've been having a dreadfully naughty giggle over everything. The Birthday, you know, and all the wheels within wheels and so on. Do join us. Or are you too grand and upright? Dear me, that sounds as if you were a piano, doesn't it?"

"It's all right," said Troy, "I won't come in, thank you. I'm on my way upstairs."

She went out, closing the door on their silence.

In the hall she found a completely strange elderly gentleman reading a newspaper before the fire. He wore London clothes, an old-fashioned wing collar and a narrow black tie. His face was thin and his hands blue-veined and knotty. When he saw Troy he dropped his newspaper, snatched off his pince-nez, and ejaculating

627

"M-m-m-mah!" rose nimbly to his feet.

"Are you waiting to see somebody?" Troy asked.

"Thank yer, thank yer, no thank yer," said the elderly gentleman rapidly. "Make myself known. Haven't had the pleasure—Introduce myself. M-mah. Rattisbon."

"Oh, yes, of course," said Troy. "I knew you were coming. How do you do?" She introduced herself.

Mr. Rattisbon vibrated the tip of his tongue between his lips and wrung his hands. "How d'do," he gabbled. "Delighted. Take it, fellow-guests. If I may so designate myself. Professional visit."

"So's mine," said Troy, picking the sense out of this collection of phrases. "I've been doing a job here."

He glanced at the painting-smock she had not yet removed. "Surely," he clattered, "Mrs. Roderick Alleyn? Née Troy?"

"That's it."

"Pleasure of your husband's acquaintance," Mr. Rattisbon explained. "Professional association. Twice. Admirable."

"Really!" said Troy, at once delighted. "You know Roderick? Do let's sit down."

Mr. Rattisbon sucked in his breath and made a crowing sound. They sat before the fire. He crossed his knees and joined his gnarled fingers, "He's a drawing by Cruikshank," Troy thought. She began to talk to him about Alleyn, and he listened exactly as if she was making a series of statements which he would presently require his clerk to come in and witness. Troy was to remember vividly this quiet encounter, and how in the middle of her recital she broke off apologetically to say: "But I don't know why I should bore you with these stories about Roderick."

"Bore?" he said. "On the contrary. Entirely so. May I add, strictly *in camera*, that I—ah—had contemplated this call with some misgivings as—ah—a not altogether propitious necessity. I find myself unexpectedly received, and most charmingly so, by a lady for whose remarkable talents I have long entertained the highest regard. M-m-mah!" Mr. Rattisbon added, dipping like a sparrow towards Troy. "Entirely so."

At this juncture Pauline and Desdemona appeared in the hall and bore down rapidly upon Mr. Rattisbon.

"We are so sorry," Pauline began. "Leaving you so long. Papa's only just been told—a little upset. The great day, of course. He will be ready for you in a few minutes, dear Mr. Rattisbon. Until then Dessy and I would be so glad if you—we feel we'd like to——"

Troy was already on her way out. They were waiting for her to get out of earshot.

She heard Desdemona's rich voice: "Just a tiny talk, Mr. Rattisbon. Just to warn you." And Mr. Rattisbon suddenly very dry and brittle: "If you desire it, certainly."

"But," thought Troy, plodding along the passage, "they won't get much change out of Mr. Rattisbon."

IV

"It's the big scene from a film script," thought Troy, looking down the table, "and I'm the bit-part lady." The analogy was unavoidable. How often had one not seen Sir Aubrey Smith at the head of such a table? Where else but on the screen was such opulence to be found? Where else such a welter of flowers, such sumptuously Edwardian epergnes, or such incredibly appropriate conversation? Never out of a film studio had characters been so well typed. Even the neighbouring squire and the parson, the one lean and monocled, the other rubicund and sleek, who apparently were annual fixtures for the event; even they were carefully selected cameo parts, too like themselves to be credible. And Mr. Rattisbon? The absolute in family solicitors. As for the Ancreds themselves, to glance at them or to hear their carefully modulated laughter, their beautifully articulated small-talk, was to realise at once that this was an all-star vehicle. Troy began to make up titles. "Homage to Sir Henry." "The Astonishing Ancreds."

"Going quite nicely, so far, don't you consider?" said Thomas at her left elbow. She had forgotten Thomas, although he had taken her in. Cedric, on her right hand, had directed at her and at his partner, Desdemona, a number of rather spasmodic and intensely artificial remarks, all of which sounded as if they were designed for the ears of his grandfather. Thomas, presumably, had been silent until now.

"Very nicely," Troy agreed hurriedly.

"I mean," Thomas continued, lowering his voice, "you wouldn't think, if you didn't know, how terrified everyone is about the Will, would you? Everybody except me, that is, and perhaps Cedric."

"Ssh!" said Troy. "No, you wouldn't."

"It's because we're putting on the great Family Act, you know.

629

It's the same on the stage. People that hate each other's guts make love like angels. You'd be surprised, I dare say. Outsiders think it very queer. "Well," Thomas continued, laying down his soup-spoon and gazing mildly at her. "What, after all, *do* you think of Ancreton?"

"I've found it absorbing."

"I'm so glad. You've come in for a set-piece, haven't you? All the intrigues and fights. Do you know what will happen after dinner?" And without waiting for her reply he told her. "Papa will propose the King's health and then I shall propose Papa's. I'm the eldest son present so I shall have to, but it's a pity. Claude would be much better. Last year Panty was brought in to do it. I coached her in the 'business' and she managed very nicely. Papa cried. This year, because of ringworm and the practical jokes, she hasn't been invited. Gracious," Thomas continued, as Troy helped herself from a dish that had appeared over her shoulder, "that's never New Zealand crayfish? I thought Millamant had decided against it. Has Papa noticed? There'll be trouble if he has."

Thomas was right. Sir Henry, when offered this dish, glanced truculently at his daughter-in-law and helped himself to it. An instant silence fell upon the table, and Troy, who was opposite Millamant, saw her make a helpless deprecating grimace at Pauline, who, from the foot of the table, responded by raising her eyebrows.

"He insisted," Millamant whispered to Paul on her left hand. "What?" asked Sir Henry loudly.

"Nothing, Papa," said Millamant.

"They call this," said Sir Henry, addressing himself to Mr. Rattisbon, "rock lobster. No more like a lobster than my foot. It's some antipodean shell-fish."

Furtively watched by his family, he took a large mouthful and at the same time pointed to his glass and added: "One must drink something with it. I shall break my rule, Barker. Champagne."

Barker, with his lips very slightly pursed, filled the glass.

"That's a big boy," said Miss Orrincourt approvingly. The Ancreds, after a frightened second or two, burst simultaneously into feverish conversation.

"There," said Thomas with an air of sober triumph. "What did I tell you? Champagne and hot crayfish. We shall hear more of this, you may depend upon it."

"Do be careful," Troy murmured nervously, and then, seeing that Sir Henry was in gallant conversation with Jenetta on his left, she added cautiously: "Is it so very bad for him?"

"I promise you," said Thomas, "disastrous. I don't think it tastes very nice, anyway," he continued after a pause. "What do you think?" Troy had already come to this conclusion. The crayfish, she decided, were dubious.

"Hide it under your toast," said Thomas. "I'm going to. It's the Birthday turkey next, from the home farm. We can fill up on that, can't we?"

But Sir Henry, Troy noticed, ate all his crayfish.

Apart from this incident, the dinner continued in the same elevated key up to the moment when Sir Henry, with the air of a Field-Marshal in Glorious Technicolor, rose and proposed the King.

A few minutes later Thomas, coughing modestly, embarked upon his speech.

"Well, Papa," said Thomas, "I expect you know what I'm going to say, because, after all, this is your Birthday dinner, and we all know it's a great occasion and how splendid it is for us to be here again as usual in spite of everything. Except Claude, of course, which is a pity, because he would think of a lot of new things to say, and I can't." At this point a slight breeze of discomfort seemed to stir among the Ancreds. "So I shall only say," Thomas battled on, "how proud we are to be gathered here, remembering your past achievements and wishing you many more Birthday dinners in the time that is to come. Yes," said Thomas, after a thoughtful pause, "that's all, I think. Oh, I almost forgot! We all, of course, hope that you will be very happy in your married life. I shall now ask everybody to drink Papa's health, please."

The guests, evidently accustomed to a very much longer speech and taken unawares by the rapidity of Thomas's peroration, hurriedly got to their feet.

"Papa," said Thomas.

"Papa," echoed Jenetta, Millamant, Pauline and Desdemona.

"Grandpapa," murmured Fenella, Cedric and Paul.

"Sir Henry," said the Rector loudly, followed by Mr Rattisbon, the Squire and Troy.

"Noddy!" said Miss Orrincourt, shrilly. "Cheers. Oodles of juice in your tank."

631

Sir Henry received all this in the traditional manner. He fingered his glass, stared deeply at his plate, glanced up at Thomas, and, towards the end, raised his hand deprecatingly and let it fall. There was evidence of intense but restrained feeling. When they had all settled down he rose to reply. Troy had settled herself for resounding periods and a great display of rhetoric. She was not prepared, in view of the current family atmosphere, for touching simplicity and poignant emotion. These, however, were the characteristics of Sir Henry's speech. It was also intensely manly. He had, he said, taken a good many calls in the course of his life as a busker, and made a good many little speeches of gratitude to a good many audiences. But moving as some of these occasions had been, there was no audience as near and dear to an old fellow as his own kith and kin and his few tried and proven friends. He and his dear old Tommy were alike in this: they had few words in which to express their dearest thoughts. Perhaps they were none the worse for it. (Pauline, Desdemona and the Rector made sounds of fervent acquiescence.) Sir Henry paused and glanced first at Paul and then at Fenella. He had intended, he said, to keep for this occasion the announcement of the happy change he now contemplated. But domestic events had, should he say, a little forced his hand, and they were now all aware of his good fortune. (Apparently the Squire and Rector were not aware of it, as they looked exceedingly startled.) There was however, one little ceremony to be observed.

He took a small morocco box from his pocket, opened it, extracted a dazzling ring, and, raising Miss Orrincourt, placed it on her engagement finger and kissed the finger. Miss Orrincourt responded by casting one practised glance at the ring and embracing him with the liveliest enthusiasm. His hearers broke into agitated applause, under cover of which Cedric muttered: "That's the Ranee's Solitaire re-set. I swear it is. Stay me with flagons, playmates."

Sir Henry, with some firmness, reseated his fiancée and resumed his speech. It was, he said, a tradition in his family that the head of it should be twice married. The Sieur d'Ancred— he rambled on genealogically for some time. Troy felt embarrassment give place to boredom. Her attention was caught, however, by a new development. It had also been the custom, Sir Henry was saying, on these occasions, for the fortunate Ancred to reveal to his family the manner in which he had set his house in order. (Mr. Rattisbon raised his eyebrows very high and made a little quavering noise in his throat.) Such frankness was perhaps ouf of fashion nowadays, but it had an appropriate Shakespearian precedent. King Lear—but glancing at his agonised daughters Sir Henry did not pursue the analogy. He said that he proposed to uphold this traditional frankness. "I have to-day," he said, "executed—my old friend Rattisbon will correct me if this is not the term'—("M-m-mah!" said Mr. Rattisbon confusedly)—"thank you—executed My Will. It is a simple little document, conceived in the spirit that actuated my ancestor, the Sieur d'Ancred when——" A fretful sigh eddied round the table. This time, however, Sir Henry's excursion into antiquity was comparatively brief. Clearing his throat, and speaking on a note so solemn that it had an almost ecclesiastical timbre, he fired point-blank and gave them a résumé of his Will.

Troy's major concern was to avoid the eyes of everybody else seated at that table. To this end she stared zealously at a detail of the epergne immediately in front of her. For the rest of her life, any mention of Sir Henry Ancred's last Will and Testament will immediately call up for her the image of a fat silver cupid who, in a pose at once energetic and insouciant, lunged out from a central globe, to which he was affixed only by his great toe, and, curving his right arm, supported on the extreme tip of his first finger a cornucopia three times his own size, dripping with orchids.

Sir Henry was speaking of legacies. Five thousand pounds to his devoted daughter-in-law, Millamant, five thousand pounds to his ewe lamb, Desdemona. To his doctor and his servants, to the hunt club, to the Church there were grand seigneurial legacies. Her attention wandered, and was again arrested by a comparison he seemed to be making between himself and some pentateuchal patriarch. "Into three parts. The residue divided into three parts." This, then, was the climax. To his bride-to-be, to Thomas, and to Cedric, he would leave, severally, a life interest in a third of the residue of his estate. The capital of this fund to be held in trust and ultimately devoted to the preservation and endowment of Ancreton as a historical museum of drama to be known as The Henry Ancred Memorial.

"Tra-hippit!" Cedric murmured at her elbow. "Honestly, I exult. It might have been so much worse."

Sir Henry was now making a brief summary of the rest of the field. His son, Claude, he thanked God, turning slightly towards

633

Jenetta, had inherited a sufficient portion from his maternal grandmother, and was therefore able through this and through his own talents to make provision for his wife and (he momentarily eyed Fenella) daughter. His daughter Pauline (Troy heard her make an incoherent noise) had been suitably endowed at the time of her marriage and generously provided for by her late husband. She had her own ideas in the bringing up of her children and was able to carry them out. "Which," Cedric muttered with relish, "is a particularly dirty crack at Paul and Panty, don't you feel?"

"Ssh!" said Desdemona on the other side of him.

Sir Henry drifted into a somewhat vague and ambiguous diatribe on the virtues of family unity and the impossibility, however great the temptation, of ever entirely forgetting them. For the last time her attention wandered, and was jerked sharply back by the sound of her own name: "Mrs. Agatha Troy Alleyn ... her dramatic and, if I as the subject may so call it, magnificent canvas, which you are presently to see——"

Troy, greatly startled, learned that the portrait was to be left to the Nation.

V

"It's not the money, Milly. It's not the money, Dessy," wailed Pauline in the drawing-room. "I don't mind about the money, Jen. It's the cruel, *cruel* wound to my love. That's what hurts me, girls. That's what hurts."

"If I were you," said Millamant with her laugh, "I think I should feel a bit hipped about the money, too."

Miss Orrincourt, according to her custom, had gone away to do her face. The ladies were divided into two parties—the haves and the have-nots. Dessy, a not altogether delighted legatee, had a foot in each camp. "It's damn mean," she said; "but after the things I've said about the Orrincourt, I suppose I'm lucky to get anything. What do you think of her, Jen?"

"I suppose," said Jenetta Ancred thoughtfully, "she *is* real, isn't she! I mean, I catch myself wondering, quite seriously, if she could be somebody who has dressed up and is putting on the language and everything as a colossal practical joke. I didn't think people ever were so shatteringly true to type. But she's much too lovely, of course, to be a leg-pull."

634

"Lovely!" cried Desdemona. "Jen! Straight out of the third row of the chorus and appallingly common at that."

"I dare say, but they *are* generally rather lovely in the chorus nowadays, aren't they, Fenella?"

Fenella had withdrawn entirely from the discussion. Now, when they all turned to her, she faced them rigidly, two bright red spots burning over her cheek-bones.

"I want to say," she began in a loud, shaky voice, "that I'm very sorry, Aunt Pauline and Mummy, that because of Paul and me you've been treated so disgracefully. We don't mind for ourselves. We'd neither of us, after the things he's said, touch a penny of his money. But we are sorry about you and Panty."

"Well, darling," said her mother, putting an arm through hers, "That's very handsome of you and Paul, but don't let's have any more speeches, shall we?"

"Yes, but Mummy——"

"Your two families are very anxious for both of you to be happy. It's like that, isn't it, Pauline?"

"Well, Jenetta, that, of course, goes without saying, but——"

"There you are, Fen," said Jenetta. "It goes, and without saying, which is such a blessing."

Pauline, looking extremely vexed, retired into a corner with Desdemona.

Jenetta offered Troy a cigarette. "I suppose," she muttered in a friendly manner, "that was not a very good remark for me to make, but, to tell you the truth, I take a pretty gloomy view of all these naked wounds. Mr. Rattisbon tells me your husband's coming back. What fun for you."

"Yes," said Troy, "it's all of that."

"Does everything else seem vague and two-dimensional? It would to me."

"It does with me, too. I find it very muddling."

"Of course the Ancreds are on the two-dimensional side anyway, if it comes to that. Especially my father-in-law. Did it make painting him easier or more difficult?"

Before Troy could answer this entertaining question, Cedric, flushed and smirking, opened the door, and stood against it in a romantic attitude waving his handkerchief.

"Darlings," he said, "*Allez-houp*! The great moment. I am to bid you to the little theatre. Dearest Mrs. Alleyn, you and the Old Person should be jointly fêted. A cloud of little doves with gilded wings should be lowered by an ingenious device from the flies, and, with pretty gestures, crown you with laurels. Uncle Thomas could have arranged it. I should so adore to see Panty as an aerial coryphée. Will you all come?"

They found the men assembled in the little theatre. It was brilliantly lit, and had an air of hopefully waiting for a much larger audience. Soft music rumbled synthetically behind the front curtain, which (an inevitable detail) was emblazoned with the arms of Ancred. Troy found herself suddenly projected into a star rôle. Sir Henry led her up the aisle to a seat beside himself. The rest of the party settled behind them. Cedric, with a kind of consequential flutter, hurried backstage.

Sir Henry was smoking a cigar. When he inclined gallantly towards Troy she perceived that he had taken brandy. This circumstance was accompanied by a formidable internal rumbling.

"I shall," he murmured gustily, "just say a few words."

They were actually few, but as usual they were intensely embarrassing. Her reluctance to undertake the portrait was playfully outlined. His own pleasure in the sittings was remorselessly sketched. Some rather naïve quotations on art from *Timon of Athens* were introduced, and then: "But I must not tantalise my audience any longer," said Sir Henry richly. "Curtain, my boy. Curtain!"

The house lights went down: the front drop slid upwards. Simultaneously four powerful floodlamps poured down their beams from the flies. The scarlet tabs were drawn apart, and there, in a blaze of highly unsuitable light, the portrait was revealed.

Above the sombre head and flying against a clear patch of night sky, somebody had painted an emerald green cow with vermilion wings. It was in the act of secreting an object that might or might not have been a black bomb.

CHAPTER VIII

Big Exit

I

This time Troy felt only a momentary sensation of panic. That particular area of background was hard-dry, and almost at once she remembered this circumstance. She did, however, feel overwhelmingly irritated. Above the automatic burst of applause that greeted the unveiling and only petered out when the detail of the flying cow was observed, she heard her own voice saying loudly: "No, really, this is too much."

At the same moment Cedric, who had evidently operated the curtains, stuck his head round the proscenium, stared blindly into the front of the house, turned, saw the portrait, clapped his hand over his mouth and ejaculated: "Oh, God! Oh, Dynamite!"

"*Darling!*" said his mother from the back row. "Ceddie, *dear*? What's the matter?"

Sir Henry, on Troy's left, breathed stertorously, and contrived to let out a sort of hoarse roaring noise.

"It's all right," said Troy. "Please don't say anything. Wait."

She strode furiously down the aisle and up the steps. Sacrificing her best evening handkerchief, she reduced the cow to a green smear. "I think there's a bottle of turpentine somewhere," she said loudly. "Please give it to me."

Paul ran up with it, offering his own handkerchief. Cedric flew out with a handful of rag. The blemish was removed. Meantime the auditorium rang with Miss Orrincourt's hysterical laughter and buzzed with the sound of bewildered Ancreds. Troy threw the handkerchief and rag into the wings, and, with hot cheeks, returned to her seat. "I wouldn't have been so cross," she thought grimly, "if the damn thing hadn't looked so funny."

"I *demand*," Sir Henry was shouting, "I *demand* to know the author of this outrage."

He was answered by a minor uproar topped by Pauline: "It was was *not* Panty. I tell you, Millamant, once and for all, that Panty is in bed, and has been there since five o'clock. Papa, I protest. It was *not* Panty."

"Nuts!" said Miss Orrincourt. "She's been painting green cows for days. I've seen them. Come off it, dear."

"Papa, I give you my solemn word——"

"Mother, wait a minute——"

"I shall not wait a second. Papa, I have reason to believe——"

"Look here, *do* wait," Troy shouted, and at once they were silent. "It's gone," she said, "No harm's been done. But there's one thing I must tell you. Just before dinner I came in here. I was worrying about the red curtains. I thought they might touch the canvas where it's still wet. It was all right then. If Panty's been in bed and is known to have been there since ten to nine, she didn't do it."

Pauline instantly began to babble. "Thank you, thank you, Mrs. Alleyn. You hear that, Papa. Send for Miss Able. I insist that Miss Able be sent for. My child shall be vindicated."

"I'll go and ask Caroline," said Thomas unexpectedly. "One doesn't send for Caroline, you know. I'll go and ask."

He went out. The Ancreds were silent. Suddenly Millamant remarked: "I thought perhaps it was just the modern style. What do they call it? Surrealism?"

"Milly!" screamed her son.

Jenetta Ancred said: "What particular symbolism, Milly, did you read into the introduction of a flying cow behaving like a rude seagull over Papa's head?"

"You never know," Millamant said, "in these days," and laughed uncertainly.

"Papa," said Desdemona, who had been bending over him, "is dreadfully upset. Papa, dearest, may I suggest——"

"I'm going to bed," said Sir Henry. "I am indeed upset. I am unwell. I am going to bed."

They all rose. He checked them with a gesture. "I am going alone," he said, "to bed."

Cedric ran to the door. Sir Henry, without a backward glance, walked down the aisle, a shadowy figure looking larger than life against the glowing stage, and passing magnificently from the

638

theatre.

The Ancreds at once began to chatter. Troy felt that she couldn't endure the inevitable revival of Panty's former misdemeanours, Pauline's indignant denials, Cedric's giggles, Millamant's stolid recital of the obvious. She was profoundly relieved when Thomas, slightly ruffled, returned with Caroline Able.

"I've asked Caroline to come," he said, "because I thought you mightn't exactly believe me. Panty's been in the sick-bay with all the other ringworms. Dr. Withers wanted them to be kept under observation because of the medicine he's given them, so Caroline has been sitting there reading since half-past seven. So Panty, you see, didn't do it."

"Certainly she didn't do it," said Miss Able brightly. "How could she? It's quite impossible."

"So you see," Thomas added mildly.

II

Troy stayed behind in the little theatre with Paul and Fenella. Paul switched on the working lights, and together they examined Troy's painting gear, which had been stacked away behind the wings.

The paint-box had been opened. A dollop of Emerald Oxide of Chromium and one of Ivory Black had been squeezed out on the protective under-lid that separated the paints from a compartment designed to hold sketching-boards. A large brush had been used, and had been dipped first in the green and then in the black.

"You know," said Paul, "this brush ought to have finger-prints on it." He looked rather shyly at Troy. "Oughtn't it?" he added.

"Well, I suppose Roderick would say so," she agreed.

"I mean, if it has and if we could get everybody's to compare, that would be pretty conclusive, wouldn't it? What's more, it'd be damned interesting."

"Yes, but I've a notion finger-prints are not as easy as all that."

"I know. The hand would move about and so on. But look! There *is* some green paint smeared up the handle. I've read about it. Suppose we asked them to let us take their prints. They couldn't very well refuse."

"Oh, Paul, *let's*!" cried Fenella.

"What do you think, Mrs. Alleyn?"

"My dear chap, you mustn't imagine I know anything about it. But I agree it would be interesting. I *do* know more or less how they take official prints."

"I've read it up quite a bit," said Paul. "I say. Suppose we did get them to do it, and suppose we kept the brush and the box intact—well—well, would—do you think——?"

"I'd show them to him like a shot," said Troy.

"I say, that's perfectly splendid," said Paul. "Look here, I'll damn well put it to them in the morning. It ought to be cleared up. It's all bloody rum, the whole show, isn't it? What d'you say, Mrs. Alleyn?"

"I'm on," said Troy.

"Glory!" said Fenella. "So'm I. Let's."

"O.K.," said Paul, gingerly wrapping the brush in rag. "We'll lock up the brush and box."

"I'll take them up with me."

"Will you? That's grand."

They locked the portrait in the property-room, and said good night conspiratorially. Troy felt she could not face another session with the Ancreds, and sending her excuses, went upstairs to her room.

She could not sleep. Outside, in the night, rain drove solidly against the wall of her tower. The wind seemed to have got into the chimney and be trying uneasily to find its way out again. A bucket had replaced the basin on the landing, and a maddening and irregular progression of taps compelled her attention and played like castanets on her nerves. Only one more night here, she thought, and then the comfort of her familiar things in the London flat and the sharing of them with her husband. Illogically she felt a kind of regret for the tower-room, and in this mood fell to revising in their order the eccentricities of her days and nights at Ancreton. The paint on the banister. The spectacles on the portrait. The legend in grease-paint on Sir Henry's looking-glass. The incident of the inflated bladder. The flying cow.

If Panty was not the authoress of these inane facetiae, who was? If one person only was responsible for them all, then Panty was exonerated. But might not Panty have instituted them with the smearing of paint on the banister and somebody else have carried them on? Undoubtedly Panty's legend and past record included many such antics. Troy wished that she knew something of modern views on child psychology. Was such behaviour characteristic of a child who wished to become a dominant figure and who felt herself to be obstructed and repressed? But Troy was positive that Panty had spoken the truth when she denied having any hand in the tricks with paint. And unless Miss Able had told a lie, Panty, quite definitely, had not been the authoress of the flying cow, though she undoubtedly had a predilection for cows and bombs. Troy turned uneasily in her bed, and fancied that beyond the sound of wind and rain she heard the voice of the Great Clock. Was there any significance in the fact that in each instance the additions to her canvas had been made on a dry area and so had done no harm? Which of the adults in the house would realise this? Cedric. Cedric painted, though probably in water-colours. She fancied his aesthetic fervour was, in its antic way, authentic. He would, she thought, instinctively recoil from this particular kind of vandalism. But suppose he knew that no harm would be done? And where was a motive for Cedric? He appeared to have a kind of liking for her; why should he disfigure her work? Bleakly Troy surveyed the rest of the field, and one by one dismissed them until she came to Miss Orrincourt.

The robust vulgarity of these goings-on was not out of character if Miss Orrincourt was considered. Was it, Troy wondered with an uneasy grin, remotely possible that Miss Orrincourt resented the somewhat florid attentions Sir Henry had lavished upon his guest? Could she have imagined that the sittings had been made occasions for even more marked advances, more ardent pattings of the hand, closer pilotings by the elbow? "Crikey," Troy muttered, writhing uncomfortably, "*what* an idea to get in the middle of the night!" No, it was too far-fetched. Perhaps one of the elderly maids had lost her wits and taken to this nonsense. "Or Barker," thought the now sleepy Troy. In the drumming of rain and wind about her room she began to hear fantastical things. Presently she dreamed of flying bombs that came out of the night, converging on her tower. When they were almost upon her they changed into green cows, that winked broadly, and with a Cedric-like flirt dropped soft bombs, at the same time saying very distinctly: "Plop, plop, *dearest* Mrs. Alleyn."

"*Mrs. Alleyn. Dearest Mrs. Alleyn, do please wake up.*"

Troy opened her eyes. Fenella, fully dressed, stood at her bedside. In the thin light of dawn her face looked cold and very white. Her hands opened and shut aimlessly. The corners of her

641

mouth turned down like those of a child about to cry. "What now, for pity's sake?" cried Troy.

"I thought I'd better come and tell you. Nobody else would. They're all frantic. Paul can't leave his mother, and Mummy's trying to stop Aunt Dessy having hysterics. I feel so ghastly, I had to talk to someone."

"But why? What is it? What's happened?"

"Grandfather. When Barker went in with his tea. He found him. Lying there. Dead."

III

There is no more wretched lot than that of the comparative stranger in a house of grief. The sense of loneliness, the feeling that one constantly trespasses on other people's sorrow, that they would thankfully be rid of one; all these circumstances reduce the unwilling intruder to a condition of perpetual apology that must remain unexpressed. If there is nothing useful to be done this misery is the more acute, and Troy was not altogether sorry that Fenella seemed to find some comfort in staying with her. She hurriedly made a fire on top of last night's embers, set Fenella, who shivered like a puppy, to blow it up while she herself bathed and dressed, and, when at last the child broke down, listened to a confused recital which harked back continually to the break between herself and her grandfather. "It's so *awful* that Paul and I should have made him miserable. We'll never be able to forgive ourselves—never," Fenella sobbed.

"Now, look here," said Troy, "that just doesn't make sense. You and Paul did what you have every right to do."

"But we did it brutally. You can't say we didn't. We grieved him frightfully. He said so."

Sir Henry had said so a great many times and with extreme emphasis. It was impossible to suggest that anger rather than grief had moved him. Troy went off on another tack. "He seemed to have got over it," she said.

"Last night!" Fenella wailed. "When I think of what we said about him last night. In the drawing-room after you'd gone up. Everybody except Mummy and Paul. Aunt Milly said he'd probably have an attack, and I said I didn't care if it was fatal. Actually! And he did *feel* it. He cut Aunt Pauline and Mummy and me and Paul out of his Will because of our engagement and

642

the way we announced it. So he did feel it deeply."

"The Will," thought Troy. "Good heavens, yes. The Will!" She said: "He was an old man, Fenella. I don't think, do you, that the future was exactly propitious? Isn't it perhaps not so very bad that he should go now when everything seemed to him to be perfectly arranged? He'd had his splendid party."

"And look how it ended."

"Oh, dear!" said Troy. "That. Well, yes."

"And it was probably the party that killed him," Fenella continued. "That hot crayfish. It's what everybody thinks. Dr. Withers had warned him. And nobody was there. He just went up to his room and died."

"Has Dr. Withers——?"

"Yes. He's been. Barker got Aunt Milly and she rang up. He says it was a severe attack of gastro-enteritis. He says it—it happened—it must have been—soon after he went up to bed. It's so awful when you think of all the frightful things we were saying about him down there in the drawing-room. All of us except Cedric, and he was simply gloating over us. Little beast, he's still gloating, if it comes to that."

The gong rumbled distantly. "You go down to breakfast," said Fenella. "I can't face it."

"That won't do at all. You can at least choke down some coffee."

Fenella took Troy's arm in a nervous grip. "I think I like you so much," she said, "because you're so unlike all of us. All right, I'll come."

The Ancreds in sorrow were a formidable assembly. Pauline, Desdemona and Millamant, who were already in the dining-room, had all found black dresses to wear, and Troy was suddenly conscious that she had without thinking pulled on a scarlet sweater. She uttered those phrases of sympathy that are always inadequate. Desdemona silently gripped her hand and turned aside. Pauline dumbfounded her by bursting into tears and giving her an impulsive kiss. And it was strange to find an unsmiling and pallid Millamant. Thomas came in, looking bewildered. "Good morning," he said to Troy. "Isn't it awful? I really can't realise it a bit, you know. Everybody seems to realise it. They're all crying and everything, but I don't. Poor Papa." He looked at his sisters. "You're not eating anything," he said. "What can I get you, Pauline?"

Pauline said: "Oh, Thomas!" and made an eloquent gesture. "I suppose," Thomas continued, "that later on I shan't want to eat anything, but at the moment I am hungry."

He sat down beside Troy. "It's lucky you finished the portrait, isn't it?" he said. "Poor Papa!"

"*Tommy!*" breathed his sister.

"Well, but it is," he insisted gently. "Papa would have been pleased too."

Paul came in, and, a moment later, Jenetta Ancred, wearing tweeds. It was a relief to Troy that, like Thomas, neither of them spoke in special voices.

Presently Millamant began to speak of the manner in which Barker had discovered Sir Henry. At eight o'clock, it appeared, he had gone in as usual with Sir Henry's cup of milk and water. As he approached the room he heard the cat Carabbas wailing inside, and when he opened the door it darted out and fled down the passage. Barker supposed that Sir Henry had forgotten to let his cat out, and wondered that Carabbas had not waked him.

He entered the room. It was still very dark. Barker was short-sighted, but he could make out the figure lying across the bed. He turned on the lights, and after one horrified glance, rushed down the corridor and beat on the door of Millamant's room. When she and Pauline answered together, he kept his head, remained outside, and, in an agitated whisper, asked Millamant if he might speak to her. She put on her dressing-gown and went out into the cold passage.

"And I knew," Pauline interjected at this point. "Something told me. I knew at once that something had happened."

"Naturally," said Millamant. "Barker doesn't go on like that every morning."

"I knew it was The Great Visitor," Pauline insisted firmly. "I knew."

Millamant had gone with Barker to the room. She sent Barker to rouse Thomas and herself telephoned Dr. Withers. He was out, but finally arrived in about an hour. It had been, he said, a severe attack of gastro-enteritis, probably brought on by his indiscretions at dinner. Sir Henry's heart had been unable to survive the attack and he had collapsed and died.

"What I can't understand," said Pauline, "is why he didn't ring. He always rang if he felt ill in the night. There was a special bell in the corridor, Dessy. The cord hung beside his bed."

644

"He tried," said Thomas. "He must have grasped at it across the bed, we think, and fallen. It had come away from the cord. And I don't think, after all, I want very much to eat."

IV

Troy spent most of that last day between her room and the little theatre, lingering over her packing, which in any case was considerable. Carabbas, the cat, elected to spend the day in her room. Remembering where he had spent the night, she felt a little shudder at the touch of his fur. But they had become friendly, and after a time she was glad of his company. At first he watched her with some interest, occasionally sitting on such garments as she had laid out on the bed and floor. When she removed him he purred briefly, and at last, with a faint mew, touched her hand with his nose. It was hot. She noticed that his fur was staring. Was he, she wondered, actually distressed by the loss of his master? He grew restless and she opened the door. After a fixed look at her he went out, his tail drooping. She thought she heard him cry again on the stairs. She returned uneasily to her packing, broke off from time to time to wander restlessly about the room or stare out of the tower window at the rain-laced landscape. She came across a sketch-book and found herself absently making drawings af the Ancreds. Half an hour went past, and there they all were, like antics on the page, for her to show her husband. Guiltily she completed her packing.

Thomas had undertaken to send by rail such heavy baggage as the Yard car could not accommodate.

She was oppressed by the sensation of unreality. She felt more strongly than ever that she was held in suspension between two phases of experience. She was out of touch, not only with her surroundings, but with herself. While her hands folded and bestowed garment after garment, her thoughts ranged aimlessly between the events of the past twenty-four hours and those that were to come. "It is I," she thought in dismay, "who will resemble the traveller who can speak of nothing but his fellow-passengers and the little events of his voyage, and it is Rory who will listen unhappily to anecdotes of these Ancreds whom he is never likely to meet."

Lunch seemed to be an uncanny extension of breakfast. There, again, were the Ancreds; still using their special voices, still expressing so eloquently that sorrow whose authenticity Troy was not quite willing to discredit. She was half-aware of their conversation, catching only desultory pieces of information: Mr. Rattisbon had been transferred to the rectory. Thomas had been dictating obituary notices over the telephone. The funeral would be held on Tuesday. The voices murmured on. Momentarily she was consulted, drawn in. A weekly paper had got wind of the portrait ("Nigel Bathgate," thought Troy), and would like to send down a photographer. She made suitable rejoinders and suggestions. Cedric, whose manner was fretfully subdued, brightened a little over this subject, and then, unaccountably, reverted to a kind of nervous acquiescence. The conversation drifted towards Miss Orrincourt, who had expressed her inability to make a public appearance and was having her meals in her own rooms. "I saw her breakfast-tray," said Millamant with a ghost of her usual laugh. "Her appetite doesn't seem to have suffered."

"T'uh!" said the Ancreds softly.

"Are we to be told," Pauline asked, "how long she proposes to——?"

"I should imagine," said Desdemona, "no longer than it takes for the Will to become effective."

"Well, but I mean to say," Cedric began, and they all turned their heads towards him. "If it's not *too* inappropriate and premature, one wonders rather, or doesn't one, if darling Sonia is in *quite* the same position *unmarried* as she would have been as the Old—as dearest Grandpapa's widow? Or not?"

An attentive stillness fell upon the table. It was broken by Thomas: "Yes—well, of course," he said, looking blandly about him, "won't that depend on how the Will is made out? Whether her share is left to 'Sonia Orrincourt,' you know, or to 'my wife, Sonia,' and all that."

Pauline and Desdemona stared for a moment at Thomas. Cedric smoothed his hair with two unsteady fingers. Fenella and Paul looked stolidly at their plates. Millamant, with a muffled attempt at easiness, said: "There's no need to jump *that* fence, surely, till we meet it." Pauline and Desdemona exchanged glances. Millamant had used the sacred "we".

"I think it's pretty ghastly," said Fenella abruptly, "to begin talking about Grandfather's Will when he's up there—lying there——" She broke off, biting her lip. Troy saw Paul reach for her hand. Jenetta Ancred, who had been silent throughout luncheon, gave her daughter a smile, half-deprecating, half-anxious. "How she dislikes it," Troy thought, "when Fenella behaves like an Ancred."

"Darling Fen," Cedric murmured, "you, of course, can afford to be grand and virtuous over the Will. I mean, you are so definitely *out* of that party, aren't you?"

"That's a pretty offensive remark, Cedric," said Paul.

"Has everyone finished?" asked Pauline in a hurry. "If so, Mrs. Alleyn, shall we——?"

Troy excused herself from the post-prandial gathering in the drawing-room.

As she entered the hall a car drew up outside. Barker, who seemed to have been expecting it, was already in the outer porch. He admitted three pale men, dressed in London clothes of a particularly black character. They wore wide black ties. Two of them carried black cases. The third, glancing at Troy, spoke in a muted and inaudible voice.

"This way, if you please," said Barker, ushering them into a small waiting-room across the hall. "I will inform Sir Cedric."

After the newcomers had been shut away and Barker had gone on his errand, Troy stood digesting the official recognition of Cedric's ascendancy. Her glance strayed to a table where, as she had observed, the senior of the three men, with a practised modesty, suggestive almost of sleight of hand, had dropped or slid a card. He had, indeed, given it a little push with his forefinger, so that it lay, partly concealed, under a book which Troy herself had brought from the library to solace her afternoon. The card was engraved in a type slightly heavier and more black than that of a normal visiting card:

"MORTIMER, SON & LOAME
    Undertakers——"

Troy lifted her book, exposing the hidden corner of the card, "——and Embalmers," she read.

CHAPTER IX

Alleyn

I

By an alteration in the rhythm of the ship's progress, suggestive almost of a physiological change, her passengers became aware of the end of their long voyage. Her pulse died. It was replaced by sounds of blind waves washing along her sides; of gulls, of voices, of chains, and, beyond these, of movement along the wharves and in the city beyond them.

At early dawn the Port of London looked as wan and expectant as an invalid already preparing for a return to vigour. Thin mist still hung about sheds and warehouses. Muffled lights were strung like a dim necklace along the waterfront. Frost glinted on roofs and bollards and ropes. Alleyn had gripped the rail for so long that its cold had bitten through his gloves into the palms of his hands. Groups of people stood about the wharves, outward signs of a life from which the passengers were, for a rapidly diminishing period, still remote. These groups, befogged by their own breath, were composed for the main part of men.

There were three women, and one wore a scarlet cap. Inspector Fox had come out in the pilot's boat. Alleyn had not hoped for this, and had been touched and delighted to meet him; but now it was impossible to talk to Fox.

"Mrs. Alleyn," said Fox, behind him, "is wearing a red cap. If you'll excuse me, Mr. Alleyn, I ought to have a word with a chap——The car's just behind the Customs shed. I'll meet you there."

When Alleyn turned to thank him, he was already walking away, squarely overcoated, tidy, looking just like his job.

Now only a dark channel, a ditch, a gutter lay between the ship and the wharf. Bells rang sharply. Men moved forward to the bollards and stared up at the ship. One raised his hand and shouted a greeting in a clear voice. Ropes were flung out, and a moment later the final stoppage was felt dully throughout the ship.

That was Troy down there. She walked forward. Her hands were jammed down in the pockets of her overcoat. She looked along the deck, scowling a little, her gaze moving towards him. In these last seconds, while he waited for her to discover him, Alleyn knew that, like himself, she was nervous. He lifted his hand. They looked at each other, and a smile of extraordinary intimacy broke across her face.

II

"Three years seven months and twenty-four days," said Alleyn that afternoon. "It's a hell of a time to be without your wife." He looked at Troy sitting on the hearth-rug hugging her knees. "Or rather," he added, "to be away from you, Troy. From you, who, so astonishingly happens to be my wife. I've been getting myself into such a hullabaloo about it."

"Wondering," Troy asked, "if we'd run short of conversation and feel shy?"

"You too, then?"

"It does happen, they say. It might easily happen."

"I even considered the advisability of quoting Othello on his arrival at Cyprus. How would you have reacted, my darling, if I had laid hold upon you under letter A in the Customs shed and begun: 'Oh, my fair warrior!' "

"I should probably have made a snappy come-back with something from *Macbeth*."

"Why *Macbeth*?"

"To explain that would be to use up all the conversation I'd saved up on my own account. Rory——"

"My love?"

"I've been having a very queer time with Macbeth."

She was looking doubtfully at him from under her ruffled forelock. "You may not care to hear about it," she mumbled. "It's a long story."

"It won't be too long," Alleyn said, "if it's you who tells it."

Watching her, he thought: "That's made her shy again. We are to re-learn each other." Alleyn's habit of mind was accurate and

649

exhaustive. He had recognized and examined in himself thoughts that another man might have preferred to ignore. During the long voyage home, he had many times asked himself if, when they met again, he and Troy might not find the years had dropped between them a transparent barrier through which they would stare without love, at each other. The possibility occurred to him, strangely enough, at moments when he most desired and missed her. When she had moved forward on the quay, without at first seeing him, his physical reaction had been so sharp that it had blotted out his thoughts. It was only when she gave him the look of intimacy, which so far had not been repeated, that he knew, without question, he was to love her again.

Now, when she was before him in the room whose very familiarity was a little strange, his delight was of a virgin kind that anticipates a trial of its temper. Were Troy's thoughts at this moment comparable with his own? Could he be as certain of her as he was of himself? She had entered into an entirely different mode of life during his absence. He knew nothing of her new associates beyond the rather sparse phrases she had allowed them in her letters. Now, evidently, he was to hear a little more.

"Come over here," he said, "and tell me."

She moved into her old place, leaning against his chair, and he looked down at her with a more tranquil mind, yet with such intense pleasure that the beginning of her story escaped him. But he had been ruthlessly trained to listen to statements and the habit asserted itself. The saga of Ancreton was unfolded.

Troy's account was at first tentative, but his interest stimulated her. She began to enjoy herself, and presently hunted out her sketch-book with the drawings she had made in her tower-room. Alleyn chuckled over the small lively figures with their enormous heads. "Like the old-fashioned Happy Families cards," he said, and she agreed that there was something Victorian and fantastic about the originals. After the eccentricities of the Ancreds themselves, the practical jokes turned out to be a dominant theme in her story. Alleyn heard of this with growing concern. "Here," he interrupted, "did this blasted kid ruin your thing in the end or didn't she?"

"No, no! But it wasn't the blasted kid at all. Listen."

He did, with a chuckle for her deductive methods. "She might conceivably, you know, write 'grandfarther' at one moment and 'grandfather' the next, but it's a point of course."

650

"It was her manner more than anything. I'm quite positive she didn't do it. I know she's got a record for practical jokes—but wait till I get to the end. Don't fluster the witness."

"Why not?" said Alleyn, stooping his head.

"To continue," said Troy after a moment or two, and this time he let her go on to the end. It was an odd story. He wondered if she realized quite how odd it was.

"I don't know whether I've conveyed the general dottiness of that monstrous house," she said. "I mean, the queer little things that turned up. Like the book on embalming amongst the *objets d'art* and the missing rat bane."

"Why do you put them together?"

"I dunno. I suppose because there's arsenic in both of them."

"You *are* not by any chance, my angel, attempting to land me with a suspected poisoning case on my return to your arms?"

"Well," said Troy after a pause, "you would think that one up, wouldn't you?" She screwed round and looked at him. "And he's been embalmed, you know. By the Messrs. Mortimer and Loame. I met them in the hall with their black bags. The only catch in it is the impossibility of regarding any of the Ancreds in the light of a slow poisoner. But it would fit."

"A little too neatly, I fancy." With a trace of reluctance he added: "What were some of the other queer little things that happened?"

"I'd like to know what Cedric and the Orrincourt were giggling about on the sofa, and whether the Orrincourt was coughing or laughing in the governess-cart. I'd even like to know what it was she bought in the chemist's shop. And I'd like to know more about Millamant. One never knew what Millamant was thinking, except that she doted perpetually on her ghastly Cedric. It would have been in her Cedric's interest, of course, to sicken Sir Henry of poor old Panty, who, by the way, has a complete alibi for the flying cow. Her alibi's a dangerous drug. For ringworm."

"Has this odious child been taking thallium?"

"Do you know about thallium?"

"I've heard of it."

"It establishes her alibi for the flying cow," said Troy. "I'd better explain."

"Yes," Alleyn agreed when she had finished, "that lets her out for the flying cow."

"She didn't do any of them," said Troy firmly. "I wish now

651

that Paul and Fenella and I had gone on with our experiment."

"What was that to be?"

"It involved your collaboration," said Troy, looking at him out of the corners of her eyes.

"Like hell it did!"

"Yes. We wrapped up the paint-brush that had been used for the flying cow and we were going to ask all of them to let us take their finger-prints for you to compare with it. Would you have minded?"

"My darling heart, I'd compare them with the Grand Cham of Tartary's if it would give you any fun."

"But we never got them. Death, as you and Mr. Fox would say, intervened. Sir Henry's death. By the way, the person who painted my banister left finger-prints on the stone wall above it. Perhaps after a decent interval I could hint for an invitation to Ancreton and you could come down with your insufflator and black ink. But honestly, it *is* a queer story, don't you think?"

"Yes," he agreed, rubbing his nose. "It's queer enough. We heard about Ancred's death on the ship's wireless. Little did I imagine you were in at it."

"I liked him," said Troy after a pause. "He was a terrific old exhibitionist, and he made one feel dreadfully shy at times, but I did like him. And he was grand to paint."

"The portrait went well?"

"I think so."

"I'd like to see it."

"Well, so you shall one of these days. He said he was leaving it to the Nation. What does the Nation do under those circumstances? Hang it in a dark corner of the Tate, do you imagine? Some paper or another, I suspect Nigel Bathgate's, is going to photograph it. We might get a print."

But Alleyn was not to wait long for the photograph. It appeared that evening in Nigel's paper over a notice of Sir Henry's funeral. He had been buried in the family vault at Ancreton with as much ceremony as the times allowed.

"He hoped," said Troy, "that the Nation would wish otherwise."

"The Abbey?"

"I'm afraid so. Poor Sir Henry, I wish it had. Ah, well," said Troy, dropping the newspaper, "that's the end of the Ancreds as far as I'm concerned."

•

"You never know," Alleyn said vaguely. Then, suddenly impatient of the Ancreds and of anything that prolonged beyond this moment the first tentative phase of their reunion, he stretched out his hands towards Troy.

This story is concerned with Alleyn and Troy's reunion only in so far as it affected his attitude towards her account of the Ancreds. If he had heard it at any other time it is possible that, however unwillingly, he might have dwelt longer on its peculiarities. As it was, he welcomed it as a kind of interlude between their first meeting and its consummation, and then dismissed it from his conscious thoughts.

They had three days together, broken only by a somewhat prolonged interview between Alleyn and his chief at the Special Branch. He was to resume, for the time being at least, his normal job at the Yard. On the Thursday morning when Troy returned to her job, he walked part of the way with her, watched her turn off, and with an odd feeling of anxiety, himself set out for the familiar room and the old associates.

It was pleasant, after all, to cross that barren back hall, smelling of linoleum and coal, to revisit an undistinguished office where the superintendent of C.I., against a background of crossed swords, commemorative photographs and a horseshoe, greeted him with unmistakable satisfaction. It was oddly pleasant to sit again at his old desk in the chief inspectors' room and contemplate the formidable task of taking up the threads of routine.

He had looked forward to a preliminary gossip with Fox, but Fox had gone out on a job somewhere in the country and would not be back before the evening. In the meantime here was an old acquaintance of Alleyn's, one Squinty Donovan, who, having survived two courts-martial, six months' confinement in Broadmoor, and a near-miss from a flying bomb, had left unmistakable signs of his ingenuity upon a lock-up antique shop in Beachamp Place, Chelsea. Alleyn set in motion the elaborate police machinery by which Squinty might be hunted home to a receiver. He then turned again to his file.

There was nothing exciting; a series of routine jobs. This pleased him. There had been enough of excursions and alarums, the Lord knew, in his three years' hunting for the Special Branch. He had wanted his return to C.I. to be uneventful.

Presently Nigel Bathgate rang up, "I say," he said, "has Troy seen about the Will?"

"Whose Will?"

"Old Ancred's. She's told you about the Ancreds, of course."

"Of course."

"It's in this morning's *Times*. Have a look at it. It'll rock them considerably."

"What's he done?" Alleyn asked. But for some reason he was unwilling to hear more about the Ancreds.

He heard Nigel chuckling. "Well, out with it," he said. "What's he done?"

"Handed them the works."

"In what way?"

"Left the whole caboosh to the Orrincourt."

III

Nigel's statement was an over-simplification of the facts, as Alleyn discovered when, still with that sense of reluctance, he looked up the Will. Sir Henry had cut Cedric down to the bare bones of the entail, and had left a legacy of one thousand pounds to Millamant, to each of his children and to Dr. Withers. The residue he had willed to Sonia Orrincourt.

"But—what about the dinner speech and the other Will?" Troy cried when he showed her the evening paper. "Was that just a complete have, do you suppose? If so, Mr. Rattisbon must have known. Or—Rory," she said, "I believe it was the flying cow that did it! I believe he was so utterly fed up with his family he marched upstairs, sent for Mr. Rattisbon and made a new Will there and then."

"But didn't he think the *enfant terrible* had done the flying cow? Why take it out of the whole family?"

"Thomas or somebody may have gone up and told him about Panty's alibi. He wouldn't know who to suspect, and would end up by damning the whole crew."

"Not Miss Orrincourt, however."

"She'd see to that," said Troy with conviction.

She was, he saw, immensely taken up with this news, and at intervals during the evening returned to the Ancreds and their fresh dilemma. "What will Cedric do, can you imagine? Probably the entail is hopelessly below the cost of keeping up Katzenjammer Castle. That's what he called it, you know. Perhaps he'll give it to the Nation. Then they could hang my portrait in its allotted place, chequered all over with coloured lights and everybody would be satisfied. *How* the Orrincourt will gloat."

Troy's voice faded on a note of uncertainty. Alleyn saw her hands move nervously together. She caught his eye and turned away. "Let's not talk about the poor Ancreds," she said.

"What are you munching over in the back of your mind?" he asked uneasily.

"It's nothing," she said quickly. He waited, and after a moment she came to him. "It's only that I'd like you to tell me: Suppose you'd heard from somebody else, or read, about the Ancreds and all the unaccountable odds and ends—what would you think? I mean——" Troy frowned and looked at her clasped hands. Doesn't it sound rather horribly like the beginning of a chapter in *Famous Trials?*"

"Are you really worried about this?" he said after a pause.

"Oddly enough," said Troy, "I am."

Alleyn got up and stood with his back turned to her. When he spoke again his voice had changed.

"Well," he said, "we'd better tackle it, then."

"What's the matter?" he heard Troy saying doubtfully. "What's happened?"

"Something quite ridiculous and we'll get rid of it. A fetish I nurse. I've never fancied coming home and having a nice cosy chat about the current homicide with my wife. I've never talked about such cases when they did crop up."

"I wouldn't have minded, Rory."

"It's a kind of fastidiousness. No, that's praising it. It's illogical and indefensible. If my job's not fit for you, it shouldn't be my job."

"You're being too fancy. I've got over my squeamishness."

"I didn't want you to get over it," he said. "I tell you I'm a fool about this."

She said the phrase he had hoped to hear. "Then do you think there's something in it—about the Ancreds?"

"Blast the Ancreds! Here, this won't do. Come on, let's tackle the thing and scotch it. You're thinking like this, aren't you? There's a book about embalming in their ghastly drawing-room. It stresses the use of arsenic. Old Ancred went about bragging that he was going to have himself mummified. Any one might have read the book. Sonia Orrincourt was seen doing so. Arsenic, used for rat poison, disappeared in the house. Old Ancred died immediately after altering his Will in the Orrincourt's favour. There wasn't an autopsy. If one were made now, the presence of arsenic would be accounted for by the embalming. That's the colour of the nigger in the woodpile, isn't it?"

"Yes," said Troy, "that's it."

"And you've been wondering whether the practical jokes and all the rest of the fun and games can be fitted in?"

"It sounds less possible as you say it."

"Good!" he said, quickly turning to her. "That's better. Come on, then. You've wondered if the practical jokes were organized by the Orrincourt to put the old man off his favourite grandchild?"

"Yes. Or by Cedric, with the same motive. You see, Panty was hot favourite before the Raspberry and Flying Cow Period set in."

"Yes. So, in short, you're wondering if one of the Ancreds, particularly Cedric, or Miss Orrincourt, murdered old Ancred, having previously, in effect, hamstrung the favourite."

"This is like talking about a nightmare. It leaves off being horrid and turns silly."

"All the better," he said vigorously. "All right. Now, if the lost arsenic was the lethal weapon, the murder was planned long before the party. You understood Millamant to say it had been missing for some time?"

"Yes. Unless——"

"Unless Millamant herself is a murderess and was doing an elaborate cover-up."

"Because I said one didn't know what Millamant thought about it, it doesn't follow that she thought about murder."

"Of course it doesn't, bless your heart. Now, if any one of the Ancreds murdered Sir Henry, it was on the strength of the announcement made at the dinner-party and without any knowledge of the effective Will he made that night. If he made it that night."

"Unless one of the legatees thought they'd been cheated and did it out of pure fury."

"Or Fenella and Paul, who got nothing? Yes. There's that."

"Fenella and Paul," said Troy firmly, "are not like that."

"And if Desdemona or Thomas or Jenetta——"

"Jenetta and Thomas are out of the question——"

"——did it, the practical jokes don't fit in, because they weren't there for the earlier ones."

"Which leaves the Orrincourt and Cedric, Millamant and Pauline."

"I can see it's the Orrincourt and Cedric who are really bothering you."

"More particularly," said Troy unhappily, "the Orrincourt."

"Well, darling, what's she like? Has she got the brains to think it up? Would she work out the idea from reading the book on embalming that arsenic would be found in the body anyway?"

"I shouldn't have thought," said Troy cheerfully, "that she'd make head or tail of the book. It was printed in very dim italics with the long "s" like an "f". She's not at all the type to pore over literary curiosa unless she thought they were curious in the specialized sense."

"Feeling better?" he asked.

"Yes, thank you. I'm thinking of other things for myself. Arsenic takes effect pretty quickly, doesn't it? And tastes beastly? He couldn't have had it at dinner, because, apart from being in a foul rage, he was still all right when he left the little theatre. And—if Sonia Orrincourt had put it in his Ovaltine, or whatever he has in his bedside Thermos, could he have sipped down enough to kill him without noticing the taste?"

"Unlikely," Alleyn said. Another silence fell between them. Alleyn thought: "I've never been able to make up my mind about telepathy. Think of something else. Is she listening to my thoughts?"

"Rory," said Troy. "It is all right, isn't it?"

The telephone rang and he was glad to answer it. Inspector Fox was speaking from the Yard.

"Where have you been, you old devil?" said Alleyn, and his voice held that cordiality with which we greet a rescuer.

"Good evening, Mr. Alleyn," said Fox. "I was wondering if it would inconvenience you and Mrs. Alleyn very much if——"

"Come along!" Alleyn interrupted. "Of course it won't. Troy will be delighted; won't you, darling? It's Fox."

"Of course I shall," said Troy loudly. "Tell him to come."

"Very kind, I'm sure," Fox was saying in his deliberate way. "Perhaps I ought to explain though. It's Yard business. You might say very unusual circumstances, really. Quite a contretemps."

"The accent's improving, Fox."

"I don't get the practice. About this business, though. In a manner of speaking, sir, I fancy you'll want to consult Mrs. Alleyn. She's with you, evidently."

"What is it?" Troy asked quickly. "I can hear him. What is it?"

"Well, Fox," said Alleyn after a pause, "what is it?"

"Concerning the late Sir Henry Ancred, sir. I'll explain when I see you. There's been an Anonymous Letter."

IV

"Coincidence," said Fox, putting on his spectacles and flattening out a sheet of paper on his knee, "is one of the things you get accustomed to in our line of business, as I think you'll agree, sir. Look at the way one of our chaps asked for a lift in the Gutteridge case. Look at the Thompson-Bywaters case——"

"For the love of heaven!" Alleyn cried, "let us admit coincidence without further parley. It's staring us in the face. It's a bloody quaint coincidence that my wife should have been staying in this wretched dump, and there's an end of it."

He glanced at Fox's respectable, grave, and attentive face. "I'm sorry," he said. "It's no good expecting me to be reasonable over this business. Troy's had one bad enough experience of the nastiest end of our job. She'll never altogether forget it, and—well, there you are. One doesn't welcome anything like a reminder."

"I'm sure it's very upsetting, Mr. Alleyn. If I could have——"

"I know, I know." And looking at Fox, Alleyn felt a spasm of self-distaste.

"Fox," he said suddenly, "I'm up against a silly complexity in my own attitude to my job. I've tried to shut it off from my private life. I've adopted what I suppose the Russians would call an unrealistic approach: Troy in one compartment, the detection of crime in another. And now, by way of dotting me one on the wind, the fates have handed Troy this little affair on a platter. If there's anything in it she'll be a witness."

"There may not be anything in it, Mr. Alleyn."

"True enough. That's precisely the remark I've been making to her for the last hour or so."

Fox opened his eyes very wide. "Oh, yes," said Alleyn, "she's already thought there was something off-colour about the festivities at Ancreton."

"Is that so?" Fox said slowly. "Is that the case?"

"It is indeed. She's left us alone to talk it over. I can give you the story when you want it and so can she. But I'd better have your end first. What's that paper you've got there?"

Fox handed it to him. "It came in to us yesterday, went through the usual channels, and finally the Chief got on to it and sent for me this evening. You'd gone by then, sir, but he asked me to have a word with you about it. White envelope to match, addressed in block capitals 'C.I.D., Scotland Yard, London.' Postmark, Victoria."

Alleyn took the paper. It appeared to be a sheet from a block of faintly ruled notepaper. The lines were, unusually, a pale yellow, and a margin was ruled down the side. The message it contained was flatly explicit:

THE WRITER HAS REASON TO BELIEVE THAT SIR HENRY
ANCRED'S DEATH WAS BROUGHT ABOUT BY THE PERSON
WHO HAS RECEIVED THE MOST BENEFIT FROM IT.

"Water-mark, 'Crescent Script'. People write these things," said Fox. "You know yourself there may be nothing in it. But we've got to take the usual notice. Talk to the super at the local station, I suppose. And the doctor who attended the old gentleman. He may be able to put the matter beyond doubt. There's an end of it."

"He will if he can," said Alleyn grimly. "You may depend upon that."

"In the meantime, the A.C. suggested I should report to you and see about a chat with Mrs. Alleyn. He remembered Mrs. Alleyn had been at Ancreton before you came back."

"*Report* to me? If anything comes of this, does he want me to take over?"

"Well, sir, I fancy he will. He mentioned, jokingly-like, that it'd be quite unusual if the investigating officer got his first statement on a case from his wife."

"Facetious ass!" said Alleyn with improper emphasis.

Fox looked demurely down his nose.

"Oh, well," said Alleyn, "let's find Troy and we'll hag over the whole blasted set-up. She's in the studio. Come on."

Troy received Fox cheerfully. "I know what it's all about, Mr.

659

Fox," she said, shaking hands with him.

"I'm sure I'm very sorry——" Fox began.

"But you needn't be," Troy said quickly, linking her arm through Alleyn's. "Why on earth should you be? If I'm wanted, here I am. What happens?"

"We sit down," Alleyn said, "and I go over the whole story as you've told it to me. When I go wrong, you stop me, and when you think of anything extra, you put it in. That's all, so far. The whole thing may be a complete washout, darling. Anonymous letter writers have the same affection for the Yard that elderly naturalists have for *The Times*. Now then. Here, Fox, to the best of my ability, is the Ancred saga."

He went methodically through Troy's account, correlating the events, tracing the several threads in and out of the texture of the narrative and gathering them together at the end.

"How's that?" he asked her when he had finished. He was surprised to find her staring at him as if he had brought off a feat of sleight of hand.

"Amazingly complete and tidy," she said.

"Well, Fox? What's it amount to?"

Fox wiped his hand over his jaw. "I've been asking myself, sir," he said, "whether you mightn't find quite a lot of circumstances behind quite a lot of sudden demises that might sound funny if you strung them together. What I mean to say, a lot of big houses keep rat-bane on the premises, and a lot of people can't lay their hands on it when they want it. Things get mislaid."

"Very true, Foxkin."

"And as far as this old-fashioned book on embalming goes, Mr. Alleyn, I ask myself if perhaps somebody mightn't have picked it up since the funeral and got round to wondering about it like Mrs. Alleyn has. You say these good people weren't very keen on Miss Sonia Orrincourt and are probably feeling rather sore about the late old gentleman's Will. They seem to be a highly-strung, excitable lot."

"But I don't think I'm a particularly highly-strung, excitable lot, Mr. Fox," said Troy. "And I got the idea too."

"There!" said Fox, clicking his tongue. "Putting my foot in it as usual, aren't I, sir?"

"Tell us what else you ask yourself," said Alleyn.

"Why, whether one of these disappointed angry people hasn't

660

let his imagination, or more likely hers, get the upper hand, and written this letter on the spur of the moment."

"But what about the practical jokes, Mr. Fox?" said Troy.

"Very silly, mischievous behaviour. Committing a nuisance. If the little girl didn't do them, and it looks as if she *couldn't* have done them at all, then somebody's brought off an unpleasant trick. Spiteful," Fox added severely. "Trying to prejudice the old gentleman against her, as you suggest, I dare say. But that doesn't necessarily mean murder. Why should it?"

"Why, indeed?" said Alleyn, taking him by the arm. "You're exactly what we needed in this house, Br'er Fox. Let's all have a drink." He took his wife on his other arm, and together they returned to the sitting-room. The telephone rang as Troy entered and she answered it. Alleyn held Fox back and they stared at each other.

"Very convincing performance, Fox. Thank you."

"Rum go, sir, all the same, don't you reckon?"

"Too bloody rum by half. Come on."

When they went into the room Troy put her hand over the mouthpiece of the telephone and turned to them. Her face was white.

"Rory," she said, "it's Thomas Ancred. He wants to come and see you. He says they've all had letters. He says he's made a discovery. He wants to come. What shall I say?"

"I'll speak to him," said Alleyn. "He can see me at the Yard in the morning, damn him."

CHAPTER X

Bombshell from Thomas

I

Thomas Ancred arrived punctually at nine o'clock, the hour Alleyn had appointed. Fox was present at the interview, which took place in Alleyn's room.

Troy had the painter's trick of accurate description, and she had been particularly good on Thomas. Alleyn felt he was already familiar with that crest of fine hair, those eyes wide open and palely astonished, that rather tight, small mouth, and the mild meandering voice.

"Thank you very much," said Thomas, "for letting me come. I didn't much want to, of course, but it's nice of you to have me. It was knowing Mrs. Alleyn that put it into their heads."

"Whose heads?" asked Alleyn.

"Well, Pauline's and Dessy's, principally. Paul and Fenella were quite keen too. I suppose Mrs. Alleyn has told you about my people?"

"I think," said Alleyn, "that it might be best if we adopt the idea that I know nothing about anybody."

"Oh, dear!" said Thomas, sighing. "That means a lot of talking, doesn't it?"

"What about these letters?"

"Yes, to be sure," said Thomas, beginning to pat himself all over. "The letters. I've got them somewhere. Anonymous, you know. Of course I've had them before in the theatre from disappointed patrons and angry actresses, but this is different—really. Now, where?" He picked up one corner of his jacket, looked suspiciously at a bulging pocket, and finally pulled out a number of papers, two pencils and a box of matches. Thomas beamed at Alleyn. "And there, after all, they are," he said. In mild triumph he laid them out on the desk—eight copies of the letter Alleyn had already seen, all printed with the same type of pen on the same type of paper.

"What about the envelopes?" Alleyn asked.

"Oh," said Thomas, "we didn't keep them. I wasn't going to say anything about mine," Thomas continued after a pause, "and nor were Jenetta and Milly, but of course everybody noticed everybody else had the same sort of letter, and Pauline (my sister, Pauline Kentish) made a great hallabaloo over hers, and there we were, you know."

"Eight," said Alleyn. "And there are nine in the party at Ancreton?"

"Sonia didn't get one, so everybody says she's the person meant."

"Do you take that view, Mr. Ancred?"

"Oh, yes," said Thomas, opening his eyes very wide. "It seems obvious, doesn't it? With the Will and everything. Sonia's meant, of course, but for my part," said Thomas with a diffident cough, "I don't fancy she murdered Papa."

He gave Alleyn a rather anxious smile. "It would be such a beastly thing to do, you know," he said. "Somehow one can't quite—however. Pauline actually almost leapt at the idea. Dessy, in a way, too. They're both dreadfully upset. Pauline fainted at the funeral anyway, and then with those letters on top of it all she's in a great state of emotional upheaval. You can't imagine what it's like at Ancreton."

"It was Mrs. Kentish, wasn't it, who suggested you should come to the Yard?"

"And Dessy. My unmarried sister, Desdemona. We all opened our letters yesterday morning at breakfast. Can you imagine? I got down first and really—such a shock! I was going to throw it on the fire, but just then Fenella came in, so I folded it up very small under the table. You can see which is mine by the creases. Paul's is the one that looks as if it had been chewed. He crunched it up, don't you know, in his agitation. Well, then I noticed that there were the same kind of envelopes in front of everybody's plate. Sonia has breakfast in her room, but I asked Barker if there were any letters for her. Fenella was by that time looking rather odd, having opened hers. Pauline said: 'What an extraordinary looking letter I've got. Written by a child, I should think,' and

663

Milly said: 'Panty again, perhaps,' and there was a row, because Pauline and Milly don't see eye to eye over Panty. And then everybody said: 'I've got one too,' and then you know they opened them. Well, Pauline swooned away, of course, and Dessy said: 'O, my prophetic soul,' and began to get very excitable, and Milly said: 'I think people who write anonymous letters are the *end*,' and Jenetta (my sister-in-law), Fenella's mother (who is married to my brother Claude), said: 'I agree, Milly.' Then the next thing was, let me see—the next thing was everybody suspecting everybody else of writing the letter, until Paul got the idea—you must excuse me—that perhaps Mrs. Alleyn being married to——"

Alleyn, catching sight of Fox's scandalised countenance, didn't answer, and Thomas, rather pink in the face, hurried on. "Of course," he said, "the rest of us pooh-poohed the notion; quite howled it down, in fact. 'The very idea,' Fenella, for instance, said, 'of Mrs. Alleyn writing anonymous letters is just *so* bloody silly that we needn't discuss it,' which led directly into another row, because Pauline made the suggestion and Fenella and Paul are engaged against her wish. It ended by my nephew Cedric, who is now the head of the family, saying that he thought the letter sounded like Pauline herself. He mentioned that a favourite phrase of Pauline's is: 'I have reason to believe.' Milly, Cedric's mother, you know, laughed rather pointedly, so naturally there was another row."

"Last night," Alleyn said, "you told me you had made a discovery at Ancreton. What was it?"

"Oh, yes. I was coming to that some time. Now, actually, because it happened after lunch. I really don't care at all for this part of the story. Indeed, I quite forgot myself, and said I would *not* go back to Ancreton until I was assured of not having to get involved in any more goings on."

"I'm afraid——" Alleyn began, but Thomas at once interrupted him. "You don't follow? Well, of course you wouldn't, would you, because I haven't told you? Still, I suppose I'd better."

Alleyn waited without comment.

"Well," said Thomas at last. "Here, after all, we go."

"All yesterday morning," Thomas said, "after reading the letters, the battle, as you might put it, raged. Nobody really on anybody else's side except Paul and Fenella and Jenetta wanting to burn the letters and Pauline and Desdemona thinking there was something in it and we ought to keep them. And by lunch-time, you may depend on it, feeling ran very high indeed. And then, you know——"

Here Thomas paused and stared meditatively at a spot on the wall somewhere behind Fox's head. He had this odd trick of stopping short in his narratives. It was as if a gramophone needle was abruptly and unreasonably lifted from the disc. It was impossible to discover whether Thomas was suddenly bereft of the right word or smitten by the intervention of a new train of thought, or whether he had merely forgotten what he was talking about. Apart from a slight glazing of his eyes, his facial expression remained uncannily fixed.

"And then," Alleyn prompted after a long pause.

"Because, when you come to think of it," Thomas's voice began, "it's the last thing one expects to find in the cheese-dish. It was New Zealand cheese, of course. Papa was fortunate in his friends."

"What," Alleyn asked temperately, "is the last thing, Fox, that one would expect to find in the cheese-dish?"

Before Fox could reply Thomas began again.

"It's an old piece of Devonport. Rather nice, really. Blue, with white swans sailing round it. Very large. In times of plenty we used to have a whole Stilton in it, but now, of course, only a tiny packet. Rather ridiculous, really, but it meant there was plenty of room."

"For what?"

"It was Cedric who lifted the lid and discovered it. He gave one of his little screams, but beyond feeling rather irritated, I dare say nobody paid much attention. Then he brought it over to the table—did I forget to say it's always left on the sideboard?—and dropped it in front of Pauline, who is in a very nervous condition anyway, and nearly shrieked the place down."

"Dropped the cheese-dish? Or the cheese?"

"The cheese? Good heavens," cried the scandalised Thomas, "what an idea! The book, to be sure."

"What book?" Alleyn said automatically.

"*The* book, you know. The one out of the glass thing in the drawing-room."

"Oh," said Alleyn after a pause. "That book. On embalming?"

"And arsenic and all the rest of it. Too awkward and beastly, because, you know, Papa, by special arrangement, *was*. It upset everybody frightfully. In such very bad taste, everybody thought, and, of course, the cry of 'Panty' went up immediately on all sides, and there was Pauline practically in a dead faint for the second time in three days."

"Yes?"

"Yes, and then Milly remembered seeing Sonia look at the book, and Sonia said she had never seen it before, and then Cedric read out some rather beastly bits about arsenic, and everybody began to remember how Barker couldn't find the rat poison when it was wanted for Bracegirdle. Then Pauline and Desdemona looked at each other in such a meaning sort of way that Sonia became quite frantic with rage, and said she'd leave Ancreton there and then, only she couldn't, because there wasn't a train, so she went out in the rain and the governess-cart, and is now in bed with bronchitis, to which she is subject."

"Still at Ancreton?"

"Yes, still there. Quite," said Thomas. His expression became dazed, and he went off into another of his silences.

"And that," Alleyn said, "is, of course, the discovery you mentioned on the telephone?"

"That? Discovery? What discovery? Oh, no!" cried Thomas. "I see what you mean. Oh, no, indeed, *that* was nothing compared to what we found afterwards in her room!"

"What did you find, Mr. Ancred, and in whose room?"

"Sonia's," said Thomas. "Arsenic."

III

"It was Cedric and the girls' idea," Thomas said. "After Sonia had gone out in the governess-cart they talked and talked. Nobody quite liked to say outright that perhaps Sonia had put rat poison in Papa's hot drink, but even Milly remarked that Sonia had recently got into the way of making it. Papa said she made it better than any of the servants or even than Milly herself. She used to take it in and leave it at his bedside. Cedric remembered

666

seeing Sonia with the Thermos flask in her hands. He passed her in the passage on his way to bed that very night."

"It was at about this stage," Thomas continued, "that somebody—I've forgotten quite whom—said that they thought Sonia's room ought to be searched. Jenetta and Fenella and Paul jibbed at this, but Dessy and Cedric and Pauline were as keen as mustard. I had promised to lend Caroline Able a book so I went away rather gladly. Caroline Able teaches the Difficult Children, including Panty, and she is very worried because of Panty not going bald enough. So it might have been an hour later that I went back to our part of the house. And there was Cedric lying in wait for me. Well, he's the head of the house now, so I suppose I mustn't be beastly about him. All mysterious and whispering, he was."

" 'Ssh,' he said. 'Come upstairs.' "

"He wouldn't say anything more. I felt awfully bored with all this, but I followed him up."

"To Miss Orrincourt's room?" Alleyn suggested as Thomas's eyes had glazed again.

"That's it. How did you guess? And there were Pauline and Milly and Dessy. I must tell you," said Thomas delicately, "that Sonia has a little sort of suite of rooms near Papa's for convenience. It wasn't called anything, because Papa had run out of famous actresses' names. So he had a new label done with 'Orrincourt' on it, and that really infuriated everybody, because Sonia, whatever anybody may care to say to the contrary, is a very naughty actress. Well, not an actress at all, really. Absolutely dire, you might say."

"You found your sisters and Mrs. Henry Ancred in these rooms?"

"Yes. I must tell you that Sonia's suite is in a tower. Like the tower your wife had, only Sonia's tower is higher, because the architect who built Ancreton believed in quaintness. So Sonia has got a bedroom on top and then a bathroom, and at the bottom a boudoir. The bedroom's particularly quaint, with a little door and steps up into the pepper-pot roof which makes a box-room. They are milling about in this box-room and Dessy had found the rat poison in one of Sonia's boxes. It's a preparation of arsenic. It says so on the label. Well!"

"What have you done with it?"

"So awkward!" said Thomas crossly. "They made me take it.

To keep, they said, in case of evidence being needed. Cedric was very particular about it, having read detective books, and he wrapped it up in one of my handkerchiefs. So I've got it in my rooms here in London if you really want to see it."

"We'll take possession of it, I think," said Alleyn with a glance at Fox. Fox made a slight affirmative rumble. "If it's convenient, Mr. Ancred," Alleyn went on, "Fox or I will drop you at your rooms and collect this tin."

"I hope I can find it," Thomas said gloomily.

"Find it?"

"One does mislay things so. Only the other day——" Thomas fell into one of his trances and this time Alleyn waited for something to break through. "I was just thinking, you know," Thomas began rather loudly. "There we all were in her room and I looked out of the window. It was raining. And away down below, like something out of a Noah's Ark, was the governess-cart creeping up the drive, and Sonia, in her fur coat, flapping the reins, I suppose, in the way she has. And when you come to think of it, there, according to Pauline and Dessy and Cedric and Milly, went Papa's murderess."

"But not according to you?" said Alleyn. He was putting away the eight anonymous letters. Fox had risen, and now stared down at their visitor as if Thomas was some large unopened parcel left by mistake in the room.

"*To me?*" Thomas repeated, opening his eyes very wide. "I don't know. How should I? But you wouldn't believe how uncomfortable it makes one feel."

IV

To enter Thomas's room was to walk into a sort of cross between a wastepaper basket and a workshop. Its principal feature was a large round table entirely covered with stacks of paper, paints, photographs, models for stage sets, designs for costumes, and books. In the window was an apparently unused desk. On the walls were portraits of distinguished players, chief among them Sir Henry himself.

"Sit down," invited Thomas, sweeping sheafs of papers from two chairs on to the floor. "I'll just think where——" He began to walk round his table, staring rather vacantly at it. "I came in with my suitcase, of course, and then, you know, the telephone rang.

668

It was *much* later than that when I wanted to find the letters, and I had put them carefully away because of showing them to you. And I *found* them. So I must have unpacked. And I can remember thinking: 'It's poison, and I'd better be careful of my handkerchief in case——' "

He walked suddenly to a wall cupboard and opened it. A great quantity of papers instantly fell out. Thomas stared indignantly at them. "I distinctly remember," he said, turning to Alleyn and Fox with his mouth slightly open. "I *distinctly* remember saying to myself——" But this sentence was also fated to remain unfinished, for Thomas pounced unexpectedly upon some fragment from the cupboard. "I've been looking for that all over the place," he said. "It's *most* important. A cheque, in fact."

He sat on the floor and began scuffling absently among the papers. Alleyn, who for some minutes had been inspecting the chaos that reigned upon the table, lifted a pile of drawings and discovered a white bundle. He loosened the knot at the top and a stained tin was disclosed. It bore a bright red label with the legend: "Rat-X-it! Poison," and, in slightly smaller print, the antidote for arsenical poisoning.

"Here it is, Mr. Ancred," said Alleyn.

"What?" asked Thomas. He glanced up. "Oh, *that*," he said. "I thought I'd put it on the table."

Fox came forward with a bag. Alleyn, muttering something about futile gestures, lifted the tin by the handkerchief. "You don't mind," he said to Thomas, "if we take charge of this? We'll give you a receipt for it."

"Oh, will you?" asked Thomas mildly. "Thanks awfully." He watched them stow away the tin, and then, seeing that they were about to go, scrambled to his feet. "You must have a drink," he said. "There's a bottle of Papa's whisky—I think."

Alleyn and Fox managed to head him off a further search. He sat down, and listened with an air of helplessness to Alleyn's parting exposition.

"Now, Mr. Ancred," Alleyn said, "I think I ought to make as clear as possible the usual procedure following the sort of information you have brought to us. Before any definite step can be taken, the police make what are known as 'further inquiries'. They do this as inconspicuously as possible, since neither their original informant, nor they, enjoy the public exploration of a mare's nest. If these inquiries seem to point to a suspicion of ill practice, the police then get permission from the Home Secretary for the next step to be taken. You know what that is, I expect?"

"I say," said Thomas, "that *would* be beastly, wouldn't it?" A sudden thought seemed to strike him. "I say," he repeated, "would *I* have to be there?"

"We'd probably ask for formal identification by a member of his family."

"Oh, Lor'!" Thomas whispered dismally. He pinched his lower lip between his thumb and forefinger. A gleam of consolation appeared to visit him.

"I say," he said, "it's a good job after all, isn't it, that the Nation *didn't* plump for the Abbey?"

CHAPTER XI

Alleyn at Ancreton

I

"In our game," said Fox as they drove back to the Yard, "you get some funny glimpses into what you might call human nature. I dare say I've said that before, but it's a fact."

"I believe you," said Alleyn.

"Look at this chap we've just left," Fox continued with an air of controversy. "Vague! And yet he must be good at his job, wouldn't you say, sir?"

"Indisputably."

"There! Good at his job, and yet to meet him you'd say he'd lose his play, and his actors, and his way to the theatre. In view of which," Fox summed up, "I ask myself if this chap's as muddleheaded as he lets on."

"A pose, you think, do you, Fox?"

"You never know with some jokers," Fox muttered, and, wiping his great hand over his face, seemed by that gesture to dispose of Thomas Ancred's vagaries. "I suppose," he said, "it'll be a matter of seeing the doctor, won't it?"

"I'm afraid so. I've looked out trains. There's one in an hour. Get us there by midday. We may have to spend the night in Ancreton village. We can pick up our emergency bags at the Yard. I'll talk to the A.C. and telephone Troy. What a hell of a thing to turn up."

"It doesn't look as if we'll be able to let it alone, do you reckon, Mr. Alleyn?"

"I still have hopes. As it stands, there's not a case in Thomas's story to hang a dead dog on. They lose a tin of rat poison and find it in a garret. Somebody reads a book about embalming, and

671

thinks up an elaborate theme based on an arbitrary supposition. Counsel could play skittles with it—as it stands."

"Suppose we *did* get an order for exhumation. Suppose they found arsenic in the body. With this embalming business it'd seem as if it would prove nothing."

"On the contrary," said Alleyn, "I rather think, Fox, that if they did find arsenic in the body it would prove everything."

Fox turned slowly and looked at him. "I don't get that one, Mr. Alleyn," he said.

"I'm not at all sure that I'm right. We'll have to look it up. Here we are. I'll explain on the way down to this accursed village. Come on."

He saw his Assistant Commissioner, who, with the air of a connoisseur, discussed the propriety of an investigator handling a case in which his wife might be called as a witness. "Of course, my dear Rory, if by any chance the thing should come into court and your wife be subpœnaed, we would have to reconsider our position. We've no precedent, so far as I know. But for the time being I imagine it's more reasonable for you to discuss it with her than for anybody else to do so—Fox, for instance. Now, you go down to this place, talk to the indigenous G.P., and come back and tell us what you think about it. Tiresome, if it comes to anything. Good luck."

As they left, Alleyn took from his desk the second volume of a work on medical jurisprudence. It dealt principally with poisons. In the train he commended certain passages to Fox's notice. He watched his old friend put on his spectacles, raise his eyebrows, and develop the slightly catarrhal breathing that invariably accompanied his reading.

"Yes," said Fox, removing his spectacles as the train drew into Ancreton Halt, "that's different, of course."

II

Doctor Herbert Withers was a short, tolerably plump man, with little of the air of wellbeing normally associated with plumpness. He came out into his hall as they arrived, admitting from some inner room the sound of a racing broadcast. After a glance at Alleyn's professional card he took them to his consulting-room, and sat at his desk with a movement whose briskness seemed to overlie a controlled fatigue.

"What's the trouble?" he asked.

It was the conventional opening. Alleyn thought it had slipped involuntarily from Dr. Withers's lips.

"We hope there's no trouble," he said. "Would you mind if I asked you to clear up a few points about Sir Henry Ancred's death?"

The mechanical attentiveness of Dr. Withers's glance sharpened. He made an abrupt movement and looked from Alleyn to Fox.

"Certainly," he said, "if there's any necessity. But why?" He still held Alleyn's card in his hand and he glanced at it again. "You don't mean to say——" he began, and stopped short. "Well, what are these few points?"

"I think I'd better tell you exactly what's happened," Alleyn said. He took a copy of the anonymous letter from his pocket and handed it to Dr. Withers. "Mr. Thomas Ancred brought eight of these to us this morning," he said.

"Damn disgusting piffle," said Dr. Withers and handed it back.

"I hope so. But when we're shown these wretched things we have to do something about them."

"Well?"

"You signed the death certificate, Dr. Withers, and——"

"And I shouldn't have done so if I hadn't been perfectly satisfied as to the cause."

"Exactly. Now will you, like a good chap, help us to dispose of these letters by giving us, in non-scientific words, the cause of Sir Henry's death?"

Dr. Withers fretted a little, but at last went to his files and pulled out a card.

"There you are," he said. "That's the last of his cards. I made routine calls at Ancreton. It covers about six weeks."

Alleyn looked at it. It bore the usual list of dates with appropriate notes. Much of it was illegible and almost all obscure to the lay mind. The final note, however, was flatly lucid. It read: "Deceased. Between twelve-thirty and two a.m., Nov. 25th."

"Yes," said Alleyn. "Thank you. Now will you translate some of this?"

"He suffered," said Dr. Withers angrily, "from gastric ulcers and degeneration of the heart. He was exceedingly indiscriminate in his diet. He'd eaten a disastrous meal, had drunk champagne,

673

and had flown into one of his rages. From the look of the room, I diagnosed a severe gastric attack followed by heart failure. I may add that if I had heard about the manner in which he'd spent the evening I should have expected some such development."

"You'd have expected him to die?"

"That would be an extremely unprofessional prognostication. I would have anticipated grave trouble," said Dr. Withers stuffily.

"Was he in the habit of playing up with his diet?"

"He was. Not continuously, but in bouts."

"Yet survived?"

"The not unusual tale of 'once too often'."

"Yes," said Alleyn, looking down at the card. "Would you mind describing the room and the body?"

"Would you, in your turn, Chief Inspector, mind telling me if you have any reason for this interview beyond these utterly preposterous anonymous letters?"

"Some of the family suspect arsenical poisoning."

"Oh, my God and the little starfish!" Dr. Withers shouted and shook his fists above his head. "That *bloody* family!"

He appeared to wrestle obscurely with his feelings. "I'm sorry about that," he said at last, "inexcusable outburst. I've been busy lately and worried, and there you are. The Ancreds, collectively, have tried me rather high. Why, may one ask, do they suspect arsenical poisoning?"

"It's a long story," said Alleyn carefully, "and it involves a tin of rat poison. May I add also, very unprofessionally, that I shall be enormously glad if you can tell me that the condition of the room and the body precludes the smallest likelihood of arsenical poisoning?"

"I can't tell you anything of the sort. Why? (*a*) Because the room had been cleaned up when I got there. And (*b*) because the evidence as described to me, and the appearance of the body, were entirely consistent with a severe gastric attack, and therefore *not* inconsistent with arsenical poisoning."

"Damn!" Alleyn grunted. "I thought it'd be like that."

"How the hell could the old fool have got at any rat poison? Will you tell me that?" He jabbed his finger at Alleyn.

"They don't think," Alleyn explained, "that he got at it. They think it was introduced to him."

The well-kept hand closed so strongly that the knuckles whitened. For a moment he held it clenched, and then, as if to

cancel this gesture, opened the palm and examined his finger-
nails.

"That," he said, "is implicit in the letter, of course. Even that I
can believe of the Ancreds. Who is supposed to have murdered
Sir Henry? Am I, by any pleasant chance?"

"Not that I know," said Alleyn comfortably. Fox cleared his
throat and added primly: "What an idea!"

"Are they going to press for an exhumation? Or are you?"

"Not without more reason than we've got at the moment,"
Alleyn said. "You didn't hold a post-mortem?"

"One doesn't hold a P.M. on a patient who was liable to go off
in precisely this fashion at any moment."

"True enough. Dr. Withers, may I make our position quite
clear? We've had a queer set of circumstances placed before us
and we've got to take stock of them. Contrary to popular belief,
the police do not, in such cases, burn to get a pile of evidence that
points unavoidably to exhumation. If the whole thing turns out to
be so much nonsense they are, as a general rule, delighted to write
it off. Give us a sound argument against arsenical poisoning and
we'll be extremely grateful to you."

Dr. Withers waved his hands. "I can't give you, at a moment's
notice, absolute proof that he didn't get arsenic. You couldn't do
it for ninety-nine deaths out of a hundred, when there was gastric
trouble with vomiting and purging and no analysis was taken of
anything. As a matter of fact——"

"Yes?" Alleyn prompted as he paused.

"As a matter of fact, I dare say if there'd been anything left I
might have done an analysis simply as a routine measure and to
satisfy a somewhat pedantic medical conscience. But the whole
place had been washed up."

"By whose orders?"

"My dear man, by Barker's orders or Mrs. Kentish's, or Mrs.
Henry Ancred's, or whoever happened to think of it. They didn't
like to move him. Couldn't very well. Rigor was pretty well
established, which gave me, by the way, a lead about the time of
his death. When I saw him later in the day they'd fixed him up, of
course, and a nice time Mrs. Ancred must have had of it with all
of them milling about the house in an advanced condition of
hysteria and Mrs. Kentish 'insisting on taking a hand in the
laying-out'."

"Good Lord!"

"Oh, they're like that. Well, as I was saying, there he was when they found him, hunched up on the bed, and the room in a pretty nauseating state. When I got there, two of those old housemaids were waddling off with their buckets and the whole place stank of carbolic. They'd even managed to change the bedclothes. I didn't get there, by the way, for an hour after they telephoned. Confinement."

"About the children's ringworm——" Alleyn began.

"You know about them, do you! Yes. Worrying business. Glad to say young Panty's cleared up at last."

"I understand," Alleyn said pleasantly, "that you are bold in your use of drugs."

There was a long silence. "And how, may I ask," said Dr. Withers very quietly, "did you hear details of my treatment?"

"Why, from Thomas Ancred," said Alleyn, and watched the colour return to Dr. Withers's face. "Why not?"

"I dislike gossip about my patients. As a matter of fact I wondered if you'd been talking to our local pharmacist. I'm not at all pleased with him at the moment, however."

"Do you remember the evening the children were dosed—Monday, the nineteenth, I think it was?"

Dr. Withers stared at him. "Now, why——?" he began, and seemed to change his mind. "I do," he said. "Why?"

"Simply because that evening a practical joke was played on Sir Henry and the child Panty has been accused of it. It's too elaborate a story to bother you about, but I'd like to know if she was capable of it. In the physical sense. Mentally, it seems, she certainly is."

"What time?"

"During dinner. She would have visited the drawing-room."

"Out of the question. I arrived at seven-thirty—Wait a moment." He searched his filing cabinet and pulled out another card. "Here! I superintended the weighing and dosing of these kids and noted the time. Panty got her quota at eight and was put to bed. I stayed on in the ante-room to their dormitory during the rest of the business and talked to Miss Able. I left her my visiting list for the next twenty-four hours so that she could get me quickly if anything cropped up. It was after nine when I left and this wretched kid certainly hadn't budged. I had a look at the lot of them. She was asleep with a normal pulse and so on."

"That settles Panty, then," Alleyn muttered.

676

"Look here, has this any bearing on the other business?"

"I'm not sure. It's a preposterous story. If you've the time and inclination to listen I'll tell it to you."

"I've got," said Dr. Withers, glancing at his watch, "twenty-three minutes. Case in half an hour, and I want to hear the racing results before I go out."

"I shan't be more than ten minutes."

"Go ahead, then. I should be glad to hear any story, however fantastic, that can connect a practical joke on Monday the nineteenth with the death of Sir Henry Ancred from gastro-enteritis after midnight on Saturday the twenty-fourth."

Alleyn related all the stories of the practical jokes. Dr. Withers punctuated this recital with occasional sounds of incredulity or irritation. When Alleyn reached the incident of the flying cow he interrupted him.

"The child Panty," he said, "is capable of every iniquity, but, as I have pointed out, she could not have perpetrated this offence with the blown-up bladder, nor could she have painted the flying cow on Mrs.——" He stopped short. "Is this lady——?" he began.

"My wife, as it happens," said Alleyn, "but let it pass."

"Good Lord! Unusual that, isn't it?"

"Both unusual and bothering in this context. You were saying?"

"That the child was too seedy that night for it to be conceivable. And you tell me Miss Able (sensible girl that) vouches for her anyway."

"Yes."

"All right. Well, some other fool, the egregious Cedric in all likelihood, performed these idiocies. I fail to see how they can possibly be linked up with Sir Henry's death."

"You have not," Alleyn said, "heard of the incident of the book on embalming in the cheese-dish."

Dr. Withers's mouth opened slightly, but he made no comment, and Alleyn continued his narrative. "You see," he added, "this final trick does bear a sort of family likeness to the others, and, considering the subject matter of the book, and the fact that Sir Henry was embalmed——"

"Quite so. Because the damned book talks about arsenic they jump to this imbecile conclusion——"

"Fortified, we must remember, by the discovery of a tin of

arsenical rat poison in Miss Orrincourt's luggage."

"Planted there by the practical joker," cried Dr. Withers. "I bet you. Planted!"

"That's a possibility," Alleyn agreed, "that we can't overlook."

Fox suddenly said: "Quite so."

"Well," said Dr. Withers, "I'm damned if I know what to say. No medical man enjoys the suggestion that he's been careless or made a mistake, and this would be a very awkward mistake. Mind, I don't for a split second believe there's a fragment of truth in the tale, but if the whole boiling of Ancreds are going to talk arsenic—Here! Have you seen the embalmers?"

"Not yet. We shall do so, of course."

"I don't know anything about embalming," Dr. Withers muttered. "This fossil book may not amount to a row of beans."

"Taylor," said Alleyn, "has a note on it. He says that in such manipulations of a body, antiseptic substances are used (commonly arsenic), and might prevent detection of poison as the cause of death."

"So, if we have an exhumation, where are we? Precisely nowhere."

"I'm not sure of my ground," said Alleyn, "but I fancy that an exhumation should definitely show whether or not Sir Henry Ancred was poisoned. I'll explain."

III

Fox and Alleyn lunched at the Ancreton Arms, on jugged hare, well cooked, and a tankard each of the local draught beer. It was a pleasant enough little pub, and the landlady, on Alleyn's inquiry, said she could, if requested, put them up for the night.

"I'm not at all sure we shan't be taking her at her word," said Alleyn as they walked out into the village street. It was thinly bright with winter sunshine, and contained, beside the pub and Dr Withers's house, a post office shop, a chapel, a draper's, a stationer's, a meeting-hall, a chemist-cum-fancy-goods shop, and a row of cottages. Over the brow of intervening hills, the gothic windows, multiple towers and indefatigably varied chimney-pots of Ancreton Manor glinted against their background of conifers, and brooded, with an air of grand seigneury, faintly bogus, over the little village.

"And here," said Alleyn, pausing at the chemist's window, "is

Mr. Juniper's pharmacy. That's a pleasant name, Fox. E. M. Juniper. This is where Troy and Miss Orrincourt came in their governess-cart on a nasty evening. Let's call on Mr. Juniper, shall we?"

But he seemed to be in no hurry to go in, and began to mutter to himself before the side window. "A tidy window, Fox. I like the old-fashioned coloured bottles, don't you? Writing paper, you see, and combs and ink (that brand went of the market in the war) cheek-by-jowl with cough-lozenges and trusses in their modest boxes. Even some children's card games. Happy Families. That's how Troy drew the Ancreds. Let's give them a pack. Mr. Juniper the chemist's window. Come on."

He led the way in. The shop was divided into two sections. One counter was devoted to fancy goods, and one, severe and isolated, to Mr. Juniper's professional activities. Alleyn rang a little bell, a door opened, and Mr. Juniper, fresh and rosy in his white coat, came out, together with the cleanly smell of drugs.

"*Yes*, sir?" Mr. Juniper inquired, placing himself behind his professional counter.

"Good morning," said Alleyn. "I wonder if by any chance you've got anything to amuse a small girl who's on the sick list?"

Mr. Juniper removed to the fancy-goods department. "Happy Families? Bubble-blowing?" he suggested.

"Actually," Alleyn lied pleasantly, "I've been told I must bring back some form of practical joke. Designed, I'm afraid, for Dr. Withers."

"Really! T't. Ha-ha!" said Mr. Juniper. "Well, now. I'm afraid we haven't anything much in that line. There were some dummy ink-spots, but I'm afraid—No. I know exactly the type of thing you mean, mind, but I'm just afraid——"

"Somebody said something about a thing you blow up and sit on," Alleyn murmured vaguely. "It sounded disgusting."

"Ah! The Raspberry?"

"That's it."

Mr. Juniper shook his head sadly and made a gesture of resignation.

"I thought," said Alleyn, "I saw a box in your window that looked——"

"Empty!" Mr. Juniper sighed. "The customer didn't require the box, so I'm afraid I've just left it there. Now isn't that a pity," Mr. Juniper lamented. "Only last week, or would it be a fortnight ago, I sold the last of that little line to a customer for exactly the same purpose. A sick little girl. Yes. One would almost think," he hazarded, "that the same little lady——"

"I expect so. Patricia Kentish," said Alleyn.

"Ah, quite so. So the customer said! Up at the Manor. Quite a little tinker," said Mr. Juniper. "Well, sir, I think you'll find that Miss Pant—Miss Pat—has already got a Raspberry."

"In that case," said Alleyn, "I'll take a Happy Families. You want some toothpaste, don't you, Fox?"

"Happy Families," said Mr. Juniper, snatching a packet from the shelf. "Dentifrice! Any particular make, sir?"

"For a plate," said Fox stolidly.

"For the denture. Quite," said Mr. Juniper, and darted into the professional side of his shop.

"I wouldn't mind betting," said Alleyn cheerfully to Fox, "that it was Sonia Orrincourt who got in first with that thing."

"Ah," said Fox. Mr. Juniper smiled archly. "Well, now," he said, "I oughtn't to give the young lady away, ought I? Professional secrets. Ha-ha! "

"Ha-ha!" Alleyn agreed, putting Happy Families in his pocket. "Thank you, Mr. Juniper."

"Thank *you*, sir. All well up at the Manor, I hope? Great loss, that. Loss to the Nation, you might say. Little trouble with the children clearing up, I hope?"

"On its way. Lovely afternoon, isn't it? Good-bye."

"I didn't want any toothpaste," said Fox, as they continued up the street.

"I didn't see why I should make all the purchases and you were looking rather too portentous. Put it down to expenses. It was worth it."

"I don't say it wasn't that," Fox agreed. "Now, sir, if this woman Orrincourt took the Raspberry, I suppose we look to her for all the other pranks, don't we?"

"I hardly think so, Fox. Not all. We know, at least, that this ghastly kid tied a notice to the tail of her Aunt Millamant's coat. She's got a reputation for practical jokes. On the other hand, she definitely, it seems, did not perpetrate the Raspberry and the flying cow, and my wife is convinced she's innocent of the spectacles, the painted stair rail and the rude writing on Sir Henry's looking-glass. As for the book in the cheese-dish, I don't think either Panty or Miss Orrincourt is guilty of that flight of fancy."

"So that if you count out the little girl for anything that matters, we've got Miss Orrincourt and another."

"That's the cry."

"And this other is trying to fix something on Miss Orrincourt in the way of arsenic and the old gentleman?"

"It's a reasonable thesis, but Lord knows."

"Where are we going, Mr. Alleyn?"

"Are you good for a two-mile walk? I think we'll call on the Ancreds."

IV

"It isn't," said Alleyn as they toiled up the second flight of terraces, "as if we can hope to keep ourselves dark, supposing that were advisable. Thomas will have rung up his family and told them that we have at least taken notice. We may as well announce ourselves and see what we can see. More especially, this wretched old fellow's bedroom."

"By this time," said Fox sourly, "they'll probably have had it repapered."

"I wonder if Paul Kentish is handy with electrical gadgets. I'll wager Cedric Ancred isn't."

"What's that?" Fox demanded.

"What's what?"

"I can hear something. A child crying, isn't it, sir?"

They had reached the second terrace. At each end of this terrace, between the potato-field and the woods, were shrubberies and young copses. From the bushes on their left hand came a thin intermittent wailing; very dolorous. They paused uncertainly, staring at each other. The wailing stopped, and into the silence welled the accustomed sounds of the countryside—the wintry chittering of birds and the faint click of naked branches.

"Would it be some kind of bird, should you say?" Fox speculated.

"No bird!" Alleyn began and stopped short. "There it is again." It was a thin piping sound, waving and irregular and the effect of it was peculiarly distressing. Without further speculation they set off across the rough and still frost-encrusted ground. As they drew nearer to it the sound became, not articulate, but more complex, and presently, when they had drawn quite close, developed a new character.

"It's mixed up," Fox whispered, "with a kind of singing."

> *"Good-bye poor pussy your coat was so warm,*
> *And even if you did moult you did me no harm.*
> *Good-bye poor pussy for ever and ever*
> *And make me a good girl, amen.*

"*For ever and ever*," the thin voice repeated, and drifted off again into its former desolate wail. As they brushed against the first low bushes it ceased, and there followed a wary silence disrupted by harsh sobbing.

Between the bushes and the copse they came upon a little girl in a white cap, sitting by a newly-turned mound of earth. A child's spade was beside her. Stuck irregularly in the mound of earth were a few heads of geraniums. A piece of paper threaded on a twig stood crookedly at the head of the mound. The little girl's hands were earthy, and she had knuckled her eyes so that black streaks ran down her face. She crouched there scowling at them, rather like an animal that flattens itself near the ground, unable to obey its own instinct for flight.

"Hallo," said Alleyn, "this is a bad job!" And unable to think of a more satisfactory opening, he heard himself repeating Dr. Withers's phrase. "What's the trouble?" he asked.

The little girl was convulsed, briefly, by a sob. Alleyn squatted beside her and examined the writing on the paper. It had been executed in large shaky capitals.

> "KARABAS,
> R.S.V.P.
> LOVE FROM PANTY."

"Was Carabbas," Alleyn ventured, "your own cat?"

Panty glared at him and slowly shook her head.

Alleyn said quickly: "How stupid of me; he was your grandfather's cat, wasn't he?"

"He loved me," said Panty on a high note. "Better than he loved Noddy. He loved me better than he loved anybody. I was his friend." Her voice rose piercingly like the whistle of a small engine. "And I didn't," she screamed, "I didn't, I didn't, I didn't give him the ringworms. I hate my Auntie Milly. I wish she was dead. I wish they were all dead. I'll kill my Auntie Milly." She beat on the ground with her fists, and, catching sight of Fox, screamed at him: "Get out of here, will you? This is my place."

Fox stepped back hastily.

"I've heard," said Alleyn, cautiously, "about Carabbas and about you. You paint pictures, don't you? Have you painted any more pictures lately?"

"I don't want to paint any more pictures," said Panty.

"That's a pity, because we rather thought of sending you a box of paints for yourself from London."

Panty sobbed dryly. "Who did?" she said.

"Troy Alleyn," said Alleyn. "Mrs. Alleyn, you know. She's my wife."

"If I painted a picture of my Auntie Milly," said Panty, "I'd give her pig's whiskers, and she'd look like Judas Iscariot. They said my cat Carabbas had the ringworms, and they said I'd given them to him, and they're all, *all* liars. He hadn't, and I didn't. It was only his poor fur coming out."

With the abandon which Troy had witnessed in the little theatre, Panty flung herself face forward on the ground and kicked. Tentatively Alleyn bent over her, and after a moment's hesitation picked her up. For a moment or two she fought violently, but suddenly, with an air of desolation, let her arms fall and hung limply in his hands.

"Never mind, Panty," Alleyn muttered helplessly. "Here, let's mop up your face." He felt in his pocket and his fingers closed round a hard object. "Look here," he said. "Look what I've got," and pulled out a small packet. "Do you ever play Happy Families?" he said. He pushed the box of cards into her hands and not very successfully mopped her face with his handkerchief. "Let's move on," he said to Fox.

He carried the now inert Panty across to the third flight of steps. Here she began to wriggle, and he put her down.

"I want to play Happy Families," said Panty thickly. "Here," she added. She squatted down, and, still interrupting herself from time to time with a hiccuping sob, opened her pack of picture cards, and with filthy fingers began to deal them into three heaps.

"Sit down, Fox," said Alleyn. "You're going to play Happy Families."

Fox sat uneasily on the second step.

Panty was a slow dealer, principally because she examined the face of each card before she put it down.

"Do you know the rules?" Alleyn asked Fox.

"I can't say I do," he replied, putting on his spectacles. "Would it be anything like euchre?"

"Not much, but you'll pick it up. The object is to collect a family. Would you be good enough," he said, turning to Panty, "to oblige me with Mrs. Snips the Tailor's Wife?"

"You didn't say "Please," so it's my turn," said Panty. "Give me Mr. Snips, the Tailor, and Master Snips and Miss Snips, please."

"Damn," said Alleyn. "Here you are," and handed over the cards, each with its cut of an antic who might have walked out of a Victorian volume of *Punch*.

Panty pushed these cards underneath her and sat on them. Her bloomers, true to her legend, were conspicuous. "Now," she said, turning a bleary glance on Fox, "you give me——"

"Don't I get a turn?" asked Fox.

"Not unless she goes wrong," said Alleyn. "You'll learn."

"Give me," said Panty, "Master Grit, the Grocer's Son."

"Doesn't she have to say 'please'?"

"Please," yelled Panty. I said 'please'. Please."

Fox handed over the card.

"And Mrs. Grit," Panty went on.

"It beats me," said Fox, "how she knows."

"She knows," said Alleyn, "because she looked."

Panty laughed raucously. "And you give me Mr. Bull, the Butcher," she demanded, turning on Alleyn. "Please."

"Not at home," said Alleyn triumphantly. "And now, you see, Fox, it's my turn."

"The game seems crook to me," said Fox, gloomily.

"Master Bun," Panty remarked presently, "is azzakerly like my Uncle Thomas." Alleyn, in imagination, changed the grotesque faces on all the cards to those of the Ancreds as Troy had drawn them in her notebook. "So he is," he said. "And now I know you've got him. Please give me Master Ancred, the Actor's Son." This sally afforded Panty exquisite amusement. With primitive guffaws she began to demand cards under the names of her immediate relations and to the utter confusion of the game.

"There now," said Alleyn at last, in a voice that struck him as being odiously complacent. "That was a lovely game. Suppose you take us up to see the—ah——"

"The Happy Family," Fox prompted in a wooden voice.

"Certainly," said Alleyn.

"Why?" Panty demanded.

"That's what we've come for."

Panty stood squarely facing him. Upon her stained face there grew, almost furtively, a strange expression. It was compounded, he thought, of the look of a normal child about to impart a secret and of something less familiar, more disquieting.

"Here!" she said. "I want to tell you something. Not him. You."

She drew Alleyn away, and with a sidelong glance pulled him down until she could hook her arm about his neck. He waited, feeling her breath uncomfortably in his ear.

"What is it?"

The whispering was disembodied but unexpectedly clear. "We've got," it said, "a murderer in our family."

When he drew back and looked at her she was smiling nervously.

CHAPTER XII

The Bell and the Book

I

So accurate and lively were Troy's drawings that Alleyn recognized Desdemona Ancred as soon as she appeared on the top step of the third terrace and looked down upon the group, doubtless a curious one, made by himself, Panty and Fox. Indeed, as she paused, she struck precisely the attitude, histrionic and grandiose, with which Troy had invested her caricature.

"Ah!" said Dessy richly. "Panty! At last!"

She held out her hand towards Panty and at the same time looked frankly at Alleyn. "How do you do?" she said. "Are you on your way up? Has this terrible young person waylaid you? Shall I introduce myself?"

"Miss Ancred?" Alleyn said.

"He's Mrs. Alleyn's husband," Panty said. "We don't much want you, thank you, Aunt Dessy."

Dessy was in the act of advancing with poise down the steps. Her smile remained fixed on her face. Perhaps she halted for a fraction of time in her stride. The next second her hand was in his, and she was gazing with embarrassing intensity into his eyes.

"I'm so glad you've come," she said in her deepest voice. "So glad! We are terribly, terribly distressed. My brother has told you, I know." She pressed his hand, released it, and looked at Fox.

"Inspector Fox," said Alleyn. Desdemona was tragically gracious.

They turned to climb the steps. Panty gave a threatening wail.

"You," said her aunt, "had better run home as fast as you can. Miss Able's been looking everywhere for you. What *have* you

686

been doing, Panty? You're covered in earth."

Immediately they were confronted with another scene. Panty repeated her former performance, roaring out strange threats against her family, lamenting the cat Carabbas, and protesting that she had not infected him.

"Really, it's *too* ridiculous," Dessy said in a loud aside to Alleyn. "Not that we didn't all feel it. Poor Carabbas! And my father so attached always. But honestly, it was a menace to all our healths. Ringworm, beyond a shadow of doubt. Fur coming out in handfuls. Obviously it had given them the disease in the first instance. We did perfectly right to have it destroyed. Come *on*, Panty."

By this time they had reached the top terrace, with Panty waddling lamentably behind them. Here they were met by Miss Caroline Able, who brightly ejaculated: "Goodness, what a noise!" cast a clear sensible glance at Alleyn and Fox, and removed her still bellowing charge.

"I'm so distressed," Desdemona cried, "that you should have had this reception. Honestly, poor Panty is simply beyond everything. Nobody loves children more than I do, but she's got such a *difficult* nature. And in a house of tragedy, when one's nerves and emotions are lacerated——"

She gazed into his eyes, made a small helpless gesture, and finally ushered them into the hall. Alleyn glanced quickly at the space under the gallery, but it was still untenanted.

"I'll tell my sister and my sister-in-law," Dessy began, but Alleyn interrupted her. "If we might just have a word with you first," he said. And by Dessy's manner, at once portentous and dignified, he knew that this suggestion was not unpleasing to her. She led them to the small sitting-room where Troy had found Sonia Orrincourt and Cedric giggling together on the sofa. Desdemona placed herself on this sofa. She sat down, Alleyn noticed, quite beautifully; not glancing at her objective, but sinking on it in one movement and then elegantly disposing her arms.

"I expect," he began, "that your brother has explained the official attitude to this kind of situation. We're obliged to make all sorts of inquiries before we can take any further action."

"I see," said Desdemona, nodding owlishly. "Yes, I see. Go on."

"To put it baldly, do you yourself think there is any truth in the suggestion made by the anonymous letter-writer?"

Desdemona pressed the palms of her hands carefully against her eyes. "If I *could* dismiss it," she cried. "If I could!"

"You have no idea, I suppose, who could have written the letters?" She shook her head. Alleyn wondered if she had glanced at him through her fingers.

"Have any of you been up to London since your father's funeral?"

"How frightful!" she said, dropping her hands and gazing at him. "I was afraid of this. How frightful!"

"What?"

"You think one of us wrote the letter? Someone at Ancreton?"

"Well, really," said Alleyn, stifling his exasperation, "it's not a preposterous conjecture, is it?"

"No, no. I suppose not. But what a disturbing thought."

"Well, did any of you go to London——"

"Let me think, let me think," Desdemona muttered, again covering her eyes. "In the evening. After we had—had—after Papa's funeral, and after Mr. Rattisbon had——" She made another little helpless gesture.

"——had read the Will?" Alleyn suggested.

"Yes. That evening, by the seven-thirty. Thomas and Jenetta (my sister-in-law) and Fenella (her daughter) and Paul (my nephew, Paul Kentish) all went up to London."

"And returned? When?"

"Not at all. Jenetta doesn't live here and Fenella and Paul, because of——However, Fenella has joined her mother in a flat and I think Paul's staying with them. My brother Thomas, as you know, lives in London."

"And nobody else has left Ancreton?"

Yes, it seemed that the following day Millamant and Cedric and Desdemona herself had gone up to London by the early morning train. There was a certain amount of business to be done. They returned in the evening. It was by that evening's post, the Wednesday's, Alleyn reflected, that the anonymous letter reached the Yard. He found by dint of cautious questioning that they had all separated in London and gone their several ways to meet in the evening train.

"And Miss Orrincourt?" Alleyn asked.

"I'm afraid," said Desdemona grandly, "that I've really no knowledge at all of Miss Orrincourt's movements. She was away all day yesterday; I imagine in London."

"She's staying on here?"

"You may well look astonished," said Desdemona, though Alleyn, to his belief, had looked nothing of the sort. "After everything, Mr. Alleyn. After working against us with Papa! After humiliating and wounding us in every possible way. In the teeth, you might say, of the Family's feelings, she stays on. T'uh!"

"Does Sir Cedric——?"

"Cedric," said Desdemona, "is now the head of the Family, but I have no hesitation in saying that I think his attitude to a good many things inexplicable and revolting. Particularly where Sonia Orrincourt (you'll never get me to believe she was born Orrincourt) is concerned. What he's up to, what both of them—However!"

Alleyn did not press for an exposition of Cedric's behaviour. At the moment he was fascinated by Desdemona's. On the wall opposite her hung a looking-glass in a Georgian frame. He saw that Desdemona was keeping an eye on herself. Even as she moved her palms from before her eyes, her fingers touched her hair and she slightly turned her head while her abstracted yet watchful gaze noted, he thought, the effect. And as often as she directed her melting glance upon him, so often did it return to the mirror to affirm with a satisfaction barely veiled its own limpid quality. He felt as if he interviewed a mannequin.

"I understand," he said, "that it was you who found the tin of rat-bane in Miss Orrincourt's suitcase?"

"Wasn't it awful! Well, it was four of us, actually. My sister Pauline (Mrs. Kentish), my sister-in-law, and Cedric and I. In her box-room, you know. A very common-looking suitcase smothered in Number Three Company touring labels. As I've pointed out to Thomas a thousand times, the woman is simply a squalid little ham actress. Well, *not* an actress. All eyes and teeth in the third row of the chorus when she's lucky."

"Did you yourself handle it?"

"Oh, we all handled it. Naturally. Cedric tried to prise up the lid, but it wouldn't come. So he tapped the tin, and said he could tell from the sound that it wasn't full." She lowered her voice. " 'Only half-full,' he said. And Milly (my sister-in-law, Mrs. Henry Ancred) said——" She paused.

"Yes?" Alleyn prompted, tired of these genealogical parentheses. "Mrs. Henry Ancred said?"

689

"She said that to the best of her knowledge it had never been used." She changed her position a little and added: "I don't understand Milly. She's so off-hand. Of course I know she's frightfully capable but—well, she's not an Ancred and doesn't feel as we do. She's—well, let's face it, she's a bit *M.C.*, do you know?"

Alleyn did not respond to this appeal from blue blood to blue blood. He said: "Was the suitcase locked?"

"We wouldn't have broken anything open, Mr. Alleyn."

"Wouldn't you?" he said vaguely. Desdemona glanced in the mirror. "Well—Pauline might," she admitted after a pause.

Alleyn waited for a moment, caught Fox's eye and stood up. He said: "Now, Miss Ancred, I wonder if we may see your father's room?"

"Papa's *room?*"

"If we may."

"I couldn't—you won't mind if I——? I'll ask Barker——"

"If he'd just show us in the general direction we could find our own way."

Desdemona stretched out her hands impulsively. "You *do* understand," she said. "You do understand how one feels. Thank you."

Alleyn smiled vaguely, dodged the outstretched hands and made for the door. "Perhaps Barker," he suggested, "could show us the room."

Desdemona swept to the bell-push and in a moment or two Barker came in. With enormous aplomb she explained what he was to do. She contrived to turn Barker into the very quintessence of family retainers. The atmosphere in the little sitting-room grew more and more feudal. "These gentlemen," she ended, "have come to help us, Barker. We, in our turn, must help them, mustn't we? You will help them, won't you?"

"Certainly, miss," said Barker. "If you would come this way, sir?"

How well Troy had described the great stairs and the gallery and the yards and yards of dead canvas in heavy frames. And the smell. The Victorian smell of varnish, carpet, wax, and mysteriously, paste. A yellow smell, she had said. Here was the first long corridor, and there, branching from it, the passage to Troy's tower. This was where she had lost herself that first night and these were the rooms with their ridiculous names. On his right,

Bancroft and *Bernhardt*; on his left, *Terry* and *Bracegirdle*; then an open linen closet and bathrooms. Barker's coattails jigged steadily ahead of them. His head was stooped, and one saw only a thin fringe of grey hair and a little dandruff on his back collar. Here was the cross-corridor, corresponding with the picture gallery, and facing them a closed door, with the legend, in gothic lettering, "*Irving*."

"This is the room, sir," said Barker's faded and breathless voice.

"We'll go in, if you please."

The door opened on darkness and the smell of disinfectant. A momentary fumbling, and then a bedside lamp threw a pool of light upon a table and a crimson counterpane. With a clatter of rings Barker pulled aside the window curtains and then let up the blinds.

The aspect of the room that struck Alleyn most forcibly was the extraordinary number of prints and photographs upon the walls. They were so lavishly distributed that almost all the paper, a red flock powdered with stars, was concealed by them. Next he noticed the heavy richness of the appointments; the enormous looking-glass, the brocades and velvets, the massive and forbidding furniture.

Suspended above the bed was a long cord. He saw that it ended, not in a bell-push, but in raw strands of wire.

"Will that be all, sir?" said Barker, behind them.

"Stop for a minute, will you?" Alleyn said. "I want you to help us, Barker."

II

He was indeed very old. His eyes were filmy and expressed nothing but a remote sadness. His hands seemed to have shrunk away from their own empurpled veins, and were tremulous. But all these witnesses of age were in part disguised by a lifetime's habit of attentiveness to other people's wants. There was the shadow of alacrity still about Barker.

"I don't think," Alleyn said, "that Miss Ancred quite explained why we are here. It's at Mr. Thomas Ancred's suggestion. He wants us to make fuller inquiries into the cause of Sir Henry's death."

"Indeed, sir?"

"Some of his family believe that the diagnosis was too hastily given."

"Quite so, sir."

"Had you any such misgivings yourself?"

Barker closed and unclosed his hands. "I can't say I had, sir. Not at first."

"Not at first?"

"Knowing what he took to eat and drink at dinner, sir, and the way he was worked up, and had been over and over again. Dr. Withers had warned him of it, sir."

"But later? After the funeral? And now?"

"I really can't say, sir. What with Mrs. Kentish and Mrs. Henry and Miss Desdemona asking me over and over again about a certain missing article and what with us all being very put about in the servants' hall, I can't really say."

"A tin of rat-bane was the missing article?"

"Yes, sir. I understand they've found it now."

"And the question they want settled is whether it was an opened or unopened tin before it was lost. Is that it?"

"I understand that's it, sir. But we've had that stuff on the premises these last ten years and more. Two tins there were, sir, in one of the outside store-rooms and there was one opened and used up and thrown out. That I do know. About this one that's turned up, I can't say. Mrs. Henry Ancred recollects, sir, that it was there about a year ago, unopened, and Mrs. Bullivant, the cook, says it's been partly used since then, and Mrs. Henry doesn't fancy so, and that's all I can say, sir."

"Do you know if rat poison has ever been used in Miss Orrincourt's room?"

Barker's manner became glazed with displeasure.

"Never to my knowledge, sir," he said.

"Are there no rats there?"

"The lady in question complained of them, I understand, to one of the housemaids, who set traps and caught several. I believe the lady said she didn't fancy the idea of poison, and for that reason it was not employed."

"I see. Now, Barker, if you will, I should like you to tell me exactly what this room looked like when you entered it on the morning after Sir Henry's death."

Barker's sunken hand moved to his lips and covered their trembling. A film of tears spread over his eyes.

"I know it's distressing for you," Alleyn said, "and I'm sorry. Sit down. No, please sit down."

Barker stooped his head a little and sat on the only high chair in the room.

"I'm sure," Alleyn said, "that if there was anything gravely amiss you'd want to see it remedied."

Barker seemed to struggle between his professional reticence and his personal distress. Finally, in a sudden flood of garrulity, he produced the classical reaction: "I wouldn't want to see this house mixed up in anything scandalous, sir. My father was butler here to the former baronet, Sir Henry's second cousin—Sir William Ancred, that was—I was knife-boy and then footman under him. He was not," said Barker, "anything to do with theatricals, sir, the old gentleman wasn't. This would have been a great blow to him."

"You mean the manner of Sir Henry's death?"

"I mean"—Barker tightened his unsteady lips—"I mean the way things were conducted lately."

"Miss Orrincourt?"

"T'uh!" said Barker, and thus established his life-long service to the Ancreds.

"Look here," Alleyn said suddenly, "do you know what the family have got into their heads about this business?"

There was a long pause before the old voice whispered: "I don't like to think. I don't encourage gossip below stairs, sir, and I don't take part in it myself."

"Well," Alleyn suggested, "suppose you tell me about this room."

It was, after all, only a slow enlargement of what he had already heard. The darkened room, the figure hunched on the bed, "as if," Barker said fearfully, "he'd been trying to crawl down to the floor," the stench and disorder and the broken bell-cord.

"Where was the end?" Alleyn asked. "The bell-push itself?"

"In his hand, sir. Tight clenched round it, his hand was. We didn't discover it at first."

"Have you still got it?"

"It's in his dressing-table drawer, sir. I put it there, meaning to get it mended."

"Did you unscrew it or examine it in any way?"

"Oh, no, sir. No. I just put it away and disconnected the circuit on the board."

"Right! And now, Barker, about the night before, when Sir Henry went to bed. Did you see anything of him?"

"Oh, yes, indeed, sir. He rang for me as usual. It was midnight when the bell went, and I came up to his room. I'd valeted him, sir, since his own man left."

"Did he ring his room bell?"

"No, sir. He always rang the bell in the hall as he went through. By the time he reached his room, you see, I had gone up the servants' stairs and was waiting for him."

"How did he seem?"

"Terrible. In one of his tantrums and talking very wild and angry."

"Against his family?"

"Very hot against them."

"Go on."

"I got him into his pyjamas and gown and him raging all the while and troubled with his indigestion pain as well. I put out the medicine he took for it. He said he wouldn't take it just then so I left the bottle and glass by his bed. I was offering to help him into bed when he says he must see Mr. Rattisbon. He's the family solicitor, sir, and always comes to us for The Birthday. Well, sir, I tried to put Sir Henry off, seeing he was tired and upset, but he wouldn't hear of it. When I took him by the arm he got quite violent. I was alarmed and tried to hold him but he broke away."

Alleyn had a sudden vision of the two old men struggling together in this grandiose bedroom.

"Seeing there was nothing for it," Barker went on, "I did as he ordered, and took Mr. Rattisbon up to his room. He called me back and told me to find the two extra helps we always get in for The Birthday. A Mr. and Mrs. Candy, sir, formerly on the staff here and now in a small business in the village. I understood from what Sir Henry said that he wished them to witness his Will. I showed them up, and he then told me to inform Miss Orrincourt that he would be ready for his hot drink in half an hour. He said he would not require me again. So I left him."

"And went to give this message?"

"After I had switched over the mechanism of his bell, sir, so that if he required anything in the night it would sound in the passage outside Mrs. Henry's door. It has been specially arranged like this, in case of an emergency, and, of course, sir, it must have broke off in his hand before it sounded, because even if Mrs.

Henry had slept through it, Miss Dessy was sharing her room and must have heard. Miss Dessy sleeps very light, I understand."

"Isn't it strange that he didn't call out?"

"He wouldn't be heard, sir. The walls in this part of the house are very thick, being part of the original outer walls. The previous baronet, sir, added this wing to Ancreton."

"I see. At this time where was Miss Orrincourt?"

"She had left the company, sir. They had all moved into the drawing-room."

"*All* of them?"

"Yes, sir. Except her and Mr. Rattisbon. And Mrs. Alleyn, who was a guest. They were all there. Mrs. Kentish said the young lady had gone to her room and that's where I found her. Mr. Rattisbon was in the hall."

"What was the business with the hot drink?"

The old man described it carefully. Until the rise of Sonia Orrincourt, Millamant had always prepared the drink. Miss Orrincourt had taken over this routine. The milk and ingredients were left in her room by the housemaid, who turned down her bed. She brewed the drink over a heater, put it in a Thermos flask, and, half an hour after he had retired, took it to his room. He slept badly and sometimes would not drink it until much later in the night.

"What happened to the Thermos flask and the cup and saucer?"

"They were taken away and washed up, sir. They've been in use since."

"Had he drunk any of it?"

"It had been poured into the cup, sir, at all events, and into the saucer for that cat, as was always done, and the saucer set on the floor. But the cup and the flask and the medicine bottle had been overturned and there was milk and medicine soaked into the carpet."

"Had he taken his medicine?"

"The glass was dirty. It had fallen into the saucer."

"And has, of course, been washed," said Alleyn. "What about the bottle?"

"It had been knocked over, sir, as I mentioned. It was a new bottle. I was very much put out, sir, but I tried to tidy the room a bit, not knowing exactly what I was doing. I remember I took the dirty china and the bottle and Thermos downstairs with me. The bottle was thrown out, and the other things cleared up. The medicine cupboard has been cleaned out thoroughly. It's in the bathroom, sir, through that door. The whole suite," said Barker conscientiously, "has been turned out and cleaned."

Fox mumbled inarticulately.

"Well," said Alleyn. "To go back to the message you took to Miss Orrincourt that night. Did you actually see her?"

"No, sir. I tapped on the door and she answered." He moved uneasily.

"Was there anything else?"

"It was a queer thing——" His voice faded.

"What was a queer thing?"

"She must have been alone," Barker mused, "because, as I've said, sir, the others were downstairs, and afterwards, *just* afterwards, when I took in the grog-tray, there they all were. But before I knocked on her door, sir, I could have sworn that she was laughing."

III

When Barker had gone, Fox sighed gustily, put on his spectacles and looked quizzically through them at the naked end of the bell-cord.

"Yes, Br'er Fox, exactly," said Alleyn, and went to the dressing-table. "That'll be the lady," he said.

A huge photograph of Sonia Orrincourt stood in the middle of the dressing-table.

Fox joined Alleyn. "Very taking," he said. "Funny, you know, Mr. Alleyn. That's what they call a pin-up girl. Plenty of teeth and hair and limbs. Sir Henry put it in a silver frame, but that, you might say, is the only difference. Very taking."

Alleyn opened the top drawer on the left.

"First pop," Fox remarked.

Alleyn pulled on a glove and gingerly took out a pear-shaped wooden bell-push. "One takes these pathetic precautions," he said, "and a hell of a lot of use they are. Now then." He unscrewed the end of the bell-push and looked into it.

"See here, Fox. Look at the two points. Nothing broken. One of the holding-screws and its washer are tight. No bits of wire. The other screw and washer are loose. Got your lens? Have a look at that cord again."

Fox took out a pocket lens and returned to the bed. "One of the wires is unbroken," he said presently. "No shiny end, and it's blackened like they do get with time. The other's different, though. Been dragged through and scraped, I'd say. That's what must have happened. He put his weight on it and they pulled through."

"In that case," Alleyn said, "why is one of the screws so tight, and only one wire shiny? We'll keep this bell-push, Fox."

He had wrapped his handkerchief round it and dropped it in his pocket, when the door was opened and Sonia Orrincourt walked in.

IV

She was dressed in black, but so dashingly that mourning was not much suggested. Her curtain of ashen hair and her heavy fringe were glossy, her eyelids were blue, her lashes incredible and her skin sleek. She wore a diamond clasp and bracelet and ear-rings. She stood just inside the room.

"Pardon the intrusion," she said, "but am I addressing the police?"

"You are," said Alleyn. "Miss Orrincourt?"

"That's the name."

"How do you do? This is Inspector Fox."

"Now listen!" said Miss Orrincourt, advancing upon them with a professional gait. "I want to know what's cooking in this ice-house. I've got my rights to look after, same as anybody else, haven't I?"

"Undoubtedly."

"Thank you. Very kind I'm sure. Then perhaps you'll tell me who asked you into my late fiancé's room and just what you're doing now you've got there."

"We were asked by his family and we're doing a job of work."

"*Work?* What sort of work? Don't tell me the answer to that one," said Miss Orrincourt angrily. "I seem to know it. They're trying to swing something across me. Is that right? Trying to pack me up. *What is it?* That's what I want to know. Come on. *What is it?*"

"Will you first of all tell me how you knew we were here and why you thought we were police officers?"

She sat on the bed, leaning back on her hands, her hair falling

697

vertically from her scalp. Behind her was spread the crimson counterpane. Alleyn wondered why she had ever attempted to be an actress while there were magazine artists who needed models. She looked in a leisurely manner at Fox's feet. "How do I know you're police? That's a scream! Take a look at your boy friend's boots."

"Yours, partner," Alleyn murmured, catching Fox's eye.

Fox cleared his throat. "Er—*touché*," he said carefully. "Not much good me trying to get by with a sharp-eyed young lady, is it, sir?"

"Well, come on," Miss Orrincourt demanded. "What's the big idea? Are they trying to make out there's something funny in the Will? Or what? What are you doing, opening my late fiancé's drawers? Come on?"

"I'm afraid," said Alleyn, "you've got this situation the wrong way round. We're on a job, and part of that job is asking questions. And since you're here, Miss Orrincourt, I wonder if you'd mind answering one or two?"

She looked at him, he thought, as an animal or a completely unselfconscious child might look at a stranger. It was difficult to expect anything but perfect sounds from her. He experienced a shock each time he heard the Cockney voice with its bronchial overtones, and the phrases whose very idiom seemed shoddy, as if she had abandoned her native dialect for something she had half-digested at the cinema.

"All upstage and county?" she said. "Fancy! And what were you wanting to know?"

"About the Will, for instance."

"The Will's all right," she said quickly. "You can turn the place inside out. Crawl up the chimney if you like. You won't find another Will. I'm telling you, and I know."

"Why are you so positive?"

She had slipped back until she rested easily on her forearm. "I don't mind," she said. "I'll tell you. When I came in here last thing that night, my fiancé showed it to me. He'd had old Rattisbon up and a couple of witnesses and he'd signed it. He showed me. The ink was still wet. He'd burnt the old one in the fireplace there."

"I see."

"And he couldn't have written another one even if he'd wanted to. Because he was tired and his pain was bad and he said he was

698

going to take his medicine and go to sleep."

"He was in bed when you visited him?"

"Yes." She waited for a moment, looking at her enamelled finger-nails. "People seem to think I've got no feelings, but I've been very upset. Honestly. Well, he was sweet. And when a girl's going to be married and everything's marvellous it's a terrible thing for this to happen, I don't care what any one says."

"Did he seem very ill?"

"That's what everybody keeps asking. The doctor and old Pauline and Milly. On and on. Honestly, I could scream. He just had one of his turns and he felt queer. And with the way he'd eaten and thrown a temperament on top of it, no wonder. I gave him his hot drink and kissed him nighty-nighty and he seemed all right and that's all I know."

"He drank his hot milk while you were with him?"

She swung over a little with a luxurious movement and looked at him through narrowed eyes. "That's right," she said. "Drank it and liked it."

"And his medicine?"

"He poured that out for himself. I told him to drink up like a good boy, but he said he'd wait a bit and see if his tummy wouldn't settle down without it. So I went."

"Right. Now, Miss Orrincourt," said Alleyn, facing her with his hands in his pockets, "you've been very frank. I shall follow your example. You want to know what we're doing here. I'll tell you. Our job, or a major part of it, is to find out why you played a string of rather infantile practical jokes on Sir Henry Ancred and let it be thought that his granddaughter was responsible."

She was on her feet so quickly that he actually felt his nerves jump. She was close to him now; her under-lip jutted out and her brows, thin hairy lines, were drawn together in a scowl. She resembled some drawing in a man's magazine of an infuriated baggage in a bedroom. One almost expected some dubious caption to issue in a balloon from her lips.

"Who says I did it?" she demanded.

"I do, at the moment," Alleyn said. "Come now. Let's start at Mr. Juniper's shop. You bought the Raspberry there, you know."

"The dirty little so-and-so," she said meditatively. "What a pal! *And* what a gentleman, I don't suppose."

Alleyn ignored these strictures upon Mr. Juniper. "Then," he said, "there's that business about the paint on the banisters."

Obviously this astonished her. Her face was suddenly bereft of expression, a mask with slightly dilated eyes. "Wait a bit," she said. "That's funny!"

Alleyn waited.

"Here!" she said. "Have you been talking to young Ceddie?"

"No."

"That's what you say," she muttered, and turned on Fox. "What about you, then?"

"No, Miss Orrincourt," said Fox blandly. "Not me or the Chief Inspector."

"Chief Inspector!" she said. "Coo!"

Alleyn saw that she was looking at him with a new interest and had a premonition of what was to come.

"That'd be one of the high-ups, wouldn't it? Chief Inspector who? I don't seem to have caught the name."

Any hopes he may have entertained that his connection with Troy was unknown to her vanished when she repeated his name, clapped her hand over her mouth and ejaculating "Coo! That's a good one," burst into fits of uncontrollable laughter.

"Pardon me," she said presently, "but when you come to think of it it's funny. You can't get away from it, you know, it's funny. Seeing it was her that—Well, of course! That's how you knew about the paint on the banisters."

"And what," Alleyn asked, "is the connection between Sir Cedric Ancred and the paint on the banisters?"

"I'm not going to give myself away," said Miss Orrincourt, "nor Ceddie either, if it comes to that. Ceddie's pretty well up the spout anyway. If he's let me down he's crazy. There's a whole lot of things I want to know first. What's all this stuff about a book? What's the idea? Is it me, or is it everybody else in this dump that's gone hay-wire? Look! Somebody puts a dirty little book in a cheese-dish and serves it up for lunch. And when they find it, what do these half-wits do? Look at me as if I was the original hoodunit. Well, I mean to say, it's silly. And what a book! Written by somebody with a lisp and what about? Keeping people fresh after they're dead. Give you the willies. And when I say I never put it in the cheese-dish what do they do? Pauline starts tearing herself to shreds and Dessy says, "We're not so foolish as to suppose you'd want to run your head in a noose," and Milly says she happens to know I've read it, and they all go out as if I

700

was something the cat'd brought in, and I sit there wondering if it's me or all of them who ought to be locked up."

"And had you ever seen the book before?"

"I seem to remember," she began, and then looking from Alleyn to Fox with a new wariness, she said sharply: "Not to notice. Not to know what it was about." And after a pause she added dully: "I'm not much of a one for reading."

Alleyn said: "Miss Orrincourt, will you without prejudice tell me if you personally were responsible for any of the practical jokes other than the ones already under discussion?"

"I'm not answering any questions. I don't know what's going on here. A girl's got to look after herself. I thought I had one friend in this crazy-gang, now I'm beginning to think he's let me down."

"I suppose," said Alleyn, wearily, "you mean Sir Cedric Ancred?"

"*Sir* Cedric Ancred," Miss Orrincourt repeated with a shrill laugh. "The bloody little baronet. Excuse my smile, but honestly it's a scream." She turned her back on them and walked out, leaving the door open.

They could still hear her laughing with unconvincing virtuosity as she walked away down the corridor.

V

"Have we," Fox asked blandly, "got anywhere with that young lady? Or have we not?"

"Not very far, if anywhere at all," Alleyn said, morosely. "I don't know about you, Fox, but I found her performance tolerably convincing. Not that impressions of that sort amount to very much. Suppose she did put arsenic in the old man's hot milk, wouldn't this be the only line she could reasonably take? And at this stage of the proceedings, when I still have a very faint hope that we may come across something that blows their damn' suspicions to smithereens, I couldn't very well insist on anything. We'll just have to go mousing along."

"Where to?" Fox asked.

"For the moment, in different directions. I've been carrying you about like a broody hen, Foxkin, and it's time you brought forth. Down you go and exercise the famous technique on Barker and his retinue of elderly maids. Find out all about the milk, trace

701

its whole insipid history from cow to Thermos. Inspire gossip. Prattle. Seek out the paper-dump, the bottle-dump, the mops and the pails. Let us go clanking back to London like a dry canteen. Salvage the Thermos flask. We'll have to try for an analysis but what a hope! Get along with you, Fox. Do your stuff."

"And where may I ask, Mr. Alleyn, are you going?"

"Oh," said Alleyn, "I'm a snob. I'm going to see the baronet."

Fox paused at the doorway. "Taking it by and large, sir," he said, "and on the face of it as it stands, do you reckon there'll be an exhumation?"

"There'll be one exhumation at all events. To-morrow, if Dr. Curtis can manage it."

"To-morrow!" said Fox, startled. "Dr. Curtis? Sir Henry Ancred?"

"No," Alleyn said, "the cat, Carabbas."

CHAPTER XIII

Spotlight on Cedric

I

Alleyn interviewed Cedric in the library. It was a place without character or life. Rows of uniform editions stood coldly behind glass doors. There was no smell of tobacco, or memory of fires, only the darkness of an unused room.

Cedric's manner was both effusive and uneasy. He made a little dart at Alleyn and flapped at his hand. He began at once to talk about Troy. "She was too marvellous, a perfect darling. So thrilling to watch her at work: that *magical* directness, almost intimidating, one felt. You must be madly proud of her, of course."

His mouth opened and shut, his teeth glinted, his pale eyes stared and his voice gabbled on and on. He was restless too, and wandered about the room aimlessly, lifting lids of empty cigarette boxes and moving ornaments. He recalled acquaintance with Alleyn's nephews, with whom, he said, he had been at school. He professed a passionate interest in Alleyn's work. He returned again to Troy, suggesting that he alone among the Philistines had spoken her language. There was a disquieting element in all this, and Alleyn, when an opportunity came, cut across it.

"One moment," he said. "Our visit is an official one. I'm sure you will agree that we should keep it so. May we simply think the fact of my wife having been commissioned to paint Sir Henry a sort of freakish coincidence and nothing to do with the matter in hand? Except, of course, in so far as her job may turn out to have any bearing on the circumstances."

Cedric's mouth had remained slightly open. He turned pink, touched his hair, and said: "Of course if you feel like that about

703

it. I merely thought that a friendly atmosphere——"

"That was extremely kind," said Alleyn.

"Unless your somewhat muscular sense of the official proprieties forbids it," Cedric suggested acidly, "shall we at least sit down?"

"Thank you," said Alleyn tranquilly, "that would be much more comfortable."

He sat in a vast arm-chair, crossed his knees, joined his hands, and with what Troy called his donnish manner, prepared to tackle Cedric.

"Mr. Thomas Ancred tells me you share the feeling that further inquiries should be made into the circumstances of Sir Henry's death."

"Well, I suppose I do," Cedric agreed fretfully. "I mean, it's all pretty vexing, isn't it? Well, I mean one would like to know. All sorts of things depend ... And yet again it's not very delicious ... Of course, when one considers that I'm the one who's most involved ... Well, *look* at me. *Incarcerated*, in this frightful house! And the entail a pittance. All those taxes too, and *rapacious* death duties. Never, never will anybody be found mad enough to rent it, and as for schools, Carol Able does nothing but exclaim how inconvenient and how damp. And now the war's over the problem children will be hurtled away. One will be left to wander in rags down whispering corridors. So that you see," he added, waving his hands, "one does rather wonder——"

"Quite so."

"And they *will* keep talking about me as Head of the Family. Before I know where I am I shall have turned into another Old Person."

"There are one or two points," Alleyn began, and immediately Cedric leant forward with an ineffable air of concentration, "that we'd like to clear up. The first is the authorship of these anonymous letters."

"Well, I didn't write them."

"Have you any idea who did?"

"Personally I favour my Aunt Pauline."

"Really! Why?"

"She prefaces almost every remark she makes with the phrase: 'I have reason to believe.'"

"Have you asked Mrs. Kentish if she wrote the letters?"

"Yes, indeed. She denies it hotly. Then there's Aunt Dessy.

Quite capable, in a way, but more likely, one would have thought, to tell us flatly what she suspected. I mean, why go in for all this hush-hush letter-writing? That leaves my cousins Paul and Fenella, who are, one imagines, too pleasurably engrossed in their amorous martyrdom for any outside activities; my Mama, who is much too common-sensical; my aunt-in-law, Jenetta, who is too grand; and all the servants led by the Ancient of Days. That, as they say in sporting circles, is the field. Unless you feel inclined to take in the squire and the parson and dear old Rattlebones himself. It couldn't be more baffling. No, on the whole I plump for Pauline. She's about somewhere. Have you encountered her? Since the Tragedy she is almost indistinguishable from Lady Macduff. Or perhaps that frightful Shakespearian dowager who curses her way up hill and down dale through one of the historical dramas. Constance? Yes, Pauline is now all compact of tragedy. Dessy's pretty bad, but wait till you meet Pauline."

"Do you know if there's any paper in the house of the kind used for these letters?"

"Gracious, no! Exercise-book paper! The servants wouldn't have had it at any price. By the way, talking of exercise books, *do* you think Caroline Able might have done it? I mean, she's so wrapped up in id and isms and tracing everything back to the Oedipus Complex. Might it perhaps have all snapped back at her and made her a weeny bit odd? It's only an idea, of course. I merely throw it out for what it's worth."

"About this tin of rat-bane," Alleyn began. Cedric interrupted him with a shrill cry.

"My dear, what a party! Imagine! Milly, the complete hausfrau (my mama, you know)"—Cedric added the inevitable parentheses—"and Dessy steaming up the stairs and Pauline tramping at her heels like one of the Fates, and poor little me panting at the rear. We didn't know what we were looking for, really. Partly rat poison and partly they thought there might be compromising papers somewhere because Sonia's quite lovely, don't you think, and *really*—the Old Person! *Hardly* adequate, one couldn't help feeling. I pointed out that, constant or flighty, a Will was a Will, but nothing would stay them. I said n fun: "You don't expect, darlings, to find phials of poison in her luggage, do you?" and that put the idea of luggage into their heads. So up into the box-room they hounded me, and there, to use the language of the chase, we 'found'."

"You yourself took the tin out of the suitcase?"

"Yes, indeed. I was petrified."

"What was it like?"

"Like? But didn't dear Uncle Tom give it to you?"

"Was it clean or dirty?"

"My dear, *filthy*. They wanted me to prise open the lid, and such a struggle as I had. Little bits of rat-bane flying up and hitting me. I was terrified. And then it wouldn't come out."

"Who first suggested this search?"

"Now, that *is* difficult. Did we, thinking of that beastly little brochure in the cheese-dish (and there, I must tell you, I see the hand of Panty), did we with one accord cry: 'rat-bane' and let loose the dogs of war? I fancy Pauline, after coining the phrase 'no smoke' (or is it 'reek'?) 'without heat,' said: 'But where would she get any arsenic?' and that Milly (my Mama), or it might have been me, remembered the missing rat-bane. Anyway, no sooner was it mentioned than Pauline and Dessy were in full cry for the guilty apartment. If you could see it, too. Darling Sonia! Well, 'darling' with reservations. The bed-chamber a welter of piercing pink frills and tortured satin and dolls peering from behind cushions or squatting on telephones, do you know?"

"I would be very glad," said Alleyn, "if the suitcase could be produced."

"Really? You wish, no doubt, to explore it for fingerprints? But of course you shall have it. Unbeknown, I suppose, to darling Sonia?"

"If possible."

"I'll trip upstairs and get it myself. If she's there, I'll tell her there's a telephone call."

"Thank you."

"Shall I go now?"

"One moment, Sir Cedric," Alleyn began, and again Cedric, with that winsome trick of anxiety, leant towards him. "Why did you, with Miss Sonia Orrincourt, plan a series of practical jokes on your grandfather?"

It was not pleasant to watch the blood sink from Cedric's face. The process left his eyelids and the pouches under his eyes mauvish. Small grooves appeared beside his nostrils. His colourless lips pouted and then widened into an unlovely smile.

"Well, really!" he tittered. "That just shows you, doesn't it? So darling Sonia has confided in you." And after a moment's

706

hesitation he added: "As far as I'm concerned, dear Mr. Alleyn, that's the end of darling Sonia."

II

"Perhaps I should explain," Alleyn said after a pause, "that Miss Orrincourt has not made any statement about the practical jokes."

"She *hasn't?*" The ejaculation was so incisive that it was difficult to believe Cedric had uttered it. He now lowered his head and appeared to look at the carpet between his feet. Alleyn saw his hands slide over each other. "How perfectly futile," Cedric's voice said. "Such a *very* old gag. Such an ancient wheeze! I didn't know but you've just told me! And in I go, as they say, boots and all." He raised his face. Its pinkness had returned and its expression suggested a kind of boyish ruefulness. "Now *do* promise you won't be lividly angry. It sounds too childish, I know. But I implore you, dear Mr. Alleyn, to look about you. Observe the peculiar flavour of Katzenjammer Castle. The façade now. The utterly unnerving inequalities of the façade. The terrifying Victoriana within. The gloom. Note particularly the gloom."

"I'm afraid," Alleyn said, "that I don't follow this. Unless you're going to tell me you hoped to enliven the architecture and decor of Ancreton by painting spectacles and flying cows on your grandfather's portrait."

"But I didn't!" Cedric protested shrilly. "That *miraculous* portrait! No, believe me, I didn't."

"And the paint on the banister?"

"I didn't do that either. Darling Mrs. Alleyn! I wouldn't have dreamed of it."

"But at least you seem to have known about it."

"I didn't do it," he repeated.

"The message written in grease-paint on the mirror? And the grease-paint on the cat?"

Cedric gave a nervous giggle. "Well——"

"Come," said Alleyn. "You had dark red grease-paint under your finger-nail, you know."

"*What* sharp eyes!" cried Cedric. "Dearest Mrs. Alleyn! *Such* a help she must be to you."

"You did, in fact——"

707

"The Old Person," Cedric interrupted, "had been particularly rococo. I couldn't resist. The cat, too. It was a kind of practical pun. The cat's whiskers!"

"And had you anything to do with the squeaking cushion in his chair?"

"Wasn't it too robust and Rabelaisian? Sonia bought it and I—I can't deny it—I placed it there. But why not? If I might make a tiny squeak of protest, dear Mr. Alleyn, *has* all this got *anything* to do with the business in hand?"

"I think it might well have been designed to influence Sir Henry's Will, and with both his Wills we are, as I think you'll agree, very definitely concerned."

"This is too subtle for my poor wits, I'm afraid."

"It was common knowledge, wasn't it, that his youngest granddaughter was, at this time, his principal heir?"

"But one never knew. We bounced in and out of favour from day to day."

"If this is true, wouldn't these tricks, if attributed to her, very much affect her position?" Alleyn waited but was given no answer. "Why, in fact, did you allow him to believe she was the culprit?"

"That devilish child," Cedric said, "gets away with innumerable hideous offences. A sense of injured innocence must have been quite a change for her."

"You see," Alleyn went on steadily, "the flying cow was the last trick of five, and, as far as we know, was the final reason for Sir Henry's changing his Will that night. It was fairly conclusively proved to him that Panty did not do it, and it's possible that Sir Henry, not knowing which of his family to suspect, took his revenge on all."

"Yes, but——"

"Now whoever was a party to these tricks——"

"At least you'll admit that I wouldn't be very likely to try and cut myself out of the Will——"

"I think that result was unforeseen. You hoped, perhaps, to return to your former position with Panty out of the picture. To something, in fact, on the lines of the Will read at the dinner-party, but rather better. You have told me that you and Miss Orrincourt were partners in one of these practical jokes. Indeed you've suggested to me that you at least had knowledge of them all."

Cedric began to speak very rapidly. "I resent all this talk of partnership. I resent the implication and deny it. You force me into an intolerable position with your hints and mysteries. I suppose there's nothing left but for me to admit I knew what she was doing and why she did it. It amused me and it enlivened the ghastly boredom of these wretched festivities. Panty I consider an abomination, and I don't in the least regret that she was suspected or that she was cut out of the Will. She probably wallowed in her borrowed glory. There!"

"Thank you," said Alleyn. "That clears up quite a lot of the fog. And now, Sir Cedric, are you quite sure you don't know who wrote the letters?"

"Absolutely."

"And are you equally sure you didn't put the book on embalming in the cheese-dish?"

Cedric gaped at him. "I?" he said. "Why should I? Oh, no! I don't want Sonia to turn out to be a murderess. Or I didn't, then. I'd rather thought ... I ... we'd ... it doesn't matter. But I must say I'd like to *know*."

Looking at him, Alleyn was visited by a notion so extravagant that he found himself incapable of pressing Cedric any further on the subject of his relationship with Miss Orrincourt.

He was, in any case, prevented from doing so by the entrance of Pauline Kentish.

Pauline entered weeping: not loudly, but with the suggestion of welling tears held bravely back. She seemed to Alleyn to be an older and woollier version of her sister, Desdemona. She took the uncomfortable line of expressing thankfulness that Alleyn was his wife's husband. "Like having a *friend* to help us." Italicised words and even phrases surged about in her conversation. There was much talk of Panty. Alleyn had been so kind, the child had taken a tremendous fancy to him. "And I always think," Pauline said, gazing at him, "that they KNOW." From here they were soon involved in Panty's misdoings. Pauline, if he had now wanted them, supplied good enough alibis for the practical jokes. "How could she when the poor child was being watched; closely, anxiously watched? Dr. Withers had given explicit orders."

"And much good they've done, by the way!" Cedric interrupted. "Look at Panty!"

"Dr. Withers is extremely clever, Cedric. It's not his fault if Juniper's drugs have deteriorated. Your grandfather's medicines

709

were always a great help to him."

"Including rat-bane?"

"That," said Pauline in her deepest voice, "was not prescribed, Cedric, by Dr. Withers."

Cedric giggled.

Pauline ignored him and turned appealingly to Alleyn. "Mr. Alleyn, what are we to think? Isn't it all too tragically dreadful? The suspense! The haunting suspicion! The feeling that here in our midst ...! What are we to do?"

Alleyn asked her about the events following Sir Henry's exit from the little theatre on the night of his death. It appeared that Pauline herself had led the way to the drawing-room, leaving Troy, Paul and Fenella behind. Miss Orrincourt had only remained a very short time in the drawing-room where, Alleyn gathered, a lively discussion had taken place as to the authorship of the flying cow. To this family wrangle the three guests had listened uncomfortably until Barker arrived, with Sir Henry's summons for Mr. Rattisbon. The squire and the rector seized upon this opportunity to make their escape. Paul and Fenella came in on their way to bed. Troy had already gone upstairs. After a little more desultory haggling the Birthday party broke up.

Pauline, Millamant and Desdemona had forgathered in Pauline's room, *Bernhardt*, and had talked exhaustively. They went together to the bathrooms at the end of the passage and encountered Mr. Rattisbon, who had evidently come out of Sir Henry's rooms. Alleyn, who knew him, guessed that Mr. Rattisbon skipped, with late Victorian coyness, past the three ladies in their dressing-gowns and hurriedly down the passage to his own wing. The ladies performed their nightly rites together and together returned to their adjacent rooms. At this juncture Pauline began to look martyred.

"Originally," she said, "*Bernhardt* and *Bancroft* were one large room, a nursery, I think. The wall between is the merest partition. Milly and Dessy shared *Bancroft*. Of course, I know there was a great deal to be talked about and for a time I joined in. Milly's bed was just through the wall from mine, and Dessy's quite close. But it had been a long day and one was *exhausted*. They went on and on. I became quite frantic with sleeplessness. Really it *was* thoughtless."

"Dearest Aunt Pauline, why didn't you beat on the wall and

scream at them?" Cedric asked, with some show of interest.

"I wasn't going to do that," Pauline rejoined with grandeur and immediately contradicted herself. "As a matter of fact I did at last tap. I said wasn't it getting rather late. Dessy asked what time it was, and Milly said it couldn't be more than one. There was quite an argument, and at last Dessy said: 'Well, if you're so certain, Pauline, look at your watch and see.' And in the end I did, and it was five minutes to three. So at last they stopped and then it was only to snore. Your mother snores, Cedric."

"I'm so sorry."

"And to *think* that only a little way away, while Dessy and Milly gossiped and snored, a frightful tragedy was being enacted. To think that if only I had obeyed my instinct to go to Papa and tell him——"

"To tell him what, Aunt Pauline?"

Pauline shook her head slowly from side to side and boggled a little. "Everything was so sad and dreadful. One seemed to see him rushing to his doom."

"One also saw Paul and Panty rushing to theirs, didn't one?" Cedric put in. "You could have pleaded with him for them perhaps?"

"I cannot expect, Cedric, that you would understand or sympathize with disinterested impulses."

"No," Cedric agreed with perfect candour. "I don't think they exist."

"T'uh!"

"And if Mr. Alleyn has no further absorbing questions to ask me I think I should like to leave the library. I find the atmosphere of unread silent friends in half-morocco exceedingly gloomy. Mr. Alleyn?"

"No, thank you, Sir Cedric," Alleyn said cheerfully. "No more questions. If I may go ahead with my job?"

"Oh, do. Please consider this house your own. Perhaps you would like to buy it. In any case I do hope you'll stay to dinner. And your own particular silent friend. What is his name?"

"Thank you so much, but Fox and I," Alleyn said, "are dining out."

"Then in that case," Cedric murmured, sidling towards the door, "I shall leave Aunt Pauline to divert you with tales of Panty's innocence in the matter of cheese-dishes, and her own incapability of writing anonymous letters."

711

He was prevented from getting to the door by Pauline. With a movement of whose swiftness Alleyn would have thought her incapable, she got there first, and there she stood in a splendid attitude, the palms of her hands against the door, her head thrown back. "Wait!" she said breathlessly. "Wait!"

Cedric turned with a smile to Alleyn. "As I hinted," he said, "Lady Macduff. With all her pretty chickens concentrated in the persons of Panty and Paul. The hen (or isn't it oddly enough 'dam'?) at bay."

"Mr. Alleyn," said Pauline, "I was going to say nothing of this to anybody. We are an ancient family——"

"On my knees," said Cedric, "on my knees, Aunt Pauline, not the Sieur d'Ancred."

"——and perhaps wrongly, we take some pride in our antiquity. Until to-day no breath of dishonour has ever smirched our name. Cedric is now Head of the Family. For that reason and for the sake of my father's memory I would have spared him. But now, when he does nothing but hurt and insult me and try to throw suspicion on my child, now when I have no one to protect me——" Pauline stopped as if for some important peroration. But something happened to her. Her face crinkled and reminded Alleyn instantly of her daughter's. Tears gathered in her eyes. "I have reason to believe," she began and stopped short, looking terrified. "I don't care," she said, and her voice cracked piteously. "I never could bear people to be unkind to me." She nodded her head at Cedric. "Ask him," she said, "what he was doing in Sonia Orrincourt's rooms that night. Ask him."

She burst into tears and stumbled out of the room.

"Oh, *bloody* hell!" Cedric ejaculated shrilly and darted after her.

III

Alleyn, left alone, whistled disconsolately, and after wandering about the cold and darkening room went to the windows and there made a series of notes in his pocket-book. He was still at this employment when Fox came in.

"They said I'd find you here," Fox said. "Have you done any good, Mr. Alleyn?"

"If stirring up a hive and finding foul-brood can be called good. What about you?"

"I've got the medicine bottle and three of the envelopes. I've had a cup of tea in Mr. Barker's room."

"That's more than I've had in the library."

"The cook and the maids came in and we had quite a nice little chat. Elderly party, it was. Mary, Isabel and Muriel, the maids are. The cook's Mrs. Bullivant."

"And what did you and Mary, Isabel and Muriel talk about?"

"We passed the time of day and listened to the wireless. Mrs. Bullivant showed me photographs of her nephews in the fighting forces."

"Come *on*, Fox," said Alleyn, grinning.

"By gradual degrees," said Fox, enjoying himself, "we got round to the late baronet. He must have been a card, the late old gentleman."

"I believe you."

"Yes. The maids wouldn't say much while Mr. Barker was there, but he went out after a bit and then it was, as you might say, plain sailing."

"You and your methods!"

"Well, we were quite cosy. Naturally, they were dead against Miss Orrincourt, except Isabel, and she said you couldn't blame the old gentleman for wanting a change from his family. It came as a bit of a surprise from Isabel, who's the oldest of the maids, I should say. She's the one who looks after Miss Orrincourt's rooms, and it seems Miss Orrincourt got quite friendly with her. Indiscreet, really, but you know the type."

"It's evident, at least, that you do."

"They seemed to be as thick as thieves, Miss O. and Isabel, and yet, you know, Isabel didn't mind repeating most of it. The garrulous sort, she is, and Mrs. Bullivant egging her on."

"Did you get anywhere with the history of the milk?"

"Isabel took it out of a jug in the refrigerator and left it in Miss Orrincourt's room. The rest of the milk in the jug was used for general purposes next day. Miss O. was in her room and undressing when Isabel brought it. It couldn't have been more than ten minutes or so later that Miss O. took it to the old gentleman. It was heated by Isabel in the kitchen and some patent food put in. The old gentleman fancied Miss O. did it, and said nobody else could make it to suit him. It was quite a joke between Isabel and Miss O."

"So there's no chance of anybody having got at it?"

713

"Only if they doped the tin of patent food, and I've got that."

"Good."

"And I don't know if you're thinking she might have tampered with the medicine, sir, but it doesn't seem likely. The old gentleman never let anybody touch the bottle on account of Miss Desdemona Ancred having once given him embrocation in error. It was a new bottle, Isabel says. I've got it from the dump. Cork gone, but there's enough left for analysis."

"Another job for Dr. Curtis. What about the Thermos?"

"Nicely washed and sterilised and put away. I've taken it, but there's not a chance."

"And the same goes, I imagine, for the pails and cloths?"

"The pails are no good, but I found some tag-ends of rag."

"Where have you put these delicious exhibits?"

"Isabel," said Fox primly, "hunted out a case. I told her I had to buy pyjamas in the village, being obliged unexpectedly to stay the night, and I mentioned that a man doesn't like to be seen carrying parcels. I've promised to return it."

"Didn't they spot you were taking these things?"

"Only the patent food. I let on that the police were a bit suspicious about the makers and it might have disagreed. I dare say they didn't believe me. Owing to the behaviour of the family I think they know what's up."

"They'd be pretty dumb if they didn't."

"Two other points came out that might be useful," said Fox. Alleyn had a clear picture of the tea-party. Fox, no doubt, had sipped and complimented, had joked and sympathised, had scarcely asked a question, yet had continually received answers. He was a pastmaster at the game. He indulged his hostesses with a few innocuous hints and was rewarded with a spate of gossip.

"It seems, Mr. Alleyn, that the young lady was, as Isabel put it, leading Sir Henry on and no more."

"D'you mean——"

"Relationship," said Fox sedately, "according to Isabel, had not taken place. It was matrimony or nothing."

"I see."

"Isabel reckons that before this business with the letters came out, there was quite an understanding between Miss O. and Sir Cedric."

"What sort of understanding, in the name of decency?"

"Well, sir, from hints Miss O. dropped, Isabel works it out that

714

after a discreet time had elapsed Miss O. would have turned into Lady A. after all. So that what she lost on the swings she would, in a manner of speaking, have picked up on the roundabouts."

"Good Lord!" said Alleyn. " 'What a piece of work is man!' That, if it's true, would explain quite a number of the young and unlovely baronet's antics."

"Supposing Miss Orrincourt did monkey with the Thermos, Mr. Alleyn, we might have to consider whether Sir Cedric knew what she was up to."

"We might indeed."

"I know it's silly," Fox went on, rubbing his nose, "but when a case gets to this stage I always seem to get round to asking myself whether such-and-such a character is a likely type for homicide. I know it's silly, because there isn't a type, but I ask myself the question just the same."

"And at the moment you ask it about Sonia Orrincourt?"

"That's right, sir."

"I don't see why you shouldn't. It's quite true, that beyond the quality of conceit, nobody's found a nice handy trait common to all murderers. But I'm not so sure that you should sniff at yourself for saying: "That man or woman seems to me to have characteristics that are inconceivable in a murderer!" They needn't be admirable characteristics either."

"D'you remember what Mr. Barker said about the rats in Miss Orrincourt's rooms?"

"I do."

"He mentioned that Miss Orrincourt was quite put-about by the idea of using poison, and refused to have it at any price. Now, sir, would a young woman who was at least, as you might say, toying with the idea of poison, behave like that? Would she? She wouldn't do it by accident. She might do it to suggest she had a dread of poison, though that'd be a very far-fetched kind of notion too. And would she have owned up as readily to those practical jokes? Mind, you caught her nicely, but she gave me the impression she was upset more on account of being found out for these pranks themselves than because she thought they'd lead us to suspect something else."

"She was more worried about the Will than anything else," Alleyn said. "She and Master Cedric planned those damned stunts with the object of setting the old man against Panty. I fancy she was responsible for the portrait vandalism, Cedric having

715

possibly told her to confine her daubs to dry canvas. We know she bought the Raspberry, and he admits he placed it. I *think* she started the ball rolling by painting the banister. They plotted the whole thing together. He practically admitted as much. Now, all that worries her may be merely an idea that the publication of these goings-on could upset the Will."

"And yet——"

"I know. I know. That damn bell-push. All right, Fox. Good work. And now, I suppose, we'd better see Mrs. Henry Ancred."

IV

Millamant was at ieast a change from her relations-by-marriage in that she was not histrionic, answered his questions directly, and stuck to the point. She received them in the drawing-room. In her sensible blouse and skirt she was an incongruous figure there. While she talked she stitched that same hideously involved piece of embroidery which Troy had noticed with horror and which Panty had been accused of unpicking. Alleyn heard nothing either to contradict or greatly to substantiate the evidence they had already collected.

"I wish," he said, after a minute or two, "that you would tell me your own opinion about this business."

"About my father-in-law's death? I thought at first that he died as a result of his dinner and his temperament."

"And what did you think when these letters arrived?"

"I didn't know what to think. I don't now. And I must say that with everybody so excited and foolish about it one can't think very clearly."

"About the book that turned up in the cheese-dish ..." he began.

Millamant jerked her head in the direction of the glass case. "It's over there. Someone replaced it."

He walked over to the case and raised the lid. "If you don't mind, I'll take charge of it presently. You saw her reading it?"

"Looking at it. It was one evening before dinner. Some weeks ago, I think."

"Can you describe her position and behaviour? Was she alone?"

"Yes. I came in and she was standing as you are now, with the lid open. She seemed to be turning over the leaves of the book as

716

it lay there. When she saw me she let the lid fall. I was afraid it might have smashed, but it hadn't."

Alleyn moved away to the cold hearth, his hands in his pockets. "I wonder," said Milly, "if you'd mind putting a match to the fire. We light it at four-thirty, always."

Glad of the fire, for the crimson and white room was piercingly cold, and faintly amused by her air of domesticity, he did as she asked. She moved, with her embroidery, to a chair before the hearth. Alleyn and Fox sat one on each side of her.

"Mrs. Ancred," Alleyn said, "do you think any one in the house knew about this second Will?"

"She knew. She says he showed it to her that night."

"Apart from Miss Orrincourt?"

"They were all afraid he might do something of the sort. He was always changing his Will. But I don't think any of them knew he'd done it."

"I wondered if Sir Cedric——"

The impression that with Millamant all would be plain speaking was immediately dispelled. Her short hands closed on her work like traps. She said harshly: "My son knew nothing about it. Nothing."

"I thought that as Sir Henry's successor——"

"If he had known he would have told me. He knew nothing. It was a great shock to both of us. My son," Millamant added, looking straight before her, "tells me everything—everything."

"Splendid," murmured Alleyn after a pause. Her truculent silence appeared to demand comment. "It's only that I should like to know whether this second Will was made that night when Sir Henry went to his room. Mr. Rattisbon, of course, can tell us."

"I suppose so," said Millamant, selecting a strand of mustard-coloured silk.

"Who discovered the writing on Sir Henry's looking-glass?"

"I did. I'd gone in to see that his room was properly done. He was very particular and the maids are old and forget things. I saw it at once. Before I could wipe it away he came in. I don't think," she said meditatively, "that I'd ever before seen him so angry. For a moment he actually thought I'd done it, and then, of course, he realized it was Panty."

"It was not Panty," Alleyn said.

He and Fox had once agreed that if, after twenty years of experience, an investigating officer has learned to recognize any

717

one manifestation, it is that of genuine astonishment. He recognized it now in Millamant Ancred.

"What are you suggesting?" she said at last. "Do you mean—?"

"Sir Cedric has told me he was involved in one of the other practical jokes that were played on Sir Henry, and knew about all of them. He's responsible for this one."

She took up her embroidery again. "He's trying to shield somebody," she said. "Panty, I suppose."

"I think not."

"It was very naughty of him," she said in her dull voice. "If he played one of these jokes, and I don't believe he did, it was naughty. But I can't see—I may be very stupid, but I can't see why you, Mr. Alleyn, should concern yourself with any of these rather foolish tricks."

"Believe me, we shouldn't do so if we thought they were irrelevant."

"No doubt," she said, and after a pause, "you've been influenced by your wife. She would have it that Panty was all innocence."

"I'm influenced," Alleyn said, "by what Sir Cedric and Miss Orrincourt have told me."

She turned to look at him, moving her torso stiffly. For the first time her alarm, if she felt alarm, coloured her voice. "Cedric? And that woman? Why do you speak of them together like that?"

"It appears that they planned the practical jokes together."

"I don't believe it. She's told you that. I can see it now," said Millamant on a rising note. "I've been a fool."

"What can you see, Mrs. Ancred?"

"She planned it all. Of course she did. She knew Panty was his favourite. She planned it, and when he'd altered the Will she killed him. She's trying to drag my boy down with her. I've watched her. She's a diabolical, scheming woman, and she's trying to entrap my boy. He's generous and unsuspecting and kind. He's been too kind. He's at her mercy," Millamant cried sharply and twisted her hands together.

Confronted by this violence and with the memory of Cedric fresh in his mind, Alleyn was hard put to it to answer her. Before he could frame a sentence she had recovered something of her composure. "That settles it," she said woodenly. "I've kept out of all this, as far as one can keep out of their perpetual scenes and idiotic chattering. I've thought all along that they were probably right but I left it to them. I've even felt sorry for her. Now I hope she suffers. If I can tell you anything that will help you, I'll do so. Gladly."

"Oh, damn!" thought Alleyn. "Oh, Freud! Oh, hell!" And he said: "There may still be no case, you know. Have you any theory as to the writer of the anonymous letters?"

"Certainly," she said with unexpected alacrity.

"You have?"

"They're written on the paper those children use for their work. She asked me some time ago to re-order it for them when I was in the village. I recognized it at once. Caroline Able wrote the letters."

And while Alleyn was still digesting this, she added: "Or Thomas. They're very thick. He spent half his time in the school wing."

CHAPTER XIV

Psychiatry and a Churchyard

I

There was something firmly coarse about Milly Ancred. After performances by Pauline, Desdemona and Cedric, this quality was inescapable. It was incorporate in her solid body, her short hands, the dullness of her voice and her choice of phrase. Alleyn wondered if the late Henry Irving Ancred, surfeited with ancestry, fine feeling and sensibility, had chosen his wife for her lack of these qualities—for her normality. Yet was Milly, with her adoration of an impossible son, normal?

"But there is no norm," he thought, "in human behaviour; who should know this better than Fox and I!"

He began to ask her routine questions, the set of questions that crop up in every case and of which the investigating officer grows tired. The history of the hot drink was traced again with no amendments, but with clear evidence that Milly had resented her dethronement in favour of Miss Orrincourt. He went on to the medicine. It was a fresh bottle. Dr. Withers had suggested an alteration and had left the prescription at the chemist. Miss Orrincourt had picked it up at Mr. Juniper's on the day she collected the children's medicine, and Milly herself had sent Isabel with it to Sir Henry's room. He was only to use it in the event of a severe attack, and until that night had not done so.

"She wouldn't put it in that," said Milly. "She wouldn't be sure of his taking a dose. He hated taking medicine and only used it when he was really very bad. It doesn't seem to have been much good, anyway. I've no faith in Dr. Withers."

"No?"

"I think he's careless. I thought at the time he ought to have asked more questions about my father-in-law's death. He's too much wrapped up in his horse racing and bridge and not interested enough in his patients. However," she added, with a short laugh, "my father-in-law liked him well enough to leave more to him than to some of his own flesh and blood."

"About the medicine," Alleyn prompted.

"She wouldn't have interfered with it. Why should she use it when she had the Thermos in her own hands?"

"Have you any idea where she could have found the tin of ratbane?"

"She complained of rats when she first came here. I asked Barker to set poison and told him there was a tin in the storeroom. She made a great outcry and said she had a horror of poison."

Alleyn glanced at Fox, who instantly looked extremely bland.

"So," Milly went on, "I told Barker to set traps. When we wanted rat-bane, weeks afterwards, for *Bracegirdle*, the tin had gone. It was an unopened tin, to the best of my knowledge. It had been in the store-room for years."

"It must have been an old brand," Alleyn agreed. "I don't think arsenical rat-bane is much used nowadays."

He stood up and Fox rose with him. "I think that's all," he said.

"No," said Millamant strongly, "it's not all. I want to know what the woman has said about my son."

"She suggested they were partners in the practical jokes and he admitted it."

"I warn you," she said, and for the first time her voice was unsteady. "I warn you, she's trying to victimise him. She's worked on his kindness and good nature and his love of fun. I warn you——"

The door at the far end of the room opened and Cedric looked in. His mother's back was turned to him, and, unconscious of his presence, she went on talking. Her shaking voice repeated over and over again that he had been victimized. Cedric's gaze moved from her to Alleyn, who was watching him. He sketched a brief grimace, deprecating, rueful, but his lips were colourless and the effect was of a distortion. He came in and shut the door with great delicacy. He carried a much be-labelled suitcase, presumably Miss Orrincourt's, which, after a further grimace at Alleyn, he placed behind a chair. He then minced across the carpet.

"Darling Milly," he said, and his hands closed on his mother's

721

shoulders. She gave a startled cry. "There now! I made you jump. *So* sorry."

Millamant covered his hands with her own. He waited for a moment, submissive to her restless and possessive touch. "What is it, Milly?" he asked. "Who's been victimising Little Me? Is it Sonia?"

"*Ceddie?*"

"I've been such a goose, you can't think. I've come to 'fess up,' like a good boy," he said nauseatingly, and slid round to his familiar position on the floor, leaning against her knees. She held him there, strongly.

"Mr. Alleyn," Cedric began, opening his eyes very wide, "I couldn't be more sorry about rushing away just now after Aunt Pauline. Really, it was too stupid. But one does like to tell people things in one's own way, and there she was, huffing and puffing and going on as if I'd been trying to conceal some dire skeleton in my, I assure you, too drearily barren cupboard."

Alleyn waited.

"You see—(Milly, my sweet, this is going to be a faint shock to you, but never mind)—you see, Mr. Alleyn, there's been a—what shall I call it?—a—well, an *understanding*, of sorts, between Sonia and me. It only really developed quite lately. After dearest Mrs. Alleyn came here. She seems to have noticed quite a number of things; perhaps she noticed that."

"If I understand you," Alleyn said, "she, I am sure, did not."

"Really?"

"Are you trying to tell me why you visited Miss Orrincourt's rooms on the night of your grandfather's death?"

"Well," Cedric muttered petulantly, "after Aunt Pauline's announcement—and, by the way, she gleaned her information through a nocturnal visit to the *archaic* offices at the end of the passage—after that there seems to be nothing for it but an elaborate cleaning of the breast, does there?"

"Cedric," Millamant said, "what has this woman done to you?"

"My sweet, nothing, thank God. I'm trying to tell you. She really is too beautiful, Mr. Alleyn, don't you think? I know you didn't like her, Milly dear, and how right you seem to have been. But I really was quite intrigued and she was so bored and it was only the teeniest flutter, truly. I merely popped in on my way to bed and had a good giggle with her about the *frightful* doings down below."

"Incidentally," Alleyn suggested, "you may have hoped to hear the latest news about Sir Henry's Will."

"Well, that among other things. You see, I did rather wonder if the flying cow hadn't been sort of once too often, as it were. Sonia did it before dinner, you know. And then at the dinner the Old Person announced a Will that was really quite satisfactory from both our points of view, and with the insufferable Panty not even a starter, one rather wished Sonia had left well alone."

"Cedric," said his mother suddenly, "I don't think, dear, you should go on. Mr. Alleyn won't understand. Stop."

"But, Milly, my sweet, don't you see dear old Pauline has already planted a horrid little seed of suspicion, and one simply must tweak it up before it sprouts. Mustn't one, Mr. Alleyn?"

"I think," Alleyn said, "you'll be well advised to make a complete statement."

"There! Now, where was I? Oh, yes. Now, all would have been well if Carol Able, who is so scientific and 'un-*thing*' that she's a sort of monster, hadn't made out a water-tight alibi for that septic child. This, of course, turned the Old Person's suspicious glare upon all of us equally, and so he wrote the second Will and so we were all done in the eye except Sonia. And to be *quite* frank, Milly and Mr. Alleyn, I should so like to have it settled whether she's a murderess or not, rather quickly."

"Of course she is," Millamant said.

"Yes, but are you *positive*? It really is of mountainous significance for me."

"What do you mean, Cedric? I don't understand——"

"Well—well, never mind."

"I think I know what Sir Cedric means," Alleyn said. "Isn't it a question of marriage at some time in the future with Miss Orrincourt?"

Millamant, with a tightening of her hold on Cedric's shoulder, said, "No!" loudly and flatly.

"Oh, Milly darling," he protested, wriggling under her hand, "please let's be civilised."

"It's all nonsense," she said. "Tell him it's all nonsense. A disgusting idea! Tell him."

"What's the use when Sonia will certainly tell him something else?" He appealed to Alleyn. "You do understand, don't you? I mean, one can't deny she's decorative and in a way it would have been quite fun. Don't you think it would have worked, Mr.

Alleyn? I do."

His mother again began to protest. He freed himself with ugly petulance and scrambled to his feet. "You're idiotic, Milly. What's the good of hiding things?"

"You'll do yourself harm."

"What harm? I'm in the same position, after all, as you. I don't know the truth about Sonia but I want to find out." He turned to Alleyn with a smile. "When I saw her that night she told me about the new Will. I knew then that if he died I'd be practically ruined. There's no collaboration where I'm concerned, Mr. Alleyn. I didn't murder the Old Person. *Pas si bête!*"

II

" '*Pas si bête*," Fox quoted as they made their way to the school wing. "Meaning, "not such a fool." I shouldn't say he was, either, would you, Mr. Alleyn?"

"Oh, no. There are no flies on the egregious Cedric. But what a cold-blooded little worm it is, Fox! Grandpapa dies, leaving him encumbered with a large unwanted estate and an insufficient, income to keep it up. Grandpapa, on the other hand, dies leaving his extremely dubious fiancée a fortune. What more simple than for the financially embarrassed Cedric to marry the opulent Miss O.? I could kick that young man," said Alleyn thoughtfully, "in fourteen completely different positions and still feel half-starved."

"I reckon," said Fox, "it's going to be a case for the Home Secretary."

"Oh, yes, yes, I'm afraid you're right. Down this passage, didn't they say? And there's the green baize door. I think we'll separate here, Fox. You to collect your unconsidered trifles in Isabel's case and, by the way, you might take charge of Miss Orrincourt's. Here it is. Then, secretly, Foxkin, exhume Carabbas, deceased, and enclose him in a boot-box. By the way, do we know who destroyed poor Carabbas?"

"Mr. Barker," said Fox, "got Mr. Juniper to come up and give him an injection. Strychnine, I fancy."

"I hope, whatever it was, it doesn't interfere with the autopsy. I'll meet you on the second terrace."

Beyond the green baize door the whole atmosphere of Ancreton was charged. Coir runners replaced the heavy carpets, passages

724

were draughty and smelt of disinfectant, and where Victorian prints may have hung there were pictures of determined modernity that had been executed with a bright disdain for comfortable, but doubtless undesirable, prettiness.

Led by a terrific rumpus, Alleyn found his way to a large room where Miss Able's charges were assembled, with building games, with modelling clay, with paints, hammers, sheets of paper, scissors and paste. Panty, he saw, was conducting a game with scales, weights and bags of sand, and appeared to be in hot dispute with a small boy. When she saw Alleyn she flung herself into a strange attitude and screamed with affected laughter. He waved to her and she at once did a comedy fall to the floor, where she remained, apeing violent astonishment.

Miss Caroline Able detached herself from a distant group and came towards him.

"We're rather noisy in here," she said crisply. "Shall we go to my office? Miss Watson, will you carry on?"

"Certainly, Miss Able," said an older lady, rising from behind a mass of children.

"Come along, then," said Caroline Able.

Her office was near at hand and was hung with charts and diagrams. She seated herself behind an orderly desk, upon which he at once noticed a pile of essays written on paper with yellow lines and ruled margin.

"I suppose you know what all this is about," he said.

Miss Able replied cheerfully that she thought she did. "I see," she said frankly, "quite a lot of Thomas Ancred and he's told me about all the trouble. It's been a pretty balanced account, as a matter of fact. He's fairly well adjusted, and has been able to deal with it quite satisfactorily so far."

Alleyn understood this to be a professional opinion on Thomas, and wondered if a courtship had developed and if it was conducted on these lines. Miss Able was pretty. She had a clear skin, large eyes and good teeth. She also had an intimidating air of utter sanity.

"I'd like to know," he said, "what you think about it all."

"It's impossible to give an opinion that's worth much," she replied, "without a pretty thorough analysis of one if not all of them. Obviously the relationship with their father was unsatisfactory. I should have liked to know about his marriage. One suspected, of course, that there was a fear of impotency, not altogether sublimated. T_e daughter's violent antagonism to his proposed second marriage suggsts a rather bad father-fixation."

"Does it? But it wasn't a particularly suitable alliance from—from the ordinary point of view, was it?"

"If the relationship with the father," Miss Able said firmly, "had been properly adjusted, the children should not have been profoundly disturbed."

"Not even," Alleyn ventured, "by the prospect of Miss O. as a mother-in-law and principal beneficiary in the Will?"

"Those may have been the reasons advanced to explain their antagonism. They may represent an attempt to rationalise a basic and essentially sexual repulsion."

"Oh, dear!"

"But, as I said before," she added, with a candid laugh, "one shouldn't pronounce on mere observation. Deep analysis might lead to a much more complex state of affairs."

"You know," Alleyn said, taking out his pipe and nursing it in his palm, "you and I, Miss Able, represent two aspects of investigation. Your professional training teaches you that behaviour is a sort of code or cryptogram disguising the pathological truth from the uninformed, but revealing it to the expert. Mine teaches me to regard behaviour as something infinitely variable *after* the fact and often at complete loggerheads *with* the fact. A policeman watches behaviour, of course, but his deductions would seem completely superficial to you." He opened his hand. "I see a man turning a dead pipe about in his hand and I think that, perhaps unconsciously, he's longing to smoke it. May he?"

"Do," said Miss Able. "It's a good illustration. I see a man caressing his pipe and I recognise a very familiar piece of fetishism."

"Well, don't tell me what it is," Alleyn said hurriedly.

Miss Able gave a short professional laugh.

"Now, look here," he said, "how do you account for these anonymous letters we're all so tired of? What sort of being perpetrated them and why?"

"They probably represent an attempt to make an effect and are done by someone whose normal creative impulses have taken the wrong turning. The desire to be mysterious and omnipotent may be an additional factor. In Patricia's case for instance——"

"Patricia? Oh, I see. That's Panty, of course."

"We don't use her nickname over here. We don't think it a

good idea. We think nicknames can have a very definite effect, particularly when they are of a rather humiliating character."

"I see. Well, then, in Patricia's case?"

"She formed the habit of perpetrating rather silly jokes on people. This was an attempt to command attention. She used to let her performances remain anonymous. Now she usually brags about them. That, of course, is a good sign."

"It's an indication, at least, that she's not the author of the more recent practical jokes on her grandfather."

"I agree."

"Or the author of the anonymous letters."

"That, I should have thought," said Miss Able patiently, "was perfectly obvious."

"Who do you think is responsible for the letters?"

"I've told you, I can't make snap decisions or guesses."

"Couldn't you just unbend far enough to have one little potshot?" he said persuasively. Miss Able opened her mouth, shut it again, looked at him with somewhat diminished composure and finally blushed. "Come!" he thought, "she hasn't analysed herself into an iceberg, at least." And he said aloud: "Without prejudice, now, who among the grown-ups would you back as the letter-writer?" He leant forward, smiling at her, and thought: "Troy would grin if she saw this exhibition." As Miss Able still hesitated, he repeated: "Come on; who would you back?"

"You're very silly," Miss Able said, and her manner, if not coy, was at least very much less impersonal.

"Would you say," Alleyn went on, "that the person who wrote them is by any chance the practical joker?"

"Quite possible."

He reached a long arm over the desk and touched the top sheet of the exercises. "They were written," he said, "on this paper."

Her face was crimson. With a curious and unexpected gesture she covered the paper with her hands. "I don't believe you," she said.

"Will you let me look at it? " He drew the sheet out from under her hands and held it to the light. "Yes," he said. "Rather an unusual type with a margin. It's the same watermark."

"He didn't do it."

"He?"

"Tom," she said, and the diminutive cast a new light upon

Thomas. "He's incapable of it."

"Good," Alleyn said. "Then why bring him up?"

"Patricia," said Miss Able, turning a deeper red, "must have taken some of this exercise paper over to the other side. Or ..." She paused, frowning.

"Yes?"

"Her mother comes over here a great deal. Too often, I sometimes think. She's not very wise with children."

"Where is the paper kept?"

"In that cupboard. The top one. Out of reach of the children."

"Do you keep it locked?"

She turned on him quickly.

"You're not going to suggest that I would write anonymous letters? I?"

"But you do keep it locked, don't you?" said Alleyn.

"Certainly. I haven't denied that."

"And the key?"

"On my ring and in my pocket."

"Has the cupboard been left open at all? Or the keys left out of your pocket?"

"Never."

"The paper comes from a village shop, doesn't it?"

"Of course it does. Anyone could buy it."

"So they could," he agreed cheerfully, "and we can find out if they have. There's no need, you see, to fly into a huff with me."

"I do not," said Miss Able mulishly, "fly into huffs."

"Splendid! Now look here. About this medicine your kids had. I want to trace its travels. Not inside the wretched kids, but *en route* to them."

"I really don't see why——"

"Of course you don't and I'll tell you. A bottle of medicine for Sir Henry came up at the same time and its history is therefore bound up with theirs. Now, as the pudding said to the shop assistant, can you help me, Moddom?"

This laborious pun was not immediately absorbed by Miss Able. She looked at him with wonder but finally produced a tolerably indulgent smile.

"I suppose I can. Miss Orrincourt and Mrs. Alleyn ..."

Here came the now familiar pause and its inevitable explanation. "Fancy!" said Miss Able. "I know," said Alleyn. "About the medicine?"

"I was really very annoyed with Miss Orrincourt. It seems that she asked Mrs. Alleyn to drive the trap round to the stables and she herself brought in the medicine. Instead of leaving it in the hall, or as you would think she might have done, bringing it in here to me, she simply dumped the whole lot in the flower-room. It seems that Sir Henry had given her some flowers out of the conservatory and she'd left them there. She's abnormally egocentric, of course. I waited and waited, and finally, at about seven o'clock, went over to the other side to ask about it. Mrs. Ancred and I hunted everywhere. Finally, it was Fenella who told us where they were."

"Was Sir Henry's medicine with theirs?"

"Oh, yes. Mrs. Ancred sent it up at once."

"Were the bottles alike?"

"We made no mistake, if that's what you're wondering. They were the same sort of bottles, but ours was much larger and they were both clearly labelled. Ours had the instructions attached. Unnecessarily, as it turned out, because Dr. Withers came up himself that evening and he weighed the children again and measured out their doses himself. It was odd, because he'd left it that I should give the medicine and I could have managed perfectly well; but evidently," said Miss Able with a short laugh, "he'd decided I was not to be trusted."

"It's a fault on the right side, I suppose," Alleyn said vaguely. "They have to be careful."

Miss Able looked unconvinced. "No doubt," she said. "But I still can't understand why he wanted to come up to Ancreton, when he was supposed to be so busy. And after all that fuss, we've had to go back to the ointment."

"By the way," Alleyn asked, "did you happen to see the cat Carabbas before it died?"

Instantly she was away on her professional hobby-horse. He listened to an exposition on Panty's fondness for the cat, and the strange deductions which Miss Able drew, with perfect virtuosity, from this not unusual relationship.

"At this stage of her development, it was really a bad disturbance when the link was broken."

"But," Alleyn ventured, "if the cat had ringworm ..."

"It wasn't ringworm," said Miss Able firmly. "I ought to know. It might have been mange."

Upon that pronouncement he left her, apparently in two minds

729

about himself. She shook hands with an air of finality, but when he reached the door he thought he heard an indeterminate sound, and turned to find her looking anxiously at him.

"Is there anything else?" he asked.

"It's only that I'm worried about Tom Ancred. They're dragging him in and making him do all their dirty work. He's quite different. He's too good for them. I'm afraid this will upset him."

And then with a rather strenuous resumption of her professional manner: "Psychologically, I mean," said Miss Able.

"I quite understand," said Alleyn, and left her.

He found Fox waiting for him on the second terrace. Fox was sitting on the steps with his greatcoat drawn closely round him and his spectacles on his nose. He was reading from the manual on poisons which Alleyn had lent him in the train. By his side were two suitcases. One of these Alleyn recognized as Miss Orrincourt's. The other, he presumed, was Isabel's. Near by was a boot-box tied up with string. As Alleyn bent over Fox he noticed an unpleasant smell.

"Carabbas?" he asked, edging the box away with his foot.

Fox nodded. "I've been asking myself," he said, and placed a square finger under a line of print. Alleyn read over his shoulder. "Arsenic. Symptoms. Manifested as progressive cachexia and loss of flesh; falling out of hair ..."

Fox glanced up and jerked a thumb at the boot-box.

"Falling out of hair," he said. "Wait till you've had a look at Carabbas deceased."

III

"You know, Fox," Alleyn said as they walked back to the village, "if Thomas Ancred can stand having his lightest cares implacably laid at the door of some infantile impropriety, he and Miss Able will probably get along together very nicely. Obviously, she's in love with him, or should I say that obviously she finds herself adjusted to a condition of rationalized eroticism in relation to poor old Thomas?"

"Courting, do you reckon?"

"I think so, Fox, I think we've had Ancreton for the moment, but I'm going to ask you to stay behind and warn the parson about an exhumation. Return to Katzenjammer Castle in the

morning and ask the inmates if they've any objection to having
their prints taken. They won't have any if they're not completely
dotty. Bailey can come down by the morning train and work
round the house for the stuff we want there. Get him to check
prints on any relevant surfaces. It'll all be utterly useless no
doubt, but it had better be done. I'll go back to the Yard. I want
to learn Messrs. Mortimer and Loame's recipe for tasteful
embalming. As soon as we get the exhumation order through
we'll come down and meet you here. There's a train this evening.
Let's have a meal at the pub and then I'll catch it. I was going to
see Dr. Withers again, but I fancy that particular interview had
better wait. I want to get the medicine bottle and poor old
Carabbas up to London."

"What's the betting, Mr. Alleyn? Arsenic in the medicine or
not?"

"I'm betting *not*."

"Routine job. It'll be a nuisance if they don't find anything,
though. Not a hope with the Thermos."

"No, damn it."

They walked in silence. Frost tingled in the dusk and hardened
the ground under their feet. A pleasant smell of burning wood
laced the air and from Ancreton woods came the sound of wings.

"What a job!" Alleyn said suddenly.

"Ours, sir?"

"Yes, ours. Walking down a country lane with a dead cat in a
boot-box and working out procedure for disentombing the body
of an old man."

"Somebody's got to do it."

"Certainly. But the details are unlovely."

"Not much doubt about it, sir, is there? Homicide?"

"Not much doubt, old thing. No."

"Well," said Fox, after a pause, "as it stands, the evidence all
points one way. It's not one of those funny affairs where you have
to clear up half a dozen suspects."

"But *why* kill him? She knew the Will was in her favour. She
wanted to be Lady Ancred. She knew he wasn't likely to live
much longer. Why incur the appalling risk when all she had to do
was marry him and wait?"

"He was always changing his Will. Perhaps she thought he
might do it again."

"She seems to have had him pretty well where she wanted him."

731

"Might she be all that keen on the present baronet?"

"Not she," said Alleyn. "Not she."

"Hard to imagine, I must say. Suppose, though, that Miss O. is not the party we'll be after, and suppose we know the old gentleman was done away with. Who's left? Not Sir Cedric, because he knew about the second Will."

"Unless," said Alleyn, "he gambled on marrying the heiress."

"By gum, yes, there's that, but what a gamble! With that fortune she could have hoped for better, wouldn't you say?"

"She could hardly hope for worse, in my opinion."

"Well, then," Fox reasoned, "suppose we count those two out. Look at the rest of the field."

"I do so without enthusiasm. They all thought the Will announced at the Birthday Dinner was valid. Desdemona, Millamant, Dr. Withers and the servants expected to do moderately well; Thomas's expectations were handsome. The Kentish family and the Claude Ancreds got damn all. In the 'haves' the only motive is cupidity, in the 'have-nots,' revenge."

"Opportunity?" Fox speculated.

"If an analysis of the medicine bottle proves negative, we're left with the Thermos flask, now sterilised, and as far as we can see, Miss O. Unless you entertain a notion of delayed action with Barker inserting arsenic in the crayfish."

"You will have your joke, Mr. Alleyn."

"You should have heard me trifling with Miss Able," Alleyn grunted. "That was pretty ghastly, if you like."

"And the exhumation's *on*," Fox ruminated after another long silence. "When?"

"As soon as we've got the order and Dr. Curtis can manage it. By the way, Ancreton Church is above the village over there. We'll have a look at the churchyard while the light still holds."

And presently they climbed a gentle lane, now deep in shadow, and pushed open a lych-gate into the churchyard of St. Stephen's, Ancreton.

It was pleasant after the dubious grandeurs of the manor house to encircle this church, tranquil, ancient, and steadfastly built. Their feet crunched loudly on the gravelled path, and from the hedges came a faint stir of sleepy birds. The grass was well kept. When they came upon a quiet company of headstones and crosses they found that the mounds and plots before them were also carefully tended. It was possible in the fading light to read inscriptions. "Susan Gascoigne of this parish. Here rests one who in her life rested not in well-doing." "To the Memory of Miles Chitty Bream who for fifty years tended this churchyard and now sleeps with those he faithfully served." Presently they came upon Ancred graves. "Henry Gaisbrook Ancreton Ancred, fourth baronet, and Margaret Mirabel, his wife." "Percival Gaisbrook Ancred," and many others, decently and properly bestowed. But such plain harbourage was not for the later generations, and towering over this sober company of stone rose a marble tomb topped by three angels. Here, immortalized in gold inscriptions, rested Sir Henry's predecessor, his wife, his son Henry Irving Ancred, and himself. The tomb, Alleyn read, had been erected by Sir Henry. It had a teak and iron door, emblazoned in the Ancred arms, and with a great keyhole.

"It'll be one of these affairs with shelves," Fox speculated. "Not room enough for the doctor, and no light. It'll have to be a canvas enclosure, don't you reckon, Mr. Alleyn?"

"Yes."

The lid of Fox's large silver watch clicked. "It's five o'clock, sir," he said. "Time we moved on if you're to have tea at the pub and catch that train."

"Come along, then," said Alleyn quietly, and they retraced their steps to the village.

CHAPTER XV

New System

I

As Troy waited for Alleyn's return her thoughts moved back through the brief period of their reunion. She examined one event, then another; a phrase, a gesture, an emotion. She was astonished by the simplicity of her happiness; amused to find herself expectant, even a little sleek. She was desired, she was loved, and she loved again. That there were hazards ahead she made no doubt, but for the moment all was well; she could relax and find a perspective.

Yet, like a rough strand in the texture of her happiness, there was an imperfection. Her thoughts, questing fingers, continually and reluctantly sought it out. This was Alleyn's refusal to allow his work a place in their relationship. It was founded, she knew, in her own attitude during their earliest encounters which had taken place against a terrible background; in her shrinking from the part he played at that time and in her expressed horror of capital punishment.

Troy knew very well that Alleyn accepted these reactions as fundamental and implicit in her nature. She knew he did not believe that for her, in love, an ethic unrelated to that love could not impede it. It seemed to him that if his work occasionally brought murderers to execution, then surely, to her, he must at those times be of the same company as the hangman. Only by some miracle of love, he thought, did she overcome her repulsion.

But the bald truth, she told herself helplessly, was that her ideas were remote from her emotions. "I'm less sensitive than he thinks," she said. "What he does is of no importance. I love him." And although she disliked such generalities, she added: "I am a woman."

It seemed to her that while this withdrawal existed they could not be completely happy. "Perhaps," she thought, "this business with the Ancreds will, after all, change everything. Perhaps it's a kind of beastly object lesson. I'm in it. He can't keep me out. I'm in on a homicide case." And with a sensation of panic she realized that she had been taking it for granted that the old man she had painted was murdered.

As soon as Alleyn came in and stood before her she knew that she had made no mistake. "Well, Rory," she said, going to him, "we're for it, aren't we, darling?"

"It looks a bit like it." He walked past her, saying quickly: "I'll see the A.C. in the morning. He'll let me hand over to someone else. Much better."

"No," Troy said, and he turned quickly and looked at her. She was aware, as if she had never before fully appreciated it, of the difference in their heights. She thought: "That's how he looks when he's taking statements," and became nervous.

"No?" he said. "Why not?"

"Because it would be high-falutin, because it would make me feel an ass."

"I'm sorry."

"I look upon this case," Troy said, and wished her voice would sound more normal, "as a sort of test. Perhaps it's been sent to larn us like acts-of-God; only I must say I always think it's so unfair to call earthquakes and tidal-waves acts-of-God and not bumper harvests and people like Leonardo and Cézanne."

"What the devil," Alleyn asked in a mild voice, "are you talking about?"

"Don't snap at me," said Troy. He made a quick movement towards her. "No. Please listen. I want, I really do want you to take this case as long as the A.C. lets you. I really want you to keep me with you this time. We've got in a muddle about me and your job. When I say I don't mind your job you think I'm not telling the truth, and if I ask you questions about these kinds of cases you think I'm being a brave little woman and biting on the bullet."

She saw his mouth twist in an involuntary smile.

"Whereas," she hurried on, "I'm not. I know I didn't relish having our courtship all muddled up with murder on the premises, and I know I don't think people ought to hang other

735

people. But you do, and you're the policeman, not me. And it doesn't do any good trying to pretend you're dodging out to pinch a petty larcener when I know jolly well what you are up to, and, to be perfectly honest, am often dying to hear about it."

"That's not quite true, is it—the last bit?"

"I'd infinitely rather talk about it. I'd infinitely rather feel honestly shocked and upset with you, than vaguely worried all by myself."

He held out a hand and she went to him. "That's why I said I think this case has been sent to larn you."

"Troy," Alleyn said, "do you know what they say to their best girls in the antipodes?"

"No."

"You'll do me."

"Oh!"

"You'll do me, Troy."

"I thought perhaps you'd prefer me to remain a shrinking violet."

"The truth is, I've been a bloody fool and never did and never will deserve you."

"Don't," said Troy, "let's talk about deserving."

"I've only one excuse and logically you'll say it's no excuse. Books about C.I.D. men will tell you that running a murderer to earth is just a job to us, as copping a pickpocket is to the ordinary P.C. It's not. Because of its termination it's unlike any other job in existence. When I was twenty-two I faced its implications and took it on, but I don't think I fully realized them for another fifteen years and that was when I fell most deeply in love, my love, with you."

"I've faced its implications, too, and once for all, over this Ancred business. Before you came in I even decided that it would be good for both of us if, by some freak, it turned out that I had a piece of information somewhere in the back of my memory that's of vital importance."

"You'd got as far as that?"

"Yes. And the queer thing is," Troy said, driving her fingers through her hair, "I've got the most extraordinary conviction that somewhere in the back of my memory it is there, waiting to come out."

"I want you," Alleyn said, "to tell me again, as fully as you possibly can, about your conversation with Sir Henry after he'd found the writing on the looking-glass and the grease-paint on the cat's whiskers. If you've forgotten how it went at any particular stage, say so. But, for the love of Mike, darling, don't elaborate. Can you remember?"

"I think so. Quite a lot, anyway. He was furious with Panty, of course."

"He hadn't a suspicion of the egregious Cedric?"

"None. Did Cedric——?"

"He did. He lisped out an admission."

"Little devil," said Troy. "So it *was* grease-paint on his finger-nail."

"And Sir Henry——?"

"He just went on and on about how much he'd doted on Panty and how she'd grieved him. I tried to persuade him she hadn't done it, but he only made their family noise at me: 'T'uh!' you know?"

"Yes, indeed."

"Then he started to talk about marriages between first cousins and how he disapproved of them, and this got mixed up in no time with a most depressing account of how he was"—Troy swallowed and went on quickly"—was going to be embalmed. We actually mentioned the book. Then I think he sniffed a bit at Cedric as his heir, and said he'd never have children and that poor Thomas wouldn't marry."

"He was wrong there, I fancy."

"No! Who?"

"The psychiatrist, or should it be 'psychiatriste'?"

"Miss Able?"

"She thinks he's quite satisfactorily sublimated his libido or something."

"Oh, good! Well, and then as he would keep talking about when he was Gone, I tried to buck him up a bit and had quite a success. He turned mysterious and talked about there being surprises in store for everybody. And upon that Sonia Orrincourt burst in and said they were all plotting against her and she was frightened."

"And that's all?" Alleyn said after a pause.

"No—no, it isn't. There was something else he said. Rory, I can't remember what it was, but there was something else."

"That was on Saturday the seventeenth, wasn't it?"

"Let me see. I got there on the sixteenth. Yes. Yes, it was the next day. But I wish," Troy said slowly, "I do wish I could remember the other thing he talked about."

"Don't try. It may come back suddenly."

"Perhaps Miss Able could screw it out of me," said Troy with a grin.

"In any case we'll call it a day."

As they moved away she linked her arm through his. "First instalment of the new system," she said. "It's gone off tolerably quietly, hasn't it?"

"It has, my love. Thank you."

"One of the things I like about you," Troy said, "is your nice manners."

III

The next day was a busy one. The Assistant Commissioner, after a brisk interview with Alleyn, decided to apply for an exhumation order. "Sooner the better, I suppose. I was talking to the Home Secretary yesterday and told him we might be on his tracks. You'd better go right ahead."

"To-morrow then, sir, if possible," Alleyn said. "I'll see Dr. Curtis."

"Do." And as Alleyn turned away: "By the way, Rory, if it's at all difficult for Mrs. Alleyn——"

"Thank you very much, sir, but at the moment she's taking it in her stride."

"Splendid. Damn' rum go—what?"

"Damn' rum," Alleyn agreed politely, and went to call on Mr. Rattisbon.

Mr. Rattisbon's offices in the Strand had survived the pressure of the years, the blitz and the flying bomb. They were, as Alleyn remembered them on the occasion of his first official visit before the war, a discreetly active memorial to the style of Charles Dickens, with the character of Mr. Rattisbon himself written across them like an inscription. Here was the same clerk with his trick of slowly raising his head and looking dimly at the inquirer, the same break-neck stairs, the same dark smell of antiquity. And here, at last, shrined in leather, varnish and age was Mr. Rattisbon, that elderly legal bird, perched at his desk.

"Ah, yes, Chief Inspector," Mr. Rattisbon gabbled, extending a claw at a modish angle, "come in, come in, sit down, slt down. Glad to see yer. M-m-maah!" And when Alleyn was seated Mr. Rattisbon darted the old glance at him, sharp as the point of a fine nib. "No trouble, I hope?" he said.

"The truth is," Alleyn rejoined, "my visits only arise, I'm afraid, out of some sort of trouble."

Mr. Rattisbon instantiy hunched himself, placed his elbows on his desk and joined his finger-tips in front of his chin.

"I've come to ask about certain circumstances that relate to the late Sir Henry Ancred's Will. Or Wills."

Mr. Rattisbon vibrated the tip of his tongue between his lips, rather as if he had scalded it and hoped in this manner to cool it off. He said nothing.

"Without more ado," Alleyn went on, "I must tell you that we are going to ask for an exhumation."

After a considerable pause Mr. Rattisbon said: "This is exceedingly perturbing."

"May I, before we go any further, say I do think that instead of coming to us with the story I'm about to relate, Sir Henry's successors might have seen fit to consult their solicitor."

"Thank yer."

"I don't know, sir, of course, how you would have advised them, but I believe that this visit must sooner or later have taken place. Here is the story."

Twenty minutes later Mr. Rattisbon tipped himself back in his chair and gave a preparatory bay at the ceiling.

"Ma-m-ah!" he said. "Extraordinary. Disquieting. Very."

"You will see that all this rigmarole seems to turn about two factors. (a) It was common knowledge in his household that Sir Henry Ancred was to be embalmed. (b) He repeatedly altered his Will, and on the eve of his death appears to have done so in favour of his intended wife, largely to the exclusion of his family and in direct contradiction to an announcement he made a couple of hours earlier. It's here, I hope, Mr. Rattisbon, that you can help us."

"I am," said Mr. Rattisbon, "in an unusual, not to say equivocal, position. Um. As you have very properly noted, Chief Inspector, the correct procedure on the part of the family, particularly on the part of Sir Cedric Gaisbrooke Percival Ancred, would have been to consult this office. He has elected not to do so. In the event of a criminal action he will scarcely be able to avoid doing so. It appears that the general intention of the family is to discredit the position of the chief beneficiary and further to suggest that there is a case for a criminal charge against her. I refer, of course, to Miss Gladys Clark."

"To *whom?*"

"—known professionally as Miss Sonia Orrincourt."

" 'Gladys Clark,' " Alleyn said thoughtfully. "Well!"

"Now, as the solicitor for the estate, I am concerned in the matter. On consideration, I find no objection to giving you such information as you require. Indeed, I conceive it to be my professional duty to do so."

"I'm extremely glad," said Alleyn, who had known perfectly well that Mr. Rattisbon, given time, would arrive at precisely this decision. "Our principal concern at the moment is to discover whether Sir Henry Ancred actually concocted his last Will after he left the party on the eve of his death."

"Emphatically no. It was drawn up, in this office, on Sir Henry's instruction, on Thursday, the twenty-second of November of this year, together with a second document, which was the one quoted by Sir Henry as his last Will and Testament at his Birthday dinner."

"This all sounds rather erratic."

Mr. Rattisbon rapidly scratched his nose with the nail of his first finger. "The procedure," he said, "was extraordinary, I ventured to say so at the time. Let me take these events in their order. On Tuesday, the twentieth November, Mrs. Henry Irving Ancred telephoned this office to the effect that Sir Henry Ancred wished me to call upon him immediately. It was most inconvenient, but the following day I went down to Ancreton. I found him in a state of considerable agitation and clothed—m-m-m-ah—in a theatrical costume. I understood that he had been posing for his portrait. May I add, in parentheses," said Mr. Rattisbon with a bird-like dip of his head, "that although your wife was at Ancreton, I had not the pleasure of meeting her on that occasion. I enjoyed this privilege upon my later visit."

"Troy told me."

"It was the greatest pleasure. To return. On this first visit of Wednesday the twenty-first of November, Sir Henry Ancred showed me his rough drafts of two Wills. One moment."

With darting movements, Mr, Rattisbon drew from his filing cabinet two sheafs of paper covered in a somewhat flamboyant script. He handed them to Alleyn. A glance showed him their nature. "Those are the drafts," said Mr, Rattisbon. "He required me to engross two separate Wills based on these notes. I remarked that this procedure was unusual. He put it to me that he was unable to come to a decision regarding the—ah—the merits of his immediate relatives, and was, at the same time, contemplating a second marriage. His previous Will, in my opinion a reasonable disposition, he had already destroyed. He instructed me to bring these two new documents to Ancreton when I returned for the annual Birthday observances. The first was the Will witnessed and signed before the dinner and quoted by Sir Henry *at* dinner as his last Will and Testament. It was destroyed late that evening. The second is the document upon which we are at present empowered to act. It was signed and witnessed in Sir Henry Ancred's bedroom at twelve-twenty that night—against, may I add, *against* my most earnest representations."

"Two Wills," Alleyn said, "in readiness for a final decision."

"Precisely. He believed that his health was precarious. Without making any specific accusations he suggested that certain members of his family were acting separately or in collusion against him. I believe, in view of your own exceedingly lucid account," Mr. Rattisbon dipped his head again, "that he referred, in fact, to these practical jokes. Mrs. Alleyn will have described fully the extraordinary incident of the portrait. An admirable likeness, if I may say so. She will have related how Sir Henry left the theatre in anger."

"Yes."

"Subsequently the butler came to me with a request from Sir Henry that I should wait upon him in his room. I found him still greatly perturbed. In my presence, and with considerable violence, he tore up the, as I considered, more reasonable of the two drafts, and, in short, threw it on the fire. A Mr. and Mrs. Candy were shown in and witnessed his signature to the second document. Sir Henry then informed me that he proposed to marry Miss Clark in a week's time and would require my services in the drawing up of a marriage settlement. I persuaded him to postpone this matter until the morning and left him, still agitated and inflamed. That, in effect, is all I can tell you."

"It's been enormously helpful," Alleyn said. "One other point if you don't mind. Sir Henry's two drafts are not dated. He didn't by any chance tell you when he wrote them?"

"No. His behaviour and manner on this point were curious. He stated that he would enjoy no moment's peace until both Wills had been drawn up in my office. But no. Except that the drafts were made before Tuesday, the twentieth, I cannot help you here."

"I'd be grateful if they might be put away and left untouched."

"Of course," said Mr. Rattisbon, greatly flustered, "by all means."

Alleyn placed the papers between two clean sheets and returned them to their drawer.

That done, he rose, and Mr. Rattisbon at once became very lively. He escorted Alleyn to the door, shook hands and uttered a string of valedictory phrases. "Quite so, quite so," he gabbled. "Disquieting. Trust no foundation but nevertheless disquieting. Always depend upon your discretion. Extraordinary. In many ways, I fear, an unpredictable family. No doubt if counsel is required ... Well, good-bye. Thank yer. Kindly remember me to Mrs. Alleyn. Thank yer."

But as Alleyn moved, Mr. Rattisbon laid a claw on his arm. "I shall always remember him that night," he said. "He stopped me as I reached the door and I turned and saw him, sitting upright in bed with his gown spread about him. He was a fine-looking old fellow. I was quite arrested by his appearance. He made an unaccountable remark, too, I recollect. He said: 'I expect to be very well attended, in future, Rattisbon. Opposition to my marriage may not be as strong in some quarters as you anticipate. Good night.' That was all. It was, of course, the last time I ever saw him."

IV

The Hon. Mrs. Claude Ancred had a small house in Chelsea. As a dwelling-place it presented a startling antithesis to Ancreton. Here all was lightness and simplicity. Alleyn was shown into a white drawing-room, modern in treatment, its end wall one huge window overlooking the river: The curtains were pale yellow, powdered with silver stars, and this colour, with accents of clear cerise, appeared throughout the room. There were three pictures

—a Matisse, a Christopher Wood, and, to his pleasure, an Agatha Troy. "So you still stick around, do you?" he said, winking at it, and at that moment Jenetta Ancred came in.

An intelligent-looking woman, he thought. She greeted him as if he was a normal visitor, and, with a glance at the painting, said: "You see that we've got a friend in common," and began to talk to him about Troy and their meeting at Ancreton.

He noticed that her manner was faintly and recurrently ironic. Nothing, she seemed to say, must be insisted upon or underlined. Nothing really matters very much. Over-statement is stupid and uncomfortable. This impression was conveyed by the crispness of her voice, its avoidance of stresses, and by her eyes and lips, which constantly erected little smiling barriers that half-discredited the frankness of her conversation. She talked intelligently about painting, but always with an air of self-deprecation. He had a notion she was warding off the interview for which he had asked.

At last he said: "You've guessed, of course, why I wanted you to let me come?"

"Thomas came in last night and told me he'd seen you and that you'd gone down to Ancreton. This is an extremely unpleasant development, isn't it?"

"I'd very much like to hear your views."

"Mine?" she said, with an air of distaste. "They can't possibly be of the smallest help, I'm afraid. I'm always a complete onlooker at Ancreton. And please don't tell me the onlooker sees most of the game. In this instance she sees as little as possible."

"Well," said Alleyn cheerfully, "what does she think?"

She waited for a moment, looking past him to the great window. "I think," she murmured, "that it's almost certain to be a tarradiddle. The whole story."

"Convince us of that," Alleyn said, "and we're your slaves for ever in the C.I.D."

"No, but really. They're so absurd, you know, my in-laws. I'm very attracted to them, but you can't imagine how absurd they can be." Her voice died away. After a moment's reflection she said: "But Mrs. Alleyn saw them. She must have told you."

"A little."

"At one time it was fifth columnists. Pauline suspected such a nice little Austrian doctor who's since taken a very important job at a big clinic. At that time he was helping with the children. She

743

said something told her. And then it was poor Miss Able who was supposed to be undermining her influence with Panty. I wonder if, having left the stage, Pauline's obliged to find some channel for her histrionic instincts. They all do it. Naturally, they resented Miss Orrincourt, and resentment and suspicion are inseparable with the Ancreds."

"What did you think of Miss Orrincourt?"

"I? She's too lovely, isn't she? In her way, quite flawless."

"Apart from her beauty?"

"There didn't seem to be anything else. Except a very robust vulgarity."

"But does she really think as objectively as all that?" Alleyn wondered. "Her daughter stood to lose a good deal through Sonia Orrincourt. Could she have achieved such complete detachment?" He said: "You were there, weren't you, when the book on embalming appeared in the cheese-dish?"

She made a slight grimace. "Oh, yes."

"Have you any idea who could have put it there?"

"I'm afraid I rather suspected Cedric. Though why ... For no reason except that I can't believe any of the others would do it. It was quite horrible."

"And the anonymous letters?"

"I feel it must have been the same person. I can't imagine how any of the Ancreds—After all they're not—However."

She had a trick of letting her voice fade out as if she had lost faith in the virtue of her sentences. Alleyn felt that she pushed the suggestion of murder away from her, with both hands, not so much for its dreadfulness as for its offence against taste.

"You think, then," he said, "that their suspicion of Miss Orrincourt is unfounded and that Sir Henry died naturally?"

"That's it. I'm quite sure it's all a make-up. They think it's true. They've just got one of their 'things' about it."

"That explanation doesn't quite cover the discovery of a tin of rat-bane in her suitcase, does it?"

"Then there must be some other explanation."

"The only one that occurs to me," Alleyn said, "is that the tin was deliberately planted, and if you accept that you accept something equally serious: an attempt to place suspicion of murder upon an innocent person. That in itself constitutes——"

"No, no," she cried out. "No, you don't understand the Ancreds. They plunge into fantasies of their own making,

744

without thinking of the consequences. This wretched tin must have been put in the suitcase by a maid or have got there by some other freakish accident. It may have been in the attic for years. None of their alarms ever means anything. Mr. Alleyn, may I implore you to dismiss the whole thing as nonsense? Dangerous and idiotic nonsense, but, believe me, utter nonsense."

She had leant forward, and her hands were pressed together. There was a vehemence and an intensity in her manner that had not appeared before.

"If it's nonsense," he said, "it's malevolent nonsense."

"Stupid," she insisted, "spiteful, too, perhaps, but only childishly so."

"I shall be very glad if it turns out to be no more."

"Yes, but you don't think it will."

"I'm wide open to conviction," he said lightly.

"If I could convince you!"

"You can at least help by filling in some of the gaps. For instance, can you tell me anything about the party in the drawing-room when you all returned from the little theatre? What happened?"

Instead of answering him directly she said, with a return to her earlier manner, "Please forgive me for being so insistent. It's silly to try and ram one's convictions down other people's throats. They merely feel that one protests too much. But, you see, I know my Ancreds."

"And I'm learning mine. About the aftermath of the Birthday Party?"

"Well, two of our visitors, the rector and a local squire, said good night in the hall. Very thankfully, poor darlings, I'm sure. Miss Orrincourt had already gone up. Mrs. Alleyn had stayed behind in the theatre with Paul and Fenella. The rest of us went into the drawing-room and there the usual family arguments started, this time on the subject of that abominable disfigurement of the portrait. Paul and Fenella came in and told us that no damage had been done. Naturally, they were very angry. I may tell you that my daughter, who has not quite grown out of the hero-worship state-of-affairs, admires your wife enormously. These two children planned what they fondly imagined to be a piece of detective work. Did Mrs. Alleyn tell you?"

Troy had told Alleyn, but he listened again to the tale of the paint-brush and finger-prints. She dwelt at some length on this, inviting his laughter, making, he thought, a little too much of a slight incident. When he asked her for further details of the discussion in the drawing-room she became vague. They had talked about Sir Henry's fury, about his indiscretions at dinner. Mr. Rattisbon had been sent for by Sir Henry. "It was just one more of the interminable emotional parties," she said. "Everyone, except Cedric and Milly, terrifically hurt and grand because of the Will he told us about at dinner."

"Every one? Your daughter and Mr. Paul Ancred too?"

She said much too lightly: "My poor Fen does go in a little for the Ancred temperament, but not, I'm glad to say, to excess. Paul, thank goodness, seems to have escaped it, which is such a very good thing, as it appears he's to be my son-in-law."

"Would you say that during this discussion any of them displayed singular vindictiveness against Miss Orrincourt?"

"They were all perfectly livid about her. Except Cedric. But they're lividly angry with somebody or another a dozen times a month. It means nothing."

"Mrs. Ancred," Alleyn said, "if you've been suddenly done out of a very pretty fortune your anger isn't altogether meaningless. You yourself must surely have resented a little your daughter's position."

"No," she said quickly. "I knew, as soon as she told me of her engagement to Paul, that her grandfather would disapprove, Marriage between cousins was one of his bugbears. I knew he'd take it out of them both. He was a vindictive old man. And Fen hadn't bothered to hide her dislike of Miss Orrincourt. She'd said ..." She stopped short. He saw her hands move convulsively.

"Yes?"

"She was perfectly frank. The association offended her taste. That was all."

"What are her views of all this business—the letters and so on?"

"She agrees with me."

"That the whole story is simply a flight of fancy on the part of the more imaginative members of the family?"

"Yes."

"I should like to see her if I may?"

The silence that fell between them was momentary, a brief check in the even flow of their voices, but he found it illuminating. It was as if she winced from an expected hurt, and

746

poised herself to counter it. She leant forward, and with an air of great frankness made a direct appeal.

"Mr. Alleyn," she said, "I'm going to ask a favour. Please let Fenella off. She's highly strung and sensitive. Really sensitive. It's not the rather bogus Ancred sensibility. All the unhappy wrangling over her engagement and the shock of her grandfather's death and then—this horrid and really dreadful business: it's fussed her rather badly. She overheard me speaking to you when you rang up for this talk and even that upset her. I've sent them both out. Please, will you be very understanding and let her off?"

He hesitated, wondering how to frame his refusal, and if her anxiety was based on some much graver reason than the one she gave him.

"Believe me," she said, "Fenella can be of no help to you."

Before he could reply Fenella herself walked in, followed by Paul.

"I'm sorry, Mummy," she said rapidly and in a high voice. "I know you didn't want me to come. I had to. There's something Mr. Alleyn doesn't know, and I've got to tell him."

CHAPTER XVI

Positively the Last Appearance of

Sir Henry Ancred

I

Afterwards, when he told Troy about Fenella's entrance, Alleyn said the thing that struck him most at the time was Jenetta Ancred's command of *savoir-faire*. Obviously this was a development she had not foreseen and one which filled her with dismay. Yet her quiet assurance never wavered, nor did she neglect the tinge of irony that was implicit in her good manners.

She said: "Darling, how dramatic and alarming. This is my girl, Fenella, Mr. Alleyn. And this is my nephew, Paul Ancred."

"I'm sorry to burst in," said Fenella. "How do you do? Please may we talk to you?" She held out her hand.

"*Not* just at this moment," said her mother. "Mr. Alleyn and I really are rather busy. Do you mind, darling?"

Fenella's grip on his hand had been urgent and nervous. She had whispered: "Please." Alleyn said: "May we just hear what this is about, Mrs. Ancred?"

"Mummy, it's important. Really."

"Paul," said her mother, "can't you manage this firebrand of yours?"

"I think it's important too, Aunt Jen."

"My dearest children, I honestly don't think you know——"

"But Aunt Jen, we do. We've talked it over quite cold-bloodedly. We know that what we've got to say may bring a lot of publicity and scandal on the family," said Paul with something very like relish. "We don't enjoy the prospect, but we think any other course would be dishonest."

748

"We accept the protection of the law," said Fenella rather loudly. "It'd be illogical and dishonest to try and circumvent justice to save the family face. We know we're up against something pretty horrible. We accept the responsibility, don't we, Paul?"

"Yes," said Paul. "We don't like it, but we do it."

"Oh," Jenetta cried out vehemently, "for pity's sake don't be so heroic! Ancreds, Ancreds, both of you!"

"Mummy, we're *not*. You don't even know what we're going to say. This isn't a matter of theatre; it's a matter of principle, and, if you like, of sacrifice."

"And you both see yourselves being sacrificial and high-principled. Mr. Alleyn," Jenetta said, and it was as if she added: "After all, we speak the same language, you and I. I do most earnestly beg you to take whatever these ridiculous children have to say with a colossal pinch of salt."

"Mummy, it's important."

"Then," said Alleyn, "let's have it."

She gave in, as he had expected, lightly and with grace. "Well, then, if we must be instructed ... Do at least sit down, both of you, and let poor Mr. Alleyn sit down too."

Fenella obeyed, with the charm of movement that was characteristic of all the female Ancreds. She was, as Troy had told him, a vivid girl. Her mother's spareness was joined in Fenella with the spectacular Ancred beauty and lent it delicacy. "Nevertheless," Alleyn thought, "she can make an entrance with the best of them."

"Paul and I," she began at once, speaking very rapidly, "have talked and talked about it. Ever since those letters came. We said at first that we wouldn't have anything to do with it. We thought people who wrote that kind of letter were beyond everything, and it made us feel perfectly beastly to think there was anyone in the house who could do such a thing. We were absolutely certain that what the letter said was an odious, malicious lie."

"Which is precisely," her mother said without emphasis, "what I have been telling Mr. Alleyn. I really do think, darling——"

"Yes, but that's not all," Fenella interrupted vehemently. "You can't just shrug your shoulders and say it's horrid. If you don't mind my saying so, Mummy dear, that's your generation all over. It's muddled thinking. In its way it's the kind of attitude that leads to wars. That's what Paul and I think anyway. Don't we, Paul?"

Paul, with a red determined face, said: "What Fen means, I think, Aunt Jenetta, is that one can't just say 'Jolly bad form and all ballyhoo,' and let it go at that. Because of the implications. If Sonia Orrincourt didn't poison Grandfather, there's somebody in the house who's trying to get her hanged for something she didn't do, and that's as much as to say there's somebody in the house who's as good as a murderer." He turned to Alleyn: "Isn't that right, sir?"

"Not necessarily right," Alleyn said. "A false accusation may be made in good faith."

"Not," Fenella objected, "by the kind of person who writes anonymous letters. And anyway, even if it was in good faith, we know it's a false accusation, and the realistic thing to do is to say so and, and ..." She stumbled, shook her head angrily and ended with childish lameness, "and jolly well make them admit it and pay the penalty."

"Let's take things in their order?" Alleyn suggested. "You say you know the suggestion made in the letters is untrue. How do you know this?"

Fenella glanced at Paul with an air of achievement and then turned to Alleyn and eagerly poured out her story.

"It was that evening when she and Mrs. Alleyn drove down to the chemist's and brought back the children's medicine. Cedric and Paul and Aunt Pauline were dining out, I'd got a cold and cried off. I'd been doing the drawing-room flowers for Aunt Milly and I was tidying up in a sink-room where the vases are kept. It's down some steps off the passage from the hall to the library. Grandfather had had some orchids sent for Sonia and she came to get them. I must say she looked lovely. Sort of sparkling, with furs pulled up round her face. She swept in and asked in that ghastly voice for what she called her bokay, and when she saw it was a spray of absolutely heavenly orchids she said: "Quite small, isn't it! Not reely much like flowers, are they?" Everything she'd done and everything she meant at Ancreton seemed to sort of ooze out of her and everything I felt about her suddenly boiled over in me. I'd got a cold and was feeling pretty ghastly, anyway. I absolutely blazed. I said some pretty frightful things about even a common little gold-digger having the decency to be grateful. I said I thought her presence in the house was an insult to all of us, and I supposed that when she'd bamboozled Grandfather into marrying her she'd amuse herself with her frightful boy-friends until he was obliging enough to die and leave her his money. Yes, Mummy, I know it was awful, but it just *steamed* out of me and I couldn't stop it."

"Oh, my poor Fen!" Jenetta Ancred murmured.

"It's the way she took it that's important," Fenella continued, still gazing at Alleyn. "I must admit she took it pretty well. She said, quite calmly, that it was all very fine for me to talk, but I didn't know what it was like to be on my beam-ends with no chance of getting anywhere in my job. She said she knew she wasn't any good for the stage except as a showgirl, and that didn't last long. I can remember the actual words she used. Fifth-rate theatrical slang. She said: "I know what you all think. You think I'm playing Noddy up for what I can get out of him. You think that when we're married I'll begin to work in some of the funny business. Look, I've had all that, and I reckon I'll be as good a judge as anybody of what's due to my position." And then she said she'd always thought she was the Cinderella type. She said she didn't expect me to understand what a kick she'd get out of being Lady Ancred. She was extraordinarily frank and completely childish about it. She told me she used to lie in bed imagining how she'd give her name and address to people in shops, and what it would sound like when they called her m'lady. 'Gee,' she said, 'will that sound good! Boy, oh boy!' I really think she'd almost forgotten I was there, and the queer thing is that I didn't feel angry with her any longer. She asked me all sorts of questions about precedence; about whether at a dinner-party she'd go in before Lady Baumstein. Benny Baumstein is the frightful little man who owns the Sunshine Circuit shows. She was in one of his No. 3 companies. When I said she would, she said 'Yip-ee' like a cow-girl. It was frightful, of course, but it was so completely real that in a way I respected it. She actually said she knew what she called her 'ac-cent' wasn't so hot, but she was going to ask 'Noddy' to teach her to speak more refined."

Fenella looked from her mother to Paul and shook her head helplessly. "It was no good," she said, "I just succumbed. It was awful, and it was funny, and most of all it was somehow genuinely pathetic." She turned back to Alleyn: "I don't know if you can believe that," she said.

"Very easily," Alleyn returned. "She was on the defensive and angry when I saw her, but I noticed something of the same quality

751

myself. Toughness, naïvety, and candour all rolled into one. Always very disarming. One meets it occasionally in pickpockets."

"But in a funny sort of way," Fenella said, "I felt that she was honest and had got standards. And much as I loathed the thought of her marriage to Grandfather, I felt sure that according to her lights she'd play fair. And most important of all, I felt that the title meant much more to her than the money. She was grateful and affectionate because he was going to give her the title, and never would she have done anything to prevent him doing so. While I was still gaping at her she took my arm, and believe it or not, we went upstairs together like a couple of schoolgirls. She asked me into her frightful rooms, and I actually sat on the bed while she drenched herself in pre-war scent, repainted her face and dressed for dinner. Then she came along to my room and sat on my bed while I changed. She never left off talking, and I suffered it all in a trance. It really was most peculiar. Down we went, together still, and there was Aunt Milly, howling for the kids' and Grandfather's medicine. We'd left it, of course, in the flower-room, and the queerest thing of all," Fenella slowly wound up, "was that, although I still took the gloomiest possible view of her relationship with Grandfather, I simply could *not* continue to loathe her guts. And, Mr. Alleyn, I swear she never did anything to harm him. Do you believe me? Is all this as important as Paul and I think it is?"

Alleyn, who had been watching Jenetta Ancred's hands relax and the colour return to her face, roused himself and said: "It may be of enormous importance. I think you may have tidied up a very messy corner."

"A messy corner," she repeated. "Do you mean——?"

"Is there anything else?"

"The next part really belongs to Paul. Go on, Paul."

"Darling," said Jenetta Ancred, and the two syllables, in her deepish voice, sounded like a reiterated warning. "Don't you think you've made your point? Must we?"

"Yes, Mummy, we must. Now then, Paul."

Paul began rather stiffly and with a deprecatory air: "I'm afraid, sir, that all this is going to sound extremely obvious and perhaps a bit high-falutin, but Fen and I have talked it over pretty thoroughly and we've come to a definite conclusion. Of course it was obvious from the beginning that the letters meant Sonia

752

Orrincourt. She was the only person who didn't get one, and she's the one who benefited most by Grandfather's death. But those letters were written before they found the rat-bane in her suitcase, and, in fact, before there was a shred of evidence against her. So that if she's innocent, and I agree with Fenella that she is, it means one of two things. Either the letter-writer knew something that he or she genuinely thought suspicious, and none of us did know anything of the sort; or, the letter was written out of pure spite, and not to mince matters, with the intention of getting her hanged. If that's so, it seems to me that the tin of rat-bane was deliberately planted. And it seems to me—to Fen and me—that the same person put that book on embalming in the cheese-dish because he was afraid nobody would ever remember it, and was shoving it under our noses in the most startling form he could think of."

He paused and glanced nervously at Alleyn, who said: "That sounds like perfectly sound reasoning to me."

"Well, then, sir," said Paul quickly, "I think you'll agree that the next point is important. It's about this same damn' silly business with the book in the cheese-dish, and I may as well say at the outset it casts a pretty murky light on my cousin Cedric. In fact, if we're right, we've got to face the responsibility of practically accusing Cedric of attempted murder."

"*Paul!*"

"I'm sorry, Aunt Jen, but we've decided."

"If you're right, and I'm sure you're wrong, have you thought of the sequel? The newspapers. The beastliness. Have you thought of poor Milly, who dotes on the little wretch?"

"We're sorry," Paul repeated stubbornly.

"You're inhuman," cried his aunt and threw up her hands.

"Well," said Alleyn peaceably, "let's tackle this luncheon-party while we're at it. What was everybody doing before the book on embalming made its appearance?"

This seemed to nonplus them. Fenella said impatiently: "Just sitting. Waiting for someone to break it up. Aunt Milly does hostess at Ancreton, but Aunt Pauline (Paul's mother) rather feels she ought to when in residence. She—you don't mind me mentioning it, Paul, darling?—she huffs and puffs about it a bit, and makes a point of waiting for Aunt Milly to give the imperceptible signal to rise. I rather fancied Aunt Milly kept us sitting for pure devilment. Anyway, there we stuck."

"Sonia fidgeted," said Paul, "and sort of groaned."

"Aunt Dessy said she thought it would be nice if we could escape having luncheon dishes that looked like the village pond when the floods had subsided. That was maddening for Aunt Milly. She said with a short laugh that Dessy wasn't obliged to stay on at Ancreton."

"And Dessy," Paul continued, "said that to her certain knowledge Milly and Pauline were holding back some tins of whitebait."

"Everybody began talking at once, and Sonia said: 'Pardon me, but how does the chorus go?' Cedric tittered and got up and wandered to the sideboard."

"And this is our point, sir," Paul cut in with determination. "The cheese was found by my cousin Cedric. He went to the sideboard and came back with a book, and dropped it over my mother's shoulder on to her plate. It gave her a shock as you can imagine."

"She gave a screech and fainted, actually," Fenella added.

"My Mama," said Paul unhappily, "was a bit wrought up by the funeral and so on. She really fainted, Aunt Jen."

"My dear boy, I'm sure she did."

"It gave her a fright."

"Naturally," Alleyn murmured, "books on embalming don't fall out of cheese-dishes every day in the week."

"We'd all," Paul went on, "just about *had* Cedric. Nobody paid any attention to the book itself. We merely suggested that it wasn't amazingly funny to frighten people, and that anyway he stank."

"I was watching Cedric, then," Fenella said. "There was something queer about him. He never took his eyes off Sonia. And then, just as we were all herding Aunt Pauline out of the room, he gave one of his yelps and said he'd remembered something in the book. He ran to the door and began reading out of it about arsenic."

"And then somebody remembered that Sonia had been seen looking at the book."

"And I'll swear," Fenella cut in, "she didn't know what he was driving at. I don't believe she ever really understood. Aunt Dessy did her stuff and wailed and said: 'No, no, don't go on! I can't bear it!' and Cedric purred: 'But, Dessy, my sweet, what have I said? Why shouldn't darling Sonia read about her fiancé's coming embalment?' and Sonia burst into tears and said we were all plotting against her and rushed out of the room."

"The point is, sir, if Cedric hadn't behaved as he did, nobody would have thought of connecting the book with the suggestion in the letters. You see?"

Alleyn said: "It's a point."

"There's something else," Paul added, again with that tinge of satisfaction in his voice. "*Why* did Cedric look in the cheese-dish?"

"Presumably because he wanted some cheese?"

"No!" Paul said triumphantly. "That's just where we've got him, sir. He never touches cheese. He detests it."

"So you see," said Fenella.

II

When Alleyn left, Paul showed him into the hall, and, after some hesitation, asked if he might walk with him a little way. They went together, head-down against a blustering wind, along Cheyne Walk. Ragged clouds scurried across the sky, and the sounds of river traffic were blown intermittently against their chilled ears. Paul, using his stick, limped along at a round pace, and for some minutes in silence.

At last he said: "I suppose it's true that you can't escape your heredity." And as Alleyn turned his head to look at him, he went on slowly: "I meant to tell you that story quite differently. Without any build-up. Fen did, too. But somehow when we got going something happened to us. Perhaps it was Aunt Jen's opposition. Or perhaps when there's anything like a crisis we can't escape a sense of audience. I heard myself doing the same sort of thing over there." He jerked his head vaguely towards the east. "The gay young officer rallying his men. It went down quite well with them, too, but it makes me feel pretty hot under the collar when I think about it now. And about the way we strutted our stuff back there at Aunt Jen's."

"You made your points very neatly," said Alleyn.

"A damn' sight too neatly." Paul rejoined, grimly. "That's why I did think I'd like to try and say without any flourishes that we do honestly believe that all this stuff about poison has simply been concocted by Cedric to try and upset the Will. And we think it would be a pretty poor show to let him get away with it. On all counts."

Alleyn didn't reply immediately, and Paul said, nervously: "I suppose it'd be quite out of order for me to ask whether you think we're right."

"Ethically," said Alleyn, "yes. But I don't think you realised the implications. Your aunt did."

"I know, Aunt Jen's very fastidious. It's the dirty linen in public that she hates."

"And with reason," said Alleyn.

"Well, we'll all have to lump it. But what I meant really was, were we right in our deductions?"

"I ought to return an official and ambiguous answer to that," Alleyn said. "But I won't. I may be wrong, but on the evidence that we've got up to date I should say your deductions were ingenious and almost entirely wrong."

A sharp gust carried away the sound of his voice.

"What?" said Paul, distantly and without emphasis. "I didn't quite hear——"

"Wrong," Alleyn repeated, strongly. "As far as I can judge, you know, quite wrong."

Paul stopped short, and, dipping his head to meet the wind, stared at Alleyn with an expression not of dismay, but of doubt, as if he still thought he must have misunderstood.

"But I don't see ... we thought ... it all hangs together——"

"As an isolated group of facts, perhaps it does."

They resumed their walk, and Alleyn heard him say fretfully: "I wish you'd explain." And after another pause he peered rather anxiously at Alleyn. "Perhaps it wouldn't do, though," he added.

Alleyn thought for a moment, and then, taking Paul by the elbow, steered him into the shelter of a side street. "We can't go on bawling at each other in a gale," he said, "but I don't see that it can do any harm to explain this much. It's quite possible that if all this dust had not been raised after your grandfather's death, Miss Orrincourt might still have become Lady Ancred."

Paul's jaw dropped. "I don't get that."

"You don't?"

"Good God," Paul roared out suddenly, "you can't mean Cedric?"

"Sir Cedric," said Alleyn, dryly, "is my authority. He tells me he has seriously considered marrying her."

After a long silence Paul said slowly: "They're as thick as

756

thieves, of course. But I never guessed ... No, it'd be too much ... I'm sorry, sir, but you're sure——?"

"Unless he invented the story."

"To cover up his tracks," said Paul instantly.

"Extremely elaborate and she could deny it. As a matter of fact her manner suggested some sort of understanding between them."

Paul raised his clasped hands to his mouth and thoughtfully blew into them. "Suppose," he said, "he suspected her, and wanted to make sure?"

"That would be an entirely different story."

"Is that your theory, sir?"

"Theory?" Alleyn repeated vaguely. "I haven't got a theory. I haven't sorted things out. Mustn't keep you standing here in the cold." He held out his hand. Paul's was like ice. "Good-bye," said Alleyn.

"One minute, sir. Will you tell me this? I give you my word it'll go no further. Was my grandfather murdered?"

"Oh, yes," said Alleyn. "Yes. I'm afraid we may be sure of that. He was murdered." He walked down the street, leaving Paul, still blowing on his frozen knuckles, to stare after him.

III

The canvas walls were faintly luminous, They were laced to their poles with ropes and glowed in the darkness. Blobs of light from hurricane lanterns suspended within formed a globular pattern across the surface. One of these lanterns must have been touching the wall, for the village constable on duty outside could clearly make out shadows of wire and the precise source of light.

He glanced uneasily at the motionless figure of his companion, a police officer from London, wearing a short cape. "Bitter cold," he said.

"That's right."

"Be long, d'yew reckon?"

"Can't say."

The constable would have enjoyed a walk. He was a moralist and a philosopher, well known in Ancreton for his pronouncements upon the conduct of politicians and for his independent views in the matter of religion. But his companion's taciturnity, and the uncomfortable knowledge that anything he said would be audible on the other side of the canvas, put a damper on conversation. He stamped once or twice, finding reassurance in the crunch of gravel under his feet. There were noises within the enclosure: voices, soft thumps. At the far end and high above them, as if suspended in the night, and lit theatrically from below, knelt three angels. "Through the long night watches," the constable said to himself, "may Thine angels spread their white wings above me, watching round my head."

Within the enclosure, but, close beside him, the voice of the Chief Inspector from the Yard said: "Are we ready, Curtis?" His shadowy figure suddenly loomed up inside the canvas wall. "Quite ready," somebody else said. "Then if I may have the key, Mr. Ancred?" "Oh—oh—er—yes." That was poor Mr. Thomas Ancred.

The constable listened, yet desired not to listen, to the next too-lucid train of sounds. He had heard them before, on the day of the funeral, when he came down early to have a look while his cousin, the sexton, got things fixed up. Very heavy lock. They'd had to give it a drop of oil. Seldom used. His flesh leapt on his bones as a screech rent the cold air. "Them ruddy hinges," he thought. The blobs of light were withdrawn and the voices with them. He could still hear them, however, though now they sounded hollow. Beyond the hedge a match flared up in the dark.
That would be the driver of the long black car, of course, waiting in the lane. The constable wouldn't have minded a pipe himself.

The Chief Inspector's voice, reflected from stone walls, said distinctly: "Get those acetylene lamps going, Bailey." "Yes, sir," someone answered, so close to the constable that he jumped again. With a hissing noise, a new brilliance sprang up behind the canvas. Strange distorted shadows leapt among the trees about the cemetery.

Now came sounds to which he had looked forward with squeamish relish. A drag of wood on stone followed by the uneven scuffles of boots and heavy breathing. He cleared his throat and glanced stealthily at his companion.

The enclosure was again full of invisible men. "Straight down on the trestles. Right." The squeak of wood and then silence.

The constable drove his hands deep into his pockets and looked up at the three angels and at the shape of St. Stephen's spire against the stars. "Bats in that belfry," he thought. "Funny how a chap'll say it, not thinking." An owl hooted up in Ancreton woods.

758

Beyond the canvas there was movement. A light voice said jerkily: "I think, if it doesn't make any difference, I'd like to wait outside. I won't go away. You can call me, you know."

"Yes, of course."

A canvas flap was pulled aside, letting out a triangle of light on the grass. A man came out. He wore a heavy overcoar and muffler and his hat was pulled over his face, but the constable had recognized his voice and shifted uneasily.

"Oh, it's you, Bream," said Thomas Ancred.

"Yes, Mr. Thomas."

"Cold, isn't it?"

"Hard frost before dawn, sir."

Above them the church clock gave a preparatory whirr and with a sweet voice told two in the morning.

"I don't like this much, Bream."

"Very upsetting, sir, I'm sure."

"Terribly upsetting, yes."

"And yet, sir," said Bream with a didactic air, "I been thinking: this here poor remains beant a matter to scare a chap, if rightly considered. It beant your respected father hisself as you might put it, sir. He's well away receiving his reward by now, and what you are called to look upon is a harmless enough affair. No more, if you'll excuse me, than a left-off garment. As has been preached at us souls regular in this very church."

"I dare say," said Thomas. "Nevertheless ... Well, thank you."

He moved away down the gravel path. The London officer turned to watch him. Thomas did not move quite out of range of the veiled light. He stood, with his head bent, near the dim shape of a gravestone and seemed to be rubbing his hands together.

"Cold and nervous, poor chap," Bream said to himself.

"Before we go any further" (that was Chief Inspector Alleyn again), "will you make a formal examination, Mr. Mortimer? We'd like your identification of the name-plate and your assurance that everything is as it was at the time of the funeral."

A clearing of the throat, a pause and then a muffled voice. "Perfectly in order. Our own workmanship, Mr. Alleyn. Casket and plate."

"Thank you. All right, Thompson."

The click of metal and the faint grind of disengaging screws. This seemed to Bream to continue an unconscionable time. Nobody spoke. From his mouth and nostrils and those of the

London constable, little jets of breath drifted out and condensed on the frozen air. The London man switched on his flash-lamp. Its beam illuminated Thomas Ancred, who looked up and blinked.

"I'm just waiting," he said. "I won't go away."

"Quite all right, sir."

"Now," ordered the voice in the enclosure, "everything free? Right!"

"Just ease a little, it's a precision fit. That's right. Slide?"

"*Oh, cripes!*" Bream said to himself.

Wood whispered along wood. This sound was followed by complete silence. Thomas Ancred turned away from grass to gravel path and walked aimlessly to and fro.

"Curtis? Will you and Dr. Withers——?"

"Yes. Thanks. Move that light a little this way, Thompson. Will you come here, Dr. Withers?"

"The—ah—the process is quite satisfactory, don't you consider, Doctor? Only a short time, of course, but I can assure you there would be no deterioration."

"Indeed? Remarkable."

"One is gratified."

"I think we'll have that bandage taken away, if you please. Fox, will you tell Mr. Ancred we're ready for him?"

Bream watched the thick-set Inspector Fox emerge and walk over towards Thomas. Before he had gone more than a few paces there was a sudden and violent ejaculation inside the enclosure. "*Good God, look at that!*" Inspector Fox paused. The Chief Inspector's voice said, very sharply, "Quiet, Dr. Withers, please," and there followed a rapid whispering.

Inspector Fox moved away and joined Thomas Ancred. "If you'll come this way, Mr. Ancred." "Oh! yes, of course. Very good. Right ho! " said Thomas in a high voice, and followed him back to the enclosure. "If I moved a bit," Bream thought, "when they opened the flaps I'd see in." But he did not move. The London constable held the doorway open, glancing impassively into the tent before he let the canvas fall. The voices began again.

"Now, this is not going to be a very big ordeal, Mr. Ancred."

"Oh, isn't it? Oh, good."

"Will you——?"

Bream heard Thomas move. "There, you see. Quite peaceful."

"I—yes—I identify him."

"That's all right, then. Thank you."

"No," said Thomas, and his voice rose hysterically, "it's not all right. There's something all wrong, in fact. Papa had a fine head of hair. Hadn't he, Dr. Withers? He was very proud of it, wasn't he? And his moustache. This is bald. *What have they done with his hair?*"

"Steady! put your head down. You'll be all right. Give me that brandy, Fox, will you? Damn, he's fainted."

IV

"Well, Curtis," Alleyn said as the car slid between rows of sleeping houses, "I hope you'll be able to give us something definite."

"Hope so," said Dr. Curtis, stifling a heavy yawn.

"I'd like to ask you, Doctor," said Fox, "whether you'd expect one fatal dose of arsenic to have that effect."

"What effect? Oh, the hair. No. I wouldn't. It's more often a symptom of chronic poisoning."

"In for one of those messes, are we?" Fox grumbled. "That will be nice. Fields of suspects opened up wide, with the possibility of Miss O. being framed."

"There are objections to chronic poisoning, Br'er Fox," Alleyn said. "He might die when he'd concocted a Will unfavourable to the poisoner. And moreover, you'd expect a progressive loss of hair, not a sudden post-mortem moult. Is that right, Curtis?"

"Certainly."

"Well, then," Fox persisted heavily, "how about the embalming process? Would that account for it?"

"Emphatically not," Mr. Mortimer interjected. "I've given the Chief Inspector our own formula. An unusual step, but in the circumstances desirable. No doubt, Doctor, he has made you conversant——"

"Oh, yes," sighed Dr. Curtis. "Formalin. Glycerine. Boric Acid. Menthol. Potassium nitrate. Sodium citrate. Oil of cloves. Water."

"Precisely."

"Hey!" said Fox. "No arsenic!"

"You're two days late with the news, Br'er Fox. Things have moved while you were at Ancreton. Arsenic went out some time ago, didn't it, Mr. Mortimer?"

761

"Formalin," Mr. Mortimer agreed with hauteur, "is infinitely superior."

"There now," Fox rumbled with great satisfaction. "That does clear things up a bit, doesn't it, Mr. Alleyn? If arsenic's found it's got no business to be there. That's something definite. And what's more, any individual who banked on its being used by the embalmer made the mistake of his or her life. Nothing for counsel to muddle the jury with, either. Mr. Mortimer's evidence would settle that. Well."

Alleyn said: "Mr. Mortimer, had Sir Henry any notion of the method used?"

In a voice so drowsy that it reminded Alleyn of the dormouse's, Mr. Mortimer said: "It's very curious, Chief Inspector, that you should ask that question. Oh, very curious. Because, between you and I, the deceased gentleman showed quite an unusual interest. He sent for me and discussed the arrangements for the interment. Two years ago, that was."

"Good Lord!"

"That is not so unusual in itself. Gentlemen of his position do occasionally give detailed instructions. But the deceased was so very particular. He—well, really," Mr. Mortimer said, coughing slightly, "he quite read me a little lecture on embalming. He had a little book. Yes," said Mr. Mortimer, swallowing a yawn, "rather a quaint little book. Very old. It seemed an ancestor of his had been embalmed by the method, *quate* outdated, I may say, outlined in this tainy tome. Sir Henry wished to ascertain if our method was similar. When I ventured to suggest the book was somewhat démodé, he became—well, so annoyed that it was rather awkward. Very awkward, in fact. He was insistent that we should use the same process on—ah—for—ah—himself. He *quate ordered* me to do it."

"But you didn't consent?"

"I must confess, Chief Inspector, I—I—the situation was most awkward. I feared, he would upset himself seriously. I must confess that I compromaysed. In point of fact, I——"

"You consented?"

"I would have gladly refused the commission altogether but he would take no refusal. He forced me to take the book away with me. I returned it with compliments, and without comment through the registered post. He replied that when the time came I was to understand my instructions. The—ah—the time came

762

and—and——"

"You followed your own method, and said nothing to anybody?"

"It seemed the only thing to do. Anything else was impossible from the point of view of technique. Ridiculous, in fact. Such preposterous ingredients! You can't imagine."

"Well," said Fox, "as long as you can testify there was no arsenic. Eh, Mr. Alleyn?"

"I must say," said Mr. Mortimer, "I don't at all care for the idea of giving evidence in an affair of this sort. Ours is a delicate, and you might say exclusive, profession, Chief Inspector. Publicity of this kind is most undesirable."

"You may not be subpœnaed, after all," said Alleyn.

"Not? But I understood Inspector Fox to say——"

"You never know. Cheer up, Mr. Mortimer."

Mr. Mortimer muttered to himself disconsolately and fell into a doze.

"What about the cat?" Fox asked. "And the bottle of medicine?"

"No report yet."

"We've been busy," Dr. Curtis complained. "You and your cats! The report should be in some time to-day. What's all this about a cat anyway?"

"Never you mind," Alleyn grunted, "you do your Marsh-Berzelius tests with a nice open mind. And your Fresenius process later on, I shouldn't wonder."

Dr. Curtis paused in the act of lighting his pipe. "*Fresenius* process?" he said.

"Yes, and your ammonium chloride and your potassium iodide and your Bunsen flame and your platinum wire. And look for the pretty green line, blast you!"

After a long silence Dr. Curtis said: "It's like that, is it?" and glanced at Mr. Mortimer.

"It may be like that."

"Having regard to the general lay-out?"

"That's the burden of our song."

Fox said suddenly: "Was he bald when they laid him out?"

"Not he. Mrs. Henry Ancred and Mrs. Kentish were both present. They'd have noticed. Besides, the hair was there, Fox. We collected it while you were ministering to Thomas."

"Oh!" Fox ruminated for a time and then said loudly: "Mr.

763

Mortimer! Mr. Mortimer!"

"Wha——?"

"Did you notice Sir Henry's hair when you were working on him?"

"Eh! Oh, yes," said Mr. Mortimer, hurriedly, but in a voice slurred with sleep. "Yes, indeed. We all remarked on it. A magnificent head of hair." He yawned hideously. "A magnificent head of hair," he repeated.

Alleyn looked at Dr. Curtis. "Consistent?" he asked.

"With your green line? Yes."

"Pardon?" said Mr. Mortimer anxiously.

"All right, Mr. Mortimer. Nothing. We're in London. You'll be in bed by daybreak."

CHAPTER XVII

Escape of Miss O.

I

At breakfast Alleyn said: "This case of ours is doing the usual snowball business, Troy."

"Gathering up complications as it goes?"

"A mass of murky stuff in this instance. Grubby stuff, and a lot of it waste matter. Do you want an interim report?"

"Only if you feel like making one. And is there enough time?"

"Actually there's not. I can answer a crisp question or two, though, if you care to rap them out at me."

"You know, I expect, what they'll be."

"Was Ancred murdered? I think so. Did Sonia Orrincourt do it? I don't know. I shall know, I believe, when the analyst sends in his report."

"If he finds the arsenic?"

"If he finds it in one place, then I'm afraid it's Sonia Orrincourt. If he finds it in three places, it's Sonia Orrincourt or one other. If he doesn't find it at all, then I *think* it's that other. I'm not positive."

"And—the one other?"

"I suppose it's no more unpleasant for you to speculate about one than about several."

"I'd rather know, if it's all right to tell me."

"Very well," Alleyn said, and told her.

After a long silence she said: "But it seems completely unreal. I can't possibly believe it."

"Didn't everything they did at Ancreton seem a bit unreal?"

"Yes, of course. But to imagine that underneath all the showings-off and temperaments *this* could be happening ... I can't. Of all of them ... that one!"

"Remember, I may be wrong."

"You've a habit of not being wrong, though, haven't you?"

"The Yard," said Alleyn, "is littered with my blunders. Ask Fox. Troy, is this very beastly for you?"

"No," said Troy, "it's mostly bewildering. I didn't form any attachments at Ancreton. I can't give it a personal application."

"Thank God for that," he said and went to the Yard.

Here he found Fox in, waiting with the tin of rat-bane. "I haven't had a chance to hear your further adventures at Ancreton, Foxkin. The presence of Mr. Mortimer rather cramped our style last night. How did you get on?"

"Quite nicely, sir. No trouble really about getting the prints. Well, when I say no trouble, there was quite a bit of high-striking in some quarters as was to be expected in that family. Miss O. made trouble, and, for a while, stuck out she wouldn't have it, but I talked her round. Nobody else actually objected, though you'd have thought Mrs. Kentish and Miss Desdemona Ancred were being asked to walk into the condemned cell, the way they carried on. Bailey got down by the early train in the morning and worked through the prints you asked for. We found a good enough impression in paint on the wall of Mrs. Alleyn's tower. Miss O. all right. *And* her prints are in the book. Lots of others too, of course. Prints all over the cover, from when they looked at it after it turned up in the cheese-dish, no doubt. I've checked up on the letters, but there's nothing in it. They handed them round and there you are. Same thing in the flower-room. Regular mess of prints and some odds and ends where they'd missed sweeping. Coloured tape off florist's boxes, leaves and stalks, scraps of sealing-wax, fancy paper and so on. I've kept all of it in case there was anything. I took a chance to slip into Miss O.'s room. Nothing beyond some skittish literature and a few letters from men written before Sir Henry's day. One, more recent, from a young lady. I memorized it. 'Dear S. Good for you, kid, stick to it, and don't forget your old pals when you're Lady A. Think the boy friend'd do anything for me in the business? God knows, I'm not so hot on this Shakespeare, but he must know other managements. Does he wear bed-socks? Regards Clarrie.' "

"No mention of the egregious Cedric?"

"Not a word. We looked at Miss Able's cupboard. Only her own prints. I called in at Mr, Juniper's. He says the last lot of that paper was taken up with some stuff for the rest of the house a fortnight ago. Two sets of prints on the bell-push from Sir Henry's room—his own and old Barker's. Looks as if Sir Henry had grabbed at it, tried to use it and dragged it off."

"As we thought."

"Mr. Juniper got in a great way when I started asking questions. I went very easy with him, but he made me a regular speech about how careful he is and showed me his books. He reckons he always double-checks everything he makes up. He's particularly careful, he says, because of Dr. Withers being uncommonly fussy. It seems they had a bit of a row. The doctor reckoned the kids' medicine wasn't right, and Juniper took it for an insult. He says the doctor must have made the mistake himself and tried to save his face by turning round on him. He let on the doctor's a bit of a lad and a great betting man, and he thinks he'd been losing pretty solidly and was worried, and made a mistake weighing the kids or something. But that wouldn't apply to Sir Henry's medicine, because it was the mixture as before. And I found out that at the time he made it up he was out of arsenic and hasn't got any yet."

"Good for Mr. Juniper," said Alleyn dryly.

"Which brings us," Fox continued, "to this tin." He laid his great hand beside it on the desk. "Bailey's gone over it for dabs. And here we have got something, Mr. Alleyn, and about time too, you'll be thinking. Now this tin has got the usual set of prints. Some of the search party's, in fact. Latent, but Bailey brought them up and got some good photographs. There's Mrs. Kentish's. She must have just touched it. Miss Desdemona Ancred seems to have picked it up by the edge. Mr. Thomas Ancred grasped it more solidly round the sides and handled it again when he took it out of his bag. Mrs. Henry Ancred held it firmly towards the bottom. Sir Cedric's prints are all over it, and there, you'll notice, are the marks round the lid where he had a shot at opening it."

"Not a very determined shot."

"No. Probably scared of getting rat-bane on his manicure," said Fox. "But the print is, you see——"

"No Orrincourt?"

"Not a sign of her. Not a sign of glove-marks either. It was a dusty affair, and the dust, except for the prints we got, wasn't disturbed."

"It's a point. Well, Fox, now Bailey's finished with it we can open it."

The lid was firm and it took a penny and considerable force to prise it up. An accretion of the contents had sealed it. The tin was three-parts full, and the greyish paste bore traces of the implement that had been used to scoop it out.

"We'll have a photo-micrograph of this," Alleyn said.

"If Orrincourt's our bird, sir, it looks as if we'll have to hand the tin over to the defence, doesn't it?"

"We'll have to get an expert's opinion, Fox. Curtis's boys can speak up when they've finished the job in hand. Pray continue, as the Immortal used to say, with your most interesting narrative."

"There's not much more. I took a little peep at the young baronet's room, too. Dunning letters, lawyer's letters, letters from his stockbroker. I should say he was in deep. I've made a note of the principal creditors."

"For an officer without a search warrant you seem to have got on very comfortably."

"Isabel helped. She's taken quite a fancy for investigation. She kept a lookout in the passage."

"With parlour-maids," Alleyn said, "you're out on your own. A masterly technique."

"I called on Dr. Withers yesterday afternoon and told him you'd decided on the exhumation."

"How did he take it?"

"He didn't say much but he went a queer colour. Well, naturally. They never like it. Reflection on their professional standing and so on. He thought a bit and then said he'd prefer to be present. I said we'd expect that, anyway. I was just going when he called me back. 'Here!' he said, kind of hurriedly and as if he wasn't sure he might not be making a fool of himself; 'you don't want to pay too much attention to anything that idiot Juniper may have told you. The man's an ass.' As soon as I was out of the house," said Fox, "I made a note of that to be sure the words were correct. The maid was showing me out at the time."

"Curtis asked him last night, after we'd tidied up in the cemetery, if he'd like to come up and watch the analysis. He agreed. He's sticking to it that the embalmers must have used something that caused the hair to fall out. Mr. Mortimer was touched to the professional quick, of course."

"It's a line defending counsel may fancy," said Fox gloomily.

The telephone rang and Fox answered it.

"It's Mr. Mortimer," he said.

"Oh, Lord! You take it, Fox."

"He's engaged at the moment, Mr. Mortimer. Can I help you?"
The telephone cackled lengthily and Fox looked at Alleyn with
bland astonishment. "Just a moment." He laid down the receiver.
"I don't follow this. Mr. Alleyn hasn't got a secretary."

"What's all this?" said Alleyn sharply.

Fox clapped his hand over the receiver. "He says your secretary
rang up their office half an hour ago and asked them to repeat the
formula for embalming. His partner, Mr. Loame, answered. He
wants to know if it was all right."

"Did Loame give the formula?"

"Yes."

"Bloody fool," Alleyn said violently. "Tell him it's all wrong
and ring off."

"I'll let Mr. Alleyn know," said Fox, and hung up the receiver.
Alleyn reached for it and pulled the telephone towards him.

"Ancreton, 2A," he said. "Priority. Quick as you can." And
while he waited: "We may want a car at once, Fox. Ring down,
will you? We'll take Thompson with us. And we'll need a search
warrant." Fox went into the next room and telephoned. When he
returned Alleyn was speaking. "Hallo. May I speak to Miss
Orrincourt? ... Out? ... When will she be in? ... I see. Get me
Miss Able, Barker, will you? ... It's Scotland Yard here." He
looked round at Fox. "We'll be going," he said. "She came up to
London last night and is expected back for lunch. Damn! Why
the hell doesn't the Home Office come to light with that report?
We need it now, and badly. What's the time?"

"Ten to twelve, sir."

"Her train gets in at twelve. We haven't an earthly ... Hallo!
Hallo! Is that you, Miss Able? ... Alleyn here. Don't answer
anything but yes or no, please. I want you to do something that is
urgent and important. Miss Orrincourt is returning by the train
that arrives at midday. Please find out if any one has left to meet
her. If not, make some excuse for going yourself in the pony-cart.
If it's too late for that, meet it when it arrives at the house. Take
Miss Orrincourt into your part of the house and keep her there.
Tell her I said so and take no refusal. It's urgent. She's not to go
into the other part of the house. Got that? ... Sure? ... Right.
Splended. Goodbye."

He rang off, and found Fox waiting with his overcoat and hat. "Wait a bit," he said. "That's not good enough." And turned back to the telephone. "Get me Camber Cross Police Station. They're the nearest to Ancreton, aren't they, Fox?"

"Three miles. The local P.C. lives in Ancreton parish, though. On duty last night."

"That's the chap, Bream … Hallo! … Chief Inspector Alleyn, Scotland Yard. Is your chap Bream in the station? … Can you find him? … Good! The Ancreton pub. I'd be much obliged if you'd ring through. Tell him to go at once to Ancreton Halt. A Miss Orrincourt will get off the midday train. She'll be met from the Manor House. He's to let the trap go away without her, take her to the pub, and wait there for me. Right! Thanks."

"Will he make it?" Fox asked.

"He has his dinner at the pub and he's got a bike. It's no more than a mile and a half. Here we go, Fox. If, in the ripeness of time, Mr. Loame is embalmed by his own firm, I hope they make a mess of him. What precisely did this bogus secretary say?"

"Just that you'd told him to get a confirmation of the formula. It was a toll-call, but, of course, Loame thought you were back at Ancreton."

"And so he tells poor old Ancred's killer that there was no arsenic used in the embalming and blows our smoke-screen to hell. As Miss O. would say, what a pal! Where's my bag? Come on."

But as they reached the door the telephone rang again.

"I'll go," Alleyn said. "With any luck it's Curtis."

It was Dr. Curtis. "I don't know whether you'll like this," he said. "It's the Home Office report on the cat, the medicine and the deceased. First analysis completed. No arsenic anywhere."

"Good!" said Alleyn. "Now tell them to try for thallium acetate, and ring me at Ancreton when they've found it."

II

They were to encounter yet another interruption. As they went out to the waiting car, they found Thomas, very white and pinched, on the bottom step.

"Oh, hallo," he said. "I was coming to see you. I want to see you awfully."

"Important?" Alleyn said.

"To me," Thomas rejoined with the air of innocence, "it's as important as anything. You see, I came in by the morning train on purpose. I felt I had to. I'm going back this evening."

"We're on our way to Ancreton now."

"Really? Then I suppose you wouldn't ...? Or shouldn't one suggest it?"

"We can take you with us. Certainly," said Alleyn after a fractional pause.

"Isn't that lucky?" said Thomas wistfully and got into the back seat with them. Detective-Sergeant Thompson was already seated by the driver. They drove away in a silence lasting so long that Alleyn began to wonder if Thomas, after all, had nothing to say. At last, however, he plunged into conversation with an abruptness that startled his hearers.

"First of all," said Thomas loudly, "I want to apologize for my behaviour last night. Fainting! Well! I thought I left that kind of thing to Pauline. Everybody was so nice, too. The doctors and you," he said, smiling wanly at Fox, "driving me home and everything. I couldn't be more sorry."

"Very understandable, I'm sure," said Fox comfortably. "You'd had a nasty shock."

"Well, I had. Frightful, really. And the worst of it is, you know, I can't shake it off. When I *did* go to sleep it was so beastly. The dreams. And this morning with the family asking questions."

"You said nothing, of course," said Alleyn.

"You'd asked me not to, so I didn't, but they took it awfully badly. Cedric was quite furious, and Pauline said I was siding against the family. The point is, Alleyn, I honestly don't think I can stand any more. It's unlike me," said Thomas. "I must have a temperament after all. Fancy!"

"What exactly do you want to see us about?"

"I want to know. It's the uncertainty. I want to know why Papa's hair had fallen out. I want to know if he was poisoned and if you think Sonia did it. I'm quite discreet, really, and if you tell me I'll give you my solemn word of honour not to say anything. Not even to Caroline Able, though I dare say she could explain why I feel so peculiar. I want to know."

"Everything from the beginning?"

"Yes, if you don't mind. Everything."

"That's a tall order. We don't know everything. We're trying, very laboriously, to piece things together, and we've got, I think, almost the whole pattern. We believe your father was poisoned."

771

Thomas rubbed the palms of his hands across the back of the driver's seat. "Are you certain? That's horrible."

"The bell-push in his room had been manipulated in such a way that it wouldn't ring. One of the wires had been released. The bell-push hung by the other wire and when he grasped it the wooden end came away in his hand. We started from there."

"That seems a simple little thing."

"There are lots of more complicated things. Your father made two Wills, and signed neither of them until the day of his Birthday party. The first he signed, as I think he told you, before the dinner. The second and valid one he signed late that night. We believe that Miss Orrincourt and your nephew Cedric were the only two people, apart from his solicitor, who knew of this action. She benefited greatly by the valid Will. He lost heavily."

"Then why bring him into the picture?" Thomas asked instantly.

"He won't stay out. He hovers. For one thing, he and Miss Orrincourt planned all the practical jokes."

"Goodness! But Papa's death wasn't a practical joke. Or was it?"

"Indirectly, it's just possible that it was caused by one. The final practical joke, the flying cow on the picture, probably caused Sir Henry to fix on the second draft."

"I don't know anything about all that," Thomas said dismally. "I don't understand. I hoped you'd just tell me if Sonia did it."

"We're still waiting for one bit of the pattern. Without it we can't be positive. It would be against one of our most stringent rules for me to name a suspect to an interested person when the case is still incomplete."

"Well, couldn't you behave like they do in books? Give me a pointer or two?"

Alleyn raised an eyebrow and glanced at Fox. "I'm afraid," he said, "that without a full knowledge of the information our pointers wouldn't mean very much."

"Oh, dear! Still, I may as well hear them. Anything's better than this awful blank worrying. I'm not quite such a fool," Thomas added, "as I dare say I seem. I'm a good producer of plays. I'm used to analysing character and I've got a great eye for a situation. When I read the script of a murder play I always know who did it."

"Well," Alleyn said dubiously, "here, for what they're worth,

772

are some relative bits of fact. The bell-push. The children's ringworm. The fact that the anonymous letters were written on the children's school paper. The fact that only Sir Cedric and Miss Orrincourt knew your father signed the second Will. The book on embalming. The nature of arsenical poisoning, and the fact that none has been found in his body, his medicine, or in the body of his cat."

"Carabbas? Does he come in? That *is* surprising. Go on."

"His fur fell out, he was suspected of ringworm and destroyed. He had not got ringworm. The children had. They were dosed with a medicine that acts as a depilatory and their fur did *not* fall out. The cat was in your father's room on the night of his death."

"And Papa gave him some hot milk as usual. I see."

"The milk was cleared away and the Thermos scalded out and used afterwards. No chemical analysis was possible. Now, for the tin of rat-bane. It was sealed with an accretion of its content and had not been opened for a very long time."

"So Sonia didn't put arsenic in the Thermos?"

"Not out of the tin, at any rate."

"Not at all, if it wasn't—if——"

"Not at all, it seems."

"And you think that somehow or another he took the Dr. Withers ringworm poison."

"If he did, analysis will show it. We've yet to find out if it does."

"But," said Thomas. "Sonia brought it back from the chemist's. I remember hearing something about that."

"She brought it, yes, together with Sir Henry's medicine. She put the bottles in the flower-room. Miss Fenella Ancred was there and left the room with her."

"And Dr. Withers," Thomas went on, rather in the manner of a child continuing a narrative, "came up that night and gave the children the medicine. Caroline was rather annoyed because he'd said she could do it. She felt," Thomas said thoughtfully, "that it rather reflected on her capability. But he quite insisted and wouldn't let her touch it. And then, you know, it didn't work. They should have been as bald as eggs, but they were not. As bald as eggs," Thomas repeated with a shudder. "Oh, yes, I see. Papa *was*, of course."

He remained sitting very upright, with his hands on his knees, for some twenty minutes. The car had left London behind and slipped through a frozen landscape. Alleyn, with a deliberate effort, retraced the history of the case: Troy's long and detailed account, the turgid statements of the Ancreds, the visit to Dr. Withers, the scene in the churchyard. What could it have been that Troy knew she had forgotten and believed to be important?

Thomas, with that disconcerting air of switching himself on, broke the long silence.

"Then I suppose," he said very abruptly and in a high voice, "that you think either Sonia gave him the children's medicine or one of us did. But we are not at all murderous people. But I suppose you'll say that lots of murderers have been otherwise quite nice quiet people, like the Düsseldorf Monster. But what about motive? You say Cedric knew Papa had signed the Will that cut him out of almost everything, so Cedric wouldn't. On the other hand, Milly didn't know he'd signed a second Will, and she was quite pleased about the first one, really, so *she* wouldn't. And that goes for Dessy too. She wasn't best pleased, but she wasn't much surprised or worried. And I hope you don't think ... However," Thomas hurried on, "we come to Pauline. Pauline might have been very hurt about Paul and Panty and herself, but it was quite true what Papa said. Her husband left her very nicely off and she's not at all revengeful. It's not as if Dessy and Milly or I *wanted* money desperately, and it's not as if Pauline or Panty or Fenella (I'd forgotten Fenella and Jen) are vindictive slayers. They just aren't. And Cedric thought he was all right. And *honestly*," Thomas ended, "you can't suspect Barker and the maids."

"No," said Alleyn, "we don't."

"So it seems you must suspect a person who wanted money very badly and was left some in the first Will. And, of course, didn't much care for Papa. And Cedric, who's the only one who fits, won't do."

He turned, after making this profound understatement, to fix upon Alleyn a most troubled and searching gaze.

"I think that's a pretty accurate summing up," Alleyn said.

"Who could it be?" Thomas mused distractedly and added with a sidelong glance: "But, then, you've picked up all sorts of information which you haven't mentioned."

"Which I haven't time to mention," Alleyn rejoined. "There are Ancreton woods above that hill. We'll stop at the pub."

P.C. Bream was standing outside the pub and stepped forward

to open the door of the car. He was scarlet in the face.

"Well, Bream," Alleyn said, "carried out your job?"

"In a manner of speaking, sir," said Bream, "no. Good afternoon, Mr. Thomas."

Alleyn stopped short in the act of getting out. "What? Isn't she there?"

"Circumstances," Bream said indistinctly, "over which I 'ad no control, intervened, sir." He waved an arm at a bicycle leaning against the pub. The front tyre hung in a deflated festoon about the axle. "Rubber being not of the best——"

"Where is she?"

"On my arrival, having run one mile and a quarter——"

"Where is she?"

"Hup," said Bream miserably, "at the 'ouse."

"Get in here and tell us on the way."

Bream wedged himself into one of the tip-up seats and the driver turned the car. "Quick as you can," Alleyn said. "Now, Bream."

"Having received instructions, sir, by telephone, from the Super at Camber Cross, me having my dinner at the pub, I proceeded upon my bicycle in the direction of Ancreton 'Alt at eleven-fifty a.m."

"All right, all right," said Fox. "And your tyre blew out."

"At eleven-fifty-one, sir, she blew on me. I inspected the damage, and formed the opinion it was impossible to proceed on my bicycle. Accordingly I ran."

"You didn't run fast enough, seemingly. Don't you know you're supposed to keep yourself fit in the force?" said Fox severely.

"I ran, sir," Bream rejoined with dignity, "at the rate of one mile in ten minutes and arrived at the 'Alt at twelve-four, the train 'aving departed at twelve-one, and the ladies in the pony-carriage being still in view on the road to the Manor."

"The ladies?" said Alleyn.

"There was two of them. I attempted to attract their attention by raising my voice, but without success. I then returned to the pub, picking up that there cantankerous bice ong rowt."

Fox muttered to himself.

"I reported by phone to the Super. He give me a blast, and said he would ring the Manor and request the lady in question to return. She 'as not done so."

"No," Alleyn said. "I imagine she'd see him damned first."

The car turned in at the great entrance and climbed through the woods. Half-way up the drive they met what appeared to be the entire school, marching and singing under the leadership of Miss Caroline Able's assistant. They stood aside to let the car pass. Alleyn could not see Panty among them.

"Not their usual time for a walk," said Thomas.

The car drew up at last into the shadow of the enormous house.

"If nothing else has gone cock-eyed," Alleyn said, "she'll be in the school."

Thomas cried out in alarm: "Are you talking about Caroline Able?"

"No. See here, Ancred. We're going into the school. There's a separate entrance back there, and we'll use it. Will you go into this part of the house and please say nothing about our arrival?"

"Well, all right," said Thomas, "though I must say I don't quite see——"

"It's all very confusing. Away you go."

They watched Thomas walk slowly up the steps, push open the great door, and pause for a second in the shadowy lobby. Then he turned and the door closed between them.

"Now, Fox," Alleyn said, "you and I will go into the school. I think the best thing we can do is to ask her to come back with us to London and make a statement. Awkward if she refuses, but if she does we'll have to take the next step. Drive back to the end of the building there."

The car was turned, and stopped again at a smaller door in the west wing. "Thompson, you and Bream wait back there in the car. If we want you, we'll get you. Come on, Fox."

They got out. The car moved away. They had turned to the doorway when Alleyn heard his name called. Thomas was coming down the steps from the main entrance. He ran towards them, his coat flapping, and waved his arm.

"Alleyn! *Alleyn!* Stop!"

"*Now* what?" Alleyn said.

Thomas was breathless when he reached them. He laid his hands on the lapels of Alleyn's coat. His face was colourless and his lips shook. "You've got to come," he said. "It's frightful. Something frightful's happened. Sonia's in there, horribly ill. Withers says she's been poisoned. He says she's going to die."

776

CHAPTER XVIII

The Last Appearance of Miss O.

I

They had carried her into a small bedroom in the school.

When Alleyn and Fox, accompanied as far as the door by Thomas, walked unheralded into the room, they found Dr. Withers in the act of turning Pauline and Desdemona out of it. Pauline appeared to be in an advanced state of hysteria.

"*Out*, both of you. At once, please. Mrs. Ancred and I can do all that is necessary. And Miss Able."

"A curse. That's what I feel. There's a curse upon this house. That's what it is, Dessy."

"Out, I say. Miss Ancred, take this note. I've written it clearly. Ring up any surgery and tell them to send the things up immediately the car arrives. Can your brother drive my car? Very well."

"There's a man and a car outside," Alleyn said. "Fox, take the note, will you?"

Pauline and Desdemona, who had backed before the doctor to the door, turned at the sound of Alleyn's voice, uttered incoherent cries, and darted past him into the passage. Fox, having secured the note, followed them.

"What the hell are you doing here?" Dr. Withers demanded. "Get out!" He glared at Alleyn and turned back to the bed. Millamant Ancred and Caroline Able were stooped above it, working, it seemed with difficulty, over something that struggled and made harsh inhuman noises. A heavy stench hung in the air.

"Get the clothes away, but put that other thing on her. Keep her covered as far as possible. That's right. Take my coat, Mrs. Ancred, please; I can't do with it. Now, we'll try the emetic again. Careful! Don't let me break the glass."

Miss Able moved away with an armful of clothes. Millamant stood back a little, holding the doctor's jacket, her hands working nervously.

There, on a child's bed with a gay counterpane, Sonia Orrincourt strained and agonised, the grace of her body distorted by revolt and the beauty of her face obliterated in pain. As Alleyn looked at her, she arched herself and seemed to stare at him. Her eyes were bloodshot; one lid drooped and fluttered and winked. One arm, like that of a mechanical toy, repeatedly jerked up its hand to her forehead in a reiterated salaam.

He waited, at the end of the room, and watched. Dr. Withers seemed to have forgotten him. The two women after a startled glance turned again to their task. The harsh cries, the straining and agonizing, rose in an intolerable crescendo.

"I'm going to give a second injection. Keep the arm still, if you can. Very well, then, get that thing out of the way. Now."

The door opened a fraction. Alleyn moved to it, saw Fox and slipped through.

"Our chap ought to be back any minute with the doctor's gear," Fox muttered.

"Have you rung for Dr. Curtis and Co.?"

"They're on the way."

"Thompson and Bream still on the premises?"

"Yes, sir."

"Bring them in. Keep the servants in their own quarters. Shut up any rooms she's been in since she got here. Herd the family together and keep them together."

"That's all been fixed, Mr. Alleyn. They're in the drawing-room."

"Good. I don't want to leave her yet."

Fox jerked his thumb. "Any chance of a statement?"

"None at the moment, far as I can see. Have you got anything, Fox?"

Fox moved closer to him, and in a toneless bass began to mutter rapidly: "She and the doctor and Miss Able had tea together in Miss Able's room. He'd come up to see the kids. She sent the little Kentish girl through to order it. Didn't fancy schoolroom tea. Tea set out for the rest of the family in the dining-room. Second tray brought from the pantry by Barker with tea for one. Second pot brewed by Mrs. Kentish in the

778

dining-room. Miss Desdemona put some biscuits on the tray. It was handed over to Miss Panty by Mrs. Ancred. Miss Panty brought it back here. Miss O. was taken bad straight away before the other two had touched anything. The little girl was there and noticed everything."

"Got the tea things?"

"Thompson's got them. Mrs. Ancred kept her head and said they ought to be locked up, but in the fluster of getting the patient out the tray was knocked over. She left Mrs. Kentish to carry on, but Mrs. Kentish took hysterics and Isabel swept it up in the finish. Tea and hot water and broken china all over the shop. We ought to get a trace, though, somewhere, if there's anything. That little girl's sharp, by gum she is."

Alleyn laid his hand swiftly on Fox's arm. In the room the broken sounds changed into a loud and rapid babbling—"Baba-ba-ba"—and stopped abruptly. At the same moment the uniformed driver appeared at the far end of the passage carrying a small case. Alleyn met him, took the case, and, motioning to Fox to come after, re-entered the room.

"Here's your case, Dr. Withers."

"All right. Put it down. When you go out, tell those women to get in touch with her people if she's got any. If they want to see her, they'll have to be quick."

"Fox, will you——"

Fox slipped away.

"I said: When you go out," Dr. Withers repeated angrily.

"I'm afraid I must stay. This is a police matter, Dr. Withers."

"I'm perfectly well aware of what's happened. My duty is to my patient, and I insist on the room being cleared."

"If she should become conscious ..." Alleyn began, looking at the terrible face with its half-open eyes and mouth.

"If she regains consciousness, which she won't, I'll inform you." Dr. Withers opened the case, glanced up at Alleyn and said fiercely: "If you don't clear out I'll take the matter up with the Chief Constable."

Alleyn said briskly: "That won't do at all, you know. We're both on duty here and here we both stay. Your patient's been given thallium acetate. I suggest that you carry on with the treatment, Dr. Withers."

There was a violent ejaculation from Caroline Able. Millamant said: "That's the ringworm stuff! What nonsense!"

779

"How the hell ..." Dr. Withers began, and then: "Very well. Very well. Sorry. I'm worried. Now, Mrs. Ancred, I'll want your help here. Lay the patient——"

Forty minutes later, without regaining consciousness, Sonia Orrincourt died.

II

"The room," Alleyn said, "will be left exactly as it is. The police surgeon is on his way and will take charge. In the meantime, you'll all please join the others in the drawing-room. Mrs. Ancred, will you and Miss Able go ahead with Inspector Fox?"

"At least, Alleyn," said Dr. Withers, struggling into his jacket, "you'll allow us to wash up."

"Certainly, I'll come with you."

Millamant and Caroline Able, after exchanging glances, raised a subdued outcry. "You must see ..." Dr. Withers protested.

"If you'll come out, I'll explain."

He led the way and they followed in silence. Fox came out last and nodded severely to Bream, who was in the passage. Bream moved forward and stationed himself before the door.

Alleyn said: "It's perfectly clear, I'm sure, to all of you that this is a police matter. She was poisoned, and we've no reason to suppose she poisoned herself. I may be obliged to make a search of the house (here is the warrant), and I must have a search of the persons in it. Until this has been done none of you may be alone. There is a wardress coming by car from London, and you may, of course, wait for her if you wish."

He looked at the three faces, all of them marked by the same signs of exhaustion, all turned resentfully towards him. There was a long silence.

"Well," Millamant said at last, with an echo of her old short laugh, "you can search me. The thing I want to do most is sit down. I'm tired."

"I must say," Caroline Able began, "I don't quite——"

"Here!" Dr. Withers cut in. "Will this suit you? I'm these ladies' medical man. Search me and then let them search each other in my presence. Any good?"

"That will do admirably. This room here is vacant, I see. Fox, will you take Dr. Withers in?" Without further ado, Dr. Withers turned on his heel and made for the open door. Fox followed him

780

in and shut it.

Alleyn turned to the two women. "We shan't keep you long," he said, "but if, in the meantime, you would like to join the others, I can take you to them."

"Where are they?" Millamant demanded.

"In the drawing-room."

"Personally," she said, "I'm beyond minding who searches me and who looks on." Bream gave a self-conscious cough. "If you and Miss Able like to take me into the children's play-room, which I believe is vacant, I shall be glad to get it over."

"Well, really," said Miss Able, "well, of course, that is an extremely sane point of view, Mrs. Ancred. Well, if *you* don't object."

"Good," Alleyn said. "Shall we go?"

There was a screen, with Italian primitives pasted over it, in the play-room. The two women, at Alleyn's suggestion, retired behind it. First Millamant's extremely sensible garments were thrown out one by one, examined by Alleyn, collected again by Miss Able, and then, after an interval, the process was reversed. Nothing was discovered, and Alleyn, walking between them, escorted the two ladies to the bathroom, and finally through the green baize door and across the hall to the drawing-room.

Here they found Desdemona, Pauline, Panty, Thomas and Cedric, assembled under the eye of Detective-Sergeant Thompson. Pauline and Desdemona were in tears. Pauline's tears were real and ugly. They had left little traces, like those of a snail, down her carefully restrained make-up. Her eyes were red and swollen and she looked frightened. Desdemona, however, was misty, tragic and still beautiful. Thomas sat with his eyebrows raised to their limit and his hair ruffled, gazing in alarm at nothing in particular. Cedric, white and startled, seemed to be checked, by Alleyn's arrival, in a restless prowl round the room. A paperknife fell from his hands and clattered on the glass top of the curio cabinet.

Panty said: "Hallo! Is Sonia dead? Why?"

"Ssh, darling! Darling, ssh!" Pauline moaned, and attempted vainly to clasp her daughter in her arms. Panty advanced into the centre of the room and faced Alleyn squarely. "Cedric," she said loudly, "says Sonia's been murdered. Has she? Has she, Miss Able?"

"Goodness," said Caroline Able in an uneven voice, "I call that

781

rather a stupid thing to say, Patricia, don't you?"

Thomas suddenly walked up to her and put his arm about her shoulders.

"Has she, Mr. Alleyn?" Panty insisted.

"You cut off and don't worry about it," Alleyn said. "Are you at all hungry?"

"You bet."

"Well, ask Barker from me to give you something rather special, and then put your coat on and see if you can meet the others coming home. Is that all right, Mrs. Kentish?"

Pauline waved her hands and he turned to Caroline Able.

"An excellent idea," she said more firmly. Thomas's hand still rested on her shoulder.

Alleyn led Panty to the door. "I won't go," she announced, "unless you tell me if Sonia's dead."

"All right, old girl, she is." A multiple ejaculation sounded behind him.

"Like Carabbas?"

"No!" said her Aunt Millamant strongly, and added: "Pauline, must your child behave like this?"

"They've both gone away," Alleyn said. "Now cut along and don't worry about it."

"I'm not worrying," Panty said, "particularly. I dare say they're in Heaven, and Mummy says I can have a kitten. But a person likes to know." She went out.

Alleyn turned and found himself face to face with Thomas.

Behind Thomas he saw Caroline Able stooping over Millamant, who sat fetching her breath in dry sobs, while Cedric bit his nails and looked on. "I'm sorry," Millamant stammered: "it's just reaction, I suppose. Thank you, Miss Able."

"You've been perfectly splendid, Mrs. Ancred."

"Oh, Milly, Milly!" wailed Pauline. "Even you! Even your iron reserve. Oh, Milly!"

"Oh, *God*!" Cedric muttered savagely. "I'm *so* sick of all this."

"You," Desdemona said, and laughed with professional bitterness. "In less tragic circumstances, Cedric, that would be funny."

"Please, all of you *stop*."

Thomas's voice rang out with authority, and the dolorous buzz of reproach and impatience was instantly hushed.

"I dare say you're all upset," he said. "So are other people. Caroline is, and I am. Who wouldn't be? But you can't go on flinging temperaments right and left. It's very trying for other people and it gets us nowhere. So I'm afraid I'm going to ask you all to shut up, because I've got something to say to Alleyn, and if I'm right, and he says I'm right, you can all have hysterics and get on with the big scene. But I've got to know."

He paused, still facing Alleyn squarely, and in his voice and his manner Alleyn heard an echo of Panty. "A person likes to know," Panty had said.

"Caroline's just told me," Thomas said, "that you think somebody gave Sonia the medicine Dr. Withers prescribed for those kids. She says Sonia had tea with her. Well, it seems to me that means somebody's got to look after Caroline, and I'm the person to do it, because I'm going to marry her. I dare say that's a surprise to all of you, but I am, so that's that, and nobody need bother to say anything, please."

With his back still turned to his dumbfounded family, Thomas, looking at once astonished and determined, grasped himself by the lapels of his coat and continued. "You've told me you think Papa was poisoned with this stuff and I suppose you think the same person killed Sonia. Well, there's one person who ordered the stuff for the kids and wouldn't let Caroline touch it, and who ordered the medicine for Papa, and who is pretty well known to be in debt, and who was left quite a lot of money by Papa, and who had tea with Sonia. He's not in the room, now," said Thomas, "and I want to know where he is, and whether he's a murderer. That's all."

Before Alleyn could answer, there was a tap on the door and Thompson came in. "A call from London, for you, sir," he said. "Will you take it out here?"

Alleyn went out, leaving Thompson on guard, and the Ancreds still gaping. He found the small telephone-room across the hall, and, expecting a voice from the Yard, was astonished to hear Troy's.

"I wouldn't have done this if it mightn't be important," said Troy's voice, twenty miles away. "I telephoned the Yard and they told me you were at Ancreton."

"Nothing wrong?"

"Not here. It's just that I've remembered what Sir Henry said that morning. When he'd found the writing on his looking-glass."

"Bless you. What was it?"

"He said he was particularly angry because Panty, he insisted it was Panty, had disturbed two important documents that were on his dressing-table. He said that if she'd been able to understand them she would have realized they concerned her very closely. That's all. Is it anything?"

"It's almost everything."

"I'm sorry I didn't remember before, Rory."

"It wouldn't have fitted before. I'll be home to-night. I love you very much."

"Good-bye."

"Good-bye."

When Alleyn came out into the hall, Fox was there waiting for him.

"I've been having a bit of a time with the doctor," Fox said. "Bream and our chap are with him now. I thought I'd better let you know, Mr. Alleyn."

"What happened?"

"When I searched him I found this in his left-hand side pocket."

Fox laid his handkerchief on the hall table and opened it out, disclosing a very small bottle with a screw top. It was almost empty. A little colourless fluid lay at the bottom.

"He swears," said Fox, "that he's never seen it before, but it was on him all right."

Alleyn stood looking at the little phial for a long moment. Then he said: "I think this settles it, Fox. I think we'll have to take a risk."

"Ask a certain party to come up to the Yard?"

"Yes. And hold a certain party while this stuff is analysed. But there's no doubt in my mind about it, Fox. It'll be thallium acetate."

"I'll be glad to make this arrest," said Fox heavily, "and that's a fact."

Alleyn did not answer, and after another pause Fox jerked his head at the drawing-room door.

"Shall I——?"

"Yes."

Fox went away and Alleyn waited alone in the hall. Behind the great expanse of stained-glass windows there was sunlight. A patchwork of primary colours lay across the wall where Henry Ancred's portrait was to have hung. The staircase mounted into shadows, and out of sight, on the landing, a clock ticked. Above

784

the enormous fireplace, the fifth baronet pointed his sword complacently at a perpetual cloudburst. A smouldering log settled with a whisper on the hearth, and somewhere, away in the servants' quarters, a voice was raised and placidly answered.

The drawing-room door opened, and with a firm step, and a faint meaningless smile on her lips, Millamant Ancred came out and crossed the hall to Alleyn.

"I believe you wanted me," she said.

CHAPTER XIX

Final Curtain

"It was the mass of detail," Troy said slowly, "that muddled me at first. I kept trying to fit the practical jokes into the pattern and they wouldn't go."

"They fit," Alleyn rejoined, "but only because she used them after the event."

"I'd be glad if you'd sort out the essentials, Rory."

"I'll try. It's a case of maternal obsession. A cold, hard woman, with a son for whom she has a morbid adoration. Miss Able would tell you all about that. The son is heavily in debt, loves luxury, and is intensely unpopular with his relations. She hates them for that. One day, in the ordinary course of her duties, she goes up to her father-in-law's room. The drafts of two Wills are lying on the dressing-table. One of them leaves her son, who is his heir, more than generous means to support his title and property. The other cuts him down to the bare bones of the entailed estate. Across the looking-glass someone has scrawled "Grandfather is a bloody old fool." As she stands there, and before she can rearrange the papers, her father-in-law walks in. He immediately supposes, and you may be sure she shares and encourages the belief that his small granddaughter, with a reputation for practical jokes, is responsible for the insulting legend. Millamant is a familiar figure in his room, and he has no cause to suspect her of such an idiotic prank. Still less does he suspect the real perpetrator, her son Cedric Ancred, who has since admitted that this was one of a series of stunts designed by himself and Sonia Orrincourt to set the old man against Panty, hitherto his favourite.

"Millamant Ancred leaves the room with the memory of those

two drafts rankling in her extremely tortuous mind. She knows the old man changes his Will as often as he loses his temper. Already Cedric is unpopular. Some time during the next few days, perhaps gradually, perhaps in an abrupt access of resentment, an idea is born to Millamant. The Will is to be made public at the Birthday dinner. Suppose the one that is favourable to Cedric is read, how fortunate if Sir Henry should die before he changes his mind! And if the dinner is rich, and he, as is most probable, eats and drinks unwisely, what more likely than he should have one of his attacks and die that very night? If, for instance, there was tinned crayfish! She orders tinned crayfish."

"Just—hoping?"

"Perhaps no more than that. What do you think, Fox?"

Fox, who was sitting by the fire with his hands on his knees, said: "Isabel reckons she ordered it on the previous Sunday when they talked over the dinner."

"The day after the looking-glass incident. And on the following Monday evening, the Monday before the Birthday when Cedric and Paul and his mother were all out, Millamant Ancred went into the flower-room and found a large bottle of medicine marked "Poison" for the school children, and another smaller bottle for Sir Henry. The bottles had been left on the bench by Sonia Orrincourt, who had joined Fenella Ancred there and had gone upstairs with her and had never been alone in the flower-room."

"And I," Troy said, "was putting the trap away and coming in by the east wing door. If ... Suppose I'd let Sonia do that and taken the medicine into the school——"

"If you'll excuse my interrupting you, Mrs. Alleyn," Fox said, "it's our experience that, when a woman makes up her mind to turn poisoner, nothing will stop her."

"He's right, Troy."

"Well," said Troy, "go on."

"She had to chip away the chemist's sealing-wax before she got the corks out, and Fox found bits of it on the floor and some burnt matches. She had to find another bottle for her purpose. She emptied Sir Henry's bottle filled it up with thallium, and in case of failure, poured the remainder into her own small phial. Then she filled the children's bottle with water and re-corked and re-sealed both Mr. Juniper's bottles. When Miss Able came in for the children's medicine she and Millamant hunted everywhere for it. It was not found until Fenella came downstairs, and who was more astonished than Millamant to learn that Sonia had so carelessly left the medicine in the flower-room?"

"But suppose," Troy said, "he'd wanted the medicine before she knew about the Will?"

"There was the old bottle with a dose still in it. I fancy she removed that one some time during the Birthday. If a Will unfavourable to Cedric had been made public, that bottle would have been replaced and the other kept for a more propitious occasion. As it was, she saw to it that she was never alone from dinner until the next morning. Barker beat on the door of the room she shared with Desdemona. She had talked to Desdemona, you remember, until three o'clock—well after the time of Sir Henry's death. She built herself up a sort of emergency alibi with the same elaborate attention which she gives to that aimless embroidery of hers. In a way this led to her downfall. If she'd risked a solitary trip along those passages that night to Cedric's room she would have heard, no doubt, that Sir Henry had signed the second Will, and she would have made a desperate attempt to stop him taking his medicine."

"Then she didn't mean at that time to throw suspicion on Sonia?"

"No, indeed. His death would appear to be the natural result of rash eating and pure temper. It was only when the terms of his last Will were made known that she got her second idea."

"An atrocious idea."

"It was all of that. It was also completely in character—tertuous and elaborate. Sonia had come between Cedric and the money. Very well, Sonia must go and the second Will be set aside. She remembered that she had found Sonia reading it. She remembered the rat-bane with its printed antidote to arsenical poisoning. So, the anonymous letters printed on the kids' paper she herself fetched from the village, appeared on the breakfast table. A little later, as nobody seemed to have caught on the right idea, the book on embalming appeared on the cheese-dish, and finally the tin of rat-bane appeared in Sonia's suitcase. At about this time she got a horrible jolt."

"The cat," said Fox.

"Carabbas!" Troy ejaculated.

"Carabbas had been in Sir Henry's room. Sir Henry had poured out milk for him. But the bottle of medicine had overturned into the saucer and presently Carabbas began to lose his fur. No wonder. He'd lapped up thallium acetate, poor chap. Millamant couldn't stand the sight of him about the house. He was one too much for her iron nerve. Accusing him of ringworm, and with the hearty consent of every one but Panty, she had him destroyed.

"She sat back awaiting events and unobtrusively jogging them along. She put the tin of arsenical rat-bane in Sonia Orrincourt's suitcase and joined in the search for it. She declared that it had been a full tin, but the servants disagreed. She forgot, however, to ease the lid, which was cemented in with the accretion of years."

"But to risk everything and plan everything on the chance that arsenic was used by the embalmers!" Troy exclaimed.

"It didn't seem like a chance. Sir Henry had ordered Mortimer and Loame to use it, and Mr. Mortimer had let him suppose they would do so. Her nerve went a bit, though, after the exhumation. She rang up the embalmers, using, no doubt, the deepest notes of her masculine voice, and said she was my secretary. Loame, the unspeakable ass, gave her their formula. That must have been a bitter moment for Millamant. Cedric's only means of avoiding financial ruin was by marrying the woman she loathed and against whom she had plotted; and now she knew that the frame-up against Sonia Orrincourt was no go. She didn't know, however, that we considered thallium acetate a possible agent and would look for it. She'd kept the surplus over from the amount she could not get into Sir Henry's bottle and she waited her chance. Sonia could still be disposed of; Cedric could still get the money."

"She must be mad."

"They're like that, Mrs. Alleyn," Fox said. "Female poisoners behave like that. Always come at it a second time, and a third and fourth, too, if they get the chance."

"Her last idea," Alleyn said, "was to throw suspicion on Dr. Withers, who's a considerabie beneficiary in both Wills. She put thallium in the milk when the tea-tray was sent in to Miss Able, knowing Withers and Sonia Orrincourt were there and knowing Sonia was the only one who took milk. A little later she slipped the bottle into Withers's jacket. With Sonia dead, she thought, the money would revert after all to Cedric."

"Very nasty, you know," Fox said mildly. "Very nasty case indeed, wouldn't you say?"

"Horrible," Troy said under her breath.

"And yet, you know," Fox went on, "it's a guinea to a gooseberry she only gets a lifer. What do you reckon, sir?"

"Oh, yes," Alleyn said, looking at Troy. "It'll be that if it's not an acquittal."

"But surely——" Troy began.

"We haven't got an eye-witness, Mrs. Alleyn, to a single action that would clinch the case. Not one." Fox got up slowly. "Well, if you'll excuse me. It's been a long day."

Alleyn saw him out. When he returned, Troy was in her accustomed place on the hearthrug. He sat down and after a moment she leant towards him, resting her arm across his knees.

"Nothing is clear-cut," she said, "when it comes to one's views. Nothing." He waited. "But we're together," she said. "Quite together now. Aren't we?"

"Quite together," Alleyn said.

To Helen, Trevor, and Shelley,
with Love

Contents

Contents

Contents

Contents

Contents

CONTRACTS

Examples and Explanations

contract as the needs of the transaction dictate. In fact, multiparty contracts are common.

§1.2.3   An Exchange Relationship

As mentioned earlier, a contract is a *relationship*. By entering into the agreement, the parties bind themselves to each other for the common purpose of the contract. Some contractual relationships last only a short time and require minimal interaction. For example, a contract for a haircut involves a fairly quick performance by the hairdresser, followed by the fulfillment of the customer's payment obligation. Other contractual relationships, such as leases or long-term employment or supply contracts, could span many years and require constant dealings between the parties, regulated by detailed provisions in the agreement.

The essential purpose of the contract relationship is *exchange*. Although the concept of exchange is discussed more fully in Chapter 7, it must be raised here because it lies at the heart of contract. Contract and trade go hand in hand: Because trading is a vital and indispensable facet of our society, contract law exists to facilitate it. Because trading is the overwhelming concern of contract law, it is not much interested in relationships that do not involve exchange.

In other words, the very essence of contract is the *reciprocal* relationship in which each party gives up something to get something. These "somethings" are as varied as one could imagine: A goatherd may promise to trade a goat to a miller for a sack of flour; a celebrity's valet may promise to reveal his employer's dark secrets to a tabloid for cold hard cash; an inventor may trade the rights to her idea for a promise by a manufacturer to develop the idea for mutual profit; a fond uncle may promise his nephew money in exchange for an undertaking not to drink, smoke, and gamble. These situations vary greatly. Some involve tangible things, others intangible rights. Some of the promises have economic value, others do not. Yet their basic format is the same—a bargain has been reached leading to a reciprocal exchange for the betterment (real or perceived) of both parties.

As discussed in Chapters 7, 8, and 9, the modern concept of contract embraces some transactions in which exchange in the traditional sense is tenuous. Nevertheless, exchange continues to be the principal motivation for contracting and the guiding rationale for the rules of contract law.

§1.2.4   Promise

As already stressed, contract is a relationship. If two people chat for a few minutes at a reception and then part with no intention of ever seeing each other again, their encounter would not likely be described as a relationship. So too, with contract: **Instantaneous exchanges,** even though consensual, do not constitute contracts. For a contract to exist, there must be a **promise**—that is, some commitment for the future, some assumption of liability lasting beyond the instant of agreement. This is because if neither party makes a commitment, there is nothing to enforce and no need for the law of contracts to be concerned with the exchange.

The concept of promise or commitment needs explanation and refinement. A promise is an **undertaking to act or refrain from acting** in a specified way at some **future** time. This promise may be made in clear and **express** words, or it could be **implied**—that is, inferred from conduct or from the circumstances of the transaction. Furthermore, as the definition indicates, only one promise needs to be made for a contract to come into existence. It may sound a little odd to say this, having just characterized contract as a reciprocal relationship. However, this does not detract from the principle of reciprocity because one party may exchange an instantaneous performance (and hence make no promise) for a promise of future action by the other. Where, at the instant of contracting, promises remain outstanding on both sides, the contract is called **bilateral.** Where, at the instant of contracting, one party has fully performed and all that remains is a promise by the other, the contract is called **unilateral.**

This sounds rather abstract. A few illustrations may help to make it more concrete:

a. An Instantaneous Exchange: No Contract. Where an exchange is entirely instantaneous, and neither party makes any promise to the other, their exchange is not regarded as a contract. For example, say that while Rocky Rapids was walking along the bank of a river he encountered Eddy M. Mersion sitting on the shore next to his kayak. Rocky took $400 in cash out of his pocket and offered to buy the kayak from Eddy "as is" (that is, without any warranty from Eddy as to its condition or quality). Eddy accepted the cash, and Rocky climbed into the kayak and paddled off. At this point, there is a simple, instantaneous exchange without any expectation that Rocky could complain if the kayak was substandard or defective. Each party has fully performed, and no promise has been made. The transaction is not a contract. In contract law, it is described as an **executed exchange.**

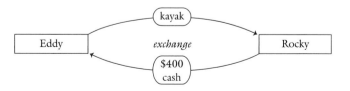

b. A Promissory Exchange: Bilateral Contract.   Change the facts in Illustration 1: Rocky said to Eddy, "I will buy that kayak from you provided that it is watertight. I will give you a check for $400 immediately." Eddy replied, "It is watertight. I accept. Give me the check and take the kayak." Even though the parties immediately exchange the check and kayak, the delivery does not end their duty of performance. By giving his undertaking Eddy has made a promise concerning the kayak's condition, which will allow recourse if it does not meet the agreed standard. Similarly, Rocky's check is not an immediate payment, but is nothing more than a commitment that his bank will pay the money upon presentation of the check. Thus, promises exist on both sides after the moment of agreement, and a bilateral contract exists. This is called an **executory exchange.**

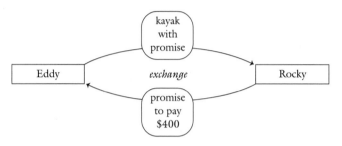

c. A Promissory Exchange by Implication: Bilateral Contract.   In Illustration 2 Eddy made an express promise that the kayak was watertight. However, it is not always necessary for promises to be stated in express terms. Often, the circumstances of the transaction, the conventions of the marketplace, or the policy of the law imply a promise even in the absence of promissory language in the agreement. Therefore, if it is commonly understood in the market that a seller warrants the fitness of what he sells, a simple exchange, without any express words relating to the kayak's condition, will give rise to an implied promise that the kayak is watertight.

d. A Promise for Performance: Unilateral Contract.   Finally, say that Rocky offered to buy the kayak for $400 and tendered his check. Eddy agreed to sell it "as is," making it clear that he made no promise about its condition or quality. Rocky agreed, handed the check to Eddy, and paddled away. Here Eddy's performance is instantaneous, but Rocky has made a promise of future performance (payment on presentation of the check). When, at the point of contract formation, only one party has a promise outstanding, the contract is called **unilateral.**[1] It is nevertheless a contract be-

---

1. This simple example serves for now. The refinements of the unilateral-bilateral distinction are covered in section 4.12.

cause only one promise is needed to classify the transaction as a contract rather than an instantaneous exchange.

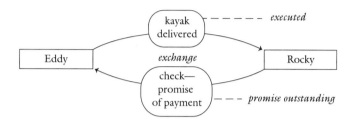

To sum up, for a contract to exist, there must be at least one promise outstanding upon execution of the agreement. This promise could be stated expressly or it could arise by implication. As you may have realized in considering the above examples, in modern society the purely instantaneous exchange is a rarity. Even when it seems that an exchange is instantaneous, such as a simple cash purchase at a store, there is a strong possibility that an implied promise (such as a warranty) will be found on at least one side. Of course, many of the most important exchanges are, by their nature, incapable of being instantaneous, simply because the performance of at least one of the parties cannot be completed immediately.

§1.2.5 Legal Recognition of Enforceability

The previous section made the point that an agreement without a promise is not a contract. However, when a promise does exist, so that contract comes into being, it is the fundamental role of contract law to ensure that the promise is upheld. The importance of this task cannot be stressed too strongly. In a world in which promises were not taken seriously, only instantaneous exchanges could occur. There could be no building, manufacturing, stable employment, or frequent flyer programs. The resulting wasteland would be far worse than any portrayed in the nastiest post-apocalyptic science fiction movie.

Contracting is often described as an act of **private lawmaking** by which persons create a kind of personalized "statute" to govern their relationship. One can only envisage contract as private legislation if it has the attribute of any law—**recognition and enforcement** through the **compulsive power of the state,** acting through its **courts.** It is therefore a hallmark of contract that it creates law binding on the parties and confers on them rights and obligations cognizable in law.

Of course, this does not mean that the compulsive power of the law has to be resorted to in every contractual relationship. In most cases, parties to

plicable rules sometimes reflects disapprobation of wrongful conduct. Outside of the realm of litigation, social pressure and business relationships frequently provide disincentives to treat contractual undertakings in a cavalier fashion.

§1.4.3   *Accountability for Conduct and Reliance*

The objective test of assent was introduced in section 1.2. In determining whether or not a person agreed to a contract or specific contractual terms, the person's manifested conduct by words or action is given more weight than her testimony about her actual intentions. An emphasis on the objective appearance of assent is important not only because of **evidentiary** considerations (that is, it is easier to prove because it is observable) but also because one of the fundamental values of contract law is that a person should be held accountable for words or acts reasonably manifesting intent to contract, and that the other party, acting reasonably, should be entitled to rely on that manifestation of assent. (Note that the perception of the conduct by the other party is also subject to an objective test of reasonableness. One who places an unreasonable and idiosyncratic interpretation on conduct has no right to expect protection of that unreasonable reliance.)

Thus, the principles of accountability and reliance qualify the value of voluntariness—volition is not measured by the true and actual state of mind of a party, but by that state of mind as made apparent to the outside world. Even if a person does not really wish to enter a contract, if she behaves as if the contract is desired and intended, that conduct is binding, and evidence of any mental reservation is likely to be disregarded. (Of course, this rule is not absolute. As we see later, where the manifestation of assent is induced by trickery, coercion, or other illegitimate means, there are grounds for going behind it.)

The value of protecting reasonable reliance is pervasive in contract law. It has both a specific and a general aspect. It is **specific** in that a person who has entered a contract has the right to rely on the undertakings that have been given. If they are breached, the law must enforce them. It is **general** because when parties in numerous specific situations feel secure in relying on promises, the expectation arises in society as a whole that contracts can be relied on, and that legal recourse is available for breach. This general sense of reliance, sometimes called **"security of contracts"** or **"security of transactions,"** is indispensable to economic interaction. If it did not exist, there would be little incentive to make contracts, which would not be worth the paper on which they are written.

In summary, accountability for conduct that induces reasonable reliance is a vital goal of contract law. This is tempered by the consideration that in some cases manifested conduct is induced by illegitimate means, and one who uses such means cannot truly be regarded as having relied on the apparent assent.

§1.4.4 Social Justice and the Protection of the Underdog

It has already been suggested, in connection with both freedom of contract and reliance, that modern contract law is sensitive to the imposition of contractual obligations as a result of coercion, dishonesty, or lack of meaningful choice resulting from power imbalance. Much of the material later in the book deals with the issue of balancing freedom of contract and accountability for manifested conduct against the need to protect vulnerable parties from unfair imposition. Because this is so pervasive a concern, it should at least be acknowledged in this overview of contract policy.

§1.4.5 Fairness

Fairness is such a loose concept that it cannot be discussed in the abstract. The fairness of any result can only be measured in the context of societal standards and expectations. In the contract setting, it must also be evaluated in light of the various goals and policies mentioned in this section. Nevertheless, it would be remiss not to at least draw to your attention that courts do not mechanically apply rules of law. Judges and juries are sensitive to the equities of individual cases and the circumstances of the parties, and where a mechanical application of rules achieves a result that seems to be unjust, there is likely to be some adjustment or even manipulation of the rule to avoid it.

Contract law has some express doctrines that address the question of unfairness, such as the doctrines of unconscionability and good faith. However, even where there is no clear and specific doctrine, you will find many cases in which the court's desire (and duty) to achieve a just result may have the effect of diverting or evading a resolution called for by a doctrinaire approach to the issues.

§1.4.6 The Economic Aspect of Contract Law

Because contracts are concerned with economic exchanges, contract law must inevitably be quintessentially economic in its purpose. Its goal is to facilitate trade and commerce, to regulate the manner in which people deal with each other in the marketplace, and to enforce commercial obligations. It should therefore be no surprise that this body of law, concerned with economic relationships, should respond to and reflect the prevailing economic conditions and philosophy. In the United States, this basic philosophy has al-

13

cash, a check is not a completed act of payment but merely an instruction by Customer 1 to his bank to pay Claire upon presentation of the check. In other words, this is a credit transaction in which Customer 1 impliedly promises that funds will be available to pay the check when it is deposited. Customer 1 has therefore made a future commitment, which makes this a unilateral contract.

4. The purchase of the fish tank is another instantaneous exchange. With regard to the broken table and glassware, Claire argues, in effect, that custom creates an implied contract to pay for broken goods. It is possible for a contract to arise by implication from conduct in light of well-accepted custom or usage. If Claire can prove such a custom (which must be done by witnesses who qualify as experts in the field of activity) she may be able to establish an implied contract, even though there is no express exchange agreement. More likely, if Customer 2 has any liability to Claire, it is for negligence in tort, based on her failure to exercise care in reversing her truck.

5. It may sound as if a contract was created between Claire and Customer 3, and this would be so if Claire promised to reserve the lamp in exchange for a promise by Customer 3 to return. Whether or not such binding commitments were made is a matter of interpretation—to be determined in light of what the parties said, and any general usage with which they reasonably should be familiar. On the brief facts given here, it is probably unlikely that Customer 3 did make any binding commitment to return and cannot therefore be liable for any lost opportunity suffered by Claire.

6. The transaction with Customer 4 appears to satisfy all the attributes of contract. Unlike the contracts in Examples 1 and 3, this one contains unperformed promises by both parties at the time of agreement, and is bilateral.

7. Even if Claire and the thrift store each made promises respectively to donate and collect the goods, there is no contract here because the element of exchange is missing. The thrift store gave nothing to Claire in exchange for the goods. This is a one-sided transaction—a donation—and the store's undertaking to collect the goods is not exchanged for the goods. It is merely a means of taking possession of the gift. In technical terms, this transaction is not a contract because it lacks consideration—a concept discussed fully in Chapter 7.

2

Facets of the Law of Contract and the Source of Its Rules, Processes, and Traditions

§2.1 The Purpose of this Chapter

Chapter 1 introduced the legal concept of contract and outlined the policies and ideological values of contract law. This chapter continues the introduction to contract by explaining a number of basic attributes of contract law, early knowledge of which will greatly assist in the full appreciation of course materials. It begins with a short note on historical perspective and then addresses some of the questions that are likely to puzzle students as they encounter unfamiliar terms and allusions in cases and other writings.

§2.2 The Historical Perspective of Contract Law

You will notice that while some of the cases in your casebook were decided in the last few years, others are quite old. Some go back to the nineteenth century or even earlier. This tells you something about the contracts course: While its primary purpose is to teach you the contemporary law of contract, it cannot do this by simply giving you a snapshot of what courts are doing right now. So much of contract law is history. Indeed, the very process by which the law is decided involves historical analysis, as the discussion of precedent in Chapter 3 shows. Most of the rules and principles of contract law were developed in the past. Some of them have remained relatively unchanged while others have been adapted or overruled as they have become superannuated. These changes tend to be evolutionary and incremental, built upon a traditional framework that is still apparent. In this respect, contract law is like a great and ancient cathedral, whose contemporary appearance reflects millennia of building, destruction, rebuilding, and addition.

Therefore, although the contracts course is not a course in legal history, modern doctrine must be studied and evaluated in its historical perspective. It is only in this way that current law can be fully understood, and a reasonably reliable prediction of the future course of the law can be made. Because a lawyer's work often centers on a prediction of how a court may decide an issue that could arise in the transaction, the ability to gauge the direction of the law is invaluable.

Although an understanding of the substantive law is one of the principal purposes of studying cases through the historical spectrum, this is not the only insight to be gained. The historical progression of caselaw is at the very heart of our common law system of jurisprudence. By tracing the development of legal rules over time, the student learns about the process of legal evolution. Familiarity with this process is essential to the analysis of court opinions and other legal materials. In section 2.4 and Chapter 3 the common law and its rulemaking process are examined.

§2.3　Classical and Contemporary Contract Law

§2.3.1　*Classical Contract Law*

It will probably not be too long before you encounter a reference to Classical Contract Law. This note explains what it is, and how it differs from contemporary law.

Although the common law of contracts is many centuries old, it did not become a systematic, interwoven body of doctrine until relatively recently. Prior to the eighteenth century the law of contract was seen not so much as a cohesive system of rules, linked by general principles, but as a collection of discrete rules, each specifically applicable to various particular types of transactions. From the eighteenth century, English legal scholars began to think of contract law in more systematic terms. They began to recognize that the specific rules reflected a general approach to contracts that could be identified and formulated as broader doctrine. This trend developed in both England and America during the nineteenth century, at a time when economic and industrial expansion called for a more sophisticated and comprehensive system of contract law. It reached its zenith in what is referred to as the **classical period.** While one could quibble about the exact dates, the classical period can be thought of as spanning the last decades of the nineteenth century and the beginning of the twentieth. The Restatement, Contracts, published in the 1930s (introduced in section 2.8) reflects the mature thinking of the classical school, but by that stage the classical conception had already begun the process of change that leads into the contemporary period.

To find a general doctrine of contract, the classicists examined decided cases, extracting from them a set of coherent and well-defined rules, which they then used as the basis for constructing more abstract general principles. The general principles formed a framework for organizing and linking the rules into a body of doctrine. Some classicists went so far as to conceive of *law as a science* in which certain and consistent results could be achieved in the resolution of cases by the rather mechanical process of selecting the right rule from the body of doctrine and applying it to the facts.

The classical school reflects the priorities of its age, which greatly valued free enterprise, private autonomy, and a laissez-faire approach to economic activity. Classical theory therefore stresses the facilitation of contractual relationships and favored a strictly **objective** approach. If parties manifested contractual intent, the inclination was to enforcement of the transaction, without too fine a probing of the actual state of understanding of either party or much solicitousness for those whose economic impotence may have curtailed the exercise of free will.

The classical approach was also heavily influenced by the legal philosophy of **positivism**, which stressed the primacy of legal rules and considered the court's principal role to be finding and applying those rules to the facts of individual cases. Because of its emphasis on clear rules and its belief in a scientific approach to adjudication, classicism tends to be relatively formalistic and rigid.

§2.3.2 Contemporary Contract Law

As the twentieth century wore on, the classical conception of contract law began to erode. Enthusiasm for the free market was tempered by a growing recognition of the need to regulate the freedom of powerful contractors, to safeguard the rights of weaker parties, and to affect social policy concerning matters such as consumer protection, employee rights, and business ethics. The formalism of the classical approach came to be perceived as too rigid and too heavily biased in favor of dominant contracting parties. The idea that law could be treated as a science sounded more and more naive as insight into human in-

codify the common law. That is, they take rules and principles already developed by judges and put them into statutory form. The purpose of this may be to reinforce or clarify the law or to make it more accessible. A statute may do more than codify, though. It may *reform, alter, or modernize* common law rules, it may intervene to hasten or mould the development of doctrine, or it may create new rules designed to deal with a problem not yet addressed by courts. As noted in section 1.3, some statutes are confined to particular contracts while others are of general application. Although there has been considerable legislative attention to contracts, the field is still regarded as part of the common law, because judge-made rules continue to predominate.

§2.4.3   "Common Law" Used to Denote a Process or Approach to Legal Analysis

The prior two meanings of "common law" are relatively easy to spot, but the term is also used in a more subtle sense. It is sometimes used to describe the mode of legal thinking and the process of judicial development inherent in a common law system.

As mentioned before, the common law develops through the decisions of judges in actual cases. Whether a rule's origin is the common law or statute, it will ultimately be applied by a judge in a specific case. In deciding the case, the judge interprets and may embellish the rule. Over time, as courts apply the rule in more and more cases, it acquires a judicial gloss that becomes part of the law. Therefore, in using *patterns of thinking* and *modes of analysis* molded by the common law tradition, judges continue to develop the law, even if the source of law is statutory. This process is as much part of the common law as the judicial creation of rules. In a civilian jurisdiction, by contrast, the judicial application of statutory rules tends to be more confined to the case under decision, and is less likely to be influential in the development of legal doctrine.

§2.5   The Distinction Between Law and Equity

The distinction between law and equity permeates the common law system. It can be confusing when first encountered and should therefore be explained as early as possible. In everyday usage, "equity" simply means fairness. In law, it is sometimes used this way as well. However, it also has a more technical meaning.

Sections 2.4.1 and 3.2 briefly discuss the way in which the Royal Courts developed the common law. As practiced in the Royal Courts during its formative period, the common law was a rigid system. It was based on forms of action called **writs.** A litigant seeking a remedy applied to court for a writ (a written order calling on someone to do something) compelling the performance claimed. The writs were narrow, specific, and formalistic. Although new writs were developed as the need arose, it often happened that a person who needed relief could not fit the case into a recognized writ, and could therefore not obtain relief at law. The Monarch had the prerogative to do justice between his or her subjects, and if the court could not give a remedy, the Monarch had the power to intervene. The Monarch did not deal with these matters personally but delegated them to the **chancellor,** the highest royal officer. Over time, the chancellor had more and more of these cases in which relief was given on the basis of fairness (equity in the usual sense) in the **absence of a remedy at law.** This eventually led to the growth of a court of chancery, which had jurisdiction over all those claims for relief that were equitable in nature. The court of chancery developed its own rules and principles and became something of a competitor of the courts of law.

This dual system of jurisdiction lasted for many centuries. Over time, it became a matter of established practice that certain claims and remedies were legal in nature and others were equitable. For example, a claim for damages for breach of contract was within the jurisdiction of the law courts, but law courts had no power to order a party to perform the contract. Therefore, a claim for specific performance of a contract or for an injunction prohibiting breach could only be granted by the equity court. Furthermore, the equity court would not assume jurisdiction unless the plaintiff could show that the legal remedy of damages was not an adequate remedy under all the circumstances of the case. Thus, the common law system, in its broad sense, incorporated a jurisdictional division between the courts of common law (used here in a narrower sense) and equity. This dual system was part of the common law of England adopted by American jurisdictions, and so it entered our legal system.

Since the nineteenth century the distinction between law and equity has been eroding both in England and in the United States. Separate courts of equity have been abolished in the federal system and in most states. Courts of general jurisdiction now hear both legal and equitable suits. Also, the substantive distinction between law and equity is fading as many principles of equity gradually become incorporated into the law as legal principles. However, the distinction is not entirely dead, and it has an impact in many areas. For example, the availability of remedies is still influenced by the rule that a party who claims equitable relief must show that the legal remedy is inadequate; the right to a jury trial is confined to actions at law and is not available in equity suits; an appellate court has a much wider scope of review in an equity suit; and some courts still confine equitable defenses and doctrines to suits in equity and do not recognize them in actions at law. Again, it must be stressed that none of these distinctions are applied with the same rigor as they used to be, and there are many cases in which courts have moved away from them. Nevertheless, the tradition is strong and its breakdown is gradual and uneven, so it must be taken into account even in modern cases. We will return to the law-equity distinction periodically as it comes up in different areas of contract law.

§2.6   State Law Governs Contracts

While there is federal legislation applicable to contracts, it is limited to federal concerns such as the regulation of interstate commerce or the provision of special rules for contracting with the federal government. There is no federal common law of contract. The common law of contract (as well as many of the statutes governing contracts) is state law. Similarly, although federal courts do sometimes have jurisdiction to decide contract cases (for example, when there is diversity of citizenship or a federal question is presented by the case), the great bulk of contract cases are decided by state courts. Even when a federal court does hear a contract case, it applies the general law of contract of the state whose law governs the transaction, and must follow state court precedents. (*See* section 3.2.2.)

It is therefore not, strictly speaking, correct to talk of *the* law of contracts. There are in fact 50 different bodies of state contract law in this country, as well as those in U.S. Territories and the District of Columbia. Each one of the states, except Louisiana, has adopted the common law of England as its basic legal system. (Louisiana adopted the civilian system, in the form of the French Code Napoleon during the short period that it was a French possession.) However, although each common law state has its own contract law, this law derives from the same source. Furthermore, because state courts and legislatures are influenced by each other, the law has tended to develop along similar lines. It is usually possible to tell from textbooks or other writings whether or not a particular rule is widely followed, and if not, what its variants are.

Notwithstanding this diversity, a generalized law of contract is studied in law school, and cases are selected based on their interest or influence rather than on the jurisdiction from which they emanate. It is probable, therefore, that some of the rules learned in law school are not followed in the state in which you will ultimately practice. This should not concern you unduly. The goal of legal study is not simply to learn rules (rules are not immutable, in any event), but to understand general policies and principles and to master the methods of reasoning and analysis that will enable you to find the answer to a specific legal problem in a particular jurisdiction.

§2.7 The Uniform Commercial Code (UCC)

§2.7.1 *The UCC as a Uniform Model Statute and State Legislation*

As mentioned earlier, contracts are generally governed by common law except to the extent that legislation has been enacted to codify, change, or add to it. The UCC is such a statute. Although all of contract law is, in a sense, commercial, the UCC is not applicable to all contracts. It covers only certain specific types of transactions including sales and leases of goods, negotiable instruments and documents (specialized types of transferrable commercial documentation that embodies rights to money or goods), and security interests in personal property (in which a creditor records an interest in the debtor's property so that if the debtor fails to pay the debt, the creditor can realize the property and use its proceeds to settle the debt). Each type of commercial transaction is provided for in a separate article of the Code. All of them except for sales of goods are beyond the scope of the contracts course and are studied in upperclass commercial law courses. However, sales of goods, governed by UCC Article 2, are given considerable attention in the contracts course because there are close parallels between the rules and doctrines applicable to contracts generally and those pertaining to contracts for the sale of goods. (Even here, many of the more complex or specialized rules of Article 2 are deferred to the upperclass commercial law course.)

The provisions of the UCC are not entirely a modern legislative innovation. Many of them are based on earlier statutory enactments, going back to the late nineteenth and early twentieth centuries and on principles and rules developed under common law. One of its goals is to **codify** (record in statutory form) well-established rules, but it is equally concerned with *clarifying* and *modernizing* the law. Therefore, while the UCC has built on principles formulated under the common law and its predecessor statutes, it has also sought to reform outdated or unsatisfactory laws and to bring the legal rules into line with contemporary commercial practice.

Apart from codifying and reforming commercial law, the other goal of the UCC is to *unify* it throughout the country. Like the law of contracts generally, commercial law is state law. There is, therefore, no national legislature that can enact a single commercial statute with nationwide application.[2] The only way to create uniform commercial law among the states is to draft a model statute and to persuade the legislature of each state to enact it. This task was undertaken jointly by two very influential national law reform orga-

---

2. Of course, Congress has enacted commercial legislation where it has felt competent to do so under the commerce clause (U.S. Const. art. 1 §8 cl. 3) which gives Congress power over interstate commerce. However, general commercial law is the law of a particular jurisdiction and is reserved to the states under the Constitution.

nizations, the National Conference of Commissioners on Uniform State Laws and the American Law Institute. Their work resulted in the completion of a model code during the 1950s. The aim of having this model code adopted has been fully successful, and it has been enacted in every state except Louisiana. (As noted in section 2.6, Louisiana has a civilian system, and the enactment of the UCC as a whole was not appropriate. Louisiana has enacted some portions of the UCC.) Of course, the law of the states can never be entirely uniform. Some states have made legislative variations from the standard model provisions, and in all states, courts often reach divergent interpretations of the code provisions.

The process of reform and updating did not end with the drafting of the current Code. Shortly after the completion of the model code, a Permanent Editorial Board was set up to review the Code and propose amendments. Since then, a number of changes have been proposed to and enacted by the states, and substantial further changes (including changes to Article 2) are under active consideration. However, the considerable debate over proposed changes and the need to convince state legislatures to enact them make the pace of legislative amendment relatively slow.

The version of the UCC used in contracts courses is the model code. However, when the UCC is cited in a case, the court typically cites the state statute in which the Code was enacted in that particular jurisdiction and it may not cite the corresponding model code section. This should not cause you trouble because the model code section number can be found incorporated within the state statute's own numbering system. For example, UCC §2.102 is cited in Connecticut as General Statutes §42a-2–102 and in Oregon as Oregon Revised Statutes §72.1020.

Another difference between the model code and most state statutes is that the model code has **official comments** following each section. These are the explanatory comments of the drafters and are not incorporated into most state enactments. They are, therefore, not legislative history in the usual sense. However, they are very influential and are often relied on by courts in interpreting UCC provisions.

§2.7.2   *The Use and Application of UCC Article 2*

As mentioned already, the UCC covers a variety of different types of commercial transactions, and each type of transaction is contained in a separate, self-contained Article. The only articles that concern us in the contracts course are Article 2, governing the sale of goods, and Article 1, which has general provisions applicable in all articles, including Article 2.

UCC §2.102 states that Article 2 applies to "transactions in goods." Although the word "transaction" is broader than the word "sale," you should not be concerned about this. You can assume for all purposes in the contracts course that if the contract is a *sale of goods*, Article 2 governs and *must be applied*. *Goods* are defined in UCC §2.105(1) to include movable things other than money and various intangible rights. A *sale* is stated in UCC §2.106(1) to consist of the passing of title from the seller to the buyer for a price.

To the extent that the provisions of Article 2 differ from the general rules of the common law of contract, the statute prevails. It would, therefore, be a serious error to try to resolve an issue arising from the sale of goods by simply applying the common law. Conversely, if the contract is not a sale of goods, Article 2 is not applicable and must not be used directly. (As explained in section 2.7.3, it could nevertheless be of persuasive weight and may be used by analogy in appropriate circumstances.)

If a contract is for the sale of goods, this *does not mean* that *common law* rules and principles are *irrelevant*. UCC §1.103 expressly states that the principles of law and equity supplement the provisions of the code unless displaced by particular code provisions. Therefore, to the extent that Article 2 is consistent with the common law, common law rules and principles are *used in conjunction* with the code provisions. In some areas, the rule of Article 2 may be the same as that of common law, so that cases interpreting the common law rule remain relevant. In addition, Article 2 is not comprehensive—it does not deal with every aspect of the law governing the sale of goods. In areas where Article 2 is silent, it is intended that the *common law fills the gap*. Therefore, even in a transaction involving the sale of goods, there is a substantial degree of interaction between Article 2 and the common law.

Quite apart from this, Article 2, like other statutes, must be interpreted and applied by courts. Therefore, when a court decides a case interpreting a section of Article 2, this case serves as precedent for later courts. Through this common law process, a judicial gloss has developed that refines the generality of code sections and creates more detailed rules by application to varied factual situations.

This abstract description of the symbiotic relationship between Article 2 and the common law will become more concrete as specific substantive topics are considered. For the present, take the point that Article 2 must be used in any case or problem involving a contract for the sale of goods, but recognize that the statute is not the only source of law. Consistent common law rules and judicial interpretations of the Code section are also applicable.

§2.7.3 The Influence of Article 2 in Cases Involving Contracts Other than Sales of Goods

Although Article 2 is not directly applicable beyond contracts for the sale of goods, it has exerted considerable influence on the development of the common law. Because the UCC is a modern, reform-minded statute, its changes in the law regarding sales are often found to be attractive by courts dealing with other contracts. The approach of Article 2 is therefore often consulted as a source of guidance when other contracts are involved, and if the court finds the issues and the purpose of the law to be *analogous* to those involved in a sale transaction, the court may decide to generalize the Article 2 resolution. As a result, there has been a trend in modern cases for older rules of common law to develop in the same direction as Article 2. This trend has been reinforced by the RESTATEMENT (SECOND) OF CONTRACTS, which has deliberately adopted many provisions of Article 2 in formulating its rules of the common law of contracts.

§2.8   What Is the RESTATEMENT (SECOND) OF CONTRACTS?

The Restatement looks like a statute. It has numbered sections that set out rules in statutory style, followed by comments and illustrations. However, unlike the UCC, the Restatement is **not a statute.** It is a **secondary authority**[3]—a textbook setting out the rules of the common law of contract as its drafters find them to be, or often, would like them to be. It is created by the American Law Institute (which, as you may recall from section 2.7.1 is one of the organizations involved in drafting the UCC).

The rules in the Restatement are largely extracted from decided cases, but this does not mean that they actually represent what the majority of courts have held. Despite its name, the Restatement **does not necessarily "restate"** the **settled law.** Indeed, given the number of jurisdictions involved, it is often not possible to find a settled law. Also, because it seeks to offer guidance on the direction that its drafters feel the law should take, it sometimes favors a legal rule that has had only minimal acceptance in decided cases. Therefore, while the Restatement is very influential and is frequently cited and relied on by courts, its "rules" have to be treated with some caution. They may not really reflect what the courts of a particular jurisdiction have actually held.

The current Restatement is the second to be published. The original was produced in the 1930s. It was the first thorough systematization of contract law, and the first comprehensive attempt to give coherent form to American contract doctrine. As such, it was immensely important in the development of the modern common law of contracts. As mentioned in section 2.3.1, it reflected classical thinking and tended towards the formalism and objectivism of the classical school. By the 1960s, the Restatement had become outdated,

---

3. The term "secondary authority" refers to legal writings like textbooks, law review articles, and commentaries that lack the binding force of official sources of law—such as statutes and court decisions (called "primary authority"). To the extent that a secondary authority is reliable and persuasive, it could be influential, but it never binds a court.

and a revision was begun, culminating in the Restatement Second, published in final form during the 1980s. The Restatement Second reflects the post-classicist thinking described in section 2.3.2, and is also heavily influenced by the UCC, which had been enacted by the time that work was begun on the Restatement Second. As mentioned before, its adoption of rules and concepts from Article 2 has helped to generalize the innovations of that statute.

The Restatement Second is cited frequently in this book. (Although its full citation form is "RESTATEMENT (SECOND) OF CONTRACTS," this is truncated here to "Restatement Second.")

EXAMPLES

1. As mentioned in section 2.7., UCC Article 2 is directly applicable only to sales of goods, even though it may have persuasive influence in cases involving other contracts. Students studying contract law often overlook this and become muddled, forgetting about Article 2 when the contract is a sale of goods or citing it as the governing law when the contract does not involve a sale of goods. These simple questions on the scope of Article 2 are included early in the book to emphasize the distinction between sales and other contracts. Which of the following contracts would be governed by Article 2?

(a) The sale of a condominium.
(b) A contract to employ someone as a sales clerk in a department store.
(c) The sale of a cow.
(d) The sale of Michelangelo's *David*.
(e) A contract under which a sculptor agrees to make a marble copy of *David* for $10,000.
(f) The sale of food in a restaurant.

EXPLANATIONS

1(a). Although this is a sale, a condominium is not goods but real property. The concept of movability distinguishes tangible personal property that is capable of being moved (even if machinery is needed to move it) from land and structures on land that are so incorporated into the land as to become united with it. Article 2 does not govern the sale.

1(b) Although the clerk will be selling goods in the course of his employment, the contract to employ him is not a sale of goods but a contract for labor (services).

1(c). Although the cow is a living animal, not an inanimate object, it still qualifies as goods. Livestock and crops (including unborn animals and growing crops) are clearly included within the definition of goods in UCC §2.105.

1(d). Although David is rather big, he is movable with some effort and therefore is goods. The fact that he is a priceless work of art is not relevant to the classification.

1(e). A contract to make a copy of David is also a sale of goods. Because the end product to be delivered under the contract—the completed copy—is the subject matter of the transaction, it is a sale of goods, even though the process of manufacture involves labor as well as materials.

1(f). The sale of food in a supermarket would clearly be a sale of goods, but a restaurant meal involves both a sale of the food and a provision of services relating to but distinct from the food, such as serving it and providing a table at which to eat it. This is distinguishable from, say, manufacturing the copy of a statue, in which all the labor is aimed at the fabrication of the item of property to be delivered. The transaction is a hybrid, involving both the supply of goods—the meal itself—and the associated services.

Many contracts involve a mix of goods and services. Other examples include contracts under which household goods such as carpets and appliances are both sold and installed; contracts for the repair of machinery involving the supply of materials and labor; and contracts between health care providers and patients for the supply of medical products such as false teeth, pacemakers, or even blood, in which the medical services associated with the transaction are as important as the health aid itself. When a hybrid transaction is in issue, courts have to decide whether Article 2 or common law should govern it. The prevalent approach to resolving this question (known as the "predominant purpose" or "predominant factor" test) is to determine whether the sale or services aspect of the transaction is predominant. If the sales component is the more significant portion of the contract and the service is incidental, Article 2 applies, but if the service is predominant and the sale of goods is ancillary, it does not. An alternative approach (known as the "gravamen test") is not to attempt to classify the contract as a whole one way or the other, but to apply Article 2 if the issue relates to the sales component and common law if the issue affects the services component.

The difference between these two approaches, and the reason why it may be important to decide whether the UCC applies, can be illustrated by *Newmark v. Gimbel's Inc.*, 258 A.2d 697 (N.J. 1969). The customer of a beauty parlor suffered severe skin irritation on her scalp and hair loss following the application of a permanent wave solution to her head by the hairdresser. The customer sued the beauty parlor for personal injury, both in tort and under a theory of breach of warranty. The tort cause of action failed because the customer could not establish that the beauty parlor had been negligent in using or applying the solution, so she had to rely on the warranty cause of action to obtain relief. However, a claim of breach of warranty could only be made if the transaction was a sale of goods, because Article 2 contains implied warranties that are not available under common law. The trial court applied the predominant purpose test. It found that the predominant purpose of the transaction was the rendition of beauty services, to which the supply of the solution was incidental. It therefore found Article 2 inapplicable so that no implied warranty existed. The Supreme Court declined to follow this approach. It considered that the policy of protecting consumers from harmful products should apply with equal force, whether those products are supplied in a sale or as part of a service. Because the predominant purpose test precludes relief in cases in which the service component dominates, it undermines this policy. The Court held instead that if it was the goods themselves that caused the injury, Article 2 warranties should apply to the claim arising from that injury.

The same approach was taken in *Anthony Pools v. Sheehan*, 455 A.2d 434 (Md. 1983), in which a homeowner sued a pool contractor for personal injury sustained as a result of falling off an allegedly defective diving board supplied with the pool. Under the predominant purpose test, the contract was principally for construction, so that UCC warranties would not be applicable. The court held that as the diving board was itself an item of goods, it was more consistent with the legislative policy of Article 2 to afford the homeowner the protection of the implied warranties with regard to any defect in the board. It therefore required the gravamen test to be applied.

3

The Doctrine of Precedent and a Contract Case Analysis

§3.1 Studying Contract Through Appellate Cases— An Introduction and a Note on Perspective

The study of case reports has been the standard teaching methodology in law schools since the latter part of the nineteenth century. In its initial use, the casebook reflected the classical conception described in section 2.3. It was thought that students could "find" the law in the cases, using the scientific approach to the study of law. While the focus of casebooks has changed to reflect the broader and more flexible post-classical view of law, case analysis is still largely used in teaching contracts. This is appropriate because case analysis is an important skill for lawyers, and the study of cases allows exposure to the common law method described in section 2.4.3. Case reports also serve as illustration of what would otherwise be abstract principles. Some casebook authors love to throw in weird cases or misguided opinions to challenge the students' critical faculties or to provoke debate.

However, it is helpful to approach this learning process with a recognition of some of its shortcomings. First, a collection of cases seldom produces a nice, concise and organized discourse on the law. That is why books like this one are needed. Second, the emphasis on caselaw gives students a rather skewed perspective because they are constantly exposed to transactions that have gone wrong—indeed, so irreconcilably wrong that the parties have felt it necessary to litigate, usually all the way to the appellate level, rather than to compromise. It is important to remember that only a fraction of contracts end up in litigation and fewer still reach the highest courts without being settled along the way. A related problem with the case method is that it focuses too strongly on contractual disputes at the expense of other lawyering skills such as counseling, drafting, and negotiation. Although there is an unavoidable emphasis on litigation when law is studied through cases, this problem can be ameliorated by paying attention to formation and negotiation issues whenever they are raised in the cases.

You may notice that most of the cases in your casebook have been decided by appellate courts. This is because most states do not publish trial court opinions. Even in those that do (and in the federal court system), the opinions of higher courts are more authoritative. Unlike trial courts, which consist of a single judge (with or without a jury), an appellate court sits in panels consisting of several judges. The exact size of the panel varies from one jurisdiction to another. If all the judges on the panel agree on the result and its rationale, the court is able to render a unanimous decision. However, it is common for members of an appellate panel to disagree on the proper disposition of the case. When that happens, the decision of the court is that adopted by the majority of judges on the panel. (The **majority opinion** is written by one of them and joined by the others.) A judge who disagrees with the reasoning of the majority but agrees with the result may write a **concurring opinion** (or, if more than one judge concurs, each may write a separate concurring opinion). A judge who disagrees with both the reasoning and the result may write a **dissenting opinion** (or, if there is more than one dissenting judge, separate dissenting opinions). Sometimes a panel is so badly divided that no majority of its judges sign onto any opinion. In that case, the opinion with the most votes becomes the **plurality opinion** of the court.

Because the analysis of cases is so central to the study of contract law, it seems really useful to include a chapter on the doctrine of precedent and to explain some of the basics of reading, understanding, and applying caselaw. In most schools, this chapter will overlap more extensive study in a legal writing and reasoning course. Nevertheless, I hope that this chapter, with an example based on a contracts case, will serve as a useful supplement, even for those who receive a thorough exposure to case analysis in class.

§3.2   How Judges Make Contract Law: Judicial Precedent

§3.2.1   *What Is Precedent?*

As mentioned in section 2.4.1, the common law developed in the Royal Courts of England. Although the Monarch was the font of justice, he or she could not deal personally with disputes between subjects, so this task was delegated to judges. As these judges decided cases over time, they came to realize that *similar situations* should be resolved in the *same way*. This allows for efficiency in the administration of justice, it enables people to predict case outcomes more accurately, and it serves one of our fundamental conceptions of justice: the equal treatment of people in like situations. As the common law developed, it became established practice for court decisions to be recorded so that they could be used as the basis of resolving later cases. This meant that a decision no longer only settled the dispute between the immediate parties. It formed a rule to be followed in the next case involving similar facts. As the number of recorded decisions grew to cover a greater variety of cases, the collection of legal rules expanded to create a compendious body of law.

The principle that a judicial decision creates a rule of law, binding upon later cases with similar facts, is known as the **doctrine of precedent** or, in Latin, stare decisis (roughly translated, "the decision stands"). The doctrine is peculiar to common law. Although civilian systems accord some weight to judicial precedent, they rely primarily on comprehensive codes and scholarly commentary as the source of legal rules. Court decisions are typically regarded as an exercise in applying the law, rather than the process of creating it, and judges conceive of their role as dispute resolution rather than lawmaking. With the exception of certain high courts and constitutional tribunals, court decisions in civilian countries are short, not very analytical, and fact-based.

§3.2.2 *Who Is Bound by Precedent?*

Obviously, the parties to a case are bound by the judicial determination of their suit. However, the doctrine of precedent deals with the binding effect of the decision beyond the parties, on later cases between other litigants. The first general rule of the doctrine has already been alluded to: The rule of a case is only binding on later cases with *substantially similar facts*. If there is a material factual difference between the cases, the earlier decision is not on point. Of course, no two cases are likely to have exactly the same facts, so the issue is one of substantial similarity—are the crucial factual elements sufficiently similar that the second case comes within the rule of the first. Even when there are notable factual differences, the later court may find the circumstances of the cases to be analogous, so that the rule may be treated as governing the second case as well.

As you can imagine, there are many instances in which the opposite also occurs. When a court does not favor applying the rule of the earlier case, it may look at the facts very narrowly and find factual differences that distinguish the cases. Often, the decision to analogize or distinguish facts is based on the judge's view on the soundness or error of the ruling in the prior case.

As a result, the issue of factual similarity is often hotly contested in argument before the court when counsel for one party wishes to bring the case within the rule but the other does not wish the precedent to govern.

A precedent does not bind every court in the country. It is binding only on the court that *decided the case* and courts of *inferior rank* in the same *judicial hierarchy*. As explained in section 2.6, the judicial hierarchy that usually deals with contract cases is the state court system. Therefore, if the state supreme court decides a case, the rule of that case is binding on the supreme court itself, as well as every other court in that state. If the case has been decided by the state's intermediate court of appeals, it binds all courts in the state except for the supreme court, which is senior in the judicial hierarchy. Therefore, if the supreme court later comes to consider a dispute with substantially similar facts (or, indeed if it comes to consider the same case on appeal), it will certainly take into account what the appeals court decided and will be influenced by that opinion if it is well reasoned. However, the supreme court is free to reject it. A case decided, even by the highest court, in one judicial hierarchy (that is, the supreme court of one state) is of no binding force on any court in another judicial hierarchy (another state). Again however, it could be of persuasive weight because courts often look to the cases decided in other states for guidance in resolving issues of first impression in their own jurisdictions.

The relationship between state and federal courts is too complex for discussion in any depth here. As a broad rule, when a *federal court* decides a matter of state law, it is treated for the purposes of precedent as being part of the judicial hierarchy of the state, so it is bound by precedent as if it was a court of that state. If the superior courts of the state have not yet had occasion to decide the particular legal issue, the federal court must try to determine from analogous or related caselaw how the state courts would decide the matter if presented with it.

The statement that a court is bound by its own decisions requires some explanation. The principle of stare decisis imposes an obligation on a court to follow its own precedents. This is true even when the membership of the court changes, so that different judges hear the later case. However, the need for flexibility and development in the law must be weighed against the policies of predictability and fairness that motivate the doctrine of precedent. Therefore, if the court believes that its prior decision was wrong or that it no longer makes sense in light of changes in society, it is at liberty to overrule the prior decision. Most judges do not do this lightly and are very reluctant to depart from precedent unless a strong case is made for doing so. A lower court does not have the same discretion to deviate from the precedent of a more senior court and is bound by it even if the lower court considers it wrong. Of course, as indicated earlier, there may be enough difference in the facts of the cases to allow the court to distinguish the unwelcome precedent. Finally, it should be remembered that (within the limits on legislative power prescribed by the U.S. and state Constitutions) the *legislature* is always free to overturn a judicial decision, even by the highest court. If the legislature does not like a rule established by a court, it can pass a statute that changes the rule.

§3.2.3 The Drawbacks of the System of Precedent

The advantages of the system of precedent—efficiency, predictability, and fairness—have already been alluded to. The system also has some drawbacks. First, it can **perpetuate unsound or unfair rules** when a later court is bound by a poor or outdated earlier decision. As just mentioned, there are means of avoiding this problem by making factual distinctions when possible, by overruling if the court is of sufficient rank, or by legislation. However, the inertia inherent in both the legislative and judicial processes often allows unsatisfactory rules to remain in force.

Second, rulemaking through court decisions tends to be **sporadic and disorganized.** When a legislature decides to enact a law, it can proceed in an orderly way to address the problem comprehensively. It can hold hearings, order staff research, and engage in debate. A statute can then be fashioned that is designed to deal with all the issues involved and to set out all the applicable rules. Caselaw develops more spasmodically. Courts have no control over the order in which cases arise, and they can respond only to the immediate issue involved in each case. They cannot legislate broadly but must confine themselves to resolving the dispute at hand. The rules that they create are very specifically tied to the facts in the case. As a result, judicial development of doctrine is haphazard. Some areas of law may be covered thoroughly because they are litigated frequently, while others may languish for decades. Some areas of the law may thus be regularly refined and updated while others are neglected. It sometimes happens that a major issue remains unresolved for years, because no party has wished to pursue it to the point of a definitive appellate pronouncement. Again, sometimes these gaps may be filled by legislative action, but they often are not.

Third, it is often **harder to find the legal rule** in a judicial opinion than in a statute. Statutes usually simply state their rules. Judge-made rules are contained in **opinions,** which can be dense, detailed, and lengthy pieces of writing. An opinion sets out the facts of the case, contains an often extended dissertation on the law, and finally reaches a decision or **judgment** resolving the issues between the parties. Somewhere in this body of writing, there are legal rules that serve as precedent. It is not always obvious what these rules are. To find them, the lawyer must study and interpret the case. To make matters worse, if the case has been decided by a divided appellate court, it can be harder still to determine the precedential weight of a majority or plurality opinion, called into question by concurrence or dissent.

§3.3   The Anatomy of a Judicial Opinion

§3.3.1   *Ratio Decidendi (Rule or Holding) and Obiter Dictum*

As mentioned before, the opinion states the facts of the case. In the opinion of a trial court, the facts are those as determined by the **factfinder** (the jury, or in non-jury cases, the judge) after weighing the evidence and resolving conflicts in testimony. The factual conclusions reached at trial are not disturbed on appeal unless they are so unreasonable that no support can be found for them in the evidence. Therefore, the recital of facts in an appellate opinion is based on the findings at trial. As the previous discussion indicates, the factual basis of the opinion is very important because the rule of the case can only be determined with reference to it.

Having laid the factual foundation for its decision, the court proceeds to resolve the *legal issues*. The judge could simply state the rule to be applied and give judgment. However, in most cases that involve significant legal issues, the judge justifies and articulates the *rationale* for the rule and its application in the case. The statement of the rule and its reasoning are the portion of the case that constitutes the precedent. This part of the opinion is called the **rule** or the **holding** or, in Latin, the ratio decidendi (roughly translated as "reasoning for the decision").

Frequently, the opinion does not confine itself to matter that is directly related to the resolution of the dispute before the court, but ranges beyond this to deal with **ancillary** or **collateral** matters on which the judge considers it necessary to express a view. These collateral discussions may be included, for example, to further explain and qualify the holding or to give guidance in future cases on how this court will view variations of the factual circumstances. This collateral matter is called obiter dictum ("said in passing") or simply **dictum.** As stated before, because it is *not necessary to the disposition* of the case, it is not binding precedent and has only persuasive value. A simple exercise in identifying the rule of a case and distinguishing it from dictum can be found in the examples.

§3.3.2   *The Process of Inductive and Deductive Reasoning in the Creation and Application of Legal Rules*

When a general rule is applied to a particular case, a process of **deductive reasoning** is followed. The general rule, accepted as true, serves as the major premise. The particular facts to which it will be applied are the minor premise. Provided that there is a necessary connection between these two premises, a conclusion is produced that must also be true. For example:

> Major premise. (The generally applicable rule of law): The contract of a minor is voidable at the instance of the minor.
>
> Minor premise. (The particular facts): June Nior is a minor who entered a contract and now seeks to avoid it.
>
> Conclusion: June has the right to avoid the contract.

Deductive reasoning, therefore, allows a rule of law to be applied in a particular case.

But where did this major premise, the rule of law, come from? In the common law, it has been created by precedent through a process opposite from deductive reasoning: The ruling in a particular case is generalized to create a rule of law applicable beyond the case. This is called **inductive reasoning.** In an earlier case another minor, Joe Venile, had entered into a contract with May Jore that he sought to avoid. In that case the court ruled that Joe, as a minor, had the power to avoid the contract. This rule then becomes generalized by the doctrine of precedent, so that it declares that not simply Joe, but all minors, may avoid contracts. The next time a minor, such as June, seeks to avoid a contract in a case with substantially similar facts, the general rule is applied by deductive reasoning to resolve it.

It must be stressed that the facts in the subsequent case (the minor premise[1]) must be substantially the same as in the prior case, otherwise there is no connection between the major and minor premise necessary to reach a conclusion. As stated earlier, material rather than absolute similarity is required. But even when there is a notable difference in the facts, the rule could be applied by analogy if the rationale motivating the first decision is equally applicable in the second. For example, say in the next case the issue arises whether a mentally impaired adult has the power to avoid a contract. The rationale for the decision in the first case was that when a person requires protection from bad judgment and exploitation resulting from youth, the values of freedom of contract and the protection of reasonable reliance in the marketplace must be weighed against the need to protect the minor. The court in the second case may find that the rule should be applied to a mentally impaired adult too, because this rationale is equally compelling in this case.

§3.3.3 The Use of Authority and Supporting Rationale in Judicial Opinions

Much has been said already on the use of precedent and legal exposition to justify the court's conclusion. The strength and extent of precedential authority and the force of the court's reasoning must be evaluated critically by

---

1. This is not a pun.

one who wishes to interpret the opinion and to evaluate its worth as precedent. It is therefore useful to take a little more time to point out some of the elements that constitute the rationale in an opinion.

When the decision is based on a prior case that serves as precedent, the earlier case is cited with some explanation of why it is controlling. The same is true if a rule of statute law is applicable. In some cases, this citation of authority may be the only justification advanced by the court for the rule. That is, in deciding in a particular way, the court may rely solely on an established rule and advance no explanation of its own. For example: "The contract of a minor is avoidable at the induce of the minor. See *Joe Venile v. May Jore.*"

However, if there is no controlling precedent or statutory provision, the court cannot simply rely on some authoritative source for its rule. It has to develop the rule itself and must explain why it does so. Even when there is authority, the court may consider it useful to bolster that citation to authority by explaining why the rule makes sense. Most policy rationales for a rule fit into one or more of three related but distinct classes:

1. A rule may be justified on the basis of **public policy** goals. The court feels that some particular social, economic, or political policy is served by the rule. For example, the court may discuss how it balanced the countervailing policies of freedom of contract and reliance against the protection of a minor.

2. A rule may be grounded in **ethics or fairness.** For example, the court may justify the minor's power of avoidance by arguing that an adult should not contract with a minor, because this is exploitive. It may also focus on the injustice of holding a person of tender years to a contractual commitment. The unfairness to the minor, combined with the unethical conduct of the major party and the likelihood that that party could tell by appearances that the other was under age, justifies the minor's power of avoidance.

3. Courts sometimes rationalize results on the basis of **institutional efficiency.** For example, the court may concede that some minors are more sophisticated than others, so that some may indeed be able to make a mature judgment. However, the court may conclude that a clear rule setting a definite age for contractual capacity is efficient because it is certain and avoids litigation over the question of actual competence.

As you read opinions, take note of their structure. You will find that one or more of these justifications appear in all of them.

EXAMPLES

1. This example provides a simple illustration of case analysis and the operation of the doctrine of precedent. It is based on an opinion in a fictitious case involving a minor's contract. Although the substantive law of contractual capacity is not discussed until Chapter 14, the principles of substantive law are not difficult to grasp and the focus is on the analysis in the opinion rather than on the rules of law. Read the opinion and consider the questions that follow it.

LORNA GREEN, Plaintiff
v.
MO MEADOWS, Defendant
Supreme Court of Suburbia, 1985.

GRASSY, Chief Justice, delivered the opinion of the court.

Plaintiff, Lorna Green, is an adult homeowner. On May 1, 1984, she entered into a contract with defendant, Mo Meadows, in terms of which defendant agreed to mow her lawn weekly during the summer of 1984 for a total fee of $400, payable in weekly installments. At the time of entering the contract, defendant was 17 years old and just two weeks short of his 18th birthday. Plaintiff did not know his age. He had a mature appearance. He lived on his own in an apartment and was financially independent, earning his living by doing odd jobs. A couple of days after making the contract, defendant was offered and accepted a more lucrative employment opportunity for the summer. He therefore called plaintiff and told her that he could no longer perform the lawnmowing services for her. At this stage the contract was fully executory—that is, no services had been performed under the contract, and no payments had been made.

After trying in vain to persuade defendant to honor his undertaking, plaintiff made inquiries and found another person to perform the same services for a fee of $600. This was the cheapest substitute available. Plaintiff then sued defendant for $200, the difference between what the services would have cost her under her contract with defendant and what they cost under the substitute transaction. This is the correct measure of damages because it compensates plaintiff for her disappointed expectation and places her in the position that she would have been in had the contract been performed. However, these damages are only recoverable if defendant's refusal to perform was an actionable breach of contract.

None of the above facts were disputed at trial. Defendant admitted entering into and subsequently refusing to perform the contract. The sole defense that he raised was that he was a minor at the time of contracting and therefore had the right to avoid the contract, which he did a couple of days later. The trial court found in favor of defendant on this issue of law and granted judgment in his favor, dismissing plaintiff's claim.

On appeal, plaintiff concedes that defendant was a minor both when entering and terminating the contract. However, plaintiff urges us to hold defendant bound to the contract under the circumstances of the case: Defendant was about 18, looked mature, lived independently of his parents, and fully understood the nature of the transaction. Plaintiff dealt fairly with defendant and had no knowledge of his age. In effect, while plaintiff acknowledges that a minor's contract is normally avoidable, she contends that the application of that rule in

2. After *Green v. Meadows* was decided, the supreme court of another state had to resolve a case with substantially similar facts. The case is one of first impression in this other jurisdiction (that is, there is no judicial precedent in the state on this issue). What impact will the *Green* decision have in the resolution of this subsequent case?

3. After *Green v. Meadows*, a trial court in Suburbia is dealing with a case in which a minor deliberately and expressly misrepresented to the major party that she was 20 years old and bolstered this misrepresentation by producing a forged driver's license. Is *Green* binding authority in this case? If not, does it offer the court any guidance on how to dispose of the case?

4. In another subsequent case before a trial court in Suburbia, the facts are almost identical to those in *Green v. Meadows*. The only material difference is that the contract was entered into three days before the minor's 18th birthday. One week after his birthday, before the services had been delivered or paid for, the minor disaffirmed the contract. How does *Green* affect the disposition of this case?

EXPLANATIONS

1(a). The holding of the case is the legal rule of the case that becomes binding precedent. It is narrowly confined to those pronouncements of law necessary to resolve the factual issues in the case. The rule in this case may be formulated as follows: A person is a minor until midnight of the day before his or her 18th birthday. A wholly executory contract entered into by a minor at any time before reaching majority is avoidable by the minor if expressly disaffirmed by the minor prior to majority. This right of avoidance continues to exist even if the minor lives apart from and is financially independent of his or her parents. A minor has no duty to disclose his or her age, and the minor's physical appearance and the major party's lack of knowledge of the minor's age are not relevant to the right of avoidance.

Notice that the holding is considerably narrower than the court's discourse on the law. For example, although the court says disaffirmance can occur expressly or by implication, before or within a reasonable time after reaching majority, the facts in the case are that disaffirmance was express and occurred before majority. Therefore, the court's recognition of implied and post-majority disaffirmance are dicta, not part of the holding. Similarly, the fact is that this contract was wholly executory—neither party had performed at the time of disaffirmance. This is a significant fact that must be reflected in the formulation of the holding. Although the absolute tone of the opinion suggests that the same rule may apply even if one or both parties had performed wholly or in part, this factor could change the equities of the case and require a different resolution. The holding must be narrowly drawn to show that this issue was not before the court in this case.

1(b). There are a number of dicta in the majority opinion. Remember that a dictum is a statement on the law that is not necessary for the resolution of the case but is pronounced on by the court in passing. A dictum is not binding precedent, but it has persuasive value. It allows the court to expound on legal doctrine and policy and provides guidance on how the court would be likely to deal with a later case having facts that present the issue discussed. Apart from the two dicta mentioned in Explanation 1(a) concerning implied and post-majority disaffirmance, the majority opinion contains the following dicta:

(i)   The discussion of plaintiff's damages is dictum because plaintiff lost the case on the issue of capacity, making the issue of remedy moot.

(ii)   The court's recognition of the exception regarding emancipation in the *L. Derly* case is dictum because the defendant in this case was not married. Note, however, that the court hints that it is not particularly well-disposed to the precedent, and this may undermine its value, as discussed in 1(e) below.

(iii)   The discussion of misrepresentation of age is holding to the extent that the court states that physical appearance combined with nondisclosure does not constitute misrepresentation. This aspect of the opinion does address facts in issue in the case. The remainder of the court's observations on this question are dicta at best. Their import is discussed in Example 3 below.

1(c). The dissenting opinion is merely the view of this individual judge. No part of it, whether directly related to the facts or not, is the holding of the case. It is not binding precedent. However, a dissent can be influential, particularly when it is the well-reasoned opinion of a respected jurist. When a court in another jurisdiction seeks persuasive authority, a dissenting opinion may be preferred to the majority approach. Even in this jurisdiction, the dissent may in time persuade the majority of the court to move away from the position adopted in this case. Alternatively, as the court's composition changes, successors to the current majority may be more sympathetic to the dissent's view. Dissents do not always have these beneficial effects. Sometimes the existence of dissent on the court can undermine the force of the majority opinion or cause confusion for lawyers trying to interpret the case.

1(d). The majority opinion uses all the elements referred to in section 3.3.3. The authoritative basis for the decision is the *Senex* case and the state statute. This recourse to authority is bolstered by rationale based on public policy, fairness, and institutional efficiency: The protection of minors from improvidence and exploitation serves both the ends of public policy and fairness; the preference for the arbitrary but certain rule is justified with reference to the goal of institutional efficiency; and the court's deference to the legislature is based on both policy and institutional grounds.

As the dissent shows, the court is not unanimous in the perception of how these different rationales come into play. The dissenting opinion finds the *L. Derly* case to be applicable authority and the statute not to be on point. It considers that the majority opinion does not serve the goals of public policy and fairness, and finds the goal of institutional efficiency to be outweighed by the policy of fairness.

1(e). The treatment of the *L. Derly* case in the majority and dissenting opinions highlights the point that a precedent is binding only when the facts of the cases are substantially similar. It seldom happens that a later case is identical to an earlier one, and it is often difficult to know whether factual differences between them are material enough to disqualify the earlier case as binding precedent. Sometimes the court's view of this issue is colored by its desire to follow or depart from the earlier decision. The majority apparently does not like the rule in *L. Derly* and does not wish to use it, so it finds the case distinguishable on the ground that the minor in the earlier case was married. The dissent feels that the independence of the minor is a relevant consideration and therefore feels that *L. Derly* should be followed. The dissenting judge therefore refuses to find the fact of marriage to be a material difference between the cases.

1(f). One of the perpetual issues confronting courts is the relationship between the judicial and the legislative role. While judges clearly do make law through the common law process, this function is circumscribed by the predominant lawmaking authority of the elected legislature. Therefore, if a statute deals with an issue, the judge must apply the statute and not disregard it. In this case there is a statute prescribing the age of minority. The difference between the majority and dissenting opinions reflects a different view on the scope and intended meaning of the statute. The majority interprets it as providing authority for a rigid rule on contractual capacity; the dissent sees it merely as altering a common law rule on age, while preserving judicial discretion to deal with the actual effect of minors' contracts. The issue of statutory interpretation can be difficult, and the extent to which the court is willing to defer to perceived legislative intent is often influenced by the judge's broad or narrow view of the court's rulemaking function.

2. This decision is not binding precedent in another judicial hierarchy. When a court deals with an issue of first impression in its jurisdiction, it is likely to seek guidance by consulting the decisions in other jurisdictions and will be influenced by the persuasiveness of supporting rationales in decided cases which should have been brought to its attention by one or the other party during the course of argument. As mentioned in Example 1(c), as the court is not bound by the majority opinion, it could find the dissent to be more compelling and may decide to use it as persuasive authority.

3. As noted in Example 1(b), *Green* is only of binding authority in its holding that physical appearance plus nondisclosure is not misrepresentation. Beyond that, the court's observations on misrepresentation are no more than

dictum. In fact, the court does not even provide clear dictum on this question. It merely refers to decisions in other states that recognize an exception for misrepresentation and then calls into question the wisdom of those decisions. Therefore, although the decision does not give clear guidance to the trial court in the later case, it does hint that if the judge recognizes the misrepresentation exception, the decision may be overturned on appeal. This signals to the judge (and to the attorneys in the case) that some careful and thorough argument should be prepared if the reliance is to be placed on the misrepresentation.

4. As noted in Examples 1(a) and (b), the holding of *Green* is confined to disaffirmance by the minor before reaching majority. In the later case, disaffirmance occurred after the age of majority, so it is not within the rule of *Green*. However, *Green* has a very clear dictum that post-majority disaffirmance is also effective if within a reasonable time. (The earlier case of *Senex* said the same thing, but we do not know if it was dictum or holding in that case. If it was holding, that case is binding precedent. If it was dictum, the fact that it was reinforced by later dictum in *Green* strengthens its persuasive force.) Therefore the trial court should take the pronouncement in *Green* very seriously. Of course, *Green* does not say what a reasonable time after majority would be, and the trial court will have to resolve that issue.

be fouled by so many different causes: The utterer's thinking may be fuzzy or confused; a poor choice of words or actions may obscure intent; a manifestation of intent may be perceived differently or misconstrued by the person to whom it is addressed; or secret reservations or deviousness may result in deliberate obfuscation. Therefore, while contracts are consensual relationships and we do like to think of them as a genuine "meeting of the minds," the minds of parties often may not be in true accord, even though their manifestations of assent appear to be congruent.

§4.1.2   *Assent and Accountability: Subjective and Objective Tests of Assent*

When imperfect communication leads to a dispute about the existence or terms of a contract, two fundamental contract policies must be accommodated. The **assent policy** dictates that contractual obligation should not be imposed on a person who did not in fact agree to be bound. However, if the need for true assent is too heavily stressed, the **policy** of **protecting reliance** is undermined. If no one could rely on words or conduct that indicate assent, it would be difficult for anyone to have confidence in the system of commercial exchange. Therefore, the assent policy must be tempered by the goal of protecting the expectations of one who reasonably relied on the appearance of assent. A person must be held accountable for behavior that signifies assent. Many nineteenth-century courts gave overwhelming weight to the assent policy and would refuse to find a contract unless there had been true mental consensus—a genuine "meeting of the minds." In other words, actual assent, determined **subjectively** by looking at each party's actual understanding, was a prerequisite to contract.

During the classical period (roughly, late nineteenth and early twentieth century) thinking changed. Courts focused more on the need to protect reasonable reliance on the apparent meaning of the manifestation. Classicists felt that a subjective approach was wrong in principle because it made transacting less dependable. It was also not workable because it placed too much store on obviously unreliable (and not easily rebuttable) self-serving testimony of actual intent. Classical contract law therefore moved to the opposite pole, refusing to see any relevance in the subjective state of mind of the parties and employing a strict **objective** or external test for assent. If agreement was apparent from the manifestations of assent, reasonably interpreted, a contract had been formed on the terms reflected in the manifestation. It was neither necessary nor permissible to receive testimony on what either party actually thought or believed.

A complete disregard of the actual state of mind of the parties gives too little weight to the assent policy and could lead to injustice where subjective evidence could cast some light on the meaning of a manifestation. For example, it could provide an alternative explanation of the meaning of words or actions, or it could indicate justifiable misapprehension induced by the other party's unfair bargaining methods. Recognizing this, modern law has moved away from the strict objectivist approach of the classical period, and is not as absolute in its focus on the manifestation of assent. It is now accepted that evidence of a party's state of mind may sometimes be helpful in interpreting or giving a context to words or conduct, provided that the subjective evidence is credible and compatible with the overt behavior. Although less rigid than it used to be, the objective test is firmly established and a subjective "meeting of the minds" is not required for contract formation. In the absence of compelling contrary indications, assent is legally sufficient if each party, by the deliberate use of words or conduct, manifested agreement to be contractually bound.

The contemporary approach is reflected in several sections of the Restatement Second. In defining a promise, §2 speaks of a manifestation of intent by the promisor that justifies the promisee in understanding that a commitment has been made; §3 describes "agreement" as a manifestation of mutual assent; §§19 and 20 stress the accountability principle by holding a party liable for deliberate manifestations by words or conduct, made with reason to know that they will create a reasonable impression of assent.

§4.1.3 The Operation of the Objective Test in Contemporary Law

Having introduced the objective test, we now look more carefully at its operation and implications. The test may be thought of as having both a substantive aspect (that is, it prescribes a legal standard for determining assent) and an evidentiary aspect (that is, it regulates what evidence is admissible to prove intent). Although these aspects are closely interrelated, it aids understanding of the objective test to articulate and describe them separately.

a. The Substantive Aspect: The Legal Standard for Determining Assent Is Objective and External

Manifestations of assent are interpreted, not in light of what the utterer actually meant or the other party actually understood, but from the standpoint of a *reasonable person in the position of the party* to whom the manifestation was made. That is, we ask not what the words or actions *did mean* to either party, but how they *should have been understood* if interpreted reasonably, in the context of the transaction, by a person with the knowledge and attributes of the party to whom they were directed. The reason for this, of course, is that the objective test is aimed at balancing the requirement of assent with the protection of reasonable reliance. It is therefore not concerned with any

In some cases, a deal may be struck very quickly, with a minimum of bargaining: One party may make a proposal that is accepted without qualification by the other. In other cases the path to contract formation may be long and arduous. Initial proposals may lead to counterproposals, negotiations, and compromise. If the transaction is complex, each step in the process may require consultation with different corporate departments, technical experts, and attorneys. In either event, where this interaction is successful, there comes a time when the parties reach agreement and bind themselves to the relationship—a contract comes into being. Sometimes this point can be clearly identified, but if there has been lengthy negotiation or several communications back and forth, it may be hard to tell if a final and binding contract actually emerged from this process, and if so, at what point it came into being.

Sometimes the creation of a contract is marked by the signing of a written memorial of the agreement.[2] When this happens, it is relatively easy to fix the time of formation and the exact terms of the contract. However, this helpful indicator of formation is not always present because the parties may have formed a contract without recording it in a formal comprehensive writing. A contract could be contained in a series of correspondence or in some other collection of interrelated documents; it could have been made orally with the intention of later drafting and signing a written memorial or it may be partly written and partly oral or entirely oral.[3] Such circumstances may create uncertainty and disputes over the question of whether a contract was formed at all, and if so, whether certain terms became part of it. The rules of offer and acceptance provide a framework for resolving these questions.

The offer and acceptance model has often been criticized as too rudimentary and artificial to cope with many contemporary methods of contract formation. For example, it bears little resemblance to what actually happens in the complex negotiations mentioned above, or where transactions involve the use of standard forms. In the latter case, the UCC has attempted a statutory modification of the rules, discussed in Chapter 6. In other situations, if there has not been legislative intervention, it is left to the courts to develop new rules or to analogize from existing ones to reach a realistic resolution.

---

2. In colloquial speech, people often talk of "signing a contract." Strictly speaking, this is inaccurate terminology. The contract is the legal relationship between the parties, and the document that is signed is actually the record or memorial of that contract.

3. Under the statute of frauds (see Chapter 11), certain types of contracts are not enforceable unless their essential terms are recorded in a signed writing. However, many contracts are not subject to this rule and are fully valid and enforceable in oral form. This does not mean that it is a good idea to dispense with a written memorial, even where the law does not require writing. It is harder to prove the existence and terms of an oral contract.

§4.2.2 When Are Offer and Acceptance Issues Presented?

Upon learning the rules of offer and acceptance, an inexperienced student may be tempted to waste time and effort in trying to unravel the sequence of offer and acceptance in every case or problem. However, not every contract dispute raises formation issues, because the parties may not be in disagreement over the facts of formation. The rules of offer and acceptance tend to be relevant in three types of dispute:

a. Was a Contract Formed?

After a series of communications or negotiations, one of the parties contends that a contract was formed, but the other denies that final agreement was reached. The rules of offer and acceptance may help to determine if a contract came into existence.

b. What Terms Were Included in the Contract?

Although the parties agree that a contract was formed (or their disagreement on this point has been resolved in favor of formation), they have a dispute about whether a particular term was included in the contract. Often, the determination of which communication was the offer and what constituted the acceptance can resolve the question of whether a disputed term became part of the contract that was ultimately formed.

c. Which Jurisdiction Governs the Dispute?

A contract is usually governed by the law of the jurisdiction in which it was formed. When parties are in different jurisdictions and have dealt with each other by correspondence or electronic means, it may be important to fix the point of formation to establish whose law applies to the transaction or which court has jurisdiction to hear the dispute. Choice of law and jurisdiction are not dealt with further. This issue is merely noted as one of the situations that may call for analysis of the formation process.

§4.2.3 The Basic Model

The rules of offer and acceptance are based on a particular conception of how contracts are formed. In the simplest terms, they envisage that one person (called the **offeror**) makes an offer to another person (the **offeree**) to enter into a contract on specified terms. The offer creates a **power of acceptance**

munication may be misunderstood. However, when intent is not clearly expressed, the communication must be interpreted **objectively.** The question is whether, taking into account the entire context of the communication, the addressee was justified in understanding that the proponent intended to be bound on acceptance.

For example, if the owner of property wishes to make an offer to a prospective buyer, she may write:

> I offer to sell you my farm "Bleakacre" for $2 million cash. If you wish to buy this property you must deliver your written acceptance to me by midnight on Friday, October 13, 1997.

The strong wording (including the use of the terms "offer" and "acceptance") leave little doubt that an offer is intended. If, on the other hand, the owner wanted to make it clear that this is not an offer, she may couch the letter something like this:

> I wish to sell my farm "Bleakacre" and will consider an offer of not less than $2 million. I invite you to make an offer if you are interested in purchasing it.

However, if the owner is less precise in her choice of language, she may come up with something like this:

> I am willing to sell my farm "Bleakacre" to you, but will not accept less than $2 million cash. Let me have your reply as soon as possible.

This flabby language does not make the offeror's intention clear. It could lead the addressee to understand the communication to be an offer, whether or not the owner meant it as such. The ambiguity could keep a couple of lawyers happily employed for some time as the parties litigate over its meaning.

One cannot be sure who will win the last "Bleakacre" dispute because I have not provided any contextual information that may clarify the ambiguity in the owner's letter. In trying to resolve disputes like this, one must weigh all the facts of the case. Courts have identified some general indicia that help to distinguish an offer from a preliminary proposal:

1. The **words used in the communication** are always the primary indicators of what was intended. Even where the language of the communication does not make its import absolutely clear, clues to reasonable meaning may be found in what was said. The use of terms of art, such as "offer," "quote," or "proposal," may be helpful but are not conclusive if the context indicates that they were not used in their legal sense. (For example, realtors' lawn signs sometimes announce that a property is "offered for sale," yet no one would seriously argue that the seller thereby makes an offer in the legal sense.)

2. Because an offer is intended to form a contract upon acceptance (and as discussed below, an offeree is not usually permitted to accept in terms that go beyond the offer), a communication that **omits significant terms** is not likely to be an offer. Therefore, the comprehensiveness and specificity of the terms in the communication are an important clue to its intent.

3. If the communication is **not specifically directed to a particular person** but is made to multiple people (for example, in a newspaper advertisement, catalog, or circular), it could be an offer, but it is more likely that it should not reasonably be seen as such. The usual expectation is that a person merely invites offers by this type of general dissemination, especially if replicants must meet certain qualifications (such as creditworthiness) or there is a limited supply of the proffered property or services.

4. The **relationship of the parties,** any previous dealings between them, and any prior communications in this transaction may cast light on how the recipient reasonably should have understood the communication.

5. Where parties are members of the same community or trade, they are or should be aware of any **common practices or trade usages,** so these are taken into account in determining reasonable understanding of a communication.

It must be stressed that these are just factors to be considered. This is not a list of firm rules and it is not exhaustive. The facts of each case must be evaluated to decide on the reasonable meaning of a communication.

§4.5   The Expiry of the Offer by Passage of Time

§4.5.1   *The Specified or Reasonable Duration of the Offer*

An offer does not last forever. It has a limited duration and lapses if not accepted in time. As the creator of the offer, the offeror is entitled to specify the time within which the acceptance must be made. If the offeror does not state the duration of the offer, it must be accepted within *a reasonable time.* The offeror takes a risk by not specifying a time for acceptance because the question of what period is reasonable for acceptance may be unclear until settled by litigation. To decide what is a reasonable time, the factfinder must ask what amount of time would be needed to receive, consider, and reply to the offer under all the circumstances of the transaction. As a rough guide, it is usually assumed that if the parties are in each other's presence, the reasonable time for acceptance concludes when they part company, but if they communicate at a distance by mail or similar noninstantaneous means, the time for transmission must be taken into account. Other factors relevant to this question include the nature of the transaction; the relationship of the parties; any course of dealing, custom, or trade usage; the means of communication used; and the stability of the market.

An offeror may not entirely eliminate the risk of uncertainty by stating a time for acceptance, if the time specified is *ambiguous*. For example, if the offer requires acceptance by 5 P.M. Pacific Daylight Time on Friday, October 13, 1997, there can be no doubt as to the exact time that the power of acceptance ends. However, an acceptance required "within five days" is ambiguous because it does not indicate if the five-day period runs from the date of the writing or receipt of the offer, or whether the offer can be accepted after business hours on that final day.

§4.5.2   *The Effect of a Late Attempt to Accept*

If the offeree attempts to accept the offer after the period for acceptance has expired, the legal effect of this late communication may be difficult to decide and depends on the circumstances and the language used. It could be a *legally meaningless act*. Alternatively, the course of dealings between the parties and the language of the late acceptance could create the reasonable understanding that it is a *new offer* by the former offeree, creating a power of acceptance in the original offeror. In some cases, especially where there is doubt about the exact duration of the offer, the offeror's *failure to object* to a late acceptance may suggest either that it was not late at all, or even if it was late, that the offeror acquiesced in the delay, making the acceptance effective despite its tardiness. There is thus no hard-and-fast rule on the treatment of a late acceptance, and its effect must be determined on the facts of each case.

§4.6   Termination of the Offer Before Its Expiry by Lapse of Time

The stated or reasonable duration should be thought of as the longest period that an offer could remain open. It may terminate even before that under four circumstances identified in Restatement Second §36:

§4.6.1   *Rejection*

The offer lapses if the offeree rejects it. Once rejection has been communicated, the offeree cannot recant the rejection and accept, because the offer has come to an end. A purported acceptance after rejection could, of course, qualify as a new offer by the former offeree.

§4.6.2 Counteroffer

As explained in section 4.8, a counteroffer is treated as a rejection of the original offer and the substitution of a new offer by the original offeree. A counteroffer therefore has the same effect as an outright rejection in terminating the offeree's power to accept the original offer.

§4.6.3 The Offeror's Death or Mental Disability

If the offeror dies before the offer is accepted, the offer lapses automatically. It does not matter that the offeree did not know about the offeror's death at the time of attempted acceptance. It is generally recognized that this long-established rule is based on the rationale that there can be no "meeting of the minds" if death intervenes before acceptance. Although the rule is inconsistent with the objective test, it is still generally followed. Note that it applies only when the death occurs before acceptance. Once a contract has been formed, the supervening death of a party does not terminate it unless the contract, by its terms, provides for termination under that circumstance. The contractual obligation remains a liability of the estate, which must perform if possible or pay damages for breach.

The mental disability of the offeror is treated by §36 in the same way as death, so that if the offeror becomes mentally incompetent between the time of making the offer and the time of acceptance, the offer lapses. But if the mental disability arises after acceptance, it does not affect the formation of the contract. Note, however, that the offeror's mental incapacity before the time of acceptance could be analyzed on a different basis. Instead of treating it as a lapse of the offer (resulting in no contract), it could be seen as creating a contract by a mentally incompetent person. As will be explained in Chapter 14, the effect of this is to create a voidable contract (one that exists but can be voided by the offeror) rather than to preclude formation at all.

§4.6.4 Revocation

a. The Offeror's Power of Revocation

Unless the offer qualifies as an option or as a firm offer under UCC Article 2 (discussed in Chapter 5), an undertaking to keep it open for a particular pe-

Time for acceptance has already been discussed. We now examine the content and mode of acceptance.

§4.8   Qualified or Equivocal Acceptance

§4.8.1   *The General Rule that an Acceptance Must Correspond to the Offer*

Under classical common law, the acceptance must correspond exactly with the offer. This is sometimes called the **"mirror image"** or **"ribbon matching"** rule. A response is not an acceptance if the offeree imposes conditions on the acceptance or seeks to change or qualify the terms of the offer. Some courts, particularly in the older cases, have applied this rule rigidly, so that any variation in the response to an offer disqualifies it as an acceptance. (In section 6.3 we return to the "mirror image" rule and discuss it in more detail in contrast to the UCC's treatment of mismatching acceptance.) The better, more contemporary approach is to tolerate minor discrepancies and to apply the rule only where the response makes *material* changes in the transaction proposed in the offer. The "mirror image" rule follows from the principle that the offeror places the final decision on contract formation with the offeree. Therefore, the offeror must be taken to invite assent only to the terms proposed and not to terms unilaterally imposed by the offeree in the course of acceptance. Were this not so, making an offer would be a risky business. The offeror could find herself bound to a contract very different from that proposed. Therefore, the rule is justified in most cases when the parties are making deliberate proposals and counterproposals, provided that the court confines it to significant discrepancies between the offer and the purported acceptance.

The rule is not as defensible where the parties seek to contract by exchanging *preprinted standard forms*, and the conflicts are between the standard terms in the forms. Because people often do not read printed terms on forms, the parties may be unaware of the conflict and may both believe that they have a contract. The application of the "mirror image" rule in such a case could lead to the conclusion that a counteroffer was made where an acceptance was really intended. UCC §2.207 attempts to address this problem, as discussed in Chapter 6, but UCC Article 2 only applies to sales of goods. Where other contracts are involved, the common law "mirror image" rule still applies. However, a court need not be inflexible in using it. Its impact can be softened by the materiality qualification and by the principles of interpretation discussed below. As we have seen, UCC rules often have a persuasive influence on the common law. Section 2.207 has many problems of its own (as you will see in Chapter 6), so it is not a very attractive candidate for too literal an adoption in a common law case. However, courts are influenced by the spirit of the section, which favors a focus on commercial reality instead of technical rules.

§4.8.2 *The Legal Effect of a Non-Conforming Response*

If an acceptance must conform exactly with the offer, what is the legal effect of a response that is not an unequivocal expression of assent? The answer to this question depends on the reasonable interpretation of the response. If, reasonably interpreted, it indicates that the offeree intends to enter a contract only as qualified in the response, it is a **counteroffer.** A counteroffer is defined in Restatement Second §39 as an offer by the offeree to the offeror, relating to the same matter as the original offer and proposing a different substitute bargain. The counteroffer is therefore both a **rejection** of the offer and a **new offer** by the former offeree for a contract on different terms. It thus terminates the original offer and creates a power of acceptance in the original offeror. Because the original offer lapses, the offeree has lost the power to accept it if the offeror rejects the counteroffer.

However, the response may reasonably suggest a different meaning. It may be an **outright rejection with an explanation,** in which case it may not give the former offeror an opportunity to accept. Conversely, it may not be a rejection at all but merely a **request for information** or a **suggestion for changes,** made with the intent of reserving the decision to accept until the offeror reacts to the request.

Some examples will illustrate these distinctions:

Say that the owner of "Bleakacre" writes to a prospective buyer, offering to sell the property to her for $2 million. The offeree replies, "I accept your offer provided you reduce the price to $1.9 million." There can be little doubt that this is a counteroffer. It causes the original offer to lapse and gives the owner the opportunity to accept the buyer's new offer.

If, instead, the offeree had replied, "I am interested in the property, but not at your price," this cannot be a counteroffer because no new proposal is made as to price. It sounds like a rejection with an explanation of the reason for the rejection, apparently encouraging the owner to make a second offer.

As a third possibility, the offeree may reply, "I am considering your offer. Do you propose a cash sale, or will you take a mortgage for the price?" This appears to be a request for elaboration or possibly a proposal for a change of terms, but it is made with the apparent intent of not foreclosing acceptance if the offeror replies in the negative. A similar intent to hold open the possibility of acceptance may be found if the offeree merely suggests a change ("I am considering your offer. Before I decide, let me know if you would be willing to throw in the living room furniture") or makes a grudging acceptance ("As I really need the property, I reluctantly agree to your excessive price").

These examples are relatively unambiguous. Often, of course, the reply may not make it clear exactly what the offeree has in mind. For example, if the reply is "Would you accept $190,000?" it is not clear if this is a counteroffer, terminating the buyer's power of acceptance, or merely a request for modification of terms, intended to keep alive the buyer's opportunity to accept the offer if the offeror sticks to the asking price. As with other communications, the ambiguity of the response leads to a greater risk of dispute and litigation.

Sometimes, a response may seem to add terms that are not expressed in the offer but that are *implicit in the offer* or would be incorporated into the offer by law or usage. If so, the response may appear superficially to be a counteroffer, but it is in fact an unqualified acceptance, because it merely articulates what was inherent in the offer.

For example, the owner of "Bleakacre" offers to sell the property to a prospective buyer for $2 million. The offeree responds, "I accept your offer, subject to your proof of clear title, payment to be placed in escrow and made to you against transfer of the deed." The offer is silent on these points. It did not warrant good title and said nothing about payment being concurrent with transfer of the deed. However, common usage and accepted legal practice implies these terms in a contract for the sale of land, so they were part of the offer in the absence of language clearly excluding them. Articulating them in the acceptance does not harm its effectiveness. I have used a fairly clear case to illustrate this distinction. It is not always that easy to decide whether terms in a response merely reflect what was unexpressed in the offer. Resolution of this question may involve legal argument on whether a term should be implied in law, or a factual dispute over the existence and pertinence of an alleged usage.

§4.9   The Mode of Acceptance

An acceptance must be manifested and communicated. The offeror has control over the manner of acceptance, and, in addition to stipulating the terms of the proposed contract, the offeror may specify what the offeree must do to accept. To be an effective acceptance, the offeree's response must be in conformity with these instructions. However, if the offer does not require acceptance to take a particular form, no special formalities are required for effective acceptance.[5] It may be signified in any manner reasonable under the circumstances. The manifestation of acceptance could be spoken, written, or by conduct, and the means of communication could be by any of a wide array of media, ranging from personal contact to singing

---

5. Subject to the qualification that if the statute of frauds applies, as discussed in Chapter 11, the acceptance must satisfy the statute's requirement of writing to be effective against the offeree.

telegram. As explained in section 4.12, the acceptance may be a promise to perform the requested exchange or the actual performance of the offeree's consideration.

To avoid confusion, it is important to distinguish the **substantive terms** of the offer (that is, the terms of the proposed contract itself) from the **instructions concerning acceptance** (that is, the procedure that must be followed by the offeree to accept). The substantive terms are central—they go to the very heart of the relationship. The instructions for acceptance are simply concerned with the most convenient and efficient way of communicating assent. The offeror's dominant concern is to make the deal, and the method of communicating assent is merely ancillary to the achievement of this purpose.

Although the manner of acceptance is ancillary to the goal of making a contract, this does not mean that the offeror is indifferent to controlling it. If the offeror is concerned about knowing of the acceptance as soon as it takes effect and of having written proof of it, the offer should prescribe an exclusive mode of acceptance that ensures acceptance only takes effect upon the offeror's personal receipt of a signed letter of acceptance. If the offeror does not care about the mode of acceptance and is willing to assume any risk of late or undelivered notice of acceptance,[6] the offeror may not specify a mode at all or may indicate a permissible but not exclusive mode. Factors such as the desire to accommodate the offeree's convenience, to encourage acceptance, or to maintain good relations with the offeree, may outweigh the offeror's desire for certainty and may dissuade the offeror from making too fine a point of the procedure for accepting. Taking this into account, the usual assumption of the law is that unless the offer clearly indicates otherwise, the offeror is more interested in attracting the acceptance than in being punctilious about the mode of acceptance.

In summary, the rules governing mode of acceptance are:

1. When the offer clearly manifests the intention that a prescribed mode of acceptance is **mandatory and exclusive,** the offeror's intent must be deferred to, and that particular manner of acceptance must be complied with exactly.

2. If a manner of acceptance is specified, but it does **not reasonably appear intended as exclusive,** any reasonable method of accep-

---

6. For example, under the "mailbox" rule, discussed in section 4.11.2, if it is reasonable to accept through the mail or a similar medium, the acceptance takes effect as soon as properly deposited in the post or introduced by the offeree into whatever other appropriate delivery system is used. It is therefore possible that the offeror will not know of the acceptance until some time after it occurred, and bears the risk of the acceptance never arriving. If the offeror does not wish to take this risk, the offer should exclude this mode of acceptance in favor of one (such as personal delivery by hand) that will ensure instantaneous knowledge of acceptance.

the manifestation of acceptance and the time that the manifestation comes to the offeror's attention—occur simultaneously. However, where there is a time lapse between these points, as happens when the parties are at a distance and do not use an instantaneous medium of communication, one of the times must be selected as the legally effective date of acceptance.

§4.11.1   *Instantaneous Communication*

Whenever the parties are in instantaneous communication—negotiating face-to-face, talking on the telephone, or communicating live by electronic means—they are in a position to hear or observe each other's manifestations immediately. The offeror is or should be aware of the acceptance as soon as it is uttered. Similarly, if the offeror should retract the offer before acceptance, the offeree should know this as it happens. Therefore, the general rule is that the acceptance occurs *as soon as it is manifested*. It could happen that there is some disruption of communication as a result of a sudden loud noise or the failure of the transmission medium. If both parties should realize this, no contract can be formed until the break is corrected and communication is restored. If only one of the parties has reason to be aware of the disruption, that party must inform the other or will be held to the other's reasonable understanding.

For example, while the owner and prospective buyer of "Bleakacre" are sitting in a room and negotiating, a kid walks past the room carrying a boom box at full volume. As a result, the owner sees the buyer's lips move but cannot hear her words of acceptance. As reasonable people, both parties should realize that communication was disrupted. When the buyer repeats the acceptance, the contract is created. If the buyer regretted her decision immediately after she spoke the first time, she may thank her lucky stars for the disruption and refuse to repeat the acceptance, in which case no contract is formed.[8]

Similarly, if the parties are speaking on the phone and the line goes dead just as the words of acceptance are uttered, the break should be obvious to the owner immediately and should become obvious to the buyer when she receives no reaction to her words. No contract comes into being until communication is restored and the acceptance is repeated.

By contrast, say that the parties are communicating by fax. The buyer transmits the acceptance and her machine shows successful contact, but the owner's machine receives an unreadable transmission. Because only the owner could reasonably be aware of the breakdown, he must inform the buyer and if he does not, he is bound to the buyer's reasonable assumption of successful communication.

---

8. Unless, of course, the owner was able to read the buyer's lips, so that the action of moving her lips was a sufficient manifestation of acceptance.

In summary, when the parties have live contact, no rule is needed to decide whether the contract takes effect on manifestation or receipt because these events are not significantly separated in time. Acceptance takes effect only when successfully communicated unless only one of the parties is reasonably unaware of the disruption. In that case, the question of whether acceptance occurred is determined from the reasonable understanding of that party.

§4.11.2 Non-Instantaneous Communication and the "Mailbox" Rule

Where the parties are at a distance and the means of communication entail a delay between the manifestation and the offeror's knowledge of it, there could be an issue of whether the acceptance became effective upon its utterance or upon its coming to the attention of the offeror. As with the mode of acceptance, the offeror has the right to *specify when acceptance becomes effective.* In many situations if a mode of acceptance is prescribed, this also implicitly establishes the effective point of the acceptance. For example, if the offeror requires acceptance to be only by the personal delivery of a signed, written acceptance, this covers both the mode of acceptance and the event (delivery) that brings it into effect. However, the offeror may not have specified a mode of acceptance or, even if having done so, may not fix the point at which the acceptance takes effect. For example, the offer may state that acceptance must be by mail, but may not make it clear if a contract comes into being upon the acceptance being mailed or only upon its being received by the offeror.

In the **absence of specification** in the offer, the acceptance takes effect as soon as it is **put out of the offeree's possession,** provided that the acceptance is made in a manner and via a medium expressly or impliedly **authorized** by the offer. Therefore, if acceptance by mail is permissible, acceptance occurs as soon as the offeree deposits a properly stamped and addressed acceptance in the mailbox. The burden is on the offeree to prove **proper dispatch,** so the offeree should make a good record of the mailing to avoid evidentiary problems. Provided that the acceptance was properly mailed before lapse of the offer, it does not matter that it was received after the offer terminated or was never received at all. The law allocates the risk of uncertainty and of lost or delayed mail to the offeror. This is often referred to as the "mailbox" or "deposited acceptance" rule. Although the mail was used as an example here, it is not confined to communication through the post office and applies whenever a non-instantaneous medium of communication is used.

Over the years, there has been some discussion of why the transmission rather than receipt of the acceptance brings the contract into effect. Probably the most convincing rationale is that the offeror could have allocated the risk of uncertainty, delay, or non-receipt to the offeree. As this was not done, it is appropriate to leave this risk to the offeror and give the offeree a reliable basis of knowing that acceptance has occurred.

What happens if the medium of transmission is not authorized or, even if it is, the offeree incompetently dispatches the acceptance, say by addressing it wrongly, attaching insufficient postage, or putting the letter in a library book-return bin in the mistaken belief that it is a mailbox? If, as a result, the acceptance is never delivered or its delivery is delayed beyond the time that a properly dispatched acceptance should have arrived, the acceptance only occurs if and when the letter is received. However, if despite the use of an unauthorized medium or the error in dispatch, the transmission is not in fact delayed beyond the reasonable time for a properly sent acceptance, it is effective on dispatch. This is because the offeror has not in fact been harmed by impropriety in communication. For example, the offeror, being highly skeptical of the efficiency of the mails, calls for the acceptance to be handed to a private courier by next Monday, for standard overnight delivery. Disregarding this instruction, the offeree mails the acceptance on Monday. To make matters worse, the offeree garbles the offeror's zip code. In fact, the post office is much more efficient than the offeror thought, and it corrects the address and delivers the letter by Tuesday, no later than the private courier would have delivered it. The acceptance took effect on Monday because the offeror's expectation of delivery was not disappointed.

As noted already, the "mailbox" rule does not apply when the parties are in instantaneous communication or if a reasonable interpretation of the offer excludes it or does not allow use of that medium of communication. In addition, the rule does not apply in two other situations:

1.   The offeree loses the benefit of the rule if the **acceptance follows a counteroffer or rejection.** Say, for example, the offeree first decides against accepting and mails a rejection or counteroffer. Immediately afterwards, she changes her mind and mails an acceptance. It would be unfair to treat the acceptance as effective upon mailing because the offeror, upon receiving the rejection, would have no way of knowing that it had been countermanded by a later acceptance which has not yet been received. Therefore the rule changes, and the acceptance only takes effect on receipt, so that if it arrives before the rejection, the offer is accepted, and if it arrives afterwards, it is ineffective.

2.   If the **offer is irrevocable** (that is, it is an option for which consideration was given), Restatement Second §63(b) treats the acceptance as effective only upon receipt. The rationale advanced for this by Comment f to §63 is that irrevocability sufficiently protects the offeree, so the "mailbox" rule is not needed to safeguard the offeree's interests or to provide a dependable basis for knowing that the acceptance has occurred. Some courts are unconvinced by this reasoning and see greater merit in having a standard, predictable rule for all acceptances.

The "mailbox" rule usually works in favor of the offeree, but it could have a negative impact on her in some cases. Because the transmission creates the contract, the offeree who changes her mind and wishes to *revoke the acceptance* cannot countermand it by sending a rejection after the acceptance, even if the rejection reaches the offeror first.

§4.11.3 Summary of the Rules Concerning the Effective Dates of Communications

Before leaving the "mailbox" rule, it may be helpful to place it in the entire context of offer and acceptance. This section summarizes the different rules that govern each of the possible communications between parties when a non-instantaneous medium is used and no contrary intent is expressed. Remember that "receipt" means that the writing comes into the possession of the addressee or the addressee's authorized representative or it is deposited in an authorized place. The addressee does not actually have to physically handle it or read it.

The offer can obviously have no effect until known to the offeree. (But the period of acceptance could run either from receipt or from the date of manifestation, depending on the terms of the offer.)

A *rejection or counteroffer* is effective only when received. However, the rejection or counteroffer does have some impact immediately upon its transmission because it makes the "mailbox" rule inapplicable in the event that the offeree changes her mind and decides to accept after all. That is, if after sending a rejection or counteroffer, the offeree decides to countermand it and accept, her acceptance is effective only upon receipt, and it must be received before the rejection or counteroffer.

A *revocation* is effective only on receipt. (But if the offeree obtains knowledge of revocation indirectly, the offer lapses even if the offeror has not communicated the revocation.)

An *acceptance* is effective upon proper transmission by an authorized medium, unless it follows a rejection or counteroffer, in which case it is effective upon receipt.

§4.12 Acceptance by Promise or Performance: Bilateral and Unilateral Contracts

§4.12.1 The Distinction in Perspective

One issue arising out of the mode of acceptance always seems to confuse students: The distinction between offers leading to bilateral and unilateral con-

mains is for the offeror to perform the promise in the offer and to transfer title and possession of "Bleakacre." Because, at the moment of formation, only one of the parties has a promise outstanding, the contract is said to be **unilateral.**

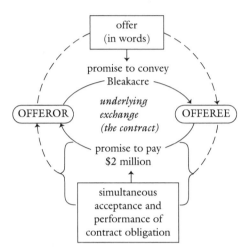

Note, therefore, that "unilateral" does not mean one-sided, in the sense that only one party has given or done something. As explained in Chapter 7, a transaction in which one of the parties has made a promise and the other has given or promised nothing in return lacks consideration and is not a valid and enforceable contract. Rather, the word "unilateral" signifies that although both parties have given consideration, only one of them has made a promise as consideration. The other has furnished consideration by rendering the required exchange performance at the very point of contract formation.

§4.12.4   *When the Offer Does Not Clearly Prescribe Performance as the Exclusive Mode of Acceptance*

In the last example, the offeror made it clear that acceptance could only be made by performance of the offeree's consideration, so there is no doubt that a unilateral contract was called for. In the occasional case, even in the absence of such clear language, the nature of the offer and the circumstances in which it is made compel the conclusion that nothing but performance of the consideration could qualify as acceptance. Perhaps the best common example is the offer of a reward. If the owner of a lost dog nails a notice to a pole offering $100 to anyone who finds and returns the cherished beast, it is hard to imagine that the offeror reasonably expected to be contractually bound to the first person who calls and promises to find the dog. Rather, the offeror appears to contemplate that the offer of reward is accepted only when a person shows up with darling Fido.

However, while an offeror could make an offer in a way that clearly permits acceptance only by performance, this is fairly uncommon. More likely, where acceptance by performance is feasible, the offer appears ambivalent on the mode of acceptance and does not clearly indicate this to be the exclusive mode. There are some older cases that devoted considerable energy to deciding if the offeror intended a unilateral or bilateral contract. This debate has largely been stilled in modern law as writers and courts have realized that an offeror who did not take the trouble to specify an exclusive mode of acceptance probably doesn't care exactly how the offer is accepted. Therefore, the general approach, as reflected in Restatement Second §32 and UCC §2.206, is to assume that unless the wording of the offer or the circumstances clearly indicates otherwise, the offeror is indifferent to whether acceptance is by promise or performance, so the offeree may choose to accept either way. As section 4.9 indicates, this approach is in keeping with the broader treatment of mode of acceptance.

For example, the offeror delivers an offer to the offeree on Monday stating, "I offer to sell you 'Bleakacre' for $2 million. If you wish to buy it, you must come to my office on Friday at 2 p.m. and pay me $2 million in cash." Clearly, it is a term of the proposed contract that the buyer's performance—the delivery of her consideration under the contract—must take place on Friday at 2 p.m. at the seller's office. However, the offer does not clearly restrict acceptance to the payment of money on Friday at 2 p.m. Therefore, if the offeree is anxious to close the deal immediately and to bind the offeror before Friday at 2 p.m., she could write to the offeror on Monday, stating "I accept." A contract immediately comes into existence on dispatch of the letter. The offeree has accepted by making a promise on Monday to perform as required on Friday, and the offeror's offer immediately becomes a promise to convey the property at some future (unspecified but reasonable) time. The early acceptance by promise creates a bilateral contract that binds both parties. The importance of this is that the offer has now become a contract, so the offeror is bound and has lost the right to revoke the offer.

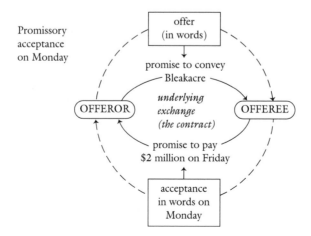

OR, at offeree's election:

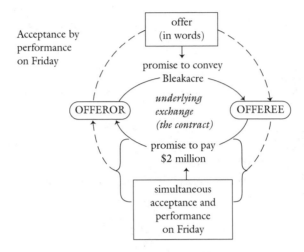

§4.12.5   When the Offer Does Not Clearly Prescribe Promise as the Exclusive Mode of Acceptance

Under the same principle, an offer that contemplates a promissory acceptance could be accepted by performance unless it is clear that acceptance can only be by promise. For example, the owner of "Bleakacre" wishes to clear some dead trees off the property to make it more attractive for sale, so she writes to a tree remover, "I need the two dead firs removed from my property as soon as possible and will pay $200 for the job. Please let me know this week if you wish to perform this work." Instead of replying, the offeree comes out the next day and removes the dead trees. The performance is an effective acceptance, creating a unilateral contract under which the owner has promised to pay $200. Although the offer contemplated a promissory acceptance, we can conclude that the offeror was indifferent to whether acceptance was by act or promise because the offer made it clear that removal as soon as possible was desired.

However, a different conclusion would be reached if the offer is for some future performance by the offeree, and it is not reasonable to believe that the offeror intended the offer to remain open for that long a time. For example, if the owner of "Bleakacre" had written in December, requesting the service in February, we can assume that she did not reasonably intend to be kept on a string until February and needs an earlier acceptance by promise.

Note that the conclusions reached here and in section 4.12.4 are really nothing more than an application of the general rules of interpretation used to find the reasonable intent of the offer with regard to the time and manner of acceptance.

§4.12.6 *Acceptance by a Performance that Cannot Be Accomplished Instantly*

In the examples concerning the offer to sell "Bleakacre," the offeree's contractual performance was cash payment, a single, relatively instantaneous act. Not all performance can be accomplished in one stroke. For example, "Bleakacre" is run-down and overgrown. The owner writes to her nephew, "If you come down and clean up the property for me this summer, I will be able to sell it for a good price in the fall and I will split my profits with you. You need not make a decision now. If you wish to accept my offer, just come down this summer and do the work."

If the nephew did respond early by making a promise, and the aunt thereafter revoked before the summer, we would have to decide if the offer called for acceptance only by performance. We would probably conclude that it did not, because neither the language used nor the circumstances reasonably indicate that performance was intended as the exclusive mode of acceptance. However, assume that the nephew did not make an early promissory reply and that the aunt did not revoke before the summer. The nephew comes down in early summer and begins the work of clearing the property. Before he has completed the task, the Aunt changes her mind about selling and revokes her offer. Traditional doctrine held that when an offer is accepted by performance, acceptance only takes effect upon completion of the performance, so that revocation is possible at any time up to point of completion. This presents less of a problem when the act of performance is the payment of cash or some other act that can be speedily accomplished, but when performance takes some time, the rule is obviously unfair because it places the offeree at great risk.

Modern law recognizes and protects the reliance interest of an offeree who has begun performance. Restatement Second §62 provides that if the **offer does not mandate acceptance by performance,** so that it can be accepted either by performance or promise, the commencement or tender[9] of performance is an **implied promise to complete the performance** within the time called for by the offer. Therefore, the commencement or tender of the performance is, in effect, an acceptance by promise creating a bilateral contract. In the present example, as soon as the nephew began work, a bilateral contract came into being under which he was committed to complete the work by the end of summer, and the aunt was committed to pay him half the profits from the eventual sale of the property.

---

9. A tender is an offer of performance by a party who is willing and able to begin it.

means of learning of his acceptance with reasonable speed and certainty. This notice is not itself the acceptance, which occurred as soon as performance began, but if it is not given (and the aunt does not otherwise hear of the performance) within a reasonable time, the acceptance becomes *ineffective* and the aunt's contractual duty is discharged.

§4.12.8   *Reverse Unilateral Contracts*

A reverse unilateral contract comes about when the offeree **accepts by promise,** but the **offeror's performance** occurs and is **completed** at the **instant of contract formation.** This is also a unilateral contract because only one party—the offeree in this case—has a promise outstanding at the point of contracting. For example, hearing that his friend is in financial difficulty, the offeror approaches the friend and holds out ten crisp $100 bills, saying "Here, I'll lend this to you for a year at 6 percent interest." If the offeree accepts by taking the money, he thereby promises to repay the loan on the offeror's terms. However, the offeror has no outstanding obligation because his performance was completed immediately upon acceptance. This type of contract presents no special offer and acceptance issues, and the offeree's response is subject to all the normal rules for acceptance.

EXAMPLES

1. Joe Kerr owns and lives in a handsome Victorian house that has been in his family for over 100 years. Every time that his friend Hume Orless has visited him, Hume has said, "Joe, I love your house. Please sell it to me right now." Joe has consistently answered, "Never!" After this had been going on for many years, Joe became irritated with it. As far as he knew, Hume had no money and had never been serious in his request to buy the house. It was simply mindless prattle. Joe decided to put an end to the annoying routine by shaming Hume into silence. He prepared a deed of sale that he placed in a drawer. The deed was on a real legal form that Joe had purchased from a stationer. He fully filled out all the blanks, included a price somewhat exceeding the market value of the house, and signed it. The next time Hume was at the house and urged Joe to sell it to him, Joe whipped the deed out of the drawer and exclaimed, "O.K. Hume. Put up or shut up! Sign this and the house is yours."

Instead of reacting with embarrassment and confusion, as Joe expected, Hume coolly read the deed, expressed satisfaction, and signed it. At first, Joe thought that Hume was playing along with him, but it is now clear that he is deadly serious and that he does have the financial means of buying the house. Joe has tried to convince Hume that the deed was intended as a bluff, but Hume refuses to accept that and insists that the transfer proceed. Joe is sick with grief at the prospect of parting with his beloved family homestead. Is he bound?

2. Professor Ivor E. Tower has spent the last three years working on his book entitled "How to Make an Ironclad Contract." The book is designed to give advice and instructions to lay people on effective negotiation and contract formation techniques. The book is finished at last, and Ivor is anxious to get it published. On July 1, he sent a copy of his manuscript to Sel Phelp Publishers, Inc., under cover of a letter that read: "I submit the enclosed manuscript for your consideration. If you would like to publish it, let me know by July 30. I want the book published as soon as possible, at least within this year. If you are willing to commit to this, I would be willing to give it to you on the customary terms, and expect the usual royalty of 15 percent of sales."

The editors at Sel Phelp read the book, which was a real page-turner. They decided that they would like to publish it. On July 24, Sel Phelp mailed a letter to Ivor, in which they accepted the book for publication, committed to have it published within the year, and enclosed their standard form contract for Ivor to sign. The terms in the form contract are those generally found in publishing contracts, including a royalty of 15 percent of sales. On July 25, before receiving Sel Phelp's letter, Ivor signed a contract with one of its competitors for the book's publication, and he immediately faxed a letter to Sel Phelp telling them that the book had been given to another publisher and was no longer available for publication by them. Ivor received Sel Phelp's letter later that day. Is Ivor now in the uncomfortable position of having made two contracts for the same book?

3. Kay Nine was going on an overseas trip for the month of July. At the beginning of June, she booked a space in a kennel for her dog, Pettodor. A few days later, she remembered that her cousin, Doug Sitter, a college student, often needed a place to stay during the summer. She thought that it would be a good idea if he could take care of Pettodor and her house while she was away. On June 10, Kay wrote the following letter to Doug:

Dear Doug,

I am going to be away from July 1 to July 30. I had planned to put Pettodor in a kennel, but it occurs to me that you may be free during July and may enjoy staying at my house for the month. You will just have to take care of Pettodor and keep an eye on things. In return, you will have free accommodation, and also, before I leave on vacation, I will give you $500 for food and other expenses.

I have booked the kennel, so I don't need to hear from you right away. If you would like to spend July here, just come down on June 29. If you are not here by the end of that day, I will assume that you cannot make it, and I will take Pettodor to the kennel on the 30th.

Best wishes,

Kay

Doug received Kay's letter on June 12. He had nothing to do during July and liked the idea of an all-expenses-paid month in Kay's house. He wrote back immediately telling her that he would be down on June 29. Doug mailed the letter on June 13, but he wrote the wrong zip code on the envelope. The post office was able to deliver it anyhow, but it was considerably delayed and Kay received it on June 20. In the interim, she had recalled what a slob Doug was and had changed her mind about having him live in her house. On June 21, she wrote back to him, telling him that she was going to kennel Pettodor after all, and no longer needed him. Doug received the letter on June 23. Doug feels aggrieved because he believes that Kay cannot simply back out of their arrangement. Is he right?

4. Art Walls owns a building whose exterior has been spraypainted by vandals with infuriating regularity. In an attempt to put an end to this expensive nuisance, he placed an advertisement in the newspaper on January 15, offering a reward of $1,000 to ". . . anyone who furnishes information leading to the arrest and conviction of those guilty of defacing the walls . . ." of his building. On January 16, the police arrested Fresco Furtive, a young man who was caught in the act of spraypainting another building in the neighborhood. Under aggressive questioning by the police, Fresco broke down and confessed to having committed several other acts of vandalism, including the spraying of Art's building. He was tried, convicted, and placed on probation.

Although Fresco was not aware of the reward offer at the time of his confession, he found out about it later that day. He claims the reward. Upon hearing this, Art is outraged. He says that he never intended to pay the culprit himself, and in any event, when he said "conviction," Art had a stiff jail term in mind and not some wimpy probationary sentence. Is Fresco entitled to the reward?

5. Assume that the police obtained no confession from Fresco Furtive. However, Fresco's nocturnal artistry had been observed by N. Former and I. Witness, two denizens of Art Wall's neighborhood who happened to be lurking separately in the area that night. Although neither of them are public-spirited enough to expose Fresco for free, they both happened to read Art's reward offer on January 15, and independently contacted Art to tell him who had vandalized his building. N. Former told him on the morning of January 16, and I. Witness told him that afternoon. As a result, Art filed charges and Fresco was arrested and tried. He was convicted of the offense and was sentenced to five years on a chain gang. Being completely delighted with this result, Art is happy to pay the reward. The problem is that both N. Former and I. Witness claim it. Art refuses to pay it twice and does not know who should receive the $1,000. To whom is he liable and for how much?

6. Last August, a country club held a golf tournament to raise funds for an organization called "Youth Golf America" that arranges and funds golf camps for troubled children. To support the charity tournament, the Caddy-Lack Golf Cart Co. donated one of its luxurious electric golf carts to be used

not precisely set. The court felt that the letter was more in the nature of a general solicitation calling for bids.

Similarly, in *Lonergan v. Scolnick*, 276 P.2d 8 (Cal. 1954), the defendant advertised some land for sale. The plaintiff made an enquiry in response to the advertisement, and the defendant wrote to him, briefly describing the property, giving directions to it, stating that his rock-bottom price was $2,500 cash, and concluding that this was a "form letter." After visiting the property, the plaintiff wrote to the defendant again, describing what he had seen and asking the defendant if he had been at the right place. He also requested a legal description of the property and suggested an escrow agent to be used if he decided to buy it. The defendant replied confirming that the plaintiff had found the right piece of land. He also provided the legal description, agreed to the escrow agent, and told the plaintiff that if he was interested, he must decide fast, because the defendant expected someone else to buy it in the next week or so. The defendant did sell it to a third party shortly afterwards and refused to recognize a subsequent purported acceptance by the plaintiff. The court found that none of the defendant's letters was an offer. The first was expressly described as a "form letter," and the second merely gave information while making it clear that the defendant intended to sell to the first comer.

Both *Nebraska Seed Co.* and *Lonergan* focus on the interpretation of the apparent meaning of the language used in the correspondence and give no indication that any contextual evidence was available to assist in establishing meaning. There is nothing to indicate that the courts were wrong in their interpretation, yet the language used is uncertain enough to admit of a contrary conclusion. A person who does not clearly express intent in negotiations runs the risk of being held to an offer when none may actually have been intended.

If Ivor did make an offer, Sel Phelp's response is likely to qualify as an acceptance. By leaving it to Sel Phelp to formulate terms in accordance with custom, Ivor implies into his offer an intent to contract on terms that are standard and usual in the trade. Provided that the terms in the standard form are indeed customary, they would not conflict with or add to his offer. With regard to the other terms regarding the publication date and royalties, the response is entirely in accord with Ivor's proposal. Ivor did not stipulate a mode of acceptance and transmitted his offer by mail. Sel Phelp's response by mail was therefore authorized, and the mailbox rule would apply, making the acceptance effective upon mailing. As a result, the revocation of July 25 was too late.

3. Doug is probably right. Kay's letter is surely an offer. It sets out the terms of the proposed transaction and gives the reasonable impression that Doug's acceptance will create a binding contract. The question is whether the offer was for a unilateral contract prescribing that the rendition of performance was the exclusive mode of acceptance. If it was, Doug's letter was

not an effective acceptance, and Kay's revocation was communicated to him before he had a chance to accept. Where an offer is for a unilateral contract, and the act of performance is instantaneous, acceptance occurs immediately that the act is performed. However, where performance cannot be instantaneous, but will take time—as in this case, where it spans a full month—acceptance is not complete until the performance is finished (on July 30). In the interim, an option is created in law as soon as Doug shows up at Kay's house on June 29, which protects Doug from revocation by Kay during the course of his performance. (As it is an option, Doug would have the right to cease performance at any time, thus terminating his act of acceptance and precluding the formation of a contract.)

In modern law, courts are not inclined to interpret offers as exclusively unilateral. This means that acceptance by promise is permissible unless an offer clearly prescribes performance as the exclusive mode of acceptance. There is no language in Kay's letter to signify that Doug can accept only by showing up at the house on June 29. In fact, the nature of a unilateral contract in giving rise to an option upon commencement of performance is inconsistent with her apparent intent. As she will be paying Doug in advance and relying on him to care for the dog, she could not reasonably have intended that he would not have been committed by an advance promise.

Doug's case is a parody of *Davis v. Jacoby*, 34 P.2d 1026 (Cal. 1934). An elderly uncle, in distress over his failing business affairs and his wife's illness, wrote to a favorite niece and her husband, asking them to come down to California from Canada to help him manage his finances and take care of his wife. In return, he promised them that they would be made the heirs of his and his wife's estates. The niece's husband replied, agreeing to come, and this undertaking was confirmed in further correspondence. While the niece and her husband were preparing to leave for California, the uncle committed suicide. They arrived there shortly afterwards and did take care of the aunt until she died. They then discovered that they had not been made heirs under either the uncle's or aunt's will. When they sued the uncle's estate in contract, the trial court held that the uncle's letter called for a unilateral contract, so it could not be accepted by promise and the nephew's letter was not an effective acceptance. Because an offer is revoked upon the death of the offeror, and the uncle died before the plaintiffs had arrived in California, they had never accepted the offer. The supreme court reversed, pointing out that the preference of the law is in favor of finding that an offer may be accepted by promise unless a contrary intent is clear. The uncle's letter was ambiguous as to the mode of acceptance, but it did contain language (". . . let me hear from you as soon as possible . . .") suggesting that a promise was contemplated. In addition, there was a close relationship of trust from which it could be inferred that the uncle would have been satisfied with a promise, and indeed, a promise would have been necessary to reassure him because he was concerned about the long-term care of his wife.

As Kay's offer did not require performance as the exclusive mode of acceptance, Doug's promise in his letter of June suffices as an acceptance. Because Kay made the offer through the mail, an acceptance via the same channel of communication is authorized, and the "mailbox" rule would apply, provided that the mailing was proper. Because Doug misaddressed the letter, the mailing was deficient and receipt was delayed, which deprives Doug of the protection of the "mailbox" rule. However, if a wrongly mailed acceptance does in fact reach the offeror, it is effective upon receipt. Kay received the offer before she communicated her intent to revoke, so the revocation is too late. A contract has been concluded, and Doug is justified in feeling aggrieved.

4. The advertisement clearly appears intended as an offer, so this issue does not require discussion. The most reasonable interpretation of public offers of reward is that they require acceptance, not by promise but by performance of the consideration called for—in this case, the furnishing of the information. If the confession qualified as an acceptance, it would have created a unilateral contract under which the only outstanding promise is Art's commitment to pay $1,000. As no time for acceptance was stated, the offer had to be accepted within a reasonable time. The next day surely is reasonable under the circumstances.

The issue is whether the confession could qualify as an acceptance. There are three arguments against treating it as such. First, Fresco was not aware of the offer when he provided the information. Even under the objective test, apparent acceptance cannot be treated as acceptance unless deliberate and made with knowledge of the offer.

In *Glover v. Jewish War Veterans of the U.S.*, 68 A.2d 233 (D.C. 1949), the Association published an offer of reward for information leading to the arrest and conviction of the murderer of one of its members. The mother of the girlfriend of one of the culprits was questioned by the police and furnished information that led to the apprehension and conviction of the murderers. As in the present case, she did not find out about the reward offer until after she had provided the information. The court held that her action could therefore not be treated as an acceptance. Her intent was merely to perform her public duty.

There is a cogent counter-argument to this approach. The rule requiring a conscious and deliberate manifestation of acceptance is intended to protect an offeree from an inadvertent manifestation of acceptance by ambiguous action. Therefore, if the offeree wishes the act to be treated as acceptance, the rationale for the rule falls away. The offeror, having made the public offer, has received what it wanted and should be made to pay.

Second, unless the offer was open for acceptance by Fresco, he has no power to accept it, even if his confession could otherwise qualify as an acceptance. As a general matter, an offer addressed to the public at large, and using the word "anyone," suggests no restriction on the class of possible offerees. Notwithstanding this broad scope, should it reasonably be understood that the offer is not open to the culprits themselves? There is no evidence of Art's intent on this issue or of pertinent custom, so the restriction would have to be implied in law as a matter of reasonable intent or on the basis of public policy. It could be argued that a restriction on acceptance by the culprit best serves the public interest by preventing the criminal from realizing a gain from the crime. A possible counterargument is that the reward is for the information, not the crime, and allowing the criminal to obtain it may encourage a confession.

Third, Art raises an issue of interpretation by contending that "conviction" requires a prison sentence. This is not convincing. Although the context in which words are uttered could have a bearing on their meaning, in the absence of evidence of some special usage, the interpretation of language is primarily based on its ordinary meaning. The conviction of a criminal is the determination of guilt in a court proceeding. The selection of the appropriate punishment is a distinct issue. If Art was concerned about a particular form of punishment, he failed to convey this in his choice of language.

5. There are three possible resolutions of this issue: Both informants accepted the offer and Art is liable to each of them for $1,000; both informants accepted and must share the reward; or the reward is due to N. Former only, because the offer was no longer open when I. Witness sought to accept. Art's offer is not clear on what happens if more than one person seeks to accept, so its reasonable intent must be ascertained by interpretation.

A person could make an offer in a way that permits multiple acceptances and thus many contracts. However, where it is clear from the offer that a single performance is all that the offeror needs, the more reasonable inference is that the offer is open to the first person who accepts by rendering the performance requested. Once that performance is given, the object of identifying and prosecuting the criminal is achieved, and it is no longer possible for another to give information that accomplishes the stated goal. If the condition of expiry is implicit in the offer, it is not necessary for the offeror to publish notice of revocation. Therefore, the best resolution is that the $1,000 must be paid to N. Former. (The possibility of sharing may have been presented if each of the witnesses provided only part of the information needed to identify Fresco, but that did not happen here.)

6. Believe it or not, something like this actually happened. This example embellishes the facts in *Cobaugh v. Klick-Lewis, Inc.*, 561 A.2d 1248 (Pa. 1989), in which a car dealer offered the prize of a free car for a hole-in-one hit during a charity tournament. The dealer failed to remove the display after the tournament, and a golfer who hit a hole-in-one demanded the prize. The facts of *Cobaugh* are somewhat easier than those in this problem because the sign

did not in any way suggest that the display related to a tournament, and it had not been removed between the fateful golf stroke and the claim of the prize. The court found that the display was an offer, reasonably understood by a person seeing it as being open for acceptance by anyone who performed by hitting a hole-in-one. Upon accomplishing this feat, the golfer accepted the offer and was entitled to the car. (The offer is for a unilateral contract because the dealer does not conceivably contemplate acceptance by promise.) Is Jock's case weaker because of the small print on the sign and the removal of the display before he claimed the prize?

The print was legible to anyone who troubled to stop and read it, so Jock is accountable for knowing what it said. He cannot claim that he thought the offer was open for acceptance if the smaller print would have signified to a reasonable reader that the offer lapsed at the end of the tournament. The language on the sign is not as clear as it could be. It does not expressly identify the tournament or confine the offer to it, but it does raise the possibility that the offer related to some charity event. A reasonable golfer, knowing the usual custom of offering prizes and promotions in connection with such tournaments, may well understand that the offer was no longer open for acceptance. If so, Jock has no claim.

The removal of the display is not legally relevant. If, contrary to what I suggest above, the wording of the offer does not reasonably indicate that it had lapsed, it had already been accepted by performance. Therefore, even if removal of the display could be treated as a sufficiently clear signal of revocation, it occurred after acceptance. When an offer is to be accepted by performance, it is the act of performance itself that creates the contract. If the act would not otherwise come to the offeror's attention, the acceptance falls away unless the offeree notifies the offeror of acceptance within a reasonable time. However, this is not a problem here because Jock did give immediate notice to Caddy-Lack's agent. A revocation between performance and reasonable notification is ineffective.

The most convincing resolution is that Jock failed to read the sign properly, and he should not reasonably have understood the offer to have been open for acceptance. He therefore cannot claim the prize.[12]

7. If Maggie's initial note is not an offer, there is clearly no contract because Minnie's responses would themselves be nothing more than unaccepted offers. However, Maggie's letter can reasonably be interpreted as an

---

12. There were two other issues in *Cobaugh* that are beyond the scope of the present discussion but are worth noting for future reference. One concerned the question of whether hitting a hole-in-one (a fortuitous event, beyond the control of the golfer) could really be treated as a detriment for the purpose of finding consideration for the promise of a prize. If it is not a detriment, the promise of the prize named would likely be treated as an unenforceable promise of a gift. The other issue involved is the question of whether the competition was an illegal gambling contract.

offer. It contains a specific proposal and appears to contemplate that a positive response by April 16 would conclude a contract.

Minnie's first response could be a counteroffer. If it is, it operates as a rejection, and the offer lapses so that there cannot be a later acceptance. However, the wording used by Minnie suggests that she did not intend an unequivocal rejection and counteroffer, but rather that she wished to explore the possibility of a change in terms. She appears to be negotiating an alternative while holding open the possibility of acceptance if Maggie refuses to budge on her initial demands. This being so, it would have been possible for Minnie to abandon her effort at securing more favorable terms and to accept the offer on April 16. Acceptance by mail would likely have been permissible because Maggie did not prescribe an exclusive medium of acceptance, and acceptance may be by any reasonable means. Also, as Maggie did not specify that acceptance would only be effective on receipt, the "deposited acceptance" or "mailbox" rule applies. The acceptance would have taken effect on April 16, as soon as Minnie deposited it in the mailbox, correctly addressed and stamped.

However, there are two reasons why Minnie's letter of April 16 does not qualify as an effective acceptance. First, it may not be an acceptance at all because it still does not completely correspond with the offer. It calls for Maggie to begin work two days later. Although this may be a minor variation, a strict application of the "mirror image" rule disqualifies it as an acceptance. The variation is less likely to be a problem if the less rigid "materiality" standard is used, because the change in dates may be too insignificant to be a material alteration of the offer's terms.[13] The problem created by the change in dates could also be overcome by interpreting the offer as impliedly authorizing Minnie to make minor adjustments in the dates.

A more serious problem is that the offer had been revoked before Minnie accepted it. Revocation is only effective when communicated to the offeree. Even if, as here, the offeror fails to communicate the revocation to the offeree, the offer may be indirectly revoked when the offeree obtains definite and unambiguous information from a reliable source that the offer is no longer open for acceptance. The case best known for establishing this principle is *Dickenson v. Dodds*, 2 Ch. D. 463 (Court of Appeal, Chancery Division, 1876). Dodds delivered a written offer to Dickenson for the sale of real property. The offer stated that it would be "left open until Friday 9 o'clock, A.M." Dickenson intended to accept but on Thursday, before he had signified his acceptance, he was told that Dodds had been "offering or agreeing to sell" the property to someone else. After hearing this, Dickenson immediately delivered his formal written acceptance to Dodds, but Dodds declined it, saying that it was too late and the property had been sold. Dickenson sued for an order compelling Dodds to deliver the property to him. The trial court

---

13. The concept of materiality is introduced more fully in section 6.5.2.

granted his relief on the basis that the offer had been accepted before Dodds had communicated his revocation to Dickenson, but this was overturned on appeal: Although Dodds did not communicate the revocation, Dickenson had indirectly obtained information that Dodds no longer intended to sell to him. (Although the headnote of the case suggests that the information was quite equivocal, the opinion accepts it as clearly indicating the fact that the property had been sold to another.) The court expressed its opinion in subjectivist terms, alluding to the fact that minds of the parties had not met. However, the real key to the case, which makes it relevant under an objective approach, is that Dickenson knew that Dodd's mind had changed. (The case also stands for the proposition that a promise to hold open an offer for a specified time does not bind the offeror unless consideration is given for that promise. This point is dealt with in Chapter 5.)

Applying this principle to Minnie's purported acceptance on April 16, we must conclude that even if it qualified as an acceptance, it was too late. Although Max may be insufferable, there is no indication that his information is unreliable. Max did not exactly say that Maggie's research for him would preclude her from working for Minnie as well, but this is certainly the tenor of his remark. The most reasonable interpretation is that Maggie was no longer available to perform and that her invitation to enter a contract had been withdrawn.

8. Flaky's arguments should be resolved as follows:

8(a). The usual assumption is that advertisements (including competitions designed to promote products) are not offers but merely solicitations for offers from the public. When a member of the public responds to the solicitation with an offer, the advertiser may then accept or reject it. Although this is what ordinarily should be understood, it does not mean that an advertisement can never be an offer. Like any other communication, its reasonable intent must be determined by interpretation. Therefore, an advertisement could qualify as an offer if it is clear, definite, and explicit; leaves nothing open for negotiation; and makes it apparent to a reasonable person that a commitment is intended without further action by the advertiser. (*See* Restatement Second §26, Comment *b*.)

In *Lefkowitz v. Great Minneapolis Surplus Store*, 86 N.W.2d 689 (Minn. 1957), a store published a newspaper advertisement stating "Saturday 9 A.M. Sharp 3 Brand New Fur Coats Worth to $100 First Come First Served $1 Each." (Lack of punctuation in the original.) The plaintiff was the first person to present himself at the store on Saturday morning. He tendered the $1 and asked for one of the coats. The store refused to sell it to him on the ground that it was a "house rule" that the offer was intended for women only. The next week the store placed another advertisement in the paper to similar effect, in which three items were listed for $1 each, "First Come First Served." One of the items was a "Black Lapin Stole Beautiful, worth $139.50." The plaintiff was again the first to show up at the store on Saturday and attempted to buy the stole. The store again refused to sell it to him because of the "house rule." The plaintiff sued for damages based on the difference between the value of the coats and the $1 price. The store contended that the advertisements were not offers but merely invitations to the public to make offers to the store. The court agreed that this may often be true, but the legal effect of the advertisement depends on the legal intent of the parties. When the terms of the advertisement are clear, definite, and explicit, and leave nothing open for negotiation, it qualifies as an offer. These advertisements were sufficiently firm to constitute offers, and they were accepted by the plaintiff. The store's "house rule" confining acceptance to women was not articulated in the offer and therefore did not restrict the power of acceptance. (The court did not address the fact that when the plaintiff sought to accept the second offer he had already been told about the house rule and therefore knew that the offer was not addressed to him.)

Although the court found that both advertisements led to binding contracts, it only awarded damages to the plaintiff for the second contract, measured as the difference between the contract price of $1 and the stated value of the stole, $139.50. The court refused damages for the first contract because the only evidence of the coat's value was the advertisement, which stated they were worth "to $100." The court said that this made damages too speculative. (This result also seems odd. The court could quite easily have held the store to its claim that the coats were worth "up to $100" and fixed damages under the first contract in that amount.)

Although there are some illogical aspects to *Lefkowitz*, it has been influential, and is still often cited by courts that must decide if an advertisement is an offer or a solicitation. If one goes behind the mechanics of the offer and acceptance rules in these cases, one senses that the real concern in many of these decisions is to hold advertisers accountable for what they appear to promise in advertisements. The court seems to have used the *Lefkowitz* rule to fire a warning shot at advertisers in *Harris v. Time, Inc.*, 191 Cal. App. 3d 449 (1987). Time made the mistake of sending a piece of junk mail to one Joshua Gnaizda, the three-year-old son of an attorney. The letter, inviting Joshua to subscribe to *Fortune* magazine, was contained in a window envelope. The text of the letter viewable through the window declared "JOSHUA A GNAIZDA, I'LL GIVE YOU THIS VERSATILE NEW CALCULATOR WATCH FREE Just for Opening this Envelope Before Feb. 15, 1985." The final sentence of this text was below the window and obscured by the envelope, but when opened, it could be seen to continue "AND MAILING THIS CERTIFICATE TODAY." Joshua's dad demanded that Time give Joshua a calculator watch without requiring a subscription, and, when it refused, he initiated a class action lawsuit on various grounds, claiming, inter alia, compensatory damages for the class of plaintiffs for the combined value of all the watches as well as punitive damages of $15 million. In addressing the cause of action based on contract, the court held the text of the mailer, as revealed through the envelope window, did constitute an offer. Like the store in *Lefkowitz*, it was clear in its terms, called for a specific act of acceptance (opening the envelope), and left nothing for further negotiation. The offer was therefore accepted by opening the envelope.

However, although the court found the existence of a contract, and hence potential liability for damages, it stopped short of imposing liability on Time. It upheld the dismissal of the case on the maxim "de minimis non curat lex"—the law is not concerned with trifles. In other words, the court considered that the proper response to junk mail is to throw it away, not to sue over it. It was therefore not anxious to reward the plaintiff. However, its finding that Time's promotion was an offer must surely have made an impression on Time and others who employ advertising of that type.

We cannot leave this discussion without alluding to the celebrated recent case, *Leonard v. Pepsico, Inc.* 88 F. Supp. 2d 116 (S.D.N.Y. 1999). Pepsi conducted a promotional campaign in which buyers of Pepsi products could earn "Pepsi points" from specially marked packages of soft drink, which could be redeemed for "Pepsi stuff" prizes. A TV commercial advertising the promotion showed various prizes (such as T-shirts and sunglasses) with the number of points required to win them. The commercial ended with a teenager landing a Harrier jet on the grounds of a high school. As he emerged from the jet, the words "Harrier fighter, 7,000,000 Pepsi Points" appeared on the screen. The commercial referred to a prize catalog that listed the prizes and contained an order form and instructions for redeeming the points. The catalog did not include a Harrier jet among the prizes. Its best prize was a mountain bike for 3,300 points. To obtain a prize, one did not actually have to earn all the Pepsi points by buying soft drinks. As long as 15 actual points were submitted with the redemption form, the balance of the points required for the prize could be purchased for ten cents a point.

The plaintiff, a self-confessed member of the "Pepsi generation," submitted a redemption form claiming the jet. He included the 15 original Pepsi points and a check for approximately $700,000 to buy the rest of the 7 million points needed. Of course, Pepsi refused to deliver the jet to him, pointing out that it was not part of the "Pepsi stuff" collection and was not included in the catalog. The jet was used in the commercial purely for humor and entertainment. The plaintiff sued on the theory that the commercial was an offer, which he accepted by properly submitting the redemption form. The plaintiff did not get past an application for summary judgment. The court distinguished this case from *Lefkowitz* and others that had found advertisements to be offers on the basis that the commercial itself was not detailed or specific enough. The full terms of the promotion could be found only in the catalog, which did not mention the jet. Furthermore, even the catalog could not be regarded as an offer because it had no words of limitation such as "first come, first served." No reasonable customer could believe that the advertiser intended to risk exposure to an unlimited number of offers. (Pepsi's argument that the use of the jet was merely a joke is discussed in Example 8(c) below.)

How should Flaky's promotion be interpreted in light of these cases? The cases show that in interpreting advertisements courts weigh two factors: On one side is the usual market expectation that few advertisements are intended to give members of the public the power to bind the advertiser simply by responding to the advertisement. However, if an advertiser uses language that reasonably indicates a willingness to give potential customers the last word on forming a contract, it could be bound immediately upon the customer's response. The crucial indicators of such an intent are clarity and completeness in the proposed terms of the transaction, and the absence of any language or circumstances that may suggest a reservation of the right to retain control over the process of contract formation. In addition, courts are mindful of the need to hold advertisers responsible to the public for promises made in their advertisements. Although false advertising is statutorily regulated, contract law can also serve as a means of policing misleading or extravagant assertions and imposing liability on those who make them.

Flaky's promotion is fully set out on the backs of its cereal boxes, which seem to describe the prizes with particularity (including an illustration) and to set out in detail the mode of responding and the performance required in exchange for the prizes. The boxes also specify an expiry date for responses and contain a limitation to protect Flaky from having to award more prizes than it has on hand. There seems to be nothing left for future resolution, so all that is called for is a response in the proper form. This may indeed be a case in which a court could find that Flaky's choice of language and format belies the normal expectation of a solicitation and creates an offer.

8(b). Flaky asserts that even if the box does create an offer, Manny could not accept it because it was open only to "boys and girls." This is a better argument than the store's claim in *Lefkowitz* because there is at least some basis for claiming that the limitation was expressed in the offer. However, even if "boys and girls" can be interpreted to mean "children," there is no language that restricts the offer to them or clearly excludes adults from claiming the prizes.

8(c). Flaky's next claim is that a reasonable person would understand that the leopard cub was not a prize, but included just a bit of hyperbole to attract attention to the competition. This argument is based on several grounds: the unsuitability of leopards as pets, the high number of box tops needed, and the huge discrepancy between the value of the cub and the cost of 1,000 boxes of cereal. This contention raises the aspect of the joke offer discussed in Example 1 and also raised in *Pepsico*. Even though the court disposed of the claim on the basis that the commercial was not an offer, it went on to address and readily accept Pepsico's argument that the use of the jet was merely for the purpose of humor. The court found that no reasonable person could have understood the commercial to be a serious offer of a jet but would have realized that the use of the jet was tongue-in-cheek, designed to add an absurd comic touch to the commercial and to exaggerate the excitement of the product. In addition, the fact that a Harrier happens to be a fierce war machine unsuitable for consumer use and costs some $23 million would alert the reasonable viewer to the fact that it was not really being offered in exchange for the equivalent of about $700,000.

Flaky's joke is certainly more apparent than that of Joe or Mr. Zehmer in Example 1, but not quite as obvious as that in the Pepsi commercial. Nevertheless, a reasonable cereal box reader (if such a creature exists) could have been alerted to the likelihood that this was not seriously intended to be part of the offer. There is at least a plausible argument that this was a joke, not a serious offer.

8(d). Flaky's final argument is that even if it did make an offer, it expressly stated that prizes were limited to quantities on hand, and it never had a leopard cub. This interpretation of the qualification gives it an evasive meaning that the advertiser should not be allowed to advance. A more reasonable understanding of the qualification is that Flaky has stocks of all prizes, based on a fair expectation of responses, but that it will be released from supplying prizes once demand for an item exceeds these expectations. To allow Flaky to claim that the language permits it to begin with no prizes of a particular kind would be to condone deceptive advertising. As noted in Example 8(a), courts are mindful of this issue when interpreting advertisements.

9. It was observed in section 4.2.1 that the offer and acceptance model, based on the concept of active bargaining between parties in person, can be quite remote from the way in which many contracts are actually created in the modern marketplace. Standard form contracting has long been recognized as stretching the model, but transactions through electronic media (particularly when part of the process is automated) strain it even further. Nevertheless, analogies can be drawn and common patterns exist no matter what process of contracting is used, so the concept of offer and acceptance can still serve as the basic framework for resolving electronic transactions. There are various ways in which we could analyze this transaction: We could find that Big Browser made an offer on its Web site to sell the camera, which Annette accepted by clicking the "confirm order" button. To reach a final conclusion on this, we would need to know exactly what language was used on the Web site. In the absence of language indicating an intent to give customers the power of acceptance, there is no reason to treat high-tech marketing differently from older means of publicity, in which the usual assumption is that a prospective seller merely solicits offers by advertising property for sale. If Big Browser's Web site does nothing more than solicit offers, Annette's clicking of the final "confirm order" button must be an offer. It surely meets all the criteria to qualify as such. If it is, a contract only comes into being once Big Browser accepts it. One could argue that the message thanking her and indicating shipment dates was an acceptance. However, if (as is probably true),

the message was generated automatically by the computer, it seems odd to think of it as an acceptance. (To treat it as such would be functionally to remove any volition from the acceptance and would be tantamount to saying that the Web site did indeed make an offer.) More likely, Big Browser will not have accepted until it responded consciously to the offer, either by a confirmatory e-mail or other communication, or by dispatching the camera. Again, this is based on what seems to be a reasonable expectation, but the language used on the Web site could lead to a contrary interpretation. If well advised, Big Browser would take trouble to reduce any uncertainty as to its intentions by making them clear on the Web site.

Finally, it should be noted that a legislature may regulate electronic commerce to control abuse and assure the security of transactions. It is therefore possible that traditional rules of contract law may be superseded by statute. However, in the absence of any statutory provision altering the general principles of contract formation, the existing rules of offer and acceptance are of use in analyzing transactions that could not even have been imagined when the rules were first devised.

5

Options and Firm Offers

§5.1 Introductory Note on the Application of the Doctrines of Consideration and Promissory Estoppel

It was noted in section 4.6.4 that an offer is revocable, even if it states that it will be held open for a stated term, unless it meets the legal requirements for an option or a firm offer under Ò Article 2. We now look at these legal requirements. Although options and firm offers may logically follow (or even be included in) the discussion of offer and acceptance, they can be difficult to understand without some knowledge of the doctrines of consideration and promissory estoppel. To minimize confusion, many casebooks defer this aspect of offer and acceptance until after those doctrines have been covered. For this reason, they are included in this short, self-contained chapter instead of being treated with offer and acceptance in Chapter 4. If your course is structured so that options are dealt with separately from offer and acceptance, you should return here when you reach this subject in class. For those who must tackle options and firm offers before consideration and promissory estoppel, this chapter has a brief preliminary explanation of those doctrines that should be adequate for present purposes.

§5.2 The Validity of Options at Common Law and Consideration Doctrine

An option is a **promise to keep an offer open for a stated period of time.** That is, the offeror undertakes not to revoke the offer for a specified pe-

101

riod, so that the offeree is assured of a set time to consider and respond to the proposal without the risk of its being withdrawn before the expiry date. As discussed earlier, an ordinary revocable offer does not bind either party until acceptance, and then binds them simultaneously when acceptance is properly communicated. However, an option binds the offeror to his promise to keep the option open, and in this sense he is committed before the offeree becomes bound. As soon as the option is communicated to the offeree, the offeror has no right to withdraw unless the offeree declines to accept in the prescribed time. The offeree is, of course, not bound until acceptance.

Under common law, an option granted for free is not binding on the offeror. This is because the common law does not treat a promise as contractual and binding unless the promisee has *given consideration in exchange* for it. As you will see in Chapter 7, the question of what constitutes consideration is complex. We cannot begin to explore that here. For present purposes it is enough to understand that in exchange for the grant of an option (the offeror's promise to keep the offer open and not revoke it for a designated period of time) the offeree has to give something to the offeror.

The most obvious "something" would be a cash payment or a promise to pay a specific sum of money for the option. But it could be a transfer of property or a promise to transfer or it could be something more abstract like the giving up of a legal right. Whatever form the consideration takes, the basic legal requirement is that the grantee must "pay" for the option by transferring or promising property or sacrificing a legal right in exchange for the promise to keep the option open.

Because an option is a form of offer, it necessarily contemplates that, if accepted, a contract will come into existence involving the exchange of performances contemplated by the offer. For example, if the offeror writes to the offeree offering to sell "Bleakacre" to her for $2,000,000, and giving her until next Friday to accept, the offeror contemplates an exchange of the farm for $2 million. Upon acceptance of the offer, the offeree promises to pay the $2 million, and that payment is surely consideration given in exchange for the farm. However, this consideration, exchanged under the contract proposed in the offer, is distinct from and does not also support the option itself. To be valid, the option must have its **own separate consideration**—the offeree must, in effect, purchase the option by providing an additional consideration, tied to the promise not to revoke. In the above example, if at the time of receiving the offer the offeree had paid the offeror

$100 in exchange for the promise to keep the offer open until Friday, the promise not to revoke would have qualified as a valid and binding option.

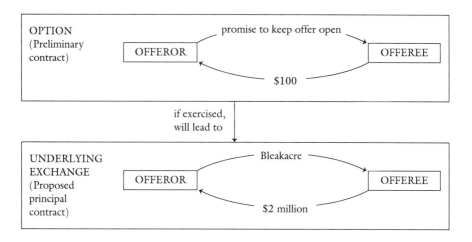

This rule requiring separate consideration for an option only applies in relation to the formation of a new contract—that is, when the option is a promise not to revoke an offer to enter into a contract. If an *option is granted within an existing contract*, it is part of the bundle of rights exchanged in the contract and is supported by the grantee's contractual consideration. This distinction may be illustrated as follows: As we just saw, separate consideration is required for the option where Seller makes an offer to sell the farm "Bleakacre" to Buyer for $2 million and promises to keep the offer open until Friday. The $2 million sale price under the proposed contract is intended as an exchange for the farm itself and is not consideration for the promise not to revoke until Friday. However, no separate consideration would be required if Buyer is the tenant of "Bleakacre" under an existing lease, and the lease contains a term granting Buyer the option of purchasing the property for $2 million at any time before expiry of the lease. This option is simply one of the rights purchased by the lessee under the lease and is supported by the consideration given by the lessee under the lease (such as the payment of rental). It does not need separate consideration to bind the lessor. This distinction may be shown as follows:

OPTION IN THE FORMATION OF A NEW CONTRACT

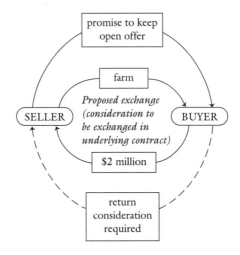

OPTION AS PART OF THE DETRIMENT EXCHANGED
IN AN EXISTING CONTRACT

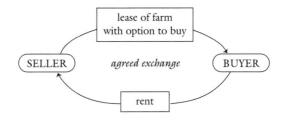

In the discussion of consideration doctrine in Chapter 7, the *rationales and justification* of the doctrine are explored. Without anticipating that discussion in any detail, we can note that two of the most significant roles that it plays are the protection of a promisor from his own (possibly ill-considered) generosity, and the provision of some formal and evidentiary basis for distinguishing a true contract from a mere non-binding expression of future intent. The requirement of separate consideration for an option is often not justified on the basis of either of these rationales.

Options are seldom intended as gifts and therefore do not commonly present the problem of protecting a donor from ill-considered generosity. They are more likely to be granted in connection with commercial exchanges in which the offeror anticipates receiving desired consideration in the ultimate contract. Therefore, although the option itself may be given without charge, this is typically motivated not by a spirit of giving, but by the offeror's desire to encourage the offeree to deal. When, in addition, the formal and evidentiary role of consideration doctrine is satisfied by a clear written and signed grant of the option, courts are hesitant to invalidate it by a rigorous and technical application of consideration doctrine. Therefore, if the option seems genuine and fairly bargained, the existence and terms of the option are evidenced by a written grant of the option signed by the offeror, there is no suggestion of underhand dealing by the offeree, and the term period of the option is not unreasonably long, a court is likely to try hard to find consideration provided that the grant gives it some basis for doing so.

Thus, where relatively short-term options are concerned, courts are much more likely to accept a purely **formal or nominal consideration** as sufficient. This means that if the option contract provides for a rather minimal payment or other performance of relatively small value, a court is likely to treat this as effective, even if the value of the payment or performance is patently lower than the value of the right to hold the offeror to the option. (If the offer is to remain open for a long period, the opportunity to speculate at the offeror's expense is greater, and the option therefore more valuable, so the apparent consideration is likely to be scrutinized more carefully.) This approach is reflected in Restatement Second §87, which acknowledges the judicial tendency to uphold an option that is couched in the form of an exchange, even if the consideration is purely formal. Section 87 requires the grant to be in writing signed by the offeror, to recite the purported consideration, and to propose an exchange on fair terms within a reasonable time.

Sometimes, purely for the sake of legal formality, the parties may recite a **sham consideration** for the grant of an option—that is, consideration is not actually given, but merely stated to have been given to make it appear that the consideration requirement has been satisfied. If the offeror later contends that the recited consideration was not actually given, a court may admit this evidence and refuse to enforce the option if the apparent consideration is shown to have been a sham. However, if the sham was not designed to perpetrate a fraud, and it was fairly agreed to purely for the sake of formally validating the option, many courts are reluctant to allow the offeror to renege on the option by contesting the presence of consideration.

Courts have used two approaches to avoid this result:[1] The first is to apply the doctrine of **estoppel** to preclude the offeror from denying that the consideration was given. Estoppel is explained more fully in section 8.4. It is a doctrine designed to prevent a person from asserting a right and taking a position that contradicts or is inconsistent with his earlier words or action on which another justifiably relied. In this context, it means that if the grantor of

---

1. This issue is taken up again in section 7.8, where it is considered in relation to nominal and sham consideration in transactions other than options.

an option signed a grant reciting that consideration was received, knowing that it was not, and having an understanding with the grantee that the recital was merely included for the purpose of validating the option, he cannot later defeat the offeree's reliance on this understanding by disregarding it and raising the defense that no consideration was in fact given. The effect of estoppel is to create the fiction that the recited consideration was in fact given. The doctrine of estoppel only applies when the offeror reasonably intended the offeree to rely on the statement or conduct and the offeree did in fact justifiably rely on it, incurring some loss or detriment. Therefore, unless the offeree can establish some form of prejudicial and justifiable reliance, estoppel cannot be used as a basis for overcoming the fact that consideration was a sham.

As an alternative to using estoppel, a court may accept that the recited consideration was not given, but may draw the inference from the recital that the parties intended it to be a *promise by the grantee to furnish* the consideration at some later time. By implying a promise to pay or deliver the consideration, the court gives the grantee the opportunity to tender the consideration at the time of suing for enforcement. If the recital was truly intended as a sham, the implication of this promise is also, in a sense, a fiction because it is not what was actually intended. However, the court may be willing to adopt this resolution because it is persuaded that by doing so it gives effect to the parties' true intent—to create a valid option. (This is an example of legal implication, or construction, discussed more fully in Chapter 10.)

§5.3   Reliance on an Option Without Consideration: The Application of Promissory Estoppel to Promises of Irrevocability

We have already seen one situation in which reliance on a revocable offer has created an option: Section 4.12.6 explains how the commencement of a noninstantaneous performance creates an option in favor of the offeree when the offer is for a unilateral contract. (That is, the offer requires performance as the exclusive mode of acceptance.) Although no consideration was given for this option (and indeed, there may not even have been an express promise to keep the offer open), an option is created by law to protect the reliance of the offeree in beginning the combined act of acceptance and performance.

Quite apart from this type of case, the doctrine of promissory estoppel has been used to create an enforceable option when *no consideration* was given for the promise of irrevocability. Promissory estoppel, discussed in Chapter 8, has developed as a basis for providing relief to a promisee under circumstances when a promise made does not qualify as contractual (because, for example, it lacks consideration), but the equities of the situation demand that the promise be enforced wholly or in part. To have a promise enforced under this doctrine, the promisee must establish that the promise was deliberately made with the reasonable expectation of inducing her to rely on it, that she did act (or sometimes, refrain from acting) in justifiable reliance, and that she suffered some detriment as a result. Once this is shown, the court has the discretion to achieve an equitable result by enforcing the promise fully or to the extent necessary to do justice.

When the promise in issue is an undertaking to keep an offer open, the offeree can use promissory estoppel to bind the offeror to honor that commitment only if she can show that despite having not given consideration for the promise of irrevocability, she was justified in relying on it.

For example, Seller writes to Buyer, offering to sell her farm "Bleakacre" to Buyer for $2 million and undertaking to hold the offer open until Friday. As noted earlier, the promise not to revoke the offer until Friday is not a binding option because Buyer has given no consideration for it. However, assume that Buyer intends to accept the offer by Friday. On Tuesday, believing he still has time to accept, he quits his miserable job in the city so that he can devote full attention to his new farm. On Wednesday, before Buyer has had the chance to communicate his acceptance, Seller revokes the offer. Buyer disregards the revocation and notifies Seller of his acceptance on Thursday morning. He claims that his reliance on the promise of irrevocability caused him to leave his job before accepting the offer, and if it is not enforced, he will suffer unfair detriment. Restatement Second §87(2) recognizes the possibility of applying promissory estoppel in this kind of situation. It sets forth requirements modeled on §90, the section that covers promissory estoppel generally (discussed in section 8.6).

Seller did make a promise to keep the offer open until Friday, and she must reasonably have expected that her promise in clear terms would in some way cause the buyer to rely on being able to delay acceptance until Friday. It also is apparent that Buyer did in fact take detrimental action on the assumption that the offer would remain open—he abandoned his job before securing his contract rights by acceptance. However, it is less clear that Buyer was justified in burning his bridges in reliance on a promise of irrevocability for which he had paid or given nothing. A court that is concerned about preserving the requirement of consideration for a valid option would be likely to require a stronger showing of justifiable reliance before enforcing the promise of irrevocability under the doctrine of promissory estoppel. But a court that questions the value of consideration doctrine in this context may be less exacting once it is convinced that the promise was in fact made with apparent serious intent.[2]

---

2. Courts are generally wary of imposing liability for promises made in the period of negotiation before contract formation. This issue is raised in connection with other types of precontractual promises in sections 8.5, 8.6, and 10.10.

§5.4   The Effect of an Option

As stated already, the principal effect of a valid option is to keep the offer open for the stated period. The offeree's power of acceptance does not expire until the end of that period and is generally not cut short by action that would terminate an ordinary offer. Most importantly, this means that the offeror *cannot lawfully revoke* the option prior to its expiration. It also means, at least in cases when the offeree has given valuable consideration for the option (as opposed to nominal or sham consideration), that the option does not come to an end if the offeree rejects it (or makes a counteroffer, which is effectively the same as a rejection) before the end of the option period. If the offeree changes her mind she is able to *countermand the rejection* by communicating acceptance before the end of the period. This rule is based on the premise that the grantee has paid consideration to acquire the effective option, which is a valid contract in itself. If so, rejection before the end of the option period amounts to a waiver of contract rights by the optionee, and such a waiver is unenforceable if the optionee did not receive new consideration for it. (This principle is expanded on in section 13.9, where modifications to an existing contract are discussed.) This rule is subject to a qualification: Although waiver needs consideration, the doctrine of *estoppel* may protect the offeror who reasonably relied on the rejection to his prejudice. Therefore, if the offeror has taken substantially detrimental action in reliance on a rejection (such as contracting with someone else for the same performance), the offeree may not reverse the rejection by later acceptance.

To accept an irrevocable offer, the offeree must *communicate acceptance* to the offeror within the option period. This usually requires that the offeror actually receives the acceptance because, as noted in section 4.11.12, some courts do not apply the "mailbox" rule to an option.

§5.5   Firm Offers Under UCC §2.205

In a sale of goods, §2.205 dispenses with the need for consideration to validate an option (called a "firm offer" in the section) under defined circumstances. The section only applies when all of its prerequisites are satisfied, namely:

1.   The offer to buy or sell goods must be made by a **merchant.** Under §2.104(1) a merchant is a person who deals in goods of the kind involved in the transaction or who otherwise, by trade or profession, represents that he has skill or knowledge in regard to the goods or the transaction. In essence, a merchant, as distinct from one whose dealings in the goods is casual or inexpert, is a

person who trades professionally in goods of that kind, either as seller or buyer. Although Article 2 does not in all cases provide different rules for merchants and casual buyers and sellers, there are some sections—§2.205 being one of them—that are applicable only to merchants or have stricter standards for them. Some of these sections are applicable only in transactions "between merchants," that is, if both parties to the transaction are merchants, but others apply if only one of them is. Section 2.205 fits into the latter category. For the rule validating firm offers to apply, only the offeror need be a merchant. (For further discussion of the merchant status, see section 6.5.2.)

2. The offer must be in **writing.**
3. It must give an **assurance** to the offeree that it will be held open.
4. If the assurance is contained on a form supplied by the offeree, the offeror must sign the assurance separately. (The purpose of this is to ensure that the offeror was aware of the term and is not bound by an assurance of irrevocability hidden in the offeree's boilerplate.)

If all these conditions are satisfied, consideration is not needed to make the offer irrevocable for the *time stated*, or for a *reasonable time* if no expiry date is specified. Section 2.205 limits the period of irrevocability to a *maximum of three months*, so that neither a stated time nor a reasonable time can exceed that period. Therefore, if the option is intended to last more than three months, the offeree must give consideration to validate it beyond the three-month period.

EXAMPLES

1. Shelly Shally had been negotiating with Reva Cation for the purchase of "Blandacre," an old farm now engulfed by suburban sprawl and zoned for housing development. By May 1, 1997, they had reached agreement in principle on the price and the other important terms on which the sale would be made, but Shelly could not decide if she really wanted the property. She said that she needed time to think about it. Reva realized that she would frighten Shelly off if she pushed too hard, but she sensed that given a little time, Shelly would probably decide to buy the property. Reva therefore agreed to give Shelly a short time to make up her mind. On May 1, she wrote out and signed the following document, which she gave to Shelly:

> It is recorded that Reva Cation is willing to sell her property "Blandacre" to Shelly Shally for $500,000, subject to the following terms . . . (the note then set out the material terms of the sale). If Shelly wishes to buy this property, she must notify Reva in writing by 5 P.M. on May 3, 1997. Reva undertakes not to sell the property to anyone else or to withdraw this offer before that date.

Shelly spent many sleepless hours agonizing over the purchase during the night of May 1. On the morning of May 2, she was pretty sure that she did want the property. She wrote a note to Reva accepting her offer, but decided that she would wait a little before delivering it to Reva, just in case she had second thoughts. Finally, on the morning of May 3, she decided finally that she would buy "Blandacre." She called Reva, and when Reva answered the phone, Shelly said, "Good news, I've decided to accept your offer. I am coming over right away with a written acceptance." Reva replied, "Sorry, I was offered a better price by someone else, and I've just sold the property."

Does Shelly have any recourse against Reva?

2. Would it have made a difference to the result of Example 1 if the last sentence of the written offer signed by the parties had instead stated, "In consideration for $1.00 received, Reva undertakes not to sell the property to anyone else or to withdraw this offer before that date"?

3. Assume that Reva had leased the property to Shelley for the period of one year at a monthly rental of $1,000. One of the terms in the lease gave Shelly the option to purchase the property for $500,000. To exercise the option, Shelly had to ". . . give written notice to Reva, to be received not later than 30 days before the expiry of the lease period."

On the fortieth day before the expiry of the lease, Shelly wrote to Reva informing her that she did not intend to exercise the option. Reva received that letter on the thirty-eighth day and immediately replied, acknowledging receipt and confirming that the option had lapsed. Shelly received the reply on the thirty-sixth day. Later on that same day, Shelly changed her mind and decided that she did want to buy the property. She wrote a second letter, countermanding the first and exercising her right to purchase the property. Reva received the second letter on the thirty-fourth day before expiry of the lease. Has Shelly bought the property?

4. Reva did not make any offer to sell "Blandacre" to Shelly. Instead, she planned to develop it herself. Because she did not intend to farm the land any more, she no longer needed her tractor, and she advertised it for sale. Harv Ester read the ad and came to see the tractor on May 1. He liked it, but wanted some time to decide whether to take it. Reva agreed to give him some time to make up his mind. On that day, she wrote and signed a note that stated, "It is recorded that Reva Cation is willing to sell her tractor [the model and make was described] to Harv Ester for $5,000 cash. If Harv wishes to buy it, he must notify Reva in writing by 5 P.M. on May 3, 1997. Reva undertakes not to sell the property to anyone else or to withdraw this offer before that date."

On May 2, Reva sold the tractor to someone else and notified Harv that she withdrew her offer. Can Harv refuse to recognize the revocation and accept the offer, thereby creating a binding contract?

5. In August, Lois Bidder, a building contractor, was invited by the owner of land to submit a bid for the construction of a new building. Lois was given until September 15 to submit the bid. To produce an accurate bid, Lois needed to know what she would have to pay plumbers, electricians, and other specialists to whom work would be subcontracted. On September 1, she sent the building specifications to a number of potential subcontractors and invited them to submit bids by September 13, explaining that she required the bids by that time to enable her to submit her own bid for the whole project on time.

S. Toppel Electricians, Inc. was one of the companies invited to bid on the electrical work. After studying the specifications, S. Toppel calculated the amount of material and labor required and submitted a written bid for $100,000. The bid stated: "This bid is open for your acceptance within a reasonable time after you have been awarded the prime contract."

Upon receiving the bid on September 13, Lois compared it to others received and saw that it was $20,000 cheaper than the next lowest bid. She therefore decided to use S. Toppel for the electrical work and included its figure in the bid to the owner. Lois submitted her bid on September 14, and the owner accepted it on September 15.

Lois immediately prepared letters to all the selected subcontractors, notifying them that their bids had been successful and that the project would proceed. Just before the letters were mailed, Lois received a fax from S. Toppel, stating that on checking its calculations after submitting its bid, it had discovered that it had mistakenly omitted the cost of electrical wire. As a result, its costs had been underestimated by $30,000 and it could not profitably perform the work for the bid price. S. Toppel apologized for the error, which resulted from having to get its bid ready in a rush, and regretted that it must withdraw its previous bid. It was willing, however, to perform the work for $130,000.

Lois faxed back, informing S. Toppel that she had already committed herself to the owner on the basis of electrical subcontracting costs of $100,000 and she considered S. Toppel bound by its original bid.

Is Lois justified in taking this position?

EXPLANATIONS

1. Reva's note is clearly an offer to sell the property to Shelly. It apparently sets out all the material terms on which she intends to enter the contract, and requires nothing more than a proper signification of acceptance to create a binding relationship. The offer contains an unequivocal promise that it will not be revoked. The problem is that Shelly has given no consideration to Reva for the promise to keep the offer open. A promise not to revoke an offer is treated as distinct from the underlying contract that would come into existence upon valid acceptance, so it needs its own separate consideration to

qualify as a binding option. Shelly cannot therefore argue that consideration for the promise of irrevocability is furnished by the $500,000 that she would have committed to pay for the property had a contract arisen. *Dickenson v. Dodds*, 2 Ch. D. 463 (Court of Appeal, Chancery Division, 1876) was used in Example 7 of Chapter 4 to illustrate the principle of indirect revocation: Before communicating his acceptance, the offeree had heard indirectly that the property had been sold to someone else. In that case, the offeror had also promised to keep the offer open for a stated time, but the court found the revocation to be effective because the offeree had given no consideration for that promise.

Shelly's case is a little different from *Dickenson*, in which the offeree heard of the revocation before making any communication of the intent to accept. Because she spoke first during the telephone conversation, Shelly did in fact signify her assent to the offer before Reva was able to tell her that the property had been sold. However, the offer clearly called for a written acceptance, and an oral acceptance by telephone does not provide the evidentiary protection of a writing and cannot be regarded as a mode of acceptance reasonably authorized by the offer. By contrast, the revocation need not be in writing, even though the offer was. As long as the revocation is in fact communicated to the offeree, it is effective and need not necessarily be in the same form as the offer. It is therefore too late for Shelly to rush over to Reva's place with a written acceptance. Finally, as Shelly took no action in reliance on the promise to keep the offer open, she has no basis for relief under the doctrine of promissory estoppel. The mere delay in acceptance on the strength of the promise is not in itself enough to constitute the type of detrimental reliance contemplated by the doctrine. (The type of reliance necessary is explored in Example 5.)

2. In this changed form, the grant of the option now records that consideration was given for it. We have no indication of what the actual economic worth may be of a three-day option to buy a piece of property for $500,000, but it is probably fair to assume that $1.00 does not and is not intended to bear any relationship to the option's actual value. Rather, it is inserted in the grant purely for the sake of formality. The parties know that consideration is required to validate the option, so they provide for it in a nominal amount for the purpose of showing their intent to create a legally binding promise. As a general rule, courts are willing to respect the parties' effort to validate an option by providing for nominal consideration, as long as there is no indication that the parties had the purpose of misleading someone else, or that the grantor was tricked or otherwise taken advantage of by the grantee. (When you deal with consideration doctrine in Chapter 7, you will recognize that this approach accords with the general principle that consideration exchanged by the parties need not be economically equivalent.)

The grant states that the $1.00 was received, but the facts do not indicate if this recital is true. If it is, we need go no further and can find the nominal consideration sufficient under the principle just discussed. However, sometimes the parties do not bother to actually transfer a consideration of nominal value and simply recite that it has been given. This is risky because if the $1.00 was not actually paid, the recital is a sham. If Reva reneges on her promise to keep the offer open, and Shelly tries to enforce it, Reva may challenge the validity of the option by arguing that the recital of consideration was false. Courts dislike the use of such a technicality to avoid a seriously-intended promise and commonly reject an argument of this kind, either by interpreting the recital as a promise to pay the $1.00 (so that the grantee can tender the $1.00 when suing) or by holding that the grantor is estopped from raising this defense. However, courts do not always take this approach. In *Board of Control of Eastern Michigan University v. Burgess,* 206 N.W.2d 256 (Mich. 1973), the defendant granted the plaintiff a 60-day option to purchase the defendant's home. The option contract acknowledged receipt by the grantor of "$1.00 and other valuable consideration," but it was conceded that neither the dollar nor any other consideration had been paid or tendered. When the grantor revoked the offer and refused to recognize the grantee's subsequent attempt to exercise the option, the grantee sued. The court found that no valid option had been created. The recital in the grant merely created a rebuttable presumption that consideration had been given, and the grantor could overturn that presumption by evidence that it had not been. The court refused to apply estoppel to preclude the defense because estoppel requires a showing of prejudicial action in reliance on the grantor's conduct, and no such reliance was established.

3. Here the option is not a self-standing promise by Reva to keep an offer open. Rather, it is one of the obligations she has assumed under the lease with Shelly in exchange for Shelly's consideration—her promise to pay the monthly rent. It is part of the collection of rights that Shelly has purchased under the lease and is enforceable like any other term of the contract. It needs no separate consideration.

In terms of the lease, Shelly had until 30 days before the expiry of the lease term to exercise her option. Ten days before this deadline, she sent a letter informing Reva that she did not intend to buy the property—in effect, rejecting the offer to sell. Her letter was received and acknowledged in writing by Reva. Had this been an ordinary offer, it would have been effectively terminated before Shelly changed her mind and decided to accept. However, when a grantee has purchased a valid option by giving consideration for it, a contract exists. As you will see in sections 7.5 and 13.9, an agreement to modify a contract or to give up rights under it is itself a contract and requires consideration to be binding. Therefore, if one of the parties gives up contract rights without receiving any consideration in exchange, the disavowal of rights does not bind her. The effect of this is that even though Reva accepted Shelly's relinquishment of her right to exercise the option, she gave Shelly no consideration in exchange for it. Shelly was therefore not bound by her abandonment of the option, and her subsequent letter was an effective exercise of the option. (There is an exception to this rule if the grantor took detrimental action in reliance of the rejection of the option, say by committing herself to sell to someone else. However, that did not happen here.) The "mailbox" rule does not apply to the acceptance of an option, but on our facts this creates no problem for Shelly because the letter exercising the option was received by Reva before the end of the option period.

4. As in Example 1, the offeree has given no consideration for the promise to hold the offer open. At common law, Reva's promise not to revoke would not bind her, and her revocation would be effective. However, this is a sale of goods, so if the requirements of UCC §2.205 are satisfied, the promise is binding as a firm offer despite the lack of consideration.

Section 2.205 only applies if the offeror is a merchant. (It is not necessary that the offeree be a merchant as well.) There may be a basis for finding that Reva is a merchant with regard to the tractor sale, but whether she has sufficient work-related expertise in transactions of this kind to qualify as a merchant under §1.104(1) is a question of fact that cannot be finally decided on the scanty information furnished here. She had apparently been farming "Blandacre" until recently, and had used the tractor for that activity. A farmer (even one who is disposing of the farm and its equipment) may qualify as a merchant with regard to farming implements, not necessarily because she deals in goods of that kind with any frequency, but because, by her occupation, she holds herself out as having knowledge or skill in relation to the goods or the transaction. The issue, in essence, is whether she has sufficient sophistication and knowledge of the trade to be subject to Article 2's more exacting rules for "professionals."

If Reva does satisfy the definition of a merchant, the offer is binding on her as a firm offer until its stated expiry time of 5 P.M. on May 3, because it meets the other requirements of §2.205: It is in a writing signed by her, and it gives assurance that it will be held open for a stated time, not exceeding three months. Harv may therefore ignore the attempted revocation and accept the offer before the time for acceptance lapses. This will create a binding contract. (Although Harv will not necessarily be able to compel Reva to deliver the tractor, he will be able to claim any money damages suffered as a result of the breach.)

5. Undoubtedly, Lois was not making an offer by soliciting bids, but was inviting a number of competing subcontractors to submit offers. It also seems clear that S. Toppel's bid was intended as and understood to be an offer. Although Lois used the offer in calculating her own bid, she did not accept it immediately. This is understandable, because Lois would not have wished to commit herself to S. Toppel until she knew that she had been

awarded the construction contract. (Indeed, S. Toppel appears to have understood this by holding the bid open until a reasonable time after that event.) The problem is that before Lois had a chance to communicate her acceptance, S. Toppel revoked the offer. Under the general rules of offer and acceptance, the revocation is effective. S. Toppel's undertaking to keep the offer open is not a valid option because Lois gave no consideration for it. (One may be tempted to argue that she did give consideration for the promise of irrevocability by impliedly promising to use the bid if S. Toppel was the lowest bidder. However, this is a real stretch, because there is no indication that Lois intended to bind herself to use the lowest bid.)

As there is no consideration to validate the promise not to revoke, it can only be made binding if relief is available under the doctrine of promissory estoppel. This raises two issues: Is it appropriate to use promissory estoppel to validate a promise not to revoke an offer? If it is, are the elements of promissory estoppel satisfied?

A. Is Promissory Estoppel Appropriate?

The facts in this example quite closely follow those in two well-known cases which reached polar opposite results. In *James Baird Co. v. Gimbel Bros., Inc.*, 64 F.2d 344 (2d Cir. 1933), Judge Learned Hand held that the contractor could not hold the errant subcontractor to its bid. In *Drennan v. Star Paving*, 333 P.2d 757 (Cal. 1958), Justice Traynor held that it could. Although there are some factual differences between the cases, the opposite outcomes reflect different approaches to the legal principles. Hand refused to apply promissory estoppel to make the bid irrevocable, while Traynor considered the doctrine to be appropriate for this purpose.

Both courts accepted that the subcontractor's bid was an offer that had not been accepted by the prime contractor before it had been revoked. Mere use of the bid was not sufficient to constitute acceptance, because in neither case did the offer dispense with the usual requirement that acceptance must be communicated to the offeror to be effective. The bid was withdrawn before this communication took place. The courts also shared the view that under traditional principles of offer and acceptance, the absence of consideration precluded the creation of a valid option. Therefore, in both cases, the only basis on which the offer could be held irrevocable was promissory estoppel. Hand was unpersuaded by the argument that the contractor's reliance should make the offer irrevocable. He questioned whether promissory estoppel should extend beyond the validation of donative promises. However, even if it was appropriately used in commercial cases, he felt that the contractor's reliance on the unaccepted offer was not justified. It would have been easy for the contractor to protect itself by doing some advance planning. It could, for example, have purchased an option by giving consideration, or it could have negotiated for an escape clause in the contract, permitting termination if it failed to obtain the prime contract. As it chose simply to rely on the bid without taking these precautions, it took the risk of committing itself before securing its sub-contract.

Traynor saw no reason to confine promissory estoppel to donative promises, but recognized the protection of justifiable reliance as a general value of contract law. He argued that the creation of an option to protect reliance on a promise not to revoke is analogous to that granted as a matter of law when an offeree commences a non-instantaneous act to accept an offer for a unilateral contract. If the law is willing to uphold reliance in that situation, it should equally do so in this one.

In part, the approach in *James Baird Co.* can be explained by the fact that the case is quite old and was decided at a time when promissory estoppel had not been much recognized outside situations involving reliance on the promise of a gift. However, the case also reflects a concern shared by many modern courts, that the application of promissory estoppel to the formation process is too intrusive. Unless an option is purchased, the assumption should be that a party does not intend to be bound before the contract is concluded, and action taken by the other in anticipation of the contract is usually at the actor's risk. The possibility that a court may decide to shift that risk by applying promissory estoppel could inhibit negotiations and undermine the reasonable expectations of the alleged promisor. The approach in *Drennan,* adopted by Restatement Second §87(2), is mindful of this concern but considers it manageable if promissory estoppel is applied carefully to avoid an overly liberal enforcement of tentative or prospective promises, while leaving room for relief where justice demands it. The doctrine must be used selectively to give relief only where the commitment is genuine, the reasonable expectation of inducing precontractual reliance is clear, and the promisee was justified in undertaking serious detriment on the strength of it.

B. If Promissory Estoppel Is Applicable, Do the Facts Satisfy Its Elements?

In *Drennan,* the court emphasized the commercial context of the bidding process and the reasonable understanding of the parties in entering the transaction. Two of the crucial factors to be considered in deciding the offeror's accountability and the offeree's reasonable reliance are any prior dealings between the parties, and common practice in the industry. If the usual practice between the parties or in the industry is for prime contractors to rely on bids in this way, Lois has a strong case for enforcing the promise to hold the offer open. If the practice is the opposite, and the assumption is that no subcontractor is bound unless an option has been purchased for consideration, it would be difficult for Lois to claim that she was not taking a risk in relying on an unaccepted offer.

If there is no clearly established general usage or course of prior dealing either way, the resolution is less certain. However, *Drennan* makes a good argument for relief based on the structure and purpose of the transaction itself:

S. Toppel knew that Lois's purpose in soliciting bids before submitting her own bid was to obtain the basis of formulating her price to the owner. The wording of S. Toppel's bid suggests that it did not expect to be notified of acceptance unless Lois both selected its bid and was then successful in being awarded the prime contract. S. Toppel must also have understood that once Lois's bid was accepted, she would be committed to the owner. If Lois could not rely on the irrevocability of the subcontractor bids used in her calculations, she would take a serious risk in making a commitment to the owner. Therefore, by submitting a bid, S. Toppel seems to have contemplated that it would be used in the way as it was, with Lois incurring potential detriment before formal acceptance. This satisfies both the elements of promise and reasonable intent to induce reliance.

Lois did rely on the bid. This reliance is justifiable if Lois was reasonable in understanding that a promise was made with the intent of inducing reliance of this kind. As suggested above, such an interpretation is reasonable given the nature and wording of the offer. However, there is a further factor to be considered: S. Toppel's price was $20,000 lower than that of its closest competitor. Even if Lois did not have any idea of the approximate cost of the electrical work, this fact could have alerted her to the possibility that there was something wrong with the price calculation in the offer. If she had reason to believe that the apparent promise was motivated by an error, her reliance should not be regarded as justifiable. It is not genuine, but a pretext for taking advantage of the offeror's mistake. It is not certain that a reasonable offeree would suspect an error because there could be many explanations of discrepancies between bids. However, to justify her reliance, Lois must explain why she was not placed on inquiry. (I have raised this issue of the palpability of the error under the head of justifiable reliance. However, it could just as well be addressed in dealing with the justice of enforcing the promise, because it affects the equities of enforcement.)

If the other elements are satisfied, we reach the selection of remedy. This is not a situation in which we are concerned only with the reimbursement of out-of-pocket expenses. The only meaningful remedy is therefore full enforcement of the promise to keep the offer open. If this relief is granted, a binding contract was formed provided that Lois accepted the offer within a reasonable time after the award of the prime contract. This appears to have happened. Immediately after being awarded the prime contract, Lois prepared her acceptance. On hearing of S. Toppel's desire to revoke, she responded without delay by notifying S. Toppel of her intent to accept. As a result, S. Toppel is contractually bound to Lois, and if it refuses to perform at the bid price, it will be liable for damages for breach of contract.

6

Offer and Acceptance Under the UCC, and the "Battle of the Forms"

§6.1 General Principles of Offer and Acceptance in the UCC

UCC §1.103 states that unless they are displaced by particular provisions of the Code, the general principles of common law apply to transactions governed by the Code. UCC Article 2 says very little about the process of offer and acceptance, so the formation of a sales contract is largely subject to the common law rules discussed in Chapter 5. While Article 2 defers to the common law on most offer and acceptance issues, it does strongly encourage courts to be realistic and to keep an eye on business practice in resolving formation disputes. As Chapter 5 indicates, this flexibility has spread beyond the UCC and is reflected in the modern common law approach to offer and acceptance generally.

The two Code sections that most directly address general formation issues are §§2.204 and 2.206. Narrower formation topics are covered in §2.207 (discussed in the remainder of this chapter) and §2.205 (discussed in section 5.5). The fundamental point made by §2.204 is that the court should *focus on the existence of agreement* between the parties, whether shown

119

by words or conduct, and if agreement is apparent, the court should *not be concerned about technicalities* but should do what it can to uphold and enforce the contract. Section 2.206 eschews technical rules on the manner and medium of acceptance and emphasizes that an offer should be interpreted as inviting acceptance by any reasonable mode unless the offer or circumstances make it clear that the mode is restricted.

§6.2   The Scope and Purpose of UCC §2.207

In dealing with the common law "mirror image" rule, section 4.8.1 stated that UCC §2.207 abolishes the rule and provides a different means of resolving conflicts in communications between the parties. Do not forget that UCC Article 2 governs only sales of goods. Although §2.207 has had some influence over the common law approach to nonconforming responses to offers, it is not directly applicable to contracts other than sales of goods.

Section 2.207 is implicated whenever one or both parties use written communications in the process of forming a contract for the sale of goods. Often, but not always, these writings are on preprinted forms that contain standard terms known as **"boilerplate."** (That is, they are standard provisions commonly employed in contracts of that kind.) As may be expected, the standard terms used by a party are usually designed to protect the interests of that party, so if seller and buyer both use standard terms, a conflict between them is likely. Because standard forms are so common, many §2.207 cases are concerned with resolving disparities between them—hence the nickname, **battle of the forms.**

§6.3   The Problem Tackled by §2.207: The Common Law "Mirror Image" and "Last Shot" Rules

The premise of §2.207 is that common law offer and acceptance rules are based on a model of individualized bargaining that does not fit the reality of most modern sales transactions. Buyers and sellers do not typically haggle over all the terms of the sale but focus on the essentials such as the description, price, and quantity of the goods. The remaining details of the contract may be left to custom or practice or they may be set out in a written order, acknowledgement, or confirmation. The use of preprinted forms is very common today, so these writings are often standardized and, as stated earlier, are designed to protect the interests of the party who produced them. In most cases, standard forms do not create problems. Even if there are conflicts in detail, the buyer and seller focus on the heart of the sale itself and do not even notice the discrepancy. The goods and money change hands, and the sale is completed without any dispute. But every so often something happens in a transaction that causes a party to lay claim to a right tucked away in the obsidian recesses of its document.

For example, Buyer sends Seller a written order for a Louden LeThal Model XZ100 Rivet Gun, for a price of $450, C.O.D. delivery in 30 days. The order is on Buyer's form that contains a preprinted indemnity provision, stating that if anyone suffers injury in operating the gun and successfully sues Buyer, Seller shall indemnify Buyer by paying the judgment and Buyer's legal fees. On receipt of the order, Seller immediately sends an acknowledgement that accords with the order in all respects, except that it also contains a preprinted indemnity provision that says exactly the opposite, requiring Buyer to indemnify Seller for any such claims that may be made against Seller.

It could happen that no problem ever arises to bring this conflict to light. Delivery and payment occur and the machine is used without incident, so that no one ever has to worry about the opposing indemnities. However, one of two things could have gone wrong in the transaction, making the discrepancy crucial.

1. One of the parties may wish to escape the transaction prior to delivery. Upon discovering the divergence between offer and acceptance, it may use it as the basis for asserting that no contract came into existence. In other words, the conflict between the writings could provide a **pretext for reneging** on the contract.

2. If this does not happen and the machine is delivered, one of Buyer's workers may be injured in operating it. At this point a dispute arises on the allocation of liability under the contract. The conflict in the writings would have to be resolved to decide **whose term** (if either) **became part of the contract.** This is, of course, not a dispute about the existence of a contract but about its content.

Under common law, these issues would be decided under the "mirror image" and "last shot" rules. Under the **"mirror image"** rule, Seller's nonconforming response prevents the acknowledgement from being an acceptance and makes it a counteroffer. Even if the parties thought that they had a contract, none came into existence upon sending of the acknowledgement, and if either party wishes to renege before performance, this could be done with impunity.

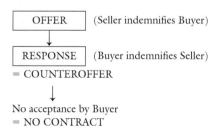

If neither seeks to escape the contract and the rivet gun is shipped and accepted by Buyer, Buyer's conduct in accepting it is an implied acceptance of the counteroffer, whether or not Buyer read Seller's reply. As a result, a contract is created subject to Seller's term, purely because Seller's was the **"last shot,"** that is, the last communication before acceptance of the goods.

The drafters of the UCC considered this result to be unduly rigid and unrealistic, especially where the conflicting terms are in standard forms. It fails to take into account that the parties really were in agreement over the essential terms of the contract, and the reply was in fact intended as an acceptance. It places too much store on a clash of boilerplate terms that are unlikely to be read. To treat the term as creating a counteroffer therefore ignores commercial reality and produces the wrong result by facilitating dishonor of the agreement up to the time of performance and by imposing an unexpected term on the offeree thereafter.

To rectify this problem, §2.207 attempts a twofold approach:

1.   It rejects the "mirror image" rule. If a response can reasonably be interpreted as an acceptance, it is recognized as such despite a variation from the offer. A contract is therefore created and the door is closed on a party who later wishes to renege. Except in narrow circumstances, the conflicting term in the acceptance falls away and does not become part of the contract.

2.   It rejects the "last shot" rule. If the response cannot fairly be interpreted as an acceptance and it is a counteroffer, subsequent performance is not deemed an acceptance by conduct. Therefore, although a contract is recognized by virtue of the mutual performance, it is not simply on the terms set out in the last communication. Rather, conflicting terms fall away and are replaced by supplementary terms in the UCC.

While §2.207 does reform these deficiencies in the common law, it has problems of its own. It is generally acknowledged to be poorly drafted, difficult to apply, and capable of achieving results just as arbitrary as those under common law. Many proposals have been made for the amendment of the section, and the Permanent Editorial Board of the UCC has been studying possible changes for some time. A redrafted provision will no doubt be proposed to state legislatures at some time in the future. Until an amended §2.207 is enacted, the current provision, ugly and misshapen as it may be, is the law. Even if we cannot learn to love it, we must try to cope with it.

§6.4 "Expression of Acceptance" and "Confirmation," the Two Distinct Situations Covered by §2.207

So far, we have considered only the offer and acceptance implications of §2.207, and indeed, most of this chapter focuses on that aspect of the section. However it is important to recognize that §2.207 has another application. One of the confusing things about §2.207 is that it does an awful job of keeping its two facets separate, and it tries to talk of both in the same breath. It is concerned not only with the question of whether a reply to an offer is an acceptance but also with cases in which, after an oral or informal agreement is reached, one or both parties sends off a written confirmation with terms different from or additional to those orally agreed. These situations present different issues:

a. Offer and Acceptance

In evaluating the effect of a reply to an offer, one is dealing with the usual offer and acceptance enquiry: Was a contract formed, and if so, what are its terms?

b. Confirmation

In considering the effect of a confirmatory memorandum following an oral or informal agreement, one is no longer concerned with offer and acceptance because this has already occurred and the contract has come into existence.[1] The issue here is whether a party's post-formation addition or change should

---

1. As discussed in Chapter 11, if the price of the goods is $500 or more, the sales contract must be memorialized in a signed writing to satisfy the statute of frauds. Therefore, an oral contract for $500 or more, while a valid contract, cannot be enforced until reduced to a writing sufficient to satisfy the statute of frauds. We need not be concerned with this for present purposes because although the oral contract may not yet be enforceable, it is in existence and any subsequent communication must be treated as a confirmation rather than an acceptance.

be given any effect. The general rule at common law is that neither party can unilaterally modify the contract simply by sending a writing with new terms to the other. Although §2.207 basically follows this rule, it does give effect to such alterations in limited circumstances.

This chapter treats these two situations separately. Offer and acceptance issues are discussed in section 6.5 and confirmations are covered in section 6.6.

§6.5   Offer and Acceptance Under §2.207

§6.5.1   Section 2.207(1): Acceptance, Rejection, and Counteroffer

The language of §2.201, relating to offer and acceptance, may be charted as follows:

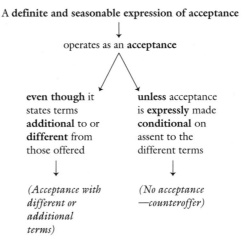

A definite and seasonable expression of acceptance

operates as an **acceptance**

even though it states terms **additional** to or **different** from those offered	**unless** acceptance is **expressly** made **conditional** on assent to the different terms
(Acceptance with different or additional terms)	*(No acceptance —counteroffer)*

a.   The Offer

Section 2.207(1) provides no guidance on whether the initial communication qualifies as an offer. This question must be resolved under the *general common law principles* set out in section 4.4. Once an offer is established under common law, §2.207(1) concentrates on the question of whether or not the response is an acceptance. It abolishes the "mirror image" rule, so the response to the offer need not match it exactly to be an acceptance. Instead, a fact-based approach is adopted to distinguish a reply that is clearly not an acceptance (so it can fairly be interpreted at best only as a counteroffer) from a reply that really is an acceptance with terms at variance with the offer. The following diagram illustrates this dichotomy:

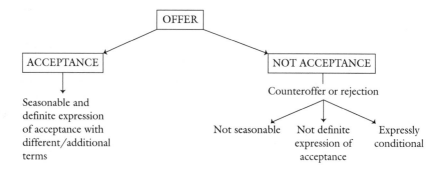

b. Replies that Are Not an Acceptance

If the response is clearly **not a definite expression of acceptance** or if it is sent after the offer has lapsed (that is, it is **not "seasonable"**) or if it **expressly states that acceptance is conditional on assent to its new terms**, then it is a rejection or counteroffer.

For example:

1. Buyer writes to Seller offering to buy a Louden LeThal rivet gun for $450, C.O.D. delivery in 30 days and requiring acceptance by Friday. If Seller sends an acceptance on the following Monday, the acceptance is not seasonable and hence ineffective.

2. Similarly, there is no acceptance, even if Seller responds in time, if the response states "Thank you for your order. Unfortunately we no longer stock Louden LeThal products, but we have a similar rivet gun made by Fierce & Fearsome which you can have on the same terms." The response proposes a sale of goods different from those ordered. This divergence from the transaction-specific terms in the offer cannot fairly be viewed as an expression of acceptance.

3. Even if the variation is not that central to the performance requested in the offer, the response is not an acceptance if it specifies that acceptance is conditional on the offeror's assent to some new or altered term. So Seller makes a counteroffer if it returns a timely acknowledgement in accord with all Buyer's proposed terms, but with the added provision: "Your order is accepted on condition that you agree to indemnify us for any claims of injury arising out of the use of the goods described above." This expressly conditional assent could be contained in preprinted standard language. Even if it is, §2.207(1) apparently gives effect to

it. This is ironical because the purpose of §2.207 is to underplay the effect of boilerplate. As mentioned in section 6.5.2, this is not the only instance in which §2.207 can be interpreted as adopting an inconsistent approach to standard terms.

As under the common law, a counteroffer terminates the offeree's power of acceptance and creates a new power of acceptance in the former offeror. If the offeror elects to exercise that power, it can *accept the counteroffer,* creating a contract on the offeree's terms. If not, no contract comes into being unless the parties go ahead and perform. As noted in section 6.3, when such *performance follows a counteroffer,* §2.207 departs from the common law. Unlike the common law, it does not assume that acceptance can be inferred merely because the offeror subsequently proceeds with performance of the transaction. The counteroffer is accepted only if it is clear that the offeror was aware of the alteration in terms and manifested assent to it by unambiguous words or action. If there is no such clear acceptance, a contract is recognized by virtue of the performance, but its terms are resolved under §2.207(3).

This may be represented as follows:

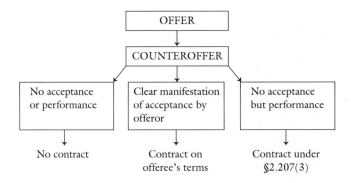

c.   A Response that Is an Acceptance with Additional or Different Terms

If the response is a **definite and seasonable expression of acceptance,** and it is not expressly conditional on assent to any new terms, it is an acceptance even though it states terms different from or additional to those in the offer.

For example, say that Seller's response in the last illustration had no language making the acceptance expressly conditional on Buyer's assent to the indemnity but had simply contained preprinted language stating, "The buyer shall indemnify us for any claims of injury arising out of the use of the goods described above." The response is likely to be an acceptance despite the new term. The fact that Seller expressed agreement with all the central terms of the offer and that the indemnity is set out in a printed standard term gives rise to the reasonable interpretation that its primary focus was on making the sale, and its intent was to accept. A contract is therefore formed, and the question of whether the indemnity becomes part of it is dealt with in §2.207(2), discussed below.

Note that §2.207(1) covers both "**additional**" and "**different**" terms—a distinction that creates problems discussed later. It is not always easy to decide if a term is "additional" or "different," and this depends on the interpretation of the offer. As a rough guideline, a term is different if it varies or contradicts something provided for in the offer, but it is additional if it adds new matter not covered in the offer.

§6.5.2   *Section 2.207(2): The Treatment of Proposals in an Acceptance*

The language of §2.207(2) may be charted as follows:

> The **additional** terms are construed as **proposals** for addition to the contract.
> ↓
> Between **merchants**
> such terms become **part of the contract**
> ↓
> **unless:**
> (a) the **offer expressly limits** acceptance;
> (b) they **materially alter** it; or
> (c) notification of **objection** to them has already been given or is given within a reasonable time after notice of them is received.

a.   The Scope and Basic Purpose of §2.207(2)

Section 2.207(2) *only applies* if the response to an offer is found to be an *acceptance*. It does not apply to a counteroffer, which only leads to a contract if accepted, or if performance occurs as contemplated by §2.207(3). Because §2.207(1) contemplates that a contract exists despite a variance between the terms of the offer and acceptance, §2.207(2) treats any such additional terms as **proposals** that do not become part of the contract unless the conditions in the subsection are satisfied.

b.   The Grounds for Excluding Proposals from the Contract

Section 2.207(2) is couched in deceptively positive terms. It says that the additional terms enter the contract *unless* one of the stated exceptions apply, but this is a very big "unless." The exceptions leave the rule applicable only to relatively unimportant terms in a small range of cases. *In most situations, the offeree does not succeed in adding terms in the acceptance,* and the general impact of §2.207(2) is to exclude most proposed additions. We now examine each of the exclusions. Note that they do not all have to be satisfied for the term to be excluded. If any one applies, the term does not enter the contract.

i. Additional Terms Do Not Become Part of the Contract Unless Both Parties Are Merchants

The **definition of "merchant"** in §2.104(1) is much broader than in common usage. It includes not only a person who deals in goods of that kind, but also one who, by following a particular occupation, has or represents having knowledge or skill concerning the goods. Therefore, as Comment 1[2] to §2.104 points out, even a person that does not trade in the goods could be a merchant if that person is a "professional" user of the goods, as opposed to a "casual or inexperienced seller or buyer." Section 2.207(2) requires that the transaction be *between merchants*. They must both be merchants, and if either of them is not a merchant, this ends the matter. The proposals do not become part of the contract, even if none of the other exclusions apply.

ii. The Term Does Not Enter the Contract If It Materially Alters It

Materiality is a complex issue, to be discussed more fully in section 17.3. Simply speaking, a term is material if it provides for an important aspect of the contractual performance. That is, it is a **significant element of the exchange bargained for by a party.** Although some terms are more obviously important than others, one can seldom decide materiality in the abstract. The contract must be *interpreted in context* to decide if the provision in question did occupy this central role in the bargain. This concept is expressed in the context of proposals under §2.207(2) by Comment 4 to §2.207. It says that a proposed alteration in an acceptance is material and does not enter the contract if it would result in "surprise or hardship" to the other party.

"**Surprise**" is determined with reference to reasonable expectations in light of common practice and usage. If a particular term is widely used, the party has reason to assume that it would be part of the contract, and its inclusion should be no surprise. (Of course if it is that common, it may be implied in the oral agreement or offer in any event.) "**Hardship**" means that the term imposes an unbargained-for burden (financial or otherwise) on, or detracts significantly from, the reasonable expectations of the other party. The concept of hardship does not do much to help resolve the question of

---

2. Section 2.7.1 introduced the role and effect of comments to the UCC. They are the drafter's explanation of the intent and purpose of code sections. They are very influential but are not part of the statute.

whether an alteration is material, because it begs the question of materiality rather than helping to answer it: A material alteration causes hardship, therefore it is material.

The Comment's use of the disjunctive "or" is misleading because the concepts of surprise and hardship are usually both elements of materiality and, in most cases, must both be satisfied to some degree. That is, even an important alteration may not be material if its inclusion should be fully expected, and a trivial alteration should not be treated as material, even if it is unexpected. The basic point of the exclusion is this: Even if the sale is between merchants, a proposed term does not enter the contract if it has more than a minimal impact on the exchange, and it is not sufficiently common to be expected.

iii. The Term Does Not Enter the Contract If the Offer Limits Acceptance to Its Terms

Even if the parties are merchants and the term is not material, it does not become part of the contract if there is *language in the offer expressly limiting acceptance to its terms.* This means that an offeror can simply eliminate the possibility of proposals entering the contract by putting appropriate standard language in the offer. This again raises the issue noted in the discussion of preprinted "expressly conditional" language in a purported acceptance. By giving effect to standardized exclusions or conditions, §2.207 breaks faith with its avowed purpose of disregarding boilerplate.

iv. The Term Does Not Enter the Contract If the Offeror Objects

If the offer did not limit acceptance to its terms, the offeror still has an opportunity to eliminate the proposal by *subsequent objection,* either in anticipation of the proposal or within a reasonable time of acquiring notice of it. This appears to contemplate not only a deliberate objection but also a standard objection issued by the offeror as a matter of course. This again raises the inconsistency displayed by §2.207 in its reaction to boilerplate.

c. The Omission of "Different" Terms from the Text of §2.207(2)

As noted in section 6.5.3, §2.207(1) refers to "additional" and "different" terms, while §2.207(2) only mentions "additional" terms. This has created two problems. First (as stated in section 6.5.1 and explored further in Examples 2 and 3), it is not always easy to tell if a term is "additional" or "different." Second, it is not clear if the omission of "different" terms was really intended or was just an oversight. The failure to include "different" terms in

§2.207(2) has led courts to adopt *divergent approaches* to the treatment of terms found to be "different":

1.   Some courts have treated the omission as **inadvertent** and have applied the subsection irrespective of whether the term may be classified as "additional" or "different." This approach has some support in Comment 3, which seems to assume that both fall within §2.207(3). (Although the Comment is apparently talking about confirmations rather than an acceptance.) It also has the obvious advantage of eliminating the problem of struggling to distinguish them.

2.   Other courts have taken §2.207(2) literally and have held that because "different" terms are not covered in the subsection, they must simply be **disregarded.** Once it is held that the response is an acceptance, there is no basis in principle for allowing this unilateral proposal to slip into the contract, and it must be excluded. The fact that "different" terms are not mentioned in §2.207(2) suggests not that they be treated more favorably than "additional" terms, but that it be treated less so. In other words, the "different" term can never become part of the contract, even if it meets all the tests for inclusion in §2.207(2).

3.   A third approach is to **treat the conflicting terms as cancelling each other out.** Some courts have reasoned that if the purpose of §2.207 is to take boilerplate less seriously, it makes no sense to prefer one of the "different" terms over the other, so they should both fall away and be replaced by whatever term the law would supply in the absence of agreement. (This has been called the **"knockout"** rule.) Although this approach seems to accord with the spirit of §2.207, there is no basis for it in the express provisions of the section. It sounds a little like the solution prescribed in §2.207(3), but that provision applies only where the parties perform despite their failure to conclude a contract. It is not directly on point and is at best justified by analogy when the offer has been accepted and the issue is whether a proposed "different" term in the acceptance is included in the contract.

§6.5.3   Section 2.207(3): The Effect of Mutual Performance When No Contract Is Formed by the Parties' Writings

The language of §2.207(3) may be charted as follows:

Conduct by both parties
that recognizes the existence of a contract

is **sufficient to establish a contract** for sale
↓
although
the writings of the parties do not otherwise establish a contract.
↓
In such a case
the terms of the particular contract consist of
those terms on which the **writings** of the parties **agree**
together with
any **supplementary terms** incorporated under any other provisions of
this Act

Section 2.207(3) only applies when there is no contract formed by the writings—typically because the offeree's response is not an acceptance with additional or different terms but a counteroffer which has never been deliberately accepted. As noted earlier, the common law "last shot" rule treated the offeror's performance as an acceptance by conduct of the counteroffer, thereby imposing the risk of inadvertent assent to the offeree's variation in terms.

Section 2.207(3) seeks to avoid this unfair imposition. If no contract was formed by the writings of the parties, but their conduct (typically in the form of tendering and accepting performance) shows that they intend a contract, the contract is recognized as existing. However, its terms are not simply those contained in the last communication. The contract includes only those terms on which the parties' writings agree, and all conflicting terms fall away. Any gaps in the contract are filled by supplementary terms recognized in the UCC. If there is any applicable trade usage or course of dealing or performance between the parties, the missing terms can be supplied as a matter of factual implication.[3] Failing that, the UCC itself provides a number of standard terms (known colloquially as **"gap fillers"**) that are implied as a matter of law into all sales of goods unless excluded by the contract. (For example, unless the parties agree otherwise, §2.308 states that delivery must take place at the seller's premises; §2.310 requires payment on delivery; and §§2.314 and 2.315 provide for minimum warranties.)

To illustrate the operation of §2.207(3) reconsider the example of Buyer's order for the Louden LeThal rivet gun for $450, C.O.D delivery in 30 days. Seller responds by accepting the order expressly on the condition that Buyer agrees to Seller's indemnity provision. It was noted in section 6.5.1 that the expressly conditional language makes the response a counteroffer. Buyer never communicates assent to this condition. In fact, having

---

3. The role of trade usage, course of dealing, and course of performance in the interpretation of contractual intent is discussed in section 10.6.2. For the present, it is enough to understand in general terms that the context in which the parties made their contract often provides much useful information on what they must have intended their contract terms to be.

not read the reply, Buyer is not even aware of the term. Seller ships the rivet gun and it is accepted and put to use by Buyer. One of Buyer's workers is injured when operating the gun and sues Seller as manufacturer of the machine. Under common law, Buyer's conduct in accepting the delivery would be deemed an acceptance of the counteroffer, making Seller's indemnity provision part of the contract. Under §2.207(3), however, a contract is recognized on the terms on which the writings agree (description, quantity, price, delivery, and payment) and the indemnity falls away. The resulting gap is filled by implication. (Whether a seller has such a right of indemnification against a buyer in the absence of agreement would be resolved by a complex interaction of contract and tort law, beyond our scope.)

§6.6   Written Confirmation Following an Oral or Informal Contract

It is impossible to decipher the provisions of §2.207(1) with regard to written confirmations. The subsection seems to say that ". . . a written confirmation that is sent within a reasonable time operates as an acceptance even though it states terms additional to or different from those . . . agreed upon, unless acceptance is expressly made conditional on assent to the additional or different terms."

However, this makes no sense. The written confirmation apparently follows an agreement. Although §2.207(1) does not say what this agreement might be, Comment 1 indicates that the drafters contemplated a situation in which an oral or informal agreement is followed by written confirmations. Presumably, this means that the parties have actually made a contract already. If so, the subsequent writing cannot be an acceptance, conditional or otherwise. The process of offer and acceptance has already been concluded.[4] If a contract already exists, the purpose of any confirmations is, of course, to confirm what has been agreed. This may be motivated by a need to satisfy the statute of frauds or simply by a desire to create a written record of the transaction.

Therefore, the references to acceptance in §2.207(1) are inappropriate in the context of confirmations and should be disregarded. This leaves us with just a few snippets of disjointed statutory language to interpret. What it seems to be trying to say is:

1.   If an oral or informal contract is formed,
2.   and if one or both parties thereafter send written confirmations,

---

4. As mentioned in footnote 1, the contract is fully enforceable in its oral form unless the price of the goods is $500 or more, in which case it does not become enforceable until reduced to writing sufficient to comply with the statute of frauds.

3. and one or both confirmations go beyond or vary what was agreed orally or informally,

4. any terms that add to or differ from the oral contract cannot simply become part of the contract,

5. but must be treated as proposals in the same way as proposals in an acceptance.

This leads to the conclusion that where confirming memoranda are involved, the only issue is whether the new terms in a confirmation become part of the contract. This question is decided using the same analysis, set out in section 6.5.2, as would be used if the additional or different term were contained in an acceptance. The one difference, of course, is that one is not so much concerned with a clash between conflicting writings (in fact, only one party may have sent a confirmation) but between one or more writings and the original oral or informal agreement.

Section 2.207(3) states that it governs where conduct establishes contractual intent but ". . . the writings of the parties do not otherwise establish a contract." If mutual performance occurs after a confirmation, a literal reading of §2.207(3) suggests that it is applicable. The contract arises, not from the writings but from the earlier oral agreement. This is surely not the intent. Section 2.207(3) is meant to deal with situations in which no contract would exist in the absence of performance and not where an oral contract has been concluded. Remember, however, that although §2.207(3) is not directly applicable, some courts have followed its spirit by adopting the "knockout" rule when a confirmation has terms "different" from the oral contract.

EXAMPLES

1. Ann Teek is an antique dealer. She has two customers, Art Deco and Bo Haus, who collect tableware from the 1920s and '30s. Whenever Ann manages to find a new item, she calls both of them to give them an opportunity to buy it. Ann recently acquired a richly decorated platter made in 1935. She called both the customers and invited them to come and see it. Art came to the store at 3 P.M. on Monday to inspect the platter, which was marked with a $499 price tag.[5] He said he was interested in buying it and would let Ann know his decision by Tuesday evening. Bo came to the store at 4:30 P.M. on the same day. He liked the platter and asked Ann if he could take it home to show it to his wife. Ann agreed and he took it away.

Just as Ann was closing the store at 8 P.M. that evening, Art called and told her that he wanted the platter. Ann agreed to sell it to him and arranged

---

5. I have no idea what an item like this might actually cost. Because all communications in this example are oral, I set the price at $499 to avoid statute of frauds problems.

for him to collect it on Wednesday. Ann then called Bo to tell him that the platter had been sold and to ask him to bring it back on Tuesday. The conversation went as follows:

> Ann: "Hello Bo, this is Ann Teek . . ."
> Bo: "Hi Ann, good news! My wife loves the plate."
> Ann: "But . . ."
> Bo: "I'll drop by tomorrow to pay for it."
> Ann: "But I just sold it to someone else."
> Bo: "Whaaat! You had no right to do that! It's ours!"

What is Ann's legal position?

2. Carr Buff's hobby is restoring vintage cars. For many years, he has been working on a 1957 Ford which he has brought to near-perfect condition. Last December, he entered it in the annual competition of his vintage car club and won second prize. Rod Hott, a banker, happened to attend the exhibition. On seeing Carr's Ford he was overcome with nostalgia, because the car was the same as the one he had owned as a teenager. He developed a strong urge to own the car and decided to try to buy it. He obtained Carr's address from the club and on January 2 he wrote to Carr as follows:

> Dear Mr. Buff,
>
> I saw your beautifully restored 1957 Ford at the car show last month and fell in love with it. Will you sell it to me? I am willing to pay you $60,000 and will pick it up at a time convenient to you. Please reply as soon as possible, but not later than January 10.
>
> > Sincerely,
> >
> > Rod Hott

Carr happens to be your cousin. (Of course you remember him . . . Aunt Millie's kid.) He is one of those annoying relatives who cannot wait for you to get your law degree before asking you for free legal advice. He comes to you on the morning of January 9 and tells you that he would very much like to sell the car to Rod. He shows you the following letter, which he proposes to mail later that day:

> Dear Mr. Hott,
>
> Thank you for your letter. I agree to sell the Ford to you for $60,000. You may collect it next week. Call me to arrange an exact time. Bring cash or a cashier's check and I will hand over the car and the title papers.
>
> As you probably noticed, the car won second prize at last month's exhibition. I have done some further detail work on it since then and I had planned to try for first prize at next December's show. Therefore, I'm only selling it to

you on condition that you maintain it in good shape and allow me to enter it in the show.

Yours truly,

Carr Buff

What should you say to Cousin Carr?

3. Tutu O'Severn decided to take up dance lessons. She needed dance shoes that were not obtainable in her town, so she obtained a catalog from Ballet de la Forms, Inc. ("Ballet"), a supplier of dance equipment in the nearest large city. After perusing the catalog, she selected a pair of shoes and entered their stock number in the order form attached to the catalog. The order form was a simple document that had blanks for the customer's name, the shipment address, the goods ordered, and the method of payment. (Tutu selected "C.O.D.") Its only printed language was the seller's name and address and a statement at the bottom which read "Please allow 4–6 weeks for delivery."

Tutu mailed the order form to Ballet. A week later she received a computer-generated note from Ballet that stated:

> Thank you for your order. It is our pleasure to serve you. Regrettably, we are out of stock of the item that you ordered. We expect new supplies from overseas in approximately two months. We apologize for the delay and will fill your order as soon as possible.

Tutu was disappointed, but felt that she did not have any choice but to wait. Two months later, she received another letter from Ballet which stated:

> We are pleased to inform you that we now have your order in stock. Unfortunately, the shoes have doubled in price since you ordered them, and we cannot deliver them at the original price. If you still want the shoes, please return the enclosed form agreeing to pay the new price.

Tutu responded to this communication by writing a letter to Ballet, stating that as far as she was concerned, she had already bought the shoes at the old price and was entitled to delivery at that price. Ballet disagrees. Does a contract exist for sale at the original price?

4. Nome's Sweet Gnomes, Inc. ("Nome") is a retailer of garden gnomes and other concrete yard decorations. Kitschcrete, Inc. manufactures these items. On May 1, Nome placed a telephone order for 15 gnomes at $20 each, to be delivered C.O.D. by May 14. Kitschcrete's telephone operator accepted the order. Immediately thereafter, each company, following its routine procedure, mailed its standard confirmation. Both forms had blanks in which the details of the transaction were filled out. Both also contained printed terms, drafted by the company's attorney. The confirmations were in accord on the transaction-specific terms written in the blanks (that is, quantity, description, price, payment, and delivery terms) and they were not significantly

different on most of the standard terms. However, they conflicted in one respect. Nome's form stated:

> Goods purchased hereunder may be returned for full refund if not resold by us within one month of delivery. Please Note: Your acceptance of this order is limited to the terms set out herein.

Kitschcrete's form stated:

> All sales are final. You are responsible for checking the goods on delivery and you may not return goods thereafter, even if found to be defective. Our acceptance of your order is conditional on your assent to all the terms stated herein.

When the confirmations arrived at the respective companies on May 3, a clerk at each company, again following routine procedure, checked only the transaction-specific terms (it was unheard of to waste time reading the boilerplate) and then filed the confirmation.

4(a). On May 10 Kitschcrete sold all its existing inventory to a large customer and is no longer able to fill Nome's order. Can it refuse delivery without liability?

4(b). Change the facts in Question 4(a). Kitschcrete did deliver the gnomes on May 14. Nome had trouble in generating customer enthusiasm for them, and by June 12 it had sold only one. Nome sought to return the 14 unsold gnomes, but Kitschcrete refused to take them back. Is it obliged to accept the return of the gnomes?

5. Change the facts of Example 4 to the following extent: Nome did not order the gnomes by telephone. Instead it placed its order by mailing a standard order form containing the same terms as its confirmation form described in Example 4. On receipt of the order, Kitschcrete's clerk read the transaction-specific terms and ignored the printed language. Kitschcrete, intending to accept the order, replied by mailing its standard order acknowledgement, containing the same terms as its confirmation described in Example 4. When Nome received the confirmation, its clerk checked only the transaction-specific terms and filed the form.

How does this change your resolution of the two situations set out in Example 4(a) (Kitschcrete reneges before shipment) and 4(b) (the parties perform and then have a dispute about Nome's right to return unsold goods)?

EXPLANATIONS

1. The facts make it clear that Ann did make an oral sales contract with Art. The issue is whether she also has a contract with Bo, leaving her liable for breach of contract to whichever of her customers ends up without the platter. This is a sale of goods governed by UCC Article 2. However, Article 2

has very few specific offer and acceptance rules, and except to the extent that they are displaced by provisions of the Code, general principles of common law are applicable. UCC §2.204(1) and (3) provide a flexible test for deciding whether a contract was formed: It may be made in any manner sufficient to show agreement, including conduct. If the parties intended to contract, missing terms do not cause it to fail for indefiniteness if the court can find a reasonably certain basis for giving a remedy.

Ann's conduct in allowing Bo to take the platter home is ambiguous. It could be an offer or merely an invitation to Bo to make an offer. It has sufficiently definite terms to qualify as an offer. The subject matter of the sale—the platter—is identified and the price is exhibited on the price tag. Because Bo has possession of the platter, delivery can be accomplished upon acceptance. Although payment terms are not expressed, there have apparently been prior dealings between the parties from which they can be inferred. If not, §2.310 makes payment due on receipt of the goods unless otherwise agreed. The fact that Ann gave Bo the plate suggests her assent to payment within a reasonable time of acceptance. Nevertheless, it is an offer only if Bo would be justified in understanding that his assent would conclude the bargain, without any need for further assent by Ann. Such an understanding may not be justified if Bo knew or had reason to know that Ann had also approached Art and that he was considering the purchase, but the facts do not indicate that he was aware of this.

If Ann made an offer, §2.206 dispenses with technicality in the mode of acceptance. It presumes that unless a particular manner and medium of acceptance is clearly required, acceptance may be by any means reasonable in the circumstances. No mode of acceptance was specified, and given the informal, oral nature of the offer, a telephonic acceptance seems appropriate. Ann may try to argue that the offer called for acceptance by performance—that is, by payment of the $499. This is not a good argument. Section 2.206 makes it clear that in the absence of an unambiguous expression of contrary intent, the offeree can choose whether to accept by performance or promise. (Section 2.206(1)(a) articulates this principle only with regard to a seller's acceptance, but the spirit and purpose of the section and the general approach of the common law supports the same rule where the buyer is the offeree.)

Although Ann called with the intent of revoking, revocation only takes effect when that intent is manifested to the offeree. Bo accepted before Ann could express the revocation. By contrast, in *Greene v. Keener*, 402 S.E.2d 284 (Ga. 1991), the buyer took a piece of furniture home to see if it fit in with his decor. The seller called later and told him that she no longer wished to sell it, thereby effectively revoking the offer before he had a chance to accept.

2. The proper response is to point out to Carr, with the appropriate degree of politeness, that you are not yet qualified or licensed to give legal advice, free or otherwise, and that he should go without delay to consult a real

lawyer.[6] Being compulsive, after he leaves, you cannot help mulling over what you would have told him had you been in a position to venture an opinion. I am sure you would have reasoned as follows:

This is a sale of goods, so §2.207 applies. Although it is nicknamed "the battle of the forms," there is nothing in the section's language that confines it to transactions in which forms are used. UCC Article 2 does not prescribe a test for deciding whether a communication qualifies as an offer, so general common law principles apply. No real issue is presented on this point because Rod's letter clearly has all the hallmarks of an offer.

Carr intends to accept, but his proposed response does not exactly correspond with the offer. His specification of the delivery date and his call for cash or a cashier's check do not conflict with the offer. The offer authorizes him to select a delivery time, and the cash payment term is implied in law by §2.310 in the absence of any contrary intent expressed in the offer. The problem is Carr's condition about maintaining the car and permitting him to exhibit it. Although §2.207(1) rejects the "mirror image" rule, it still requires the response to express intent to accept. The language used by Carr in imposing this new term makes it sound as if no acceptance is intended unless this condition is agreed to. Although courts generally require very clear language to make acceptance expressly conditional on assent to the new term, Carr's letter seems to satisfy this standard. Even if one could interpret the reply as falling short of imposing an express condition on acceptance, it still does not seem to meet the more general requirement of a definite expression of acceptance. It is therefore a counteroffer, and if Carr's desire for the sale outweighs his interest in exhibiting the car, he should think twice about including this term in his response.

If his predominant concern is to make the sale, he may decide not to abandon the term entirely, but to include it with watered-down language that emphasizes his intent to accept. However, this will not be of much use to him. The term would simply become a proposal for an "additional" term. (It adds to rather than contradicts the offer, so it does not seem to be a "different" term. The distinction is not necessarily this easy, as shown by Examples 2 and 3.) As such, it would only enter the contract under §2.207(2) if the sale is between merchants (which means, under §2.104(3) that both parties are merchants) and none of the three bases for exclusion apply. Our enquiry need not proceed beyond the initial requirement because neither Carr nor Rod is a merchant as defined in §1.104(1). Although Carr has skill relating to the goods, the restoration of old cars is his hobby, not his occupation, and there is nothing to indicate that he regularly deals in them. Rod is a banker and purchases the car as a consumer. As the sale is not between mer-

---

6. An alternative but regrettable response is to tell him that you have no clue, but you will craftily disguise his problem as a hypothetical and see if you can worm an answer out of your contracts professor.

chants, the term would not become part of the contract, and Rod can disregard it. We do not have to consider the other exclusions in §2.207(2), which are taken up in Example 3.

If Carr's primary intent is to make the sale, he must accept the offer promptly because it lapses tomorrow. Section 2.207(1), like the common law, requires "seasonable" (that is, timely) acceptance. Carr should be safe as long as he properly mails the letter by tomorrow. Unless the offer clearly prescribes a particular mode of acceptance, §2.206 permits acceptance by any manner and medium reasonable in the circumstances. Rod's offer was by mail, and a response by the same medium is certainly reasonable. The "mailbox" rule is not excluded by Article 2, and the acceptance will take effect immediately upon its deposit, correctly stamped and addressed, in the mailbox.

3. Except in unusual circumstances, a catalog is not likely to be intended as an offer by the seller or reasonably interpreted as such by a prospective buyer. It is more properly seen as inviting offers by those who receive it. Tutu's order form has enough specificity to be an offer, and it can reasonably be understood as such. It does not matter that Ballet supplied the form with the preprinted delivery term. By completing it without alteration, Tutu adopted it as her offer.

Under the "mirror image" rule, Ballet's response would be a counteroffer, not an acceptance, because it extends the delivery period. (The analysis of this exchange of correspondence under common law is discussed below.) Section 2.207 rejects the "mirror image" rule, If Ballet's response is a definite expression of acceptance, it operates as an acceptance even if it contains an additional or different term. We must therefore distinguish a response that is an acceptance despite some variation in terms from one whose variations preclude it from being an acceptance. For the response to fail as an acceptance, it must make it clear to a reasonable offeror that the offeree declines to contract on the offeror's terms. This could be done by using the expressly conditional language contemplated by §2.207(1), or by otherwise making it clear that the offeree does not propose to bind itself on the terms of the offer.

Ballet has not expressly made its acceptance conditional on Tutu's assent to its new delivery terms, so we must decide if the response otherwise fails as a definite expression of acceptance. If the response is interpreted as an acceptance with a proposal for a variation in terms, the new delivery date would simply be a proposal that (as discussed below) would not likely become part of the contract. For this reason, although Ballet indicates its delight at the prospect of filling Tutu's order and seems to assume that it will have the opportunity of supplying shoes to her, it really cannot be assenting to her terms. The response indicates that it cannot meet those terms, and it surely does not intend to set itself up for a probable breach by committing itself to an obligation that it states to be beyond its ability to perform. The most reasonable interpretation of the response is that it does not intend to be bound unless Tutu acquiesces in extending the delivery date proposed in the offer. Concededly, Ballet's response is on an impersonal computer-generated form, and it could be a standardized acknowledgement. Although the purpose of §2.207 is to underplay the impact of standardized terms in a response and to prefer treating them as proposals, this response does not seem like the usual mindless boilerplate. It reacts to a particular transaction-specific (albeit preprinted) aspect of the offer. Therefore, in this situation, the fact that forms are exchanged does not seem to point in the direction of treating the response as a definite expression of acceptance.

On this analysis, the result is the same as it would be under common law: A counteroffer was made. Unless Tutu accepted it, there is no contract, and Tutu would have to agree to the new price if she still wants the shoes. There is a good argument that Tutu did accept the counteroffer. She reluctantly acquiesced in the new delivery date, but she never communicated this to Ballet. Normally an acceptance must be communicated to be effective, and silence is not treated as assent. This is particularly true under §2.207, which generally demands a deliberate expression of acceptance to bind the offeror to the offeree's terms. However, this rule is for the offeror's protection, and it should not be used against her if the counteroffer creates the reasonable impression that acceptance need not be communicated, and her silence was induced by this understanding. Ballet's response does not expressly invite acceptance by inaction, but this can be reasonably inferred. It follows Tutu's initiation of the transaction and indicates that shipment will follow in due course, suggesting that performance will proceed on these terms unless the customer objects. This justified Tutu in assuming that she had no need to communicate further if she was willing to accept these terms. Because Tutu's interests are served by treating her silence as an acceptance of the counteroffer, it should be so regarded, and Ballet is committed to deliver the shoes at the old price.

This analysis disposes of the case and we need not go further, but for the sake of exercise, we will consider what would have happened if Ballet's response had been viewed not as a counteroffer but as an acceptance with additional or different terms. Section 2.207(2) seems to be the only place to go for the answer to this question, but there is a preliminary puzzle to be resolved. While §2.207(1) refers to both "different " and "additional" terms, §2.207(2) only covers "additional" terms. This raises three questions: What is the distinction between "additional" and "different" terms; why are only "additional" terms mentioned in §2.207(2); and what happens to "different" terms if they fall outside §2.207(2)?

At the simplest level, it is not difficult to see the distinction. A term is "additional" if it introduces new matter not covered in the offer, and it is "different" if it conflicts with a term in the offer. The distinction can get more complicated, as Example 3 shows, but on the present facts, the delivery term is best characterized as "different" because it seeks to change a term expressed in the offer.

It is not clear why §2.207(2) does not mention "different" terms. Some courts have considered this omission to be an oversight and have applied the subsection to "different" terms as well. Comment 3 to §2.207 supports this view because it assumes that the subsection covers them. If this approach is correct, then we may simply apply §2.207(2) without worrying about the distinction. The proposed term only becomes part of the contract if none of the exclusionary circumstances in the subsection applies. As in Example 1, we do not have to go beyond the requirement that the sale is between merchants. Tutu is a consumer and a casual buyer and not a merchant as defined in §2.104. Therefore, the proposed term does not enter the contract and the delivery date in the offer governs. Ballet is not only contractually bound to sell at the original price, but also is in breach for late delivery. (Tutu may have waived that breach, but we need not go into this now.)

Other courts have taken the language literally and have held it inapplicable if the term is "different" rather than "additional." If this view is correct, §2.207 provides no guidance on what to do with the term. Two approaches have been used. Some courts eliminate the proposed term on the basis that there is nothing in §2.207 to justify doing otherwise. On this basis, the contract is on Tutu's terms. Other courts agree that the proposal should not become part of the contract, but go one step further, and also "knock out" the conflicting term in the other form. This would mean that the delivery terms cancel each other out, and the delivery obligation is based on the UCC's supplementary terms. Under §2.309, delivery must be in a reasonable time if the time for delivery is not specified. To decide what is reasonable, general usage and normal customer expectations would have to be considered. Although the "knockout" approach seems sensible, it has no support in the language of §2.207. It is analogous to the solution in §2.207(3), but that provision is not directly pertinent because this is not a case where parties perform despite the failure of prior contract formation.

In summary, the most convincing answer is that there was an accepted counteroffer. However, if Ballet's response was an acceptance, its alteration in the delivery time is a "different" term. Whichever analysis is used to decide what to do with it, it does not become part of the contract so that there is either a contract on Tutu's terms or one with an unspecified time of delivery. Under the circumstances of this problem, as the dispute centers on the question of whether Tutu gets the shoes for the original price, Tutu wins, whichever analysis is used.

If you thought that this example was not gruelling enough, try Example 4.

4(a). This example involves an oral agreement followed by confirmations. Because offer and acceptance occurred at the time of the telephone call, there is no longer an issue of whether the offer has been accepted. Because there is already an enforceable contract between the parties,[7] the only

---

7. The price of the goods is less than $500, so we do not have to worry about the statute of frauds (see footnotes 1 and 4 above). If the price had been $500 or more, the oral agreement would not have been enforceable on its own, but the confirmations would satisfy the statute of frauds.

question is whether the contract is on Nome's or Kitschcrete's terms. Question (a) can therefore be resolved easily: Kitschcrete cannot escape the transaction by claiming that its confirmation was an unaccepted counteroffer.

4(b). In this question the parties do not disagree that a contract exists but dispute one of its terms. The question is designed to demonstrate just how incoherent §2.207 is, especially when applied to confirmations following an oral agreement.

To begin with, note that while §2.207(2) is supposed to apply to both confirmations and acceptances, its language focuses on the response to an offer and it is awkward when applied to confirmations. To make matters worse, we have to confront the problem again of deciding what to do with the distinction between "different" and "additional" terms. The nature of the term in Example 2 made it relatively easy to draw this distinction and to conclude that the term must be "different" because it varied the offer rather than adding to it. But matters become more complicated if the new term does not vary any express term in an offer or an oral agreement, but it changes what would otherwise have been implied in fact or law. The oral agreement did not expressly address the question of returns, so at face value, both confirmations have "additional" terms. However, when an agreement is silent on the question of a buyer's right to return goods, the UCC's standard provisions fill this gap. Under these provisions, broadly speaking, in the absence of contrary agreement, the buyer has a reasonable time to inspect the goods and to reject any that fail to conform to the contract (see §§2.513 and 2.601) but otherwise has no right to return unsold goods (see §2.326). This implied term conflicts with both confirmations in that Kitschcrete seeks to narrow Nome's right of inspection and rejection and Nome seeks to broaden it. Therefore, they both should be considered as proposing "different" rather than "additional" terms.

If this is correct, we must again contrast the three approaches to dealing with the omission of "different" terms from § 2.207(2).

A. If §2.207(2) Applies to "Different" Terms:

In this example, both parties do qualify as merchants, so the terms enter the contract unless excluded on one of the three grounds in §2.207(2)(a), (b), or (c). They are so excluded. The contradictory terms in the confirmations serve as objections to each other under §2.207(2)(a) and (c). This disposes of both terms, and no further analysis is needed. However, for the sake of completeness, note that unless there is some particular usage that comports with either of the terms, they both appear to materially alter the oral agreement and would be excluded on this ground even in the absence of objections. Nome's term imposes an unusual duty on Kitschcrete to take back the goods, hence losing the benefit of having a completed sale to that extent. Kitschcrete's term reduces Nome's normal opportunity to identify and reject defective goods, thereby increasing its risk of having to pay for substandard performance.

Thus, if §2.207(2) is applied, neither provision survives and the buyer's right to return the goods is subject to the general rule stated above.

B. If §2.207(2) Does Not Apply to "Different" Terms:

There is no difference in result whichever of the alternative analyses is used. On the "knockout" approach, the terms cancel each other out. However, this also happens if the court treats a "different" proposal as falling away, because the term in each confirmation is discarded.

Upon seeing that we got identical results on all three approaches to "different" terms, you may also realize that we must inevitably reach the same conclusion, mutual annihilation, if the terms were handled as "additional" under §2.207(2). This may lead you to wonder why you wasted all that time struggling with the distinction between "different" and "additional" terms. Do not feel too badly. This happened here only because of a factual quirk. By coincidence, there were two confirmations with precisely opposite terms. In other situations, identical results would only be assured if the court follows the approach of treating both "different and "additional" terms under §2.207(2).

The simple result of this tortuous process is that new matter in a confirmation by either party is typically disregarded, as well it should be. Neither party should be able to impose unexpected and unbargained-for terms in a boilerplate confirmation. The difficult interpretational contortions that had to be performed to get this result show why §2.207 needs a serious overhaul.

5(a). *Kitschcrete Reneges Before Shipment.* Although it seems a little absurd to reach this result, given the non-formalistic spirit of §2.207, the expressly conditional boilerplate in Kitschcrete's form makes the acknowledgement a counteroffer. Therefore, even though no one (except, perhaps, Kitschcrete's lawyer) was paying any attention to the form, and the parties thought that they had a contract, the language of the form gives Kitschcrete a pretext for evading its obligation. This does not mean that Kitschcrete has a very clever lawyer because the clause could just as well have been used against Kitschcrete if Nome had wished to renege.

5(b). *The Parties Perform, Notwithstanding that the Writings Never Formed a Contract.* Because Kitschcrete's response is a counteroffer, the common law "last shot" rule would hold Nome's acceptance of delivery as an acceptance of the counteroffer by conduct. Section 2.207(3) is intended to avoid this random result. It recognizes the existence of a contract and treats the conflicting terms as cancelling out each other, leaving a gap to be filled by the UCC's supplementary terms. The result is that neither the term in the original offer nor the counteroffer enter the contract. Instead, as stated in Example 4, the supplementary terms supplied by Article 2 permit Nome to return defective goods within a reasonable time, but otherwise give it no right to return unsold goods.

On the particular facts of this case, Kitschcrete wins this dispute because the parties are fighting over Nome's right to return unsold goods, an issue on which Kitschcrete's form happened to correspond with the UCC's position. However, if the dispute had been over Nome's right to return defective goods, the reasonableness standards of §§2.513 and 2.601 could have provided a different result than the more rigorous requirements in Kitschcrete's form.

7

Consideration

§7.1 Consideration as the Basis of Contract Obligation

Consideration can be fun.[1] It has a network of interlocking rules that can be applied to all kinds of silly cases featuring beneficent aunts, sanctimonious uncles, hypothetical tramps, mysteriously illusory promises, and detriments that are actually beneficial. Yet at the same time, consideration doctrine can be a huge pain in the neck. How often have poor students (and poor professors) cursed the quirk of history[2] that left us with so sad a legacy. It is not that the basic rules of consideration are difficult, arcane, or unfathomable. The real problem lies in rationalizing these rules, understanding how courts are likely to use them, and justifying them in light of the policies of contract law.

One thing is clear: Consideration doctrine is in a state of flux. It has evolved away from the more rigid and certain classical form. Courts have long recognized that an inflexible insistence on doctrinaire rules can undermine freedom of contract by precluding the enforcement of serious promises, fairly and voluntarily made. As a result, they have manipulated the rules, created exceptions and legal fictions, and have increasingly recognized alternative theories for enforcing promises that lack consideration. It is therefore not enough simply to learn the rules of consideration and to attempt to apply them mechanically to a set of facts. Consideration must be studied with an awareness of the purpose of these rules, a focus on their impact in each transaction, and an understanding of the way in which consideration doctrine fits

---

1. Obviously, depending on your idea of fun. It does help to be deranged.

2. Apart from the odd historical allusion, I will spare you the history of consideration. It arose from and is peculiar to the common law tradition. It is either unknown or scoffed at by civilian lawyers, who have always managed quite well without it. (If you do not know what is meant by "common law" and "civilian," see section 2.4.1.)

in with the broader principles and policies of contract law. You will not be fully able to appreciate this complex interaction between consideration and other elements of contract law just yet, but it will become more apparent as your study of contract law proceeds. At this stage it may be helpful to alert you to some themes that you will begin to see:

1. Often you will find that although consideration doctrine is the basis of a decision, the court is really concerned with the *legitimacy of the transaction* in issue and is in fact using the doctrine to achieve an appropriate result in the case. Therefore, a court may stretch to find consideration when the promise appears to be seriously intended and fairly obtained, but may more readily apply the doctrine to invalidate a promise that appears to have resulted from advantage-taking or unfair dealing. In this respect, consideration often serves a purpose parallel to other doctrines such as fraud, duress, or unconscionability (discussed in Chapter 13) in the *policing* of *bargaining behavior.*

2. Consideration is an essential element of contract, and a promise is not recognized or enforced as contractual unless consideration has been given for it. However, an obligation assumed without consideration may be enforceable under an *alternative theory* such as promissory estoppel, restitution, or moral obligation, discussed in Chapters 8 and 9. Therefore, although we may decide in this chapter that a promise or assumption of duty is not a contract because of lack of consideration, this may not mean that the person to whom it is owed is without remedy. Under appropriate circumstances there may be grounds for full or partial relief under one of those other theories, developed to avoid the injustice of turning away an obligee[3] empty-handed where the lack of consideration precludes contractual liability.

§7.2   The Essence and Scope of Consideration

When "consideration" entered the legal lexicon many centuries ago, its usage by lawyers was apparently close to its lay meaning of "reflection," "contemplation," or "thinking." It was a vague concept that probably did no more than assert the general principle that a promise must be seriously contemplated and deliberately intended to be legally binding. As courts expounded on this principle over the years, they gradually embellished it so that it came to require something more than a serious and deliberate intent to be bound. It demanded, in addition, that some quid pro quo be given for the promise by the **promisee** (that is, the person to whom it was made).[4] In

---

3. An obligee is a person to whom an obligation is owed.

4. In discussions of consideration, the person who makes the promise is called the **promisor** and the person to whom it is made, the **promisee.** This terminology is clear where only one party has made a promise, and the issue is whether some immediate performance of the other is consideration. However, in many contracts, both parties make promises and each is therefore both promisee and promisor. In such a case, common usage is that the word "promisor" denotes the person whose promise is

other words, a purely gratuitous promise—one that is not "paid for" in some way—cannot be enforced as a contract. This is the essence of consideration doctrine. From this, we can draw some initial inferences about the scope of our subject:

1. We are concerned with the validity of promises. Consideration is only an issue when there is an outstanding promise to be enforced, and it does not affect the validity of an **executed** gift, that is, a gift that has already been given or a gratuitous action that has been completed. If a donor has second thoughts about the gift after it has been made, it is too late to claim that no consideration was received.

2. Although consideration issues may potentially arise in connection with any unexecuted promise, there are two types of cases in which it presents no problems, simply because its absence or presence is so obvious. At the one end of the scale, we have the unquestionable **donative promise,** in which the promisor, motivated by kinship, friendship, or generosity, unconditionally undertakes to make a future gift. There is no point in agonizing over consideration here because it is obviously absent, and the promise is not legally binding. For example, following his 300th nosedive into the snow, Al Pine has become terminally frustrated with the sport of skiing. He decides to give his skis to his friend Buster Legg and promises to drop them off at Buster's home as soon as he gets out of traction. Until the skis are handed over to Buster, this is simply an unexecuted promise. There is no suggestion that Buster gave Al any quid pro quo for the promise, which is purely gratuitous. On these facts, consideration is not in issue because it is so obviously absent. If Al changes his mind and fails to deliver the skis, Buster can sulk or pout or even have a massive tantrum, but he has no legal recourse.

At the other end of the scale, we have the straightforward **commercial exchange** in which the promise is clearly purchased for an economically equivalent price, so that there is no plausible argument that consideration was lacking. For example, instead of promising to donate the skis to Buster, Al agrees to sell them to him for $100, their market value. Buster pays Al $100 in cash immediately, and Al promises to deliver the skis as soon as he leaves the hospital. On these facts, there is no issue that Al's promise was not paid for.

Between these two obvious cases is the happy hunting ground of consideration doctrine, in which apparently commercial promises are made for an unclear or questionable exchange, and apparently gratuitous promises have strings attached to them. Unless you are using very boring class materials, most of the consideration cases that you study will fall within this range.

---

sought to be enforced, and "promisee" refers to the recipient of that promise whose return promise is challenged as insufficient to constitute consideration.

§7.3   The Elements of Consideration: Detriment, Benefit, and Bargained-for Exchange

The broad statement was made above that a promise must be paid for to be contractually binding. As you will soon see, "payment" for the promise is much more complicated than you might first have suspected. In the earlier cases, it was said that the quid pro quo for the promise could be furnished by anything that was either a **detriment to the promisee** or a **benefit to the promisor.** The promisee suffers a detriment if she is left poorer in some way, because property, money, or some legal right has been given up to the promisor. It follows that from the perspective of the promisor, the receipt of such property, money, or rights from the promisee is a benefit. Therefore, in most situations, the benefit to the promisor is just the mirror image of the promisee's detriment.

Older cases stated that only one of these need be shown for consideration to exist. During the late nineteenth century, courts began to recognize that it was not enough simply to look for detriment or benefit. It also had to be apparent that the promisee's detriment was suffered in **exchange** for the promise: The parties must have **bargained for** (that is, agreed to) an exchange of the promise for the detriment, so that each induces the other. This became known as the **"bargain theory"** of consideration.[5] Because benefit to the promisor is simply a natural consequence of having the promisee suffer whatever detriment was sought in the exchange (that is, the benefit is simply getting what was bargained for), the bargain theory obviates any need to focus on benefit to the promisor as a distinct element of consideration. (As explained in section 7.3.2, the fact that some tangible benefit was received may have evidentiary value in showing that an exchange was intended.)

So far, the words "detriment," "benefit," and "bargained-for exchange" have been used in an abstract way. These are terms of art that can easily be misinterpreted. Their scope and meaning must now be explored.

§7.3.1   What Is a "Detriment"?

A legal detriment is any **relinquishment of a legal right.** In the legal sense, "detriment" does not mean that the person has suffered some horrible harm, loss, or injury. In fact, a detriment could even be something that benefits or advances the interests of the sufferer. The important element is not

---

5. Justice O. W. Holmes is credited with being primarily responsible for articulating the bargain theory, but it has been plausibly argued that he simply recognized what was already happening in the cases, rather than created a new requirement for consideration.

harm but the yielding of a legal right. It could take the form of an immediate **act** (that is, doing or giving something), a **forbearance** (refraining from something), or the **partial or complete abandonment of an intangible right.**

It could equally be a *promise* to act, forbear, or abandon a right in the future. Provided that an immediate performance is a detriment, a promise of that performance creates a future liability to perform, which is also a detriment. Consideration doctrine does not discriminate between the immediate suffering of detriment and a commitment to suffer that detriment at a later time. To be a promise, and hence a detriment, the undertaking must be a genuine commitment. If it is hedged with qualifications, it may not qualify as a promise. This is discussed in section 7.9.

In the example of the sale of skis by Al to Buster for $100, Buster's payment of $100 was an act constituting his detriment. It would equally have been a detriment if, instead of paying the money, Buster had promised to pay $100 to Al on delivery of the skis. As the act of payment is consideration, the promise to perform that act is also consideration. (Al's detriment is, of course, the promise to deliver the skis. This is a standard bilateral contract, in which the promise by each party is exchanged for and induces the promise by the other.)

If instead of paying or promising to pay $100, Buster had accepted the promise of the skis in settlement of a prior overdue claim of $100 that he had against Al, Buster's detriment would be the abandonment of his right to sue on the claim, or alternatively, his forbearance from exercising that right.

In these examples, the exchange of Buster's detriment for Al's promise can be shown as follows:

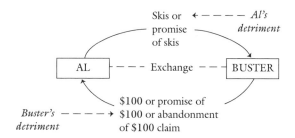

Because both the skis and the money (or the claim for money) have economic value, it is not hard to see that each party suffers a detriment by giving them up. If instead of asking for $100 for the skis, Al had agreed to give them to Buster in exchange for Buster's promise to quit smoking, the detriment to Buster is less obvious. Unanimous medical opinion is that giving up smoking is decidedly not detrimental but is beneficial. Notwithstanding, because Buster has the legal right to smoke, his promise to refrain from doing so (forbearance) is a legal detriment and can qualify as consideration for Al's promise of the skis. Restatement Second §79(a) reflects this principle by stating that if the requirement of consideration is met, there is *no additional requirement of loss or disadvantage* to the promisee.

This concludes our first look at the concept of detriment. Specific applications of this subject are discussed below.

§7.3.2   *How Does Benefit to the Promisor Fit In?*

Benefit to the promisor is even more prone to misunderstanding than detriment to the promisee. As stated earlier, it used to be one of the alternative tests for consideration, but under the bargain theory, it plays only an *evidentiary* role. In many cases, the promisee's detriment translates easily into a benefit to the promisor. In the exchange of the promise of skis for money, the detriment to Buster (a loss of $100) is obviously a benefit to Al (a gain of $100). By contrast, when Al's promise of skis is exchanged for Buster's promise to quit smoking, it is not as clear that Buster's detriment of giving up the legal right to smoke translates into any benefit to Al. However, in the same way as "detriment" has a very broad meaning, "benefit" is seen as meaning simply that Al *got what he bargained for.* It does not need to be shown that Al received any tangible or economically valuable gain. Restatement Second §79(a) states that a gain or advantage to the promisor is not a requirement for consideration.

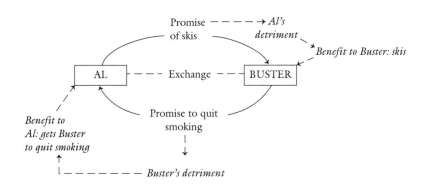

Thus, we need not ask why Al wished for Buster to quit smoking, nor need we speculate what is in it for him. His *motive* in making the exchange is not of central concern, as long as it is apparent that he intended to exchange his promise of skis for the promise to quit. This does not mean that Al's motive is entirely irrelevant, because it could be evidence of his intent to make the exchange. If a gain or advantage to Al can be identified, this bolsters the argument that he did in fact bargain for the detriment suffered by Buster. This issue is discussed further in the next section.

§7.3.3 The Bargained-for Exchange

As stated in section 7.2, the bargain theory was formulated around the turn of the century and it is now thoroughly well-established in our law. It is reflected in Restatement Second §71, which requires that a performance or return promise must be bargained for to constitute consideration. That is, it must be **sought by the promisor** and **given by the promisee** in exchange for the promise. Section 33 reinforces this by defining a **bargain** as an agreement (in turn defined as a manifestation of mutual assent) to exchange promises, performances, or promise for performance. The bargain theory recognizes that contracts are voluntary exchange relationships involving reciprocal promises or performances. It means nothing if a party suffers a legal detriment unless the parties agree that it is the price for the promise.

Be careful not to get too carried away by all this talk of bargain and inducement. "Bargain" simply means "agreement" and does not suggest that the parties have to dicker back and forth or to negotiate at length. If each agrees to a performance desired by the other, the bargain can be struck instantly without any fuss. Also, the **objective test** (discussed in section 4.1) applies to the determination of contractual intent, so "inducement" is gleaned from the manifestation of intent rather than from a probing of the party's actual state of mind. The motive for the transaction is therefore the *apparent motive,* as evidenced by the nature of the exchange in context.

In the example of the sale of the skis for $100, the fact that Al and Buster had agreed to an exchange seems obvious. In most commercial transactions the existence of a bargained-for exchange is not in question. Exchange also seems to be quite clear in the case of the promise of skis for the promise to quit smoking. Even though the motivation is apparently not commercial, we can still understand an incentive for the exchange based on friendship. However, what if Al had said to Buster, "If you walk over to my car, I will give you the skis that I have on my rack." Under the broad concept of legal detriment, Buster's act of walking to the car is a detriment: He gave up his legal right to remain where he was and undertook the perambulation across the parking lot. However, this detriment seems incidental to Al's promise. Common experience suggests that the parties did not see it as the price for the skis but simply as the act needed to take delivery of the gift. That is, it is a *condition of the gift.* This conclusion is based, not on a probing of Al's innermost thoughts but on the apparent purpose of his request, based on our understanding of human motivation. There is no evidence from which one could reasonably understand that Al was so desirous of having Buster walk across the lot, that he felt it was worth promising him skis to induce him to do it.

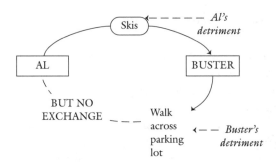

The same conclusion would follow if Al had said to Buster, "Put out your hand, and I will place a $10 bill in it." It would be hard to argue with a straight face that the act of extending the hand was bargained for as the exchange for the money. Al's apparent purpose is to give a gift to Buster, and the request to position the hand is merely intended as a means of its efficient delivery—better than cramming it in his ear or casting it on the ground.

However, there may be some additional evidence that makes this conclusion less obvious, so that under all the circumstances, Buster may reasonably understand from Al's words and conduct that the extension of his hand was a bargained-for detriment. (Note the objective test used here: It is not what Buster in fact understood, but what he has reasonably understood. We measure Buster's interpretation of Al's words and conduct from the perspective of a reasonable person in Buster's position.) Say, for example, that Buster was one of those sidewalk performers who strikes a pose and tries to stand dead-still like a statue. Al's offer of money may well be in exchange for the hand movement, because Buster could reasonably infer that Al is bargaining for the pleasure of seeing Buster abandon his art for filthy lucre. (Is that pleasure worth $10? We do not usually need to inquire. As discussed in section 7.6, once exchange is determined, it is not necessary to evaluate the adequacy of consideration.)

This example again confronts the awkward fit between benefit to the promisor, motive, and the objective test of intent. When no benefit to Al was evident, we concluded that the detriment was not bargained for. When additional facts were supplied that suggested a motive, albeit not an economic one, the conclusion was that the detriment was bargained for. Yet we did not try to seek Al's actual motive for the exchange, but rather his apparent motive. The benefit to the promisor, measured objectively, is purely the satisfaction of having his apparent desire fulfilled. This is sufficient to support a finding of exchange. (As we will see later in this chapter, the exchange requirement has many facets.)

§7.4 The Purpose and Function of Consideration Doctrine

So far we have looked at the basic principles of consideration and have identified the grounds of some of its rules but have not sought any comprehensive explanation of the rationale of the doctrine. Such a discussion is vital to an understanding of consideration and to a critical appraisal of its appropriate use in individual cases. This important discussion has been deferred until now because it is difficult to appreciate before an exposition of the doctrine itself.

Some people doubt that consideration has any useful purpose at all. They consider it an historical relic that could disappear unmourned, its functions being more effectively performed by other doctrines of contract law. Yet consideration is still a dominant force in contract law. Unless this can be attributed solely to the inertia of the common law, it must mean that courts still find consideration doctrine to be more useful than harmful. What are the most convincing justifications for the retention of this old common law doctrine? In 1941, Lon Fuller wrote his celebrated article, *Consideration and Form* (41 COLUM. L. REV. 799), which has ever since formed the starting point for all discussion of the modern role of the doctrine. Fuller identified both formal and substantive bases for consideration.

§7.4.1 Formal Functions of Consideration

Fuller recognized that legal formalities serve three interrelated functions: "**Evidentiary**" (i.e., provide evidence of the existence and terms of a contract), "**cautionary**" (i.e., make the parties aware that they have made a serious legal commitment), and "**channelling**" (i.e., provide an objective basis for a court to determine that the promise is contractual, rather than a mere generous impulse or a tentative or informal expression of intent). The functions are interrelated in that a formality that satisfies one of them is likely to satisfy all.

At least up to a point, consideration serves the functions of legal formalities. For example, when Al exchanged his promise to deliver his skis for Buster's payment of $100, the fact that $100 was given for the promise tends to prove that it was made (why else would Al be sitting with $100 of Buster's money?); it forces Al to realize that he has made a binding commitment to part with his skis; and it tells the court that this truly is meant as a legally enforceable exchange transaction.

Recognize that the argument that consideration satisfies formal functions is at best a partial answer. If its role were purely formal, it could easily be dispensed with because these formal functions could be accomplished simply by having a rule that upholds written, signed promises. However, this is not the law. A promise of a gift, even if executed in writing with due formality, is not treated as binding.[6] Even if the parties go to the trouble of reciting a formal or nominal consideration for the sake of trying to validate the gift, this is not usually recognized as sufficient to support the gratuitous promise. (*See* section 7.8.)

Therefore, parties cannot be assured of avoiding consideration problems by clearly and soberly executing a document that satisfies the functions of legal formalities. If consideration serves only the functions of legal formality, this result makes no sense. To justify it, there must be some substantive basis for requiring consideration.

§7.4.2   *The Substantive Basis for Consideration*

If legal formalities are thought of as procedural in nature, substantive justifications of consideration are based on the goals and policies of substantive contract law. Because the concerns generated by gift promises are quite different from those arising in gratuitous commercial promises, we should begin by distinguishing the substantive rationale for non-enforcement in these separate contexts. We can then consider more general rationales, applicable to both.

a.   The Reasons for Not Enforcing Gift Promises

The substantive basis of consideration is often expressed in market terms: Exchange transactions are enforced as contracts because society has a vital interest in the reliability of commercial exchanges, but gift promises are **"sterile"** and of little commercial utility. This rationale has the ideological undertones of the Victorian work ethic and conjures up images of slothful remittance men, lolling about on some tropical veranda, wasting their lives away in booze, and other unmentionable pursuits. In truth, few gifts are economically sterile. The donee's use, expenditure, or saving of the gift surely has some impact on the marketplace, and a charitable gift has social as well as economic utility.

---

6. In this respect, modern law has moved away from older common law which did have a formal device—the **seal**—that could be used to make a promise binding without consideration. The promisor could create a binding gratuitous promise by sealing the document. Originally, the seal was made by dripping sealing wax on the document and impressing the hot wax with a signet ring. In time it became acceptable simply to append the letters "L.S." (*locus sigilli*—meaning "in place of a seal") to a signature. The seal did not develop as an exception to consideration doctrine but predates the doctrine, which applied only to "informal" (i.e., unsealed) promises. Today, the seal has been abolished or given only residual evidentiary effect in most jurisdictions. In only a few states has the formal device of the seal been replaced by a statutory method of formally validating a gift promise.

A more convincing rationale lies in the *equities between donor and donee,* contrasted with those between parties to a commercial transaction. Gifts tend to be motivated by affection, gratitude, or altruism and usually have a stronger emotional impetus than commercial exchanges. There may be some moral obligation to keep the promise, but nothing was given in exchange for it, and the donee has lost nothing except the prospect of a gift.[7] The donor should therefore be able to recant without legal liability. This protects the donor against improvidence and also indirectly protects his or her creditors who did give value for their claims. For example, a person, much inspired by an evangelist, promises a large donation to his ministry. The next day the promisor realizes that the donation would leave her so short of money that she will not be able to pay her bills. If she could not renege on the promise, the evangelist would have the same claim to her assets as any creditor from whom she has purchased goods or services. However, consideration doctrine assures that while the creditors can hold her to the promises for which she received value, the preacher's recourse must be sought in some celestial forum. The terrestrial courts will not enforce the promise.

This rationale is the substantive echo of the formal **cautionary** function. That is, while the presence of consideration cautions the promisor that a legal duty is being assumed, its absence creates the expectation that the promise can be revoked without legal liability. In a circular way, this expectation itself bolsters the need to retain the requirement of consideration: Because gift promises have not been enforced, a donor may make a promise in the reasonable expectation that it will not be binding, and the continued insistence on consideration protects this reasonable expectation. In other words, the fact that the rule has existed for so long, in itself justifies its continuation.

Although it is widely accepted that gift promises should not be enforced, this rule is not applied absolutely. Sometimes the equities of a case call for the enforcement of a gratuitous promise, and courts have the means of finding a basis for enforcement either by a manipulation of the broad concept of bargained-for detriment (as introduced in section 7.3.1) or under the alternative doctrines discussed in Chapters 8 and 9.

b. The Reason for Not Enforcing Commercial Promises Without Consideration

A commercial promise without consideration may sound like a contradiction in terms. After all, one may think that a promise without consideration must by definition be a gift. However, there are many examples in this chapter of promises lacking consideration even though motivated by commercial ends.

---

7. If the donee has suffered some loss in reliance on the promise, the alternative theory of promissory estoppel, discussed in Chapter 8, may provide relief.

For example, an apparent promise may in fact be illusory; or the promise may have been made during negotiations, before the other party made a firm return commitment; or the promise may have been made in recognition of some economic benefit that is not given in exchange because it predates the promise or is expected but not actually promised.

In a commercial transaction, in which altruism, affection, or gratitude is not a motivating factor,[8] the rationale relating to the nonenforcement of gifts is inapplicable. Therefore, to refuse enforcement of the promise as a contract, the court must be satisfied that the parties did not intend it to be such. That is, that the promise was in fact an **informal, non-binding expression of intent,** or it was **otherwise not reasonably expected to create a legal duty.** If, on the other hand, the court is persuaded that serious legal commitment was reasonably intended, it is likely to make great effort to give effect to that intention by scouring the transaction to find consideration for it.

c.   Consideration as a Means of Policing for Unfair Bargaining

In both donative and commercial settings, consideration continues to be useful to courts as a means of refusing to enforce a promise that was extracted by unfair or illegitimate means. This is hardly a unique function of the doctrine in that there are many other principles of contract law designed to prevent the enforcement of promises induced by fraud, duress, and other unfair bargaining methods. Indeed, as noted earlier, it is often claimed that these other means of policing contract formation are more direct and efficient than consideration doctrine. Nevertheless, the requirement that there must be consideration has historically played an important role in this area of contract law, and it has continuing value as one of the tools available to the court for this purpose.

§7.5   Detriment and "Pre-Existing Duty"

§7.5.1   *The Basic Rule*

If a detriment is the relinquishment of a right, it follows that one does not suffer a detriment by doing or promising to do something that one is *already obliged to do* or by forbearing to do something that is *already forbidden.* Therefore, the rule is often stated that the performance of, or promise to perform, a pre-existing duty is not consideration. For example, say that Al and

---

8. Of course, I do not suggest that these impulses are always absent in the commercial setting. There may be situations in which gratitude is the overwhelming or possibly the only motive for an apparently commercial promise, and affection or friendship may play some role in a commercial exchange. To the extent that these motives are strongly present, the transaction may in fact be a gift and hence subject to the policy relating to gratuitous promises, even if the context is commercial.

Buster contracted last week for the sale of Al's skis to Buster for $100, C.O.D. delivery to be effected at a specified future time. Before the date due for delivery and payment under the contract, Al discovers that he has undercharged for the skis. He approaches Buster and asks him to agree to change the price to $150. Buster believes that he did underpay and feels that the skis are still a good buy at $150. Not wishing to take advantage of Al's mistake, he agrees to pay the extra amount. This second agreement does not create a binding contract because Al gave Buster no consideration for his promise to pay $50 more. Al already had a duty to deliver the skis under the original contract, and he neither gives nor promises anything new. It cannot be a legal detriment to promise what he is already obliged to do. As a result, Buster's second promise is not binding, and if he later regrets it, he can insist on delivery of the skis for the original price of $100.

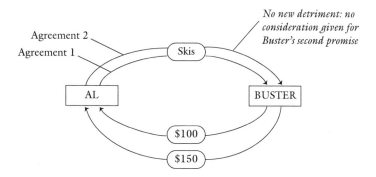

The pre-existing duty rule only applies if the performance of the promisee is completely encompassed by the pre-existing duty. Therefore, if Al had in any way added to his performance or obligation as an incentive to Buster's agreement to pay more (for example, Al offered to throw in a set of used thermal underwear), this *new increase in his detriment* would be sufficient to constitute consideration for Buster's promise of more money. The fact that the underwear is not worth anywhere near $50 will usually not matter because, as explained in section 7.6, economic equivalence is not normally required in the exchange.

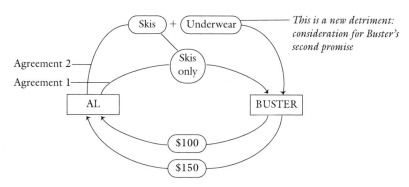

§7.5.2   *The Justification for the Rule: Coerced Modifications*

It is quite easy to express the pre-existing duty rule in its basic form, but application of the rule is seldom this simple. In some cases, the problem may be factual. For example, it may be unclear if a pre-existing duty exists or if the detriment in the later agreement really is coextensive with this duty. However, the bigger problem is a conceptual one. Why have the rule at all? True, it is consistent with and simply a specific application of the concept of detriment, so the rule is doctrinally justifiable. But what policy does it serve?

The rule makes most sense when, after a contract has been made, one of the parties takes advantage of the other's dependence on his performance, by threatening to breach the contract unless the other promises to increase her payment or other return performance. When a modification of an existing contract has been coerced in this way, the court can employ the pre-existing duty rule to void the unfair modification. Although we will return to the subject of contract modification in section 13.9 in connection with a broader study of the doctrines governing unfair bargaining, we must deal with it here as well, because it has a significant connection to consideration doctrine. To illustrate, say that a traveller, on arriving at the airport of a large city, contracts with a cab driver to pay him $35 to take her to a hotel on the other side of town. Halfway through the journey, as they are driving through a dark and frightening part of town, the cab driver jams on the brakes, turns to the passenger, and says, "Sorry, but unless you agree to pay me $100 for my fare, I am going to dump you off here." Of course the passenger agrees to this modification of the contract. However, the cab driver had a pre-existing duty to complete the trip. He has therefore given the passenger nothing more than what he originally promised—transport to the hotel. Because he has suffered no further detriment in exchange for the passenger's promise to pay another $65, this promise of additional payment lacks consideration and the passenger can refuse to pay any more than $35 when they reach the hotel.[9]

Although the justification of the rule is the prevention of this kind of coerced modification, it has been applied more widely to cover all modifications, even those, such as the price increase in the contract between Al and Buster, that are legitimately agreed to. In these circumstances, application of the rule precludes parties from ever being able to make a binding agreement to modify the obligations of one of them, even when circumstances justify a modification and the promisor genuinely agreed to it without unfair pres-

---

9. Furthermore, she need not tip him, either.

sure. Such an *unquestioning use* of the rule *undermines freedom of contract* and has led many commentators and courts to believe that the rule is unnecessary and undesirable. Coercion can be more directly dealt with under doctrines such as duress and bad faith, and unless the modification has been induced by illegitimate pressure, there is no reason to refuse its enforcement by a mechanical application of the rule.

In fact, the UCC has abolished the rule and replaced it in §2.209 by a **good faith** test. (This is discussed more fully in section 13.9.) Under the common law, courts are usually more oblique in avoiding application of the rule to legitimate modifications. Although some courts may be willing to take a bold approach, adopting the UCC test of good faith in a common law case, others consider themselves bound by consideration doctrine. They will therefore only uphold a modification, even though genuinely consensual, if, on examining its terms, the court can find some new detriment suffered by the promisee. Of course, if the court is convinced of the legitimacy of the modification, it will make great effort to find a new detriment, even if slight in relation to the value of the modification (such as the sacrifice of used underwear for a promise to pay an extra $50). The disparity in value of the exchange can be disregarded under the rule that the court does not inquire into the adequacy of consideration.

Another possibility is that the modification may fit into an exception to the rule: If the modification was motivated by supervening difficulties that so affect the basic assumption under which the contract was made, the modification is enforceable, even in the absence of consideration. The underlying rationale for this exception is that a modification to take account of an unexpected burden on the promisee is less likely to be coercive. As doctrine has developed, the concern over upholding legitimate modifications has manifested itself in this specific exception, rather than in a more general one.

§7.5.3   Pre-Existing Duty to a Third Party

So far, we have talked only about a pre-existing duty owed by the promisee to the promisor. What if the duty is owed to someone else? For example, Al has contracted with Ava Lanche to sell his skis to her for $200; C.O.D. delivery is to take place next week. Ava has promised her friend Buster that when she gets her new skis, she will give him her old ones. Buster is therefore most anxious for the sale to go through, and he promises Al that if Al delivers the skis to Ava as arranged, Buster will give Al his almost-new thermal underwear. Al has already made a commitment to Ava to deliver the skis. The pre-existing duty rule would appear to apply, in that he has incurred no new detriment in exchange for Buster's promise.

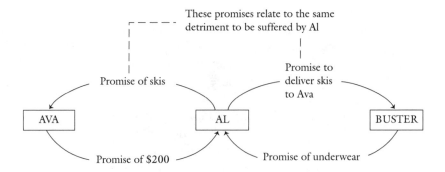

Note however, that the concern about extorted contract modification is not present in a case like this, so the rule may not be appropriate. Some courts (and Restatement Second §73) simply confine it to cases in which the duty is owed to the promisor. An alternate way of looking at the situation is to say that Al does incur a detriment in that he forbears from the right to negotiate with Ava for the cancellation of the contract. (He also forbears from the power but not the right to breach the contract with Ava, but as detriment is the relinquishment of a legal right, forbearance from breach is not a very kosher detriment.)

A pre-existing duty may be owed, not to the promisor or a third party, but to the state. This type of duty presents slightly different policy concerns because the public interest may demand that external incentives to obey that duty must be discouraged. This is particularly so when the promisee is a public official, and an additional reward for performing the public duty may create the danger of corruption or favoritism.

§7.6   The Measurement of Detriment: Adequacy of Consideration

When skis are exchanged for money, items of ascertainable economic worth are involved, so it is usually not difficult to determine if there has been equivalence in the exchange. It is a lot harder to value the right given up by Buster in promising to quit smoking. However, this generally does not matter, because consideration doctrine does not require that the performances or promises exchanged be of equal value. As long as a legal detriment has been suffered in exchange for the promise, the court *does not inquire* into its *value in relation to the promise*. (Restatement Second §79(b).) A related principle is that there does not have to be an *equivalence* in the *number of promises or performances* provided by each party. One party can exchange a single promise or performance for multiple promises and performances by the other. For example, Al could have given Buster the skis in exchange for Buster's payment of $100 plus his promise to stop smoking and his forbearance from asserting a claim that he has against Al. For the purposes of finding consideration, we need not worry that Buster has given up three rights to one of Al's, nor need we fret about whether the promise of the skis is worth more or less than Buster's detriment.

The rule that the court will not inquire into adequacy of consideration is based on the policy of enforcing the voluntary exchange on the terms agreed by the parties. Once consideration has been found to exist, the court should not second-guess the value placed on the exchange by the parties at the time of contracting, even if it now appears that one of them received a great bargain and the other was underpaid. Therefore, if Al's skis are actually worth $500, and he agreed to sell them to Buster for $100, the court should not allow him to escape the contract and disappoint Buster's expectations. This argument has even more force when the economic value of one of the performances is hard to determine (or was so at the time of contracting). For example, one really cannot place an economic value on Buster's promise to stop smoking, so one cannot even be sure that this promise was an inadequate exchange for the skis. (Indeed, some smokers feel that a thousand times that amount would be insufficient recompense for the pain of abnegation.)

This principle makes sense where the agreement is the product of fair bargaining, because the parties bear responsibility for setting the value of the exchange. The disparity in value may be the result of many and varied factors such as poor judgment, inaccurate cost calculations, bad luck in market predictions, or even deliberate underpricing. Whatever the reason, the party who received less than the value of his or her performance has no basis to complain. However, this general rule does not apply in two situations: First, adequacy of consideration does become an issue when the disparity in the exchange results from **oppressive** or **underhand bargaining** or **justifiable mistake.** When assent is negated by such a defect in the bargaining process, doctrines such as fraud, duress, unconscionability, or mistake allow the court to take cognizance of the disparity in exchange and to overturn the transaction or to adjust its terms to equalize it. (These doctrines are dealt with in Chapters 9 and 15.) Second, if the consideration given for a promise has so small a value in relation to the promise that it is obviously **nominal,** it may fail to satisfy the requirement of exchange, and the transaction may be viewed as a gift. This is discussed further in section 7.8.

§7.7 Past Performance

Because exchange is the basis of consideration, each party's detriment must induce and be induced by the other's. Therefore, if the promisee suffered the detriment before the promise was made, it cannot be said that the detriment was exchanged for the promise. Although the *detriment may have induced the promise,* it was *not itself induced by the promise* which had not yet been made. This means that if a person makes a promise to compensate another for some prior performance, that prior detriment cannot be consideration for the promise. The promise is seen as gratuitous and non-biding, even if it was seriously and freely made, and even if the prior detriment conferred a valuable benefit on the promisor.

The prior detriment is often referred to as **past consideration,** but this is a misnomer, because it is not consideration at all. For example, say that Al had fallen into a crevice while skiing, and Buster, risking horrendous peril, saved him. After being extracted from the crevice, Al gasped to Buster, "In consideration for saving my life, I promise to give you my skis." This promise is not supported by consideration because Buster's detriment had already been suffered and was not truly exchanged for the promise. This result could be justified by the cautionary function of consideration. Buster probably did not act for commercial motives, and Al's promise can reasonably be seen as a gift, impulsively induced by feelings of gratitude. Conversely, it is not hard to see the merit in making Al give poor Buster the measly reward, and some courts have responded to this type of situation by formulating an alternative theory, commonly called "moral obligation," to enforce the promise. This is discussed in Chapter 9.

§7.8   False or Nominal Consideration

It was stated in section 7.6 that courts do not normally inquire into the adequacy of consideration, but leave it to the parties to decide what their promises or performances are worth. This is an important principle, because it protects the autonomy of the parties and upholds the security of transactions by preventing the evasion of contractual duties by the party who made the wrong economic judgment. However, as mentioned already, this general rule is subject to two exceptions. The first, relating to policing doctrines such as fraud or duress, is discussed in Chapter 13. We turn to the second here.

A person promising a gift may know enough about the law to realize that consideration is needed to validate the promise. To make the gift binding, the promisor may **falsely recite** that consideration has been received (provide for a **sham** consideration) or may provide for some **nominal detriment** to be given by the promisee. Provided that the promisor has not been tricked into this pretense of consideration and it is not designed to defraud some third party, it seems consonant with the policy of contractual autonomy to allow the parties to use this device to validate the promise. However, Restatement Second does not take this approach. While it asserts the general rule that courts should not inquire into adequacy of consideration, it states several times that the *pretense of a bargain* does not satisfy the exchange element, so that a false consideration, which does *not in fact induce* the return promise (or, at least, cannot reasonably be conceived as doing so), should not be treated as sufficient. (*See* §71, Comment *b*; §72, Comment *c*; §79, Comment *d*; and §81, Comment *b*.)

Because the nominal or sham consideration satisfies the formal functions discussed in section 7.4, the rationale of the Restatement's position must lie in the substantive justifications for consideration. We have already disposed of the policing function by excluding situations in which the promisor has been deceived or the parties have some ulterior motive of misleading a third party. This leaves the justifications relating to the nonenforcement of gratuitous promises. Sometimes, the circumstances may suggest that the goal of protecting against generosity may outweigh the policy of upholding private autonomy, but in other situations, despite what the Restatement says, the better approach may be to take the apparent consideration at face value. This is particularly so when the formal functions of consideration are fully satisfied by a clear document and there is no suggestion of advantage taking or underhand conduct by the promisee, and no indication that the promisor acted impulsively and with immediate regret.

Although some cases do refuse to recognize consideration when it is clearly nominal or false, others decline to question the adequacy of nominal consideration, and counter an allegation of sham (falsely recited) consideration by interpreting the recital as an implied promise to provide the stated act or forbearance at some future time, or by estopping[10] the promisor from denying receipt of recited consideration. Many courts do not follow one or the other of these approaches rigidly but may select whichever one seems appropriate on the facts of the particular case. That is, adequacy is not questioned if there is no indication of impropriety or rashness, but nominal or sham consideration may be treated as insufficient if circumstances suggest that the promisor needs protection from generosity, impulsiveness, or unfair imposition.

Both Restatement Second and the courts adopt a more lenient attitude to purely formal consideration in **options.** An option is a promise to keep an offer open (that is, not to revoke it) for a specified period of time. Like other promises, it must have consideration to be binding on the promisor. However, as explained more fully in section 5.2, because an option is granted to induce the grantee to enter a contract desired by the grantor, the common law more readily accepts nominal consideration to validate options. Furthermore, a false recital of consideration may be more readily interpreted as a

---

10. Estoppel is explained in section 8.4. In short, its impact in this context is that because the promisor has participated in setting up the pretense of consideration, he or she cannot now deny that consideration was given. The promisor's earlier conduct induced the promisee reasonably to rely on the validity of the promise and the promisor is therefore held accountable for that conduct and is precluded from asserting that the consideration is a sham.

promise to furnish the consideration or may be more easily found to estop the grantor from asserting that the recital was a sham. UCC Article 2 has gone even further and (as discussed in section 5.5) dispenses with consideration for options (called "firm offers") for the sale of goods under certain circumstances.

§7.9　The Quality of a Promise as Consideration: "Mutuality of Obligation," Illusory, Conditional, and Alternative Promises

§7.9.1　Mutuality and Illusory Promises

The requirement of mutuality of obligation is expressed in the old maxim "both parties must be bound, or neither is bound." Taken too literally, the concept of mutuality can be confusing and misleading, because it seems to suggest that one could never have an unilateral contract, or a contract in which one of the parties has the legal right to escape liability. Yet, both types of contract are well recognized in law. It has been explained in section 4.12 that a promise can be exchanged for an immediate performance, resulting in a unilateral contract in which only the promisor has an outstanding obligation at the instant of contract formation. Elsewhere in this book many other situations are described in which only one of the parties is bound because the other has the right to end the contractual relationship. This is true, for example, in an option contract (see section 5.4) or a contract that is voidable by one party on such grounds as minority (see section 14.2.1), incapacity (see section 14.3.3), bargaining impropriety (see section 13.3), or mistake (see section 15.5). It is also quite valid to provide in a contract for any one of the parties to have the right to terminate the contract by giving notice.

Therefore, in modern law, "mutuality" does not mean that both parties must make a future commitment or, if they do, that each must be bound with the same degree of firmness. It also does not mean that the parties must have equal and coextensive obligations under the contract. Because there need not be economic equivalence in the exchange, it is permissible and common for one party to incur far more numerous, extensive, or onerous obligations than the other.

If "mutuality" does not carry any of these implications, what does it mean? In modern law, it is nothing more than a specific application of the general principle of consideration: When consideration consists of the exchange of **mutual promises,** the **undertakings** on **both sides** must be **real and meaningful.** If the promise of one party has qualifications or limitations so strong that they negate it, it is really no commitment at all. Because it does not bind that party, this lack of consideration voids the apparent contract, so neither party is bound. For example, Buster promises to buy Al's skis for $100, and Al promises to sell them to Buster unless Al changes his mind. This qualification reserves such unlimited discretion to Al that he has really promised nothing. His apparent promise is said to be **illusory** and hence cannot be consideration.

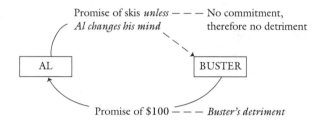

Using the language of mutuality, we could say that because Al is not bound, Buster is not bound either. However, we do not need to formulate it this way. The real problem is that Al has suffered no detriment because he has neither given nor actually promised anything to Buster. Therefore, Buster's return promise lacks consideration and is not binding. (Al may have thought that he was being very clever in getting a promise from Buster while keeping his own options open, but his lack of commitment removes binding force from Buster's promise too, so Al cannot hold Buster to his promise if Al decides to exercise his discretion to go through with the sale.) Because "mutuality" is redundant and misleading, Restatement Second §79(c) and Comment f disavow the concept and stress that it should not be thought of as a separate or additional requirement for consideration.

In the above example, Al's promise was illusory because he retained unlimited discretion to perform. This is the most common type of illusory promise, but not the only one. It would also be an illusion to promise something based on a condition that cannot occur. For example, Al gives his skis to Buster. In return, Buster promises to pay $100 for them if, by the end of the week, Elvis is returned to earth by the aliens who stole him.[11]

§7.9.2 Interpretation and the Use of Implied Terms to Cure an Apparently Illusory Promise

The examples given so far try to provide obvious illustrations of the absence or presence of commitment. It is not always this easy to tell if a qualification so eviscerates a promise as to make it illusory: The promise could be subject

---

11. Of course, some people do not believe this to be an impossible condition.

to some degree of discretion that may not be broad enough to negate commitment. For example, Al and Buster agree that Buster will buy Al's skis for $100 C.O.D. next Monday if Buster can borrow the money by then. Al's promise to sell the skis is firm, but Buster's promise to buy is subject to a condition. It could be argued that Buster has made no real commitment. He can prevent fulfillment of the condition simply by not trying to borrow the money. However, if we **imply** into Buster's undertaking a **promise to use best efforts** to secure a loan, we impose a detriment upon him and cure the lack of commitment. This promise to make best efforts is not the same as a promise to buy the skis, so that Buster has no obligation to consummate the sale if he tries conscientiously but unsuccessfully to secure the loan. But if he makes no effort at all, he is liable for breach of contract.

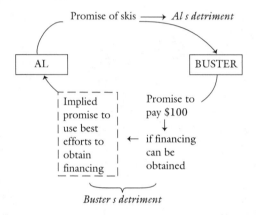

This brings to mind one of the most cherished cases in the contracts repertoire—*Wood v. Lucy, Lady Duff-Gordon*, 222 N.Y. 88 (1917)—in which Judge Cardozo implied an obligation to use best efforts to validate an exclusive dealing contract between Lucy, a fashion maven of her time, and Wood, her business agent. Wood had agreed to pay her Ladyship half the profits earned from placing her endorsements and selling her designs, but had not, in so many words, promised to promote her wares. When Lucy breached the exclusive agency by endorsing products on her own and keeping all the profits for herself, Wood sued for his share. Lucy argued that there was no contract: Although Wood had undertaken to pay half the profits to her, he had not actually promised to do anything to earn those profits. In light of the obviously commercial intent of the agreement, the court concluded that Lucy's grant of an exclusive agency necessarily gave rise to the implication that Wood was obliged to use best efforts in generating profits. UCC §2.306(2) follows this approach by implying an obligation of best efforts in exclusive dealing contracts involving goods.

We look more closely at the principles of interpretation—including the implication of terms by a court—in Chapter 10. The point to note here is that in most transactions with a commercial purpose, apparently discretionary promises can fairly be interpreted as subject to some implied limitation. When contracting, the parties usually intend their promises to be meaningful, and a later assertion that one of them is illusory is probably just a pretext to escape a bargain that is no longer desired. However, there are some situations in which absolute discretion is exactly what was intended, because one of the parties takes the gamble that the attractiveness of the product or service will be enough to motivate the other to exercise discretion favorably. In such a case, if a court unthinkingly implies unintended limitations on that discretion, it creates a contract out of an informal relationship that was not intended to be one. The process of implying terms to give content to apparently meaningless prose comes up in many types of cases, and you will find many examples of this as you read through this book.

§7.9.3 *"Mutuality" in Requirements and Output Contracts Under UCC §2.306*

Most sales contracts involve a single item or a specified quantity of goods. In some situations, however, it may suit the parties to leave the *quantity* of goods open-ended on the understanding that the quantity to be supplied under the contract will be determined either by the buyer's requirements or by the seller's output. The parties are likely to find a requirements contract most desirable if the seller is confidant that it can produce enough to satisfy the buyer's demands, and the buyer is unsure of its exact needs and wishes to avoid the risk of ordering a specified quantity which may turn out to be short or excessive. An output contract suits the parties when the seller wishes to dispose of its full production in one transaction, and the buyer is confident that it can use all that the seller can supply.

For example, assume that the seller is a persimmon grower and the buyer is a manufacturer of persimmon jam. The buyer is not exactly sure how much jam it will make next year, because consumer demand is erratic.[12] Buyer does not want the headache of trying to find persimmons on the market if it turns out that it did not order sufficient quantities, and it does not want a warehouse full of rotting persimmons if demand for jam is low. The buyer therefore makes a **requirements** contract with the seller under which the buyer promises to buy and the seller to supply the buyer's total demand for persimmons during a specific period. By contrast, assume that persimmon jam is so popular that the buyer cannot get enough persimmons and it can use all the fruit the seller can grow. The seller is happy to sell its entire crop to the buyer, because this saves the costs of multiple transactions with different buyers.

---

12. If you have ever tasted persimmon jam, you will know why.

The parties therefore enter an **output** contract under which the seller promises to sell and the buyer to take all the persimmons grown by the seller during a specified period.

Some earlier cases refused to uphold requirements and output contracts because the flexible quantity term was regarded as too vague and also because such contracts lacked "mutuality." That is, the broad discretion given to the party who determined quantity made that party's promise illusory because a requirements buyer could elect to have no requirements and an output seller could decide to produce no goods. In time, it came to be generally accepted that requirements and output contracts served a valuable commercial purpose, and that this approach was untenable. The problems of vagueness and lack of mutuality were solved by recognizing that even if the contract did not say so expressly, the discretion to determine quantity is limited by an implied obligation of good faith or reasonableness, and by an implied obligation of exclusive dealing. (The obligation of exclusive dealing could be absolute, or could relate to a particular portion of the requirements or output. Obviously, a promise to buy requirements or sell output is meaningless if the party has an unrestricted right to deal elsewhere.)

This relationship may be illustrated as follows, using the requirements contract as an example. (In an output contract, the discretionary performance would be on the seller's side of the exchange.)

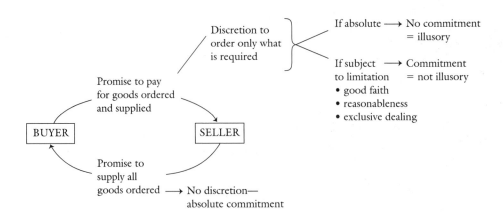

This approach forms the basis of UCC §2.306(1) that implicitly recognizes the **exclusive dealing** obligation and imposes both a good faith and a reasonable expectations test on the party who determines quantity. It states that when a contract measures quantity by the seller's output or the buyer's requirements, this means the **actual output or requirements** as may occur in **good faith**. In addition, it provides that the quantity tendered or demanded may not be **disproportionate** to any estimate, or if no estimate was stated, to any **normal** or otherwise **comparable** output or requirements.

UCC §2.306(1) is structured so that the good faith test is applicable in all transactions of this kind. Good faith is an elusive standard because the concept is so vague, but courts take much trouble to give it content.[13] Its general definition in the UCC is subjective "**honesty in fact** in the conduct or transaction" (UCC §1.201(19)) but a **merchant** is held to a higher standard that includes an objective element: "honesty in fact and the observance of **reasonable commercial standards of fair dealing in the trade**" (UCC §2.103(1)(b)).

Because parties to output or requirements contracts typically satisfy the definition of "merchant" in UCC §2.104(1),[14] the latter formulation of good faith usually applies. This means that the party setting quantity is held not only to a standard of honesty, but its conduct is also evaluated in light of what would be considered fair in the commercial context. In addition, when expectations of quantity are circumscribed by estimates or comparable data on quantity, this objective measure of the range of quantity further limits the party's discretion. Thus, as Comment 2 to UCC §2.306 states, these limits on discretion cure the "mutuality" problem.

§7.9.4 *Conditional Promises*

In the example in which Buster promised to pay for the skis if Elvis is returned by the aliens, the promise was illusory because it was conditional on an event that could not occur. However, a promise is not illusory merely because it is conditional. A qualified or conditional promise is good consideration provided that the contingency is genuine. That is, it is an uncertain future event within the realm of possibility and outside the complete and discretionary control of the promisor. If these requirements are satisfied, the conditional promise is a commitment. A legal detriment is suffered, even though the obligation to perform the promise only comes into effect upon satisfaction of the condition. For example, Al promises to give his skis to Buster tomorrow, and the parties agree that Buster need not pay for them unless he wins this week's state lottery, in which he has already bought a ticket. Buster promises that if he does win the lottery, he will pay Al $100 for the skis. Although Al's promise is absolute, and he must deliver the skis as promised, Buster's return promise is conditional. If he wins, he must pay. If not, he gets the skis free. The contingent nature of his promise does not prevent it from being consideration, because he suffers the **detriment** of **binding himself** to pay on the happening of an **uncertain future event outside his control.** This is different from the condition involving Elvis' return or from a case in which the fulfillment of the

---

13. It is discussed further in section 10.8.2.
14. The merchant status under UCC Article 2 is explained in sections 5.5 and 6.5.2.

condition is left by the agreement wholly within the control of the party who made it, so that the unbridled discretion in bringing about the condition makes the apparent commitment an illusion.

§7.9.5   *Promises of Alternative Performances*

A form of discretionary promise is one involving alternative performances. For example, Al promises to sell his skis to Buster in exchange for Buster's promise, in his discretion, to pay $100 or to mow Al's lawn for two months. Provided that each of the promises, on its own, would be consideration, there is nothing objectionable in permitting a party to select between alternative promises.

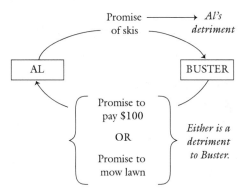

The case is more difficult if *one of the alternatives* imposes so small a burden on the party who has the choice that it *would not likely have induced the promise on its own.* For example, Buster may make the alternative promises either to buy the skis for $100 or to give Al notice of cancellation of the sale. The purpose of this is to give Buster the discretion to escape the contract if he so desires, and he is really no more firmly bound than if he promised to buy the skis if he feels like it. Although the obligation to give notice is a detriment, it is such a slight detriment that it would not on its own be likely to have induced Al to commit himself to sell the skis. Nevertheless, seen as a package with the more burdensome alternative, one can understand that the parties could have been satisfied with the commercial utility of this arrangement, and Al may have bargained for the chance that Buster would exercise his discretion in favor of completing the sale. By refusing to inquire into the adequacy of Buster's alternative detriment of giving notice, a court can uphold the transaction. This may seem like the exultation of form over substance when compared to the invalid purely discretionary promise, but the provision of notice gives the court a basis for validation, if it deems the agreement to have been fairly bargained for.

EXAMPLES

1. Penny Less entered college two years ago at the age of 22. At the time, her Uncle Rich, concerned about reports of excessive drinking by college students, promised her that if she did not drink any alcoholic beverages in her first year of college, he would give her $5,000 at the end of that year. Penny thanked Uncle Rich, stating that it would be easy money because she hated the taste of alcohol.

Penny did not consume any alcohol during her first year of college. When she reported this to Uncle Rich at the end of the year and asked for her reward, he said, "I have changed my mind about giving you the money. Don't be disappointed. Sobriety is its own reward." Was Uncle Rich free to change his mind?

2. Would your answer to Example 1 change if Penny was 19 years old at the time that she made her agreement with Uncle Rich? At that time she was old enough to be a major for the purposes of contracting but below the state's minimum drinking age of 21.

3. Chip A. Hoy borrowed $100,000 from Patience N. Vestor to finance his new startup business. The loan fell due for repayment last week. On due date, Chip told Patience that his business was failing, and he could not find the money to pay his many debts. He felt, however, that if his creditors would give him a break, he could save the business and survive. On the other hand, if his creditors would not help him, he would have to file for bankruptcy and because his debts greatly exceeded his assets, creditors would receive only a small fraction of their claims. Chip proposed that Patience give him a six-month grace period and then a further year to pay off the debt in monthly installments. He told Patience that he intended to make this proposal to all his creditors.

Patience agreed to the proposal. Chip and Patience signed a written memorandum reflecting their agreement that Chip would pay Patience $100,000, with interest at the market rate, in 12 equal monthly installments commencing six months later. Has Patience received consideration for her agreement to extend Chip's debt?

4. When Chevy K. Marro was 20 years old, his Aunt Charity expressed the intention of buying him a new car for his 21st birthday. Chevy's mom, who knew that Aunt Charity always talked big but never did what she promised, suggested that if Charity really meant what she said, she would write out the promise and sign it. Charity agreed, and Mom (known for her shrewd business sense) drew up the document. It stated that Charity, "in

consideration for value received" from Chevy, undertook to deliver the car (which was specifically described by make, model, and year) to Chevy on his 21st birthday. Mom had Charity and Chevy sign the writing. True to form, Aunt Charity gave Chevy a sweater for his 21st birthday and did not deliver the car.

(a)   Is Aunt Charity obligated by her promise of the car?

(b)   When Chevy threatened to sue her for the car, Aunt Charity became very annoyed. She would like to take back the sweater on the basis that Chevy gave her no consideration for it. Does she have the right to reclaim it?

5. Hunter Fortune used to work as a gardener on the country estate of Buck Plentiful, a billionaire. After Hunter was discharged by the groundskeeper for incompetence, he sued Buck for $1 million, alleging that he was sexually harassed and emotionally abused by the groundskeeper while in Buck's employ. Buck believed that the claim was without substance but did not want any scandal in his household, so he offered to settle the claim out of court for $10,000. Hunter accepted, and a settlement agreement was executed. After the agreement, Buck had second thoughts and refused to pay Hunter. Does Hunter have a valid claim arising from the agreement?

6. Ivor E. Keyes is a gifted pianist. On hearing him play, his beloved Aunt Charity determined to do something to help him advance his career. Ivor told her that he needed to get some training from a really fine pianist to improve his interpretation and style. He had contacted the celebrated Maestro Molto Bravissimo but had not engaged him as a teacher because he could not afford his fee of $150 an hour. Aunt Charity declared: "You shall have him as your teacher. I will send you a check for $15,000 tomorrow. That should cover 100 lessons." Ivor thanked her and said, "Auntie, if I ever make it to Carnegie Hall, I will get you the best seat in the house." She replied, "Yes, that will be nice, dear. I'll hold you to it." Do Ivor and Aunt Charity have a contract?

7. Save Our Slugs (SOS) is a citizens' organization formed to advance the interests of common garden slugs and to lobby for legislation to prevent assault on their natural habitat. One evening an articulate and persuasive fund raiser for the organization called on E. Z. Tutch to solicit a contribution. The fund raiser's impassioned and heart-rending plea for support convinced E. Z. Tutch that the poor creatures were under siege, and that urgent action was needed to save them from extinction. He therefore signed the following pledge card:

In consideration of my love for my ancient and venerable mother, the earth, and all her little creatures,

And in consideration for the promise of SOS to use my contribution in its tireless struggle to advance the noble cause for which it was constituted,

And in consideration of others subscribing with me to support this worthy endeavor,

E. Z. Tutch *hereby pledges the sum of* $ 500 ⁰⁰/₁₀₀ *to SOS, payable in* 10 *equal monthly installments, beginning on* Dec 1, 1997

Signed: E.Z.-Tutch

Date: Nov. 30, 1997

The next day, E. Z. Tutch realized that he had been overcome by his emotions the prior evening and had acted thoughtlessly. He has had many large expenses lately and really cannot afford the amount pledged. He regrets his decision to make the pledge and wishes to cancel it. May he do so without incurring legal liability?

8. Gutter Press, Inc. is a publisher of paperback books. Bonzo Steele, a famous bodybuilder and action-movie hero, was recently indicted for the gruesome murder of his agent, and the case has attracted enthusiastic public attention. Gutter Press plans to publish a book on Bonzo's seamy past and his present predicament. It wishes to produce the book as quickly as possible so that it hits the stands at supermarket checkouts before the inevitable lapse of the public attention span.

Gutter Press engaged Tabb Lloyd, a journalist, to write the book. The parties signed a written agreement which included the following terms:

(a)   Tabb promised to submit a completed manuscript within four weeks.

(b)   Gutter Press promised to publish the manuscript provided that it found it to be satisfactory.

(c)   If the manuscript was published, Gutter Press would pay Tabb a royalty of 15 percent of gross receipts.

(d)   During the first week following execution of the agreement, Gutter Press had the right, for any reason, to cancel it by delivering written notice of termination to Tabb. After the first week, Gutter Press could cancel at any time before completion of the manuscript by delivering the notice to Tabb and paying him a fee of $1,000 for all work done up to that time.

The day after signing the agreement, Tabb told his friends about it. They were disgusted and accused him of selling out and perverting his art for the sake of a quick and dirty buck. This so shamed Tabb that he no longer wishes to write the book. Can he escape his commitment to Gutter Press?

9. Constance De Votion decided to retire after working for the Turn Coat Corporation for 40 years. On her last day of work, the president of the company called her into his office and presented her with the following letter, signed by all the members of the Board of Directors:

> In recognition of your long and faithful service to this company, we are honored to give you an all-expenses-paid, two-week vacation at the hotel of your choice anywhere on the North American continent. When you have decided on your destination, please call the company's travel agent to make the arrangements. We hope that this vacation will be a joyful beginning to your richly-deserved retirement.

Constance spent a happy couple of weeks planning her vacation and settled on a lavish coastal resort. When she called the travel agent, he denied any knowledge of this arrangement and said that he had not been authorized by Turn Coat to book a trip for her. Constance called the president of Turn Coat, who told her with obvious discomfort that, a few days after she left, the Board had to meet in emergency session to approve drastic cutbacks because of a downturn in profits. One of the savings approved was the withdrawal of its promise to her.

Can Constance hold Turn Coat to its promise?

10. Gerry Atrick, another employee of the Turn Coat Corporation, had worked for it for 35 years. Although he used to be a superb worker, he had recently become absentminded and slow. His work was incompetent and had to be redone by others. Gerry was an employee at will, which meant that he could be summarily dismissed. The president was going to fire him, but the president's secretary dissuaded her from doing so by pointing out that the dismissal of such an old and loyal employee would be cruel and would upset and demoralize his coworkers. The president therefore offered Gerry a year's pay if he would retire. Gerry accepted and submitted his resignation. That night, as the

president was thinking about the events of her day, she suddenly realized that she did not really care if the staff was upset and would now have to justify this decision to the tightfisted Board. The next day, she called Gerry into her office, revoked the promise, and dismissed him. Is Turn Coat's promise binding?

11. Peters Pickled Peppers manufactures pickled peppers.[15] Last fall it made an agreement with Hal Apeno, a farmer, under which Hal undertook to supply all the peppers it would need for its bottling operations next season. During negotiations preceding the agreement, Peters told Hal that its average needs in the last five years had been between seven and ten tons of peppers. Hal was satisfied that he could grow sufficient quantities to meet this range of demand.

A short time later, Peters' Board met to discuss disappointing sales in the prior year. Studies showed that new and aggressive competitors had gained the lion's share of the pickled pepper market, and all indications were that next year would be even worse. The Board decided to switch from peppers to persimmons, for which there was very little competition. Peters' existing plant was suitable for the processing of persimmons, so the conversion could be achieved at small cost.

Because of this decision, Peters had no need for peppers, and it wrote to Hal telling him so. Hal sued Peters for breach of contract and Peters defended the suit on the basis that it had the right under the contract to order no pickles if it had no requirements. The trial court granted summary judgment to Peters on the theory that there was no contract because the transaction lacks mutuality of obligation. Is the judge right?

EXPLANATIONS

1. This example pays homage to those great Victorian cases in which a well-to-do family member promises some reward for specified behavior. The facts here are inspired by *Hamer v. Sidway,* 124 N.Y. 538 (1891), in which sanctimonious Uncle William Story promised $5,000 to his nephew, William II, if the nephew refrained from drinking, using tobacco, swearing, and playing cards or billiards for money until he reached the age of 21. Young Willie complied but had not been paid by the time that his uncle died. The court enforced Willie's claim against the uncle's estate. It rejected the estate's argument that Willie had not given consideration for his uncle's promise. Defining consideration as either a benefit to the promisor or a detriment to the promisee, the court found that Willie's abstention from the stated activities pursuant to the promise was sufficient detriment, because it was the abandonment of his legal right to engage in them. The legal benefit to the uncle did not need to be economic. His benefit lay in having his expressed desire fulfilled. Although the court in *Hamer* used the older definition of

---

15. Really? Who would have guessed!

consideration, the result is consistent with the bargain theory in that Willie's conduct seems to have been intended as the exchange for the promise.

Like Willie, Penny's detriment is not "detrimental" in the usual sense because it is really in her best interests. In fact (apparently unlike Willie) she does not even "suffer" in the usual sense because she has no desire to engage in the activity. Notwithstanding, she suffers a legal detriment simply by forgoing something that she is entitled to do. She exchanges this for Uncle Rich's promise of payment, providing him with a non-economic but identifiable benefit.

Because the benefit to Uncle Rich has no commercial purpose and is apparently motivated by his concern for Penny's well-being, one may be tempted to see his promise as the promise of a conditional gift. However, even a non-commercial promise may be bargained for if it reasonably appears intended to induce particular action desired by the promisor.

Another factor that may make Uncle Rich's promise appear to be a conditional gift is that it is hard to imagine that he could sue Penny to enforce her obligation not to drink. However, this can be explained if we recognize that Uncle Rich's offer proposed a unilateral contract, in which Penny gave no undertaking but accepted Uncle Rich's offer by rendering the performance, which was not complete until the end of the semester.[16]

2. As Penny's state of residence prohibits consumption of alcohol by people under the age of 21, she does not have a legal right to drink, so her forbearance is not the relinquishment of a legal right and hence no legal detriment. (The law distinguishes the power to do something from the legal right to do it.) Stated alternatively, she had a pre-existing legal duty to the state not to drink.[17]

However, the pre-existing duty rule should not be applied here. The rule is best confined to cases in which the duty is owed to the promisor. When the duty is owed to society or to a third party, the principal rationale of the rule—protection from coerced modification—is not implicated. Therefore, unless there is some other justification for it, the rule should not be used to invalidate Uncle Rich's voluntary promise. It could be argued that a public duty should be obeyed of its own force, and a promise given as an incentive to obedience should not be enforced as a matter of public policy. This is justified when the

---

16. The acceptance of an offer for a unilateral contract is explained in section 4.12. In short, if Uncle Rich's offer could be accepted only by the completion of Penny's performance (forbearing from drinking for the entire semester), no contract comes into existence until completion of Penny's performance. Once the performance is complete, a unilateral contract arises in which only Uncle Rich's obligation remains outstanding. If Penny does not perform, she never accepts the offer, and Uncle Rich has no contractual right to enforce. To protect Penny from having the offer revoked after she has begun her performance in reliance on it, the law deems the offer irrevocable as soon as Penny begins her performance.

17. This issue did not come up in the *Hamer* case.

promise is made to a public official as an incentive to the performance of his or her duty, because this leads to danger of corruption or favoritism. However, when the promise is merely an incentive to a private person to obey the law, the corruption problem is absent. Provided that the purpose of the contract is not extortionate (such as the payment of protection money to a mobster), there seems to be no public interest in refusing enforcement of the promise.

3. The principal focus of this example is the pre-existing duty rule and its application in contract modification. This is just a first look at modification, which is dealt with again in section 13.9.

The general rule is that a creditor's promise to accept less than the amount owing on an admitted debt or to extend the due date of the debt is not binding, because the debtor incurs no legal detriment in exchange for that promise. (*See* Restatement Second §73.) The debtor had a pre-existing duty to pay the debt now, and his promise to pay it over time adds nothing to that duty.

If the release or reduction of a debt is intended as a gift (say, when the parties are family or friends), the pre-existing duty rule guards against generosity. In a business context, the function of the rule is less likely to be aimed at protecting the promisor from charitable impulses, but more at the prevention of extortionate modifications. It is hard to justify the rule if the modification was fairly obtained. UCC §2.209 has tackled this problem directly by validating good faith modifications, even if without consideration. This approach is not as clearly established in common law, and courts that consider themselves bound by consideration doctrine have to find consideration in order to uphold a fairly agreed modification.

A court could find consideration if the promisee incurs some new detriment by giving something or undertaking any new obligation in exchange for the extension of the debt. Because the court does not ordinarily take account of the adequacy of consideration, even a slight new detriment enables the court to find consideration where it feels that the agreement was fairly made. There are a few possible bases for finding consideration in this case, but they are not without problems. First, Chip's undertaking to pay interest is probably not a new detriment unless he was not previously obligated to pay interest on the overdue debt (unlikely), or the previous rate of interest was lower. Second, detriment could be found if Chip's statement about intending to approach other creditors could be interpreted as a promise. However, it seems too vague to qualify and does not indicate a firm commitment.[18]

---

18. Had Chip entered into a multilateral agreement with a group of creditors under which they had all agreed to reduce or extend payment of their claims, this would have been recognized as a valid contract with consideration. Although the debtor gives no new consideration, the mutual forbearance of the creditors is treated as sufficient consideration for the contract as a whole. The policy for recognizing such an arrangement (known as a composition and extension) is that it facilitates the debtor's ability to manage and restructure debt by cooperative arrangement with creditors.

Third, Chip's warning about the possibility of bankruptcy could likewise be interpreted as an implied promise not to file (or at least to use best efforts not to have recourse to bankruptcy). A promise not to file bankruptcy has been held to be valid consideration for a promise to reduce or extend a debt provided that the debtor is really in financial difficulty, he would be justified in seeking bankruptcy relief, he is otherwise acting in good faith, and his indication of intent to file bankruptcy is not a thinly veiled threat to embark on an abuse of the court system for vexatious or dilatory purposes. However, the vague words used by Chip do not really seem to be strong enough to amount to a promise.

Even if no detriment can be found, consideration doctrine recognizes an exception that may be invoked here. If a contract modification is a response to unforeseen economic difficulties that have imposed an unexpected burden on the promisee, the modification may be upheld despite the lack of new detriment to the promisee. The rationale for the exception is that the unforeseen difficulties justify the modification, which is more likely to be fair and uncoerced. (Of course, unforeseen diffficulties do not necessarily eliminate the possibility of coercion, so it may not always be sensible to apply it.) In the context of an agreement to extend an undisputed debt, the poor performance of Chip's business may not, in itself, be sufficient to constitute unforeseen economic difficulties. Financial adversity is commonly foreseeable, and if it, alone, was enough, there would be very few debt adjustments that would not qualify for the exception. Chip should have to show some dramatic and unusual external cause for the difficulties, such as an economic crisis or market disruption.

4(a). Chevy has given no consideration to Aunt Charity for her promise, which is clearly intended as a gift, not an exchange. At Mom's instigation, the parties have attempted to validate the transaction by reciting that an unspecified consideration has been given. Restatement Second §71, comment *b*, regards such a false recital as ineffective. Some courts may be more sympathetic to this kind of effort at satisfying the formal function of consideration, but in most cases courts are only likely to uphold a formal recitation of consideration if a promise to furnish the recited consideration can be implied (which cannot be done when the recital does not specify what the purported consideration is), or the promisee's reliance on the promise creates grounds for estopping the promisor from denying the receipt of consideration.

This example is inspired by *Dougherty v. Salt*, 227 N.Y. 200 (1919), in which an aunt gave a promissory note for $3,000 to her eight-year-old nephew. The note was on a printed form that stated that it was given "for value received." Despite this language, it was clear that no consideration had been given for the note. The court refused to enforce it merely on the basis of the false recital.

4(b). The gift of the sweater has already been given, and there is no longer a promise to be enforced. Although the absence of consideration precludes enforcement of a promise, it is not grounds for recovering an executed gift. (Of course, there could be other grounds for reclaiming the gift. For example, the gift would be recoverable if it was induced by fraud or mistake, or if it was given subject to a condition that was not honored by the donee. However, these bases for recovery are distinct from consideration.)

5. The settlement agreement in this case compromises a claim that is disputed on the merits and unliquidated in amount. It is therefore distinguishable from the contract between Chip and Patience in Example 3, where the debtor's liability was undisputed. If a claim is in contention, an agreement to settle it is supported by consideration because each party forbears from asserting his full claim or defense. As a matter of policy, settlements of this kind are encouraged because there is a public interest in facilitating the consensual resolution of claims and lawsuits.

However, the dispute must be genuine and in good faith because it hardly serves the public interest to uphold an agreement to settle a dishonest claim or to abandon a dishonest defense. To allow this would be to encourage spurious claims, made purely for the purpose of coercing a nuisance payment, or of advancing groundless defenses, purely to hinder the collection of debt. Therefore, when consideration consists in the forbearance of a claim or defense, courts do, in effect, enquire into the adequacy of the consideration to the extent of determining whether the dispute is legitimate. This does not mean that the claim or defense must be valid. Obviously, the existence of a dispute must mean that the position of one of the parties will turn out to have been wrong. The test for legitimacy, as set out in Restatement Second §74, is either that the claim or defense is doubtful because of uncertainty in fact or law or that the party forbearing from the claim or defense believes that it may fairly be determined to be valid. That is, either the claim or defense must be objectively doubtful, or, even if it is not, the person asserting it must have an honest and genuine belief in its merits. (The formulation of the test in the First Restatement was stricter. It required both an honest and a reasonable belief in the validity of the claim.) In many cases, these alternative tests may amount to the same thing because it may be hard to convince a jury that a claimant had an honest belief in the genuineness of a claim that has no objective basis of support. However, the subjective alternative does allow account to be taken of honest ignorance. Under either test, the viability of the claim or the party's state of mind is measured at the time of the agreement, even if later events show that the claim or defense would not have succeeded if litigated.

In the present case, Hunter seeks enforcement of the settlement, so the issue will be whether his forbearance from asserting the full claim is consideration for Buck's promise of payment. Hunter's claim is not uncertain in law. His cause of action is well established and not based on some innovative and untried legal theory. Therefore, any uncertainty must relate to the factual viability of the case. These facts are deliberately left ambiguous. It is not clear if Hunter's claim is genuine or merely fabricated in revenge for his dismissal or to extort a payment from his rich ex-employer. To establish consideration, he must show that the claim is not merely an abuse of the legal process. From the perspective of what was known at the time of contracting, the claim must have had some objective grounds of support, or, based on his own understanding, he must have honestly believed himself to have been injured.

6. Aunt Charity clearly has suffered a detriment in promising to pay $15,000 to Ivor. However, this is nothing more than a gratuitous promise, like her promise to Chevy in Example 4, unless Ivor has given consideration in exchange for it. The only undertaking that could conceivably qualify as consideration is his assertion that he will get her the best seat in the house if he ever makes it to Carnegie Hall. (His implicit undertaking to use the money for piano instruction is merely a condition of the gift and cannot qualify as consideration.)

It is not clear that this really is a serious promise at all. It has several problems. First, it is very vague. It does not make it clear what is meant by the "best seat," nor does it specify the concert or concerts for which it will be obtained. Second, it is contingent on a very uncertain future event. A conditional promise could qualify as consideration provided that the fulfillment of the condition is not entirely at the will of the promisor, and the contingency is not so remote as to make it unlikely that the event would occur. (A promise subject to such a remote contingency would be nothing more than a sham.) Third, unless Ivor can be interpreted to have promised a large number of free concerts, the value of his apparent consideration is disproportionately small in relation to Aunt Charity's promise. (It is worth even less than the face amount of a ticket because its value must be discounted to take account of the uncertainty of the condition occurring.) Courts normally do not evaluate the adequacy of consideration, and a court may decline to do so in this case. However, sometimes (especially when there are other indications of gratuitous intent) a court could take a significant discrepancy in values into account, and may find that the transaction is really not an exchange but a gift formalized by a nominal return.

Finally, even if Ivor did make a promise and Aunt Charity accepted it by her response, it does not seem that his promise was in exchange for Aunt Charity's promise. He made it after she had already told him she would give him $15,000, so it cannot be said to have induced her promise.

The basis for holding that Ivor gave consideration for Aunt Charity's promise is therefore quite thin, and the transaction really seems to be nothing more than a promise of a gift. An argument for consideration is not inconceivable, but it is shaky.

7. The pledge recites three forms of purported consideration, but none of them qualifies as consideration.

7(a). E. Z. Tutch's love of nature may have motivated him to make the pledge (and even this is suspect, given that it is a standard recitation on the pledge form), but motive must be distinguished from consideration that must consist of a legal detriment suffered by SOS in exchange for his promise.

7(b). The commitment by SOS may be a promise, but it is also not consideration. Rather, it is merely an undertaking to use the gift for the purpose for which it was given. That is, it is a condition of the gift. In some cases it can be difficult to distinguish a bargained-for exchange from a gift with conditions, and the intent of the parties (evaluated objectively) is determinative. This is not one of the difficult cases, however. There really is no exchange. The only detriment suffered by SOS relates to its use of the money promised by E. Z. Tutch. This cannot qualify as a legal detriment because SOS has no legal right to use the money until it receives it, and it therefore gives up no legal right that it has at the time of the pledge. (SOS has a duty to prior donors to pursue its goals, so the "pre-existing duty" rule could be used as an additional argument. However, a duty to a third party may not preclude this promise from being consideration.)

7(c). The fact that others have subscribed or will do so is not consideration because the legal detriment is suffered by those parties and not by SOS. Like the situation with compositions, noted in Example 3, SOS may have provided consideration by promising to seek other subscribers, but no such promise is expressed or implied. Similarly, if a group of donors get together and all pledge to make a donation to an organization, the multilateral commitment of the donors could be sufficient to constitute consideration even if the organization has itself suffered no detriment. However, this did not happen here. The pledge form merely refers to other subscribers.

Because no consideration has been given by SOS for E. Z. Tutch's pledge, he may cancel it without liability. In this case, consideration doctrine fulfills its cautionary function by allowing the donor to escape his generous impulse and to allocate his income to the payment of creditors who gave him something in return for his debts.

8. In this contract, there has been an exchange of promises. The issue is whether Gutter Press's discretion to escape its commitment to publish the book and to pay royalties is so wide as to make its promise illusory.

A. The Condition of Satisfaction

On the face of it, Gutter Press can simply evade its promise by claiming that the manuscript is unsatisfactory. However, unless the contract makes it clear that a provision like this is in fact intended to reserve unbridled discretion to the party, it will be interpreted to impose an obligation on the party to exercise either good faith or reasonable judgment in determining if the performance is satisfactory. Unless the agreement itself indicates the standard to be applied, the rule of thumb is that dissatisfaction must be in good faith when the performance involves a matter of taste, and it must be reasonable when the performance has a technical or commercial purpose.

If an individual had ordered the book for his own amusement, he could legitimately claim that satisfaction with the book is a matter of taste (or, in the present case, distaste). The question would then be: Did this reader genuinely dislike the book? However, the book is a commercial venture, and the proper inquiry is whether a reasonable publisher would find the manuscript up to standard and capable of gainful exploitation. Because writing is not a purely technical venture such as pouring a concrete foundation, some subjective evaluation is inevitable—after all, even the production of a penny-horrible calls for some aesthetic judgment. But the focus is on a trade standard, oriented toward an evaluation of artistic merit and salability, as viewed by a reasonable publisher of this kind of material.

B. Gutter Press's Right to Terminate

Here again an unfettered termination right removes all commitment and makes the promise illusory. However, if Gutter Press undertakes to incur any detriment in terminating, consideration is present. The agreement may be viewed as giving Gutter Press the right to choose between alternative performances, and as long as each one would be consideration on its own, this right to select between alternatives does not negate the consideration.

Is each consideration on its own? There can be little doubt that the promise to publish and pay royalties and the promise to pay $1,000 are detriments. The termination on notice in the first week may seem to be an unbridled right to escape the contract, but courts usually uphold agreements subject to such termination provisions provided that notice of termination must be given. The giving of the notice is regarded as a detriment because it is a new duty assumed under the agreement. This may sound a little flimsy and Tabb surely would not have bargained for this as the exclusive consideration for his promise. However, courts are disinclined to inquire into adequacy of consideration unless it clearly appears to be sham or there is some indication that the disparity resulted from deceit or coercion.

If Gutter Press had reserved the right to terminate without any notice at all, the ability to escape the agreement without any detriment would make the promise illusory. Some courts avoid this fine distinction between no detriment and marginal detriment by implying a promise of reasonable notice when the agreement is silent on the question of notice and the implication is consistent with the express language of the agreement.

9. This example is based on retirement bonus cases such as *Feinberg v. Pfeiffer Co.*, 322 S.W.2d 163 (Mo. 1959). The problem in such cases is that the promise of reward for faithful service is made after the service has been rendered. Although the relationship between the parties is commercial and the promise may be in recognition of valuable work, the exchange element is missing. The employee's service was rendered in the past in return for wages and other contractual benefits. This "past consideration" cannot be thought

of as bargained for in exchange for the promise, and Constance has suffered no new detriment in return for it.

Because Turn Coat has breached its faith to Constance, the court may make great effort to find some new detriment on her part, however slight, to validate the promise. However, this would be a real strain on the present facts. Her assent to call the agent is some detriment, but it is obviously a condition of receiving the gift rather than bargained for as the price of the promise. If Constance had taken any action in reliance on the promise, the doctrine of promissory estoppel could afford a remedy, as discussed in Chapter 8, but no such action is suggested here. (In *Feinberg,* the court found no consideration for the promise of a pension made by the employer after years of service. However, it did apply promissory estoppel to enforce the promise because the employee had relied on the promise to her detriment. This aspect of the case is discussed in Example 3 of Chapter 8.)

10. The fact that Turn Coat contemplated some benefit—worker morale—from the resignation is not in itself consideration. This is merely the motive for the promise. However, the fact that some benefit would be gained by the company does serve as evidence that the resignation was bargained for in exchange for the promise. The issue in this case is whether the resignation was a legal detriment to Gerry. If Turn Coat could fire him at will, it could be argued that Gerry gave up no legal right by retiring because he had no right to continued employment. However, he did have the right to stay on the job until dismissed. Although this is not a very valuable right, equivalence in consideration is not required, and his sacrifice of the right should be sufficient to support the promise. As noted already, there is a reasonable basis for finding that the company did bargain for the advantage of not having to exercise its power to dismiss him.

In *Katz v. Danny Dare, Inc.,* 610 S.W.2d 121 (Mo. 1980), a longstanding employee suffered a head injury in trying to stop a thief who had stolen money from his employer. The injury impaired his ability to work competently, and the president of the employer (who also happened to be the employee's brother-in-law) tried to persuade the employee to retire by offering him a pension. The employee eventually agreed and left the company with the Board's promise of a life pension. Like Gerry, the employee could have been dismissed at will. A dispute later developed over the employer's obligation to continue paying the pension. Contrary to the resolution that I suggest above, the court held that an employee-at-will gives up no legal right by retiring. This seems to be an unduly narrow view, especially given the obvious desire of the employer to avoid the embarrassment of firing an old employee, injured in the line of duty, and related to the president. Nevertheless, the case turned out satisfactorily, because the court found that the employee had relied on the promise, and it enforced the promise under the doctrine of promissory estoppel. Again, his aspect of the case is taken up in Example 3 of Chapter 8.

11. Shame on the judge for using that naughty phrase that has little meaning in modern law. What the court means, of course, is that it considers Peters' promise to be illusory because Peters has the discretion to have no requirements for peppers. In this too, the judge betrays a sadly old-fashioned state of mind. Many years ago, some courts did take this approach to requirements and output contracts, but this view died out as it became accepted that contracts for flexible quantities have commercial utility and should not be found to lack consideration. Today, UCC §2.306 places this matter beyond doubt by limiting the discretion of the buyer in a requirements contract and the seller in an output contract. Peters' requirements must be its actual requirements as may occur in good faith. Furthermore, as there is a stated estimate, this sets the range of permissible variation. (Even had there not been an estimate, Peters' normal or prior comparable requirements would set the range.)

The fact that an estimate has been made suggests that this case can simply be resolved on the disproportionality test. Although Peters can order as little as approximately seven tons and as much as approximately ten tons, these estimates set the outer limits of its discretion, and it would be a breach to order substantially less than the bottom end of the range. However, there are some cases—for example, *Empire Gas Corp. v. American Bakeries Co.*, 840 F.2d 1333 (7th Cir. 1988)—that have said that the disproportionality test applies only to increases in demand and not to decreases.

If this is so, Peters' elimination of its requirements must be measured on the good faith standard. Because Peters deals in peppers and has knowledge and skill relating to them, it is a merchant under UCC §2.104 and is subject to the definition of good faith in UCC §2.103(1)(b). It is held not only to actual honesty but must also observe standards of fair dealing in the trade. Is Peters' decision, based on a business judgment to discontinue production of pickled peppers, in good faith? Comment 2 to UCC §2.306 indicates that the good faith standard permits an honest discontinuance of requirements resulting from lack of demand. It draws a distinction between the justifiable shutdown of the buyer's plant for lack of orders, and an impermissible shutdown merely to curtail losses. This suggests that the good faith standard is not satisfied merely because Peters has made a sensible business judgment based on profitability. There must be hardship serious enough to overcome Peters' duty to honor Hal's reasonable expectations. This seems to be a matter of degree, and it is not clear from the facts whether the threat of competition is so severe as to necessitate the change in product line as a matter of survival.

8

Promissory Estoppel as the Basis for Enforcing Promises

§8.1 Introduction

As Chapter 7 shows, consideration is a prerequisite to a valid contract. A promise that has not been bargained for in exchange for some detriment cannot be enforced as a contract. Of course, as we have seen, consideration doctrine has a degree of flexibility that enables courts to stretch the concept of bargained-for exchange to accommodate some deserving cases. But this only works up to a point. Sometimes the facts are such that no manipulation of consideration doctrine could produce a realistic argument that consideration was given for a promise. In many cases the resulting nonenforcement of the promise is an appropriate consequence, but this result can be unfair when the promisee incurred some loss in justifiably relying on the promise. Promissory estoppel has developed to provide relief in such cases. When all its elements are satisfied, a promisor may be held accountable for a promise without consideration, and the court may enforce it to the extent necessary to remedy the unfair result of reliance on it.

Promissory estoppel was first articulated as a distinct basis of liability in §90 of the First Restatement. The original formulation, with subtle revisions, survives in §90 of Restatement Second. Although the Restatement section does not itself call the doctrine promissory estoppel, this name is firmly established by long usage.

Several factors must be considered in deciding whether promissory estoppel relief is appropriate, as will be discussed shortly. However, its essential elements can be stated simply: A **promise** coupled with **detrimental reliance** on that promise. Although these two prerequisites do not always receive the same emphasis, a combination of them must be present for relief to be granted.

§8.2   The Ancillary and Independent Basis of Promissory Estoppel

Although some writers argue that promissory estoppel is growing in importance and that it may one day eclipse consideration as the ground for contractual liability, it remains an *ancillary basis for relief.* If a promise is supported by consideration and there are no other problems disqualifying the promise as contractual, promissory estoppel is not needed. When analyzing a problem, it is therefore logical to first consider if a contract has been formed and to turn to promissory estoppel only if that question is answered negatively.

Because it allows for the enforcement of a promise without consideration, promissory estoppel is sometimes called a **substitute for consideration.** One must approach this phrase carefully, because there is disagreement over the categorization of promissory estoppel and its relationship to contract. This debate is partly philosophical, reflecting contrasting opinions on the way that the law should be conceived, and partly empirical, based on different interpretations of how the courts actually treat promissory estoppel. One's view of the nature of promissory estoppel can have significant practical consequences because it has an impact on the approach to relief, as discussed below, and could also affect questions such as the appropriate statute of limitations[1] or matters of procedure.

Those who argue that promissory estoppel is truly a consideration substitute take the view that if the elements of promissory estoppel are satisfied the promise must be treated as a contractual undertaking. That is, when consideration is lacking, promissory estoppel is an alternative basis for finding contractual liability. This approach is favored by Restatement Second, Comment *d* to §90 declares that a promise binding under that section is a contract.

The opposing view is that promissory estoppel does not result in enforcement of the promise as a contract but is an alternative and independent

---

1. Statutes of limitation specify the period within which a person must commence action on a claim. If suit is not brought within the specified period, it is barred. Different types of claim have different limitation periods. For example, in most states a suit on contract must be commenced within six years of the claim arising but the limitation period for tort is only two years. Therefore, if promissory estoppel is regarded as a contract-based doctrine, its limitation period should correspond to the longer period for contract, but if it is seen as derived from tort, the shorter period may apply.

basis for enforcing the promises—a separate theory of obligation, based not on bargain but on accountability for conduct that induces reliance. This conception of promissory estoppel emphasizes its affinity to tort and sees it more as a redress for injury suffered in reliance than as a consensual relationship.

It seems to me that the truth lies somewhere in the middle of these positions. The existence of a voluntary promise surely provides some link between promissory estoppel and contract. Yet, the need for demonstrated injurious reliance and the approach to relief makes promissory estoppel quite distinct from contract. It is therefore more coherent to conceive of promissory estoppel as a basis for relief separate and distinct from contract.

§8.3 The Difference in Remedial Emphasis Between Contract and Promissory Estoppel

Whether or not one views promissory estoppel as an independent theory of liability, it is generally recognized that the remedy for promissory estoppel is subject to different concerns than those affecting contractual relief. However, the difference between contract-based and tort-based approaches does affect one's view of the most appropriate remedial goal for promissory estoppel. As discussed more fully in section 8.7, if promissory estoppel creates contractual liability, the normal relief for promissory estoppel should be the *full enforcement* of the promise, and it is only appropriate to limit relief under special circumstances. Conversely, if one focuses on the protection of reliance, the remedy should usually be confined to *reimbursement of actual loss,* with fuller enforcement reserved for cases when justice so demands. This could make a substantial difference in recovery: Contract damages look toward the future and try to place the promisee in the position he or she would have been in had the contract been honored. They aim at giving the promisee the benefit of the bargain by awarding the money equivalent of what the promisee would have gained as a result of the contract. On the other hand, tort-like damages look toward the past and merely try to restore the status quo by reimbursement of expenses and losses.

§8.4 An Introduction to Equitable Estoppel and Its Link to Promissory Estoppel

As intimated above, the essential function of promissory estoppel is to provide relief for justifiable reliance on a promise given without consideration. Promissory estoppel, a relatively modern doctrine, derives from the much older principle of **equitable estoppel,** also known as **estoppel in pais.** It is therefore helpful to understand the basic idea of equitable estoppel. Equity was introduced in section 2.5. Because a court of equity exercises its discretion to do justice between the parties, it is a general principle of equity that the litigants must themselves behave equitably in seeking the court's assistance. Relief that may otherwise be available is barred by the claimant's unworthy conduct.

Equitable estoppel reflects this principle. Its basic purpose is to **preclude** (i.e., "estop") a person from asserting a right when, by **deliberate words or conduct,** he or she has **misled** the other party into the justifiable belief that the right does not exist or would not be asserted. Like many equitable doctrines, estoppel involves a *balancing of the equities* between the parties and a comparative evaluation of the fault and responsibility of the parties. Therefore, it generally only bars relief when the party asserting the rights deliberately engaged in the misleading behavior with *knowledge or reason to know* it was misleading and would likely induce reliance by the other. In addition, the other, unaware of the true facts, must have *relied* on the misrepresentation in a way that would result in some *loss or prejudice* if the claimant is permitted to assert the right.

For example, Jack Black had just won $2,000 at cards, an activity that his wife, Prudence, firmly forbids. To conceal his ill-gotten gains, he hid the cash in an unused cookie jar. One day, while their niece, Penny Less, was visiting, she dipped her hand into the jar, thinking that it contained cookies. When, instead, she pulled out the wad of bills, Aunt Prudence's suspicious nature was aroused. She demanded to know of Uncle Jack where the money came from. Always a cool customer, Uncle Jack had little trouble coming up with a plausible story to get Aunt Prudence off his back: "Oh . . . well . . . Penny's dad sent the money to me as a surprise gift for Penny. I specially hid it in the jar because I knew that she would find it when she felt in the jar for cookies, which she always does." Although this explanation satisfied Aunt Prudence, it turned out not to have been a clever tactic because Penny scooped up the cash with a squeal of joy, exclaiming, "Now I can take that vacation that I dreamed of and couldn't afford!" Before Uncle Jack could take Penny aside to explain where the money really came from, she left and went directly to a travel agent, from whom she bought a non-refundable air and hotel excursion package. A short while later, Uncle Jack arrived in a breathless frenzy at Penny's door, told her the truth, and asked for the money back.

If Penny refuses to repay Uncle Jack and he is foolish enough to publicize his nefarious activity to Aunt Prudence by suing for it, he would likely be estopped from asserting that it was his own money. He deliberately misinformed Penny that it was hers. Upon realizing that she believed him, he did not reveal the truth to her and allowed her to rely on his statement. She apparently had no reason to doubt the truth of what he said, and incurred an irreversible commitment on the strength of the belief that she was $2,000 richer. She cannot easily find the money to reimburse him. It does not matter that Uncle Jack made the statement without intent to cheat Penny. Estoppel is not based on fraud but on accountability for deliberate words or conduct that induce reliance and consequent injury. A person who is estopped from asserting a fact is treated as if that fact does not exist, so the falsehood becomes true in the eyes of the law.

This is a case of **equitable,** not promissory, **estoppel** because Uncle Jack made an incorrect **factual assertion** and not a promise. Indeed, estoppel was originally held not to be applicable to promises. During the nineteenth century, some courts began to recognize that reliance on a *promise* was just as worthy of protection as reliance on a factual assertion, and they began to apply equitable estoppel to promises. (The theory of these cases was that the promisor was *estopped from asserting a lack of consideration* for the promise, hence consideration was present. Therefore the early cases did treat estoppel as a consideration substitute.) Not all courts followed this approach. Some refused relief despite reliance if consideration was absent, and others sought to protect reliance indirectly by bending over backwards to find consideration in the most tenuous of detriments.

By the time of the drafting of the First Restatement, there was enough caselaw to support the inclusion of a new doctrine that came to be called promissory estoppel. The Restatement's formulation (in §90) did not treat the promise as estopping the denial of consideration, but simply recognized **detrimental reliance** on the promise as a basis of enforcing it. Therefore, while the drafters of the Restatement did not necessarily conceive of promissory estoppel as a theory of liability separate from contract, they planted the seeds of this idea. Following publication of the Restatement, the judicial recognition of promissory estoppel grew, and the doctrine has become well-established, even though courts differ on its scope and range. Its formulation in Restatement Second §90 follows that of the original Restatement quite closely but makes changes to reflect its development over the intervening years.

§8.5 The Range of Promissory Estoppel: Gifts and Commercial Transactions

When promissory estoppel first developed, its primary role was to validate **gratuitous promises** such as family gifts and charitable donations. It was not thought to be applicable to promises made during the course of commercial interaction. It continues to have application to donative promises, but the tendency has been to expand it. Promissory estoppel is now commonly invoked as a basis for enforcing a commercial promise. Of course, promissory estoppel has no role in most commercial transactions. No gift is intended and once agreement is reached, consideration is present. However, we have already seen that consideration problems do sometimes arise in the commercial setting, or other factors may prevent a promise from being enforceable as a contract.

As this suggests, the decision to enforce a promise involves an evaluation of the conduct and reasonable understanding of each party and the fairness of holding the promisor accountable for a promise that would not otherwise be binding in contract law. While separate elements can be identified, their nature is such that they flow into and affect each other. Thus, for example, if the promise is clear and express, it is easier to infer intent to induce reliance and to justify reliance, and enforcement is more likely to be needed to avert injustice. Conversely, if there is doubt about the apparent promise, it is harder to show these other elements convincingly. We now survey each of the factors outlined above.

§8.6.2 *A Promise Must Have Been Made*

The meaning of promise was introduced in section 1.2.4, where it was pointed out that not every assertion or statement of intent qualifies as a promise. Unless clear language of commitment is used, it can be difficult to decide if a promise has been made. Words and conduct must be interpreted in all the relevant circumstances of the case to determine if the alleged promisor *manifested an intent to commit* to a particular performance or course of action.

Note that it is manifested, rather than actual, intent that is determinative. As in contract, intent for the purpose of promissory estoppel is gauged by an *objective* test. The question is not what the promisor actually intended, but what the promisee was justified in understanding that intent to be, based on the promisor's utterances and conduct. This could not be otherwise because promissory estoppel aims to protect reliance that necessarily is based on a reasonable perception of exhibited intent rather than on the undisclosed thoughts and beliefs of the promisor. Notwithstanding this, the promise must be voluntarily and deliberately made. As in the case of contract, the promisor's accountability for the reasonable meaning of his manifestation is tempered by doctrines that allow the court to look behind apparent intent when there is some question as to whether the promisor's volition had been undermined by trickery, coercion, or mistake. Therefore, doctrines such as fraud, duress, and mistake (covered in Chapters 13 and 15) may be used to avoid liability based on promissory estoppel in much the same way as they may be used by one whose apparent assent to contract was improperly extracted.

Also bear in mind the evidentiary, cautionary, and channelling functions served by consideration doctrine. The fact that consideration was not given for the promise means that these functions are not fulfilled by any act of exchange. Therefore, a court must exercise particular care before finding a promise when there is little or no formality in its execution or the circumstances suggest that the promisor may have acted on impulse or with rash generosity.

§8.6.3 The Promisor Should Reasonably Have Expected the Promise to Induce Action or Forbearance by the Promisee

This element is so closely connected to the inquiry into promise that it is a little artificial to treat it separately. However, it is helpful to split the evaluation of promisor accountability into two issues for the purpose of building a framework for analysis. Because the promisor is accountable only for a deliberate and voluntary promise, one must go beyond simply interpreting the meaning of the manifestation and must also evaluate the promisor's *justifiable understanding* of the likely impact of the promise. The circumstances must be such as to warrant holding the promisor accountable for creating the situation leading to reliance and the resulting loss.

This means that the promisor knew or reasonably should have realized that the promisee would likely understand that a promise had been made and would thereby be induced to take or refrain from action of the kind that occurred. (Thus, not only the likelihood of reliance but also the general nature and extent of the response must have been reasonably foreseeable by the promisor.) Again, an objective standard is used, so the promisor is held to a standard of reasonableness, whether or not he actually intended the promise to be relied on.

§8.6.4 The Promise Must Have Induced Justifiable Action or Forbearance by the Promisee

We now move from the promisor's accountability to the promisee's reliance. In dealing with inducement, the text of §90 does not expressly require the reliance to be justifiable, but this principle is referred to in the comments. In any event, it is inherent in the purpose of promissory estoppel. Thus, the evaluation of the promisee's response also splits into two inquiries:

a. Did the Promise Induce the Action or Forbearance?

There must be a **cause and effect** between the promise and the promisee's conduct. Therefore, any loss or expense incurred before the promise was made cannot be said to have been induced by the promise. Even if the conduct followed the promise, it is not induced by the promise if it would have occurred even in the absence of the promise.

b. If There Was Inducement, Was the Promisee Justified in this Response?

The promisor should not indiscriminately be held accountable for any action or forbearance induced by the promise. Sometimes it is appropriate to leave the risk with the promisee for having made the judgment to incur a loss or expense on the strength of a noncontractual promise. This is particularly true if the promisee's reaction to the promise could not reasonably be expected because it was a gamble, ill-considered, or quirky. Therefore, the promisee's response to the promise is also judged by a **reasonableness standard.** Relief is denied to the extent that this response was not justified under all the circumstances of the case. As usual, the evaluation is not absolutely objective and takes into account the personal attributes and situation of the promisee, so the question is not simply whether an abstract reasonable person would have so responded, but whether this was a reasonable response from a *person in the promisee's position.*

It should be obvious that there is a very close link between the factors that determine the promisor's accountability and the promisee's justifiable reliance, and that they are frequently just different aspects of the same overall pattern: The stronger the sense of commitment, the greater likelihood of a reasonable expectation of inducement and, consequently, of justifiable reliance.

Section 90 dispenses with proof of reliance for **charitable pledges** and **marriage settlements.** By eliminating the requirement of reliance, §90 makes a promise binding purely on the basis that it was made, effectively abolishing the requirement of consideration in these two classes of gift. This dispensation has had some influence, but it has not been widely accepted. The policy arguments for and against enforcing charitable promises without consideration are considered in section 7.4.2.

§8.6.5   The Promise Is Binding if Injustice Can Be Avoided Only by Its Enforcement

This element reflects the total balance to be drawn by the court after evaluating the equities, so that a decision can be reached that achieves a fair result in all the circumstances. (This balancing is an aspect of the equitable roots of promissory estoppel.) It takes into account not only the issues of promise and reliance discussed above, but also any other factors that bear upon the appropriateness of enforcing the promise.

The most significant of these is the **detriment or harm** suffered by the promisee in relying on the promise. If one accepts the protection of reliance as the fundamental purpose of promissory estoppel,[2] it is not enough that the promisee had merely a generalized expectation of gain which has been disappointed. The promisee must have suffered some **specific** and **measurable loss** by relying on the promise. Therefore, "detriment" in this context is usually not used in the attenuated sense associated with consideration doctrine but describes a real economic loss such as an expenditure, a sacrificed opportunity, a commitment or some other prejudice of a substantial kind. While some courts may accept less, especially if the other equities strongly favor enforcement, the need to avert injustice by enforcement of the promise is not very strong if there is no loss that needs redress and the only effect of nonenforcement is the failure to receive the promised benefit.

Another important factor that weighs in the balance was mentioned earlier in connection with the promise in section 8.6.2, but should be reemphasized here in dealing with the general equities of enforcement. Comment *b* to §90 stresses that the promisor needs protection from an **ill-considered promise** or a **bogus claim of promise.** Because consideration is absent, its safeguards—the channelling, cautionary, and evidentiary functions—are missing. The court should therefore weigh the lack or presence of formality and the apparent deliberateness of the commitment in deciding whether the equities favor enforcement, and if so, to what extent.

§8.7 The Remedy When Promissory Estoppel Is Applied

Restatement Second §90 states that the remedy for breach of the promise may be limited as justice requires. Although Comment *d* to that section says that a promise binding under the section is a contract, this limitation of remedy means that the promisee is not necessarily entitled to **full contractual relief.** While the court may grant the promisee full expectation damages to compensate for the loss of bargain resulting from the breach, it has the discretion to provide a lesser remedy. Typically, this lesser remedy would be focused on the **reimbursement** of the **actual loss or expense** incurred in reliance on the promise.

Although §90 suggests a range of damages and makes it clear that the balance of the equities affects the extent of relief, there is some debate on the

---

2. It was noted in section 8.2 that some writers argue that the enforcement of a deliberate promise is the true basis of promissory estoppel. On this view, the protection of reliance has a less central role, and the proof of actual loss is less important.

correct emphasis to be placed on the choice of remedy. Those who see promissory estoppel as a contractual doctrine (a consideration substitute) believe that full contractual relief should be the normal measure of relief and a lesser remedy is appropriate only in exceptional cases. Those who argue that promissory estoppel is an independent tort-like theory of liability consider that reimbursement of actual loss should be the normal relief, with full enforcement confined to cases in which the lesser remedy is clearly inadequate. Some studies suggest that courts do in fact incline to full enforcement except when there is some problem in proving expectation damages. In short, it is difficult to say for sure where the primary focus is, given the spectrum of damages available to courts. It is important to recognize, however, that courts have a discretionary range of relief. This gives a court the flexibility to avoid an "all or nothing" resolution. The court need not confine itself to the question of whether the promise should be enforced at all. It may also consider the possibility of a lesser level of enforcement, and in a close case, it can reach a median position by granting partial relief.

To illustrate the possible range of remedies and the distinction between full contractual damages and reliance recovery, consider Penny's enrollment in college on the strength of Uncle Rich's promise to give her $20,000: Penny's expectation is $20,000, and full contractual enforcement would give her this amount. By contrast, reliance damages would depend on the extent of her actual loss or prejudice. Therefore, if the year's tuition is $20,000, injustice may be averted only by full enforcement of the promise because she has committed herself for that amount. However, if annual tuition is only $5,000 and Penny is committed for only one year's tuition, enforcement to the extent of $5,000 (or maybe $5,000 plus living expenses) may be enough to prevent injustice. Although Penny, in a sense, may have relied on having tuition for more than one year, the broken promise of future funding disappoints her expectation but does not constitute an actual out-of-pocket loss. The facts become more complicated if, in addition to committing herself for $5,000 tuition, she gave up a job to attend college, because her sacrificed earnings are also a reliance loss and should be taken into account in deciding her recovery.

The following examples focus on general principles of promissory estoppel but do not end our study of this topic. It is also covered in Chapter 8 (promissory estoppel as an alternative to restitutionary recovery); section 5.3 (promissory estoppel in the context of options); section 11.4 (the application of promissory estoppel to the statute of frauds); and section 13.9 (promissory estoppel in relation to contract modification).

EXAMPLES

1. Tina Terrible owned a large motorbike that she persisted in dumping against the front door of the family home. One day, her father, having grown

tired of nagging her to park the bike neatly in the driveway, issued an ultimatum: He told Tina that the next time he found the bike obstructing the front door, he would take it away and lock it in the basement for a month. True to form, Tina ignored this threat and left her bike at the door the next day. When her father returned from work, he saw the bike and resolved to take it to the basement after dinner. Unluckily, while he was eating his dinner, the bike was stolen.

Tina has no comprehensive insurance on the bike. She blames her father for her loss because had he locked up the bike as threatened, it would not have been stolen. Is she entitled to claim the value of the bike from her father?

2. Assume facts different from those stated in Example 1: Tina, a sweet and conscientious daughter, dutifully parks her motorbike in the driveway every night. She has always had comprehensive insurance on the bike, but she has a low-paying job and it has been a real struggle to find the money for the very high premiums. When she received the current renewal notice, she thought of terminating her comprehensive coverage, but worried that if she did so, she would be unable to replace the bike if stolen.

One evening, a few days before the premium was due, she told her father of her difficulties. He generously offered to pay the premium for her and took the policy renewal notice from her, promising to pay it the next day. Sadly, Tina's father talks big, but he almost never does what he promises. True to form, he did not pay the premium. A few days later, Tina received a warning of cancellation from the insurer and asked her father if he had paid. He apologized for the delay, but assured her that the check would be mailed to the insurer the next morning. Hearing nothing further from the insurer, Tina assumed that matters had been taken care of. A couple of weeks later, the bike was stolen. She then discovered that her father had never paid the premium.

Can Tina recover from him? If so, what can she claim?

3. Examples 9 and 10 of Chapter 7 identified a consideration problem in which promises of reward for long service were made to retirees at the point of retirement. Under the "past consideration" rule, prior service is not consideration because it has already occurred and is not therefore bargained for in exchange for the promise. Both cases involved the fickle and ungrateful company, Turn Coat Corporation. In summary, the facts were:

3(a). In Example 9, when Constance De Votion retired after working for Turn Coat for 40 years, the company promised her an all-expenses-paid vacation in recognition of her faithful service. She planned the vacation, but when she tried to book it, she discovered that the company had revoked its promise as part of an economy drive. She could not enforce the promise under consideration doctrine because she had suffered no new detriment in exchange for it.

3(b). In Example 10, Gerry Atrick was a longstanding employee who had become incompetent. Although he could have been summarily dismissed as an employee at will, the company decided that worker morale would best be served if he could be persuaded to retire. The company offered and he accepted the promise of a year's wages in exchange for his voluntary retirement. The company then changed its mind and fired him. It is arguable that his agreement to retire is sufficient legal detriment to be consideration for the promise of a year's wages. However, the contrary argument could be made that an employee at will gives up no legal right in agreeing to resign because the company can dismiss him summarily.

Assuming that the court finds no consideration for the company's promises to these employees, do these facts support recovery under promissory estoppel?

4. Since graduating from the Elmo Mater College a few years ago, Al Lumnis has been very successful in business. Toward the end of the financial year, he decided to share a little of his wealth with his old college. As he thought back to his days on campus, he remembered how difficult it had been to find a good cup of coffee. The bilge in the cafeteria was undrinkable, and the closest source of espresso was ten blocks away. He therefore decided that his gift to the college would be a fully equipped espresso bar. He wrote a letter to the president in which he stated: "In consideration of my desire to enhance and ennoble the quality of campus life at the Elmo Mater College, I hereby pledge to the College the sum of $20,000 to be paid as soon as the College submits plans to me for the construction of a fully equipped espresso bar in the Student Union building. The bar shall be known as the 'Al Lumnis Mochamorial'."

The president of the college wrote back, thanking Al for the pledge and undertaking to begin work immediately on planning the coffee bar. The president appointed a joint faculty-student committee to consult with architects. She also instructed the editor of the alumni magazine to prepare a flattering article on Al and his gift for the next edition of the magazine.

It is now a couple of weeks later. The committee has met a couple of times and has had one consultation with an architect. Copy has been written for the magazine which has not yet been published. The president has just received another letter from Al which states: "My offer to fund an espresso bar was a bad idea. The trouble with kids today is that life is too easy. My character was built by trudging through the snow to get my cappuccino. This hardship gave me the resilience to succeed in business. Please disregard my last letter. I withdraw my pledge."

Can the College hold Al to his pledge?

5. Chilly Winters lived in a cold and congested northern city. Sonny Climes, his college roommate, moved south a few years ago and lives in Tropicana, a balmy southwestern metropolis. Over the years, Sonny has frequently enticed Chilly with his accounts of the good life under the palm trees. Sonny has established a flourishing high-tech business and often told

Chilly that if he ever decided to escape the snow and smog, a job would be waiting for him at Sonny's company.

After suffering through a particularly harsh winter, Chilly decided that it was time to move south. He called Sonny and asked if a job was still available. Sonny responded, "You bet! Get down here as soon as you can and I'll put you to work." When Chilly tried to discuss the terms and nature of the proposed employment, Sonny said, "Don't worry about the details. We can work that out when you get here. After all, we're old friends and I know that you'll fit right in." Chilly told Sonny that he would give notice to his present employer and would be in Tropicana in a month.

Chilly immediately gave notice to his employer and his landlord and bought a one-way air ticket to Tropicana. When he called Sonny a week later to tell him his exact time of arrival, he received an unpleasant surprise. Sonny told him that he had just received an offer for the sale of his business that was too good to resist. He had accepted it and planned to retire. He was sorry, but he could no longer employ Chilly.

Chilly tried to retract his notice to his employer and his landlord, but his employer had already hired a replacement and his apartment had been relet. Chilly found a new apartment at a higher rental. After two months searching, he found a new job that paid the same salary as the old one. He cannot obtain a refund of his airfare, but airline policy allows him to cancel his booking and to use the ticket for travel within the U.S.A. at any time within the next year.

What recourse, if any, does Chilly have against Sonny?

EXPLANATIONS

1. Tina clearly has no contractual basis for recovery. There is no hint of a bargained-for exchange under which father undertook to remove Tina's bike in consideration for some performance by her.

Are the elements of promissory estoppel satisfied? It would be outrageous to think so. It is a real stretch to find father's ultimatum to be a promise. His intent, even from an objective perspective, was not to commit himself to a course of action, but to threaten punishment for disobedience to his wishes. It follows that there was no apparent intent to induce reliance on the threatened action. Just the contrary—the statement was made for the obvious purpose of motivating Tina not to take the action that led to the loss. It would be a patent misinterpretation of father's statement to suggest that he reasonably expected Tina would rely on his statement as an undertaking to store the bike safely.

Having found no promise or reasonable intent to induce reliance on father's part, we need not proceed further. The crucial element of accountability is not satisfied, so there was nothing for Tina to rely on. However, for the sake of completeness, let us deal with the issue of justifiable reliance. Looked at from Tina's perspective, father's statement cannot reasonably be perceived as conveying a sense of commitment. Nothing in her particular circumstances justifies her interpreting it as a promise to safeguard the bike. In any event, Tina was not induced to act by anything that father said. The parties were not contemplating theft (which could just as easily have occurred had Tina obeyed her father and parked in the driveway) and understood that the real issue was proper parking. (This example illustrates that a reasonable interpretation of the statement and its motive from the perspective of the alleged promisor is often congruent with the reasonable perception of the alleged promisee.)

These facts are a parody on cases involving a promise to procure insurance, such as *East Providence Credit Union v. Geremia,* 239 A.2d 725 (R.I. 1968). The credit union financed a car purchase and took a security interest in the car to secure the debt. The credit agreement obligated the borrower to keep the car insured and provided that if he failed to do so, the lender could pay the insurance premium and add the premium plus interest to the balance due on the loan. When the borrower failed to pay the premium, the insurer sent a notice to the borrower and the lender warning that the policy would be cancelled if payment was not received in two weeks. In response, the lender wrote to the borrower stating that unless it was notified in five days that the premium had been paid, it would exercise its right to renew the policy and charge the borrower for the premium and interest. The borrower did nothing and the lender neglected to renew as well, so the policy lapsed. A few weeks later, the car was stolen, and the question of liability for the loss had to be decided.

The court said that the lender made a promise when it threatened to pay the premium for the borrower's account, and it found that the borrower had given consideration for this promise by agreeing in the loan contract to pay interest. Because the court found consideration for the promise, the obligation was contractual, and promissory estoppel was not needed for enforcement. Nevertheless, in dictum the court said that had consideration been absent, the promise would still have been enforceable under promissory estoppel: It was intended to induce reliance, it was relied on, and injustice could only be avoided by its enforcement. (The extent of enforcement is discussed in Example 2.)

Although one can sympathize with the plight of the borrower, who has lost his car and would otherwise still be liable for the loan balance, the result feels odd. The claim of liability is not as outrageous as Tina's. At least in this case protection against loss was contemplated by the intended action. However, it seems unlikely that the lender's statement was a promise intended to induce reliance. It was really a threat intended to induce renewal of the policy. Furthermore, the justification of the borrower's reliance seems to be shaky, given that he had already breached his contractual obligation and omitted to rectify this after warnings from the insurer and the lender. Is justice really served by rewarding this behavior?

2. Tina gave no consideration for father's undertaking to pay the premium. It was simply a gift promise motivated by family relationship and cannot be enforced as a contract. Promissory estoppel was developed to provide a basis for enforcing this kind of gratuitous promise, relied on by the promisee to her detriment.

Are the elements of promissory estoppel satisfied? Whether or not father subjectively intended to honor his undertaking, his words, interpreted objectively, convey a clear commitment to pay the premium. There can be little doubt that he did or reasonably should have expected Tina to rely on it. It was an unequivocal response to her appeal for financial assistance, made with knowledge of her circumstances and reiterated when the cancellation warning was received.

The promise apparently induced forbearance on Tina's part. There is a suggestion that financial difficulty may have compelled Tina to let the comprehensive coverage lapse had father not undertaken to help. This suggests the argument that she did not really forbear from renewing that coverage on the strength of the promise—she would have let it lapse anyhow. However, she may not have adopted this course. Her concern about the consequences of possible theft could have motivated her to make the sacrifices necessary to find the money for the premium. The mere possibility that she may have forborne even without the promise is not strong enough to break the causal link between the promise and her forbearance.

Her reliance must have been justified. When a promise is stated in clear and unequivocal terms, it is easier to find that reliance was justified. However, this does not mean that a promisee can unquestioningly react in blind faith. Tina must have known about father's bad habit of breaking his promises, yet she accepted his word without checking on payment, even after a cancellation notice was received. This weakens the quality of her reliance and weighs against her when all circumstances are balanced to determine the injustice of nonenforcement.

Can injustice be avoided only by the enforcement of the promise? All the above elements go into the balance and are considered along with Tina's detriment and the concern for protecting the gratuitous promisor. The consequences of Tina's reliance are severe. She suffered a real harm in losing the right to be indemnified for the stolen bike. The injustice of making her bear this loss must be weighed against the fact that the promise was gratuitous. Because consideration is absent, the circumstances of the promise must be examined to see if they fulfill the evidentiary, cautionary, and channelling functions that would otherwise have been performed by consideration. By taking the renewal notice, father did engage in conduct that evidenced his intent. While not a legal formality in the strict sense, his action is helpful in showing serious intent to be bound. Furthermore, he never indicated a desire to retract the promise and in fact, subsequently reiterated it. This tends to show that it was not an impulsive and immediately regretted act of generosity.

How does the balance come out? It could go either way, but I think that the equities favor holding father accountable for his promise. True, Tina was not fully justified in trusting his word, but he did make a clear commitment and its breach caused her great harm. Maybe it is time for him to learn that promises cannot be broken with impunity. (Yes, the morality of keeping one's word is certainly a factor in the balance.)

What should the remedy be? The court has flexibility in formulating relief for promissory estoppel and need not enforce the promise as if it were a contract. Depending on the circumstances, relief could range from the simple reimbursement of wasted expenses to full enforcement. The equities balanced by the court in validating the promise flow into the determination of the appropriate scope of relief. The least measure of recovery for promissory estoppel is the reimbursement of wasted expenses, but this is inapplicable on the facts, because Tina incurred no expenses in reliance on the promise. An award of the cost of the premium is the literal enforcement of the promise, but this is insufficient, because Tina suffered a serious consequential loss as a result of the failure to pay it. Therefore, the only remedy that would completely restore Tina to the position she occupied before relying on the promise is reimbursement for the value of the stolen bike. This is a substantial burden on father. Maybe it is appropriate to impose it on him. However, this could be too harsh given the gratuitous nature of the promise and Tina's failure to safeguard her own interests. The advantage of remedial flexibility is that the court can find father's promise binding, yet adjust the extent of his liability. In the *Geremia* case, cited in Example 1, the court did award the full value of the stolen car, but this case is distinguishable from Tina's. It involved a commercial transaction and the court found consideration for the promise, leading to enforcement as a contract.

3. There have been a number of cases in which courts have used promissory estoppel to validate a promise of retirement benefits when the promise was found to lack consideration under the "past consideration" rule. This happened in both cases cited in Examples 9 and 10 of Chapter 7, *Feinberg v. Pfeiffer Co.*, 322 S.W.2d 163 (Mo. 1959), and *Katz v. Danny Dare Inc.*, 610 S.W.2d 121 (Mo. 1980). In each of those cases, the court found that a promise had been made with the intention of inducing reliance, that the promisee acted detrimentally in reliance, and that full enforcement of the promise was necessary to prevent injustice.

In *Feinberg*, while the employee was still working, the employer's board, on its own initiative, passed a resolution honoring her 37 years of service by granting her a life pension whenever she should decide to retire. She retired about 18 months later. The pension was paid for a few years until the management of the employer changed. The new management, being advised by its attorney that the promise of the pension was not legally binding, sought to reduce the pension. The employee refused to accept the reduction and sued. Although the court found that no consideration had been given for the promise, it held that the promisee's retirement in reliance on the promise caused her irreversible detriment because her age made it unlikely that she could find another job. The court therefore concluded that the employer, having intentionally influenced the employee to alter her position for the worse, must in fairness be held to its promise. The court followed the theory that promissory estoppel is a consideration substitute in that it estops the employer from asserting the absence of consideration. On this basis, it fully enforced the promise as a contract.

In *Katz*, the longstanding employee was also induced to retire by the promise of a life pension but was found not to have given consideration for the promise because he could have been summarily dismissed. Relying on *Feinberg*, the court found that Katz, being of advanced age, was induced by the promise to give up the opportunity of continuing in full-time employment. (The strange quirk of the case is that while the court did not find this to be a sufficient detriment to constitute consideration, it did find it prejudicial enough to support promissory estoppel.) In the result, the court fully enforced the promise.

It should be recognized that when an older employee retires on the strength of the promise of a pension, the reliance on the promise increases as the years pass, because it becomes harder for the employee to reenter the work force. This factor may not be strictly relevant to the initial inducement, but it must surely be weighed in the equities. Both *Feinberg* and *Katz* involve this situation. Ms. Feinberg's case was made more poignant by the fact that she had developed cancer by the time of trial.

Not all cases end so happily for the retiree. In *Hayes v. Plantation Steel Co.*, 438 A.2d 1091 (R.I. 1982), the court refused to use promissory estoppel to uphold a promise of a pension. The employee decided to retire after 51 years of service. After this decision was made, the employer told him that it would "take care of him" in appreciation of his long service. No formal agreement was made and no figure was mentioned, but an annual payment of $5,000 was made for the next several years. Payments stopped when the employer got into financial difficulty and the management changed. The court found no consideration for the promise and also refused to enforce it under promissory estoppel. The promise was made after the employee's decision to retire and therefore could not have induced it. Furthermore, there was evidence that the employee himself had been unsure about the stability of the commitment because of its vagueness as to amount and term.

How do the claims of Constance and Gerry fare under these principles?

3(a). Constance can probably not recover. She retired before the promise, so it did not induce that decision. Her only other action was planning her vacation and communicating with the travel agent. Apart from wasting some of her free time, she incurred no loss or expense. Unquestionably, her expectation of a vacation has been dashed by her ingrate ex-employer, but if promissory estoppel is aimed at protecting reliance, the enforcement of this expectation interest is beyond the scope of the doctrine. A gratuitous promise was made, and in the absence of detrimental reliance, it simply fails because consideration is lacking. This unpleasant result could be avoided by underplaying the element of detriment in promissory estoppel. However, the real policy question is whether the "past consideration" rule has any justification at all in a case like this.

3(b). Turn Coat Corporation did make a definite promise to Gerry with the clear intent to induce action. Gerry relied on it, suffering the detriment of giving up his job. His actual loss is very small because he had no right to long-term employment. Because substantial actual loss is a significant factor in weighing the justice of enforcement, the lack of detriment for consideration purposes could also make the harm too trivial to support promissory estoppel. The court in *Katz* did not seem to see this irony. Nevertheless, promissory estoppel does add flexibility to the court's decisionmaking. Although a court may feel the need to be rather literal-minded in deciding on legal detriment for consideration purposes, the general balancing of the equities inherent in promissory estoppel allows the court to underplay the detriment element in weighing the justice of giving promissory estoppel relief. This could justify the court in enforcing the promise to its full extent (a year's salary) to avoid the injustice of nonenforcement.

4. Again, this problem treads that uncertain line between a promise with consideration and a gift with conditions, but it more likely falls on the latter side of the line. The recited "consideration" is not consideration at all but merely expresses Al's purpose in giving the donation. Although the president replies by promising to use the fund for this purpose, as a matter of strict doctrine, the college suffers no legal detriment in undertaking to use a gift for its designated purpose. It had no right to the money in the absence of the gift, and hence gives up no legal right by promising to use it in a particular way.

However, doctrine is not always applied rigorously where the circumstances allow some fudging and enforcement seems appropriate. This happened in *Allegheny College v. National Chautauqua County Bank*, 159 N.E. 173 (N.Y. 1927). A donor pledged $5,000 to the college on condition that the fund be named after her and be used to educate students for the ministry. Although payment was due only after the donor's death, she did pay $1,000 while she was alive. The college set this money aside for a scholarship fund as stipulated but did nothing further in reliance on the promise. The donor later repudiated the pledge. After she died, the college claimed the balance of the pledge from her estate. Justice Cardozo found consideration for the pledge. He did not rely on the college's obligation to use the fund for the purposes stipulated, because that is rather too obviously a condition of the gift. Rather, he found that by accepting the $1,000, the college impliedly promised to memorialize the donor's name.

To find consideration in such a situation requires rather a stretch of doctrine, and it can only work if the donee has expressly or impliedly made some promise. Could promissory estoppel be used to avoid so tortured an application of consideration doctrine? In a dictum in *Allegheny College*, Cardozo suggested that promissory estoppel could have been used in the case had consideration not been found. However, the facts do not present a strong case for promissory estoppel either. Although the donor surely made a promise, there seems little indication of an intent to induce reliance or of prejudicial action in reliance on the promise. The parties did not contemplate that anything would be done until the full sum was paid following the donor's death, and all the college did was to bank the down payment. The need for detrimental reliance was recognized in *Congregation Kadimah Toras-Moshe v. DeLeo*, 540 N.E.2d 691 (Mass. 1989), in which the donor promised $25,000 to the synagogue for the conversion of a storage room into a library, to be named after the donor. The gift had not been paid by the time of the donor's death and the synagogue sued his estate for payment. The court refused enforcement of the promise. The undertaking to name the proposed library after the donor was simply a condition of the gift. It was not a legal detriment and did not induce the gift, so the promise was without consideration. Promissory estoppel did not allow for enforcement because all the synagogue had done was to allocate the fund to the library renovation in its budget. This was simply an accounting entry, having no prejudicial effect. The synagogue had not yet taken any action to begin the renovation.

The facts of our problem are a little stronger than both these cases. Al stipulated that planning must take place before payment and the college did begin this process in reliance on the promise. The college should at least be able to recover the fee paid to the architect. It could possibly also receive reimbursement for the value of the time spent by committee members in planning (to the extent that the time of faculty and students has any value at all).[3] If it was reasonably foreseeable that the donation would generate an article in the alumni magazine, the cost of the wasted production effort may also be claimable. Even if all these expenses are awarded, this recovery cannot be more than a fraction of the $20,000 promised, but promissory estoppel is primarily aimed at the reimbursement of reliance expenses and should not extend to full enforcement of the promise unless that is the only way that injustice can be avoided. That is, the commitment or expenditure must be so extensive that the prejudice cannot be undone except by full enforcement. For example, in *Estate Timco v. Oral Roberts Evangelical Ass'n*, 215 N.W.2d 750 (Mi. 1974), a promise to pay the balance of the price of a building was

---

3. Just kidding, of course.

vague prospect. There is no indication that he had an unusual dependency on Sonny. He had a job and was not desperate for employment or under some other compelling pressure. He has attended college (the facts indicate that he was Sonny's college roommate) and is a current participant in the labor market. He should be worldly enough to realize that even when parties desire to contract, they may not be able to reach common ground. He tried to initiate discussion about the terms of employment but, on meeting resistance, was content to defer decision until later. These considerations weigh in the direction of leaving Chilly with the risk of his losses, but they must be balanced against Sonny's accountability.

In *Hoffman v. Red Owl Stores, Inc.,* 133 N.W.2d 267 (Wisc. 1965), the court did use promissory estoppel to impose liability on Red Owl, a store chain, for statements made to Hoffman during the period leading up to an abortive contract. Hoffman wished to open a store with a Red Owl franchise and approached Red Owl to set him up in business. After reviewing and expressing approval of his proposed financial arrangements, Red Owl encouraged Hoffman to take a series of actions to prepare for opening a store. Hoffman allowed himself to be guided by Red Owl and incurred expenses in following its instructions. Negotiations eventually collapsed, primarily because the company had not been entirely straight with Hoffman on the financing requirements for the business. Although there had been no clear and express commitment by the chain to set up the business, the circumstances of its relationship with Hoffman in building toward a contract showed that Hoffman had placed faith in Red Owl's expertise and good faith, and it had been careless of his interests. The chain's superior expertise and its shoddy indifference to Hoffman's welfare outweighed his naiveté in unquestioningly relying on the precontractual undertakings. Commentators have pointed out that *Hoffman* has a definite tort flavor and stresses accountability for careless assurances.

Viewed broadly, *Hoffman*'s principles could be applied to hold Sonny accountable for Chilly's reliance on his promise. But if the facts of *Hoffman* are emphasized, Chilly seems less deserving of solicitude and Sonny's single vague promise is quite different from Red Owl's pattern of dealing. A strict approach to Chilly's reaction would result in a finding that reliance was not justified. However, given the background of friendship and Sonny's expectation of reliance, this may be too harsh. If it is too difficult to adopt a win-or-lose approach, the court does have the flexibility of granting a limited remedy.

What should the remedy be? As noted before, there cannot be full enforcement of a promise to employ Chilly because his expectation interest cannot be divined. Full reimbursement for reliance would include:

(1)   Two months' salary lost in reliance on the promise. This loss should be recoverable provided that Sonny can show that he would have had the right to remain on this job for two months

had he not been induced to resign. In addition, the delay in finding a replacement job must have been reasonable. If Chilly had not made a reasonably diligent effort to mitigate his loss by expeditiously seeking new employment, Sonny cannot be held liable to the extent that Chilly exacerbated his damages. (This is the principle of mitigation of damages, discussed in section 18.6.3.)

(2) The additional rental payable (that is, any increase in rent that he would have to pay) for equivalent premises for the period that would have remained on the lease had Chilly not been induced to give notice. (If Chilly's tenancy was month-to-month, loss may be difficult to show.)

(3) Any money wasted on the air ticket. To the extent that the promisee is able to salvage an expense, it is not a loss and is not recoverable. If the promisee fails to take reasonable steps to salvage, the mitigation principle precludes recovery of that portion of the loss aggravated by the promisee. In this case, the ticket can be used within a year, so the fare is salvageable provided that it is reasonable to expect Chilly to have use for it or it can be sold.

If full reimbursement is an unfair burden on Sonny, the court may cut down recovery by making distinctions between the various items of expense, based on factors such as the extent that they were foreseeable or justified, and the degree to which they can be proved. It is worth noting that in both *Hoffman* and *Grouse*, the court permitted recovery of all losses and expenditures that could be proved with reasonable probability.

9

Restitution: Unjust Enrichment and "Moral Obligation"

§9.1 Introduction

Chapter 8 explained how promissory estoppel can sometimes be used to ameliorate the harsh consequences of consideration doctrine by enforcing a promise that induced justifiable reliance. Although the remedy of restitution is available in a variety of different situations, both within the bounds of contract law and beyond them, in one of its aspects it serves a purpose similar to promissory estoppel by allowing for the enforcement of obligations that do not qualify as contractual. Having drawn this general parallel, it must be stressed that restitution and promissory estoppel have very different conceptual bases. Restitution is not predicated on accountability for promise. In fact, its usefulness is greatest when no promise has been made. Its purpose is the restoration of an unfair gain. Its focus is on cases in which one party has obtained a benefit at the expense of another under circumstances that make it unfair for the recipient to retain the benefit without paying for it.

§9.2 Unjust Enrichment, the Basis for Restitution

It is common to confuse restitution, a **remedy,** with unjust enrichment, the **cause of action** that gives rise to the remedy. **Restitution** is the **act of**

211

restoring something or its value. When a court grants restitution, it adjudges that the recipient of a benefit is obliged to give back that benefit or to pay its value to the person who conferred it. The basis of this judgment is that the recipient has been **unjustly enriched** at the expense of grantor. That is, there is **no legal justification for retention of the benefit without pay.** In short, when the elements of the cause of action, unjust enrichment, are satisfied, the remedy of restitution is the relief awarded. Some writings and court opinions are not punctilious about correct terminology and use the word "restitution" in reference to both the cause of action and the remedy.

Unjust enrichment is not a subcategory of contract law. It is a distinct and *independent basis of obligation,* occupying a place alongside contract, promissory estoppel,[1] and tort. The following illustration attempts to emphasize this relationship between different causes of action and remedies.

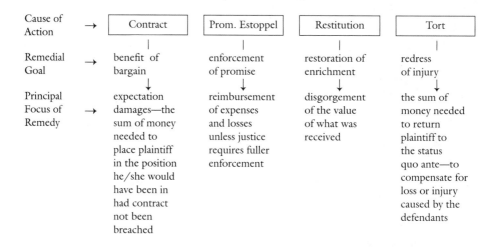

Cause of Action →	Contract	Prom. Estoppel	Restitution	Tort
Remedial Goal →	benefit of bargain	enforcement of promise	restoration of enrichment	redress of injury
Principal Focus of Remedy →	expectation damages—the sum of money needed to place plaintiff in the position he/she would have been in had contract not been breached	reimbursement of expenses and losses unless justice requires fuller enforcement	disgorgement of the value of what was received	the sum of money needed to return plaintiff to the status quo ante—to compensate for loss or injury caused by the defendants

§9.3   The Relationship Between Unjust Enrichment and Contract

Unjust enrichment is a complex field, covering many situations that have nothing to do with contract. It falls within our scope in two broad areas. These two different roles of unjust enrichment in the contractual context must be distinguished to prevent confusion. The diagram and brief general description is followed by explanatory illustrations:

---

1. But remember that one view of promissory estoppel is that it is not an independent theory of liability but a subcategory of contract law. *See* section 8.2.

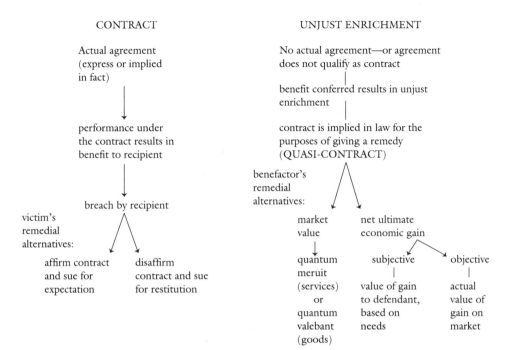

Unjust enrichment serves as an independent theory of liability in cases when *no contract* has come into existence, either because something went wrong or failed to happen in the process of formation, or because the parties simply did not attempt to make a contract. Yet they had some interaction that resulted in the one party obtaining a gain from the other. In situations like this, there is no basis for contractual relief, but unjust enrichment permits restitutionary recovery. The link to contract could be close here because there could be strong contractual elements in the interaction. However, some of these situations have only a marginal relationship to contract, based on the legal fiction called "quasi-contract" explained in section 9.4. This chapter is concerned with cases like these, when no contract exists and unjust enrichment is the basis of obligation.

Unjust enrichment also plays an important role when a *valid contract* does exist but has been *breached*. One of the parties may have conferred a benefit on the other in the course of performing the contract before its breach, and restitution of that benefit may be a better option than enforcement of the contract. (In some cases it may be the only option because, for example, contractual expectation damages cannot be proved.) Even though there is a valid contract, the plaintiff may elect to forego contractual relief in favor of restitution. This role of restitution is an issue of damages for breach of contract. Apart from this brief mention of it and the illustration below, this question is deferred to the discussion of remedies for breach in section 18.9.

The following examples illustrate the range of the restitutionary remedy by showing its application in a number of situations. The first involves restitution when a valid contract exists, the next two show the use of restitution when the parties aimed to enter a contract but their dealings did not result in a valid contract, and the fourth demonstrates the use of restitution when there has been no contractual interaction between the parties.

Illustration 1.   *Restitution as an alternative remedy when a valid contract has been breached*

Buyer and Seller make a contract for the sale of Seller's house. Buyer pays a deposit of $5,000 to Seller. Seller later reneges on the contract and refuses to close. Because a valid contract exists, Buyer has the right to claim expectation damages for breach of contract that would place her in the position she would have been in had the contract been performed. If the price under this contract is less than the cost of buying an equivalent house on the market, Buyer's expectation damages would be the difference between the contract price and what she would have to pay for a substitute.[2] However, assume that Seller's house was overpriced, and it turns out that Buyer can purchase an equivalent house for less on the market. Expectation damages are zero because Buyer would have paid more had Seller not breached. Enforcement of the contract does not help her. However, Buyer has enriched Seller by the $5,000 down payment that Seller no longer has any right to keep. His enrichment is unjust and if he fails to repay, the remedy of restitution is available to Buyer to recover the down payment.

Illustration 2.   *Restitution when a benefit is conferred pursuant to an invalid or unenforceable contract*

Assume that the parties in the above illustration had made an oral agreement for the sale of the house. Under the statute of frauds, a sale of real property must be in writing and the oral agreement is unenforceable as a contract.[3] Therefore, if Seller reneges, Buyer does not have the option of suing for enforcement of the contract. But because Seller no longer has any right to keep the money, Buyer can, nevertheless, obtain restitution of the down payment on the theory of unjust enrichment.

Illustration 3.   *Restitution when a benefit is conferred on the strength of a promise without consideration*

The principle of Illustration 2 applies in other situations when no valid contract came into existence. For example, say that Owner made a written promise to donate the house to Charity, a non-profit organization that provides shelter for victims of abuse. Before taking transfer of the house, Charity

---

2. The measure of expectation damages is fully discussed in section 18.3.

3. *See* section 11.2.

obtains Owner's permission to install a security system on the premises and to build a wall around it. After Charity has done this work, Owner reneges on the promise and refuses to transfer the house. Charity's enhancement of the property was obviously not intended as consideration for the promise of the house and was not bargained for by or owed to Owner. It was simply done to enable Charity to make proper use of the gift. Because the promise is not supported by consideration, Charity cannot enforce it as a contract. But it has improved the house that now remains Owner's property. This unjustly enriches Owner, so Charity can obtain restitution for the value of the wall and security systems.

This illustration raises a number of points that will be discussed later:

1. Unlike the prior illustrations, it involves not the restoration of a fixed sum of money but the value of labor and materials. This is common. When the value of a benefit is not fixed and certain, evidence of value is required as discussed in section 9.6.

2. Owner may not particularly want a security system and wall on the property, but because he changed his mind about giving the house to Charity, he is stuck with paying for them. Under the circumstances, this result is justifiable because Owner authorized the work. However, principles of unjust enrichment ensure that this will not happen when a benefit is imposed on a recipient.

3. These facts appear to support recovery under promissory estoppel: Acting in reliance on the promised donation, Charity incurred a loss in installing the security system and wall on the property. Injustice may be averted only by enforcing the promise, if not in full, at least to the extent of the costs incurred in supplying the materials and doing the work. Although it does not always happen that the same circumstances support relief either in restitution or in promissory estoppel, this is not an uncommon situation. When the claimant has a choice of remedies, the selection between them is based on factors such as ease of proof and extent of recovery. The elements of one may be easier to establish than the other. In addition, the relief for each may be quite different, because restitution focuses on the restoration of the value of the benefit conferred, while promissory estoppel is more concerned with the costs incurred by the claimant.

Illustration 4.   *Restitution in cases when no contractual interaction occurred*

Victim slips on a banana peel and falls down a flight of stairs. Doctor, a stranger who happened to be walking by, administers emergency treatment to unconscious Victim. Doctor has never entered into a contract with Victim who could not consent to treatment because he was unconscious. The only basis on which Doctor could recover a fee for her services is unjust enrichment, on the theory that Victim would have had to pay for them in the marketplace, and it is unjust that he should receive them for free. (The merits of this argument will shortly be explored in more detail.) Although this is not a contract case, it is historically linked to contract law through a quaint legal fiction known as "quasi-contract."

§9.4   The Meaning of "Quasi-Contract"

Although the claims of Buyer, Charity, and Doctor in Illustrations 2, 3, and 4 are not based on contract, and recovery is premised solely on the policy of preventing unjust enrichment, our legal tradition has created a peculiar fiction that makes the cases sound as if they have something to do with contract. In early common law, courts were bound by a rigid set of writs called **"forms of action."** To obtain relief, the plaintiff had to fit his or her claim into one of these recognized categories of suit. There was no writ for unjust enrichment, so the court needed to fit enrichment claims into some other writ. It chose the contract writ of assumpsit, and squeezed enrichment into a contractual form by pretending that the benefit was conferred on the recipient pursuant to a contract with the grantor. Thus, to use Illustration 4 as an example, the court would act as if Victim had asked Doctor to treat his injuries, so that Doctor could recover the value of her services under the writ of assumpsit. Claims for unjust enrichment based on this fictional contract were said to arise **quasi ex contractu,** and the restitutionary remedy based on this fiction has come to be called **quasi-contract, or contract implied in law.** It is easy to be confused by this terminology, so it is important to remember that a quasi-contract or a contract implied in law is not a real contract. Legal implication is a fiction created for remedial purposes. It must be distinguished from a contract **implied in fact.** This is an actual contract in which agreement is inferred from conduct rather than express words.[4] For example, if Victim had not been unconscious, but had been mentally alert, emotionally stable, and capable of making a decision when Doctor began treatment, his failure to refuse the treatment may be interpreted as an implicit agreement to pay for it. His silence is evidence from which the factual conclusion can be reached that he made an actual contract for medical services.

To sum up and to put all the terminology together, we can describe the general principle of unjust enrichment as follows: When a benefit has been conferred on a recipient under circumstances in which it is unfair to permit

---

4. In section 10.4 a similar distinction is explained between a term implied into a contract as a matter of legal construction, and one implied in fact based on evidence that the parties agreed to it.

him to retain it without payment, the **cause of action of unjust enrichment** is available to the person who conferred the benefit. Using this cause of action, the conferrer can claim the **remedy of restitution,** under which the court will restore the benefit or its value to her. In order to fit this newly recognized cause of action into existing legal forms, earlier common law courts used various **fictions.** The one that we are concerned with here (there are others that are beyond the scope of a contracts course, but are commonly covered in upperclass Remedies courses) was based on the fiction that the benefit had been contracted for. That is, the court **implied a contract in law,** even though no contractual relationship actually existed between the conferrer and the beneficiary. Restitutionary recovery based on unjust enrichment was therefore described as "quasi ex contractu," and the term **"quasi-contract"** has come down to us as an alternative name for this form of relief.

When it comes to enforcement of the obligation, **relief** for unjust enrichment (quasi-contractual relief) can be very different from that for contract. For example, if Doctor had made a real contract with Victim, she could enforce its actual terms and could recover whatever fee was agreed on for the treatment. As no contract was made and the cause of action is a quasi-contract, there cannot be an agreed fee, so recovery is based on the value of the benefit, typically determined by market value as discussed in section 9.6. (In many circumstances, there will be little or no difference between restitutionary and contractual recovery. In a contract, the parties may not have agreed to an express price, so that the contract is deemed to be at the market price. Even when they do agree, it is more likely than not that the agreed amount is what would typically be charged in the market.)

§9.5   The Elements of Unjust Enrichment

As stated earlier, the remedy of restitution is aimed at restoring money, property or the value of property, or services when it would be unjust to permit the recipient to retain what was received without paying for it. As its name suggests, unjust enrichment is predicated on two elements: The recipient must have been enriched at the expense of the claimant, and the circumstances must be such as to make this enrichment unjust.

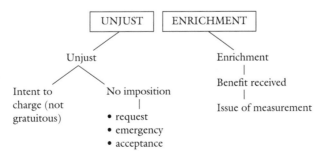

§9.5.1 *Enrichment*

Enrichment is an **economic benefit.** When a person receives and retains money or property, it is easy to see that the recipient has been enriched to the extent of the payment or the value of the property because the recipient's net worth has been increased by that amount. However, a person could also be enriched by consuming goods or receiving intangible services that result in no long-term financial advantage. One is not obviously made wealthier by consuming a free bag of pretzels or getting a free haircut, but one has saved the cost of buying these items in the marketplace. Naturally, the existence or absence of lasting economic advantage and its extent are factors taken into account in deciding on relief, as discussed in section 9.6. However, it is necessary to recognize the general principle that enrichment occurs whenever something of value is received, even if it does not directly enlarge the recipient's net worth.

§9.5.2 *When Is Enrichment Unjust?*

To receive restitution, it is not enough that the claimant has conferred an uncompensated benefit on the recipient, because it is not always unjust for a person to receive a benefit without paying for it. Justice is only offended if the conferral of the enrichment meets two criteria: The claimant must have intended to charge for it, and must not have imposed it on the recipient.

a.   Intent to Charge

Enrichment is not unjust if the benefit was conferred with gratuitous intent. It is not unfair to allow a donee to keep a gift.[5] Quite the contrary, it would unfairly disrupt the donee's reasonable expectations by allowing the donor to demand payment for something originally given for free. A person who confers a benefit gratuitously is sometimes called a **volunteer.** In the context of unjust enrichment, this word carries more than its common meaning. It connotes not only that something was done or given by free choice, but also with the intent not to seek compensation.

As usual, intent is not measured subjectively but is based upon apparent intent, as manifested by the conduct of the person conferring the benefit in light of all the circumstances. An objective test is used, not only because it is difficult to divine a person's true state of mind, but also because the recipi-

---

5. Of course, there is no consideration issue once the donation has been given. Consideration doctrine only applies to the enforcement of unexecuted promises.

ent's reasonable expectations should be protected. Therefore, if a reasonable person in the recipient's position would perceive the grantor as not expecting compensation, the intent is gratuitous, no matter what the grantor claims to have been thinking.

Benefits are sometimes conferred in an emergency when it is unlikely that the benefactor was thinking about compensation at all when taking the beneficial action, so it is sometimes artificial to talk of intent. Therefore, intent is likely to be determined by inference from the circumstances. One of the significant considerations in deciding whether or not the benefit was conferred with gratuitous intent is the relationship of the benefit to the trade or profession of the conferrer. For example, unless she is particularly crass and cold-blooded, a doctor probably does not think of her fee as she is administering emergency aid to a victim. Nevertheless, if the general expectation is that a doctor would charge for services in these circumstances, intent to charge is attributed to her. Because the doctor rendered professional services, it is conceivable that she had a reasonable expectation of payment. The reasonableness of this expectation would have been even stronger if the doctor was not a passer-by but attended to the victim after he was rushed, unconscious, into her consulting rooms for emergency treatment.

By contrast, if the aid was provided by a lay person, the general expectation is likely to be that there was no intent to charge. We normally think of amateur emergency intervention as public spirited and gratuitous. There is a difficult policy question to be considered when deciding whether services rendered by a nonprofessional should be presumed as gratuitous: We should expect people to respond to crises altruistically without expectation of reward. But a strict presumption of voluntarism could be unfair and could discourage intervention in emergencies, especially if loss or injury was suffered in the course of conferring the benefit.

Sometimes, although there was an intent to charge for the benefit, the intent may not have been to charge the recipient. If so, from the recipient's perspective, the benefit is gratuitous. For example, say a suitor orders flowers on credit for his paramour. If the suitor fails to pay after the florist has delivered them, the florist cannot claim that the recipient was unjustly enriched. Although it had intended to charge for the flowers, it had never intended to charge her.

b. Imposition

If restitution was available for any benefit conferred with intent to charge, this would open the way for all kinds of imposition from busybodies and sleazy operators. Imagine how a homeowner would feel if, upon returning from work one day, she found that her overgrown yard had been weeded and trimmed without her knowledge. On the front door is a note that reads:

Your yard was a mess, so we cleaned it up for you. Our charge is $300. Please send a check right away.

> Your friendly neighbors,
>
> O. Fishus
> N. Termeddler

Alternatively, it may not be the neighbors who did the yard work, but some roving landscaper who makes a living by seeking out unkempt yards, beautifying them without permission, and then demanding payment. In either case, the law treats these claimants as **officious intermeddlers.** Even though they did not intend to confer the benefit gratuitously, they were not justified in imposing a benefit on someone without asking first, so they are not entitled to restitution.

Although the above examples are obvious, it is not always so easy to decide if a benefit was conferred officiously. In the clearest case, a benefit is not officious if it was **requested** by the recipient.[6] When the benefit has not been requested by the recipient, it is likely to be officious unless there was some good reason to confer the unasked-for benefit. This is usually satisfied only when an **emergency** has arisen and the following conditions are satisfied:

1.   Immediate action is required.
2.   Advance assent is impracticable, and
3.   The claimant has no reason to believe that the recipient would not wish for the action to be taken.

The greater the urgency and the more at stake, the more likely that unrequested action will be justified. Threats to life or health are generally regarded as giving greater cause for unsolicited action than threats to property. Thus, the doctor in the earlier example is likely to obtain restitution. Not only was she not a volunteer, she was also not an officious intermeddler. Although the protection of the person of the beneficiary is the strongest justification for unrequested emergency action, an emergency response to avert harm to property is also of value to the property owner and to society. Therefore, if a person, in response to an immediate threat, takes lawful and appropriate action to save or preserve the property, he is not likely to be treated as an officious intermeddler. However, whether the threat is to person or property, if the actor knows or reasonably should know that the beneficiary would not want the benefit, intervention is meddlesome and should not be reimbursed. For example, if the injured victim was a member of a religious sect

---

6. Where the benefit was requested, an actual contract may have been created (so that restitution serves the role as an alternative remedy) but if the request falls short of a contractual commitment, unjust enrichment is the basis of obligation.

that forbids medical intervention and the doctor happened to know this, the doctor's medical services would be intermeddling despite the emergency.

Even if a benefit is imposed on the recipient, restitution may still be appropriate if, being able to reject it and return the benefit, the *recipient accepts* it. In the yardwork example, the owner of the unkempt yard cannot return the benefit, even if undesired, because it is incorporated into the land. To deem acceptance would eviscerate the rule against intermeddling because there is no means of rejection. However, some benefits can be easily returned. For example, if instead of weeding and trimming, the neighbors beautified the yard by installing a garden gnome, it would be a simple matter for the homeowner to reject the gnome and to allow the neighbor to remove it. If the owner chooses to keep the gnome, acceptance of the unrequested benefit justifies compensation.

§9.6   Measurement of Benefit

§9.6.1   *The Remedial Aim of Restitution*

As noted in section 9.2, the remedial focus of restitution is different from contract. Contractual damages are based on the breach victim's expected gains under the contract and are calculated to approximate the monetary value of the benefit that he or she would have realized had the contract not been breached. By contrast, the primary focus of restitutionary damages is not the grantor's loss of expectation, but the *recipient's gain*. They are calculated to approximate the monetary value of what has been given to the recipient. Damages for breach of contract and the distinction between contractual expectation damages and restitution are dealt with in some detail in Chapter 18. However, because restitutionary relief is so tied into the subject matter of this chapter, it seems convenient and logical to deal with the nature and measurement of restitution here.

§9.6.2   *Alternative Methods for Measuring Enrichment*

The following illustration suggests the two principal ways in which enrichment can be measured:

Maggie Zine owns a newsstand in an office lobby. As she was opening the booth early one morning, she fainted and was rushed to the hospital. She spent the day there for observation and tests and was discharged that evening. Sam Aratan, Maggie's friend, happened to be in the lobby coffee bar when he heard that Maggie had been taken away in the ambulance. As he had the day off, he decided to help Maggie by keeping her booth open. He ran the booth the whole day, making $600 in sales, of which $200 is profit. The going wage for a kiosk clerk is $7 per hour. Sam ran the newsstand for ten hours.

Assume that Sam is neither a volunteer nor an intermeddler, so that he should receive restitution for his services. There are two alternative means of calculating Maggie's enrichment:

1. The market value of Sam's service, represented by the going wage of kiosk clerks, $70, or
2. Maggie's net economic gain—her profit for the day, $200. (Not her net sales, of course, because she had to buy $400 worth of goods to generate the $600 income.)

Market value of the benefit and the recipient's ultimate net fiscal gain are the two alternative choices for measuring enrichment. Market value tends to be the standard measure, but net gain is used when the circumstances make recovery of market value either excessive or inadequate. If net gain is the basis of measurement, the gain could be valued differently depending on whether it is measured objectively—that is, in the abstract (what it is reasonably worth in general) or subjectively—with regard to the beneficiary's particular circumstances. This breakdown may be represented as follows:

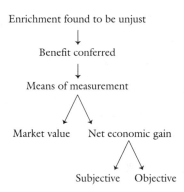

We will now look more closely at each of these means of measurement.

§9.6.3   *Market Value*

When the benefit is the payment of money, value is readily apparent, but if the benefit consists of the receipt of property or services, their value must be established by evidence of their price on the market. If services are involved, the term **quantum meruit** ("as much as deserved") is used to express market value. The term used to describe the market value of goods is **quantum**

valebant ("as much as they are worth").[7] Market value is most reliably determined by testimony of an expert who is familiar with the market and can provide objective information about customary pricing. However, if such evidence is not available, the plaintiff may be able to make a prima facie showing of value by providing evidence of his own usual price. This is not the most convincing evidence, but if the defendant offers nothing to rebut it, and the plaintiff's basis for calculating it appears reasonable, it may be sufficient. If there is no evidence of either the objective market value or the plaintiff's usual price, evidence of the plaintiff's costs in providing the property or services may be accepted as the best evidence of value, provided that it appears that the plaintiff acted efficiently and that costs were not higher than they should be. (Of course, the reimbursement of cost is likely to be a less attractive basis of recovery for the plaintiff, because market price usually consists of cost plus profit.)

§9.6.4 The Recipient's Net Gain

The net actual enrichment of the recipient—that is, the actual amount by which the recipient's wealth is increased—could be more or less than the market value of the services. For example, although the market value of hiring Sam was $70, Maggie actually gained $200 from his services. Conversely, had it been a slow day, her takings from the booth could have been less than $70.

In this example, net gain is relatively easy to determine. This is not always true. Net gain could be speculative or difficult to quantify. Consider the example of the doctor who came to the aid of the victim in an emergency. Say that the customary fee for the doctor's services is $200. If, as a result of her prompt efforts, the victim was saved from death or crippling injury, this is surely worth more than $200 but it is difficult to value the gain. If restitution were to be based on the victim's net gain, testimony would have to be given on the monetary value of his life and health. Conversely, if despite the doctor's valiant effort the victim died soon after the fall, he received no ultimate benefit and has no net gain. In this particular case, the victim's benefit would not be measured on the basis of his net gain, for reasons explained in section 9.6.5, but the illustration does make the point that valuation can be a tough issue.

A further problem with net enrichment is that it can be perceived in two different ways. If it is determined *subjectively*, it is measured with reference to

---

7. This terminology is not confined to restitution, but is also used in connection with contracts in which the parties have left the price open. In fact, the terms derive from contract law and enter the language of restitution through the fiction of quasi-contract.

the actual recipient, taking into account the recipient's needs, circumstances, and intentions. *Objective* valuation is based on the worth of the benefit in market terms. (This is not the same as market value of the service, because it is the ultimate gain that is measured by the market standard.) For example, Contractor builds a patio on Owner's property without authorization, but under circumstances that make contractor neither an intermeddler nor a volunteer. The market value of the work is $1,000. The patio enhances the value of the house by $400. However, Owner has no intention of selling the house, and she hates sitting outside, so she has no use for the patio. Owner has received labor and materials worth $1,000 on the market, but her objective net gain is $400 and her subjective net gain is zero.

§9.6.5   *Choosing Among Market Value, Objective, or Subjective Net Gain*

As the above illustrations show, the means of measuring the benefit can make quite a difference to recovery. The selection of the most appropriate measure is within the court's discretion, exercised to achieve a result that is fair under all the circumstances. The goal is to reach a figure that neither over- nor under-compensates the claimant while imposing liability on the recipient that is realistic and not excessive. While one cannot state hard-and-fast rules in an area involving discretion, there are some guidelines that are commonly followed:

1. **Market value** tends to be the **preferred** measure of recovery because it is likely to be the fairest and most balanced basis of compensating the conferrer at a rate that could reasonably be expected by the beneficiary. Also, because quantum meruit (or quantum valebant) approximates what the contract price would have been, had the parties made a contract for the services or property, it is conceptually most consistent with the underlying theory of quasi-contractual recovery, which is based on a fictional contract. This basis of calculation is therefore particularly appropriate when the benefit had been requested (even though there is no contract), or circumstances indicate that it likely would have been had the beneficiary had the opportunity to do so.

Maggie would thus be liable to Sam for the $70 reasonable wage, rather than the $200 profit, and the victim would have to pay the doctor $200 for the successful treatment, rather than the value of life and health.

2. If there is some other *fault or impropriety* in the conduct of the *conferrer* that is not serious enough to preclude relief, the court may award the lowest measure of relief. For example, when a party materially breaches a contract after having partially performed, the breacher cannot recover under the contract but can obtain restitution for what has been given. Because the breacher is at fault for breaking the contract, restitutionary recovery is limited to the smaller of the market value of what was done or the portion of the

price allocated to the performance under the contract. For example, say that a builder wrongfully abandons work after erecting part of a building. The market value of what has been done before abandonment is $5,000, but because the builder underbid, the amount of the contract price attributable to that work is only $4,000. The builder cannot recover more than $4,000, and that amount may be further reduced if the owner has suffered damages as a result of the breach. (This is discussed more fully in connection with material breach in section 17.6.2.)

3. Even in the absence of imposition or fault, if one measure is *disproportionately large or small,* fairness or reasonable community expectations may require that it not be selected. For example, irrespective of the concern for imposition, there would never be any basis for awarding the doctor the value of the victim's life. Not only could this be a gargantuan recovery, imposing great hardship on the victim and grossly overcompensating the doctor for her work, but it is not customary for doctors to be rewarded for services in this way.

4. If the *recipient* has been guilty of *dishonest or improper conduct,* the *highest measure* is likely to be used. To illustrate, recall the example in which Sam managed Maggie's kiosk after she fainted. Instead of paying over the $600 proceeds to Maggie, Sam used it to buy lottery tickets and won $100,000. Sam is now the recipient of enrichment by using Maggie's property without authority, and his wrongful act in misappropriating it justifies holding him liable for the full extent of his gain. That is, he is treated in law as having won the $100,000 on Maggie's behalf so that he has to disgorge the full amount of his winnings. If he won nothing in the lottery, so that he has no ultimate gain, the value of what he took, $600, is the higher measure and the most appropriate one to be used.

5. If the benefit was *requested* (that is, when there is a contract, but the conferrer elects restitution, or the request does not qualify as a contract), any price agreed to by the parties is probitive *evidence of value* and may be used in preference over other measures.

6. In some cases, none of the more common bases of measurement work at all, and the court may have to use its discretion to make an award more in keeping with the circumstances. For example, say that a climber is stranded on a cliff. A passerby sees this and climbs the cliff and rescues the climber. In doing so, the rescuer falls and is injured. She does not claim a fee for the rescue (which she most likely will not get for reasons stated in section 9.5.2), but she does claim reimbursement of her medical expenses on the theory that it would unjustly enrich the climber if he did not pay them. Although it is possible that the rescuer would be held to have been performed with gratuitous intent, a court may feel that it would be unjust to deny relief altogether. However, the medical expenses do not fit into any of the categories mentioned—they are not the market value of the service, nor the net enrichment of the climber, objectively or subjectively determined. To give relief, the court would have to use its discretion to create a remedy based on plaintiff's

post-benefit medical expenditure. This resolution may be fair if the medical expenses are not too high, but if they are substantial, the concern is raised about imposing massive liability on the climber.

§9.7   "Moral Obligation": Restitution When a Promise Is Based on a Prior Benefit

§9.7.1   *Introduction*

As we have seen, restitution is not dependent on the obligor having made any promise. It is predicated on unjust enrichment rather than commitment. The doctrine traditionally known as "moral obligation" is something of a hybrid, in that it covers situations in which the facts do not fully support restitutionary recovery, but the justification for giving relief is bolstered by a promise made after receipt of the benefit. In other words, it blends restitutionary concepts and promise.

To illustrate, add a fact to the example of the busybody neighbors, O. Fishus and N. Termeddler, who cleaned up the unkempt yard while the owner was at work and left a bill for $300. As officious intermeddlers, they are not entitled to restitution. However, instead of tossing the bill in the garbage, the homeowner wrote back to them thanking them for their effort and promising to pay the $300 at the end of the month. This promise is not contractual because the neighbors' detriment was "past consideration." It was not exchanged for, but preceded, the promise. Similarly, the sequence of action followed by promise precludes promissory estoppel relief because the neighbors' action was not induced by the homeowner's promise.

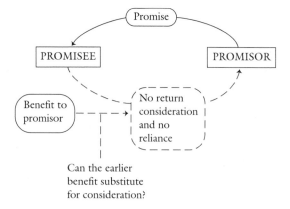

Can the earlier
benefit substitute
for consideration?

The question addressed in this section is whether the *prior benefit plus the later promise* should create a ground for enforcing the promise independent of consideration, restitution, and promissory estoppel.

§9.7.2 Terminology

Under the influence of Lord Mansfield, the great English jurist, a movement grew in eighteenth-century English courts to enforce promises without consideration, purely on the basis that they were morally binding. As Chapter 8 amply demonstrates, this trend did not take root. In the absence of consideration, an obligation cannot be enforced as a contract even if it is morally binding. Relief under promissory estoppel and restitution likewise require more than moral obligation. Indeed, when people say that an obligation is morally binding, they usually mean that the obligor should honor it despite the lack of legal duty to do so.

Notwithstanding this general sense in which "moral obligation" is understood, it has also come to be used as a term of art to describe a particular doctrine under which a promise without consideration may be enforced in a narrow range of circumstances. It is important not to confuse this technical use of "moral obligation" with its wider and more general meaning. Although promises are not enforced simply because they are morally binding, a promise that satisfies the prerequisites of the doctrine of "moral obligation" is enforceable despite the absence of consideration. Because the name of this doctrine is so easily confused with the general meaning of moral obligation, many courts and commentators prefer to use a different label for it. The most common is the **material benefit rule,** or, following the wording of Restatement Second, **promise for benefit received.**

§9.7.3 The Traditional Scope of "Moral Obligation"

Although Lord Mansfield's efforts did not lead to the general substitution of moral obligation for consideration as the basis of contract, some vestiges of this idea remain in our law in the form of narrow exceptions to consideration doctrine. These exceptions apply only to a small number of specific situations in which a debtor makes a promise to pay an earlier unenforceable debt. Although the later promise lacks consideration, the moral obligation to pay the pre-existing unenforceable debt is treated as sufficient to make the promise enforceable.

This is best explained by an illustration using one of the specific situations: the barring of a debt by the **statute of limitations.** Because witnesses disappear and memories fade over time, and because claims should not be allowed to fester indefinitely, all claims are subject to a time bar called a statute of limitations. The claimant must initiate suit before the expiration of a specified period after it arises, failing which the right to sue is lost. The legal effect of expiry of the limitation period is not elimination of the claim, but only of the right to sue on it. For most purposes, this distinction does not mean much, but the vestigial obligation is enough to support a later promise by the obligor to pay the debt.

Say, for example, that Debtor borrowed $5,000 from Creditor seven years ago. The loan should have been repaid six months later, but Debtor never paid and Creditor never got around to suing for recovery of the money. The statute of limitations for contractual claims is typically six years, so the claim is now barred. Upon realizing that the limitation period had run, Debtor was at first jubilant, but then his conscience troubled him. He therefore wrote to Creditor and promised to pay the old loan. Although there was no new consideration given by Creditor for this promise, the pre-existing valid but barred debt is recognized as furnishing a moral obligation sufficient to dispense with the need for new consideration. The new promise is therefore binding on the debtor and can be enforced if he declines to perform it.

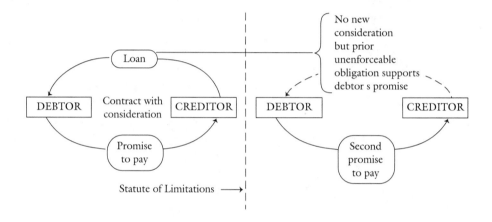

In addition to obligations barred by the statute of limitations, courts have applied this concept of moral obligation in a few other specific situations involving a subsequent promise to honor a pre-existing but unenforceable legal obligation. The two most familiar are prior debts discharged in bankruptcy and prior voidable debts. When a debtor becomes **bankrupt,** his or her prebankruptcy debts are usually paid only in part by a distribution from the bankrupt estate. The balance is discharged and creditors are forbidden by law to take any steps to try to collect it. However, the doctrine of "moral obligation" validates a later promise by the debtor to pay the discharged debt. (This common law rule is now heavily regulated by statute. To prevent creditors from undermining the discharge, the Bankruptcy Code imposes a strict procedure for reaffirmation of discharged debts that makes it difficult for a creditor to obtain a valid promise to pay such a debt.)

A **voidable** debt is one that can be avoided by the debtor because of some defect in formation or contractual capacity such as fraud, mistake, or minority. A voidable obligation must be **distinguished from** a **void** one. When a putative contract is void (as happens when consideration is lacking), it is a legal nullity and neither party can enforce it. However, if a contract is voidable by one of the parties, that party has the choice of treating the contract as fully valid and enforceable, or relying on the defect to escape the contractual relationship.[8] Under the doctrine of "moral obligation," if the party with the right of avoidance ratifies the contract by a second promise after becoming aware of the defect or after the basis for contractual incapacity has ended, the later promise is binding despite the lack of new consideration.

These discrete situations form the core of the traditional doctrine of "moral obligation," and have become well-accepted exceptions to the "past consideration" rule. The difficult question is whether the doctrine should be broadened beyond this narrow range to create a more general basis for enforcing promises motivated by prior benefits.

§9.7.4 The Broad "Material Benefit" Rule

In addition to reaffirming the specific situations in which courts have accepted the enforceability of a promise based on a pre-existing unenforceable obligation, Restatement Second §86 advocates broad recognition of promises based on a benefit previously received. It sets forth the following requirements:

1. The promisor has been **unjustly enriched** by a **benefit previously received** from the promisee.
2. The benefit was **not given as a gift.** (However, according to Comment *d*, the later promise shifts the burden of showing gratuitous intent to the recipient. The effect of this is to allow relief, even if the benefit was gratuitous, unless the recipient (promisor) can prove that the benefit was intended as a gift.)
3. The promisor subsequently makes a **promise in recognition** of the benefit.

If these requirements are satisfied, the promise is binding to the *extent necessary to prevent injustice.* One of the factors to be taken into account in exercising this discretion is the relationship between the value of the benefit and the amount promised. This factor is expressly identified by §86, which specifically requires enforcement to be limited to an amount proportional to the value of the benefit. Beyond this, the general discretion to prevent injustice allows the court to weigh whatever other factors bear upon the appropriate extent of relief.

To illustrate how this doctrine may work, return to the example of the neighbors' claim for the yardwork in which the homeowner made a subsequent promise to pay the $300 bill: The making of the subsequent promise

---

8. We return to the distinctions between void and voidable obligations in section 13.3.

could remove the objection that the neighbors were officious intermeddlers. The comments to Restatement Second §86 say that a clear, well-considered, and uncoerced subsequent promise to make restitution lessens the concern about imposition by demonstrating the utility of the benefit. Thus, clear and voluntary ratification of the benefit acts as a counterweight to the meddling and changes the equities in favor of enforcement. The facts indicate that the other prerequisites for relief, a prior benefit, enrichment, and an intent to charge are satisfied, so we turn to the question of relief.

The market value of the yardwork is not stated, so we do not know if $300 is disproportionate to the value of the benefit. If it is, the court may reduce recovery. Therefore, although a valuation issue arises here, as it does in a restitutionary claim based on unjust enrichment, the existence of a promise changes the dynamics of the valuation issue. The promise is at least evidence of what the promisor considered the worth of the benefit to be, and evidence of market value is relegated to a subsidiary role of policing the promise to ensure that it is not too generous. Proportionality is a rough equivalence between the amount promised and the value of the benefit, and does not require an exact match. The proportionality requirement is congruent with the goal of restoring only the enrichment gained by the promisor. It is also related to the cautionary function of consideration doctrine, in that it protects the promisor from a promise that is too generous or rash.

In addition to ensuring proportionality, the court exercises a broad discretion (similar to the overall balancing employed in promissory estoppel cases) to evaluate all the circumstances of the case to decide what must be done to achieve justice. The nature and circumstances of the enrichment and the quality of the promise must both be taken into account. In a case like this one, in which the original imposition was outrageous, the promise must be looked at carefully to ensure that it was a voluntary commitment, unaffected by the manipulations of the intermeddler. The degree to which the promise satisfies the evidentiary and cautionary functions of legal formality is relevant here. In addition, the court must take into account the danger of reinforcing meddlesome behavior and may conclude that even a subsequent promise should not validate the actions of the neighbors.

Although a broad principle of restitution based on a subsequent promise is advocated by Restatement Second, the courts of many states have refused to follow this lead and have not extended "moral obligation" beyond the few narrow situations involving prior unenforceable legal obligations.

EXAMPLES

1. Sarah Nade is a violinist. One evening, as she was walking home after playing at a symphony concert, she approached a sidewalk cafe. She noticed a young couple at one of the tables, sipping wine, talking softly, and gazing

lovingly into each other's eyes. Then a point of contention must have arisen between them because their voices were sharply raised and anger flashed in their eyes. Upset that the beautiful moment had been shattered by this unexpected strife, Sarah tore her violin from its case, hurried over to the couple's table, and played a poignant love song. Her intervention worked. The couple paused in their argument, looked at each other wistfully, and, murmuring sweet nothings, fell into each other's arms. When the song ended, Sarah asked the couple if they would like another, and they requested a romantic favorite that Sarah played with exquisite passion. At the end of the second piece, Sarah extended her hand to the couple and said, "That will be $20 please." They refused to pay, claiming that they had no idea that Sarah intended to charge for the serenade.

Does Sarah have a claim for the $20?

2. Benny Fishery has been involved in a longstanding feud with his neighbor, Sam Aratin, arising out of the alleged excretory habits of Sam's dog. Matters have become so bad that Benny has purchased a shotgun and vows to use it on Sam or his dog if either sets foot on his property.

Last Saturday, Benny locked up his house and left on a two-week camping trip in the wilderness. On Saturday evening a faulty appliance caused a fire to break out in his kitchen. Sam saw the fire through the kitchen window. Having seen Benny set off that morning with his camping gear, Sam realized that immediate action was called for. He grabbed his disposable fire extinguisher, smashed the window, and discharged its contents into the flames, dousing the fire. Afterwards he made inquiries and ascertained that Benny was incommunicado for the next two weeks. Sam was concerned that a burglar could easily enter the vacant house through the broken window, so he hired a contractor to replace it for $200. Sam had to pay the contractor because he insisted on cash and refused to wait for his money until Benny returned.

Sam left a note on Benny's charred kitchen counter, telling him what had happened and asking for payment of $300, made up as follows:

(a)   Cost of the disposable fire extinguisher, $30.
(b) $200 paid for the window.
(c)   Sam's fee for services rendered, $70.

On his return from vacation, Benny sent back Sam's note, having scrawled on it some unpleasant suggestions on what Sam should do with it. Should Sam follow these suggestions, or does he have a right to payment?

3. Change the facts in Example 2 as follows: The fire was so fierce that the extinguisher did not douse it. Sam entered the kitchen through the broken window and tried valiantly to stamp out the flames. He eventually succeeded, but burned his legs badly in the process. As a result, he incurred

$4,000 in medical expenses and had to take three weeks unpaid sick leave, losing an additional $2,000. He has no medical or disability insurance. Apart from the financial loss, he has suffered excruciating pain.

When Benny returned from vacation and heard of Sam's sacrifice, he was overcome with gratitude and felt deep remorse for his hostile attitude to Sam's dog. He visited Sam in the hospital and tearfully promised to pay Sam $200 per month for the next three years to compensate Sam for the medical expenses, loss of earnings, and pain. Sam accepted this offer in an emotional display of reconciliation.

Benny paid installments for two months until, looking out of his window one morning, he saw Sam's dog busy decorating his lawn. This rekindled the old feud, and Benny refuses to pay another cent to Sam. Is his promise enforceable?

4. Rhoda Hogg began hearing noises from her car when she accelerated beyond 85 m.p.h. on the freeway. She took the car to Mark Price, a mechanic, to have the trouble determined and repaired. She told Mark that he was to call her for authorization if the repair would cost more than $200. Mark neglected to communicate this instruction to his assistant, who completed an expensive repair without checking with Rhoda. When Rhoda was presented with a bill for $650, she refused to pay it, and insists that she is liable for no more than $200. Mark admits his mistake, but argues that the repair was necessary and $650 is a fair charge for the parts and labor. This is in fact true.

Is Rhoda obligated to pay the $650?

5. Val N. Teer and Justin Richmond entered into a contract of sale under which Val purchased Justin's house. The contract was conditional on Val obtaining a mortgage loan to finance the purchase. Justin knew that Val had a poor credit record and did not qualify for a loan, so he encouraged her to apply to a particular lender that had a reputation for lenience in evaluating borrower qualifications.

Val applied for the loan. While she was waiting to hear the decision on her application, she began to plan her move. One of the items that had to be moved to her new house was a hot tub. As the house had no suitable firm area on which to place it, Val realized that a concrete slab would have to be built on which to install it. She had ascertained from the moving company that she would save considerable costs if the tub could be moved and installed in one operation, because this would eliminate moving the tub to storage and then transporting it and setting it up on site. Because she was anxious to have the slab in place by closing, Val felt that she could not wait for the decision on the loan application. She discussed the matter with Justin, who expressed confidence that Val would get the loan and told her that he would have no objection if she laid the slab immediately. The parties did not discuss what would happen if the loan was refused.

Val's cousin is a contractor and he agreed to build the slab for her for the special price of $1,000. (His normal charge would be $2,000.) A few days after the slab was completed, Val was notified by the loan company that her application had been rejected. As there were no other prospects for financing, the sale fell through.

Justin now has a slab on his property at Val's expense. He has no use for it and it does not enhance the value of his house. Val would like to be reimbursed for the slab. Can she recover? If so, how much?

EXPLANATIONS

1. Although there was no express contract, the first question to ask is whether the parties may have entered into a contract implied in fact. A factually implied contract is an actual contract inferred from conduct. It arises when the parties do not utter or fully articulate words of agreement, but their behavior, reasonably interpreted, indicates an intent to be bound to each other. The ultimate effect of a factually implied contract is no different from an express one: They are both real contracts. A contract implied in fact must not be confused with a contract implied in law, or quasi-contract, which is not based on evidence of intent to enter an actual contract, but is a legal fiction— a remedial device used by the court to provide relief for unjust enrichment.

For a contract to be implied in fact, deliberate conduct of each party, viewed reasonably from the perspective of the other under all the circumstances, must manifest an intent to enter an exchange relationship under which each delivers or promises a performance to the other (Restatement Second §19). In the present case, there was deliberate overt conduct: Sarah played her violin for the couple, who accepted her performance by listening and selecting an encore. If it was common practice for street musicians to charge for their services and the couple knew or should have known this, their conduct in acquiescing to the service could give rise to the inference that they intended to pay the reasonable or customary fee for it. However, if this is not the practice, or the couple should not be held accountable for knowing of it, their conduct in listening to her and making a request does not create the implication of a promise to pay.

If no actual contract was made, Sarah's only basis for claiming compensation is unjust enrichment: Despite the absence of true contract, the court may use the procedural fiction of implying a contract in law to give restitution to Sarah for the value of her services. To qualify for quasi-contractual relief, Sarah must have been neither a "volunteer" nor an "officious intermeddler."

A volunteer is one who confers the benefit without intent to charge for it. Although Sarah's actual intent is unknown, her decision to play the serenade was apparently a spontaneous altruistic reaction, intended to quell the looming crisis between the lovers. The idea of requesting compensation may have been an afterthought. However, gratuitous intent is objectively determined, based on apparent intent as perceived by a reasonable person in the position of the recipient. For this reason, unless Sarah manifested an intent to charge, or it is common practice to pay street musicians, she is likely to be deemed a volunteer. (Unlike the doctor who conferred emergency treatment on the sidewalk, Sarah's status as a professional musician cannot plausibly be used to create the inference of intent to charge. Sarah was too far beyond the range of normal professional activity for her status to have any relevance to her action. Intent to charge must be judged in the context of the reasonable expectation of having to pay for street music.)

You probably noticed that the factors from which we would imply an objective intent to charge for purposes of quasi-contract are very similar to those relevant to the determination of an actual implied contract. In some cases the dividing line between factual and legal implication is subtle, especially when the recipient is aware that the benefit is being conferred and does not protest. The distinction between factual and legal implication is more obvious when (as in Example 2) the recipient did not become aware of the benefit until after it was conferred. In such a case, there is no basis for arguing a contract implied in fact, and quasi-contractual relief is the only option.

If Sarah was a volunteer, this ends the matter. She cannot recover. But even if she satisfies the test of intent to charge, restitution is not available if she was an officious intermeddler. As she conferred the benefit on the couple without being asked, this is an imposition unless the crisis demanded immediate response and made it impractical to get advance authorization for her action. Although this was apparently something of a crisis, it is hard to imagine anything more meddlesome than the intervention in a lover's quarrel between complete strangers. (Indeed, some diners at a sidewalk cafe would consider Sarah's serenade an intrusion under any circumstances.)

Although a benefit may have been conferred officiously, enrichment may still be unjust if the recipient, having the easy option of rejecting it, accepts it in the reasonable realization that compensation is expected. The couple could have waved Sarah away or otherwise have shown that they did not care for her attentions, but they listened to her and requested an encore. Again, the issue of reasonable expectations becomes relevant. If Sarah can show a general understanding that street musicians do not perform for free, the couple's conduct can be reasonably interpreted as an acceptance of the benefit, curing the problem of imposition. If not, they are a captive audience and their toleration of her playing cannot be taken to imply an acceptance of a benefit with an understanding that it must be paid for.

Although Sarah is not assured of establishing a case either in contract or in quasi-contract, she does have arguments for both. If she succeeds in establishing liability under either, what relief should she obtain? A factually implied contract entitles her to the contract price of the performance, but because no contract price was settled (Sarah's demand for $20 was first made only after she had performed), the usual inference is that the parties contracted for a reasonable price based on the market value of the performance. That is, quantum meruit is the usual measure of the contract rate when the price is not fixed in the contract. Twenty dollars may or may not be the market price for Sarah's musical services. This must be established by testimony from a witness familiar with the trade.

Restitutionary recovery, also generally based on quantum meruit, coincides with the contract price in this case. However, restitution may be restricted to actual net economic gain when fairness so dictates. In this case, there is no indication that the serenade enhanced the wealth of the couple, so there is no ultimate economic gain, and use of this measure would be tantamount to denying relief. Therefore, if relief is justified, market value must be used to measure recovery.

2. Unlike Example 1, there is no basis for arguing here that Sam and Benny have a contract implied in fact. However, even in the face of a clear absence of actual contract, the fiction of quasi-contract is employed to remedy unjust enrichment.

A. Was Sam a Volunteer?

If Sam did not intend to charge for his efforts, he is a volunteer and cannot receive restitution. As usual, intent is not determined purely on the basis of Sam's actual state of mind but in light of his reasonable expectations. Compensation may not have been Sam's focus as he rushed out to fight the fire, so the idea of asking for reimbursement probably occurred to him only after the crisis had passed. Nevertheless, the requirement of intent to charge should be satisfied if Sam would reasonably have expected payment had he thought of this issue when rendering the service.

It is reasonable to attribute to him the intent to seek reimbursement for the extinguisher. It is less likely that a court would accept that he intended to charge for his services. Although such intent is plausible when a person renders professional services in an emergency, intervention by a neighbor, even a hostile one, is typically regarded as altruistic and gratuitous.

There is no question of gratuitous intent when Sam hired the window repairer. He clearly intended to seek reimbursement for that cost. In short, Sam provided his services gratuitously but was not a volunteer with regard to the costs of the extinguisher and window repair. To succeed on those claims, Sam must also not have been an officious intermeddler.

B. Was Sam an Officious Intermeddler?

Apart from intent to charge, RESTATEMENT OF RESTITUTION §117[9] lists several requirements that Sam must satisfy to avoid being characterized as an intermeddler in preserving Benny's property without his knowledge and consent:

---

9. Note that the citation is to the RESTATEMENT OF RESTITUTION which is a different publication than the RESTATEMENT OF CONTRACTS. It is also published by the American Law Institute and is confined to principles of restitution. It was published in 1937 and has not been revised.

(1)   Sam took possession of the property lawfully.

(2)   It was not reasonably practicable to get Benny's authority before conferring the benefits.

(3)   Sam had no reason to believe Benny did not desire him to act.

(4)   Benny in fact obtains the benefit of the expenditures.

Benny had made it very clear that Sam was not permitted on his property, but this was a serious emergency threatening Benny's home, and Sam could reasonably assume that Benny's prohibition did not go so far as to forbid entry onto the property to save it. Given the urgency of attending to the fire, Sam could not have communicated with Benny before extinguishing it. Sam's efforts were successful, and Benny received a substantial benefit as a result. Restitution for the cost of the extinguisher is appropriate.

The window is a harder case.[10] Although Benny was still in the wilderness and could not be reached, the extreme urgency had passed and Sam could no longer assume that Benny would desire his presence on the property or his assistance. Even if this objection is overcome, it is not clear that the window replacement was so pressing that it had to be done before Benny's return. The risk of burglary could have been reduced by a cheaper temporary measure such as boarding up the window. Of course, Benny would have had to replace the window anyhow, and Sam has saved him this cost. This fact reduces the concern about imposition. When combined with others such as the risk of burglary, the inability to communicate with Benny, and the fact that Sam actually disbursed money to confer the benefit, it could shift the equities in favor of relief.

C. Measurement of Relief

If Sam is to obtain restitution for the extinguisher and the window, how are these benefits measured? Benny's ultimate gain is substantial because his house was preserved and protected. However, as in the case of the doctor who saved the life of the injured victim, this net gain is not the appropriate measure of relief because it is too burdensome to Benny and overcompensates Sam. Gain by the recipient beyond the market value of the benefit is normally not restored unless the recipient has committed some wrongful act that merits disgorgement of consequential profit. The market value of the extinguisher and the window repair is the proper measure. The cost to Sam is probitive but not conclusive evidence of market value.

3. Benny's later promise raises the possibility of enforcement on the basis of moral obligation, also known as the material benefit rule. This theory of liability is useful when a promise to compensate for a prior benefit bolsters

---

10. Because Sam broke the window, there is the added complication of Sam's possible liability for causing the damage in the first place. Assume that breaking the window was the minimum degree of force needed to confront the fire, and there is no issue of Sam being responsible for unjustifiable damage.

an otherwise weak restitutionary claim. (That is, restitution in the absence of the promise would be difficult because some element of unjust enrichment is hard to prove or missing.)

Had Benny not made the promise, Sam would have had an uncertain prospect of recovering compensation for his injuries on the basis of unjust enrichment. That cause of action does not comfortably fit situations in which a person incurs injury in conferring the benefit: As in Example 2, Sam's services in fighting the fire are likely to be regarded as gratuitous. In addition, his injury is incidental to the act of conferring the benefit and is not really a value conferred on Benny. Recognizing the unfairness of leaving Sam uncompensated for his injuries, a court may feel that justice demands that the concept of enrichment be stretched so that the cost of compensating Sam for his injury can be awarded. Even if it does this, the value of Benny's benefit has nothing to do with the normal principles of valuation. In this case, the medical expenses are relatively small. But they could be extensive and, without a voluntary assumption of liability by a promise, a court may be unwilling to impose huge liability on the beneficiary—especially if this exceeds the value of what was saved. Sam would have difficulty in establishing the value of Benny's benefit.

The premise of the material benefit rule is that Benny's subsequent ratifying promise shifts the equities in Sam's favor by conceding the reality of the benefit, diminishing the concern of intermeddling and creating the presumption that he did not act with gratuitous intent. (Comment *d* to Restatement Second §86 says that the promise excuses the claimant from showing intent to charge and requires proof of gratuitous intent to defeat restitution.) The promise also fixes the monetary value of the benefit. This does not entirely eliminate the problem of determining its worth, because the promise must not be disproportionate to the value of the benefit, but it does diminish this difficulty.

In *Webb v. McGowan,* 168 So. 196 (Ala. 1935), the court validated a promise like Benny's by manipulating consideration doctrine. Webb, working on the upper floor of a mill, was at the point of dropping a large wooden block to the ground when he noticed McGowan in its path of fall. To divert it from crushing McGowan, he held onto the block and fell with it. He thereby saved McGowan at the cost of severe and disabling injury to himself. In gratitude, McGowan promised a life pension to Webb. It was paid for several years until McGowan died. His estate discontinued payment. The court realized that the "past consideration" rule would bar enforcement, but it avoided application of the rule by using a legal fiction. By legal implication, it deemed the promise to have been contemporaneous with Webb's act of saving McGowan. Although Webb had not acted with compensation in mind, the court stressed the great value of what he had done for McGowan in saving him from death or terrible injury. This material benefit created a moral obligation on McGowan, which demanded enforcement of his promise.

Webb has always been a controversial case because it extended the narrow confines of the "moral obligation" exception to the "past consideration" rule. It moved beyond the handful of cases involving promises to pay prior unenforceable legal obligations and recognized a broader doctrine of more general application. Many later courts have declined to follow this lead. For example, in *Harrington v. Taylor*, 36 S.E.2d 227 (N.C. 1945), plaintiff saved defendant (an abusive husband) from death or injury by catching an axe wielded by his wife during a violent domestic confrontation. In the process, plaintiff's hand was badly damaged. Defendant promised to compensate her for the injury but never paid more than a small amount. The court refused to enforce the promise on the basis that it lacked consideration and was binding in conscience only.

Despite judicial resistance to a broad material benefit rule, Restatement Second §86 does advocate relief in cases like these. Unlike *Webb*, it does not fit enforcement into consideration doctrine by using the fiction of implying the promise as contemporaneous. Instead, it recognizes a distinct cause of action when a promise is made for a prior benefit and justice demands enforcement. Because there is a strong restitutionary element in these cases, the justice of binding the promisee lies in the fact that the promise was motivated by some enrichment that would not otherwise be paid for.

This is what happened in the present case. Sam has been injured in preserving Benny's property, and yet, as noted earlier, would have difficulty with a claim based on a pure unjust enrichment theory. Benny's promise is not a contract because it is not supported by contemporaneous legal detriment, yet it is an acknowledgment of the benefit. It reinforces the conclusion that the benefit was not imposed on Benny and shifts the burden of showing lack of intent to claim compensation.

One of the factors balanced by the court in deciding on enforcement is whether the promise was exacted by unfair pressure or was made in circumstances where emotion overcame judgment. There is no question of coercion in this case, but a promise made in the hospital so soon after the incident must be looked at warily. This may indicate the kind of rash undertaking addressed by the cautionary function of consideration doctrine. However, Benny's subsequent payments reaffirm his commitment and reduce the concern that his promise was a pure emotional impulse. The policy of protecting the promisor from a rashly generous or coerced undertaking is also reflected in the rule that the promise is not binding to the extent that it is disproportional to the benefit. Given the high potential value of the benefit (preservation of the house) and the close correlation between Sam's injury and the amount promised, it would be difficult to argue disproportionality.

4. In contrast to the previous examples, there is a contract in this case under which services were requested by Rhoda. The problem is that Mark negligently exceeded his authority under the contract. As the repair was necessary and reasonably priced, refusal to award its value enriches Rhoda by giving her a $650 repair for $200.

If asked, Rhoda may have authorized the repair, but she was given no opportunity to exercise this choice and had the repair imposed on her. She cannot return it because it is incorporated into her property. This imposition makes Mark an intermeddler as much as if he had made the repair without any request. Rhoda's enrichment is not unjust, and Mark is not entitled to quantum meruit relief. He is bound by the maximum price settled by the contract, $200.

In *Deck v. Jim Harris Chevrolet-Buick*, 386 N.E.2d 714 (Ind. 1979), the case on which this example is based, the court reached this conclusion. Although the mistake may have been honest, the repairer was in a better position than the customer to prevent it and must take responsibility for the negligence that led to the customer's enrichment.

5. The principal purpose of this example is to emphasize the point, made in section 9.3, that some facts may give rise to alternative theories of liability. This case invites consideration of possible recovery under contract, promissory estoppel, or restitution, and a comparison of the remedies under each theory. Unfortunately for Val, her prospects for relief are not good under any of them.

A. Contract

The claim for contractual relief is tenuous at best. The parties had a contract for the sale of the house, but made no express contract concerning the slab. Val clearly intended it for her own benefit and made no commitment to Justin to build it. If she had changed her mind and had not laid the slab, Justin could not have claimed that he had breached any obligation to him. Because the parties apparently did not contemplate failure of the sale, they made no agreement on what would happen in that event. There is no evidence from which to infer a commitment by Justin to pay for the slab if the property remained his.

B. Promissory Estoppel

Val's claim for relief on the basis of promissory estoppel runs into difficulty on the issues of both promise and justifiable reliance. Justin's only express promise, to transfer title to the house, was discharged because Val could not satisfy the condition of financing. While there is some hint that Val relied on Justin's recommendation of a lender and his permission to build the slab, there is not enough here to support a finding that Justin promised that Val would be able to make use of the slab or that he reasonably intended to induce her to build it. By laying the slab in anticipation of a successful loan application, without resolving liability if the sale fell through, Val assumed the risk of wasting her money. In the absence of a clear promise of reimbursement or of circumstances that impose some special duty of care on Justin, Val must take responsibility for poor judgment in the precontractual period.

C. Restitution

Restitution is not available, for related reasons. Although Justin has been enriched by the building of a slab on his property, his grant of permission to
build was not a request for this benefit. Had he been told that he would have
to pay for the slab if the sale fell through, he may well have refused permission. To treat his permission as a request would unfairly impose on him a useless concrete slab that adds no value to his property. Val's failure to resolve his
liability in the event of the sale's failure makes her a volunteer. She assumed
the risk that if the sale collapsed, she would have conferred a gratuitous benefit on Justin.

D. Relief

Although Val has had no luck under any theory of liability, it is a useful exercise to consider briefly the different forms of relief that would have been
available to her under each theory: If a contract had been established, she
would have been entitled to enforce it and to recover the agreed price of the
slab. If no price had been agreed, she would be entitled to a reasonable price
based on quantum meruit. If the contractor's normal price reflects market
value, the market price is $2,000, and the fact that Val obtained the work for
$1,000 because of family connections does not detract from the market
value. She is entitled to retain this profit unless it could also be implied that
she undertook to furnish the slab at her cost. Promissory estoppel would aim
primarily at reimbursing Val for her expenditure in reliance, the actual cost of
$1,000. Restitution is based on Justin's enrichment, which is normally mea-
sured on the basis of quantum meruit in the same way as it would be under a
contract with an open price term. It could be as high as $2,000 if that is the
true market value of the construction work. But if the slab did not add a full
$2,000 value to the property, the award may be reduced to the extent of
Justin's actual economic gain. Because he had no use for the slab and it added
no value to his property, his ultimate gain is zero, whether measured subjectively or objectively.

10

Interpretation and Construction: Resolving Meaning and Dealing with Uncertainty in Agreements

§10.1 The Problem of Indefiniteness in an Agreement

If the terms of an agreement are expressed clearly and comprehensively, the fact of contract formation and the extent of each party's commitment can be ascertained with relative ease by the interpretation of their language in context. However, parties sometimes fail to express their assent adequately, in that they have left a material aspect of their agreement vague or ambiguous, or because they have failed to resolve it or to provide for it at all. When the agreement suffers from this kind of uncertainty, it is said to be **indefinite.**

There could be many different causes of indefiniteness. For example, the parties may not take the trouble of discussing all aspects of the proposed relationship, they may not give enough attention to detail, they may be unclear in their thinking or articulation of what is expected, or they may avoid confronting thorny issues that threaten to collapse the deal. Sometimes it is clear that the parties genuinely intended a contract despite the indefiniteness, but in other cases the lack of resolution means that they had not yet achieved consensus.

The general rule is that no contract comes into being if a **material** aspect of the agreement is left indefinite by the parties and the uncertainty cannot be resolved by the process of interpretation or construction. The existence of such an irresoluble key aspect of the relationship means that the parties never reached sufficient consensus to conclude an enforceable contract.

This statement of the general rule suggests two central issues that must be confronted in dealing with problems of indefiniteness:

1.   For an apparent contract to fail for indefiniteness, there must be an *incurable uncertainty* about what the parties agreed to, so that their intent to enter a contract is in doubt, or the court is at a loss in establishing a basis for enforcing what was agreed. This first issue involves many considerations that form the basis of the remainder of this chapter.

2.   The uncertainty must relate to a *material aspect* of the relationship. Although an indefinite non-material term does need to be settled by the court if it is relevant to the dispute, the uncertainty does not preclude contract formation.

A term is material if it is an important component of the contract. It is so central to the values exchanged under the contract that it is a **fundamental basis of the bargain.** Although materiality is sometimes obvious, it is not always easy to decide because the significance of a term in any particular relationship can only be gauged by interpreting the facts of the case to uncover the reasonable expectations of the parties. (This broad definition of materiality is enough for present purposes. The question of when a term is important enough to be material is considered in greater detail in sections 6.5.2 and 17.3.)

§10.2   The Appropriate Judicial Response to Problems of Indefiniteness

If the unclear or unresolved terms do indicate that the parties never reached final, coherent consensus, a court should not try to concoct a contract for them. This would overstep the proper bounds of judicial power. It is the court's job to enforce contracts, not to make them up simply because the parties have engaged in negotiation. However, this does not mean that the court should refuse contractual enforcement unless every material term of the agreement has been expressed with piercing clarity. Such a rigorous standard would err in the opposite direction by failing to recognize a contract when the evidence suggests that the parties reasonably expected to be bound, did intend to enter a contract despite the indefiniteness, and had relied on the existence of a contract.

The balance between these poles results in a general principle that tolerates some degree of indefiniteness provided that the evidence indicates that the parties did intend a contract, and there is some means of resolving the uncertainty, so that a breach can be identified and a remedy provided. Both UCC §2.204(3) and the Restatement Second §33(2) adopt this approach by emphasizing that a contract should be treated as reasonably certain if the language of agreement, interpreted in context and in light of applicable legal rules, provides enough content to establish an intent to contract, a basis for finding breach, and a means of providing a remedy.

Although remedies are not discussed until Chapter 18, it is useful to focus on the *relationship between definiteness and remedy* suggested by the UCC and Restatement Second. Definiteness is not absolute but relative, and the degree of certainty required may be different depending on the nature of the controversy and the relief claimed. For example, if the plaintiff claims enforcement of a clear obligation due by the defendant, and the defendant contends that the contract is too indefinite because of vagueness in the plaintiff's obligation, the court does not have to establish the plaintiff's obligation with as much certainty as it would have to do if that was the obligation in issue. Similarly, if the plaintiff is claiming damages for the breach of an unclear obligation of the defendant, the court needs just enough information to determine a monetary award. However, if the plaintiff was seeking specific performance of the obligation (that is, a court order compelling the defendant to perform the contract), the court would need a greater degree of certainty to grant the order because the court must be able to define the obligation clearly if it is going to order its performance.

Although it is relatively easy to identify the general range of appropriate judicial intervention to cure indefiniteness, it is much more difficult to know if an individual case falls within that range: Whether the indefiniteness is properly remediable or should preclude contractual enforcement. As in so many other situations, the answer can only be reached by finding the mutual intent of the parties through the process of interpretation (evaluating the facts) and construction (applying appropriate legal rules that are used to determine presumed intent). Interpretation and construction are explained in section 10.4. Before we examine them in detail, it is useful to further define indefiniteness by looking at the different ways in which it may be manifested.

§10.3 Different Forms of Indefiniteness

Indefiniteness in an agreement could be caused by vagueness, ambiguity, omission, or irresolution. These different shortcomings have much in common, but they may raise different concerns that call for separate treatment. It is therefore useful to begin by articulating this distinction.

§10.3.1 *Unclear Terms: Vagueness and Ambiguity*

A term is **vague** (or **uncertain**) if it is stated so obscurely or in such general language that one cannot reasonably determine what it means. For example, Lessor agrees to let certain business premises to Lessee for one year in exchange for "a periodic rental payment based on a fair percentage of Lessee's earnings." One cannot determine on the face of this language the amount and the due date of the rent. The wording fails to convey a certain and concrete meaning.

A term is **ambiguous** if it is capable of more than one meaning. Ambiguity can lie in a word itself or in the structure of a sentence. Ambiguity in a word may be illustrated by a term in a lease that confines the use of the premises to "the purpose of conducting a bookmaking business." The word "bookmaking" could refer either to the manufacture of books or to the making and placing of bets on horses and sporting events. Ambiguity can also result from inept sentence construction. For example, although the lease makes it clear that "bookmaking" is used in the latter sense, it goes on to provide that Lessor "shall be entitled to ten percent of Lessee's profits from all gambling activities that shall be lawfully conducted on the premises." The clumsy sentence construction may mean that Lessor is entitled to ten percent of all profits earned by Lessee from gambling, and that Lessee is obliged to conduct only lawful activity on the premises, or it may mean that Lessor is entitled to ten percent of the profits from lawful gambling but gets no share of illegal gambling proceeds.

A term that is not readily comprehensible on its face may not be incurably vague or ambiguous, because it *may become clear if interpreted in context.* Evidence of what the parties said or did in negotiations, correspondence, or dealings prior to the agreement or during the period following it may help to clarify what they meant by the language used. In addition, clarity may be supplied by a custom or usage in the commercial environment in which the parties made the agreement, or by standardized terms recognized by law. We will shortly turn to these matters in detail. For the present, simply note that language that seems vague or ambiguous in isolation may become more certain if interpreted in the wider environment of the transaction. In the first example above, the vague rental provision may not be as unclear as it sounds if its meaning is embellished by facts in the context. Say, for example, that these clauses are regularly used in the commercial real property market, in which "fair rental" is widely understood to be based on an index published by an association of landlords, and rent is customarily paid monthly in advance. Similarly, the ambiguous word "bookmaking," while unclear in isolation, may become more definite if other provisions in the lease, discussions during negotiations, or other facts are available to show what the parties meant.

But contextual evidence cannot always save a vague or ambiguous term. Sometimes unclear language defies interpretation, even in context, because the circumstances of the transaction are devoid of helpful indicators of meaning. If a central component of an apparent agreement suffers from this degree of incurable indefiniteness, one can only conclude either that no contract was intended or, if it was, that the parties failed to form a clear intent or failed to communicate it well enough to create an enforceable relationship.

§10.3.2   Omitted Terms

If a term is omitted, it simply is not there. The **agreement has a gap** regarding that particular aspect of the relationship. Say that Lessor and Lessee discussed and wrote out most of the terms of the lease, but did not address the amount of the rent orally or in writing. This could mean that they failed to reach agreement on this crucial term, so that no lease came into being. However, it could also mean that the parties did not consider it necessary to articulate the amount of the rent, because they assumed that the rent would be reasonable, based on the fair market rental for commercial property of this kind. In other words, the apparent gap in their agreement indicates not a lack of consensus, but an intent to adhere to some "off-the-shelf" market or legal standard that they thought of as too obvious to need articulation. To decide which of these two possibilities is the right one, their intent must be determined by looking at the language of the agreement as a whole in light of all the circumstances of the transaction.

§10.3.3   Unresolved Terms

An unresolved term differs from a vague or omitted term in that the parties have **raised the issue** in their agreement but have **not yet settled it,** leaving it to be resolved by agreement at some later time. For example, when Lessor and Lessee negotiated the lease, they reached agreement on all the terms of a ten-year lease, including the rent to be paid for the first year. However, neither of them wished to commit to a fixed rental figure for the remaining years of the lease, and they could not agree on the method for calculating the annual rent increases. They became tired of arguing about this issue and were anxious to get the lease signed. They therefore executed a written lease setting out all the agreed terms, including the first year's rent, and providing that the rent for the remaining period of the lease would be negotiated further in the week before Lessee took occupation of the premises.

In this situation, the indefiniteness results from the deliberate postponement of agreement on the amount of consideration to be paid by Lessee for the bulk of the lease period—certainly a material aspect of the lease. Therefore, at this point there is no lease in existence despite the consensus on most of its provisions. A material term is left unresolved, and the parties clearly do not intend it to be supplied by some external standard. They have simply not yet reached final agreement. It could be that their undertaking to negotiate further imposes some obligation on them to try to reach consensus, but such an "agreement to agree" is not regarded as definite enough to create a firm and final contract. (As discussed in section 10.11, it could, however, create an ancillary commitment to bargain in good faith.)

§10.4   Ascertaining the Meaning of an Agreement: Interpretation Distinguished from Construction

§10.4.1   *Introduction to the Distinction*

The processes of interpretation (inferring meaning from facts) and construction (inferring meaning as a matter of law) have been alluded to in earlier chapters.[1] If you have read them already, the basic point of the present discussion will not be entirely unfamiliar. This section more closely examines and differentiates the methods and uses of the related but separate functions of interpretation and construction. To begin, a broad distinction may be drawn:

Restatement Second §200 describes **interpretation** as the ascertainment of the meaning of a promise or agreement. It is an **evaluation of facts** (that is, evidence of what the parties said and did and the circumstances surrounding their communications) for the purpose of deciding their mutual intent.

Construction, also called **implication in law,** is likewise concerned with the ascertainment of meaning, but it goes beyond available facts to find, not necessarily what the parties did mean, but what they **probably would (or should) have meant** in making the manifestations that were made. In other words, although the facts do not go far enough to establish the meaning of an indefinite term, the court uses a legal rule to create a meaning for it.

Although this point is expanded upon in section 10.4.2, it must be stressed at the outset that the distinction between interpretation and construction can be subtle and is often not of great practical significance. Nevertheless, it is worth understanding. When possible, it is preferable for a court to find the intended meaning of terms in actual evidence, rather than to construe it, because the courts' preliminary role is to enforce what the parties actually agreed. However, there are two situations in which a court is justified in inferring meaning as a matter of law:

1. As a general matter, construction is appropriate only when the existing evidence supports the reasonable conclusion (based on objective manifestations of assent) that the parties did intend to make a contract, but there is little or no evidence from which a factual inference can be drawn on their

---

1. For example, section 7.9.2 discusses the implication of a promise to use best efforts or to exercise reasonable judgment as a means of giving content to an apparently illusory promise, and section 4.1 discusses the interpretation of objective manifestations of assent in the context of offer and acceptance. This is not a definitive list. The issue of interpretation comes up often.

intent regarding a particular aspect of that contract. In seeking to effectuate the parties' intent, the court builds on what it knows of the transaction to provide a meaning that seems most reasonable in the circumstances and tries to simulate what the *parties probably would have agreed, had they focused on the issue.* This is preferable to an approach that would defeat contractual expectations by demanding clear proof of intent for every gap and uncertainty. It must be emphasized again that implication of meaning in law is based on the premise that the evidence at least points to an intent to be bound. If not, the court should not construe agreement as a matter of law.[2]

2. In addition to this general scope of construction, there is a narrower and more aggressive use of the process. In certain limited situations, a term may be implied in law even though it *overrides or conflicts with the evidence of what was agreed.* (But even here, the court will not construe a term to give effect to a contractual relationship unless the evidence reasonably supports the conclusion that the parties manifested intent to contract.)

This stronger form of construction is appropriate when the term must be implied to effect some public policy, or is so fundamental to fair dealing that the law insists that it be incorporated into the contract despite the parties' actual intent. In effect, legally implied terms of this kind are *mandatory* and cannot be varied by contract. Construction of this kind is more a matter of regulation than interpretation. It is discussed further in section 10.9.

§10.4.2   *The Distinction in Perspective*

The distinction between interpretation and construction is much easier to draw in theory than in practice. Sometimes it is fairly clear that the court is

---

2. There is potential for confusion between what has just been said—that a court should not construe an agreement as a matter of law—and the concept of quasi-contract discussed in section 9.4. Chapter 9 is concerned with unjust enrichment, a cause of action distinct from contract, in which relief is based on the fact that the defendant has been enriched at the plaintiff's expense as a result of receiving some benefit from the plaintiff, and justice requires that the benefit should be returned or paid for. The remedy for unjust enrichment is restitution—the restoration to the plaintiff of the benefit or its value. Because early common law courts were bound by rigid forms of action, they could not simply recognize unjust enrichment as a new basis for relief, so they fit it into the form of action for contract. To do this, they used a legal fiction under which they deemed the benefit to have been contracted for. As a result, restitutionary relief based on this legal fiction has come to be known as arising out of quasi-contract, or contract implied in law. This was purely a procedural form devised for the purpose of remedying unjust enrichment and had nothing to do with actual contract. Although courts are no longer constrained by this formalism, the terms "quasi-contract" or "contract implied in law" are still commonly used in connection with restitution. However, the purpose of quasi-contract is the remediation of unjust enrichment. The creation of a legal fiction to remedy unjust enrichment is, of course, very different from what is being discussed here—the inference that the parties did in fact make a contract. It would be improper for a court to draw that inference as a matter of law—to construe it—in the absence of some factual basis for believing that this comports with what the parties must have intended.

engaging in one or the other, but in many cases the line between them is fuzzy because they lie on a spectrum. At one end of the spectrum, evidence of intent is clear enough to require nothing beyond factual implication to determine the meaning or existence of a term. At the other end, there is no evidence at all from which to derive meaning for a term or to establish its existence, so the parties' intent is necessarily determined via implication in law. However, many cases lie somewhere in the middle of the spectrum, so that the resolution of contractual meaning is based partly on interpretation of and partly on extrapolation from evidence. It may be hard to tell where factual inference ends and legal implication begins. Although this may sound very abstract now, it will become clearer as you read on.

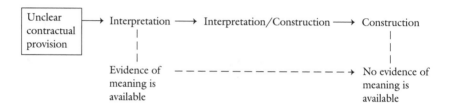

Luckily, it is not necessary for most purposes that this distinction be identified precisely because the end result—the establishment of meaning—is the same. However, it is important for courts and attorneys to understand the distinction. A judge who does not bear it in mind may move too far from established intent and impose obligations that were not reasonably expected or intended. An attorney who is unclear on the difference will have difficulty assessing the strength of an argument concerning meaning and predicting the court's likely response.

§10.5   Who Ascertains Meaning: Judge or Jury?

There is some confusion over the proper roles of the judge and jury in deciding the meaning of agreements, and cases offer conflicting views on whether the ascertainment of meaning is a matter of fact or law. Because **interpretation** is a **factual process,** the general approach should be that the factfinder (the jury, unless the case is being tried without one) must ascertain meaning after evaluating all pertinent evidence. Conversely, as **construction** is the process of supplying meaning as a **matter of law,** this is a legal question for the judge.

This simple theoretical dichotomy has become blurred. In part, this is because of a longstanding judicial mistrust of juries, which has motivated judges to retain many interpretational issues by characterizing them as matters of law. However, the problem goes beyond this historical lack of faith in juries. Confusion is inherent in the very subtlety of the distinction between interpretation and construction, which often makes it difficult to tell where factual inference ends and legal implication begins. As a result, there are no watertight rules, but there are some general guidelines that are helpful in deciding on the likely roles of judge and jury in the ascertainment of meaning:

1. When there is **no factual dispute** requiring an assessment of **credibility,** but interpretation involves nothing more than establishing the **ordinary grammatical meaning of words,** interpretation is the function of the **judge.** Therefore, when an agreement is written, and all that is required is the determination of meaning by consulting a dictionary or grammar book, it is the judge, and not the jury who pulls the book off the shelf.

2. If meaning has to be decided by the **evaluation of oral testimony** concerning what the parties expressed, or relating to the context from which meaning must be derived, this is more appropriately left to the **factfinder.** This is particularly so if disputes in meaning must be resolved by deciding on the credibility of witnesses.

3. If there is **no pertinent evidence of meaning,** and it can only be divined by legal implication, this is clearly the **judge**'s function.

Of course, as indicated earlier, meaning is often based on a combination of the grammatical meaning of words, contextual evidence, and legal implication. In such cases, it can be very difficult to unravel the proper roles of judge and jury, and concern about control over decisionmaking tends to push in the direction of entrusting the judge to balance the relative probity of these different elements.

Apart from the question of who decides meaning, the fact–law distinction has significance beyond the trial phase of the case. If meaning is determined as a matter of law, it can be reversed on appeal on the **standard of review** for legal questions: that the judge erred in the application of the law. However, if the determination is a question of fact, it can only be reversed if it satisfies a much stricter standard: The evidence must provide no reasonable basis for supporting the factfinder's conclusions. Also, a legal determination has weight as precedent, but a factual one does not.

§10.6 Interpretation: Deriving Meaning from Evidence

§10.6.1 The Meaning of "Interpretation"

This section looks more closely at the process of interpretation and examines the type of evidence that may be available to cast light on the meaning of manifestations of apparent intent. As stated earlier, interpretation first focuses on the normal, accepted meaning of the words used by the parties, but it involves more than an evaluation of language in isolation. The words are used in a context that often provides useful evidence of what the words meant.

The process of interpretation was introduced in section 4.1 on offer and acceptance, where it was noted that agreement is manifested by the use of outward signals: words—whether written or spoken; actions; and, even in appropriate situations, a failure to speak or act. As the parties move towards developing consensus in the process of contract formation, intent thus communicated by each party is necessarily interpreted by the other. If a dispute later arises about whether consensus was reached or about what was agreed, the communications of the parties must again be interpreted—this time in court—to determine which party's interpretation is correct. It is the *objective or reasonable meaning,* and not the subjective understanding of either party that must be sought.

§10.6.2   *The Sources of Evidence Used in Interpretation*

Manifestations of intent are always made in some context. Depending on the circumstances, this context may be quite sparse, or it may provide extensive information pertinent to meaning. If no information on meaning is available beyond the actual words used by the parties, interpretation of those words is necessarily limited to ascertaining their ordinary grammatical meaning. However, if the context does provide a background from which indicators of meaning can be drawn, interpretation can move beyond the confines of the dictionary and grammar book.[3]

There are four principal areas of factual inquiry generally thought of as comprising the context for interpreting an agreement—the language and conduct of the parties in forming the agreement, their conduct in performing the contract after it was formed (course of performance), their conduct in prior comparable transactions with each other (course of dealing), and the customs and usages of the market in which they are dealing with each other (trade usage). Notice that in each of these four areas we are concerned with objective evidence, in the form of words or conduct manifested by the parties, or verifiable facts in the contractual environment. The evidence of one party concerning what she may have thought or believed is only marginally helpful or relevant. Obviously, not all of these components are present in every transaction. However, the more that exist in a transaction, the richer the background from which meaning can be ascertained. In a fortunate case, all the evidence drawn from these different aspects of the context will point to the same meaning. If they conflict, the general rule (reflected in both UCC §§1.205(4) and 2.208(2) and in Restatement Second §203(b)) is to give greatest weight to the express terms of the parties, followed in order by

---

3. When the ultimate agreement is recorded in writing, the parol evidence rule places limits on the use of contextual evidence to supplement or vary the writing. This problem is deferred for now and is discussed in Chapter 12.

any course of performance, course of dealing, and usage. Let us now examine each of these four factual indicators of intent.

The Environment for Contractual Interpretation

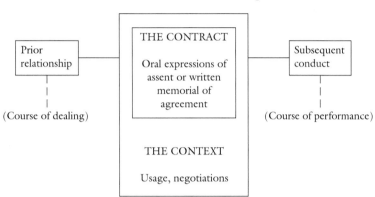

a. **The Express Words and Conduct of the Parties Signifying Intent**

The words used by the parties in formulating their respective obligations and expectations are always the principal facts to be consulted in establishing meaning. Both UCC §§1.205(4) and 2.208 and Restatement Second §203(b) give greatest weight to express terms. Interpretation therefore begins with an examination of what was actually said by the parties when they formulated their agreement. The parties' final expression of agreement may be oral—an oral agreement is fully effective unless the statute of frauds (discussed in Chapter 11) applies. However, even if the transaction is not subject to the statute of frauds, parties commonly follow the sensible practice of executing and signing a written memorial of agreement. In this way they avoid later disputes about what words were actually used in expressing their agreement. Of course, unless the language used is absolutely clear, comprehensive and unambiguous, the writing will not guarantee that problems of interpretation will not arise, but it will at least obviate disputes about what was actually said. (When the agreement is wholly or partially recorded in a writing, the parol evidence rule places very strong emphasis on the writing, and restricts the admissibility of contextual evidence. This is fully discussed in Chapter 12 and is not addressed here.)

When a court seeks the meaning of a particular provision, it does not simply confine itself to the wording of that term in isolation, but looks at the **language of the agreement as a whole**—that is, it reads the whole document or considers the entire oral agreement. A term that may in itself be uncertain or may suggest a particular meaning could become clearer or take on a different

251

meaning if considered in light of the rest of the expressed provisions, with an eye on its relationship to the underlying purpose of the agreement.

Because the words used by the parties are of primary significance, very clear language makes recourse to extrinsic evidence (that is, evidence beyond the actual words expressed) less important. In fact, earlier cases were disinclined to entertain broader contextual evidence at all if the words used by the parties appeared capable of interpretation without it. Heavy emphasis was placed on the common grammatical meaning of the words used by the parties. This approach was particularly rigorous if the agreement was written, and it was generally held that the court should not look beyond the "four corners" of an apparently clear writing.

Although a firm focus on plain meaning has the advantage of speedy and clean disposition, it can lead to the wrong result when words having an obvious meaning to an outside observer (like the court) may have been understood by the parties in a different sense. Modern courts are therefore more willing to accept that superficially clear language could have a different meaning when viewed in the entire context of the parties' dealings and will recognize an interpretation that departs from the dictionary meaning of a word when the evidence convincingly establishes that the parties meant it in a different sense. However, the **ordinary sense** of the language used by the parties remains the **primary focus** of interpretation, and extrinsic evidence at odds with the plain meaning of the language is not likely to be very persuasive if it cannot be reconciled with the apparent meaning of the words, or the discrepancy credibly explained. Of course if the language used is obscure, vague, or ambiguous, this primary source of meaning cannot resolve the interpretational question, and contextual evidence is more readily received and more crucial.

Apart from the actual words spoken or written to express agreement, there may be a history of communication and negotiation leading up to the execution of the contract. If the contract is recorded in writing, the parol evidence rule affects and may exclude evidence of what was said or written by the parties in the phase before final execution of the writing (as is discussed in Chapter 12). Subject to that reservation, evidence of what was expressed by the parties during the period leading up to contract formation could be useful and relevant to establish the meaning of what was ultimately provided for in the agreement.

b. Any Conduct by the Parties in the Course of Performing Under the Agreement

If the uncertainty to be resolved by interpretation only becomes an issue after the parties have begun performing the contract, their conduct in proffering and accepting, or otherwise reacting to performance may provide evidence of what was intended by an indefinite term. This post-formation behavior is called the "**course of performance**" and its relevance to interpretation is based on the assumption that the actual performance tendered and accepted without objection is a strong indicator of what must have been intended. The evidentiary value of the course of performance is recognized by UCC §2.208, mimicked by Restatement Second §202(4).

For example, a lease provides that "dogs, cats, and other animals may not be kept on the premises." Lessee owns a pet duck that he thinks of as a bird, not an animal. He has kept it on the premises for several months. Lessor has seen it on several occasions and has never complained. The mutual conduct of the parties creates the fair inference that they were in agreement that "animals" does not include ducks.

Not all post-formation conduct necessarily reflects what the parties intended at the time of contracting. The conduct may simply not be pertinent to the meaning of the term in issue, or, even if it is, it may reflect a subsequent change of mind or a disinclination to enforce rights under the contract.[4] Therefore it is possible to draw the wrong inference from behavior that is ambiguous or does not really have a bearing on the term in issue. There are several guidelines that help to avoid misconstruing conduct as a course of performance:

1. For a course of performance to be valid as a source of interpretation, it must be *pertinent to the meaning* of the term in controversy. For example, if the term in dispute concerned the date on which the rent payments were due, lessor's tolerance of the duck does nothing to clarify the uncertainty.

2. The conduct must show that the party performed or accepted performance *without a protest or reservation of rights*. Therefore, if on each occasion that Lessor saw the duck, she protested that it was not allowed, Lessor's failure to take stronger action does not clarify the meaning of "animals."

3. Conduct by only one of the parties, *not known and acquiesced in* by the other (for example, if Lessee kept the duck inside and Lessor never saw it or knew about it), may show what the performing party understood the agreement to be, but does not prove that the other party shared this view.

4. The more *extensive or repetitious* the conduct, the stronger the inference that it does reflect what was intended by the parties. By contrast, isolated or single instances of conduct are more ambiguous and could simply be a waiver of or disinclination to enforce rights on a particular occasion. For ex-

---

4. It can be difficult to distinguish a course of performance, which casts light on what the parties meant at the time of contracting, from post-formation conduct that is either a waiver of rights or a modification of the contract. For example, the lessor's failure to complain about the duck could indicate that the parties did not include it in the definition. However, it could mean instead that the lessor has simply chosen not to enforce the ban on ducks, or that the parties have implicitly agreed by conduct to eliminate the restriction on animals. If it is not a course of performance but a waiver or modification, it is subject to different rules, which are discussed in sections 13.9 and 16.11.2.

ample, merely because Lessor sees the duck on one occasion and does nothing about it, does not necessarily show that she shares Lessee's view of the meaning of "animals."

c. Any Prior Course of Dealing Between the Parties in Similar or Analogous Contractual Relationships

While "course of performance" means the parties' post-contractual relationship, the term **"course of dealings"** refers to any relationship they may have had in the **period before the transaction** in question. The parties may have dealt with each other on prior occasions, and the current transaction may be the latest in a series of similar ones that have taken place over a period of time. If so, the parties' conduct in prior dealings may provide information that helps to interpret a term that has generated a dispute in the present transaction. This is recognized by UCC §1.205(1) and Restatement Second §§202 and 203.

For example, Lessee previously rented premises from Lessor under a lease that had the identical clause forbidding animals. During the prior lease term, Lessor discovered the duck and told Lessee to get rid of it or face eviction. He sadly obeyed and boarded it with his mother. When the parties enter into a new lease with the same term, it is reasonable to infer that they intend its wording to have the meaning established under the prior relationship. If they intend otherwise, they must make this clear in the new lease. If they do not, Lessee cannot claim that "animals," as used in the new lease, does not include ducks.

A course of dealings is only pertinent if the earlier relationship is *comparable or analogous*. The transactions must be substantially similar, the term in controversy must have been present in the earlier dealings, and past conduct must be relevant to the meaning in issue. As with course of performance, *repetition strengthens the inference*, so multiple transactions with consistent, pertinent behavior more clearly establish intended meaning.

d. Any Trade Usage, Common Usage, or Custom that Is Reasonably Applicable to the Parties' Dealings

Although the ordinary or general sense of words must be the starting point in any exercise of interpretation, both UCC §1.205 and Restatement Second §202(5) emphasize the significant impact of trade usage on the meaning of language. Parties usually deal with each other in the context of a larger community. This may be a **particular market** (whether international, national, or more local), or it may be a **specialized trade or industry.** If the market has a well-accepted custom or practice that explains language or supplements an omission in an agreement, this customary usage is of value in ascertaining the parties' intent.

The UCC and Restatement Second refer only to *trade usage,* which may give the impression that custom or usage is only pertinent where the parties are members of a particular vocation, industry, or profession. However, usages exist even in the general marketplace, and "trade usage" should be taken to encompass any applicable commercial custom, whether it derives from a specific trade or from a broader market in which the parties are involved.

Older common law did not recognize any practice as a usage unless it was so firmly established as to be notorious, universal, and ancient. The modern approach is more flexible. UCC §1.205, Comment 5 explicitly rejects any requirement of great longevity and universality and admits of the possibility of new usages. The UCC test is simply whether the usage is **currently observed by the great majority of decent dealers.** In common law transactions, while some courts may still apply the stricter test, modern common law tends to follow the broader recognition of usage advanced by the UCC.

A party who alleges that usage explains or supplements an agreement must prove four things:

1. The usage must be *pertinent* to the term in issue.

2. The usage *does in fact exist* in the trade or market in which the transaction occurred. Before any usage can be said to apply, the party alleging it must prove that it exists. This is a factual question with two components. The party must prove what the usage is (that is, its terms and scope) and also that it is widely accepted in the trade or market. Proof of usage normally requires expert testimony by witnesses who are familiar with the customs and practices of participants in the trade or market.

3. Both parties must be *sufficiently connected to the trade or market* in question to make the usage fairly attributable to their interaction. This means that once a usage is proven:

    (a) If the usage pertains to a specialized vocation or industry of which *both parties are members,* they are bound by it unless the contract excludes it. As members of the trade, they are deemed to know of it and to intend it to apply unless their agreement provides otherwise.

    (b) If *only one of the parties is a member* of the trade, the usage does not apply unless the non-member party knew or had reason to know of it and the parties reasonably expected it to apply to the transaction.

    (c) Similarly, usages in a *non-specialized market* apply only if both parties are sufficiently familiar with the market that they knew or reasonably should have know of it and expected it to apply.

Note that an objective standard is used to hold a party accountable for knowledge that it should have had, even if it did not actually know of the usage. When a usage is incorporated into an agreement based on presumed, not actual knowledge, this is not really interpretation but construction. (Indeed, such objectively attributed knowledge is called "constructive" knowledge.) The usage becomes part of the contract because the parties are deemed reasonably to have intended it to apply. (The fact that we have slipped into construction in this discussion of interpretation shows how easily they flow into one another.)

4.   The usage *must not be excluded by or incompatible with the express terms* of the agreement. The presumption that parties intended to contract in light of accepted usage cannot stand if the parties make clear their intent not to be subject to it.

To illustrate a possible application of usage, consider again the lease that bars "dogs, cats, and other animals" from the premises. To support her contention that ducks are included, it would be helpful for Lessor to prove that the word "animals" is generally understood by all participants in the residential rental market to include all living creatures other than homo sapiens. By contrast, it would not be helpful for Lessee to show that among some specialized group of people, say zookeepers, the word "animal" is used to refer only to mammals, and "birds" is used to denote our feathered friends.

§10.7   General Rules of Interpretation (or Construction)

When a term is omitted or its meaning is uncertain, this indefiniteness can often be resolved by having recourse to one of a variety of general principles that have been developed by courts as guidelines in the ascertainment of reasonable but unexpressed intent. Many of these rules are based on *commonsensical inferences,* but some are dictated by policy or a perception of fairness. Some of the rules are old enough to be in the form of Latin maxims and are still commonly known by their Latin names that are noted below.

These rules are sometimes called rules of interpretation, and sometimes rules of construction—again reflecting the subtle distinction mentioned so frequently before. The important point, from a practical standpoint, is that they are guides to enable the court to draw the proper inferences of meaning from whatever facts may be available. Typically, they are used only when there is some uncertainty in the intent of the agreement. They should not be applied mechanically and must take into account the reasonable expectations of the parties and the underlying purpose of the agreement.

There are many rules of interpretation. They are not all of equal strength, and some are more compelling than others. Obviously, they are not all relevant to every case. Although most of the common ones are included here, no attempt is made to catalog them all. These examples sufficiently illustrate the range and kind of rules covered under this category:

1. If possible, the court should try to interpret an agreement in a way that gives effect to all its terms.

2. *Ut res magis valeat quam pereat,* "The thing should rather have effect than be destroyed." If one interpretation would make the contract invalid and another would validate it, the court should *favor the meaning that validates the contract.* In the same spirit, there are allied rules that prefer an interpretation that would make a term reasonable and lawful over one that would have the opposite effect, and an interpretation that positively rather than negatively impacts public policy or the public interest. For example, recall the lease that was ambiguous because it provided for the lessee to conduct a bookmaking business on the premises. If there is no factual basis for interpreting the word "bookmaking," and gambling is illegal, the preferred interpretation would be that it means the manufacture of books.

3. Specific or precise provisions should be given greater weight than general provisions. For example, one clause in a lease says that "ducks shall be kept on leashes at all times" and another clause says "no dogs, cats, or other animals may be kept on the premises." The specific provision concerning ducks makes it clear that the general rule on animals does not apply to them.

4. Where an agreement consists of both standardized and negotiated terms (or printed and handwritten or typed terms), any conflict between them should be resolved in favor of the *negotiated* or *handwritten terms.*

5. *Ejusdem generis,* "of the same kind." When specific and general words are connected, the **general word is limited by the specific one,** so that it is deemed to refer to things of the same kind. For example, a lease states that "skateboards, rollerskates, rollerblades, and other means of locomotion are prohibited in common areas and hallways." The common denominator here is that all these items make use of wheels under the feet. On this reasoning, the general words "other means of locomotion" do not include wheelchairs or motorbikes. However, if the common denominator is taken to be wheels, these two items would be included in the general language, but a camel would not be.

6. *Noscitur a sociis,* "known from its associates." This rule is similar to *ejusdem generis,* but is not confined to linked general and specific words. Whenever a series of words is used together, the **meaning of each word in the series affects the meaning of others.** For example, if a term in a lease provides that "no dogs, cats, or primates may be kept on the premises," the meaning of "primates" is qualified by the others. It would therefore cover only primates in the sense of apes and monkeys, and would not forbid the lessee from having his uncle, a bishop, move in with him.

7. *Expressio unius est exclusio alterius*, "The expression of one thing excludes another." This is in some sense the opposite of the *ejusdem generis* rule. When a **thing or list** of things is specifically mentioned **without being followed by a general term,** the implication is that **other things of the same kind are excluded.** For example, a term that prohibits "dogs, cats, and primates" impliedly does not prohibit ducks.

8. *Contra proferentum* (or stated in full, *omnia praesumuntur contra proferentum*), "All things are presumed against the proponent." When **one party has drafted or selected the language** of an unclear provision, the **meaning is preferred that favors the other party.** This rule is often said to be a tie breaker, in that it should be used as a last resort when no more direct and pertinent guide to meaning is applicable. It is not always used as a last resort, however, and tends to be much favored when the proponent of the terms is a party with relatively strong bargaining power who has produced a preprinted standard form for the other's signature.

§10.8   Gap Fillers—Implication by Law to Effectuate the Parties' Reasonable Intent

§10.8.1   Introduction

It was stressed in section 10.1 that construction is an extension of interpretation, employed to reach the reasonable intent of the parties. Normally (subject to the exceptions discussed in section 10.9), a court does not use construction to establish a contract when the evidence indicates that none was intended, nor does it construe a meaning inconsistent with the apparent intent of the parties. Therefore, gap fillers are used to supplement contracts, not to override the parties' probable intent. This means that the parties can "contract out" of a legally implied standard term (that is, they can avoid its application) by expressing a contrary intent.[5]

A gap filler is a provision **legally implied** into a contract to **supplement** or **clarify** its **express language.** As its name suggests, the principal purpose of a gap filler is to supply a logically inferable contract term when it is clear that the parties intended a contract, but have failed to provide adequately or at all for the question in issue. Of course, some apparent gaps in an express agreement could be filled by contextual evidence, so a legally implied gap filler is usually only used when no pertinent contextual evidence is available to establish the existence of a term as a matter of fact.

Gap fillers are thus **standard terms supplied by law.** Some have been

---

5. The exception to this general rule is discussed in section 10.9.

developed by courts and others are provided by legislation. Courts and legislatures do not pick them out of the air but base them on common expectations, commercial practice, and public policy. For this reason, the standardized term supplied by law should not usually take the parties by surprise and should genuinely reflect what they likely would have agreed had they discussed the issue. The contract was entered into in the very milieu from which the law developed the standardized term, and so the reasonable (and possibly even the actual) expectations of the parties are likely to be congruent with it.

For example, Buyer agrees to buy Seller's house, subject to Buyer being able to secure the necessary financing. Nothing is said in the written agreement or in the negotiations about Buyer having the duty to make a conscientious effort to obtain the financing. If Buyer does nothing to seek financing, he will likely be held to have breached a legally implied promise to make reasonable efforts to apply for and secure the financing. The implication of such a promise is a logical extension of the express provisions of the agreement and gives effect to the presumed intent of the parties. It recognizes that they probably did not contemplate that Buyer could slip out of his obligations simply by not bothering to apply for a loan. In this way, the implied term *constructs what the parties must have intended,* had they been *acting fairly* and *reasonably,* and it gives effect to their reasonable expectations and to the underlying purpose of the agreement. Note the affinity between legally implied terms and usage, because legally implied terms typically do (or should) reflect the custom of the marketplace. Therefore, this same term requiring best efforts in seeking a loan could probably have been established by evidence of the customary practices pertaining to the sale of a home subject to the contingency of financing. However, the difference is that if a usage is so well-established that it has reached the point of being recognized as a legal standard term, it becomes part of the contract as a matter of law, not of fact. It is therefore not necessary to establish it by evidence.

Some gap fillers are well-established and others have been recognized more recently. Additional ones will continue to develop in the future as new legal implications are drawn from changing market expectations. Of course, there cannot be standardized terms for every conceivable gap, so there are some omissions that cannot be cured by legal implication. Some gap fillers supply generalized obligations that are likely to be implied in all kinds of contracts, and some are very specific, relating to particular types of term in specialized contracts. The following samples of general and specific gap fillers illustrate their range and nature.

§10.8.2 *Gap Fillers that Supply General Obligations*

When a contract does not clearly specify a level of performance but it is clear that the parties' purpose can only be achieved if the obligor puts some energy and dedication into the performance, the law implies an obligation to make **best efforts (reasonable efforts)**[6] to affect the contract's purpose. The above example of the house sale subject to financing illustrates this. Another illustration is provided by *Wood v. Lucy, Lady Duff-Gordon,* 22 N.Y. 88 (1917), discussed in section 7.9.2, in which the court found that an exclusive distributorship contract impliedly required the distributor to make best efforts to sell the product. This general principle is likely to apply in any type of contract under which the grantor of a license, distributorship, or dealership relies on the conscientiousness of the grantee to market a product effectively.

The problem with the legal implication of broad, generalized obligations is that they are vague in themselves. Therefore, although they may go part of the way in curing a vagueness or omission in the agreement, they do not settle the scope and content of the obligation. That is, a concept such as "best efforts" is mushy and non-specific, so that it is not enough simply to imply the obligation. The further step must be taken to determine with some precision what degree of effort is required by the obligation. It may be easy to find a breach when no effort is made at all, but more clarity is needed to decide if some greater degree of effort is an adequate performance. To define the obligation more acutely, a further inquiry must be made into the underlying purpose of the contract and the reasonable expectations of the parties.

§10.8.3   *Gap Fillers that Supply More Specific Rights and Duties*

Both the UCC and the common law supply gap fillers that relate to specific aspects of particular kinds of contracts. Some of these are concrete and precise, but others include generalized concepts, such as reasonableness, that present interpretational problems similar to those discussed above. The following selection illustrates the kind of supplementary terms available to fill gaps left by the parties. These are merely random examples. No attempt is made to be comprehensive. Remember, they are only used if the contract has a gap or uncertainty that has not been resolved by contextual evidence.

The **common law** has developed many gap fillers through the process of judicial decision. For example:

---

6. There may be a difference between "reasonable efforts," which appears strongly objective, and "best efforts," which suggests some blend of subjective and objective standards. However, the distinction is probably not substantial. Whichever term is used, the decision on what constitutes an acceptable effort should take into account both the objective market standards and the subjective honesty and particular circumstances of the party who is to exert the effort.

1. If the parties to an employment contract do not specify its duration, it is deemed to be terminable at will.

2. If the parties do not state that rights under a contract are personal to the obligee, the obligee may transfer (assign) those rights to another person.

3. If the contract does not provide for the sequence of performance, it is presumed that when both performances are a single instantaneous act, they must be made concurrently. But if one performance is instantaneous and the other needs time to perform, it is presumed that the longer performance must take place first. (Therefore, in the sale of a house, unless otherwise stated in the contract, it is implied that transfer of title and payment occur at the same time, but in a contract to build a house, the builder must complete the construction before the owner has to pay.)

UCC Article 2 also has a number of gap fillers. Because they are set out in the statute, they are easier to find than those provided by common law. For example:

1. Unless the agreement expresses otherwise, §§2.312, 2.314, and 2.315 imply certain minimum warranties that a seller makes under defined circumstances regarding the title to and quality of the goods.

2. If the parties do not specify the price of the goods, §2.305 infers that they agreed to a reasonable price unless the apparent intent of the agreement is otherwise. Furthermore, if payment terms are not expressed, §§2.307 and 2.310 assume a C.O.D. sale. (This is the Article 2 equivalent of the third example of common law gap fillers, implying concurrent instantaneous performances.)

3. Several sections supply the terms governing delivery in the absence of contrary agreement. Sections 2.307, 2.308, and 2.309 require that the goods be delivered in a single lot at the seller's place of business within a reasonable time.

4. Sometimes a gap filler supplied for certain types of contracts may be a specific application of a more generalized implied term of the type discussed in section 10.8.2. In a requirements or output contract,[7] §2.306(1) implies both a good faith and a reasonableness obligation on the party who is to determine the quantity of goods ordered or supplied. Section 2.306(2) implies an obligation of

---

7. *See* section 7.9.3 for an explanation of this type of contract.

best efforts on both parties when the contract imposes an obligation on one of them to deal exclusively with the other.

§10.9   Implication in Law Irrespective of the Intent of the Parties

§10.9.1   Supplementary Terms that Cannot Be Excluded by Agreement

There is an exception to the general rule, stated in section 10.8, that terms supplied by law are intended to bring out the perceived reasonable intent of the parties and will not be included in the contract unless consistent with that intent. Some legally implied obligations are so fundamental to fair dealing or so strongly demanded by public policy, that they are mandatory and are part of the contract irrespective of the parties' actual intent. Even if they wish to, the parties cannot effectively agree to exclude such a term.

Construed terms of this kind are not properly called gap fillers. They are not default rules, but enter the contract whether or not there is a gap or uncertainty about the parties' intent. Although such strongly construed terms are raised here as part of the discussion of the process of finding meaning in agreement, they are more a *matter of regulation than of seeking intent*. The law's true purpose in such a firm imposition of standard terms is not so much to ascertain what the parties reasonably must have intended, but to limit contractual autonomy in the interest of public policy. Sometimes the policy in question is not directly related to contract law, but is concerned with the undesirable effect of particular contract terms on some other field, such as tort, antitrust, or criminal law. Often, however, the underlying public policy is that of protecting a weaker party from one-sided and unfair terms. In this respect, mandatory construed terms are part of the broader subject of regulating the formation and content of contracts, discussed in Chapter 13.

One of the most important and pervasive mandatory construed terms is the general obligation of both parties to perform the contract reasonably and in good faith. Whether or not the agreement expressly articulates this obligation, and even if it expressly excludes it, the law implies it into every contract.[8] This duty is recognized in both UCC §1.203 and Restatement Second §205.

---

8. There is a link between this principle and the second rule of construction mentioned in section 10.7, which favors a reasonable, effective, and lawful interpretation of unclear provisions. However, it goes even further than that rule by imposing a duty of fair dealing on the parties.

§10.9.2 Construed Terms that Can Be Excluded Only by Express or Specific Language

Below this level of absolute legal implication, there is another category of construed terms that are important enough to be more strongly implied than other gap fillers. Although public policy does not preclude the parties from contracting out of them, it requires the intent to exclude them to be clearly expressed. Stated differently, while most gap fillers enter the contract only when necessary to resolve an uncertainty or omission, there are some that are so strongly implied as a matter of policy that they *become part of the contract unless its express terms clearly exclude them*. In some cases, even a clear exclusion is not good enough unless it complies with specified rules that may prescribe the use of particular language or format.

For example, UCC Article 2 has a policy in favor of providing warranties in certain types of sales of goods. Therefore, although §2.316 allows the seller to contract out of them, it only recognizes a warranty disclaimer as effective if it satisfies certain formalities. To disclaim the merchant[9] seller's warranty of merchantability (that is, that the goods meet minimum trade standards), the sales contract must mention "merchantability" and, if in writing, the disclaimer must be conspicuous. When goods are sold for a particular purpose, the seller gives an implied warranty of fitness for that purpose unless it is disclaimed conspicuously in writing. The goal of these rules is to make it more likely that the buyer notices the disclaimer, and to prevent the seller from hiding it in a mass of boilerplate.

§10.10 Terms Left for Future Determination

Say, for example, that Owner has completed the plan for a new commercial building and construction is about to begin. Owner has been negotiating with Lessee for a lease of space in the building upon its completion. The parties have reached agreement on the period of the lease, the location and size of the premises, and all other terms except for the rent to be paid. They wish to enter the lease agreement now, even though the premises will not be ready for occupation for two years. However, neither wishes to agree to a set figure because they do not know what the rental market will be like when the building is completed. If they cannot agree on a firm figure, they have a number of alternatives:

---

9. *See* sections 5.5 and 6.5.2 for the definition of "merchant."

§10.10.1   Determination by an Objective Standard

The parties could decide on a formula or an external source or standard, so that the rent will be fixed at a specified future time by some objective criterion. For example, they could provide for the rent to be calculated by applying a published economic indicator to a base figure, or they could base the rent on a market standard derived from average rent charged for comparable buildings in the area at the time of occupation, or they could provide for binding arbitration by an independent arbitrator. In this way they are able to make a valid and effective contract now, but avoid the hazards of trying to predict an appropriate rent figure for the future.

Provided that the formula or standard is properly drafted to furnish a clear and workable method of ascertainment, the term for the future ascertainment of rent is valid and enforceable. At the time selected, the criterion is applied, and the rent figure determined. But if the formula or standard is poorly drafted, so that method of calculating the rent is vague or ambiguous and incapable of clarification by interpretation or construction, no contract has been made because a central term of the contract is unresolved.

§10.10.2   Determination Within the Discretion of One of the Parties

The parties may decide to leave the determination of the rent to the discretion of one of them. Although such a provision is quite risky for the party who defers discretion to the other, a provision like this is not necessarily too indefinite or lacking mutuality. As we have seen, the discretion can be limited and subjected to acceptable market standards by construing an obligation of good faith and fair dealing.

§10.10.3   Omission of the Term

The parties could simply not mention the rent at all in their agreement. The omission of a central term could mean that the parties have not yet reached final agreement, and so a contract has not yet been formed. In this case, there may be evidence indicating that the parties committed themselves to negotiate further in good faith, in which case the principles discussed in section 10.10.4 below, are applicable. However, the circumstances may indicate that the parties did consider themselves committed to the lease already, in which case it may be appropriate to infer that they implicitly agreed to a reasonable rent based on the rental value of the premises on the market.

§10.10.4 Deliberate Deferral of Agreement: "Agreement to Agree" or to Negotiate in Good Faith

If the parties have purposely left the term unresolved, this presents a different issue. As noted in section 10.3.3, parties may reach the stage of settling most of the terms of a proposed contract, but may not be able to achieve consensus on some aspect of their relationship. They may therefore acknowledge their commitment to the settled terms and undertake to reach agreement on the unresolved term at a later time. The general approach of the common law is that *no contract comes into existence until all its material terms have been settled*. It would be premature to find a contract before negotiations are complete, merely because the parties have settled some or even most of the terms.

In many cases it is appropriate to find that all commitment is postponed until agreement can be reached on every material term of the relationship. However, in some situations, even though no final commitment has been made on the ultimate contract, the parties may at least have undertaken, expressly or impliedly, to **continue negotiations in good faith.** They have, in essence, made an **"agreement to agree"**: Although they have not yet reached agreement, they commit themselves to continue making honest efforts to work toward agreement.

Some courts are resistant to the idea that parties can legally bind themselves to negotiate in good faith, while others are more receptive to it. A principal concern is that negotiating parties normally assume that either of them is free to break off negotiations at will and has no legal duty to try to reach agreement. Therefore, recognition of such liability could inhibit negotiations because the fear of premature commitment could make the parties wary of expressing agreement to anything. It could also give rise to specious claims if promising negotiations collapse. This concern can be addressed by ensuring that such an obligation is recognized sparingly. Because a commitment to continue bargaining is atypical, the party claiming the obligation must provide credible evidence that this was not an ordinary negotiation, but one in which the parties had reason to expect that each would do their best to strive for final agreement.

Even if a commitment to bargain in good faith is conceded as a possibility, some courts consider the very concept of good faith negotiation too indefinite to be enforced. As is always true with good faith, it is often hard to be sure what state of mind and attendant conduct is required. The standard clearly does not require a party to reach agreement at all costs, or even to make undesired concessions. However, it does at least suggest a duty to make an open-minded and cooperative effort to resolve differences. Of course, it could be difficult to prove an absence of good faith if the party, having secretly decided not to make a contract, takes care to go through the motions of negotiation. However, if the party refuses to negotiate at all, makes unrealistic demands, or otherwise behaves in a patently obstructive way, bad faith may be convincingly demonstrated.

Even if a breach of faith could be proved, the victim may have trouble proving the fact and extent of the loss suffered, and may therefore not be able to establish **damages.** The principles governing damages are discussed in Chapter 18. Depending on the organization of your contracts course, you may or may not have studied remedies for breach of contract by the time you read this. However, the general principles applicable in this context can be set out in simple form: When one party materially breaches a contract (including a contract to bargain in good faith), the other may seek expectation damages—an amount of money sufficient to make up the gain that the plaintiff lost as a result of the breach. Stated differently, expectation damages are a monetary award designed to put the plaintiff into the economic position it would have occupied had the defendant not breached. To obtain these damages, it is not enough for the plaintiff to prove that the defendant breached the contract. The plaintiff must also show that the breach led to an injury that can be proved with reasonable certainty.

A promise to negotiate in good faith is merely a commitment to make honest efforts to reach agreement—it is not a promise that agreement will be reached. It is therefore not guaranteed that had the defendant negotiated in good faith, a contract would have resulted. The plaintiff may therefore have trouble proving that the defendant's bad faith left him in a worse position than he would have been in had the defendant made a good faith effort to reach consensus. Even if this can be shown on the balance of probabilities, the plaintiff may have trouble proving what gain would have been made from the contract. For this reason, some courts consider such damages too speculative and are resistant to awarding expectation damages for breach of an obligation to bargain in good faith. However, other courts are willing to afford such relief if the plaintiff can show that agreement would have been probable in the absence of the defendant's bad faith, and can make some plausible showing of probable loss. Even if expectation damages are not capable of proof, the court may be amenable to granting lesser relief, such as the reimbursement of losses incurred in reliance on the promise of genuine negotiation.

§10.11   Agreements to Record in Writing

Say that representatives of a corporation and an advertising agency meet to negotiate a contract for the production of a promotional video. By the end of the meeting they have reached oral consensus on all the broad terms of the relationship. They agree that the corporation's attorney will draw up a written contract reflecting the agreed terms and providing for matters of detail not fully addressed in the negotiations. Upon completion of the document, it will be presented to both parties for approval and signature. A couple of days later, before the writing has been prepared, the corporation changes its mind and no longer wishes to use the agency's services. Can the corporation cancel without legal liability?

If the parties had clearly stated the intended effect of their oral understanding, this question would be easy to answer. However, if they failed to express its legal significance, it may mean one of three different things:

1. The parties intended a contract to arise immediately upon concluding the oral agreement, so they are already bound. The reduction to writing is *just a formality,* and they are obliged to sign it if it properly reflects their agreement.

2. The oral agreement in principle is not yet a contract, and the parties did not intend to be bound until the detail has been settled in the writing to their satisfaction and they have signed it.

3. Because the detailed terms must still be resolved in the course of drafting, the parties have not yet reached final agreement. However, they have committed themselves to negotiate over those terms in good faith. (This alternative raises the issues discussed in section 10.10.)

The uncertainty over the parties' intentions must be resolved by the process of interpretation and construction discussed in this chapter, in which the entire circumstances of the agreement are evaluated and the appropriate factual and legal inferences of intent are drawn. Examples 6 and 7 illustrate some of the factors that may help to reveal their intent.

§10.12 Misunderstanding: Total Ambiguity

As discussed in section 10.6, interpretation is based on the objective meaning of the language of an agreement, viewed in its context. We do not seek to ascertain what each party thought or believed, but what they reasonably appeared to intend. Therefore, when the parties have different understandings of their agreement, the party with the more reasonable understanding prevails.

However, it sometimes happens that while the parties have diametrically opposite understandings of a term, each of their interpretations is entirely reasonable, and there is no basis for preferring one over the other. In such cases, interpretation and construction cannot resolve the uncertainty in the apparent agreement. If the uncertainty relates to a material aspect of the agreement, the only conclusion to be reached is that no contract came into being.

The classic illustration of this problem is provided by a mid-nineteenth century English case, *Raffles v. Wichelhaus,* 159 Eng. Rep. 375 (Ex. 1864). A buyer and seller agreed to the sale of cotton on board the ship *Peerless* sailing from Bombay. It so happened that there were two ships named *Peerless* due to leave Bombay with a cargo of cotton in October and December, respectively. The seller had the later ship in mind and the buyer the earlier. Neither of them knew of the existence of the second ship. The ship contemplated by the buyer arrived in England first, but the seller did not tender delivery from that ship. In fact, he apparently did not even own that cotton. When the second ship arrived and the seller tendered delivery, the buyer refused to accept the goods, contending that he had bought the cotton on the earlier ship. The seller sued for breach of contract, but the court granted judgment in favor of the buyer on the ground that the misunderstanding prevented a contract from arising.

The doctrinal basis of the opinion is obscure, so it can be (and has been) interpreted simply as an outmoded subjectivist case, in which the court refused to find a contract in the absence of an actual meeting of the parties' minds. However, the case is now widely accepted as illustrating the kind of situation in which even an objective approach cannot resolve the misunderstanding. As each party was reasonable in believing that the agreement referred to a particular ship, and neither had any reason to know of the other's contrary understanding, there is no way to decide whose meaning should be preferred. That is, there is *no objective criterion* for deciding which ship must have been intended, and a contract on reasonable terms cannot be established. Hence, assuming that the date of delivery is a material term, no contract came into being.

Restatement Second §§20 and 201 seek to convey this principle in language so convoluted that it boggles the mind. In essence, the Restatement's rule boils down to this: A material misunderstanding precludes contract formation when the parties were *equally innocent* in not reasonably realizing the misunderstanding *or equally guilty* in realizing it but saying nothing. However, if on balancing the degree of fault of the parties, it appears that *one is more accountable than the other* for knowing of the misunderstanding, a contract must be found to exist on the terms understood by the more innocent party.

EXAMPLES

1. Claire Cutter decided to remove a large oak tree in her front yard. She hired Jack Lumber, a tree remover, to cut it down. Jack has no liability insurance, so he requires his customers to sign a simple one-page written contract that includes the following standard term, drafted by his attorney:

"By signing this contract, the customer assumes sole responsibility for any loss, damage, or injury caused by the performance of work under this contract and indemnifies Jack Lumber for any such claims."

Claire read and signed the contract. Jack began work a few days later. He negligently failed to take proper precautions to ensure that the tree would fall safely. As a result, it crashed down onto Claire's driveway, pulverizing Jack's truck that was parked there. Jack says that the indemnity clause in the contract makes Claire liable to him for the cost of replacing his truck. Is he right?

2. Fairest Fowls, Inc., is a poultry supplier. Gordon Bleu is a trained chef who owns and operates a restaurant. Gordon had often ordered duck and chicken from Fairest Fowls before. Although he had always ordered the cheaper quality "regular" birds, rather than the more expensive "gourmet" quality, he had always been well satisfied.

Gordon decided to begin serving more exotic game birds at his restaurant. He found a recipe for pheasant and checked Fairest Fowls' price list to see what it cost. The list showed "regular" pheasant for $5.00 per pound, and "plump deluxe" pheasant for $12.50 per pound. Gordon ordered and received 50 pounds of the "regular" quality.[10] He prepared the birds according to his recipe. When they were cooked, he tasted them and discovered that they were tough and uneatable. He called Fairest Fowls to complain. Fairest Fowls' representative expressed surprise that Gordon did not know what was "common knowledge" in the trade—that "regular" pheasants were old, scrawny birds, sold only for making soup. The more expensive "plump deluxe" variety were intended for eating.

After being told this, Gordon asked six chefs and four poultry suppliers if they knew about the distinction between "regular" and "plump deluxe" pheasant. Four of the chefs had never heard of the distinction. However, one of these had never cooked pheasant, and the other three had always bought pheasant at around $12.00 per pound. The remaining two were not familiar with the names used by Fairest Fowls, but they knew that old pheasant could be bought cheaply for soup. The four suppliers contacted all knew that the flesh of old pheasants was not suitable for eating, and said that they would have understood "regular" pheasant at $5.00 per pound to mean pheasant for soup.

In light of this, did Fairest Fowls breach the contract by delivering uneatable birds to Gordon?

3. Beau Teek operates a clothing store in a shopping mall under a five-year lease. One of the terms of the lease gives Beau the option to renew the lease for a further period of five years "at a rental to be agreed at the time of renewal in light of the prevailing economic conditions."

Beau properly exercised his option to renew within the time specified in

---

10. The order was oral, but as the total price of the birds was $250, the statute of frauds is not applicable. Also, because there is no written memorial of agreement, the parol evidence rule does not apply to complicate matters. This same contract, in written form, is used in Example 4 of Chapter 12 to illustrate the impact that the parol evidence rule would have on the resolution of this interpretational issue.

the lease. Although the parties tried to agree on rent for the renewal period, they were unable to reach consensus. The lessor called on Beau to vacate the premises, but he refused to leave and commenced suit for specific performance, requesting that the court order the lessor to extend the lease for a five-year period at a rent determined by the court to be reasonable.

Should the court grant the order and determine a reasonable rent?

4. Jill Loppy agreed to sell her old car to Carr Less. They wrote out the following on a piece of paper and both signed it: "Jill Loppy agrees to sell her 1984 Chev to Carr Less for 90 percent of its retail bluebook value."

The next day, Jill changed her mind and no longer wished to sell her car. She claims that she does not have a binding contract with Carr, and points out that the piece of writing is too skimpy to be a contract because it does not fully describe the car, has an indefinite price term, and omits many essential terms. In particular, it makes no mention of the delivery and payment obligations and warranties. Furthermore, these issues were not discussed by the parties.

Is this a good argument?

5. Chic A. LaMode is a budding fashion designer. She entered into an agreement with Deadwood Enterprises, Inc., under which Chic granted Deadwood the exclusive right for two years to sell her fashion designs. In consideration, Deadwood promised to pay Chic half of all profits and revenues that it earned from any such sales. Chic delivered all her latest designs to Deadwood, representing well over a thousand different garments.

Hearing nothing from Deadwood for a month, Chic called to find out how sales were going. She was told that sales were slow, but she should be patient because things would pick up soon. After waiting another month, Chic received a check for $300 from Deadwood, representing 50 percent of earnings for the sale of two designs for small garments. In a note accompanying the check, Deadwood apologized for the small return, saying that it hoped to do better in the future.

About two weeks later Chic ran into one of her classmates from design school. The classmate told Chic that he had been approaching manufacturers directly, and had sold over $2,000 worth of designs in the last six weeks. Chic would like to dump Deadwood. Can she do so without breaking the contract?

6. Empire Building Products Co., wished to buy a sawmill. A few months ago, it heard that Woody Cutter, a lumberman, was in severe financial distress and had to sell off one of his two sawmills to pay his debts and remain in business. Empire approached Woody and negotiations for the purchase began. After several weeks of meetings, involving attorneys, accountants, and technical advisors, the parties had reached agreement on all the terms of the sale except price. They were deadlocked on this issue. Empire had refused to pay more than $2.5 million. However, Woody refused to take less than $4 million for it. The parties therefore felt that a cooling-off period would be useful, and

they agreed to meet two weeks later to see if they could resolve their differences on price. They signed a joint memorandum drafted by their attorneys, setting out the terms on which they agreed so far, and recording simply that they would meet on a stated day to continue discussions on price.

Empire's board met just before negotiations were to resume. Realizing that Woody was under pressure to sell and that he had no other prospective buyer, the board decided not to budge on the $2.5 million price. They knew that this would be a bargain because they had reliably appraised the mill at a value of $3.5 million. At about this same time, Woody, reviewing his precarious financial position, decided not to hold out for his asking price but to come down as low as $3 million (which he realized was below the mill's true value).

When the meeting took place as arranged, Woody made great efforts to persuade Empire to close the gap between the price proposals, but Empire refused to consider anything above $2.5 million. As a result, the negotiations terminated in failure.

Woody had run out of time. Before he could look for another buyer, his creditors petitioned to put him in bankruptcy, so that his assets could be liquidated to pay his debts. As a result, he lost both his sawmills as well as most of his other property. He blames Empire for this calamity because its stubbornness prevented the sale of the one mill that would have allowed him to keep his creditors happy while he tried to make his other mill profitable and to turn his business around. Does Woody have any basis for holding Empire liable for his loss?

7. Molly Fido owned a profitable and successful restaurant. She decided to sell the business and she solicited inquiries by placing an advertisement in a trade journal. Faith Fullness responded and they met to discuss the possible sale. At their initial meeting, Faith examined the premises, equipment, and financial records and the parties had extensive but inconclusive discussions about price. Faith expressed strong interest in buying the business and they agreed to meet again in a week. During that week, Faith visited the restaurant several times to observe the operations, service, and customer traffic. She visited her bank to discuss financing and spoke to a couple of potential investors to see if she could raise some capital. Everything looked promising, and she became enthusiastic about buying the business.

At their next meeting, Faith and Molly discussed the sale in earnest. After some hours they had reached agreement in principle on the basic terms of the sale, which Faith wrote down on a yellow legal paid: Faith would pay Molly $300,000 for the equipment, name, goodwill, lease rights, and transferrable licenses. A third of the price would be paid upon the signing of a written agreement, and the balance would be paid in installments over two years. Faith would take over the business and receive transfer of its assets as soon as possible after the agreement was signed, and Molly would remain on as an employee of the business for six months at a salary to be mutually decided. Faith would immediately instruct her attorney to draw a written contract reflecting these terms and dealing with any necessary matters of detail that the parties had not thought of. Later that day, Faith consulted her attorney and gave her the pad with the notes of the meeting. The attorney promised to set to work as soon as possible on drafting the memorandum of agreement.

The next day, Molly received a call from Ruth Less who had also read the advertisement. Molly told Ruth that she had almost certainly sold the business already, but agreed to meet with Ruth anyhow. After a whole day's negotiations, during which Molly disclosed to Ruth the terms of the understanding with Faith, Ruth made a very attractive offer. She is willing to buy the business for $350,000 cash. Molly would like to accept the offer but is unsure if she has legally committed herself to Faith. Has she?

8. Pierre Less came across the following advertisement in a magazine:

> Miss Communications, Inc.
> ADULT VIDEO CLOSEOUT!!!
> XXX Assorted titles in boxes XXX
> Formerly $25 to $35 each
> NOW ONLY $150 per box of 30 different titles.
> ORDER NOW—QUANTITIES LIMITED
> Payment must accompany order. All sales final.

Pierre enjoys a little spicy viewing, so he placed an order for two boxes and sent a check for $300 to Miss Communications at the address shown in the advertisement. When his boxes arrived and he opened them, he found that they contained ordinary, common, older R-rated movies of the kind that can be found in bins at any video store, and can usually be bought for about $5.00 or less. Pierre understood from the advertisement that he was buying hardcore pornography and wishes to return the insipid videos and get his money back. Miss Communications refuses to return his money. It disagrees that the advertisement suggests that the tapes are pornographic—the word "adult" simply means "suitable for persons over 18" and triple X's are merely the Roman numeral for 30, being the number of tapes in each box. Who is right?

EXPLANATIONS

1. The question here is whether the indemnity clause is broad enough to impose liability on Claire for loss suffered by Jack as a result of damage he negligently inflicted on his own property in the course of his performance. Do not be too quick to scoff at Jack's claim—remember that he is handy with a chainsaw. To ascertain the scope of the indemnity provision in the contract, its wording must be examined within the context of the language and purpose of the agreement as a whole and in light of any pertinent extrinsic evidence.

In this case, there is no extrinsic evidence, so the import of the clause must be determined by interpreting its language in the context of the writing as a whole. We are not told of anything in the other terms of the writing that bears upon the indemnity, so we are left with nothing to go on except the bare language of the clause. There are a number of arguments that Claire could make against Jack's claim based on the language of the clause itself and on general principles of interpretation:

1(a). In its narrowest meaning, the clause sounds like a third-party indemnity provision, designed to do no more than protect Jack from claims of neighbors, passers-by, and other strangers who may be injured or whose property may be damaged by accidents during the removal of the tree. This narrow meaning has some support in the wording of the clause: The sentence in which the owner assumes responsibility for loss, damage, or injury ends with the words ". . . and indemnifies Jack Lumber for any such claims." The reference to "such claims" suggests a focus on demands by other people against Jack, and the word "indemnity" is often used to refer to reimbursement for liability to third parties. However, the wording of the clause is not clear and conclusive, because Jack's demand is also a claim (albeit not a claim against Jack) and "indemnify" is not confined to third-party liability and is often used in a wider sense to cover any reimbursement of loss.

The difficulty of trying to decide on the scope of an indemnity that is not written precisely is illustrated by *Pacific Gas and Electric Co. v. G. W. Thomas Drayage & Rigging Co.*, 442 P.2d 641 (Cal. 1968). The owner of a steam turbine entered into a contract for removal and replacement of its metal cover. The contract provided that the repairer would perform the work at its "own risk and expense" and would "indemnify" the owner "against all loss, damage, expense, and liability resulting from . . . injury to property, arising out of or in any way connected with the performance of this contract." The repairer also agreed to take out liability insurance for damage to property. During the course of work, the cover fell onto the turbine rotor. When the owner claimed reimbursement for the damage, the repairer contended that the indemnity clause was intended to apply only to loss or injury to third parties and did not cover any damage to the owner's property. The trial court, which interpreted the contract purely on the face meaning of the document,[11] acknowledged that the language used in the indemnity was the

---

11. Unlike our case, the repairer in *Pacific Gas* (the party liable under the indemnity provision) did seek to introduce extrinsic evidence to support the interpretation that the indemnity was confined to third-party claims. (This evidence included evidence of discussions between the parties and their conduct in prior dealings.) The trial court excluded the evidence under the parol evidence rule because the court considered the meaning of the written indemnity to be a complete, final, and unambiguous expression of the term. This was overturned on appeal, and the case was remanded for consideration of the extrinsic evidence. (The parol evidence issue in the case is discussed in Example 6 of Chapter 12.) Because the trial court had excluded the contextual evidence, its initial resolution of the case was based on its perception of the plain meaning of the written indemnity clause. Its conclusion is of interest in a case like ours, in which the lack of contextual evidence leaves the court with no choice but to confine its interpretation to the bare language of the clause.

"classic language for a third party indemnity provision." It nevertheless found that the plain meaning of the words did not restrict it to liability for harm to third parties. Although the trial court's decision was overturned on appeal on the issue of whether it should have admitted extrinsic evidence in interpreting the contract, its resolution based on the face meaning of the language is of interest in our case, where that language is the only evidence available. It shows that when sparse and obscure language could possibly point to a broad liability, one cannot be too confident in predicting that the court will readily read restrictions into it. Not withstanding, it may be that the language in Jack's contract is more conducive to a restrictive interpretation than that used in *Pacific Gas*. In addition, to make Claire liable for Jack's own negligence seems to offend the general rule that favors an interpretation that is reasonable.

1(b). Jack's failure to control the falling of the tree was clearly negligent and possibly even reckless. Quite apart from the point about reasonable interpretation in (a) above, a disclaimer of negligence raises public policy concerns relating to accountability for wrongful conduct. Therefore, although a contractual disclaimer of liability for negligence is usually lawful and enforceable, if fairly bargained, courts do not readily find such a release unless it is very clearly expressed. The language of this provision does not merely inadequately express Claire's assumption of liability for Jack's negligence. It points in the opposite direction.

If Jack's conduct was reckless, the likelihood of enforcing the clause (even if it could be interpreted to exist) is even more remote. The law may absolutely forbid a disclaimer of liability for reckless or deliberate injury, but even if it does not, it would require the disclaimer to be very articulate about its coverage. (The policy over disclaimers of wrongful conduct is discussed again in Example 6 of Chapter 13.)

1(c). Finally, if doubt still remains over the proper interpretation of the clause, the contra proferentum rule may be used to resolve the doubt against Jack, who is the proponent of the indemnity.

2. This is a sale of goods under the UCC, but interpretation of the agreement is based on principles not significantly different from those applied in modern common law. UCC §1.205 recognizes the primacy of express terms but also articulates the importance of trade usage and course of dealing in the ascertainment of meaning.

The example is loosely based on the famous chicken case, *Frigaliment Importing Co. v. B.N.S. International Sales Corp.*, 109 F. Supp. 116 (S.D.N.Y. 1960). The buyer, a Swiss importer, ordered a large quantity of chicken from the seller. The contract called for "U.S. fresh frozen chicken, grade A" of two different sizes and prices per pound. The seller contemplated that the larger, cheaper birds would be older stewing chickens, but the buyer expected all the chicken to be younger, more tender chicken, suitable for broiling and frying. When the chicken was delivered, and the larger birds were stewing chicken, the buyer protested. He eventually sued the seller for breach of warranty, claiming that the stewing chicken delivered did not conform to the description "chicken" in the contract. The case turned on the question of whether "chicken" included stewing fowl or meant only fryers.

After examining the agreement's wording in context and weighing evidence of trade usage, the court concluded that the normal usage of "chicken" was broad enough to cover both stewing and frying chicken. Because the buyer contended that the word was used in the poultry trade in a narrower sense to cover only frying chicken, the buyer bore the burden of proving that usage. The buyer had failed to establish the usage as a question of fact, and therefore the complaint was dismissed. The case has a detailed analysis of both the language of the agreement and the alleged trade usage. The principles set out are helpful in resolving a number of the issues raised by Gordon's claim, which we will now consider.

A. The Plain Meaning of "Regular" in the Context of the Whole Agreement

The ordinary meaning of the language is the point of departure. In *Frigaliment*, the court found "chicken" to be ambiguous, in that it was capable of both the meanings contended for by the parties. For this reason, normal usage favored the broader sense understood by the seller, and the buyer therefore had the burden of proving that trade usage supported the narrower meaning. "Regular" has many meanings. In this context it probably connotes "normal" or "usual." This suggests that the pheasant is of the normal kind and quality sold in the market. The ordinary meaning therefore supports Gordon's position because the evidence suggests that the better quality eating birds are more commonly sold, a reasonable person would think of those as the "regular" variety.

Beyond the term itself, there is not much in the rest of the agreement to cast light on the meaning of "regular." In *Frigaliment*, the price term was relevant to interpreting "chicken" because the cheapness of the price suggested that the stewing birds were being sold. However, in Gordon's case he does not claim the right to deluxe birds, but merely challenges the quality of the cheaper variety.

B. Prior Dealings

Gordon's meaning is bolstered by the fact that in prior transactions, Fairest Fowls sold him eatable ducks and chickens under the description "regular." The earlier sales are not exactly of the same kind as the present transaction, because they involved different birds, but their application of the word "regular" to describe eatable birds does call into question Fairest Fowls' contention that "regular" should be understood to mean "suitable only for soup."

C. Trade Usage

The meaning of an ambiguous word may be clarified by trade usage provided that the parties are members of the trade or are otherwise chargeable with knowledge of the usage. A party who seeks to establish the binding effect of trade usage must show a number of things. First, the trade must be identified and defined. Second, at the time of contracting the parties must have been members of the trade, or must have had knowledge or reason to know of the usage and to expect it to apply. Third, the usage must be proved.[12]

It is not always easy to define the trade, and the way in which it is defined can have a significant impact on the outcome of the case. In this example, the trade could be defined narrowly to include only poultry suppliers, or it could be defined more broadly to include suppliers and restaurants. A narrow scope gives Fairest Fowls the advantage of making the usage stronger (all suppliers recognize it) but the disadvantage of excluding Gordon from the trade, making it more difficult to hold him to the usage. A wide scope would include Gordon in the trade, but weaken the usage because it is less well-known to chefs.

In *Nanakuli Paving & Rock Co. v. Shell Oil Co.*, 664 F.2d 772 (9th Cir. 1981), a case discussed further in Example 4 of Chapter 12, the court dealt with the problem of defining a trade and holding an outsider accountable for knowledge of its practices. One of the issues to be decided in the case was whether a seller of asphalt could be treated as a member of the asphalt paving trade, thereby being subject to usages in the paving trade. Pointing to the UCC's policy of flexibility, adherence to the realities of the market, and broad recognition of usage, the court gave broad scope to the meaning of "trade." It found that as sellers of asphalt had a close relationship with pavers in the particular locality, they could properly be seen as members of a common trade. However, even if the trades were seen as distinct, the close relationship gave the seller reason to know of the usages in the paving trade.

On this reasoning, the trades of supplying and preparing poultry seem to be sufficiently connected to make usages among suppliers relevant. These usages are not a secret code, used only by suppliers among themselves, but are communicated to their customers. This means that evidence of trade usage must be gathered not only from chefs, but from suppliers too. If the evidence supports the existence of a usage, Gordon is bound by it, either because he is a member of the trade, broadly defined, or because he is closely enough connected to it that he has reason to know its usages.

---

12. Of course, usage would only have to be proved if Gordon sued—which he may not do, considering the small size of his claim. Also, Gordon is a customer of Fairest Fowls, which has an incentive not to alienate him by resisting his claim. Therefore, settlement is likely. However, in evaluating Gordon's claim, we must try to predict his prospects of successful suit. This calls for an assessment of the question of establishing usage.

This was the first time that Gordon had ordered pheasant. Is it fair to expect him to know about the distinction between cooking and soup pheasant? An analogous issue came up in *Frigaliment,* because the seller was a newcomer to the trade. The court indicated that a "knowledge or reason to know" standard was therefore more appropriate than the more stringent standard applicable to a fully-fledged member of the trade. The UCC does not make this distinction between experienced and inexperienced trade members, so this may not be a pertinent distinction. In any event, Gordon was not new to the trade, but merely ordered goods that he had not previously bought.

Based on Gordon's inquiries, is there likely to be evidence to establish the usage? Usage is a factual question, to be established on the balance of probabilities. In *Frigaliment* there was conflicting testimony by several expert witnesses on the accepted meaning of "chicken" in the trade. Because the evidence on usage was inconclusive, the buyer, as the bearer of the burden of proving the usage, failed to make a case for breach of contract. Likewise, in the present case, Fairest Fowls has the burden of proving the specialized usage of the word "regular." If it satisfies the factfinder that the usage exists, it will likely succeed on this important element of its case. If not, it will lose on this issue.

On balance, the plain meaning of "regular" and the prior dealings favor Gordon. The issues concerning trade usage could go either way but appear to support the meaning understood by Fairest Fowls. If the usage can be established, Fairest Fowls should prevail; if not, the outcome is difficult to predict.

3. The term relating to the rental for the renewal period is unquestionably vague. It suggests an "agreement to agree" but it does seek to limit the parties' discretion in negotiating by stating a standard: the economic conditions prevailing at the time of renewal. A similar (but even more tortured) renewal provision was the subject of litigation in *Walker v. Keith,* 382 S.W.2d 198 (Ky. 1964). In that case, the renewal option provided that "rental will be fixed in such amount as shall actually be agreed upon by the lessors and the lessee with the monthly rental fixed on the comparative basis of rental values as of the date of the renewal with rental values at this time reflected by the comparative business conditions of the two periods." After the parties could not reach agreement on the rent to be paid for the renewal period, the lessee commenced suit for a declaratory judgment, in which he asked the court to declare that the option had been effectively exercised, and to determine a reasonable rent. The trial court gave judgment in favor of the lessee and fixed the rent at a reasonable figure, based on factors such as the consumer price index. The appellate court reversed, holding that the term was too indefinite to be enforced. The court recognized that it would have been valid for the parties to leave the actual amount of the rent for future determination, had they set a formula or objective standard by which rent

could be determined. However, the language used did not achieve this purpose. It combined an "agreement to agree" with an incoherent and ambiguous reference to comparative business conditions. This indicated that the parties had not in fact agreed to rent, and it is not the proper function of the court to make an agreement for them by fixing it. The court noted that there was case authority under which a court could fix a reasonable rent when parties have expressly or impliedly agreed to it. However, the court refused to follow that practice because it was not convinced that the parties had in fact agreed to a reasonable rent. Even if they had, the court expressed disapproval of the idea of recognizing the validity of a term providing for "reasonable rent" because it is too indefinite. It is hard to say whether the rental provision in Beau's lease is better or worse than that in *Walker*. It is less convoluted, but also seems to have even less content. At least the renewal clause in *Walker* expressed the concept of comparing conditions.

The resolutions of the trial and appellate courts in this case reflect a dichotomy in judicial thinking on this issue. Some courts take the view that when the parties apparently intended to be bound, but inadequately express the means of calculating rent, the court should attempt to give effect to their purpose by implying agreement to a reasonable rent and taking evidence of the market to fix it. Other courts are more insistent that the parties must have agreed to a figure or at least to a clear formula from which the figure can be objectively calculated. Restatement Second leans in favor of the more liberal approach. Section 33 recognizes terms of a contract as reasonably certain if they provide a basis for determining the existence of a breach and giving an appropriate remedy, and §204, Comment *d*, hints that a court might supply a reasonableness standard in appropriate cases.

In Beau's case, a refusal to give effect to the renewal term is harsh, and the appellate court in *Walker* seems unduly rigid. After all, the rental provision was not simply an "agreement to agree," and it did make reference to what could be seen as a market-based standard, albeit poorly expressed. It is not a great leap beyond their expressed intent for a court to determine and apply a reasonable market standard if they cannot reach agreement. In so doing it upholds an apparent serious intent to be bound, and conforms to the rule of interpretation that favors an effective meaning over one that renders the term ineffective.

The vague suggestion of a market standard may allow a court to uphold the renewal option. Had the parties simply provided for a rent to be agreed, there is less justification for the judicial fixing of a reasonable rent. In *Joseph Martin, Jr., Delicatessen, Inc. v. Schumacher,* 417 N.E.2d 541 (N.Y. 1981), the court refused to find a valid renewal option where the parties had specified only that the rental was to be agreed upon, and provided no standard for fixing it. Restatement Second §33, Illustration 8, takes the same view, stating that a provision for future agreement on price strongly indicates a lack of intent to be bound.

4. No. This is a sale of goods, and the UCC is very clear on the question of omitted terms. Section 2.204(3) states that a contract for sale does not fail for indefiniteness, even though terms are left open, provided that the parties intended to make a contract and there is a reasonably certain basis for giving a remedy. In addition, Article 2 contains a number of gap fillers that apply to any agreement of sale in the absence of contrary provisions expressed by the parties. As a result, this skimpy-looking contract is much fuller than Jill suggests.

The goods sold need not be fully described in the writing. The identity of the car is not uncertain, and it can be established by oral testimony. (It would have been different if Jill owned two 1984 Chevs and the parties had not yet agreed on which would be bought.)

The parties need not fix a specific price, as long as they have indicated an objective market standard or some other reasonably certain means of determining it. In fact, the UCC's approach to open price terms is much more flexible than reflected in the *Walker* case, discussed in Example 3. Section 2.306 validates express agreement for a reasonable price and implies such agreement whenever appropriate. In this case, there is no need to have recourse to a reasonable price, because the parties have expressed a workable market standard. (Even if they cannot agree on adjustments to base value provided for in the book, an appraiser could make this determination.)

If any of the remaining terms had been settled orally by the parties and just not stated in the writing, oral evidence of their actual agreement would establish these terms. In the absence of any such agreement (and any applicable usage and course of dealing or performance), the UCC provides the following supplementary terms:

(a) The seller is obliged to transfer and deliver the goods, and the buyer must accept and pay for them (§2.301).

(b) The seller accomplishes her tender of delivery by holding the car available for collection by the buyer at her home at a reasonable hour and for a reasonable period (§§2.308 and 2.503). In addition, because the state requires registration of transfer of title for motor vehicles, the certificate of title must be tendered with proper endorsement.

(c) The delivery must take place within a reasonable time (§2.309).

(d) The buyer must pay for the goods (in cash) on receiving them (§2.310).

(e) The seller warrants that she has good title to the goods (§2.312). (A full discussion of UCC warranties is beyond our scope. It is enough to note that no other warranties are implied in law. The two other implied warranties, set out in §§2.314 and 2.315, are not applicable on the facts of this case.)

5. As you may have suspected, this is a cleverly disguised ripoff of *Wood v. Lucy, Lady Duff-Gordon*, discussed in section 10.8.2. As in *Wood*, we can easily infer from the underlying commercial purpose of the contract that Deadwood impliedly promised to make best efforts to place Chic's designs. However, it is a harder case because it requires us to give content to the obligation to use best efforts. The court did not have to do that in *Wood* because it was not Wood's duty to Lucy that had to be enforced, but Lucy's duty to Wood. (She had sold designs herself in violation of the agreement, and Wood sued her for his share of the profits.) Because the court needed to imply the obligation of best efforts only for the purpose of finding that Wood gave consideration for Lucy's promise, it did not have to decide what would have constituted best efforts. Since Chic asserts that Deadwood has fallen short of best efforts, we need to tackle the question of what level of effort would satisfy Deadwood's obligation.

To decide what constitutes best efforts, we must examine both the reasonable expectation in the trade and the scope and resources of Deadwood's operation. The standard seems to be a blend of reasonable efforts (evaluated objectively) and honest efforts (measured subjectively). We do not have enough information to make a decision on whether Deadwood's efforts would qualify. Deadwood apparently had very little success, and Chic's classmate did better without representation. But that, on its own, is not enough to prove that Deadwood breached its obligation of best efforts. The test is not one of result but of endeavor.

6. The parties clearly did not have a final contract at the end of their first set of negotiations. The price term was unresolved and there is no indication that they intended to be bound unless it was settled. This is not a case in which it would be justifiable to infer that they agreed to a sale at a reasonable or market price.

Therefore, the only basis of liability is that Empire had a duty to continue negotiating in good faith, and that it breached it by standing firm and refusing to negotiate further on the price. Negotiations are normally precursors to legal commitment, and they do not in themselves usually give rise to any legal obligations. In most cases, until the parties actually reach agreement and conclude a contract, neither has any duty to persist in negotiations or to pursue consensus. Both are free to terminate discussions at any time for any reason, to lose interest, make unreasonable demands, or refuse reasonable offers. The only sanction for unreasonable behavior is that it could mean loss of the deal. This has to be the general rule, because otherwise it would be too risky to participate in negotiations. Commercial activity would be greatly curtailed if people feared being trapped as soon as they embarked upon preliminary dealings.

However, in some situations, the negotiating relationship may be such as to impose on the parties a duty to continue negotiating in good faith. This could occur when the parties expressly commit themselves to make this effort, but it could also arise by implication from the circumstances. In this case the parties have agreed to meet again to discuss price. This, in itself, is not enough to create a binding legal commitment that curtails the parties' normal right to drop further negotiation. (If this were so, a car dealer would have a cause of action against a potential customer who expressed enthusiastic interest in a car, promised to return to the showroom later, but changed her mind and never came back.) In short, the promise to meet is no more than an informal and nonbinding arrangement unless the nature of the relationship is such as to establish a shared intent, not only to continue talking but to do so with the commitment to make honest efforts to reach agreement.

What kind of factors must be present to give rise to an implication that the parties committed themselves to negotiate in good faith? The case of *Hoffman v. Red Owl Stores,* 133 N.W.2d 267 (Wisc. 1965), is a good example. *Hoffman,* discussed in Example 5 of Chapter 8, is a promissory estoppel case that does not directly focus on the duty to bargain in good faith, but that is the underlying premise of the case. Red Owl, the grocery chain, was held liable to Hoffman, a small-town baker, for expenses he incurred in preparing to open a Red Owl store. During a lengthy period of negotiations, Hoffman had placed heavy reliance on Red Owl's expertise and guidance in setting him up in a store. Realizing this, and with complete indifference to his trust, it strung him along, involving him in successive expenditures. In the end, the parties could not reach final agreement on a contract. However, the combination of trust and indifference justified the imposition on Red Owl of liability for Hoffman's wasted costs.

Another example of this type of special circumstances is *Channel Home Centers v. Grossman,* 795 F.2d 291 (3d Cir. 1986). The parties had been negotiating a lease on premises to be purchased by the lessor. The lessee gave the lessor a letter of intent setting out the proposed terms of the lease, and the lessor used this letter to obtain financing for the purchase of the building. The lessee also spent $25,000 in preparation for assuming the lease, based on the lessor's assurances that agreement would be reached. The lessor then let the premises to a third party for a higher rental. The court found that the lessor had breached its duty to continue good faith bargaining because the terms of the lease were largely settled, the parties had acted as if the contract was very likely to be concluded, the lessor had actually promised not to negotiate with others, and the lessor had used the letter of intent provided by the lessee to secure financing.

The equities favoring the implication of the promise in both these cases seem to be reflected in the facts of the present situation. Empire knew that Woody was in trouble, he needed to sell, and his options for preserving his business were running out as time passed. It deliberately used his distress to obtain bargaining leverage. A great deal of energy had gone into negotiations already, and substantial consensus had been reached. Given Empire's apparent interest in the transaction and its willingness to meet again, Woody could reasonably have expected Empire to return to the bargaining table in a spirit of honest compromise.

If an obligation to bargain in good faith is implied in this case, what must Empire have done to satisfy it? Bad faith is easy to identify in situations where there has been outright crookery, but it is much more difficult to define in close cases where there is a thin dividing line between bad faith and acceptable commercial hardball. This distinction was addressed in *A/S Apothekernes Laboratorium for Specialpraeparater v. IMC Chemical Group, Inc.*, 873 F.2d 155 (7th Cir. 1989), a case that should be cited in full as often as possible, just for the sake of keeping one's cite-checker amused. The court pointed out that the duty to negotiate in good faith does not require a party to abandon its interests or to make undesired concessions. Rather, it contemplates that parties make a genuine and sincere effort to build on what has been settled in an attempt to resolve differences. It would therefore be a breach of faith for a party to renounce the deal or abandon negotiations; to raise new conditions and objections regarding settled terms; or to remain obstinate with the ulterior motive of killing the deal in favor of a more lucrative opportunity.

It would not in itself have been bad faith for Empire to make a business decision to stick to its price limit. A party should not be compelled to pay more than it desires. However, when Empire's knowledge of Woody's circumstances and its motive for the refusal to budge are taken into account, its insistence on the low price looks decidedly less wholesome. This is particularly so given Woody's concessions that considerably narrowed the price gap between them.

If Empire did breach its duty to bargain in good faith, what is Woody's remedy? The obligation to bargain in good faith is contractual in nature in that Woody and Empire have made a preliminary contract to continue their negotiations. The consideration exchanged is the mutual detriment of giving up the right to abandon negotiations.[13] This being so, Woody should be able to get expectation damages designed to put him into the position that he would have been in had Empire not breached its duty of good faith negotiation. However, expectation damages may be too difficult to prove because Woody would have to make a convincing showing of two uncertain facts to establish a link between Empire's breach and his harm: He must prove not only that a contract probably would have resulted had Empire bargained in good faith, but also that the sale of the mill would likely have enabled him to prevent the loss of his business. In addition, Woody must show the amount of the alleged loss, which could present many problems when the present

---

13. If one cannot find an exchange of detriment, the theory of recovery for the breach of a promise to negotiate in good faith is promissory estoppel, which would normally confine relief to the reimbursement of reliance expenses. As mentioned above, *Hoffman v. Red Owl Stores* was decided on the basis of promissory estoppel because no contract had been established.

value of the business is in doubt, and any value it may have would depend on future management and economic conditions. If such expectation damages cannot be proved, a court is able to award Woody any loss incurred in reliance on the contract to bargain in good faith. These damages would be the same as reliance damages under the theory of promissory estoppel. No reliance expenses are indicated in the facts.

7. When parties have agreed in principle to the essential terms of a contract, but contemplate a signed writing, are they yet bound? They may have intended no commitment whatever until the writing is signed. Conversely, they may have concluded a contract already, subject merely to the formality of writing. As a third possibility, even if they have not yet made a final commitment, they may at least have undertaken to bargain over the unresolved issues in good faith. Simply by stating the intended effect of their oral understanding, parties may make clear which of these alternatives applies. However, if, as in this case, they do not express their intentions on this issue, their purpose must be determined from all the circumstances of their interaction.

All the usual avenues should be explored for helpful indications of intent: the language of agreement itself, statements or actions during negotiations, trade usage, and course of dealings or performance. No facts are given to suggest that there is any specific trade usage, and there is no indication of prior dealing or subsequent performance, so the only source of information is the circumstances of the transaction itself, evaluated in light of usual commercial standards. Comment *c* to Restatement Second §27 suggests some of the factors that may help in deciding if a contract was concluded orally. They include considerations such as the extent of the express agreement; the nature and extent of unresolved issues; whether it is normal practice—or, stronger still, legally required—to put a contract of this kind in writing; and the value and complexity of the transaction.

There are some indications that suggest that the parties did not yet intend to be fully bound in contract. The sale of a business is a commercial exchange of a relatively complex and valuable nature, and it seems reasonable to assume that parties would normally expect to sign a written memorandum before being bound. This assumption is strengthened by the fact that a number of known or possible issues were left unresolved. Not only did they deliberately leave open the salary to be paid to Molly for her work in the six months following the sale, but they also anticipated further unidentified issues to emerge when Faith's attorney drafted a comprehensive writing. Some of these may be trivial, but some could be significant and contentious.

Of course, these are merely indications. They are not conclusive, and an argument can be made for the opposite result. *Texaco v. Pennzoil,* 729 S.W.2d 768 (Tex. 1987), illustrates that a firm oral contract can be found before an intended written memorial is drafted and signed, even when the transaction is complex and the negotiations did not resolve all issues. Pennzoil had been negotiating to purchase stock in the Getty Oil Company and reached an agreement in principle with certain Getty stockholders for the creation of joint ownership of the company. A press release was issued by Getty stating that there was an agreement in principle for acquisition of its stock, subject to execution of a definitive agreement and the approval of other Getty shareholders. Following this, but before the writing was executed, the sellers continued negotiations with Texaco, a competing buyer. Texaco ultimately offered them a better deal, and they contracted to sell the stock to it. The case involved a suit by Pennzoil against Texaco for the tort of interference with Pennzoil's contract rights. To decide that issue, the court had to determine if Pennzoil had in fact acquired any contract rights upon conclusion of the negotiations. At trial, the jury found that a contract had been made at the close of negotiations, despite the absence of a final writing. This was upheld on appeal. The court said that although the press release referred to an agreement in principle, subject to execution of a writing, and the transaction was complex enough to necessitate writing, the general tone of the negotiations and public statements could lead a jury reasonably to conclude that the parties considered themselves bound immediately, and that the writing was intended merely to memorialize their contract.

It is therefore conceivable that Molly and Faith had entered a binding contract of sale at the conclusion of negotiations. If so, Molly risks legal liability if she reneges. Because this is a close question, let us consider what would happen if there was no final commitment at that stage. Would this mean that there is simply no contract, or do the circumstances suggest that the parties at least agreed to bargain in good faith on unresolved issues, promising to sign unless they encounter a genuine dealbreaker? The circumstances are ambiguous and may not be strong enough to deprive Molly of her normal right to abandon these negotiations in favor of a better deal. The facts do not indicate the level of trust, commitment, or reliance discussed in Example 6. Nevertheless, Faith's dealings with Molly are quite far advanced, oral agreement has been reached on all apparently material terms, and Molly has at least given some implicit assurance that there are no obstacles to the completion of the transaction. It is therefore possible that a court may find that they had reached a stage that precluded Molly from walking away from the deal.

If this is so, it does not invariably mean that Faith is entitled to relief, because she has to prove economic loss. As stated in Example 6, this means that she will have to prove both that the contract probably would have resulted but for Molly's refusal to proceed further, and that following the purchase of the business, she would have been reasonably likely to have made profits in a reasonably certain amount. In the absence of this proof, she may be awarded reliance damages if any reliance loss was suffered. She may have incurred some expenses relating to her inquiries before the second meeting, but no such losses are indicated following the implied promise to bargain in good faith.

8. Whenever a question involving consumer advertising is raised, there is a possibility that the case may be subject to policies or statutory rules, regulating against deceptive practices, which may impose a higher standard of clarity on the advertiser and a stronger presumption in favor of consumer relief than may be otherwise required under the common law of contract. For the sake of discussion, assume that the advertisement does not offend any bar on dishonest advertising and that Miss Communications was not trying to deceive the public. It genuinely believed that the advertisement adequately described its R-rated offerings and intended the triple X's to refer to quantity.

The word "adult" is ambiguous. When used in connection with other words, such as "bus fare" or "admission," it means "grown-up," but when used to qualify words such as "book," "video," and "theme," it usually signifies sexual content. Even in this use, it is ambiguous, because it is applied to a wide array of publications, ranging from pornography to publications that are not solely concerned with explicit sex, but have enough erotic content to make some arbiter feel they should not be viewed or read by minors. Under the objective test, we are not concerned with the different subjective understanding of the word held by each of the parties, but hold them to its reasonable meaning, as understood in the community. Given the ambiguity of the word, there may be no way to select a single reasonable meaning or to chose between the different meanings attributed to the word by the parties. If we had nothing to go on beside the word "adult," we might conclude that this is a situation analogous to *Raffles v. Wichelhaus*, 159 Eng. Rep. 375 (Ex. 1864), in which there was no basis for the court to decide which of the two ships named *Peerless* was designated by the contract. *Raffles* stands for the proposition that no contract can be found where the double-meaning of a word used cannot be settled by recourse to its most reasonable meaning, because there is no objective means of choosing between the meanings held by each party. The *Peerless* principle may be illustrated by a more modern case involving computer accessories rather than ships sailing from Bombay. In *Konic International Corp. v. Spokane Computer Services, Inc.*, 708 P.2d 932 (Idaho 1985), a Spokane employee was instructed to investigate the purchase of a surge suppressor. After making inquiries of several sellers, in which he was quoted prices ranging from $50 to $200, he had a telephone conversation with a Konic representative, who had a product suitable for the purpose. When asked the price of the suppressor, the Konic salesman said, "fifty-six twenty," by which he meant $5,620. However, the Spokane employee, having been used to hearing prices in the $50 to $200 range, assumed he meant $56.20. The suppressor was ordered and installed before this misunderstanding was discovered. Upon realizing what had happened, Spokane tried to return the suppressor, but Konic refused to take it back. Applying "Peerless" and Restatement Second §20, the court held that no contract had been concluded because there had been a complete failure of communication. Each party attached a materially different but reasonable meaning to the manifestation, and neither knew or had reason to know the meaning attached by the other.

However, the advertisement by Miss Communications contained more than the irreparably ambiguous word "adult." The two sets of triple X's, while not actually words in the usual sense, are symbols whose meaning tips the balance in favor of Pierre's understanding of the contract. In some contexts (such as in the date chiseled in the side of a building or in the chapter numbering of a learned book), this symbol is commonly understood in the sense intended by Miss Communications—as a Roman numeral. But this meaning is far too literate to be reasonably expected in an advertisement of the kind in issue here. Indeed, the use of that symbol anywhere in the vicinity of the word "adult" is commonly understood to be a qualifier to that word, making it clear that the adult theme in question is not simply R-rated, but full-blown, hard-core pornography. If, as suggested at the beginning of this explanation, we charitably assume that Miss Communications was not being deliberately misleading, it was certainly being quaintly pedantic and naive in selecting Roman numerals for the purpose of indicating quantity.

Therefore, on an objective evaluation of the meaning of the advertisement, the triple X's, combined with the words "adult video," reasonably convey the impression that hard-core pornography was being sold. Even if Miss Communications did not actually realize what meaning Pierre attached to its advertisement, it should reasonably have done so. Pierre's interpretation must therefore be preferred, and a contract exists on the terms understood by him. As Miss Communications did not deliver what was promised, it is in breach of the contract.

Had we found a misunderstanding of the kind in *Raffles* or *Konic,* there would have been no contract. As Pierre wants nothing more than to return the tapes and get a refund, that conclusion is all that he needs. However, it is important to recognize that finding a contract on his terms gives him stronger rights if he should choose to pursue them. As will be discussed more fully in Chapter 18, when a contract is breached, the aggrieved party can choose between rescinding the contract and getting his money back, or enforcing the contract by purchasing a reasonable substitute for the performance (60 pornographic videos of a quality equivalent to those that should have been delivered) and holding the breaching seller liable for the cost in excess of the contract price of $300.

11

The Statute of Frauds

§11.1 Introduction

As a general rule, the law gives effect to oral contracts. Although it is almost always a good idea to record a contract in writing to facilitate proof of the fact and terms of agreement, for many contracts this written record is not a prerequisite to validity. However, certain types of contract fall outside this general rule and must be written and signed to be enforceable. The requirement of a written record for specified types of contracts entered the law of England just over 300 years ago, through a statutory enactment during the reign of King Charles II.

The original motivation for the rule was a concern over fraudulent testimony, hence the original name of the statute, "An Act for Prevention of Fraud and Perjuries," which came to be shortened to "the statute of frauds." Its principal function was to ensure that a person could not seek to enforce a contract of the kind covered by the statute purely on the basis of unreliable and possibly perjured oral testimony, but would have to produce some adequate written record of the contract. American jurisdictions have adapted a statute modeled on the original statute of frauds, covering much the same types of contracts. Over the years, many states have enacted additional statutes requiring writing for further types of contracts. (For example, a writing is required for a contract granting a security interest in personal property under UCC Article 9. Often, consumer protection statutes require a written and signed contract for particular sales of goods and services, and may even specify that the writing must set out the terms governing certain aspects of the transaction.) Therefore, although one usually refers to "the statute of frauds" in the singular, there could be a number of statutes in existence in a jurisdiction, each prescribing writing for a different kind of contract. In this discussion, we are concerned only with the general common law statute of frauds and with that prescribed by UCC Article 2.

The *basic rule* of the statute of frauds (referred to from now on as "the statute") is that a contract within its scope **may not be enforced** unless a **memorandum** of it is **written and signed by the party to be charged.** This gives rise to a few initial observations:

1.   The statute does not require the entire contract to be written, but only a memorandum of it. The degree to which a writing must set out the detail and content of the contract to qualify as a sufficient memorandum is discussed below.

2.   Only the party who is to be charged, that is, against whom enforcement is sought, needs to have signed it. The signature of the other party is not needed. The question of what constitutes a signature is discussed below.

3.   The consequence of non-compliance is usually unenforceability, not invalidity. This distinction is explained more fully in section 11.5.

The statute is intended to prevent a person from enforcing a falsely alleged contract through perjured testimony. However, when a contract was really made orally, the statute can equally be used by the party seeking to evade it. For this reason, there is some concern that the benefits of the statute are outweighed by its potential for abuse. It may be better policy to have no requirement of writing and to allow the fact finder to evaluate the credibility of the oral evidence. These considerations led to its repeal in England some time ago, but it continues to survive in U.S. jurisdictions. The principal focus of the courts has been on making it more flexible to better ensure that it efficiently achieves its purpose while cutting down on the opportunities for abuse. Sometimes this has been done by legislation, as happened by the enactment of a reformed version of the statute relating to the sale of goods in UCC §2.201, but more often, reforms develop in the process of judicial application of the original statutory provisions. Restatement Second §§110-137 seek to reflect contemporary judicial thinking on the statute.

To determine whether problems of enforcement exist under the statute, it is useful to ask three questions in the order represented by the following flow chart:

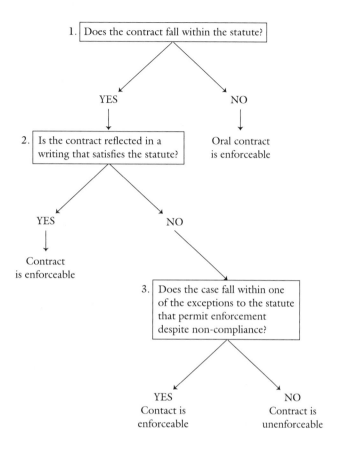

§11.2 The First Inquiry: Is the Contract of a Type that Falls Within the Statute?

The original statute covered six types of contract. Although others have been added in different jurisdictions, these six largely continue to make up the core of modern versions of the statute. This shows remarkable durability, since they are more reflective of the commercial priorities of seventeenth-century Englishmen than of today's economy. It is not necessary to mention all six categories here because three relate to specialized transactions beyond our scope. The other three, more useful for the purpose of discussing general principles, are contracts for the sale of land or an interest in land, contracts that cannot be performed within a year of being entered into, and contracts for the sale of goods. As noted already, the original statute's coverage of sales of goods has been superseded by the enactment of UCC §2.201.

§11.2.1 Contracts for the Sale of Land or an Interest in Land

Like many rules derived from older English law, this rule reflects the importance of land as the principal means of wealth in English society at the time. The statute applies not only to a contract to sell land, but also to any promise to transfer an interest in land, such as the grant or transfer of an easement or mortgage. A lease is also an interest in land and must be in writing, but the statute commonly exempts short-term leases from its purview.

§11.2.2   *Contracts that Cannot Be Performed Within a Year*

Any contract, irrespective of its subject matter, must comply with the statute if it cannot be performed within a year of its execution. Note that the rule is not confined to contracts in which the performance itself will take over a year, but includes any contract—however short the period of performance may be—in which the performance *will not be completed within a year of contracting.* Therefore, if on July 1, 2000, a customer makes a contract with a popular resort to rent a room for the July 4 long weekend in 2001, the contract falls within the statute, even though the performance will last only three days.

The idea behind the one-year rule is probably to ensure that longer-term contracts are recorded. In part, this reflects the concern that parties cannot be expected to remember unrecorded terms as time passes, but it could also be motivated by the expectation that a long-term contract may involve greater economic value. Commentators have pointed out that if the rule is motivated by this goal, it does not achieve it very effectively because the one-year period does not relate to the length of performance but the period between the making of the contract and the end of performance. Therefore, the rule just as much governs a short, inexpensive transaction (such as the hotel booking used in this illustration) as a long, expensive one. Whatever the thinking behind the rule, it is obviously arbitrary and if rigidly applied, could result in absurd distinctions. For example, if an employment contract is entered into on Monday, for a year's employment beginning that day, the statute is not implicated. However, if the employment period is to begin on Tuesday, the statute applies. Courts try to avoid this kind of absurdity when the evidence strongly suggests that a contract really was made orally, and the court does not wish to refuse enforcement by technical application of the rule.

To get around the rule in such a case, one device is to be rather literal-minded about the requirement that the contract cannot be performed in a year. Therefore, if there is *any possibility* that performance *could be completed before a year,* the statute is held to be inapplicable. For example, a contract entered into on July 1, 2000, provides that a builder must complete the construction project by August 1, 2001. Although it may be shown to be impossible, as a practical matter, for the builder to complete the work ahead of schedule, the contract does not *require* performance of more than a year, because it would not be a breach for the builder to complete ahead of schedule. Hence, the application of the statute is avoided. Another common example shows just how tortured the reasoning can be when a court is intent upon finding the contract enforceable: If a young, healthy, fitness freak purchases a lifetime membership in a gym, the contract clearly contemplates a long-term relationship, extending for many years. However, such a contract is typically treated as performable within a year because at the time of contracting there is a possibility that performance will last less than a year—the customer's remaining lifetime may terminate before the year is over despite (or maybe as a result of) all that physical exertion. Of course, some contracts do not admit of this reasoning, so the flexibility provided by this approach only works in some cases. In the example regarding the resort booking, the contract does not contemplate that the resort could complete its performance within a year by making the room available earlier than the July 4 weekend.

§11.2.3   Contracts for the Sale of Goods

Not all sales of goods must be in writing. UCC §2.201 only applies if the contract price of the goods is $500 or more. This refers to the total price under the contract, so if several items, each individually costing less than $500, are sold under a single contract, the statute applies if their combined price exceeds the limit. The price includes not only cash, but also the value of any trade-in or other property exchanged. The $500 figure was fixed some decades ago, so inflation has reduced its present buying power way below what was originally intended.

§11.3   The Second Inquiry: If the Statute Applies, Is the Contract Reflected in a Writing that Satisfies Its Requirements?

To satisfy the general statute, the written memorial of agreement must satisfy a number of requirements. The requirements of UCC §2.201 are similar, and any significant differences are noted below. The requirements are:

a.   A Written Memorandum

Although the statute requires a written memorandum of the contract, there is *no particular formal requirement* beyond this, so a penciled note on a piece of bathroom tissue would be just fine. There is also no requirement that the memorandum be in one document, so it is possible to satisfy the statute by a series of correspondence or other linked writings. The writing need not be made with the deliberate intent of satisfying the statute, or even for the purpose of evidencing the contract, as long as it actually has this effect. Because as discussed below, the writing need only be signed by the party against whom it is to be enforced, it need not be the joint product of the parties or even delivered to the other party by its maker. This means that the internal recordkeeping of one of the parties could contain a document that would be sufficient to satisfy the statute against that party. Although the written memorandum is often made at the time of contracting, there is no requirement that it be made at that time. A later record, even one made after litigation has commenced, could satisfy the statute.

Provided that the writing was made, the statute is satisfied even if it has been *lost by the time of litigation.* Its prior existence and its contents can be proved by oral testimony. This may sound like a strange rule, given that the principal purpose of the statute is to require a written record to prevent a false allegation of contract. It could be just as difficult to detect perjured evidence of a lost writing as it is to expose a bogus claim that a contract was made. Nevertheless, when there is convincing evidence that a writing did exist at one time, this is one further safety valve that prevents abuse of the statute by a party who seeks to escape a genuine contract.

Writing is normally thought of as the making of intelligible marks on a tangible surface, such as paper, whether this is done with a traditional handwriting instrument like a pen or a machine like a typewriter. Today, much recorded information has no such tangible form, but may consist of a recorded voice message or electronically transmitted illuminations on a screen. *Technology must be accommodated* in the statute if it is not to become an archaic impediment to transacting through the use of current technology. Therefore, even if they have not been printed out, technological analogs of writing must be held to satisfy the statute provided that they serve its evidentiary purpose. (The problem of signature in these media of communication is discussed below.)

b. The Memorandum Must Contain Enough Information to Show that a Contract Has Been Made

Evidentiary adequacy for the purpose of satisfying the statute is set quite low. All that is needed is enough writing to sufficiently show the existence of a contract. Therefore, the writing does not have to contain every term of the contract, nor need it be completely clear and unambiguous in all respects. The common law and UCC have different standards for sufficiency of the memorandum, but, as usual, the looser UCC test tends to influence courts even in common law cases. Therefore, in some jurisdictions, the difference is fading.

At common law, it is generally required that the writing must at least *identify the parties* and the *nature of the exchange,* and it must set out all or at least most of the *material terms.* Provided that there is enough substance to show a contract, missing or unclear terms can be proved by oral evidence or otherwise resolved by the process of interpretation and construction discussed in Chapter 10.

UCC §2.201 provides for a less stringent standard. The only term that must be stated in the writing is the *quantity* of goods sold, so that the contract is not enforceable beyond the stated quantity. Beyond that, §2.201 demands only that "there is some writing sufficient to indicate that a contract for sale has been made between the parties." It expressly states that a writing is not insufficient merely because it omits any term other than quantity, or incorrectly states any term.

Because the level of writing needed to satisfy the statute is quite minimal, it is important to recognize that a writing sufficient for the purposes of the statute may not be clear and full enough to ultimately convince the factfinder that a contract was made on the terms alleged. Compliance with the statute is a *different issue from adequate proof of the contract for the purpose of relief.* If the writing is skimpy or uncertain, the statute of frauds may be only the first hurdle to be jumped by the party seeking enforcement. Thereafter, the gaps or indefiniteness in the writing will have to be supplemented or cured by interpretation and persuasive extrinsic evidence.

c. The Writing Must Be Signed by the Party Against Whom the Contract Is to Be Enforced

It is not necessary that the enforcing party signed the writing, because the evidentiary role of the statute is satisfied as long as the *party disputing the existence of the contract* has signed it in person or through an agent. A signature is any **mark or symbol** placed by the party on the paper with the **intention of authenticating it,** so a full and formal signature is not needed. Initials, a logo, or even an "x" is enough. The signature does not have to be placed on the paper after the terms are written down, so if a party's symbol (such as a logo at the top of the page) is already on the paper, that party can adopt the symbol by writing the terms of the contract on the page. UCC §1.201(39) codifies this principle by defining "signed" to include "any symbol executed or adopted by a party with present intention to authenticate a writing." Restatement Second §134 is to the same effect.

When the writing consists of *several pieces of paper* (such as a series of notes or letters), it is not necessary that every piece has been signed, provided that it appears from the writings themselves that they all refer to the same transaction. Some courts require that the signed writing actually makes some reference to the unsigned one, but other courts require only that the writings, on their face, relate to the same transaction.

When the writing is not in tangible form, but consists of a *voice recording or electronically generated images,* the concept of signature requires some adaptation, because the existing definitions were formulated in light of the traditional notions of a mark on paper. In developing an approach to this issue, courts will likely bear in mind the purpose of requiring a signature: It provides evidence that the party, by affixing an identifiable symbol on the writing, manifested agreement with its contents. Where technology substitutes some different means of identifying authorship, this must be viewed as the equivalent of signature, provided that it serves to authenticate the communication. New means of communication may raise new problems of establishing the genuineness of an apparent identifying symbol, but the possibility that a signature was forged is not a new problem.

Section 2.201(2) recognizes one situation in which a writing can be enforced against the party who did not sign it. All the following requirements must be met:

1. Both parties are **merchants.**
2. Within a **reasonable time** of the oral contract, one of the parties sends a written confirmation to the other, which is **signed by the sender** and otherwise **satisfies the statute as against the sender.**
3. The recipient has **reason to know** its contents.
4. The recipient does not give written notice of **objection** to it within ten days of receipt.

In other words, although the contract could normally be enforced only against the sender, as signatory, when both parties are merchants, the nonsigning recipient is also bound by the conduct of failing to protest after receiving a writing that should have been read.

§11.4   The Third Inquiry: If the Statute Applies and Is Not Complied with, Does the Oral Contract Fall Within Any of Its Exceptions?

When a contract falls within the statute and fails to comply with it, the contract is unenforceable as discussed in section 11.5. However, there are a few exceptions that permit enforcement despite the lack of a sufficient signed writing. The exceptions are justified on one or both of two broad grounds. The one (which is a predominant basis for the first exception and the sole basis for the second) is that circumstances following contract formation provide evidence that a contract was indeed made, so that it is unduly technical to insist on compliance with the statute. The other (which strongly motivates the third exception, but may play some role in the first too) is the protection of the interests of a party who suffered a detriment in justifiable reliance on the oral contract.

§11.4.1 The Part Performance Exception

Following an oral contract, the parties may begin performance, which may provide *reliable evidence that a contract was made*. Even if the statute applies to the transaction, the performance satisfies its function, so that refusal of enforcement would be too rigid and would allow a party to renege on an established contract through a technical application of the statute. Despite the logic of this reasoning, courts do not wholeheartedly embrace this exception in common law cases. It is not applied to all contracts subject to the statute. Even when it is used, courts usually require a very clear showing that the conduct does in fact refer to and demonstrate the existence of a contract. In addition, they often require some degree of *prejudice* to have been *suffered in reliance* on the agreement by the party seeking enforcement, and impose other limitations that are too detailed to discuss here. Some courts recognize an exception only if the party seeking enforcement has fully performed. The broad point is that at common law, part performance may allow enforcement of a contract that does not satisfy the statute, but you should not assume that this principle will be readily applied without qualification.

Two subsections of §2.201 give limited recognition to the part performance exception when the contract is for the sale of goods. The two exceptions are narrow and apply only in specific circumstances. The first, in §2.201(3)(a), covers cases in which the seller has begun the manufacture of **goods that are specially made for the buyer** and not otherwise easily saleable. The second, in §2.201(3)(c), allows enforcement of the contract **only to the extent payment** for the goods has been **made and accepted,** or **goods** have been **delivered and accepted.** This means that if one party has performed and the other has accepted that performance, the party who performed can enforce the contract to recover the consideration due for the performance rendered. If only part performance has been made (that is, only part of the goods have been received, or only part of the price has been paid), the contract is only enforceable with respect to what has been done, but cannot be enforced with regard to the balance.

§11.4.2 The Judicial Admission Exception

As the statute is intended to guard against a fraudulent assertion of contract, it would seem logical that a party who admits the contract in pleadings or testimony should not be allowed to raise the statute as a defense. Nevertheless, the *common law* has been loath to embrace such a rule because of a *concern of its impact on litigation*. First, it has been perceived as creating an incentive for perjury because a party may choose to deny the contract to avoid losing the defense by an admission in litigation. Second, because a party can be compelled to disclose information in litigation, the admission may not be truly voluntary. These arguments have been criticized as inadequate to overcome the obvious relevance of admissions in litigation. The UCC has not followed them, and it does recognize an exception for judicial admissions under certain conditions. Under the UCC's influence, the exception is gaining wider recognition in common law too.

The exception is specific and narrow. Section 2.201(3)(b) permits enforcement of a contract against a party, despite non-compliance with the statute if that party **admits in "pleading, testimony or otherwise in court"** that a contract was made. The contract is enforceable only to the extent of the *quantity* of goods admitted. Note that the admission must be made in connection with litigation, and the exception does not extend to admissions in other circumstances. (Of course, a written admission outside of litigation may itself be a memorandum satisfying the statute, but an oral admission in those circumstances has no effect.)

One of the more difficult issues that has arisen in connection with this exception is what constitutes an admission. Clearly, if the party breaks down under cross-examination and concedes the contract, an admission has been made. However, it could also be taken as an admission if a party's pleadings raise a defense on the merits (such as claiming that the other party breached by failure to deliver), rather than clearly denying the existence of a contract. There are also a number of procedural complexities, not addressed here, raised by the question of whether a party can be compelled to admit or deny the contract.

§11.4.3   *The Protection of Reliance: Estoppel and Promissory Estoppel*

Under some circumstances, **equitable estoppel** may be used to protect reliance on a **false factual assertion.** For example, if one of the parties represents to the other that she has made a signed written note of the contract, and the other reasonably relies on this assertion. However, as equitable estoppel is traditionally confined to an assertion of fact, it is generally only helpful in a narrow range of situations.[1]

Promissory estoppel is more useful when there is no factual representation inducing reliance, but one of the parties justifiably relies on the oral contract as a promise, thereby suffering some detriment. While some courts are reluctant to apply the doctrine beyond the area of donative promises, we have seen that there has been a trend toward using it to enforce promises made during negotiations.[2] This trend toward the expanding use of promissory estoppel has also been reflected in its occasional application to enforce a promise in an oral contract that is otherwise unenforceable because of non-compliance with the statute of frauds.

Restatement Second §139, a modified version of §90, recognizes

---

1. The elements and purpose of equitable estoppel are explained in section 8.4.

2. Promissory estoppel is discussed fully in Chapter 8, and section 8.5 discusses the use of the doctrine in the negotiating setting.

promissory estoppel in this context. The elements of promissory estoppel in this situation are similar to those in §90: **A promise reasonably expected to induce reliance,** the inducement of **justifiable reliance** on the promise by the other party, and the need to enforce the promise to **prevent injustice.** Section 139, by its express language, appears to be stricter than §90 because it specifically stresses the need for reliance of a substantial character, reasonableness by the promisee, and foreseeability of the reliance by the promisor. Despite the articulation of these requirements, §139 is not really that different from §90 in this respect, because, as the discussion in Chapter 8 shows, these elements are implicit in §90 as well.

Nevertheless, the emphasis of these requirements in §139 highlights the principle that promissory estoppel is not intended to be applied routinely to circumvent the statute. In the routine case, a party is not usually justified in relying on a contract that violates the statute, even if she was ignorant of the law. Furthermore, the mere fact that she performed wholly or in part (assuming that the performance is insufficient to qualify it for the part performance exception) does not necessarily constitute a reliance of a substantial character. To be substantial, the reliance must lead to a detriment that cannot be avoided except by enforcement of the promise. Because the remedy of restitution can be used to recover the benefit conferred, a detriment consisting of nothing more than an unmerited performance is usually reversible by restitution, and therefore does not require the recourse of enforcement of the promise. Thus, the intent is to confine promissory estoppel to cases where the one party is clearly accountable for inducing reliance, the circumstances justify the other in relying on an oral promise despite the applicability of the statute, the detriment is serious enough that it cannot be rectified by restitution, and application of the statute would cause great hardship.

There is one element unique to §139, because it derives from the evidentiary purpose of the statute: One of the factors to be taken into account by the court in deciding to give relief is the extent to which the promisee's conduct in reliance or any other available evidence *corroborates the existence of a contract.* This suggests that promissory estoppel could be useful as a supplementary basis for enforcement when there is some evidence of performance, but the evidence is not sufficient to invoke the part performance exception.

§11.5   The Impact of Non-Compliance with the Statute

There is some variation in the statutes of different states and some confusion in the caselaw about the effect of failure to satisfy the statute. The non-compliant contract is sometimes said to be **invalid** or **void**—that is, a legal nullity, of no force or effect. Sometimes it is called **unenforceable**—that is, a contract that is valid, but cannot be sued on and enforced in court. Some cases use these words interchangeably. It is more generally accepted that non-compliance with the statute does not void the contract, but merely makes it unenforceable. In many cases, this distinction is only of theoretical interest. A plaintiff with an unenforceable right cannot get relief from the court, so it is cold comfort to know that the contract is not an absolute nullity. However, there are a few situations in which consequences do follow from the distinction, because an existing but unenforceable contract does have more legal effect than a legal non-entity. For example, although an unenforceable contract cannot be used as the basis of a suit, it can be raised as a defense if one of the parties is sued by the other for doing something that is permitted under the contract: Say that an oral contract for the sale of land permits the buyer to enter the land. Although the buyer cannot enforce the right to acquire the land, if the seller found the buyer on the land and sued for trespass, the buyer could prove the contract as a defense to liability for tort.

If the contract is unenforceable for non-compliance with the statute, the party seeking to rely on the statute as a defense cannot raise it by a general denial. It must be specifically pleaded as an **affirmative defense,** otherwise it is waived. If the defense is raised and succeeds, the contract cannot be enforced. If neither party has given or done anything under the contract, the practical effect of non-enforcement is to terminate any obligation that either party orally assumed. However, sometimes a party may have rendered some performance before the contract was declared unenforceable. (Obviously, this partial performance could not have been sufficient to except the contract from the statute as discussed above.) Once the contract is unenforceable, the party who received the performance no longer has a right to keep it. It must therefore be returned under principles of **restitution.** If it was a money payment or the delivery of property still in the hands of the beneficiary, the money or the property itself must be restored. If it was services or property that has been consumed, restitution is usually measured based on its market value, but the court has the discretion to value it differently if fairness so dictates.[3]

§11.6   The Effect of the Statute of Frauds on Modifications of a Contract

Obviously, neither party can unilaterally change the terms of a contract after it has been made, but a contract can always be modified by agreement between the parties. A modification is a contract in itself, distinct from the original contract that it changes. As a separate contract, it is subject to most of the usual requirements of contract law for formation and validity.[4] As a general rule (un-

---

3. The measurement of restitutionary benefits is discussed more fully in section 9.6.

4. This principle is reflected in the common law rule that a modification needs consideration to be binding. However, that rule has changed under the UCC and is probably in decline at common law too. *See* sections 7.5 and 13.9.

less the statute of a particular state provides otherwise), this means that *the statute of frauds applies to modifications*. Therefore, whether or not the original contract was subject to the statute, if the contract as modified falls within the statute, the modification must be recorded in a writing sufficient to satisfy it. For example, under an original contract, entered into on July 1, 2000, a customer booked a room at a resort for the July 4 weekend in 2001. As the contract cannot be performed in a year, it is subject to the statute. Two weeks after making the contract, the customer calls the resort and the parties agree to change the booking to the Christmas holiday in 2000. The statute no longer applies to the modified contract. The opposite would occur if the original booking was for Christmas 2000, and was changed to Thanksgiving 2001, a date more than a year after the modification. The statute did not apply to the original contract, but it does apply to the modification.

EXAMPLES

1. On May 15, Viva Voce, the president of Ritten Records, Inc., interviewed Juan Annum for the position of sales manager. The parties reached agreement on a one-year period of employment, beginning on June 1 at an annual salary of $75,000. At the end of the interview, Viva tore a piece of paper from a blank pad and wrote "Call pers. dept. to enroll Juan Annum as a sales mgr.—1-yr contract starting 6/1. Pay $75,000 p.a." She told Juan that the purpose of the note was to remind her to call the personnel department so that they would put him on the payroll from June.

After the meeting, Juan resigned from his current employment by giving the required two weeks' notice. On May 17, he received a memo in the mail from the personnel department of Ritten Records, Inc. It was written on the company's letterhead and said simply, "We understand that you will be joining us on June 1. Please come in as soon as convenient to fill out the necessary tax forms."

On May 23, before he had a chance to go to the personnel office, Juan received a letter in the mail from Viva on the company's letterhead. It read:

Dear Juan,

I was happy to be able to extend an offer of employment to you last week. I regret, however, that since then we have reevaluated our earnings for the last quarter and find them disappointing. We have therefore decided not to hire any new employees at this time. I am sorry that we cannot use your services. I am sure that a person of your talents will have no difficulty in finding a suitable position elsewhere.

Sincerely,

Viva Voce
President

Can Ritten Records, Inc. get away with this?

2. Change the facts of Example 1 as follows: Viva did not send the letter of May 23 and Ritten Records still wished to employ Juan. However, on May 23 Juan received a better job offer and is no longer interested in working for Ritten Records. Apart from this, all the facts are the same as in Example 1. Can the company enforce the contract against him?

3. Clay Potter owns a small pottery in which he manufactures ceramic ovenware and crockery. Terry Cotta sells such items in his retail store. On June 1, Terry called Clay and spoke to his assistant who accepted his order of 100 ceramic mugs of various designs at $5.10 each, for immediate delivery. Later that day, Terry mailed the following printed form to Clay, with the blanks filled out by hand (the handwriting is denoted here by italics):

TERRY'S HOUSEWARES

Terry Cotta, proprietor.

PURCHASE ORDER

Date *June 1, 2000*

Ordered from *Clay Potter*

Please ship immediately:

Quantity *100*

Price *$5.10 each*

Description *assorted mugs as discussed by phone*

On June 6, Terry received the following letter from Clay:

Dear Mr. Cotta,

I have received your order of June 1. I am sorry that I am out of mugs at present and cannot supply them right now. I am in the process of making a new batch and should have them in stock next month. Due to increased costs, I am going to have to raise the price to $5.50 each. If you would like me to hold your order until that time let me know. Also, tell me which designs you want. Your order refers to an assortment as discussed by phone, but no one here remembers talking to you and we have no record of your call.

Yours truly,

Clay Potter

Terry claims that he already has a contract for immediate delivery at the old price. Can he enforce it against Clay?

4. Sally Dally is a famous, top-selling artist. Ore Alloys, Inc. (ORAL) was building a new headquarters and commissioned Sally to paint a large picture of its ore smelter for the lobby. Sally submitted a preliminary sketch that was approved by ORAL's board. The parties then agreed orally that Sally

would deliver a completed painting in time for the building's dedication 18 months later, and would be paid $50,000 on delivery.

Sally purchased a canvas of appropriate size and began to rough in the outlines of the painting. Before she had proceeded much further, the president of ORAL called to tell her that the corporation had changed its mind and no longer desired the painting.

Does Sally have an enforceable contract with ORAL?

5. Example 9 of Chapter 4 raised the issue of applying the rules of offer and acceptance to a transaction conducted on the Internet. In summary, Annette X. Plorer visited the Web site of Big Browser and selected a digital camera for $600. She ordered it by clicking on various links; keying in her name, address, and credit card particulars; and finally clicking a "confirm order" button to confirm her order. After she did this, a message appeared on her screen thanking her for her order and stating that the goods would be shipped in 10 to 20 days. Assuming that a contract was formed through this process, does it satisfy the statute of frauds?

EXPLANATIONS

1. Although the letter of May 23 suggests that the company is revoking an unaccepted offer, it is clear that an oral contract was made between Juan and the company, represented by its president, on May 15.

A. Is the Contract Subject to the Statute of Frauds?

The only applicable provision of the statute is that covering contracts not to be performed within a year. Although the performance itself will take exactly one year, it is not the length of actual performance that is crucial, but the time between making the contract and the end of performance. This period is approximately two weeks longer than a year. When there is some flexibility in the length of performance, the contract is not treated as falling within the statute if performance could conceivably be completed within the year, but this is not the case here because this is a fixed-term contract. Could it be argued that the performance could end before a year because the employee might die before that time? Although a court is more likely to accept this reasoning when the contract contemplates termination by death (for example, a lifetime employment term), it may be more hesitant to do so if death would merely be a discharge of the duty to perform. However, given the resistance to the one-year rule, it is possible that a court would be willing to entertain an argument that the mere possibility of death makes the contract performable within a year. Of course, such an interpretation would go a long way towards gutting the rule.

B. Is There a Writing Sufficient to Satisfy the Statute?

To satisfy the statute, there must, at a minimum, be a written record, signed by the party against whom enforcement is sought, identifying the parties, setting out the nature of the exchange, and containing most, if not all, of the material terms. The writing need not be contained in a single document, but can be made up of a set of linked documents. Three documents are referred to in the question: Viva's note to herself, the memo from the personnel department, and the letter from Viva. None of these documents on its own is sufficient to satisfy the statute:

(1) Viva's Note to Herself.   The note probably has enough content to show that a contract was made for a year's employment, and it seems to contain the central terms that were agreed. However, it lacks two elements needed to satisfy the statute: It identifies Juan, but not Ritten Records. Worse still, the absence of any identification of Ritten Records means that even on a liberal definition of signature, there is no symbol placed on the paper to authenticate the document on its behalf. Had Viva written its name on the note, or had the notepad had a company logo on it, an argument for signature could have been made, but nothing like this exists.

Therefore, the absence of Ritten Records' signature prevents the note from being an adequate memorial of agreement. Had the note been signed, it would not have mattered that the note was intended as an internal document. The writing need not be addressed or given to the other party. The facts do not state if the note is still in existence, so it is possible that Viva may have crumpled it up and thrown it away after calling the personnel department. However, this would not necessarily be fatal to Juan's case because as long as he can prove the existence and contents of the note at an earlier time, it need not still be extant at the time of suit. (Of course, if Viva denies writing the note or disputes what it said, Juan's success in his suit will be heavily dependent on his credibility. This is not a happy situation for a plaintiff, who could easily fail to discharge his burden of proof.)

(2) The Memo from the Personnel Department.   The memo was written on company stationery and exhibits its logo. Although we normally think of a signature as a symbol made on the document at the time of writing, a pre-existing printed name or logo should qualify as a signature because the party adopts it when using the preprinted stationery. Therefore the logo probably qualifies as a signature. The memo also identifies Juan and suggests the existence of a contract. However, the memo does not set out the terms of the contract. Although some degree of omission is tolerated, an indication of the central terms is usually required. In particular, there is no way to tell that this was not a contract for employment at will because of the lack of reference to the period of employment.

(3) Viva's Letter of May 23.   The letter is signed, but it is of little help to Juan because it does not in any way evidence a contract. In fact, it is written to suggest just the opposite because it is phrased like the revocation of an unaccepted offer.

It is not necessary for a single document to contain all the elements needed to satisfy the statute. Its requirements can be met by a set of writings in combination. *Crabtree v. Elizabeth Arden Sales Corp.*, 110 N.E.2d 551 (N.Y. 1953), discusses the test for deciding whether a group of writings may be looked at together for this purpose. Ms. Arden, the president of the company, orally agreed on its behalf to employ Crabtree as a sales manager for a two-year period with a salary increase every six months. After their negotiations, Ms. Arden's secretary made a note of the agreement on an order blank. The note was headed "Employment agreement with Nate Crabtree." It set out the date, the salary scale, and the phrase "two years to make good," followed by the words "Arrangement with Mr. Crabtree by Miss Arden." Crabtree began work and during the course of the next six months two payroll cards were filled out and signed by company officers. The first stated the parties' names, Crabtree's job classification, and his salary, but said nothing of the period of his employment. The second reflected his first biannual salary increase "per contractual arrangements with Miss Arden."

However, Ms. Arden apparently refused to approve the increase, and a dispute followed, resulting in Crabtree leaving the company and suing for damages for breach of the two-year employment contract. The company denied that a two-year term was agreed and also invoked the statute. The court held the statute to be satisfied. Although the initial note was found to lack the company's signature,[5] it showed that a contract had been made and set out its essential terms. While the payroll cards did not mention all the essential contract terms, they had been signed by company representatives. Taken together, these writings met the statute's requirements. While some courts require that the signed document actually refer to the unsigned one, so that the signature can be attributed to the unsigned document without extrinsic evidence, this court found such a test unnecessarily rigorous. It is enough that it is apparent from the writings that they refer to the same transaction. Oral testimony can then be used to prove that the signature on the one writing was intended to signify assent to the contents of the other.

Applying this test to Juan's case, it seems that he has a chance of showing compliance with the statute. If Viva's note exists or can be convincingly shown to have existed, and the logo on the personnel department's memo is accepted as a signature, these two writings should be viewed in combination because they both refer to the same transaction. (Although Viva's letter of May 23 has a stronger form of signature, it does not help Juan. Its implicit denial of a contract disqualifies it as referring to the transaction in a probative way.)

---

5. Although the court found the note not to have been signed, it seems that an argument could be made that the secretary, by writing "By Miss Arden" on the note with her authority, did in fact sign it on behalf of the company. The company's name itself was not written on the note but the "By" preceding the president's name identifies it as the company's signature.

C. If There Is Insufficient Writing to Satisfy the Statute, Does Any Exception Apply?

If Juan does not succeed in establishing compliance with the statute, he cannot enforce the contract unless he can fit it into one of the recognized exceptions to the statute. The only exception that might apply is promissory estoppel, based on the argument that Ritten Record made a promise in the oral contract, reasonably expecting to induce Juan's reliance, he did justifiably rely on the promise and suffered a substantial detriment in resigning from his existing job. The problem with this argument is that Juan is responsible for knowing the law, and there is no apparent justification for his reliance on an oral contract. If ignorance of the need for a writing is enough to invoke promissory estoppel, the statute would be routinely circumvented.

In *McIntosh v. Murphy,* 469 P.2d 177 (Hawaii 1970), the plaintiff, living in California, interviewed for a job with a car dealer in Honolulu and eventually received an oral offer of employment by telephone. He was discharged a couple of months after beginning work and claimed that he had been wrongfully dismissed because the oral contract was for a year's employment. The employer denied this, contending that the employment was at will, and also argued that had a year-long contract been made, it would have been unenforceable under the statute of frauds. The trial court tried to avoid application of the statute by finding that the contract was accepted by the commencement of performance on the first day of employment, making it performable within a year. Alternatively, the trial court felt that even if the offer had been accepted when made on the telephone, that had happened on the weekend immediately before the Monday on which employment began, and it would be unfairly technical to apply the statute. The appellate court found this reasoning to be too artificial. Instead, because the plaintiff had moved to Hawaii in reliance on the oral contract, it enforced the contract on the basis of promissory estoppel. A dissent in the case points out that the plaintiff had not satisfactorily proved that the contract was for a year, and the judicial circumvention of the statute defeated its very purpose of assuring adequate proof of such contracts. The case, which is based on Restatement Second §139, could also be criticized for too easily finding the element of justifiable reliance to have been satisfied.

Juan had not begun work before Ritten Records sought to escape the contract, but the plaintiffs in both *Crabtree* and *McIntosh* had. It is therefore worth asking if the commencement of employment would have invoked the part performance exception. It should not, unless the performance serves to prove the alleged oral agreement. The rationale of the exception is that part performance is good evidence that the parties did in fact make the contract, so that the goal of the statute is achieved by the parties' conduct in performing. However, when (as in both these cases) the performance is ambiguous, it does not help to prove the contract. It is just as consistent with an employment at will as it is with a long-term contract. (Notwithstanding, the court in

McIntosh notes a link between part performance and estoppel and seemed willing to treat the employment as satisfying the exception.)

2. Although Juan may be able to enforce the contract against Ritten Records either on the basis of the combined writings or under promissory estoppel, the company has no corresponding right. When the writing has been signed by just one of the parties, the statute makes the contract enforceable against that party only. If the rule were otherwise, the statute would have little purpose because it would be too easy for one of the parties to write and sign a bogus document and to claim a contract binding on the other. (The UCC has a limited exception to this rule, discussed in the next example.) Juan has not signed anything, and Ritten Records has taken no action in reliance on his oral promise. It cannot enforce the contract.

This means, of course, that Juan might be able to enforce a contract against Ritten, but Ritten has no basis to enforce a contract against him. Does such a result give rise to a problem of mutuality of obligation (both parties must be bound, or neither is) discussed in section 7.9.1? The answer is no. In contemporary law, mutuality is just another way of describing the requirement of consideration doctrine that when promises are exchanged, both must be genuine. Beyond this, there is no general rule that prevents one party from being bound, even though that party itself has no right of enforcement.

3. Although the price of each item of goods is only $5.10, they are sold together in a single contract, so the price of the sale is their total price of $510. The contract is therefore subject to the statute of frauds in UCC §2.201. Terry's order form does not satisfy §2.201(1) as against Clay because it must be signed by the party against whom enforcement is sought. Clay's letter does have his signature (defined in §1.201(39) as "any symbol executed or adopted by a party with present intention to authenticate a writing"), but it fails to satisfy §2.201(1) because it does not indicate that a contract has been made. In fact, phrased as a counteroffer, it suggests just the opposite.

We saw in Example 2 that under the general statute, a writing sufficient to satisfy the statute against one party does not bind the other in the absence of the other's signature. The same rule applies in many cases under the UCC, but §2.201(2) provides an exception to it. If one of the parties sends a confirmation of the oral contract to the other, the statute is satisfied as against the recipient if all the following conditions are satisfied:

(a)   Both parties are merchants

(b)   The writing is sufficient under §2.201(1) to satisfy the statute as against the sender

(c)   It was sent within a reasonable time

(d)   It was received by the other party who has reason to know its contents

(e)   The recipient does not give written notice of objection to it within ten days of receipt

Both parties are merchants under §2.104(1) because they both deal in goods of that kind. For the writing to be sufficient against Terry, the sender, it must indicate that a contract of sale has been made between the parties and must be signed by Terry. Beyond this, it need not accurately or fully state all the terms agreed, but it is not enforceable beyond the quantity stated. The order form does set out the essential terms of the contract, including the quantity of the goods. Terry's printed name at the top should qualify as his signature because it was adopted by him to authenticate the form when he filled out the blanks. The only problem is that the form is described as an order, which suggests not a contract, but an offer. It would have been clearer if the form had been headed "order confirmation." Nevertheless, this difficulty can be overcome by the reference to the telephone call that, on a reasonable interpretation, suggests a prior oral order accepted by or on behalf of Clay. This was the approach taken by the court in *Harry Rubin & Sons v. Consolidated Pipe Co.*, 153 A.2d 472 (Pa. 1959) to a form similarly headed "order" that referred to a prior telephone call.

The form was sent on the same day as the telephone call, surely with a reasonable time, and Clay's response shows that it was received and its contents read. All is well for Terry so far, but the final requirements seems to be his undoing. To be an effective objection to the contents of the writing, the response must challenge the existence of a contract. Although the letter from Clay does not say in so many words that it denies Terry's claim of a contract, its import is clearly to that effect. It treats the order as an offer and claims no knowledge of the telephone call. It is in writing and is given within ten days of receipt of Terry's form.

4. Is the contract within the statute? If it is a sale of goods, UCC §2.201 will apply, but if it is not, it would not likely fit any category recognized by the general statute of frauds.

(a). *Common Law.* Although Sally was given 18 months to complete the painting, there is no contractual bar to her finishing it much sooner, and ORAL's performance is due on delivery, so the contract can be performed within a year. This would be true even if Sally's other commitments or the scale of this painting make it unlikely that she would be able to finish it that quickly. The statute is not treated as applicable unless the contract itself requires performance that cannot be completed within a year of its execution.

This approach, which declines to find the one-year rule applicable unless the contract, by its terms, clearly obliges the party to extend performance beyond a year, is illustrated by *C. R. Klewin, Inc. v. Flagship Properties, Inc.*, 600 A.2d 772 (Conn. 1991). The developer of a major construction project (consisting of a hotel, a convention center, and a large number of commercial and residential buildings) contracted with a general contractor to manage the construction. A written contract was executed for the first phase of the construction, but the contract for the second phase was oral. The developer dismissed the contractor at the end of the first phase. When the contractor sued for breach of contract, the developer applied for summary judgment on the basis that, given the scale of the project, the contract clearly could not be performed in a year. (The contractor conceded that the project would take between three to ten years to complete.) The trial court found that the statute of frauds barred enforcement of the oral contract and granted summary judgment to the contractor. The Supreme Court reversed. It observed that the one-year rule was difficult to justify and should therefore be confined as narrowly as possible to apply only where the contract expressly specifies that performance is required to extend more than a year beyond its execution. However, when the contract does not contain such a clear obligation, it should be treated as legally performable within a year, even if, as a matter of fact, performance cannot be completed within that period and the parties did not expect it to be.

(b). *Article 2.* Is the painting of a commissioned artwork a sale of goods or a contract for services? While it may seem as if it is Sally's talent that is being bought, the parties contemplate the creation of a tangible end product that is self-standing and moveable (even if special equipment may be needed to move it). This makes the transaction a sale of goods. It is very different from, say, the hiring of an orchestra to play music at the building's dedication, which would be a contract for services. Sally's case can be distinguished from that of her even more celebrated colleague, Salvador Dali. In *National Historic Shrines Foundation v. Dali,* 4 UCC Rep. Serv. 71 (N.Y. 1967), Dali, the famous, eccentric surrealist artist, had made an oral contract with the foundation to appear on a television show during which he would execute a painting of the Statue of Liberty. The painting would then be sold to raise funds for a museum. When Dali reneged and was sued, he raised the statute of frauds as one of his defenses. In an argument as outlandish as his pictures, he reasoned that as the painting was the end product of the exercise, and his work was worth vastly more than the $500 minimum in §2.201, this was a sale of goods subject to §2.201. The court rejected this contention, pointing out that the true purpose of the contract was to have Dali perform a service by doing his show on TV. The creation of the painting for later sale was merely incidental to this.

As Sally's contract is a sale of goods over $500, §2.201 must be complied with. There is no writing at all, so the statute is not satisfied unless one of the exceptions in §2.201(3) applies. (Luckily, Sally did not sign her preliminary sketch, so we do not have to worry if it could constitute a writing that satisfies the statute of frauds.[6]) The only exception that has any possible relevance is the version of the part performance exception set out in §2.201(3)(a). It has the following requirements:

---

6. I am only half joking. This might make an intriguing argument.

(a)   The goods are to be specially manufactured for the buyer.

(b)   They are not suitable for sale to others in the ordinary course of the seller's business.

(c)   Before receiving notice of the buyer's repudiation, the seller made a substantial beginning on their manufacture or commitments for their procurement.

(d)   The circumstances reasonably indicate that the goods are for the buyer.

Very clearly, the exception has its basis in the principle, recognized to some extent at common law too, that the statute should not be applied to defeat relief to a party when post-formation conduct both indicates detrimental reliance on the oral contract and provides evidence of the contract's existence. By commencing performance or procurement of goods that are specific to the buyer's needs and not readily resalable, the seller incurs prejudice and her actions demonstrate the existence of a contract.

In Sally's case, the painting is especially commissioned by and reflects a theme of particular interest to the buyer. This, together with the submission and approval of the preliminary sketch, strongly indicate that the painting is for the buyer. Could Sally sell the painting to anyone else? It may be that no other person on earth would buy a painting of ORAL's smelter, but art is art after all, and collectors are remarkably easygoing about the themes and subject matter of well-executed paintings. (Indeed, the "Precisionist" school of the 1930s delighted in the portrayal of machinery and their paintings are worth a fortune.) It is therefore not clear that the painting would not be easily saleable in the ordinary course of Sally's business.

Sally bought the canvas and began the painting before the repudiation. Is this a substantial enough beginning? This requirement, combined with that of difficulty of resale, is intended to confine the exception to cases in which non-enforcement would cause hardship to the seller. It is difficult to draw a definite line at which the commitment of time and materials passes from insubstantial to substantial, but Sally could make a respectable argument that the purchase of the canvas, a major component of the materials to be used, the time spent in conceiving the painting, and the preliminary blocking work is enough to be substantial. However, as the canvas has not been consumed and could be used for another painting, this is not an overwhelming argument.

In short, the performance seems to serve the evidentiary function well, but is less compelling on the question of detriment. Sally has a chance of success, but this is not an easy case to predict.

5. This is a sale of goods for a price over $500, so UCC §2.201 applies, and there must be a written memorandum of agreement, signed by the party against whom enforcement is sought, sufficient to show that a contract has been formed.

The question does not indicate whether any of the communications were printed out. However, this should not be relevant. Although the traditional concept of writing involves the inscription of words on paper or some other tangible object, it would make no sense to disregard new forms of storing and preserving data. The crucial issue should not be whether the contract has been incorporated onto a piece of paper, but whether there is a record of it that constitutes reliable evidence of its content. Even if no hard copy was made by either party, Big Browser's electronic records no doubt will contain all the crucial terms of the contract—the identity of the parties, the description and quantity of the goods ordered, the price, and the delivery terms.

The concept of signature has to be adjusted when electronic communications are involved. Both Article 2 and the common law are amenable to flexibility in this regard because they have long recognized that a signature could be any symbol executed or adopted with the intention of authenticating the writing. Therefore, for example, the use of a company logo or name on the Web site could serve as Big Browser's signature, and Annette may have signed the order by inserting her name or e-mail address in her order. The forgery of signatures is a longstanding concern affecting all forms of writing or recording. However, it seems to be particularly acute in the disembodied world of the Internet. There are means, such as encryption, to guard against the unauthorized use of an electronic "signature," but this method is not yet universally used, especially in consumer transactions. In the end, whether the signature is some more traditional mark or an identifying characteristic such as an e-mail address, the basic questions are the same: Is this truly the mark of the party against whom enforcement is sought, and, if so, was it placed on the writing or other record with the intention of authenticating it?

12

The Parol Evidence Rule

§12.1 The Relationship Between the Parol Evidence Rule and Interpretation

It was said in Chapter 10 that when an agreement is recorded in writing, the meaning of its terms must be determined, not by interpretation of the written language in isolation, but within the entire context of the transaction. Although the writing is the primary source for establishing meaning, further relevant evidence of meaning may be found in the environment of the contract, including the negotiations, the dealings between the parties, and accepted usages. The parol evidence rule qualifies this general principle by imposing restrictions on the extent to which the context of a writing may be used to establish what the parties agreed.

§12.2 A Basic Statement of the Rationale and Content of the Rule

The parol evidence rule is based on the principle that when the parties reduce their agreement to writing, they often intend the written record to be the final version of what was agreed. If this is so, the final draft must have been *intended to supersede* earlier negotiations and communications to the extent that its terms depart from or do not include what was formerly agreed. As a result, *evidence of any earlier agreement is irrelevant and misleading,* and should be *kept from the factfinder.* (This rationale is taken up again and illustrated in section 12.3.)

Restatement Second §213 sets out the common law parol evidence rule, as it is applied by many contemporary courts. The UCC rule, in §2.202, is worded somewhat differently, but is largely similar in effect. In essence, both versions of the rule provide that to the extent that the parties execute a **writing that is and is intended to be a final expression** of their **agreement,** no parol evidence may be admitted to **supplement, explain, or contradict** it. However, to the extent that the writing is **not a final and complete expression** of agreement, **consistent, but not contradictory** parol evidence may be admitted to supplement or explain those parts of it that have not been finally expressed.

§12.3   What Is Parol Evidence?

"Parol" is derived from the French *parole,* meaning "a word"—more particularly a spoken or oral word. It has the same etymological root as the more familiar modern English word "parole," which has now developed the specialized meaning of a prisoner's early release from jail subject to conditions. Because contract lawyers do not like in any way to be associated with criminal activity, it is a grave breach of etiquette to use that final "e" when referring to parol evidence.

Although the roots of "parol" may suggest that it refers only to evidence of oral terms, the parol evidence rule extends to written terms as well. It covers all evidence of alleged terms not incorporated into the written memorial of agreement, but claimed by one of the parties to have been agreed to, either **in writing or orally,** at some time **before its execution.** For example, Seller and Buyer sign a written agreement under which Seller sells her car to Buyer for $5,000 cash, to be paid on delivery of the car. When Seller thereafter tenders delivery of the car, Buyer refuses to pay the $5,000, claiming that on the day before the agreement was signed, Seller had orally agreed to give him 30 days' credit. If this matter should eventually be litigated, Buyer's testimony about the *prior oral agreement* would be parol evidence. (As we will shortly see, it most likely satisfies all the elements of the parol evidence rule, and the court would therefore refuse to allow Buyer to testify about the prior oral agreement.) The rationale for filtering such evidence through the parol evidence rule is that an allegation of prior consensus on an oral term is suspect when the oral term is not incorporated into the writing executed for the purpose of recording the agreement. Its absence from the writing suggests either that it is a complete fabrication by Buyer, or even if it was agreed to, that the parties intended to supersede it by the written term. Therefore, the evidence should be evaluated with special care by the judge before it is admitted for the factfinder's consideration.

Say that the parties had not negotiated orally, but by correspondence. Their correspondence shows agreement on a 30-day credit term, but their final written contract of sale reflects the C.O.D. term. The *written evidence of prior agreement* is also parol evidence. Although the presence of objectively verifiable written evidence of prior agreement reduces concern that Buyer made up the claimed agreement on the credit term, its absence from the final writing still suggests that the parties must have intended to supersede it by the cash term.

The parol evidence rule therefore applies to both oral and written evidence of agreement allegedly made prior to execution of the writing. When oral evidence is in issue, the same reasoning excludes testimony of claimed *oral agreement* made *contemporaneously* with the execution of the writing. For example, say that Buyer wishes to testify that when the parties got together to sign the sales contract, he raised the issue of credit and Seller agreed to give him 30 days to pay for the car. However, this agreement is not reflected in the writing. Such an assertion is just as much suspect (or maybe even more so) as that concerning a prior oral agreement and is therefore equally subject to the parol evidence rule.

Written evidence of *contemporaneous agreement* presents a trickier issue because the effect of contemporaneous writings is more ambiguous. When two writings are executed at approximately the same time, it is not always obvious that either is *the* final written memorial of agreement. For example, say that when Buyer and Seller met to sign the written contract of sale, Buyer raised the question of being given credit and Seller agreed to allow him 30 days to pay. Although the parties signed the written sales agreement reflecting the C.O.D. term, they also executed a short document containing the credit term. This could suggest that their actual agreement is contained, not in one document, but in two. (Of course, it would have made life easier had they instead made their intention clear, either by removing the C.O.D. term from the sales agreement or by labeling the second writing as an amendment or addendum.) Because of this ambiguity, some courts and commentators say that the parol evidence rule does not apply to a contemporaneous writing. The result of this is that both writings are freely admissible. This does not guarantee that Buyer will ultimately win, but he has no restriction on placing the evidence before the factfinder, which will decide if the writing reflecting the credit term was intended by the parties to qualify the sales agreement.

The parol evidence rule does not affect evidence of either *oral or written* agreements claimed to have been made *after the execution of the writing*. The theory behind the parol evidence rule is that the writing is likely to have subsumed all prior understandings, and this presumption cannot have any relevance to an agreement entered into subsequent to the writing. This is in fact a modification, which is subject to its own particular rules[1], but it is not affected by the parol evidence rule. (The written memorial of agreement may

---

1. Modifications are dealt with in sections 7.5.2 and 13.9.

itself seek to prevent future oral modifications by requiring that all modifications must be in writing and signed by the parties. The effectiveness of such a provision is discussed in section 12.12.) The range of the parol evidence rule may be shown as follows:

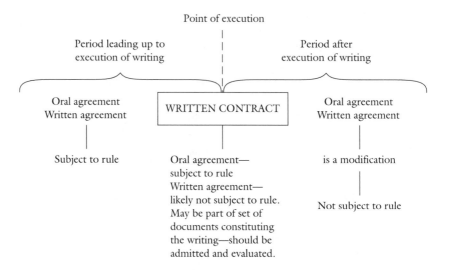

§12.4   A Closer Look at the Purpose and Premise of the Parol Evidence Rule

The basic concept of the parol evidence rule is quite simple and its premise is grounded in common sense. Sadly, however, this basic simplicity is completely overwhelmed by the considerable difficulties that emerge when one tries to define the scope of the rule and to apply it to inconclusive facts. The complexity and confusion generated by the rule result largely from the dilemma it presents to courts: The rule serves **a useful role** in permitting the **exclusion of evidence** that is probably **unreliable or dishonest,** but it also has the **potential of producing injustice** by **preventing a party** from **proving what was actually agreed.** A firm rule is more efficient at keeping out undesirable evidence, but is also more likely to exclude legitimate evidence. A more flexible rule allows the court greater discretion in evaluating and determining the reliability of evidence, but it weakens the protection against undesirable evidence and detracts from the certainty and clarity of the law. If you think of the rule as a door to the witness box, its ideal design would keep out the perjurer and irrelevant waffler, but would admit the honest and pertinent witness. The current state of the rule aspires to that design but has not achieved it and probably cannot.

The following illustration indicates the premise of the rule:

Homer M. Provement wishes to build an addition to his house. He enters into negotiations with Archie Tekt and eventually agrees to hire Archie to draw the plans. They write out a memorandum of agreement that describes the work to be done by Archie and simply states that the fee for the work is $1,500, payable by Homer in advance. Homer pays the fee and Archie draws the plans. Although the plans are well executed and conform exactly to Homer's wishes, Homer is very unhappy. The proposed alteration will cost $25,000 to build, and Homer cannot afford more than $20,000. He says that during their negotiations he specifically told Archie that he had no more than $20,000 to spend and that he did not wish to waste time and money having plans drawn up if the addition could not be built within this limit. Archie assured him that the job could be done for well under $20,000 and said to him, "If I am wrong and it would cost more, I won't charge you for the plans and I'll refund the fee." Archie denies that he ever made that commitment and refuses Homer's demand for a refund.

Because the writing says nothing about Archie's alleged promise of a refund, Homer has no case unless he is allowed to testify about the alleged oral promise. The law could simply allow all the evidence to be presented, leaving it to the factfinder (typically, the jury) to decide if Homer is telling the truth. If the jury believed Homer, it would conclude that the parties did actually agree to the term and would find it to be part of their contract even though it was left out of the writing. However, the common law has not taken this approach. Instead, it has developed the parol evidence rule to allow the judge to make an initial evaluation of the proffered evidence and to decide if the jury should be allowed to hear it.

Like many evidentiary principles in our law, the primary purpose of the parol evidence rule is to restrict the information given to the jury. By excluding evidence, the judge is able to *shield the jury from apparently unreliable or irrelevant matter,* and thereby to exercise some control over its decision making. A secondary rationale for the rule is the *efficient use of court time:* If evidence is of dubious value and relevance, a decision to exclude it saves considerable time in examination and cross-examination. It is also probable that the rule has a less direct benefit by affecting the way that people act in the marketplace and encouraging *more efficient transacting:* Because it exists, more people are likely to make an effort to record their agreement fully, thereby cutting down on uncertainty and disputes.

As the parol evidence rule relates to the admissibility of evidence, one might be forgiven for assuming that it is a rule of **evidence.** However, it is generally thought of as a rule of **substantive law.** The distinction is subtle: If it were evidentiary, it would be an exclusionary rule based on a presumption that the writing is the best evidence of agreement. Seen as a rule of substantive contract law, it nullifies parol agreements when a writing is executed as a final expression of agreement. This rule of law then leads to the exclusion of the evidence as irrelevant. Happily, one does not usually have to worry about this distinction, because it makes no difference for most purposes. Its principal impact is on matters of procedure. For example, if a federal court deals with a contract case, it follows its own rules of evidence but is bound by the state's parol evidence rule because it is a matter of state substantive law. Similarly, if it were a rule of evidence, a party would waive it by failing to object to the evidence at trial. As a rule of substantive law, it can be raised on appeal despite the failure to object at trial.

Let us return to the reasoning behind the rule, introduced in section 12.2, and use Homer's case to illustrate it: It is self-evident that Archie and Homer went to the trouble of writing down their agreement because they wanted a reliable and accurate record of what they agreed. The written terms must be taken to be definitive to the extent that they can fairly be regarded as having dealt dispositively with a particular issue, and they must surely be intended to supersede any discussions on that issue that did not make it into the writing. In other words, if Homer and Archie had really agreed to the refund term, surely they would not have recorded an unqualified payment term in the writing. This must mean either that Homer is wrong in thinking they had agreed to it, or worse still, he is making it up. If the alleged term is his fabrication, the court certainly does not wish to assist him in perjury. Even if he is not lying, the best that can be said for him is that he was very sloppy in safeguarding his own interests by not ensuring that the writing fully and accurately set out what Archie had promised. In either event he merits no help from the court.

Therefore, the general approach is to view with suspicion any attempt by a party to introduce evidence that embellishes or contradicts a recorded term. Unless the judge is satisfied that the extrinsic evidence is plausible and congruent with the writing—that is, that the writing was not intended to supersede it—the alleged term cannot be regarded as part of the agreement. Evidence concerning it may wrongly influence the jury, and must be excluded. This is just a broad description of the thinking behind the parol evidence rule. As you will see shortly, the rule itself is more intricate. However, even this general description suggests some of the important features of the rule and the issues that it presents. They should be articulated before we go deeper into the details of the rule:

1. The rule only applies when a *written agreement* has been executed. The rule applies whether the writing is a comprehensive or incomplete record of the agreement. However, the more complete the written memorandum, the more rigorous the application of the rule.

2. The writing must have been *adopted by both parties.* It need not be signed by them as long as it is shown to be a mutual document. Naturally, the presence of signatures more strongly proves that it is a joint memorandum, but a letter written by one party and received by the other without objection qualifies. A memorandum written by only one of the parties and not disseminated to the other does not bring the rule into effect. To invoke the parol evidence rule, a writing must therefore have qualities beyond those needed to satisfy the statute of frauds. This is because the statute is concerned with the

minimal amount of writing needed to establish the existence of a contract, while the parol evidence rule is concerned with the degree to which the writing should be used to exclude extrinsic evidence of what was agreed.

3. Remember that the word "parol" suggests that the rule is *primarily concerned with oral communications* between the parties before or at the time of execution of the writing. However, the rule is not confined to oral communications, and it also covers *prior written communications.*

4. The rule *does not absolutely bar all parol evidence.* If it did, our job would be much easier, but the results of the rule would be bizarre. The purpose of the rule is to exclude presumptively irrelevant or concocted testimony, but not honest and pertinent evidence of what was actually agreed. The rule must therefore be sufficiently fine-tuned to allow the court to make this distinction. Herein lies the greatest complexity and difficulty in devising and applying a rational rule.

5. The rule contemplates a *two-stage process.* When the parol evidence is proffered, the judge must make an initial finding of admissibility. If the judge finds that the evidence is admissible, it is presented to the factfinder (the jury unless the trial is before a judge alone) that hears the testimony and makes the ultimate finding on credibility. The judge's initial determination is characterized as a *question of law,* but it is not necessarily devoid of factual evaluation. This is one of the confusing aspects of the rule. Although the factfinder may eventually have to decide if the evidence is believable, the judge, in making the initial decision on admissibility, is also concerned with the plausibility of the proffered evidence, a preliminary issue of credibility.

§12.5   The Degree of Finality of the Writing: Total and Partial Integration

The impact of the parol evidence rule depends on the degree to which the writing executed by the parties constitutes a comprehensive and final written memorandum of their agreement. In short, if the writing is full, complete, unambiguous, and clear, the rule excludes all parol evidence. But to the extent that the written memorandum does not fully and unequivocally cover all of the agreed terms, parol evidence is admissible to supplement it. Even here, however, the parol evidence cannot contradict what has been written or add to those aspects of the agreement that have been fully dealt with in the writing. As discussed in section 12.6, it can be a difficult question of interpretation to determine whether and to what extent the memorandum is comprehensive and final.

If the written memorandum is a complete and final and certain record of the parties' agreement (that is, it unambiguously and clearly expresses every term in the agreement, and it is intended to be the exclusive statement of everything that was agreed), it is said to be **totally (or completely) integrated.** If the writing is truly a total integration, then, by definition, no terms can exist beyond those set out in the writing. It follows that neither party should be allowed to offer parol evidence tending to prove terms extrinsic to the writing, because such evidence is irrelevant or incredible.

It must be emphasized that a writing, even if apparently intended as a total integration, does not exclude parol evidence to the extent that it is *unclear or ambiguous*. Even if the parties intended to create a watertight, self-contained memorial of their agreement, their attempt to do so fails to the extent that language used is capable of more than one meaning or conveys no precise meaning at all. Parol evidence will be necessary and admissible to resolve such ambiguity or to explain what was meant by unclear language. One of the difficult issues in applying the parol evidence rule is to decide what constitutes ambiguity or uncertainty in the language of an apparent integration. This is discussed in section 12.7.

If the writing is not a complete and final record of the agreement it is said to be **partially integrated,** or **unintegrated,** depending on the extent to which it reflects the agreed terms. If one or more terms of the agreement have been fully, finally and clearly expressed in the writing, it is a partial integration—that is, it is a final statement of those terms. However, if the writing does not set out any term in full, final and certain form, it is unintegrated. It is not worth expending much energy on the rather elusive distinction between a partially integrated or unintegrated writing. In either event, the issue always involves a particular term, and the real question is whether the writing fully disposes of the subject matter to which the term relates. Therefore, if the writing as a whole is anything short of a complete integration, the parol evidence rule applies to each individual term that is fully, finally and clearly expressed in the writing, and no parol evidence on the subject matter of that term may be admitted. With regard to other aspects of the agreement that are not integrated in the writing—either because they are not dealt with at all, or because they are not expressed with sufficient clarity—parol evidence is admissible to **supplement** or explain the writing, provided that it does *not contradict or vary* anything that has been recorded in the writing. If there is some explicit or implied reference to the subject matter of the disputed term in the writing, and the parol evidence is offered to clarify an ambiguity or uncertainty, consistency requires that the meaning supported by the parol evidence is reconcilable with what has been provided in the writing.

§12.6   The Process of Dealing with Parol Evidence

The issue of the admissibility of parol evidence could arise early in the suit if one of the parties applies for summary judgment in response to a claim or defense based on an alleged parol term. Because the admissibility of parol evidence is a legal question, a dispute on admissibility is often appropriate for summary adjudication. If the case is not disposed of on the pleadings and it goes to trial, the admissibility of the evidence may be challenged when an attempt is made to introduce it. As noted before, the evaluation of parol evidence at trial involves two stages. In the first, the judge decides admissibility as a legal matter. If the evidence is admitted, the factfinder evaluates its credibility. We now look more closely at the process involved in each of these two stages, which may be charted as follows:

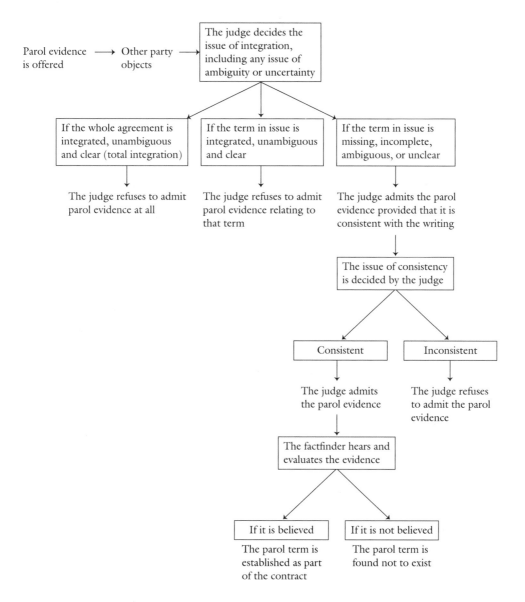

Stage 1: The judge's determination

In making the finding of admissibility, the judge conducts an inquiry that may itself be split into two sequential components:

1. The first issue to be resolved by the judge is the question of *integration*. Is the writing a full, final, and certain record of the agreement as a whole (that is, a complete integration) or of the particular term in issue (a partial integration). If so, we do not get beyond the first inquiry, because the parol evidence may not be admitted.

2. If the writing is neither a complete integration nor a partial integration covering the term in issue (whether it simply does not address the term at all, or its treatment is ambiguous or unclear), consistent supplementary parol evidence is admissible. The judge's inquiry then turns to whether the proffered parol evidence is in fact *consistent* with and not contradictory to what has been written. If it contradicts the writing, it may not be admitted, and it still never reaches the jury.

Having drawn this distinction between the judge's two inquiries, it is useful to express a word of caution: It is easy enough to separate the issue of integration from the issue of consistency for the purpose of theoretical analysis, and it is logical that the first must be resolved before the second is reached. However, as a practical matter, the inquiry into integration is often influenced by the question of whether the alleged parol term is consistent with the writing, and these two stages often meld into one another. That is, unless the intent to integrate is so clear that there can be no doubt on the matter, the extent to which the alleged parol term is reconcilable with the writing may affect the court's decision on whether an integration was reasonably intended by the parties.

Stage 2: The factfinder's determination

If the judge's preliminary inquiry into the evidence leads to the determination that the subject matter covered by the alleged term has not been integrated into the writing and that the proffered parol evidence is consistent with what has been written, the judge rules the evidence admissible. It may then be presented to the factfinder, which is responsible for the ultimate decision on whether the term was agreed to. If the case is to be tried by a jury, the dichotomy between judge and factfinder is clear. However, if the parties have agreed not to try the case before a jury, the judge is the factfinder, and the dichotomy becomes quite artificial. The judge, in the role of legal arbiter, makes the initial finding as a matter of law. If she rules the evidence inadmissible, she must then exercise the professional objectivity of not being influenced by it in her role as factfinder. This is probably not as difficult as it sounds—the fact that the judge excluded it as a matter of law means that she could not have found it very convincing to begin with—as explained further below.

§12.7   Determining the Question of Integration

Integration is a question of intent—truly a factual question, although characterized as one of law for the reasons of judicial control, as discussed above.

Therefore, to decide if the parties intended the writing to be a full and final expression of their agreement, the court must interpret it. During the classical period of contract law, courts tended to emphasize the objective test of assent and to place great importance on the reasonable meaning of language. This heavy emphasis on *objectivity* made the question of determining integration relatively easy: If the writing, interpreted as a whole in accordance with the plain meaning of the language used, appeared to be a full, final, clear and unambiguous expression of the agreement, it was deemed to be integrated. Thus, the judge decided the parties' intent to integrate their agreement in the writing purely on the basis of the **"four corners"** of the written document, without recourse to any extrinsic evidence. If the document *appeared* complete and there was no obvious ambiguity or lack of clarity in the language pertaining to the matter in issue, this intent was established and no parol evidence was admissible to add to or alter its reasonable meaning. (This earlier emphasis on the "four corners" test explains why courts felt justified in thinking of integration as a legal question. A purely grammatical evaluation of meaning involves no assessment of the credibility of extrinsic evidence.)

The trend has been to move away from a strong "four corners" approach. Most modern courts recognize that even when a writing appears at face value to be clear and comprehensive, inquiry into the context in which it was written may dispel this impression. Therefore, in deciding the question of integration, a contemporary court is likely to go beyond the face value of the writing, and to entertain *extrinsic evidence* that may be helpful in revealing that an *apparently integrated writing* was in fact *not intended as such*, or contains an *ambiguity that is not otherwise obvious*. The judge's evaluation of this extrinsic evidence is preliminary, and treated as a legal exercise despite the obvious factual and credibility issues involved. If the judge concludes that the evidence is admissible as a matter of law, the factfinder (whether a jury or the judge herself in that role) will be the final arbiter of its factual truth.

When the term sought to be proved by the parol evidence is omitted from the writing, one of the key questions in determining integration under the contextual approach is to ask whether the circumstances offer an explanation of why the term may not have been included in the writing. Restatement Second §216(2)(b) expresses this concept by asking whether the term is such as *might naturally be omitted* from the writing. UCC §2.202, Comment 3, suggests a similar inquiry: Would the term *certainly have been included* in the document had it been agreed to? The UCC test sounds more favorable to admission because it excludes the evidence only if it clearly would have been part of the writing if the parties had agreed to it. However, in most cases, this test would not likely give a different result than the Restatement's inquiry into whether the term might naturally have been agreed separately.

When the parol evidence is offered to clarify an alleged ambiguity in an apparently unambiguous integrated writing, a court adopting the contextual approach will hear the evidence as an initial matter and decide whether the language of the writing reasonably admits of the interpretation. If so, the evidence tending to prove the interpretation should be admitted for the factfinder's evaluation.

The movement away from the plain meaning of the writing should not be exaggerated. Even under the contextual test, if the document does appear to be clear, unambiguous and complete, the court is likely to assume that it is integrated unless the extrinsic evidence is reconcilable with the apparent intent and plausibly demonstrates a justification for going beyond the writing. Also, one should not simplistically relegate the "four corners" approach to history. It still has some sway, and courts have not moved beyond it at a uniform pace. You still find today a range of approaches to the issue of integration that are based both on the strength of the evidence of integration and on the conservatism of the court.

The range of possibilities involved in the inquiry into integration may be charted as follows:

DESCRIPTION OF CONTENT OF WRITING	TEST	QUALITIES OF WRITING	RESULT
1. All terms fully and clearly expressed = Total Integration	*4 corners:* Decided on face of document. *Contextual:* Parol evidence is considered by judge to determine integration.	• all terms included • terms fully expressed • no vagueness or ambiguity • apparent comprehensiveness— possibly expressed in merger clause	No parol evidence may be admitted
2. Some terms fully and clearly expressed = Partial Integration	As in 1	• some terms written in full and final form • those terms are clear and unambiguous • other terms are not included at all, or are not in final and comprehensive form	Parol evidence is admissible to supplement or explain missing or incomplete terms, but cannot contradict them. Parol evidence is not admissible to supplement final terms
3. Some or all terms purport to be fully and finally expressed, but the language of the term in issue is unclear or ambiguous	*4 corners:* Existence of ambiguity/uncertainty decided on plain meaning of language in writing. *Contextual* Parol evidence is considered by judge to decide if meaning of writing is unclear or ambiguous.	• term in issue may or may not be intended as final expression of assent, but its language admits of more than one interpretation or its meaning cannot be determined on the basis of the writing alone	Parol evidence is admissible to explain the uncertainty or to establish the correct meaning of the ambiguity

4. No terms are fully and clearly expressed = Unintegrated Writing	As in 1 and 2	• writing is only a partial memorandum, and does not fully, finally and clearly reflect any of the terms	Parol evidence is admissible to supplement or explain the writing, but cannot contradict what is written down

Some of the difficulties in deciding the question of integration can be illustrated by returning to the contract for architectural services between Homer and Archie. Assume that their memorandum of agreement reads as follows:

MEMORANDUM OF AGREEMENT

Between

Archie Tekt (Archie)

and

Homer M. Provement (Homer)

1. In consideration for $1,500, payable by Homer on the signing of this contract, Archie agrees to draw plans for the alteration of Homer s residence in accordance with the attached rough sketch.

2. The plans will be completed within one month of the date of this agreement.

3. This is the entire agreement between the parties. No representations or promises have been made save for those set out in this memorandum.

Signed _Archie Tekt_   Date _September 1, 1997_

Signed _Homer M. Provement_   Date _September 1, 1997_

(The annexure referred to in the memorandum is not set out here. It is a fairly complete drawing with a plan and elevation. It sets out the dimensions, shape, and appearance of the alteration and includes notes on materials and finishes desired by Homer. It is sufficiently detailed to enable Archie to draw the plan.)

Assume the same facts as stated earlier: Archie allegedly made an oral undertaking that the alteration could be done for less than $20,000 and said that if he was wrong, he would waive his fee. After the plans are drawn and bids obtained, it becomes clear that the alteration cannot be built for less than $25,000. Based on Archie's promise during negotiations, Homer claims that he is entitled to a refund of the fee. The evidence that he offers relates to a parol agreement that has been *omitted* from an apparently integrated writing. Under the "four corners" test, evidence of the promise would certainly be excluded. The writing appears comprehensive. Not only does it set out all the terms one could reasonably think of as necessary for the transaction, but it specifically states in clause 3 that the parties intend it to reflect their entire agreement. This is called a **merger clause** because it "merges" all the terms into the writing. Provided that the writing does appear to be complete, a merger clause removes any doubt over integration under the "four corners" test. Furthermore, the payment clause is clear enough to convey a plain meaning, so Homer cannot convincingly argue that the proffered evidence is needed to clarify any ambiguity or vagueness in the language used.

Even under the more flexible approach favored in contemporary law, Homer is not likely to have much success in his attempt to introduce evidence of the oral promise. The apparent intent to integrate the agreement in the writing carries considerable weight, and Homer cannot explain why he signed a writing that has a merger clause and makes no reference to the alleged promise. Although a merger clause is not given quite as much deference under the contextual approach, it still carries great weight as an articulation of the parties' intention to execute an exclusive writing. Its influence may be diminished if it is a standard term, tucked away in a field of boilerplate, but Archie's form is not that dense.

If the writing did not contain the merger clause, the question of integration would be harder to resolve because the intent to integrate is not as clear. A stricter approach would probably still point in the direction of total integration, because the writing seems to be complete on its face, in that it apparently contains all the terms needed for the transaction. A looser test may be more receptive to Homer's evidence, because there is no clearly expressed intent to integrate and this particular issue is not addressed in the writing at all. Nevertheless, there is something fishy about Homer's allegation: The writing is not very long and complicated, so the omission of this rather significant and unusual term is glaring. If it was really agreed to, surely it would have been recorded in the writing. (This illustrates the inquiry suggested by the "might naturally be omitted" test of Restatement Second and its UCC analog, the "certainly would have been included" test.) In a sense, Homer's allegation lacks credibility, and this may affect the court's decision to admit the evidence. As noted earlier, although ultimate credibility is for the jury, the court's decision to admit the evidence is also based in part on a determination of plausibility.

The above example illustrates the use of the parol evidence rule when a term is completely omitted from the written memorial of agreement. To illustrate the application of the rule when the term is included in the writing, although it may be ambiguous, change the facts of the example as follows: Assume that the memorandum contains all the provisions set out above as well as the following additional clause relating to the refund: "Archie undertakes that he will design the alteration so that it can be built for a total cost not to exceed $20,000, failing which Archie will refund the fee of $1,500 paid by Homer." Archie completes the plans. The cheapest bid for the construction that Homer is able to find from a competent builder is for $19,500. Nevertheless, Homer demands a refund of the fee on the grounds that the parties meant by "total cost" the combined amount of the building cost and Archie's fee. This would place the total cost at $21,000. Homer seeks to testify about a conversation with Archie during negotiations in which he expressed this meaning and Archie agreed to it. Of course, Archie now denies any such conversation and objects to the admission of the testimony as parol evidence. On its face, the clause seems to deal only with the total cost of building—so it seems not to cover the architect's fee, which is paid separately in advance. However, even a court that favors a "four corners" approach may balk at finding such clarity in the plain language of the writing. A court that is willing to consider extrinsic evidence would surely find Homer's evidence pertinent. It does suggest an ambiguity that, while not necessarily obvious from the language of the writing, is at least not entirely at odds with it. The court could conclude that even if the parties intended to integrate their agreement in the writing, they did not succeed in doing so because they failed to express their intentions clearly. The ambiguity undermines the completeness of the written memorandum, and it cannot really be thought of as integrated on this issue. It must be stressed again that even if the court recognizes the relevance of the evidence and admits it as pertinent to the proper interpretation of the writing, the final decision on whether to believe Homer or Archie will ultimately be made by the factfinder.

§12.8   Distinguishing Consistency from Contradiction

The determination that the writing is not a total integration is not the end of the judge's admissibility inquiry. The next question to be decided is whether the proffered evidence fits in with what has been written. If it supplements or explains the writing, it should be allowed in, but if it clashes and cannot be reconciled with the writing, it must be excluded. Without attempting to cover all situations that may arise, the following diagram attempts to represent the possible range of parol evidence that may be offered to supplement or explain a writing that has been found not to be fully integrated, and the court's likely response to that evidence:

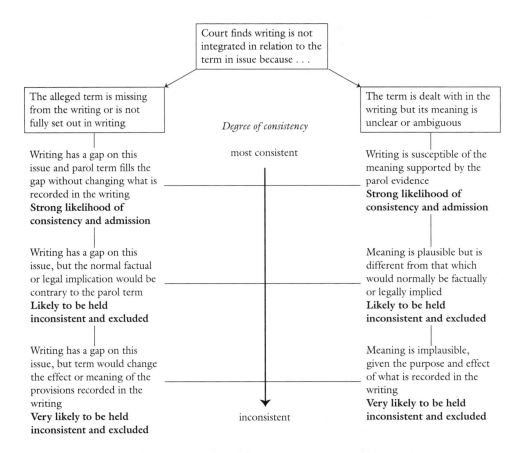

Inconsistency is easy to identify when the parol evidence seeks to establish a term or meaning that is the antithesis of what is recorded in the writing, or at least it provides for something that *cannot be reconciled with the terms expressed in the writing.* For example, say that the contract between Homer and Archie was silent on the question of when payment would be made, but it did have a provision stating that Homer would be entitled to a refund of the $1,500 paid if Archie did not complete the plans by the due date. It would be inconsistent with the writing for Homer to allege a parol agreement that payment was due only on completion of the plans, because this cannot be reconciled with the refund term. However, it would not appear to be contradictory to the writing for Homer to offer parol evidence that the parties agreed to payment, not on signing but two weeks after signing. This is reconcilable with the refund term and with what is expressed about payment. However, even here, there could be a more subtle inconsistency. Even though an alleged parol term does not contradict anything expressed in the writing, it could still be in conflict with the normal legal or factual implications of the contract. Say that it is common usage in contracts for architectural services that the fee must be paid immediately upon execution of the contract. This trade usage will normally be incorporated into the contract unless the parties have made it clear that they intend a different rule to govern this transaction. Therefore, parol evidence of a term providing for payment two weeks after signing conflicts with the usual import of the writing by contradicting a term that arises from the silence on that point. Some courts find inconsistency only if the express words of the writing are contradicted, but other courts look beyond this to implied terms.

If the meaning of the writing is *unclear or ambiguous,* its meaning may be explained by parol evidence, but again, the proffered evidence must be reconcilable with what has been written. For example, it seems that there could be an ambiguity in the term "total cost" in Homer's contract with Archie, because it is not clear if this phrase was intended to include Archie's fee. Therefore parol evidence that it was intended to include the fee is reconcilable with the language expressed in the writing. However, the mere fact that the phrase is ambiguous would not allow Homer to testify that the parties agreed to a figure of $18,000, because this cannot be reconciled with the existing language. Although the ambiguity may compromise the apparent integration of the writing, it does not give Homer carte blanche to offer evidence at odds with a reasonable interpretation of the meaning of what has been written.

§12.9 The Effect of the Rule on Evidence of Trade Usage, Course of Dealing, and Course of Performance

The formulation of the rule in both UCC §2.202 and Restatement Second §213 refers only to parol terms that were allegedly agreed to between the parties during the interaction leading up to execution of the writing. Although the Restatement does not expressly exclude course of dealing or performance and trade usage from the rule, it does not appear to cover them. UCC §2.202(a) goes further by specifically permitting an otherwise integrated agreement to be supplemented by evidence of course of dealing, trade usage, and course of performance.

This suggests the argument that testimony of a course of dealing or performance or of trade usage is not parol evidence at all. It therefore should be admitted without restriction and evaluated by the jury to determine if it is part of the contract. This approach is more readily explained when a **course of performance** is concerned, because it necessarily takes place after the writing has been executed.[2] However, a **course of dealing** and a **trade usage** are

---

2. Furthermore, if evidence is offered to show a course of performance rather than to claim a modification of the contract, its purpose is merely to serve as evidence of the parties' intent at the time of contracting. It therefore should not be affected by a provision in the writing (discussed in section 12.12) that bars oral modifications.

facts in existence at the time of contracting, so are stronger candidates for the rule. Despite the impression created by UCC §2.202(a), the general assumption is that the rule does apply to such evidence. The best approach is therefore to treat it as being subject to the rule, but to recognize that it is parol evidence treated with particular favor and given much more weight than understandings arising from negotiations or communications between the parties. Specially favorable treatment of a course of dealings or a usage is justified because it is more credible than evidence of negotiations and communications. It is shown by objective evidence and is less vulnerable to self-serving perjury.

UCC §2.202 states that evidence of usage, course of dealings, or course of performance is admissible to explain or supplement a writing *even if it is intended as a final expression* of agreement. That is, although a writing may appear to be integrated and may have a merger clause, the court should not exclude this evidence. This makes sense if the writing does not address the matter covered by the extrinsic evidence, because unless the parties express a contrary intent, they are assumed to contract in light of their own and the market's customary practices and to take them for granted. Therefore, one would not normally expect to find such customary understandings articulated in the writing.

However, if the parties did truly intend the writing to be a final expression of their agreement, the admission of any extrinsic evidence defeats their purpose. If the court follows an approach that places strong reliance on the "four corners" of the writing, a detailed and apparently complete document, preferably with a merger clause, may persuade the court to exclude evidence of any course of dealing or trade usage not incorporated into it. However, this may not be enough for a court with a more flexible approach to integration, particularly if the transaction is a sale of goods. To such a court, if the usage or course of dealing can be reconciled with the writing, it will be admitted to explain or supplement it unless the writing expresses a clear intent to exclude it. Therefore, if the parties really mean to exclude a usage or course of dealing, they should not rely on an apparent integration with a general merger clause, but should ensure that their intent is made plain by express written terms.

§12.10   Exceptions to the Parol Evidence Rule: Evidence to Establish Grounds for Avoidance or Invalidity, or to Show a Condition Precedent

The primary purpose of the parol evidence rule is to keep spurious or irrelevant evidence from the factfinder, but there is always a danger that it may be used to exclude truthful evidence of genuine agreement that was, for some reason, not encompassed within the writing. If the parol evidence relates to an alleged term that was in fact agreed to but is not reflected in a completely integrated writing or is not consistent with what was written, the party seeking to present the evidence is out of luck. By failing to ensure the accuracy of the writing, that party exposed itself to the risk of not being able to prove the term.

However, in some situations, this result may be too harsh, and may play into the hands of an unscrupulous operator who has deliberately taken advantage of the other party. To cater for such situations, there is a well-recognized exception to the rule that permits the introduction of parol evidence to show **fraud, duress, mistake, and other bases for invalidating or avoiding the contract.** The exception creates the risk that the parol evidence tendered to show mistake or misconduct may itself be perjured, thereby defeating the rule's purpose of protecting the integrity of a final writing. However, this risk is seen as necessary to ensure that the rule is not used as a means of defeating a party's right to avoidance.

Along similar lines, parol evidence is also admissible to show that **a fact recited in a writing is false.** Therefore, if the first clause of the memorandum executed by Homer and Archie stated, "In consideration for $1,500 paid by Homer, Archie agrees to draw plans . . . ," Archie would be permitted to introduce evidence that the money was never in fact paid. The purpose of this, of course, is to prevent Homer from evading his payment obligation and to allow Archie to recover what is due. The parol evidence turns the recital of consideration into an implied promise to pay. You may remember from section 7.8 that parties sometimes use a false recital of consideration in an attempt to validate gifts. That is, Archie may have agreed to draw the plans for free, and the parties merely recited the fact of payment to make it appear as if Archie received consideration for his promise. In this situation, although the parol evidence does not exclude evidence of nonpayment, the circumstances may make it appropriate to estop Archie from denying receipt of the payment.

Another exception to the rule permits parol evidence to be admitted to show that the **agreement was subject to a condition.** Conditions are explained more fully in Chapter 16. For the present, it is sufficient to understand that the parties may reach agreement on an exchange of performances, but provide that one or both parties' performance obligation will take effect only if a future uncertain event occurs (or does not occur). For example, say that when Archie and Homer were negotiating their contract, Archie told Homer that he was waiting to hear if he had secured a contract to supervise the construction of an office building in another city, and if he got that contract he would have to leave town for a year and could not take on Homer's project. The parties therefore signed the memorandum subject to the oral understanding that their contract was contingent on Archie not being awarded the other contract. Archie is then awarded the other contract and seeks to escape his obligation to Homer by testifying to the oral condition.

If the court finds the writing to be an integration, the parol evidence rule would normally exclude this testimony. However, because the testimony relates to a condition precedent to Archie's performance, the rule does not apply. This exception has long been recognized by courts and is reflected in Restatement Second §217. Comment *b* to §217 seeks to rationalize it on the basis that if a condition exists, the writing cannot be said to be integrated. This is rather flimsy reasoning, which could just as well be applied to any other alleged term. A point of distinction could be that if a contract is subject to a condition, no obligations come into existence unless the condition is met. However, this is not a convincing rationale either, because a contract subject to a condition precedent is a contract nevertheless. There is no reason to treat the allegation of a parol condition with any less suspicion than some other term claimed to have been left out of the writing. Nevertheless, the exception is well-established.

§12.11   The "Collateral Agreement" Rule

Evidence is not subject to the parol evidence rule if it relates, not directly to the subject matter of the agreement reflected in the writing, but to some collateral agreement. Although this is sometimes called an exception to the rule, it is not really an exception at all, but simply follows from an application of the general principles of the rule: It is based on the determination that the collateral agreement is **sufficiently distinct from the scope of the writing** that it was **not integrated into it,** and that the subject matter of the collateral agreement is **consistent** with the writing.

The collateral agreement rule developed during the period when the "four corners" approach was more firmly followed, and it was one of the means of softening its rigors. The rule still exists, but the broadening of the scope of inquiry under the contextual approach has tended to meld the concept of collateral agreement into the more general inquiry into integration and consistency. Even when the writing is an apparent integration, it may appear that agreement on an ancillary or related matter could conceivably have been made separately. That is, the alleged parol terms cover a matter distinct enough that it does not appear to be included in the integration, it is consistent with what has been written, and it logically could have been agreed to outside the writing.

How can one tell if a parol term is sufficiently separate that it could conceivably be a collateral agreement? Traditionally, courts have focused on whether its *subject matter and consideration can be separately identified,* and Restatement Second §216(2)(a) and Comment *c* acknowledges this test. An alternative more general approach is that discussed in section 12.7. The court evaluates the plausibility of the assertion of separate agreement by asking if it would have been rational and expected for the parties to agree to the term outside of the writing. That is, whether (in the restatement formulation) the term might naturally be omitted or (in the UCC formulation), whether it certainly would have been included in the writing if agreed to.

It is one thing to identify the focus of a test, but quite another to achieve consistent results with it. The problem with the collateral agreement concept is that the question of whether an agreement is collateral is quite relative. It depends on the way in which the court views the relationship between the writing and the parol term. For example, when Archie and Homer made their written contract for the drawing of the plans, they also orally agreed that after the plans were completed and a builder was hired, Archie would supervise the construction of the alteration for a fee of five percent of the building costs. One court could see the oral supervision contract as collateral to the written contract for the plans. It has its own consideration, it deals with a distinct subject, and it might rationally be made separately. However, another court may see it differently: The right to supervise the construction is much more valuable than the drafting of the plans and would surely have been an important incentive to Archie in accepting the drafting work. Therefore, if the parties had agreed to it, surely they would have provided for it in the writing. The fact that it is not mentioned suggests that it was never agreed to.

§12.12   Restrictions on Oral Modification

As stated before, the parol evidence rule does not exclude testimony relating to agreements made after the writing. These are not part of the environment in which the writing was executed, and they cannot be superseded by it. However, the parties may wish to avoid disputes over possible future allegations of oral modification, and may therefore insert a **"no oral modification" clause** in the writing, stating that no modification will be binding unless written and signed by both parties. Such clauses are difficult to enforce because courts do not usually consider that the parties can effectively restrict in advance their right to modify orally. The parties' power to modify the contract must include the power to modify the "no oral modification" clause, and the fact that they made an oral modification in itself indicates that they did so. Therefore, courts are generally willing to admit evidence of an alleged oral modification despite the existence of the restriction in the writing, and to leave it to the jury to decide whether the modification was in fact made.

UCC §2.209(2) appears to change this approach by expressly recognizing the effectiveness of "no oral modification" clauses. However, the recognition is half-hearted because §2.209(4) provides that even if the later oral modification is ineffective because the original contract requires written modification, the attempt at oral modification may still operate as a waiver of rights under the original contract. Under §2.209(5) the waiver is generally effective. It can only be retracted in relation to future performance if it has not been detrimentally relied upon by the other party, and it cannot be retracted to the extent that it covers performance that has already been rendered.

EXAMPLES

1. Ann Cestor owns a farm by a lake in a beautiful valley. It has been in her family since her great-grandfather's time and she had operated it since her youth. For the last couple of years, her granddaughter Bertha Wright had been helping her on the farm. Bertha had often expressed interest in buying it, and last year Ann decided to sell it to her. They settled on a price and Ann called her lawyer to have the contract drawn up. When the document was ready, Ann and Bertha drove into town to sign it. On the way, Ann told Bertha tales of the hardships that her forebears had endured in taming the land, and expressed how important the farm was to her. She made Bertha promise that she would never allow the farm to pass into the hands of a stranger as long as there was a family member who was willing to buy it from her. Bertha said that she could not imagine ever selling the old place, but assured Ann that if she ever had to sell, she would contact all surviving family members and give them the right of first refusal.

Upon arriving at the lawyer's office the parties were presented with a routine land sale contract that described the property and stated the price and a standard set of terms about the discharge of encumbrances and transfer of title. As the parties signed the document, Ann said to Bertha, "Remember what you promised, now," and Bertha replied, "Of course, Grandma."

A year later, a developer visited Bertha at the farm and told her of a wonderful plan to build a world-class golf course with a resort and condos on the farm and adjacent lakefront land. The developer offered to buy the farm for a handsome price including cash and shares in the project. Bertha accepted with alacrity. When Ann heard about this, a terrible confrontation took place between grandmother and granddaughter. Ann claimed that Bertha had breached their contract, and demanded that Bertha resell the farm to her. In response, Bertha waved the memorandum of agreement in Ann's face and yelled, "You show me where this says I cannot sell it to anyone that I please!" Does Bertha have a point?

2. Klaus Merger owned two adjoining quarter-acre lots. One had a house on it and the other, overgrown and neglected, had been used by Klaus as a dumping ground for assorted bits of junk, including a couple of broken-down cars. A few months ago Klaus placed the quarter-acre with the house on the market. Andy Gration expressed interest in buying it and negotiations ensued. Andy eventually agreed to buy it for the asking price on condition that Klaus cleared up the adjacent lot and removed all the junk. Klaus agreed to do this.

Klaus then produced a standard-form agreement of sale that he had procured from a legal stationer. The form had the usual provisions found in transactions of this kind, with blank spaces for details such as the property description and price. It also had a large blank at the end of the form, headed "Additional terms." One of its standard terms was a merger clause, stating "This is the entire agreement between the parties. No agreements or representations have been made save for those stated herein." Klaus filled out all the blanks except the last one headed "Additional terms," and the parties signed it. The form made no reference to Klaus being obliged to clear the adjacent lot.

Of course, Klaus never bothered to clear the lot and now denies ever agreeing to do so. Does Andy have any prospect of proving and enforcing the oral agreement?

3. Di Aquiri owns a tavern. Margie Rita runs a small, exclusive distillery that makes a variety of health-conscious, socially responsible, non-alcoholic versions of popular liquors. Di entered into a written contract with Margie under which Di bought 100 bottles of Margie's "fat-free, sugar-free, sodium-free,[3] non-alcoholic, non-animal-tested, all natural faux tequila." In addition to this description of the goods, the writing stated the names and addresses of the parties, the price of "$10 per bottle, subject to discount for cash," payment terms (30 days after delivery) and delivery date. It also contained a merger clause stating that the writing was intended to be "the complete, exclusive and final expression of all terms agreed to by the parties." Both parties signed the writing and Margie delivered the liquor on due date.

Consider how the parol evidence rule would affect the following different disputes that arose after delivery.

(a) Upon delivery, Di gave Margie's driver a check for $900, this being the stated contract price of $1,000 less a ten percent discount for early payment. Margie refuses to allow Di a ten percent discount. She says that the parties discussed the amount of the discount orally, and she told Di that it was five percent. Di claims that they agreed to a ten percent discount.

(b) Di did not pay the driver. Five days later she sent a check for $900 in payment, less a ten percent discount. Margie's problem is not with the amount of the discount, but with Di's right to it at all. She says that "cash payment" means cash on delivery, so Di is not entitled to any discount. Di says that Margie told her orally that payment within a week of delivery qualifies as cash. Margie denies ever discussing the question.

---

3. It is also taste-free, but the agreement did not specify that.

(c)   After delivery Di, who is very fussy about the quality of what she serves to her customers, conducted her usual chemical analysis of the faux tequila. She found that it has traces of fat and sugar (about 0.5 percent of each). Di's tests also revealed that the faux tequila contains about 0.08 percent alcohol. She wishes to reject the goods as nonconforming to the contract and to get her money back. Margie claims that she is not entitled to do this for two reasons. First, Margie has sold liquor to Di in the past with similar small traces of fat, sugar, and alcohol, and Di has never objected before. Second, it is widely accepted in the make-believe-liquor industry that one can never completely remove the good stuff, and beverages described as free of a substance may acceptably contain up to one percent of it.

4. Gordon Bleu, a chef who owns and operates a restaurant, decided to begin serving game birds to his customers. He found a recipe for pheasant and checked the catalog of his regular supplier, Fairest Fowls, Inc., to see what it cost. The catalog showed "regular" pheasant for $5.00 per pound, and "plump deluxe" pheasant for $12.50 per pound. Gordon decided that "regular" pheasant would be fine, and he called Fairest Fowls and placed an order for 50 birds.

A couple of days later Fairest Fowls delivered the birds, accompanied by its written delivery invoice. The invoice contained the parties' names and addresses, the date, and the statement "Delivered as per order, 50 regular pheasants @ $5.00 per pound. Cash on delivery." The invoice was signed by a representative of Fairest Fowls. Gordon signed the form as requested and paid the driver.[4]

Gordon prepared the birds exactly in accordance with his recipe, but they were tough and uneatable. Gordon complained to Fairest Fowls, which explained that it used the word "regular" in its catalog to denote scrawny birds useful only for soup, and that the more expensive "plump deluxe" variety had to be used if the flesh was to be eaten. Fairest Fowls said that "everyone knew this about pheasants," and it was surprised that Gordon, as a trained chef, was unaware of the distinction.

---

4. If this example sounds familiar, it is because it is based on Example 2 of Chapter 10. That example involved the interpretation of an oral contract. In the present example, the contract is recorded in the invoice, which is a written memorial of agreement for parol evidence purposes. The goal of this example is to allow you to consider the parol evidence issue that was absent from Example 2 of Chapter 10. After working through this example, you may find it helpful to review Example 2 of Chapter 10 to compare interpretational issues in the absence of the parol evidence rule. (Note that some of the facts concerning the evidence have been simplified in this example.)

Gordon insists that there is no reason why he should have understood "regular" in the sense used by Fairest Fowls and he points out that the dictionary meaning of "regular" is "usual, normal or customary." Fairest Fowls claims that it can produce several experts in the restaurant trade who would attest to the fact that "regular" pheasants are commonly understood to be suitable only for soup.

If Gordon and Fairest Fowls cannot settle their dispute and Gordon decides to sue Fairest Fowls for the return of his money, would Fairest Fowls be able to introduce the testimony of its expert witnesses over Gordon's objection?

5. Beverly Hill, a movie producer, offered a leading role in a new movie to Holly Wood, an actress. The parties met with their lawyers and agents and spent the full morning negotiating the terms of the contract. By noon they had reached agreement. Their attorneys spent the rest of the day drafting the written agreement.

The parties met again on the following morning and signed the agreement. After signing, they remained in Beverly's office to celebrate making the deal. As she was sipping her champagne, Holly said, "You know, I am really unhappy about that advance of $2 million that you agreed to pay me next week. I think that it should be higher, say $2.5 million. After all, I have to live until the box office receipts come in." Beverly replied, "No problem, I'll send you a check for $2.5 million instead." The parties did not amend the figure of $2 million in the written contract, and this agreement was not otherwise recorded in writing. The next week, Beverly sent a check of $2 million to Holly as specified in the written agreement. She denies ever agreeing to pay more. The written agreement does not have a "no oral modification" clause.

Holly immediately sued for the additional $500,000. Beverly applied for summary judgment on the ground that the written contract clearly calls for a payment of $2 million, and no parol evidence can be tendered by Holly to support her claim for more money. Should Beverly be granted summary judgment?

EXPLANATIONS

1. Yes, faithless Bertha does have a point, because if Ann decides to sue on the basis of Bertha's undertaking, she is confronted with two hurdles. She must first convince the judge to admit her evidence of the oral term that qualified the writing, and if she succeeds, she must then convince the jury that such a term was in fact agreed to. A written memorandum of agreement was executed, and Ann seeks to testify about a prior and contemporaneous oral agreement (In this case, both prior and contemporaneous oral agreements were made, because the oral understanding was not only made on the car journey, but was actually confirmed orally while the writing was being

signed.) Bertha may object to admission of the evidence under the parol evidence rule, and the judge must determine as a question of law whether the evidence is admissible. If not, it is excluded and the jury does not hear it, leaving Ann with no case. If Ann can jump this hurdle by satisfying the judge that the evidence is not barred by the rule and is admissible, she may then testify about the conversation before the jury. The next hurdle is to convince the jury that the conversation occurred. If Bertha denies it, Ann will only win if the jury believes her over Bertha.

In the first stage of this process, the judge considers two questions. The first concerns the issue of integration and involves two possibilities: First, the writing may have been intended as the full and final expression of the parties' agreement (that is, a total or complete integration). If it is, parol evidence is inadmissible. Even if the writing is not a total integration, the alleged parol term may concern a subject that is itself fully and unambiguously dealt with in the agreement, so that it is intended as a complete expression on this issue (that is, the agreement is a partial integration that fully and finally sets out this term). If so, the evidence is likewise excluded.

If the writing is neither a complete integration, nor a partial integration concerning the subject of the alleged parol term, the judge goes to the next level of the preliminary inquiry to decide the issue of consistency. The parol evidence may be admitted to the extent that it is consistent with what has been recorded in the writing. Thus, the evidence may explain an ambiguity or vagueness, or it may fill a gap, but it may not contradict the writing.

Let us apply these principles to the present facts.

A. Integration

There is no question of partial integration in this case, because the writing does not deal at all with Bertha's right to transfer the property. Therefore, if there is any integration at all, it must be based on the finding that the parties intended the writing to fully express everything that they agreed, so that no additional undertakings were made. Under the strictly objectivist "four corners" test, integration is found if the writing appears complete and unambiguous, and there is no obvious gap or inadequacy. Although we are not given the terms in detail, the writing is described as a routine land sale contract with all the usual terms. At face value, it seems final and complete and would be perceived as integrated under this test.

The contextual approach to integration, more favored by modern courts, goes beyond the face of the writing and evaluates contextual evidence to decide the question of integration. The only contextual evidence here apart from the parol evidence itself (Ann's testimony of the conversation) is the fact that the parties were close relations who had lived together for some years and were members of the family that had owned the farm for generations. This has a bearing on the question of integration. If the parties were strangers, dealing at arms length, one would expect a term of this importance to be stated in the apparently complete writing. However, the trust and perceived mutual sentiment engendered by the family relationship might plausibly explain why the parties in this case would be happy to allow the writing to reflect only the routine legal formalities and to omit this more personal aspect of their agreement. The point, as expressed in Restatement Second §216(b) is whether the circumstances are such that the term might naturally be omitted from the writing.

In *Masterson v. Sine*, 436 P.2d 561 (Cal. 1968), the majority of the court found this test to be satisfied under circumstances considerably less sympathetic than those of the present case. Masterson and his wife owned a ranch. They sold it to the Sines, his sister and her husband, subject to an option to repurchase. Masterson later became bankrupt and his trustee attempted to exercise the repurchase option to bring the property into Masterson's estate for the benefit of his creditors. The Sines resisted this, claiming that the parties intended the property to remain in the family and had orally agreed at the time of the sale that the option was personal to the Mastersons and could not be transferred to or exercised by anyone else. The majority found that such an agreement might naturally be made outside of the writing in a family transaction. The dissent criticized this as too loose and open-ended, and argued that it would have been a simple matter for the parties to have included the term in the writing had they agreed to it. The allegation of a parol restriction on transfer was particularly suspicious, given that its effect would be to keep the property out of Masterson's bankruptcy estate.

B. Consistency

If the judge finds that the writing is not fully integrated, Ann's evidence is admissible provided that it does not contradict the writing. The majority in *Masterson* adopted the approach that unless the alleged parol term directly contradicts a term expressed in the writing, it is consistent. On the basis of this test, Ann's evidence does not contradict the writing, which is silent on the question of the family's right of first refusal.

The dissent in *Masterson* argued that consistency must be determined not merely on the basis of what is expressed in the writing, but also in light of terms implied in the agreement. In *Masterson*, this test would have excluded evidence of the term restricting transfer because the usual implication of law is that contract rights are fully transferable unless the agreement specifies otherwise. The restriction on transfer did in fact contradict the import of the writing. The same would be true in Ann's case, because the law's usual implication is that in the absence of an express restriction in the contract, the buyer acquires all rights in the property, including the power to dispose of it as she desires.

The majority's test more readily allows evidence to be evaluated by the factfinder and would enable Ann to go to trial on the dispute. The dissent's approach results in a stricter standard for admission, and would mean that Ann may never get past an application for summary judgment. Courts are divided on these two views of consistency, but one can probably assume that if a court found Bertha to be a sympathetic party with a plausible explanation for the omission, it would be likely the find for her as a matter of law so that she has the opportunity to place her evidence before the jury.

2. The analysis of this problem is the same as that in Example 1, but Andy's problem is worse than Ann's. To begin with, there is a merger clause in the writing, and an unfilled blank suitable for inserting a term like this. Courts tend to be wary of standard-form merger clauses, because they may not have been conspicuous or understood, but this does not mean that such clauses are invariably treated as ineffective. A signatory has a duty to read the document before signing it, and one who fails to exercise that duty cannot expect relief unless the bargaining circumstances compel the conclusion of unfair imposition. (More on this in section 13.12.) There is nothing in the facts of this case to indicate that Andy could not be expected to read and understand the writing or that Klaus had a bargaining advantage that allowed him to impose unfairly one-sided terms.

On a "four corners" test the apparent completeness of the document, the unfilled blank space, and the merger clause will surely lead to the conclusion of integration. Even on a contextual approach, the terms of the writing, including the merger clause, are taken seriously. However, the contextual approach at least gives Andy a shot at explaining why the apparent integration was not intended as such. In other words, Andy is given the opportunity to persuade the court that despite the existence of an apparently complete and final writing, this term might naturally have been agreed to separately. On these facts, this does not seem like an easy task. One basis for making this argument is that a standard form was used which does not admit the addition of special terms tailored to the transaction. However, that will not work here because there was space for its insertion on the form. Family connection or some other relationship may explain an informal approach to some special term of a contract, as discussed in Example 1, but Andy had no prior connection with Klaus.

The only conceivable argument that Andy could make is that the agreement to clear the lot is so distinct from the sale that it is in fact a collateral oral agreement, not intended to be integrated into the written sale contract. This argument is recognized under both the "four corners" approach and the contextual approach—but the "four corners" test is, as usual, more strictly focused on the language of the writing, while the contextual approach may look at surrounding circumstances to decide if the lot-clearing agreement might naturally be made as a separate collateral contract. To be viewed as collateral to the writing, the oral agreement must usually deal with a distinct matter and have a severable consideration. Although the first aspect may be satisfied because the lot to be cleared is a neighboring property not subject to the sale, there is no separate consideration provided for in the oral agreement. It sounds as if Klaus induced Andy to pay his asking price by giving an undertaking to clear the lot, but there no evidence from which one could identify what portion of the price (if any) is attributable to this. If a separate consideration had been agreed to and the obligation to clear the lot had been made as a collateral agreement, one would expect the consideration also to be provided for and identified separately. As it is, the writing merely sets out the full price without qualification. In the end, the question of whether the oral agreement was collateral is resolved by an assessment of the plausibility of the allegation that the parties really did agree to a term omitted from the writing—that it might naturally be made as a separate contract. Andy seems to fall short of making a convincing case.

In *Mitchell v. Lath*, 160 N.E. 646 (N.Y. 1928), the seller orally agreed to remove an unsightly ice house on land adjacent to the property purchased by the buyer, but this undertaking was not included in the written contract of sale. The writing appeared comprehensive and it included a number of terms ancillary to the sale. Therefore, the court disagreed with the buyer's argument that this was a separate agreement that might ordinarily be made separately. It was closely enough related to the subject matter of the contract that had it been agreed to, one would expect to find it in the writing. The dissent took the opposite view, based on the fact that the purpose of the writing was to convey the property that had been bought, and the ice house was on adjacent land. The dissent felt that the evidence did show that the oral agreement was made, so even if the writing integrated the terms of the sale, there was no reason to believe that the parties intended it to preclude recognition of this ancillary oral undertaking. These different perceptions of the intended scope of the integration demonstrate that it can be quite difficult to predict if a judge will find an oral agreement to be collateral to an apparently complete writing. Inevitably, the determination depends on the strength of the judge's conviction that the oral agreement was made.

3. This example involves a sale of goods, so UCC §2.202, the Article 2 version of the parol evidence rule, applies. In general principle, it is substantially similar to the contemporary common law rule, so many courts would not answer these questions differently had this not been a sale of goods. The writing in this case is apparently intended as a complete integration. It contains all the terms essential to a sales contract and it has a merger clause. Notwithstanding, it is not a watertight final and complete memorial of agreement, so most of the parol evidence suggested by the questions should be admissible.

3(a). Despite the attempt at integration, the parties did not fully express their agreement. They provided for a discount but failed to specify its amount. With regard to this term, the writing cannot be a complete and final expression of their agreement, so evidence of what they agreed orally is admissible to supplement it. Note that neither denies making an oral agreement, but they argue about what was agreed. Neither party's evidence is inconsistent with the writing, so it will all be admitted and the factfinder will have to decide whose version of the discussion is correct.

3(b). Although the amount of the discount was omitted, the existence of that gap does not give Di license to produce parol evidence on other terms on which the writing is the full and final expression. On a "four corners" test, the agreement is apparently integrated on this issue, and Di would probably prevail on the plain meaning of the word "cash." However, Comment 1 to §2.202 makes it clear that the "four corners" approach is not to be used and that meaning must be determined in the commercial context in which the words were used. This does not mean that we abandon all restrictions on admissibility merely because one of the parties is willing to testify as to a meaning different from the obvious ordinary meaning of the writing. The contextual evidence must point to a meaning of which the writing is reasonably susceptible—it must persuade the court that there is some basis for going beyond the apparent clarity of the writing. If not, the evidence should not be admitted because the party offering it has not shown that the apparently integrated writing suffers from an ambiguity or vagueness that renders the writing incomplete and in need of explanation. (Alternatively, even if there is no integration, the contended meaning does not explain, but contradicts, the writing.)

One of the best-known examples of a broad approach to ambiguity is not a UCC case, but an opinion on the common law rule by California Chief Justice Traynor (who was also responsible for the *Masterson* opinion discussed in Example 1). In *Pacific Gas & Electric Co. v. G. W. Thomas Drayage & Rigging Co.*, 442 P.2d 641 (Cal. 1968), the issue was whether an indemnity clause in a repair contract covered damage by the repairer to the customer's property or was intended only to hold the customer harmless for damage to third-party property. Although the contract on its face had no such limitation and provided generally for indemnity for all loss or damage, the repairer sought to offer evidence (including that of prior dealings) to prove that it was intended to cover only damage to third-party property. The trial court refused to admit the evidence because it found the language in the writing to be clear and unambiguous, but the Supreme Court criticized this approach, saying that words do not have an inherent meaning. What appears plain in the abstract may become ambiguous when viewed in light of contextual evidence that indicates a meaning to which the words may be reasonably susceptible.

In the present case, the only contextual evidence of the meaning of "cash" is the disputed parol evidence itself: Di's allegation about what was said during negotiations. This self-serving testimony is apparently not corroborated by more objective evidence, such as usage or course of dealing. In the absence of some indication that there is a common understanding or a practice between the parties that "cash" means credit of up to a week, it is difficult to reconcile Di's evidence with the word's normal meaning. Even under the more liberal rule of the UCC (and Restatement Second), the evidence should be excluded.

3(c). Margie is trying to establish both a course of dealing and a trade usage to show that her faux tequila conforms to the contract even though it has traces of fat, sugar, and alcohol. Section 2.202(a) makes it clear that even if a writing appears fully integrated and has a merger clause, evidence of usage and dealing should always be allowed to supplement or explain the writing. However, they may not contradict it. The rationale for this more liberal rule is twofold. First, parties normally take it for granted that this transaction is subject to well-established custom or their own prior practices, so they are unlikely to trouble spelling them out in the writing. Second, the evidence to establish these facts is objective and harder to make up than an account of what was said in negotiations. Therefore, unless the parties negate usages or prior understandings by clear wording (in which case the evidence would contradict the writing), they are assumed to apply despite the silence of an apparently complete agreement.

There is nothing in the writing to indicate that the parties deliberately excluded the usage or practice claimed by Margie, so the general merger clause does not keep out the evidence, and it is admissible unless it is inconsistent with the writing. The writing unqualifiedly describes the tequila is free of fat, sugar, and alcohol, so it could be argued that the writing is contradicted by testimony that small quantities of these substances are acceptable. This again raises the difficult question of deciding whether a qualification to an absolute undertaking is a supplementation or a contradiction. There is no sure dividing line, but courts tend to favor admission of this kind of objective evidence in cases of doubt, requiring quite strong wording of negation to exclude it. A classic example is *Columbia Nitrogen Corp. v. Royster Co.*, 451 F.2d 3 (4th Cir. 1971), in which the written contract provided for the purchase of a specific minimum tonnage of phosphate. The buyer failed to take the minimum and claimed that because of market uncertainties in the industry it was accepted in the trade that quantity specifications were mere projections. Prior transactions between the parties were also alleged to support that reading of the quantity term. The court of appeals held the evidence admissible, reversing the trial court's determination that it contradicted the writing. Do not forget that the decision to admit the evidence is just the first step in the process. Margie must then convince the factfinder that the course of dealing and trade usage did exist and that they support her position.

4. The issue here is the meaning of the word "regular." Gordon contends that its plain meaning is self-evident, but Fairest Fowls argues that it is

ambiguous if understood in light of trade usage. If Fairest Fowls is right, we need not be concerned about whether the parties expected the writing to be an integration. The ambiguity of the word means that, at least insofar as the quality of the pheasant is concerned, the writing is not a complete and final expression of what the parties agreed. Evidence may therefore be admitted to explain the meaning of "regular" provided that the evidence supports a meaning reconcilable with the writing.

A court adopting a "four corners" approach may be inclined to find that there is no ambiguity about "regular" in the context of the writing as a whole, and that it can only have the meaning contended by Gordon. However, such an approach is clearly not appropriate in a sale of goods, because UCC §2.202, Comment 1, rejects it and calls for consideration of the commercial context in establishing meaning. The evidence of trade usage will be admitted provided that it is consistent with the writing. As nothing else in the writing even remotely pertains to the quality of the pheasant, the only language that must be reconciled with the proffered evidence is the word "regular" itself. If looked at from the patterns of normal speech, it is hard to think of "regular" as meaning "old and scrawny." However, from the perspective of the trade in which the parties are engaged,[5] the evidence suggests that there is no inconsistency. That is, having decided that trade usage may support such an esoteric meaning, rendering the word ambiguous, we must necessarily conclude that the meaning is not inconsistent with the word.

Section 2.202 gives very strong credence to trade usage, which is presumed to enter the contract unless the parties clearly indicate a contrary intent. Therefore, §2.202 discourages application of the parol evidence rule to trade usage unless the intent to exclude the usage is unequivocally expressed. The strength of trade usage, and the likelihood that it will be found to be consistent with the writing in all but the most overwhelming cases of direct conflict, is illustrated by *Nanakuli Paving & Rock Co. v. Shell Oil Co.*, 664 F.2d 772 (9th Cir. 1981). The written contract between Shell, which supplied asphalt, and Nanakuli, a paver, stated that the price Nanakuli would pay Shell for asphalt purchases would be "Shell's posted price at the time of delivery." Nanakuli argued that this term was qualified by a trade usage, forming an unstated part of their agreement, that the supplier of asphalt would "price protect" its customer. This meant that when the customer committed itself to do work on the basis of the price prevailing at that time, Shell would supply the customer at that price, even if the posted price had increased by the time of delivery.

After finding that the trade usage did exist and did apply to the activities in which the parties were involved, the court held that the parol evidence rule

5. In Example 2 of Chapter 10, the issue of defining the trade and holding Gordon accountable for the usage was discussed. This issue is not duplicated here, and the facts indicate that the expert evidence covers the restaurant business, of which Gordon is a member.

did not exclude proof of it. Although the writing contained an apparently clear and unequivocal price term, pegging price at the time of delivery, the price protection term was not inconsistent with that. The only reasoning used by the court to support this conclusion was that the price protection term had been incorporated into the agreement by usage. This does suggest that the concept of consistency is very marginal when the evidence strongly supports the existence of the usage. A term qualifying a written provision that is absolute and unqualified does seem inconsistent with it, but this was not enough for the court. The conclusion must be that little short of an express disclaimer of the usage would have made it irreconcilable with the writing.

5. The alleged oral term for the payment of $2.5 million directly contradicts the clear and unambiguous provision in the writing for payment of $2 million. Whether or not the agreement is fully integrated, it does definitively express the amount of the advance, and there is no way in which the written and alleged oral terms can be reconciled by interpretation. Therefore, if the oral agreement is contemporaneous with the writing, evidence of it would be barred by the parol evidence rule. However, if the oral agreement was made subsequent to the writing, the parol evidence rule does not apply, and there is no provision in the agreement barring oral modifications. This example focuses on what is meant by a subsequent agreement for the purposes of the parol evidence rule. If we take a literal approach, the oral agreement was unquestionably made after the writing, and the evidence is admissible. However, such a technical distinction may lead to an absurd result that places too much emphasis on the sequence of events in a single interaction. The alleged amendment was made almost immediately after the execution of the writing, while the parties were still together following the meeting at which it was signed. If the parties really did agree to change the amount of the advance, it would have been easy and natural for them to alter the writing to reflect the change. The fact that the writing was not amended casts suspicion on the claim that the parties agreed to the change. (This argument would be even stronger if the parties' lawyers and agents were still present when the alleged oral agreement was made.)

This was the approach taken by the Superior Court in *Kehr Packages, Inc. v. Fidelity Bank*, 710 A.2d 1169 (Pa. 1998). The bank had agreed to finance the purchase of shares in a corporation. The closing of the transaction took all day and consisted of the signing of a number of documents. During the course of the closing the borrowers realized that they would need more funds than originally had been contemplated. After conferring privately with their attorney, they asked for an increase in the loan amount. The borrowers alleged that the bank agreed to an additional advance, but this was not reflected in the loan agreement or in any other document. The loan agreement had been signed before the request for further funds but prior to the end of the closing process, which then proceeded to its conclusion. The bank never advanced the additional funds, and the borrowers sued for breach of contract.

The trial court admitted the evidence of the oral agreement on the basis that it was subsequent to the writing and not covered by the parol evidence rule. This was reversed on appeal. The court said that the closing must be viewed as a single, ongoing transaction, and that it was artificial to focus on the fact that the loan agreement was signed before the alleged oral agreement. The alleged oral agreement therefore should be treated as contemporaneous with the writing and was barred by the parol evidence rule as a contradiction of the integrated writing. The court noted that the parties were sophisticated and legally represented. It would have been both easy and expected for them to change the writing to reflect any alteration in terms.

The facts in *Kehr Packages* make a stronger case for treating the alleged oral agreement as contemporaneous. The credit agreement was just one component of a complex financing transaction, and the parties were still in the process of executing various closing documents when they made the alleged oral agreement. Nevertheless, even in our case, the proximity in time and place between the writing and the claimed oral agreement suggest that the premise of the rule—that the writing can be fairly deemed to incorporate all that was agreed—should apply.

13

The Judicial Regulation of Improper Bargaining and of Violations of Law and Public Policy

§13.1 Introduction

The doctrines covered in this chapter and the next have at least one thing in common: They are all concerned with the courts' ability to refuse the enforcement of an apparent contract or a contractual provision that offends some basic public policy.

The public policies most widely involved are the two familiar fundamental policies of contract law: the **assent policy** inherent in **freedom of contract** and the policy of **protecting reliance** and ensuring the **security of transactions.** Contractual freedom encompasses not only the right to enter and have the state enforce consensual relationships, but also the right not to be bound in contract in the absence of meaningful voluntary assent. This right is constrained by the reliance policy that requires assent to be measured by objective and observable criteria that focus on the manifested intent of the parties rather than on their subjective states of mind. It is therefore possible that a party may be bound by appearing to assent to a transaction, even though she did not truly desire or intend to be bound.

However, the reliance policy does not demand an unquestioning accountability for the apparent meaning of words or actions. In committing a party to manifested intent, the objective test presupposes that the party exercised a sufficient degree of autonomy or at least that the other party had no reason to believe that she did not. This requires that the party making the manifestation was at liberty to choose whether or not to do so, and that she exercised that choice voluntarily. If her actions were induced by improper pressure or successful deception, or if she was mentally incapable of forming genuine intent, it would offend the policy of freedom of contract to hold her to the false manifestation of contractual intent. To the extent that the other party was responsible for or reasonably realized her inability to give genuine assent, the reliance policy is not undermined by refusal to enforce the contract. Therefore, the basic premise underlying most of the discussion in these two chapters is that the objective meaning of words and actions can only be treated as a valid indication of contractual assent if they are based on at least a *minimally acceptable degree of volition.* The tension between these goals of protecting autonomy and reliance may be represented as follows:

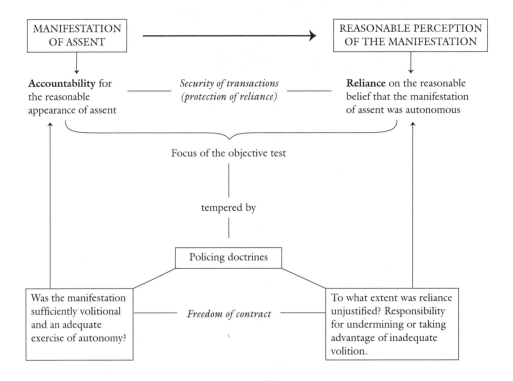

The topics centering around the policies of freedom of contract and the protection of reliance fall into one of two themes. Those dealt with in this chapter—misrepresentation, duress, undue influence and unconscionability—concern the problem of the undermining of a party's will by the oppressive or dishonest conduct of the other. In addition, this chapter concludes with a discussion of public policies beyond those underlying contract law, and examines the way in which other concerns of public policy may affect the validity and enforceability of an otherwise fully consensual and effective contract. The topics covered in Chapter 14 focus on the accountability for apparent assent by those whose ability to form contractual intent is hampered by immaturity or mental incapacity. The discussion in Chapter 14 implicates not only the contract policies of freedom of contract and the protection of reliance, but also the policy of protecting children and mentally disabled people from exploitation.

§13.2   The Objective Test and the Viability of Apparent Assent

The discussion of the objective test of assent in section 4.1 stressed that although contract is based on consensus, the law does not require a genuine subjective "meeting of the minds." The focus is on apparent assent, as it would reasonably be perceived by one party from the manifested words and actions of the other. This has to be the general rule, otherwise no one could ever rely on overt indications of assent, and the one party's reasonable expectation of agreement could be defeated by a showing that the other really did not mean what those indications reasonably conveyed.

The principal purpose of the objective test is therefore the protection of reasonable expectations. Although a consistent and unbending application of the test would have the merit of certainty, it could lead to great injustice. For example, Lilly Livered signed a memorandum of agreement to sell her casino to Attila "The Animal" Axehacker. She agreed to the sale because Attila shoved the muzzle of his revolver up her left nostril and indicated his intent to pull the trigger if a signature was not immediately forthcoming. No doubt the signature is a first-class manifestation of assent, but no judge (except for Judge "Greasy" Palmer, who was seen taking a brown paper bag from Attila the other day) would hold Lilly accountable for the reasonable import of her conduct. Not only should she not be held accountable for a manifestation of assent forced out of her, but Atilla was responsible for undermining her free will and cannot legitimately claim that he relied on her assent being volitional. That is, a rigid focus on Lilly's manifested assent—her signature—would serve neither justice nor the goals of contract law. Policing doctrines allow the court to go behind the appearance of assent in cases like this. The policing doctrine applicable in this particular example is duress because Attila induced Lilly's apparent assent by illegitimate threat. Other facts may satisfy the elements of one of the other doctrines discussed below. As a general observation, it can be said that all the doctrines are safety valves for the objective test, so that it cannot be used as a tool of oppression, deceit or advantage-taking.

The evil at which these doctrines aim is *improper behavior in the bargaining process:* trickery, pressure, or unfair persuasion that undermines the victim's free will. For this reason, the principal focus of the doctrines is on the *process of formation* rather than on the unfairness of the resulting terms, and even if the terms of the contract are reasonable, improper bargaining may render it unenforceable. For example, because the means used by Attila to induce assent are wrongful, it would not much matter that he had purchased the casino for a fair price and otherwise on fair terms. However, the *unfairness of the resulting exchange* can be a significant factor in the determination of enforceability. In a case where impropriety is not clearly established, the unfairness of the terms serves as evidence to bolster the claim of wrongful bargaining. Indeed, if the terms are outrageous enough, a court may require only a minimal showing of procedural impropriety as a basis for refusing enforcement.

§13.3   General Note on Remedy: Avoidance and Restitution or Adjustment of the Contract

The remedies available under the doctrines discussed here form another general thread that runs through this chapter. While there is some variation between them (noted in the discussion of each doctrine), the effect of a successful claim under any of these doctrines tends to be the same.

§13.3.1   *Avoidance and Restitution*

The usual effect of improper bargaining is to make the resulting contract **voidable** at the instance of the aggrieved party. A voidable contract must be distinguished from a **void** contract. If a contract is void (as it would be, for example, if one party failed to give consideration), it is a legal nullity—in fact it is not a contract at all, so the phrase "void contract" is anomalous. Therefore, neither party can sue to enforce the relationship. By contrast, a voidable contract is a valid contract that remains fully effective unless the aggrieved party elects to exercise the right to terminate it. ("Avoidance" is a term of art in contract law, and it is usually confined to situations in which a voidable contract is terminated by the aggrieved party.) In the above example, Lilly, as the victim of duress, has the right to avoid the contract. However, if despite her initial reluctance she now thinks that the transaction is attractive, she may choose not to avoid it. If she desires to keep it in force, Attila is bound. He cannot claim the contract's avoidability as a defense. That power belongs solely to Lilly. However, if the contract had been void, either party would have been able to seek relief on that basis.

The aggrieved party may use the right of avoidance **affirmatively,** for example, by suing for a declaratory judgment terminating the contract, or

defensively, by raising it as a defense when sued on the contract. When a contract is avoided, the general rule is that both parties are entitled to **restitution.** Any benefit received before avoidance by one party from the other must be returned. As the benefit was conferred under a contract that has been brought to an end, retention of the benefit would unjustly enrich the recipient, who no longer has any right to retain it. However, as discussed below, restitution may not be required from an aggrieved party if the benefit received provided no lasting enrichment.

§13.3.2 Excision or Modification of the Offending Term

Although avoidance of the entire contract is usually the remedy sought, in some cases the aggrieved party may prefer to keep the contract but to have its terms adjusted to remove the effects of the other party's improper bargaining. This alternative may not be possible when the problem affects the very basis of the contract, and it is not available in all situations. In other cases, it may be the only remedy available because the problem is not serious enough to merit avoidance. However, in many situations the aggrieved party has a choice between asking the court to avoid the contract or to alter or eliminate the improperly imposed terms.

§13.3.3 The Availability of Damages

Avoidance of the contract or the adjustment of its offending terms are the more conventional remedies for improper bargaining, but in some cases the victim has the alternative of leaving the contract fully in force but claiming damages to compensate for the economic consequences of the wrongful bargaining. This alternative is not available in all cases, but courts do have remedial discretion to award such relief where appropriate. This is most commonly true when the wrongful act is a tort as well as a bargaining impropriety. Thus, if Lilly afterwards decides to keep the contract in force, she could still sue Attila (if she dares) for the tort of battery. Similarly, as fraud is a tort, the victim of a fraudulent misrepresentation may decide not to avoid the contract, but instead to claim damages in tort for the difference in value between the performance represented and that actually received.

§13.4 The Nature and Relationship of the Doctrines Regulating Bargaining

The doctrines considered here are **regulatory** in nature and are often described as **policing** mechanisms. When there is an allegation of unfair bargaining, they allow the court to go behind objective indications of assent to determine if apparent agreement was cajoled by trickery or unfair pressure. This power of regulation must be used with restraint so as to intrude as little as possible on normal and legitimate commercial activity. It is important to recognize that it is not the point of these doctrines to eliminate the advantages of forceful bargaining, savvy decision making or favorable market position. They operate in a free-market economy in which contracting parties are expected to try to serve their own interests and to use their available information and resources to obtain the best deal possible. There is nothing inherently wrong in the resourceful use of superior information, clever sales techniques, and the exploitation of advantage. Furthermore, it is to be expected that transactions routinely occur between parties having great disparity in power, sophistication and resources. Regulation aims, not at "leveling the playing field" by cutting down economic advantage, but rather at allowing the court to step in when behavior crosses the line from hard bargaining to unacceptable exploitation. In obvious cases, such as Attila's gun up Lilly's nostril, it is clear that the line has been crossed. But in more equivocal cases opinions differ on the appropriateness of intervention. Some courts and commentators favor policing for only the more extreme cases and see judicial regulation as leading to inefficiency and market interference. Others advocate a more aggressive role for courts as protector of the underdog.

In classical contract law the policing doctrines were very clearly distinguishable and each had relatively firm and specific elements, making it applicable to a narrow range of situations. As they have developed in more recent times (some courts having moved further away than others from the categorizations of classical law), the doctrines have become more fluid so that they have a greater tendency to meld into each other. While they still retain many of their characteristic elements, their points of connection have become more obvious. This means that although the facts of some cases may support the invocation of only one of the doctrines, others may permit alternative analyses under more than one of them. Together, the doctrines form a network of rules that permit courts to deal with a variety of sins that might be committed during the formation of a contract. As we examine the doctrines individually, we will keep an eye on their common ground and interconnections.

§13.5   Misrepresentation Generally: The Meaning of "Misrepresentation" and the Distinction Between Fraudulent and Non-Fraudulent Misrepresentations

A "misrepresentation" is defined in Restatement Second §159 as an **assertion not in accord with the facts.** It is a factually incorrect representation made by one of the parties at the time of contracting. Misrepresentations fall into one of three categories, each of which has different rules. If the assertion is made with knowledge that it is false (that is, a deliberate lie) and with the intention of inducing the other party's agreement, it is **fraudulent.** If the misrepresentation is not a deliberate lie, but reflects a genuine, albeit erroneous, belief by the party making the assertion, it is either **negligent** (the misinformation results from that party's failure to check facts that he had a duty to ascertain) or **innocent.**

The severity and consequences of a misrepresentation depend on the state of mind of the party making the assertion. A fraudulent misrepresentation is the most serious deviation from legal and ethical obligations, which not only violates the contractual obligation of fair dealing, but is also tortious and could have criminal sanctions, too. In addition, a party guilty of fraud cannot be said to have justifiably relied on the other's manifestation of assent. The elements of fraudulent misrepresentation reflect the law's disapprobation of deliberate falsehood: If a fraudulent assertion is proved to have been made, the remaining prerequisites for relief are comparatively lenient. The consequent inducement is evaluated on a largely subjective standard and the perpetrator's accountability for purposeful deceit usually outweighs any culpability the victim may have for gullibility or carelessness. A negligent or innocent misrepresentation is not as morally reprehensible and may not entirely defeat the perpetrator's reliance interest. Therefore, the decision on whether or not to grant relief involves a closer balancing of the relative culpability of the parties, and a stronger focus on the objective importance (materiality) of the misrepresentation and the victim's duty to verify the facts. Obviously, a negligent misrepresentation weighs more heavily against the perpetrator than an innocent one, and negligence may give rise to tort liability, too.

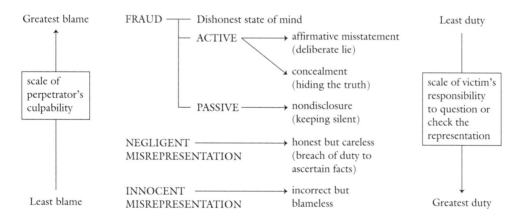

When a contract is recorded in writing, the misrepresentation could be made in the writing itself. However, it is quite possible that the misrepresentation was made either orally or in writing before the contract was signed, and was not recorded in the final written memorial of agreement. If so, the evidence of the misrepresentation is parol evidence. As a matter of policy, the parol evidence rule may not be invoked by a party to *exclude evidence* of a *fraudulent misrepresentation.* To permit this would allow him to use the parol evidence rule to shield his fraud. However, because *negligent* and *innocent* misrepresentations are not as morally indefensible, the parol evidence rule *does apply* to exclude evidence of a prior oral negligent or innocent misrepresentation.

§13.6   Fraudulent Misrepresentation

§13.6.1   Introduction

To qualify as fraudulent, a misrepresentation must be made with deliberate dishonest intent. The person making it must know it is false and must intend to induce the other party to enter the contract. The most common type of fraud, called **fraud in the inducement,** is a fraudulent misrepresentation concerning a fact that forms the basis of the contract, giving the party to whom it is made a false incentive to enter it. A less common type of fraud, **fraud in the factum,** is a misrepresentation relating to the nature or effect of a document to be signed (for example, persuading someone to sign an order for goods by asserting that it is merely a request for a catalog). The principal difference between them is that fraud in the inducement is generally treated as rendering the contract voidable, but fraud in the factum voids it completely. The discussion and examples in this section are concerned only with the more common fraud in the inducement.

The elements of fraudulent misrepresentation are:

1.   A false representation of fact;
2.   made with knowledge of its falsity and with intent to induce the other party to enter the contract;
3.   which does in fact deceive the other party;
4.   to the other party's injury or detriment.

§13.6.2   A False Representation of Fact

a.   The Meaning of "Fact": Facts, Opinions, Predictions, and Promises

The very basis of all misrepresentations is an untrue assertion of *fact*. It is sometimes said, particularly in older cases, that a misrepresentation can only relate to an objectively ascertainable fact, so that it is not fraud to misrepresent one's *opinion*. This distinction holds true in some cases, not only because it is often hard to prove that a person lied about his state of mind (opinion being, by definition, entirely a matter of personal attitude and preference) but also because the expression of opinion should usually be understood as nothing more than a personal view (sometimes exaggerated for the purpose of hype) not to be given undue weight by the other party. For example, we would treat it as fraud if the seller of a vinyl sofa knowingly misrepresents it as made of leather, but we would be likely to think differently if he falsely asserted that he thought it was a beautiful piece of furniture.

However, contemporary courts do not rigidly distinguish misrepresented fact and opinion. First, it is not always that easy to separate fact from opinion because most opinions have a factual basis. Thus, if the seller of the sofa says, "this sofa is exquisitely crafted by skillful workers," the opinion on quality suggests some familiarity with facts concerning the method of manufacture. Second, in some contracts, the opinion of one of the parties is clearly a decisive factor in persuading the other to enter the transaction, so a misrepresentation of that opinion goes right to the heart of the contract. It has as serious an effect as the misrepresentation of an external fact. Therefore, when one of the parties has or claims expertise or superior knowledge, and the other justifiably expects and relies on his recommendation, a misrepresentation of opinion is fraud. For example, an attorney who believes that a client has a weak case makes a fraudulent misrepresentation if he expresses a contrary opinion to the client.

A distinction is also drawn between a factual assertion, which necessarily relates to a state of affairs in existence at the time it is made, and a **promise of future performance** or a **prediction of future events.** As a general matter, a promise or prediction cannot be a statement of fact and hence does not qualify as an actionable misrepresentation. However, it would again be erroneous to treat this distinction rigidly. Although the event or performance may be in the future, the state of mind of the party making it, like an opinion, exists at the time of the assertion. Thus, while it is not fraud simply because a prediction turns out to be untrue, or a promised performance is not rendered, it is fraud if **at the time of the assertion,** the party making it has **no genuine belief** in the correctness of the prediction, or **no intention of performing** as promised.

As discussed below, to claim fraud, the victim of a misrepresentation, whether of fact, opinion, prediction, or promise must prove that the misrepresentation was dishonest. It tends to be easier to prove dishonesty when factual misrepresentations are concerned, because proof of the fact and knowledge of it usually lead to a conclusion of fraud. With opinions, predictions, and promises, proof may be more difficult because there may be little or no objective external evidence from which to draw an inference of dishonesty.

b. Types of Fraudulent Misrepresentation: Affirmative Statements, Concealment, and Silence

A fraudulent misrepresentation is most often an affirmative statement in the form of *words,* either written or oral, but it could be made by *conduct* or even by *silence*. For example, if the seller of a house knows that the old beams underneath the porch are rotten and about to collapse, but she says to the buyer, "we recently replaced the beams supporting the porch, and they are solid," that is an **affirmative false statement.** This is the most readily identifiable form of misrepresentation. Although sometimes more ambiguous and harder to prove, deliberate conduct to hide a fact is also an affirmative act, just as grave as a verbal lie. Say that the beams under the porch were so weak that it had begun to sag and wobble. If the owner does not actually say anything about the beams, but before the buyer came to look at the house, she had temporarily placed some jacks under the porch to remove the sagging and to stabilize it, she has taken **deliberate action to conceal the truth.**

However, sometimes a representation may be implicit in silence. Even if the owner takes no action to hide the defect and says nothing at all about the porch, if she does not actually tell the buyer of the problem, her failure to speak could be a misrepresentation by silence. **Non-disclosure** presents the most difficult case for deciding on whether there has been fraud, because a free market operates on the assumption that a party is entitled to use the advantage of superior information and need not alert the other to all the facts that have motivated entry into the transaction. A home buyer, having studied the market carefully, is not obliged to point out to a seller that the seller's house is underpriced, and a purchaser of commodities is not expected to hand over research data suggesting that a world shortage will shortly drive up the price.

However, there is not an absolute right to keep information secret from the other party, and at some point the line is crossed between information of a private or proprietary nature, and information that must fairly be passed on. The difficult question is to know when that line is crossed. Restatement Second §161 suggests some specific situations in which non-disclosure amounts to an assertion that a fact does not exist—for example, when the party knows that disclosure is needed to correct a previous assertion or to correct a mistake, or when there is a relationship of trust between the parties. It also states the more general principle that disclosure is required when it is demanded by reasonable standards of **fair dealing.** This is, of course, a very vague and open-ended standard, which requires a case-by-case analysis of the ethics of non-disclosure. Another yardstick, suggested by some commentators, is that information need not be disclosed if it can legitimately be regarded as the property of the party who failed to disclose it (for example, because that party had "bought" the information by spending effort or money in acquiring it). Courts also sometimes ask whether the information was reasonably accessible to the other party by diligent inquiry. If so, that party cannot complain about lack of disclosure. Thus, in the example about the porch, if the structural problem could be discovered on inspection, the information is readily accessible, even if the porch was not yet patently unstable. No matter how characterized, the tests all center around the question of fair dealing, which is difficult to define with any precision.

§13.6.3 Knowledge of Falsity and Intent to Induce the Contract

A guilty state of mind is essential to fraud. This state of mind has two components—**knowledge of falsity** (called "**scienter**") and an **intent to mislead.** Although it may be possible for one but not the other to exist, in most cases they go hand-in-hand. In defining knowledge of falsity, Restatement Second §162 covers not only an assertion made with the actual knowledge that it is not in accord with the facts, but also an assertion made without confidence in its truth or without a known basis in fact. This means that there is some blurring of the line between fraudulent and negligent misrepresentation, because reckless disregard for the truth or an extreme degree of negligence in ascertaining information before making an assertion may qualify as fraud.

§13.6.4 Deception of the Victim and Justifiable Inducement

In addition to establishing deliberate fraud, the victim must also show that the misrepresentation is causally linked to the resulting contract: It must have played a significant role in the victim's decision to enter a contract on these terms. Although morally wrong, if the lie played no part in inducing assent, it had no practical impact and does not merit avoidance. Justifiable inducement has two ingredients. First, the false representation must be of a kind sufficient to be an inducing factor and second, the victim must have acted justifiably in relying on it.

This suggests both an examination of the **significance** (that is, materiality) of the misrepresentation and an evaluation of the **victim's reaction** to it. However, these matters are not tested objectively because this would give too great an advantage to the perpetrator of the fraud, whose reprehensible conduct is more wrongful than any objective lack of vigilance by the victim. Therefore, inducement is *evaluated subjectively,* taking into account the victim's own perception of the importance of the misrepresented fact and her own credulity. If the misrepresentation did in fact induce the victim to contract, the perpetrator cannot avoid liability by showing that a reasonable person would not have been influenced by the misrepresentation or would have been less gullible. This approach is adopted by Restatement Second §162, Comment *c,* and §164, which require merely a showing of subjective inducement and do not place the burden on the victim to establish objective materiality or reasonable reliance to obtain relief for fraud.

As is always true, the difference between a subjective and objective test of intent is not a matter of drawing bright lines of distinction but is more a matter of emphasis. To convincingly assert subjective inducement, the victim must satisfy the factfinder that there is a link between the misrepresentation and her motivation to enter the contract. It is hard to do this if the victim's reliance is irrational or the alleged inducement makes little sense in light of normal patterns of thinking. Therefore, some degree of objective assessment must inevitably enter the evaluation of inducement. However, the test does strongly emphasize the victim's personal attributes, so that an ignorant and unsophisticated victim may be able to demonstrate inducement that would be incredible if asserted by a person who has the resources and training to be more suspicious. For most people, therefore, the objective materiality of the misrepresentation and the reasonableness in relying on it are of strong evidentiary value, so that a trivial or incredible misrepresentation may not convincingly establish genuine subjective reliance.

§13.6.5   *Injury or Detriment and the Remedies of Rescission or Damages*

When the effect of the fraud is to induce the victim into paying for a valueless or overpriced performance, the resulting economic injury is palpable and the requirement of detriment is easily satisfied. For example, a seller, by fraudulently representing a vase to be antique, induces a buyer to purchase it for $1,000. It is in fact a modern replica, worth only $10, so the detriment suffered is measurable and obvious. In other cases, there may be nothing wrong with the terms of a contract induced by fraud, judged from the perspective of a reasonable outsider, but the victim has nevertheless suffered the detriment of having been tricked into entering an unwanted contract. Say, in the above example, that although the vase is a modern replica, it was made by a famous potter and is worth just as much as the antique. There is no economic detriment because the actual exchange is on equivalent terms. Nevertheless, the buyer's intent was to purchase an antique, not a modern vase, and he would not have bought the vase in the absence of the fraudulent representation. His injury is that he was tricked into spending his money on a vase that he did not want. This is sufficient detriment, and the victim does not usually have to show an actual economic loss to establish injury. However, the nature of the injury affects the choice of remedy. In the first example, the buyer may elect either to rescind the contract and obtain restitution or to keep the $10 vase and sue for damages, measured as the difference between the value as represented ($1,000) and the actual value ($10). In the second example, the buyer's only remedy is rescission and restitution. If he decides to keep the modern vase he has no damages because he has suffered no economic loss.

As the above examples indicate, a contract induced by fraud is *voidable* by the victim. If, on discovery of the fraud, the victim wishes to terminate the contract, he may **disaffirm**—that is, avoid the contract by rescinding it and claiming restitution of all benefits conferred. As noted in section 13.3, voidability must be distinguished from voidness. The contract is not a nullity, and only the victim has the right to seek avoidance. If, despite the fraud, he decides to keep the contract, he may *affirm* it, and if the fraud caused any economic loss, he may sue the perpetrator for damages to compensate for the difference between the actual value of the performance and its value as represented. Theoretically, the only remedy recognized by contract law is disaffirmance, and the remedy of affirmance and damages is supplied by tort law (fraud being a tort as well as a breach of contract). This theoretical difference is not always apparent from the cases, and it seems to be of little practical significance. The important point is that fraud gives the victim the election to affirm or disaffirm.

If the victim seeks avoidance, he recovers any consideration given to, and must return any benefit received from, the perpetrator. The perpetrator, having acted wrongfully, has a qualified right of restitution, and any doubts over value are resolved in favor of the victim. The victim need not make restitution of property or its value to the extent that it was worthless when received or it deteriorated as a result of its own defects, but must generally pay the value of property that he consumed or used. (*See* Restatement Second §§164, 376, and 385.)

§13.7   Negligent or Innocent Misrepresentation

A misrepresentation made without the deliberate intent to mislead is classified either as negligent or innocent. (As mentioned earlier, a grossly negligent misrepresentation may qualify as fraud, because knowledge of falsity could be inferred where an assertion is made without confidence in its truth or a known basis in fact.) The distinction between negligence and innocence is not always easy to make, and it depends on the circumstances of each case. A misrepresentation is negligent if the person making it failed to act with reasonable care in ascertaining and communicating the truth, but it is innocent if no such duty was breached.

Although negligent and innocent misrepresentations do not carry the same degree of disapprobation as a deliberate lie, they do permit avoidance if they are material and have induced justifiable reliance. Restatement Second §§162, 163, and 164 make only one significant distinction between fraudulent and non-fraudulent misrepresentations: When the element of deliberate and knowing misstatement is absent, the *materiality* of the misrepresentation becomes crucial. Thus, an innocent or negligent misrepresentation only gives grounds for relief if it relates to a fact central to the transaction, and the party making the misrepresentation knew or had reason to know of its importance. It follows from this that the **test of justifiable reliance** is correspondingly strengthened, because materiality to the victim is seen from the reasonable perspective of the other. This approach accords with the general idea that some balance must be struck between the fault of the misrepresenting party and the reasonable expectations of the victim. To the extent that the misrepresenter is less culpable, one would expect a stronger showing of the importance of the misrepresentation and the victim's reasonable reliance.

It can be difficult to distinguish an innocent or negligent misrepresentation from a *contractual promise*. For example, the seller of a house, having inspected it and found no termites, informs the buyer that the house is termite-free. If termites are present this could qualify as a misrepresentation, or it could be a warranty—a contractual promise that the house does not have termites. If it is the former, the remedy of avoidance is appropriate, but if it is the latter, the failure of the house to comply with the warranty is a breach of contract, giving rise to the remedies discussed in Chapter 18. The distinction is largely factual and interpretational. It depends on whether the assertion was merely a statement inducing the contract or was actually incorporated into the contract to become one of the promises made as part of the seller's consideration for the price of the house.

§13.8   Duress

§13.8.1   *The Nature of Duress*

In older contract law, duress was available as a ground of avoiding a contract only in extreme circumstances. A party claiming duress had to show that the other had induced the contract by using **actual force** or an **unlawful threat of death or bodily harm** (not merely property damage). In addition, the test of inducement was objective: The threat must have been such as would overcome the resistance of a person of "ordinary firmness." The example in section 13.2, involving Lilly Livered's sale of her casino at gunpoint to Attila "The Animal" Axehacker is a classic case of duress in this sense. Even under these strict standards, Lilly should be able to avoid the contract by showing that Attila engaged in the threatening conduct, that it was unlawful and constituted a credible threat, and that she was not being unduly wimpy in giving in to it.

During the last several decades duress has moved beyond these narrow confines. It is generally accepted that a person's free will can be undermined by unfair pressure short of physical compulsion or a threat of looming personal injury. "**Economic duress**"—an illegitimate threat to proprietary or economic interests—is well-recognized as a basis for relief. Also, the strongly objective test of "ordinary firmness" has been abandoned in favor of a less rigorous standard that combines objective and subjective factors: Did the victim have no reasonable alternative but to agree? Duress has thus become a much broader doctrine, better able to accommodate situations in which one party uses subtle threats or improper pressure to gain the other's acquiescence to a transaction. As with fraud, the basis of avoidance is consistent with, but an exception to, the general objective test of assent. The underlying rationale is that the victim should not be held accountable for her apparent assent when it is not genuine, and the other party, having improperly induced it, does not have a compelling reliance interest.

The contemporary approach to duress is set out in Restatement Second §§174, 175, and 176. Section 174 deals with the rare situation in which a person's manifestation of assent is *physically compelled,* so that the act of manifesting assent is completely lacking in free will. For example, instead of Attila placing his gun up Lilly's nostril, inducing her to sign, he actually clasps her fingers around a pen and forces her hand across the paper to make a signature. Because Lilly is rendered like an automaton by the physical compulsion, §174 treats such an apparent contract as **void.** We need not be further concerned with this unusual situation, and turn to the more common forms of duress, covered by §§175 and 176, in which an **improper threat** has the effect of making the contract **voidable.** In essence, these sections set out the following elements:

1. One of the parties must make a threat
2. The threat must be improper
3. The threat must induce the apparent assent, in that it leaves the victim no reasonable alternative but to agree.

§13.8.2 The Threat

Although the contemporary doctrine of duress still requires an improper threat, the modern concept of threat has expanded well beyond the confines of its original scope. Today, a threat may be defined as an indication of intent to do or refrain from doing something so as to inflict some harm, loss, injury, or other undesirable consequences that would have an adverse effect on the victim's person or personal or economic interests. This encompasses a wide range of behavior, including not only **explicit** intimidation, but also subtle or even unspoken threats. The presence of an **implied** threat is determined by interpretation in the usual way, taking into account the circumstances of the relationship between the parties. The transaction is examined in context to ascertain if the words or actions of the one party show a reasonable intent to make a threat, reasonably so understood by the other. The threat may either be to take positive **action** or to **refrain from acting,** and the **harm** may consist of any adverse consequences sufficient to overcome the victim's resistance to the contract. A threat could even be implicit in the transaction when one party knows that the other will suffer undesirable consequences if the contract is not made, and uses this knowledge to take unfair advantage of the other's need.

While this wider and more realistic scope allows courts to police less obvious forms of duress, it is less certain and stable than the earlier, more rigid approach. As a result, it presents the danger of undue judicial interference in borderline cases where the line blurs between **legitimate hard bargaining** and **improper coercion.** In this area it must be used cautiously, because duress doctrine should be used only when there has been wrongful bargaining conduct, and should not be misapplied to overturn a tough or burdensome contract simply because one of the parties has managed to use bargaining advantage effectively.

An example will illustrate how difficult it can be to distinguish legally acceptable market behavior from unfair pressure: Say that Lilly needs to sell her casino quickly because she urgently needs money to pay for an operation to cure a dangerous medical condition. Attila knows of her trouble and also knows that she will have difficulty finding a buyer quickly. He therefore offers her less than market price for her casino. Because her need for the money is desperate, she sees no alternative but to sell to Attila for that price. Clearly, Attila has taken advantage of her plight, but the only threat he has made is that unless she meets his terms, he will not contract with her. Such a threat is implicit in all contract negotiations, so it can hardly be viewed as duress. This could simply be treated as a case in which Attila has used his market position to obtain a favorable deal. Conversely, one could take the approach that the circumstances render illegitimate this otherwise routine bargaining strategy. (As an alternative, the doctrine of unconscionability, discussed in section 13.11, may provide relief to Lilly.) In this example, Lilly's bargaining weakness was caused by her need for an operation, so her case invokes easy sympathy. Some needs are less compelling and thus move away from the borderline of duress, more clearly falling into the realm of legally acceptable market interaction. Say, for example, that Attila desperately craved to own Lilly's casino, but Lilly refused to sell it unless he paid an exorbitant price. If Attila succumbs to his desires and agrees to buy at that price, he cannot claim that he acted under duress.

Because relief for duress is premised on wrongful coercion by one of the contracting parties, that party must be responsible for the threat. If the threat is made by a *non-party,* the victim cannot avoid the contract unless the other party is implicated in the threat or knowingly took advantage of it. Outside pressure cannot defeat the legitimate expectations of an innocent party who relied on the transaction in good faith and without knowledge of the threat. For example, Attila made several fair and increasingly generous offers to buy Lilly's casino but Lilly steadfastly rebuffed him every time until, one day, she received a visit from his godfather, Bull "The Butcher" Bloodbath, who threatened to smash her kneecaps unless she sold to Attila. Duress is present if Attila is in some way implicated in his godfather's threat. However, in the unlikely event that Attila's godfather acted entirely independently and without his knowledge, the doctrine of duress cannot appropriately be applied to defeat Attila's honest reliance interest in the fair contract. (But as the outside pressure in this case is a criminal threat by a gangster, the public policy of protecting citizens from extortion may overwhelm Atilla's reliance interest, justifying non-enforcement of the contract on grounds of public policy. See section 13.13.)

§13.8.3 Impropriety

When is a threat improper? In addition to the obvious threats of criminal or tortious conduct, modern law tends to take a broad view of impropriety, so that it could include any threatened behavior that **goes beyond the legitimate rights** of the party applying the pressure, or that constitutes an abuse of those rights. This would include, for example, a threat to engage in vexatious litigation, to withhold a performance or property to which the victim is entitled, to disclose information that would embarrass the victim, or otherwise to do something spiteful or vexatious purely for the sake of hurting the victim. It is, of course, not duress to threaten consequences, even dire ones, that may lawfully and properly be pursued in the absence of agreement. For example, at the time for renewal of an employment contract, an employee who has become indispensable may legitimately threaten to quit unless the employer agrees to a substantial raise. Similarly, a person with a colorable tort claim may justifiably threaten to sue unless the tortfeasor agrees to a settlement. However, a threat to file criminal charges is regarded as improper, even if prosecution is warranted, because it is against public policy for a person to use the threat of criminal prosecution as a bargaining chip.

§13.8.4 Inducement

As noted earlier, the older test for inducement was objective. It required not only that the threat was credible, but also that it would have overcome the resistance of a person of "ordinary firmness." The contemporary test is not so rigorous. Although it has an objective element, it also takes the *subjective attributes of the victim* into account, recognizing that a bully should not be able to enforce a contract merely because his victim is easily intimidated. The inquiry is whether, under all the circumstances, the duress *substantially overcame the free will of this party,* leaving him *no reasonable alternative* but to acquiesce. Inducement is therefore considered not in the abstract, but in light of the victim's needs, personality, and circumstances.

An alternative is only reasonable if it is a feasible and practical means of evading the consequences of the threat. If it would be unduly burdensome or risky, or would not likely avoid the threatened consequences, the victim cannot be said to have had a reasonable alternative to manifesting assent. For example, say that Attila owes Lilly $1 million from a prior transaction. He threatens not to pay her unless she agrees to sell her casino to him. Lilly does have the alternative of refusing to sell and commencing suit against Attila for the debt. However, this alternative is not reasonable for Lilly if she needs the money immediately and cannot afford the cost and delay of litigating to enforce payment.

§13.8.5   *Remedy*

It is sometimes said that when a contract is induced by an extreme degree of duress, such as actual physical force or a threat of physical violence, the contract is void, because there has been no assent. However, because duress doctrine is designed to protect the victim, the more common and logical approach is to treat it as *voidable* at the victim's election. The victim may choose to abide by the contract despite the duress, or may decide to avoid it, claim restitution of any benefit conferred, and tender restoration of any benefit received. The remedy of avoidance and restitution is subject to the same general principles discussed in connection with misrepresentation.

Although in most cases the victim must choose between keeping the contract, subject to all its terms, or avoiding it entirely, there are circumstances in which courts allow a middle path—retention of the contract subject to an **adjustment** of its terms. For example, if a party desires to keep property purchased, but can show that she was forced to pay an excessive price for it, the court may enforce the contract, subject to a refund to the victim of the amount in excess of fair value. If the act of duress is a tort, the victim is able to obtain *damages in tort* in addition to any relief under contract law.

§13.9   Duress in the Modification of an Existing Contract

Section 7.5 deals with the **pre-existing duty rule,** a rule of consideration doctrine declaring that a party does not suffer a legal detriment by promising to do what he is already bound to do under an existing contract. It follows from this rule that the modification of one party's contractual performance is not binding unless it is supported by new consideration given by the other. The principal purpose of the rule is to invalidate a one-sided contractual modification extracted by a party who threatens not to perform unless his compensation is increased. It was pointed out in section 7.5.2 that consideration doctrine is a clumsy tool for policing coerced modifications. It does not allow for easy discrimination between legitimate and improper modifications, and it can be circumvented if the party demanding the modification undertakes some new detriment of relatively small value in relation to the gain to be received, or if the parties go through the ritual of terminating the original contract and executing a new one. It is more efficient to focus directly on the problem of coerced modification by evaluating it under the rules of duress.

That is, the modification should be upheld if it was fairly bargained, but it should be avoided if the one party's assent to provide increased compensation was induced by the other's improper threat to otherwise withhold his promised performance.

UCC §2.209 adopts this solution. It abolishes the requirement of consideration for a modification and subjects it to a test of **good faith.** Comment 2 to §2.209 makes it clear that the extortion of a modification by duress offends the obligation of good faith. As is always true of the good faith standard, the test is rather vague and difficult to apply in close cases. It involves an evaluation of the state of mind of the person requesting the modification, in light of the overall commercial circumstances and the business justification for it. Say, for example, that a manufacturer agrees to make a machine for a buyer at a fixed price. Halfway through the job, the manufacturer realizes that it has underbid and the agreed price will not even cover its cost. It tells the buyer that it will have to abandon the project unless the buyer agrees to pay a higher price. Because it needs the machine immediately and cannot waste time dealing with another supplier, the buyer reluctantly agrees to the price increase. After the machine is delivered, the buyer reneges on its promise to pay more, claiming that the modification was extorted by the manufacturer's bad faith threat of breach. This is a plausible argument, because the manufacturer extracted the modification when it had the buyer "over a barrel." However, the counterargument could be made that the manufacturer made an honest mistake in pricing, resulting in a bargain for the buyer at its expense. It was not such a heinous act to approach the buyer with a request to alter the contract. Although there is a genuine business justification for the modification, bear in mind that the manufacturer had committed itself to deliver the machine for the price originally agreed. While there is nothing wrong with seeking a modification on discovery of the error, the factor that likely tips this conduct over the line into bad faith is that the manufacturer did not merely ask for more money, but, at a time when its performance was indispensable to the buyer, threatened to breach its obligations by abandoning the project. That is, the seller's ability to harm the buyer by breach was used to gain bargaining leverage over the buyer. The UCC's good faith test has had an impact on the common law, because courts recognize the value of articulating the true basis for objecting to modifications.

Even when consideration doctrine is applied to a modification in a common law case, there are two situations recognized by Restatement Second §89 in which the modification may be enforced despite the absence of consideration. The first is when the party benefitted by the promise of modification has acted to her detriment in reliance on it, under circumstances in which it would be unjust to refuse enforcement—in other words, in appropriate circumstances—the doctrine of **promissory estoppel** may be applied to enforce a modification fully or in part. The second is when the modification was motivated by unforeseen **supervening difficulties**. That is, where a change in circumstances so alters a basic assumption of the contract, that the performance of the party seeking the modification becomes more burdensome than originally expected. Say that the manufacturer in the prior example did not underbid at the time of contracting. However, after the contract is executed, the price of the metal from which the machine is to be made escalates beyond all expectation, making the machine considerably more expensive to build. If the manufacturer then persuades the buyer to modify the contract, a court may uphold the modification under this exception to consideration doctrine because the adjustment was a response to unforeseen supervening difficulties.[1] (If the contract was for the sale of goods, this situation would be analyzed in the same way as any other modification and the supervening event would be just one of the factors taken into account in deciding if the modification was fairly bargained.)

§13.10   Undue Influence

The doctrine of undue influence was developed by courts of equity to deal with situations in which duress was not present, but one of the parties had a particularly **strong influence** over the other and **abused this position of dominance** to persuade the subservient party to enter a disadvantageous contract. Thus, while duress provides relief to one whose apparent assent has been induced by an unlawful threat, undue influence is concerned with cases of abuse of trust. Like duress, undue influence makes the contract voidable at the instance of the victim. In most jurisdictions, the doctrine has not been extended beyond its original confines and is not available to redress unfair persuasion in arms-length transactions. Restatement Second §177 reflects this narrow scope by confining the doctrine to *relationships of dependence and trust*. Although it would have been possible for courts to enlarge the scope of undue influence, making it available in all cases of unfair persuasion, the expanded concept of duress and the growing use of unconscionability provide a sufficient basis for the general regulation of bargaining, eliminating the need for a broader application of undue influence. As a result, undue influence has retained its specific character.

To obtain relief for undue influence, the victim must establish two elements:

1.   He had a relationship of dependency and trust with the other party that gave the other party dominance over him and justified

---

1. As you will see in section 15.7, there is an affinity between the supervening difficulties doctrine and the defense of impracticability of performance. The difference, however, is that impracticability applies when the party suffering from the changed circumstances has not obtained a modification of the contract, but seeks to be excused from performance.

him in believing that the dominant party would not act contrary to the victim's interests.

2.   The dominant party improperly abused this position of trust and psychological advantage by unfairly persuading the victim to enter the contract adverse to his interests.

For example, say that Lilly's father had established and built up the casino. Lilly had never been involved in the business. When her father died and left the casino to her, she had to keep this large and complex enterprise running. Because she had no clue about casino management or business in general, she turned to her father's longtime bookkeeper, Sel "The Skimmer" Short, for assistance in running it. Taking advantage of her inexperience and faith in him, Sel persuaded Lilly to sell him a large amount of stock at a bargain price.

The law does not absolutely bar contracts between the dominant and subservient parties to a trust relationship, and relief is available only if the weaker party can show that the dominant party abused his power by unfair persuasion. Unfair persuasion is an elastic concept. When the relationship of dependency is strong and the resulting contract is clearly disadvantageous to the weaker party, unfair bargaining may be inferred from those facts alone, and it may not be necessary to point to any specific underhanded bargaining strategy. However, if the degree of dependency is not as intense or the terms of the contract are not patently unfair, evidence of improper bargaining or oppressive circumstances may be needed to bolster the claim of undue influence. Unseemly bargaining can, as usual, take many forms, including the use of high-pressure tactics, the failure to disclose information, concealment of self-interest, or discouraging recourse to other advisers.

§13.11   Unconscionability

§13.11.1   *The Role of Unconscionability*

As noted earlier, duress does not cover situations in which there is no threat, express or implied. This means that it does not provide a mechanism for policing contracts that are not induced by threat, yet are the result of unfair pressure or abuse of power. Similarly, unless there is some relationship of trust between the parties, undue influence is not available in most jurisdictions to redress an imposition of terms on a weaker party. Even when imposition is accompanied by some degree of dishonesty, fraud cannot be claimed unless the misrepresentation and its consequent inducement are serious enough to satisfy the elements of fraud. Nevertheless, meaningful and genuine assent may be just as badly undermined when one party is able to impose an unfair contract on the other, using a strong bargaining position or unethical tactics to take advantage of the other's weakness, ignorance, or distress. The law therefore needs a more general doctrine under which courts may provide relief in cases that do not clearly fall within any of the more specific doctrines. The concept of unconscionability helps to cater to these situations.

§13.11.2   *The Nature and Origins of Unconscionability*

Unconscionability originated as a discretionary bar to **equitable** relief in a contract suit. It is the function of a court of equity[2] to do justice between the parties, and it would therefore decline relief to a plaintiff who had behaved inequitably. For example, if a party to a contract sued for equitable relief (such as specific performance) under a contract that was harsh or unfairly bargained, the court would refuse to enforce it on the ground that to do so would offend its conscience. Even after the courts of law and equity were combined, many courts did not recognize unconscionability as generally available and would only consider using the doctrine when the relief sought in the case was equitable in nature. Because most contract cases involve claims for damages or other relief at law, and claims in equity are less common, relief for unconscionability was often unavailable.

This changed dramatically when the UCC was enacted because §2.302 adopted the doctrine as a general rule, applicable to all contracts for the sale of goods. As a result of the strong influence of the UCC on the common law, courts have increasingly applied unconscionability doctrine in cases at law involving contracts other than sales of goods. This trend was recognized and bolstered by Restatement Second §208, which closely follows the wording of UCC §2.302.

Juries are not used in cases at equity, so unconscionability, being equitable in its origins, is *decided by the judge*. Of course, the UCC could have changed this when it codified the doctrine, but because a finding of unconscionability has such a strong discretionary content, the drafters of the UCC chose to keep it within the realm of the judge. Section 2.302 therefore characterizes it as a matter of law. The Restatement Second adopts the same approach.

§13.11.3   *The Elements of Unconscionability*

The UCC and Restatement Second simply acknowledge that the court has the power to refuse enforcement of an unconscionable contract or to adjust

---

2. The distinction between law and equity is explained in section 2.5.

the contract by removing or modifying the unconscionable provision. Neither section attempts to say what constitutes unconscionability, but the comments to §2.302, largely echoed in those to §208 of Restatement Second, suggest a two-part test that has become widely accepted. For relief to be granted on grounds of unconscionability, the transaction must exhibit both **bargaining unfairness** (referred to as **procedural unconscionability**) and resulting **unfair or oppressive terms** (called **substantive unconscionability**). In most cases, both improper bargaining and oppressive terms are present, at least to some degree, but there is some balance between these two elements, so that if one of them is strongly shown, the court is likely to be less finicky in finding the other. In fact, there are some cases in which relief has been granted when only one of the elements has been established, but this usually happens when that element is so overwhelmingly present (typically, substantive unconscionability in the form of outrageously unfair terms), that the other can be assumed to have been present as a matter of course.

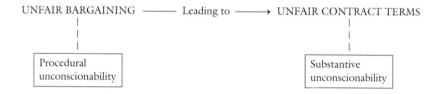

It is one thing to identify the dual elements of procedural and substantive unconscionability, but quite another to describe them with any certainty. As a result, courts and writers continue to struggle with the scope and content of the doctrine. We will now look more closely at each of these elements.

§13.11.4 *Procedural Unconscionability*

This element focuses on the *bargaining behavior* of the party alleged to have acted unconscionably. While Comment 1 to UCC §2.302 does not provide much guidance on what constitutes unconscionable bargaining, it states that the aim is to prevent **"oppression and unfair surprise,"** but not to disturb the "allocation of risks because of superior bargaining power." Restatement Second Comment *d* to §208 makes a similar observation and expands on it by noting that gross inequality of bargaining power may satisfy the requirement of unconscionability if combined with substantively unfair terms. The Restatement comment also lists some indicia of oppressive bargaining, such as some degree of deception or compulsion, or an awareness by a dominant party of infirmity, ignorance, or lack of understanding on the part of the other.

As noted earlier, unconscionability doctrine is most useful when there are some elements of pressure, deception, or unfair persuasion present in the formation process, but these are not sufficient to qualify as duress, fraud, or undue influence. It is difficult to be more concrete, because unconscionability, by its nature, is intended to be an open-ended doctrine, allowing the court discretion to examine each case on its facts and to decide if underhanded or oppressive conduct by one of the parties is severe enough under the circumstances to merit the avoidance or adjustment of the contract.

The comments emphasize that mere *disparity of bargaining power* is not enough to constitute unconscionability. It is not the purpose of the doctrine to place the parties on a level of equality by eliminating the advantages enjoyed by a more powerful or sophisticated party. If this were so, most contracts could be challenged by a dissatisfied party on the basis that the other was bigger, or had better lawyers or more money or power. But this does not mean that the relative strength of the parties is irrelevant to the issue of unconscionability. Often it is only because of a disparity in power that a dominant party is able to behave in an unfair or oppressive manner or to insist on unfair terms. Thus the key is not whether one party was more powerful or knowledgeable than the other, but whether it abused its power to impose its will on the other party.

Having said this, it must be acknowledged that there are situations in which the abuse of power is quite subtle. There is no obvious dishonesty or unfair persuasion, yet it is nevertheless clear that one of the parties used its position of dominance to impose the contract (or unfavorable contract terms) on the weaker. That is, one of the parties enters the transaction with such bargaining power relative to the other, that the stronger party has enough control over the transaction to leave the weaker with no choice but to enter it on the terms proposed by the dominant party. Contracts entered into under these circumstances have come to be known as **contracts of adhesion** because the weaker party is seen as adhering without choice to terms dictated by the stronger. Contracts of adhesion are examined more fully in section 13.12, but it is useful to anticipate and emphasize the point made in that discussion, that a contract does not become adhesive or unconscionable merely because one of the parties has greater bargaining power. Comment 1 to UCC §2.203 specifically states that the purpose of unconscionability doctrine is not to disturb the allocation of risks resulting from superior bargaining power and contemplates that some procedural impropriety—an abuse of that power—should normally be present as well. Nevertheless, when substantively unfair terms are present and are attributable to the bargaining dominance of the party favored by the terms, it is relatively easy to conclude that the weaker party was deprived of free choice by a degree of dominance that, in itself, amounted to procedural unfairness.

§13.11.5   Substantive Unconscionability

It should be apparent from the discussion of procedural unconscionability that there is a close relationship of cause and effect between the procedural and substantive elements: By engaging in unconscionable conduct during formation, one of the parties has been able to impose a substantively unconscionable contract or contract term on the other. It is not usually enough to show merely that the contract is substantively unfair, because it is not proper for a court to adjust a contract simply because one of the parties overpaid, underbid, or otherwise made a disadvantageous or unwanted deal. Unless this unfortunate state of affairs was caused by the behavior that qualifies as procedurally unconscionable, the parties should both be held to their manifested agreement. Once again, this general rule must be qualified by the caveat that the substantive and procedural elements do not have to be present to an equal degree. When the contract terms are grossly oppressive, procedural unfairness may be found simply in the opportunistic use of a position of dominance.

Most commonly, a contract is substantively unconscionable when its terms are **harsh, unfair, or unduly favorable to one of the parties.** One could think of endless examples of unfair terms, such as an excessive price for goods or services; exorbitant interest rates; harsh penalties in the event of default; the waiver of legal protection or of the right to seek legal redress in a proper forum, and so on. The test suggested by Comment 1 to §2.302 calls on the court to decide whether, "in the light of the general commercial background and the commercial needs of the particular trade or case, the clauses involved are *so one-sided as to be unconscionable under the circumstances* existing at the time of the contract." This is a hopeless circumlocution, but it does at least suggest that a contract or term is unconscionable if it favors one of the parties more than should reasonably be expected, given the commercial context in which the contract was made. The comment goes on to identify one of the goals of the doctrine as the prevention of *oppression*, which, while also rather vague, gives some further hint of the direction of the inquiry.

Although the conclusion that a contract is substantively unconscionable is normally based on the presence of unfair terms, it is possible for this element to be present even when the contract appears fair and reasonable from an objective standpoint. The unfairness could lie in the fact that the weaker party did not desire the transaction but was unfairly persuaded to enter it. For example, say that the conduct of a door-to-door sales representative is procedurally unconscionable because high-pressure techniques and smooth talk are used to bamboozle a hapless householder into buying an unneeded home appliance. Even if the price of the appliance and the other terms are reasonable, the contract as a whole may nevertheless be unconscionable, because it was unwanted by and imposed on the buyer.[3] As you can see, we are again looking at that balance between the substantive and procedural aspects of unconscionability.

---

3. Home solicitation sales are legislatively regulated, so the buyer may have statutory grounds of avoidance as well.

A number of unconscionability cases involve the substantive unfairness of *excessive price,* so that particular form of unfairness may be used to illustrate the difficulty in deciding on the proper balance between the substantive and procedural components. In many cases, although there is no clear showing of bargaining unfairness, the buyer of goods or services (typically a consumer) has agreed to pay an excessive price for the purchase. Excessive price, on its own, should not normally be a basis for finding unconscionability if the disparity in exchange cannot be attributed to bargaining misbehavior. As emphasized in the discussion of consideration in section 7.6, the courts do not normally inquire into the adequacy of the exchange, but leave it to the parties to make their own judgments on the relative value of the performances. However, in some cases the disparity in value is so gross that courts refuse to enforce the contract at the price on which agreement was manifested. This has led to some debate about whether courts should exercise regulatory power over excessive pricing, even in the absence of proof of unfair bargaining. However, in most of the cases in which courts have intervened on the grounds of excessive price, there is at least some indication from the evidence that the high price would not have been obtained without improper bargaining methods, or at least an exploitation of the buyer's weakness, ignorance, or lack of choice.

§13.11.6   *The Remedy for Unconscionability*

As noted already, both the UCC and the Restatement Second leave it to the discretion of the court to devise the most appropriate response to an unconscionable contract or term. In exercising its discretion, the court is influenced, but not bound, by what relief the victim requests.

In some cases, the unconscionability so profoundly affects the quality of the victim's assent that she no longer desires the contract and should not be held to it. This is what would happen in the example of the consumer who was cajoled into buying the unwanted appliance. Here, the most appropriate remedy is for the court to refuse enforcement of the contract as a whole. This is tantamount to *avoidance and restitution.*

In other cases (particularly where the victim would like to keep the contract with appropriate adjustments), the better remedy may be to enforce the basic bargain but to change its terms to *eliminate its unconscionable aspects.* This may involve either eliminating the unconscionable provision entirely or altering it to remove the unfairness. For example, if the consumer who bought the home appliance paid an excessive price but would like to keep the appliance, the court may enforce the sale at a reasonable market price. By adjusting the contract to get rid of the unconscionability, the court remakes the bargain assented to by the parties. In most cases this is justified as not being an unreasonable burden on the party guilty of the unconscionable conduct, who gets what he would have received had he behaved equitably. However, if the adjustment of terms would place an undue hardship on him, avoidance may be the more appropriate remedy. For example, say that it is the buyer of goods that imposes an unconscionably low price on the seller. If the buyer cannot afford to pay the fair market price so that adjustment of terms would be an undue hardship on her, it may be more equitable to end the contractual relationship and to order restitution of any benefits conferred.

§13.11.7 The Temptation to Overuse Unconscionability Doctrine: A Final Note on Perspective

Because unconscionability is such a vague and relatively formless doctrine, students are often tempted to haul it out at every opportunity. In reality, despite its apparent breadth, unconscionability is not an appropriate argument whenever one of the parties has second thoughts about a disadvantageous contract. It is therefore worth reiterating some of the realities that inhibit its successful use in many cases:

1. Remember that courts only have statutory power to give relief for unconscionability when the contract is a sale of goods. At common law, despite its adoption by the Restatement Second, there are still some courts that are reluctant to extend it to cases that do not involve equitable relief.

2. Even when the doctrine is available, most courts use it sparingly. It is most commonly used in consumer transactions when a relatively unworldly individual has entered a disadvantageous or unwanted contract as a consequence of having been subjected to high-pressure or otherwise disreputable marketing practices by a larger, more sophisticated business entity. Although it is sometimes applied in transactions between commercial entities, courts are usually quite circumspect in using it in this context, particularly if both parties have the resources to take care of their own interests.

3. Although it has been stressed that unconscionability is concerned with improper bargaining and unfair terms, rather than with a disparity in bargaining power, the discrepancy in bargaining power is by no means irrelevant. In many cases, it is the existence of bargaining inequality that allows unconscionable advantage-taking. This means that if the parties are of relatively equal strength and sophistication, it is much harder for one of them to make a convincing case of unconscionability, and a court will be less inclined to interfere with their bargain.

§13.12 Standard Forms and Contracts of Adhesion: The Role of Unconscionability in Redressing a Power Imbalance

There has already been some general discussion of the proper judicial response to a contract when it is not possible to pinpoint specific bargaining impropriety, but the one party has used its dominant position to impose an unfair contract on the other. As noted before, the difficulty in such situations is to separate the legitimate use of market power from the kind of unfair exploitation and imposition that makes the contract adhesive. Although this problem could occur in any type of transaction, it most commonly comes up in connection with standard form contracts, because standard form contracts are widely used and are the routine means by which enterprises enter repetitive transactions. If the enterprise is large and powerful, the danger of large-scale imposition is more acute.

Although some commentators have urged that standardized contracts of adhesion be regulated under a separate doctrine, most cases of real or alleged adhesion are resolved under principles of unconscionability.[4] A standard contract becomes adhesive and unconscionable only if the doctrine's two-part test is satisfied. Procedural unconscionability lies in the fact that one party was able, by using its overwhelming dominance, to deprive the other of any meaningful choice on the terms of the contract. Substantive unfairness is present if the resulting contract has terms that are unduly harsh and one-sided, or if the contract as a whole was forced on the weaker party.

It must be stressed that standard form contracts are not wicked per se, nor are they even presumptively unconscionable. They are common and efficient means of contracting when a party enters many transactions of a similar kind, and it would be ridiculous to expect routine contracts to be individually drawn in every case. The drafter of the form obviously benefits from using a standard form, not only because it reduces transaction costs and permits more centralized control over the scope and terms of its commitments, but also because the form is composed with its interests in mind. However, the standardization often also benefits the persons with whom it contracts. They, too, may save the time and expense of negotiation, and the price of the product may reflect the savings in transaction costs. Furthermore, standard terms often become familiar in the marketplace, so that they are less alien and more readily expected and understood. Remember, too, that one should not jump to the conclusion that a disparity in bargaining power inevitably leads to adhesion. In a market economy, we assume that transactions are commonly entered into by parties of disparate wealth, sophistication, and strength, but that competition acts as a restraint on power. So the law generally leaves parties free to make the best contract that they can, given their own wiles and the prevailing market forces.

---

4. In some cases, a similar result can be achieved by analyzing the problem as one of economic duress, because some courts have expanded duress doctrine broadly enough to encompass circumstances in which the threat of not contracting, except on dictated terms, is sufficient to compel assent. Of course, it is usually within the rights of a party to refuse to contract except on stated terms, so such a threat can only be duress if the circumstances make it wrongful. This means that the weaker party's need for the goods or services must be compelling, and it must be immoral for the stronger to exploit this need by demanding assent to the terms in question.

This being acknowledged, it is also widely recognized that sometimes one of the parties (typically a large enterprise) is so dominant, and its attitude to those with whom it deals is so rapacious, that the give-and-take of the market is inadequate to control its self-serving conduct. It uses its substantial power to impose its will on weaker parties by presenting them with non-negotiable standard form contracts that unfairly favor its interests. If the enterprise is indeed powerful enough to get away with this kind of imperious behavior, the contract imposed qualifies as a contract of adhesion. Such standard contracts have been likened to a form of private legislation in which the powerful party acts like a kind of dictator, in effect creating general rules of law that bind all the little people who need to deal with it.

An example may help to illustrate this kind of situation. Say that Megalomarketing Corp., Inc. owns and operates the only shopping mall in town and there are no competing retail businesses for 200 miles around. Anyone who wishes to buy anything at any of the shops in the mall must sign a standard form acknowledging profound and perpetual delight in the quality of the goods purchased, and forever waiving all rights to return or complain about them or to seek legal recourse for any defect in them. No member of Megalomarketing's sales force has authority to negotiate a change in these terms and is in fact instructed to refuse to sell to any customer who makes a fuss about signing. Megalomarketing has, in effect, enacted a local law that eliminates all warranties on its goods and abolishes any right of rescission that its customers may otherwise have had. Because there is no effective competition in the region, customers who cannot travel 200 miles to shop have no choice but to do without new goods or to adhere to the standard term.

A number of methods have been developed to deal with companies like Megalomarketing: Laws prohibiting anticompetitive behavior (such as the antitrust laws) may make it difficult for Megalomarketing to create a situation in which it has such control of a market. If it is too difficult to ensure competition, or if competition does not eliminate the problem of unfair imposition (as has happened with utilities and the insurance industry), the legislature may impose regulation that requires approval of standard terms and other oversight by a government agency. Alternatively, the legislature may simply focus on particular undesirable provisions and make them unenforceable as contrary to public policy. If the legislature has not intervened, the courts have several means of refusing to give Megalomarketing its way. If there is any ambiguity or uncertainty in the term, its harsh effect may be avoided by interpretation; or the court may itself refuse enforcement on the basis of public policy, as discussed in section 13.13; or it may use policing doctrines such as duress or unconscionability. In the latter case, the basis for relief is not that Megalomarketing employed any specific deceptive or high-pressure tactics to force assent by its customers (although if such tactics were used, they strengthen the case for intervention), but rather that it abused its market power to achieve a substantively unfair result.

Note, however, that the Megalomarketing example is extreme. In most cases, customers dealing with a large enterprise are not so thoroughly deprived of choice, and the presence of competition may make even the most powerful contractor susceptible to negotiation. Think of the purchase of a car by an individual consumer from massive automobile dealership. Although the consumer's resources may be meager compared to those of the dealer, competition in the market is stiff, and this gives the consumer considerable leverage. Therefore, if an average consumer signs a standard form with a particularly ungenerous limited warranty, it will not be easy to show that the contract was adhesive. The consumer would have to show not only that limitation is unfair in light of reasonable expectations and the price paid, but also that it was not possible to go elsewhere for a better deal, and that circumstances precluded efforts to read, understand, and negotiate over the term, or that such negotiations were attempted without success.

§13.13   Policing Contracts for Illegality or Contravention of Public Policy

§13.13.1   *Illegality, Public Policy, and Freedom of Contract*

It was noted in the introduction that the assent and reliance policies of contract law are not the only policies that may be implicated in the enforcement of a contract. Even when the contract is a full and genuine exercise of both parties' freedom of contract, it may break the law or so offend public policy that the court refuses to enforce it. This distinguishes regulation on grounds of illegality and public policy from the other doctrines discussed in this chapter: The issue here is not that one of the parties dealt wrongly with the other or that one party's assent is deficient (even though this factor could also be present in some cases), but that the contract is forbidden or does some damage to the public good. Therefore, the goal of policing here is different from that in cases where the only issue is bargaining impropriety. The court's concern goes beyond doing justice between the parties, to the *protection of the public interest.*

Although illegality and the violation of public policy are often dealt with as falling within the same general rules, there is a significant difference between them. A contract is illegal if making it contravenes a statute or the common law. Although a violation of law inevitably offends public policy as well because laws are enacted to effectuate public policy, not every public policy is covered by a rule of law forbidding contracts that violate it. Yet, even if the contract is not illegal, it may seriously undermine or harm the public interest. If so, courts have the discretion to refuse to give effect to the contract or an offending term.

§13.13.2 Illegal Contracts

Illegal contracts are not all of the same degree of turpitude. Some forms of illegality are so serious that the contract is invalid and its making is a criminal act. In other cases, the illegality is of less moral culpability and the law's purpose is satisfied simply by making the contract ineffective. To illustrate, return to the sale of the casino by Lilly Livered to Attila "The Animal" Axehacker. Say that Attila has been associated with organized crime for many years. A statute has been enacted that precludes casino ownership by a person with connections to a criminal organization and declares that any attempted sale to such a person is void. Even if Attila had put no undue pressure on Lilly, and the parties had bargained freely and reached agreement on a reasonable price and fair terms, their contract is ineffective. However, this is the only consequence of their violation of the law. By contrast, assume that the consideration given by Attila in exchange for the casino was his promise to tie a rock to the feet of one of Lilly's non-paying customers and dump him into the East River. The contract moves beyond the mere disobedience of gaming regulations and becomes a criminal act, subjecting the parties to prosecution.

In either event, the consequences for the contract itself are the same: It infringes the law, and its enforcement would make the court an accessory to the illegal act. No matter how genuine the parties' assent, the contract cannot be given effect. The law has already struck the balance between the other public policy and freedom of contract, and has determined that the protection of the public from corrupt casinos (or, even more so, from murder) outweighs the contractual autonomy of Lilly and Attila.

§13.13.3 Contracts Contrary to Public Policy

If a contract is not actually illegal, but it nevertheless offends public policy, the consequence of nonenforcement is not as inevitable. A decision on whether or not to enforce the contract involves a **balancing of policy concerns** and of the **equities** between the parties. Assuming that the contract suffers from no deficiencies in assent, the regulation of contracts on the basis of broader public interest creates a **tension between the policy of enforcing contracts** and the **other public policy** that would be frustrated by enforcement. To resolve this dissonance, the countervailing policies must be balanced. If the harm to the public interest outweighs the benefit of enforcement to the public and the parties, enforcement must be refused.

How does the court identify the existence and force of a public policy affected by the contract? In the easiest case, the policy may be expressed by legislation or well-established common law precedent. Of course, if the statute or rule of common law clearly prohibits a contract in violation of a particular policy, we have a case of illegality, as discussed above. But sometimes the law does not actually forbid a particular contract, yet it is apparent that the law's policy goals are incompatible with the recognition and enforcement of a contract of this kind. For example, assume that there is no legislation forbidding casino ownership by persons associated with criminal organizations. However, the legislative history of the existing regulatory statute contains reports of and expressions of concern over the unhealthy influence of criminal organizations in the gambling industry, or there is a well-established judicial policy against corrupt casinos in prior case law. In the absence of a clear and express legislative or common law policy, the court has a more difficult task in deciding if some compelling public interest is implicated in the transaction and necessitates non-enforcement of the contract. Because this often amounts to *judicial policymaking,* most courts are cautious about identifying public policy that does not have a firm base in statute or precedent. A court may try to seek guidance in other governmental policy pronouncements and may entertain policy arguments by the parties. If it should conclude that such a policy exists, it must then weigh it against the policy of upholding contracts.

§13.13.4   *The Effect of Contracts that Are Illegal or Contrary to Public Policy*

If a contract violates the law, a court will not make itself a party to that illegal act. Therefore (apart from any criminal or civil sanctions that may be applicable under the law that has been broken), the consequence of illegality is *nonenforcement* of the contract. If one or both parties has previously rendered some performance under the illegal contract, *restitution* becomes an issue. The basic rule is when the parties *share the guilt* of having entered an illicit contract, the court will keep aloof from their dispute and will not intervene to help either of them. Not only will it refuse enforcement, but it will leave the parties as it finds them, and decline to assist either in obtaining restoration of any benefit conferred under the contract. This is known as the **"in pari delicto"** rule, an abbreviation of the maxim, *in pari delicto potior est conditio defendentis.* (When the parties are in equal guilt, the defendant's position is stronger.)

The maxim refers to equal guilt, but it applies not only when the party seeking restitution is equally guilty, but also when he is *more at fault* than the other in entering the illegal contract. It does not bar restitutionary relief when the claimant is less morally and legally responsible for the illegality. This gives the court some discretion to conduct an equitable balancing, and to order restitution when the relative blame of the parties and the public interest favor it. In some cases it is quite easy to differentiate the parties' degree of culpability, in others it is difficult to decide which party, if either, was more at fault. In deciding relative guilt, courts look not only at the role played by each party, but also at the purpose of the violated law and goals it is intended to achieve. Therefore, the decision on whether to refuse restitution is often based, in part at least, on the question of whether that remedy would advance or undermine the purpose of the law. This can be a difficult evaluation, as a couple of examples will illustrate:

In contravention of a statute forbidding the ownership of casinos by mobsters, Lilly sold her casino to Attila, a gangster, for $10 million. Both parties knew about the prohibition. At the time of executing the agreement, Attila made a down payment of $100,000 to Lilly. A few days later she repudiated the contract. Clearly, the contract is unenforceable, and Attila cannot sue for relief on the contract, whether in the form of specific performance or damages for breach. Can he get the $100,000 back? There is no obvious answer: It could be argued that, as the mobster seeking to acquire the casino, he is more to blame than the seller. But the contrary argument could be made that people like Lilly, by deliberately violating the law, make possible the very harm that the statute seeks to avert. The determination of which of these alternatives best serves the public interest is also difficult to make: Is it better to allow her to keep a windfall profit from her deliberately wrongful transaction, or to allow the court's process to be used by a thug to recover the down payment made in an attempt to violate the law? Unless it is demonstrated that judicial intervention is the more appropriate alternative, the thrust of the *in pari delicto* rule is to leave the parties as they are.

As a second example, a liquor store sells a case of scotch to a 20-year-old minor, violating a statute (known to both parties) that prohibits the sale of alcohol to persons under the age of 21.[5] The buyer paid for the scotch in cash, but the seller now refuses delivery. Again, the buyer clearly cannot enforce the contract, but can he get his money back? One could argue that the buyer had no business trying to purchase the liquor and deserves no help from the court in recovering the payment. However, it seems intolerable to allow the seller to keep his money. If the whole idea of barring the sale of liquor to young people is that they do not have the maturity to use it responsibly, it would seem that this lack of maturity also diminishes blame vis-à-vis the adult seller. It is relevant that a central purpose of the law is to protect people like the buyer. The law sees him more as a victim and therefore less to blame for the illegal transaction.

When the contract is not illegal, but offends *public policy*, the same rules are generally applicable, but not with the same degree of force: Although such contracts are usually unenforceable, the fact that they are not actually illegal gives the court greater flexibility in tailoring relief. Therefore, in appropriate circumstances, *enforcement on adjusted terms* may be a better solution when the equities favor the party who seeks enforcement and the harm to the

---

5. Although the general rule is that a person must be over 21 to buy liquor, in most states a person acquires contractual capacity at 18. The contract is therefore not avoidable for lack of capacity.

public interest can be averted or minimized by eliminating the offensive terms. If enforcement is refused, the *in pari delicto* rule may be applied to deny restitution, but because the wrongfulness is less grave, the equities are more likely to favor restoration of any benefit conferred.

An example based on a **covenant not to compete** illustrates the *adjusted enforcement* of a contract that offends public policy: A covenant not to compete is an undertaking by a person associated with a business that, upon leaving the business, he will not, for a specified period and in a specified area, engage in activity that competes with the business. Such covenants may be found in employment or partnership agreements or in contracts for the sale of a business. Say that a well-established pediatrician takes in a newly-qualified doctor into her practice as a junior partner. The established doctor is concerned that her new partner may work with her just long enough to get experience and a following among her patients, and that he will then terminate the partnership and set up practice on his own. To avoid this, she demands a provision in the partnership agreement in terms of which the junior partner undertakes that upon leaving the partnership, he will not practice medicine within a ten-mile radius of the partnership premises for a period of five years.

There is a long-established public policy against agreements that stifle competition or that restrict a person's freedom to earn a livelihood by full participation in the market. This policy underlies the antitrust laws, which prohibit various kinds of anticompetitive behavior. But even in situations not covered by the antitrust legislation (such as the present case) courts apply the policy when a contract unduly hampers competition. The covenant not to compete is not per se invalid, but the court will assess its impact on competition under all the circumstances of the case, taking into account factors including the legitimate interests (such as patient goodwill) of the established doctor, the mores of the medical profession, the hardship on the junior doctor, the patients' right to use a doctor of their choice, and the fairness of the bargaining process leading to agreement on the provision. If, on balance, the deleterious impact of the clause outweighs the interests of the established doctor, the court may refuse to enforce the clause altogether. Alteratively, it may cut down the restraint to a level that goes no further than necessary to protect those interests, reducing the time or geographic limit of the restraint or defining the prohibited activity more narrowly (for example, to cover pediatrics, rather than medical practice generally). In this case, therefore, a violation of public policy does not usually render the entire contract unenforceable, but more likely results in the elimination or adjustment of the offending provision.

EXAMPLES

1. Cookie Racha owns a house built in 1915. The house has been plagued with chronic cockroach infestation. Although Cookie fumigated it

regularly, roaches reappeared in ever increasing numbers within a few weeks of treatment. Also, the house was slowly sinking into soft ground on one side. The sinking can only be corrected by an expensive process that requires the side of the house to be jacked up while a firm concrete foundation is laid. The sinking has caused deep cracks in the living room wall. Cookie has re-plastered the wall a few times, but the continuing movement reopened the cracks soon afterwards. Cookie had already become quite sick of the house when she recently read in the newspaper that the neighboring property had been bought by the state for use as a halfway house for paroled sex offenders. This was the final straw and she decided to sell.

Acting on the advice of her realtor, Chic "The Snake" Canery, she fumigated the house, plastered the cracks, and repainted the wall just before the house was placed on the market. Each time that the house was shown, Chic ensured that all the lights were on. Not only did this present the house in a more attractive manner, but the brightness discouraged the regenerating population of roaches from venturing into full view. Chic brought Bugsy Crawley to see the house. Cookie happened to be present and saw that Bugsy seemed to be very interested in buying the house. During their brief conversation Bugsy said to Cookie, "Does the house have termites?" Cookie had never seen signs of termites in the house, so she simply answered, "No."

A week later, Cookie happened to notice signs of termite damage in the basement. On the very next day she received an offer from Bugsy to buy the house for the full asking price. She accepted immediately. The terms of the contract of sale were set out in Bugsy's offer, made on a standard form provided by the realtor. One of the standard terms was a merger clause that stated that no representations had been made save for those expressed in the writing. The writing simply set out the basic terms of the transaction and made no representations concerning the property. The transaction closed a short while later, and Bugsy moved into his new home. It did not take very long before the roaches reappeared, the wall cracked, the sex offenders moved in next door and the termites were discovered. Does Bugsy have grounds for avoiding the sale?

2. Tuttu Tango is a 65-year-old retired tax lawyer. Her life had become quite dull since retirement, and she was looking for excitement. One day she was invited to accompany a friend to a free introductory dance lesson at the Fraud Astaire Dance Studios. During the lesson, she fell into the clutches of Gig Aloe, a suave and unctuous dance instructor employed by Fraud Astaire. Gig subjected Tuttu to all the charm and flattery that he had perfected by taking Fraud Astaire's super sales course. After observing Tuttu's inept and clumsy cavortings on the dance floor, he pretended to be very impressed. He told her enthusiastically that she had a wonderful natural talent and ageless grace. He said that he was convinced that with proper training, she had the potential of becoming an elegant and alluring dancer. Tuttu had been around the block a few times, so she didn't really believe a word of this. But Gig was cute and he would be her instructor, so she agreed to sign up for a month's

worth of lessons at a cost of $100. Gig produced a form and asked her to sign it. He cleverly positioned his hand over the top of the form so Tuttu could not see the top few lines. This little trick worked, because Tuttu did not pay much attention to the form and signed it without trying to read it. Had she been more astute, she would have seen that Gig had given her a life membership contract form to sign, in which she irrevocably purchased a lifetime of lessons for a fee of $10,000, payable within seven days of signing.

A few days later Tuttu went to the studio for her first lesson. She discovered that Gig had been fired and replaced by a decidedly uninteresting instructor—a beefy middle-aged man who wore a string tie. Tuttu went to the manager to tell him that she wanted to cancel her month's lessons. She was shocked when the manager corrected her, showing her the contract form in which she had signed up, not for a month, but a lifetime. He told her that it was studio policy never to release customers from their commitments, and pointed out that her payment was due within the next few days.

Does the common law give her the right to cancel? (Answer on common law principles only, and disregard any consumer protection legislation of which you may have heard.)

3. Sweaty Shoppe, Inc. is a retailer of sports and fitness clothing. It sells a wide variety of all brands of merchandise including goods marketed under its own "Du Resse" trademark. The Du Resse products are made by Sweaty Shoppe's manufacturing division that operates a factory in a small undeveloped country. Brute Force, Inc. makes very expensive weightlifting equipment. Sweaty Shoppe considers these products overpriced and has steadfastly refused to carry them despite several requests by Brute Force.

The president of Brute Force has a friend who works for an organization that monitors violations of human rights. This friend gave him a copy of a secret report that convincingly describes shocking conditions at Sweaty Shoppe's factory, including the virtual enslavement of child workers who are forced to labor in the cruelest conditions for pitifully low wages. If this information is made public, it would cause incalculable harm to Sweaty Shoppe's reputation and customer relations. Also, because a federal law makes it a criminal offense to import goods fabricated by child laborers, the publication of the report would attract a government investigation, possibly leading to prosecution. Realizing this, the president of Brute Force showed a copy of the report to Sweaty Shoppe and threatened to leak it to the press unless Sweaty Shoppe agreed to buy, maintain stocks of, and vigorously promote a full line of Brute Force's products.

Although Sweaty Shoppe knows the report is untrue, it is concerned that many customers would believe it. Also, the government would be bound to initiate an investigation that would be messy, intrusive, and burdensome. Sweaty Shoppe therefore decided to accede to Brute Force's demand and entered the purchase and promotion contract. A week later, the report surfaced anyway because the human rights organization released it.

(a)   As Sweaty Shoppe no longer has an incentive to deal with Brute Force's goods, it would like to avoid the contract. Does it have grounds?

(b)   Would your answer change if the report was in fact true?

4. D. Fense Contractors, Inc. was awarded a contract by the Air Force to manufacture an early warning system for detecting invasions of alien space-craft. The system had been designed in an underground lab by a brilliant sci-entist, and the contract had very precise specifications. D. Fense was obliged to give this endeavor absolute priority and was to deliver the completed ma-chine in one year. The contract provided that if delivery was late, the Air Force would be entitled to claim liquidated damages in a horrendous amount for each day of delay. Also, it was well known in the defense industry that a contractor who has proved unreliable would have great difficulty in obtain-ing further government contracts in the future. D. Fense's plant was not suf-ficiently secure for work of a top secret nature, so it needed to find suitable premises. After some investigation, it discovered that an obscure company, Clandestine Industries of America, Inc. (CIA) had an idle plant that was ideal for the project. CIA agreed to let the premises to D. Fense for one year at an annual rent of $1 million. Six months later, after D. Fense had set up opera-tions in the premises, CIA's auditors surveyed the market and discovered that it had undercharged for the use of the premises, which could have been let for $1.25 million a year. CIA approached D. Fense with these figures and re-quested an additional $250,000 rent. When D. Fense refused, CIA threat-ened to terminate the lease and evict D. Fense from the plant. D. Fense knew that even if it defended eviction proceedings, the litigation would be disrup-tive and the outcome uncertain. It could not seek new premises and begin operations elsewhere without considerable trouble and delay, and it faced real danger of being prevented from honoring its delivery commitments to the Air Force. D. Fense reluctantly decided not to fight CIA on the demand for a price increase and gave in, promising to pay the additional $250,000 at the end of the lease term.

When the lease term had run, D. Fense refused to pay any more than the originally agreed rent. Can CIA enforce the modification?

5. One afternoon, Hardy Ticker developed intense chest pains while digging in his garden. His neighbor, Sam Aritan, noticed his distress and came over to see if he was alright. On being told the problem, Sam put Hardy into his car and rushed him to the nearest hospital, The Sisters of Good Con-science. The receptionist insisted that admission forms be completed before Hardy could be sent to the emergency room. Sam was concerned that Hardy needed urgent attention and begged the receptionist to admit Hardy while he completed the forms. The receptionist agreed. Sam completed as much of Hardy's biographical information as he knew and handed the form to the re-ceptionist. She told him that he had to sign it, which he did. He noticed that

the form had about half a page of printed text above the signature blank, but he did not read it. Had he done so, he would have found that he had signed a standard form contract with a provision that obligated the signatory to pay all the hospital's charges for treatment administered to the patient.

Sadly, Hardy died despite the efforts of the emergency room doctors. It was then discovered that he was insolvent and there is nothing in his estate. The hospital therefore demands payment of its fees from Sam, based on his signature on the form contract. Must Sam pay?

6. Mary Maker, a resident of California, decided to go on a cruise. After studying the brochures of several cruise lines, she settled on a seven-day package from Los Angeles to Mexico on the ship S.S. Briny Binge, owned and operated by Party Lines, Inc. Party Lines has its headquarters in Miami, Florida, and operates cruises out of Miami and Los Angeles. Mary called her local travel agent and booked. A week later she received her ticket, printed on one side of a single sheet of paper. She checked to make sure that the dates and cabin booking were correct. She did not otherwise read the printed matter on the ticket, despite a warning, printed on the ticket in large red letters, that stated "PASSENGER: THIS DOCUMENT AFFECTS YOUR LEGAL RIGHTS. READ IT!" Had she read the document, she would have found the following provision:

"This ticket is issued subject to the following terms and conditions:

1.   Party Lines, Inc. shall not be responsible for any loss or injury suffered by the passenger while on board the ship, whether or not caused by the negligence of Party Lines, Inc. or any of its employees or agents.
2.   In the event that any dispute should arise between Party Lines, Inc. and the passenger arising out of this transaction, the courts of the State of Florida shall have exclusive jurisdiction to hear and resolve such dispute."

Mary embarked on the ship. Three days into the cruise, while making her way to her cabin in the small hours of the morning, she did not notice a steep, poorly illuminated staircase. She tumbled down the stairs and injured herself. Upon returning home, she sued Party Lines in a California court, alleging that the company was negligent in failing to light the staircase, and claiming medical expenses and damages for pain and suffering. Party Lines requests summary judgment on the grounds that the California court has no jurisdiction in terms of the contract and that, in any event, Mary had contractually waived any claim that she may otherwise have had. Should summary judgment be granted?

7. Hi Rate Gems, Inc. operates a retail jewelry store in a less affluent neighborhood and draws most of its customers from the local area. They are typically quite poor and do not have the means to buy jewelry for cash, nor

could they qualify for credit under the usual market standards. To make sales, Hi Rate has found it necessary to provide financing to its customers under a lenient credit policy. As a result, its losses from uncollectible debt are much higher than those of more conservative lending institutions. To compensate for this, it prices its jewelry about 20 percent higher than the prevailing market and charges interest five percent above the market rate. To obtain credit, a customer is obliged to sign a standard form contract under which Hi Rate retains a security interest in the items purchased. This means that if the customer should default in payments, Hi Rate has the right to repossess the jewelry, to credit its value against the balance owing, and to institute collection action against the customer for any remaining deficiency.

Rock Sparkler bought a diamond nose stud with matching earrings from Hi Rate for $2,000. Rock did not have the $2,000, and his terrible credit record assured that no sensible lender would advance him a penny. He therefore applied for credit from Hi Rate. One of the questions on the form asked if any judgments had been granted against the applicant. Rock knew of at least five such unsatisfied judgments, but he feared that disclosing them would be fatal to the application. He did not wish to lie, so he simply ignored the question and left the space blank. Luckily, the credit clerk did not notice the omission because he did not look at the application very carefully before approving the financing. The sales assistant then filled out the details of the items purchased and the monthly payment rate on the standard form purchase agreement, and handed it to Rock for his signature. The assistant made no attempt to explain the form's printed terms to Rock, who did not read it before signing. He then took the jewelry and left.

A few weeks later, Hi Rate's credit manager was reviewing the applications and noticed that Rock had not answered the question about judgments. He checked the public record and discovered the unsatisfied judgments. Hi Rate wishes to rescind the contract and get the jewelry back. Has it the right to do so?

8. All the facts regarding the formation of the contract are the same as in Example 7. The only factual difference is as follows: Hi Rate did not check the public record. It is happy with the transaction and has no desire to avoid the contract. However, a short time after the purchase, Rock had misgivings about buying the jewelry. He would like to cancel the sale and return it. May he do so?

9. Rob Graves plundered a 3,000-year-old bronze figurine from the tomb of an ancient king. He smuggled it into the U.S. and used his contacts in the world of art collecting to find a buyer. He was put in touch with Ann Tiquity, a wealthy collector. Ann asked Rob how he acquired the figurine, and he told her that he had inherited from his grandfather, who found it while participating in an archeological dig in the late nineteenth century. Ann knows a great deal about art and had little trouble identifying the bronze as genuine. However, she comes from a very wealthy family and has always as-

sociated with rich people. She is therefore quite used to the idea that art treasures and other valuables are inherited from relatives, and Rob's explanation seemed quite reasonable to her. She purchased the figurine from him for $5 million cash, a remarkably low price for so rare a piece. In fact, after buying it, Ann had it appraised at $7 million.

Assume that federal law forbids the smuggling and sale of plundered artifacts and permits their confiscation and return to the country of origin. The statute does not apply to artifacts imported before 1900. Both parties knew about the law at the time of the transaction. A few weeks after the sale, U.S. Customs agents traced the figurine to Ann, took it from her and returned it to the government of the country from which it was smuggled. Ann has sued Rob for the return of the $5 million. Assuming that the federal statute contains no provisions dealing with the rights between the parties to the forbidden sale, should she be given restitution of her payment?

EXPLANATIONS

1. There are a number of statements, acts, or silences that could qualify as misrepresentations. Before examining them, we must address a preliminary issue raised by the merger clause in the written agreement: Even if the agreement is fully integrated, the parol evidence rule does not bar evidence of oral or prior written fraudulent misrepresentations. As stated in *Hill v. Jones,* 725 P.2d 1115 (Ariz. 1986), one of the several entomological cases discussed below, a party may not use a merger clause to exclude evidence of her fraudulent conduct. However, a completely integrated writing with an effective merger clause does bar parol evidence of innocent or negligent misrepresentations. The merger clause is on a standard form, but before you rush to judgment on the question of whether this may make the merger clause less effective in excluding evidence of innocent or negligent misrepresentations, remember that it is Bugsy, not Cookie, who made the decision to adopt the form. As the party responsible for the use of the form, Bugsy can hardly contend, now that his interests would be served by invalidating the clause, that Cookie imposed it on him.

Let us now consider each of the possible misrepresentations.

A. The Cockroaches and the Sinking

Cookie did not make any statement asserting that the house was free of cockroaches or that it was stable. However, concealment of the truth by conduct is as much an affirmative misrepresentation as a verbal misstatement. When the truth is known and the act of concealment is intended to induce the contract, the requisite scienter is present and the misrepresentation is fraudulent. It seems clear that Cookie's motive in fumigating and performing the cosmetic repairs to the wall went beyond acceptable preparations for sale and were deliberate steps to conceal serious problems that would have made the house less marketable.

The misrepresentation must have induced Bugsy to enter the contract on the agreed terms. When fraud is involved, the test for inducement is largely based on a subjective standard. Bugsy must show that the misrepresented fact was influential to him and that, given his circumstances and personal attributes, he was justified in relying on the false words or appearance. Of course, it is easier to show subjective inducement if the misrepresentation concerns a fact that would have been regarded as material and would have been relied on by a reasonable person. Although we do not know what motivated Bugsy to make the offer, the concealed facts are important even if viewed objectively, so it should not be difficult for him to show that they influenced him to make the offer. Bugsy probably should have had the house inspected for structural soundness and pests, or should at least have asked about more than just termites. His reliance on appearances may not have been justified. His lack of vigilance could weaken his case, but a court is likely to weigh his neglect against Cookie's active dishonesty, and her deliberate concealment will likely outweigh Bugsy's omission. Finally, prejudice is obvious. Not only does the house have a chronic cockroach problem, but it requires expensive repairs. Bugsy probably overpaid by agreeing to the full asking price, which we can assume was at least equal to the market price of the home in the condition represented. In any event, he does not want a home with these problems at any price.

In *Weintraub v. Krobatsch,* 317 A.2d 68 (N.J. 1974), the concealment was not as extensive and the problem not a serious as in this example, yet the court recognized the possibility of fraud. Before buying a home, the buyers always saw it with the lights on. Upon entering the house one evening just before the sale closed, they encountered a veritable cockroach convention. The fact that so many roaches had survived a recent routine fumigation showed that this was an especially bad infestation. The buyers refused to proceed with the closing, so the seller sued for damages and sought summary judgment. The buyers argued that the seller had committed fraud because she knew of the infestation (a fact that she denied) and deliberately kept the lights on to conceal it. They contended, in the alternative, that she had a duty to disclose it and even silence would have amounted to fraud. The court said that if the seller had known of the cockroach problem and it was not readily observable, fair dealing may have required her to disclose it and not to take steps to hide it. Furthermore, a cockroach infestation, while apparently curable by extensive further fumigation, could so badly put a buyer off a house that its concealment may have induced the sale. Because these factual issues needed to be resolved, the court refused the seller's motion for summary judgment and remanded for trial.

B. The Termites

When asked by Bugsy if the house had termites, Cookie answered incorrectly that it did not. Because she did not know about the termites at the time that she made the misrepresentation, it was innocent or, at worst, negligent. In *Halpert v. Rosenthal,* 267 A.2d 730 (R.I. 1970), the seller made a similar representation without knowledge of a termite infestation, but the court pointed out that even an innocent misrepresentation is grounds for avoidance if it is material and justifiably relied on by the other party. This rule does not apply in the present case because the integrated writing with a merger clause precludes Bugsy from introducing parol evidence of a non-fraudulent misrepresentation.

However, this does not end the matter. Before the contract was concluded, Cookie discovered the termites and acquired information that showed her previous representation to be false. She had a duty to disclose this to Bugsy before accepting his offer. As she did not, her newfound knowledge removed the innocence from her misrepresentation and made it fraudulent. She is in no better a position than if she had deliberately lied at the time of being asked the question, and the fact that Bugsy asked is good evidence that he relied on the answer in deciding to enter the contract.

C. The New Neighbors

Cookie's sin here is her failure to tell Bugsy that a halfway house for sex offenders was to be opened on the adjacent property. Although the nondisclosure of known information is not as obviously fraud as an affirmative act of lying or concealing the truth, it can be fraud if the duty of fair dealing imposes an obligation to speak. It can be difficult to decide when disclosure is required, because the law recognizes that fair dealing does not compel a party to bare all information pertinent to the transaction. Furthermore, even if there was a duty to speak, the omission may not be as culpable as a positive act. As a result, the prerequisites for relief are not as heavily weighted against the perpetrator, and the victim is more readily held accountable for failure to make diligent inquiry.

As a general guide, a party is only required to disclose information if four conditions are satisfied:

(1)   She knows that the other is unaware of it.
(2)   It would be reasonably likely to influence the other's decision to enter the transaction.
(3)   The information is not readily accessible to the other by diligent inquiry.
(4)   The information is not fairly regarded as the party's own property, having been acquired by special efforts or study.

Another termite case, *Hill v. Jones,* 725 P.2d 1115 (Ariz. 1986), illustrates the application of these principles. The sellers of a house did not tell the buyers that it had been infested by termites in the past. Although the termites had been eradicated and were no longer present, they had caused some damage to the house. Having kept quiet about this before the contract was concluded, the sellers were dumb enough to leave tell-tale brochures about termites in the kitchen drawer. Upon finding them after moving in, the buyers became suspicious, investigated, and discovered the history of termite problems. They sued for avoidance, and the sellers applied for summary judgment on the basis that they had no duty to disclose this fact. The appellate court reversed the trial court's grant of summary judgment and remanded the case for trial on the issue of whether the seller had a duty to speak. The court said that even if there were currently no termites in the house, the existence of termite damage could be a sufficiently material fact to dissuade a reasonable person from buying a house, and if the termite damage was not reasonably observable by diligent examination, fair dealing may require disclosure. The court mentions some additional facts that probably influenced its decision to submit the case to a factfinder and would later become significant at trial: The buyers knew something about termites and suspected damage at the time of viewing the house, but they employed a termite inspector who did not discover signs of prior infestation. This is relevant to the question of whether they were in fact induced by the nondisclosure and exercised due care. In addition there were some strategically-placed boxes and a potted plant that conveniently happened to cover some holes in the floor. It was not clear who had put the boxes down, but the plant was the seller's so there was a possibility of deliberate concealment. Finally, the buyers did notice and asked about a ripple in the parquet floor, which they recognized as being consistent with termite damage. The sellers told them that it was water damage. There had in fact been water damage in that area, so the assertion may have been true, but the question may have required a fuller answer. There was, therefore, the possibility of a false assertion, or at least a heightened duty to speak.

Cookie's silence about the halfway house seems less difficult to resolve. Given the outcry when a released sex offender takes up residence in a neighborhood, a reasonable person would assume that this information would be material to a homebuyer. The information is not proprietary, so Cookie cannot claim that she had the right to keep it to herself. However, the proposed home is a public project that has already been reported in the press. The information is freely available and for all Cookie knows, Bugsy has also read the paper. If not, it would be easy enough for him to gain access to the information. On balance, if he did not know about the halfway house, his lack of inquiry should preclude relief on this ground despite Cookie's silence.

2. This example is a factual variation of a couple of infamous Arthur Murray cases decided in the 1960s. In *Vokes v. Arthur Murray, Inc.*, 212 So. 2d 906 (Fla. 1968), and *Syester v. Banta*, 133 N.W.2d 666 (Iowa 1965), Arthur Murray franchisees employed the deliberate tactic of ongoing and excessive flattery to induce untalented elderly women to sign up for astoundingly large quantities of dance lessons at grotesque total cost. In both cases

the importuning, begun at first contact, was reinforced and accelerated during a long period of continuing lessons. The courts found that the fulsome praise, unremitting sweet talk, undeserved medals and awards, and untrue claims of progress were so extreme as to pass beyond good customer relations and become outright fraud.

The fraud in these cases was not the misrepresentation of an external objective fact, but of an opinion. By pretending that they believed the victims to have talent and potential, the studio employees lied about what they thought, inducing the victims to buy copious quantities of lessons. Although false opinions do not always qualify as factual misrepresentations, a deliberate misstatement of opinion can be fraud when the party expressing it claims to have the knowledge and expertise to form a judgment and should realize that the victim is relying on an honest assessment. As the brief description of the case suggests, the behavior of the Arthur Murray studios went far beyond the expression of a dishonest opinion. The transactions were thoroughly unsavory. Lonely and gullible elderly women were cruelly manipulated for a long period and induced to spend substantial amounts of their savings on extended courses of dance lessons that were unlikely to be used up in their lifetimes.

Fraud was the basis for relief in both cases, but the facts make an overwhelming case of unconscionability as well: As a result of the studios' slimy bargaining methods, their victims were induced to enter contracts for lessons well in excess of their needs at a ludicrous cost. Unconscionability doctrine is not needed when the elements of fraud are satisfied. However, if there is any doubt about establishing fraud, unconscionability serves as an alternative theory for avoidance. Tuttu's case may be an example of this.

Fraud Astaire's conduct was not as egregious as that of the Arthur Murray studios, and Tuttu, being a worldly former tax lawyer, is not as sympathetic a victim as the plaintiffs in those cases. Nevertheless, there were two instances of dishonesty by Gig, acting on behalf of Fraud Astaire, that could provide an argument for fraud. First, he deliberately misrepresented his opinion. However, this may not be a good basis for establishing fraud because his misrepresentation apparently did not induce Tuttu to enter the contract. Tuttu was not taken in by his flattery and was motivated by deeper urges. (Although he turned out not to be the instructor, there is no indication that he realized that this was an inducing factor or that he knew of and failed to disclose his impending dismissal.)

Second, he concealed the true nature of the form by placing his hands over it. If this is fraud, it would be in the factum, not in the inducement, because it relates to the document being signed rather than to a motivating fact. Note also that the misrepresentation is by concealment, not affirmative assertion. Although his intent is dishonest, Tuttu is probably damned by her sophistication and training. While an illiterate or naive person may be able to convince a factfinder of having been bamboozled into unwittingly signing a lifetime contract, Tuttu, a trained lawyer, should have known better than to sign something without reading it. The strategically placed hand adds no force to her case. Although the writing was concealed, it was easily discoverable (in fact, the attempt at concealment should have excited her suspicion). While inducement is based on a largely subjective standard, her attributes affect the credibility of any claim that she was actually induced to sign as a result of the clumsy deception. Having said this, it must be acknowledged that an argument of fraud is not entirely inconceivable if Tuttu can show an intent to defraud. Even extreme neglect may be outweighed by clear proof of the perpetrator's dishonesty.

If fraud is not a promising avenue for attack, unconscionability may be more successful. Bargaining unfairness short of actual fraud may be sufficient to show procedural unconscionability, and it should not be too difficult to demonstrate the substantive unfairness of a $10,000 contract for lifetime dance instruction. Unconscionability is less potent a weapon in the hands of a well-educated and commercially proficient party, but even former tax lawyers can be caught off guard by predators in the marketplace.

3(a). Sweaty Shoppe should be able to avoid the contract on grounds of duress because it has been induced to enter the contract by Brute Force's wrongful threat. The threatened action would lead to economic harm rather than physical injury, but it is well accepted in contemporary law that duress encompasses a wrongful threat of economic damage. There is nothing subtle about the threat in this case. It is blackmail pure and simple. Even if the disclosure had been motivated only by an honest desire to keep the public informed, the dissemination of false allegations could be wrongful in itself and may result in liability for defamation. When the threat of dissemination is meant to gain a private economic advantage, the wrongfulness is beyond debate.

The facts indicate that Sweaty Shoppe was in fact induced to enter the contract by the threat. Although modern law rejects the objective test of "ordinary firmness," the victim must still show justification for giving in to the threat. The test is whether, given all the circumstances, the victim had no reasonable alternative but to acquiesce. Sweaty Shoppe did have alternatives. The most obvious would have been to refuse to contract with Brute Force and to deal with the consequences of the disclosure by suing for defamation, mounting a publicity campaign to correct the public perception, and averting prosecution by convincing the government of its compliance with the law. However, this is not likely to be regarded as a reasonable alternative given the cost and expense as well as the strong likelihood that Sweaty Shoppe would probably never be able to fully redeem its public image. Another possible alternative may be to try to avert the harm by seeking an injunction against release of the information. However, even if a court could be persuaded to enjoin publication, the proceedings would inevitably engender the very publicity sought to be avoided. There are probably other alternatives that could be suggested, but the court is likely to be sympathetic to the victim's claim that they all seemed risky and harmful.

The compelling effect of potential harm to customer goodwill is illustrated by *S. P. Dunham & Co. v. Kudra*, 131 A.2d 306 (N.J. 1957). Unknown to its customers, when a department store accepted their fur coats for cleaning and storage, the store did not keep the coats itself, but entrusted them to a concessionaire, who in turn stored the coats with a rival store. The concessionaire became bankrupt and did not pay storage charges due on these and other garments. The rival store wrongfully refused to release the coats unless the department store agreed to pay the concessionaire's debt. Although it was not legally responsible for the debt, the department store agreed to pay it to avoid the embarrassment of not being able to return its customers' coats and having to reveal that they were being stored with a competitor. The court held that although the store had the alternative of refusing to pay and suing for return of the wrongfully retained coats, this alternative was not reasonable because the publicity and delay of litigation would result in the very harm to customer relations that the department store was anxious to avoid.

3(b). The result of the case may have been different had the allegations about the working conditions been true. The truth of the allegations does not change the conclusion that the threat is wrongful. Because the facts are true, the act of publication is no longer wrongful in itself if motivated by the desire to serve the public interest. However, even a proper act loses its legitimacy if performed for the ulterior motive of blackmail for private advantage. Knowing the truth, Brute Force chose not to reveal the facts to the public, but rather to conceal it for a price, using the power of its knowledge to coerce Sweaty Shoppe into a contract.

In addition, as the importation of goods manufactured with child labor is a crime, Brute Force has done more than merely threaten adverse publicity. It is essentially agreeing not to report the criminal activity in exchange for the commitment to purchase its products. This is a dereliction of duty and a violation of public policy. Knowledge of criminal activity cannot be used as a bargaining chip in contract negotiations. This is illustrated by *Germantown Mortgage Co. v. Rawlinson*, 491 A.2d 138 (Pa. 1985). After discovering that its employee had been embezzling money, the employer persuaded the employee's wife to undertake repayment of the funds. In addition to other questionable bargaining tactics, it intimated that it would not press charges against the employee if she agreed to the commitment. Although the act of prosecuting the employee would have been justified, the court found a wrongful threat because the employer used its power to prosecute for the purpose of inducing the contract.

The element of inducement is, if anything, strengthened by the fact that the allegations are true. It weakens or eliminates the alternative of allowing the dissemination of the information and trying to counter it. As the court pointed out in *Germantown Mortgage*, the threat is improper, whether or not the party is guilty of the alleged action. But if the party is guilty, the threat is even more intimidating, and the apprehension of the threatened disclosure is more likely to cloud judgment and volition.

There are a number of public policies implicated in this case. Brute Force has offended two policies: Its attempt at blackmail violates the assent policy of contract law, and its illegitimate use of the threat of criminal prosecution harms the public interest in the proper investigation and punishment of criminal activity. Sweaty Shoppe has also violated policy by using child labor. This mutual misbehavior leads to the additional consideration of whether the public welfare is best served by refusing enforcement of the contract. The answer must be that it is. To refuse enforcement directly serves two of these policies and is at least consonant with the third. It upholds the assent policy by not binding Sweaty Shoppe to a coerced transaction. By refusing to recognize the binding effect of a commitment not to prosecute, it reduces the incentive to use bargain over criminal prosecution. A contrary argument may be that a refusal of relief to Sweaty Shoppe would further the policy against child labor by punishing it for its nefarious foreign activity. However, this consideration is outweighed by those in favor of non-enforcement because the law provides other penalties for addressing this problem.

Although nonenforcement favors Sweaty Shoppe in this case, the result may not always benefit the lawbreaker. A manufacturer in a future case who may genuinely desire to make a binding cover-up agreement is forewarned that it cannot lawfully buy silence, and a promise not to disclose the information would not likely be binding on the informant.

4. This contract does not involve a sale of goods, so the common law applies. In traditional common law analysis, the modification is unenforceable because CIA had a pre-existing duty to let the premises for the original rent, and it suffered no new detriment in exchange for D. Fense's promise to pay more money. (The undertaking not to breach does not qualify as a legal detriment because although CIA has the power to breach, it has no legal right to do so.) Therefore, while the real reason for refusing enforcement is that the modification was coerced, consideration doctrine achieves this purpose indirectly by focusing on the lack of exchange in the modification. This indirect approach to policing modifications is illustrated by *Alaska Packers Assn. v. Domenico,* 117 F. 99 (9th Cir. 1902). A cannery contracted with a group of fishermen to harvest salmon during the short Alaskan season. After the fishermen had been transported to Alaska and the season had begun, they refused to continue work unless their wages were increased. (Their demand was based on the pretext that working conditions were more burdensome than expected, but this contention was disputed by the employer and not accepted at trial.) The employer had to acquiesce because it would have been impossible to get a replacement crew to Alaska in time for the harvest, but when the fishermen claimed the extra wages at the end of the season, the employer refused to pay. The court found against the fishermen on the basis that they had incurred no new detriment in exchange for the promise of a wage

increase. However, the opinion makes it clear that the true reason for nonenforcement was that the court considered the demand for more money to have been extortionate and unjustified.

Although consideration doctrine can serve the purpose of policing for unfair modifications, it does not assure correct resolution, because it focuses on the exchange rather than on the justification for the modification. It could therefore lead to the enforcement of an unfair modification if some small detriment is given for it, or conversely, it could result in the nonenforcement of a fair modification simply because no new detriment was suffered by the party who was benefited by the change. Recognizing this, a court may decide to move away from consideration analysis in a common law case, and to adopt the approach of policing more directly on the basis of duress. Although not directly applicable, UCC §2.209 may be used as a persuasive analogy. It is therefore useful to consider how this case would be resolved if it involved a sale of goods.

Had this contract been a sale of goods rather than a lease of premises, consideration doctrine would have been inapplicable. UCC §2.209 rejects the doctrine as a means of policing modifications and replaces it with a good faith test. Under §2.209 the court must directly deal with the question of whether the modification was extortionate, or was fair and justified under all the circumstances of the case. In *Austin Instrument Co. v. Loral Corp.*, 272 N.E.2d 533 (N.Y. 1971), Loral had been awarded a Navy contract to supply radar equipment. Like D. Fense, it was subject to strict delivery terms and a substantial liability for late delivery. It subcontracted with Austin for the supply of components. After performance had begun, Austin realized that it had underbid. It threatened not to deliver the parts ordered unless Loral agreed to a price increase. (The extent of the extortion was aggravated by the additional demand that Loral agree to use Austin as the subcontractor in another contract Loral had just made with the Navy.) Loral tried to find another supplier, but it could not obtain the components elsewhere in time. Faced with inevitable delay, liability for damages to the Navy, and harm to its reputation as a reliable contractor, Loral unsuccessfully tried to negotiate with Austin and eventually, under protest, gave in to its demands. After the completion of performance Loral refused to pay the extra price and Austin sued. The majority of the court held that Loral's free will was undermined by the pressure induced by Austin's threat of breach, so the modification was voidable on grounds of duress. However, a dissent expressed the view that the demand for a higher price was commercially reasonable because there had been a genuine escalation of costs, and agreements for price increases were not uncommon under such circumstances.

This difference in view shows that the distinction between a fair modification and an extortionate one is not always self-evident, but involves a careful evaluation of the motivation and business justification of the demand, the commercial expectations and practices, the force with which the demand is asserted, and the pressures to which the acquiescing party is subject. A subtle line separates opportunism and abuse of power from a fair request for an adjustment of terms. As noted earlier, *Austin Instrument* is not exactly on point here because the present case is not a sale of goods. But even in common law cases, courts have increasingly recognized the shortcomings of consideration analysis as a policing mechanism and have favored a more direct inquiry into the question of whether the modification was coerced.

5. A similar situation occurred in *Phoenix Baptist Hospital v. Aiken*, 877 P.2d 1345 (Ariz. 1994). After rushing his wife to the hospital, a husband signed a form contract obliging him to pay the hospital's charges. In the absence of this undertaking he would not have been personally liable for his wife's medical expenses. The hospital sued him and applied for summary judgment on the basis of his signature on the form. The court refused summary judgment and held that the husband was entitled to go to trial on the question of whether the contract was unconscionable. The court said that the contract appeared adhesive, signed under traumatic and hurried circumstances in which the husband had little realistic opportunity to know what he was signing. Even if he did know, the emotional stress and the need for the hospital's immediate services would likely leave him without power to bargain, and give him no choice but to acquiesce in order to ensure that his wife received medical attention. Adhesion of this kind could make the contract procedurally unconscionable, but this on its own is not enough. In addition, he must prove substantive unconscionability, which could lie in the fact that he assumed liability for which he would not otherwise be responsible, and that he could not reasonably have expected to be provided for in the form that he signed. Note that this was not a sale of goods, so unconscionability doctrine does not derive from UCC §2.302. This is one of the many modern cases that recognizes unconscionability as a doctrine applicable to contracts under common law.

As discussed more fully in Example 6, adhesion and procedural unconscionability are not present merely because the contract is a standard form drafted by the party with greater bargaining power, or because the choices of the weaker party are limited. However, when the services contracted for are desperately and urgently needed, and the party to perform the services presents a form without explanation or a reasonable opportunity to read, in circumstances that make bargaining burdensome or futile, it should not be very difficult to make a case for procedural unconscionability. It is not required that the hospital purposely used unfair bargaining methods to trick or coerce Sam into signing. The procurement of apparent assent under these circumstances should be enough. Sam's emotional stake in the rendition of the services to Hardy is not as strong as that of a spouse, but the stress and urgency of the situation is patent. Sam would not have to show that the terms were objectively unfair—for example, that the hospital charged an excessive price. The substantive unconscionability lies in the fact that Sam incurred an obligation that he would not otherwise have, for services from which he received no personal gain. In this respect, his case is stronger than that of a spouse. There is thus an adequate showing of substantive unconscionability—but even if a court may question this conclusion, the strong showing of procedural unfairness would seem to place beyond doubt the need to give Sam relief.

Unconscionability is the most appropriate basis for relief in this case. Could it also have been argued under a theory of duress? Duress doctrine has expanded enough to make this a possibility, in that the threat to withhold medical services for Hardy undermined Sam's free will and coerced him into signing. However, this strains the concept of improper threat because the hospital did nothing more than indicate intent not to enter a contract except on its own terms. This cannot be a threat unless it can be concluded that the hospital had a duty outside of contract law to render services to any patient brought in.

6. Mary was not even told about these standard terms when she booked, so that "adhesion" alarm is probably flashing in your brain. Yet it cannot be that simple because we all know that cruise lines, airlines, hotels, credit card issuers, insurance companies, and other businesses often accept telephone bookings or simple application forms, and only afterwards send a formal document with boilerplate terms that were not even hinted at the time of booking or application. As they keep on doing it, it must work, at least some of the time. This case involves two standard terms that affect Mary's right to sue for her injury. The liability disclaimer is the most serious. If it is effective she cannot sue for her injury at all. The forum selection clause is less devastating, but if valid, it will lead to dismissal of her present suit in California and subject her to the inconvenience and expense of litigating in Florida. This presents four separate but closely interconnected inquiries:

(1)   Can Party Lines' standard terms be part of a contract if they were not communicated to Mary at the time of formation? This raises an issue of contract formation.

(2)   If the terms are part of the contract, do they have the legal effect contended for by Party Lines? This is an interpretation issue.

(3)   If this is also answered affirmatively, are one or both terms unconscionable?

(4)   Is public policy offended by one or both terms?

A. The Formation Issue

In some situations, the facts could show that the booking is just a preliminary communication, and the actual contract is formed only when the customer receives and accepts the document (such as the ticket or insurance policy) fully setting out its terms. However, in the typical case this is clearly not the intent, and the parties consider the contract to arise when the booking or application is accepted. If the customer is given a record of the terms only after formation of the contract, this seems to be the worst kind of imposition. Not only has the dominant party prepared standard terms, but it does not even bother to show them to the other party at the time of contracting. This really should not work, and it often does not. Although it is not required that the parties actually bargain over terms, it is at least necessary that the proposed terms be on the table and available for reading at the time the contract is formed. Even if one of the parties intends terms to be part of the contract, it can hardly claim that the other assented to them if they are not revealed until after the contract has been made.

Nevertheless, there are situations in which it is reasonable to infer that the non-drafting party impliedly assented to standard terms that were not presented to her at the time of contracting. For such assent to be inferred, it must be well known in the marketplace that contracts of that kind are likely to be subject to standard terms, and the terms in issue must be so commonly used and familiar that the non-drafting party should reasonably expect them. Of course, the terms must have been in existence and on record at the time of contracting. They cannot have been unilaterally created afterwards. It must be stressed that courts do not routinely sanction this practice, and circumstances in the market must justify the conclusion that the non-drafting party actually or reasonably should have anticipated in the terms. Because disclaimers of tort liability present strong public policy concerns (as discussed later), courts are resistant to upholding them unless they are shown to have been consensual. This means that disclaimers in standard forms are generally regarded with disfavor and are even less likely to be tolerated when the term was not brought to the attention of the non-drafting party at the time of contracting. A forum selection clause, being less devastating to the rights of the non-drafting party, has a better chance of sympathetic consideration.

Therefore, the basis for refusing to enforce terms not made available at the time of contracting may simply be that they were not agreed to and did not become part of the contract. If you read the above reasoning astutely, you would have been struck by its similarity to unconscionability analysis. The imposition of the terms is oppressive and unfairly surprising unless the terms are usual and reasonably anticipated. If they are too harsh or one-sided, the inference that they were unexpected is very strong. Therefore, unconscionability could be used as an alternative rationale for refusing the enforcement of terms that are not made available at the time of contracting. However, we do not need to test the terms for unconscionability unless we first decide that they entered the contract. This is why the discussion of unconscionability is left for later in this explanation.

We do not know enough about market practices to reach a firm conclusion on whether these two terms should reasonably have been expected by Mary. If it is indeed routine practice for cruise lines and other providers of tourist services to issue tickets with terms and conditions only after the contract has been formed, Mary may be held accountable for knowledge that the transaction is subject to standardized terms. If the terms themselves are routine and familiar, she may be taken to have assented to them tacitly by her failure to ask about them and to negotiate different terms at the time of booking. If this is so, they become part of the contract and bind her unless they can be overturned on one of the three following grounds.

B. Interpretation

Even if the terms are part of the contract, it is possible that their language may not be entirely clear, so that any adverse effect on Mary's rights could be avoided by restrictive interpretation. The language of the disclaimer creates some doubt about its scope. It exonerates Party Lines from "loss or injury," but does not specifically state that this includes personal injury. The juxtaposition of the words "loss" and "injury" may suggest that only economic harm is covered. If there is any doubt, the *contra proferentum* rule favors interpretation against the drafter, so if Party Lines seeks to subject its passengers to a standard disclaimer, it had better make sure that its language leaves no doubt as to scope in the mind of the reasonable customer. Thus, the term could simply be gutted by interpretation.

The forum selection clause may also be susceptible to interpretational challenge. The argument could be made that the language "any dispute . . . arising out of [the] . . . transaction" is not broad enough to cover tort claims for personal injury and should be confined to issues concerning the proper performance of services promised in the contract.

C. Unconscionability

As noted earlier, the unconscionability of the terms need not be addressed unless it is found both that they became part of the contract and that they have the meaning contended for by Party Lines. In this case, the analysis of procedural unconscionability closely mirrors the inquiry into whether the terms were part of the contract, and if that issue was resolved in favor of Party Lines, this one should be as well. Any bargaining unfairness would lie in the adhesive nature of the terms. Mary must show that she had no meaningful choice but to accept the terms, which were imposed on her without her reasonable awareness, and with no possibility of negotiation. It is not enough for her to base this assertion on the mere fact that these were standard terms; improper imposition must have occurred. There is no unfair surprise if a reasonable customer would have anticipated the terms as a result of commercial usage (such as the widespread use of disclaimers or the marketing and promotion of separate insurance coverage) or Party Lines' own efforts at alerting customers of the existence of the term. If, in light of this reasonable expectation, Mary did not bother asking to see the terms or haggling over them, she would have difficulty in showing a lack of meaningful choice.

To establish substantive unconscionability, Mary must show more than that the terms are adverse to her interests. They must be unfair or unduly one-sided in relation to what she paid for the cruise. The clauses could be fair, despite their unfortunate consequences for Mary, if they are justified by business realities, and are part of a reasonable exchange for her payment. For example, it could be that without the disclaimer and forum selection clauses, Party Lines would have such a large exposure to liability and litigation costs that the price of cruise tickets would have to be considerably higher.

These concerns were discussed by the U.S. Supreme Court in relation to a forum selection clause in *Carnival Cruise Lines, Inc. v. Shute*, 499 U.S. 585 (1991). Like Party Lines, Carnival is based in Florida, and its cruise tickets contained a clause designating the Florida courts as the agreed forum for resolving disputes. (There was no disclaimer of liability in issue in the case.) The Shutes, residents of Washington, booked a cruise to Mexico from Los Angeles. Only after booking did they receive their tickets with the forum selection clause. During the cruise, Ms. Shute slipped on a deck mat and injured herself. She later sued in federal district court in her home state of Washington. (Federal court was selected because it was an Admiralty case.) On the motion of Carnival, the district court granted summary judgment dismissing the suit on the basis that it should have been brought in Florida. The Ninth Circuit reversed on the grounds that the clause was not freely bargained, but the Supreme Court disagreed, reinstating the trial court's summary judgment.

The plaintiff conceded notice of the clause, so the court did not have to deal with the issue of whether printing it on the ticket was sufficient to make it part of the contract. Therefore, the opinion concentrates on the question of whether the standard clause was unfair and was imposed on Ms. Shute without her meaningful assent. The majority noted that standardized forum selection clauses should be scrutinized for fairness, but this does not mean that they are presumptively invalid. Form contracts are efficient and serve a useful purpose in routine cases. It would be absurd to expect a cruise line to negotiate the terms of the ticket individually with each passenger. Therefore, the fact that Ms. Shute had no real power to negotiate the clause does not, in itself, make it invalid. She must also show that the forum selection was unreasonable or was primarily intended not to ease the cruise line's burden, but to discourage or hamper suit. This was not true in the present case because Carnival had a legitimate interest in selecting the courts of Florida: It would save litigation costs by ensuring that all claims were brought in its home courts, and by removing doubt about the choice of forum. Passengers may also benefit in that a reduction in legal expenses could be passed on to customers in the form of lower fares. Finally, because Carnival was based in Florida and many cruises departed from there, the forum selection was reasonable and not alien or selected for purposes of frustrating claims. The dissent argued that efficiency and a reduction in Carnival's litigation costs were not a good enough reason to bind a passenger to a clause that was unlikely to be noticed at all (it was one of 25 paragraphs on the ticket) and was not even made available at the time of contracting. Apart from the adhesive nature of the clause, the dissent felt that it was substantively unfair because it deprived the passenger of the ability to enforce her rights in the least expensive and most convenient forum.

D. Public Policy

Quite apart from the assent and reliance policies of contract law, other public policies are implicated in both liability disclaimers and forum selection clauses. These policies have already been taken into account indirectly, because they influence the decisions discussed above. However, concerns of public policy may be so strong that the contract's violation of policy may be an independent ground for refusing enforcement.

The forum selection clause affects Mary's fundamental right to seek redress in a court that would otherwise have jurisdiction. It thereby impairs an important public interest in uninhibited access to justice. The majority in *Carnival Cruise Lines* held that this policy does not absolutely invalidate an agreement restricting this right of access. However, it stressed that the agreement must be genuine and freely made and that the selected forum must be reasonable. Thus, the assent policy of contract law is congruent with and reinforced by the policy of protecting access to relief from an appropriate and convenient court. These policies call for specially careful scrutiny of forum selection clauses to ensure not only that apparent assent was genuine, but also that the basis for choosing a particular court was justifiable. This is particularly so where the clause is in a standard form and the circumstances suggest the strong possibility of imposition. Having asserted this principle, the majority found the clause to be consensual and fair, a conclusion with which the dissent disagreed.

Even if the majority's conclusion appeals to you more than the dissent's, it may not be helpful to Party Lines because of the important factual difference noted above. Unlike Ms. Shute, Mary has not conceded notice of the clause. Therefore, although the public policy disfavoring forum selection clauses is not, on its own, a basis for invalidating the clause, it does serve as a bolstering argument for the grounds of nonenforcement discussed above.

Disclaimers of liability implicate a different policy. There is a strong public interest, reflected in the rules of tort law, in holding people accountable for loss or injury caused by their negligent or intentional conduct. A contractual provision that exonerates a party from tort liability infringes upon this policy of accountability. The effect of such a clause depends on the extent to which it harms the public interest. Some disclaimers are regarded as so pernicious that they are not upheld at all, even if they are genuinely consensual. For this reason, a disclaimer of liability for intentional or reckless injury is generally regarded as unenforceable, whether or not it was freely bargained. It offends public policy to permit a person to obtain advance immunity from deliberate or reckless wrongful conduct.

A disclaimer of liability for negligence is seen as less harmful to the public good, and it is generally allowed if it is truly consensual. However, this is not invariably true. In *McCutcheon v. United Homes Corp.*, 486 P.2d 1093 (Wash. 1971), a standard form lease indemnified the lessor for injury suffered by tenants on the premises. A tenant was injured when she fell down an unlighted flight of steps. Upon being sued by the tenant for negligence in tort, the lessor sought and obtained summary judgment on the basis of the exculpatory clause in the lease. The judgment was overturned on appeal, not on the basis that the disclaimer was nonconsensual or unconscionable, but on grounds of public policy. The court considered it to be in the vital public interest that lessors be obliged to maintain safe conditions in residential buildings, and that they should not be able to contract out of this duty. The court was unpersuaded by the argument that parties should be able to order their relationship by contract. It said that because so many people rent apartments, their safety and protection is a matter of public concern, passing beyond the realm of private ordering. Of course, one cannot fail to notice that the disclaimer in the case was on a widely used standard form, so elements of adhesion and inadequate consent were present and influenced the decision. Nevertheless, the court chose the broader basis of public policy to invalidate the disclaimer.

Party Lines' disclaimer is not confined to negligent conduct, but it would be so limited on public policy grounds. However, there is no indication that liability here resulted from anything beyond simple negligence. The safety of the cruising public is arguably as much a matter of public concern as that of tenants, so the *McCutcheon* approach may be an appealing means of disposing of this case. However, many courts would find *McCutcheon's* per se invalidation of the disclaimer to be too strong an assertion of the policy of public protection at the expense of the policy of freedom of contract. For those courts, the policy becomes nothing more than an added factor in deciding whether to refuse enforcement on one of the other bases discussed above.

7. Rock's failure to disclose the judgments likely qualifies as a fraudulent misrepresentation. Even though he did not affirmatively lie, he declined to disclose known information when asked. In some situations it may be difficult to decide if a party has the duty to disclose facts pertinent to the transaction, but this is not such a case. It is generally accepted that a duty of honest response does arise if the other party asks a direct question, particularly when the information sought is not of a proprietary nature. By ignoring the question with knowledge that a true answer would imperil the credit application, Rock makes a deliberate misrepresentation of fact with knowledge of its falsity and intent to induce the contract.

It is more difficult to say whether the misrepresentation did in fact induce the contract. A debtor's unreliability in other transactions is generally a crucial factor in the decision to grant credit. However, Hi Rate's cursory look at the form suggests that its standard for granting credit is very low indeed. If it really cared about the applicant's credit history or was truly interested in the answers on the application, it would have taken more trouble to read the form. Furthermore, judgments are a matter of public record, easily accessible to the prospective creditor. A creditor who regards this information as crucial would not simply rely on the applicant's disclosure and would check. Normally, when fraud is involved, the serious malfeasance of the perpetrator outweighs any lapse of care by the victim in failing to check the facts. But actual inducement must still be shown, and where the victim is sophisticated enough to know better, careless gullibility may break the chain of justified reliance.

In addition, there is some suggestion in this case that Hi Rate is not being entirely responsible or socially conscious in selling expensive luxury items to people who cannot afford them, and that it has ameliorated its risk of loss by padding its prices and interest rates. Although this does not excuse Rock's dishonesty, Hi Rate cannot comfortably don the mantle of innocent dupe. It can fairly be expected to take care of its own interests. In short, without condoning Rock's deceitful silence, a court may be indisposed to allow Hi Rate out of the contract. As long as Rock continues to make his payments as promised, Hi Rate must live with the risk of his lack of creditworthiness.

8. There is nothing to suggest that Hi Rate made any misrepresentation to Rock, or that it applied any threat to make him enter the contract. Therefore, if Rock is to have any right of avoidance, it must be based on unconscionability.[6] Avoidance of the contract, as opposed to enforcement on adjusted terms, is within the range of relief available to Rock at the court's discretion.

Because Hi Rate seems to have a captive market and it imposes higher prices and adverse terms on its customers under standard form contracts, one may jump to the conclusion that Hi Rate is a predatory mass contractor subjecting a whole section of the community to its harsh contracts of adhesion. This conclusion is even more tempting if one perceives it as socially harmful to sell luxury items on credit to people who cannot afford them. However, it is important to resist the knee-jerk reaction, and to look at the facts of the transaction soberly.

These issues are raised in one of the earliest cases dealing with the modern approach to unconscionability, *Williams v. Walker Thomas Furniture Co.*, 350 F.2d 445 (D.C. Cir. 1965). Ms. Williams (and other plaintiffs) had pur-

---

6. As the following discussion shows, the public policy of consumer protection is inherent in the unconscionability analysis and is one of the motivations for unconscionability doctrine. One could therefore say that the right of avoidance is based on public policy, but this is always true because all contract doctrines have a policy basis.

chased several appliances and items of furniture from Walker Thomas over the years. Each sale was on credit, secured by the store's retention of a security interest in the item sold. However, the standard form contract went further than this. By structuring payments so that no prior sale was ever paid off, the store extended the security interest not only to the most recent purchase, but to every item bought on credit in the past. The effect of this "cross-collateralization" clause (as it is known) was that default would mean not merely repossession of the new goods, but also of all the aging and much depreciated past purchases. The realizable value of these older bits of household property was small, so they would likely generate little proceeds on resale and were not worth much as collateral. However, the debtor probably still needed them and would have an added incentive not to default.

Ms. Williams' most recent purchase was a new stereo. When she failed to make her payments, the store sought to enforce the cross-collateralization clause. Although the case involved the sale of goods, the UCC was not yet applicable because it had not been enacted in the District of Columbia at the time of the transaction. Therefore, the lower courts expressed disapproval of the store's business practices, but found no basis for granting relief. The court of appeals recognized unconscionability as a ground for relief under common law as well and disagreed that the courts were powerless to act in the absence of statutory authority. Suggesting that the case had the hallmarks of unconscionability, it remanded it for a determination of this issue. To guide the trial court, the court of appeals described the essence of unconscionability as an absence of meaningful choice by the one party, resulting in contract terms unreasonably favorable to the other. To decide whether the one party was deprived of meaningful choice, the entire circumstances of the transaction must be examined, including the personal attributes to the parties (such as their relative education and sophistication) and the stronger party's bargaining techniques.

Would these principles permit relief for Rock? This is a sale of goods and the UCC is now firmly in place, so whether or not the jurisdiction has accepted it as a doctrine of general application under common law, unconscionability applies by virtue of UCC §2.302. *Williams* foreshadows the well-accepted elements of unconscionability. The lack of meaningful choice evokes the concept of procedural unconscionability, and the unreasonably one-sided terms suggests the element of substantive unconscionability. These elements need not be exhibited with similar strength, so that if one of them clearly exists, the other may be present in minimal form. In Rock's case, however, neither is overwhelmingly demonstrated.

A. Procedural Unconscionability

Hi Rate has not employed high-pressure selling techniques or behaved deceptively. Notwithstanding, *Walker* suggests that procedural unconscionability could be present simply because Rock had no meaningful choice—that is, that Hi Rate had the power to dictate the terms and because Rock had no means of acquiring the jewelry otherwise, he had no choice but to adhere. The fact of adhesion may, in itself, constitute procedural unconscionability, even when no specific instance of improper bargaining conduct can be identified. However, it must be clear that the situation truly is adhesive. The dissent in *Williams* warns of the danger of finding unconscionability too readily when the economic underdog cannot point to any specific sharp practice. It noted that this could open the door to judicial tampering with transactions whenever a more powerful contractor makes standard-term credit sales to consumers on the lower end of the economic scale. Such a paternalistic approach, motivated by the desire to protect consumers, could have the effect of discouraging credit in that market and depriving the customers of the opportunity to purchase what they desire. Therefore, courts must proceed cautiously and with full recognition that the realities of the market may inevitably reduce the range of choices for the weaker party.

There were factors limiting Rock's choices in the present transaction, but Hi Rate is not selling something essential to sustain life, or even services or goods basic to decent living. The "absence of choice" analysis becomes tenuous when applied to luxury goods like jewelry. It is plain silly to suggest that Rock really had no meaningful choice. Hi Rate's contracting procedure seems more insouciant than pushy. Procedurally, its greatest fault may lie in its failure to take pains to draw its customers' attention to its higher price and interest rates and to adequately alert them to the existence and meaning of its standard terms, such as the grant of the security interest, incorporated into preprinted boilerplate. It is not clear if Rock knew that he could find the goods more cheaply elsewhere, or that he understood what he was signing. However, it is not alleged that Hi Rate attempted to conceal this information or to divert him from ascertaining it, and he surely has some duty to survey the market and to read and understand what he is signing. Because he did not object to any proposed terms or attempt to negotiate over them, it cannot be concluded that negotiation would have been unavailing. It must be stressed that this last remark is directed at Rock's situation. It is not intended as a general standard applicable in every case. Under the right circumstances, a dominant party may have a stronger duty to alert the weaker and less sophisticated party to the content of the written standard forms. The idea that there is an absolute duty to read—no matter what the circumstances—has diminished in our law as it has moved away from a rigid objectivity.

We should also not forget that Rock was sly enough to practice his own bit of deception. Because unconscionability is derived from equity, his wrongful conduct could be taken into account when he asks the court for relief. In addition, his conduct reveals a degree of sophistication that belies the image of a downtrodden consumer. His failure to read or quibble over the terms may have been motivated by an eagerness to conclude the deal before his omission on the application was noticed and queried.

B. Substantive Unconscionability

The contract terms may sound adverse to the customer, but the facts suggest that they may be based on sound business practice and may be commercially reasonable under the circumstances. The excess price and interest rate could be justified by the increased cost and risk of extending credit in this market (but we need further evidence to be sure that they are not appreciably higher than justified). The retention of a security interest is widely used as a means of protecting a creditor from default, and as long as its terms are not unduly harsh, it is not objectionable. The term may be unduly harsh if, for example, it encumbers property of value well beyond the debt or waives rules designed to protect the debtor from improper foreclosure. A cross-collateralization clause such as that used in *Williams* is also commonly perceived as beyond the realm of commercial legitimacy in consumer transactions, particularly when the additional collateral consists of used household goods with little realizable value. In such a case, the strong inference is that the creditor's true motive for including these goods is not to ensure that the debt is fully covered by adequate collateral, but to terrorize the debtor into avoiding default.

9. This example involves issues of fraud and illegality. Rob made a fraudulent misrepresentation by lying about the way in which he acquired the figurine. Two elements of fraud, scienter and prejudice, are surely satisfied. Scienter is present because Rob knew the statement was false and must have realized that Ann, as a collector, probably knew the law, and would likely not have bought the figurine if she thought it had been illegally smuggled into the U.S. He therefore deliberately made a false statement with intent to induce the contract. Injury to Ann is obvious because she has paid for the piece that has been lost as a result of the flaw in title, concealed by Rob's lie.

The element that is in doubt is inducement. Normally, the test for inducement in a fraud case is largely subjective—it tries to glean the actual state of mind of the victim, and to determine whether the misrepresentation did in fact induce her to enter the contract. A subjective test would give Ann some hope of convincing the factfinder that she truly was as naive and unworldly as the facts suggest. However, even under a subjective test, her claimed innocence strains credulity. Given her knowledge of art dealings and law, a more likely explanation is that she deliberately avoided inquiry because the bargain was too good to miss, and she did not want to know the truth.

Therefore, even under the usual subjective standard, Ann could have trouble showing inducement. However, in this particular case, there is a strong argument for not using a subjective test of inducement, but of objectively evaluating her reliance on the misrepresentation. On an objective test, her chance of success is remote. Although we do not have evidence of acceptable market behavior, we can at least make the preliminary assumption that a reasonable collector, knowing the risk of confiscation, would not likely spend $5 million on an artifact without verifying the truth of Rob's assertion.

The reason for moving to an objective test in this case lies in the fact that reliance on Rob's fraudulent misrepresentation would lead Ann to violate the law, so we are no longer concerned only with the assent and reliance policies of contract law, but also with the policy reflected in the federal statute. If the only matter at stake was Ann's duty to herself, we could accept her genuine reliance, even if she had been sloppy in failing to probe further. Her fault in lack of vigilance pales before Rob's venality, and a subjective standard meets the need of balancing the assent and reliance policies of contract law. However, by making the purchase of smuggled artifacts unlawful, the statute imposes a public duty on Ann that goes beyond her responsibility to safeguard her own interests, and it demands a higher level of justification for her conduct. By buying the property, she makes its smuggling worthwhile and she frustrates the goals of the law. Her role is similar to that of a fence receiving stolen goods, and public policy may demand that she be held accountable for her (objective) reason to know of the figurine's origins. She may even have an affirmative duty to verify the seller's assertion. If this is so, she fails the test of inducement and is not entitled to relief.

Ann may therefore have difficulty establishing fraud and probably cannot base her claim for avoidance of the contract and restitution on that theory. However, illegality may provide an alternative ground on which to claim restitution. The federal statute, although it does not expressly declare the contract void, does have that effect by confiscating the artifact despite its sale by the smuggler. When illegality affects the contract, a party who has performed under it is normally granted restitution unless the court determines her conduct to have been so contrary to law and morality that it refuses to come to her aid and decides to leave the parties as it finds them. This principle is expressed in the *in pari delicto* rule, under which the court weighs the relative guilt of the parties and will refuse to order restitution if Ann is as much or more at fault than Rob. In applying the rule, the court does not look only at relative blame, but also considers whether restitution will advance or harm the policy goals of the law. As mentioned before, the allocation of blame between a thief and the buyer of the stolen property who makes the theft worthwhile is not self-evident. However, Rob seems to be the guiltier of the two. Not only did he steal and smuggle the figurine, but he then lied to Ann about the origin of his possession, leading her (even if not entirely innocently) into the illegal transaction.

On the question of policy, it is difficult to say if the statutory goal of discouraging these transactions is better served by leaving the buyer with the loss or by making the smuggler restore his ill-gotten gains. Unless the former situation clearly appears more helpful to the statutory purpose, the balance favors restitution. It is important to bear in mind that the decision on restitution takes the public interest into account and is not simply a matter of doing justice between the parties, so the mere fact that Rob was unjustly enriched at Ann's expense is not conclusive. This principle is illustrated by

Homami v. Iranzadi, 211 Cal. App. 3d 1104 (1989). Although the case involved a claim to enforce an illegal agreement, not restitution, its lesson applies here too. A lender wished to avoid paying income tax on interest to be earned from a loan. The parties therefore agreed orally on the payment of interest, but signed a promissory note stating the loan to be interest-free. When the borrower reneged on his agreement to pay interest, the lender sued, but the court refused to give him judgment for the interest because the contract had the illegal purpose of tax evasion. The court found the parties to be *in pari delicto* and was unsympathetic to the lender's argument that nonenforcement gave the borrower a windfall. The court pointed out that its focus was not simply on what was fair between the parties, but on the protection of the public by discouraging such transactions.

14

Incapacity

§14.1 The Scope and Focus of the Doctrines Discussed in this Chapter

Chapter 13 considered the courts' ability to police contracts for improper bargaining. Although improper bargaining may have some impact on the transactions discussed here (and the introductory sections of Chapter 13 set out some general themes that are applicable in this context too), the principal basis of the regulation of the contracts in this chapter is the *legal status* of one of the parties. The law generally assumes that all persons enjoy the freedom to contract and have the capacity to enter binding consensual relationships. However, there are two classes of persons who lack this capacity: minors and mentally incompetent adults. A minor's lack of capacity is relatively easy to establish because it is largely based on the objectively ascertainable fact of age. The conclusion that an adult is incompetent is more complex, because it requires investigation of the adult's subjective state of mind. This does not mean, however, that the state of mind is determined by subjective evidence. On the contrary, it is usually ascertained by evidence of manifested conduct, observed by both lay people and experts, and diagnosed by those experts.

Protection from exploitation is the central rationale for permitting avoidance by a minor or mentally incompetent person. However, this chapter must be distinguished from Chapter 13 in that the core basis for relief is incapacity, not improper bargaining. This means that avoidance for incapacity is often possible even when the other party did not try to take advantage of the immaturity or disability. It is only when the incapacity is less extreme that a showing of inequitable conduct and unfair terms becomes relevant.

§14.2   Minority

§14.2.1   *The Basis and Nature of a Minor's Contractual Incapacity*

A person attains majority at the age of 18 in most states. Before that time, the minor[1] does not have the legal capacity to be bound in contract, and the contract is **voidable** at the minor's instance. As explained in section 13.3. a voidable contract is not absolutely void, but may be annulled or affirmed at the instance of the party entitled to invoke that election. This means that the minor may **disaffirm** it at any time before reaching the age of majority, or within a reasonable time thereafter. Because a minor has no capacity to contract, it follows that she does not have the capacity to affirm the contract while still a minor. This is why the right to make the election extends for a reasonable time past the attainment of majority. This right is not compromised or waived until majority, even though the minor never tried to disaffirm. Even a fully performed contract can be disaffirmed within a reasonable time after majority. If, upon reaching majority, the minor expressly ratifies the contract or fails to exercise the right of disaffirmance within a reasonable time, she becomes fully bound.

The legal incapacity of a minor is based on the policy of protecting minors from their own immaturity and preventing their exploitation by adults. Of course, any law protecting a party from contractual liability also places that party under a *disability* because sensible and informed people will decline to contract with one who lacks capacity. Incapacity is therefore not always a desirable state, and the law should not impose it unless the duty to protect outweighs the liberty interests of the protected class. In the case of minors, society has long been satisfied that this is true, and the rule has beneficial effects in most cases. However, it inevitably has some negative impact on the autonomy of an older and more independent minor.

Although the basis of incapacity is the policy of protection from immaturity and exploitation, this does not mean that the minor has to prove bad judgment, predatory behavior by the adult party, or unfair terms to avoid the contract. A minor's incapacity is a purely *objective* fact, in the sense that it is based solely on the minor's age, and not on subjective attributes such as intelligence or sophistication, or on transactional circumstances such as the other party's unfair bargaining or the harshness of the contract's terms. Because minors typically look young enough to alert a prudent person to the possibility that they are under age, a person contracting with one of youthful appearance is deemed to be placed on inquiry. A party who does not bother

---

1. The word "infant" is sometimes used in legal texts to refer to a person below the age of majority. The word sounds odd in contemporary usage, because we now take it to mean a baby.

to inquire therefore cannot argue that the minor looked older than her years. Similarly, it does not matter that the minor was close to majority at the time of contracting. It may be arbitrary to fix a particular birthday as the date on which a person comes of age, in that a person does not magically acquire full wisdom at the stroke of midnight. Nevertheless, the law generally prefers the certainty of treating majority as an objective fact, over the uncertainty of a more personalized inquiry into the minor's actual maturity and judgment. The objective test leads to a simple dichotomy, so that unless the official age of majority was reached before the contract, it is voidable. (These issues concerning a minor's contract were raised in the examples in Chapter 3 to illustrate the doctrine of precedent.)

§14.2.2   *Situations in Which a Minor May Incur Legal Liability*

There are some limited situations in which a minor can incur legal liability as a result of having entered a contract. However, this liability may not be equal to the minor's full contractual commitment and may be confined to restitution for benefits received:

1. If the contract is for the supply of **"necessaries"** to the minor (that is, goods or services reasonably needed for the minor's livelihood), the minor is liable to pay for them. However, the theory of recovery is not contract, but unjust enrichment, so if the reasonable value of the necessaries is less than the contract price, the minor's liability is confined to that reasonable value. A necessary is not quite the same as a necessity. It need not be shown that the goods or services were vital to the minor's continued survival, but merely that they were needed, useful, and unobtainable by her unless she contracted for them herself. A necessary may go beyond bare subsistence, as long as it is suitable to the minor's social position and station in life and is not purely luxurious.

2. **Marriage** is generally regarded as terminating minority, so a married minor is fully liable in contract. However, in the absence of marriage, it is not generally considered sufficient that the minor has set up a household independent of her parents (this is traditionally called **"emancipation"**—a word that would be regarded as apt by most teenagers).

3. A minor may be precluded from disaffirming if she **deliberately misrepresented** that she was a major, thereby inducing the other party to enter the contract with her. The other party must have been reasonable in believing the misrepresentation of age and must actually have given value to the minor or suffered a detriment as a result of the misrepresentation. The basis for holding the minor to the contract under these circumstances is **estoppel.**[2]

---

2. Estoppel is explained in section 8.4.

As an alternative, a court may base the relief for misrepresentation on *tort*. Deliberate misrepresentation is a tort, and accountability for tortious conduct could begin at an age earlier than majority. Recovery in tort aims at restoring loss, rather than enforcing the expectations under the contract, so the relief awarded could be quite different.

4. Apart from these common law exceptions, there are specific kinds of contracts made binding on minors by **legislation** where deemed desirable to facilitate the minor's entry into those types of transaction, or to bind the minor to contractual obligations recognized as important.

§14.2.3   *Restitution or Other Relief Following Disaffirmation*

If the minor's contract is purely executory—that is, nothing has changed hands between the parties—disaffirmance simply terminates it. However, if the minor had given or received some performance before disaffirming, the effect of disaffirmance is more complex. The general rule is that restitution must be made by both parties. The major party must return what was given by the minor or its value, but the minor is generally treated more leniently. Her responsibility for restitution is usually confined to whatever property she still retains at the time of disaffirmance. The minor is therefore shielded from liability beyond the duty to return her *present economic advantage* and does not have to pay the market value of services or of property consumed, lost, or dissipated. This is based on the reasoning that the minor is not harmed by giving back what she still has, but should not suffer monetary liability, because this would defeat the law's purpose of protecting the minor from improvidence. Say, for example, that the minor bought a car on credit and then disaffirms the contract. She merely has to restore the car itself in its present condition. She need not reimburse for any deterioration in the car, and if it has been lost completely (say, it was stolen), she has no liability. If, instead, the minor contracted for services or consumed goods (for example, she contracted to receive a course of windsurfing lessons on credit and had two lessons before disaffirming), she does not have to restore the value of what was received, because it conferred no ultimate economic benefit on her.

There is some movement away from this strongly sheltering approach toward minors. Provided that the adult party acted fairly and reasonably, did not take advantage of the minor, and the minor enjoyed a benefit at the adult's expense, some courts have permitted an offset against the minor's recovery for the reasonable value of the minor's use of what was received and consumed. The same approach may be taken if property given to the minor was damaged or destroyed through the minor's fault. Some courts have confined the exception to cash transactions because the adult's recovery can be offset against the minor's restitution, so the minor does not actually have to find the money to pay for this value. Although the distinction between cash and credit transactions seems to be fortuitous and not well-grounded in principle, it can be justified on the basis that a major who enters a credit transaction with a minor is more culpable than one who sells goods and services for cash and is thus less worthy of protection.

Apart from this, the minor could be liable in *tort* if the action causing the loss to the adult was more than a breach of contractual duty and constituted a tort. As mentioned above, responsibility for tortious injury could begin before the age of majority. For example, if the minor received a car on credit and wrecked it by wild driving, she could be liable to compensate the major for that loss as a result of her failure to exercise reasonable care in using the major's property. Tort recovery, based on compensating the major for loss, is different from restitutionary recovery, based on the value of what the minor received.

§14.3   Mental Incapacity

§14.3.1   *The Basis and Nature of Voidability Due to Mental Incapacity*

In contrast to the objective incapacity of a minor, based on the fact of age alone irrespective of the minor's actual state of mind, the mental incapacity of a major is based purely on his *subjective* attributes. As has often been stressed, when a contracting party is of full age, the objective test of intent holds him accountable for manifested assent. The law does not excuse people from contractual obligations merely because they are of below average intelligence, misguided, or weird. However, the policy of protecting persons who are mentally disabled places limits on this emphasis of objectivity. If a party suffers from a mental disability so severe as to preclude formulation of the requisite contractual intent, he cannot be held to his apparent agreement. Mental incompetence is determined at the *time of contracting*. If it can be proved to have existed at that time, it is a basis for avoidance even if the condition was temporary or has since been cured.

The common law has long recognized mental incapacity as a basis for avoiding a contract, but the issue in contemporary law revolves around the standards for avoidance. The established test for incapacity is strict and narrow, covering only the most severe and debilitating forms of mental disability. But in more recent times, there has been a trend toward broadening the test to include a wider range of psychological disturbances that impair a person's ability to make rational decisions.

When a person has been declared incompetent by a court and a guardian has been appointed to administer his property, the fact of incapacity is clear.

However, if there has been no adjudication of incapacity prior to the contract, the presumption is that adult parties were fully capable of contracting. The **burden** therefore lies on the allegedly incompetent party (or those representing his interests) to prove a disabling mental condition. This requires a demonstration both that the condition existed, and that it was in nature and extent severe enough to preclude an adequate degree of assent. To show this, it is usually necessary to produce expert psychiatric evidence as well as testimony by people who observed the behavior of the party at the time of the transaction. As noted earlier, a person dealing with a youthful party is placed on inquiry and cannot claim that she believed the minor to be older. By contrast, when the mental capacity of an adult is concerned, the *presumption is in favor of capacity,* so the other party is entitled to rely on apparent capacity unless some behavior or other circumstances signal a problem. As a result, the *other party's knowledge or reason to know* of the incapacity is an important factor when mental incompetence is claimed. Some forms of mental disability produce behavioral symptoms that are readily observable, leading to an easy conclusion that the other party did know or should have realized that she was dealing with a mentally incompetent person. However, this is not invariably true. The effect of the illness may be subtle and not easily detected— especially when negotiation is brief, and the parties do not have a prior relationship.

The purpose of permitting avoidance is the protection of the disabled person and his estate, but the observation concerning minors' contracts applies even more strongly here: The benign motive of protection carries a risk of **paternalism and intrusion.** It could mean that a person diagnosed with or suspected of having a mental disease is deprived of his freedom to contract because others will not risk dealing with him. Even if that problem were overcome and a contract were made, a finding of incapacity might still undermine the party's autonomy. In many cases, it is not the contracting party himself who desires to escape the contract, but his friends or relatives who seek to have him declared incompetent so that the contract can be avoided. In situations like this, a court has to be particularly careful that it is truly serving his best interests and not unduly interfering with his contractual liberty.

§14.3.2   *The Test for Mental Incapacity*

As mentioned earlier, the established test for mental incapacity is strict. The contract can only be avoided if, at the time of contracting, the party was *unable to understand the nature and consequences of the transaction.* This standard, called the **cognitive** test, confines avoidance to cases in which the party was so profoundly disabled that he did not know what he was doing. Because the lack of capacity is so serious, it is usually likely to have been quite apparent to the other party, who should have realized that there was a problem. Therefore, the equities strongly favor avoidance because the other party cannot fairly claim to have reasonably relied on the genuineness of manifested intent. For this reason, and because a narrow test is easier to apply, some courts still prefer it.

However, other courts consider it to be outdated and too rigid. Growing insight into psychology over the last few decades has shown that there are many forms of mental incapacity that fall short of cognitive disability, but that nevertheless so affect a person's *judgment, self-control, and motivation,* that he is incapable of genuine assent. This has led to a broader test that recognizes not only cognitive disorders, but also an illness or defect that impairs the party's ability to transact in a reasonable manner. Because this type of incapacity may be less apparent to the other party, it is only grounds for avoidance if the other had reason to know of the condition. Restatement Second §15(1) adopts the broader test.

Although the broader test is more congruent with contemporary thinking on the effect of mental disorders, it is perilously open-ended and could greatly expand the availability of mental incapacity as a means of escaping a contract. After all, there are all kinds of eccentric people out there, with all kinds of peculiar ideas and twisted motives. Can you get out of a contract because you had an unhappy childhood, or because you are a compulsive shopper, or because you believe that the Speaker of the House of Representatives was beamed to earth from an alien spacecraft? Courts that use the wider test seek to keep it under control by insisting on both psychiatric testimony, establishing a clinically recognized condition, and factual evidence, showing irrational or peculiar behavior during the period of and relevant to the transaction. As an added safeguard, the test emphasizes a balanced approach that takes into account not only the protection of the incompetent party, but also the rights and reasonable expectations of the other party. This means that even if the court finds some disturbance in the mind of the party seeking avoidance, it may conclude that the resulting disability is outweighed by the injustice of upsetting a fair contract entered into in good faith by the other party.

Neither test is premised on the requirement that the party seeking avoidance shows that the terms of the contract are unfair. The basis of avoidance is lack of meaningful assent, not harshness in the terms of the contract. Therefore, even a contract with perfectly reasonable terms can be avoided if the elements of the test are satisfied. Of course, if the terms are so unfair or so heavily in favor of the other party that they would not have been agreed to by a rational person in the position of the party seeking avoidance, this can be persuasive supporting evidence of incompetence. It also affects the equities in favor of avoidance, as mentioned earlier.

§14.3.3   *Avoidance and Its Consequences*

Like a minor's contract, the contract of a mentally incompetent person is voidable, not void. Unlike minority, however, mental disability does not disappear on a set and certain date, after which the fact of disaffirmance or ratification can be settled. The fate of a contract by a mentally incapacitated person may therefore hang in the balance until either it is disaffirmed or the incapacity abates, and the formerly incompetent party affirms it. (Or a guardian is ultimately appointed and does so.) In the interim, there may be performance or the other party may have otherwise changed his position in reliance on the contract. If that party had not taken unfair advantage of the other's mental incapacity—that is, he contracted on fair terms without awareness of the incapacity, Restatement Second §15(2) acknowledges his interests. It provides for termination of the power of avoidance to the extent that the contract has been so performed, or circumstances have so changed that avoidance would be unjust.

If the contract is avoided, the parties must be *restored to the status quo ante*. Both must return money or property received under the contract, or the value of property consumed or dissipated, or of services rendered. However, if the other party knew of and took advantage of the incompetence, the disabled party may be excused from paying to the extent that benefits received did not ultimately enrich him.

§14.3.4   *Incapacity Induced by Alcohol or Drug Abuse*

Incapacity caused by intoxication is viewed less sympathetically than that resulting from age, illness, or injury, because the incapacitated party is seen as having some blame for the problem. However, courts are aware of the compulsive nature of alcoholism and drug abuse. They therefore recognize that if intoxication is severe enough, its impairing effect can be just as profound as mental illness. Furthermore, that degree of inebriation is usually obvious enough to be apparent to the other party, so a strong inference can be drawn that he deliberately took advantage of it. Therefore, despite any moral reprobation that a court may feel about the conduct of the intoxicated party, courts do generally permit avoidance on the ground of incapacity if the level of intoxication is sufficient to deprive him of understanding or of the ability to act rationally, and the other party had reason to know of this. Restatement Second §16 follows this approach. The case for relief is even stronger if the terms of the resulting contract are unfair or unduly favorable to the other party.

EXAMPLES

1. Hardy Culturalist, age 19, was about to leave his hometown to attend college. Up to that time, he had operated a very successful part-time yard maintenance business on weekends. As he would no longer be able to service his

customers, he wished to dispose of his lawnmower, trimmer, wheelbarrow, and other garden tools. Lon Mower, a 16-year-old high-school junior, who lived with his parents next door to Hardy, was interested in filling the gap that would be left by Hardy's departure. He wanted to buy the equipment and try to take over Hardy's customers. Hardy and Lon began negotiations, and eventually reached agreement on the sale of all the equipment for $800. This is a fair price, somewhat below its market value. Lon did not have that much money in his savings account, so he paid $300 to Hardy and undertook to pay the balance in installments of $50 per month, which he expected would be generated from his yardwork. Lon had just taken a business law course in high school, so he knew that a sale of goods over $500 had to be recorded in writing and signed. He therefore drew up a simple document reflecting their agreement, and they both signed it.

After taking delivery of the equipment and paying Hardy the $300, Lon began work. He successfully groomed about five yards in the first week, but did not enjoy the hard labor very much and began to regret having undertaken this new venture. In the second week, he had a disaster. He lost control of the lawnmower, which ran over the trimmer, completely mangling it, and then plunged off a steep embankment and exploded. This experience convinced Lon that yardwork was not for him. He wishes to cancel the sale, get his $300 back, and return all the surviving equipment to Hardy. May he do this?

2. Bonna Petite is a precocious 17-year-old with an appetite for *haute cuisine*. For a while she had been dying to eat lunch at Trés Cher, the most elegant and expensive restaurant in town. One day she put on her mother's best business suit and groomed herself meticulously, succeeding in making herself look like a young executive of around 25 years of age. She set off for the restaurant, where she was seated and served a magnificent lunch. At the end of the meal she summoned the waiter and said, "*Garçon*, this has been an excellent repast. It is therefore with some sadness that I must inform you that I am a minor. I hereby disaffirm my contract to purchase this lunch from you." (By the way, she did not leave a tip either.) The age of majority in Bonna's state is 18, so she is a minor. May she do this?

3. Price Slasher, a man of 82, had lived in his house for 45 years. During the last ten years of that period, following the death of his wife, he had lived alone. As he got older, it had become increasingly more burdensome for him to maintain the house and to take care of domestic chores. He therefore decided that the time had come for him to sell it and to move to an assisted living complex. Price had always been a stubborn, impatient, and difficult man, and this had become worse as he aged. He hated asking anyone for help, and he rarely sought or listened to advice. His insistence on self-reliance had become quite worrisome to his daughter lately, because he did not seem to manage his affairs very well. He was constantly losing things, could not keep his bank account balanced, forgot to pay some bills, and double-paid others without realizing it.

When he told his daughter that he planned to sell the house, she offered to help him, but he declined her assistance. She then begged him to get it appraised and to list it with a reputable realtor. He refused, insisting that he was fully aware of the market, knew exactly how much the house was worth, and was perfectly capable of negotiating the sale himself. In this he was quite wrong. His information about the market was years out of date, and he had never been much of a negotiator.

Price advertised the house for sale at a figure that was about 25 percent lower than its true market value. Lowe Ball saw the advertisement and came to see the house. It did not take him long to make an offer at the full asking price, which Price accepted. Lowe's contact with Price during the transaction was quite minimal. The parties had a short conversation when Lowe inspected the house, and another when the written offer was submitted and accepted. Lowe did not attempt to negotiate the price because he realized that Price's price was good (although he did not realize that it was so far below the market value of the house). His only impression about Price was that he was an elderly man of few words who seemed to know exactly what he wanted.

After the contract of sale had been signed, Price told his daughter about it. She was appalled because she knew that he had let the house go for a patently inadequate price. A long family meeting took place that evening, at which his daughter and other relatives finally convinced Price that he had sold too cheaply. He now wishes to rescind the sale. Does he have grounds to do so?

4. Bourne Tushop, age 20, bought an expensive luxury car on credit. He negotiated effectively with the salesman, beating the price down by $1,500. He then spent over 30 minutes reading the sales contract before he signed it. After driving the car for two weeks he decided that he did not like it any more, and he wished to return it. Dr. Heddy Shrinker, prominent psychiatrist, has done some studies of young adults who have been raised by indulgent, status-conscious parents. She has identified a form of dysfunctional conduct in many of them that she calls "Preyupss" (premature young professional spending syndrome). As part of this syndrome, the young people compulsively purchase fashionable, expensive, and unneeded consumer products. Very shortly afterwards, they realize the futility of what they have done and experience deep regret and depression. Dr. Shrinker has examined Bourne and has concluded that he suffers from the syndrome. He has had it since his mid-teens and can only be cured by several years of therapy and counseling.

May Bourne rely on his disorder to avoid the contract?

EXPLANATIONS

1. This is a sale of goods, but apart from the statute of frauds issue, which Lon has cleverly identified, there are no special rules applicable in this

case. UCC Article 2 does not deal with minors' contracts, which are therefore governed in sales transactions by general principles of common law.

Because Lon is a minor, he may disaffirm the contract. It does not matter that he may have been smart and sophisticated enough to understand exactly what he was doing, that he was knowledgeable about the statute of frauds, or that he planned to use the equipment for a moneymaking venture. The protection from contractual commitment afforded a minor is based on the objective fact of age and does not take account of the subjective attributes of the minor. The objective criterion of minority also makes it irrelevant that Hardy was little over the age of minority himself, or that the contract was on fair terms. He does not fit the stereotype of the grasping, advantage-taking adult who should know better than to exploit a kid, but Lon's right to disaffirm does not depend on a showing of bargaining impropriety.

When the minor elects to disaffirm the contract, each party must restore what was received from the other. However, if the minor has lost, consumed, or damaged property obtained under the contract, the established rule is that he is responsible to restore only what he has at the time of disaffirmance and need not compensate the major for any shortfall. Under this rule, Lon is entitled to his $300 back and must return the surviving equipment to Hardy. In more recent years, courts have begun to recognize that a rigid rule to this effect may not be fair in every case, and have been willing, in proper circumstances, to hold the minor liable for more than the mere return of existing enrichment.

There are two separate theories of liability. If the property was destroyed tortiously, the minor may be liable in tort for the loss in value, provided that the minor is old enough to be accountable for negligence under the state's tort law. If Lon was negligent in losing control of the mower, this approach would make Lon responsible to reimburse Hardy for the value of lost mower and trimmer, in addition to returning the other equipment.

As an alternative to tort liability, some courts have adopted the approach that if the minor has benefitted from the use of the property, the value of that benefit may be recoverable from the minor. Some courts confine recovery to an offset against any restitution due to the minor, but others are willing to grant a money judgment against the minor, imposing liability on him greater than any offset against restitution. The court did this in *Valencia v. White*, 654 P.2d 287 (Ariz. 1982), where a minor engaged in a trucking business incurred substantial costs in contracting for the repair of the trucks and resisted paying those costs on the basis that he was a minor. Lon was not benefitted by the destruction of the mower and trimmer, so he cannot be held liable for their value. However, he did earn money by using the equipment for a week. He may therefore be responsible, in addition to restoring the remaining tools to Hardy, for payment of the rental value of all the equipment for a week

If the court does not apply either of the above principles to compensate Hardy for the loss, he may try the argument that the mower and trimmer were necessaries, because Lon used them to earn money. If this argument is accepted, Lon would, in addition to returning the remaining equipment, be liable to pay for the mower and trimmer, based on the lesser rate of the contract value or fair market value at the time of sale. In this case, fair value was apparently above the contract price, so the contract price of the destroyed mower and trimmer would be the proper measure of recovery. However, to avoid watering down the protection of minors, courts tend to be conservative in classifying property or services as necessaries. Lon was still in school and living with his parents and did the yardwork part-time. As this was not his livelihood, the equipment is unlikely to be regarded as a necessary. In *Valencia*, the minor lived with and was supported by his parents. Although the court imposed liability as noted above, it made it clear that the basis of its judgment was not that the repairs to the minor's trucks were necessaries. Similarly, in *Bowling v. Sperry*, 184 N.E. 2d 901 (Ind. 1962), the court held that a car was not a necessary, even though a car may be regarded as a vital necessity by every teenager of driving age, and there was at least some suggestion that the minor would have found the car useful as a means of transport to his summer job.

2. A minor may disaffirm her contract at any time before or within a reasonable time after attaining majority. The general rule is that she must restore any benefits that she still retains at the time of disaffirmance, but is not accountable for the value of property that has been consumed or dissipated. (In a sense, she does still have Trés Cher's property and will retain it until the process of digestion is complete, but Trés Cher would probably not be too interested in the "disgorgement" of this benefit.)

The general rule places the burden on Trés Cher to inquire about the age of its youthful-looking customers, and it bears the risk of failing to do so, even if she looked older than she was. On the other hand, Bonna has behaved very badly, and the law should not encourage our young citizens to do this kind of thing. The following arguments could be made to hold her accountable to pay for the meal, but they probably will not work:

(a)   Trés Cher could invoke the rule that a minor is liable to pay the value of a necessary. Food required for sustenance surely qualifies as a necessary. But even a good meal, going beyond the minimum needed to sustain life, could be a necessary, because the concept goes beyond bare subsistence and takes into account the minor's reasonable and accustomed style of living. A fine meal in a top restaurant may be a little excessive unless Bonna is an actual member of the House of Windsor. Apart from this, goods are only deemed necessaries if the minor had no means of obtaining them unless she contracted for them herself. There is no indication that Bonna was in this position. She lived with her parents and had access to their refrigerator. In *Webster St. Part-*

nership v. Sheridan, 368 N.W.2d 439 (Neb. 1985), the court considered whether an apartment leased by a minor was a necessary. Although shelter is surely needed and useful, indeed vital for a reasonable level of survival, the apartment was not a necessary because the minor could have moved back to his parents' home whenever he wanted.

(b) A minor may be liable for deliberately misrepresenting her age. A misrepresentation could occur by conduct or concealment, but where minors are concerned, courts generally require an affirmative lie about age. Dressing up is not enough to constitute a deliberate misrepresentation.

(c) If a minor has used or consumed a benefit purchased for cash, some courts permit recovery of the value of its use as an offset against the minor's restitution, provided that the contract was fair and the major party was not aware of the minority. Grounds for applying this rule are particularly strong if the minor was in some way negligent or wilful in causing the loss. For example, in *Dodson v. Schrader,* 824 S.W.2d 545 (Tenn. 1992), the court recognized that a major party may be entitled to offset the value of use and depreciation on a truck sold to a minor for cash, where the minor's neglect caused severe engine damage. Because Bonna is such a brat, it is tempting to try to apply this rule to her, but she has not paid cash, and it may be difficult to convince a court to extend the rule. After all, we assume that Bonna is improvident, and we must protect her from the fiscal consequences of her rash and antisocial behavior.

In sum, it does not seem that contract law offers any relief to Trés Cher. However, do not overlook the possibility that a 17-year-old could be held responsible in tort or criminal law for intentional wrongdoing.

3. The facts concerning Price's mental capacity are deliberately vague but suggestive. It appears that he has certain character traits, such as stubbornness, resistance to advice, weak negotiating skills, and impatience, that are likely to place him at risk of entering into a disadvantageous contract. These flaws in his nature may indicate that he probably lacks skill in contracting, but do not, on their own, constitute the kind of mental incompetence that would give rise to a claim for avoidance. However, there are indications that the effect of these shortcomings have been aggravated by mental infirmity, manifested in symptoms such as loss of memory and confusion. His family has noticed a deterioration in his mental capacity, but this is not necessarily something that was obvious to Lowe.

A person is presumed to be competent to contract. If Price seeks to avoid the contract on the basis of incapacity, he must prove that he was mentally incompetent at the time of entering the contract. The degree of incompetence to be established depends on whether the jurisdiction follows the older cognitive test—that he could not understand the nature and consequences of the transaction; or has accepted the looser motivational standard—that his mental defect impaired his ability to transact in a reasonable manner. The motivational test is satisfied by a much less serious degree of infirmity, but for that reason it more strongly protects the reasonable reliance interest of the other party, and is not a basis for avoidance unless Lowe had reason to know of Price's inability to conduct the transaction rationally.

Evidence of Price's behavior during the transaction is the most probitive indication of his mental state, and is also relevant to the question of whether Lowe had reason to know of his incompetence. However, evidence of his conduct immediately before and after the transaction is also a pertinent indicator of his state of mind at the time of contracting. Price's daughter can testify about his confused and disoriented behavior during the period surrounding the transaction, but Lowe was the only person who observed Price during the transaction, and he claims to have found nothing amiss. Both of them could be telling the truth, because Price's condition seems to have manifested itself in lapses. The anecdotal evidence may therefore be quite inconclusive, and it may not be possible for Price to make a case for avoidance unless he can offer expert testimony by a psychiatrist who has examined him, diagnosed his condition, and can convince the factfinder that it is serious enough to have impaired his ability to contract under the applicable test.

Although evidence of Price's mental state is the most directly relevant to the decision on whether to permit avoidance on grounds of incapacity, courts are concerned with balancing the protection of the incapacitated party against the need to treat the other party fairly and to foster the security of transactions. Therefore, testimony about the transacting environment is often of great relevance, particularly when the mental incapacity falls short of a palpable cognitive disorder. Such factors as the adequacy of consideration given to the incompetent party, the fairness of the contract terms, any abuse of trust or confidence by the other party, and any other bargaining impropriety could influence the outcome of the case. In the present case, if Lowe is believed, he was guilty of no deliberate underhand dealing and had no reason to notice anything peculiar in Price's demeanor that may have alerted him to a problem. He offered what was asked for the property, and his only sin was that he made an attractive bargain. However, a 25 percent shortfall from the market price is quite extreme, and (even though Lowe may not have known how good a price it was) this could in itself be regarded as an indication to a reasonable buyer that something was wrong with Price. A person who makes a particularly favorable exchange with one who suffers from a mental disability is not in a particularly strong position.

In *Heights Realty Ltd. v. Phillips*, 749 P.2d 77 (N.M. 1988), an 84-year-old woman entered into an exclusive listing agreement with a realtor, and then refused to sell the property when the realtor found a willing and able buyer. Although there was nothing unfair or extraordinary about the contract terms, and the realtor testified that the seller was "sharp as a tack" during their negotiations, the seller had been in a gradual and subtle mental decline for some years. Her deteriorating mental condition was described by a number of family members, who had noticed erratic and confused behavior, memory lapses, and mismanagement of her affairs. A psychiatrist testified that although it could not be stated conclusively that she was mentally incompetent, this could be asserted as a matter of medical probability. He believed that she probably realized that she was contracting for the purpose of selling her property, but could not have understood the detailed terms of her contract. During the course of the suit, she was in fact adjudged incompetent and was represented by a conservator. The court, applying the stricter cognitive test followed in the jurisdiction, found that the combination of psychiatric and anecdotal evidence was sufficient to satisfy the seller's burden of establishing mental incompetence under that standard.

4. Bourne surely fails the cognitive test of mental incapacity because there is no indication that he could not understand and appreciate the nature and consequences of his acts when entering the transaction. A court that accepts the looser test of Restatement Second §15 would allow him to avoid the sale if he can show that a mental illness or defect affected his ability to act in a reasonable manner in the transaction and that the car dealer had reason to know of his condition.

For the first element, a mental disease or defect must be established. Even under the more lenient test, a person cannot claim mental incapacity just because he made a quirky or unreasonable judgment, or because he was motivated by irrational desires. Dr. Shrinker has identified something that may be called a mental condition, but even if the conclusions of her research are correct, this may not be a profound enough problem to qualify as an incapacity. Of course, even if we accept Dr. Shrinker's opinion, the dealer will probably be able to find its own equally qualified expert to contradict everything that she says. In the end, the question of whether the disease exists, and if so, whether Bourne suffers from it so as to impair his rationality, will come down to a battle of the experts. One of the problems with the more open test is that conflicting psychiatric opinion evidence must be evaluated by lay people. This is ameliorated somewhat if the disease has any observable symptoms, because evidence of Bourne's behavior would be available to bolster the psychiatric evaluation. As Bourne bears the burden of proof, any uncertainty must be resolved against him.

Even if a mental condition is established, relief is still not granted unless the need to protect Bourne from his incapacity outweighs the dealer's right to enforcement of its reasonable expectations. Therefore, Bourne must also show that the dealer knew or had reason to know of his incapacity. Some mental conditions are made obvious by the patient's conduct, but others are more subtle. The brief facts given here do not suggest any observable conduct that may have put the dealer on notice that Bourne could not make rational judgments or exercise control over his actions. In the end, the court would have to strike a balance, based on all the circumstances of the transaction. It seems unlikely that avoidance would be permitted. Bourne's disease, if it exists at all, is rather self-indulgent, and the dealer's reliance interest appears to be strong and legitimate.

Of course, if Bourne succeeds in avoiding the contract, he must return the car to the dealer and is entitled to restitution of his payments. However, as discussed in Example 1, he may in addition be liable to the dealer for the value of his use of the car for the two weeks.

15

Mistake, Impracticability, and Frustration of Purpose

§15.1 The Common Themes and the Differences Between Mistake, Impracticability, and Frustration of Purpose

The three doctrines considered in this chapter have common themes that make it useful to consider them together. They are each concerned with a situation in which the exchange between the parties turns out to be very different from what was expected. In the case of mistake, this is caused by a serious factual error made by one or both parties at the time of contracting, so that the contract is premised on incorrect information. By contrast, impracticability and frustration arise when there is no false premise at the time of contracting, but events change drastically enough after formation to belie the original expectation of the parties. An issue of mistake, impracticability, or frustration may be raised at various stages after formation of the contract and for the purpose of achieving different ends. For example, before performance is due, it may be used to excuse the prospective performance. After performance has been rendered, it could be used as a defense to a claim that the performance fell short of that called for by the contract. Most commonly, its effect is termination of the contract, but sometimes adjustment of the contract terms is the more appropriate remedy.

Each of the doctrines pose two central questions that will be constant themes in our discussion:

1. *Materiality—How fundamental is the discrepancy between the expected and the actual exchange?*   This question is concerned with the impact of the mistake or altered circumstances on the bargain reasonably anticipated by the parties. Relief is only available when the impact is so material that it changes the very basis of their bargain.

2. *Risk—Which party should be made to bear the consequences of this defeat of the original expectations?*   The fact that original expectations have been fundamentally upset only justifies relief if the party seeking it does not bear the risk of this upset. The allocation of risk may be clear from the terms of the contract, or it may have to be established by interpretation from the circumstances of the transaction. The determination of risk allocation is a crucial aspect of the judicial inquiry in all these cases.

Having identified common themes, it is important to stress the difference between mistake, on the one hand, and impracticability and frustration on the other. As noted earlier, the doctrine of **mistake** applies when the contract is based on an **erroneous belief at the time of contracting** that certain facts are true. The error causes one or both parties to manifest assent that would not have been given had the true facts been known. When the error is later discovered the mistaken party—or one of them, if the parties shared the mistake—may have grounds to avoid (or in a special case, to claim adjustment of) the contract. In this sense, mistake causes a *defect in assent* similar to that resulting from fraud, duress, or unconscionability so that the basis for relief is that *apparent assent is not genuine.* Even under the objective test, a party is not held accountable for a manifestation of assent when the error is grave and justifiable enough. Because mistake has this commonality with the doctrines discussed in Chapter 13, it could have been dealt with there. However, it differs from them in that the defect in assent is *caused by misinformation, not by deception, improper pressure, or other bargaining misbehavior.* Of course, sometimes the error of one party may have been induced by or deliberately taken advantage of by the other. If so, this strengthens the case for mistake and it may also allow the party to invoke alternative grounds for relief based on fraud or unconscionability. Notwithstanding, bear in mind that the elements of mistake do not include a requirement of improper bargaining, so relief is possible even when the other party has not behaved wrongfully.

In contrast to mistake, **impracticability and frustration** are concerned with the impact of **supervening events** on the transaction. These doctrines are not based on any defect in assent at the time of contracting, but aim to provide relief when the basis of a **fully consensual transaction is pro-**

foundly altered by some external event that occurs **afterwards.** (In this discussion I adopt the position that impracticality and frustration are always concerned with supervening events, and that the distinction between these doctrines and mistake is primarily based on chronology. There are cases that have found impracticality or frustration where, unknown to the parties, the event had already occurred at the time of contracting. The cases could just as well have been handled under the rules of mistake, with no difference in the ultimate result. The notion of *contemporaneous impracticability* or frustration therefore seems to serve no purpose, except to duplicate and create confusion with mistake, and it is best disregarded in favor of the clarity of drawing a firm temporal line between a mistake and supervening impracticability or frustration.)

§15.2 The Meaning of Mistake and the Distinction Between Mutual and Unilateral Mistake

§15.2.1 *The Legal Meaning of Mistake: An Error of Fact*

In lay terms, "mistake" has quite a wide range of meaning. It could refer to a factual error, but it might also include a bad judgment, a rash decision, or simply a situation that did not work out well. For example, it may have been a real mistake to buy that ugly chair, to invest in your cousin's harebrained enterprise or to drive to town instead of taking the bus. The legal meaning of "mistake" is much narrower. It is confined to **errors of fact,** that is, to errors about some **thing or event that actually occurred or existed** and can be **ascertained by objective evidence.** This leads to a number of important observations on the scope of mistake doctrine:

a. An Error in Judgment Does Not Qualify as a Mistake

A party cannot escape a disadvantageous or regrettable contract resulting from poor judgment. Say, for example, that a buyer of a plot of land purchases it in the belief that it is worth more than the asking price, but then finds that this is untrue. Or a buyer of stock believes wrongly that the company is undervalued and the stock is considerably more valuable than its price. If these parties were to be allowed to avoid their obligations simply because they had judged wrongly, no transaction could be secure. Although this distinction can be drawn in principle, it is not always a simple matter to distinguish an error in judgment from a mistake of fact. Judgments are usually based on fact, and less obvious cases could require some unravelling.

b.   An Incorrect Prediction of Future Events Is Not a Mistake

A future event may one day become a fact, but until it has happened, it cannot be thought of as a fact by anyone except Nostradamus. Therefore, as a rule, it is generally accurate to say that the mistake must relate to a fact in existence at the time of contracting. A party cannot claim relief for an erroneous prediction. This is often closely related to point *a* above, because most predictions at the time of contract are speculations concerning the future value of the transaction and are therefore in the nature of judgments. For example, if a buyer of oranges purchases them in the belief that the market will rise, he cannot complain if it later turns out that he was wrong. This is not a mistake in the legal sense, but simply an erroneous prediction (or misjudgment) of profitability. Again, although the distinction between fact and prediction is easy to draw in some cases, there are situations in which a contractual assumption may have both factual and speculative elements. When that happens, it can be difficult to decide if the error should be treated as a mistake.

c.   Mistake Doctrine Is Not Concerned with Mistaken Understandings Between the Parties

We saw in Chapter 10 that one party may be mistaken as to the meaning of the words or conduct of the other, and that for purposes of interpretation, meaning is usually regarded as a question of fact. However, this kind of error is not covered by the doctrine of mistake. A misunderstanding about the meaning of a manifestation is a matter of interpretation, governed by the principles discussed in Chapter 10.

d.   The Law Is a Fact, so that a Mistake in Law Is Covered by Mistake Doctrine

After taking some pains to learn the difference between fact and law, you may be disappointed to find that this is one area in which the distinction does not apply. Although older cases did not regard an error in law as a mistake of fact, it is now accepted that the legal rules governing or pertinent to the transaction do qualify as facts. They constitute an existing state of affairs that can be objectively ascertained. For example, a piece of beachfront land is sold to a buyer who intends to build a vacation home on it. The parties are unaware that the land is in an environmentally protected zone and a state statute prohibits all building on it. Their ignorance of the law is a mistake of fact.

e. Situations that Appear to Call for the Application of Mistake Doctrine May Be More Properly Treated as a Breach of a Contractual Commitment

This is not so much a new point as a reinforcement of two prior observations that merit strong emphasis: It has already been noted that many mistakes in the lay sense do not constitute mistakes in the legal sense, and that risk allocation is a crucial consideration in deciding whether a mistake should be grounds for relief. A party's responsibility for her own judgments and the parties' understanding about risk allocation may mean that a mistake does not call for application of mistake doctrine, but should be treated as the breach of a contractual promise (that is, a warranty) or as a misrepresentation.

For example, a buyer purchases a painting for $5 million, based on the seller's claim that it is a genuine Van Gogh. It turns out to be a forgery. Only by carefully examining the facts of the transaction and weighing the closely related issues of judgment and risk allocation can we decide which party must be assigned responsibility for the problem. Some of the questions to consider would be: Did the seller knowingly or unwittingly give false information to the buyer or conceal facts? If so, there may be a misrepresentation. Did the seller promise that this was a genuine Van Gogh? If so, there may be a breach of warranty. Was this an uncertain fact on which both parties gambled? If so, the buyer may be stuck with the bad judgment. Was the genuineness a basic premise of the contract? If so, maybe an actionable mistake was made. The characterization is important, because the remedies are very different, ranging from no remedy at all to rescission for mistake or innocent misrepresentation, to expectation damages for breach of warranty, to expectation damages plus possible punitive damages for fraud.

§15.2.2 *Mutual and Unilateral Mistake*

Established doctrine draws a distinction between mutual mistake, in which the error is shared by both parties, and the unilateral mistake of only one of the parties. This sounds like a simple distinction, but it can be quite subtle and elusive. This is because a mistake is only **mutual** if it relates to a factual assumption so shared by the parties, that it is a **joint premise** of their bargain. A mistake is **unilateral,** not only in the obvious case where **one party knows the true facts and the other does not,** but also where both parties may be unaware of the truth, yet the fact in issue affects the decision of only one of the parties and is of no interest or relevance to the other. In other words, although neither knows the truth, the erroneous fact is a **basic assumption of only one of the parties** because the other is neutral on it. This means that the distinction between mutual and unilateral mistake is not necessarily merely a matter of deciding whether one or both parties had been misinformed. The contract must be interpreted in context to decide if it was built around the mutual assumption that a particular fact was true.

The relativity of the distinction may be illustrated by a couple of examples: A builder buys some land from a person claiming to be the owner of the land. The builder intends to build a house on it for resale. He makes a subcontract with an earthmover to clear and excavate the land. Immediately afterwards, and before any work is started, the builder discovers that the seller did not have title to the land. The builder therefore does not own it and cannot build on it. It could be said that the builder and earthmover entered their contract under the mutual mistake of fact that the builder owned the land. That is, the builder's ownership was a shared basic assumption of the contract. However, it could also be said that the earthmover does not care who owns the property, and any mistake as to the existence of valid title is purely the builder's affair. If so, the mistake is properly treated as unilateral on the builder's part.

Assume that the mistake does not relate to the ownership of the property. Instead, the earthmover made an arithmetical error in calculating the number of hours required to perform the excavation and accordingly submitted a bid 25 percent lower than its actual cost of doing the work. The builder, not realizing the error, accepts the earthmover's figure. Again, one could see this as a mutual erroneous assumption that the earthmover's calculations are correct, or alternatively, as a unilateral error of the excavator. The correct choice can only be made by carefully analyzing the relationship of the fact to the contract.

These examples are intended merely to illustrate the relativity of the mutual–unilateral distinction. The decision on whether or not relief should be granted for the mistake is based on the considerations discussed in the following sections. When you read them you will find that unilateral and mutual mistake involve essentially the same basic inquiry—that is, their elements are the same in many respects. However, in addition to sharing the elements of mutual mistake, unilateral mistake has its own further prerequisites. This is because a party who has made a unilateral mistake must make a stronger case for relief by demonstrating that the unfairness of enforcing the contract outweighs the need to protect the reasonable reliance of the other party.

In other words, unilateral mistake calls for a stronger focus on the relative equities of enforcement or nonenforcement. In a sense, this is an additional element but, as you will see, it follows quite logically from and is really inherent in the elements held in common with mutual mistake. Thus, the difference between the elements of mutual and unilateral mistake are largely a matter of emphasis and focus. This is just as well, considering that it is sometimes difficult to decide if the error was a shared assumption or purely one-sided. Misclassification need not be fatally wrong if the elements are properly analyzed because, in the end, both types of mistake must be resolved by deciding who should suffer the consequences of the error, in light of the factual indications of contractual intent and the surrounding equities. UCC Article 2 does not deal with the doctrine of mistake, so a mistake in a contract for the sale of goods is governed by principles of common law.

§15.3 The Elements of Mutual Mistake

According to Restatement Second §152 (read with §§151 and 154), a mutual mistake is avoidable by the adversely affected party if the following prerequisites are satisfied:

1. *At the time of contracting, the parties must have shared an erroneous belief concerning a fact.* As noted already, a mistake in the legal sense is an error relating to a fact. The error must be made at the time of contracting and it must relate to a state of affairs existing at the time, rather than one predicted to occur in the future.

2. *The erroneous fact was a basic assumption on which the contract was made.* The mistaken fact must be so *fundamental to the shared intent and purpose* of *both parties* that it is reasonable to conclude that they would not have made the contract at all or on the present terms had they known the truth. For example, the seller sells a whitewater raft to the buyer for $1,000. Both seller and buyer wrongly believe that it was once owned by President Bill Clinton, and used by him in his famous whitewater adventure. The seller understands that the buyer does not indulge in whitewater rafting and is only buying the raft because he has always been a devoted follower of President Clinton. The mistake is the very basis of their bargain.

3. *The mistake must have a material effect on the agreed exchange of performances.* This sounds like a repetition of the prior element, because it would seem to follow that an erroneous basic assumption of the contract will inevitably have a material effect on the exchange. This is often true, but the focus of these elements is different. Sometimes, the materiality of the effect on the exchange is obvious. For example, if the raft would otherwise have a market value of $200, and the higher price reflects the erroneous belief that it belonged to President Clinton, the mistake not only forms the basis of the contract, but it also has a material effect on the exchange. However, if the raft is worth $1,000 anyhow (there being no enhancement of market price merely because the raft is a relic of the esteemed president), the mistake still forms the basis of the contract, but the materiality of the error is more subtle and harder to identify. It is arguable that as the buyer suffers no economic

loss, the mistake should not be grounds for relief. The buyer suffers no hardship and can recoup any loss by reselling the raft. However, if such recoupment is not possible and the buyer ends up with something substantially different from what was expected, the mistake may be material notwithstanding the absence of identifiable economic loss.

Thus, the test of **basic assumption** examines the aggrieved party's **motivation,** as shared with the other party, but **materiality** calls for an assessment of the **mistake's impact on the balance of the exchange** to see if it substantially deprived the adversely affected party of the value expected. Restatement Second §152, Comment *c,* suggests that the test is whether the error creates an overall imbalance between the parties by making the exchange less desirable to the adversely affected party and more advantageous to the other. This element thus contains a component of equitable balancing, in which the court examines the effect of the mistake on both the parties to decide the fairness of enforcing the contract despite the mistake.

4.   *The adversely affected party must not have borne the risk of the mistake.* Although this question is commonly phrased so as to focus on the assumption of risk by the adversely affected party, the issue is to *allocate the risk of error to one party or the other.* There is no such thing as a neutral decision on risk because a determination that one party did not bear the risk inevitably means that the other did. (Although it is possible to find that the parties shared the risk, this does not seem to happen very often.) The allocation of risk is often the dispositive element in mistake cases. Despite everything that has been said up to now, and no matter how serious the error, if the adversely affected party bore the risk of mistake, there can be no avoidance of the contract.

How can one tell who assumed the risk of the mistake? The first place to turn for an answer to this question is the contract itself. The resolution is clearest if the *contract expressly addresses the risk.* There can be no doubt about risk allocation if, for example, the contract for the sale of the raft stated, "While the seller believes the raft belonged to President Bill Clinton, he neither represents nor warrants that this belief is correct. The buyer may not terminate this contract if it proves to be wrong." Even if the contract is not that clear, risk allocation may be *inferred from the contract terms* in context by the usual process of interpretation or construction. As always, **factual interpretation** is attempted first, but if no evidence of actual agreement can be found, the court must assign the risk in the way most reasonable under the circumstances, based on general expectations and practices in the market or community. That is, the court must resolve the question by **construction,** determining how the parties would reasonably have allocated the risk, had they thought of the issue.

Many different factors may come into play in the process of construing risk allocation. If a pertinent commercial practice exists, it is a strong indicator of the parties' reasonable expectation or risk. For example, it would be useful to know if buyers of presidential memorabilia normally conduct their own research into authenticity. If so, this buyer's failure to investigate President Clinton's ownership would be an assumption of the risk of error. Similarly, if loss or liability can be insured against in transactions of this type, it would be helpful to know which party normally takes out the policy. In some cases, there may be a legal rule that dictates or suggests risk allocation in the absence of contrary agreement. This would be true in the present example if the contract described the goods as "President Bill Clinton's whitewater raft" without any disclaimer. The unqualified description is treated by UCC §2.313(1)(b) as an express warranty by the seller that the goods conform to the description, thereby placing the risk of error on the seller.

§15.4 The Elements of Unilateral Mistake

The elements of unilateral mistake are set out in Restatement Second §153. Relief for unilateral mistake has basically the same prerequisites as mutual mistake, but because the mistake is one-sided, the common elements are phrased somewhat differently and an additional concern must be taken into account: Because only one party has made a mistake, the expectations of the non-mistaken party must be protected insofar as they are reasonable and legitimate. Therefore, unilateral mistake is grounds for relief only if the equities favoring release of the mistaken party outweigh the need to uphold the rights of the non-mistaken party. As noted in section 15.2.2, this additional concern is really implicit in the other elements that unilateral mistake shares with mutual mistake.

The elements for unilateral mistake are:

1. *The error concerns a fact.* This requirement is no different from mutual mistake.
2. *The fact is a basic assumption on which the mistaken party made the contract.* Of course, we are concerned here not with a shared assumption, but with the individual motive of only one of the parties, which has not necessarily been communicated to the other. Nevertheless, the subjectivity of this requirement is not a threat to

the reliance interest of the other party, which is taken care of by the other elements.

3. *The mistake has a material effect on the exchange, adverse to the mistaken party.*   As with mutual mistake, this element concerns the mistake's objectively determinable impact on the exchange of values.

4. *The mistaken party must not bear the risk of the mistake.*   The allocation of risk involves issues of interpretation and construction the same as those in mutual mistake, but this element has a particular twist in unilateral mistake cases because there is often some degree of *negligence* involved in a one-sided error. If negligent conduct inevitably placed the risk of error on the mistaken party, unilateral mistake would seldom permit relief. However, a serious degree of negligence, or worse, a recklessness or a dereliction of duty owed to the other party, is likely to lead to the conclusion that the mistaken party took the risk of mistake. Quite apart from its role in the element of risk allocation, the carelessness of the mistaken party could have an impact on the balance of the equities discussed below. That is, even if there has not been enough sloppiness or serious negligence to dispose of the case on the question of risk allocation, the mistaken party's fault could tip the balance in favor of the other party.

5. *The equities must favor relief for the mistake.*   While equitable balancing takes into account factors beyond the first four elements, it obviously cannot be performed in isolation from them. In other words, the degree to which the first four elements are satisfied forms a vital component in the overall balance. Beyond this, the balance involves consideration of two more general questions:

   (a)   Would enforcement of the contract result in such severe *hardship on the mistaken party* that it would be *unconscionable* to uphold it, and

   (b)   Would avoidance impose an *unfair hardship on the non-mistaken party?*

These questions are partly concerned with the economic impact of the avoidance decision on each of the parties, but it also takes into account their relative innocence or fault.

Therefore, the balance weighs most heavily in favor of the non-mistaken party when the mistake involved a degree of negligence by the other, the non-mistaken party had no reason to realize the mistake, and took action in reliance on the contract. In such a situation, her good faith reliance on the apparent assent of the mistaken party has led her to incur some commitment or expense, so that avoidance would go beyond depriving her of the good bargain, but would actually cause her loss. The protection of good faith reliance is the central issue, but the principle may be articulated in different ways—for example, it is sometimes expressed as a rule to the effect that a contract cannot be avoided for unilateral mistake unless the innocent non-mistaken party can be restored to the status quo. It is sometimes stated that relief should be denied unless the mistaken party promptly notifies the other upon becoming aware of the error. This rule is aimed at ameliorating any prejudicial reliance on the mistake, and it also reflects another factor in the balance—the degree of diligence exercised by the mistaken party. At the other end of the scale, if the non-mistaken party realized the error and kept quiet in order to jump at the bargain, or worse, if the non-mistaken party actually caused the error, her reliance interest is at its weakest. Between these extremes, there are countless variations in relative fault and hardship, so that the balance may be harder to find.

A simple example may make this more concrete. Say that the owner of an apartment complex decides to install new drapes in all the apartments. He contacts a decorator, who measures the windows and shows him a sample book, from which he selects a fabric. The book does not have current prices, so the decorator contacts the manufacturer, who gives her a quote (in the form of an offer of sale) for making the curtains. The decorator adds a profit of 100 percent and makes her offer to the owner, which he accepts. The decorator in turn accepts the manufacturer's offer. Shortly afterwards, the manufacturer discovers that it had misread its price list and had incorrectly based its quote on an inferior material that costs half of the one ordered. As a result, the manufacturer has agreed to a sale price below its cost and, given the size of the order, will lose a substantial sum of money if it fulfills its contractual obligation. Assume that the first four elements for unilateral mistake are satisfied and consider only the equitable balancing: The manufacturer will clearly suffer hardship if the contract is enforced because the price is less than its cost and it will actually lose money. However, the decorator has committed herself to a contract with the owner based on the manufacturer's quoted price. Avoidance shifts the loss to her, but maybe it is less of a hardship because she has such a high profit margin and will just break even, rather than lose money. The determinative factor will be the relative fault of the parties. The manufacturer appears to have been negligent in not properly reading its price list. If the decorator could not have known of the mistake, her commitment based on the quoted prices gives her a strong reliance interest. However, as a professional decorator, she may have been familiar with the general range of prices for fabric of the quality ordered and may have fully realized that a mistake had been made. If so, by keeping silent, she took advantage of the manufacturer's error, and her reliance interest is not worthy of protection. Her impressive profit may be evidence of this advantage-taking. We do

not know the customary markup in the decorating industry, but if it is notably less than 100 percent, her high profit tends to show that she knew the
fabric price was way below market, and that she charged her customer what
he would have expected to pay, thereby keeping the gain for herself. (Notice
the close connection here between unilateral mistake and fraudulent nondisclosure. It was stated in section 13.6.2 that silence could amount to a fraudulent misrepresentation if a party keeps quiet on becoming aware that the
other has made a mistake. Fraud may therefore be an alternative ground for
relief in a case like this if she knew there was something wrong with the quote
and deliberately said nothing.)

§15.5   Relief for Mistake

The principal remedy for mistake is **avoidance** of the contract at the instance of
the mistaken party. There is only one mistaken party when the mistake is unilateral, but if the mistake is mutual the parties share the error. If both wish to
avoid the contract, it can simply be rescinded by agreement. However, if only
one is hurt by the mistake and the other benefits from or is unaffected by it, it
stands to reason that the claim for avoidance will be made by the adversely affected party. Avoidance brings the contract to an end and both parties must **restore any benefit** resulting from performance that was rendered prior to termination. If the benefit is property still in existence, the property itself must be
returned, otherwise restitution must be made of the value of services or property consumed or incapable of return. Value is normally based on the market
worth of the property or services (of which the contract value may be probitive
evidence). However, the court has some discretion in determining the basis of
valuation, and it may use some other measure appropriate under the circumstances. For example, if the party who conferred the benefit was more to blame
for the mistake, the value of consumed goods or services could be confined to
the actual ultimate economic benefit enjoyed by the other party.

Because relief for mistake derives from equity, the court has some flexibility in remedy and could provide relief other than avoidance and restitution
if the equities so dictate. For example, avoidance on the grounds of unilateral
mistake could be ordered subject to the payment of *reliance expenses* designed
to restore the non-mistaken party to the status quo. In relatively rare cases,
the court may keep the contract in force with an *adjustment to its terms* to
counter the effect of the mistake. This alternative is not widely recognized in
the caselaw, and even if a court is willing to allow it in principle, it is not appropriate if the mistake is so fundamental that the entire character of the
transaction is altered, or its basic purpose is defeated. It is also seldom the
best solution if the contract is entirely executory, and neither party performed or otherwise relied on it before the mistake was discovered. However,
in some cases, if avoidance would be disruptive and the error relates to an as-

pect of the contract that can be adjusted (say to a price calculation), an alteration of terms may be a fair remedy. Even here, adjustment of terms must be approached with caution because the court should not readily remake the contract on terms that were not agreed to, especially if that subjects one of the parties to an unexpected and more burdensome obligation.

§15.6 Mistake in Transcription: Reformation

Some mistakes may relate, not to a factual premise of the agreement, but to **the way in which the agreement is expressed in writing.** For example, a memorandum of agreement reflects the price of a piece of land as $280,000. The buyer contends that the parties had orally agreed to a price of $250,000, and that the written price is a typographical error not noticed by the buyer when signing the document.

Mistakes in transcription are completely different in nature from those discussed in the prior sections. The "fact" that is wrong is **not one that motivated the transaction,** but one **inherent in the written record** of the transaction. The problem is not that the manifestation is based on a faulty premise, but that it is false in itself. Nevertheless, an error in expression has one thing in common with a mistake of underlying fact: In both cases one of the parties seeks to avoid the apparent meaning of a manifestation of assent by showing that it was induced by error. In the case of mistake as to an underlying fact, the goal is to negate assent and avoid the contract. When the mistake is in transcription, the desired relief is to have the writing changed to reflect what was actually agreed.

If both parties recognize that an error has occurred in transcription and they act honestly, the problem can be disposed of simply by amending the writing and initialling the change. But life is not always that simple because the party benefiting from the error may claim (whether genuinely or disingenuously) that the writing is correct. If so, the other party is able to seek the equity-based remedy of reformation to have the court correct the writing so that it accurately reflects what was agreed. This remedy involves both a declaration by the court that the contract is on terms other than reflected in the writing, and enforcement on those terms.

Because a signed writing is usually regarded as the most reliable evidence of what was agreed, a party seeking reformation has a difficult burden. He must convincingly show that an error was indeed made in recording the terms agreed, and must also plausibly explain why the error was made and why he failed to notice it when signing the document. Because the right to reformation cannot be shown except by recourse to evidence extrinsic to the writing, the parol evidence rule does not bar the introduction of evidence for the purpose of showing a mistake in transcription. If it did, the remedy of reformation could never be used.

A question of reformation could also be presented when the parties chose words in their writing that do not have the legal effect intended. For example, a written contract for the sale of a car states that it is sold "as is." This is a legal term of art that means that it is sold without any warranties. However, the buyer contends that the parties were unaware of that meaning and did not intend it at all. The seller had added a number of accessories to the car, and the words "as is" were used merely to reflect their agreement that these accessories were to be included. This kind of transcription error is more complicated than the error in the previous illustration involving the incorrect reflection of price, because it is more difficult to distinguish the problem of misrecording from an error in understanding that would need to be resolved by interpretation on the principles discussed in Chapter 10. If the dispute centers around what the parties meant by the term "as is," it is a question of interpretation. However, if the argument is that they agreed on what it was supposed to mean, but the objective appearance of the document, in employing this term, is different from intended, it is a case for reformation. In either event, the party who argues for the idiosyncratic meaning will probably have an evidentiary headache (including possible problems under the parol evidence rule because this is less obviously a simple matter of reformation) if the other now denies that the meaning was intended. Note also that there is a subtle difference between the erroneous expression of agreement by the incorrect use of a legal term and a mutual mistake of law. By using the phrase "as is" the parties do, in a sense, make a legal error—but that error relates not to what the law is, but to the legal meaning of the word-symbol used in the writing.

§15.7   Impracticability of Performance

§15.7.1   The Nature of Impracticability Doctrine, Contrasted with Mistake

Mistake concerns an error of fact in existence at the time of contracting, so fundamental to the premise of the contract that it precludes the formation of true assent. Impracticability applies when events following contract formation[1] are so different from the assumptions on which the contract was based, that it would be unfair to hold the adversely affected party to its commitments. Although there are close affinities between mistake and impracticability, as you will see when comparing their elements, they have an important

---

1. As noted in section 15.1, there are cases in which the circumstances causing the impracticality existed at the time of contracting. This situation is unusual, and impracticality is more commonly associated with supervening events. This discussion is therefore confined to supervening impracticability.

difference in scope and purpose. A mistake causes a defect in contract formation, permitting a party to be excused from accountability for a manifestation of assent. Impracticability has nothing to do with any problem in formation and presupposes that a binding contract was made. Rather, it is concerned with whether a **post-formation change of circumstances** has such a **serious effect** on the **reasonable expectations** of the parties, that it should be allowed to **excuse performance.**

An example will illustrate this difference: The owner of a beachfront cabin makes a contract to sell it. Unknown to both parties at the time of contracting, a tidal wave swept the cabin into the sea just a few hours before the contract was executed. They are mutually mistaken that the cabin exists. However, if the tidal wave hits after the contract was made, but before the seller transfers and delivers the cabin to the buyer, there was no error about its existence at the time of contracting. Instead, the issue is whether this supervening event should permit the seller to escape liability for failure to deliver the cabin as promised in the otherwise valid and enforceable contract.

Note that the issue is not whether the seller can be forced to deliver the cabin. Obviously, he cannot do so because it has been reduced to flotsam on the ocean. The issue is whether, by failing to deliver, he has breached the contract. If failure to deliver is excused on grounds of impracticability, the seller is not in breach and is therefore not liable to pay damages to the buyer. On the facts of this example, impracticability would completely excuse the seller's performance. It follows, of course, that the buyer would not be required to perform either, so the effect of impracticability is to terminate the contract. If either party has partly performed before this (say, for example, that the buyer made a down payment), the benefit of that performance must be restored.

§15.7.2 The Early Form of the Doctrine: Impossibility of Performance

In older common law, once a contract had been made, the parties were absolutely bound and remained committed even if a change in circumstances made it extremely difficult or even impossible for one of them to perform. (As just noted, the party was not expected to work a miracle by performing the impossible, but the failure to perform was not excused by the supervening event and was a breach giving rise to a damages claim.) By the mid-nineteenth century, the harshness of this rule was ameliorated by judicial recognition of the doctrine of impossibility of performance. In its original form, as articulated by the English case of *Taylor v. Caldwell*, 122 Eng. Rep. 309 (Queens Bench, 1863), the doctrine was quite narrow: If, when making the contract, the parties reasonably contemplated that its **performance was dependent** on the **continued existence of a person or thing,** the post-formation **death** of the person or **destruction** of the thing, **not**

caused by the fault of the party seeking relief, would **excuse performance** by that party, and hence, also the return performance, resulting in termination of the contract without liability for breach.

In *Taylor*, the contract was for the hire of a music hall that burned down after the contract was made and before the time for performance. Although the obligation to provide the hall was not qualified by any express term of the contract, the court found the continuing existence of the hall to have been a basic assumption of the contract. This led to the legal implication of a term that the destruction of the hall excused performance. As originally formulated, the defense of impossibility was confined to situations in which the change of circumstances made the contract *objectively* impossible to perform. That is, the event must have completely defeated the ability to deliver the performance, not only by this party, but by a reasonable person in his position. Say, for example, that the fire merely damaged the music hall. If a reasonable owner could have restored it sufficiently in time for the performance, this owner could not claim the defense of impossibility merely because he did not have the resources or energy to do so.

§15.7.3   The Contemporary Doctrine of Impracticability of Performance

During the course of this century, the doctrine of impossibility has come to be perceived as too restricted. There are situations in which events do not make performance absolutely impossible, yet they place such a great and unexpected burden on the party that fairness demands relief. As a result, the scope of the doctrine has broadened and has been renamed "impracticability" to reflect this change. As in so many other areas of contract law, a strong impetus for change in the doctrine came from the UCC. Section 2.615 enacted the broader concept of impracticability as the standard for sales of goods, and this has been influential in reinforcing change in common law doctrine too. By embracing a formulation based on the UCC, Restatement Second §§261 to 272 reinforces the common law's movement away from the stricter impossibility standard. There are a number of differences between UCC §2.615 and the provisions of the Restatement Second, but the basic concepts are the same. This discussion focuses on general principles applicable to both.

If all of its elements are established, the excuse of impracticability is available to the party who is adversely affected by the change in circumstances. (UCC §2.615 assumes that it will always be the seller who claims impracticability, but this need not necessarily be so, and courts have recognized that a buyer can use the excuse in appropriate circumstances.) Although these elements are identified and discussed separately, the defense of impracticability is better understood if one recognizes that they are very much interwoven and that the facts affecting one are often relevant to the others. All the elements must be satisfied for the defense to be available. As in mistake, risk allocation is usually the predominant and pervasive consideration. We now examine each of the elements:

a. After the Contract Was Made, an Event Occurred, the Non-Occurrence of Which Was a Basic Assumption of the Contract

This concept is very much like its equivalent element in mistake doctrine, except that the basic assumption relates not to an existing but to a future state of affairs. The idea here is that when the parties entered the contract they expressly or impliedly made assumptions about the future course of events and these assumptions were a *central motivation of the contract.* Whether or not a basic assumption is articulated, it must be patent enough from the circumstances and the apparent purpose of the contract that it is reasonable to conclude that the parties must have shared it.

Having entered the contract on this basic assumption, the parties are then faced with an event so contrary to the assumption that it *changes the very basis of the exchange.* Comment 1 to UCC §2.615 describes this occurrence as an "unforeseen supervening circumstance not within the contemplation of the parties at the time of contracting." This suggests that the event must be so unexpected that the parties did not think of it at the time of contracting, or if they did, that they did not consider it to be a realistic likelihood.

The comment uses the word "unforeseen," which must be distinguished from "unforeseeable." An event is **unforeseen** by the parties if they themselves **did not contemplate it as a real likelihood.** That is, although it could be imagined, the parties did not expect it to happen and contracted on the assumption that it would not. It may be a possibility, but is not treated by the parties as a probability. An event is **unforeseeable** if it **could not have been conceived of by a reasonable person.** To require unforeseeability would impose too stringent a test, making the defense of impracticability available only when the supervening event is beyond human experience. For example, it is unforeseeable that a music hall could be demolished by a rampaging dinosaur or other large beast,[2] but its destruction by fire is certainly within the range of possibility. Therefore, fire was foreseeable at the time of contracting, but it was not foreseen by the parties if, under all the circumstances, it is shown that they did not think of it at all or, even if one or both may have realized the possibility, it was not considered a strong enough likelihood to be raised and

---

2. Of course, the fact that I (and several talented "B" movie creators) have contemplated this possibility may mean that it is indeed foreseeable.

dealt with as a contingency. Of course, the fact that the event was unforeseen does not, on its own, mean that the defense of impracticability will succeed. This is only the first of the elements that must be satisfied. Often, even though the non-occurrence of the event was a basic assumption of the contract, the risk of the occurrence may have been impliedly assumed by the party claiming impracticality. That is, if the parties foresaw the likelihood of the event, they probably allocated the risk of its happening (expressly or impliedly) in the contract. However, even if they did not foresee it, commercial practice or other surrounding circumstances may give rise to an implication of risk assumption.

Impracticability arises from the occurrence of an event, so we must identify **what types of happening might constitute an event.** Again, there is an analogy to mistake, in that an event is a factual situation, albeit one that arises after the contract. Most **occurrences external to the contract** qualify as events: war, a natural disaster, a strike, and so on. A **change in the law or government regulation** is also an event. Therefore, if the law changes to prohibit a performance that was lawful at the time of contracting, the change in the law defeats a basic assumption of the contract. UCC §2.615(1) and Restatement Second §264 expressly recognize this by providing that good faith compliance with governmental regulation excuses performance, even if the regulation is later found to be invalid. Say, for example, that the music hall did not burn down, but shortly after the contract was made, the city council strengthened its public safety regulations so that the hall no longer satisfied them and cannot be lawfully let for public performances. If the council's action was unexpected and was given no advance publicity, this would be an unforeseen contingency that defeats the basic assumption that the hall could be used. This example highlights the development of the law from impossibility to impracticability. It would still be possible for the lessor to make the hall available and for the buyer to pay the rent, but the contract is made impracticable because its basic assumption has been overturned.[3]

A **change in market conditions** is generally not regarded as a contingency beyond the contemplation of the parties because the very purpose of setting a price or committing to a future delivery of goods or services is based on the possibility that prices or demand may change. Therefore, the basic assumption of most contracts is not that the market will remain constant, but that it might change. However, the basic assumption of any particular con-

---

3. In anticipation of the discussion in section 15.8, it is also worth pointing out that these facts would support an argument that the purpose of the contract has been frustrated: Although the lessor can still deliver possession of the hall and the lessee can still pay the rent, the purpose of the hiring—the use of the hall for a public concert—has been negated by the new regulations. This illustrates the observation in section 15.8 that impracticality is broad enough to cover most, if not all, situations that would have required a separate doctrine of frustration in earlier law.

tract is a factual question, so this general approach should not be treated as an invariable rule. It is possible that a constant market was assumed in a contract, or even if not, that the market variation results from a disruption which causes changes way beyond reasonable expectations. This is particularly so if some unexpected calamity, such as a sudden war, embargo, or natural disaster is the cause of the market changes. This has happened a number of times, and there are cases arising from events such as the Suez crisis, the Vietnam War, and the OPEC oil embargo, in which the supplier of a commodity or service has claimed impracticability based on greatly added expense or burdens on performance caused by the crisis. In some of the cases, the international disturbance was found to render performance impracticable, but in others, the defense did not succeed, either because the disruption was foreseen by the parties or because one of the other elements of the defense (such as extreme hardship or risk allocation) was not satisfied.

b. The Effect of the Event Is to Render the Party's Performance "Impracticable," that Is, Unduly Burdensome

A loss in certainty is the price paid for the law's movement away from the more discernible standard of impossibility, toward the vaguer and more relative concept of impracticability. Once a party no longer has to establish that performance is objectively incapable of being rendered, we are left with the task of deciding how extensively the performance must have changed to qualify as impracticable. If impracticability merely required a showing of inconvenience, lack of profitability, or the loss of a better opportunity, it would be too easy for a party to escape a contract that turns out to be disadvantageous because of a change in the market or commercial environment. Therefore, relief is only appropriate if the change is extreme or very burdensome. In a sense, this requirement is similar to the element of *materiality* in mistake. The event must have such a severe impact on the performance that it cannot be rendered without great loss, risk, or other hardship. Unfortunately, this is as vague as it sounds, but it necessarily must be so, because impracticality is relative and must be assessed on all the facts of the case.

In the easiest case, an event that creates objective impossibility also renders the performance impracticable, because the wider doctrine includes cases that would have satisfied the narrower standard. Therefore, if the parties contemplated the rental of a specific music hall, the destruction of the hall makes performance impossible and hence also impracticable. However, as the facts move beyond this clearer case, the determination becomes more difficult. Say that the music hall did not burn down, but after the contract is made, the premium payable by the lessor for liability insurance increases tenfold because of a large number of theater fires in the region over the last year.

As a result, if the lessor is to permit use of the premises by the public, he must pay a huge insurance premium that will exceed the earnings he will make from renting the hall. Both parties can still perform—the lessor can make the hall available and the lessee can pay the rent—but the increase in insurance rates has imposed a financial burden (or a massive risk of liability, if the policy is not renewed) on the lessor that may make its performance impracticable.

Consider another example: The hall does burn down, but there is another hall in the same block owned by a competitor of the lessor. The hall is about the same size, is equally suitable for the performance, and it is available for the night of the concert. The lessee contends that the lessor's performance is therefore still possible, because the exact identity of the hall is immaterial, and the lessor can still provide appropriate premises by hiring the second hall and making it available to the lessee as a substitute for the destroyed hall. The problem is that the owner of the surviving hall demands a rental from the lessor far higher than that which the lessor is to be paid by the lessee under the contract, so the lessor will lose money by doing this (or by paying the rental difference to the lessee as damages if he refuses). If the lessee's contention is correct and the identity of the hall was not a central term of the contract, the lessor's performance is not impossible, so the question becomes whether the loss to be incurred in finding a substitute renders it sufficiently burdensome to constitute impracticability.

There is no definitive answer to the question in these cases. However, they point to the focus of the inquiry—the economic impact of the unforeseen supervening event. A prospective loss that is not negligible could satisfy this element. The magnitude and effect of the loss is obviously of crucial significance, and a huge loss that threatens the lessee's financial survival is more likely to be seen as making the performance impracticable, than a manageable smaller loss. This may make it sound as if the defense of impracticability can be easily invoked whenever a serious prospective loss is shown. But remember that this element is only one of several that must be satisfied, and proof of the most devastating loss is not enough to assure relief if the other elements are not also present.

c.   The Party Seeking Relief Was Not at Fault in Causing the Occurrence

A person should not be able to take advantage of his own wrongful or negligent act, and a party who disables himself from performing, or makes performance more difficult, cannot expect to be excused from liability. Thus, the lessor of the music hall would have a nerve claiming impracticability if he deliberately set the fire. Similarly, a person cannot be excused from liability just because it turns out that he is incompetent and cannot perform as promised. However, the issue of fault could be more subtle. Should the lessor be denied relief if the fire was caused by an antiquated and improperly maintained electrical system in the music hall? In less obvious cases, the degree to which the party was in some way responsible for his troubles, or could have surmounted them with reasonable effort, is a relevant factor to be taken into account.

d. The Party Seeking Relief Must Not Have Borne the Risk of the Event Occurring

As with mistake, the risk allocation is often the dispositive issue in impracticability cases. In many ways, the other elements foreshadow the question of risk allocation and seem to be no more than components of it. (In fact, as you may have sensed, the issue of risk allocation was constantly lurking in the discussion of the other elements and had to be restrained from jumping out.) The analysis of risk allocation is basically the same as for mistake: If the party adversely affected by the event had *expressly or impliedly assumed the risk of its occurrence,* the non-performance cannot be excused even though all the other elements are satisfied.

The first place to look in determining risk allocation is the contract itself. If the parties realized that a particular future event could affect performance, the contract may have an express and specific term assigning risk. For example, a consignor of goods and a shipping company may contemplate the possibility that a war may break out along the route, requiring a diversion of the ship. If so, they may specifically state in the contract which party will bear the loss and expense of the diversion. Even if the parties do not have a particular contingency in mind, the contract may have a more general provision allocating the risk of disruptions or calamities. This is known as a **force majeure** clause. It may provide, for example, that the shipping company shall have the right to charge for the cost of any diversion or delay of the ship resulting from war, revolution, national disasters, governmental action, and so on.

Even in the absence of these more direct types of risk allocation clauses, the contract may impliedly place risk on a party by means of a provision such as a warranty, an undertaking to obtain insurance, or some other commitment from which the assumption of risk may be inferred. In fact, a term expressly allocating the risk of certain events to one party may give rise to the inference that the other assumed the risk of events not enumerated. For example, a clause states that the shipping company may charge for additional expenses caused by war, revolution, and governmental action. If the ship is seized by pirates and held hostage for ransom, the loss of this disruption is not apparently covered by the contract, so it could be inferred that the consignor of the freight was intended to bear it. It is good planning for the parties to consider potential risks and to provide for them clearly in the contract. This reduces the possibility of later disputes and litigation. Of course, as the last example suggests, no risk allocation provision is foolproof. It may fail to contemplate the actual event that occurs.

If the contract terms do not settle the issue, its *context,* including normal *commercial practices and expectations,* must be examined to decide where the risk should lie. On this basis, we can reconsider some of the prior examples, to show that risk allocation may preclude relief even though the other elements may be satisfied. The lessee of the music hall will probably not be able to claim impracticability on the basis of poor ticket sales. Unless the contract provides otherwise, commercial practice in the entertainment industry probably places this risk on the promoter of the concert and will not allow him to foist it on the lessor by cancelling the booking if sales are weak. Practices concerning insurance can often help to settle risk allocation where the contract does not deal with the issue. Therefore (contrary to the result in *Taylor),* the lessee may be able to argue that the fact that the owner has an insurable interest in the hall suggests that the burning of the hall was the owner's risk, and he cannot use this calamity as the basis for escaping liability to the lessee. Finally, it is worth reiterating a point made in the discussion of basic assumption, and to emphasize that the assumptions underlying the contract are closely intertwined with the question of risk allocation: For example, unless the contract provides otherwise, the usual commercial assumption is that a party takes the risk of market fluctuations unless the change is so dramatic and unexpected as to be beyond the normal range of risk.

§15.7.4   *Relief for Impracticability*

When impracticability fully defeats the feasibility of performance by a party, it is a **complete defense** to that party's failure to perform, **relieving** him of the **duty of performance** and liability for **damages.** Release of that party also discharges the contractual duties of the other. If any performance had been rendered by either party under the contract prior to the finding of impracticability, the benefit or its value must be returned, measured in accordance with the same restitutionary principles applicable to mistake.

If impracticability does not go to the entire basis of the contract, the court has the discretion to award relief short of fully excusing performance. This is recognized in general terms by Comments 6 and 7 to UCC §2.615, and in more detail by Restatement Second §§269 and 270. It may be more appropriate to adjust the terms of the contract, to excuse a portion of the performance (with a reciprocal reduction in counterperformance), or simply to permit a delay if this would enable the difficulties to be surmounted.

§15.8   Frustration of Purpose

The doctrine of frustration of purpose developed as an extension of impossibility. It was designed to provide relief when a party could not show that an unexpected supervening event rendered his performance impossible, yet it so destroyed the value of the transaction for him that the contract's underlying purpose was frustrated. Because contemporary doctrine has expanded beyond the confines of impossibility, there is probably no longer a need for a separate doctrine of frustration of purpose. Frustration could simply be treated as a class of impracticability and subsumed into that doctrine. Notwithstanding, these two closely-linked defenses continue to coexist and are treated by courts (and by Restatement Second §265) as separate but allied. It is therefore necessary to understand the difference between them. However, if you should find it difficult to decide whether a particular case involves impracticality or frustration, take comfort in the thought that misclassification probably will not make much difference in result. They involve essentially the same issues and lead to the same type of relief. The only difference between them lies in the sometimes subtle distinction between an event that makes a party's performance unduly burdensome, and one that makes it pointless. (UCC Article 2 doesn't provide for a separate doctrine of frustration.)

Like impracticability, frustration is concerned with a **post-formation event**, the **non-occurrence** of which was a **basic assumption** on which the contract was made. This event must not have been caused by the fault of the party whose purpose is frustrated, and that party must not have borne the risk of its occurrence. The essential difference lies in the effect of the event. It does not directly affect the performance of the adversely affected party by making it unduly burdensome. Rather, its impact is on the benefit reasonably expected by that party in exchange for the performance. The event so **seriously affects the value or usefulness** of that benefit that it **frustrates the contract's central purpose** for that party. This cannot be a secret or obscure purpose, because a party's private motivation is not relevant to the contract and cannot be the basis of disappointing the other party's reliance. Therefore, the purpose must be so patent and obvious to the other party that it can reasonably be regarded as the *shared basis* of the contract.

The classic illustration of frustration is supplied by another beloved English case, *Krell v. Henry*, 2 K.B. 740 (1903). Krell owned a flat on the route to be taken by the coronation procession of Edward VII. Krell was out of the country and instructed his solicitor to attempt to let the premises while he was away. A sign was placed in the window stating that the flat was available to be let for viewing the procession. Henry responded to the sign and contracted to hire the flat on the two days of the coronation celebrations. The King became ill before the coronation and it was postponed, so Henry was left with no need for the premises on the days in question and he did not use them. Krell sued him for the balance of the agreed rental. (Henry had made a down payment but apparently did not pursue a counterclaim for a refund of the deposit.) The court resolved the case by using an adaptation of the impossibility defense of *Taylor v. Caldwell*. Although the contract did not expressly state the purpose of the rental of the flat, both parties understood that Henry's sole purpose in making it was to view the coronation procession. This purpose was the very foundation of the contract. The postponement of the coronation was a supervening event that had not reasonably been contemplated by the parties at the time of contracting. Although it did not make either party's performance impossible (Henry could still pay the agreed rent and Krell could give him possession of the flat), it so defeated the purpose of the contract that it should excuse Henry's performance. A concurring opinion in the case agreed with this analysis but raised the question of whether Henry would have been the more appropriate party to bear the risk of the coronation's postponement. This is a fair question and it again raises the point that when the contract does not itself provide for risk allocation, it is not always easy to know who should suffer the loss caused by the frustration. It is by no means self-evident that the court was right in imposing it on the lessor rather than the lessee.

EXAMPLES

1. Tiffany De Canter owned an ornate silver jug. She bought it some years ago for a substantial amount of money, believing it to be the work of Maestro Da Silva, an important nineteenth-century silversmith. Since she acquired it, Tiffany has had it examined by several experts. Although some of them thought that it might have been made by Da Silva, the prevailing view among them is that it was the product of one of his pupils. It has therefore been appraised at $10,000. Had it been authenticated as the work of Da Silva, it would be worth $1 million. Based on its appraised value, Tiffany grossly overpaid for the jug. She hates it and gets irritated every time she sees it. She therefore decided to sell it.

Sterling Silverman, an art collector, has seen the jug and is familiar with Da Silva's work. He has a hunch that the experts may be wrong in concluding that it was not made by Da Silva. Upon hearing that Tiffany wished to sell it, he immediately made an offer to buy it at her full asking price of $12,000. Tiffany accepted his offer and a written contract of sale was executed. The writing was a simple document that identified the parties, set out the physical description of the jug, and stated the price and delivery obligation. A few months after the sale was completed, a scholar unearthed some previously unknown notebooks and sketches by Da Silva that conclusively proved that he had made the jug.

Can Tiffany avoid the sale to Sterling?

2. Manny Lisa recently became wealthy through the exercise of his stock options. All his newfound rich friends owned portraits of themselves painted by the celebrated society portraitist Leonardo De Fancy. Although he is clueless about art, Manny decided to get hold of the divine Leonardo and commission a portrait. He looked in the yellow pages under "Painters, por-

trait" and found a listing for De Fancy, Leonardo. He called the number and spoke to Leonardo, who agreed to paint his portrait for $250. Manny was astounded at how reasonable this was, and he accepted. The parties arranged a date for a sitting at the end of the week.

A couple of days later, Manny discovered from a more worldly friend that the person who is listed in the yellow pages is not *the* Leonardo, but his father, Leonardo De Fancy the Elder, a talentless hack who ekes out a meager living by painting the children of middle-class suburbanites. Being unschooled in the ways of the art world, Manny had not known that a famous celebrity portraitist like the real Leonardo does not advertise in the yellow pages and only accepts commissions on referral. Furthermore, his charge for a portrait would be about 40 times what Manny had agreed to pay Leonardo the Elder.

Understandably, Manny no longer desires the portrait for which he contracted. Can he avoid the contract?

3. Reliabuild Contractors, Inc. was invited by the owner of property to submit a bid for the erection of a new building. Reliabuild planned to do all the work itself except for the excavation of the land. It needed to know the cost of excavation before it could complete its bid, so it sent the building plans to Bill Dozer, an earthmover whom it had used with satisfactory results on several prior projects. Bill studied the plans and calculated his own cost. Unfortunately, he did this while watching his favorite afternoon talk show, and he did not concentrate properly. As a result, he added wrongly and miscalculated his cost as $500,000 instead of $800,000. He then added a ten percent profit of $50,000 and submitted a written bid of $550,000 to Reliabuild. Reliabuild calculated its own bid on the basis of this figure and submitted it to the owner. Reliabuild's bid was about $400,000 less than the lowest competing bid, so the owner accepted it. Reliabuild then accepted Bill's bid.

A few days before Bill was to begin his performance, he reviewed his bid and discovered his miscalculation. The error would not only deprive him of his expected profit, but would result in a loss of $250,000. He could not absorb such a loss, which would put him out of business. Bill called Reliabuild immediately, explained the error, and withdrew from the contract. Reliabuild told Bill that it regarded this as a repudiation and would hold him liable for damages. Reliabuild then sought other bids and accepted the lowest one of $900,000. As a result, Reliabuild had to pay $350,000 more than it originally expected and lost about 80 percent of the profit it had anticipated on the project.

Reliabuild claims the $350,000 from Bill as damages for breach of contract. Does Bill have a defense?

4. Change the facts of Example 3 as follows: Assume that when Bill explained the mistake, Reliabuild did not wish to drive him out of business by insisting that he perform at a great loss. It therefore took pity on him and agreed to release him from his obligation. Reliabuild does not itself wish to

assume the extra cost of employing a more expensive subcontractor, so it in turn seeks to withdraw from its contract with the owner. The owner is not so kind and threatens suit if Reliabuild does not perform as agreed. Can Reliabuild escape its contract with the owner?

5. Merlin Magnifico, Master of the Impossible, is a magician. On July 1 he entered into a contract with Showstopper Promotions, Inc. under which he agreed, for a fee of $10,000, to perform a magical extravaganza at the Pyro Palace Theater on August 30. This contract forms the basis of the separate and distinct factual variations set out in the following questions.

(a)   On July 20, Merlin tried to perform the most daring escape trick ever attempted. He jumped out of a plane all trussed up like a turkey, allowing himself two minutes to free himself and pull his parachute cord. He succeeded in loosening his bonds, but in his feverish unravelling, also mistakenly untied his parachute harness.

(i)   Is the estate of the late Merlin Magnifico liable to Showstopper for the substantial profits it lost as a result of having to cancel the show and refund the price of tickets sold?

(ii)   This sad event had an impact (no, I would not be so callous as to intend a pun) on a transaction between two other parties: By July 15, all the tickets to Merlin's show had been sold, and people were clamoring to buy tickets from those who had been lucky enough to get them. Buck Fast had managed to buy a ticket for $50 when they first went on sale. His friend Fanny De Voted adored Merlin and desperately wanted to see the show. She nagged Buck to sell the ticket to her, offering an increasingly higher price each time he refused. Eventually he gave in and sold it to her when her offer reached $150. When Merlin was killed, Showstopper cancelled the show and announced that ticketholders should return their tickets for a refund. Naturally, Showstopper will only refund the face value of the ticket, so Fanny demands that Buck repay her the excess of $100. Buck refuses. Is Fanny entitled to the return of her money?

(b)   Change the facts so that Merlin did succeed in accomplishing the parachute trick. As a result, he became an instant worldwide sensation. He is now able to command a fee of $500,000 for a booking. He does not wish to perform for Showstopper at the measly rate of $10,000. Can he escape the contract?

(c)   Merlin survived his parachute prank, only to be apprehended by grim-faced F.A.A. officials for failing to obtain the permits needed for exiting an aircraft in a state of physical restraint. To avoid prosecution and stern punishment, Merlin entered into a consent decree with the F.A.A. in which he undertook never again to perform magic tricks on land or sea, or in the air. When Merlin told Showstopper that he could no longer perform on August 30, Showstopper sued him for breach of contract. Does he have a defense?

(d) The trick of July 20 did not happen. (In fact, Merlin is terrified of heights and can only undertake air travel under deep sedation with his seatbelt firmly fastened.) Merlin was therefore willing and able to give his show at the end of August. On August 15 the Pyro Palace burned down.

    (i) Showstopper had sold almost all the tickets to the extravaganza and did not wish to cancel or postpone it. It therefore hired a smelly but capacious high school gym for the performance. Merlin says that it is beneath his dignity to do his act in a school gym, and he wishes to cancel the contract. Does he have grounds for doing so?

    (ii) Assume that Showstopper could not find a replacement hall and it had no choice but to cancel the show. Merlin accepts the cancellation of the performance and does not demand payment of the fee. However, he has spent $1,000 on a costume and special props that were specifically made for this performance and cannot be used elsewhere. He would like to be refunded for these expenses. Is he entitled to them?

(e) None of the above catastrophes happened. However, ticket sales for the show were appalling. Despite intensive promotion, Showstopper had filled only 30 percent of the house by August 20. It is clear that Showstopper will incur a substantial loss if the show goes on. Showstopper takes the position that, known to Merlin, its obvious purpose in entering the contract was to make a profit. The supervening lack of interest on the part of the public has frustrated this purpose, and Showstopper is therefore entitled to cancel the contract with Merlin. Is this a good argument?

6. Professor Goldbrick hates grading exams. One day he saw an advertisement by Slacker Software, Inc., in which it claimed that it could design computer programs to meet any educational need. Goldbrick contacted Slacker and asked if they could devise a program that would enable him to feed essay exams into his computer so that the machine could grade them for him. Slacker took full details of what Goldbrick would need and said it would consider the matter and get back to him. A few weeks later, Slacker sent him a written proposal in which it undertook to create a program of the kind he required. In essence, the program would have a highly sophisticated and revolutionary means of identifying key words and phrases so that the computer

could make a comparison between student answers, scanned into the computer, and a model answer entered into the computer by the professor. Because the program was so innovative, Slacker wanted the obscene price of $100,000 for producing it. Goldbrick hated grading so much that he decided it was worth it, even though it meant that he would have to sell all his assets to come up with the money. The parties entered a contract under which Slacker undertook to deliver the program within six months.

Slacker set to work on the program immediately. After struggling with it for four frustrating months, it became apparent to Slacker that its original conception was too simplistic and that the program would need considerable refinement and expansion. Slacker is not sure that a workable program can be created at all, but if it could, it would require so much extensive further research and experimentation that its cost would be prohibitive. It therefore told Goldbrick that it could not produce the program and cancelled the contract. Goldbrick is deeply disappointed. He would like to contract with another programmer and hold Slacker liable for any difference in price. Would Slacker be liable?

7. Crystal Springer owns land that has a pristine spring on it. In 1992 she made a contract with Hale & Hearty Bottling Co., under which she agreed to sell it one million gallons of water a year for ten years. The contract provided for an initial base price for the first year, to increase by ten percent at the beginning of each succeeding year. This annual increase was calculated on the basis of market trends over the last ten years. During that period there had been a steady increase in demand for bottled water, resulting in an upward pressure on prices. This, combined with annual inflation, had led to a fairly steady price growth, averaging around ten percent per year. At the time of the contract, all indications were that this trend would continue because people still distrusted municipal water supplies and the progress in cleaning them up was slow.

The pricing formula worked very well for the first three years of the contract. However, in the fourth year, a dramatic breakthrough was achieved in the technology for treating municipal drinking water. This led to a cheap, effective, and completely safe means of purifying public water supplies. Water districts across the country implemented it as quickly as possible. People began to have confidence in municipal water and came to realize that they no longer had to pay steep prices for something they could get for pennies from their own faucets. Gradually everyone except for the diehards and incurable cynics began to stop buying bottled water. As a result the market price for spring water did not increase at all in the fourth year of the contract, and it began to plummet by the beginning of the fifth year. By the middle of that year, the price paid to Crystal by Hale & Hearty was four times the market value of her water. To make matters worse, Hale & Hearty no longer needed a million gallons a year, because it could not sell more than 100,000. It predicts that this downward trend will continue until the market all but disappears, and it will soon be forced to cease bottling water altogether. May Hale & Hearty cancel its contract with Crystal?

8. Bill Dozer seems to have ongoing problems in filling out forms. He was completing an order for some standard quotation blanks to be used in giving bids to customers. The quotation blanks were to be customized with his logo, name, and address. He planned to order 1,000 blanks, but because he was watching his favorite afternoon soap opera while completing the order, he made a mistake and filled in the quantity as "100,000." He then mailed the order to the supplier. (This was the first time he had ordered forms from the supplier, which is located in another city.) In due course, he received a crate of forms. He cannot use up that many forms in his lifetime and would like to avoid the contract and return them to the supplier on the basis of mistake. Does he have a case for claiming mistake?

EXPLANATIONS

1. Tiffany is a sophisticated seller who made her judgment without any reliance on a representation by Sterling or under any pressure from him. In the absence of deception or other improper bargaining, the only possible basis for avoidance is mistake. (It may be tempting to find unconscionability in the grossly inadequate price. Although there is some recognition that a gross disparity in exchange could, on its own, be grounds for unconscionability, the generally accepted view is that this substantive unfairness must have resulted from wrongful bargaining conduct or at least from an environment that would allow advantage to be taken of a vulnerable party. This is discussed in section 13.11.) This is a sale of goods, but mistake is not specifically dealt with in UCC Article 2, so it is governed by common law rules.

The error in this case does not concern the actual identity of the jug, but its authorship. The identity of its maker is a fact, and the low price reflects an erroneous shared basic assumption (that is, a mutual mistake) about it. However, both parties were aware of the possibility of incorrect attribution, and if they were wrong, this is more a question of incorrect judgment. Tiffany gambled that she was correct in believing it to be a work of Da Silva's pupil, in which case, she obtained a good price, somewhat above its true market value. Sterling speculated that the experts might be wrong, in which case he would make a killing. When parties deal with each other in an arms-length market transaction, their respective reliance interests are entitled to protection. One of them cannot be deprived of his bargain because it later turns out that the other made a poor judgment.

Thus, the case can be disposed of quickly by treating it as a misjudgment on Tiffany's part and not an error of fact at all. However, even if, as an initial matter, it was to be conceded that there was a mistake of fact, the analysis of risk allocation leads to the same result: Tiffany must be held responsible for her own judgment. The written contract simply describes the jug without making any representation of authorship, and there is no other term that expressly allocates the risk of error. In the absence of guidance in the contract itself, risk must be allocated to the party who should most appropriately bear it under all the circumstances of the transaction. When the parties knowingly enter a contract for the sale of a work of art of uncertain attribution, the risk must lie with the party whose judgment proves to be wrong. This is the resolution suggested in *Firestone & Parson, Inc. v. Union League of Philadelphia*, 672 F. Supp. 819 (E.D. Pa. 1987). The case involved the sale of a painting attributed to Albert Bierstadt, the celebrated nineteenth-century American landscape painter. At the time of the sale, the painting was accepted by art experts to be a Bierstadt, and the parties had no reason to believe otherwise. As a result, it was sold for $500,000. About four years after the sale, scholarly opinion began to change, and doubt was expressed about its attribution. This debate led to further research and an article was published about two years thereafter demonstrating that the painting was the work of a lesser-known artist. This meant that it was worth only a tenth of what was paid for it. The buyer sued for avoidance of the contract on the grounds of mistake. Because the suit was brought such a long time after the contract, the central issue in the case was whether the buyer's suit was barred by the four-year statute of limitations provided for in UCC Article 2. The court held that it was, and the suit was dismissed on this ground. Although the court did not have to deal with the mistake issue, it observed that even if the buyer had been able to overcome the statute of limitations problem, the parties' assumption that the work was a Bierstadt would not necessarily permit avoidance. In essence, the court suggested that where the contract is based on prevailing views on the authorship and value of an artwork, this is more in the nature of a judgment than a mistake of fact.

This example also invokes the infamous cow case, *Sherwood v. Walker*, 33 N.W. 919 (Mich. 1887). A cattle breeder, believing a highly pedigreed cow to be infertile, sold it as a beef cow for a fraction of its value. Before delivery, the seller discovered the cow to be pregnant and he refused to deliver it to the buyer. When the buyer sued to compel delivery, the court allowed the seller to avoid the contract for mistake because the sale was based on the mutual belief that the cow was fit only for beef and could not breed. The court said that relief was appropriate because the cow's infertility was a mistake as to its very substance and not merely as to its quality. The distinction between "substance" and "quality" is quite obscure and is no longer regarded as particularly helpful. It probably translates, under the contemporary test, to a conclusion that the infertility was a basic assumption of the contract, and that the seller did not assume the risk of the assumption being wrong. The dissenting opinion challenged this conclusion and reached a result consonant with that suggested above: Neither party knew for sure that the cow could not breed, and the seller's loss should be treated more as a matter of misjudgment. The buyer won on the gamble and should not be deprived of the fruits of his successful speculation.

2. There are two possible arguments that Manny could make for avoidance, but both would be difficult to establish on these facts. He could claim that Leonardo the Elder made a fraudulent misrepresentation by nondisclosure when he advertised under the name shared with his celebrated son and failed to indicate that he was not *the* Leonardo. This argument seems tenuous. Although there is some chance of confusion, and maybe a possibility that Leonardo was consciously taking advantage of his son's name recognition, the two painters operate in different spheres. Leonardo the Elder has not misrepresented his name and he made no claim to be a society painter. His advertising in the yellow pages and the modesty of his fee suggest that he may not even have imagined that there would be any reasonable confusion. Furthermore, any duty that he may have had to alert potential customers to the fact that he was not *the* Leonardo seems to be outweighed by Manny's carelessness in not making proper enquiries to obtain easily ascertainable information, especially in light of the low price.

Manny's other possible argument is that the contract was induced by unilateral mistake. A mistake as to the identity of the other party is treated as a factual error. The mistake did relate to Manny's basic assumption in entering the contract. It is harder to say whether the error materially affected the exchange of values. There is unlikely to be a market for a portrait of Manny, and this portrait does not really fulfill Manny's purpose of acquiring a fashionable decorative item, so the materiality element may be satisfied.

The resolution of this issue may not be crucial, because Manny is likely to lose on the allocation of risk and the equities. Manny may have been untutored in the ways of the art world, but he had ready access to information and advice and should have proceeded more carefully before committing himself to ordering a painting from the wrong artist. There do not seem to be strong equities for shifting the risk to Leonardo. There is nothing to suggest that Leonardo had reason to suspect an error and exploited it, and he has a legitimate reliance interest worthy of protection.

3. The facts here are similar to those of Example 5 in Chapter 5. The difference between them is that in that case, the subcontractor discovered the error before the builder had accepted its offer, and the issue was whether promissory estoppel could be used to protect the builder's reliance on the bid, making it irrevocable until the builder had a reasonable opportunity to accept it after being awarded the prime contract. On those facts, the subcontractor was held to its bid on the authority of *Drennan v. Star Paving Co.*, 333 P.2d 757 (Cal. 1958), which recognized the use of promissory estoppel to create an option. This issue does not come up on the present facts, because the error was discovered only after Bill's offer had been accepted by Reliabuild. Mistake is therefore the only basis on which Bill can resist liability for Reliabuild's expectation damages.

This mistake is not mutual, but unilateral on Bill's part. In a sense, Reliabuild has also been in error over the correct price for the earthmoving, but this does not make the mistake mutual. The calculation of Bill's price is solely within his realm and forms his individual basic assumption. Reliabuild was not involved in the determination of Bill's price. It simply reacts to the end result of Bill's calculations, which it will accept or reject. Are the requirements of unilateral mistake satisfied? Bill should not have much trouble with the first three: His cost in doing the work is a fact. It was a basic assumption on which he entered the contract. It materially effects the exchange, in that it causes him to undercharge so badly that his expected profit becomes an unbearable loss.

He is not likely to do as well with the issues of risk allocation and equitable balancing. His miscalculation is not simply a matter of conscientious error, but results from sloppy inattention to his work.[4] This, on its own, may be enough to preclude relief in that his degree of negligence amounted to an assumption of the risk of mistake. Even if this does not dispose of the matter, the cause and nature of the mistake will weigh against him in the balance of the equities. On the other side of the balance is the hardship he will suffer if the contract is enforced. The damages may put him out of business, but shifting the loss to Reliabuild will apparently have a less devastating effect because it has a bigger profit margin and may be able to better absorb it. When the potential impact of the mistake is so severe to the mistaken party as to threaten his livelihood, and only reduces the gains of the other party, a court may be swayed by the balance of hardship.

Nevertheless, the relative depth of the parties' pockets, while a relevant consideration, may not be weighty enough to be the overriding factor in the decision to foist the loss onto one of them. Relative blame and innocence must be considered as well. In this case, Bill's carelessness must be weighed against Reliabuild's justifiable reliance on his contractual commitment. It could be that Reliabuild, as an experienced prime contractor, should have realized that the bid was too low, but there are no facts to indicate this. If it had no reason to have suspected the mistake, it made its own commitment to the owner in reasonable reliance on Bill's manifestation of assent. Bill cannot be released from his obligation without subjecting Reliabuild to the substantial harm of either reneging on its obligation to the owner, with the probability of ensuing litigation, loss of reputation and loss of profit, or of having to pay the additional cost of a substitute. In other words, Reliabuild cannot be restored to the status quo if Bill is allowed to escape liability under their contract.

The refusal of relief does find some support in *Drennan*. After finding

---

4. Assuming, of course, that he or one of his employees reveals that the TV was absorbing his attention while he was doing his calculations.

the subcontractor's bid binding on the basis of promissory estoppel, the court turned to the question of whether the unilateral mistake in calculation should relieve the subcontractor of liability for damages. The court found that it should not, because the equities favored enforcement of the bid: The mistake was caused by the subcontractor's negligence (although, unlike Bill, it had not been trying to mix business and pleasure), the prime contractor had no reason to know of the error, and it had committed itself to the owner on the strength of the bid. Admittedly, the facts in *Drennan* do not indicate that the subcontractor was facing a loss as dire as that to be borne by Bill, but, as mentioned earlier, this may not be strong enough to be dispositive where the equities otherwise so heavily favor enforcement. (A final comment on this explanation is made at the end of the explanation of Example 4.)

4. If Reliabuild releases Bill from his subcontract, the question becomes whether Reliabuild itself could use mistake as the basis for seeking relief under the prime contract. That is, Reliabuild could argue that it made an error in its own cost calculations, based on having been given incorrect information by Bill. The argument would run as follows: Bill's charges are a fact forming Reliabuild's basic assumption in entering the prime contract, and the mistake has a material effect in the exchange of values. As Reliabuild had no reason to realize that Bill had made a mistake, and because it had used Bill before without trouble, it did not lack diligence in assuming that his bid was accurate. For this reason, it did not assume the risk of mistake, and there is no carelessness to be weighed against it in balancing the equities. Enforcement of the contract would have a harsh impact on Reliabuild, which would lose 80 percent of its profit, and the only impact on the owner is that it loses its bargain price. Finally, the fact that the lowest competing bid was $400,000 more means that the owner was unfairly benefitted by the mistake and may reasonably have been alerted to the possibility of error by the wide discrepancy.

There is a reasonable argument to the contrary: It may not be appropriate to allocate the risk of this error to the owner, who did not deal with Bill and had no means of evaluating his bid. Furthermore, the owner had no role in releasing Bill, and Reliabuild took it upon itself to forgive Bill's negligence and to abandon any recourse against him. Notwithstanding, Reliabuild's argument could succeed on all the equities of the case. It worked on similar facts in *Wil-Fred's Inc. v. Metropolitan Sanitary District*, 372 N.E.2d 946 (Ill. 1978). The prime contractor was working on a rehabilitation project at a water reclamation plant. Its price for the work was based on a miscalculated bid by its excavation subcontractor. When the subcontractor discovered its mistake, it asked the prime contractor to be released from its subcontract. The prime contractor permitted the subcontractor to withdraw, because the subcontractor would have been forced into bankruptcy had it been made to perform the work at the price bid. The prime contractor in turn sought to avoid its own contract with the Sanitary District, and the court granted relief on the ground that the prime contractor's mistake was not grossly negligent (the subcontractor had been used on several prior occasions and had always been reliable) and the Sanitary District had lost nothing but its unduly cheap bargain. There was an additional bolstering fact, in that the specifications for the work were badly drawn and could have been partly to blame for the subcontractor's error.

This example involves an error in the bid at the time of contracting, so it is best characterized as an issue of mistake. However, it could conceivably be treated under the doctrine of impracticability. Bill's withdrawal after formation of the contract could be seen as an unforeseen supervening event, the non-occurrence of which was a basic assumption of the contract between Reliabuild and the owner. As a result, Reliabuild's performance becomes unduly burdensome. However, even if the case is analyzed under impracticability, the result should not change, because fault and risk allocation are again the dispositive considerations and they should be resolved in the same way.

An Observation on the Relationship Between Examples 3 and 4

These two questions present a conundrum. If Reliabuild could get out of the contract with the owner, as suggested in the answer to Example 4, it may not necessarily have been correct to assume in Example 3 that Reliabuild had prejudicially relied on Bill's contract. That is, the possibility of Reliabuild's right to avoid the prime contract could affect the balance of the equities vis-à-vis Bill. Although this could have some influence on the resolution of Bill's defense of mistake, it does not seem strong enough to change the result. Reliabuild's successful avoidance cannot be assured, and is at best a prospect that may only be established by expensive litigation. Apart from this, Reliabuild may consider it undesirable to seek release from its commitment, because of the impact this could have on an ongoing business relationship with the owner, or on its general reputation for reliability.

5. All the factual variations in this example involve supervening events—occurrences after contract formation that may be grounds for a claim of impracticability or frustration of purpose.

5(a)(i). Even under the original doctrine of impossibility, performance was excused by the death of a party whose continued existence was necessary for the performance. This may seem ridiculously obvious, but remember, as the question indicates, the issue is not whether Merlin's corpse can be made to do magic tricks, but whether his estate is liable for damages. The initial two elements of impracticability (which now encompasses impossibility) are satisfied: As the contract was for Merlin's personal services, it was clearly dependent on his continued vitality. His death is a supervening event contrary to the contract's basic assumption.

The more difficult question is who bore the risk of his death. The contract itself does not assign the risk, so the allocation must be made in light of the parties' reasonable expectations, determined from all the circumstances surrounding the transaction. These circumstances may include a particular practice in the entertainment industry that may help to determine the normal incidence of risk when an artist dies before a show. (For example, promoters may regularly insure the lives of performers who have been booked.) If not, general community expectations must be determined and any pertinent considerations of public policy must be taken into account. It is difficult to be sure what result would be reached. Many contracts do not end with the death of a party, so that performance or damages becomes an obligation of his estate. As noted above, this may not be the reasonable expectation when the contract is for personal services. In this case, however, the risk allocation is also influenced by the circumstances of Merlin's death. Impossibility or impracticability cannot be used as a defense by a party who is at fault in causing the supervening event, and it could be argued that Merlin recklessly caused his own death. This may, in itself, be grounds for withholding relief from his estate. If not, it may tip the balance in the determination of risk.

5(a)(ii). Fanny's demand for refund of the $100 is, in effect, a claim of restitution based on the implicit contention that the cancellation of the magic show frustrated the purpose of her contract with Buck. (As you may recognize, these facts are a less regal adaptation of *Krell v. Henry*.) These facts show how difficult it can be to distinguish impracticality and frustration. The latter seems more appropriate here because the contractual performance—the exchange of a ticket for $150—has not been altered by the supervening event. Rather, the goal and purpose of the exchange have been defeated. (However, it could just as plausibly be argued that the supervening event so devalued the exchange for Fanny that her performance was rendered unduly burdensome, and impracticality doctrine is applicable.)

The first three elements of frustration are clearly satisfied: Merlin's death and the ensuing cancellation of the show were supervening events that defeated a shared basic assumption of the parties entering the contract, and neither was at fault in causing the event. Therefore, once again, risk allocation becomes the determinative issue.

In the absence of any assignment of risk in the contract itself, the risk of the show's cancellation must be placed where the parties reasonably would have expected it. The show's promoter has readily undertaken to refund all amounts it has received for tickets, which suggests that it is common practice for the promoter of an event to assume the risk of cancellation. However, it does not follow that a consumer seller would similarly assume that risk. In a consumer-to-consumer sale, it may be more consonant with common practice to conclude (in the absence of a warranty) that the buyer assumes the risk that the item or service purchased will be worth less than its price, and the seller assumes the countervailing risk that it will be worth more.

Thus, although a contrary argument could be made, Fanny may be the more appropriate party to bear the risk of cancellation. If so, she cannot recover the $100 paid to Buck. (This is contrary to the result in *Krell v. Henry*, but the concurring opinion in that case questioned the issue of risk allocation.) If the opposite result is reached and Buck bears the risk, she can terminate the contract on grounds of frustration of purpose. In that case, any benefit conferred by either party on the other must be restored as unjust enrichment. Fanny still has the ticket worth $50 (the amount of the refund), so that value given by Buck must be offset against the $150 paid by Fanny, leaving her with a net recovery of $100.

5(b). The only basis on which Merlin could escape the contract is to contend that his new-found fame is a supervening event that defeats the basic assumption on which the parties contracted for his services at the relatively modest sum of $10,000. As a result, his loss of the opportunity to earn 50 times that amount is such a burden as to make his performance impracticable. He should not get away with this because he does not show either that performance has become unduly burdensome or that Showstopper bears the risk of the change in circumstances. Impracticability should not be permitted as an excuse when the change in market conditions merely has the effect of making the performance more valuable than anticipated, especially when the harm to Merlin is nothing more than the loss of an opportunity to sell his services at greater advantage. In addition, the argument made in Question 5(a)(ii) is applicable here too: Each party made a judgment in assenting to the price of $10,000, and neither can complain if that judgment turns out to have been wrong.

5(c). Compliance with a change in the law or government regulation or with a judicial or administrative order is generally regarded as a basis for excusing performance on grounds of impracticability. The F.A.A.'s prohibition on Merlin's further career as a magician could fall into this category, but because the bar on his performance resulted from his violation of the law, he should be denied relief. Even had he not entered a consent decree, the event precluding his performance arises from his own fault, and he must be held to have assumed the risk of its occurrence. This resolution is made more compelling by the fact that the F.A.A. may not unilaterally have imposed the prohibition, and Merlin acquiesced in it by entering a consent decree to avoid other punishment.

These are sufficient grounds to defeat a claim of impracticability, but one further issue should be noted: I have no idea if the F.A.A. has the authority to dispose of Merlin's case in this way. If it does not, the order may be invalid. This would not in itself prevent a claim of impracticability, provided that compliance with the order is in good faith. Therefore, if Merlin were able to overcome the problems of fault and risk allocation, he could still not claim impracticability without showing that the order was valid or, if not, that he acted in good faith in complying with it.

5(d)(i). At last, we get to the fiery destruction of the Pyro Palace, but with a twist on *Taylor v. Caldwell* in that Showstopper, the impresario, is willing to provide a substitute but the star of the show objects and suggests that the fire has rendered performance impracticable. The key consideration on these facts is whether the destruction of the Pyro Palace defeats a basic assumption of the contract, rendering Merlin's performance unduly burdensome. (The other elements are not in issue because it cannot be said that Merlin was at fault in causing the fire, and Showstopper, as the promoter and renter of the hall, is more likely than Merlin to bear the risk of its destruction.)

The contract apparently contemplated the use of the Pyro Palace for the show, but this is not quite the same as saying that the theater's continued existence was a basic assumption of the contract. If an alternative venue is equally suitable and may be obtained without undue hardship, the destruction of the Pyro Palace does not defeat a basic assumption of the contract. Even if a substitute hall is permissible under the contract, it may have been a basic assumption that the hall would be of a particular quality or be equipped with special facilities. If this is so, the school gym may so badly fall short of the contemplated standard that performance in it would cause Merlin severe hardship or loss. This may be the consequence if the hall does not have the facilities he needs to stage his show, or if performance in it would damage his reputation or standing as an artiste. However, a mere claim of offense to his dignity does not suggest a problem of these proportions.

5(d)(ii). In this question, the parties accept that performance has become impracticable, and the only issue is Merlin's right to reimbursement of wasted expenses. The normal relief when a contract is terminated for impracticability is mutual restitution: Each party must restore to the other any benefit received from performance rendered prior to termination of the contract. Showstopper has conferred no benefit on Merlin, so it has no restitutionary claim. However, Merlin has spent $1,000 on props and costumes in preparation for his performance. The problem is that Showstopper has received no economic gain from this expenditure.

In *Albre Marble & Tile Co. v. John Bowen Co.*, 155 N.E.2d 437 (Mass. 1959), a contractor for a hospital building hired a subcontractor to do the tile and marble work. Following execution of the subcontract, the subcontractor began preliminary planning required under the contract, such as sample preparation, drawings, and tests. Before actual work had commenced on the building itself, the prime contract was declared invalid by a court because of improper bidding procedures. The subcontractor did not contest the fact that cancellation of the prime contract rendered performance of the subcontract impossible, but it claimed restitution of the value of its preparatory work. The contractor argued that because nothing had yet been incorporated into the building, it had not in fact received any benefit from the performance. The court conceded that this should be the general rule when the performance has been precluded by an event not caused by the fault of either party. In such a case, the absence of fault requires restitution to be confined to actual economic gain and should not be measured by the market value of services (quantum meruit) that do not result in ultimate enrichment. However, the court said that the rule should not be applied rigidly because the equities in some cases call for restitution based on quantum meruit, even when there is no resulting economic gain by the other party. The court found this to be such a case, because the contractor was partially to blame for the legal problems that caused the invalidity of the prime contract. Although its degree of fault was not enough to preclude termination of the contract on grounds of impracticability, it was sufficient to shift the equities in favor of the subcontractor in its restitutionary claim.

There are factual distinctions between *Albre Marble* and Merlin's claim that make it doubtful that this principle supports his recovery. The facts do not indicate that Showstopper had any blame for the destruction of the theater, so there do not seem to be any equities that favor making it pay for expenditures that resulted in no economic gain to it. In addition, the tiling subcontractor's preparatory work was required by its contract, so it was actually part of its performance, rather than a preparation for performance. This gives its restitutionary claim greater strength. It is not clear that Merlin's expenditures were an obligatory part of his performance. Finally, even if restitution were to be allowed on the basis of quantum meruit, remember that it is the market value of the benefit that must be measured. Although Merlin's cost may be evidence of market value, it is not necessarily the same thing.

5(e). Most commercial contracts are motivated by the prospect of profit, so if Showstopper's argument was taken seriously, no party could ever be held to a contract once it becomes apparent that its expectation of profit will be disappointed. Therefore, although profitmaking may, in a sense, be the purpose of a contract, the doctrine of frustration is not intended simply to focus on this underlying "bottom-line" purpose. Rather, it looks at the primary purpose—that is, at the goal to be achieved by the parties, from which the possibility of profit may flow. In this light, the primary purpose of the contract was to stage a public entertainment. The generation of profit from this purpose is better thought of as the desired consequence—the ultimate result—of achieving the contract's purpose.

This distinction was pointed out in response to a similar argument made in *Karl Wendt Farm Equipment Co. v. International Harvester Co.*, 931 F.2d 1112 (6th Cir. 1991). Wendt had a contract with International Harvester under which it had a dealership in I.H. products. Following losses resulting from a serious downturn in the farming economy and, consequently, in the farm equipment market, I.H. sold its farm equipment division. As the buyer already had a distributor in Wendt's area, Wendt's distributorship was terminated. It sued I.H. for breach of contract, and I.H. raised the defenses that the recession in the farm economy was a supervening event rendering the contract impracticable, and that the lack of profitability frustrated the contract's purpose. The court disposed of the impracticability argument by finding, first, that the poor market conditions were not so severe as to pass beyond the range of the normal risk to be borne by I.H. Second, that the impact of the recession was not so severe as to result in undue hardship to I.H. The court then addressed the alternative argument of frustration and concluded, reaching the conclusion indicated above, that the primary purpose of the contract (to sell farm equipment) could still be achieved, even if the desired goal of profitability may not be fulfilled.

6. This is one of those ambiguous situations that sounds like a case of impracticability, but is better characterized as a unilateral mistake. The only supervening event is the discovery that the program is not capable of production for the price quoted. However, this is not really a supervening event at all, but rather Slacker's post-contractual realization that it never had the ability to deliver on its promise. Luckily, incorrect labelling should not have any practical consequence because risk allocation, the element common to both defenses, points to the same result.

Let us consider mistake first. Slacker, the expert, is approached by Goldbrick, a lay customer who desires an end product and has no idea about what may be involved in creating it. Slacker makes its own evaluation of what would need to be done to create the product and then makes an unqualified promise to deliver the program in six months. We may simply describe this as an error in judgment, or we could say that Slacker assumed the risk that it could not perform for the price quoted (or at all). However phrased, the point is that Goldbrick had no way of knowing that Slacker had misjudged the complexity of the project, and Slacker was foolishly overconfident in giving him an absolute promise. When a manufacturer undertakes to create an innovative custom-made product—a prototype—it cannot know for sure what may lie ahead in its development. To protect itself from unpleasant discoveries, it should draw the contract so as to articulate the experimental nature of the project and provide for a price increase, a delay in delivery, or a right to terminate if production difficulties are encountered. By not doing this, it assumes the risk of unforeseen problems.

The consequences for Slacker are unclear. If Slacker is lucky, it may be impossible for anyone to create a program like this on the basis of existing technology (which I suspect, with profound sadness, to be the case). This would mean that Goldbrick could not have it made and would therefore not suffer any economic loss. (He cannot claim compensation for his pain, suffering, and mental distress in having to grade all those exams. As discussed in section 18.13.1, damages of this kind are not generally available for a breach of contract.) However, if the program can be developed by someone else, the lack of excuse would make Slacker liable for the difference between its contract price and the higher price charged by the other programmer. It sounds as if this could be a horrendous figure, but the equities should not be balanced to take this hardship into account if risk assumption is clearly resolved against Slacker.

It was noted earlier that this is not properly viewed as an impracticability case, but that even if it was analyzed as such, the same result would apply because Slacker assumed the risk of post-contractual difficulties in production. An impracticability defense was raised unsuccessfully in *United States v. Wegematic Corp.*, 360 F.2d 674 (2d Cir. 1966), a case with facts analogous to those here. An electronics manufacturer made a contract with the Federal Reserve Board for the supply of a computer system (touted as "revolutionary") by a specified date. The manufacturer encountered numerous difficulties in building the system, and eventually notified the Board that it could not produce it. The Board ordered an equivalent system from another vendor and sued the manufacturer for damages. The court rejected the manufacturer's defense of impracticability on the grounds that it had assumed the risk of technical difficulties in the fabrication of the system. Although the system may have been an experimental prototype, the manufacturer's promise was simply to deliver a working computer by a specified time. (The court also found that performance was not impracticable because the element of undue hardship was not satisfied. Problems in the system could have been rectified by costly but not overwhelmingly burdensome redesign.)

7. As in the previous example, there is some ambiguity about whether this is a mistake or impracticability case. It could be said that the parties made a mutual mistake about an existing fact—the reliability of their pricing formula and the market. However, these are really both predictions of future trends, so the problem is really one of impracticability—they failed to foresee future events that would overturn the assumptions they made at the time of contracting. Although there may be an argument to the contrary, assume that the water sold under the contract satisfies the definition of "goods" under UCC Article 2. If so, impracticability must be resolved under UCC §2.615. That section refers only to impracticability affecting the seller's performance, but it has been interpreted to apply to a buyer as well. Although the following analysis is based on §2.615, the contemporary doctrine of impracticability under common law is substantially the same.

It stands to reason that unpredictability is a particular problem in long-term contracts because the longer the relationship, the greater the likelihood of change in the environment in which performance will take place. Parties usually realize this when contracting, and try to build some flexibility or protection into the contract to accommodate expected events as well as those of which they may have no forewarning at the time of contracting. However, parties are not always sufficiently cautious, or even if they try to be, changes may be so dramatic as to surpass the maneuverability built into the contract. When that happens, the adversely affected party may seek refuge in the doctrine of impracticability.

In this case, Hale & Hearty made the assumption that it could use a million gallons of spring water a year and the parties tried to make an accurate prediction of future price, based on past trends. Although advances in water purification would have been reasonably foreseeable, the issue is whether they were foreseen—contemplated it as a realistic possibility—by the parties at the time of contracting. It appears that they were not. Therefore, the technological advance does appear to qualify as a supervening event, the non-occurrence of which was a basic assumption of the contract. Neither party can be blamed for causing the event, so fault is not a relevant consideration on these facts.

While Hale & Hearty is still capable of performing, the change in circumstances imposes a substantial burden on it. Not only is it already paying four times the market price of the water, but it is also compelled to buy quantities considerably beyond its needs. In the remaining years of the contract, this burden will likely become even greater as the market dries up.[5] It is never easy to tell how severe market changes must be for a court to consider them so burdensome as to constitute impracticability. All one can say is that more is required than mere lack of profit or even manageable loss. Hale & Hearty's current and prospective loss may be large and devastating enough to satisfy this element. However, this on its own is not a sufficient basis for relief. We must still consider the closely linked question of risk allocation, which is frequently determinative.

By committing themselves to a fixed annual quantity and a rigid price escalation, the parties made a deliberate choice. They picked certainty and stability over flexibility. Had they chosen differently, Hale & Hearty could have better protected itself from a drop in demand by making a requirements contract, and both parties could have avoided the risk of buying or selling above or below market price by using a price formula tied to an index or other market standard. Thus, by their selection of terms, they allocated the risk of low demand and reductions in market price to Hale & Hearty, while Crystal assumed the risk that her contract price might be outpaced by the market. Even when parties have allocated the risk of market fluctuations in their contract, the market could be so severely disrupted as to cause hardship to one of the parties (and a resulting windfall to the other) that goes beyond the level of risk anticipated by the contract. That is, even if the contract does assign risk, the effect of a supervening event may be so extreme that it cannot fairly be said to have been encompassed in the risk reasonably anticipated. One cannot say for sure whether this has happened here. Hale & Hearty have a tenable case, but remember that courts are quite resistant to excusing performance when the alleged impracticability relates to a market change that is conceivably within the range of the reasonable risk assumed by the adversely affected party.

This example is loosely based on several cases concerning long-term contracts. One of the most interesting of these is *Aluminum Company of America v. Essex Group, Inc.*, 499 F. Supp. 53 (W.D. Pa. 1980). In 1967,

---

5. Warning: Feeble pun alert.

Alcoa made a contract with Essex to smelt its alumina for a base period of 16 years, with an additional five years at the option of Essex. The parties went to a great deal of trouble to work out a formula for the escalation of the price over the period of the contract. One aspect of it related to Alcoa's non-labor production costs. The parties selected the Wholesale Price Index—Industrial Commodities (WPI) as the basis for escalating this element of the formula. They chose it because it had reliably corresponded to Alcoa's actual non-labor costs in prior years, and they believed that it would continue to do so. The intention of the formula was to assure Alcoa of a four-cent profit per pound of alumina processed, with a possible variation of three cents either way. (That is, the parties contemplated that their pricing formula would assure Alcoa of a profit of between one cent and seven cents per pound.)

A few years after the beginning of the contract period, electricity prices increased steeply as a result of the combined effect of the OPEC oil embargo and the increasing cost of producing electricity in compliance with pollution regulations. A large amount of electricity is used in the smelting of alumina, but electricity charges formed only a small part of the costs that made up the WPI. As a result, the high increase in electricity costs pushed up Alcoa's actual non-labor costs out of proportion to the WPI, which ceased to be an accurate predictor. This meant that Alcoa began to suffer huge losses, which promised to get worse and may have reached about $60 million over the life of the contract.

The court resolved the case in favor of Alcoa on the basis of mistake. It found that the suitability of the WPI was not a prediction of the future, but a fact in existence at the time of contract. The parties had been in error in selecting the formula in the belief that it was appropriate and would achieve their pricing goal. (This result, although possibly tenuous, is more justifiable than it would be in Hale & Hearty's case, because in *Alcoa* it could be argued that the error related to the relationship, as at the time of contracting, between the chosen index and Alcoa's operations.)

Although the court based its decision on mistake, it discussed impracticability as an alternative justification for its conclusion. The court acknowledged that market changes and increased cost do not in themselves constitute impracticability. However, it felt that the scale of the loss and the disproportion between the anticipated profit range and the prospective loss distinguished this case from others that had declined relief. Alcoa had assumed some risk of cost increase, but the escalation formula shows that the parties intended to shield it from increases as dramatic as this.

The most controversial aspect of the case was the relief granted. The court reasoned that it would be unfair to terminate the contract because this would deprive Essex of its assurance of long-term performance and give Alcoa the windfall of complete release. The court therefore left the contract in effect, but modified its terms to assure Alcoa its minimum contractual expectation of a profit of at least one cent per pound.

8. As Example 3 indicates, if this is a mistake in the legal sense (which I do not think it is, as discussed below), it is unilateral on Bill's part. As in Example 3, his negligence seems inexcusable and should leave him with the risk of error. In addition, the equities are even less in his favor. The supplier had no prior dealings with Bill, and there is nothing to suggest that the supplier knew anything about the scale of his business or otherwise would have been alerted to the possibility that the quantity ordered was in error or way in excess of Bill's needs. Also, Bill cannot restore the supplier to the status quo by returning the forms because they have been customized and cannot be placed back into stock and resold. Therefore, there seems to be no justification for shifting the loss to the supplier.

This was the resolution in *Monarch Marketing System Co. v. Reed's Photo Mart*, 485 S.W.2d 905 (Tex. 1972). The photo store had meant to order 4,000 adhesive custom labels. The letter "M" was understood by trade usage to signify 1,000. As he was filling out the form, the representative of the store was interrupted, and he wrote "4MM" instead of "4M," erroneously ordering 4 million labels. The store refused to accept the 4 million labels when they were delivered, and the supplier sued to recover their price. The court found that the store was liable on the basis that it had made a unilateral mistake and could not restore the supplier to the status quo. (The opinion indicates that the jury found that Monarch did not know of the mistake. The court did not find error in the fact that the jury was not instructed to enquire into whether it should have known. This would be a relevant consideration under the Restatement Second formulation.)

The result of the case seems right, but the legal analysis is odd. When a party makes a mistake, not as to some external fact but in expressing his intent, this is not a mistake in the legal sense. Rather, it is a miscommunication that results in a manifestation of intent contrary to what the party had in mind. Such a situation should not be resolved under mistake analysis but should simply be decided on the basis of the objective test: When a person's word or actions manifest an intent to contract on stated terms, the person making the manifestation is bound by the reasonable meaning of his apparent intent, even if it does not accurately reflect his true state of mind. That is, Bill and Reed's Photo Mart are bound simply because the supplier reasonably understood their manifestations at face value.

16

Conditions
and Promises

§16.1　The Structure of a Contract: An Introduction
to Promises and Conditions

Most terms in a contract are promises or conditions—or both. The meaning, nature, and effect of a promise is very familiar by now. The concept of promise was introduced right at the beginning of this book, and its central role in all contractual relationships has been emphasized ever since. Although conditions are just as much a fundamental component of contracts, their presence and function have not been much discussed in previous chapters. It is the purpose of this chapter to introduce the concept of conditions and to examine their functions. In doing this, we will look more carefully at the structure of a contract and explore the way in which conditions and promises interact to form the basis of the contractual relationship. We will then proceed, in this chapter and the next, to consider the performance obligations created by the network of promises and conditions, and to address the problems that are created when those obligations are violated. You will encounter some unfamiliar terminology, but this does not mean that we are entering some new and alien field of contract law. Most, if not all, of the substantive principles discussed here have been covered already, and the breakdown of a contract into promises and conditions is simply the means by which its structure is studied. As is so often the case, you will find that the key to analysis is interpretation—the determination of the parties' intent, as expressed by them in their contract or as inferred from surrounding evidence and reasonable expectations.

We begin with a set of definitions and some simple examples to introduce terminology and to provide an initial insight into the reason for differentiating promises and conditions.

A **promise** was defined in section 1.2.4 as an **undertaking to act or refrain from acting in a specified way at some future time.** As we have seen repeatedly since then, the exchange of promises (or of at least one promise for a performance) is what contracts are all about. Thus, for example, when parties make a contract for the sale of land, the buyer promises to pay the price in exchange for the seller's promise to convey title and possession of the land. This can be illustrated by a diagram similar to those used to explain the exchange element of consideration:

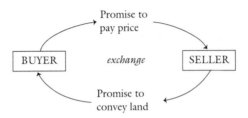

A **condition** is an **event** that is **not certain to occur.** A promised performance under a contract is subject to a condition if the **parties agree** that the **performance** is **contingent** on the **occurrence of the uncertain event.** That is, when making the contract, the parties agree that a particular promised performance or set of performances will not become due until and unless a particular uncertain event occurs. As this suggests, conditions commonly concern *future events* because, in most cases, the uncertainty no longer exists once the event has happened. However, there are situations in which a useful purpose is served by making performance conditional on a *past event.* Although the event in question may have occurred, the parties themselves may be uncertain about whether it took place, and it may be inconvenient or impossible for the parties to find this out at the time that they wish to execute their contract. To avoid the risk of having the agreement unravel while they delay to get the information, they could enter the contract immediately subject to the condition that their agreement—or the obligation of one of them—is contingent upon the event having occurred. (This is illustrated in section 16.2.)

The following example provides a simple illustration of the way in which conditions and promises may be combined to structure a contract in a way that binds the parties, yet allows them to deal with the risk of uncertainty: Buyer is interested in acquiring land to build a housing tract. At the time of negotiations, the land is zoned for agricultural use, but Seller has applied for rezoning for residential development. If the application succeeds, the land can be developed profitably. If not, it can be used only for farming. The parties do not know how the zoning authority will rule on the application, but neither wants to delay contracting until its outcome for fear that the other will lose interest in the transaction. Buyer does not wish to commit himself absolutely at this stage, because he does not wish to be stuck with farmland. To solve this problem, the parties can make a contract now for the sale of the land and include a provision in the contract stating: "Buyer's obligation to purchase this property is conditional upon the grant of the pending rezoning application within 60 days of the date of this agreement." The success of the rezoning application within the next 60 days—a future uncertain event—is therefore a condition of Buyer's promise to pay and take transfer of the land. (Or stated differently, Buyer's promise to pay and take transfer of the land is conditional upon the grant of the application.[1]) Until the condition occurs, Buyer's duty to perform is suspended. If it occurs, the duty becomes due and must be performed, but if the condition is not satisfied by the time that the 60 days has passed, the Buyer's obligation to perform never takes effect, and it falls away. This can be represented as follows:

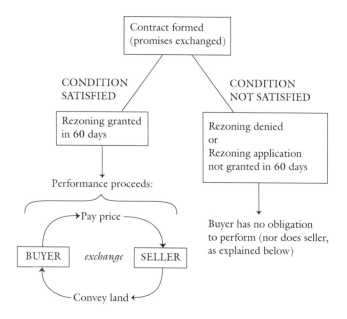

The parties' purpose in structuring the transaction in this way is to *allocate the risk* of the denial or inaction by the zoning authority. If Buyer had simply purchased the property unconditionally, he would have taken the risk

---

1. This variation in terminology can be confusing, so make a point of recognizing that these statements mean the same thing, whether made in the active voice (rezoning **is a condition of** Buyer's performance) or the passive voice (Buyer's performance **is conditional on** the rezoning).

of being saddled with an unwanted farm or a costly delay in the ability to develop it. Because Buyer does not wish to assume this risk, he uses a condition as an escape clause.

§16.2   The Meaning and Scope of "Uncertain Event"

As noted earlier, uncertainty most commonly relates to future events, but it is possible for parties to be unsure about an *event that has already happened* at the time of contracting. Although a past event is not uncertain in a general sense—someone probably knows that it did or did not occur and the parties themselves can find out about it—it may nevertheless be unknown to and not readily ascertainable by them at the time they are ready to form the contract. If they wish to avoid the inconvenience or risk of suspending formation until the information is obtained, they can enter the contract immediately, but make performance conditional on the event's currently unknown outcome. For example, say that Buyer and Seller know that the zoning authority made a decision late on Friday afternoon, but it is now Saturday, and the decision cannot be discovered until Monday morning. The parties would like to sign their contract before Seller leaves on vacation on Sunday morning. By making Buyer's obligation to purchase conditional on the application having been granted, they can execute the contract on Saturday without subjecting Buyer to the risk of having bought farmland incapable of development. Although this condition is based on a past event, there is still some element of futurity in that the knowledge cannot be obtained until Monday. The outcome therefore does qualify as uncertain as far as the parties are concerned.

Most conditions, however, do not relate to unknown past events, but are based on something that has not happened at the time of contracting. All future events may be thought of as uncertain to some degree, so in the broadest sense, everything that has not yet occurred must be a *future uncertain event*. But the law regards an event as uncertain if, in light of human experience, its occurrence would not be regarded as *strongly predictable*. Therefore, although a pessimist may fear otherwise, it is regarded as certain that the sun will rise tomorrow morning, or that Friday will follow Thursday, or that January 1 of next year will arrive. A provision in a contract that calls for performance upon the occurrence of so certain an event is not thought of as a condition at all, but merely fixes the time for performance. The passage of time is not regarded as a condition. (Or, if you prefer it is a condition with such a strong probability of occurrence that its legal effect is insignificant.) By contrast, the grant of the rezoning application is not so sure a thing. Even if it was carefully prepared, complies with the prescribed procedures, and makes a compelling case on the merits, we cannot say with the same degree of confidence that its success is inevitable. It therefore qualifies as uncertain.

Although uncertainty about the happening of the event is necessary to qualify the event as a condition, this does not invariably mean that a condition is intended merely because the contract links performance to some uncertain future event. It could be that the parties do not really contemplate the event as uncertain, assume that it will occur, and merely use it as a means of *setting the time for performance.* If, as a matter of interpretation, the parties do not intend the performance to be contingent upon the event, it should not be treated as a condition. This distinction is explained in section 16.10.

Although a condition is spoken of as an **event,** the contingency need not be an **affirmative happening.** It could also be a negative contingency—a **non-happening.** In the above example, the zoning authority's approval of the application is an affirmative event. But it would just as much be a condition if the buyer's performance was subject to something not taking place: Say that the zoning authority had approved the application at the time of contracting, but irate neighbors had threatened to appeal the decision. The contract of sale could provide that the buyer's obligation to purchase is conditional on the approval not being successfully appealed.

§16.3 The Intent to Create a Condition: Express, Implied, and Construed Conditions

Like all terms of a contract, a condition exists because the parties have agreed to it. Similarly, like all other contractual provisions, the mutual intent to create a condition and the condition's scope and meaning are matters of interpretation. Sometimes the language used by the parties to express this intent is clear, express, and unambiguous, but it could just as likely be obscure and uncertain. In some contracts, the intent to create a condition is not articulated at all, but such intent may be established by evidence extrinsic to the express words used by the parties, or it may be construed by the court. These issues are resolved by applying the general principles of interpretation discussed in Chapter 10.

§16.3.1 *Express Conditions*

We have already seen an example of an express condition in the land sale contract described above: The contract expressly stated that Buyer's obligation to purchase the land was contingent on approval of the zoning application within 60 days of the date of the agreement. A condition is express if the **language of the contract, on its face** and without reference to extrinsic evidence, **articulates** the **intent** to **make performance contingent on the**

event. Commonly, conditions are expressly denoted by using conditional language such as "on condition that," "subject to," "provided that," or "if," but no special incantation is required as long as the intention of establishing a condition arises from the language itself. For a term to be an express condition, it is not enough that the term itself is expressed. Its *conditional nature* must also be *apparent from the language* used. Thus, if a contractual provision states "Seller shall transfer title to the land," this is an express term—an express promise by the seller—but as the obligation is not stated to be contingent on any event, it is not expressly conditional. (It is, however, likely to be subject to an implied condition, as discussed below.)

Because it is the function of courts to give effect to apparent contractual intent, the general approach to express conditions is to apply them strictly, even if this may have a harsh result on one of the parties. Provided that the meaning of the condition is clear, the fact that the parties have articulated it must mean that they intended it to be satisfied exactly as stated. This principle is reflected in the rule that there must be *strict compliance* with an express condition. For example, an insurance policy states that the insurer's duty to reimburse for loss is conditional upon the insured giving it written notice of the loss within ten days of the loss occurring. If the insured does not give notice until the morning of the eleventh day, the condition is not satisfied. Even if the few hours delay may seem insignificant, and enforcement of the condition means that the insured loses the right of reimbursement for which she has paid a hefty premium, the rule of strict enforcement precludes an argument that there was substantial compliance with the condition of notice. (As section 16.11 will show, there are some circumstances in which harshness of such a result may be ameliorated.)

§16.3.2   *Conditions Implied in Fact*

Even if there is **no express language** creating a condition, **contextual evidence** may **support the inference** that the **parties intended a performance** to be **conditional.** Like other terms in a contract, a condition can be implied in fact by interpreting the words used by the parties in light of the circumstances surrounding the formation of their contract. As with other terms, there is no difference in legal effect between an express and an implied condition. The difference lies in the nature of the evidence available to establish its existence. An express condition is apparent from the language of the contract itself—the actual words of the parties are the best evidence of what they intended. However, an implied condition is not ascertainable simply from the wording of the contract, but is established once contextual evidence is introduced to cast light on what was meant. Because this contextual evidence may be less firm and more equivocal that express language, a court may have some greater flexibility in interpreting an implied condition in a way that avoids the harsh results that would have been more inevitable had the condition been clearly expressed. That is, although strict compliance with the condition is still required, the less direct and absolute nature of contextual inference may permit an interpretation that the action or event did in fact satisfy the condition.

As with all terms implied in fact, if the agreement is recorded in writing, the parol evidence rule may preclude contextual evidence of a condition that varies an integrated term or conflicts with the writing. However, as noted in section 12.10, there is a traditionally recognized exception to the parol evidence rule when the evidence is offered to establish that the contract as a whole was subject to a condition precedent.

§16.3.3 *Constructive Conditions*

Although a condition may not be expressed or inferable from contextual evidence, it could be implied in law. The process of legal implication of conditions is the same as for any other contractual term, and is subject to the general principles discussed in Chapter 10: In essence, although there may be no evidence that the parties actually agreed to the condition, a court will imply it as a matter of law if the circumstances and nature of the contract compel the conclusion that the condition should exist as a matter of *policy,* or that if the parties had addressed the issue, they *reasonably would have intended* it to be part of their contract.

Construed conditions may be illustrated by returning to the example involving the sale of land subject to the express condition that the rezoning application would be granted. If you think about the exchange of performances contemplated in that contract, you will realize that while the express condition may be the only one visible, there are surely two more lurking under the surface of the express agreement: In promising to pay the price of the land, Buyer must reasonably have expected that his obligation to pay was conditional on Seller conveying the land, and Seller surely did not expect to transfer the land to Buyer without getting paid. Thus, each party's performance must reasonably be intended as a condition of the other's. Buyer's duty to pay is contingent on Seller's transfer and vice versa. (The respective performances do qualify as uncertain events, because the honoring of a contractual commitment is not inevitable and assured.)

These conditions are construed rather than implied in fact, because there is apparently no actual evidence that the parties discussed the question or expressed this intent to each other. But remember that the dividing line between factual interpretation and legal implication is not always easily discernable, and they tend to blur into each other at the edges. In other words, the conclusion that each performance is conditional upon the other could be reached as a question of fact if there is evidence (such as trade usage, prior dealings, or statements made during negotiations) to support it. But even in the absence of any such evidence, it may be possible to reach the same conclusion by implication of law from the nature of the exchange relationship. In an exchange transaction, unless the language of the contract or its surrounding circumstances clearly indicate a contrary intent, the parties must almost always be taken to have expected that the principal promises exchanged would be **dependent** on each other—that they would be what are known as **constructive conditions of exchange.** If they were not, this would lead to the bizarre situation in which a party could be forced to perform even when the other has failed or refused to do so.

The effect of this is that there is an initial condition that the rezoning must be approved. If it is not, Buyer has no obligation to pay and because Buyer's payment is a condition of Seller's obligation to convey, the nonfulfillment of the condition of payment releases Seller too. If the rezoning is approved, we are left with the two conditions relating to the performances, and each party must tender performance (that is, show a readiness, willingness, and ability to perform) in order to be entitled to performance by the other. We must therefore expand the previous diagram to look like this:

So far we have identified the mutual performances as conditions of each other, but as the diagram shows, we have not dealt with the sequence in which the conditions must be satisfied, or with some other important distinctions between these two conditions and the one that relates to the rezoning. These matters will be discussed in succeeding sections.

§16.4   A Condition of One Party's Performance, as Distinct from a Condition of the Contract as a Whole

In the prior section, the success of the rezoning application was described as a condition to Buyer's obligation. Because Buyer's performance is, in turn, a condition of Seller's obligation, it follows that if the rezoning is denied and Buyer does not perform, Seller is also relieved of her obligation to perform. As a result, the entire contract falls away. That is,

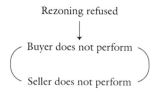

Rezoning refused
↓
Buyer does not perform
Seller does not perform

Why is this two-stage analysis necessary? Could it not simply be said that both parties' obligations are conditional on the grant of the application? That is,

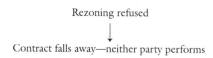

Rezoning refused
↓
Contract falls away—neither party performs

This sounds like the same thing, with one less step in the analysis, but the situations are significantly different. If the *contract as a whole* was *conditional* on the rezoning approval, this would mean that if the application is denied, *neither party is bound* to the transaction. Even if Buyer decided that he wanted the land despite the failure of the application, he could not disregard the condition, tender his payment, and hold Seller to the contract. This is probably not what was intended. Rather, the purpose of the condition is to affect only Buyer's obligation—it is *included purely for Buyer's protection,* and not for Seller's benefit. If Buyer decides that he still wants the land with its present zoning, he should be able to waive the condition and proceed with the transaction.[2] Seller is not in any way deprived of her expected exchange and has no cause for complaint.

However, if the terms or circumstances of the transaction were otherwise, we may reach a different conclusion on the intent of the condition. Say that the sale price of the land was fixed at a base amount of $100,000 (being its current market value as farmland) plus ten percent of Buyer's profits upon selling off the subdivided lots. If the condition of rezoning is not satisfied, Buyer could not subdivide, and Seller would be deprived of her expected share of the profits. If Seller's incentive for selling the land was to share in the profit of development, and she would not have sold the property for its price as farmland, the condition can no longer be seen as merely for Buyer's benefit. It affects the contract's value to Seller as well. It must surely have been intended that neither Buyer nor Seller could unilat-

---

2. Waiver of condition is discussed further in section 16.11.2.

erally waive the condition and hold the other to the contract despite its non-fulfillment. This means that the condition was an event upon which the duties of *both* parties were *contingent*—the entire contract was subject to the condition.

In short, if a condition is intended to relate only to the performance of one of the parties, that party can chose to perform despite its non-occurrence and may fully enforce the contract against the other. But if the condition relates to the contract as a whole, its non-occurrence discharges the right of both parties to demand performance, and neither can unilaterally waive it. To decide the intended scope of the condition, its purpose must be ascertained by the usual process of interpreting the contract's wording in context.

§16.5   Pure Conditions and Promissory Conditions

It has already been stated that when the operative terms of a contract are analyzed, each can be classified as either a promise or a condition. Some terms may be classified as **pure promises**—they are not conditions at all, but merely undertakings.[3] Others may be **pure conditions**—they contain no promise but merely describe an event that must occur for a duty of performance to arise. However, some terms in a contract combine both these elements. They not only identify an event that must occur for performance to become due, but they also contain a promise by one of the parties that the event will take place. A term that is not only a condition, but is both a condition and a promise that the condition will occur, is called a **promissory condition.** This concept often confuses students on first exposure, but it is not as strange and esoteric as it sounds.

The usual process of interpretation and construction must be followed to decide if a term is a pure promise, a pure condition, or a promissory condition. If the express language of the contract does not clearly settle this question, it must be resolved with reference to any factual evidence of intent or, failing that, by construing the parties' reasonable intention. Our land sale example may be used to illustrate:

In agreeing to the sale of the land conditional upon the success of the rezoning application, the parties apparently intend to place the fate of the transaction on an event beyond their control. The application has been made, nothing more can be done by either to influence the result, and there is no indication in the contract that either of them guarantees the outcome of the application. From this it must be inferred that they intended the rezoning to be a pure condition. By contrast, the conditions that make the performance

---

3. The role and effect of pure promises is explained in sections 16.6 and 16.8.4.

of each party contingent on that of the other are promissory conditions. Each party does have control over the satisfaction of the condition that he or she will perform, and each, by committing to perform, has promised that the condition will be satisfied. The payment and conveyance of the land are not simply conditions, but promises as well. This distinction may be portrayed as follows:

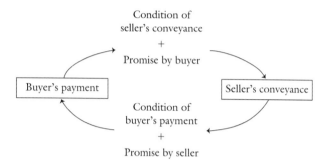

In the above example, the event constituting the condition of each party's performance is the actual performance of the other. When a party's own performance is the condition, that party has some ability to ensure that the promised condition will occur, and can make the commitment with some confidence that the condition will be satisfied. However, if the condition is some event that is beyond her control, she takes a greater risk in promising that it will occur. Therefore, in cases of doubt, it is generally assumed that a pure condition is intended when a party has no power to influence the happening of the event, but a promissory condition is intended if she can play a role in affecting the outcome. It must be stressed that this is merely an assumption—a rough guide. It is not a firm rule. The agreement could expressly or impliedly indicate that the parties intended otherwise. If she is willing to take the risk, there is no barrier to a party assuming responsibility for the happening of an event that she cannot control. For example, instead of simply making their land sale contract conditional on approval of the rezoning application, the parties could have included a warranty by Seller that the application would be granted. Although the disposition of the application is beyond her control, Seller promises that it will succeed. If it does not, there is both a failure of the condition and a breach of Seller's contractual promise.

The significance of the distinction between a pure and a promissory condition lies in the *different effect of promises and conditions.* If a condition is not satisfied, the performance contingent on that condition does not become due. If it is a **pure condition,** the **performance obligation falls away** and there is no basis for claiming breach of contract. However, if a contractual *promise is broken,* the promisor is liable for *breach* of contract. It follows that if a **promissory condition** is not fulfilled, the party whose performance was contingent on it is entitled **both to withhold counter performance** and to seek a **remedy for breach.** Therefore, in examining the language of a contract in context to interpret a term as a pure or promissory condition, it is helpful to ask two questions:

1. Did the parties intend a performance to be excused if the event does not occur? If the answer is "yes," the event is a condition of that performance.

2. If the answer to Question 1 is yes, did the parties intend that one of them is responsible for the event's occurrence and would be liable for breach of contract if it does not occur? If the answer is "no", the event is a pure condition. If it is "yes," it is a promissory condition.

§16.6   The Time Sequence: Conditions Precedent and Concurrent Conditions

Another difference between the conditions in the land sale example is that the condition relating to rezoning must occur before Buyer's (and consequently, Seller's) performance becomes due. Because its fulfillment must precede the performance contingent upon it, it is known as a **condition precedent.** However, the contract does not indicate a sequence for fulfillment of the conditions of paying and conveyance of the land. If no such order of performance is expressed, it must be determined by interpreting the parties' intent in light of any contextual evidence or, in the absence of such evidence, by construing what must reasonably have been intended. When a contract provides for counter-performances in exchange for each other, and the contract does not prescribe a sequence of performances, the general presumption is that if the performances are **capable of being rendered simultaneously,** they are due at the same time. They are **concurrent conditions.** Thus, the promissory conditions of payment and conveyance of the land, each being capable of exchange by a single act, are concurrent conditions. Each is a condition of the other and they must be performed at the same time. This means that the parties must get together at an appointed place and perform simultaneously. If this had been the sale of goods, there could have been a physical exchange of the goods and cash, but in a real estate transaction, the funds would be deposited in escrow and released to the seller upon recording of the transfer. Because the performances are concurrent conditions of each other, both parties must show up for the exchange ready, willing, and able to tender performance. If one of them is available to tender performance but the other can or will not, the tendering party is excused from delivering his performance and may sue for breach. Our diagram now looks like this:

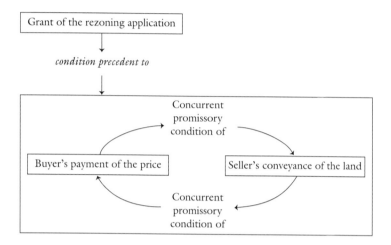

If performances are **not capable of being rendered simultaneously** because one of them requires a period of time to perform and the other can be rendered instantly, the general presumption, unless the contract indicates a different sequence, is that the performance that takes time must go first and must be concluded before the instantaneous one is due. That is, the completion of the longer performance is a **condition precedent** to the instantaneous one. For example, when Seller originally decided to make application for the rezoning of her land, she hired an attorney to prepare and submit the rezoning application for her. Unless that contract provided otherwise, the attorney's fee would only have been due after the attorney had completed the work. Her performance in handling the application takes time to complete, and it is therefore deemed to be a condition precedent to Seller's instantaneous action of paying the fee.

When one party's performance is a condition precedent to the other's, their mutual promises are still dependent in a broad sense. They are exchanged for each other, and both parties are motivated to perform by the incentive of receiving the other's performance. However, they are not mutually dependent in the same way as concurrent promissory conditions in that one of the parties—the attorney—must go first. Therefore while the client's promise of later performance is fully dependent on the attorney's earlier performance, the attorney's performance is subject to no condition at all. Her duty to perform is absolute and not contingent on the happening of any prior event.

The effect of this is that the attorney's performance is a promissory condition precedent to the client's payment, but the client's payment is not a condition of anything. It is the last performance in the chain and no further contractual duties are contingent on it. It is therefore a **pure promise**. In short, although the promises may still be thought of as dependent in the exchange sense (and as we will see in section 17.7.2, the attorney would not have to perform if the client repudiated his obligation in advance), the nature of the performances has the effect of making the attorney's promise a condition.[4] This may be shown as follows:

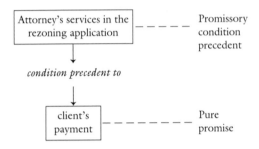

§16.7   Conditions Precedent and Subsequent

In our land sale example, the contract stated simply that Buyer's obligation to purchase the land was conditional on the grant of the rezoning application. This led us to the interpretation that the rezoning is a condition precedent to Buyer's obligation. However, our path to this conclusion is made a little more complicated as a result of a rather arcane and technical distinction in doctrine. Properly speaking, it is only correct to describe this as a condition precedent if the parties intend that Buyer's obligation to purchase does not become due until and unless the application is granted. However, if they intend that the obligation to purchase falls due immediately upon execution of the contract and is then discharged if the application is not granted, the condition is not precedent but subsequent. The difference is that a **condition precedent** is a **prerequisite to the duty arising,** while a **condition subsequent terminates a duty** that came into existence when the contract was formed. That is, when a performance is subject to a condition precedent, the duty to perform, although created at the time of contracting, exists in only potential or contingent form. If the condition occurs, it is converted from a potential to an actual duty. By contrast, if a performance is subject to a condition subsequent, the duty to perform arises immediately upon contracting but is discharged if the condition occurs. This can be portrayed diagrammatically as follows:

---

4. This is expanded upon further in section 16.8.4.

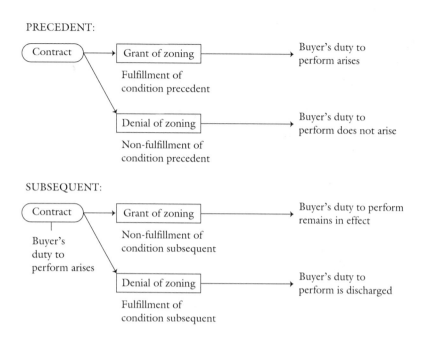

PRECEDENT:

SUBSEQUENT:

The distinction is frustrating because it is so much dependent upon the way in which the *condition is phrased* in the contract. It depends on the interpretation of often subtle nuances in the contract's wording that were probably not intended by the parties. (Indeed, even courts and writers often speak of a discharge of a duty by non-fulfillment of a condition precedent.) Luckily, the distinction can be disregarded for most purposes because it makes *no difference to the substantive result.* In the case of both types of condition, the ultimate effect is that the conditional duty need not be performed. That is, whether we treat the approval of the zoning application as a condition precedent, or its disapproval as a condition subsequent, the end result is that Buyer need not proceed with the purchase.

The principal significance of the distinction lies in its impact on the *burden of proof.* The fulfillment of a condition precedent is regarded as an element of the plaintiff's case in suing on the contract and must be proved by the party seeking to enforce it. Conversely, the occurrence of a condition subsequent is a defense to non-performance and must be proved by the party whose performance obligation has allegedly been discharged. (Therefore, if the grant of the rezoning application is a condition precedent, Seller would have to prove that rezoning was granted in order to enforce the contract, but if the failure of the application is a condition subsequent, Buyer would have to prove refusal of the application to escape the obligation to purchase the land.)

Although the distinction's principal significance relates to the burden of proof, one should not underplay its possible importance. When the happening of the condition is difficult to prove, the incidence of the burden can make the difference between winning or losing the case. Given the likely confusion and unintended results that could flow from subtleties in wording, there is a good argument for abolishing the distinction entirely, or at least for not finding a condition subsequent unless the contract makes it clear that the parties really did intend it. The Restatement Second tends in this direction. It disfavors the concept of conditions subsequent and does not even refer to such conditions in the text of any of its sections. In defining the term "condition" in §224, it confines it to an event that must occur before a performance becomes due. Although it concedes, in Comment *e* to §224, that a contract may provide for the discharge of a duty upon the happening of a specified event, it does not consider such a term to be a condition at all. The comment indicates a preference for interpreting contractual language as creating a condition precedent and suggests that a condition subsequent should not be found merely because the contract speaks of a duty being "discharged" or "extinguished." Section 227(3) reinforces this by stating that in cases of doubt, a condition should be interpreted as precedent. The overall effect of this thinking is that the condition subsequent has declined in importance in modern cases.

§16.8   The Purpose of Using Conditions in a Contract

The preceding discussion has already provided several indications of the role played in the contract by conditions. In this section, attention is focused more directly on that subject. It is important to remember that conditions are contractual terms, available to be used or avoided by the parties in formulating their agreement. By properly using conditions, they can provide for contingencies, allocate risks, and generally control the way in which their bargain is to be performed. To the extent that they can do this clearly and expressly, they are less likely to have disputes later on. However, as we have already seen, in the absence of clear provisions, unexpressed conditions may still be found by applying principles of interpretation and construction to determine what the parties had or reasonably must have intended. The following are the most common purposes achieved by conditions.

§16.8.1   The Use of a Condition as a Complete or Partial "Escape Clause"

The land sale example demonstrated Buyer's purpose in making his commitment conditional upon the granting of the rezoning application—he did not wish to buy the land if it could not be developed. Used in this way, a nonpromissory condition enables the parties to enter into a contract now, while permitting one (or both) of them to terminate the relationship and escape the commitment if a contemplated event does not occur. (In this example, as explained in section 16.4, the condition is interpreted as relating to Buyer's performance only, so it is his escape clause, not Seller's. The facts of the example were then varied to illustrate a condition intended to allow both parties to escape the transaction.)

In the land sale contract, the rezoning has been interpreted as a pure condition, so that Buyer escapes his obligation simply because the condition is not satisfied. He has no obligation to make any effort to bring about its fulfillment. However, some conditions create an escape that is less absolute, because they expressly or impliedly require the party to *take steps to try and make the event happen*. If so, the party is released from performance only if the condition is unfulfilled despite his efforts to make it come about. This can be illustrated by changing the facts of the example. Say that at the time of sale, the application for rezoning had not yet been made. Buyer is willing to submit an application, but does not wish to gamble on its success. The parties could enter a contract in which Buyer undertakes to make and conscientiously pursue the application, but is excused from proceeding with the purchase if the application is declined. In this contract, Buyer makes an initial promise to apply for the rezoning, but the success of the application is a condition precedent to his obligation to buy the land. This is not completely a promissory condition, because Buyer does not promise that it will be satisfied. However, he does make a *promise to take all reasonable steps in good faith to try to get it fulfilled*. If he does this and fails, he escapes the contract, but if he does not make a conscientious effort to get the rezoning, he has broken his promise and will be liable for breach of contract.

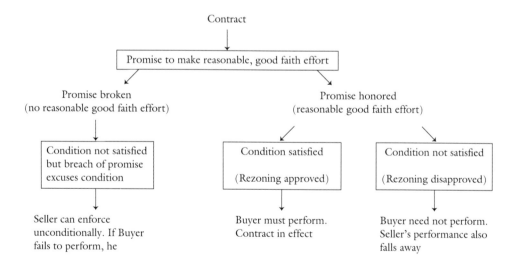

The same characteristics can be found in a common contract to buy a home, under which the buyer's obligation to proceed with the purchase is subject to his being able to obtain a mortgage or to sell his current home. The buyer undertakes to make reasonable efforts to satisfy the condition and cannot escape the promise to buy unless the condition is unfulfilled despite those efforts. In some cases, the promise to make reasonable or good faith efforts to satisfy the condition is expressed in the contract, but it may not be. If not, the contract must be interpreted to decide if such a commitment can be implied in fact or law.

§16.8.2 *The Use of a Condition to Permit the Exercise of Judgment by One of the Parties or a Third Party*

One of the parties to a contract may wish to have some discretion in evaluating a future state of affairs (whether this relates to circumstances external to the contract or to the other party's performance) before rendering her own performance. To achieve this, the party could have a term included in the contract making her satisfaction (or her agent's satisfaction) with the specified state of affairs a condition precedent of her performance. This type of term, known as a **condition of satisfaction,** is useful to a party who does not wish to take the risk of performing until she is sure that circumstances are as desired or that the other party has properly done what the contract requires. A few examples will illustrate conditions of this kind and show how they may be employed:

A person contracts to have her portrait painted. In the contract, she undertakes to buy the portrait for $1,000 upon its completion, on condition that she likes it. The condition gives the buyer a means to escape the contract if she is not satisfied with the portrait, and places the risk of making her happy on the artist. In this illustration, the future state of affairs to be evaluated by the buyer is the adequacy of the painter's performance.

A buyer contracts to purchase an old building for the purpose of restoring it and making it into shops, but she is not sure if this kind of development would be successful. She therefore makes her promise to buy the building conditional on her determination, following a feasibility study, that it can be profitably renovated. The risk to be managed by the condition of satisfaction in this case is not related to the adequacy of the other party's performance, but to an external state of affairs—the economic environment—on which the buyer has inadequate information at the time of contracting.

In some cases, the evaluation is not to be done by the party herself, but by some expert third party. For example, a buyer may contract to buy a building subject to the condition that her engineer finds it to be structurally sound, or the owner of property may promise to pay a builder for construction work on condition that her architect certifies the work as competent.

In dealing with consideration doctrine in section 7.9, we saw that if a promisor reserves unrestrained discretion to perform, the apparent promise is

illusory and cannot be consideration. Therefore, a promise conditional on the satisfaction of one of the parties could fail as consideration unless there is some limitation on that party's ability to claim dissatisfaction. The contract may itself express the *standard by which to measure satisfaction,* but if it does not, it is usually possible to imply such standards, either as a matter of factual interpretation or legal implication. As a general rule, in the absence of the expression of a contrary intent, an *objective* test is used to limit discretion if, based on the underlying purpose and nature of the contract, the reason for the evaluation is to ensure that *commercial or technical standards* are satisfied. Under such an objective test, the question is whether the party is reasonable in being dissatisfied. In the above examples, it is a fair assumption that the market feasibility of the renovation, the soundness of the building, and the quality of the construction work would all fit into this category. Conversely, if the goal of the contract is to provide a performance that satisfies *personal preference involving matters of taste or aesthetics,* satisfaction is judged on a *subjective* standard: Is the party's dissatisfaction *honest and genuine?* The painting probably falls into this category, and the buyer may be able to show honest dissatisfaction with her portrait, even if art critics consider it to be a fine piece of work.

Of course, as is usually true, objective and subjective standards may not always give different results because it could be quite hard to make a convincing showing that unreasonable dissatisfaction is honest and genuine. Nevertheless, the good faith test is more oriented to personal judgment, while reasonableness focuses more on market or mechanical factors. Restatement Second §228 expresses a preference for use of the objective standard in case of doubt, because it is obviously fairer and more predictable. A party should not be taken to have subjected herself to the risk of the other's purely subjective foibles unless this is made clear in the contract or is necessarily inferred from the nature of the transaction.

Like the conditions discussed at the end of section 16.7.1, the promise inherent in a condition of satisfaction is not a promise to ensure that the condition is fulfilled, but only a promise to act in good faith or reasonably to cooperate in achieving its fulfillment. It provides an escape from the contract, but only if the condition is unfulfilled despite the reasonable or honest evaluation of the party with the conditional obligation. Therefore, if a party refuses to perform on the basis of unreasonable or false dissatisfaction, the condition of satisfaction is deemed fulfilled, and the refusal of performance is a breach.

§16.8.3 The Use of a Condition to Provide for Alternative Performances

In the example involving the sale of land subject to rezoning, the denial of the application completely released Buyer from his promise to buy the land.

However, a condition need not invariably result in the total termination of a party's performance obligation. Because a condition is a contractual term, the parties can agree that some other consequence will follow its non-fulfillment. To illustrate, reconsider the land sale example with slightly changed facts: As before, at the time of contracting, Seller's application for rezoning was pending. If it succeeds, the land can be used for a housing development, but if not, it can only be used for farming. Buyer wishes to have the land irrespective of the outcome, but the parties recognize that its value will be very much higher if the zoning is changed. To accommodate the uncertainty of the application's outcome, they may contract for the sale, but may provide in the contract that its purchase price is $100,000 (its market value as farmland), yet if the rezoning application is successful, the price will be $300,000 (its value as a tract capable of residential development). Here, as before, the parties agree to make Buyer's performance contingent on an uncertain future event—the change in zoning. However, the condition does not operate to release Buyer, but to commit him to an alternative promise that changes the extent of his performance. The condition is used as a *channeling device*, not as an escape clause.

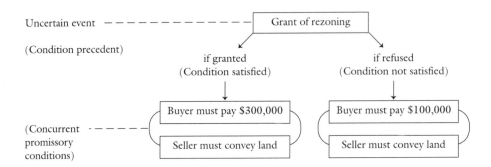

§16.8.4   The Use of a Condition to Regulate the Sequence of Performance

In the land sale example, the two dependent promises—Buyer's promise to pay and the seller's to convey the land—were construed as concurrent. This meant that the performances were conditions of each other and had to be exchanged simultaneously. This conclusion was reached because the contract did not indicate a contrary intent, and concurrent performance was the most reasonable construction under the circumstances. As noted in section 16.5, when a *contract is silent on the sequence of performance*, the law recognizes two *default rules:* If the performances are capable of being rendered simultaneously, the presumption is that the parties intended concurrent performance. However, if one of the performances is capable of being rendered instantaneously and the other needs time to be accomplished, the completion of the longer performance is deemed to be a condition precedent of the instantaneous one. This means that the party with the longer performance must go first. Of course, these are only default rules, so the *parties can change them by providing differently* in their contract. They can set up any sequence of performances that they think fit, and can even split up one or both parties' performances to provide for portions of each to be rendered serially. Sometimes this intent is spelled out expressly, but it could also arise by factual implication from the nature and structure of the contract. Because the promises are dependent, it follows that the earlier performance to be rendered by one of the parties is a promissory condition precedent of the next performance in the sequence, to be rendered by the other.

We begin with the simplest illustration: Buyer and Seller contract for the sale of a piece of land on credit. The contract states that Seller will convey the land immediately, and Buyer will pay for it in six months. The promises are still dependent, in the sense that Seller would not have to convey the land if Buyer repudiated his promise before conveyance fell due. But it is clearly no longer true that performances must be simultaneous, so they are not, in that sense, conditions of each other. Instead, even though the parties have not said so expressly, the sequence prescribed for performance leads to the reasonable inference that conveyance of the land is a **condition precedent** to payment of the price in six months. (As noted in section 16.2, the passage of the six months after conveyance is not itself a condition because the mere affluxion of time is not regarded as an uncertain event.) Note that once Seller has performed, Buyer is committed to pay in six months. This is the last promise to be honored in the transaction, and as such it is a **pure promise**. It obviously cannot be a promissory condition because it is not a condition of anything—no further performance is contingent on it.

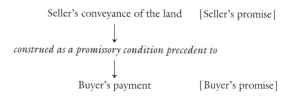

This example illustrates the point made in section 16.3. Even though the promises are express, the conditional nature of the seller's promise is not articulated, so the condition itself is not express, but construed—it is inferred as being what the parties reasonably must have intended by providing for the order of performances. (For it to be both an express promise and an express condition, the contract would have to have contained language stating that the seller undertakes to convey the land, and that this conveyance is a condition of the buyer's payment.) It makes no difference to the ultimate legal effect of a condition whether it is express or construed. However, as a matter of planning, when parties intend to sequence their performances, it makes more sense to set this out clearly in the contract, rather than to argue about it before a court.

We now consider a second, more complex illustration (a further embellishment of the previous land sale example) to see how the parties are able to use sequential conditions to break up their performance obligations into stages and to provide for several consecutive performances as well as a set of simultaneous performances. The contract so structured has a combination of pure conditions, promissory conditions precedent, promissory concurrent conditions, and pure promises. Say that the contract commits Buyer to purchase the land for $300,000 on condition that the zoning application is granted. However, it does not simply provide, as before, for the simultaneous transfer of price for title. Instead, it specifies that if the application does succeed, Buyer will pay a down payment of $30,000 to Seller immediately upon the grant of the application; a further $250,000 will be paid concurrently with Seller's transfer of title to Buyer; and the remaining balance of $20,000 will be paid one month after the transfer. The purpose here is not simply to give Buyer an escape if the rezoning is refused, but also to distribute the risk of breach between the parties and to extend credit to Buyer for part of the price.

The initial condition that the rezoning must be approved is an **express condition precedent** to the buyer's promise to purchase the land. As before, this is likely to be interpreted as a **pure condition**. There is nothing from which to conclude that it was intended as promissory, because the fate of the application is out of the buyer's control, and the language of the contract does not indicate that he intended to guarantee that it would happen, or that he has to do anything to try to bring it about. Therefore, if the rezoning is refused, the buyer has the right to escape the contract, and the seller's dependent promise falls away too.

If the rezoning is approved, the contract requires Buyer immediately to pay a deposit of $30,000 to Seller. This payment is performance of part of Buyer's consideration and it is expressly promised. Although the parties have not expressly called this a condition of the subsequent transfer of the land, this is the reasonable construction of what was intended. The apparent purpose of the deposit is to show Buyer's earnest (that is, to indicate his commitment) and to alleviate Seller's risk that Buyer may breach, so it can reasonably be inferred that if payment is not made, Seller is relieved of her subsequent obligation to perform by tendering conveyance of the property. Furthermore, if Buyer should breach by not causing the condition to be satisfied, he would also be liable to Seller for breach of contract. The undertaking is therefore not only an **express promise**, but also a **construed promissory condition precedent** to Seller's performance.

If both the conditions of approval and payment of the deposit are satisfied, the next set of terms involve the simultaneous conveyance of title and payment of $250,000. As in the earlier example, these are **express promises,** construed as dependent on each other, to be performed simultaneously—that is, **construed promissory concurrent conditions.** If either party fails to tender performance at the time appointed for the exchange, the other has the right both to withhold the return performance and to treat the failure as a breach of contract.

If all the above conditions are satisfied, one promised performance remains following the transfer of the land against payment of the $250,000—Buyer's payment of the final installment of $20,000. This is a **pure promise.** Although payment is an event, there is no later performance that is contingent on it, so it is not a condition. If Buyer fails to pay, Seller has nothing to withhold, but she can enforce the promise by suing for breach. A diagram of the contract's structure looks like this:

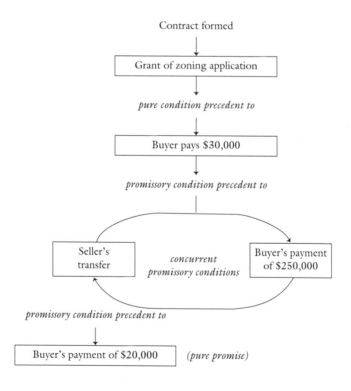

It is worth stressing again that the distinction made in the above example between promises, conditions, and promissory conditions was a matter of interpretation and construction, based on any express language used by the parties, or in the absence of such clear language, on their apparent intent as evidenced by any contextual evidence, or failing that, as reasonably inferred. In this case, there was no extrinsic evidence of negotiations, trade usage, or other facts, so reasonable meaning was construed from nothing more than the language and structure of the writing itself.

This analysis makes it clear why conditions are useful in establishing a particular sequence of performances, requiring obligations to be satisfied serially or concurrently. The party who performs first takes the *risk of not receiving the return performance* when it later becomes due. By using conditions, the parties can structure the contract so that risk goes to the party who is willing to bear it. If neither party wishes to assume the risk of relying on the other's credit, concurrent performances may be the answer. In the above example, the exchange of title and money could have been performed concurrently, but the parties chose to break up Buyer's performance obligation and to provide for it in stages.

In other contracts it may not be possible for parties to perform simultaneously because one party's performance will take time, while the other's can be rendered instantaneously. As noted above, unless the parties provide differently, the presumption in such a contract is that completion of the longer performance is a condition precedent of the instantaneous one. A final example, involving a construction contract, demonstrates how parties may use conditions to avoid this result and allocate risk more evenly. If the owner of property contracts with a builder to build a house on it, the builder's performance—constructing the house—will take several weeks or months, while the owner's performance—payment—could be accomplished in a single instant. In the absence of a different sequence set out in the contract, the completion of construction is construed as a promissory condition precedent to the payment. This places the entire risk of the owner's non-payment on the builder. If the builder does not wish for this result, she could ensure that the contract prescribes a different order of performance. The owner will probably not agree to pay in advance, because that shifts the whole risk of the builder's non-performance to him. But the parties may be able to agree on a sequence that shares the risk of default and ensures that neither party is exposed to the full burden of trusting the other. To do this, the parties may use promissory conditions to break the performance into stages. For example, the contract may require the owner to pay a ten percent deposit one week after the contract is signed; one week thereafter, the builder must begin to excavate and build the foundation; on completion the owner must pay a further ten percent of the price; the builder must then frame the house; when that is done the owner must pay another ten percent. This sequence of alternating performances goes on until the entire house is built and the builder has received periodic payments of 90 percent, upon which the owner must pay the final installment. Each of the incremental performances is a promise by the one party and also a condition precedent to the next stage of performance by the other, so that if any one stage of performance is not rendered, the party entitled to that performance can refuse to render the consequent return performance and claim breach. For instance, if the owner fails to pay after the excavation and foundation, the builder has the right to refuse to do the framing and may also sue the owner for breaching the contract. The sequence looks like this:

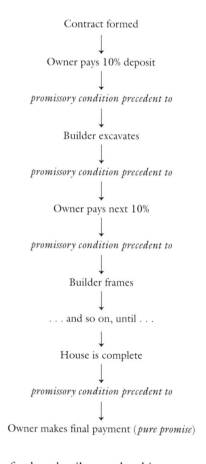

Contract formed
↓
Owner pays 10% deposit
↓
promissory condition precedent to
↓
Builder excavates
↓
promissory condition precedent to
↓
Owner pays next 10%
↓
promissory condition precedent to
↓
Builder frames
↓
. . . and so on, until . . .
↓
House is complete
↓
promissory condition precedent to
↓
Owner makes final payment (*pure promise*)

We could add a further detail to make this contract a little more complex: The parties agree further that the owner's obligation to make the deposit and to proceed with the construction is conditional on the owner obtaining a building permit. They also agree that before the owner has to pay for any stage of construction, his architect will inspect the work and certify it as in accordance with specifications and competently performed. By agreeing to these terms, the parties have added an initial condition precedent that allows the owner to escape the contract if the city refuses a permit, but impliedly requires the owner to make reasonable efforts to obtain the permit. They have also conditioned the owner's second and later payment obligations on his architect's satisfaction with the builder's performance. Because this involves a matter of technical judgment, the dissatisfaction must be reasonable. I am not sure if my sanity (or yours) can withstand another diagram, but here goes:

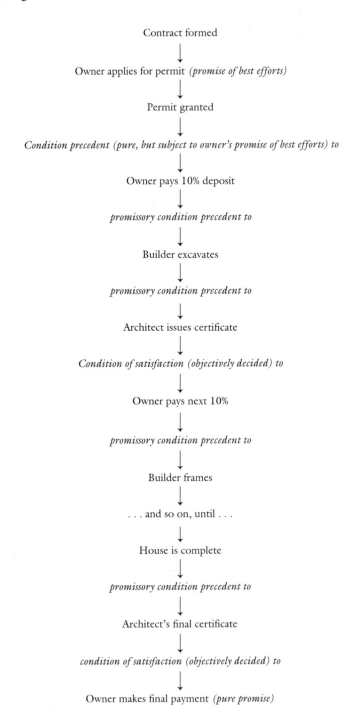

Contract formed

↓

Owner applies for permit *(promise of best efforts)*

↓

Permit granted

↓

Condition precedent (pure, but subject to owner's promise of best efforts) to

↓

Owner pays 10% deposit

↓

promissory condition precedent to

↓

Builder excavates

↓

promissory condition precedent to

↓

Architect issues certificate

↓

Condition of satisfaction (objectively decided) to

↓

Owner pays next 10%

↓

promissory condition precedent to

↓

Builder frames

↓

. . . and so on, until . . .

↓

House is complete

↓

promissory condition precedent to

↓

Architect's final certificate

↓

condition of satisfaction (objectively decided) to

↓

Owner makes final payment *(pure promise)*

§16.9 Strict or Substantial Compliance with a Condition: The Different Rules of Interpretation Governing Express and Construed Conditions

The fundamental rule has been stated that when a performance is subject to a condition, the duty to perform does not arise unless the condition is fulfilled. If the parties have taken the trouble to create an express condition by clear language in the contract, this rule is regarded as absolute: Unless the *express condition* is exactly satisfied, the conditional duty does not become due. The justification for this doctrine of *strict compliance* is that the parties have clearly chosen to make performance subject to the stated event, and the court should honor this intention by upholding the beneficiary party's right to demand nothing less than exact fulfillment of the condition. Therefore, even if it seems that the condition is rather technical and apparently unimportant, or even if it has been substantially satisfied, so that the shortcoming in compliance is rather unimportant or trivial, the court should not second-guess the parties by treating the condition as having been met.

To illustrate, recall that in our land sale example, the contract expressly stated that Buyer's obligation to purchase the property was conditional upon the grant of the rezoning application within 60 days of the date of the agreement. If the rezoning has not yet been approved by the 60th day, but it is granted on the 61st, the condition has not been fulfilled. Because the condition is express, Buyer is entitled to demand that it is strictly complied with. Seller should not be able to claim its fulfillment by arguing that a one-day delay in the grant is unimportant and the short delay has no real impact on the value of the transaction to Buyer. This could be a harsh result for Seller, particularly if Buyer is using technical non-fulfillment as a pretext to avoid a contract that he no longer desires. Nevertheless, the rationale is that Seller agreed to a condition on these express terms, and if the event does not occur precisely as contemplated, she has no basis for complaint.

In some cases, the harsh results of this approach may be ameliorated by *excusing* the condition on one of the grounds discussed in section 16.11, but only if the facts fit into one of the recognized bases for excuse. It is also sometimes possible to avoid an unfair result by interpreting the condition so as to find that it was in fact satisfied, but this solution is only available if the language of the condition admits of such a meaning. It would not, for example, be easy to interpret the clear wording "within 60 days of the date of this agreement" to mean "within 61 days." However, if the condition was for approval of the rezoning "within a reasonable time," the less precise language of this express condition provides greater flexibility in interpretation and makes it easier for a court to conclude that the condition was in fact fulfilled.

A similar flexibility in interpretation occurs when a condition is not expressly stated, but it is **implied in fact.** Although the factually implied condition is, in legal effect, no different from an express one and just as much merits rigorous enforcement, the process of deciding on exactly what the condition was gives the court some leeway. If alternative interpretations are possible, the court may be able to avoid the one that would lead to a harsh result, and favor the one that supports the conclusion that the condition was in fact satisfied.

As we have seen, many conditions are neither express nor implied from factual evidence, but are **construed** as a matter of law, based on what the parties reasonably must have intended. A construed condition is found by the court, in the absence of clearly established actual intent, for the purpose of giving reasonable effect to the parties' agreement. For fairly obvious reasons, a *standard of strict compliance is not appropriate* where a condition is construed: Because the condition is not established by a clear manifestation of assent, the parties' intent to agree to strict compliance is not as certain. Furthermore, construction is a search for the apparent expectations of the parties, measured in light of what would be reasonable. The court is therefore unlikely to construe a condition so strictly that it would require exact compliance and admit of no flexibility.

The distinction between strict compliance with an express condition and substantial compliance with a construed condition may be illustrated by looking again at the example involving the building contract under which the owner undertook to make a ten percent down payment a week after execution of the contract, and the builder committed to begin construction a week thereafter. The owner has expressly promised to make the down payment. If the language of the contract clearly articulates that this is also a condition precedent to the builder's duty to commence performance, the owner's failure to pay the full amount of the deposit by due date constitutes nonfulfillment of the condition, so that the builder's obligation to perform does not arise. Because strict compliance is required, the owner will not be deemed to have satisfied the condition if, say, he pays the deposit one day late. However, if the promise's role as a condition is not expressly stated but is construed as a matter of reasonable intent from the way in which the contract has set out the sequence of performances, the court has more flexibility. It may employ the doctrine of substantial compliance and decide whether the delay in payment is good enough to constitute fulfillment of the condition.

Of course, we must not forget that the owner's down payment is not simply a condition, but *also a promise* (that is, a promissory condition). Therefore, late payment of the deposit raises not only the question of whether strict compliance with the condition is required, but also whether the owner's breach of his promise to pay at the time specified is a serious or minor breach. This issue is deferred to Chapter 17, but it is useful to note at this stage that where a promissory condition is involved, the impact of the deficiency in performance must be evaluated from both perspectives. As Chapter 17 will show, there is usually a close coordination in the results of these two enquiries, so that a minor breach that qualifies as *substantial performance* of the *promise* is likely to be also a *substantial compliance* with the *condition*, and a material breach will likely be a non-fulfillment of the condition as well. The effect of this may be illustrated by returning to our example: If late payment is a serious violation of the contract, the builder would be entitled to withhold performance and also to rescind the contract and claim the full extent of relief necessary to compensate for the lost expectation. However, if the delay is trivial, substantial compliance with the condition does not discharge the builder's duty to perform, and the minor breach does not permit rescission. The builder must perform and is confined to claiming compensation, in the form of a monetary allowance, for any loss caused by the inadequacy of performance.

§16.10 Distinguishing a Condition from an Event that Sets the Time for Performance

In requiring a down payment from the owner, the construction contract specified that the payment must be made one week following the execution of the contract. As stated already, the passage of time is not a condition because this is not regarded in law as an uncertain future event. The purpose of the provision is merely to set a time for the owner's performance, not to impose a condition on it. However, sometimes it is trickier to differentiate between a time-setting event and a condition. Say, for example, that the contract required the owner to make the down payment on payday, which is at the end of the month. Two days after the contract was signed, the owner's employer filed bankruptcy. It is clear that the employer is so badly insolvent that its estate will not have enough funds to pay salaries due to employees—payday will never dawn.

If the parties intended simply to fix a time for payment, the owner is obliged to make the down payment at the end of the month, the day on which the employer's debt to him was due, whether or not he actually collects it. But if the parties intended the owner's obligation to be conditional on his receiving his salary, the non-occurrence of that event discharges his duty. Unless the contract makes it clear which of these alternatives was intended, the import of a term like this must be determined by interpretation or construction. In most cases, in the absence of evidence of a contrary intent, the most reasonable construction is that the promisor, not the promisee, bore the risk that the funds would not become available, so that the term merely postpones payment for a stated period and does not make performance conditional on the event occurring.[5]

---

5. We will not consider here the question of whether the owner would be able to use the excuse of impracticability to avoid liability for failing to perform.

§16.11   The Excuse of Conditions: Wrongful Prevention, Waiver or Estoppel, and Forfeiture

If a performance is subject to a condition, it does not fall due unless that condition is satisfied. However, circumstances may change after the contract is entered into, making it unfair or unreasonable to require the condition to be satisfied, or the inequitable conduct of the beneficiary of the condition may preclude his assertion of its non-fulfillment, or the impact of the condition may otherwise be so harsh that its enforcement would be unjust. To take account of this, the law recognizes certain limited and defined situations in which the condition may be excused to prevent injustice. If grounds for excuse exist, the condition falls away and the contingent obligation becomes absolute. That is, it is no longer conditional and must be performed despite the non-occurrence of the event originally contemplated in the contract. In this section we look at three of the most common and important bases for excuse.

§16.11.1   The Party Favored by the Condition Wrongfully Prevents or Hinders Its Fulfillment

Some conditions are completely beyond the control of the promisor, and she has no power to do anything to facilitate or to hinder their occurrence. For example, if a lessor promises the lessee that she will install air conditioning in the premises next year if the average temperature for this August reaches 100 degrees, there is little that the lessor can do to manipulate the weather so as to influence the fulfillment of the condition. If a party has no capacity to influence the happening of the condition, she cannot, of course, wrongfully prevent its fulfillment. But some conditions are, to a greater or lesser extent, capable of being influenced by one or both parties.

a.   When a Party Has a Duty to Take Active Steps to Facilitate Occurrence of the Condition

We have already seen that even if a party does not promise that the condition will be fulfilled, she may at least have some role to play in affecting it, and may expressly or impliedly promise to make a *reasonable or good faith effort* to attempt to bring it about. For example, the buyer of a home may undertake to purchase it on condition that she is able to obtain a mortgage loan for 90 percent of the purchase price. She does not promise that she will obtain the loan, but she does have the duty (even if this is not expressly stated) to make best efforts to get it. Although fulfillment of the condition is not entirely within her control, she does have a role to play in bringing it about. If she makes adequate efforts to obtain the financing, but fails, the condition is not fulfilled and she has no duty to proceed with the purchase. However, if she does not try to get the loan, or makes only a halfhearted or token attempt, she violates her duty to deal fairly with the seller. She is therefore taken to have hindered fulfillment of the condition. This allows the seller to claim that the condition is excused, so that he can enforce her promise to purchase the house as if the condition had not existed.

b. Obstructive Conduct

Even if a party has no duty to cooperate actively in the condition's fulfillment, the *obligation of fair dealing* may require her not to do anything to obstruct fulfillment of the condition. The example involving the sale of farmland subject to rezoning may be used again to illustrate this point. Because the rezoning application had already been submitted by Seller and was awaiting disposition by the zoning authority, Buyer had no duty to take any action to prosecute the application or to ensure the condition's occurrence. (That is, it is a pure condition, without any promissory elements.) Nevertheless, Buyer's general obligation of fair dealing does create an implied promise not to act in bad faith to prevent its occurrence. Therefore, the condition may be excused if its non-occurrence resulted from some wrongful action by Buyer to negatively influence the local authority's decision. (For example, he persuaded a neighboring landowner to file an objection to the application, or he lobbied members of the board to vote against it.)

To be wrongful, the action need not break the law. It is enough that it *faithlessly undermines the contract*, betraying the other party's reasonable expectations. In the above example, the obligation not to obstruct fulfillment of the condition is an obvious implication because Buyer's actions would be inconsistent with the contract's purpose. However, one should not assume, as a matter of course, that every contract imposes an implied duty not to act in a way that obstructs fulfillment of a condition. This is a matter of interpretation, dependent on the apparent intent of the parties, and some contracts may contemplate that the promisor does have the right to try to avoid satisfaction of the condition. For example, if a buyer promises to purchase goods from the seller on condition that he cannot find them cheaper elsewhere, the buyer obviously has the right to try to avoid satisfaction of the condition by seeking cheaper goods, and these efforts would not be a wrongful obstruction of the condition.

c. The Link Between Conduct and Non-Fulfillment

When the promisor has wrongfully failed to make a good faith and reasonable effort to facilitate occurrence or has acted in an obstructive way, it may not be clear if that conduct was directly responsible for non-fulfillment of the condition. For example, the buyer of the house may not have obtained a mortgage, even had she made a genuine and conscientious effort, or the re-zoning board may have refused the application even without Buyer's interference. Some courts have imposed a strict test of causation, excusing the condition only if it can be shown that the condition would have been fulfilled, but for the promisor's obstruction. A less rigorous test, favored by other courts, does not require the promisee to demonstrate as strong a causal link, but merely to show that the promisor's conduct played a significant role in the condition's non-fulfillment.

§16.11.2   *Estoppel or Waiver*

Estoppel and waiver are distinct doctrines, but they are quite muddled in the context of excuse of conditions because conduct is often ambiguous enough to be classified as giving rise to either of them. As a result, courts sometimes do not take the trouble to differentiate them, and Restatement Second §§84 and 230(3) combine them into a general principle of excuse. The basic idea is that after the contract is entered into, the promisor whose duty is conditional indicates by *words or conduct* that he will perform even if the condition does not occur. This indication of *intent not to require compliance with the condition* may take place either before the time on which the condition is to occur, or after that time has passed and the condition has not been satisfied. Although there are some differences in legal analysis depending on whether the condition is dispensed with before or after it is due to occur, these will not be explored here. This discussion is confined to an explanation of the basic principles applicable in either case. Although the two doctrines of estoppel and waiver are intermingled in this area, they do give rise to distinct justifications for excusing a condition, so it is useful to describe them separately and to show why they are so easily mixed up.

a.   Estoppel

Estoppel, an equitable doctrine, was introduced in section 8.4. Its purpose is to prevent the unfair assertion of rights by a person who has acted inconsistently with those rights. The basic effect of the doctrine is to preclude a person from asserting a right when, by *deliberate words or conduct,* and with *knowledge or reason to know* that the words or conduct will *likely be relied on* by another, the actor causes the other party *detriment* by *inducing* the *justifiable belief* that the *right does not exist* or that it *will not be asserted.* In the context of conditions, the party who is the beneficiary of the condition may be estopped from claiming its non-fulfillment if, by her words or conduct, she induces the other party to act to his detriment by causing him justifiably to believe that the condition has been satisfied, or that compliance with it will not be required. (If, instead of misrepresenting a fact, the beneficiary party promises that she will not require compliance with the condition, the basis for relief is promissory estoppel rather than equitable estoppel, but the elements for relief are so similar, that the analysis is the same.)

To illustrate, consider again the example involving the sale of land subject to the condition that the rezoning application is granted within 60 days of execution of the contract. Fifty-five days after execution of the contract, the zoning authority tells Seller that it will not be ready to make a decision for at least two weeks. When Seller informs Buyer of this, he responds by stating that he is willing to wait an additional two weeks. On the strength of this, Seller forgoes an opportunity to sell the land to someone else. If, on the 61st day, Buyer sought to escape the contract by asserting non-fulfillment of the condition, he would likely be estopped from doing so, because he deliberately indicated to Seller that he would not insist on compliance with the 60-day provision and Seller justifiably relied on that assertion to her detriment.

b. Waiver

A waiver occurs when, after the contract has been made, the beneficiary of a condition agrees to perform even if the condition is not satisfied. In essence, the waiver is a **voluntary abandonment of a contractual right.** (Naturally, a party can only waive a condition that is solely for his benefit. One party cannot waive rights belonging to the other.) For example, after the rezoning application is denied, Buyer informs Seller that he wishes to proceed with the transaction despite the denial. If Buyer then refuses to perform, Seller can claim that Buyer's performance obligation became unconditional because the condition was excused by the waiver. A waiver must be distinguished from a contract modification. A modification is a contract in itself—a mutual agreement under which one party agrees to relinquish rights in return for consideration given by the other. A waiver is one-sided—one of the parties *unilaterally* gives up a contractual right without asking for or receiving anything in exchange. Because consideration is required for a valid modification, the general rule is that if the right to be given up is an important part of the exchange under the contract (that is, it is a material right) it cannot be validly relinquished by a unilateral waiver. Its abandonment must be exchanged for consideration in a fully-fledged contractual modification. However, if the right relinquished is **non-material**—ancillary, and not a central part of the contractual exchange—the consideration requirement is dispensed with and it can be validly waived. To decide if the grant of the rezoning application was a material part of the exchange and therefore not validly waivable without consideration, the role of the condition and its significance in the exchange must be determined by interpretation. (This is, of course, the common law rule, because UCC §2.209 does not require consideration for a modification. Therefore, even the waiver of a material part of the exchange would be valid despite a lack of consideration.)

The issue of consideration for a waiver only arises when it is the party entitled to the conditional performance who seeks to excuse the condition and to enforce the performance against the beneficiary of the condition. It does not apply when it is the beneficiary of the condition who elects to abandon his right to protection of the condition. For example, it was mentioned in section 16.4 that if the grant of the rezoning application is solely for Buyer's benefit, he can decide to proceed with the sale of the property as farmland, even if the application is denied. In such a case, Buyer is not attempting to enforce rights arising out of the excuse of a condition, but is merely enforcing his original rights for which he gave consideration under the contract. Seller cannot resist this by arguing that she gave Buyer no consideration for his waiver.

c.   Distinguishing Waiver from Estoppel

As noted earlier, it can be difficult to distinguish waiver from estoppel. The estoppel example given above can be used to show just how ambiguous the distinction can be. In that example, it was stated that Buyer's conduct in indicating that he would wait a further two weeks for approval estopped him from asserting non-fulfillment of the condition on the 61st day. It could just as well be said that Buyer waived his right to have the condition fulfilled within 60 days. If the time for approval is not a central component of the exchange (which it appears not to be, but that is a question of interpretation), the waiver without consideration is valid and binding. Thus, in most situations, conduct by the party benefitted by the condition could equally well support an estoppel or waiver argument, so they should generally be regarded as alternative bases for excuse. Selection of the theory to be used would be based on the issues of reliance and materiality. Estoppel is more appropriate if detrimental reliance can be shown and there is some question about whether the right relinquished is material enough to require consideration. Waiver is a better argument if no prejudicial reliance can be established, but there is an argument that the abandoned right is ancillary, not central to the exchange.

d.   Retraction of a Waiver

Although, as stated earlier, we will not go into the details of the distinction between waivers prior to and after the due date for occurrence of the condition, there is one point on which it is useful to indicate a difference in approach. Because a waiver is not supported by consideration, a waiver made prior to the due date for the condition's fulfillment can be retracted. But here again, principles of estoppel and waiver intermingle, making the right to withdraw the waiver subject to protection of the other party's reliance. The ability to retract the waiver is lost if notice of the retraction is not received by the other party in time to allow him to take any action necessary to bring the condition about, or if he has taken detrimental action in reliance on the waiver. If the waiver is made after the time for occurrence of the condition has passed (so that it is clear that the condition has failed to occur), it cannot be retracted because the party benefitted by the condition is treated as having made a final election to proceed with the transaction despite non-occurrence of the condition.

§16.11.3 Forfeiture

In a sense, any finding of liability under a contract, or any conclusion that a party is not entitled to performance because of the non-fulfillment of a condition, results in some forfeiture of money or expected benefits. Therefore, when forfeiture is raised as a basis for excusing a condition, it must mean more than this. As a general matter, forfeiture is an appropriate basis for excusing a condition only if its enforcement would result in an **unfair, disproportionate, and harsh deprivation** of the rights or property of the party who expects performance, and a **windfall or unfair benefit** to the party whose performance is subject to the condition. Thus, in deciding forfeiture, the court *balances* the *relative hardships* between the parties. It weighs the burden on the party who would suffer if the condition was enforced against the harm that excuse would do to the beneficiary of the condition.

This ground for excusing a condition is really a safety valve that ameliorates the harsh results that may follow from the rule of strict compliance with express conditions. It is therefore most useful when the condition is express and unambiguous, and is not needed when the court has flexibility in construing the terms and scope of the condition, or when ambiguous language can be interpreted in a way that avoids an unfair result. (In setting out standards of interpretation, Restatement Second §227 expresses a general preference in favor of interpretation that will avoid forfeiture in cases when there is doubt about the existence, scope, or nature of a condition.)

The principal purpose of the forfeiture doctrine, set out in Restatement Second §229, is to allow the court to disregard an express condition of a *technical or procedural nature* where the *strict enforcement* of the condition would have the *unfair impact* described above. It should therefore not be used if the occurrence of the condition is a material part of the exchange. To illustrate, say that an insurance policy provides two express conditions to the insurer's liability. The first is that the insured must pay the annual premium, and the second is that the insured must notify the insurer of loss within five days of its occurrence. Payment of the premium is surely a material part of the exchange—it is the entire consideration bargained for by the insurer. Therefore, if the insured suffers a loss after failing to pay the premium, he cannot claim unfair forfeiture of his right to reimbursement and ask the court to excuse the condition of payment. However, if he has paid the premium, and he does give notice of loss, but is one day late in giving it, the court is more likely to be sympathetic to an argument that the insurer's insistence on strict fulfillment is a technicality, and the insured's deprivation of his right of reimbursement would be an unfair forfeiture.

EXAMPLES

1. This first example is an exercise in classification. Identify the promises, conditions, and promissory conditions in the following contracts. Having identified the conditions, consider whether they are express or construed and precedent or concurrent.

1(a). A lessor and a lessee entered into a lease of real property for a two-year term at a rent of $1,200 a month, payable in advance by the first day of each month. The lease gave the lessee the right to renew the lease for a further two years provided that she delivered written notice of renewal to the lessor not later than 30 days prior to the end of the second year of the lease. The rent for the renewal period would be $1,500 per month, but if the lessee satisfactorily repainted the premises in the first month of the renewal period, the rent would be $1,400 per month.

1(b). An insurance policy provides that in consideration for an annual premium, payable in advance, the insurer will reimburse the insured for any loss by fire occurring on the insured premises, provided that the insured furnishes satisfactory proof of loss to the insurer within 30 days of the loss.

1(c). On June 1, the owner of land granted an option to purchase the land. The prospective buyer had until June 30 to exercise the option. On June 10, a second buyer expressed interest in purchasing the land, and the owner entered into a contract with him under which she agreed to sell it for $100,000 if the grantee of the option failed to exercise it by its expiration on June 30.

1(d). Following discussions on the possible sale of a car, the owner of the car writes to the prospective buyer, stating, "I will sell you my car for $5,000 on condition that you communicate your acceptance to me within five days of the date of this letter."

2. Wendy Vendee entered into a contract with Homer Sellar for the purchase of Homer's house for $200,000. The contract, recorded on a standard form, provided that Wendy would pay $50,000 in cash on closing and would pay the balance of the price in installments over 15 years. To secure

payment of the balance, Homer would take a first mortgage in the property, to be recorded at the time of transfer. In a blank space at the end of the form, Homer wrote the sentence, "This contract is contingent on seller's approval of buyer's credit report." Both parties initialed this handwritten addition.

Shortly after the contract was signed, Homer obtained a credit report on Wendy. It showed that Wendy had gone on a credit-card spending binge five years ago and had to file a voluntary bankruptcy petition to discharge unmanageable debt. The report also showed that since obtaining her bankruptcy discharge, Wendy apparently no longer used credit cards and had not defaulted on any other debts. Homer considers bankruptcy to be shameful and thinks it immoral for a person to go on a spending spree and then file bankruptcy to get out of paying her debts in full. He no longer wished to deal with someone as unworthy as Wendy, and he certainly did not trust her enough to give her credit. Homer therefore disapproved the credit report and declared the sale to be terminated.

Wendy objected and said that Homer had no basis to reject her credit report. Wendy can show that Homer's attitude is tougher than that prevailing among financial institutions in the consumer credit industry, which would be likely to approve Wendy's credit under these circumstances. The reasoning in the industry is that a five-year-old abuse of credit and bankruptcy filing should not be held against a borrower who has behaved responsibly since then, particularly when the loan applied for is fully secured by a mortgage on real property. Did Homer have the right to disapprove the report and cancel the sale?

3. Assume that the contract between Wendy Vendee and Homer Sellar was on slightly different terms: Like the contract in Example 2, it provided for the sale of the home to Wendy for $200,000, of which $50,000 would be paid in cash on closing, and the balance would be paid over 15 years, secured by a mortgage on the property. The contract had no condition concerning a credit report. Instead, in the blank space at the end of the form contract, the parties had included the following handwritten term:

> This contract is subject to the buyer's sale of her present home for not less than $165,000 within 30 days hereof.

The reason for including this term was that at the time of the contract Wendy already owned a smaller house that she needed to sell, so that she could use the proceeds to pay the $50,000 cash due on closing. Wendy's old home was subject to a mortgage of $100,000, so she had to sell it for at least $165,000 to pay the mortgage, broker's fees, and other costs, leaving $50,000 clear for her cash payment to Homer.

Consider the following separate and distinct factual variations:

3(a). After signing the contract, Wendy decided that she would save having to pay realtor's commission by marketing the house herself. She bought one of those "for sale by owner" kits, erected "for sale" signs, and placed advertisements in the paper. Unfortunately, Wendy is overbearing and insensitive and has no skill in dealing with people. Although several prospective buyers responded to her advertising, she managed to scare all of them away by her rude and aggressive sales technique. As a result, she had not managed to sell her house by the end of the 30-day period. Wendy therefore claims that she is no longer obliged to buy Homer's house. Is she correct?

3(b). On the 25th day after signing the contract with Homer, Wendy received an offer to sell her house for $165,000. In terms of the offer, the offeror's commitment to proceed with the purchase was contingent on the offeror being able to obtain financing. Wendy accepted the offer on the next day. The offeror immediately submitted a loan application to a mortgage company, but no decision had been made on the application four days later, the expiry date of the 30-day period under the contract between Wendy and Homer. What is the status of Wendy's contract with Homer?

3(c). After signing the contract with Homer, Wendy decided that she would not sell her existing house as planned, but would keep it as rental property. To raise the down payment, she would instead borrow the $50,000 from her sister. She immediately called Homer, explained this, and told him that she waived the condition. Does Homer have any grounds for objection?

4. Consider a third variation of the contract between Wendy and Homer. As before, it provided for the sale of the house to Wendy for $200,000, of which $50,000 was to be paid in cash on closing. However, unlike the prior examples, the contract did not provide for Homer himself to extend credit for the sale on security of a mortgage (Wendy was to seek her own financing) and Wendy did not currently own a home. The contract was therefore not contingent on a satisfactory credit report or on the sale of existing property. Instead, it contained the following provision:

> This sale is subject to the buyer obtaining a loan from a bank or other lending institution, secured by a first mortgage on the property purchased hereunder, in an amount of not less than $150,000, extending for a term of at least 15 years, and at a rate of interest not exceeding eight percent per annum. If, after the exercise of due diligence, the buyer is unable to obtain financing on these terms, this contract shall terminate, and neither party shall have any liability to the other.

Immediately after Wendy signed the agreement, she consulted a mortgage broker. Upon reviewing Wendy's truthful and accurate financial statement, the broker told Wendy that her income was insufficient and her indebtedness too large to qualify her for a loan of $150,000 from any lender that he knew. This made Wendy realize that she had bought a house beyond her means, and she was relieved that the financing contingency had been included in the agreement of sale. She promptly notified Homer of termination of the sale on the ground that the condition had not been satisfied. On hearing that Wendy had given up after an interview with a single broker and had done nothing more to seek financing, Homer claimed that Wendy had not exercised due diligence in trying to satisfy the condition. Is he correct?

5. Primo Contracting Co. is a small general contractor. It was engaged in the construction of an office building under a contract with the owner of the property. Primo entered into a subcontract with Precedent Conditioning, Inc. (PC), a large multinational corporation, for the supply and installation of the building's air conditioning unit. The subcontract between Primo and PC required the unit to be installed by July 1, and further stated: "The price due to PC under this contract shall not be payable until the project's architect has certified that the air conditioning unit has been properly installed in working order and, following such certification, Primo has received payment for this work from the owner."

PC competently installed a fully operational air conditioning unit by June 15. On June 17, before the unit had been inspected by the architect, the owner of the property filed for bankruptcy. The bankruptcy trustee reports that the estate is hopelessly insolvent. It has so few unencumbered assets that no funds will be available to pay any of the debts arising from the construction. The project was abandoned and the architect resigned. Primo has not been paid for any work done during the last month, including the air conditioning. (Although both PC and Primo are entitled to file mechanics' liens on the property, there is a large pre-existing mortgage on the property, and the liens are worthless.[6])

PC has demanded payment from Primo, but Primo has refused on the grounds that neither of the two conditions to its obligation to pay—the architect's certification and the owner's payment—have been fulfilled. Is this a good argument?

6. Larson E. Grand owned an old vacant office building in a bad part of town. Because the building was unoccupied, he did not see the point of paying for burglary insurance, but he did need insurance for destruction to the building itself by fire, vandalism, and other disasters. He therefore bought an insurance policy covering these risks from Equity & Fidelity Indemnity Co., Inc. (E. & F.) The relevant terms of the policy stated:

---

6. Any person who supplies labor or material in connection with the construction of an improvement on real property is entitled by statute to a lien on the property—known as a mechanics' or construction lien—to secure the value of the work or materials. The lien is created by statute, not by contract, so PC would be entitled to file a lien even though it has no contract with the owner. The lien creates a right to payment of the claim from the proceeds of the property, so that the property can be sold in foreclosure and its proceeds used to pay contractors and subcontractors. However, the lien is subject to any rights that existed in the property before construction began. On the facts of this case, there is a large pre-existing mortgage on the property which leaves no value in the property for lien claimants. As a result, the lien will not help PC, and its only hope of payment is from Primo.

(a)   In consideration for the premium paid, Insurer undertakes to reimburse Insured for any loss resulting from damage to or destruction of the above-described premises caused by fire, storm,
explosion, nuclear accident, civil commotion, or vandalism.

(b)   For the purposes of this policy, "vandalism" is restricted to and
includes only wilful and malicious physical injury to the premises
and excludes any loss by pilferage, theft, or burglary.

(c)   This policy does not cover damage resulting from flooding, tidal
wave, volcanic action, earthquake, landslide, or mudflow.

(d)   No claim shall be paid under this policy unless Insured notifies
Insurer of loss within seven days thereof, and submits proof of
loss within a further 14 days. No action taken by Insurer to investigate such claim shall operate as a waiver of any of the terms
of this policy.

The plumbing in the building was copper pipe that has some value as
scrap. A few months after the policy was issued, someone broke into the
building and methodically removed all the copper pipe. To extract the pipe,
the thief ripped open walls and floorboards, causing extensive damage to the
building. In addition, because the thief did not bother to turn off the water
before removing the pipe, the basement and first floor of the building were
flooded and further damaged.

Neighbors noticed the flooding the next morning and called the city to
turn off the water, but because the building was unoccupied and Larson did
not go to it often, more than a week passed before he heard about the damage and discovered the theft. He immediately informed E. & F., which sent
out a loss adjuster the next day. After completing an inspection of the
premises, the adjuster said to Larson, "Well, you may as well go ahead and
get estimates of the cost of fixing this mess and get them to me as soon as you
can. However, I must warn you that the company will probably reject your
claim because this looks like theft, not vandalism, and flooding is not covered
either." Larson protested that, as far as he was concerned, ripping out plumbing was vandalism of the worst kind, and all the damage was caused by that
act. The investigator responded, "I don't think that my boss will see it that
way, but there is no point in our arguing about it because that's not my decision. Put in your estimates and see what happens."

Larson obtained estimates the next day and submitted them immediately. A few days later he received a letter from E. & F. refusing reimbursement of the loss on the basis that it was not covered by the policy. Should
Larson accept this?

7. Sue Burbanite owned a piece of land in a fast-growing suburb.
Sprawling Malls, Inc., a developer of shopping malls, had some interest in
building a mall on Sue's land. However, it needed to study more carefully the
economic feasibility of the project, and to raise adequate funds from in-

vestors. In 1999, Sprawling Malls entered into negotiations with Sue to acquire an option to purchase the land. Sprawling Malls believed that it could conduct a comprehensive feasibility study and attract investors within a year. It therefore proposed buying a year's option to purchase the property. Sue was amenable to this, and the parties ultimately entered into an option contract on December 1, 1999, under which Sprawling Malls was given the option to purchase the land for $1.5 million. The provisions of the contract concerning the option itself were as follows: Sprawling Malls agreed to pay Sue $10,000 for the year's option, payable on the signing of the contract. If Sprawling Malls wished to exercise its option to purchase the property it was required ". . . by not later than November 30, 2000, to deliver to Sue Burbanite written notice of its intention to exercise the option."

After the contract was signed, Sprawling Malls paid Sue the $10,000 and began its feasibility study. By June 2000 the study had been completed at a cost of $300,000. It showed the shopping center development to be a viable project. Armed with the study, Sprawling Malls began to solicit investors. After some considerable effort, it finally managed to raise the necessary capital by late November 2000. On November 29, it mailed written notice to Sue, exercising its option to purchase the land. The letter was delayed in the mail and not received until December 1.

Sue had wanted to escape her contract with Sprawling Malls because the value of the property had increased since December 1999, and she would now be able to sell it for more than $1.5 million. She therefore rejected the attempted exercise of the option on the basis that it was received after the expiry of the option period. Does Sprawling Malls have a basis for challenging this?

EXPLANATIONS

1(a). The lessee's payment of rent and the lessor's obligation to give the lessee use and occupation of the premises are dependent promises. That is, each party's performance is a promissory condition of the other's. Even if the conditional nature of the promises is not expressly stated in the lease, it is easily construed as being what the parties reasonably must have intended. The parties have structured the lease so that the performance of each is broken into monthly segments. The lessee's payment of the month's rent is a condition precedent to that month's tenancy, and the lessor's making the premises available for that month is in turn a condition precedent to the next rent payment. (So, if either party breaches his obligation, the other can withhold the next performance in the sequence in addition to suing for damages for breach of the lease.)

With regard to the lessee's renewal option, her delivery of notice of renewal within the prescribed time is an express condition precedent to the extension of the lease for another two years. (Its conditional nature is expressed in the language of the lease by use of the term "provided that.") It is not a promissory condition, nor even a condition subject to an implied promise to use best efforts, because the lessee has no obligation to renew and need not deliver the notice unless she wishes to extend the lease. If she does want to extend, she must comply exactly with the terms of the condition. As an express condition, it will be strictly enforced.

If the lessee does exercise the renewal option, the same set of promissory conditions—payment of rent and occupation of the premises—continue through the renewal period. In addition, the lease contains another condition intended to give the lessee a choice of alternative performances: If she paints the premises in the first month of the renewal period, her rent is reduced by $100 per month. Although this condition does not use clear language of condition such as "on condition that" or "provided that," its conditional nature is clear enough to qualify it as express. It is not a promissory condition, in that the lessee has no obligation to paint the premises if she would rather pay the extra rent.

Finally, if the lessee does elect to paint the premises, she implicitly promises to do so in a workmanlike manner. The rent reduction is contingent on the paint job being satisfactory to the lessor. This condition of satisfaction is subject to a promise (implied in law, if not expressed) that the lessor will act reasonably or in good faith in assessing whether the painting is satisfactory. The preference is for an objective standard to measure satisfaction, particularly if the work is commercial or technical in nature. However, a subjective good faith standard is used if it is clear from the wording of the contract or from the nature of the performance that the parties intended satisfaction to be measured by the individual taste of the party who is to make the judgment.

1(b). The insurer's obligation to indemnify the insured is subject to four conditions precedent. The first is that the insured has paid the premium due under the policy. The second is that a loss by fire on the premises occurs, the third is that the insured gives proof of loss within the time specified, and the fourth is that the insurer is satisfied with the proof.

Payment of the premium appears to be a condition precedent to coverage. The language of the payment term, as suggested by the question, simply denotes the premium as consideration and does not, in so many words, expressly call it a condition of coverage. However, this does appear to be the import of the wording. The insured may or may not have promised to pay the premium. If he committed himself to pay it, it is a promissory condition. However, the application for coverage may not have obliged him to pay, but may merely have provided that coverage would not be extended unless it was paid. In that case, it is a pure condition.

The condition of loss does not use expressly conditional terminology, but there can be no doubt that loss must be a condition precedent to indemnity. This is so obvious that the implication of a condition is inevitable. It is also obvious that this cannot be a promissory condition. It would be a bizarre policy indeed, under which the insured committed himself to suffer a loss.

The condition of notice is express. It is also a pure condition because the insured has no obligation to submit the proof if he does not wish to claim under the policy. That is, the insurer would have no claim for breach if the insured failed to notify of loss. It would simply have no duty to indemnify.

The condition of satisfactory proof, like the condition of satisfaction in Example 1(a), is subject to an implied promise that limits the insurer's discretion to be dissatisfied. Because the adequacy of proof of loss is a matter of commercial judgment, not taste, the insurer promises to exercise reasonable judgment in deciding if the proof is satisfactory.

1(c). The owner's obligation to sell the land to the buyer is subject to an express condition precedent that the option-holder does not exercise the option by June 30. This is not a promissory condition, because the seller makes no promise that the option will not be exercised. The purpose of the condition is to allow the parties to execute the sale agreement immediately, but to protect the seller from having committed to sell the property to two people. The condition enables the seller to escape the second contract if the grantee of the option (the first offeree) binds her by exercising the option. If the grantee of the option does not exercise it, the seller's obligation to convey the property becomes due, and accordingly, so does the buyer's obligation to pay for it. Even in the absence of expressly conditional language, these mutual promises of performances are construed as conditions of each other. Unless a different sequence is prescribed by the contract, they are deemed to be concurrent conditions because both are capable of instantaneous performance.

1(d). The letter is an offer, and one could say, broadly speaking, that the creation of the contract is conditional on acceptance within the time prescribed. However, despite the use of the word "condition" in the letter, the acceptance within five days is not a condition at all, in the sense used in this chapter. It is simply the time specified for acceptance. If the offer is accepted in time, a contract will be formed, under which the car is exchanged for $5,000. At that point, conditions in the contract will come into effect. The seller's promise to deliver the car and the buyer's promise to pay for it are dependent promises. Even if not expressly stated to be conditions of each other, they are construed promissory conditions. As in Example 1(c), they can be performed at the same time and are therefore deemed concurrent unless the contract specifies an order of performance.

2. The provision concerning the credit report is a condition of satisfaction. It is an express condition precedent to Homer's obligation to sell the property to Wendy on credit. The purpose of the condition is obvious: It is intended to protect Homer from having to extend credit to Wendy if she proves to be uncreditworthy. Of course, Homer could have checked Wendy's credit before making the contract, but this would have delayed execution of the contract and risked loss of the deal. Homer avoided this risk by entering the contract immediately, subject to a satisfactory credit report.

A condition of satisfaction is not fully a promissory condition because Homer does not promise that he will be satisfied. However, this does not mean that Homer has unfettered discretion in deciding whether to be satisfied. Even if nothing is expressed in the contract to restrict his discretion, the law implies an obligation on him to exercise judgment honestly or reasonably. Unless the contract indicates differently, the objective standard is preferred, especially if the judgment involves matters of technical or commercial quality. The subjective standard of good faith is confined to contracts in which it is clearly contemplated that the performance must appeal to the party's aesthetic sense or personal taste.

Creditworthiness is quintessentially a matter of commercial utility, capable of being judged by market standards. Therefore, unless the contract clearly calls for a subjective evaluation, a buyer who submits to a credit check is not likely to have assumed the risk of subjecting herself to the seller's idiosyncrasies. Therefore, the fact that Homer has atypically strong moral qualms about bankruptcy is probably not good enough a basis for his dissatisfaction. He must judge Wendy's credit history purely on the basis of whether a person with her credit history presents a risk of default beyond a reasonably acceptable level.

However, even if we hold Homer to an objective standard, that does not automatically mean that we should apply the industry standard suggested by Wendy. Homer is not a member of the consumer financing establishment, but a simple homeowner who is selling his home on credit. A large and wealthy institution, which can distribute risks of default among many customers, is likely to be less risk-averse than a private seller. For this reason, the question is not what would constitute a reasonable credit report for the consumer credit industry, but what would be an acceptable report for a self-financing private seller. In other words, the answer suggested here is that an objective test be used, but the reasonable person evaluating the report should not be a professional lender, but a lender in Homer's position.

This issue came up in *Forman v. Benson,* 446 N.E.2d 535 (Ill. 1983), but it was resolved on a different basis from that suggested above. The self-financing seller rejected a credit report on the basis that it showed the buyer to be in shaky financial condition. The uncontroverted evidence of a loan officer was that his financial institution would regard the buyer's credit as excellent on the basis of that report. The trial court applied an objective standard and held that the seller had been unreasonable in rejecting the report. The appellate court agreed that if satisfaction was to be based on an objective standard, the seller's rejection of the report was not justified. It also recognized that the objective standard is to be preferred when matters of commercial quality are in issue. However, it found that a subjective standard was more appropriate in this case because it was likely intended by the parties, given the purpose of the condition, as interpreted in the context of the contract as a whole: The seller was concerned about giving credit to the buyer, so the condition was included to allay his concerns and to induce his agreement. It was reasonable to infer that he would not be held to commercial standards with which he was unfamiliar, but would have some degree of personal discretion in evaluating the report.

Even though the court used the subjective standard, the seller lost under that standard because there was evidence that he had tried to negotiate with the buyer for an increase in price before he rejected the report. This gave rise to the conclusion that he was not motivated by genuine concern over the buyer's credit, but used his claimed dissatisfaction as a pretext for rejecting the report after being unable to renegotiate the price.

Although the subjective test in *Forman* could give a different result from the more objective test that I have suggested, it is worthwhile to point out once again, that the line between reasonableness and good faith can be blurred. If the factfinder finds a judgment to be unreasonable, it will not readily be convinced that it is honest. Thus, in many cases, there may not be much difference between honest dissatisfaction and dissatisfaction reasonable to a person in the party's position.

3(a). Because Wendy cannot afford to buy Homer's property without first selling her existing home, she has sensibly made her obligation to Homer contingent on selling it. That is, to avert the risk of being committed to Homer without any prospect of raising the $50,000, Wendy has agreed with Homer that her obligation to purchase his property is subject to the express condition precedent that Wendy can sell her home in 30 days. Although this is not a fully promissory condition, in that Wendy does not absolutely commit to ensuring that the house will be sold, it is subject to the implied promise that Wendy will make a diligent effort to try to fulfill the condition. Diligence is not to be judged entirely subjectively, because Homer cannot be taken to have assumed the risk of idiosyncratic or irrational behavior.

Therefore, the test is whether Wendy made an honest and genuine effort, as may reasonably be expected from a person in her position. Wendy may have tried hard to sell her house, but that does not seem good enough. Quite apart from Wendy's unfortunate personality, she was apparently not an experienced dealer in real estate. Given the short time provided in the contract for the satisfaction of the condition, she should not have attempted to sell the house on her own. This conclusion is reinforced by the fact that the price to be realized to satisfy the condition took broker's commission into account, indicating that the parties' reasonable expectation was that a broker would be used.

If it is found that Wendy did not satisfy her implied obligation to use best efforts, this would be a ground for excusing the condition, so that the condition is deemed fulfilled. Homer can insist on her performance. If she fails to render it, she is in breach and Homer can sue for appropriate relief.

3(b). The condition is that Wendy must sell her house within 30 days of the date of her contract with Homer. Because the contract expressly requires the conditional event to occur within a stated time, exact compliance with the time period is required, and failure of occurrence within that time is non-fulfillment of the condition. However, the problem raised by this question centers on the meaning of the condition: What is meant by "sale"? The question serves as a reminder that even where a condition is express, it may be stated in ambiguous language that requires interpretation or construction. If the "sale" is accomplished upon execution of the sale agreement, the condition has been satisfied. But if the "sale" is regarded as suspended until the contingency of financing is met, it occurred beyond the 30-day period.

There is no evidence that the parties discussed or otherwise manifested what they intended by use of the word "sale," so there may be no factual basis for interpretation unless some pertinent and applicable market usage can be shown. In the absence of evidence of meaning, the court must construe the meaning of the term so as best to give effect to what the parties reasonably must have intended. Legally, when Wendy accepted the offer from her buyer, a complete and binding contract of sale was formed. Although that sale was itself subject to a condition precedent, it is an effective contract. A binding contract came into being upon execution, even though her buyer's duties of performance would not become due until the condition was satisfied. On this view, the sale did occur within the 30-day period. This means, of course, that Wendy took a risk by entering into a contingent sale of her existing house, because if her buyer cannot get financing, she is stuck. Possibly, this is a good ground for arguing that the parties must have intended that Wendy's house be unconditionally sold within the 30-day period. But even if that argument is persuasive, may Wendy not have waived the condition by entering into a contingent transaction? Alternatively, could it be argued that her obligation to make best efforts required her to reject this offer, and to spend the few remaining days in seeking a better offer?

3(c). Although Wendy could have abandoned this condition had it been solely for her benefit, the condition was not necessarily intended for her protection alone, and she therefore should not be able to waive it unilaterally. In addition to allowing her an escape if she cannot sell her house, the condition ensures that upon buying Homer's house, Wendy will have discharged the mortgage debt on her prior home. As the person financing Wendy's purchase of his house, Homer has an obvious stake in the level of her debt and may reasonably have taken this into account in agreeing to extend credit to her for the balance of the price. If she keeps her existing house and borrows money for the down payment, she increases her debt load, which may heighten the risk that she will default on her mortgage payments to Homer. (Although his mortgage in the property does secure his right to payment, foreclosure is inconvenient and costly, and there is always a danger that the proceeds of a foreclosure sale will not fully cover the balance of the mortgage.)

4. Like the conditions in Examples 2 and 3, the financing contingency is not fully a promissory condition, but the beneficiary party (Wendy) does commit to make best efforts to attempt its satisfaction. As long as she diligently applied for financing, she can escape the contract without liability for breach if she fails to obtain it. Unlike the previous example, Wendy's promise of due diligence is expressed in the contract and need not be construed. The sole question is whether her single discouraging interview with a mortgage broker was enough of an effort to qualify as due diligence.

In *Luttinger v. Rosen,* 316 A.2d 757 (Conn. 1972), the buyers of a home bought it subject to a similar financing contingency. They were told by their attorney (whose information was apparently reliable) that only one lending institution would accept an application for a home mortgage in the amount specified in the contract. They therefore applied only to that lender, which was willing to give them the loan, but at an interest rate higher than that specified as the maximum in the contract. They declined the loan on those terms and notified the seller of their withdrawal from the transaction on the basis that the condition had not been satisfied. They persisted in refusing to proceed with the purchase, even though the seller offered to compensate them by making up the difference between the interest rate specified in the contract and that to be charged by the lender.

The court held that the condition had not been satisfied, so the buyer could escape the contract without liability. It accepted as accurate the buyer's information that no other lender would consider a home mortgage of the amount required. This being so, the buyer had acted with due diligence in making the single application, and it was senseless to insist that the buyer go to the trouble of making pointless and futile further applications. Furthermore, as the express condition of obtaining a mortgage at the specified interest rate had not been exactly fulfilled, the buyer's obligation had not become due. The seller could not alter this result by offering to compensate for the higher rate, and the buyer was free to reject this offer. (In its holding on the latter point, the case serves as an example of the principle of strict compliance with an express condition, and of the harsh result that could ensue. If the seller's offer would have entirely eliminated the cost of the higher interest rate, the buyer is in no way prejudiced by the shortfall in compliance with the condition, and the continued refusal to proceed with the transaction appears to be based on a technicality.)

With regard to the issue of due diligence, the resolution of the case is justifiable if it really was unquestionably certain that further effort would have been futile. However, if there was a reasonable chance of success or even some uncertainty about the fate of an application to other lenders, the single application seems like a feeble effort, falling short of what the seller would be entitled to expect of a conscientious buyer.

In Wendy's case, the facts are ambiguous. If the broker's conclusion was well informed and accurate, and the lenders known to him represented the full range of the market, further efforts at obtaining financing may have been a futile waste of Wendy's time. If so, they should not be necessary for an exercise of due diligence. However, unless Wendy is sure about this, she takes the risk that her single interview with a broker falls short of what is required, and could lead to excuse of the condition. The question of whether a party exercised due diligence (or best efforts) in attempting to satisfy a condition is factual, to be decided under all the circumstances. The test has both objective and subjective elements and is concerned not only with what effort would be reasonable, but also with the genuineness and honesty of the effort. For this reason, we should not forget that Wendy lost the incentive to pursue financing when she realized that the house was too expensive for her. She developed an ulterior motive for avoiding a burdensome transaction. This suggests that her lack of further effort was not solely motivated by a conviction that it would be unavailing, but that her claim of futility may be a pretext for escaping a contract that she no longer desired.

It may be helpful to conclude this discussion of the test for due diligence by considering another case that is the opposite of *Luttinger* in both its facts and result. *Fry v. George Elkins Co.*, 327 P.2d 905 (Cal. 1958), also involved the purchase of a home subject to a financing contingency. The buyer was told by the seller that the holder of the existing mortgage on the property would be likely to approve the financing sought by the buyer, but that other lenders would be unlikely to do so. (That is, the buyer was told that the best chance of getting the mortgage was to apply to the seller's mortgagee.) Despite this, the buyer did not apply to the existing mortgagee, but made applications to two other lenders, both of whom refused to lend him the funds. The buyer terminated the contract on the grounds of non-fulfillment of the condition of financing and sued for return of his deposit. At the trial, the existing mortgagee testified that it would have approved the loan had it been applied for. The buyer claimed that he had declined to apply for that loan because it would have been subject to a prepayment penalty. The court found that the buyer's two applications did not constitute a diligent effort in light of his failure to seek financing from the source that he was told would be the most likely prospect. His excuse concerning the prepayment penalty did not avail him, because the financing condition did not include the absence of such a penalty as one of the requirements for a qualifying loan. The court's conclusion was bolstered by evidence that the buyer had lost interest in proceeding with the sale and was looking for a means to escape it.

5. The contract expressly makes payment conditional upon the *architect's certification* of proper completion of PC's performance. It necessarily follows from this express condition that the proper performance itself is also a condition precedent to payment. Although the architect has not given the certificate, it is clear that the condition of proper completion of the work has been satisfied. Primo does not contend otherwise. The certification is a condition of satisfaction under which the performance must meet a standard of competence to be evaluated by a third-party expert. Although the architect

was employed by the owner of the property and is its agent, her role in this contract between Primo and PC is to act on behalf of Primo.

Obviously, Primo cannot evade fulfillment of the condition simply because the architect is no longer available to inspect the work. Although it is not Primo's fault that the architect resigned, its implied duty to cooperate in the fulfillment of the condition requires it to ensure that inspection takes place within a reasonable time of completion of PC's performance. Its failure to facilitate occurrence of the condition is a wrongful hindrance of fulfillment which excuses the condition. (Alternatively, excuse could also be based on the argument that Primo waived the condition by declining to have the work inspected within a reasonable time. Another alternative is to argue excuse on grounds of unfair forfeiture because PC would surely be grievously harmed if the technicality of non-certification could be allowed to deny payment for satisfactory work. However, forfeiture is a discretionary doctrine that is not needed if there are more concrete bases for excuse.)

Primo argues that its receipt of the *owner's payment* for the air conditioning is a condition precedent to its obligation to pay PC. If this is so, Primo would be justified in not paying, because it has not been (and will not be) paid for the air conditioning. The parties' intent on this matter is a question of interpretation. If there is extrinsic evidence that casts light on the meaning of the clause (such as evidence of trade usage or of discussions between the parties), this would help to determine the intent of the language. If no such evidence is available, the reasonable meaning of the wording of the contract must be sought in light of the purpose of the contract as a whole. As we are told of no usage or other contextual evidence, our interpretation will be based solely on the language used in the contract.

At first sight, the language seems relatively clear. Payment from the owner does sound like an express condition precedent. It follows the condition of certification in the same sentence. This suggests that both of these events must occur before Primo's payment obligation falls due. However, courts interpreting payment provisions like this one tend to be skeptical of the argument that they are intended to be conditions. Unless the language (read in light of any contextual evidence that might be available) makes it very clear that the owner's payment was intended as a condition precedent, the assumption is that a term like this is more likely to have been intended as merely fixing a time for payment. Therefore, even if the owner does not pay the contractor, the contractor must pay the subcontractor within a reasonable time. The reasoning behind this interpretation is that, unless the parties express such an intention unequivocally, they cannot be taken to have placed the risk of the owner's non-payment on the subcontractor, who has no contractual relationship with the owner but is employed by the prime contractor. Risk is more rationally left with the prime contractor, who has dealt with the owner and had the opportunity to evaluate its creditworthiness.

Such a conclusion was reached in *Thos. J. Dyer Co. v. Bishop International Engineering Co.*, 303 F.2d 655 (6th Cir. 1962), despite contractual language that suggested that the owner's payment was a condition. (The term in question stated that no part of the price to be paid to the subcontractor ". . . shall be due until five (5) days after Owner shall have paid Contractor therefor . . .") Similarly, in *Peacock Construction Co., Inc. v. Modern Air Conditioning, Inc.*, 353 So. 2d 840 (Fla. 1977), the court interpreted a provision as setting a time for payment, and not as a condition where the contract stated that final payment would be made to the subcontractor ". . . within 30 days after the completion of the work included in this subcontract, written acceptance by the Architect, and full payment therefor by the Owner." Although the language in these contracts, like the wording of the contract between Primo and PC, does admit of interpretation as a condition, the courts felt that the language was not strong enough to remove all doubt, and to overturn the usual assumption that the contractor bears the risk of the owner's default.

In *Peacock Construction*, the court made much of the fact that subcontractors are typically small businesses that would be driven into insolvency if forced to bear the risk of owner default. This is not necessarily true. It is quite possible (as in PC's case) that the subcontractor could be larger, richer, and more capable of bearing loss than the contractor. However, the relative wealth of the parties is not the issue. The interpretation is based on the reasonable meaning of the language used by the parties, in light of their relationship with each other and to the owner.

6. Two express conditions precedent are implicated in this dispute. The first is that a loss must occur of a kind covered by the policy. The second is that the insured must follow the prescribed claim procedure.

Has there been fulfillment of the condition precedent that a covered loss occurred? The policy covers loss by vandalism, which it defines as wilful and malicious damage to the premises. However, it specifically excludes coverage for pilferage, theft or burglary, and flooding too. Therefore, the first issue is one of interpreting the language of the policy to determine if the losses are encompassed within the risk that is insured. Because this is a standard form insurance policy drafted by the insurer, the contra proferentum rule is particularly applicable. Any doubt in the meaning of a provision in it will be resolved against the insurer.

There are three separate items of loss caused by the removal of the pipe: The loss of the pipe itself, the damage caused to walls and floors in removing it, and the ensuing flood damage. Does this loss result from vandalism? Vandalism is commonly thought of as the deliberate harming or defacement of property, purely for its own sake. However, the concept is broad enough to include purposeful damage motivated by economic gain. It is beyond doubt that the thief acted wilfully (deliberately) and maliciously (with intent to violate the law and Larson's rights) in causing the loss. This applies not only to the taking of the pipe, but also to the concomitant destruction. The problem is that the policy draws a distinction between loss from vandalism and that from theft or flood, so when a wrongful act gives rise to injury of all three kinds, the apparent conflict in terms must be reconciled.

In *United States Fidelity & Guaranty Co. v. Bimco Iron & Metal Corp.*, 464 S.W.2d 353 (Tex. 1971), an insurance policy similarly distinguished vandalism, which it covered, from theft, which it excluded. Burglars entered the insured premises and stole electrical transformers and wiring, causing damage to the building. The court interpreted the policy to include any wilful and malicious damage to the building (extending not only to damage to the structure itself, but also to the value of the stolen wire), even if caused by burglars. It held that the exclusion for burglary applied only to unaffixed personal property removed from the premises. This conclusion was made easier because the clause in the policy covering vandalism specifically included damage to the building by burglars, even though another clause excluded loss by theft. Larson's policy does not have a similar provision, making it somewhat more ambiguous. However, if we understand "vandalism" to be broad enough to include wilful and malicious damage to the premises, for whatever motive, this is a fair interpretation of the policy, and the more specific language is not needed to reach the same result. A concurring opinion in *Bimco* felt that the majority was too generous in finding that the vandalism coverage included the value of the stolen wire and considered that once property was removed, even if it had been part of the building, the loss is more correctly characterized as theft. On this view, only the cost of fixing the damage to the building should be recoverable, and not the value of the electrical components (or, in our case, the copper pipe) that was taken from it. It is hard to decide which is the better view. Once a building has been vandalized, the insurer should compensate for the damage even if incorporated materials have been taken away. On the other hand, removal is more in the nature of theft than vandalism.

Bimco thus leads to the conclusion that the policy covers the damage to the floors and walls caused by the pipe removal, and it suggests that the value of the pipe is covered too. There was no issue of flood damage in that case, so the decision is not helpful in resolving this issue. A fair argument can be made that the exclusion of flood damage is not intended to cover this situation. The exclusionary provision refers to flooding in the context of a series of other causes of loss, all of which are related to natural disasters. Under the *noscitur a sociis* rule, the meaning of an ambiguous word is ascertained by words associated with it (*see* section 10.7), and "flooding" should be restricted to floods caused by nature, rather than by vandalism. This interpretation best gives effect to full protection from vandalism where water damage results from a wilful and malicious act.

Has the insured followed the prescribed claim procedure? Even if the loss is covered by the policy, satisfying the first condition precedent, E. & F. is still not obliged to indemnify Larson for the loss unless the second condition—

notice within seven days of loss and proof of loss 14 days thereafter—is also fulfilled. Because the condition is express, strict compliance is required. Larson's late notice failed to satisfy the condition exactly. This would preclude recovery under the policy unless there is a basis for excusing strict compliance.

Larson may succeed in arguing that E. & F. tacitly waived the requirement that notice must be given within seven days of the loss. The facts do not state if Larson told E. & F. or its adjuster when the theft occurred, or if this became apparent during the investigation. If the insurer or its agent realized or should have known that the loss was more than a week old, its action in accepting and investigating the claim and then rejecting it on other grounds could constitute a waiver of the delay. A waiver does not have to be by express words. It can be inferred from conduct if the party knows or has reason to know of non-compliance with a condition and yet acts as if the condition is satisfied. (Such conduct could also give rise to an estoppel, but waiver is a better theory because Larson has taken no detrimental action in reliance on the representation.) A waiver of rights without consideration is effective provided that the condition is ancillary and technical, rather than a material component of the exchange. Although prompt notice is important to an insurer, who needs the opportunity to investigate a claim while it is fresh, a relatively short delay in notice is likely to be interpreted as a waivable ancillary matter.

The policy states that the insurer does not waive rights under the policy by investigating a claim. Non-waiver clauses (or non-waiver agreements made after the loss has occurred) provide only limited protection to the insurer. They prevent an inference of waiver merely from the insurer's action in investigating or processing the claim, but they do not annul words or actions that more forcefully point to waiver. For example, in *Connecticut Fire Insurance Co. v. Fox*, 361 F.2d 1 (10th Cir. 1966), a fire damaged the aptly-named Firebird Motor Hotel. The insurer's agent had the insured sign a non-waiver agreement prior to investigating the loss, which stated that investigation would not constitute a waiver of any conditions of the policy, and also that no company representative had authority to waive conditions orally. Despite this clause, the court found that an adjuster had in fact waived timely proof of loss through an ongoing course of interaction with the insured and by settling a claim made by a motel guest. E. & F.'s actions do not as strongly point to waiver, but they did go beyond the narrow range of investigation covered by the non-waiver clause. Neither the adjuster nor the person who processed the claim raised the issue of delay, and the claim was rejected solely on the grounds that the loss was not covered by the policy.

In *Bimco*, the insured had also filed its proof of loss late, so the issue of waiver came up in that case as well. Although the court found that the insurer had waived the condition of timely proof of loss, the case has stronger facts than are present in Larson's claim. In *Bimco*, the insurer had conceded some liability for loss. While it rejected the claim for the stolen electrical equipment, it did accept a claim for damage to a door caused by the burglars. The court said that had the insurer completely denied liability on any grounds, even if it failed to mention the delay, this would not have constituted a waiver. But the fact that it accepted some liability must be taken as a waiver of the tardiness of the proof. Because the insurer had not merely investigated the claim but had sought to settle it by agreeing to pay for the door, the court found that it could not claim protection under a non-waiver agreement which stipulated that investigation of the claim would not operate as a waiver. In our case, E. & F. made no concession of liability at all. On the basis of *Bimco,* the mere fact that it denied liability on grounds other than a delay in notice, is not in itself sufficient as a waiver. However, it could be argued that the approach in *Bimco* is too restrictive, and that a failure to raise or rely on the issue of late notice in denying the claim should be enough to constitute a waiver. This argument is particularly attractive when there has been substantial compliance with the condition, the delay has caused no apparent harm to the insurer, and refusal of payment seems to be based on nothing more than a technicality.

7. The delivery of the notice by November 30, 2000, is an express condition precedent to Sue's obligation to sell the land to Sprawling Malls. It is not a promissory condition—Sprawling Malls has no commitment to ensure that it is satisfied. The purpose of the condition is to give it the discretion to send the notice if it wishes to exercise its option and purchase the land, but imposes no obligation on it to do so if it decides to allow the option to lapse.

Sprawling Malls did decide to exercise its option, but its notice of intent arrived a day late. Because the delivery of notice by November 30 is an express condition, it must be complied with strictly. If Sprawling Malls wanted the land, it had to deliver its notice to Sue within the time stated. Although the notice was mailed before November 30, the contract specified delivery— that is, receipt—by that date, and delivery occurred a day after the deadline. Although a day's delay may be a small deviation from the terms of the condition, this is not taken into account under the rule that requires strict compliance with express conditions. The rationale is that once the parties have taken the trouble to articulate and define the condition, the court should not tamper with their expressed intention. Of course, if the language used to describe the condition is unclear, the court may have some flexibility in interpreting what the condition required, but the language of this condition concerning the manner and time of exercising the option is unambiguous and provides no basis for an interpretation favorable to Sprawling Malls. Therefore, unless there is some ground for excusing exact compliance with the condition, the day's delay in delivery results in non-fulfillment of the condition, and Sprawling Malls has lost its right to buy the land.

The only possible ground for excuse presented by these facts is forfeiture. Courts have the discretion to excuse exact compliance with a condition (or to excuse the condition altogether, if appropriate) when strict enforcement of the condition would result in a disproportionate and unfair forfeiture by one of the parties and a windfall gain by the other. The policy of preventing unfair forfeiture acts as a counterweight to the rule of strict compliance, allowing courts some flexibility in averting particularly harsh and unfair results where there has been a minor or technical non-compliance with a condition. This does not mean, of course, that courts routinely excuse express conditions on the basis of forfeiture. To do so would eliminate the rule of strict compliance. For forfeiture to apply as a ground for excuse, the strict enforcement of the condition must result in undue hardship to the party seeking excuse and inappropriately extensive gain to the beneficiary of the condition. The balance of hardship against unfair gain must be evaluated in light of the relationship of the condition to the exchange as a whole.

In this case, the short delay in delivery of the notice certainly results in considerable hardship to Sprawling Malls: It loses its right to buy the land, gets no benefit from the $10,000 that it paid for the option, and no chance to recoup its substantial expense in conducting the study, or to enjoy the fruits of its efforts in securing financing for the project. True, it bought an option for a year, not a year and a day, so the effect of excusing exact compliance would be to give it a longer option than it purchased. Sprawling Malls was at fault in entrusting such an important communication to the vagaries of the mails, but this was not an egregious sin. It is more the result of poor judgment than of some deliberate attempt to prolong the option period for the purpose of speculating for an additional time at Sue's expense. Looking at the delay from Sue's perspective, we must recognize that she bargained on being bound to the option until no later than November 30. The exact duration of an option is generally regarded as material, and a day's extension should not be assumed to be a trivial matter. However, the equities do not strongly favor strict compliance: She received a substantial payment for the option; the price of the land itself is apparently fair, based on its market value at the time of contracting; she has not yet taken any action in reliance on the lapse; and her motivation in refusing to accept the notice is that she can do better reselling the land. There may be enough here to tilt the balance in favor of excusing the failure of exact compliance with the condition.

This was the conclusion reached on similar facts in *Holiday Inns of America v. Knight*, 450 P.2d 42 (Cal. 1969). Holiday Inns had purchased an option to buy land. The initial period of the option was one year, but it could be extended annually for a further four years. To extend it, Holiday Inns had to pay a renewal fee of $10,000 per year, to be made by July 1 of each year. Holiday Inns had renewed the option for two years and had developed adjacent land over this period, thereby increasing the value of the property subject to the option. It intended to renew the option for a third time, and mailed its check for the renewal fee just before due date. However, the grantor did not receive it until July 2 and refused to extend the option. Holiday Inns successfully sued for a declaratory judgment that the option had been validly extended. The court excused the failure of strict compliance on the ground that it would be an unfair forfeiture for Holiday Inns to lose its option because of a short delay. The court based this conclusion on the fact that the delay did not have a material impact on the exchange, Holiday Inns had not been attempting to take advantage of the grantor by extending the option beyond the period purchased, and it would be unfair to make it sacrifice the $30,000 in option fees that it had already spent for the first three years of the option. (Although the development on the adjacent land could be seen as further justification for excusing the condition, giving Holiday Inns a stronger case on the equities than Sprawling Malls, the court did not base its determination on this fact.)

17

Breach and Repudiation

§17.1 The Scope of this Chapter: Non-Fulfillment of a Promise

The distinction was drawn in Chapter 16 between the non-fulfillment of a condition, which excuses the conditional performance, and the failure to honor a promise, which results in liability for breach of contract. If a term is a promissory condition—that is, one of the parties undertook that it would be satisfied—its non-fulfillment has the combined effect of entitling the other party both to withhold performance and to seek a remedy for breach. Chapter 16 concentrated on the effect of conditions and their non-fulfillment. This chapter considers the impact and consequences of the breach of a promise. Because promises are so often conditions as well (promissory conditions), a failure to perform often constitutes both a breach of the promise and non-fulfillment of a condition. Therefore, while we can make this distinction for the purpose of analysis, it is important to understand that in many cases a single default in performance raises the question of both breach and non-fulfillment.

An example will help to frame the issues and make the discussion less abstract: Violet Ultra decided to add a deck to the back of her home so that she could enjoy her favorite leisure activity—sunbathing. On July 1, Violet entered into a contract with Woody Sawyer, a carpenter, under which Woody undertook to build a 20′ × 15′ deck onto Violet's home for $5,000. The contract, written on a sheet of paper and signed by the parties, states that Violet will make an initial cash payment of $2,000 to Woody by 5 P.M. on July 6. Woody will begin work on July 7 and will complete the deck by July 9, upon which Violet will pay him the balance of $3,000 in cash. Although no express language of condition has been used, it is easily inferable from the sequence set out in the contract that the parties intend Violet's down payment on July 6 to be a promissory condition precedent—the payment is not only expressly promised, but is also impliedly a condition precedent to Woody's performance. Woody expressly promises to begin the work one day later on July 7 and to complete it within three days, by July 9. The fact that final payment is to be made on completion gives rise to the inference that Woody's performance is not merely a promise, but also an implied condition precedent to Violet's final performance, the $3,000 payment. As there is no further performance contingent on this payment, it is a pure promise.

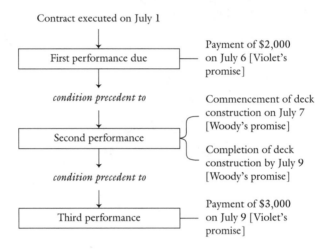

If both parties perform as undertaken, the promises are honored, the conditions fulfilled, and the transaction ends happily. As Restatement Second §235(1) says (maybe somewhat self-evidently), a contractual duty is discharged by full performance. However, all kinds of things could go wrong: At some point before performance is to commence on July 6, one of the parties may renege or indicate an intention to breach the contract; or Violet may not make the down payment at all, or in full, or on time; or Woody may not show up for work on July 7, or may not complete the deck by July 9; or Woody may begin and complete the deck on time, but may make it one foot too short. The purpose of this chapter is to discuss the legal effect of breaches like this relating both to pure promises and to promissory conditions. Sections 17.2–17.6 deal with breach proper (that is, a violation of a promise that occurs at or after performance is due) and section 17.7 examines the particular issues that arise when a party repudiates the contract in advance of the time of his performance. The importance and extent of the breach is a crucial factor throughout this chapter, so we begin by differentiating breaches of different degrees of gravity.

§17.2   The Nature of Breach

As intimated above, a party breaches a contract by failing, for whatever reason, to honor a promise of performance when that performance falls due. Therefore, to establish that a breach of contract has occurred, one needs to ask four questions:

1. **Was a promise made, and if so, what was promised?**

    That is, what was the exact nature and extent of the performance that was undertaken? This is, of course, a matter of determining the existence and content of the contractual undertaking through the process of interpretation discussed in Chapter 10.

2. **When was the promised performance due?**

    It stands to reason that until a performance falls due, the promisor has no duty to render it, so failure to perform cannot be a breach.[1] It is therefore crucial to ascertain the due date of the performance, which may be clearly stated or, if not, must be established by interpretation in context or construction. In the absence of a specified date, performance is due within a reasonable time, as determined under all the circumstances of the contract. Furthermore, as discussed already, if the promise is subject to a condition, its performance is only due upon satisfaction of the condition.

3. **Was the performance in compliance with the promise?**

    Once the promise is identified and its meaning and due date established, it must be decided if the performance was rendered in accordance with the promise. Any shortfall from the promised performance is a breach. Sometimes, breach is clear because the promisee has not performed at all or has done so in a glaringly inadequate manner. In other cases, the matter is not that simple, either because the exact scope and extent of the promise is unclear, making it difficult to be sure that a performance is in compliance with the contract, or because there is some disagreement on the quality and sufficiency of what was performed.

---

1. As mentioned in section 17.1, this statement is subject to the significant qualification that a party might repudiate a contractual obligation before it falls due. If a party commits an anticipatory repudiation by making it clear before the time for performance that she will not honor her promise when the date to do so arrives, the promisee does have the right to take action immediately in response to the repudiation and is not required to wait until the due date. This issue is discussed in section 17.7. Because a repudiation is an advance indication of breach and an exception to the general rule that a breach can only occur when performance is due, it is subject to special rules designed to protect the promisee from precipitate action by the promisor.

stantial performance is nevertheless a breach, because it does fall short of what was promised, so the promisee is not without remedy. However, the promisee is obliged to stick to the contract and perform his side of the bargain, but is entitled to a *monetary adjustment* to compensate for the deficiency in the performance received from the breacher. This measure of damages is usually based on the cost of rectifying the deficiency, or possibly on the actual loss in the value of the performance, as discussed in section 17.3.3. Such damages could be substantially less than what would be awarded for a total and material breach.

The words **"total" and "partial" breach** could be just another way of describing a material breach and a trivial one that results in substantial performance. That is, when a party has substantially performed, the deficiency in performance is said to be a partial breach. However, the reference to total and partial breach is also used to identify a somewhat different but allied issue: A breach is called partial when, even if it may become material in time, it is not yet important enough to so qualify, because there is a possibility of **cure.** That is, the deficiency may be rectified to prevent it from reaching the level of total and material breach. Thus, a partial breach could be one that is potentially serious enough to give rise to a right of termination, but that may be averted if the breacher remedies it in time. This is why the diagram shows that when a breach is partial, there is not yet a right to termination. The victim's recourse is to suspend his own performance while waiting to see if the breach will be cured. If it is, the breach is over (or, at worst, it is a trivial one, resulting in substantial performance) and the only remedy the victim has is to recover any loss that may have been occasioned by the delay in proper performance. However, if the potentially serious partial breach is not cured, it becomes a total, and because it is now material, it gives rise to all the rights and remedies available for such a breach. The concepts of partial breach and cure are discussed more fully in section 17.3.4.

Before leaving this topic, it may be helpful to make one more observation on the slippery semantics of the phrase "partial breach": It is also sometimes used to describe the situation mentioned earlier, in which a *material breach has occurred,* but the victim has elected not to terminate and to give the breacher a chance to remedy it. When that happens, it is often said that the *victim has treated the breach as partial.* In this sense, the breach may have been interpreted as total rather than partial, based on the manifested intent of the parties at the time of contracting, but the victim has decided to treat it as partial. He may therefore have committed himself to proceed as if it were partial, and will be entitled to termination only if there is no subsequent cure.

§17.3.2   What Makes a Breach Material?

The gravity and extent of a breach is a matter of interpretation that can only be resolved by examining the language of the contract in context and evalu-

ages simply involves money changing hands, and Violet could invest her damages award or spend it more productively. The real point is unfair forfeiture. When cost of rectification is not used, damages are based on loss in value. It may be that Violet can establish that a deck of 19'8" × 14'7" has a market value less than a deck of the size promised. If so, that is her loss. More likely than not, there is no difference in value, which would mean she is entitled to no damages at all.

§17.3.5   *Partial Breach and Cure*

Some breaches have such an immediate, irreparable, and significant impact on the promisee's rights that they are material as soon as they occur, and there is nothing that the promisor can do to rectify them. Other breaches are by nature so trivial that they could never result in a total breach of the contract, even if no attempt was made to remedy them. However, between these poles, there are breaches that are *potentially material* when they occur, but at that stage they are still regarded as partial because they are not yet serious enough to be total. The breacher can prevent such a breach from becoming total by *curing the deficiency* within a reasonable time.

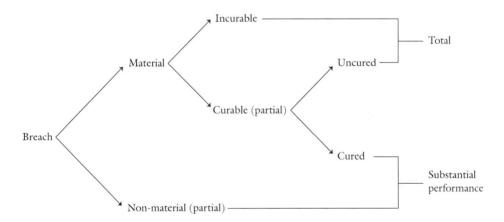

For example, say that the contract for the deck specified that the down payment of $2,000 was to be paid no later than 5 P.M. on July 6. Violet failed to pay by that time. If Woody called shortly afterwards to ask where the payment was, and Violet told him that she no longer wanted the deck and would not pay, the breach would be material and total. Non-performance is absolute and Violet indicates no intent to cure it. However, if Violet's response was that she was running late and would deliver the cash to Woody as soon as she could get out to his place, the issue is more difficult. Failure to pay on time is a breach, but unless payment by precisely 5 P.M. is a material term of the contract (or, to use the well-worn phrase, "time is of the essence"), a short delay in payment may be only a trivial breach. If so, Violet's failure to pay by 5 P.M. is a partial breach, and as there is a prospect of cure, it will only become total once a reasonable time has passed and she has still not paid.

Therefore, if Woody refuses to wait and terminates immediately, he must be able to show that the exact time for payment was such a material term of the contract that even a short delay in payment is a total breach. It cannot be cured because the clock cannot be turned back to eliminate the delay. However, if payment exactly on time was not a material term, Woody must give Violet the opportunity to cure by showing up with the money within a reasonable time. To decide materiality, the contract's language must be interpreted in context. The basic inquiry is whether a delay in payment would have a significant negative impact on Woody's reasonable contractual expectations by seriously affecting the transaction's value to him. Here again, the question of whether the delay is willful or caused by circumstances beyond the promisor's control is not directly relevant to the inquiry into the totality of the breach, but the promisor's state of mind has some bearing on the issue. If the breach was not deliberate, this may signal a greater likelihood of a genuine desire to cure it and could persuade a court in a close case to treat the breach as partial.

On the facts given in the present example, it seems unlikely that payment by exactly 5 P.M was "of the essence," so Woody probably must afford Violet an opportunity to cure. If he does so, and Violet does attempt a cure, the next difficult question may be whether Violet's cure was *complete* and accomplished within a *reasonable time*. This, again, must be decided with reference to Woody's reasonable expectations under the contract. A few hours' delay may be a trivial breach. But if Violet is a day late, or she shows up a couple of hours later with a check instead of cash, the impact of the delay is more serious. A promisor who waits too long to cure, or whose performance is still not substantially compliant, loses the right to cure. The partial breach thereupon becomes total. It must be reiterated that the promisor does not invariably have the right to cure a breach. Some breaches are fundamental enough that they cannot be fixed at all, or even if they could be reversed, given time, the delay in performance would itself be a material breach.

§17.4   The Relationship Between the Materiality of Breach and the Non-Fulfillment of a Condition

The above discussion has intimated how the analysis of conditions, set out in Chapter 16, ties into the issue of breach of promise. Students often struggle with this relationship, so it may be helpful to set out the basic principles in point form.

breached one part to isolate the breach and confine it to the affected part, so that the remainder of the contract is not sullied by the breach. This will enable him to treat the unaffected portion of the contract as if no breach had occurred and to enforce rights that have accrued in that portion. That is, if a contract is divisible, a material breach relating to only part of it is confined to that part, and the breacher can enforce the remainder without being subject to the general rule precluding action on the contract by the party who has materially breached it.

Sadly, the contract between Violet and Woody, no doubt a source of such intense fascination up to now, cannot be used to illustrate the concept of divisibility. The parties contemplate an exchange of two single, unitary performances—a deck for $5,000. Would the contract be divisible if it broke up performance into sequential stages (similar to the construction contracts discussed in section 16.8.4) and allocated payment of a specified portion of the price to each stage of work? That is:

Violet pays $1,000, and Woody then delivers the lumber
↓
Violet pays a further $1,000, and Woody then builds the supports
↓
Violet pays another $2,000, and Woody then lays the decking
↓
Violet pays the final $1,000, and Woody then completes the deck by installing the railing

We now have a series of matched sequential performances, in which the parties have broken down the price into installments, each of which is identified with a specific stage of the construction. However, this alone will not make the contract divisible unless the parties intended to enter into a group of four self-contained discrete exchanges. In seeking their true intention, we must ask if the contract manifests a reasonable expectation that each of the sequential exchanges could be treated as a complete performance of an independently valuable transaction. To answer yes, we would at least have to be satisfied that the payment provided for each piece of the construction was exactly equivalent to its proportional value under the contract, and we would have to be sure that if Woody ceased work after completing any one component, Violet would receive the full value contemplated by the contract for that component. If this is not so, the likely purpose of breaking performance into stages was simply to alternate the risk of credit between the parties.

A better argument for divisibility could be made if Violet was a home builder who had erected four new houses in a subdivision. She entered into a contract with Woody under which he agreed to build a deck onto each of the houses for $5,000 apiece. After completing two of them, he materially breached by abandoning the job. Because each of the four components of the contract are distinct, the payment provided is exactly equivalent to the contractual value of the performance, and the breach affects only the two uncompleted decks, in no way detracting from the value of the finished ones, this contract can be interpreted as divisible. Of course, this does not affect Violet's right to claim damages from Woody for losses resulting from his failure to build the two decks, but it does affect his ability to recover for the work that he has done. If Violet has not paid him for the completed decks, he can sue her on the contract for payment of the contract price. He is not simply relegated to a restitutionary claim for the work done, which would, at best, require him to prove the less certain (and possibly lower) value of the benefit. In those jurisdictions which deny restitutionary relief to a breacher, a finding of divisibility is even more important, because a claim on the contract may be the only basis of recovery.

§17.7   Anticipatory Repudiation

§17.7.1   *The Distinction Between Breach and Repudiation*

It was stated in section 17.2 that a breach, properly speaking, can only occur when the promised performance falls due. However, it is possible for a party to breach in advance of performance—to repudiate her obligation in anticipation—if, before the time for performance, she **makes it clear by words or actions** that she **will breach when performance falls due.** A repudiation may occur between the time that the contract is made and the time due for its performance—that is, one of the parties repudiates before either party has begun performance under the contract. It may also occur after performance under the contract has begun, but before the due date of the repudiated performance.

To illustrate, recall that in the contract between Violet Ultra and Woody Sawyer, executed on July 1, Violet did not have to make her down payment of $2,000 before July 6, Woody did not have to begin work until July 7, and Violet did not have to pay the last installment of $3,000 until the deck was complete on July 9. It stands to reason that Violet cannot be in breach for not paying until July 6, and Woody cannot be in breach by failing to perform before July 7. However, if the conduct of a party goes beyond mere passive waiting for the due date, and he manifests the intent in advance that he will not perform when that date arrives, he repudiates the contract. For example, Woody would be guilty of repudiation if, on July 2, he tells Violet that he no longer intends to build the deck for her and will not show up to begin work July 7. In this case, Woody has repudiated in the period before performance was due by either party.

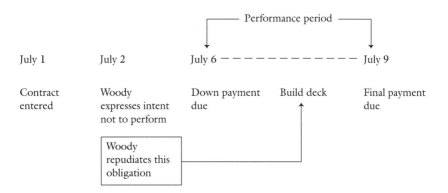

However, say that Woody did not repudiate, Violet paid the deposit on July 6, and Woody began work on July 7. On the evening of July 7, Violet confesses to Woody that she is broke and cannot find the $3,000 that she is supposed to pay upon completion of the deck. Although the performance of the contract is already underway, Violet's statement is still a repudiation, not a breach, because she made it before her payment was due.

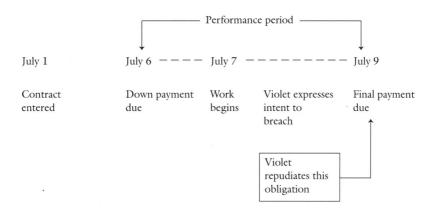

§17.7.2 *The Purpose and Value of the Doctrine of Anticipatory Repudiation*

Older common law did not recognize the concept of anticipatory repudiation, so the promisee had no right to react to such an advance indication of breach. He had to wait until the time of performance to see if breach would in fact occur. In the interim, he had to hold himself available to tender his return performance when it fell due. Under this rule, if Violet told Woody on July 2 that she no longer wished him to build the deck, he could not have responded to Violet's statement of intent on July 2, but would have been required to wait until July 6 to see if Violet would in fact not make the down payment. To hold himself available to do the work on July 7 in the event that Violet repents, Woody would be obliged to refuse any other offers of work for the period of July 7–July 9, thereby losing any opportunity to mitigate his loss. Under the old approach, the situation would be even worse if the victim of the repudiation had to perform first, because the law did not allow him to suspend his performance while waiting to see if the other party carried through with the threatened breach. So, if it had been Woody who repudiated on July 2 by telling Violet that he would not show up on July 7 to begin work, Violet would not have been allowed to react to this by withholding the payment of $2,000 due on July 6. On the facts of these examples, the victim of the repudiation only had to wait a few days to know if a breach would occur, but the harm could be even worse if the period before the due date of performance had been longer.

During the nineteenth century, courts came to recognize that this approach was both unfair to the promisee and inefficient. The English case of *Hoechster v. De La Tour*, 118 Eng. Rep. 922 (Q.B. 1853), is generally regarded as the preeminent judicial pronouncement that when one of the parties clearly repudiates a material promise in advance, the other may treat this as a breach immediately and may seek relief for breach without delay. The doctrine of anticipatory repudiation is now well established in common law and under the UCC. Although the UCC does not define what constitutes a repudiation (thus leaving this issue to the common law, even in sales of goods), it does codify and make some refinements to the doctrine in UCC §§2.609–2.612. As in other areas, the changes brought about by the UCC have been influential in developing common law rules, and their spirit is reflected in the treatment of repudiation in Restatement Second §§243 and 250–257.

The basic approach is that a *clear, unequivocal, and voluntary repudiation* by one of the parties is recognized as the equivalent of a material and total breach, provided that the threatened action or failure to act *would be a material and total breach* if it happened at the time due for performance. As the non-breaching party's promise of performance is dependent on the repudiator's promised performance (whether expressly or impliedly), the advance indication of prospective breach also amounts to an *advance failure of the condition*. This is so, whether or not the repudiated performance would, in the normal course, have been due before and thus a condition precedent to, the return performance.

For example, Woody's promise to build the deck is a dependent promise—a construed condition of Violet's performance. But because it is required to be performed only after Violet has paid the $2,000 deposit, it is not a condition precedent to Violet's payment of the deposit. In fact, the opposite is true: The payment is a condition precedent to the work. However, if Woody repudiates the contract on July 2, it would be absurd to argue that Violet is nevertheless compelled to pay on July 6, because the contract does not make her payment conditional on Woody performing first. It must necessarily be implicit in the contract that Violet's obligation to render the first performance is contingent on Woody not repudiating before her performance falls due. In other words, a repudiation has the effect of accelerating the due date of the breacher's promissory condition for the purpose of allowing the victim of the repudiation to withhold any return performance that would otherwise have been due first.

§17.7.3 *The Response to a Repudiation*

When a repudiation has occurred, the other party has a choice between two alternatives. Her one option is to *accept the repudiation* by *treating it as an immediate breach.* This entitles her to refuse to render her own performance, to terminate the contract, and to sue for relief for total breach. Her other alternative is to *delay responding* to the repudiation to see if the repudiating party repents. She may even take affirmative steps to encourage retraction of the repudiation by notifying the promisor that he has a specified time to recant, failing which the repudiation will be accepted. If she does this, she *may change her mind at any time before retraction* and accept the repudiation.

Whichever choice the victim of an apparent repudiation makes, she incurs some risk. If she responds by terminating, she takes the chance that the other party will deny that he repudiated, and declare her termination to be a breach. The more equivocal or unclear the alleged repudiation, the greater this risk becomes. If her response is to delay accepting the repudiation, she runs the risk of a court ultimately finding that she aggravated her damages by not terminating immediately and taking action to mitigate her loss. The clearer and firmer the repudiation, the greater this risk becomes. This point will become more apparent as the nature of repudiation is discussed more fully in section 17.7.5.

§17.7.4 *The Elements of Repudiation*

As stated already, for a prospective non-performance to constitute a material and total repudiation of the contract, the promisor must clearly, unequivocally, and voluntarily communicate an intention not to render the promised performance when it falls due. This intention could be communicated by words or conduct. This definition indicates that words or conduct must satisfy a number of prerequisites to qualify as a repudiation:

a. The Prospective Action or Inaction Indicated by the Promisor Must Be Serious Enough to Qualify as a Material and Total Breach of the Contract

An advance repudiation cannot itself give rise to a right of termination, withholding of performance, and damages unless the threatened deviation from what was promised would constitute a material and total breach if it occurred at the time performance falls due. It is obviously a material repudiation if the promisor manifests the intent by words or conduct of not performing at all, but it would also constitute a material repudiation if the promisor communicates the intent to render a substantially deficient performance, or to refuse performance unless the promisee agrees to do or pay more than the contract requires. But an indication of intent to deviate in some minor way from the promised performance, while it may ultimately lead to a claim for damages for substantial performance, cannot be grounds for the extreme reaction of termination.

b. The Promisor's Statement or Conduct Must Clearly Indicate to the Reasonable Promisee that the Promisor Intends to Breach Materially When the Time for Performance Arrives

The question of whether words or action indicate a clear and unequivocal intent to breach is one of interpretation. The meaning of the words and actions must be ascertained. As is true in other matters of interpretation, an *objective test* is used. The law is not so much concerned with the promisor's actual intent or the promisee's subjective interpretation of the statement or action, but with the way in which the promisee should reasonably have understood it.

As we have often seen, verbal expressions of intent can be obscure or ambiguous, presenting difficulties in interpretation. But the meaning of conduct can be even more difficult to divine. For this reason, a court is unlikely to find a repudiation by conduct unless it is unquestionably so inconsistent with an intent to perform as promised, that the promisor's purpose of abandoning the contract is beyond doubt. It is sometimes said that the promisor's conduct must be such as to make her future performance impossible. This is something of an overstatement, but it does convey the need for very unambiguous behavior. For example, if, on July 2, Violet has the deck built by another contractor, her conduct clearly indicates an intent to repudiate. However, if, on July 2, she puts her house on the market, her intent is not as clear. It is possible that she has changed her mind and will fail to perform on July 6, but it could also be that she still intends to build the deck to make the house more saleable. Although faced with this uncertainty, Woody would be taking a risk in declaring a repudiation. However, he may be able to clarify

Violet's intentions by asking for an assurance of performance, as discussed in section 17.7.7.

c. The Promisor's Statement or Conduct in Repudiating Must Be Voluntary, That Is, It Must Have Been Deliberate and Purposeful Rather than Inadvertent or Beyond the Promisor's Control

This may seem to contradict what was said in the immediately preceding point, which focuses on the objective meaning of the manifestation of the promisor's intent rather than on his state of mind. However, even under an objective test, there must be an adequate degree of volition underlying the manifestation. The requirement that the promisor's words or conduct must be deliberate and voluntary means only that he makes the statement or takes the action purposefully. It does not mean that the promisor must have acted in bad faith, or must have realized that the threatened course of conduct or the assertion of rights would constitute a breach. It is thus possible for a promisor to repudiate purposefully in the belief that he is acting fully within his rights. For example, Woody may firmly believe that he is entitled by trade usage to begin work, not on July 7, but within a reasonable time after the promised date of performance. He therefore tells Violet on July 3 that he is running behind schedule and expects to start her deck on July 14. If Woody is wrong in his understanding of the contract, and a week's delay is a material breach, his statement is a deliberate expression of intent to deliver a materially deficient performance and a repudiation. His innocent state of mind does not justify it.

A **statement of intent** not to perform does not usually present this problem because a verbal expression of intent is usually deliberate unless it was coerced. Therefore, when a statement is made, the primary issue is one of interpreting its meaning: Is the promisor saying that she will not perform, or is she merely expressing a lack of confidence in her ability to perform, or complaining about the terms of the contract?

It can be considerably more difficult to establish deliberateness when prospective breach is indicated by **conduct** because action is sometimes inadvertent or compelled by circumstances beyond the promisor's control. For this reason, it is only when the conduct demonstrates an unwillingness to perform that it is regarded as a repudiation. If the action does not lead to the conclusion of willful abandonment of the contract, it is premature for the promisee to declare a repudiation, but again, there may be grounds to demand an assurance of performance.

This principle applies even more strongly when the promisor has *taken no action and made no statement* at all, but a *change of circumstances makes it likely that a breach will occur* when the time for performance arrives. For example, if a large judgment is recorded against Violet on July 2, this creates the possibility that she may not be able to pay the deposit on July 6. Similarly, if Woody has to finish another project before beginning Violet's job, and his other work is considerably behind schedule on July 2, this may indicate that he will not be able to begin performance as promised anytime close to July 7. Even though these circumstances may indicate the possibility of breach, there has not been any statement or conduct indicating an unwillingness to perform, and the promisee cannot treat the contract as repudiated. This is because the promisor should be given the opportunity of trying to overcome the obstacles to performance. After all, the performance is not yet due and there is no indication of a lack of desire to proceed with the contract, despite the adversity. There are not yet grounds to hold the promisor to an advance breach. Again, if it appears that the obstacles to performance may be insurmountable, the promisee's remedy is to demand an assurance of performance.

§17.7.5   *The Dangers of Dealing with Possible Repudiation*

The three rules explained above inhibit the promisee's ability to react to a prospect of future breach. This is an appropriate control because a repudiation, by definition, occurs before performance is due, and there must be some restraint on the promisee's ability to declare breach in advance. If this could be too easily asserted, the promisor would be vulnerable to an unjustified or premature claim of prospective breach whenever any uncertainty arose about his future performance. This protection is not so crucial when the repudiation is conscious and knowledgeable: The repudiating party knows that he no longer wishes to or is able to perform, and he makes it clear that he is abandoning the contract, with full awareness that he will be liable for breach. But risks arise, both to the promisor and the promisee, *when there is any degree of uncertainty* about the existence and extent of the right claimed to have been repudiated, or when it is unclear if the conduct amounts to a repudiation, or when there is doubt about the appropriate level of response. It may take litigation to resolve whether the promisor's indication of intent really was a repudiation of an important contractual duty, and if the promisee *overreacts in response,* this could *itself amount to a repudiation.*

For example, the contract between Woody and Violet said nothing about the wood to be used for the deck. On July 5, the day before Violet was to make her down payment, Woody mentioned to her that he intended to use a pressure-treated fir. She objected and told him that she had assumed that he would use cedar, which is reputed to be the best material for decking and is the wood most commonly chosen. Woody said that pressure-treated fir is less expensive than cedar and is just as good in appearance and durability. He was willing to use cedar if she wished, but that would add $750 onto the price.

Violet insisted on cedar but refused to pay more. A dispute followed that resulted in the termination of the transaction amidst mutual recrimination. At this point both parties believe that they are in the right, but one is wrong and is going to be found to have repudiated the contract. It may take litigation to finally resolve the uncertainty.

In the above example, it was at least clear what Woody planned to provide as his performance (Violet knew he was going to use fir), so the uncertainty was confined to the question of whether the use of fir would be a material breach of the contract. However, the uncertainty could be even worse, because it could happen that there is not even clarity about the promisor's intentions. Say that Violet discovered on July 3 that Woody left town to interview for a job in another city and is expected back on the morning of July 8, the day after he is supposed to begin the deck. This makes her dilemma more difficult. She must make a judgment on whether the information is correct. If it is, does Woody's conduct reasonably mean that he has abandoned the job entirely, or will he just be late? If delay seems more likely than abandonment, is a day's delay a material breach? Even if the breach would be total, his performance is not due for a few days, so should she find another contractor or should she give Woody a chance to repent? If the latter, should she put him on terms or just wait? If she follows that course and it turns out that Woody has in fact repudiated, would her delay in arranging a substitute increase her loss and if so, would a court refuse to compensate her for this increased loss on the basis that her delay aggravated her damages?[5] She may be able to resolve some of these problems by calling for an assurance of performance as discussed in section 17.7.7, but even that procedure carries some risk.

§17.7.6 *Retraction of Repudiation*

It was stated in section 17.7.3 that (subject to the duty to mitigate damages) a promisee is not obliged to accept a repudiation when it occurs, and can wait to see if the promisor repents. She is entitled, but not obliged, to give notice to the promisor demanding retraction of the repudiation within a specified time. It follows from this that the promisor has the ability to retract a repudiation. This should not be too startling a proposition, because, after all, a repudiation is by definition a prospective breach that occurs before the due date of performance. However, repudiation is a wrongful act, and the ability to recant is not absolute. As the promisee does have the option of not waiting for a retraction, the promisor's ability to retract is *lost* as soon as the promisee *notifies* the promisor that the *repudiation has been accepted*. Even in

---

5. Mitigation of damages is discussed in section 18.6.3.

the absence of such notification, the promisor cannot take back the repudiation if the promisee has treated it as final and has taken *action in reliance* on it, resulting in a significant change in her position. This principle recognizes that once the promisor has committed the wrongful act of repudiation, he does not deserve an express response to it. The promisee is entitled to act on the strength of the repudiation without further communication, and this reliance interest is protected, whether or not the promisor is aware that the opportunity for repentance has passed.

§17.7.7   *Prospective Non-Performance and Assurance of Performance*

It has already been stressed that a prospective inability or apparent reluctance to perform may not be strong enough to constitute a repudiation, so that the promisee takes a considerable risk in treating it as such. Yet if the uncertain prospect of repudiation does ultimately ripen into an actual repudiation or breach, inaction may result in inconvenience or even in loss that may have been preventable by an early response. The promisee who does not wish to remain passive, but would like to try to avoid overreaction, has one further option—to demand an assurance of performance. Both UCC §2.609 and Restatement Second §251 give some power to a promisee to try and safeguard his rights by taking a median response to words, conduct, or circumstances that suggest, but do not firmly establish, a likelihood of future breach. Although such a response ameliorates the risk of passivity or an inappropriately aggressive reaction to possible repudiation, it does not entirely eliminate it.

UCC §2.609 provides that if a party has *reasonable grounds for insecurity* regarding the other's performance, she may make a *written demand* for an *adequate assurance of due performance*. Until that assurance is received, the party requesting it may, *if commercially reasonable, suspend* any of her *own performance* for which she has *not already received the agreed return*. The *party receiving a justified demand* for assurance *must provide an adequate assurance* within a *reasonable time, not exceeding 30 days*. If he fails to do so, he has repudiated the contract. Restatement Second §251 differs in its wording to some extent, but is largely to similar effect. As is always true of rights codified in the UCC, the ability to demand an assurance in appropriate circumstances is more certain where a sale of goods is concerned because the right has a statutory base and is not dependent upon judicial adoption.

Although UCC §2.609 and Restatement §251 set out the broad rules under which a party who feels insecure about the prospect of receiving performance may demand an assurance of adequate and due performance, they leave many questions to the judgment of both the party demanding the assurance and the party responding to the demand. An error in judgment by either party could lead to serious consequences for that party. To begin with, the party requesting the assurance must be satisfied that her grounds for insecurity are reasonable. In making the demand, she must decide what assurance would solve the insecurity and whether it is reasonable to ask for it. When she receives the response, she must decide whether it cures the problem. If she misjudged and asked for too little, the assurance may be meaningless. If her misjudgment was to make a demand that was unjustified or went beyond her rights, she would herself commit a breach by insisting on the assurance and in suspending her own performance. The party from whom the assurance is requested must make a judgment on how to respond. If she believes the demand to be unjustified or excessive, she will not want to sacrifice her rights by giving in to it. But if it is proper, her refusal to comply, or a response short of what was demanded, may convert the formerly equivocal situation into a clear repudiation.

To illustrate, take the example again of the contract between Violet and Woody under which Woody is to build a deck for Violet for $5,000, of which $2,000 is to be paid in advance on July 6 and the balance upon completion. After receiving the down payment on July 6, Woody begins work on July 7. While he is working at the house on that day, the sheriff arrives with a writ of execution and levies on Violet's living room furniture. A couple of hours later, a repossessor from a finance company shows up and takes away Violet's car. This is, of course, very disconcerting to Woody, who begins to wonder if Violet will be able to pay the $3,000 due upon completion of the deck. He cannot treat the execution and repossession as a repudiation of Violet's promise to pay him, because Violet herself has not said or done anything to indicate an intent not to perform, but he hates the idea of continuing work in the face of a serious possibility of non-payment.

If the activity at Violet's home on July 7 gives Woody reasonable grounds to believe that Violet will breach when her performance falls due, he may demand an adequate assurance of performance from Violet.[6] Violet must respond satisfactorily within a reasonable time. While Woody is waiting for her response, he may stop work on the deck, and if he does not get an adequate assurance in time, he may treat the contract as breached. This is all very well, but you can probably see immediately that there could be serious issues for dispute, some of which may be: Does Woody really have reasonable grounds for feeling insecure? If not, his suspension of performance is itself a breach. If he is justified in demanding assurance, what should he ask for? Merely asking Violet to reaffirm that she will pay is not very helpful, because the assurance could just be a hollow promise and Violet may not admit that

---

6. This contract is a hybrid because Woody is both selling goods (the materials) and performing services, so there may be a question of whether the transaction falls within UCC Article 2. However, unless the jurisdiction does not follow Restatement Second §251, the broad principles are not notably different under the UCC and common law.

she is in financial trouble. It would be much more reassuring if Violet would pay right now, but is Woody entitled to demand that? In effect, this would be a revocation of the credit that he agreed to give her, and such a stringent demand could be a violation of his duties under the contract. Maybe Woody could ask Violet to deposit the payment in escrow, or for a financial statement showing that the funds are available, but this first alternative may ask too much, and the second too little. Once Woody settles on his demand, Violet has to decide how to respond. If she feels that he is not justified in feeling insecure, she could refuse the assurance. If she feels that it is excessive, she could offer a more modest assurance. But if she is wrong, her refusal to comply with the demand crystalizes the uncertainty into a repudiation.

There are no easy answers to these fact-based questions, but this example highlights the kinds of concerns that may arise when a prospective breach is perceived. Of course, not all cases end up in a morass of uncertainty, and the ability to demand assurances does often enable a party either to obtain adequate security or to establish a repudiation.

§17.7.8   *Transactions Involving Installments*

Issues of repudiation and total breach are highlighted in contracts that call for performance in installments. When a breach occurs in the performance of an earlier installment, it can be difficult to know if the breach *affects only the defective installment* or is *so serious as to undermine the contract in its entirety,* operating as a *repudiation* of all *remaining installments.*

For example, Seller, a manufacturer of machinery, contracts with Buyer for the sale of three of its machines to be used by Buyer in its factory. Under the contract, the machines are to be delivered a month apart from each other. Because Buyer is depending on prompt delivery to avoid disruption of its business, the contract requires delivery of the machines on the exact dates specified. The first machine is delivered on time and is installed. After two days of operation it breaks down as a result of a defect that cannot be repaired without removal of the machine. Because timely delivery is important in the transaction, the defect in the first machine is likely to be a material and total breach of Seller's performance obligation with respect to the first installment, but does this also constitute a material and total repudiation of the future installments and hence a breach of the contract as a whole? That is, does the delivery of a defective first installment so seriously impair Buyer's expectations concerning the remaining machines that it is a repudiation of the performance promised in the future? If so, Buyer may use the present breach as the basis for terminating the entire contract. If not, the breach does not impact future performance, so that Buyer continues to be obliged to accept and pay for the later two machines, and is confined to a remedy for breach of the current installment.

As this is a sale of goods, the principles governing these questions are set out in UCC §2.612, which qualifies the perfect tender rule of §2.601 in contracts providing for delivery in installments. It states that a non-conformity in an earlier installment can only be treated as a breach of the entire contract if the deficiency in that installment *"substantially impairs the value of the whole"* contract. This means that when a breach occurs in an earlier installment, it must be determined whether this is a breach so fundamental to the whole contract as to constitute not merely a partial breach, but a total and material breach of the contract as a whole. If it does, the breach operates not only as a breach of the current installment, but also as an advance breach (that is, repudiation) of the performance obligations due in the future. The question is whether it is pervasive and irreparable enough to make it clear that the promisor is incapable of rendering, or unwilling to render, substantially compliant performance in the future.

An express rule governing installment sales is particularly necessary when a sale of goods is involved because the perfect tender rule does not permit application of the doctrine of substantial performance. At common law there is less need for having a special rule for installment contracts because the result of §2.612 can be achieved by applying the general principles of substantial performance, under which the breach relating to one installment will only be a total breach if it results in an incurable material violation of the contract as a whole. This is reflected in Restatement Second §243(4), which, in dealing generally with total breach (and not with specific reference to installment transactions), adopts language similar to that used in UCC §2.612.

EXAMPLES

1. Sue Burbanite had just bought a newly built home on a small suburban lot. The builder had not landscaped the lot, which was uneven, bare, and muddy. Sue therefore hired Holmes Wrecker, a landscaping contractor, to level and shape the ground and to form contours and beds so that Sue could later plant trees, shrubs, and grass. Holmes drew up a landscaping plan that was incorporated into a written contract. In terms of the contract, Holmes undertook to begin the work on May 1 and to complete it by May 5. Sue promised to pay the price of $5,000 in two equal installments due on May 3 and 5.

Holmes began work on May 1. The earthmoving proceeded well until the afternoon of May 2, when Holmes lost control of his bulldozer as he was trying to negotiate a narrow section of the lot at the corner of the house. The machine smashed into a pillar supporting an upper-floor deck, causing the entire deck to collapse. Sue, who happened to be sitting on the deck at the time, was thrown to the ground and would have been seriously injured had her fall not been cushioned by a pile of mud. Enraged, Sue chased Holmes off the premises, hurling abuse and mud clods at him.

On the morning of May 3, Holmes arrived at Sue's property. He apologized for ruining her deck and explained that he misjudged the space available for maneuvering. He told her that he was insured, and that his insurer would pay for the rebuilding of the deck. In the interim, he said he was willing to resume work. Sue had calmed down by this time, and she agreed to let him continue. He then reminded her that her first installment was due on that day. Sue was astounded at the man's nerve. She pointed out that he had a large and unpaid liability to her for the damage to the deck, and until that was settled, he had no right to expect any money from her. He responded that his insurer would handle the deck, and that payment under the contract was a separate matter altogether. As the parties could not resolve this impasse, Holmes left without doing any further work.

Holmes's insurer did eventually pay to have the deck rebuilt and Sue had the landscaping completed by another contractor. The second contractor charged more than she would have paid Holmes under the contract, so she sued Holmes for the difference. Holmes contested liability and counterclaimed for the cost of the work performed prior to termination, plus the profit that he lost by being denied the opportunity to complete his performance. Who should prevail?

2. Standard Home Construction, Inc. builds houses for individual homeowners. It usually works from one of its stock plans, which may be modified to suit the needs or desires of a particular customer. Standard entered into a contract with Lofty Lanky to build a ranch-style house on a lot owned by Lofty. The price of the completed house was $180,000. The contract called for the house to be built in accordance with a stock plan and specifications, a copy of which was annexed to the signed memorandum of agreement. However, one change was made in the specifications, increasing the ceiling height from the standard 8′ to 9′. This change was recorded in the contract itself and in the specifications, and it was reflected in the price of the house, which was $10,000 more than normal. Lofty desired this change because he is 7′2″ tall and feels claustrophobic in a house with low ceilings.

The contract required Lofty to make a down payment and provided for periodic further payments during the course of construction. He made the down payment and construction began. Building proceeded on schedule with periodic payments being made as required. It was not until the house was fully framed and the roof was constructed that Lofty first noticed that the base of the roof seemed lower than it should be. On taking some measurements he realized that when the ceilings were installed, they would be only 8′ from the floor. He immediately contacted Standard and a meeting was held on site. Standard conceded that the house was a foot too low. Apparently the foreman was very familiar with the stock plan, having built many houses like this one. He therefore failed to consult the plan carefully and had simply not noticed the change in the specifications.

The only way to correct the error is to demolish most of the existing work and start again. The roof would have to be dismantled and the supporting walls taken down and rebuilt with taller studs. Although some of the lumber could be saved and reused by a painstaking effort at disassembly, a considerable amount of material would be destroyed. The cost of wasted labor and materials would be so high that Standard's final cost would be $240,000, which would exceed the contract price by about $60,000.

Notwithstanding this sacrifice, Standard is so mortified by the error and so concerned about preserving its reputation that it is willing to remedy the mistake and take the loss. However, Lofty points out that the demolition and rebuilding will delay completion of the house by a month beyond the date specified in the contract. In addition, he feels that Standard was so incompetent and cavalier in not examining the plans, that he wonders what other stupid mistakes may be made. He also fears that it will try to reduce its losses by cutting corners, trying to reuse materials, and otherwise doing a "patch-up" job. He is not convinced that the house will ultimately conform to specifications or that it will have the structural soundness and integrity of a brand-new house. He therefore wants to rescind the contract, get his money back, and enter into a completely new transaction with another builder for the demolition and rebuilding. Naturally, he intends to hold Standard liable for any loss arising from the delay and for the considerable additional cost to be incurred in getting the existing structure removed and building a house according to specifications. Is he entitled to this relief?

3. All the facts are the same as in Example 2, except for Standard's reaction upon discovering the foreman's oversight. Although Standard is apologetic for the error, it considers it a ridiculous waste and a great hardship to demolish and rebuild the house. Standard can prove that although higher ceilings may be an attractive feature to some buyers, others would consider them a drawback. As a result, the higher ceilings would not make the house more saleable and would not increase its market value. Standard also feels that Lofty is making a big fuss for nothing—after all, there will still be several inches of clearance between his head and the ceiling. It therefore refuses to rebuild the house and insists that Lofty allow it to complete the house with the lower ceilings. It would, of course, deduct the extra charge of $10,000 from the price. Lofty does not find this solution attractive. He demands that Standard rectify the error itself, and if it refuses to do so, he threatens to terminate the contract, hire someone else to bring the house into conformity, and hold Standard liable for his damages. Is he entitled to make this demand?

4. Sandy Shaw owns a small motel (called "Sandy Shaw's Motel," as you may have guessed) a few blocks off the main strip of a seaside town. Sandy entered into a contract with Bill Board, a signwriter, under which Bill undertook to paint four signs for Sandy. Two of the signs, measuring 6' long and 4' high, were to read, "Sandy Shaw's Motel—elegance and comfort by the sea. Turn just three blocks ahead." The price of these signs was $500 each. Sandy planned to erect them facing incoming traffic at either end of the

town's main road. The third and fourth signs were to be arrow-shaped, measuring 5′ long and 2′ high, bearing the legend, "This way to Sandy Shaw's Motel." The price of these signs was $400 each. Sandy planned to place them facing opposite directions on the main road at its intersection with the street leading to the motel. The contract required all four signs to be delivered together two weeks after execution of the contract, and payment was due on delivery.

Bill delivered all four signs as promised. On inspecting them, Sandy finds that the two signs meant for erection at the ends of the main road are only 5′ high and 3′ wide. She demands that Bill must either redo these signs or pay her the cost of having them redone by someone else. Is this demand tenable?

5. Change the facts of Example 4 to the following extent: Bill made the two signs for erection at each end of the main road and delivered them on time. These signs fully conformed to the contract and Sandy has put them up. Bill failed to deliver the other two signs on time, but Sandy was willing to forgive this on the strength of Bill's promise that they would be delivered shortly. Despite several weeks of constant nagging by Sandy, Bill never got around to doing the other two signs. Eventually, Sandy lost patience with him, terminated the contract, and had those signs painted by another sign-writer. She had not paid Bill for the first two signs and when he asked for his money, Sandy told him that he was not entitled to payment because he never finished the job. Is Sandy right? Although this is a sale of goods, consider the question under both the common law and UCC Article 2.

6. Consider another variation of the contract between Sandy Shaw and Bill Board. The terms of the contract concerning the goods and the price are the same as before. However, it has a different delivery term. It calls for Bill to deliver the four signs in installments. The first is to be delivered within a week of the contract, and the remaining three at weekly intervals thereafter. Sandy is to pay for each sign on delivery. Following formation, Bill made the first sign and delivered it to Sandy exactly on time. Sandy was unimpressed. It read:

Sandy Shors   Motel eligence and cumfert by thesea. Just three   bloks ahed.

Furthermore, the lettering was uneven and not placed symmetrically on the board. The paintwork was sloppy and there were runs and dribbles all over the sign.

Sandy pointed out these faults with some forcefulness. Bill apologized and admitted that he had trouble with spelling. He told Sandy that if she wrote out the message for him, he would redo the sign properly and deliver it within a day. Sandy cannot imagine that Bill could do a decent sign, even if she helped him with his spelling. She sees nothing but aggravation and conflict as she battles with him over this and the other three signs, and she is sure that if she allows him to try again, she will end up with unusable garbage and will have to hire someone else to redo the job. Does she have the right to cancel her contract with Bill?

7. Here is another factual variation of the contract between Sandy Shaw and Bill Board: As before, Bill agreed to make four signs for the prices stated earlier. However, Bill did not simply undertake to deliver them, but also agreed to erect them in position. In addition, because the town requires a permit to be obtained before any new signs are placed next to the roadway, Bill promised to obtain the necessary permit from the town council before erecting the signs. Bill was obliged to have the signs completed, authorized, and installed within four weeks of signing the contract. Sandy agreed to pay 25 percent of the price of the signs within a week of signing the contract, and the balance after erection of the signs.

Two days after the contract was entered into (and therefore 26 days before the date specified for the completion of Bill's performance), Sandy read in the local newspaper that the town council had just refused a permit application made by Bill for another customer. The refusal was based not only on the fact that the application was sloppily handled and full of errors and omissions, but also on the ground that the design of the proposed sign violated the town's ordinance. Apparently Bill responded to this denial by ranting and making threatening gestures at the councilors. As a result, he was forcibly ejected from the hearing and told not to return.

On the day that she read this, Sandy wrote to Bill, expressing alarm at the report of his behavior, and voicing concern that his prior conduct would make it impossible for him to secure a permit for her signs. The letter concluded that unless Bill could allay her fears by getting a permit within the next week, she would consider the contract at an end. In the interim, she would withhold her 25 percent payment until she received notice that the application had been granted. Bill wrote her a reply on the very same day, saying that it was neither convenient nor necessary for him to get the permit so quickly, but assuring her that it would be in hand by the time that the signs are due for erection. He reminded her that he was expecting her payment of 25 percent of the price in five days, as agreed. What should she do now?

8. In May, Cleaver Carnage, a famous chef, entered into a contract with Televicious, Inc., the owner and operator of a television network, to produce and star in a weekly cooking show, to be called "Cleaver's Critter Cookout." The show was to run for a trial season from September 1–October 30. Each weekly installment was to begin with live video footage showing Cleaver hunting and slaughtering various woodland creatures. The scene would then change to Cleaver's well-equipped studio kitchen, in which he would prepare a delectable dish from the day's catch.

In July, Televicious came under great pressure from various consumer groups and government agencies to reduce the level of violence in its broadcasts. In attempting to respond to community concerns, it reviewed its fall programming and decided to cancel several shows that seemed unnecessarily gruesome. Cleaver's cooking show was one of them. Televicious proposed to replace it with a program entitled "Longevity with Legumes," to be hosted by Lena Lofatt, a widely published author of health-conscious recipe books. Televicious wrote to Cleaver on July 30, informing him that his services were no longer required. Cleaver responded immediately by writing a letter to Televicious, pointing out correctly that the contract gave Televicious no right to cancel unilaterally, and notifying it that he continued to hold it to the contract.

By August 10, Cleaver had heard nothing more from Televicious. On that day he received an offer to work during September as camp chef for a culinary safari of central Africa. Although he was quite attracted by the invitation, he decided that it was not nearly as beneficial to his career as a television program would be. Because he still hoped that Televicious would repent if given some time, he declined the offer of the safari and waited for its response to his letter. His optimism was in vain. A week later, he received a terse note from Televicious, stating that the decision was final. By now, it is too late for Cleaver to find anything else to replace his aborted television venture. What are his rights?

EXPLANATIONS

1. Holmes's commencement of work is an express promise and a construed condition precedent to Sue's payment of the $2,500 on May 3. Sue's performance of this promise is, in turn, a construed condition precedent to Holmes's continued performance. If Holmes materially breached his promissory condition precedent, Sue would have been entitled to refuse the payment, but if he did not, her refusal to pay would have been a material breach of her promise and also a non-fulfillment of the condition to Holmes's further work. Therefore, if Holmes breached materially, Sue's non-payment was justified, Holmes had no right to leave the job, and Sue can terminate and claim damages for total breach. Conversely, if he did not breach materially, Sue's refusal of payment was a material and total breach, giving Holmes the right to terminate his own performance, to end the contract, and to claim full expectation damages from Sue.

Was Sue entitled to refuse payment? Although the contract does not say so expressly, it is implied that Holmes would not simply begin work on May 1, but that he would continue to perform in a satisfactory and workmanlike manner in the period before payment fell due. This performance was a construed condition precedent to Sue's payment, so that if he materially and totally breached his promise, Sue had the right to withhold her performance, terminate, and claim expectation damages. Apart from demolishing the deck, there is no suggestion that Holmes did anything wrong, so our determination of the respective rights of the parties must begin by deciding how that unfortunate incident ties into his contractual obligations. In the absence of a more specific yardstick set out in the contract, the question of whether the quality of the work is sufficient to be reasonably workmanlike is judged by prevailing commercial standards—it must be so regarded by reasonable participants in the market. A small deviation from this standard would be a minor breach, resulting in substantial performance, but a significant departure would be material, and if not curable, total.

One does not need extensive evidence of commercial expectations to accept the proposition that a landscaper's duty of workmanlike performance includes an obligation to exercise reasonable care in the use of heavy equipment and to avoid demolition of the structures erected on the land. Holmes apparently failed in this duty, with grave consequences. The materiality of a breach is a factual question, to be determined with reference to the terms of the contract in context. Given the extent of the damage caused by the breach and Holmes's apparent inability to manage his equipment properly, the deviation from his contractual duty should qualify as material.

But even if the breach was material, Sue elected not to treat it as total. She was willing to allow Holmes back on the job. However, she refused to render her own performance until her claim against him for the damage to the deck had been paid. If a party chooses to treat a breach as partial, she must normally render her own performance when it becomes due. By electing not to pursue her right to declare total breach, she forgoes the remedies for total breach, including the right to withhold her own performance. However, she is entitled to an offset for the damages caused by the breach, so when, as in this case, those damages for partial breach are likely to be extensive, and may well equal or exceed her obligation to Holmes, it would be unfair to expect her to pay Holmes first and later struggle to recover for her loss. Under these circumstances, it is makes sense to allow her to hold back her payment for the purpose of set off. As she was justified in not paying, Holmes's abandonment of the job converted his partial breach into a total breach and entitled Sue to terminate and claim damages.

This example is based on *K & G Construction Co. v. Harris,* 164 A.2d 451 (Md. 1960), in which an excavation subcontractor damaged the contractor's house by driving a bulldozer too close to it. The pertinent facts of the case are quite similar to those here, except that the contract expressed the subcontractor's duty to perform in a workmanlike manner, and the subcontractor was not as willing to concede liability for the damage (and in fact only paid for it after an adverse judgment). In dealing with the contractor's refusal to pay the subcontractor when payment fell due, the court characterized the promises of payment and performance as dependent—that is, conditions of each other. Based on the sequence of performance set out in the contract, the court construed proper performance by the subcontractor to be a condition precedent to payment. Because the damage to the house was negligent and exceeded the amount of the payment due at that stage, the court had no doubt that the damage was a material breach of the promise to perform in a workmanlike manner. By permitting the subcontractor to continue work, the contractor did not treat the breach as total. Nevertheless, the court held that the material nature of the breach entitled the contractor to withhold payment. As a result, the subcontractor had no right to abandon the job on the ground of non-payment. When he did so, he turned the partial breach into a total one, entitling the contractor to terminate and claim damages. The opinion focuses on the distinction between material and total breach, and does not articulate the offset rationale suggested above. But that is the basic point of the case. Although the contractor treated the breach as partial, its material nature meant that appreciable damages had been suffered. It was the existence of that significant damages claim that justified the withholding of performance.

2. Standard has breached the contract by failing to comply with the specifications. If the breach is material and total, Lofty has the right to respond as he intends, seeking termination of the contract and compensation for any expectation damages that may be suffered. (The damages would be measured as the difference between the contract price and the higher cost of employing another contractor to achieve the end result promised by Standard in the contract. Because the attainment of Lofty's contractual expectations will require demolition of part of the existing structure and rebuilding, the cost of completing the house to specifications will considerably exceed the contract price. As Lofty's total outlay will include not only what will be paid to the new contractor, but also what he has already paid to Standard, his expectation recovery will include reimbursement of his down payment and the periodic payments to date.)

Standard does not claim that it has substantially performed, and it has undertaken to demolish and rebuild. It, in effect, concedes that the breach is material. We therefore do not have to consider this question on the present facts. (It is raised by the facts of Example 3.) The only issue is whether the breach is total—that is, whether Lofty can terminate immediately without giving Standard the opportunity to perform the tendered cure. Standard proposes to give Lofty his exact contractual expectations, but because rectification of the defect involves considerable work, it cannot be completed for a full month after the date specified in the contract for completion of construction. Lofty objects to the cure not only because of the delay (which is by now inevitable, even if Lofty rescinds) but also because he claims to have lost faith in Standard and does not believe that he will ultimately get a house of the quality contemplated by the contract.

When the contract involves a sale of goods, the right to cure a defective performance has a clear statutory basis under UCC §2.508. However, the common law concept of partial breach also envisages the possibility of cure when the breach is not so immediately and irrevocably material as to be incapable of reversal, and the breaching party shows a desire to remedy the defective performance within a reasonable time. There are two issues that must be considered to decide if the breach is curable. The first is whether delay on its own would be a total breach. If so, the breach became total as soon as the work was not completed on time. If delay is not itself a total breach, the second issue is whether the error was so grave that it undermined Lofty's reasonable expectation of ultimate proper performance. If it did, it is incapable of cure, irrespective of any flexibility in the time of performance.

A. Is Standard Permitted to Take Time to Cure?

Of course, by the time that the foreman's error is discovered, nothing can be done to complete the house on time. Delay is inevitable, whether Standard is given the opportunity to cure or the contract is immediately terminated and a new builder is hired. In either event, Lofty will be entitled to recover any loss resulting from the delay. The real issue in deciding whether this is a curable breach is to determine if Standard may be fired immediately or should be given the chance to rectify the problem and complete the construction.[7]

The issue of whether a delay in completion is, on its own, serious enough to be a total breach requires analysis of two consecutive questions. First, it must be decided if any delay at all would be permissible. If completion of performance on the specified date is a central element of Standard's undertaking—that is, the time of completion is "of the essence"—even a small delay would be a material breach. As a result, the defect in performance could not be cured by any efforts after the completion date. Missing the contractual due date for conforming performance would, in itself, be a material and total breach. However, if the completion date is not that crucial, failure to meet it would be only a partial breach, leaving some further time to affect a cure.[8] If this is so, the question becomes: How much time does the breacher have to complete the cure before the breach does become total? These are factual questions, to be decided by a contextual interpretation of the contract's time provisions.

---

7. Why would Standard prefer to cure itself, rather than to pay damages to Lofty so that he can have someone else to do the work? When the cost of cure and completion is less than the contract price, the breacher is able to earn at least some of the profit that it had hoped for under the contract. But this is not true here because the cure is so expensive that it will more than wipe out any gain from the transaction. It seems that Standard is motivated in part by pride in its work, but it would also have the advantage of keeping some control over the extent of its liability by managing the work and expenditures required for rectification.

8. Note that the common law approach to the materiality of performance dates differs from that under UCC §2.508. At common law, the question of whether time of performance is material involves the usual factual evaluation of the importance of the time provisions of the contract. By contrast, because perfect tender is required under §2.601, once the due date for delivery has passed, §2.508 places greater restrictions on the seller's ability to cure. Not only must the cure be accomplished in a reasonable time, but the seller must have had reason to believe that the nonconforming tender would have been acceptable. This usually means either that the seller was unaware of the non-conformity, or that it believed that the buyer would not object to the nonconformity if a money allowance was made.

In some contracts, the timing of the performance is so vital that even a short delay could seriously damage the promisee's reasonable expectations. For example, if a contract with a caterer calls for delivery of the food by 6 P.M., the time scheduled for the wedding reception, it is quite obvious that the caterer materially breaches by showing up with the food at midnight. However, unless a building must be finished in time for a specific event, a delay in completion, not excessive under the circumstances, is unlikely to be so material a breach as to justify termination.[9] We are given no facts in this example to indicate that time was "of the essence," so a reasonable delay is not likely to be treated as a material breach. Is a month's delay reasonable? Obviously, the longer the delay, the greater the chance that it will have a material impact on the value of the transaction to Lofty by increasing his inconvenience and possibly having a negative effect on related transactions, such as his financing arrangements or the sale of an existing house. We do not have enough facts to reach a firm conclusion.

Although the materiality of delay is largely based on an interpretation of contractual expectations, one cannot disregard the cause of the problem and the response of the breaching party. Although these matters are seemingly unrelated to the magnitude of breach, some degree of equitable balancing comes into the decision on whether the promisee should be able to visit the consequences of total breach on the promisor. Standard is placed in a more sympathetic light by the fact that this delay resulted from an honest mistake and is necessitated by an apparently sincere effort to remedy it. This point also has a bearing on the second consideration, which is the adequacy of the cure.

B. Even If a Month's Delay Is Permitted, Is this a Breach that Could Be Cured, Given Time?

Even if it is found that a month's delay in completion is not itself a material and total breach, the resulting efforts at cure must produce a performance in compliance with the contract. Therefore, if we decide that Standard should be given a month to cure, its performance will be evaluated when the effort to cure is complete. If the finished product remains significantly deficient, the failure to cure properly will itself be a material breach. (Conversely, if the cure falls short of the promised performance in only a minor respect, it will con-

---

9. It is, of course, a breach nevertheless, and, as noted earlier, may give rise to a claim for damages even if no termination is allowed. If the building is to be used for commercial purposes, the damages may include any increase in expenses and any loss in revenue or profits. If it is a residence, lost revenue is not usually in issue, but the homeowner may have a claim for the reimbursement of such wasted expenses as additional rent or storage charges.

stitute substantial performance.) However, Lofty does not wish to give Standard any opportunity to attempt a cure. He claims the right to terminate immediately on the basis that the proposed cure (quite apart from the time it would take) will not give him the benefit of his bargain. He bases this assertion on the conviction that Standard's pre-existing incompetence and sloppiness will be exacerbated by its incentive to compromise the quality of its performance, leaving him with a patchwork job.

Although Lofty's concerns may be genuine, if he rejects the offer of cure, he may later have some trouble establishing that they were realistic and reasonable. There is no indication that Standard is incapable of following a plan, or that it would approach the rectification of performance grudgingly. If cure is feasible and the will to cure is apparent, the promisee takes a risk that a court may later disagree with his prediction of inadequate performance, and may find him to have acted unreasonably in preventing rectification of the breach. In *Wilson v. Scampoli*, 228 A2d 848 (D.C. 1967), a case decided under UCC §2.508, the buyer of a defective television set refused to allow the seller to take it back and attempt to ascertain the cause of the problem, claiming that she was entitled to a new set, not a repaired one. The court disagreed. It said that although the buyer of a new television was not obliged to accept a substantially repaired article, she had to give the seller the opportunity of curing the defect, either by minor repair or by replacement. Because she refused to allow the seller to take the set away for inspection, she deprived it of a reasonable opportunity to determine what was needed to affect a cure. She therefore had no right of termination.

3. Although Standard does not articulate the legal basis of its proposed resolution of the problem, it is in fact contending that the erection of a house with 8′ ceilings would be substantial performance of its contractual obligations. If this is correct, Lofty would have no right to terminate and would be left with no choice but to accept the defective performance with a monetary allowance. Standard argues, furthermore, that the appropriate measure of this allowance is a reduction in the contract price by removal of the extra charge for 9′ ceilings.

The question of whether performance is substantial is factual and must be determined by interpretation of the parties' reasonable expectations. The mere specification of 9′ ceilings in the contract is not enough. This term must be so central to the bargain that its breach will deprive Lofty of the value reasonably anticipated. The importance of the term is most strongly demonstrated by the fact that, of all the standard specifications, Lofty elected to change only that relating to the ceiling height. The reason for his doing so—his tallness—is patent, even if his claustrophobia may not have been. Lofty bought the house for his own use and comfort, so the claim that the higher ceilings do not add to its market value is beside the point. For this reason, the non-compliance with the contract must surely be material. Lofty should therefore be entitled to insist on proper cure and, failing that, to terminate and seek the relief he demands.

The result may possibly have been different if Lofty had not bought the house for his own use, but for the purpose of resale. His goal would then have been profit, and if the lower ceilings would not have adversely affected the house's marketability or value, the breach would not have had a notable impact on the contract's value to him. In addition, because Standard's breach was inadvertent, a court may have been more sympathetic to a claim that the breach was immaterial so as to shield Standard from the severe consequences of total breach. However, even if the facts were changed in this way, a good argument could be made that the breach is still not trivial. Lofty did go to the trouble of specifying and paying for this change in the standard specifications, and a court will not lightly dismiss a term that is so pointedly added to the contract.

One of the best-known cases involving substantial performance is *Jacob & Youngs v. Kent*, 129 N.E. 889 (N.Y. 1921). A builder had completed the construction of a grand country home for a total price of $77,000, a considerable sum in 1914. The owner refused to pay the balance of the contract price, approximately $3,500, on the ground that the builder had breached the contract by installing the wrong plumbing pipe in the house. The builder had apparently overlooked a contract specification calling for pipe of Reading brand, and over half the pipe installed was of another make, although of equal quality. The owner demanded that the builder remove and replace the non-conforming pipe. Because the pipe was encased within the walls, this would have involved demolition and rebuilding of a significant portion of the house. The builder would not do this, so the owner refused to make the final payment under the contract. The builder sued for the balance of the contract price. Judge Cardozo, writing for the majority, treated the breach as trivial. Although the specification of the brand name was an express promise in the contract, and the performance of such an express promise could be construed as a condition precedent to the owner's obligation to make final payment, Cardozo felt that such a construction would result in unfair forfeiture. There was nothing in the contract to indicate that the parties considered the brand name to be a significant term, as long as the quality of the pipe was up to the specifications. Therefore, he described the brand specification as an "independent promise." This terminology sounds confusing, but it is really just another way of saying that where a breach is trivial (so that substantial performance has been rendered), the non-breaching party's remaining obligation of performance is not treated as dependent on exact fulfillment of the breached promise. The non-breacher can therefore not withhold the return performance and claim total breach, but continues to be obligated to perform, subject to an offset for damages caused by the breach.

Although Cardozo was confident that the breach was trivial and inadvertent, this is not self-evident. The dissent took the view that there was no justification for the builder's failure to install the correct pipe, and it may have done so deliberately. Furthermore, as the owner had specified the use of Reading pipe, the court should not assume that the pipe brand was unimportant to him, thereby depriving him of what he bargained for.

The facts of Lofty's case are reminiscent of, but distinguishable from, those in *Plante v. Jacobs*, 103 N.W.2d 296 (Wis. 1960). In that case, the court found that a builder had substantially performed when he misplaced the wall dividing the living room and the kitchen, making the living room about a foot smaller than required by the plan. Although this could have been a material breach in some circumstances, the house was built to stock specifications, and there was nothing to indicate that the exact dimensions of the rooms were of importance. The placement of the wall did not affect the market value of the home.

The crucial difference between Lofty's contract and those involved in the two cases above lies in the significance of the breached term. In finding the breach in *Jacob & Youngs* to be trivial, Cardozo stressed the importance of weighing the breach in light of the contract's language and purpose, and of distinguishing between those deviations from performance that go to the heart of the contract, and those that do not. On the facts given here, Standard's breach falls into the former category. Similarly, although Lofty's house was to be built in accordance with a stock plan, as in *Plante*, the vital distinguishing fact is that the ceiling height was the one individualized feature of the plan.

The conclusion that the breach was material disposes of this case: Lofty is entitled to the relief that he demands. However, it is useful to consider what the result would have been had this issue been decided otherwise. Say, for example, that Lofty was in the business of building houses for immediate resale, and it was understood between the parties that Lofty would market the house on completion. As the lower ceilings would have no effect on Lofty's purpose, it would be fair to conclude that the non-conformity had no material impact on his reasonable expectation of full value under the contract. Such a finding of substantial performance would have raised the issue of the extent of relief necessary to compensate Lofty for the shortfall in performance. In most cases, the preferred measure of damages for a partial breach when there has been substantial performance should be the cost of remedying the defect. In this case, such a measure would lead to artificially high damages, because of the cost of tearing down and rebuilding the structure. As we are now operating on the premise that the breach was found to be minor, such a large award of damages would be disproportionate to the actual harm suffered by Lofty. That is, the defect makes no difference in the resale potential or value of the house, and hence does not harm Lofty's ultimate expectations. Yet the cost of rectifying it is so big that it will not only eat up Standard's anticipated profit, but will leave it with a loss of $60,000 beyond that. To award damages on that scale therefore gives Lofty more than he would actually lose as a result of the non-conformity, while imposing a hardship on Standard beyond what is merited by its minor breach. To avoid such an unfair forfeiture, the court is likely to choose an alternative measure, based on the actual loss in value suffered by Lofty as a result of the breach.

Because the majority in *Jacob & Youngs* found that the contract had been substantially performed, Cardozo went on to deal with this issue of unfair forfeiture. Noting that the cost of rectification is the normal measure of damages, he found the enormous expense of reconstruction in this case to be grossly out of proportion to the benefit that it would attain. He therefore limited the owner to an offset against the price equal to the difference in value between a house with Reading pipe, and one with other pipe of equivalent quality—a difference that he considered to be nominal or nothing. A similar analysis was followed in *Plante*. The cost of putting the wall into the right place would have involved extensive demolition, rebuilding, and redecorating, making it disproportionate to the value of the gain to be achieved. The owners were therefore confined to an offset for diminished market value, which was zero. Like those cases, there would be no ultimate market loss to Lofty. However, there is an additional factor to consider. He paid an extra $10,000 for the higher ceilings, and it would not be appropriate for Standard to retain that overpayment. Therefore, his true loss in value is not zero, but the $10,000 that he would not have had to spend to build a house of the kind that he received.

4. As if you haven't already had enough of the substantial performance issue, this question raises it again. If the common law applied to this contract, the analysis of this question would be very much like that in prior examples: We would have to decide if the size of the signs was a material term of the contract. If it was, Bill has materially breached. A breach of that magnitude[10] would give Sandy the right to demand compliant performance or, failing that, to claim expectation damages measured by the cost of placing her in the position that she would have been in, had the breach not occurred. One cannot reach a definitive conclusion about the materiality of the sign's dimensions on the facts available, but as the purpose of the sign is to advertise the motel to passing motorists, size may well be material. However, if the size of the sign is not material, the otherwise competent performance may be substantial, in which case the cost of rectification may not be an appropriate remedy, because it will presumably require nothing less than scrapping the signs and making new ones. This may constitute an unfair forfeiture to Bill, so Sandy may be confined to a claim for the difference in value (if any) between what she contracted for and what she received.

However, this contract cannot simply be analyzed under common law. Bill's undertaking to make the sign is not a contract to perform a service for

---

10. This sounds like a subtly clever pun, but it's not.

Sandy, but a sale of goods. The transaction involves the exchange of an end product—the completed signs—for money. (It is, of course, common for a manufacturer to sell goods that it has fabricated, and this is no less a sale because the goods are custom-made.) As this is a sale, the doctrine of substantial performance does not apply. Under §2.601, the buyer may reject the goods if they fail in any respect to conform to the contract. This right of rejection is mitigated by the seller's right to cure under §2.508, but this does not help Bill very much because Sandy is willing to allow him to cure, and his problem is with the excessive cost of cure. The UCC therefore seems to point in a very different direction from the common law when the issue of unfair forfeiture arises, because the UCC simply does not countenance an adjustment for specific performance when the buyer makes a timely rejection of non-conforming goods.

However, this absolute statement should be tempered by the general observation that a court that really does not like the result mandated by the perfect tender rule does have some room to wriggle. It is beyond our scope to go into the intricacies of rejection, but we can note that the buyer has to follow the proper procedure and act in a timely way to effectively reject the goods. If the buyer slips up, the goods are deemed to have been accepted, and the remedy for a non-conformity in accepted goods (set out in §2.718) gives the court more flexibility in fixing damages in an amount reasonable under the circumstances. Also remember that the common law is only displaced by the UCC to the extent that it is inconsistent with the provisions of the statute, and this interface could, on the right facts, give a court some scope for the creative incorporation of common law principles into a sales case.

5. There is no issue here of perfect tender, substantial performance, or rejection with regard to the two signs delivered. They are apparently satisfactory and in use. Nor is there any doubt that Bill has totally breached his outstanding performance obligations, giving Sandy the right to terminate that portion of the contract relating to the remaining performance. We are spared the issue of Sandy's damages because she claims none. She apparently incurred no demonstrable loss as a result of the delay in getting the signs up, or on account of having to pay more for a substitute. Therefore, the only issue is whether Bill's breach permits Sandy to keep his signs without paying for them.

A. Common Law Analysis

Although this is a sale of goods, the question asks for an analysis under the common law for comparison purposes. The common law requires a determination of whether failure to deliver half the signs was a material and total breach. This would most likely be answered in the affirmative, especially after the failure persisted beyond a reasonable cure period. As a material breacher, Bill has no right to sue on the contract unless it is divisible. If it is divisible, he may enforce those portions of the contract that he has fully performed (subject to an offset for any damages suffered by Sandy, had she incurred loss or expense relating to the breached portion). If it is not divisible, he has no claim in contract. In some jurisdictions, he may obtain relief on the theory of unjust enrichment (again, subject to any offset for Sandy's damages), but there are courts that refuse even restitutionary relief to a breaching party. Others permit it only when the breach is not willful. Even in those jurisdictions that permit restitutionary recovery, it is likely to be a more difficult and less attractive claim than contractual relief, because the breacher must prove the value of the ultimate economic enrichment actually conferred on the non-breaching party, which could well be lower than the contract price.

Is this contract divisible? In *John v. United Advertising, Inc.*, 439 P.2d 53 (Colo. 1968), the owner of a motel contracted with an advertising agency for the installation and upkeep of seven signs. The contract was structured as a lease and maintenance agreement, not a sale of the signs. The monthly rent payable for each sign was reflected separately. Although five of the signs were properly installed and maintained, one was not erected at all and another was put in the wrong place. The court emphasized that divisibility is a question of fact, to be determined by interpreting the contract in context. The issue to be decided is whether the parties assented to the exchange as a complete whole, so that there would be no bargain at all if any set of promises were eliminated. The motel owner argued that the signs formed a unit, in that they were designed to lead tourists to the motel. As a result, if one was missing, the value of the others was lost. The advertising agency countered that the language of each sign was self-sufficient and did not refer to another sign. In addition, separate consideration was identified for each sign, the contract actually stated that each of the items in the contract could be terminated or modified without affecting others, and billings were made on a "so much per sign basis." The court concluded that the evidence was sufficient to support a finding of divisibility.

In the present case, the contract likewise specifies a separate price for each sign, so it is capable of being broken into subparts. There is some interdependence between the signs in that those in the middle of the strip are intended to guide motorists to the motel after they have seen it advertised at the entrance to the town. The absence of the directional signs makes the signs at the town limits less valuable because prospective customers may zip through without knowing where to turn, and may not bother to come back to look for the motel. However, the signs that have been erected are not rendered meaningless or completely valueless, because they are self-sufficient advertisements. Division of the contract may therefore not seriously damage the value of these signs to Sandy. If so, Bill should be able to enforce the contract with regard to these signs and recover their contract price. Since Sandy suffered no loss as a result of Bill's breach of the remainder of the contract, there is no offset against his recovery.

B. Analysis Under Article 2

Does this analysis change because this is a sale of goods? No section of UCC Article 2 speaks directly to this question, so the above principles of common law are applicable. To the extent that Article 2 deals indirectly with the issue of severability, its approach is consistent with these principles. There are several provisions that recognize the concept of divisibility where the language and purpose of the contract, viewed in its commercial context, indicate that division of the goods into separate units would not impair the value of performance. Section 2.601 suggests that contracts for the sale of goods are normally divisible if the goods can be broken down into "commercial units." It contemplates that a buyer has the right to accept a "commercial unit" of goods that comply, and to reject the rest. To constitute a "commercial unit," an item or collection of goods must be regarded as a unit in commercial usage and must be capable of being traded as a unit without any impairment of value on the market. (*See* §2.105(6).) This approach is also reflected in the general remedy provisions in §§2.702 and 2.711; in §2.709, which allows the seller to recover the price of accepted goods; and in Comment 2 to §2.612, in which the drafters make it clear that when the parties apparently intended delivery in installments, a commercially reasonable fact-based interpretation must be used to apportion price to deliveries, and to break the contract into a set of self-standing exchanges.

6. Because the contract ". . . authorizes the delivery of goods in separate lots to be separately accepted . . ." it satisfies the definition of an installment contract in §2.612. That section allows the buyer to reject any installment that has a non-conformity that substantially impairs its value. If cure is possible and permissible, the buyer may not reject the installment if the seller gives an adequate assurance of cure. In other words, to be able to reject this installment, Sandy must show three things:

(1) The goods are non-conforming.
(2) The non-conformity is serious enough that it substantially reduces the value of that installment. (Thus, where an installment sale is concerned, the perfect tender rule does not apply, and the test for rejection is more equivalent to the common law substantial performance standard.)
(3) The non-conformity cannot be cured.

There can be little doubt that the sign is materially deficient, so the determinative issue is whether the defect is curable. Although the standards of §2.508 may be applicable to the cure of an installment sale, there is some question about whether its specific requirements have been replaced by a more general and looser test set out in Comment 5 to §2.612. That comment indicates that an installment delivery must be accepted if the non-conformity is curable by a price adjustment or later delivery and the seller gives adequate assurance of cure. It could be, therefore, that in an installment sale, we need not be concerned with the rule in §2.508(2) that only permits cure after the time for delivery if the seller had reasonable grounds to believe that the non-conforming tender would be acceptable. (This rule would otherwise apply here because the sign was delivered on its due date, and the time for Bill's performance had expired before he could attempt to redo it.) In any event, under both §2.508 and Comment 5 to §2.612, cure is only permitted if effective remediation is assured and is affected within a reasonable time.

Is Bill's assurance of cure adequate? Although Bill, in his incompetent fog, may have thought that his sloppy work would have been acceptable to Sandy, it is unlikely that he was reasonable in this belief. Furthermore, even if he earnestly intends to make a better sign, bad spelling is not his only shortcoming. Given the atrocious quality of the work tendered, Sandy has no reasonable expectation that cure will be adequate. She should therefore be entitled to reject this installment.

But Sandy does not wish simply to reject this sign. She would like to end the entire contract. Even if a non-conformity allows rejection of the installment under §2.612(2), the breach does not give Sandy the right to cancel the entire contract unless a further element, required by §2.612(3) is satisfied: To terminate the entire contract on the basis of a non-conformity in one or more installments, the buyer must show that the breach "substantially impairs" the value of the contract as a whole. That is, the breach relating to an installment is usually regarded as a partial breach, giving rise only to relief for that non-conformity. The buyer cannot use it as a basis of terminating the entire contract unless it so fundamentally undermines the exchange of values that it defeats the buyer's reasonable expectations concerning the remaining performance.

Therefore, even a serious defect in the sign delivered would not entitle Sandy to terminate the contract relating to the remaining signs unless the defective sign was so interlinked with the others that the defect substantially diminished their value too. This could happen, for example, when the goods in the deficient installment are such a major component of the sale that the other installments have little purpose without it, or when the goods delivered in each installment must be combined to provide the benefit bargained for, and have little use to the buyer on their own. A situation like this does not seem to be involved here. It was already suggested in Example 5 that the contract is probably divisible.

However, the whole contract could also be substantially impaired if the defect is due to such incompetence that the buyer has no reason to expect that the seller is capable of proper performance in future. Comment 6 to §2.612 indicates that the reasonable perception of failure of performance must go beyond insecurity. If the buyer merely has doubts about future installments, the proper course is to demand an assurance of performance under §2.609. However, if the defect in the installment strongly demonstrates that the seller will never be able to deliver what was promised, so that the prospect of adequate future performance is so remote as to be tantamount to a repudiation, the buyer should be able to declare a breach of the entire contract based on the defective installment. Bill's amateurish attempt at signwriting and his apparent obliviousness to its deficiencies should entitle Sandy to use this breach as the basis for termination of the entire contract.

7. Because this contract involves the performance of services in connection with the sale of the signs, it is no longer as obviously subject to the UCC. In a mixed transaction, some courts decide this scope issue by looking at the dominant purpose of the contract. Others apply Article 2 to the sales component, but not to the service aspect. (See Example 1 of Chapter 2.) On the dominant purpose test, this probably still qualifies as a sale of goods, because the services are ancillary to the sale and do not appear to have increased the price. For the purpose of discussion, assume that Article 2 is applicable to the transaction. However, it would not make any substantive difference in many jurisdictions if this conclusion is wrong, because the relevant UCC section, 2.609, is mirrored in Restatement Second §251.

Bill's performance is not due for 26 days, so he cannot yet be in breach of his obligations. Furthermore, his actions before the council cannot be treated as a repudiation, because he has not made an unequivocal statement or taken clear action to indicate an intention not to perform this contract when the time comes. Notwithstanding, his conduct in an unrelated contract of a similar kind has made Sandy feel insecure about his ability to perform his obligations to her in the near future. This has caused her to write to him, making a demand that goes beyond what she is entitled to under the contract, and threatens suspension of her own performance unless the demand is met. If she is unjustified in this demand, then either her failure to pay in five days or her termination at the end of a week would itself be a repudiation of her contractual obligations. Indeed, the very act of making the demand could constitute an unequivocal repudiation, if the demand states the intention to withhold performance unless its unjustified terms are met.

When one party has reasonable grounds to feel insecure about the other's performance, §2.609 permits the insecure party to suspend her own performance and to make a written demand for an adequate assurance of due performance. Upon receiving a justified demand, the other party must provide an adequate assurance within a reasonable time, not exceeding 30 days, failing which, he has repudiated. Both the demand and the response must be reasonable, so this process imposes a duty of careful judgment on each of the parties: The party making the demand must not overreact to the possible threat of breach and must decide not only if the circumstances warrant a demand, but also what assurance is needed. If she is unreasonable in her perception of potential breach, the act of making the demand could itself indicate intent to repudiate. Even if not, repudiation could occur if she follows up by withholding a due performance. In addition, the demand must be carefully aimed. If she asks for too little, the assurance may be useless, but if she asks too much, she could be taken to have repudiated the contract herself by refusing to perform unless the other party agrees to a forced modification. Upon receiving the demand, the other party must react to it within the time prescribed by §2.609. If it is unjustified, he has the right to refuse it altogether. If it is justified but excessive, he may offer a more modest assurance. But if it is justified, failure to give the demanded assurance is a repudiation.

This danger of excessive demand is illustrated by *Pittsburgh-Des Moines Steel Co. v. Brookhaven Manor Water Co.*, 532 F.2d 572 (7th Cir. 1976). A contract for the manufacture and installation of a water tank provided for payment after completion of the job. After the contract was executed, but before the construction of the tank (and hence, some considerable time before payment was due), the seller heard that the buyer was experiencing delay and difficulty in obtaining the loan needed to pay for the tank. The seller had, in any event, begun to regret having agreed to construct the tank on credit, and it therefore used the information about the hitch in the loan as a basis for demanding that the buyer deposit funds in escrow to cover the price of the tank. It later made the additional demand that the buyer's president guarantee the debt until the escrow was established. The seller also stated that it would suspend its own performance until the demands were met. When the buyer did not accede to these demands, futile negotiations followed, and the tank was never made. The seller sued the buyer, and both parties claimed that the contract had been repudiated by the other.

Although the tank was a very large item, to be fabricated and installed on site by the seller, the court found that the contract was a sale of goods. Therefore, §2.609 governed the seller's demand for the escrow and guarantee. The court found the seller to have repudiated by making a demand unjustified by that section. The fact that the buyer had not secured the loan at that stage, some several months before payment would have been due, was not grounds for insecurity. It was by no means clear that there would be a problem in raising the funds by the time payment had to be made. Even if the seller did have some basis for concern, its demand was excessive. The court hinted that while some lesser demand may have been appropriate, such as a request for a letter of intent from the lender, the seller went beyond what was reasonable in the circumstances. Not only did it require the buyer's president to forgo the protection of limited liability, but it also sought to alter the payment terms unilaterally, effectively depriving the buyer of the advantage of credit.

It seems likely that Sandy was acting reasonably in her concern about Bill's likelihood of obtaining a permit. His conduct in a similar transaction for another customer suggests not only that he has some difficulty in complying with

the permit requirements, but also that he lacks self-control and the political finesse to deal with public officials. In addition, he has no doubt alienated the
very people who must decide his next application. If we accept that Sandy had
the right to demand an assurance, did she go too far in requiring the permit to
be obtained in a week? Sometimes, particularly when the other party has said or
done something to cast doubt on the desire to perform, it may be enough to
ask for verbal reassurance. In a case like this, a mere reaffirmation is not likely to
be very helpful. Bill really cannot alleviate her concerns simply by stating that he
is still committed to perform, because he may be incapable of doing so. However, by insisting on an immediate successful application, Sandy seeks to force a
modification of the contract by accelerating Bill's performance (and possibly
doing so at a rate that makes it difficult or impossible for him to comply with
the demand). A demand that requires the other party to assume more onerous
performance obligations is seldom permissible. To justify it, the prospect of
breach must be particularly strong, and there must be no less intrusive way of
eliminating the insecurity. In this case, performance is still some time off and
Bill has given no indication that he will not make the application. A more appropriate demand may have called on Bill to give a prompt and explicit account
of how he plans to avoid a similar outcome in Sandy's application.

If the demand was appropriate, Bill's refusal to honor it would be a repudiation, and Sandy could immediately terminate. Conversely, if as suggested above, the demand was excessive, Sandy may have repudiated simply
by making it. However, we do not have to resolve that issue, because Bill has
not treated it as a repudiation. He has given a response that he sees as adequate and reminded Sandy about her payment due in a few days. This requires a further judgment by Sandy. She could simply back down and pay on
due date, hoping that Bill will perform as required. Alternatively, she could
try a different and less stringent demand, suspending payment until Bill responds, or she could press her original demand and withhold her payment. If
she takes either of these latter courses, she goes out on a limb and can only
hope that if the matter is litigated, the court shares her view that the response
was inadequate and the demanded assurance was no more than she needed to
remove her insecurity.

8. On July 30, Televicious unequivocally repudiated the contract. This
gave Cleaver the option either of accepting the repudiation and immediately
pursuing his remedy for total breach, or of declining to act on the repudiation and giving Televicious the opportunity to repent within a reasonable
time. He chose the latter course. After about ten days had passed without any
sign of retraction from Televicious, Cleaver was given the chance to recoup
some of his potential loss by agreeing to join the African safari during September. Despite his initial decision, Cleaver has the right to change his mind
and accept the repudiation at any time before retraction is communicated to
him. He therefore could have accepted the offer to be a chef on the safari. He
would have had no obligation to notify Televicious of this, because the repu-

diation cannot be retracted once Cleaver has made another commitment on the strength of it. Having accepted the repudiation, Cleaver would no longer have had to hold himself available to perform for Televicious, and could have sued immediately for damages based on the difference between what he would have received under the contract with Televicious, and what he would have earned from the substitute employment. (We leave to Chapter 18 the question of whether someone in Cleaver's position could also have claimed any damages resulting from the loss of potential fame and fortune as a TV celebrity.)

However, Cleaver decided to pass up the opportunity in the hope that Televicious would have a change of heart. When he is eventually left with nothing to do in September, his decision to wait may be held against him. If, when he ultimately sues Televicious for damages, he is found to have acted unreasonably in continuing to await a retraction, his recovery from Televicious will be reduced to the extent that he should have acted to avoid the loss. That is, under the principle of mitigation of damages, he will not be able to hold Televicious liable for the amount that he could have recouped had he resigned himself to the repudiation and gone on the safari.

The crucial question is therefore whether Cleaver was reasonable in continuing to hold out hope for a retraction on August 10. Reasonableness is always a factual issue, to be decided in light of the nature and clarity of the repudiation and the likelihood of repentance under all the circumstances of the case. Televicious clearly and unconditionally expressed its intention to breach and completely ignored Cleaver's invitation to reconsider. He was given no reason to believe that Televicious would change its mind and was unduly optimistic in waiting further. He did not even attempt another communication before refusing the substitute employment. Under these circumstances, he would have quite a difficult task in convincing a court that he reasonably acted to cut down his loss. (Let us assume for now that the safari was indeed an appropriate substitute contract. This question will be discussed further in Chapter 18.)

This principle may be illustrated by *Oloffson v. Coomer*, 296 N.E.2d 871 (Ill. 1973). This case involved a sale of goods, so it is governed by UCC §2.610. However, the analysis under the UCC is the same as under the common law because §2.610 codifies the above principles. It allows the victim of a repudiation either to act immediately on the repudiation or to await performance for a commercially reasonable time. The contract, entered into in April, was for the sale of corn by a farmer to a grain dealer, to be delivered in October and December. In June, the seller told the buyer that he had decided not to plant corn that season and suggested that the buyer make a substitute purchase. Despite being told on several further occasions in the succeeding months that the corn would not be delivered, the buyer persisted in demanding performance until the date due for delivery. By that time the market price of corn had increased beyond that on the date of repudiation, and the question was whether the buyer could recover damages based on the higher price at the delivery date. The court refused to award damages at that rate and confined the buyer to the difference between the contract price and the market price at the time of repudiation. It found that because the repudiation was unequivocal and it would have been easy for the buyer to make a substitute purchase on the market at that time, it was unreasonable for him to await performance any longer.

18

Remedies for Breach of Contract

§18.1 The Scope of this Chapter

Because a contract creates obligations enforceable in law, its breach by one of the parties entitles the other to commence suit to enforce it. This does not mean, of course, that the victim of a breach will inevitably sue. Breaches are often settled by negotiation or by methods of resolution other than litigation, such as mediation or arbitration. Even if not, the victim may decide not to sue because the amount at stake is too small to justify the expense of litigation, or because of the difficulty of proving economic injury, or because it seems clear that the breaching party has no funds or other assets available to pay any judgment that may be obtained. Although the possibilities of informal or *non-judicial enforcement,* the *economic feasibility of litigation,* and the *problem of actually collecting on the judgment* should always be borne in mind, they are not addressed here. It is the concern of this chapter to set out the policies, general principles, and rules that govern the choice of remedy for breach and the measurement of compensation. We therefore focus on the judicial enforcement of the contract following its breach. (This does not mean that the principles discussed here are applicable only in litigation. The rules governing the nature and extent of judicial relief are obviously also relevant to, and form the basis of, any alternative method of resolving liability for breach.)

This is not the only part of the book in which judicial remedies are covered. There are many examples in prior chapters of remedies available to a party to redress a wrong that arises in the context of a transaction. For example, the remedy of avoidance has been discussed repeatedly in connection with topics such as duress, fraud, and mistake. This chapter is distinct in that it deals only with remedies for breach of contract. The discussion here *pre-*

supposes that a *valid and enforceable contract* has been entered into and that one of the parties has *materially breached* that contract. We are not concerned at this point with the issue of what is required for the creation of a valid and enforceable contract, nor with what constitutes a breach, whether a breach occurred, or if that breach is material or trivial. Those matters are considered in prior chapters. For present purposes, the fact of material breach of a binding contract is treated as a given.[1] Therefore, whether you are reading this chapter at the end of the course, after having dealt with the issue of breach, or your contracts course deals with damages at or near the beginning of the year, just accept as a premise that the question of material breach must be settled as a precursor to the determination of damages.

Once these initial issues concerning the formation and breach of a contract have been disposed of, and it is established that the plaintiff does have a claim against the defendant, the remedial issues fall into three distinct but interrelated inquiries:

1. The *nature and extent* of the plaintiff's *compensable loss* must be determined. This requires consideration not only of the plaintiff's injury—the harm suffered as a result of the breach, but also the extent to which the law recognizes the availability of recompense for it.

2. Having established the existence and nature of the injury, we must then decide upon the *remedy that most effectively redresses* it. This involves a consideration of the different means that may be available to rectify the harm, and the rules that govern the calculation or measurement of compensation. If there is more than one way to address the loss, a decision must be made on which remedy is the most efficient and comprehensive.

3. Finally, we must consider if there are any *policies or principles* that may apply to *limit* the *defendant's liability* for the loss.

§18.2   The Basic Goal of Remedies for Breach: Enforcement of the Expectation Interest

§18.2.1   *The Nature of the Expectation Interest*

A valid and enforceable contract justifies a *future expectation* by each of the parties. They are both entitled to expect that the other will honor the contractual promise made and will perform as undertaken. If one of the parties fails to do so, thereby breaching the contract, the expectations of the other

---

1. Damages for non-material breach are discussed in section 17.3.

have been disappointed. Therefore, the fundamental goal of the remedy for breach is to cure that disappointment by giving the victim of the breach exactly what was promised and justifiably expected under the contract. This starkly contrasts contract damages from those for tort: While tort damages seek to compensate for something lost—to restore the victim to the pre-injury position, contract damages aim at compensating for something that was not gained—what the plaintiff should have had. This goal of enforcing contractual expectations is the beacon that guides contract remedies. The principle is described in a number of alternative ways, all of which have essentially the same meaning: Sometimes it is said that the goal is to protect the plaintiff's **expectation interest**; sometimes it is described as giving the plaintiff the **benefit of her bargain**; and sometimes it is said that the purpose of contract remedies is to place the victim of breach in the **position** that she **would have been in had no breach occurred**. This goal of damages applies both at the common law and under the UCC, which codifies it in §1.106.

A party's expectation interest is the value of the performance to her, based on the purpose of the contract, as gleaned from its wording and the circumstances surrounding the contract's formation. However, even though the expectation interest is based on the contractual expectations of the particular party aggrieved by the breach, it is not determined on the purely subjective criterion of her privately held, subjective belief about what she would derive from the contract. Contracts are interpreted *objectively*, so her expectations must be in accordance with what a reasonable person in her position would have expected as the benefit of the transaction, given the language used by the parties to express their agreement, and the circumstances surrounding it.

§18.2.2 An Introduction to the Means of Enforcement: The Primacy of Monetary Compensation over Specific Relief

The most direct and accurate way of enforcing the plaintiff's reasonable expectations under the contract would be for the court to grant an order of **specific performance** of the contract. This is an order to the defendant requiring him to perform as promised. For example, Harpo C. Cord owns the only extant piano known to have been used by Chopin. He entered into a contract with Nick L. Odeon under which he agreed to sell it to Nick for $25 million. Harpo breached the contract by refusing to go through with the sale. Nick's expectation is to gain the piano in exchange for depleting his bank account by $25 million, so the most accurate means for the court to ensure that he achieves that expectation is to compel Harpo to deliver the instrument against payment of its price. This seems like the most obvious solution, and on these facts—because the piano is unique—the court may see this as the most effective and desirable resolution. However, specific performance is not the norm. It is reserved for unusual cases where damages seem to be incapable of adequately compensating the plaintiff. More commonly, the plaintiff's disappointed expectations are compensated for by an award of money.

Why does the law prefer a *money equivalent of expectation* over the real thing? The answer lies partly in considerations of *practicality and policy,* and partly in the *traditional dichotomy between law and equity.* The practical and policy issues may be illustrated by the following example: Sara Nade, an aspiring singer, had entered a singing competition in the hope of winning first prize, the chance to sing the national anthem at an important sports event. To give herself the best chance of winning, she contracted with Harmony R. Peggio, a voice coach, to receive an intensive period of voice training in the week before the competition. Under their contract Harmony undertook, for a fee of $1,500, to give Sara four hours of coaching every day in that week. A few days before the course of instruction was to begin, Harmony notified Sara that she would be leaving town to do a last-minute concert tour, so she could not give the lessons as promised. Sara's expectation interest is to have the lessons for $1,500, and therefore the most accurate way of ensuring that Sara gets exactly what she expected would be for a court to compel Harmony to decline the tour and to give the promised lessons. However, in this situation the remedy of specific performance presents a number of problems: It would be difficult for the court to ensure that Harmony put her best efforts into a job that she is forced to do; the compulsion takes on the aspect of involuntary servitude; and the solution is not very efficient if another teacher could be found instead. For these reasons, it makes sense to allow Harmony to go on her tour, but if her breach results in a loss to Sara, to hold her liable to compensate for that loss.

As noted earlier, the preference for monetary relief is not based only on concerns of practicality, forced labor, and efficiency. Even if none of these problems exists, our legal tradition tends to emphasize damages as the standard remedy for breach of contract and disfavors specific relief in all but the most compelling circumstances. This is because the award of money *damages* was a remedy that could be granted by courts of *law,* whereas *specific performance* was granted only by a court of *equity.* (The distinction between law and equity is explained in section 2.5 and is discussed further in section 18.10.1.) Courts of equity were intended to intervene only when the available remedies at law were inadequate, and therefore a plaintiff who sought the equitable relief of specific performance was required to show that the nature of the expectation interest was such that the only means of achieving adequate relief was by the specific enforcement of the contract. Although courts of law and equity were merged some time ago, this ancient distinction still haunts our decisionmaking. As a result, even if it is practicable to give the plaintiff precisely what she expected, a money substitute is used in the great majority of cases: The plaintiff is awarded a sum of money that aims, as closely as possible, to put her into the economic position she would have been in had the contract been performed.

What is the basic principle on which this monetary award is calculated? To illustrate it, let us add some facts to the case of Harmony's breach of the voice-training contract: After Harmony's breach, Sara was able to find another voice coach, who was available to give her equivalent lessons for the same amount of time, but who charged $1,800 for the course. By hiring him, she got the lessons expected for $300 more, so to place her in her expected position, damages of $300 must be awarded against Harmony. Of course, this is not exactly Sara's expectation, because the teacher was different. However, we can seldom achieve the plaintiff's exact position by paying her money. The aim is to get as close possible. It should also be apparent that the concern here is only with economic loss, so if Sara could obtain the equivalent lessons at exactly the same price as Harmony charged under the contract, she has suffered no financial loss at all and is entitled to no damages for the breach.

§18.2.3 Fundamental Principles of Expectation Relief

The above examples suggest a number of important basic principles which will be recurring themes of the discussion that follows.

a. The Achievement of the Plaintiff's Expectation Is an Aspiration Seldom Precisely Realized

It is the aim of contractual remedies to place the plaintiff in the position she would have been in had there been no breach, but because specific performance is available in only limited circumstances, the precise attainment of that expectation is seldom achieved. The best a court can do, in most cases, is to try to determine, as closely as possible, what monetary award will approximate that result.

This is already clear from the discussion of Sara's employment of a substitute trainer. The monetary award provides her with the compensation of getting the same hours of instruction for the same price, but it does not give her the less tangible benefit of being instructed by the teacher that she bargained for. The facts of the example, having been drawn with deliberate simplicity, do not illustrate some of the additional difficulties that may get in the way of an accurate measure of the value of the expectation. We will consider these later. For the present just bear in mind that the more complex the facts become, and the more uncertain the consequences of breach are, the harder it is to determine the amount of damages necessary to approximate the plaintiff's rightful position. Sometimes the amount awarded may undercompensate the plaintiff, and sometimes it may overcompensate her. It is important to remember that the burden of proving damages is on the plaintiff, who bears the ultimate risk of failing to persuade the factfinder about the fact or extent of loss. This burden is alleviated in some situations by evidentiary presumptions or inferences.

b.   The Economic Nature of Contract Remedies

In the discussion of Harmony's breach, no mention was made of any award for Sara's aggravation, inconvenience, or emotional distress in trying to cope with this last-minute letdown and in finding a replacement for Harmony. Unlike tort law, which is very solicitous of injured feelings and damage to the psyche, contract law is dry-eyed and coldly *commercial*. It does not, except in the most unusual cases, take any account of non-economic injury.

It is implicit in the principle that contract law *compensates only for economic injury;* that there is usually no sanction for a breach that causes no economic loss.[2] This may be disturbing to one who approaches this chapter after having spent so much effort learning that contractual obligations are binding and legally enforceable. Nevertheless, this is a basic truth of contractual remedies. If the contract is not one of the few that qualifies for specific enforcement, and no economic loss can be established, a breach normally results in no legal liability. (Of course, a breach may nevertheless carry some adverse non-legal consequences, such as loss of goodwill or reputation.) It follows naturally from this that damages measured purely by the extent of the plaintiff's loss do not generally distinguish between breaches that are *inadvertent* and those that are *willful and purposeful*. Because the focus is on rectifying harm and not on sanctioning improper conduct, punitive damages are not typically available for a breach of contract (except in unusually egregious cases), even when the violation of the contractual duty was deliberate.

c.   The Moral Dimension of Contract Remedies

The strong emphasis on the compensatory nature of contract remedies suggests that contract law approaches breach quite amorally: The law does not care if a party fails to honor her contract, provided that she compensates the other for any loss resulting from her faithlessness. A contractual promise

---

2. There are limited exceptions to this rule—discussed in section 18.3—when the defendant's conduct in breaching is particularly outrageous or the contract is especially aimed at giving the plaintiff a non-economic benefit.

means nothing more than a **commitment either to perform or to pay compensation** for not doing so—a party may usually feel free to renege on her obligations and "buy out" the other party's rights by paying damages. Although this is largely true, one cannot entirely dismiss the fact that most judges and jurors recognize it as wrong to break a promise, and this moral sense must play some role in the deliberation over relief.

Therefore, although the focus is on compensation, the court's attitude to the need for and extent of that compensation is often affected by the degree of the *defendant's moral blame* in breaching. This means that even though a sanction for breach is not expressly included in an award of damages, there are ways in which the defendant's fault can be taken into account. It is sometimes expressed in rules governing issues such as the allocation of the burden of proof, but it may also be an unarticulated factor in the factfinder's determination of damages. As damages are often not merely a matter of making arithmetical calculations on undisputed facts, the factfinder commonly has considerable discretion to weigh evidence on the fact and extent of the plaintiff's loss, and may be inclined toward greater generosity if the defendant's conduct was unsavory. (And because findings of fact need not be explained in the verdict, and factual determinations are not overruled on appeal unless there is no reasonable basis for them in the evidence, the factfinder's reaction to evidence of the defendant's moral blame is not easily divined or challenged.)

d. The Economic Justification for Confining Damages to Financial Loss: The Concept of Efficient Breach

Although the principle of confining damages to financial loss predates the widespread resort to economics to explain, criticize, or justify legal rules, in recent times it has become popular to analyze the rule in economic terms. It is now commonly rationalized by the concept of efficient breach. A *breach* of contract is said to be *efficient* if the *defendant's cost to perform* would *exceed the benefit that performance* would give to *both parties*. Where this is so, the defendant saves enough money by breaching to enable her to pay compensatory damages to the plaintiff and still come out ahead. Provided that one looks only at the *economic impact* of the breach, one can say in such a case that the defendant's breach does not harm the plaintiff, who receives the financial benefit of his bargain, and yet it improves the defendant's position. In this sense, it satisfies the criterion of economic efficiency in that it makes the defendant better off without making the plaintiff worse off. If this is true, it follows that a *rational contracting party* with *full information* will choose to breach where circumstances make the breach efficient. The law should not discourage this because a legal rule that permits efficient breach—such as the rule that a plaintiff is entitled only to damages for economic loss—is itself efficient and thus best serves the interests of society.

Although analysis of this type is of some help in understanding and justifying the approach to contract damages, it has many limitations. The most significant is, of course, that it takes into account neither important non-economic values (such as reliability, fair dealing, or faithfulness), nor those consequences of breach that are not measurable in economic terms (such as inconvenience, disappointment, or frustration). As a result, a conclusion that a breach imposes no harm on the plaintiff or on society may be misguided if based purely on quantifiable financial considerations.

Furthermore, economically efficient decisionmaking can only be achieved if all the conditions are right: The market must be competitive and stable, so that the relative costs and benefits of performing and breaching can be gauged. The party contemplating breach must be capable of acting voluntarily and rationally, and must have sufficiently full and reliable information to enable her to make a prediction of likely losses and gains. In addition, the **transaction costs** involved in terminating this contract and making substitutes must be small enough so as not to eliminate any advantage achieved by the breach. (Transaction costs are those costs incurred by both parties in dealing with the breach and any substitute transactions. They would include such expenses as the cost to the breaching party of entering into the other transaction perceived as more profitable, the aggrieved party's costs in finding and making a substitute contract, and the costs of litigating or otherwise resolving the breach issue between the parties.) Such ideal conditions are seldom likely to exist, which means that it will often be difficult to know at the time of breach whether it will turn out to have been economically efficient. To the extent that a theory of efficient breach is predicated on an unrealistic assumption of rational, voluntary, and informed behavior in a perfect market, with negligible transaction costs, it is likely to be unreliable, and more an academic model than a reflection of reality.

§18.2.4   *The Enforcement of a Damage Award*

The illustrations in section 18.2.2 do not indicate what happens after Sara gets her judgment of $300 against Harmony. The means of collecting payment on a judgment is beyond our scope, but it is useful to describe it briefly to provide an overall picture of the enforcement process. After the judgment is obtained (or if appealed, once it is affirmed on appeal),[3] Harmony may pay it voluntarily, thereby ending the matter. If she does not, Sara's only means of enforcing the judgment is to have a **writ of execution** issued by the clerk

---

3. The claim in the example is for $300. Although it is used here for the purposes of illustrating the process of collection, it should be noted that when the amount in issue is that small (or indeed, even considerably larger), very few plaintiffs would incur the legal expense of pursuing it. It would not take long for legal costs to exceed it.

of the court to the sheriff (or equivalent official), calling on that official to find, seize, and sell property owned by Harmony to satisfy the judgment. The sheriff tries to execute the writ by finding property sufficient to satisfy the amount of the judgment, taking custody of it (known as levying upon it), and selling it at public auction. The proceeds of the sale are then paid to Sara, less the costs of execution. There are variations of this procedure that need not concern us here.

The point is that a **judgment** itself is **merely a finding of liability.** It does not guarantee that the plaintiff will get paid. If the defendant fails to satisfy it, and no assets can be found to execute upon, the plaintiff may never see her money. This sobering reality must be taken into account by anyone who decides to initiate litigation, and it means that being able to establish breach and damages are only part of the problem of enforcement. A judgment in law for damages is said to be *in rem*—it is enforceable only against the property of the defendant, and if the defendant has no property, the plaintiff loses in the end, having incurred substantial legal costs in the process.

§18.3 The Calculation of Expectation Damages

It is essential to bear in mind that the aim of expectation damages is to *simulate as closely as possible* the *plaintiff's economic situation* in the *absence of breach*. To determine the amount of money needed to approximate that position, a comparison must be made between what the plaintiff had the *right to expect and what she actually got*. Although the facts needed to calculate these two points of comparison can be very complicated and sometimes immensely difficult to prove, the basic concept of the comparison is straightforward. If one does not keep it in sight and use it constantly as a yardstick, one risks getting lost and confused.

Different formulas have been devised for use in making the comparison. These formulas are really just checklists to remind one of the factors to be taken into account, and they are only helpful to the extent that they do reliably cover every component of the calculation and signal clearly what figures go into each of them. A particular formula may be specific to certain kinds of cases and may not work well in others. In general, there are two essential elements to any formula, no matter how it structures the calculation: One part of it will *count up the plaintiff's losses* caused by the breach, and the other will *take into account* any *gains or recoupments* that she has made as a result of rescission of the contract. Damages consist of the losses less the gains. The Restatement Second §347 suggests the following general formula:

Damages =
Plaintiff's loss in value caused by the defendant's non-performance
    (This is determined by deducting the contractual value of what the plaintiff received from what she was promised)

Plus
Any **other loss**
>(This includes consequential and incidental damages)

Less
Any **cost or loss** the plaintiff **avoided** by not having to perform

The principles and method of calculation are best explained by some concrete illustrations that describe some different types of situations and the various considerations that must be taken into account under each of them. Note that the actual ingredients of the calculation shift in accordance with the nature of the contract in question, but that the basic inquiry is always the same—the determination of damages always revolves around a comparison between the plaintiff's rightful position under the contract and her actual situation as a result of the breach.

a. Cases Involving a Substitute Transaction Made by the Plaintiff: Damages Are Based on the Loss Incurred as a Result of Having to Make the Substitute Contract

We have already seen that in her simple contract for the purchase of voice training services, Sara's damages could be calculated by measuring the difference between what it would have cost her to receive the services under the contract, and what it ultimately cost her to obtain equivalent services elsewhere. That is, had the contract not been breached by Harmony, she would have had 28 hours of voice training for $1,500. As a result of the breach, she had 28 hours of training for $1,800, so damages of $300 puts her in the position she would have been in had the contract been performed.

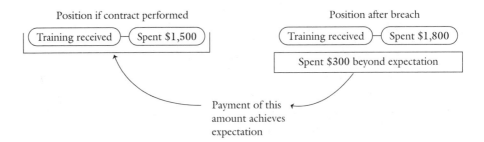

Exactly the same calculation and result would occur if, instead of purchasing lessons for $1,500, Sara had bought a car from Harmony for that price, Harmony breached by refusing to deliver, and Sara managed to find an equivalent substitute on the market for $1,800. UCC §2.712 codifies this by expressing the buyer's damages as the difference between the cover (i.e., repurchase) price and the contract price.

Change the facts: It is Sara who breached by canceling the lessons, and Harmony entered a substitute transaction by taking on a new student to fill the slot left open by Sara's breach. The same principle applies, but because the plaintiff is the provider of services, damage results only if the gains from the substitute transaction are less than those expected from the breached contract. For example, assume that Harmony could not find a replacement student at Sara's advanced level, and so she accepted a more junior student at the lower rate of $700 for the 28 hours. Harmony would be entitled to damages of $800, calculated by deducting the $700 earnings under the substitute contract from the $1,500 she expected to earn under her contract with Harmony. Similarly, a seller of goods who reasonably resells the goods at a lower price following the buyer's breach is entitled under UCC §2.706 to the difference between the contract price and the lower resale price.

b. Cases in Which the Plaintiff Could Have Made a Substitute Transaction, but Did Not Do So or Failed to Do So Reasonably: Damages Are Measured by a Comparison Between the Contract Price and the Market Value of a Substitute

Under both the common law and the UCC, if the aggrieved party did not enter into a substitute transaction, she is entitled to sue for loss based on a *hypothetical substitute,* valued at the market rate (which would have to be established by testimony, typically of an expert witness). Therefore, if, after Harmony's breach, Sara decided not to find a replacement teacher, and if the market value of the lessons is higher than what Harmony charged her, she could still sue Harmony for the difference between the market value of 28 hours of equivalent instruction and the contract price. Similarly, following Sara's breach, Harmony could have decided not to book the other student and could have claimed the difference between the contract price and the market rate she would have earned had she taken the substitute student. The same principle applies under the UCC. Section 2.713 allows the buyer the market-contract difference as damages, and §2.708(1) provides for contract-market damages for the seller.

The market price may also be used as the basis for calculating damages when the plaintiff did enter a substitute transaction, but the principle of mitigation, discussed in section 18.6.2, makes it inappropriate to award damages based on the actual cost of the substitute because the cost of the substitute transaction was higher than it needed to have been. This may happen when the market was rising and the plaintiff waited too long before making the substitute contract, or she chose an unreasonably expensive substitute. For example, following Harmony's breach, Sara hired a substitute teacher for $1,800, but that teacher charges more than the market rate of $1,600. If Sara could reasonably have found a teacher at the market rate, her damages will be confined to $100. This principle applies under the UCC as well and is reflected in UCC §§2.706 and 2.712, which require resale or cover to be without unreasonable delay and on reasonable terms.

When market value is used as the basis of determining damages, it must be decided at which *place and time* the value must be determined. If the parties reside in the same place and the performance was to occur in that place, there is no problem in deciding on the locality of the market, but if more than one location is connected to the contract, it must be decided which one should be used to measure market value. In addition, a market may fluctuate, so it is necessary to decide the date on which value is to be measured. There are different views on the most appropriate choice of market, and some inconsistency on this issue between the common law, the treatment of the seller under UCC §2.708, and the treatment of the buyer under UCC §2.713. Without getting into that complexity, it may simply be observed that the most sensible approach is to use the time and place that most closely approximates the market that the aggrieved party would reasonably have entered to obtain the substitute.

c. Cases Involving a Contract for Services, in Which Breach Results in Lost Income that Cannot Be Recouped: Damages May Be Equivalent to the Full Value of the Expected Performance

Sometimes it may not be possible for the victim of a breach to find a substitute transaction. If the contract is for services, such as an employment contract in which the employee's only performance is her labor, and if the employee cannot find another job, a breach by the employer results in the employee's loss of her entire expectation under the contract. In such circumstances, the only way to compensate for the employee's disappointed expectation is to award damages equivalent to the full consideration due to her under the contract. For example, a few days before the voice training lessons are to begin, Sara reneges on her contract with Harmony because she decides that she does not need voice training. At this late date, Harmony cannot find another pupil to substitute for Sara, so she loses 28 hours of gainful employment. Sara would have come to Harmony's home for the lessons, and Harmony would not have incurred any costs in performing the service. That is, the full $1,500 would have been profit to her. Had the contract been performed she would have spent nothing and gained $1,500; now she still spends nothing, but gains nothing. Therefore, a payment of $1,500 is needed to give her the benefit of her bargain. Of course, this award really puts her in a better position than the contract would have done, because she does not have to work for it. But this is not taken into account when her savings—avoiding the act of working—have no monetary significance.

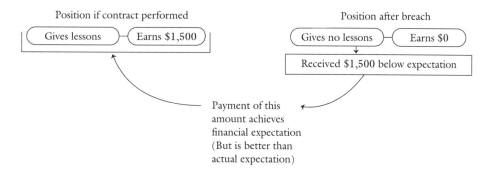

d. Cases in Which the Breach of a Contract Results in the Plaintiff's Losing Income but Also Saving Costs: Damages Are Measured by Deducting Savings from Expected Returns

The result in the above example would be different if Harmony would have had to incur costs to perform. Say that she would have needed to hire an accompanist for $600 to play the piano during the lessons and she is able to avoid doing so as a result of the breach. This cost, which is incurred solely in the process of and for the purpose of performing, is known as a **direct or variable cost.** It must be distinguished from **fixed cost or overhead,** such as Harmony's rent or utilities, which would have to be paid whether or not she performed this contract, and is hence not saved by the breach. Because direct costs would have reduced her expected profit had the contract been performed, it stands to reason that as they are actually saved as a result of the breach (or could have been saved if the plaintiff acted reasonably), they must be deducted from gains to achieve true expectation.

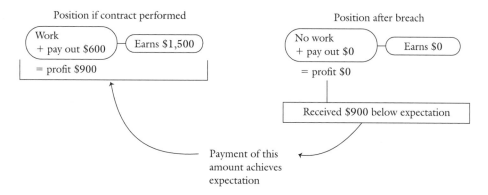

Of course, she *must have been able to save the costs* by reasonable action. The above example assumed that Harmony had the right to cancel her contract with the accompanist, thereby avoiding that direct cost. However, if she could not cancel without incurring liability to him for his fee (that is, she had made an irrevocable contractual commitment to him) she would not save these costs as a result of Sara's breach, and they would not be deducted.

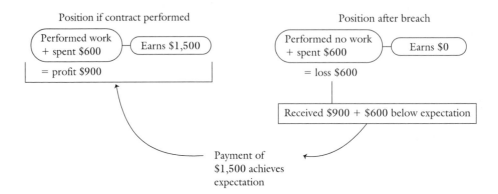

The same result would be reached if, instead of a contract for the provision of services, we were dealing with a sale of goods to be manufactured by the seller. If the buyer breached before the fabrication has begun, so that the seller avoids the direct costs of making the goods, the seller's damages are its lost profits on the sale, calculated by deducting the costs saved from the contract price.

As noted earlier, fixed costs (overhead expenses) are not saved by the breach and are not therefore deducted from damages. The above calculations therefore do not take into account costs such as the rent that Harmony paid for her studio or any other expenses that she had to incur in the course of her business, whether or not she taught Sara. Therefore, when we talk of the recovery of profit in a case like this, we mean gross, not net, profit.

In the first of the above illustrations, Harmony could avoid the direct cost of hiring the accompanist, so her damages are pure profit. But in the second, because she could not save this direct cost, her recovery includes both her *expected profit* and the *reimbursement* of the *wasted expenditure* that she incurred (or was committed to pay) in *reliance* on the contract. In a situation like this, when the plaintiff has incurred the expense of partial performance before the breach, a convenient formula for calculating expectation damages is therefore:

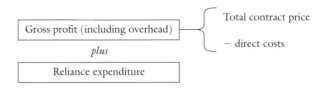

If the plaintiff has received any *part payment* under the contract or has managed to salvage any of the expenditure, that would be *offset* against recovery, and any *consequential or incidental losses* would be *added* to the recovery. Thus the full formula is:

> Gross profit
>
> + reliance
>
> − payments or proceeds
>
> + other loss (consequential or incidental damages)

Discussion of consequential and incidental damages is deferred for later, but the other three elements of the formula may be illustrated by the following further examples involving a construction contract and a sale of goods:

Some months before the singing competition, and in anticipation of winning it and becoming an internationally renowned star, Sara decided to build a fully-equipped recording studio onto the back of her house. She had the plans drawn, and entered into a contract with Ken Tractor to construct it for a total price of $75,000. The contract required Sara to make a down payment of $5,000 and to pay the remainder of the price in installments as the construction proceeded. Sara made the down payment, and Ken began work about two weeks before the competition. On the eve of the competition, he had reached the stage of completing the foundation and the framing of the new studio. Sara did not win the competition, and she immediately terminated the contract for construction of the studio. As she had no right to do this, she has breached. At that point, Ken had received only his initial payment of $5,000. His costs in material, laborer's wages, and subcontractor charges to date were $10,000. He can show that had he completed the studio, his total direct cost would have been $60,000. The above formula leads us to a damage recovery of $20,000:

Gross profit	Contract price	$75,000
	− total direct cost	$60,000
	=	$15,000
Plus **reliance expenditure**	+	$10,000
Total **(profit + reliance)**	=	$25,000
Less **payments received**	−	$5,000
Recovery	=	$20,000

If you make the comparison between Ken's expected position and his position following breach, as we have done in prior illustrations, you will find that the payment of $20,000 achieves his expectation.

Consider a different case: Sara decided to have a special evening gown made for her appearance at the competition. She contracted with Cadenza La Scala, a dressmaker, for the manufacture of the dress for $1,500. Sara paid a deposit of $150 to Cadenza. After Cadenza had begun work, Sara decided that she had been profligate in ordering such an expensive outfit and decided to use an old prom dress instead. She immediately told Cadenza to stop work, thereby breaching the contract. At that stage, Cadenza had spent $200 on fabric that she had cut according to the pattern designed for Sara. In its present form, the cut fabric could be sold as scrap for $5. If Cadenza completes the dress, she will have to spend a further $50 on materials, but it would be very hard to sell the completed product because it was cut to fit Sara and it reflects her peculiar and rather eccentric fashion sense. This contract is a sale of goods, and UCC §2.708(2) codifies the formula set out above. Before looking at §2.708(2), we should note that as a manufacturer of the goods, Cadenza has the option under §2.704(2) of either scrapping the dress or of completing it and selling it to someone else. In making this choice, she must exercise commercially reasonable judgment. She would be justified in completing and attempting to resell the dress if she reasonably believed that by doing so, she could recoup all or most of the profit lost by Sara's breach, thereby reducing or eliminating her damages. As there is unlikely to be a ready market for such an idiosyncratic piece of clothing, the more reasonable judgment would be to scrap it and to seek damages under our formula, which is adopted in §2.708(2). Her recovery would be:

Gross profit	{	Contract price	$1,500
		− total direct cost	−$250
			=$1,250
Plus	reliance expenditure		+$200
Total	(profit + reliance)		=$1,450
Less	payments made ($150)		
	and salvage ($5)		−$155
Recovery			=$1,295

Sara's down payment is of course an offset, as it was in the prior example, but the salvage must also be included in the deduction because it is, in a sense, a substitute transaction. Cadenza gains the $5 because she was able to sell the fabric—something she would not have been entitled to do in the absence of breach.

Having labored through this rather exhausting set of illustrations, you should by now be quite convinced of the basic point of this section: There are different ways of expressing the formula for measuring expectation damages. To be helpful, any formula employed must be geared to the facts of the particular type of case, and it must enable you to deal with the fundamental task of calculating the shortfall between what was reasonably expected under the contract and what was received.

§18.4 An Overview of Expectation Damages Under UCC Article 2

§18.4.1 The Basic Principles

The discussion of expectation damages in section 18.3 covers both the common law and UCC Article 2, and includes illustrations concerning sales of goods. You are therefore already familiar with the pertinent Code provisions. Notwithstanding, it may be helpful to review the Article 2 provisions on expectation damages as a whole to show their organization, the symmetry between buyer's and seller's remedies, and their basis in common law principles.

The concept of expectation relief under Article 2 is essentially the same as that under the common law. Like the common law, it reserves the remedy of specific performance for special cases and treats damages as the primary remedy for breach. The award of damages is meant to achieve, as closely as possible, the economic position the plaintiff would have been in had there been no breach. This principle is strongly articulated in §1.106(1), which declares that UCC remedies ". . . shall be liberally administered to the end that the aggrieved party may be put in as good a position as if the other party had fully performed. . . ." Article 2 provides statutory formulas for calculating compensation. It organizes them into seller's remedies for the buyer's breach (§§2.703–2.710) and buyer's remedies for the seller's breach (§§2.711–2.717). Although there is necessarily some variation between these two sets of remedies, they are largely mirror images of each other, providing approximately equivalent rights to buyers and sellers, but taking into account the somewhat different remedial needs of each.

§18.4.2 The Seller's Remedies

Sections 2.706, 2.708, and 2.709 contain the core of the seller's expectation remedies. Section 2.709 is the seller's specific performance remedy for payment of the price of the goods. Like the common law, Article 2 sees specific enforcement of the contract as a limited and secondary remedy, available only when damages are inappropriate. Section 2.709 therefore allows the seller to claim the price of the goods only when the goods have been accepted by the buyer or they are incapable of being resold because they have been lost or damaged or are just not resalable.

The other two sections contain the primary remedies of the seller's expectation damages where the buyer breaches by failing to accept conforming goods tendered by the seller. Section 2.706 permits an aggrieved seller to enter a *substitute transaction* by reselling the goods and, provided that the resale is made in good faith and in a commercially reasonable manner, to recover the shortfall between the contract price and the resale price. Section 2.708(1) recognizes that damages may be based on a *hypothetical resale* as an alternative to actual resale. It allows the seller to calculate damages based on the difference between the contract price and the market price of the goods at the time and place at which delivery was to have been tendered under the contract. This may be used, for example, when the seller elects not to resell, or when the resale was not conducted reasonably, resulting in too low a resale price. Some, but not all, courts even allow it as an alternative when the seller has resold above the market price, so that the contract-market difference provides a more advantageous recovery.

When it is inappropriate to use the contract-market difference as a basis for measuring damages (such as cases in which the seller decides not to manufacture the goods following breach, or suffers a loss in volume of sales as explained in section 18.6.3), §2.708(2) permits recovery of the seller's *gross profit plus reliance expenses, less allowance for payments or salvage received.*

§18.4.3   The Buyer's Remedies

The buyer's specific performance remedy is set out in §2.716. It, too, is a secondary remedy, available only when damages cannot adequately compensate because the goods are fairly regarded as unique under the circumstances of the case. In other situations in which the buyer has rejected nonconforming goods or the seller has failed to deliver any goods at all, the buyer is confined to substitutionary damages, based on an actual good faith and reasonable **repurchase** of the goods (**cover**) under §2.712 or a **hypothetical repurchase** under 2.713, calculated as the difference between the market price at the time the buyer learned of the breach and the contract price. (Note that the language identifying the buyer's hypothetical market is different from that set out for the seller in §2.708(1). This provision has caused interpretational difficulties that are not considered here.) Article 2 prefers the cover-contract difference as the more realistic measure, but the buyer is permitted not to cover, and instead use the market price of the goods as a basis of recovery. The market standard is also used if the buyer did not act reasonably in covering, so that the cover price is excessive. As in the case of sellers, there is some controversy over whether a buyer who has covered at a price lower than the market may nevertheless elect to sue for damages based on the more advantageous market-contract difference.

In some cases, a buyer may not be able to make a substitute transaction and may suffer **consequential damages** as a result of the breach. If so, §§2.714 and 2.715 permit their recovery. (The nature of consequential damages and the prerequisites for their recovery is discussed below.) Finally, when the seller has breached by delivering goods that are defective or not in conformity with what was promised under the contract, but the goods have been *accepted* by the buyer, damages based on an actual or hypothetical repurchase are not appropriate. Section 2.714 therefore measures damages for accepted goods based on the loss suffered by the buyer as a result of the *deficiency* in the goods. This principle ties in with the discussion of partial breach in Chapter 17.

§18.5 The Distinction Between Direct and Consequential Damages

In all the examples used up to now, we have been concerned only with damages that are a direct result of the breach. That is, they can be readily and easily attributed to the breach and are designed to compensate for the very performance that has been promised. Thus, for example, after Harmony breached her promise to coach Sara, Sara's cost of hiring a substitute trainer does no more than substitute for the performance of the contract itself. The same is true when Ken Tractor or Cadenza La Scala seek their outlay and expected profit in their construction or manufacturing contracts. These cases are all characterized by the fact that the award of damages goes no further than the confines of the contract itself to compensate for the breach. The payment of money is designed to give nothing more than the benefit of performance, whether in the form of the costs of a substitute or the lost gains under the contract. The payment of damages thus acts as a **direct equivalent** for the **expected performance** and thereby fully cures the disappointed expectation. For this reason, the compensation paid is called **direct damages.**

In some cases, however, it is not enough to award only these direct damages, because the breach has had more far-ranging consequences. Not only has it disappointed the direct expectations under the contract, but it has *caused further losses* in *other transactions or endeavors* that were *dependent upon the contract.* For example, recall that Harmony had undertaken to give Sara a series of voice training lessons in the week before the competition. In our first illustration, she reneged just a few days before the lessons were to begin, but Sara was able to find another teacher. What if no other teacher was available, so that Sara could not obtain the training? As a result of being deprived of coaching in the crucial period before the competition, she was not adequately prepared for it. A whole horde of voice experts are available to testify, based on meticulous scientific tests, that Sara has talent of almost superhuman dimensions, and she would have been able to sing circles around the other competitors had she received the week's intensive training. If this can indeed be shown, a mere award of the cost of a substitute teacher comes nowhere near to compensating for her contractual expectations. Her loss consequent upon the breach is far more serious and must take account of all the opportunities for fame and fortune that would have flowed from her success in the competition. These losses, consequent on the breach, are called **consequential damages.**

This example graphically portrays the difference between direct and consequential damages, but it also suggests some of the particular problems that a plaintiff must deal with to obtain consequential damages. Even if she has a bevy of experts to attest to her genius and the certainty of victory that would have followed proper training, Harmony can probably summon an equivalent phalanx of experts who will conclude differently. Even if Sara succeeds in convincing the factfinder of the important role that training would have played in her success, she must also establish the probability that Harmony's breach was the only reason why she did not win, that Harmony should reasonably have understood that this consequence was likely, and that Sara could not herself have taken some reasonable action to prevent it. Finally, Sara would also have to make a credible showing of the actual harm she suffered—that is, the opportunities that she lost, and would have to be able to place a plausible money value on her injury. All these considerations are commonly referred to as limitations on her recovery, and they are discussed more fully in the next section.

§18.6   Limitations on Expectation Recovery

§18.6.1   *The Nature and Goals of the Limitations*

As just intimated, a number of factors, often referred to as limitations on expectation damages, must be taken into account in reaching a final decision on the extent of the proper monetary award. Although called limitations, these factors are not, for the most part, external checks on damages, but are simply an expression of principles inherent in the goal of compensating for the loss of reasonable expectations. They represent the following specific values and practical considerations that are listed briefly before being examined in detail:

1.   In determining damages for the breach of a contract, we must be careful to remember that the extent and scope of damages should be consistent with what was reasonably contemplated by the parties at the time of contracting. This gives rise to the concept of **foreseeability.**

2.   Although the law sympathizes with the victim of a breach, it does not allow her to hold the breacher responsible for increased losses resulting from her own irrational or unfair behavior. Therefore, if the plaintiff unreasonably or dishonestly worsens the loss following breach, the damages will not include compensation for such aggravated loss. This is the principle of **mitigation.**

3.   Because damages are intended to compensate for losses resulting from the breach, it follows that the plaintiff can claim only those damages caused by the breach. She must therefore show a causal link between the breach and the loss. This is the principle of **causation.**

4.   As contract remedies are concerned with economic loss, it is not enough for the plaintiff to prove that a breach occurred. She must also show that the breach resulted in financial loss, and must provide adequate evidence of the monetary extent of the loss. This is the principle of **reasonable certainty.**

5.   We have already seen in several different areas of contract law (for example, in sections 9.6.5, 14.2.3, 16.11.1, and 17.3.4) that courts exercise a general discretion to temper the enforcement of contract rights when rigid enforcement would have an unjustifiably harsh effect on the party against whom those rights are asserted. This general concept of **unfair forfeiture** is also applied when damages, otherwise available on a strict application of the rules, would unfairly harm the defendant and result in a windfall to the plaintiff.

§18.6.2   *Foreseeability*

An event or consequence is foreseeable when a reasonable person would realize the likelihood of its occurrence. Foreseeability is thus an *objective* concept, concerned not with what a particular person actually did foresee, but what she would have foreseen had she reasonably contemplated the course of likely future events. Applied in the context of liability for breach of contract, damages are foreseeable when, at the **time of making the contract,** the party who ultimately breached **reasonably should have realized** that those damages would be **a likely consequence of the breach.** Because contractual liability is based on the breach of a consensual relationship, it is a firm principle of our law that a breaching party should not be held accountable for losses unless, at the time of making the contract, she reasonably should have conceived of those losses as a *probable result* of her breach. The reasonable foresight of probable consequences depends on the extent of information available to a party, and it is not fair to impose liability on a breaching party if she could not reasonably have anticipated the loss when making the contract, because she did not have access to information at that time that would have alerted her to the probable result of her breach. The time of contracting, and not the time of breach, must necessarily be the point at which foreseeability is gauged if the crucial issue is whether the breaching party should be taken to have predicted and risked liability of the kind suffered.

Foreseeability is not likely to be an issue when direct damages are concerned. When parties enter a contract, they do or should understand that if one of them breaches, the other may lose a profit that would have been earned under the contract, or may suffer a loss or added expense in entering a substitute transaction. This does not mean that a party actually has to foresee the amount or exact nature of the loss or the precise way in which the other party would elect to attain his expectation, but merely that she reasonably understands that if she breaches, she will be responsible for lost profits or the cost of a reasonable substitute.

However, the breach could have consequences beyond the actual deprivation of the contracted performance because other transactions or ventures are dependent upon it. Unless the other party has some reason to know that her breach will have an impact beyond the simple deprivation of the immediate contract performance, it is not fair to hold her accountable for such **consequential losses**. This is the focus of the principle of foreseeability. It confines liability for consequential damages to those losses that a party reasonably should have contemplated, based on information to which she had access at the time of contracting, as a probable result of her breach.

The foreseeability principle is regarded as having been firmly established in the common law by the English case, *Hadley v. Baxendale,* 156 Eng. Rep. 145 (Exchequer 1864). The owners of a mill delivered a broken millshaft to a carrier for shipment to the manufacturer so that it could be used as a model for a new one. There was a delay in the shipment. Because this was the mill's only shaft, the delay idled the mill for longer than necessary. The owners sued the carrier for damages based on the profit that they lost when the mill could not operate during the period of delay. Although the court acknowledged that the delay did in fact directly result in the loss of profits, it declined to award those lost profits as damages. The court found the carrier not to be accountable for that loss because it was not told that this was the only shaft and had no way of knowing that a delay would cause the mill to lie idle.[4] The court enunciated the rule of foreseeability that is still current today and is reflected in modern formulations in language that deviates little from

---

4. The headnote in the case always confounds students because it clearly states that the clerk was told that the mill was stopped. This has been explained by commentators on the basis that the headnote does not accurately reflect the facts, or that communication to the clerk was not sufficient to bind his employer.

that used in the case: It held that damages for breach may only be recoverable if one of two conditions is satisfied: Either the loss must be one that may fairly and reasonably be considered to arise naturally—*in the ordinary course of things*—from the breach, or it must be one that *may reasonably be supposed to have been contemplated by the parties* at the *time of contract* as a *reasonable consequence* of breach. (Although *Hadley* refers to the parties' contemplation, we are, of course, principally interested in the reasonable contemplation of the party who breached. By referring to the common contemplation, the court merely denotes the objective standard—not what the breaching party actually knew and realized, but what he should reasonably have contemplated.)

The rule in *Hadley* may be found in both Restatement Second §351 and UCC §2.715. In essence, it breaks damages into two categories:

a. General Damages

Damages that arise naturally, in the ordinary course, are called "general damages." They include not only all easily imaginable direct damages, but also those consequential damages that should be *obvious* to the breacher *without any special or particular knowledge* of the other party's circumstances or affairs, because such a loss would be a *normal and well-accepted likelihood* of the breach of a contract of this kind. Of course what is generally understood as a likely consequence of breach is not decided in the abstract, but in light of the market in which the parties are dealing.

For example, the roof of a home is damaged by a falling branch. The homeowner contracts with a roofer to repair the roof without delay, and the roofer promises to make the repair on the very day of the damage. If the roofer breaches the contract by not showing up, he must surely contemplate the probability of direct damages—that the owner may try to engage another roofer and to hold him liable for damages if the reasonable substitute is higher-priced. However, the breaching roofer must also reasonably realize that the owner may not be able to get someone else out immediately and that if it rains, there could be water damage to the interior of the house under the broken roof section. Any damage to the interior is consequential—it is not a cost of achieving the promised performance, but a loss resulting as a consequence of (I could have said "flowing from," but that sounds too much like a pun) the breach. This consequential damage would fall into the first category identified in *Hadley* because the possibility of rain damage is something that may reasonably be considered as arising naturally in the normal course of human experience. One needs no special information about the homeowner's affairs to recognize this risk of breach. (Of course, if the owner could have taken temporary measures to prevent water damage but did not do so, the owner's failure to mitigate could be a different basis for the denial of consequential damages.)

b.   Special Damages

The second category, called "special damages," can be illustrated by embellishing the facts of the last example. Say that the area beneath the broken roof happened to contain an expensive piece of electronic equipment that is affixed to the floor and cannot be moved or otherwise protected.[5] Unless the roofer was told or otherwise had reason to know about the equipment at the time that he made the contract, it would not be fair to hold him liable for damage to it because he had *no basis for expecting this loss.* Had he known about it, he may well have declined the contract or he may have decided to undertake it only if the owner paid a higher price to cover the cost of extra precautions or as a premium for the assumption of the greater risk of liability. By not giving the roofer the information, the homeowner deprives him of the means to make a rational decision on risk or to take additional steps to minimize the chance of breach. He therefore should not be able to hold him accountable for the unusual loss. Not only does the rule protect the roofer from surprise liability, but the fact that the rule exists is likely to be an incentive to a party in the owner's position to provide adequate information, which is likely to increase the *efficiency of transacting* and may even lessen the chance of breach. The foreseeability principle can therefore be justified as economically efficient as well as fair.

The concept of **reasonable contemplation** is central to the foreseeability of special damages, but its scope and meaning are elusive. To begin with, recognize that it does not require that a reasonable person in the breacher's position would have foreseen the exact loss with great precision and specificity. All that is required is that a loss of that **nature and approximate extent** could be conceived of as a **probability.** In requiring the contemplated loss to be probable, **rather than just possible,** the law does not cover every possibly imagined serendipitous or outlandish consequence, but it does cover more than those outcomes that are obvious inevitabilities. This means that it can be a subtle exercise to decide on the strength of the link between the information available to the breacher and her reasonable accountability for the ultimate consequences of her breach.

There is also some obscurity in the question of the relationship between the *nature of the exchange* under the contract and the *loss*—the extent to which the test of reasonable contemplation should take into account the type and value of the contractual exchange. There was a time, earlier this century, when courts described the test as one of *tacit agreement:* The circumstances of the contract must justify the conclusion, not merely that the breaching party should have foreseen the probability of loss, but must have tacitly ac-

---

5. Again, if it could be moved, protected, or sheltered by a makeshift covering, the owner's failure to take action to safeguard it would raise the issue of mitigation of damages in addition to the foreseeability question.

cepted liability for it. That is, had the likely consequences of the breach been brought to her attention at the time of contracting, she would have agreed that she had assumed liability for them. The tacit agreement test would go beyond an evaluation of the information available to the breaching party at the time of contracting, and would also examine the question of whether the consideration given to her reflected the extent of risk assumed. The tacit agreement test is generally regarded as *too restrictive by modern courts,* and it is expressly rejected by Restatement Second §351, Comment *a* and UCC §2.715, Comment 2. In contemporary law, the focus of reasonable contemplation is therefore more on the relationship between the information available to the breacher and the loss, and less on the relationship of the loss to the extent of risk and the consideration received. In other words, it is possible that a party could be held to have contemplated great liability despite the modest value of what she was to gain from the contract. This does not mean that the value of the consideration given to the breacher is invariably irrelevant. A court may always take the equities into account (as expressly recognized by Restatement Second §351(3)) and if the consequential losses are greatly disproportionate to the value of the consideration paid to the breacher, a court may exercise its equitable discretion to curtail liability for them.

§18.6.3 Mitigation

a. The Purpose and Policy of Mitigation

In most cases, a rational party, faced with a breach by the other, will naturally take whatever action is necessary to avoid or minimize loss. Unless the victim of a breach is particularly stupid, litigious, or spiteful, her self-interest will propel her in the direction of keeping her loss as small as possible, rather than aggravating it in the hope that she will ultimately be able to recover it from the breaching party. This means that it happens only rarely that the plaintiff deliberately and maliciously sets out to increase her damages, just for the satisfaction of punishing the defendant with a large claim. More commonly, the defendant's allegation that the plaintiff failed to mitigate is likely to turn on the question of whether the plaintiff's response to the breach was an unreasonable or poor judgment that aggravated damages.

The basic principle of mitigation is that if the **plaintiff** has, through **bad faith** or **unreasonable** action (or inaction) **aggravated** her **damages,** the **defendant is not held responsible for the increase in loss** caused by the plaintiff. This is often described as the plaintiff's *duty to mitigate damages.* Of course, this is not a duty in the normal sense, because the plaintiff owes it to no one but herself to keep her losses down. But if she fails in that duty to safeguard her own economic welfare, fairness dictates that she must be left with the added loss and the defendant should not be called on to pay it. It may be obvious from what has just been said that a failure to mitigate damages does not deprive the plaintiff of all relief, but affects recovery only to the extent that the damages were increased as a result of the plaintiff's conduct. The plaintiff is therefore still entitled to recover those damages that she could not have avoided by good faith or reasonable conduct.

It must be stressed that the question is not merely whether the plaintiff's response to the breach turned out, with hindsight, to be a wrong judgment that worsened the harm. Nor is it enough that a different response would have been preferable. The words "bad faith" and "unreasonable" indicate that there must be some *element of fault* on the plaintiff's part. It must be apparent that the plaintiff's behavior in reacting to the breach was dishonest, opportunistic, or vindictive, or that it so deviated from what would be expected, that it failed to conform to community standards of rationality. It must be borne in mind that the defendant has breached the contract, leaving the plaintiff in the unhappy position of having to salvage the benefit of her bargain. For this reason, the plaintiff, herself the victim of the defendant's wrong, should be given some leeway when her response is judged. It must be clear, under all the circumstances, that the plaintiff's reaction to the breach is sufficiently improper that it would be wrong to make the defendant bear the increased loss. Restatement Second §350 expresses this approach by stating that losses are not recoverable if the plaintiff could have avoided them without "undue risk, burden or humiliation," but the plaintiff should not be precluded from recovery to the extent that she made "reasonable but unsuccessful efforts to avoid harm."

The general principles of mitigation recognized in common law are applicable to UCC Article 2. Although there is no section specifically devoted to the principle, it is inherent in the Code by virtue of §1.103, which incorporates consistent common law principle, and in the general remedial principle expressed in §1.106. In addition, it is reflected throughout the remedies provisions of Article 2. Sections 2.706 and 2.712 require an aggrieved seller or buyer to act reasonably, in good faith, and within a reasonable time when making a substitute transaction; §2.715 bars a buyer from obtaining consequential damages that could have been prevented by cover or otherwise; §2.704(2) reflects the seller's duty to mitigate in deciding whether to complete the manufacture of specially ordered goods; and §2.709 requires the seller to make reasonable attempts at resale before claiming the price of the goods from the buyer.

The principle of mitigation makes perfect sense on its own merits because the defendant should not be accountable to the extent that the consequences of breach are exaggerated by the plaintiff's fault, and because a rule that encourages the plaintiff to control loss is efficient and sensible. In addition, however, it is congruent with two other limitation principles: A loss caused by the plaintiff's improper actions is not reasonably foreseeable, and the plaintiff's conduct breaks the chain of causation between the breach and the loss.

b. The Reasonableness Test for Determining Whether the Plaintiff Violated the Duty to Mitigate

As stated earlier, unless bad faith is evident, the plaintiff's accountability for aggravated loss depends upon the reasonableness of her response to breach. As always, reasonableness is a factual matter. The plaintiff's action (or failure to act) must be evaluated by an *objective standard* under all the circumstances of the case: Was it reasonable for a person in the plaintiff's position to have acted as she did? This inquiry takes into account a whole range of factual questions such as: what the plaintiff did or did not do; what choices were available to her; what risks, hardships, or inconveniences were involved in each choice; what her motivation was in choosing as she did; how much time she had available to respond; and how quickly she took action. All of these facts are looked at with a sympathetic eye on the plaintiff. As the breach compelled her to take action to safeguard her interests, courts are inclined to respect her judgment if it had an honest and rational basis, even if the defendant can point to a different response that may have been more effective in fully or partially preventing the loss. Because the plaintiff is the wronged party, she is not expected to take heroic or exhaustive action to keep damages at a minimum. The defendant cannot complain of a failure to mitigate if the action required to reduce loss would have been *unduly burdensome, humiliating, or risky* to the plaintiff. Similarly, the plaintiff cannot be expected to explore every conceivable possibility of avoiding loss or to try methods that reasonably appear to be futile.

The sympathetic approach to the plaintiff is reflected in the way in which the burden of proof is typically allocated when mitigation is in issue. The plaintiff bears the overall burden of proving her damages. But if she establishes loss and the defendant raises the issue of mitigation, the defendant must show that there was a reasonable means available to the plaintiff to curtail her loss and that if she had followed that course, a reduction in the loss would have been likely.

Once it is established that the plaintiff's reaction to the breach unjustifiably increased her loss, the next task is to calculate what the damages would have been had the proper response been made. This is also a factual issue, involving an inquiry into the causal link between the plaintiff's conduct and the loss.[6]

c. The Substitute Transaction as Mitigation

The most obvious form of mitigation is the substitute transaction. We saw an example of this right at the beginning of this chapter when, a few days before

---

6. *See also* section 17.7.3 in which the issue of mitigation is discussed in relation to the decision by the victim of a repudiation on whether to accept and act on the repudiation immediately, or to await the possibility of retraction.

the voice training was to begin, Harmony repudiated her contract with Sara to provide the lessons for a fee of $1,500. Sara hired another voice coach for $1,800 and claimed the $300 difference as expectation damages. The decision to hire another coach is itself an act of mitigation in that it prevented any consequential loss that Sara may have suffered by entering the competition without the training. (The fact that such a consequential loss may have been speculative and very difficult to prove increases Sara's incentive to avoid it.)

Although the hiring of a substitute coach avoided more serious consequential damages, this does not mean that Sara had carte blanche to engage the services of any coach that she liked, and to hold Harmony accountable for the full additional cost. To mitigate fully, she must also act *reasonably* and in *good faith* to *select among available substitutes,* and to find the one that *most closely compares* in price and quality to what she would have received from Harmony. That is, if Sara could, with reasonable effort, have found a substitute coach for less than $1,800, she may have aggravated her damages by using a more expensive substitute than necessary and will not be able to recover any unreasonable excessive cost. To decide if her action in hiring this coach was honest and reasonable, we would need to know who else may have been available, what their rates of compensation were, whether they were at least as qualified and reputable as Harmony, and what steps Sara made to find the most economical appropriate substitute. Her inquiries need not have been exhaustive, so long as they were *adequately diligent,* given the urgent need to find a replacement in a short time. Nor would she necessarily be obliged to take the cheapest substitute if there was a rational basis for believing that she would not thereby get the equivalent of what she bargained for. As noted earlier, Sara is given leeway for making a judgment under the difficult circumstances created by Harmony's breach, and her damages will not likely be reduced as long as she cannot be faulted for bad faith or unreasonableness.

What if the second coach was the only one available, but the reason that his fee was $300 more than Harmony's is because he is a more experienced and effective teacher. If Sara is awarded damages of a full $300, she ends up with coaching beyond her expectations under the contract with Harmony. As a general rule, the substitute must be a *reasonable equivalent* of the performance that was due under the contract. The plaintiff cannot obtain a windfall by holding the defendant responsible for the full cost of a replacement performance superior in quality or extent to that promised. (Therefore, when the seller of a 1985 Ford breaches the contract, the buyer can obviously not argue that she is entitled to buy a new BMW and hold the seller liable for the full cost of the substitute.) However, if the only appropriate substitute available is of greater value than the contract performance, so that it is the closest reasonable replacement for the breached performance, the plaintiff is likely to be given the benefit of it at the defendant's expense. After all, it is fairer to place this added cost on the defendant who caused the problem, than on the plaintiff who did not particularly seek the more valuable performance and cannot otherwise approximate the performance promised by the defendant. Of course, the plaintiff must make a convincing case that the more expensive substitute is in fact the only means of achieving her expectation interest.

In Sara's case, the issue of a reasonable substitute comes up in connection with her claim for damages for its added cost. However, the issue also arises when the breach releases a plaintiff from performance, so that a *substitute transaction* becomes available to *reduce the plaintiff's loss*. For example, say that a few days before the voice training lessons were to begin, Sara repudiated the contract. Harmony now finds that she has 28 hours of free time in which she will not be gainfully employed. If she does nothing about this, she will lose her full profit from the transaction—the contract price of $1,500 less any costs. However, if she is able to take another student or otherwise use this time to generate income, she will reduce or possibly eliminate completely her loss from Sara's breach. It therefore stands to reason that if Harmony sues Sara for her lost profit, she will have to deduct whatever she earned in the time freed by Sara's breach. If she failed to use the time gainfully at all, she would have to show that, despite reasonable efforts, she was not able to mitigate damages by productively redeploying this time. If she used some or all of it but did not fully reduce her loss, she would have to show that she was not reasonably able to reduce her loss to a greater extent.

Assume that as soon as Sara repudiated, Harmony put up notices at local schools and colleges advertising her availability, and she also called all the people she knew who may have referrals. However, no one expressed interest in lessons for the week in question. Harmony also noticed a sign in the neighborhood hamburger joint that they were looking for part-time help. When she sues Sara for her full profit under the contract, two issues are likely to be raised: First, were her efforts in seeking other students reasonable under the circumstances? It sounds as if she did everything reasonably possible considering the short time available to fill the slot left empty by Sara's breach. Second, should she have tried to recoup her loss by taking a part-time job at the hamburger joint? It may be that by doing this work in the times set aside for Sara's lessons, she could have earned back part of her loss. However, as the victim of a breach, she is not expected to take every conceivable step to avoid loss. She is allowed *reasonable discretion* in *declining* to pursue *alternatives that are unsuitable*, and should not be deprived of recovery as a result. As a music teacher, she surely should not have to suffer the indignity of moonlighting at a greasy fast-food place.

d. Post-Breach Transactions that Are Not Appropriately Treated as Substitutes: The "Lost Volume" Situation

In the last example, it was assumed that any lessons given by Harmony would take place in the hours allocated to Sara under the contract. If this is so, and if Harmony was otherwise fully booked, the new student would truly be a substitute for the contractual performance because Harmony could not have taken on an additional student in the absence of a breach by Sara. That is, the only time available to take on extra work was time that would have been committed to Sara had she not broken the contract. However, if Harmony was not fully booked, she could have taken on new students even if Sara had not breached. Therefore, a new student accepted after Sara's breach does not substitute for Sara. It would make no difference if Harmony schedules the new student for the time formerly devoted to Sara because Harmony would have simply booked the student at a different time had Sara not breached. Therefore, one should not automatically assume that a similar transaction after the breach must be a substitute for the broken contract. It should only be so treated if it is clear that the plaintiff *would not or could not have entered* it in the *absence of breach*. Failure to maintain this distinction carefully could lead to an unfair and unwarranted reduction of the plaintiff's recovery by offsetting the proceeds of an entirely independent transaction.

Consider a second illustration, based on a sale of goods: A homeowner sells her used fridge for $200, but the buyer breaches the contract by failing to take delivery and pay for it. The seller then sells it to someone else for the same price. Obviously, the second sale is a substitute because the seller had only that one fridge to sell. However, if the seller was not a homeowner trying to sell a single fridge, but a huge appliance store with a whole warehouse of fridges of this exact make and model, the resale of the fridge to the second buyer is not so clearly a substitute transaction. Because the seller has a stock of identical products, it had another one to sell to the second buyer even had the first buyer not breached. It could therefore have sold two fridges instead of one, and the breach has the effect of *reducing its volume of sales.* If the seller can establish such a lost volume situation, the second sale is *not a substitute,* its proceeds should not be treated as reducing the loss from the breach, and the seller is entitled to *recover its full profit* expected under the breached transaction. In a sale of goods, §2.708(2) caters for lost volume. It provides in essence that when the usual measure of damages—the difference between the contract price and the market price on resale—is inadequate to fully compensate the seller, the seller's lost profit on the sale is the appropriate measure.

This illustration has been kept simple to demonstrate the concept, but it lacks the sophistication that some commentators feel is necessary. It may not be enough for the seller to show merely that it had enough stock to supply all prospective buyers. To recover its full profit, it may also have to produce an economic analysis that demonstrates that *additional sales* would have *continued to generate profits of an equal extent.* Factors such as increases in the seller's marginal costs, competition in the marketplace from used goods, and other factors may reduce and ultimately eliminate the profitability of successive sales. Of course, it should be borne in mind that loss must be proved only on a preponderance of the evidence (as discussed in the next section), and a seller who merely shows the availability of a sufficient stock may be held to have satisfied this standard, or at least to have made a prima facie showing of lost volume.

Even when a seller has a plentiful supply of the goods, it can only claim profit based on lost volume if the next buyer is someone who would likely have bought from the seller whether or not the first sale was breached. Therefore, if, after breaching, the buyer brought his friend into the store for the purpose of buying the fridge sold under the broken contract, the second buyer is clearly a substitute if he would not have made the purchase from the seller in the absence of the breach.

§18.6.4 Causation

The concept of causation is not as prominent in contract law as it is in tort because it is usually more self-evident and its function can largely be accommodated within the principles of foreseeability, mitigation, and certainty. It is therefore not given much separate attention by courts and commentators. Nevertheless, it is worth articulating as a distinct limitation on relief. A breaching party cannot be accountable for loss that was not caused by her breach. There must be a **link between the breach and the loss.** Causation is not usually an issue when direct damages are concerned. Unless the plaintiff has broken the chain of causation by aggravating damages, there is invariably a clear causal link between the breach and the loss of the contractual bargain. However, consequential damages are by definition more remotely connected to the breach, and when they are claimed, it must be established that they were indeed a consequence of the breach.

To illustrate, consider again one of the variations of the example concerning Harmony's breach of her contract to give voice training lessons to Sara: Harmony reneged on the contract just before the lessons were to begin, and Sara could not find a replacement teacher, so she had no choice but to sing in the competition without having had any coaching in the prior week. She loses the competition and sues Harmony for a huge amount of damages to compensate her for the loss of a career as a singing star. Her theory is that Harmony's breach prevented her from winning and deprived her of the career opportunities that would have resulted. It does not take much imagination to realize that she has serious difficulties in establishing a cause and effect between the breach and her alleged loss. She may not be able to show a probable link between her failure to win and the lack of coaching because there are too many variables that could have intervened: She may not have been as talented as her competitors, she may have had a bad night, or the judges may have been wrong. Even if she could show a strong likelihood of success in the competition, she cannot go on to show that she would have had opportunities as a result, or that she would have acted successfully in pursuing them.

As you will readily recognize, some of the problems that Sara faces in proving her case may be described in terms of mitigation (did she make reasonable efforts to prevent or staunch the negative consequences of the breach?), or foreseeability (could Harmony have reasonably contemplated this huge loss?), or reasonable certainty (can Sara establish the fact and extent of loss?). Nevertheless, the question of causation is also present in the inquiry, and it is a useful adjunct to the other limitations in analyzing the issue of liability and justifying the result.

§18.6.5   *Reasonable Certainty*

As the party seeking to enforce the contract, the plaintiff bears the burden of proving her loss. If she is unable to show on the *preponderance of the evidence* the fact and extent of her loss, she will not be able to recover damages. The limitation of reasonable certainty is really nothing more than the embodiment of this principle—the evidence must be sufficient to persuade the factfinder that the loss is more likely to have occurred than not, and must give the factfinder enough basis for calculating a monetary award. As this suggests, reasonable certainty involves two inquiries: The threshold question is whether the plaintiff has proved *injury*. If injury is shown, the next question is whether the plaintiff has provided sufficient evidence to enable the factfinder to determine the *amount* of the loss.

As a general rule, the *more clearly* the *plaintiff can demonstrate* the first element (the fact that some *injury* was suffered), the *greater effort the factfinder will make* to come up with some kind of *compensation figure*. This is because it has now become clear that the plaintiff has indeed suffered as a result of the defendant's wrongful violation of her rights, and the court should strive, insofar as possible, to come up with a figure to compensate for the loss. This does not mean that the plaintiff will receive damages even if no relevant and plausible evidence is presented on the amount of her loss, but the court will try to do the best it can to fix damages with reference to whatever evidence is available.

This means that the second element is not a matter of all or nothing. Even if the evidence does not establish loss in the full amount claimed, it may be sufficient to justify an award of some lesser amount of compensation. This approach is reflected in Restatement Second §352, Comment *a*, which notes that although damages cannot be recovered for loss beyond the amount established with reasonable certainty, the policy of holding the breacher accountable for her wrongful act requires that doubts should generally be resolved against her once it is established that a significant injury has occurred. Therefore, the determination of damages is an approximation, not an exercise in mathematical precision. UCC §1.106, Comment 1, expresses a similar sentiment.

Problems of certainty often affect direct damages, but they are even more likely to arise when the plaintiff seeks consequential damages. Direct damages may be difficult to prove, for example, when the plaintiff seeks his expected profit from the contract, but cannot prove what that profit would have been. Say that an engineering firm enters a contract with a paper mill to design and manufacture an innovative system for the safe disposal of chemical wastes. The contract price for the system is $2 million. Before work begins, the mill reneges on the contract. The engineering firm's direct damages are its lost profits on the job, which must be established by deducting its expected costs from the contract price. However, the system would have been so revolutionary that the engineering firm has no reliable evidence of what its costs would have been. If it cannot establish those prospective costs with reasonable certainty, it will not be able to show that it expected a profit from the contract and will not recover any direct damages. Of course, if the engineering firm had done its planning properly before quoting a price for the work, it would have made a cost projection that, if it appears reasonably accurate and reliable, will be sufficient evidence to establish loss on the preponderance of the evidence.

Although direct damages can present problems of reasonable certainty, difficulty of proof is most commonly encountered when consequential damages are in issue. Sara's alleged loss of career opportunities, raised in the context of causation, is an extreme example of this. She would not only have trouble showing a causal link between her claimed loss and Harmony's breach of the voice training contract, but she would also have great difficulty in establishing the fact and amount of that loss. Some courts may regard those difficulties as insuperable. Others may be willing, upon being satisfied that the breach did remove all chance of her winning the competition, to allow the jury to place a value on her chance of winning.

Sara's claim is plagued with particularly troublesome issues of certainty, but even in less extreme cases, whenever an *expected gain is conjectural* the plaintiff must be concerned about whether she will be able to convince the factfinder that a gain of any credible amount would have been made. This is best illustrated by the recurring problem of trying to determine consequential losses when the defendant's breach prevents the plaintiff from opening a *new business*. Older cases often adopted a fairly rigid rule that when the defendant's breach prevented or delayed the plaintiff's opening of a new business, the plaintiff could not collect damages for lost profit, because the profitability of a new business is necessarily too speculative. Contemporary courts are more flexible and are willing to look at each case on its merits to decide if the available evidence provides a reasonable basis for determining a likely loss.

For example, say that an imaginative young entrepreneur, having just graduated from college, decides to open a new video store in a neighborhood that does not yet have one.[7] He enters into a lease with a shopping mall for premises in which he will conduct his new business, but the mall breaches the lease and lets the space to someone else just before he is about to move in. It takes him six months before he can find equivalent premises in the neighborhood. Although he will pay the same rent for the replacement premises, and therefore suffers no direct damages, he claims his consequential loss of profit for the six months during which he was unable to do business. He can produce evidence of his own projections of costs and sales, and also has witnesses who can testify about the average profits made during that period by other video stores in the area. In addition, because it takes some time for the case to come to trial, he has, in the intervening months, been able to accumulate figures on his profits for the period following the commencement of his business.

This evidence does not, of course, fix his damages with precision because it leaves a number of questions unanswered: His projections are just predictions, and they may be more or less thorough; the profits of competing video stores may not be exactly comparable, especially if they are branches of large chains or well-established businesses run by experienced people; and his post-opening profits were earned at a different time of year than the period of breach, and may be effected by seasonal factors. Nevertheless, a court should not demand greater precision. He is the victim of a clear breach and it is undisputed that he was delayed by six months in opening his business, so his evidence should be accepted as sufficient to establish loss. However, if he does not have this kind of evidence, or if he only has some of it, or if there are notable discrepancies between the different components, he may fail to establish loss on the balance of probability. The court cannot make up a figure out of thin air. For example, he would probably lose his action if, say, he abandoned the project after the lessor breached, so that he has no post-breach track record, his projections were not very scientific, and the evidence of similar businesses is all based on profits earned by well-established chain operations (most smaller stores having gone out of business).

§18.6.6   Unfair Forfeiture

The principle of unfair forfeiture has already been discussed in connection with damages for substantial performance (see section 17.3.3) and is restated briefly here. The basic concept is that where expectation damages, calculated in accordance with the principles stated above, would have the absurd and unfair result of placing a **great burden of liability** on the de-

---

7. Assuming that such a neighborhood could be found anywhere other than on the moon.

fendant **far in excess of the real loss** suffered by the plaintiff, the court has the discretion to confine damages so as to reflect the plaintiff's true economic loss. That is, the normal measure of damages, while technically correct, has the effect of giving the plaintiff a **windfall** because it is unduly expensive to achieve the plaintiff's contractual expectations, and that expense is **disproportionate** to any actual advantage that the plaintiff has lost as a result of the breach.

The most difficult issue in applying the principle of unfair forfeiture is to decide when the burden on the defendant reaches the level that merits use of the doctrine. It is obviously not enough that the defendant would suffer expense or even hardship in compensating the plaintiff for the breach. In most cases, the fact that the defendant has breached her obligation and that the plaintiff is entitled to this relief will outweigh any adverse effects on the defendant. It is only when the defendant's sacrifice in providing compensation is extraordinarily great in relation to the insignificance of the plaintiff's violated rights that an assertion of unfair forfeiture is tenable. To decide if this situation exists, one must interpret the contract to determine the materiality of the breach. A useful guideline for assessing this question is to ask whether, upon receiving the damages claimed, the plaintiff might rationally use the money awarded to achieve the contractual expectations or would be more likely to pocket the money instead. (This is not intended to suggest that a plaintiff does not have the right to bank an award of damages instead of spending it to achieve the equivalent of the contractual performance. It is simply a gauge of the importance placed by the plaintiff on completely compliant performance.)

For example, a roofer entered into a contract with a homeowner to install brown composition tiles on a roof for $3,500. The roofer came out early in the morning and took a day to install the new tiles. The tiling material cost the roofer $2,000 and he spent $1,000 on labor, so his expected profit for the job is $500. Regrettably, he erroneously used scarlet tiles instead of brown. When the customer returned from work that evening, she was apoplectic and refused to accept the work. This is surely justifiable because it is safe to say that most homeowners would regard such a drastic nonconformity in color to be a *material deviation from the contract.* To get the roof that she ordered, the owner will have to pay $500 in labor to remove the red tiles. The tiling material has no salvage value because it cannot be reused and must be discarded. The owner would then have to have the roof redone at a cost of, say, $3,500. The owner's total cost to rectify the job is $4,000, and her damages are this amount less the original contract price of $3,500—that is, $500. As the roofer materially breached and conferred no benefit on the owner by the first job, he is not entitled to any recovery for the work that he did. This means that he is not only liable for the $500 damages, but also has an unreimbursed cost of $2,500 on the flawed job. His breach has caused him a total out-of-pocket loss of $3,000, instead of his hoped-for profit of $500. This is a horrible forfeiture, to be sure, but because the deviation from the promised performance is material, it is not an unfair one.

However, what if, instead of installing scarlet tiles, the roofer mistakenly used tiles of a slightly darker brown than that ordered. Although this is a breach, an interpretation of the homeowner's reasonable expectations under the contract would probably lead us to the conclusion that it is a breach of considerably less magnitude—it is non-material. In other words, the roofer has *substantially performed*. If so, the loss of $3,000 to give the homeowner exactly what she ordered now seems to be an unfair and excessive imposition on the roofer, and the doctrine of unfair forfeiture would likely be applied. If it is, the owner's damages would be confined to the reduction in the house's value caused by the breach, which is probably zero. (Bear in mind the guideline suggested above: If the owner would be more likely to pocket the money than to retile the roof, thereby ending up with a free roof and $500 in the bank, it makes sense to interpret the color deviation as non-material.) The basic point, therefore, is that the discretion to reduce damages to avoid unfair forfeiture is typically exercised only when the court concludes that the failure to perform in accordance with the contract involves an incidental or ancillary aspect of the exchange so that performance may fairly be treated as substantial. As such, the rule against unfair forfeiture must be seen as a narrow exception to the general rule that the plaintiff is entitled to full expectation damages.

§18.7   Reliance and Restitution as Alternatives to Expectation

Although expectation damages are the primary remedy for breach of contract, they can only be recovered to the extent that the plaintiff can prove that the breach deprived her of an economic gain that would have resulted from the performance promised by the defendant in the contract. She must be able to show that she received less than her entitlement under the contract or was otherwise precluded from realizing an expected gain. It can happen that *a breach causes no economic loss* because, say, a substitute transaction can be found at the same or a lower cost, or because the contract was not profitable. If no loss can be shown, the plaintiff has no recourse for the defendant's wrongful act because there is no need for monetary compensation and contract remedies are not aimed at penalizing breaches. For example, if the seller of a house breaches the contract, but the buyer can purchase an equivalent house for the same or less money, the seller suffers no legal sanction for the breach.

However, the plaintiff's inability to prove expectation damages does not always end the matter of relief, because she *may be able to show that she has suffered losses other than her defeated expectation.* For example, even if a replacement house costs the same or less, the buyer may have partly performed before the breach by, say, paying a deposit to the seller. The buyer may also have incurred expenses in anticipation of receiving the benefits of the contract, say, by paying an architect to plan an alteration to the house. Damages of this kind may be recoverable under one or both of the alternative remedies of reliance and restitution.

The basic difference between reliance and restitution is that **reliance,** like expectation, is conceived of as a remedy based on **affirmation** of the contract—it is an enforcement of the contract, but **restitution** is premised on the theory of **disaffirmance**—it treats the breach as having caused the contract to fall away. This distinction, which will be made clearer as the remedies are discussed below, affects the aim and focus of the remedies. While the goal of expectation damages is to place the plaintiff in the position she would have been in had the contract been performed, reliance and restitutionary damages have more limited goals. **Reliance** damages aim to **refund expenses wasted or equivalent losses** by the plaintiff in reliance on the contract, thereby restoring her to the **status quo ante**—the position she would have been in had no contract been entered. **Restitution** seeks to return to the plaintiff the **value** of any **benefit conferred** on the defendant under the breached contract. It focuses not on the plaintiff's expectation or expenditure, but on the extent of the defendant's **enrichment** at her expense.

To illustrate, let us slightly embellish the above example of the house sale: The seller contracted to sell the house to the buyer for $150,000. After the contract was signed, the buyer paid $5,000 to the seller as a deposit. She also hired an architect to draw a plan to enlarge the living room and paid him a fee of $1,000. If, after the seller breaches, the buyer finds a reasonable replacement house for $155,000, she will claim and be entitled to expectation damages in the total amount of $11,000 because this is what she must receive to be in the position of having a house for $150,000. She gets not only the $5,000 extra cost of a substitute, but also reimbursement of her costs of $6,000 expended in reliance on the contract. Part of that reliance is the $5,000 she actually paid to the defendant—called **"essential"** (or sometimes **"direct"**) reliance, and part is the $1,000 wasted in having plans drawn that are now useless to her—called **"incidental"** (or sometimes **"consequential"**) reliance.[8]

However, assume that the buyer is able to purchase a replacement house for the same or less than the contract price, so she has suffered no loss in expectation. She would still be able to obtain reliance damages of $6,000 that would restore her to the status quo ante. If she chose to, she could instead recover restitutionary damages, but the benefit conferred on the seller is only

---

8. These terms are expanded upon below with qualifications that are not raised at this stage.

$5,000. (Although the plans relate to the seller's house, she is not enriched by them because she did not ask for them to be drawn and presumably does not even have them.) Therefore, the buyer has no incentive to chose restitution in preference over reliance.

Notice that some items of damage are recoverable no matter which form of relief is sought. In this case: The $5,000 deposit is both a reliance expense (and consequently also part of expectation damages) and a benefit subject to restitution. Others may be consistent with only two (here, the wasted architect's fee is counted in both expectation and reliance) or available only under one (the cost of a substitute is claimable only under expectation). Naturally, the plaintiff will select as her first choice whichever of the alternative remedies provides the widest relief. The basic distinction can be represented as follows:

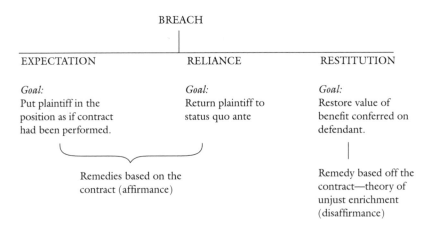

BREACH

EXPECTATION	RELIANCE	RESTITUTION
Goal: Put plaintiff in the position as if contract had been performed.	*Goal:* Return plaintiff to status quo ante	*Goal:* Restore value of benefit conferred on defendant.

Remedies based on the contract (affirmance)

Remedy based off the contract—theory of unjust enrichment (disaffirmance)

We will now proceed to a more detailed examination of reliance and restitution as alternatives to expectation and to each other.

§18.8   Reliance Damages

§18.8.1   *The Distinction Between Essential and Incidental Reliance*

It was noted earlier that when a loss or expense is incurred in performing an obligation under the contract, the reliance motivating it is called "direct" or "essential" because it is directly based on the contract and essential to fulfilling the party's contractual commitment. However, if a loss or expense is incurred as a consequence of and incidentally to the contract, for the purpose of enjoying or taking advantage of the benefit expected from the contract, it is called "consequential" or "incidental." Sometimes this distinction is easy to draw, as in the case of the deposit and of the architect's plan in the prior illustration. However, the question of whether something is essential or incidental to a party's contractual performances requires an *interpretation* of the party's obligations under the contract. In some cases the distinction may be harder to draw.

For example, the owner of a store hires a signmaker to execute a large neon sign and to install it on a pylon to be erected by the owner in front of the building. In the contract, the signmaker guarantees that it will obtain approval for the sign from the city. The owner erects the pylon, but the signwriter is unable to obtain approval for the sign. Because he promised to do this, he has breached the contract. If we interpret the owner's erection of the pylon as necessary to enable the signmaker to perform, the expenses incurred in building it are essential reliance. However, if we interpret the purpose of the pylon merely as a means for the owner to obtain the benefit of the signmaker's performance, then the erection costs are incidental reliance. In some cases, the distinction may not have any significant effect on the result, but as discussed below, different rules apply to these different types of reliance, and the characterization could be significant.

There is one important point to bear in mind no matter how reliance expenses are classified. The basis of awarding reliance damages is **waste.** The expense or loss must cause prejudice to the plaintiff in that something of value has been wasted and cannot be salvaged. Thus, in the above example, it is indicated that the pylon is useless because the city will not approve it. If, following the breach, the owner finds another signmaker who is able to get the sign approved, the expense of constructing the pylon will not be wasted and cannot be recovered. (If the second signmaker charged more than the first, the owner would be able to recover the reasonable extra cost of the substitute as expectation damages.)

§18.8.2 *Essential Reliance Damages*

We have already seen in section 18.3 that in many types of contracts (especially when the aggrieved party's performance consisted of the supply of work or work and materials), expectation damages are made up of expected profit on the whole contract plus expenditure already incurred in reliance on the contract. In cases like this, essential reliance expenses are therefore a *component of expectation recovery.* For example, a builder contracts to build a house for $150,000. After the builder has performed about half of the work and spent $60,000, the property owner breaches by terminating the project. The builder can prove that his total cost to build the house would have been $120,000. His expectation damages are $90,000, consisting of his lost profit of $30,000 as well as the reimbursement of the expenses of $60,000 already incurred. Both these components must be included to give him the benefit of his bargain—a net gain of the $30,000 profit.

On the above facts, the builder could prove that his total cost would have been less than the contract price, so he can show that he expected a profit. However, this is not always the case. A plaintiff may have no reliable evidence from which to project his total expected costs, or he may have underbid so that projected total cost exceeds the contract. If the *plaintiff cannot prove that he would have made a profit* on the contract had it been fully performed, he *cannot claim a loss of profit.* He is nevertheless *still entitled* to recover the *essential reliance component* of his damages—the $60,000 actually spent in performing. (As these examples show, a plaintiff who can prove profit has no reason to confine his claim to reliance damages.)

When the plaintiff **would have made a loss** in full performance of the contract—that is, he had a **negative expectation**—the defendant's breach is a lucky break. It allows him to cease performance and curtail his loss. This means that if he is awarded his full reliance damages, he actually does *better than he expected.* For example, say that the builder agreed to build the house for $100,000, but his total cost to complete it would have been $120,000 so that he has an expected loss of $20,000. The owner breaches about halfway through the construction. At that point the builder has spent $60,000. If he is given the full amount of his reliance damages, he fully recovers his cost. Yet he only expected to recover five-sixths of his cost. A convincing argument could be made that this should not be the basis of any adjustment. The defendant breached and cannot be heard to complain if the breach enabled the plaintiff to avoid expected losses. However, because the law is concerned with trying to give the plaintiff true expectation, many courts consider it appropriate to take negative expectation into account when reliance damages are claimed. However, they qualify this rule by shifting the burden of proving negative expectation to the defendant so that in cases of doubt, the plaintiff does end up with full reimbursement.

Therefore, the general rule is that when the *defendant can prove* that the *plaintiff would have suffered a loss* in the event of complete performance, the plaintiff's reliance damages should cut back to bring his recovery into line with his expectations. Although some courts speak merely of the deduction of expected loss from the award of expenses, the better approach is to reduce the recovery *proportionally.* That is, to *prorate* the loss and to reduce the recovery of expenses by a percentage of the total loss equal to the ratio of expenses incurred to total expenses. Thus, on our facts, the builder has incurred half the costs, so his recovery should be reduced by half the loss, $10,000. This means that he recovers only $50,000 of the $60,000 spent. This is justified as being *consistent with his expectation.* Of course, it is still better than he expected, because he really anticipated being not $10,000 but $20,000 out of pocket. However, as he is the victim of the breach, we don't want to be too zealous in placing him in exactly his correct position, because that rewards the breacher by giving her full credit for the plaintiff's prospective loss.

It was mentioned earlier that to get reliance damages reduced, the defendant must prove that the plaintiff would have suffered a loss. The allocation of this burden of proof to the defendant is an accommodation to the plaintiff in recognition of the fact that the defendant was in the wrong for breaching the contract. Therefore, a plaintiff seeking recovery of reliance damages need only prove his expenditure and need not show that he would not have made a loss on the contract. If the defendant seeks a pro rata reduction, it is she who must show that it would have been a losing contract. This means that when projected costs are uncertain and the fact of loss unclear, the plaintiff will obtain full reimbursement of expenses.

A *pro rata reduction* of reliance is *not appropriate in every case.* Even if the defendant can prove that the plaintiff will ultimately have lost money on the contract, reliance expenses should not be reduced if the *purpose of the contract was not to make a profit.* For example, a homeowner contracts with an artist to execute a large and colorful mosaic at the entrance to his property. A vertical concrete slab must be built so that the artist can do the mosaic on it, and the owner undertakes to have the slab erected a month after execution of the contract so that the artist can begin work by that time. A couple of weeks after entering the contract, when the owner has half finished the slab, the artist repudiates the contract. The owner particularly wanted the work of this artist and does not wish for a substitute, so the hunk of concrete is now useless. Having no expectation damages, the owner claims his wasted expenses from the artist. Even if the artist can produce testimony from a bevy of realtors that the mosaic would have been so flashy that it would have reduced the market value of the property, this is not a proper case for reducing reliance recovery. Enhancement of the property value was not the purpose of the contract, and the possibility of economic loss is not relevant to the reimbursement of the wasted costs.

§18.8.3 *Incidental Reliance Damages*

As stated earlier, incidental reliance expenditure or loss is **incurred in consequence** of having made the **contract** and for the purpose of **using or enjoying the benefits expected** under it. Because these damages are premised on the plaintiff's reliance on the contract, they must necessarily have been induced by the contract and incurred after it was entered into. A loss or expense incurred in anticipation of the contract, but before it is actually formed, is therefore not included in incidental reliance damages. (Whether it may be recovered under the independent theory of promissory estoppel is discussed in Chapter 5.)

Incidental reliance may be illustrated and distinguished from essential reliance by using a variation of the example of the young entrepreneur who entered into a lease of business premises for the purpose of opening a video store. At the time of signing the contract, he paid a deposit of $5,000 to the lessor as required under the contract. In addition, a short time before the business was due to open he spent $1,000 on flyers which he planned to distribute to advertise the opening of his store. A few days after he had incurred this expense the lessor breached the lease by letting the premises to someone else. Say that no other suitable premises are available, so the lessee is forced to abandon his attempt to open the store. Because he is entering a new business and has scant evidence to show what his profit would have been, the lessee decides not to try claiming his lost expectation, but instead confines himself to reliance damages. He has suffered both essential reliance damages—the deposit paid to the lessor as required by the contract, and incidental reliance damages—the **wasted expense** of the useless flyers. The former expense qualifies as essential reliance because it was incurred as part of his performance obligation. However, he had no contractual duty to have the flyers printed. He did this solely for his own purpose of attracting business. Even so, the expense was incurred in reliance on the contract, and the breach has defeated that reliance and made the expenditure useless.

Most commonly, incidental reliance takes the form illustrated above—an expenditure or outlay that is wasted as a result of the breach. But sometimes it is in the nature of a *lost opportunity or other gain sacrificed*. For example, after executing the lease of the premises, the lessee had given up his job so that he could operate his new video store, or he had declined an offer of other premises on the strength of this lease. Lost gains and opportunities are, of course, harder to prove and quantify than wasted expenditure, but they are recoverable if properly established, subject to the qualifications discussed below.

Because incidental reliance is ancillary to the contract, there must be a limit on it to protect the breaching party from liability for expenses that it could not fairly have expected, or that were not incurred reasonably. Therefore, incidental reliance is only recoverable if the defendant *foresaw or reasonably should have foreseen* the possibility of the loss or expenditure being incurred, and both the amount and nature of the loss or expenditure were *reasonable*. The mitigation principle applies here too, but it need not be stated as a separate requirement because it is inherent in the concept of reasonable reliance. As with all other types of damage, the loss or expense must be proved with reasonable certainty. As noted before, incidental reliance is only compensable to the extent that it had been **wasted.** Therefore the lessee could not claim wasted expenditures for the flyers if the breach occurred before they were printed and he had the ability to cancel the order. Similarly, if the loss can be salvaged or the items reused, any recoupment of the waste will limit the claim. (Again, this is consonant with the mitigation principle.) For example, say that in addition to flyers, the lessee had bought shelving on which to display the videos. Unlike the flyers, the shelving can be resold and the proceeds of resale will curtail the loss.

Where the incidental loss or expense would not be deducted from earnings to determine profit, the fact that the plaintiff would have made a loss upon fully performing the contract is not relevant to the reimbursement of reliance. Therefore, the incidental reliance damages are not subject to the *rule of proportionate reduction*. However, if the contract involves a money-making enterprise and the defendant can show that the venture as a whole would have resulted in a loss to the plaintiff, this reasonable expectation of loss could be taken into account and incidental reliance recovery could be reduced proportionately.

§18.9   Restitutionary Damages

Restitutionary damages were explained in section 9.6, in which the basic premise of the remedy and measurement of relief were introduced. While the pertinent aspects of that discussion will be restated briefly in the course of this section, you should refer back to it if you want more detail. The purpose of restitutionary damages is to **restore to the plaintiff** the **value** of a **benefit unjustly conferred** on the defendant.[9] Section 9.6 focused on unjust enrichment as a theory of liability alternative to contract and dealt with situations in which the remedy of restitution is granted when a benefit was conferred on the defendant in the absence of contract. However, restitution is also available when a valid contract has been entered into and breached, because the plaintiff has the option of either suing on the contract for expectation or reliance, or of **disaffirming** the contract (that is, operating under the legal fiction that it does not exist) and suing in restitution for the recovery of benefits conferred under the now-defunct contract.

Stated differently, when the defendant commits a material breach, the plaintiff will, when possible, usually seek full enforcement of the contract to recover the value of her expectation. However, if the plaintiff cannot recover expectation damages either because she cannot prove them or because she has a negative expectation (that is, she would have lost money on the contract), she will be able to chose to recover in either reliance or restitution. If she claims reliance damages, she is still suing on the contract because, as explained above, reliance expense is a component of expectation damages. However, if she claims restitution, she proceeds on the theory that the *breach ended the life of the contract,* so that the defendant is no longer justified in retaining the benefit of any performance that the plaintiff rendered to her under it, and the value of that performance unjustly enriches her.

To understand why restitution often provides a different measure of recovery from reliance, one needs to remember their different goals, as mentioned in section 18.7: Reliance is aimed at the recovery of wasted expenses,

---

9. This section discusses only restitution in favor of the victim of the breach. It does not consider restitution in favor of a breaching party, which is discussed in section 17.6.2. That section explains that, as a general rule, when a contract is rescinded for breach, the breaching party is also entitled to the restitution of any benefits that she conferred on the other party prior to her breach. However, the breaching party's restitution is subject to limitations and is offset by any damages due to the victim.

while restitution is designed to restore the value of a benefit that the defendant has unjustly retained. Sometimes the plaintiff's expenditure may be exactly equal to the defendants's enrichment, so it would make no difference which basis of recovery was used. This is true, for example, when the benefit to the defendant is simply the payment of money. Therefore, if the seller of a house breaches the contract of sale after the buyer has paid a deposit of $5,000, the value of the benefit conferred is precisely equivalent to the plaintiff's expenditure (and interest on the money would be claimable in both restitution and reliance). However, in other situations the plaintiff's *outlay could be considerably different* from the *value of what it produced*. Say that a painter entered into a contract to paint a house, and the owner breached after the painter had stripped and primed the walls. If the painter had incurred expenses of $100 in doing this preparatory work, that is all he can recover in reliance. However, restitution based on the value of what has been done for the owner—commonly measured by the market value (quantum meruit) of the service—is likely to be more than what was actually spent. This is because it includes not only the cost of performance, but also the value of the plaintiff's labor or a reasonable profit. Conversely, restitution could be lower than reliance where the expenditure, although justifiable and reasonable, does not result in a benefit to the owner. This is particularly likely when the reliance is incidental so that nothing is actually given to the breacher.

Although *market value* is the *preferred measure* of value, the *recipient's net gain* is sometimes more appropriate. The factors that are taken into account in selecting the means of measurement are discussed in section 9.6 and are not repeated here. However, when restitution is based on the disaffirmance of a breached contract, there is one further question concerning the measurement of the benefit: If the market value of the benefit exceeds the value placed on it in the contract (that is, its contract price), should the *contract price* be an *upper limit on recovery*? For example, in the above contract to paint a house, say that the portion of the contract price attributable to stripping and priming the walls is $500, but the painter underbid and this price is lower than the market value of the work, which is $600.

The issue here is not quite the same as that of prorating reliance recovery where the plaintiff would have sustained a loss had the contract not been breached. However, depending on one's view, it can be seen either as analogous or distinguishable. If one emphasizes the difference in the underlying theories of reliance and restitution, disparate treatment is justified. Unlike reliance damages, restitution is not based on enforcement of the contract, but on the assumption that the contract no longer exists. There is no reason to give the defendant any right to rely on the breached contract for the purpose of curtailing the extent of the plaintiff's restitution. Conversely, if one sees the distinction between affirmance and disaffirmance as artificial—a contract does exist after all, and restitution is based on a legal fiction—consistency demands that the plaintiff's expectation should limit restitution in the same way as it does reliance.

§18.10 Equitable Remedies: Specific Performance and Injunctions

§18.10.1 Specific Performance

It was noted in section 18.2.2 that the remedy of specific performance—a court order commanding the defendant to perform the contract as promised—would seem to be the most precise means of achieving the plaintiff's expectation. Yet, for a number of reasons, some historical and some based on practicality and principle, damages are the primary form of relief for breach of contract, and specific performance is reserved as an extraordinary remedy. The historical basis for the primacy of the damages remedy lies in the *dichotomy between law and equity*. As it was originally formed, the court of equity was a court of special resort, presided over by the Lord Chancellor, acting under the sovereign's prerogative power. The Lord Chancellor would intervene to do justice when the regular courts of law had no power to provide an adequate remedy to the plaintiff.[10] In the context of contract, the law courts were confined to awarding damages for breach and had no power to order the defendant to perform the contract. If damages were not an adequate remedy, the plaintiff had to approach the court of equity to request it to use its discretionary power to compel the defendant's performance. As one of the prerequisites for obtaining this equitable relief, the plaintiff had to show that the *normal legal remedy* of *damages would not provide adequate relief.* The most common examples of such situations are contracts for the sale of unique property that cannot be substituted for on the market; cases in which damages would be very difficult to prove with reasonable certainty; and cases in which the defendant is financially incapable of satisfying a money judgment.

Although courts of law and equity have long been combined, and the same judge decides on the alternative remedies of damages and specific performance, the requirement of establishing the inadequacy of the damage remedy still exists in our law. It is, of course, not as firm or rigid as it may once have been, and courts tend to focus more on the relative efficiency or effectiveness of the remedies. Nevertheless, the rule is still widely followed and is reflected in both Restatement Second §359 and UCC §§2.709 (the

---

10. *See* section 2.5 for a fuller explanation of the distinction between law and equity.

seller's action for the price) and 2.716 (the buyer's remedy for specific performance).

The primacy of the damages remedy is not based purely on tradition, and there are often good practical and policy reasons for preferring damages over specific performance. Because specific performance is an equitable remedy, a court will only grant it if, on balancing the equities between the plaintiff and the defendant, and taking into account the societal interests at stake, the justification of affording the plaintiff this relief outweighs its drawbacks. This requires the court to evaluate a number of different factors, including the following issues and concerns:

a.   In Many Cases It Is Simply More Efficient to Award Damages

If the plaintiff is able to purchase substitute property or services on the market, it is just easier to award a sum of money to her to enable her to do that, rather than ordering the defendant to perform. It is only when there is no reasonable possibility of acquiring a substitute or no reasonable prospect of being able to establish or collect a monetary award that specific performance becomes a preferable remedy.

It is relatively easy for the buyer or lessee of *real property* to obtain specific performance on the basis that damages would be inadequate, because the common law has long assumed that land is unique. This assumption still holds, although possibly with less force when the property is standardized commercial space or tract housing. The opposite assumption applies to *goods*. Under UCC §2.716, a buyer is relegated to a claim for damages and cannot get an order compelling the seller to perform unless she can show that the goods are unique or that the circumstances otherwise justify the order. Comment 2 to that section explains that to be unique, an item does not necessarily have to be the only one of its kind in existence. The concept is broader than that and covers any situation in which it is not commercially feasible to obtain a substitute.

b.   It Could Be Unnecessarily Intrusive and Harsh to Force the Defendant to Perform as Promised

Unlike an award of damages, which operates *in rem* (as explained in section 18.2.4, it is simply a money judgment enforceable against the defendant's property), an order of specific performance operates *in personam*. This means that it is a command of the court directed at the person of the defendant. If she disobeys it, she can be sanctioned for contempt of court and jailed or fined.

c. When the Performance Involves Personal Services—Such as a Contract of Employment—an Order Directing the Provider of the Services to Perform Is Tantamount to Involuntary Servitude

Even if damages are not an adequate remedy, the constitutional bar on involuntary servitude precludes a court from ordering specific performance of a contract for personal services.

d. Practicality of Enforcement

Even if an order compelling performance does not amount to involuntary servitude, if the performance involves something more than the mere delivery or conveyance of property or documents, *problems of supervision* may arise. That is, the performance may require judicial monitoring to ensure that a reluctant defendant does not provide a grudging performance that falls below the reasonable standards required under the contract. The problem of supervision of performance is one of the factors that a court weighs in deciding whether it should grant specific performance, but it is not dispositive. If the court otherwise feels that specific performance is the best remedy, it will undertake to supervise the performance if necessary. This can be accomplished by appointing a special master or some other person accountable to the court who will evaluate performance and possibly mediate any disputes that might arise in the course of carrying it out.

e. Vagueness

It is a general principle of equity that when a court orders the defendant to do something, it must be clear in its command so that the defendant is able to tell exactly what must be done to obey and avoid sanctions for contempt. This principle, combined with the courts' reluctance to invent contract terms for the parties, leads to the rule that specific performance will not be decreed unless the *contract is definite enough to form the basis of a clear order*. In Chapter 10 it was noted that if the parties are too vague or indefinite in their agreement, their arrangement may fail to qualify as a contract at all. However, even if the uncertainty is not so severe as to defeat a claim that a contract was made, it could render the contract sufficiently unclear to support an order of specific performance.

f. Specific Performance May Be a Partial Remedy

Specific performance does not have to be an all-or-nothing remedy. In the proper circumstances, a court has the discretion to order *performance of part* of the contract in *combination with an award of monetary damages* for the remainder. In many cases, specific performance is obviously an alternative to damages, so the plaintiff cannot get both remedies. However, when the breach has already caused a loss that will not be recouped by the specific performance, it is appropriate for the court to award damages to compensate for that irretrievable loss in addition to granting specific performance. For example, if the defendant refuses to convey business premises purchased by the plaintiff, the court could decree specific performance and also award the plaintiff whatever loss in profits she can show to have been suffered for the period of delay between the date for delivery under the contract and the date on which the order is finally complied with.

g.   The Plaintiff's Return Performance

It probably goes without saying that a plaintiff who seeks specific performance must render the return performance to the defendant, and the court may grant its order conditional on the plaintiff doing so.

§18.10.2   *Injunctions*

An order of specific performance is *mandatory* in its effect—it compels the defendant to perform an *affirmative act*. Sometimes, even if the court will not affirmatively order the defendant to perform, it may be willing to issue a **negative order**—an injunction **prohibiting** the defendant from doing **some particular act.** In the context of contract remedies, a prohibitory injunction may be helpful to a plaintiff who cannot get specific performance, when the defendant has breached for the purpose of entering a more lucrative or desirable transaction. By enjoining the defendant from performing that second transaction, the plaintiff is able to defeat the defendant's purpose in breaching, thereby encouraging her to relent and perform as promised.

For example, say that Sara Nade entered a contract with Smalltime Productions, Inc. under which Sara agreed to perform at a concert. Sara thereafter received a much more attractive offer from Worldwide Promotions, Inc. to sing somewhere else on the same evening. She decided that she would prefer the second transaction and therefore repudiated her contract with Smalltime. The court will not grant an order of specific performance of this personal services contract, but it may be willing to enjoin Sara from singing for Worldwide. This remedy does not directly help Smalltime, but it does remove the motive for the breach and may therefore provide the indirect benefit of persuading Sara to sing for Smalltime after all.

The *drawbacks* of enjoining Sara from pursuing the desired second contract are self-evident. The injunction prevents her from employing her talents and skills as she desires and affects her ability to earn a livelihood. If she has already contracted with Worldwide, and Worldwide was unaware of her commitment and was not guilty of deliberate interference with her contract, an injunction defeats with its legitimate contractual expectations. Furthermore, there is always a danger that an aggrieved plaintiff may seek an injunction out of spite rather than from a genuine desire to encourage repentance. For this reason, courts are cautious and quite reluctant to put their power behind such an order and will do so only when the equities strongly favor the plaintiff. (Like an order of specific performance, a prohibitory injunction is an equitable remedy subject to the same process of balancing the equities between the parties.) Therefore, the plaintiff will not likely succeed in obtaining an injunction unless she can demonstrate that the less intrusive remedy of damages is inadequate (which it would be if Smalltime cannot obtain a substitute and would have difficulty proving or collecting damages from Sara), and that the need to protect the plaintiff's rights under the contract outweigh any hardship the injunction might impose on the defendant and any harm that it might do to innocent third parties and the public interest.

§18.11 Liquidated Damages

A liquidated damages provision is a term in a contract under which the parties agree that in the event of a breach by one of them, the breacher will pay damages in a specified sum or in accordance with a prescribed formula. If such a clause is valid, it has the effect of **settling in advance** what **damages will be due in the event of a breach.** The contract could liquidate damages for the breach of either party or for only for one of them. (If the liquidated damages clause covers breach by only one party, a breach by the other will require proof of damages in the usual way.) The exact meaning and effect of a liquidated damages provision is a matter of *interpretation,* but unless the language or context indicates otherwise, it is generally assumed that when damages have been validly liquidated in the contract, the fixing of the amount binds not only the defendant who is responsible for it, but also the plaintiff. That is, even if the breach causes the plaintiff greater loss than that provided, the plaintiff's *recovery is limited to the amount agreed.* However, unless the provision makes it clear that the liquidated damages are the plaintiff's *exclusive remedy,* Restatement Second §361 assumes that it does not prevent the plaintiff from electing to claim specific performance instead of damages.

There are a number of reasons why the parties may agree to commit themselves in advance to a set amount of damages in the event of breach: The principal one is that if damages are stipulated in the contract, it is *easier and more efficient to obtain relief* if a breach occurs, particularly if the transaction involves a venture that is speculative. The plaintiff avoids the problem of establishing foreseeability, mitigation, and certainty, and the defendant has a predetermined liability so that she can predict the cost of breaching. In fact, if one of the parties is particularly concerned about protecting itself from the problem of establishing damages in the event of breach, the ability to stipulate damages in the contract may be a significant incentive to entering the contract.

However, liquidated damages have an obvious negative aspect. They are nothing more than *a forecast of probable loss.* Even if the parties try hard to make as precise and thoughtful a prognostication as possible, they can never prophesy exactly what the actual losses will be. If the outcome of the transaction is uncertain or speculative, reasonably accurate prediction of the impact of breach becomes more unlikely. The problem of unreliable prediction is, of course, increased to the extent that the parties are less careful in their projections. It may therefore turn out that the forecast of damage is very different from the loss that ultimately results from a breach, and that the agreed damages greatly overcompensate or undercompensate the plaintiff.

Liquidated damages have enough problems of accuracy, even when they are intended to be a reasonable forecast of harm. But sometimes their purpose is not to approximate anticipated harm, but to *discourage breach* by imposing a *penalty* designed to make breach too costly. That is, although the term is set out in the form of a pre-estimate of damages, its real goal is to make breaching so unattractive that the promisee will try to avoid it. Because the remedial system of contract law is based on the premise of compensation, courts have long followed the practice of refusing to enforce a provision that purports to liquidate damages, but in reality imposes a penalty for breach. While this approach is well-established, it continues to be controversial because it tries to accommodate two countervailing policies. The policy of *freedom of contract* pulls in the direction of enforcing the parties' agreement on damages, even if it provides for relief that goes beyond actual loss. However, the policy of confining contractual relief to *economic compensation* dictates that a provision that goes beyond that should not be enforced. To one who places stronger emphasis on freedom of contract, there is little justification for a court to interfere with fairly bargained liquidated damages provisions, and policing should be confined to fraud, duress, or other bargaining impropriety.[11] To one who more highly values the compensation policy, the goal of achieving an accurate expectation

---

11. Note that the issue of whether to enforce a liquidated damages provision is independent of questions such as duress, fraud, unconscionability, adhesion, or other bargaining unfairness discussed in Chapter 13. Of course, if assent to a liquidated damages clause is obtained by one of these improper means, that would in itself provide grounds for invalidating it.

award demands a more rigorous examination of the purpose and effect of such clauses. The issue of *fairness* also comes into the question of whether or not agreed damages should be enforced despite their penal effect, but this issue tends to be resolved based on one's view of the relative primacy of the contract freedom or compensation principle. One could say that it is fair to hold the defendant to her commitment, even if this results in over-compensation of the plaintiff, but one could also say the opposite. Arguments based on the economic impact of agreed damages can be used to support either side of this debate: If such clauses overcompensate, they discourage efficient breach and should therefore be overturned. Conversely, the refusal to enforce agreed damages may deter and interfere with trans-actions by making it more difficult for parties to effectively allocate risk in their contract.

Despite the controversy, courts do continue to draw a distinction be-tween enforceable liquidated damages provisions and unenforceable penal-ties. Given the uncertainty inherent in any prediction, the most difficult practical problem created by the distinction is to devise standards for decid-ing when to treat the provision as legitimate and when to refuse enforce-ment. Because it is well known that courts will not enforce penalties, few contracts openly admit that the purpose of the clause is to penalize and dis-courage breach. When all such clauses profess to be true liquidations of damage, it can be hard to tell if a provision was a genuine attempt to settle damages or a penalty. To deal with this problem, courts have developed a policing mechanism in the form of a set of guidelines that look at the cir-cumstances existing both at the time of executing the contract and at the time of breach. The purpose is, first, to evaluate whether, at the time of con-tracting, the parties genuinely intended to make a genuine pre-estimate of loss, and second, to compare the agreed damages to any actual damages that were in fact suffered.

Restatement Second §356 and UCC §2.718 reflect this bipartite test in almost identical language: Damages for breach by either party may be liqui-dated in the contract, but the provision will not be enforced and will be void as a penalty unless the amount it fixes as damages is *reasonable in light of an-ticipated or actual harm* caused by the breach.

§18.11.1 *Anticipated Harm—Evaluation of the Liquidated Damages as at the Time of Contracting*

To decide the reasonableness of the anticipation of harm, the court must consider two factors: the *expected difficulty of proving loss* and the degree to which the estimate of harm was a *reasonable advance estimate of that loss*—a principled and genuine attempt to predict likely loss. On their face, these two factors *appear contradictory* because the more difficult it is to prove loss, the harder it must be to make any kind of reasonable pre-estimate of damages. However, the factors are not treated as rigid co-equal requirements, but as flexible considerations to be balanced against each other. Therefore, the more uncertain and speculative the damages, the less rigorous the court will be in examining the reliability of the pre-estimate. However, if anticipated damages would be relatively mechanical and routine, the parties are held to a stricter standard in trying to estimate them.

For example, if the contract relates to an innovative new business venture, it will likely be difficult to prove damages for breach with reasonable certainty, so the court should be rather accepting of the amount of agreed damages settled on by the parties, even if it is quite speculative. However, if the contract involves the sale of property for which there is an active market, substitutionary damages should be quite easy to prove, so the parties' means of determining the amount of agreed damages is more rigorously examined.

The general approach is to *place the greatest emphasis on this first stage* of the evaluation, so that if the clause was really not intended as a penalty and the parties were truly concerned about avoiding the uncertainty of a later dispute over loss, their genuine and principled attempt at estimation is worthy of respect. It may therefore be appropriate for the court to uphold the clause even if it appears that the actual loss suffered is smaller than predicted. This is reflected in both Restatement Second §356 and UCC §2.718, which call for reasonableness of the liquidated damages to be assessed in light of anticipated *or* actual harm. That is, it is not always necessary for the provision to satisfy both the test of reasonable prediction and the test of proportionality to actual loss.

§18.11.2   *Actual Harm—Comparison Between Anticipated and Actual Loss*

Although the comparison between anticipated and actual loss may be of secondary importance when evidence of genuine estimation is strong, courts are not likely to be oblivious to a substantial discrepancy between damages as agreed and as actually suffered. Of course, if, after breach, it turns out that damages are truly difficult to prove, this second stage of the inquiry becomes marginal or falls away. The uncertain and speculative nature of the loss vindicates the parties' judgment in trying to settle it in advance, provided that they made enough effort to satisfy the test of reasonable estimation. However, when it is possible to prove actual damages, courts balk at enforcing agreed damages that clearly and substantially exceed the plaintiff's loss. In fact, a gross disproportionality may in itself be evidence that the estimate was not a reasonable forecast of harm.

It may be helpful to represent these guidelines diagrammatically:

TIME OF CONTRACTING
The issue: Was this intended as a genuine liquidation of damages?

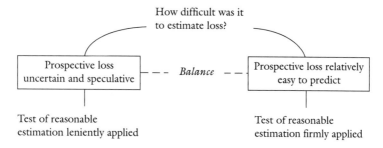

TIME OF BREACH
The issue: How does the estimate compare to the actual loss suffered?

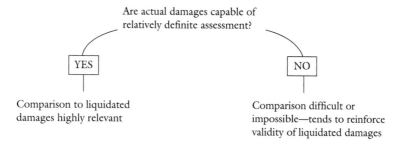

The principles stated above apply to liquidated damages that may be unenforceable as a penalty because they overcompensate the plaintiff. However, a different approach is taken to a contractual provision that seeks to *limit damages*. In that situation, there is no concern about penal provisions undermining the compensation principle. As a result, Restatement Second §356, Comment *a*, UCC §2.718, Comment 1, and UCC §719 indicate that damage limitation provisions are enforceable unless they are *unconscionable*. A limitation of remedy that grossly undercompensates the victim of a breach and deprives her of meaningful relief could, of course, be substantively unconscionable. However, as the discussion of unconscionability in section 13.11 explains, a finding of unconscionability requires more than a harsh result. There must also be some evidence that the unfair term resulted from procedural unconscionability—that it was imposed on the plaintiff by improper bargaining.

§18.12   Incidental Damages, Attorney's Fees, and Interest

In addition to the principal remedies discussed above, there are ancillary monetary awards that are often needed to fully compensate the plaintiff for a breach of contract. They are noted briefly here.

§18.12.1   *Interest*

When a *contract itself provides for the payment of interest* on an amount due by a party, the claim of interest is simply part of the plaintiff's damage recovery and is included in the claim. For example, if a lender makes a loan and the borrower breaches the contract by failing to repay it, the lender is entitled to sue for both the principal and for the full amount of accumulated interest at the rate provided in the contract. Interest continues to accrue until the debt is paid.

Even when the contract does not provide for the payment of interest, the general rule is that a plaintiff may recover interest on a *performance with a fixed or ascertainable money value* from the time that the performance became due to the time that payment is ultimately made. Such an award of interest may be seen as a form of consequential damages—because the plaintiff has lost the benefit of investing the money during the period between breach and recovery, or as a form of restitution—because the defendant has benefitted by its retention.

Even when damages are *uncertain until finally fixed in the judgment,* interest is commonly awarded to the plaintiff from the time between rendering of the judgment and its ultimate payment.

§18.12.2   *Incidental Damages*

Incidental damages are those expenses **reasonably incurred** by the plaintiff after the breach **in attempting to deal with the breach.** They are essentially the administrative costs of coping with the breach and taking whatever action is necessary to **protect and enforce the plaintiff's rights under the contract.** They include such items as the costs incurred in making arrangements to obtain substitute performance and to mitigate damages. For example, say that the buyer of goods breaches the contract by refusing to accept the goods when the seller tenders delivery. As a result, the seller has to transport them back to a warehouse, store them, and negotiate for their resale. All the additional costs of transport, storage, and negotiation are incidental damages and may be recovered by the seller, provided that they were incurred reasonably. (As this example involves a sale of goods, incidental damages are defined in UCC §§2.710 and 2.715, but they are also available under common law.)

Although incidental damages do, in a sense, follow as a consequence of the breach, they are distinguishable from and should not be confused with consequential damages: They do not arise as a result of the impact of the breach on some other transaction or activity dependent on the contract, but are expenses directly related to the plaintiff's attempt to manage the effects of the breach.

§18.12.3   *Attorney's Fees*

Based on the above definition of incidental damages, one might assume that the plaintiff should be able to recover her attorney's fees incurred in suing to enforce the contract after breach. They are, after all, expenses that the plaintiff was forced to undertake in dealing with the breach and seeking to enforce her rights under the contract. Despite this, attorney's fees are *not usually recoverable* by the winner of a lawsuit *unless the contract specifically allows them,* they are authorized by *statute,* or the case falls within one of a few narrow categories of exception recognized at common law. The *common law exceptions* apply to *bad faith and vexatious litigation* and to other specific situations that need not concern us here, and there is no statute that generally provides for the recovery of attorney's fees in contract cases (but individual states may have statutes that allow fees in certain types of contract suit). Therefore, the general rule is that attorney's fees are not recoverable by the winner of a suit on contract unless the contract itself makes provision for this.

The United States is one of the few countries in the world in which the prevailing party in litigation is not routinely entitled to recover attorney's fees from the loser. The debate over the merits of this approach is complex and beyond our scope. It is important to recognize, however, that unless one of the exceptions to the general rule applies, our system, by not reimbursing the plaintiff for the considerable expenses of litigation, does not really achieve its goal of placing the plaintiff in the position she would have been in had the contract been performed.

In tort cases, where a jury has a fairly wide discretion in deciding on the amount of non-economic damages (such as those awarded for mental distress or pain and suffering), it has some ability to increase the plaintiff's compensatory damages to take account of attorney's fees. If the case merits punitive damages, overcompensation may go far beyond this. By contrast, because contract damages are focused on provable economic loss, the jury has much less flexibility to inflate the award to cover the plaintiff's attorney's fees. This difference in approach between contract and tort can be justified on the basis that, unlike a tort victim, a contracting party is capable of providing in the contract for the award of attorney's fees (if she has the bargaining power to do so).

§18.13 Non-Economic Damages and Punitives

§18.13.1 Non-Economic Damages

Because contract damages are geared to economic loss, they do not typically take account of any *mental distress, inconvenience, humiliation,* or other *psychic harm* caused by the breach. This principle is applied firmly, whether the aggrieved party is a corporation without heart or soul, or some poor individual who really is traumatized and distressed by the breach. Therefore, for example, cold-hearted compensation for financial loss is all the comfort available to an employee who suffers anguish after being fired in breach of her employment contract, or the buyer of a dream home who weeps for months after being denied transfer by a faithless seller, or the apoplectic homeowner who cannot get the carefree and unreliable contractor to come out to finish the remodeling job.

There are two situations in which courts have recognized exceptions to this rule. First, if the *breach of contract is also a tort,* the tortious nature of the breach permits compensation for whatever non-economic damages that the plaintiff suffered. However, this is not really much of an exception at all, because the true basis of recovery is tort, not contract, since a tort was in fact committed. For example, if a surgeon negligently performs an operation, thereby both breaching a contractual duty of competent performance and committing the tort of battery, the patient can recover not only any economic losses, but also damages for pain and suffering and emotional harm.

The second exception concerns situations in which, according to Restatement Second §353, the *contract or breach is of a kind* that makes *serious emotional disturbance* a *particularly likely result.* Although the text of the section seems to contemplate either a contract or a breach that is likely to cause emotional distress, the comments and caselaw suggest that the nature and purpose of the contract are the determinative factors. For the exception to apply, the contract must be one in which the *clear and principal purpose* was not to satisfy any economic pursuit by the plaintiff, but to provide her with *some emotional or psychic benefit.* The plaintiff's non-economic expectation must be clear and obvious enough that it can fairly be said that the defendant should reasonably have realized at the time of contracting that her breach would likely inflict serious emotional distress on the plaintiff.

There is, of course, a strong link between this principle and the concept of foreseeability, but it goes beyond mere foreseeability. It is not enough for the defendant to have reasonably foreseen the likelihood that her breach would cause the plaintiff serious emotional distress. If that was all that was required, mental suffering damages would be commonly available, because likelihood of mental distress is easily contemplated whenever it is clear that the contractual performance is important to the plaintiff. Rather, courts tend to focus on the nature of the contract and to confine emotional distress damages to those contracts that have a *specially sentimental aim.* A classic example is the breach of an interment contract by a funeral home which so badly botches the burial ceremony that the plaintiff is tormented instead of being comforted by the last rites.

§18.13.2   *Punitive Damages*

As their name suggests, the purpose of punitive damages is to **punish** the defendant for particularly egregious conduct and to **deter** her from similar conduct in the future. Because the fate of the defendant is also likely to make an example of her and thereby have a deterrent effect on others, punitives are also sometimes called **exemplary.** Punitive damages are principally available in *tort* law. They are not appropriate when the tort involves ordinary negligence and are confined to cases in which the defendant *deliberately and maliciously injured* the plaintiff, or sometimes when the defendant acted in *callous and conscious disregard* of the plaintiff's rights. Although punitive damages are aimed at punishing the defendant, they are not in the form of a fine payable to the public treasury, but are awarded to the plaintiff in addition to whatever she is entitled to as compensatory damages. They are therefore a windfall that have the effect of overcompensating her. Because punitive damage awards can be large, the degree of overcompensation can be astounding.[12] Even in the area of tort law, where the jury's discretion to award punitive damages in appropriate cases is well-established, their scope and appropriateness is a matter of continuing controversy.

As emphasized many times in the preceding pages, the orientation of contract law is to the *compensation* of the plaintiff's economic loss, *not* to the *punishment and deterrence of breach.* As a result, it has long been seen as inappropriate to augment any compensatory award by punitive damages, even when the breach was deliberate and faithless. Restatement Second §355 reflects this attitude by taking the position that punitive damages are not recoverable for a breach of contract *unless* the *breach consists of tortious conduct* for which punitives would be available under tort law. This approach is commonly followed by courts, and punitives are rarely awarded in contract cases. (But recall that we have seen some examples of more subtle means of signifying disapprobation of the defendant's conduct, such as rules that shift the burden of proof to the defendant, that assist the plaintiff in overcoming problems of reasonable certainty, or that provide a less generous restitutionary recovery to a breacher. In addition, a jury often has some discretion in calculating the amount of damages and could take account of the defendant's conduct when it decides on the award of compensation.)

Although the general rule requires the breach to be a malicious tort as well for punitive damages to be awarded, some courts have been willing to broaden the basis for awarding punitives, either by recognizing that certain types of wilful breach constitute torts in themselves or by permitting punitives where, although the breach does not actually qualify as a recognized tort, the defendant's conduct was so *egregiously wrongful* that punishment and deterrence is merited. Cases of this kind have most commonly involved insurance contracts in which the insurer has so unjustifiably violated its contractual duty to indemnify the insured, that the breach constitutes a violation

---

12. The degree of overcompensation is reduced by the fact that a portion of the award will be used to pay attorney's fees and the costs of preparing for and conducting the litigation.

of the insurer's obligation of *good faith and fair dealing.* The insurance contracts in question are typically contracts of adhesion[13] in which the insurer has strong control over the terms, the insured is in a comparatively weak economic and bargaining position, and the insured relies heavily on proper and prompt indemnification so that the breach has a disastrous effect. Accordingly, the insurer's deliberate or cavalier treatment of the insured can be set apart from other wilful breaches and treated as particularly deserving of punishment. In addition, because the insurer would have little at stake in resisting or delaying indemnification if the only consequence would be an ultimate judgment of compensatory damages, punitives can also be justified as necessary to deter the conduct by increasing the financial risk of such behavior. Although there has been some judicial recognition that a bad faith breach may deserve punishment and deterrence in other types of contract, especially when the defendant had a particular duty of trustworthiness or dependability, courts have been slow to expand the availability of punitives in contract actions.

EXAMPLES

1. In January, the city council of Barbarian Bluffs decided to erect a monument to Barb Aryan, its founder. It commissioned Percy Vere, a local sculptor, to carve a giant bust of Barb into the granite bluff overlooking the town. In terms of his contract with the city, Percy undertook to begin work on the massive carving project in February and to complete it in time for the dedication in March of the following year. The town agreed to a fee of $250,000 for his work, to be paid upon completion of the carving. In February, Percy spent $50,000 to buy dynamite and other materials needed for his performance, and he hired two assistants at a monthly wage of $2,000 each. He began work immediately, and by April he had completed the blasting, erected scaffolding, and had begun the carving with jackhammers.

The project had been controversial from the beginning, but as it proceeded, hostility to it intensified. A growing number of citizens became persuaded that Barb Aryan did not deserve a monument at all because she had been fierce and ruthless in the way that she had forced the aboriginal inhabitants to vacate the area. Many others felt that it was a sacrilege to despoil the natural contours of the bluff. By the end of April, the outrage of the townfolk had reached such a pitch that the council members realized that it would be politically unwise to proceed any further with the monument. They therefore voted to abandon it and in early May they told Percy to stop work. This was a material and total breach because the town had no right to cancel the contract. Percy pointed this out and refused to accept the town's cancellation, which offended both his rights and his artistic sensibilities. Having em-

---

13. Contracts of adhesion are discussed in section 13.12.

barked upon the great enterprise of creating a masterpiece, he would not stop short of consummation of his artistic vision. He therefore ignored the town council's instruction to cease work and pressed on for another two weeks, until forcibly ejected from the site by the sheriff.

Had Percy stopped work when he was told to, he would already have paid $2,000 each to his assistants for wages earned to that stage and would have been required to pay them an additional $1,000 each as severance pay. As he had not used up all the materials bought for the job, he could have recouped $20,000 of the $50,000 spent by selling what remained of them. Because he refused to stop, he incurred an additional wage expense of $2,000 and used up a further amount of the materials, reducing their resale value by $5,000. Had the council not breached its contract, and had Percy been permitted to complete his performance, his total cost for the job would have been $150,000. What are his damages?

2. Buddy Beautiful is a celebrated supermodel, best known for his extremely seductive advertisements for men's fragrances and designer denim jeans. He decided to capitalize on his fame by becoming a movie star. Following intensive negotiations, his agent managed to secure a contract for him with Medea Mogul, an important movie producer. In terms of the contract, Buddy would be paid $10 million for taking the lead role in a movie to be called *Buddy's Big Budget Adventure*, an expensive and riotous new comedy, full of cute jokes and romantic scenes in which Buddy would have the opportunity to remove some or all of his clothing. Production of the film was to begin two months after the contract was signed, and would last for six months.

About a month after entering the contract, Medea decided not to produce the film. She wrote to Buddy, informing him of the film's cancellation and offering him the leading role in another movie called *Hamlet* that would be produced instead during the same period. Although Medea assured him that this film would do his career far more good than *Buddy's Big Budget Adventure*, Buddy was unconvinced. He read the script, which was written in strange, complicated, old-fashioned language. It was difficult to follow and would be even harder to learn. From what he understood of it, it also seemed very sleazy and definitely "R" rated. It was about this dysfunctional Danish family who are rather lacking in traditional family values and are heavily into sex and violence. The character to be played by Buddy talks too much, never has any fun, and does not conform to the sexy, but cute and wholesome image Buddy wanted to project. Furthermore, in her letter Medea described *Hamlet* as an "art film," which apparently meant that its box office draw would be small. As a result, the letter regretted to inform him, his fee for starring in it would be only $5 million.

Despite his misgivings, Buddy decided that *Hamlet* was better than nothing, so he accepted the offer. Does he have any claim for damages against Medea? If so, how much?

3. Change the facts of Example 2 as follows: Buddy did not feel that playing Hamlet offered a suitable role, so he declined Medea's offer and insisted that she make the original movie as promised. Medea refused and their relationship broke down. Buddy put his agent to work seeking other movie opportunities. Despite a year's conscientious and persistent effort, the agent was unable to secure any film roles for Buddy. In the interim, Buddy had done no other work because he felt that he should hold himself available to perform whatever new film contract his agent should find. What damages, if any, should Buddy receive?

4. How would your answer to Example 3 change if two weeks after Medea's repudiation, Buddy entered into a contract with Dee Ziner, a designer of men's fashions, to model her new line of summer clothing? Buddy's performance under the modeling contract began immediately after execution of the contract and lasted one month. Buddy earned a fee of $1 million.

5. Because Buddy's agent could not find another film contract for him, his hopes for a movie career ended in failure. Buddy is convinced that had he made the comedy for Medea, he would have established himself as a star and enjoyed unlimited opportunities for further movies. He has now sued Medea for the $10 million payable under their contract, as well as $200 million in damages for the destruction of his movie career. Should he be awarded these damages?

6. Harpo C. Chord is a young and ambitious pianist. After struggling for many months to find work, he finally received an offer to play dinner music at Trés Trendi, a fancy restaurant. This was not quite what he had in mind as a career opportunity, but his financial reserves were much depleted and he was becoming desperate. He also realized that because the restaurant was in the theater district, many of its patrons were influential in the arts, so there was a good chance that someone important might notice his talent and offer him something better. He therefore accepted the offer and on January 15 he entered into a contract with Trés Trendi under which he would play the piano during dinner from 8 P.M. to midnight every night for a month. His performances would begin on February 1, and he would be paid "the going rate" for his services. Because neither party knew at the time of contracting what the current market rate was for a dinner pianist, Trés Trendi said that it would make inquiries and tell Harpo as soon as it found out.

Having heard nothing from Trés Trendi for a week, Harpo called the manager to find out what rate of compensation had been established by the promised market survey. He was stunned when the manager told him that inquiries had shown that the market rate for a pianist was much higher than she had anticipated, so she had decided to scrap the idea of having live music in the restaurant. This is a clear breach of contract, and despite Harpo's fervent pleas, the manager refuses to relent.

Having just gone through the agonizing process of looking for work, Harpo realizes that he has little chance of finding other employment for February. Besides, he wants to work for Trés Trendi so that he can showcase his talents to any useful diners that may be present. What recourse does he have?

7. Barney Sellers owned an acre of land in the suburbs. The land was once part of a farm that has long since been subdivided into smaller lots for housing. However, the original barn is still located on Barney's acre, which is otherwise vacant. When Barney retired last year, he decided to move from his home in the city to his suburban acre. He had plans drawn for a new house to be constructed on the eastern portion of his lot. The existing barn was on the western side of the lot, so it did not interfere with his building plans, but it was quite an unsightly structure and would occupy space that Barney wished to use as a garden. The barn was in reasonably good condition and was easily removable, so he decided to sell it instead of demolishing it. He advertised it for sale and ultimately sold it to Penny Pincher for $5,000. In terms of the contract, Penny agreed to pay all the costs of removing the barn and also to break up its concrete foundation and remove the debris.

A few weeks later, Penny removed the barn. She was going to hire someone to break up and remove the concrete foundation, but when she discovered that the cheapest quote for the job was $7,000, she decided that it was a waste of money and refused to do it. The existence of the concrete slab will spoil Barney's landscaping plans and leave him with an eyesore in his backyard. However, because suburban land is scarce and of prime value, the presence of the slab would apparently not dissuade a typical buyer from purchasing the property at its full worth. As a result, the removal of the slab would not enhance the property's market value. What damages, if any, can Barney recover for Penny's breach?

8. To satisfy the demand for its required course on professional ethics, a law school offers a summer school ethics course every year. The course is usually in great demand and attracts about 50 students each summer. Last November, the law school contracted with Bill A. Billhours, a prominent local attorney, to teach the summer ethics course for a fee of $8,000. The contract obliged him to teach four evenings a week for eight weeks, beginning on June 1. On May 15, Bill was given the opportunity of advising a new client in connection with a huge international transaction. Participation in the proposed transaction promised to be both stimulating and lucrative, so Bill grabbed the chance of working on it. Unfortunately, the work required him to be out of the country for much of June and July, so it was no longer possible for him to teach. He called the dean of the law school on May 17 and told him that he could not teach summer school as planned.

8(a). Not wishing to disappoint the students who were relying on taking the course that summer, the dean immediately set to work finding a replacement. After making several unsuccessful calls, she was finally put in touch with Professor Wise, a world-famous expert on legal ethics and the author of several definitive books on the subject. Professor Wise had just retired, so he had no plans for the summer, but he was unwilling to teach for less than $10,000, plus his traveling and living expenses, which amount to a further $4,000. Desperate, the dean agreed to his terms. Can the law school recover all or any of the $14,000 from Bill?

8(b). Assume that the dean was unable to find anyone to teach the course because it is too late to find a teacher on such short notice. The dean cannot bear to let down all those students who are relying on taking the course during the summer. Is there anything she can do to force Bill into teaching?

8(c). Assume that the dean can neither find a substitute teacher nor compel Bill to teach. As a result, the summer ethics course has to be canceled. Based on enrollment before cancellation, the law school can show that it would have made $75,000 in tuition from the course. In addition, the law school was sued by one of the students who had enrolled in the course. The student had been relying on the course to complete his requirements for graduation in the summer so that he could graduate in August. He had a job beginning in August, but now he cannot begin work until after he graduates at the end of December. He therefore claimed three months' salary from the law school. To avoid adverse publicity and a negative impact on alumni relations, the law school paid the student's claim. What recourse, if any, does the school have against Bill?

9. Nat Atorium hired La Goon Pool Co. to build a swimming pool in his backyard. As the yard was small, the pool had to be placed not more than five feet from the rear wall of the house. La Goon brought its excavating equipment into the yard and one of its workers began to dig the hole. After spending some hours on the job and having excavated to a depth of about six feet, the operator started to become weary and careless. As a result, he dug too close to the house, undermining its foundation and causing the rear of the house to collapse. At the time, Nat was in one of the rear rooms and he could have been severely injured or killed had he not had the presence of mind to dive out of a door just as the room began to cave in. Although he escaped physical injury, he was badly traumatized by the close call and the destruction of half his house.

This experience has removed Nat's desire for a swimming pool. La Goon concedes that it is liable for the cost of repairing Nat's house, the fair market value of all personal property lost in the collapse, and the cost of filling in the hole and restoring the yard. However, Nat says this is not enough. He demands in addition:

(a)   Compensation of $150,000 for the shock and distress that he suffered as a result of La Goon's incompetence.

(b)   Compensation of $50,000 for the loss of irreplaceable family records and photographs that were among the personal property destroyed. Although they have no economic worth, they were of immense sentimental value to Nat.

(c)   Punitive damages of $1 million.

Is Nat likely to succeed on any of these further claims?

10. Chic Canery has managed to train a troupe of chickens to perform amazing tricks. She has appeared on several TV shows with them and has attracted a lot of public attention. Asi-9 Productions, Inc., a show promoter, decided the market was ready for a live show featuring Chic and her chickens. It approached Chic with a proposal to produce such a show. Following negotiations, in January Chic and Asi-9 entered into a contract for the production of a show on July 4. The show was to be staged in a sports stadium with a capacity of 100,000 seats. Asi-9 would make all arrangements for the show and would be entitled to all proceeds from the event, save for a fee of $1 million to be paid to Chic. An advance of $100,000 on this fee would be paid to Chic on the signing of the contract, and the balance would be paid a week before the show.

Immediately after the contract was signed, Asi-9 paid the $100,000 to Chic and it began preparations for the show. It booked the stadium, hired a special staff to work exclusively on publicity and sales, and committed itself to the purchase of television advertising. On March 1, Chic changed her mind about doing the show and she repudiated the contract. After trying unsuccessfully to convince her to recant, Asi-9 had no choice but to accept the fact that Chic would not perform. As the theme and concept of the entire show were built on Chic's unique chicken act, it was too late to begin afresh by changing the theme and trying to find a new starring attraction. Asi-9 stopped all further work on the show and laid off its special staff. It exercised its cancellation right under the contract with the stadium and terminated its booking, forfeiting a $50,000 deposit. It had no right to cancel the television advertising slots. At the time of Chic's repudiation, Asi-9 had incurred the following expenses and commitments:

(1) Before making a final decision to enter the contract with Chic, it had spent $30,000 on a market analysis and profit projection for the show.

(2) It paid the $100,000 advance to Chic.

(3) It paid $25,000 in salary and severance pay to its special staff.

(4) It forfeited its $50,000 deposit on the stadium.

(5) It committed itself to pay $500,000 for television advertising.

According to the market analysis and projections made by Asi-9 before it entered the contract with Chic, it expected the show tickets to be sold out, generating income of $5 million. It expected further earnings of $3.5 million from the sale of T-shirts, souvenirs, and food. Its projected costs, including Chic's fee, were $5.5 million, so it expected a profit of $3 million. What damages is it likely to recover from Chic?

11. Benny Fishery Co. entered into a contract with Reliant Renovations, Inc. under which Reliant agreed to build an addition to Benny Fishery's processing plant. The contract required Reliant to excavate the site,

build a foundation, and erect an aluminum structure on it. The total price for the project was $230,000. Reliant began work and encountered trouble immediately because the ground was much rockier than expected. As a result, it had to hire a subcontractor to blast the rock and had to use much heavier equipment than anticipated. This greatly increased its costs of excavation from an expected $50,000 to $100,000, and its total projected cost from $200,000 to $250,000. This meant that it now projected a loss of $20,000 on the contract. (Had Reliant conducted a proper inspection of the lot, it would have discovered this problem before bidding, so the underbidding is its own error in judgment. It acknowledges this and has not tried to use it as a basis for avoiding the contract for mistake or requesting a price modification.)

Soon after the excavation had been completed and before Reliant could proceed any further, Benny Fishery decided that it no longer needed the addition to its plant. It terminated the contract. As it had no right to do this, the termination was a total breach. The excavation work constitutes exactly one-quarter of Reliant's performance under the contract, and Benny Fishery has therefore offered to pay Reliant $57,500, which is exactly one-quarter of the contract price. Should Reliant accept this payment or demand more?

12. Gracie Spooner owns a busy hamburger joint. She recently decided to replace her grungy ketchup pumps with little plastic sachets of ketchup. To ensure a ready and stable supply of this vital ingredient in her cuisine, she entered into a one-year contract with Sauce Source, Inc., a wholesaler. Under the contract, Gracie committed herself to buy a minimum of ten boxes of sachets a month, at a price of $25 a box. The contract contained the following provision:

> The parties record that the pricing of the product sold under this contract is based on Buyer's commitment to take the minimum quantities specified above. Therefore if Buyer should breach this contract by failing to take the prescribed minimum quantity, Seller shall be entitled to damages based on the difference between the amount actually paid by Buyer for purchases of the product and the total minimum price payable for the full period of this contract. The parties expressly agree that this provision does not constitute a penalty, but is a genuine attempt to estimate damages and to avoid the uncertainty and difficulties of proof.

Gracie bought and paid for the minimum quantities required by the contract for seven months, but she found that she had grossly overestimated the amount of ketchup that she needed. Unopened boxes of sachets were beginning to pile up in her small storeroom, and it was clear to her that she already had enough ketchup to last her for more than a couple of years. She therefore declined to order or accept delivery of any more ketchup from Sauce Source. When the year-long contract period ended, Sauce Source sent an invoice to Gracie for $1,250, based on the price of the minimum quantity that she had failed to take during the last five months of the contract. Gracie protested to the manager of Sauce Source. She pointed out that ketchup had gone up in price since they made their contract, and she suggested that Sauce Source simply sell the remaining boxes at a better price to someone else. The manager told her that they had enough ketchup to keep all their customers supplied, with plenty over, so her breach actually reduced their volume of sales for the year. In any event, he reminded her that she did agree to this payment in the contract. Gracie feels that the invoice is ridiculous. Should she pay it?

EXPLANATIONS

1. Had the town not breached the contract, Percy would have spent $150,000 and earned $250,000, leaving him with a profit of $100,000. This is his expectation interest. Had he incurred no costs, an award of $100,000 would fully compensate for the loss of this expectation, but as he has already made expenditures and commitments in reliance on the contract, these must be returned to him as well. Thus, his full expectation recovery is his reliance losses plus his expected profit.

Had Percy stopped work immediately upon the town's breach, his outlay in reliance on the contract would have been $56,000. (The $50,000 spent on materials, the $4,000 paid in wages, and the $2,000 severance pay for which he was committed.) However, not all his reliance expenditure is wasted, because he can recover $20,000 as salvage for the unused materials; therefore this amount must not be included in his reliance loss, which is reduced to $36,000. This, added to his expected profit, leaves him with expectation damages of $136,000.

We get the same answer if we use the formula of awarding him full contract recovery ($250,000) less costs saved as a result of the breach. By not completing the work, he saved $94,000 (total cost of $150,000 less costs already incurred, $56,000) and then recouped a further $20,000 of what he would have spent, making his total savings $114,000. This amount, deducted from $250,000, leaves $136,000.

Although $136,000 would have fully compensated Percy had he ceased work when told, it does not in fact give him his full expectation because he continued performing for an extra two weeks, incurring additional losses of $7,000 by using up more material and paying more wages to his assistants. He was not justified in obstinately persisting in his performance following the town's clear and unequivocal breach. In doing so, he unnecessarily increased his loss, and the mitigation principle precludes him from holding the town responsible for the resulting aggravation of his damages. In *Rockingham County v. Luten Bridge Co.*, 35 F.2d 301 (4th Cir. 1929), the county breached its contract for the construction of a bridge by terminating the project and telling the contractor to stop work. The contractor disregarded the instruction and continued to build the bridge. It was held

entitled to recover its anticipated profit as well as those losses incurred up to the date of breach, but was denied any compensation for expenditures made after the breach.

2. Buddy's acceptance of the offer to star in *Hamlet* could be seen as a modification of the contract. If it was, there is no issue of breach or damages—the parties have simply changed their terms. However, when one party seeks to substitute a performance different from that originally agreed, the circumstances are also consistent with breach and offer of mitigation. It is important to distinguish these situations by interpreting the words and conduct of the parties in context; otherwise a party accepting an offer of a mitigating substitute from the breacher could lose his claim for damages to compensate for the difference in value of the original and substitute performances.

In Buddy's case, the facts indicate that Medea breached and then offered a substitute in mitigation. This seems a more appropriate conclusion given Medea's attitude (she informed Buddy of her decision rather than seeking to negotiate a change) and Buddy's reluctant acquiescence. Since Medea terminated the contract before performance was due, this is an anticipatory repudiation. It is unequivocal, material, and total. (This issue is discussed in section 17.7.2.) Upon Medea's total breach, Buddy is entitled to sue for his lost profit under the contract, less any amount recovered in mitigation. (In an employment contract, lost profits are commonly equal to the full salary because employees usually do not have to incur costs to perform, but any earnings from substitute employment must be deducted from damages as mitigation.)

Hamlet is surely a substitute contract, because Buddy would not have been able to do both films, since the production dates are the same. (In fact, Medea's decision to produce the second was apparently based on her decision to cancel the first.) When, as a result of the breach, the plaintiff is released from his performance so that he can undertake other work that could not have been done in the absence of breach, any earnings from that other work must be treated as a gain from the breach and offset against damages. Therefore, his earnings from *Hamlet* ($5 million) must be deducted from his damages for the breach of the initial contract.

3. Buddy has rejected the opportunity to reduce his damages by starring in *Hamlet* for $5 million. Because he could find no other substitute film contract, he has been idle for a year. It must therefore be decided if Buddy's refusal of Medea's offer and his failure to perform other work was a violation of his duty to mitigate, resulting in aggravated loss for which Medea should not be held accountable. If so, there must be an offset against his damages of the $5 million that he could have earned from *Hamlet*, or of whatever other amount he should have earned by other substitute work in the period that would have been occupied by filming *Buddy's Big Budget Adventure*.

A. Did Buddy Fail to Mitigate by Refusing to Take the Hamlet Role?

One's first reaction may be that it seems outrageous to require the victim of a breach, on pain of losing part of his damages claim, to mitigate by dealing with the very person who violated the contract and caused the loss. However, the breach victim cannot invariably make this argument. His reasonableness and honesty in failing to accept the mitigation offered by the breacher is subject to the same general rules as apply to any other available substitute. Therefore, he would not have to contract with the breacher if to do so would be unduly risky, burdensome, or humiliating. For example, he would have been justified in refusing to accept an offer of a mitigating transaction from the breaching party if it was a term of the proffered substitute that he waived rights to damages under the broken contract. Alternatively, the fact that the mitigation is offered by the breacher may justify the victim's feeling insecure about getting reliable performance under the substitute.

Quite apart from these concerns, the victim of a breach is not expected to enter a mitigating contract (whether with the breacher or a third party) if the substitute transaction is inconsistent with or, worse, damaging to the victim's reasonable expectations under the breached contract. This is illustrated by *Parker v. Twentieth Century-Fox Film Corp.*, 474 P.2d 689 (Cal. 1970). Shirley MacLaine (Parker) had a problem similar to Buddy's. The studio had contracted with her to star in a musical called *Bloomer Girl* for a fee of $750,000. The studio canceled the production and, in its stead, offered her a leading role in another film, *Big Country, Big Man* for exactly the same compensation. She refused it and sued for the full amount of her promised fee. The studio admitted the breach, but argued that she should be denied recovery because she could have mitigated her damages in full by taking the other role offered. This argument failed, and the court upheld summary judgment in favor of the plaintiff for the full amount of the earnings lost. The court noted the general rule that a wrongfully dismissed employee must make a reasonable effort to recoup her lost earnings by taking other employment in substitution for that promised under the breached contract. However, the duty to mitigate requires only reasonable effort and does not impose on the victim the obligation to take action that is prejudicial or unduly burdensome. Where an employment contract is concerned, the court must be solicitous of the employee's dignity and career goals, and should not penalize her for refusing to take work that would humiliate her or damage her professional development. Therefore, the court should not find that the plaintiff failed to mitigate when she declined an opportunity for substitute employment that was different and inferior to that under the breached contract. The court concluded that *Big Country* was different and inferior to *Bloomer Girl* not only because the role was an inferior vehicle for the plaintiff's talents, but also because the substitute contract eliminated her rights to approve personnel and screenplay. The dissent stressed that it is not enough that the available substitute is merely different from the employment under the breached contract. It must also be inferior. The dissent felt that the majority had superficially identified differences in the two films, but the question of whether these differences were serious and detrimental enough to make the substitute inferior could not be resolved in summary judgment proceedings.

Like the offer from Fox to Shirley MacLaine, Medea's offer of a role in *Hamlet* is clearly different from the movie promised under the contract. It may be hard to think of *Hamlet* as inferior to *Buddy's Big Budget Adventure*, but we are not simply evaluating this as movie critics. A substitute can be inferior for the plaintiff's purposes, even it if may be as good or better for someone else. *Hamlet* is inconsistent with Buddy's career goals, his talents, and his expectation of reaching the right audience. In fact, the profound brilliance required to portray even an acceptable Hamlet makes that role inferior employment to an actor who has neither the talent nor the understanding to realize it adequately. The fact that Buddy would be paid less under the substitute transaction is not itself an indication of the substitute's inferiority because the difference in earnings can be compensated for by a damages award. Therefore, inferiority is measured by the quality of the substitute employment in relation to his reasonable interest in career development and personal dignity.

B. Did Buddy Fail to Mitigate by Remaining Idle for the Period During Which Performance of the Contract Would Have Taken Place?

If Buddy's duty to mitigate would have required him to accept the role of Hamlet, our inquiry is at an end. His failure to accept the contract for $5 million is an aggravation of his damages, and the money that he would have earned from *Hamlet* must be deducted from his damages. However, if Buddy's refusal to play Hamlet was justified, the next question is whether he failed to take other action to mitigate his loss.

Buddy did make an effort to find another film role, and his agent apparently worked persistently and conscientiously on his behalf. It is therefore likely that his inability to obtain a substitute film part will not be held against him. His effort to mitigate in this respect was probably reasonable, even though unsuccessful. However, it is not clear that Buddy was justified in confining his energies to seeking employment as a lead actor. Although he would not be obliged to humiliate himself by taking different and inferior work, there seems to be no good reason why he could not have tried to look for modeling jobs. A modeling contract would present none of the career hazards that performing a bad Hamlet may have had. In fact, given his success as a supermodel, a little further public exposure would likely have a beneficial effect on his reputation and his future ability to pursue a film career. If Medea can show that a reasonable means was available to Buddy to curtail his loss, his damages will likely be reduced by whatever amount he could reasonably have earned during the six-month period that became free as a result of the breach.

4. If Buddy should have accepted the Hamlet role, the answer does not change—the full $5 million that he should have earned must be deducted from his damages. However, if his refusal of *Hamlet* was justified, the fee earned from the modeling job must be offset against the $10 million loss. The performance of Dee's modeling job took place during the period reserved for the filming, and Buddy could not have accepted it and earned the modeling fee had Medea not breached the movie contract. It is therefore a substitute transaction and the $1 million fee is a gain that would not have been made but for the breach. (If Buddy incurred any direct costs to perform for Dee, those would be subtracted before his earnings are offset. But in the typical employment contract it is the employee's time and labor that are being contracted for, and he does not usually have to spend much in rendering that performance. As a result, the employee's direct costs are likely to be small or even nonexistent.)

The effect of this is that Buddy can claim damages for breach in the amount of $9 million—his full contract salary, less the $1 million earned in mitigation. This means that Buddy will, in a sense, be overcompensated because he will receive his full contract fee, but will work only one month instead of six. However, this is in accordance with principle because his gain from not having to work for his money is not of economic value.

Note that the issue of whether the substitute is different and inferior does not come up with regard to the modeling job that Buddy accepted. It is only an issue when the question is whether the plaintiff was justified in not taking a substitute. If the substitute is accepted, the mitigatory amount is actually earned, and the only question is whether it was a true substitute, in the sense that it could not have been earned absent a breach of the contract.

5. Buddy's claim for consequential damages is based on the theory that by losing his opportunity to star in *Buddy's Big Budget Adventure*, he was deprived of a successful movie career and lost $200 million. The mitigation issue would arise here again, because his failure to accept the Hamlet role may have precluded an opportunity to prevent this consequence. However, Buddy may argue that this consequential loss would have occurred whether or not he had accepted the Hamlet role, because *Hamlet* would not have advanced his career at all and may even have ruined it.

It is arguable that a movie producer should reasonably foresee that her failure to produce a budding (honestly, no pun intended) actor's first film—especially if it is planned as an expensive blockbuster—could have an adverse impact on his career and deprive him of future opportunities. However, even if this is so, the overwhelming barrier to recovery is the highly speculative nature of the claim. It is unlikely that Buddy could prove with any degree of plausibility that the proposed movie would have been successful and would have advanced his career. There are just too many imponderables: Would he have performed well? Would good judgments have been made about publicity and promotion? Would the public have been attracted to the film and to him? Would it have made enough money to make him desirable to other producers? More uncertainties could be listed, but the point is made. Even if he could overcome this burden of showing a probability that opportunities would have been created, a further level of uncertainty would be encountered in trying to decide if he would have been lucky and clever enough to use them to advantage. In short, he cannot even prove what would have happened had the film been made, let alone establish a monetary value of the loss. The consequential damages claim must fail under the principles of certainty and causation.

The difficulty in establishing quantifiable loss when the breach results in a lost opportunity for publicity and its consequent career advancement is shown by another case springing from the entertainment industry: *Ericson v. Playgirl, Inc.,* 140 Cal. Rptr. 921 (Ct. App. 1977). *Playgirl* had featured Ericson, another budding actor, as the nude centerfold in one of its monthly editions. Subsequent to that publication, the magazine contracted with Ericson to rerun his pictures in its "Best of *Playgirl*" annual. In the contract, the magazine undertook to include Ericson as one of four models on the cover of the annual. It breached this term of the contract by failing to put him on the cover at all. Ericson sued for damages based on the contention that his absence from the cover cost him valuable publicity. To support his claim he produced witnesses who testified generally on the benefits of publicity to an aspiring actor, and he also attempted to establish a figure for his loss by introducing evidence of the cost of advertising space in the magazine as well as some opinion evidence of the economic worth of appearing on a magazine cover.

The court found that *Playgirl* had breached the contract, but awarded Ericson nothing more than nominal damages because he had failed to establish any measurable injury. The advertising rates for the internal pages of the magazine were irrelevant because the case concerned cover publicity, and the other evidence of loss was pure conjecture. Although the court accepted that, as an abstract matter, exposure (if you will permit the double entendre) is valuable to an actor, it is impossible to divine what beneficial effects, if any, would have been derived from it.

6. Although Harpo's remuneration has not been settled, this should not affect the validity of the contract, because the parties have agreed on a market standard for determining it. A contract for a reasonable fee, to be based on an objectively ascertainable standard, is sufficiently definite for enforcement.[14] If Harpo has no reasonable opportunity to mitigate his loss by

---

14. This issue is discussed in section 10.10.1.

finding appropriate substitute employment, he will at a minimum be able to sue for what he would have earned under the contract (less direct costs saved, if any). To establish what this amount would have been, he would have to produce evidence of the market rate paid to a pianist of his experience for equivalent work in a restaurant of similar standing. Such evidence is apparently available. However, Harpo was expecting more than a mere month's employment. He was hoping to make contacts and to open opportunities by playing in the restaurant. Although unlike Mr. Ericson, whose case is discussed in Example 5, Harpo plans to keep his clothes on during performance, that example shows that it is difficult to establish measurable injury as a result of the loss of publicity. Therefore, an award of money damages would most likely cover only his direct damages and would fail to compensate him for speculative consequential damages.

When a plaintiff can show that a monetary award cannot adequately achieve his expectation, he establishes one of the essential grounds for the remedy of specific performance. It could be quite unpleasant for Harpo to work in a place that does not want him and begrudgingly employs him under a court order, but if Harpo considers the opportunities arising from the employment important enough, he may decide to pursue this remedy. To get the order, Harpo must satisfy the court, in addition to showing the inadequacy of the damages remedy, that the court's burden of supervision is outweighed by the need for the remedy and that the balance of the equities favor granting the order. In addition, when there is some indefiniteness in the contract terms, even if the indefiniteness is not serious enough to invalidate the contract, the court may confine the plaintiff to damages unless the terms can be clearly established to support a precise and comprehensible order.

An order compelling Trés Trendi to employ Harpo as promised would entail some burden of supervision to ensure that he is properly treated and allowed to work unmolested. However, this is not an overwhelming task. It is not likely necessary to appoint an official to oversee the employment, and the court can rely on Harpo to bring any alleged impropriety to its attention. If he does so, the court can conduct a hearing to determine if his complaint is justified. The risk of misunderstanding and later dispute is minimized if the court specifies the employer's duties in its order.

If Harpo had breached, the restaurant could not have obtained an order compelling him to perform, because there is a strong policy against forcing an individual to work against his will. However, modern law recognizes no doctrine of mutuality of remedy, and the fact that the restaurant could not get an order against Harpo is no basis for refusing an order in his favor. There is no general public policy that is offended by compulsion leveled against the employer, and such orders are widely recognized in employment law and are commonly granted when the equities favor them. In this case, the equities do appear to favor Harpo. It imposes no great hardship on Trés Trendi to permit Harpo to play the piano in its restaurant, and the only disadvantage it suffers is the payment of money that would in any event be claimable as damages. (Indeed, specific performance would benefit Trés Trendi more than an award against it of direct damages because it will still get Harpo's music in exchange for its payment.) By contrast, the refusal of the order would leave Harpo uncompensated for any value that the month's public exposure would have given him. The fact that Trés Trendi's breach was deliberate, inconsiderate, and motivated by penny-pinching must also have some influence on the equities.

Finally, the indefiniteness in the contract should not be a bar to relief because it concerns only the calculation of payment for Harpo's work—a matter that can be easily established with reference to the market. Because it is only the defendant's monetary obligation that was left unresolved in the contract, the indefiniteness has no greater impact on specific performance than it would have had in a suit for damages. Matters would be different if the indefiniteness related to some less tangible commitment. Say, for example, that the contract obliged Trés Trendi to erect a suitable podium in the center of the restaurant and to furnish a piano of concert quality. Vagueness of that type, while not likely severe enough to preclude contract formation or to thwart a determination of damages, may form too uncertain a basis for resolving performance standards in an order for specific performance. (However, even when the vagueness is of this greater degree, a court may be willing to resolve the uncertainty if damages would be an inadequate remedy and equity dictates the need for specific relief.)

This point is illustrated by *City Stores Co. v. Ammerman,* 266 F. Supp. 766 (D.D.C. 1967), a case in which the court granted specific performance even though the uncertain performance obligations were quite extensive and complex. In exchange for assistance in getting some open land rezoned for the purpose of building a shopping mall, the developer granted an option to a department store to become a major tenant in the proposed mall. As the mall had not yet been constructed at the time that the option was granted, the contract left open the amount of rent to be paid and all the details concerning the design, location, and quality of the premises. The contract simply provided that these terms would be at least as favorable as those to be granted to other major department store tenants. After construction began and two of the three department store spaces had been rented, the developer sought to let the last remaining area to one of the department store's competitors.

The store immediately applied for an injunction to restrain the developer from entering into that lease, and it then asked the court for an order of specific performance. The developer opposed it on the basis that the option contract was too indefinite to be specifically enforced. The court disagreed. As there were by then leases in existence with the other two major tenants, there was an objective basis for settling the precise terms of the plaintiff's lease. The court also acknowledged that although courts do not normally relish the idea of supervising the performance of construction contracts, this could be done with the assistance of a special master who could mediate differences between the parties on points of detail. In this case, any burden of supervision imposed on the court was outweighed by the strong equities favoring a decree of specific performance: The defendant would suffer no undue hardship by honoring its contract with the plaintiff and would suffer nothing more than having to give up the more lucrative deal that it hoped to close by breaching. On the other hand, damages could not adequately compensate the plaintiff for the breach because it would not be possible for the plaintiff to prove with adequate certainty what losses it would suffer as a result of being deprived of a long-term lease in this large a regional shopping complex.

7. It is easy to identify the measure of damages required to place Barney in the position he would have been in had Penny not breached. It is the reasonable cost of demolishing the slab and removing the concrete debris, apparently $7,000. However, the facts show that although damages of $7,000 would give Barney the equivalent of performance in compliance with the contract, the breach did not actually cause him economic harm, if his loss is instead measured by the diminution in the value of the property on which the work was to have been done. This raises the issue of whether the proper basis for recovery is the cost of giving him what was promised (which is $7,000) or the actual reduction in his wealth (which is zero). Stated differently, when the cost of giving the plaintiff his contractual expectation exceeds his actual ultimate financial loss, should his damages be confined to reimbursement of that ultimate loss?

The general principle, as reflected in *Jacob & Youngs, Inc. v. Kent*, 129 N.E. 889 (N.Y. 1921), is that when a contract has been substantially performed, so that the cost of rectifying a trivial breach exceeds the value of the benefit that full performance will confer on the plaintiff, principles of fairness dictate that diminution in value is the proper measure. However, this principle is premised on a finding that the breach was not material and involved some minor aspect of performance, incidental to the essence of the values exchanged. When the breach relates to a central purpose of the contract—it is apparent from an interpretation of the contract that the performance in question was a material aspect of the exchange—it would be wrong for the court to defeat the plaintiff's expectations merely because the cost of providing them exceeds the enhancement of the objective market value of the plaintiff's property.

This was the rationale of *American Standard, Inc. v. Schechtman*, 427 N.E.2d 512 (N.Y. 1981). The owner of an industrial site closed its plant and sold the buildings and other moveable property in exchange for $275,000 plus a promise to grade the property and remove foundations and other remaining structures to a foot below grade level, leaving the vacant land in a reasonably attractive state for resale. After the buyer took what it purchased but failed to perform its restoration obligations, the seller sued it for $110,000, the cost of doing the work. The buyer contended that the damages should not be awarded based on the cost of restoration, because it would be economically wasteful to do the work. To support this argument, the buyer attempted to offer testimony that the seller had resold the land for only $3,000 below the fair market value that it would have had if restored. The court refused to admit this evidence on the basis that the ultimate diminution in value was irrelevant because, on its interpretation of the contract, the restoration of the land was a significant part of the consideration exchanged for the property sold and not merely incidental to the contract's main purpose. It was also of some significance to the court that the breach, unlike that in *Jacob & Youngs*, was deliberate and not inadvertent.

A similar approach was adopted in *Groves v. John Wunder Co.*, 286 N.W. 235 (Minn. 1939), in which the lessee of a gravel quarry failed to level and grade the land after removing the gravel. Although the cost of the leveling and grading far exceeded the market value of the land, the court refused to limit the lessor's damages on this account. *Peevyhouse v. Garland Coal & Mining Co.*, 382 P.2d 109 (Okla. 1963), reached a result opposite from *Groves*. Because the court expressly distinguished its facts from *Groves*, the opinions are frequently cited as foils to each other. After strip mining the plaintiffs' land, the defendant failed to restore it as required by the contract. The court refused to award damages to the plaintiffs based on the cost of restoration because this cost was disproportionately larger than the amount by which the work would enhance the market value of the land. The court's justification for this decision was that the main purpose of the contract was the extraction of coal for mutual profit, and the remedial work was merely an incidental obligation. For that reason, it would be unfair and an "economic waste" to hold the defendant liable for the full expectation damages.

Peevyhouse has always been a controversial case, not only because the scars of strip mining fail to drive us to poetic ecstasies, but also because it appears that the plaintiffs did indeed negotiate firmly for the land's rehabilitation and this was likely understood by the parties to be a material aspect of the bargain. Twenty years after *Peevyhouse*, the Tenth Circuit Court of Appeals had to resolve a similar dispute under Oklahoma law. In *Rock Island Improvement Co. v. Helmerich & Payne*, Inc., 698 F.2d 1078 (10th Cir. 1983), a mining lease required the lessee to restore the land after mining. When it failed to do so, the lessor sued for the cost of restoration. The lessee argued, on the basis of *Peevyhouse*, that as the cost of restoration ($375,000) greatly exceeded the diminution in the land's value (about $6,000), the plaintiff should be confined to the loss in value. The court felt that the Oklahoma Supreme Court would no longer apply the rule in *Peevyhouse* because state policy relating to land reclamation had changed, and state law required mine operators to rehabilitate the land. The failure to perform this aspect of the contract could no longer be considered immaterial, and it is more logical to assume that the parties intended the reclamation provision to be a significant aspect of the consideration exchanged.

This does not mean that cost of restoration will inevitably be the proper measure of damages. In fact, one could question the result in *American Stan-*

dard because the plaintiff in that case did appear to have been primarily concerned with the ultimate resale value of the land and had allegedly resold it at only a small loss. Because materiality is a matter of interpretation, it is not always easy to predict how a court may view the fundamental purpose of the parties' bargain.

In Barney's case, the facts do not indicate what the barn was worth, or how much its cash price was reduced on account of the promise to remove the concrete. This information would be useful in deciding on the significance of the breach. However, even in its absence, there is nothing that Penny can point to as an indication that removal of the concrete was not a material aspect of the exchange. Had Barney in fact sold the property and received its full value, there would be a basis for arguing that the primary purpose of the contract with Penny was simply a sale, that removal of the concrete was merely incidental, and that Barney's true loss is zero. (Even if this was so, however, it should not be forgotten that a court may decline to apply the unfair forfeiture principle if the breach was deliberate.) However, these are not the facts, and the lack of impact on the property's market value should not be relevant. Unless sale of the property is clearly the ultimate goal, the owner's contractual right to performance should not be defeated merely because the performance would not translate into an equivalent increase in the objective value of the property.

8(a). When, following a total breach, the plaintiff obtains a reasonable substitute performance, expectation damages are the difference between what the plaintiff had to pay for the substitute and what it would have had to pay under the contract for the equivalent performance. When the substitute is not only more expensive in itself, but also involves the plaintiff in the extra expense of having to go outside the local market, the additional cost of transportation or (as in this case, travel and living expenses) is also included in determining the replacement cost. Therefore if Professor Wise is a reasonable substitute for Bill, the law school will be able to recover from Bill the $6,000 difference between what it paid to Wise, $14,000, and what it would have paid him, $8,000.

Although it is seldom likely that a substitute performance will exactly match that promised under the contract, both the compensation and the mitigation principle require that the replacement be as close as possible. If the plaintiff is awarded the added cost of a more valuable or better-quality replacement, it is overcompensated, and its damages must be reduced to reflect the lower cost of a nearer substitute. However, this principle is not rigidly applied so that the plaintiff is invariably precluded from receiving reimbursement of the full cost of a superior replacement. As the victim of breach, the plaintiff has the burden foisted on it of finding a substitute to effectively counter the ill effects of the breach, sometimes within a very short time. When the only reasonable option open to the plaintiff under all the circumstances is to select a better replacement, it may be appropriate to hold the defendant accountable for the full cost, even if this means that the plaintiff profits somewhat by a performance superior to that expected. This is particularly so when the better substitute gives the plaintiff no realizable economic advantage.

In this case, Bill breached about two weeks before classes were to begin, and the dean had little time to find a substitute. She did make immediate efforts and only hired Professor Wise when it was apparent that she would be unlikely to find anyone else. She has no duty of exhaustive inquiry, but need only make such good faith and reasonable efforts called for by the circumstances. Even if Professor Wise is more experienced, has greater prestige, and may possibly be a better teacher, he may be the most reasonable substitute.

This was the conclusion reached on analogous facts in *Handicapped Children's Education Board v. Lukaszewski*, 332 N.W.2d 774 (Wis. 1983). A speech and language therapist was hired by the board under a one-year contract for a salary of $10,760. She had to commute a long distance to work, which she did not like. Therefore, when another position became available closer to home, she decided to take it. She resigned, claiming ill health, but the court found this to be a pretext, so her quitting was a breach. Following her resignation, the board sought a replacement. The only qualified applicant was a person with lower educational qualifications but greater seniority. In accordance with the union rates, her level of seniority required that she be paid about $1,026 more than the defendant. When sued for this difference, the defendant argued that she should not be liable for the increased cost because the board got a more experienced teacher for its money. The court disagreed, pointing out that it is not the objective value of the services that is important, but the fact that the plaintiff received no more than it bargained for—a special education teacher for the year. It neither needed nor desired a more experienced teacher, but, having taken reasonable steps to find a substitute, it was forced into the position of having to hire one as a result of the breach. Any benefit of her increased experience was imposed on it.

8(b). A court will not decree specific performance of personal services. Quite apart from the obvious difficulty in supervising the performance of teaching duties, the compulsion of personal services is rather too much like involuntary servitude. Therefore, even though the plaintiff may have no adequate remedy at law, the considerations disfavoring specific enforcement outweigh the plaintiff's interest in performance.

If specific performance is not available, a court may be willing to grant the plaintiff a prohibitory injunction, restraining the defendant from entering into the transaction that motivated the breach. The concerns about involuntary servitude and difficulty of supervision are not present in such a negative order. Of course, preventing Bill from participating in the international transaction does not, in itself, achieve the school's expectation, but the idea is that by removing the motivation for the breach, the order will induce Bill to perform as promised. However, even when a prohibitory injunction is sought, courts are very wary about using their power of compulsion to prevent an individual from selling his labor and earning his livelihood as he sees fit. It is therefore in only the most compelling cases that a court will issue such an order.

Like specific performance, an injunction is an equitable remedy, subject to the same general prerequisites: The plaintiff must show that the legal remedy of damages is inadequate, and that the balance of equities favor the grant of the order. In this case, given the fact that no substitute is available, the possibility of substitutionary damages does not exist. This would lead to lost profits and consequential damages that (as Question 8(c) discusses) could be very speculative and difficult to prove. Furthermore, no monetary award can compensate for the immeasurable harm caused by the disruption of the law school's program, its inability to provide planned educational services, and the disappointment or even hostility of its students. Overall, a good argument can be made that the school has no adequate remedy at law. If this is so, the equities of trying to protect the law school's expectation weigh heavily in the balance. They are given further weight by the fact that Bill's breach is deliberate and motivated by ambition and financial reward. Nevertheless, Bill's primary professional pursuit is legal practice and the service of his clients' needs. It may simply be too harsh on Bill to restrain him. Also, there is a strong public interest in allowing people access to an attorney of their choice, so an injunction may improperly interfere with the attorney-client relationship. This would be particularly so if Bill has already agreed to represent the client. In short, without reaching a definitive conclusion, we can recognize that an injunction may be feasible, but there may not be enough here to overcome the court's disinclination to issue such an order.

Some of the complexities in this kind of balancing are illustrated by *American Broadcasting Co. v. Wolf,* 420 N.E.2d 363 (N.Y. 1981). Wolf worked for ABC as a sportscaster. The contract of employment obliged him, during the last 90 days of the employment period, to enter into good faith negotiations with ABC for renewal of the contract. He also agreed that if they could not reach consensus on renewal, he would not accept an offer of employment as a sportscaster from anyone else in the three months following termination of the contract, without first giving ABC the option of employing him on substantially similar terms. During the final months of his employment by ABC, Wolf committed himself to work as a producer for CBS. This meant that he could not genuinely negotiate a renewal with ABC. Although he continued to go through the motions of meeting with ABC executives, the discussions were a sham and a breach of his obligation to seek agreement in good faith. Furthermore, to evade ABC's three-month right of first refusal, he made a separate sportscasting agreement with CBS, structured as an option to be accepted by him as soon as the three-month period expired.

Although the court accepted that Wolf had breached his undertaking to negotiate in good faith, it refused ABC's claim for specific performance on the basis of the policy against involuntary servitude. The majority of the court also refused an injunction restraining Wolf from working for CBS. The majority opinion acknowledged that a restraint on employment may be appropriate when the contractual period of employment has not yet ended and the employee attempts to defect to a competitor, irreparably harming the plaintiff by depriving it of unique skills. An injunction may also be granted after the end of the term of employment if the employee violates an express, valid, and properly limited covenant not to compete. However, the majority found that neither of these conditions were satisfied in the case. The period of employment had expired, and the first-refusal in the three months after expiration of the contract was not equivalent to an express covenant not to compete. The dissent disagreed with these conclusions, arguing that although the contract had ended, the breach in issue—violation of the duty of good faith negotiation—did occur during the term of the contract. In addition, the second basis for an injunction was also satisfied because the 3-month right of first refusal was, in effect, a covenant not to compete.

8(c). Because the law school is unable, after reasonable effort, to replace Bill and avert the loss resulting from cancellation of the class, its net loss is claimable as direct damages. Of course, it cannot claim the full lost earnings of $75,000. First, it must establish that its forecast of tuition income is reasonably reliable and takes into account what likely proportion of enrolled students may exercise any available right to drop the course and be excused from paying tuition. Thereafter, it must deduct its savings from the breach and any recoupment of that loss. The most obvious saving is Bill's salary of $8,000. Although the facts do not indicate them, there may be some other variable (direct) costs that are saved. They probably do not amount to much—a few sticks of chalk, some photocopying, and items of that kind. Overhead expenses such as maintaining the buildings and paying support staff are likely not reduced at all by the breach and are not deducted as costs saved. In addition, there may be some recoupment of the lost earnings if some of the students decide to switch to another summer school class instead, or if the law school's fee structure is such that the students end up paying more tuition in the semester for having to take the ethics course then. Once all these savings and recoupments are calculated, the law school is entitled to claim its lost profit—expected earnings less savings and recoupment—from Bill.

The payment to the student who sued for lost salary is a consequential loss. When a breach of contract causes the plaintiff to breach a dependent contract with a third person, the plaintiff's liability to the third person could be recoverable provided that the requirements of causation, reasonable certainty, foreseeability, and mitigation are satisfied. Certainty could have been a problem had there been unresolved potential claims for lost employment opportunities, but as we are concerned with only one claim of a defined amount, the loss is quantifiable and defined. However, many questions are raised by the other prerequisites.

For the loss to be foreseeable, Bill must have had enough information to reasonably realize that his breach could result in cancellation of the class, making the law school liable to some students for postponed graduation and loss of employment. It is not clear what Bill was told about the plans of class members and the possible impact on them of having the class canceled, but he did know that he was to teach a law school summer class. As a legal practitioner and visiting professor, he probably was familiar enough with legal education that he should have been aware that some students enroll in summer school to complete their graduation requirements and that inability to take a required course (assuming that he had reason to know that it was a required course) may result in a delay in graduation and employment.

Even if all this is reasonably foreseeable, it is not clear from the facts that the law school would have been responsible for any losses suffered by students as a result of cancellation. If the law school, expressly or by common practice, reserved the right to cancel the course, the cancellation would not have been the breach of a contractual commitment to the enrolled students, and any payment would have been a purely voluntary act, for which Bill could not be held accountable. If the law school had made a firm contractual commitment to the students, Bill would either have needed to be told this, or it must have been so generally known to be the practice that he should have been aware of it.

Finally, even if the law school was liable for losses suffered by its students, it would still have to show that its action in paying the claim in full, instead of contesting it, was reasonable. Given the cost, uncertainty, and harm to goodwill that would have resulted from litigation, this may have been reasonable action provided that the student did in fact have a colorable claim. In short, an argument can be made for the recovery of this consequential loss, but the law school's success is dependent upon a number of uncertain questions.

9(a) & (b). *The claims for shock, distress, and sentimental loss.* The focus of contract damages is on economic loss, so the general rule is that no compensation is claimable for emotional distress or sentimental loss resulting from the breach. In some cases, losses of this nature could be excluded simply on the basis that they were not reasonably foreseeable. But even when there may have been some basis for contemplating them as a probable consequence of breach, the policy of confining contract damages to economic loss usually outweighs any sympathy for the plaintiff's suffering. There are, however, two situations in which courts are willing to countenance a claim for emotional or sentimental damages:

A. When the Clear Goal of the Contract Is to Provide the Plaintiff with a Performance that Is Not Intended to Serve the Plaintiff's Economic or Commercial Ends, but Is Aimed Purely at Alleviating His Suffering or Enhancing His Psychic Well-Being

It may seem, at first thought, that the construction of a swimming pool in Nat's backyard, for his own personal use and enjoyment, is such a contract. However, courts constrict this exception more narrowly. It is not enough, to remove the contract from the commercial realm, that the plaintiff's desire for the performance was motivated by personal pleasure rather than profit. For example, in *Chrum v. Charles Heating & Cooling, Inc.*, 327 N.W.2d 568 (Mich. 1982), a furnace bought from the defendant caught fire and destroyed the plaintiff's home. The court refused to award damages for mental distress on the basis that the contract was not one involving a "deep personal human relation," or a matter of "mental concern and solitude," but was simply a commercial transaction, the breach of which led to property loss. The reason for this rather cold-hearted approach is probably quite obvious: If the exception were extended to cases like this, it could cover almost every consumer transaction in which it is clear that the primary motivation is the use of the property or services purchased to enhance quality or enjoyment of life. A similar approach is taken to employment contracts. For example, in *Valentine v. General American Credit*, 362 N.W.2d 628 (Mich. 1984), the court conceded that when an employer discharges an employee in violation of their contract, the negative impact on the employee's security and peace of mind is readily foreseeable. However, the fact that emotional distress may be foreseeable is not enough because the contract is primarily economic and not to secure the protection of personal interests. Any psychic satisfaction gained from employment is secondary.

If the above types of contract do not qualify for the exception, what does? In *Chrum*, the court gave the examples of a nursing home that failed to notify the plaintiff of her mother's pending death, and of a funeral home's mutilation of the body of the plaintiff's daughter. In *Deitsch v. Music Co.*, 453 N.E.2d 1302 (Ohio 1983), a band that failed to show up at a wedding was held liable for damages for distress, inconvenience, and diminution in the value of the reception. These illustrations suggest the kind of personal and sentimental attributes that a contract must have before a court is willing to consider awarding emotional distress damages, but the dividing line is quite fuzzy and not always easy to draw.

B. When the Breach of Contract Also Qualifies as a Tort

This is not so much an exception to the rule barring emotional distress damages in contract, as a recognition that some breaches of contract may involve conduct that is also a violation of duty under the law of torts. The non-economic damages are therefore not really awarded for the breach of contract, but are independently compensable in tort. After concluding that the contract did not involve the kind of personal interests that merited mental distress damages, the court in *Chrum* observed that negligent installation of the furnace could give rise to an independent tort action, for which mental suffering damages may be awarded. The court remanded the case to allow the plaintiff to pursue a claim in tort. The damage to Nat's house was also apparently caused by negligent operation of the earthmoving equipment. If this is so, the negligent performance is likely to constitute not only a breach of contract, but also a tort, allowing Nat to go forward with his claim for mental distress damages. (Whether he satisfies the requirements of tort law for award of these damages is beyond our scope.)

9(c).   *Punitive damages.* The compensation principle also precludes punitive damages in most contract suits. Although some courts are willing to consider an award of punitive damages where the breach is so egregious a violation of good faith and fair dealing that punishment and deterrence are called for, the most common approach is not to award punitives unless the breach is also a tort for which such damages are appropriate. Punitives are not generally available in tort law unless the injury was deliberate and malicious, or was at least the result of reckless and callous disregard for the plaintiff's rights. Therefore, even if LaGoon's employee did commit a tort by damaging Nat's house, this sounds more like a case of common negligence than the kind of conduct that warrants punitive relief.

10.   If Asi-9's projections are credible, its expectation damages are its anticipated profit of $3 million plus the reliance expenses that it has already spent or committed for which it would have been reimbursed out of its earnings under the contract. (These expenses are discussed below.) One cannot be sure how convincing the projections are. It is conceivable that they are so carefully done by analysts of profound expertise and experience that they may overcome the natural skepticism with which such forecasts are normally treated. More likely, however, they will fail to satisfy the requirement of reasonable certainty. It is generally very difficult to establish prospective lost profits from a canceled entertainment event. Public taste often surprises even the most seasoned promoter, and it is quite common for the most promising projects to lose vast sums of money at the box office—as most movie studios and performing arts groups could readily attest. The prospect of profit is even less certain when the show centers on something as odd as a performing chicken act. Given the substantial projected costs of mounting the show, Asi-9 would have to do remarkably well in selling both its tickets and its associated knick-knacks. Its prediction that it could sell out a stadium of 100,000 seats shows laudable, but possibly (I hope) misplaced, faith in the artistic sensibilities of the American public.

If Asi-9 cannot prove lost profits, what other alternatives does it have? Restitutionary relief would be available to reclaim Chic's unjust enrichment, but that would cover only the $100,000 down payment. None of the other expenditure enriched her in any way. However, a plaintiff who cannot prove lost profit may nevertheless still recover as reliance damages the expense component of its expectation claim. A claim of reliance damages would permit the recovery of not only the $100,000 down payment, which qualifies as essential reliance, but also some of the other losses incurred in reliance on the contract. Provided that they were reasonably necessary to Asi-9's performance under the contract and were not profligate, the forfeited stadium deposit and the staff salaries are recoverable in reliance. (They are probably best classified as essential reliance, in that they were expended in furtherance of Asi-9's contractual obligation to arrange and promote the show.)

The debt for television advertising would also fall into this category, but only to the extent that the expenditure is wasted and not salvageable. Although the advertising slots cannot be canceled, they may be assignable or diverted to use for other purposes. Therefore, to the extent that Asi-9 can recoup its expenditure by selling the slots or using them for another show, it is not claimable as a reliance loss.

The cost of the market survey and profit projection were incurred before the contract was entered into, so even though these expenses were a waste in the end, they cannot, by definition, be treated as having been incurred in reliance on the contract. This seems to be the general approach to precontractual expenses, notwithstanding that the breach cut off any prospect of earning income that may have reimbursed them.[15]

As noted above, Asi-9 would claim reliance only if it could not prove its larger claim of lost profit. The plaintiff does not have to prove that the contract would have made a profit to recover reliance damages. However, when the purpose of the contract was profit, and the defendant is able to prove that the plaintiff would have made a loss in the event of complete performance, the court will reduce the reliance recovery pro rata to take account of this expectation of loss. In a case like this one, where profit is highly speculative, the risk of uncertainty therefore falls on the defendant. Chic probably has about as much chance of proving loss as Asi-9 has of proving profit, so she probably cannot satisfy her burden, and Asi-9's recovery is not likely to be subject to reduction.

If you think that a chicken act is silly, consider the case of *Wartzman v. Hightower Productions, Ltd.*, 456 A.2d 82 (Md. 1983). A group of bright en-

---

15. There have been some situations in which courts have been willing to include precontractual expenses in reliance recovery. For example, if the defendant knew that the plaintiff was incurring the expenses in anticipation of the contract and had strongly indicated an intention to enter the contract, promissory estoppel relief may be available for the precontractual expenses. Also, the expenses take on the character of lost opportunity reliance if the plaintiff could have recouped them by entering a similar contract with a third party but gave up that chance by entering the contract with the defendant.

trepreneurs conceived of the gimmick of making some money out of breaking the world flagpole-sitting record. They planned to lodge an entertainer in a specially constructed perch atop a hydraulic lift mounted on a flatbed trailer. (This sounds like cheating to me, as it was nothing like any flagpole I have ever seen, but the case does not address this issue.) He would live on the perch for about nine months, being hauled around the county and exhibited at exciting events like supermarket openings and talk shows, and would ultimately descend to great acclaim in Times Square on New Year's Eve. This culturally significant venture required capital, so the promoters consulted the defendant, an attorney, to have it incorporated so that investments could be solicited. Unfortunately, the defendant did not know much about securities law and he failed to prepare the legally required memorandum and disclosures.

The promoters immediately proceeded to solicit investments and to set their enterprise in motion. By the time that it was discovered that they were in violation of the law, they had already incurred substantial expenses. They could not proceed any further without rectifying the legal problem, which would require the hiring of an expensive securities lawyer, the payment of improperly solicited investments into escrow, and the suspension of all fundraising activity until compliance with the law was achieved. Because the promoters could afford neither the expense nor the delay, the venture collapsed. The court, acknowledging that profits were too speculative to prove, awarded the corporation reliance damages to compensate for the wasted expenditures incurred in justifiable reliance on the defendant's contractual commitment to incorporate the enterprise properly.

In case you are tired of infantile entertainments and would like to end on a more elevated plane, *Chicago Coliseum Club v. Dempsey*, 265 Ill. App. 542 (1932), a suit arising out of the manly art of pugilism, may be used to reinforce the concepts discussed above. Jack Dempsey, the world-champion heavyweight boxer, entered into a contract with the Chicago Coliseum Club to engage in a bout with Harry Wills, another well-known boxer. After the club had incurred costs in organizing the match, Dempsey repudiated the contract and set about preparing for another fight instead. The club initially obtained an injunction restraining Dempsey from engaging in the other fight. It thereafter sued for damages. Although the club sought to prove lost profit, its evidence on profit projections was excluded because the court held that profitability was subject to too many contingencies and lacked the necessary "stability."[16] However, the court did remand the case to the trial court to allow the club to establish its reliance claim for all post-contractual expenses that had reasonably and necessarily been incurred in furtherance of its performance. (There had also been some costs incurred in anticipation of,

---

16. To satisfy the prerequisite for an injunction, the club alleged that because damages were too difficult to prove, it had no adequate legal remedy. This admission in the earlier case hardly helped its effort to prove those damages in the subsequent suit for lost profits.

but prior to the execution of the contract. The court pointed out that even if the plaintiff could establish these costs, they are were not incurred in reliance on the contract and were not recoverable.)

11. Had Reliant's cost been as it had estimated, it would have had a reasonable expectation of profit. Benny Fishery's material breach would have entitled it to full expectation damages, calculated by adding its reliance expenditure, which would have been $50,000, to its anticipated profit of $30,000. However, Reliant's miscalculation of its cost has defeated its expectation of profit and its claim for expectation damages. Its only reasonable expectation from full performance is a loss of $20,000. As a result, its claim is confined to reliance or restitutionary damages. Its reliance damages are its cost of $100,000, but they may be even less than this if the defendant can make a case for prorating them, as discussed below. Restitution is measured by the market value of the work performed (quantum meruit). Unless Reliant performed inefficiently, incurring costs in excess of what would be normal on the market, the value of its performance is likely to be higher than its cost, because it would include a reasonable profit. For the sake of illustration, if the costs are indeed efficient and the industry norm is to have a 10 percent profit margin on excavation work, the market value of the performance is $110,000. This being so, Reliant would elect to sue for the higher restitutionary relief. However, the question of whether restitution turns out to be the more advantageous measure of relief depends on whether the court allows unrestricted restitutionary recovery or imposes a limit on it based on the contract value of the performance.

When the defendant can prove that the plaintiff's reasonable expectation under the contract was to lose money, the plaintiff's reliance recovery may be reduced proportionately to adjust it for that expectation of loss. Note that the burden of proving the losing expectation is placed on the breaching defendant, and the plaintiff's reliance recovery is unaffected if the defendant cannot sustain the burden. It would unfairly undercompensate the plaintiff to deduct the full amount of the expected loss from a reliance recovery that constitutes only a portion of its performance. The deduction must therefore be pro rated so that it is no more than a share of the loss proportionate to the performance rendered. The most rational way of allocating the loss to completed performance is to determine its proportion of the total contractual performance based on the relationship of the cost incurred to the total cost of performance. In the present case, Reliant had incurred costs of $100,000 out of a total anticipated cost of $250,000—that is, two-fifths of the total. Therefore (provided that Benny Fishery can prove this anticipated loss), the $100,000 reliance expenses must be reduced by two-fifths of the total expected loss of $20,000, that is $8,000, leaving a recovery of $92,000.

The possibility of prorating makes reliance damages an even less attractive alternative to restitution if no equivalent principle applies to restitutionary recovery. Some courts feel that it should not. One such case is *United States ex rel. Coastal Steel Erectors, Inc. v. Algernon Blair, Inc.*, 479 F.2d 638 (4th Cir. 1973). The defendant, a prime contractor, had entered into a subcontract with the plaintiff for the erection of steel. A dispute arose between the parties as to which one of them was responsible for the payment of rental for cranes used on the job, and when the contractor refused to pay for them, the subcontractor terminated its performance. It was found that the contractor had been obliged to pay the rental, so its failure to do so was a material breach, entitling the subcontractor to rescind the contract. At the time of termination, the subcontractor had done about 28 percent of its work and had already been paid the full portion of the contract price for what had been done. It therefore had no claim based on its contractual expectation. However, the subcontractor had underbid, so the contract price was considerably less than the market value of the work. It sued in restitution, claiming the difference between what it had been paid and the market value of its performance. The defendant urged the court to confine the plaintiff to the contract value of its work, but the court permitted the higher quantum meruit recovery, reasoning that a breaching defendant forfeits the right to retain the benefit of a good bargain under the contract that it broke. This approach is based on the theory that if the plaintiff elects to disaffirm the contract and sue for unjust enrichment, it should not be limited to the value placed on the performance in the contract. In the present case, it would mean that by choosing restitution, Reliant could recover the full market value of its work, which we have assumed to be around $110,000. A much more advantageous choice than reliance, which would, at best, yield $100,000 and, at worst, $92,000.

Some courts, uncomfortable with the anomaly of achieving different results in reliance and restitution for exactly the same breach, do treat the contract value of the performance as a limit on restitution. In the present case, as two-fifths in value of the work was done, a court following this rule would confine Reliant to two-fifths of the contract price of $230,000. This works out to a recovery of $92,000.

12. We will first deal with the question of whether Sauce Source should be awarded agreed damages, and will then consider what relief it should receive if the agreed damages provision is held invalid.

A. Should Sauce Source Be Awarded the Agreed Damages?

Sauce Source is attempting to enforce what purports to be an agreed damages provision.[17] We should note briefly, as an initial matter, that the term

---

17. When a party promises to take a specified quantity of goods or to pay for that quantity even if it is not taken, the term is sometimes characterized not as an attempt to liquidate damages, but as a "take or pay" provision. As such, it is seen as a promise of the alternative performances of either taking the goods or paying for them. If so interpreted, the provision is not subject to regulation as agreed damages and is upheld even if it does not satisfy the prerequisites for a valid agreed damages provision. "Take or pay" clauses are typically found in long-term supply contracts where the supplier incurs the bulk of its costs at the outset. The buyer's commitment to pay for a minimum quantity is justified because it is needed to enable the supplier to recoup that cost. Such facts are not present in our case, and we need not concern ourselves with this ethereal distinction. The clause is both described in the contract as, and functions as, a liquidation of damages.

sounds rather like boilerplate, so it may be a standard term printed on all Sauce Source's supply agreements. There is nothing wrong, per se, with a standard-form liquidated damages clause, but the fact that it is standardized may raise two issues for inquiry. First, it may create the suspicion that the apparent agreement to pay liquidated damages was not freely bargained. Second, the very fact of standardization may cast some doubt on whether the term could be a genuine estimate of the likely harm that would result from a breach of any particular transaction.

Although the first point is more fully discussed in section 13.12, and it is not given any detailed attention here, it is worth noting that if assent to the term was tainted by adhesion, unfair imposition, or other bargaining impropriety, that may furnish a separate and distinct basis for challenging it. However, the facts here do not suggest any claim of improper bargaining.

Even if there is no issue arising out of the legitimacy of the means by which assent was obtained, the compensation principle requires study of an agreed damages provision to ensure that it is a genuine attempt to liquidate damages and not an unenforceable penalty. Because this is a sale of goods, the validity of the provision is tested under UCC §2.718(1), which employs a two-point test, later adopted for the common law by Restatement Second §356. The agreed damages are examined in light of both the anticipated harm at the time of contracting, and the actual loss following breach. (Both §§2.718 and 356 speak of "anticipated or actual" loss, which makes it sound as if one looks at either one or the other. However, both are relevant, as discussed below.)

The first point of the test requires that the liquidation of damages must be a genuine attempt to reasonably estimate loss at the time of contracting. The more difficult the prospect of proving loss appeared at that time, the greater leeway the parties should be given in coming up with a figure. However, if the basis of determining loss would reasonably have seemed relatively straightforward at the time of contracting, the parties are held to a higher standard in calculating a figure that approximates expected loss. Because the court must give substantial deference to the expressed will of the parties, it should be loath to avoid the clause if it was a genuine attempt to estimate damages in advance and to save the uncertainty and burden of establishing actual loss. Therefore, the first point of the test, focusing on the time of contracting, should be given greater weight.

In addition to evaluating the clause in the context existing at the time of contracting, the court must also take into account the relationship between the agreed damages and the actual loss that was caused by the breach. When actual loss is apparent following breach, this second point of the test serves as a safety valve to prevent unfair overcompensation. If the plaintiff's true loss is disproportionately lower than the agreed damages, the policy of providing no more than compensation may call for a reduction of the defendant's liability to a more realistic level.

In the present contract, we are given no facts about how the agreed damages were calculated. In fact, as noted earlier, it may be that the clause does not in any way represent any attempt to estimate loss in this particular transaction, but may be no more than a piece of boilerplate inserted routinely into all Sauce Source's supply contracts. Although it is conceivable that a standardized estimate of loss may be valid for multiple transactions of the same kind, it is more likely that the use of a standard clause strongly suggests an absence of meaningful estimation.

In any event, even if it was not a standard form, the basis of determining damages under the clause cannot be justified as being a realistic prognostication of harm. In most sales of goods, the seller's damages are relatively easy to predict and calculate. If the goods are resold after breach, the difference between the contract and resale price is quite easily ascertainable. If they are not resold or the resale is unreasonable, the contract-market difference can be established. If there is no substitute sale (for example, because the seller loses volume of sales), the seller's lost profit can be proved without too much difficulty. Finally, if the goods are perishable and they cannot be resold, the seller is able to sue the buyer for their price. Although there could be uncertainties and disagreement on a number of issues, such as the reasonableness of resale, the market price, or the issue of lost volume, these difficulties are not comparable to, say, the problems of proving lost profits for a speculative venture. There is enough predictability to require the plaintiff to show a sensible basis for coming up with an estimate that bears some relationship to reality. Instead, Sauce Source has used a formula that assures it of full recovery of the sale price, no matter how much it actually delivers to Gracie. If there ever was a term designed as a disincentive to breach—that is, a penalty—this is it.

Furthermore, the amount of damages is quite random in its relationship to loss and ensures that Sauce Source is always overcompensated. To demonstrate, consider the following calculations based upon arbitrarily selected, but generous, actual damage figures: Gracie breached after taking her minimum requirements for seven months, so she is liable for agreed damages of $5 \times $250 = $1,250$, representing her failure to take 50 boxes of sachets.

If the ketchup can be readily resold at full price, the damages may overcompensate Sauce Source by a full $1,250 (less any incidental damages). But even if it resells at a huge loss, say at $5 a box, its actual damages would still be considerably less than what was agreed: They would be $1,000, the difference between the contract price of the 50 boxes ($1,250) and their resale price of $250.

Even if we assume that it makes no substitute transaction because it has more ketchup than it can sell, so it loses volume of sales, the agreed damages must still exceed its lost profit, no matter how big its profit margin may be. To illustrate, let's say that its total cost of selling each box is only $2, so that makes a generous profit of $23 per box. Its lost profit is still only $50 \times 23 = $1,150$—$100 below the agreed damages.

In fact, there seem to be only two situations in which it could have anticipated a loss equal to the damages provided. Both are highly unlikely. First, if its costs are zero and it has suffered loss of volume, its lost profit would be equal to the agreed damages. Second, if it could not resell at all and the ketchup would spoil and have to be discarded, it would lose the entire contract price. Although this could occur where perishables are sold, the life expectancy of ketchup in sealed packages exceeds that of the average human.

This set of calculations is based on Gracie's breach in the seventh month of the contract. If you care to do some further arithmetic, you will see that the earlier the breach, the greater the discrepancy between the damages fixed and the reasonably likely harm. However, at no point, not even in the last month, does this disproportion entirely disappear. Having decided that the agreement on damages was not a reasonable forecast of harm, it is not necessary to proceed to the second stage by examining the discrepancy between actual and anticipated harm.

A somewhat similar analysis was undertaken by the court in *Lake River Corp. v. Carborundum Co.,* 769 F.2d 1284 (7th Cir. 1985), to demonstrate the penal nature of agreed damages in a more complex, but roughly analogous, case. The plaintiff and defendant had entered a contract under which the plaintiff would bag ferro carbo (an abrasive powder used in steelmaking) for the defendant. The plaintiff had to install special equipment for the work, and therefore insisted on a contract for a term of three years. The contract provided that the plaintiff would ship to the defendant, and even if not, would pay for a specified minimum tonnage. A downturn in steel production led to a reduced demand for ferro carbo, and by the end of the contract term, the defendant had shipped just over half of the minimum quantity. The plaintiff sued for damages under the agreement, equal to about half the total amount that would have been due had the full minimum performance taken place.

The court (while expressing reservations over the wisdom of interfering with contract provisions fairly negotiated by sophisticated commercial entities, but considering itself bound by precedent on the issue) invalidated the clause as a penalty. This contract involved the rendering of a service, not a sale of goods, so common law applied. As it was a service contract, the plaintiff's damages would normally be its lost profit. Therefore, because the formulation of agreed damages did not take into account any costs saved by the breach, it would inevitably exceed the plaintiff's lost profit and its actual loss. The earlier in the period that the breach occurred, the greater the cost savings would be, and the higher the disproportion between realistic and agreed damages.

B. If Agreed Damages Are Invalid, What Are Sauce Source's Actual Damages?

When an agreed damages provision is invalidated, the plaintiff does not lose all remedy. It may still recover whatever actual damages it suffered. If Gracie is correct in saying that the market value of ketchup rose since the contract was entered into, Sauce Source would not be able to claim contract-market damages. Further, if it did enter a substitute transaction by reselling in a commercially reasonable way, it probably sold at the higher price and cannot claim damages based on resale. It does make the argument, however, that even if it did make a subsequent sale, this was not a substitute because it has enough ketchup in stock to satisfy all demand. If it can establish that the breach caused it a reduction in volume of sales, it is entitled to claim lost profits under UCC §2.708(2).

The application of this section is illustrated by *Neri v. Retail Marine Corp.*, 285 N.E.2d 311 (N.Y. 1972). The buyer of a boat breached by canceling the contract. When he later requested and was refused the return of his deposit, he sued for its return. (Remember, a breaching party is entitled to restitution, offset by any damages suffered by the other.) Although the seller had resold the boat for an amount equal to the contract price, it argued that it had damages to offset against the buyer's refund claim. It contended that had the buyer not breached, it would have sold another boat to the second buyer and would have made two sales instead of one. The court agreed and found that the contract-resale difference could not adequately compensate the seller, who was therefore entitled to its lost profit under §2.708(1). The court (rather extravagantly) observed that the seller had an "unlimited supply of standard-priced goods," so the second sale was not a substitute.

Although *Neri* has been criticized as too superficial in its evaluation of whether a loss in volume of sales truly loses the seller its full profit, a facile approach may be appropriate to aid the aggrieved seller. The seller should at least be treated as having made a prima facie case for lost profit if it can establish that it did have access to a supply of the goods in excess of its demand and that the second sale was not in any way motivated by or connected to the breach. (That is, the second buyer would probably have bought similar goods from the seller if these particular goods had not been available.) If Sauce Source can satisfy this burden and it can prove its profit on the 50 boxes, it should be awarded the profit lost as a result of Gracie's breach.

19

Assignment, Delegation, and Third-Party Beneficiaries

§19.1 Introduction

During the entire course of this book, it has been emphasized that contract is a consensual relationship created by agreement between the parties. In dealing with the enforcement of contracts, it has been taken for granted that contractual rights and duties arise only between the parties and that the power of enforcement resides in each against the other. In the great majority of contracts, this assumption is accurate. A person who is not a party to a contract cannot be bound by it and acquires no rights under it. However, this chapter deals with two situations in which this rule is qualified. Although these situations have in common the fact that a non-party to the contract obtains the right to enforce a promise under it, they are otherwise quite distinct and are based on very different premises:

1. A contract may create rights in a third party when the parties to the contract expressly or impliedly agree, at the time of making it, that the performance of one of them will be rendered to or for the benefit of a person who is not a party to the contract, and that the non-party will have the right to enforce that commitment. The creation of the third-party rights is contemplated by the parties and occurs at the time of contract formation.

2. The assignment of contractual rights and the delegation of contractual duties does not involve any conferral of rights on a non-party at the time of contracting. Rather, it is the transfer of rights or obligations by one of the parties at some time after the contract has been executed. Each party's right to performance under the contract is an asset belonging to that party. As a property interest, it is generally capable (with exceptions to be noted later) of being transferred (assigned) by sale, donation, or other means of disposition. When a party assigns rights under a contract (thereby becoming the assignor), ownership of those rights passes to the recipient (assignee) who is substituted for the assignor as the person entitled to performance. Instead of, or in addition to, assigning rights under a contract, a party may wish to transfer (delegate) all or some of her obligations under the contract. Unlike assignment, delegation is not based on any concept of ownership—one cannot own a duty. Nevertheless, it is also generally permissible provided that it does not impair the reasonable expectations of the party to whom the performance is due.

§19.2   Third-Party Beneficiaries

§19.2.1   The Distinction Between Intended and Incidental Beneficiaries

Contracts routinely benefit people who are not parties. For example, neighbors are benefitted by the aesthetic enjoyment of a well-groomed yard, resulting from a landscape maintenance contract between a homeowner and a gardener; adjacent hotels are benefitted by a contract between a property owner and builder to erect a new convention center. In fact, in a complex interactive economy, vast numbers of contracts between strangers allow people to enjoy facilities and services that would otherwise not be available. However, even though these bystanders may derive some advantage from the contract, and even have an important stake in its performance, they have no legal rights under the contract. Therefore, if the landscaper or builder breaches the contract by failing to perform, the adjacent property owners have no cause of action to enforce it. They are known as **incidental beneficiaries**—the benefit they anticipated was purely a fortuitous and incidental result of a transaction between others. The contracting parties may have been pleased, indifferent, or resentful to see someone else derive benefits from their contract, but they did not make the contract for the purpose of conferring those benefits.

However, in contrast to these more commonplace situations in which the positive effects of the contract on a third party occur merely by happenstance, a contract may be entered for the *deliberate purpose of bestowing a benefit*—and more importantly, a *power to enforce that benefit*—on a third party. That is, a contract is properly described as for the benefit of a third party only if it manifests the intent to give a benefit to a third party, directly enforceable by that third party against the contracting party who undertakes to perform it. It is the creation of this directly enforceable right that is the hallmark of a contract for the benefit of a third party. For example, Debbie Tor owes $20,000 to Len Der. Debbie enters into a contract with Wendy Vendee under which Debbie sells a plot of land to Wendy for $20,000, and the contract stipulates that Wendy will pay the $20,000 to Len. Debbie's purpose, of course, is to have the proceeds of the property transmitted directly to Len to settle the debt. In this case, the payment to Len does not occur as a fortuitous result of the contract but is specifically called for by it. Len's benefit is not merely incidental, but is clearly contemplated and deliberately conferred. If it is expressed or can be reasonably inferred that the parties, in contracting for the performance to be rendered to Len, also intended to give Len the right to enforce Wendy's promise of performance directly and independently of Debbie, Len acquires the status of **intended beneficiary.**

When a contract is intended to confer a benefit on and create enforcement rights in a third-party beneficiary, the contracting party who is to render the performance to the beneficiary (in the example above, Wendy) is usually referred to as the **promisor,** and the contracting party whose right to performance has been conferred on the beneficiary (in the above example, Debbie) is usually called the **promisee.** This nomenclature could be confusing because in a bilateral contract the terms "promisor" and "promisee" are relative—each party is both a promisor with regard to his own performance and a promisee with regard to the performance promised by the other. However, as we look at the contracting parties from the perspective of the third-party beneficiary, "promisor" means the party who has committed to perform in favor of the beneficiary. The following diagram illustrates the basic relationship and the terminology:

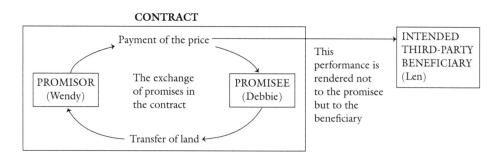

Normally, if the parties intend to confer the status of intended beneficiary on someone, that person is likely to be specifically named or identified in the contract. If this is not so, the strong inference is that the benefit is merely incidental. However, this conclusion is not inevitable. Intent to benefit is a matter of interpretation. Provided that the beneficiary will be *identifiable* when the *time for performance falls due*, it could be apparent that the parties did intend to create rights in his favor, despite the lack of specific identification at the time of contracting.

§19.2.2   *The Essence of Intended Beneficiary Status: The Right of Independent Enforcement*

As indicated above, when a contract confers the status of intended beneficiary on a third party, this does not mean only that performance must be rendered to or for the third party's benefit. It also means, as Restatement Second §304 provides, that the contract manifests the intent to grant the beneficiary an independent cause of action to enforce the promise. The grant of this enforcement right in the beneficiary is the central point of the third-party beneficiary doctrine and the distinguishing feature of a contract for the benefit of a third party. The beneficiary's direct cause of action against the promisor can be of great importance in making the benefit meaningful. He can pursue the right to performance on his own and does not have to depend on the promisee to take action on his behalf.

In the above example, if Len had no independent right of enforcement, he would not be able to sue Wendy, the promisor, if she failed to perform in his favor as promised. Debbie, the promisee, would be the only person who could sue Wendy for the payment, and Len's only claim would be against Debbie, his debtor under the loan contract. However, as an intended beneficiary, Len can sue Wendy directly if she fails to pay. He has this right of direct enforcement in addition to his right to sue Debbie under the loan contract, so he has two people against whom he can seek recourse for the unpaid loan. This may be represented as follows:

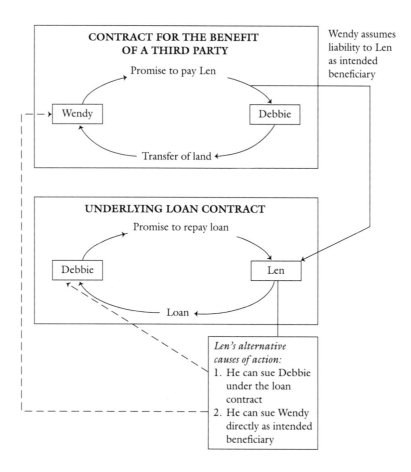

English common law did not recognize such a direct cause of action in the beneficiary unless the beneficiary could establish either that the promisee was acting as his agent, or that the contract created a trust. However, in the mid-nineteenth century, the concept of direct enforcement by the beneficiary developed in American law. *Lawrence v. Fox,* 220 N.Y. 268 (1859), is recognized as the groundbreaking case. A man named Holly lent $300 to Fox. Holly was indebted to Lawrence for the same amount, and so Holly and Fox agreed that Fox would repay the loan amount to Lawrence. When he failed to pay, Lawrence sued Fox, who defended the suit on the basis that Lawrence had no standing to sue because he was not a party to the contract—there was no privity between them. The court rejected this defense and articulated the principle that even where no agency or trust is established, the parties to a contract do have the power to create rights enforceable by a person who is not a party to a contract, and that person can sue the promisor to enforce the performance undertaken to the promisee for his benefit.

§19.2.3   The Intent to Confer an Independent Right of Enforcement

The recognition of enforcement rights in a non-party may seem like a radical departure from the general concept of contract as a private consensual arrangement that creates rights only between those who have bound themselves to each other. However, the third-party beneficiary doctrine is consistent with that concept because the third party only acquires the right to enforce the benefit if it is apparent that the parties intended to give him that right—they have elected to create the beneficiary status as part of their agreement. As stressed already, it is not enough that the contract calls for performance to be rendered to the third party. It must also manifest the intention to give the third party the right to enforce the performance if it is not rendered. This is reflected in Restatement Second §302(1), which recognizes a "right to performance" (which means the right to enforce the performance) in the beneficiary only when it is *appropriate to effectuate the intention of the parties.*

Like all other contract terms, the intent to establish third-party enforcement rights is a matter of interpretation. If this intent is expressly stated or otherwise clearly apparent, the matter is relatively easy. However, as we have seen so often, the parties may not be so articulate in expressing their intent, so that their purpose has to be gleaned by *interpretation or construction.* As always, the determination of meaning is based on whatever factual evidence may point to the parties' intent, but when this is inconclusive, the court will attempt to construe meaning in light of what is reasonable and most in accord with public policy.

The determination of intent is, as usual, based upon an *objective standard.* The import of their agreement is not governed by what the parties may actually have intended, but by the reasonable perception of their intent, as it appears from their manifestation of agreement *judged from the perspective of the beneficiary:* Would the third party's reliance on the promise be reasonable and probable?

Because it is the promisee who is channeling a performance to the beneficiary that would otherwise be due to him, the promisee's desire to confer the benefit must be apparent from the language of the contract or its circumstances. However, as important as the promisee's intent might be, it is not enough on its own. For mutual intent to exist, the promisee must have communicated this intent to the promisor sufficiently for the promisor to have reasonably understood that she was assenting to it. Although the promisor may not much care who is to receive the performance, she does potentially incur liability to the non-party beneficiary, and this cannot be imposed on her unless it can be fairly regarded as a risk that she assumed under the contract.

§19.2.4 The Relevance of the Relationship Between the Promisee and the Beneficiary: Creditor and Donee Beneficiaries

As just mentioned, Restatement Second §302(1) sets forth a broad standard to guide the determination of whether a non-party to the contract should be treated as an intended beneficiary: The recognition of the beneficiary's right to enforce performance must be appropriate to give effect to the parties' intent. The intent to confer the benefit is the central criterion and the focus of the inquiry. This is possibly all that needed to be said. However, motivated by a long tradition that it neither wishes to follow nor to abandon, §302(1) goes on to suggest what appears to be a second requirement: There must in addition be some *relationship* between the *promisee and the beneficiary* from which it can be *inferred* that the *parties had the beneficiary's interests in mind* when entering the contract. Although this seems to be set out as a prerequisite in addition to intent, it is really just a subset of the general inquiry into what the parties intended. If a relationship between the promisee and beneficiary can be identified to explain the motivation for conferring the benefit, the conclusion of intent to benefit is reinforced.

This bipartite inquiry originates from the established conception, reflected in the first Restatement, that a beneficiary can be regarded as intended, rather than incidental, only if one of two conditions is satisfied. Either the beneficiary must be a creditor of the promisee, or it must be clear that the promisee intended to make a gift of the benefit to the beneficiary. The situation involving a **creditor beneficiary** has already been illustrated by both *Lawrence v. Fox* and our example involving Debbie, who made a contract with Wendy under which Wendy would render performance to Debbie's creditor, Len. This set of relationships may be represented as follows:

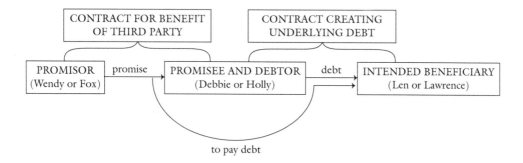

to pay debt

By contrast, if the promisee owes no debt to the third party, but intends to make a gift of the performance, the third party is a **donee beneficiary.** Although *Lawrence v. Fox* expressly dealt only with a creditor beneficiary, its basic principle was broad enough to be extended to cases in which the promisee was not indebted to the beneficiary. As a result, later cases recognized that a person could qualify as an intended beneficiary when the purpose of conferring the benefit was not to pay any debt, but to give her a gift. *Seaver v. Ransom,* 120 N.E. 639 (N.Y. 1918), is the most famous of these cases. A dying woman intended to bequeath a house to her niece. Upon being presented with a will that omitted this bequest, she agreed to sign on the strength of a promise by her husband, the residual legatee, that he would cure the omission by making provision in his own will for a bequest to the niece of equivalent value. When the husband eventually died, it was discovered that he had not made the bequest as he had promised his late wife. The niece sued his estate. The trial court gave judgment in favor of the niece on the theory that her uncle had held the house from his wife in constructive trust. Although it affirmed the judgment in favor of the niece, the court of appeals rejected the trust theory. Instead, basing its decision on *Lawrence* and subsequent cases, it found that there was no reason in principle to confine the third-party beneficiary doctrine to cases involving creditor beneficiaries. The uncle and aunt had made a contract under which the niece was an intended beneficiary, and she could enforce the promise against the uncle's estate.

As another illustration, say that Don Nation entered into a contract with Wendy Vendee under which he sold a plot of land to her for $20,000. His purpose in selling the land was not to pay a debt, as in the example involving Debbie, but to realize funds to be donated to his niece, Charity. Don therefore stipulates in the contract with Wendy that the sale price be paid directly to Charity. (Although the fact that Charity gave no consideration to Don for the benefit would preclude her from enforcing the promise against Don, the lack of consideration from Charity does not bar her suit against Wendy. The contract being enforced by Charity as an intended beneficiary is that between Don and Wendy, and consideration was exchanged between the parties to that contract.) This set of relationships may be shown as follows:

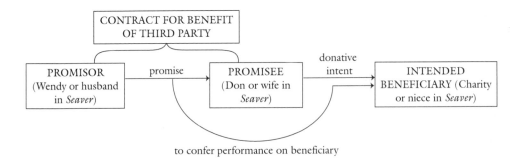

Section 302(1) attempts to move away from the creditor-donee dichotomy, which it finds too rigid and restrictive. However, it recognizes that the distinction is well-ingrained in the case law and cannot be ignored. It therefore acknowledges the distinction but alters it to make it more flexible. Many courts have followed its lead. Section 302(1) identifies two types of situations in which it recognizes a relationship sufficient to bolster the conclusion that the beneficiary was intended: The first, set out in §302(1)(a), approximates the concept of creditor beneficiary by covering cases in which performance of the promise will *satisfy a monetary obligation* due by the promisee to the beneficiary. This is somewhat narrower than the original category, which included not only monetary obligations, but also situations in which performance of the promise would satisfy an actual, supposed, or asserted duty of the promisee to the beneficiary. The narrowing of this category is more than compensated for by the widening of the second. The second, set out in §302(1)(b) is based on, but more expansive than, the older category of donee beneficiaries. It encompasses not only situations in which gratuitous motives are apparent, but any case in which the *circumstances indicate* that the *promisee intends to give the benefit of performance to the beneficiary.* As just noted, this would include cases in which there is some supposed or asserted duty that is not clear enough to fall into §302(1)(a) as an actual liquidated monetary obligation. This sounds very vague and open-ended, but that is what is intended. The idea is to let courts decide case by case, with a strong focus on the parties' intent, as bolstered by some relationship between the promisee and the beneficiary that plausibly points to a motive for conferring the benefit.

§19.2.5 Vesting of the Benefit and the Parties' Power to Modify or Terminate It

In the same way as parties have the power to make a contract, they have the power to modify or terminate it by subsequent agreement. The alteration or discharge of a contract, like its creation, is dependent on the parties' assent.[1] It would therefore seem to follow that as the parties to the contract have created the beneficiary's rights, they could agree to change them or take them away entirely. However, if they had the unrestricted power to do this, the status of intended beneficiary would be very uncertain and unreliable. To protect the beneficiary's actual or potential reliance on the contract, the rule has been developed that at some point after the contract is made, the benefit **vests** in the beneficiary—it becomes **irrevocably settled** on her so that it cannot be changed or withdrawn by the contracting parties without her consent. If the parties do agree to modify or discharge the contract after the benefit has vested, this agreement binds the parties between themselves, but it binds only them. It does not affect the rights of the beneficiary, who can enforce the performance as it vested under the original agreement. It is therefore possible that the promisee could agree to give up her own rights of enforcement or to change them so that they are less extensive than those that have vested in the beneficiary.

---

1. Of course, consideration is generally required too, as discussed in sections 7.5.2 and 13.9.

Over the years, different courts have adopted various approaches to the question of *when the benefit vests*. Some have treated it as vesting immediately upon formation of the contract, but others have required some manifestation of acceptance or some act of reliance on it by the beneficiary. The original Restatement had different rules for vesting depending on whether the beneficiary was a donee or a creditor. Restatement Second §311(3) makes no such distinction. It seeks to clarify and standardize the rule for vesting, irrespective of the nature of the underlying relationship between the promisee and the beneficiary. It provides that the benefit vests in the beneficiary when she *manifests assent* to it at the request of one of the parties, or she *sues on it*, or she materially changes her position by acting in *justifiable reliance* on it. This formulation clearly shows the analogy between vesting and the formation of other promissory obligations. Its basis is quite akin to that for offer and acceptance or promissory estoppel: The right vests in the beneficiary either when she "accepts" it by manifesting assent to it, or when she has detrimentally relied on it. Once that has occurred, the contracting parties are committed to the conferral of rights, and the beneficiary's independent cause of action on the promise is secure.

This rule is subject to a qualification: As creators of the benefit, the contracting parties can confer it subject to whatever limitations and conditions they see fit. By so stipulating in the contract, they *can retain the power to modify it or take it away* even after it has vested in the beneficiary. These limitations will inhere in the right created in favor of the beneficiary, and it will vest subject to them. However, unless the parties clearly reserve the power to alter the rights conferred on the beneficiary after vesting, they lose it as against the beneficiary as soon as vesting occurs.

§19.2.6   The Promisee's Parallel Rights of Enforcement Against the Promisor

Notwithstanding the conferral and vesting of rights in the beneficiary, the promisee continues to be a party to the contract. As such, except to the extent that the beneficiary has enforced and obtained satisfaction of the performance, the promisee has the right to enforce the promise just as she would have had in an ordinary bilateral contract. (As explained below, the promise to be enforced is the promise to render performance to the beneficiary, not to the promisee.) Restatement Second §305(1) reflects this by stating that the promisor has a duty of performance to the promisee, even though he has a similar duty to the beneficiary. This does not mean that promisor has to perform the obligation twice. The promisee's right against the promisor is discharged to the extent that the promisor performs in favor of the beneficiary. If full performance is not rendered to the beneficiary, the promisee may enforce the obligation to perform any remaining balance.

The nature of the relief available to the promisee depends on the circumstances. When a claim for damages is not an adequate remedy, she may request specific performance—an order compelling the promisor to render the performance to the beneficiary. Alternatively, the promisee may have a claim for damages based on her contractual expectation. This will at least consist of her direct damages, measured by the loss in value of the promised performance. In addition, if the failure to perform results in a foreseeable and unavoidable increase in the promisee's liability to the beneficiary or other consequential loss, consequential damages may also be claimed.

§19.2.7 The Promisor's Ability to Raise Defenses Against the Beneficiary

The beneficiary's rights derive from the contract, so it stands to reason that they are limited by any defense arising out of the contract. Therefore, the basic rule, as reflected in Restatement Second §309, is that unless the contract makes it clear that it confers rights on the beneficiary free of defenses, the beneficiary's rights are *subject to any limitations inherent in the contract.* The promisor may raise against the beneficiary any defense that would have been available against the promisee, arising out of a defect in the formation of the contract (such as invalidity due to lack of consideration, voidability on grounds of fraud, duress or some other bargaining defect, or unenforceability for failure to comply with the statute of frauds); or based on the promisee's breach of contract; or arising out of post-formation occurrences that affect the very basis of the contract, such as supervening impracticability and the nonoccurrence of a condition. (The beneficiary's position is very much like that of an assignee, discussed in section 19.3.3.)

Although a wrongful act of the promisee (such as breach or fraud) can be raised by the promisor as a defense against the beneficiary, it *does not impose any liability* on the *beneficiary.* He does not, by accepting the benefit, assume any responsibility for proper behavior or performance by the promisee. Any recourse that the promisor has must be pursued against the promisee.

Unless the contract expresses a contrary intent, the promisor cannot raise against the beneficiary any *defense* that is *purely personal against the promisee,* such as a defense that the promisee owes money to the promisor in another transaction. Similarly, as we saw in section 19.2.5, if the promisee and promisor make an agreement to modify or discharge the performance after vesting, this agreement would be a defense to enforcement by the promisee, but it would not avail against the beneficiary.

§19.2.8 The Beneficiary's Rights Against the Promisee in the Event of the Promisor's Non-Performance

As has been stated already, once the benefit has vested in the beneficiary, he has a direct claim against the promisor and may proceed to enforce it if the promisor fails to perform. However, it may occur that the beneficiary is unsuccessful in obtaining satisfaction of his claim against the promisor either because the promisor has no money or assets to satisfy the claim, or because she is able to raise a defense available against the beneficiary. When that happens, the question is whether the beneficiary may then proceed against the promisee. The answer depends on whether the beneficiary is a creditor or donee.

If the beneficiary is a donee, his relationship with the promisee is not supported by consideration. Therefore, the beneficiary has no enforceable claim against the promisee in the event that he is unable to recover from the promisor. However, if the beneficiary is a creditor of the promisee, he may, upon being unsuccessful in pursuing his claim against the promisor, proceed against the promisee to enforce the promisee's debt.

Some courts have not allowed the creditor beneficiary to sue the promisee after unsuccessfully trying to enforce rights against promisor. They have held that once the beneficiary elects to proceed against the promisor, the right of action against the promisor is substituted for and eliminates the cause of action on the original debt due by the promisee. (This is called **novation.**) However, the more common contemporary view, as expressed in Restatement Second §310, is that the beneficiary *surrenders no rights against the promisee* by seeking to enforce the benefit against the promisor. Instead, the promisee becomes a **surety** for the promisor, so that to the extent that the promisor fails to perform, the promisee remains liable for the outstanding amount of her undischarged debt to the beneficiary. (And, of course, the promisee may then attempt to recover from the promisor, based on the promisor's breach of her contract with the promisee.) This may be shown as follows:

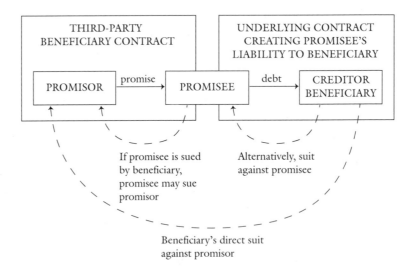

§19.2.9 Citizens' Claims as Intended Beneficiaries of Government Contracts

The government represents the public. In a broad sense, it can therefore be said that whenever the government enters a contract, it has the intention of conferring a benefit on the citizenry at large, or on a group of citizens whose interests are furthered by the contract. However, this does not mean that an individual citizen can sue to enforce the performance promised to the government. As with other contracts that result in a benefit to a non-party, the crucial question is not simply whether there was an intent to provide the benefit, but whether there was an intent to create an independent right of enforcement in the non-party. Therefore, as Restatement Second §313(1) makes clear, government contracts are to be *treated the same as contracts by private parties* in deciding whether a third party was an intended beneficiary: The terms of the contract must be interpreted in context to determine if it manifests the intent to confer a direct cause of action on the beneficiary.

Because many government contracts are made in pursuance of a specific statutory policy, the question of whether a private right of action was intended is often answered, not only by examining the terms of the contract, but also by interpreting the *legislation* that authorizes the contract, and the underlying public policy. In fact, the question of whether *citizen enforcement* is an *appropriate means of effectuating government policy* is often the dominant consideration in deciding if the plaintiff is an intended beneficiary.

Because of concern that bedlam would result if courts too readily recognized private suits to enforce government contracts, the general assumption is that *citizens are merely incidental beneficiaries* of government contracts unless a private right of enforcement is clearly conferred by the contract or the authorizing statute, or the government has a specific legal obligation to provide the performance to the citizen (making the citizen, in effect, a creditor beneficiary). Comment *a* to §313 reflects this approach by suggesting that in cases of doubt, the contract should be interpreted as not making citizens intended beneficiaries.

§19.3 Assignment and Delegation

§19.3.1 *The Basic Concept and Terminology*

Section 19.2 was concerned with cases in which the parties to a contract intend, at the time of entering it, to confer an enforceable benefit on someone who is not a party to the contract. Although assignment and delegation also involve the introduction of a third party into the contract, the circumstances under which that happens and the legal relationship that arises is very different from that of a third party beneficiary. We are concerned here with the transfer by one party of his rights or obligations under an existing contract, and the rules and limitations governing that transfer. It is useful to begin with the terminology used to describe such a transfer and its participants: The **transfer of rights** is called an **assignment,** and the **transfer of duties** is a **delegation.** The person who **assigns a contractual right** is the **obligee** under

679

the contract and becomes the **assignor.** The person to whom it is assigned is the **assignee.** The other party to the contract, whose duty is transferred to the assignee by the assignment, is referred to as the **obligor.** A person who **delegates her contractual duty** is the **obligor** under the contract and becomes the **delegator** of the duty. The person who assumes the duty is called the **delegate** (not delegatee). The other party to the contract, whose right to performance has been delegated, is called the **obligee.** In the following set of diagrams, assume that Party 2 is the person who decides to assign her obligations or delegate her duties. The relationships may be drawn like this:

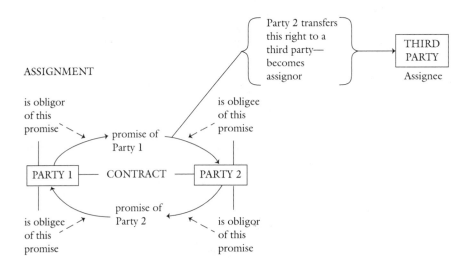

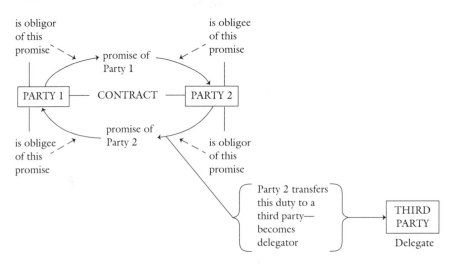

The possibility that a party may wish to transfer contractual rights and duties could arise in all kinds of transactions, and the rules described here could apply to any ordinary contract. We are no longer considering situations in which, as with the third-party beneficiary doctrine, a particular type of contract was created by the parties, designed from the outset to confer enforceable rights on a non-party. There are a number of reasons why a party may wish to transfer his rights, duties, or both rights and duties. Some of these motives will become apparent in the following discussion.

The law favors the free transferability of contractual rights and obligations and inclines to uphold the right of a party to make such a transfer. Therefore the general rule is that *unless a contract specifically prohibits* a party from *transferring her rights* acquired and *duties assumed* under it, or the *nature of the contract* is such that the transfer would *impair* the other party's *reasonable expectations* or would *offend public policy,* a party has the *power to transfer* contractual rights and obligations. This principle is well-established under common law, and is reflected in Restatement Second §317(2). It is also recognized in relation to sales of goods by UCC §2.210(2).

It is probably self-evident that because we are dealing with the transfer of contractual rights and obligations, the issue of whether transfer is permitted can only arise *subsequent to the formation of the contract* that created those rights and obligations. That is, assignment and delegation are only possible once a contract has been made and those rights and obligations have come into existence. This must be distinguished from the rule that applies in the pre-contract period. As it was noted in section 4.7, the power to accept an offer is personal to the offeree and cannot be transferred unless the offer so authorizes.[2]

§19.3.2   *The Nature of an Assignment*

An assignment may be defined as a voluntary manifestation of intention by the holder of an existing right to make an immediate transfer of that right to another person. This definition breaks down into two essential components:

> (1)   The assignor must voluntarily manifest intent to assign the right; and

---

2. This rule does not apply to a valid option—a promise exchanged for consideration not to revoke the offer. As explained in section 5.4, the option is a contract in itself and the right to accept the offer in the option period is a binding contractual right. It can therefore be assigned.

(2)   The right must be in existence at the time of assignment, and its transfer must take effect immediately.

a.   A Voluntary Manifestation of Assent to Assign

The act of assignment is between the assignee and assignor. Unless the contract forbids assignment without his assent, the obligor need not be involved in that transaction. An assignment is a voluntary transfer of a right that comes about by consensus between the assignor and assignee.[3] This means not only that the *assignor* must *manifest the intent* to *assign* the right, but also that the *assignee must indicate a willingness to accept* the assignment.

In many cases, this willingness is apparent because the assignment is itself a contract between the assignor and the assignee. However, not all assignments are contracts. An obligee may make a gratuitous assignment (which would lack the consideration necessary for a contract), or may assign rights to settle a pre-existing debt to the assignee. In such a case, the assignee must signify acceptance of the assignment by words or conduct. The question of whether there is a valid contract of assignment is subject to the usual rules of contract law, and the issue of whether mutual assent was manifested is resolved by the usual principles of interpretation.

There are some specialized types of assignment involving rights evidenced by commercial paper (such as negotiable instruments or documents) for which prescribed formalities must be satisfied. Apart from these transactions, which are beyond our scope, there are no particular formalities needed for an assignment of ordinary contract rights, but the transaction may be subject to the statute of frauds.

b.   The Immediate Transfer of an Existing Right

As section 19.3.4 explains, the effect of an assignment is to extinguish the assignor's right to performance from the obligee and to transfer it to the assignee. For such a complete transfer to occur, the right must be in existence and transferred immediately. Furthermore, the transfer must be a *complete relinquishment* of the right by the assignor in favor of the assignee, so that the

---

3. It is possible for a right to be transferred without the assent of the holder. For example, it could be seized by a creditor in satisfaction of a judgment debt through the process of garnishment, or it could pass to the holder's trustee if the holder becomes bankrupt. Although such transfers are legally effective if the right itself is capable of transfer, they are not considered here. Our discussion is confined to consensual transfers.

assignor retains no control over it and no power to revoke it. This absolute and unequivocal transfer is necessary for the protection of the obligor, who must be able to rely on the fact that performance in favor of the assignee will discharge her obligation.

A right comes into existence as soon as the contract creating it has been formed. As long as it exists in this sense, the right *need not be unconditional or immediately due*. It is perfectly valid, and very common, for a right to be subject to a condition or not yet due at the time of assignment. Of course, the assignee takes the right subject to the terms governing it, and can only obtain performance from the obligor when the time for performance falls due and any condition is satisfied.

The assignment of a conditional or unmatured right must be distinguished from the transfer of a right that has not yet been created, but is *expected to arise in the future*. This does not qualify as an assignment. It may be a valid contract between the transferor and transferee, but it lacks the hallmark of an assignment—enforceability against the obligor. Similarly, a *promise to assign an existing right in the future* does not constitute an assignment. To constitute an assignment effective against the obligor, the transfer of the right must actually be accomplished, so that the transferee acquires it immediately.

§19.3.3 *Restrictions on Assignment*

As noted earlier, the general approach of the law is that contract rights should be freely assignable. The obligee's right to performance under the contract is one of his assets—an item of property with some value. It is property of a nature different from, say, his car or his house, in that it has no tangible physical existence. (It is called a "chose in action.") Nevertheless, it is his property all the same, and he should be able to dispose of it if he so desires. However, this right of disposition is subject to a qualification that arises from the nature of this particular kind of property. Unlike a car or house, a contract right represents a relationship with the obligor, who also has rights under it. Therefore, the obligee's power to deal with this property is tempered by the need to assure the obligor of her contractual expectation. Accordingly, the right cannot be assigned if doing so would violate the terms of the contract or otherwise materially impair the obligor's rights under it.

This means that an assignment cannot be validly made *if the contract prohibits it*. Because the law generally favors assignment, the contractual bar must be clearly expressed. Restatement Second §322 and UCC §2.210(3) call for a *restrictive interpretation* of contract provisions that appear to preclude assignment. Any doubt or ambiguity should be resolved in favor of transferability, and a clause that prohibits "assignment of the contract" should, if possible, be taken to forbid only the delegation of duties. Even if a provision of the contract definitely does prohibit assignment, a court should assume, unless the contrary intent is clear, that although the assignment would be a breach (giving the obligor grounds for seeking a remedy for breach), the transfer of rights is itself effective.

This general presumption in favor of transferability does not apply to all situations, and there are some types of contract for which the opposite presumption holds. Even in the absence of a clear prohibition, Restatement Second §317(2) and UCC §2.210(2) recognize that unless the contract specifically authorizes assignment, rights may not be assigned if this would *materially change the obligor's duty, increase the burden or risk* imposed by the contract, *impair her prospects of getting return performance,* or otherwise *substantially reduce its value to her.* Every assignment is likely to have some effect on the obligor's duty, even if that is nothing more than having to make a payment to someone other than the person she contracted with. The requirement of material impact prevents the obligor from resisting an assignment on the basis of some trivial change in her performance obligation.

To decide whether an assignment may have any of these materially adverse consequences, the contract must be *interpreted in context.* In many cases, especially when the performance in question is nothing more than the payment of money or the delivery of property, an assignment of rights is unlikely to have any negative impact on the obligor. It is a matter of indifference to her whether she pays or delivers to the original person with whom she contracted or to someone else designated by that person. However, in some contracts, the identity of the party who is to receive performance is important, and the obligor does have a *stake in performing only for the original obligee.* This may be true, for example, when performance is subject to a condition of satisfaction involving personal taste, or when the obligor reasonably expected to get some special advantage or credit by being associated with the obligee. (Cases like this may alternatively be viewed not as pure assignments, but as also involving a delegation of duty, on the ground that the obligee has a contractual duty to evaluate performance in good faith or to receive performance personally.)

Apart from any contractual barrier to assignment, the transfer of certain types of contract rights are *contrary to the public interest,* and therefore prohibited by statute or public policy. A common example is the statutory prohibition on the assignment of a claim for wages, intended to protect workers from disposing of earnings in advance of receiving them.

§19.3.4   The Effect of Assignment

After a valid assignment is made, the assignee substitutes for the assignor as the person to whom performance must be rendered. It therefore follows that although the obligor need not be a party to or assent to the assignment to make it effective, she must be *notified* of it so that she knows the person to whom performance is now due. There is no particular formality required for the notice, provided that it coherently indicates what right has been assigned, and to whom. The notice must be *received by the obligor*—that is, it must either come to her attention, or be delivered so that she reasonably should be aware of it. Either the assignor or the assignee may give the notice, but if it comes from the assignee, the obligor is entitled to adequate proof of the assignment.

If the obligor performs in favor of the assignor before receiving this notification, her obligation is discharged and she has no responsibility to the assignee. However, after receiving clear and adequate notification, the obligor, in effect, *holds the performance in trust for the assignee* and is obliged to ensure that he receives it. If the obligor disregards the assignment and performs for the assignor, she incurs *personal liability to the assignee* and will be obliged either to perform again or pay damages. (Here again, there are special rules concerning the transfer of negotiable instruments and documents, for which notification alone is not enough.)

The following simple example illustrates the basic effect and purpose of an assignment: Lender lends $10,000 to Borrower, who undertakes to repay the loan with interest in six months. After the loan is advanced, Lender no longer wishes to wait six months to get her money back. She therefore sells her contractual right of repayment to Finance Co. In this case, Lender is simply treating her contract right as a saleable asset and seeks to realize its economic worth.[4] Unless there is a term in the contract that forbids assignment, the transfer will surely be permissible, because it is not likely to have any materially adverse effect on Borrower's contractual burdens or expectations. Borrower has already received the performance of Lender's promise (advance of the loan funds) and his remaining duty is clear and not subject to any discretion or cooperation by the obligee. Borrower must simply pay a specified sum of money on a stated date. Lender falls out of the transaction and Finance Co. is substituted as the obligee. When the time for repayment comes, Borrower will pay Finance Co. Of course, Borrower must be notified of the assignment so that he knows (or reasonably should know) this. If he is not, his payment to Lender will discharge his duty. This transaction may be represented as follows:

---

4. Of course, as it is an intangible right, its value is dependent on Borrower's creditworthiness. Unless Lender can satisfy a prospective buyer that there is a strong likelihood that the loan will be repaid, she will not be able to sell it. Even if the right is saleable, it will not likely be sold for its face value of $10,000 but will be discounted to take account of the risk of default. This discount, together with the prospect of earning the interest payable by Borrower under the contract, may make this an attractive purchase for a buyer like Finance Co. that is willing to take the risk of default in the hope of gaining more than it paid.

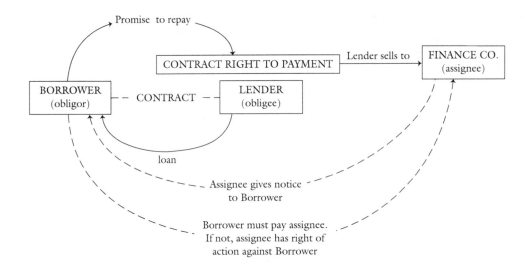

In this example, Lender assigned her contract right by sale, but sale is not the only reason for transferring rights. They may also be transferred for security—that is, used as collateral to secure a loan,[5] used to settle a preexisting debt, or simply donated as a gift. Also, Lender assigned her entire right in the example, but she could have assigned just a portion of the performance, provided that a partial assignment would not materially burden Borrower.

§19.3.5   Defenses Against the Assignee

As a general rule, when rights are assigned, the assignee can get no greater right against the obligor than the assignor had. This is in accordance with the rather obvious proposition that when a person disposes of property, he *cannot validly transfer more than what he owns.* (Again, there are some important exceptions to this rule in the case of negotiable instruments and documents, but these are beyond our scope.) This means that the assignee takes the rights *subject to any conditions and defenses* that the obligor may have against the assignor *arising out of the contract.* For example, if the contract is avoidable by

---

5. Assignment is commonly used for the purpose of securing a loan. While an important aspect of commercial transacting, the transfer of intangible rights as security is subject to complex and detailed rules that are beyond our scope. However, a brief description of the basic structure of such a transaction may be helpful: The owner of the contract right does not sell it outright, but instead borrows the needed funds and transfers the right to the lender as security for his promise to repay the money. In such a case, the transfer is not absolute. The secured creditor retains an interest in the contract right until such time as the loan is repaid, but has the right to foreclose on the security and collect payment of the contract performance in the event that its debtor defaults. There are variations on this format that need not concern us here.

the obligor or unenforceable because of a defect in formation of the contract, or the obligor's duty is subject to an unsatisfied condition, or the assignor breached the contract, or the obligor's performance has become impracticable, these defenses can be raised against the assignee in the same way as they could have been against the assignor.

As in the case of a third-party beneficiary, the obligor may only use the assignor's breach *defensively* against the assignee. That is, the assignor's breach operates as a defense to the assignee's claim, and damages due to the obligor by the assignor may be offset against the assignee's claim. However, the assignee has no liability for the obligor's damages to the extent that they exceed the amount of the offset.

The obligor's right to assert *defenses arising out of the contract* is *not cut off by the notice of assignment,* so the defense is available against the assignee whether the basis for it (for example, the assignor's breach) arose before or after the obligor received notice. However, the notice does affect any *claim of set off* that the obligor may have against the assignor, *arising out of a different transaction.* The rule is that the assignee's rights are subject to any such right of set off that arose before a notice of assignment, but cannot be defeated by one that arose afterwards. For example, say that Lender lent $10,000 to Borrower. In a completely separate contract, entered into a short while later, Borrower sold her car to Lender for $5,000. Lender took delivery of the car but failed to pay Borrower. When the time comes for Borrower to repay the loan, she has the right to deduct the $5,000 owed to her by Lender—she may set off the debt due to her under the car sale transaction against the debt that she owes Lender. If Lender has assigned his rights under the loan contract, Borrower's right of set off may be asserted against the assignee provided that the right had not been assigned and notice of assignment received by her before the set off right arose. However, if she received notice of assignment before the set off right was created, the claim of set off may not be raised against the assignee.

Unless the assignment indicates an intent to the contrary, the *assignor impliedly warrants* to the assignee that the rights assigned are *valid* and *not subject to any defenses.* Therefore, if the obligor successfully raises a defense against the assignee, the assignee usually has a cause of action against the assignor for breach of this warranty.

§19.3.6 Delegation

Restatement Second §317 and UCC §2.210(1) set out the basic principles of delegation: An obligor is *entitled to delegate* his contractual duties unless this *violates* the *contract* or *public policy.* As this suggests, the law's general approach to delegation is much like that toward assignment. A party should be given the freedom to engage someone else to perform his contractual duties unless the contract prohibits this or the delegation otherwise impairs the obligee's reasonable expectations. However, it stands to reason that while a mere assignment of rights will often make little difference to the other party's contractual expectations, a delegation of duty will quite likely have a direct impact on them. This is particularly true if the contract is founded on the personal attributes or skills of the obligor.

Irrespective of whether the performance involves special skill or attributes, if the *contract makes it clear* that delegation is *forbidden,* this expressed intent will be given effect. A party is entitled, by so stipulating in the contract, to absolutely preclude the delegation of any duty owed to her. In the absence of a clear prohibition, delegation is allowed unless the obligee has a *substantial interest* in having the *obligor himself perform or control the duty.* This would be the case where the contract contemplates personal performance by the obligor or the obligor was chosen because of some particular attribute, skill, or talent relevant to performance. An impermissible delegation may in itself be a *repudiation* of the contract by the delegator, which may allow the obligee to declare advance breach and claim damages. If the obligee gives the delegator an opportunity to retract the delegation and he fails to do so in time and to render personal performance, this becomes a breach.

The effect of a permissible and effective delegation is that the delegator commits no breach of the contract by having his duty performed by the delegate, and the delegate's conforming performance discharges the delegator's contractual obligation. If a performance is properly delegated but the obligee refuses to accept it, this will be a breach by the obligee in the same way as it would have been to refuse the delegator's own performance.

Unlike assignment, *delegation does not result in a complete substitution* of the *delegate for* the *delegator.* Unless the obligee agrees (either in the contract or subsequently) to release the delegator from any further responsibility, he *remains obligated* under the contract. He cannot unilaterally release himself from his commitment to the obligee. Therefore, if the delegate fails to perform or renders a defective performance, this is as much a breach by the delegator as his own deficient performance would have been.

The delegate's nonperformance or defective performance could also render the delegate himself liable to the obligee but this is not inevitably so. It depends on whether the delegate has assumed the duty to the obligee by promising to perform it. Such a promise could be made directly to the obligee, or it could arise where the delegate has promised the delegator to perform, and this can be interpreted as a contract for the benefit of the obligee, as an intended third-party beneficiary. It is possible, therefore, that both the delegator and the delegate will be liable to the obligee in the event of the delegate's breach.

The following example illustrates how delegation may operate: Owner enters into a contract with Painter under which Painter undertakes to repaint the exterior of Owner's home for $5,000. Just before the work is due to begin, Painter decides that he does not wish to do the painting himself, so he hires Friend to do it. (There is no assignment here because Painter does not transfer his payment right to Friend, but makes a separate contract to pay him an hourly wage.) The delegation is established by a separate contract between Painter and Friend—Painter, in effect, subcontracts with Friend to do the job. (Painter may keep a profit from the transaction by paying Friend less than the price to be paid by Owner.) Assuming that Owner's contract with Painter does not expressly prohibit delegation, Painter's delegation of the performance is permissible unless the contract contemplated that he had to do the work himself. If Painter had been engaged to paint a mural on the side of the house, or if the house is one of those intricately detailed, multicolored Victorian "painted ladies," there would be a strong argument that the contract is based on his individual craftsmanship. But if it is just a routine house-painting job, the importance of Painter's personal attention to the job is less clear, and his performance is likely delegable unless the circumstances indicate that the contrary was intended.

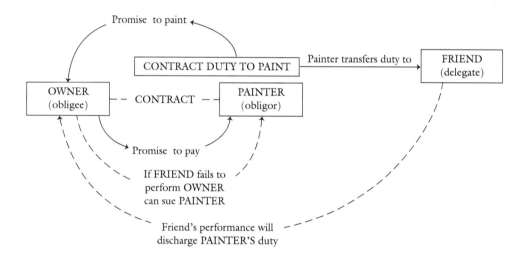

§19.3.7 "Assignment" of the Contract: The Assignment of Rights and Delegation of Duties

In the immediately preceding example involving the housepainting contract, Painter did not assign his rights against Owner. He retained his right to her contractual performance (payment of the $5,000) and made a separate arrangement to remunerate Friend. However, Painter could have decided to transfer his entire package of rights and duties under the contract. This is sometimes referred to loosely as an assignment of Painter's contract. Restatement Second §328(1) more properly characterizes it as both an assignment of Painter's rights under the contract and a delegation of his duties. (UCC §2.210(4) provides similarly for the assignment of a contract for the sale of goods.) Painter is an obligor who delegates *and* an obligee who assigns. Friend is the assignee of his rights *and* the delegate of his duties, and Owner is both the obligee as regards the delegated duty *and* the obligor as regards the assigned rights. The transaction is subject to the rules governing both assignment and delegation.

§19.3.8   Grounds for Insecurity Following Assignment or Delegation

When the assignment of a right or the delegation of a duty does not clearly impair the obligee's expectation of performance, but it gives the obligee reasonable grounds for insecurity, Restatement Second §317, Comment *d*, and UCC §2.210(5) recognize the obligee's right to demand adequate assurances of performance. In an assignment, the assignor could be called upon to assure the obligor that the transfer of rights will not impair the obligor's prospect of return performance. In a delegation, the obligee may demand the assurance of proper performance, as appropriate, either from the delegator or the delegate. This process is equivalent to the demand for assurances discussed in section 17.7.7, when a promisee is concerned about the possibility of repudiation. If, following a justifiable demand, the person to whom it is addressed gives an adequate assurance that the performance will be rendered in accordance with the contract, the reasonable concern about impairment is resolved. If adequate assurances are not given, the assignment or delegation may be objected to. In some circumstances, the lack of assurance of performance may go beyond precluding effective transfer. It could amount to a repudiation by the assignor or delegator, permitting the other party to seek relief for anticipatory breach.

EXAMPLES

1. Tess Tatrix consulted Mel Practice, an attorney, for the purpose of drawing up a will. She instructed Mel to provide a bequest of $100,000 to her old friend, Des N. Herited. Mel forgot to include the bequest to Des in the will. Tess signed it without reading it carefully, so she did not notice the error. She had told Des about his inheritance, so when she died a couple of years later, Des was very surprised to find that he was omitted from the will. Upon being confronted by Des, Mel looked up his records. They show that Tess did tell him to include the bequest in her will, but he must have overlooked that instruction in error. Does Des have any cause of action against Mel?

2. Every year, Fair City holds a week-long celebration to commemorate its founding. This year it decided to set up a funfair in one of the city parks. It contracted with Meandering Merriment Co., to erect and operate the funfair for the week. Carr Parker owns a plot of vacant land a couple of blocks away from the park. When he heard that the fair was to be held so

close to his property, he realized that parking would be at a premium in the area and that he could make a considerable amount of money by using his land as a parking lot. A month before the fair was due to open, he cleared the weeds and debris off the lot and leveled it so that cars could drive onto it. He painted signs and built a little booth to erect at the entrance. Two weeks before the fair was to begin, Meandering Merriment notified Fair City that it had double-booked for the week in question and could not set up the fair as agreed. It thereby repudiated its contract with Fair City. It was too late for the city to be able to make alternative arrangements, so it canceled the funfair.

Carr has made careful projections of his expected profits for the week of the fair, based on the anticipated attendance at the fair and the number of cars that could be accommodated on the lot on each day. Assuming that he can establish his lost profits with reasonable certainty, should he be able to recover them from Meandering Merriment?

3. After Rock Sparkler and Di Amond had been dating for about a year, they decided to become engaged. They visited the showrooms of Belle Bijoux, a jewelry dealer, to pick out a ring. After examining the selection for some time and receiving solicitous guidance from Belle, Di and Rock agreed on a diamond ring priced at $4,500. Rock purchased the ring, took delivery of it, and placed it on Di's finger.

About six months later, Rock fell in love with another woman and broke off his engagement to Di. To assuage his guilt at abandoning her, Rock told Di that he did not want the ring back. Di no longer wished to keep the ring, and she decided to sell it. She took it to an appraiser to get an accurate assessment of its value. On examining the stone, the appraiser told her that it was not a diamond at all, but merely a piece of cut glass.

Di is very bitter about the breakup of her engagement to Rock, and she does not want to ask for his help in making a claim against Belle. Does Di have any basis for proceeding directly against Belle?

4. N. Solvent Contracting Co., Inc., a general contractor, entered into a contract with Landowner, Inc., to erect a building on Landowner's property. Landowner knew that N. Solvent would be using subcontractors on the project. It was also aware that under the state's construction lien statute, any subcontractor who is not paid by the general contractor has the right to file a lien on the owner's property. Under the statute, the subcontractor is entitled to the lien whether or not the owner has already paid the general contractor. [6]

---

6. These statutory liens are known as "mechanic's" or "construction" liens. They are available to any person who has furnished work or materials for a construction project under a contract with the contractor. If the contractor fails to pay for the work or materials, the supplier is entitled, by following a statutory filing procedure, to place a lien on the owner's property. This means that even though the owner has not contracted with him directly, he may acquire an interest in the owner's property to secure the reasonable value of what he has provided for the property under the contract with the

To protect itself from exposure to such liens, Landowner included a term in its contract which obliged N. Solvent to obtain a payment bond. This is a form of insurance policy under which an insurance company becomes surety for any debts due by the general contractor to subcontractors, suppliers, and laborers. It guarantees that if the contractor fails to pay for work or materials, the insurer will do so.[7]

N. Solvent obtained a payment bond from Steadfast Surety Co., Inc., and construction began. After the project had proceeded about halfway, N. Solvent did collapse financially and abandoned the job. It is so badly insolvent, that its business cannot be rehabilitated. It will be liquidated, and its creditors will receive no distribution from the estate. N. Solvent had been paid in full by Landowner for all work done up to the time that it stopped work. It now appears that Benny Fishery, a subcontractor hired by N. Solvent to work on the building, has not been paid what is due to him for work done on the project under his contract with N. Solvent. Had Benny filed a construction lien, he would have been able to extract payment from Landowner by threatening to foreclose on the lien. However, the statute has very rigorous time limitations for recording the lien, and Benny did not comply with them. As a result he has lost his lien right. Can he nevertheless claim the price of his work from Landowner or Steadfast?

5. Ben Derfender was slightly injured in a car accident. The other driver's insurer paid him the cost of repairing his car, but it would not as readily settle his claim for personal injury. He retained Patty Foggery to pursue his personal injury claim against the insurer. Although Patty assured him that the insurer was likely to settle his claim eventually, Ben was impatient and did not wish to wait for ultimate payment. He therefore asked his friend, Lon Shark, to lend him $5,000, promising to pay it back as soon as his pending personal injury claim was settled. Lon called Patty, who told him that Ben's case was straightforward, the other driver was clearly at fault, and she expected the claim to be settled shortly for an amount in the range of $6,000 to $10,000. On the strength of this, Lon made the loan to Ben. To ensure that he would be paid upon settlement, Lon had Ben sign a letter which stated:

> I, Ben Derfender, acknowledge that I am indebted to Lon Shark in the amount of $5,000. I undertake to pay this amount plus interest at 12 percent per

---

contractor. If the owner does not pay the claim, the lienholder has the right to foreclose on the property—to have it sold to generate funds to pay what is due.

7. The purpose of the bond is, of course, to protect the owner from construction liens. If the owner has not paid the contractor, it suffers no real harm from a lien, because it can just pay the claimant directly and have the lien discharged. However, if the owner has already paid the contractor for the work or materials, and the contractor failed to pay the subcontractor and has become insolvent, the owner may end up paying twice. This is because the construction lien statute does not permit an owner to contest a construction lien on the basis that it has already paid the contractor for the work or materials. By guaranteeing the contractor's debts, the surety ensures that the owner will not be placed in this position.

annum as soon as my attorney, Patty Foggery, has settled my personal injury claim and received the settlement proceeds. I authorize my attorney to pay Lon directly out of those proceeds.

Ben sent a copy of the letter to Patty.

A few months later, Patty settled the claim on Ben's behalf for $6,000. Before she disbursed the proceeds of the settlement, Ben wrote to her, revoking his authorization to pay Lon and asking her to remit the money directly to him. In compliance with this letter, Patty deducted her one-third contingency fee of $2,000 and sent Ben a check for $4,000. Ben promptly flew down to Las Vegas, where he blew the entire sum in one night.

Lon has no prospect of recovering the loan debt from impecunious Ben. Has he the right to demand it from Patty?

6. Manny Quinn owns and operates a business that makes purses, belts, and other high-quality leather fashion accessories. Dell E. Gator, Manny's old friend, cures and supplies alligator hides. Because of Manny's long friendship with Dell, and because Dell is obsessively exacting about the quality of his skins, Manny has relied on Dell for many years to supply all of his needs for alligator skins. Last year, the friends decided to formalize this arrangement, and they executed a requirements contract under which Dell became Manny's exclusive supplier of alligator skins for the next five years. Manny agreed to buy, and Dell agreed to supply all of his requirements for alligator skins for that period.

One year after the contract was executed, Dell decided to retire to his cabin in the Everglades. He sold his business to Skin Traders, Inc., a large dealer in real and synthetic leather, with manufacturing plants in several states, all controlled by a centralized head office in a foreign country. After buying Dell's business, Skin Traders wrote a form letter to all his customers, including Manny, saying that it would take great pleasure in honoring all Dell's supply agreements and would continue to provide the same excellent quality products and service. In Manny's mind, Skin Traders is a trashy operation that stoops to the production of tons of imitation leather, so he cannot imagine that they will take quality control as seriously as Dell did. He also knows that he will never get the same personal service and attention to detail that he came to expect from Dell. He would prefer to terminate his requirements contract and to look for another small supplier. Does he have the right to do so?

7. Percy Nality is a celebrity by profession. He entered into a contract with Hall Carnegie, an entertainment promoter, under which Percy would be paid $100,000 to deliver a speech at a special "Celebrity Lecture Series" that Hall intended to organize in the grand ballroom of a plush big-city hotel. Percy was paid his fee in advance upon signing of the contract. A few weeks before the speech was to be given, Hall decided that Percy had probably been a bad choice for his series because he was quite a boring person and had very little of consequence to say. He therefore booked another speaker for the event.

To recover some of what he had paid Percy, Hall sold his contract with Percy to Rich X. Centric, who notified Percy that he had bought the right to Percy's performance. Rich informed Percy that instead of speaking in the "Celebrity Lecture Series," Percy was to come to Rich's home on the night set for the lecture, so that he could deliver his remarks to Rich and his wife in their living room. Percy refused and demanded that Hall allow him to speak at the event originally agreed upon. Hall declined this demand and warned Percy that if he did not deliver the speech to Rich, he would be in breach of contract. Percy did not show up at Rich's house on the evening set for delivery of the speech. What are the parties' respective rights and liabilities?

8. A lessee entered into a five-year lease of premises. The lease had a clause that provided, "The lessee may not assign this lease or any rights or interest in it without the express written permission of the lessor. Any such unauthorized assignment shall be void and shall give the lessor the right to terminate this lease immediately." A year after entering the lease, the lessee wishes to sublet the premises, but the lessor refuses to give permission. Is there anything that the lessee can do?

EXPLANATIONS

1. Tess was not indebted to Des, so even if her expression of intention to leave him the $100,000 was a promise, it lacked consideration and cannot be enforced against her estate. (There is also no indication that Des relied on the promise to his detriment, so no basis for promissory estoppel is shown.) Des's only possible recourse is against Mel. He could consider suing Mel for malpractice, but the courts are reluctant to recognize a cause of action for negligence in one who is not a client of the attorney. An attorney's obligation to act with reasonable competence runs to his client, and courts will not usually extend it to others who may suffer economic loss as a result of his incompetent handling of his client's affairs.

However, Mel's undertaking to draw a will for Tess was his promised performance under a contract entered into between them. Des will be able to claim damages arising from Mel's non-compliant performance if he can establish that he is an intended beneficiary of the contract. In *Hale v. Groce*, 744 P.2d 1289 (Or. 1987), the court found, on facts very similar to those here, that the legatee was a classic example of an intended beneficiary of the contract between the testatrix and her attorney. The attorney's duty to draw the will as instructed therefore extended to the legatee as well as the client, and the legatee could sue for damages when the attorney breached that duty.

The same conclusion was reached in *Guy v. Liederbach*, 459 A.2d 744 (Pa. 1983), in which an attorney had the named beneficiary of a will sign it as a witness, thereby voiding her entire legacy and her appointment as executrix. The court stressed that it was not enough that the legatee was named in the will, because the will is not the contract and does not in itself show that the parties intended to confer the status of intended beneficiary. It must be apparent from the contractual relationship between attorney and client that the recognition of the beneficiary's right is necessary to give effect to the parties' intention. The court found that this test was satisfied because the estate had no incentive to sue the attorney, and the testator was dead and could not enforce the contract herself. Therefore, the recognition of an independent right of action in the beneficiary was the only way that the attorney's contractual duty to the testator could be enforced. (Although there was no direct evidence of the parties' intent, the court construed this intent to give effect to what they reasonably would have intended, had they addressed the issue.)

In both these cases, the courts addressed the plaintiff's alternative cause of action based on professional malpractice, and they rejected it because there was no contractual privity between the legatee and the attorney. Therefore, the third-party beneficiary doctrine was the only basis for recourse.

2. Carr has no grounds for claiming his loss from Fair City because he had no contract with it to provide parking. His only possible basis for relief is to proceed against Meandering Merriment on the theory that he is an intended beneficiary of its contract with Fair City. Unfortunately, Carr is a prime example of an incidental beneficiary. True, Fair City, as a government entity, intended the funfair for the benefit of its citizens. No doubt the benefit contemplated was not only the enjoyment of fairgoers, but also the economic gain by businesses and entrepreneurs in the vicinity. In planning festivals and civic events, governments usually have an eye on the positive effect that such activities have on the local economy. However, intent to benefit is not enough. There must also be an intent to create a power of enforcement in the beneficiary. Even though a governmental unit may contract for the benefit of its citizens, it does not necessarily follow that it contemplates conferring a private right of action on any individual citizen to enforce the contract. In fact, the usual assumption, in the absence of a strong indication to the contrary, is that such a private enforcement right was not intended. It is only likely to be found where the contract (or any legislation authorizing it) makes it clear that citizen enforcement is intended, or where circumstances or considerations of public policy require the recognition of third-party rights to give effect to the governmental purpose. None of these considerations are suggested here.

By contrast, *Zigas v. Superior Court,* 174 Cal. Rptr. 806 (Cal. Ct. of App. 1981) is a good example of a case in which a citizen's right of action was recognized for the breach of a government contract. An apartment building had a federally insured mortgage. Under its financing agreement with HUD, the owner of the building committed to keep its rent charges within prescribed limits. It violated this agreement and the tenants brought a class action against it on the theory that they were intended beneficiaries of its contract with HUD. The court found that the government's specific intention, in both the contract and the legislation that underlay it, was to benefit tenants by keeping rents at a reasonable level. There was really no other purpose for the provision. This intent must have been shared by the owner, who, in contracting with HUD, reasonably must have understood and acquiesced in it. The court found several reasons why the purpose of the agreement and the statute would be best effectuated by recognizing that the tenants have the right to sue the owner for breach of its contract: It is the tenants, not the government, who lose by the breach; the statute provided no other procedure for the tenants to seek redress of the wrong; the suit did not interfere with any remedial or administrative proceedings prescribed by the statute; and there was nothing in the contract to suggest that the owner was induced to enter the agreement on the understanding that it would be protected from liability to members of the public, or that it had any reasonable expectation of being shielded from exposure to tenant suits.

As *Zigas* shows, when a government contract is in issue, considerations of public policy, especially when they are expressed in an authorizing statute, are a very important aspect of the decision on whether to recognize a third party as an intended beneficiary. However, it is worth remembering that the basic test of intent in government contracts is no different from that relating to contracts between private persons: The recognition of the right of enforcement must be consistent with and necessary to give effect to the parties' intention. There are no facts in Carr's case that point to such an intention. Had Fair City been committed to Carr under a contract to provide parking (so that he was a creditor of the city) this may have suggested a purpose of conferring enforcement rights on him. But the opposite is true: The city had no obligation to Carr and there is nothing to suggest that it contemplated donating a right of action to him, or that Meandering Amusements had any basis for expecting liability to third parties. Carr is not identified in the contract and there is not even an indication that the parties knew of his plans to open a parking lot. Although identification in the contract is not crucial as long as the beneficiary is identifiable at the time performance is due, the absence of identification tends to suggest an absence of intent to benefit.

If you think that Carr's claim is flaky, consider the even more outrageous case of *Bain v. Gillispie,* 357 N.W.2d 47 (Iowa 1984). Bain was a basketball referee who called a foul on a University of Iowa player, resulting in victory for the opposing team. This caused him to be held in rather poor regard by the Iowa partisans. Amongst these were the Gillispies, who owned a store that specialized in Iowa sports memorabilia. They began to sell a t-shirt that suggested a sticky end for Bain. He sued the Gillispies to enjoin its sale and was met by a counterclaim in which they contended that Bain had committed malpractice by incompetently officiating at the game. As a result, they claimed that he had caused them substantial lost profits by depriving them of sales that would have been made had Iowa won the game and qualified for the championships. (They also claimed damages for emotional distress and anxiety as well as punitive damages!) Their counterclaim was based on the alternative theories that

Bain's malpractice was a tort, and that they were third-party beneficiaries of his contract with the league, which he breached by incompetent performance. They did not make it past Bain's application for summary judgment. They had no cause of action in tort, because like the attorney in Example 1, a referee, even if incompetent, has no duty of care to those who are not in contractual privity with him. Their claim as third-party beneficiaries was also held to be untenable. It was not even clear that there had been a contract between Bain and the league, but if there was, the Gillispies were nothing more than its incidental beneficiaries. There was nothing to indicate that the parties intended them, or anyone else, to acquire enforceable rights under it.

3. If Belle knew that the diamond was fake, she is guilty of fraud. Even if she honestly believed the diamond to be genuine, the delivery of a piece of cut glass was a breach of her warranty that it was a diamond—whether such a warranty was given in so many words or arose by necessary inference from the price and description of the ring. There is no doubt that Rock would have a cause of action against her for breach of contract, but the issue is whether Di can proceed against her directly without relying on Rock to assert the claim. Although Di visited the showroom with Rock and helped select the ring, she was not a party to the contract for its sale. Her only basis for a direct claim against Belle (in the absence of some consumer protection statute that may extend rights to her) is as an intended beneficiary of Belle's contract with Rock.

It is clear that Rock intended Di to have the ring. This was obviously apparent to Belle at the time of contracting because she knew Rock was buying an engagement ring and saw Di participate in its selection. Of course, this is not enough on its own, because there must also have been an understanding between the parties that Di would acquire an independent right to enforce Belle's contractual warranty. Although it is unlikely that the parties would have discussed this, or even thought of it at the time, intent to confer a right of action on the beneficiary need not be articulated if, under all the circumstances, it is, in the words of Restatement Second §302(1), "appropriate to effectuate the intention of the parties." In this case, given Di's close involvement in the selection of the ring and the fact that she was to receive and own it, the recognition of her right to enforce Belle's warranty does seem consistent with the parties' intent.

The facts of this example are adapted from those in *Warren v. Monahan Beaches Jewelry Center, Inc.*, 548 So. 2d 870 (Fla. 1989). In that case, the plaintiff did not participate in the selection of the ring and was not known to the seller at the time of its purchase. However, the seller did know that its customer, the plaintiff's fiancée, was buying it as an engagement ring. After her fiancée gave her the ring, the plaintiff noticed a chip in it and took it back to the seller, who undertook to replace it as soon as new inventory came in. While she was waiting for the new stock, the plaintiff decided to have the ring appraised and discovered that the diamond was not genuine, but was cubic zirconia. The plaintiff then sued the seller directly. The seller responded by moving to dismiss her complaint on the basis that it did not allege sufficient facts to show that she was an intended beneficiary of the seller's contract with her fiancée. The appellate court found that the complaint did set out a cause of action. By alleging both the seller's pre-contractual discussions with the plaintiff's fiancée and its post-contractual dealings with the plaintiff herself, it adequately pleaded an intent to confer an enforceable benefit on the plaintiff. (The post-contractual dealings in *Warren* were useful bolstering evidence because they constituted a course of performance that helped to establish that the contracting parties intended to confer a right of enforcement on the beneficiary. Although no such evidence exists in Di's case, her evidence of the pre-contractual dealings is stronger than in *Warren,* and should be enough, on its own, to establish intent.)

4(a). *Does Benny have any claim against Landowner?* As Benny failed to record his lien claim in time, he has lost his lien rights against Landowner and has no statutory basis for recovering from it. He has no claim against Landowner under a theory of unjust enrichment, because Landowner has already paid N. Solvent for Benny's work, so it has not been unjustly enriched. There is no contractual privity between Landowner and Benny because Benny's contract was with N. Solvent and not with Landowner. Nor is there anything in the facts to suggest that Benny was an intended beneficiary of the contract between Landowner and N. Solvent. The contract contemplates that Landowner's performance (payment) was to be rendered to N. Solvent. There is no provision for direct payment to subcontractors. The clearly apparent intent was that N. Solvent would decide whom it would employ as subcontractors, and would make its own arrangements to pay them. This conclusion is bolstered by the contract's recognition of the possibility of statutory lien rights and its provision for a payment bond to protect Landowner in the event that N. Solvent breaches any of its subcontracts or supply contracts.

4(b). *Does Benny have any claim against Steadfast?* As Benny has no basis for recovering from Landowner, his only hope for reimbursement is against Steadfast. To recover from Steadfast, Benny must show that he is an intended beneficiary of Steadfast's undertaking to pay subcontractors who were not paid by N. Solvent. This undertaking was not made directly to Benny, but was made to Landowner under the payment bond. (Although N. Solvent procured and paid the premium for the bond, assume that it was structured as a contract between Landowner and Steadfast.)

Does Benny have a basis for contending that he is an intended beneficiary of the bond? The purpose of the bond has already been indicated in the facts of the example: to protect Landowner from lien claims in the event that N. Solvent failed to pay for work or materials provided for the construction. Although the bond has the incidental effect of benefitting any unpaid claimants, this was not its central motivation. In fact, the parties obviously understood that these claimants were already protected by the statutory mechanics' lien, and the bonding requirement was meant, not to assist claimants who were already catered for by statute, but to ensure that the owner was not harmed as a consequence of that statutory protection.

On this reasoning, it does not appear that recognition of a third-party enforcement right would effectuate the parties' intent in contracting for the bond. On the contrary, given the goal of Landowner's protection, it would seem that the parties contemplated that Steadfast would only be responsible for paying claims that threatened Landowner's interests (that is, claims supported by valid liens on Landowner's property), and did not expect Steadfast to be liable for claims that could not be asserted against the property. This suggests that to allow Benny to sue as a third-party beneficiary would undermine rather than advance the parties' intent and impose a liability on Steadfast for which it had not assumed the risk. Therefore, as a matter of contractual interpretation, the reasonable conclusion is that Benny is not an intended beneficiary. This conclusion is reinforced by faithfulness to the public policy reflected in the construction lien statute. It limits the owner's liability by demanding timely compliance with its filing procedures, and its balance between the relative protection of the owner and the claimant is undermined by giving Benny a claim after he neglected to take proper action under the statute.

Notwithstanding this reasoning, courts tend to be rather sympathetic to laborers and small subcontractors and suppliers who claim that they are intended beneficiaries under a payment bond. Even though its principal purpose is typically to protect the owner, the argument that it is also intended for the claimant's protection has some persuasive force. After all, the bond does guarantee payment to this very class of beneficiaries. It is therefore quite possible that a court may reach a conclusion opposite from that suggested above, particularly when the language of the bond is ambiguous and admits of an interpretation favoring the claimant's position. (This result is even more likely if the owner of the property is the government, because mechanics' liens cannot be claimed on public property. The government therefore does not need protection from liens, and it is much easier to draw the conclusion that the bonding provision was intended primarily for the protection of subcontractors, workers, and suppliers.)

A couple of cases will help to show the range and subtlety of this type of inquiry. In *The Cretex Companies, Inc. v. Construction Leaders, Inc.*, 342 N.W.2d 135 (Minn. 1984), the contract between the owner and contractor required a performance bond. In contrast to a payment bond, which guarantees payment to laborers, subcontractors, and suppliers, a performance bond guarantees to the owner that if the contractor fails to finish the job, the surety will pay for another contractor to complete it. A performance bond is therefore even more clearly focused on the owner's protection. The contractor obtained the bond and began work. It later became insolvent and defaulted.

One of its suppliers had not been paid for materials used before the default. It had failed to file a lien, and so it tried to recover on the theory that it was a third-party beneficiary of the performance bond. The court found that the supplier was not an intended beneficiary of the bond, which was furnished solely for the owner's protection. However, the court did suggest that if the bond had been a payment bond, the intent to benefit the supplier would have been more easily inferred.

In *Alaniz v. Schal Associates*, 529 N.E.2d 832 (Ill. 1988), the court similarly found that a construction worker was not the intended beneficiary of rights of quite a different nature. A roofer was injured when an extension ladder collapsed. He was employed by a roofing company that was working on the site under a contract with a subcontractor. In both its contract with the prime contractor and that with the worker's employer, the subcontractor had assumed the duty to maintain scaffolding in a safe condition. The injured worker sued the subcontractor on the ground that he was an intended beneficiary of these contracts. The court held that he was not. The purpose of the provision in the contract was simply to allocate responsibility for the scaffolding between the parties. (This conclusion was bolstered by the fact that in the same contract, the plaintiff's employer had indemnified the subcontractor for any injury resulting from the use of the scaffolding.) The court observed that parties to a contract usually include provisions for their own benefit and not for the purpose of benefitting others. Therefore, strong evidence is needed to overcome this normal assumption.

5. Unlike the situation in Example 1, there is no question here of Lon being an intended beneficiary of the contract under which Patty agreed to represent Ben in his personal injury case. Ben's obligation to him had not arisen at that time, and the parties did not in any way indicate the intention of conferring a benefit on him. Also, although Lon did communicate with Patty before lending the money to Ben and he sent her a copy of Ben's letter, there is no basis for finding a contractual relationship between Lon and Patty. Nor could Lon claim against Patty on the basis of promissory estoppel, because he was not induced to lend the money to Ben in reliance on any undertaking by Patty to pay the loan from the settlement proceeds. It has already been noted, in Example 1, that even if Ben could establish that Patty was negligent in paying Ben, he would have difficulty in showing that she owed a duty of care to him sufficient to establish a malpractice claim. Therefore, the only basis on which he could assert a claim against her is by arguing that he is the assignee of Ben's contract right against her to receive the proceeds of the settlement, and that she improperly performed in favor of Ben after receiving notice of the assignment.

An assignment is a voluntary manifestation of intent by the owner of a right to transfer it immediately and irrevocably to another. When general contract rights are concerned (as distinct from rights embodied in negotiable instruments or documents), this manifestation of intent need not be in any particular form. The letter signed by Ben does not, in so many words, assign his right to payment or make it clear that he irrevocably relinquishes control over the fund. However, he does acknowledge a debt to Ben, promise to repay it from the settlement proceeds, and authorize direct payment by his attorney. The reasonable import of that language is that he did intend to make an assignment of his right to the settlement proceeds in an amount of $5,000 plus interest. This is the assignment of a present right, not the transfer of a future right—the tort giving rise to Ben's claim has already occurred, and his contract with Patty has been executed. Although his claim is not yet liquidated and payment by Patty is conditional upon her receiving the settlement proceeds, his right does exist. One can assign an unliquidated, contingent, and unmatured claim.

Apparently, Ben had hoped that the settlement would exceed the amount of the loan, and he must have intended to make a partial assignment of his right against Patty. This would have been valid provided that the splitting of the right would not have imposed a substantial risk or burden on her. As it turned out, the right was less valuable than he expected because the settlement was not large enough to leave more than $4,000 after Patty had deducted her fee. An assignor cannot transfer greater rights than he has, and provided that Patty had the right against Ben to deduct her fee from the proceeds (which would most likely have been their arrangement), this right avails against Lon as well. As a result, if the assignment is effective against Patty, it is limited to the $4,000 that she owed Ben.

Although the assignment may be a valid contract between Lon and Ben, enforceable against Ben, it must still be established that it bound Patty. Provided that the assignment does not violate the contract or materially burden or affect the rights of the obligor, it is binding on the obligor as soon as she receives notice of it (and she is given adequate proof of the assignment, if she requests it). At that point the assignee is substituted for the assignor as the party entitled to performance, and the obligee can only discharge her contractual duty by rendering performance to the assignee. We have already decided that the letter manifests Ben's intent to assign his rights. There is no indication that the contract between Ben and Patty, either by its terms or by its nature, barred the assignment. Patty's obligation is simply the payment of money, and she suffers no risk or hardship by paying a person designated by her client. The assignment was therefore effective against her as soon as she received notice of it (she did not call for proof of it), and her payment to Ben was therefore improper. She is liable to Lon for the $4,000.

In *Herzog v. Irace*, 594 A.2d 1106 (Me. 1991), a person injured in a motorcycle accident owed money to a doctor for medical treatment received after (but unrelated to) the accident. He signed a letter to his attorney requesting that payment be made to the doctor from his settlement proceeds. The attorney was aware of the letter, but when the client later countermanded his instruction, the attorney paid the proceeds to him and failed to remit any payment to the doctor. The client never paid, so the doctor sued the attorney. The court found that the client's letter of request was sufficient to manifest an intent to assign the right of payment to the doctor. The attorney argued that he had an ethical obligation to honor his client's instructions and had to obey the client's countermand. The court pointed out that while an attorney must comply with the client's instructions, the client, by assigning his right to payment, had already irrevocably instructed the attorney to pay the doctor and had given up the power to countermand that instruction.

As a matter of policy, there are reasons to have some misgivings over the assignment of tort claims for personal injury. This could lead to the irresponsible advance expenditure of speculative awards, and could also harm the public interest by promoting the trafficking in claims. (There is an age-old policy in the common law against maintenance and champerty—the promotion of litigation for profit by persons who finance it in exchange for receiving part of the proceeds.) These policies do not act as a barrier where, as in *Hernandez v. Suburban Hospital Assn., Inc.*, 572 A.2d 144 (Md. 1990), the assignment is necessary to allow the victim of injury to pay hospital bills resulting from the accident. Nor did it preclude assignment in *Herzog*, even though the medical treatment did not relate to injuries suffered in the accident. However, they may feature more strongly in a case like Lon's, where the assignment is made to repay a loan that was not compelled by urgent necessity. However, the policy concerns do not overwhelmingly demand invalidating the assignment. Although Ben was profligate in borrowing money, and Lon was probably taking quite a risk in lending it to him on the basis of an unsettled tort claim, there does not appear to be any hint of maintenance and champerty. Lon has not taken assignment of the tort claim, but merely of Ben's contractual rights against his attorney.

6. Upon selling his business to Skin Traders, Dell assigned to it his entire contract with Manny—he both assigned his rights and delegated his duties. Because this is a contract for the sale of goods, the rules governing its assignment and delegation are set out in UCC §2.210: As no mention is made of an anti-assignment clause in the contract, that section allows Manny to resist the assignment and delegation only if it would materially affect his rights and obligations under the contract, or the contract gives him a substantial interest in having Dell personally render or control the performance. (The applicable rules would not be different under common law.)

The contract is purely a commercial arrangement for the supply of materials used by Manny in his business. Although there are surely variations in quality between suppliers of animal skins, there is no reason to assume that Dell's product is so skillfully made and unique that no other supplier could come up with an equivalent. At this stage, Manny is convinced that Skin Traders will not match Dell in quality or service, but he has not given it a chance to prove itself. If its performance does, in fact, turn out to be below the standard reasonably expected under the contract, Manny will have the right to deal with that as a breach when it happens. However, he cannot simply assume that the delegated performance will be inadequate. Under §2.210(5), Manny is entitled to treat the delegation as creating reasonable grounds for insecurity, and he may demand assurances from the assignee. Skin Traders has already offered a general assurance in its form letter, but Manny may be able to call on it to provide more specific assurances on aspects of performance that concern him.

Is the answer affected by the fact that this is a requirements contract under which Manny is committed to get all his alligator skins exclusively from this source for the remaining four years of its term? The assignment of a requirements contract was discussed in *Crane Ice Cream Co. v. Terminal Freezing & Heating Co.*, 128 A. 280 (Md. 1925). In that case it was the buyer, not the seller, who was the assignor. The buyer owned a small business that made ice cream. He entered into a contract with the seller for the supply of all his needs for ice (up to a stated limit) for renewable fixed periods. After the contract had been renewed once and was in its second term, the buyer sold his business to a much larger ice cream maker and assigned the contract to it. The seller objected and refused to deal with the new owner of the business. The court held that it was justified in terminating the contract because (in addition to other reasons discussed below) the size and scale of the new owner's operations disrupted the seller's established expectations of the quantity of ice that the buyer would be likely to order, and the existence of other manufacturing facilities made it possible for the new owner to manipulate its requirements at this plant. The case is not directly relevant to our problem because it is the seller, Dell, and not the buyer, Manny, who has assigned the contract. A seller in a requirements contract does not have the discretion that would allow such uncertainty or manipulation. In any event, even in the case of a buyer's assignment, *Crane Ice Cream Co.* should come out differently today because UCC §2.306 imposes a duty of good faith and reasonableness on a requirements buyer that would prevent an assignee from making disproportionate demands or manipulating its requirements. This control on the buyer's discretion makes the buyer's personal attributes and scale of business less significant.

It seems, therefore, that if the contract is looked at purely in its commercial dimensions, it is not one that is so dependent on the personal services of Dell that Manny has a substantial interest in having him render or control performance, and at this stage, Skin Traders has done nothing to suggest that it will not perform satisfactorily. Does it make a difference that the assigned contract was based on a close personal relationship between Manny and Dell, as well as a long background of business dealings that stressed Manny's satisfaction and Dell's personal attention? This kind of comfortable congeniality would be hard to duplicate with any stranger who had not been chosen by Manny, but it is even less likely to be present in dealings with a large, centrally-controlled multinational corporation.

If the quality of the relationship is at the core of the contract, then an argument could be made that delegation is not appropriate. However, while the personal connection was obviously a happy incident of the contract, it may or may not have been a central component and underlying assumption of the contract. Manny may have been induced to enter a five-year requirements contract because of his relationship with Dell. But if Dell had not been in business, Manny would still have needed to buy his alligator skins from someone, and he could just as well have seen the advantage of assuring his source of supply from another seller whom he did not know as well. It is therefore not clear whether the personal choice of Dell as a supplier went to the basis of this contract.

In *Crane Ice Cream Co.*, the court found the personal attributes of the buyer—such noble traits as creditworthiness, reliability, and probity, well-established over a period of prior dealing—to have been a crucial factor in inducing the seller to make the contract. Despite the fact that the new owner of the business was willing to pay cash for deliveries, the court did not feel that this would be enough to overcome the barrier to assignment. In so deciding, the case seems to be more inclined to non-assignability than §2.210 would be.

The question of choice of party and personal relationship arose in connection with a contract between corporations in *Sally Beauty Co., Inc. v. Nexxus Products Co., Inc.*, 801 F.2d 1001 (7th Cir. 1986). Nexxus had an exclusive distributorship agreement with a company called Best Barber and Beauty Supply Co., Inc. Best was acquired by Sally, which was a wholly-owned subsidiary of a competitor of Nexxus. Nexxus objected to the assignment of the distributorship to Sally on the basis that the contract was for personal service and was founded on a relationship of trust and confidence between officers of Best and Nexxus. The court found that the contract did not call for special or unique services. Nor did it feel that the personal relationship between corporate officers was relevant—after all, one is never assured of being able to deal with particular corporate employees. (A corporation's claim of special relationship, based on the interaction of individual officers, is obviously weaker than a similar assertion where the parties are sole proprietors like Manny and Dell.) However, the majority of the court did consider that delegation of the duties of exclusive distributorship to this particular company did deprive Nexxus of the benefit of its bargain. Although the performance by Sally would have been subject to the duty to use best efforts, as implied into the contract by UCC §2.306(2), this general standard could not adequately protect Nexxus against the pressure on Sally to promote the sales of its owner's products at the expense of those of its competitors. The dissenting opinion made the argument that there is no reason to assume that merely because the delegate was owned by a competitor, it would not apply best efforts to sell Nexxus products. Its self-interest in maximizing profits and maintaining good business relationships would be an incentive to sell all its suppliers' products successfully.

It therefore seems that there are good arguments for and against the assignment of the contract—particularly insofar as it entails Dell's delegation of his duties to Skin Traders. Although it is hard to know how the case would be resolved, it is useful to bear in mind that the essence of the answer lies in balancing the protection of Manny's contractual expectations against Dell's right to sell his contract as part of the sale of his business. The value that he will receive for the business is based in part on the expectation that his buyer will be able to take over and perform profitable contracts. Therefore, unless it is relatively clear that this transfer will violate Manny's rights, Dell should be able to dispose of his property, which includes his right to receive the profit of rendering performance under the contract for the next four years.

Do not forget that unless Manny releases him, Dell remains responsible for proper performance of the delegated duties. Therefore, if Skin Traders breaches the contract, Dell will be liable to Manny for any losses resulting from the breach. Quite apart from this, Skin Traders appears itself to have assumed responsibility for performance, so Manny is probably in the strong position of having performance commitments from both delegator and delegate.

7. If Hall's obligation under the contract is interpreted to be nothing more than the payment of the speaking fee, then his sale of the contract is merely an assignment of his right to have Percy blabber for an hour or so. If this is the correct interpretation, then the performance due to Percy in return for the speech is not jeopardized because it has been paid, and unless Rich's house is substantially less accessible than the plush hotel, there seems to be little burden imposed on his ability to render his performance. The assignment of the right would therefore be unobjectionable.

However, it is more than likely that Percy did not bargain only for the fee, but also had a reasonable expectation of enjoying the prestige and exposure of participating in the lecture series. This right may or may not have demonstrable economic value, but its economic worth is not the issue. Even intangible psychic benefits can be a material part of the bargain if they are reasonably contemplated by the parties. On this interpretation, the sale of Percy's performance also entails the delegation of Hall's duty to stage the speech, which is no longer capable of being performed in conformity with the contract. (Or, to put it differently, Hall's assignment of his right to receive the speech materially reduces the value of the return performance due to Percy or impairs his chance of receiving it.)

If this is so, it follows that the assignment of the contract was a repudiation, and when Hall refused to retract before the due date for performance, he materially violated his contractual promise. This gave Percy the right to withhold his own performance and to sue Hall for damages. Presumably at that late date Percy had no opportunity to mitigate by finding another lucrative engagement, so he can at least keep the $100,000 as direct damages. It may be possible for him to establish some economic loss for being deprived of the ability to speak in the lecture series, but such a loss is probably too uncertain and speculative, so consequential damages are unlikely to be provable. In addition, Hall is liable to Rich for failure to perform that contract. In transferring his right to Rich, Hall impliedly warranted the existence and validity of the right assigned. Therefore, if it was non-assignable, Rich can sue Hall for breach of this warranty. As he is unlikely to have suffered any consequential loss, his claim is probably confined to restitution of what he paid for the right.

By contrast to Percy's case, a right to the performance of personal services was held to be assignable in *Evening News Assn. v. Peterson*, 477 F. Supp. 77 (D.D.C. 1979). Peterson, the defendant, was employed as a news anchor by a television station. The station was sold to Evening News, who took assignment of Peterson's employment contract. Peterson stayed on for about a year, and then broke the contract and went to work for a competitor. When Evening News sued to enjoin his employment by its competitor, he raised the defense that his employment contract was non-assignable because he had a close personal relationship with the prior management. The court characterized his claimed relationship with the prior management as highly subjective and not part of what he was entitled to under his contract. As his working conditions had not themselves been changed in any material way since the sale of the station, the assignment of the right to his services and the delegation of the duty to employ him had not increased his burden of performance or endangered his prospects of return performance. (The court noted that Peterson probably waived his right to object to the assignment by working for a year before raising the issue. However, as the contract was assignable in any event, the court did not need to address this issue.)

8. Because the law has a general preference in favor of the assignability of rights and the delegation of duties, courts interpret anti-assignment clauses as narrowly as possible. In *Allhausen v. Caristo Construction Corp.*, 103 N.E.2d 891 (N.Y. 1952), a subcontract provided that the subcontractor could not assign the contract, or any interest or payment due under it, without the consent of the contractor, and that any such assignment would be void. The subcontractor did assign its right to payment (but did not delegate its duties) without permission. The court upheld the prohibition on assignment because the non-assignment clause was clear and it expressly stated that an unauthorized assignment would be void. However, the court stressed that its decision was based on the fact that the intent to prohibit an effective assignment was so clearly expressed. Had the contract merely prohibited assignment and had not specifically stated that it would be void, the court would have treated the assignment as a breach by the assignor, but would have upheld it as effective as between the assignee and the obligor. That is, it would have been regarded as a personal covenant by the assignor, which could make it liable for any damages suffered by the obligor, but it would have been effective to transfer the rights to the assignee. (Because it is difficult to think of any financial loss to the obligor arising from the assignment of his payment obligation, no damages are likely to be provable.)

The provision in the lease involved here is just as clearly worded as the non-assignment clause in *Allhausen*, and it therefore must be taken to preclude effective transfer without the lessor's permission. As the lessee needs permission to sublet, we must now consider if there is anything that can be done to compel the lessor to give its permission. The general approach, as reflected in *Julian v. Christopher*, 575 A.2d 735 (Md. 1990), is that unless the lease makes it clear that the lessor reserves absolute discretion to refuse permission, the law implies an obligation on the lessor to act reasonably in refusing it. This accords with the normal marketplace expectation of commercially reasonable conduct and is consistent with the law's general policy of requiring parties to deal with each other fairly and in good faith. Therefore, to legitimately refuse permission to sublet, the lessor must show that it has reasonable grounds for objecting to the subtenant. For example, that it is financially unstable, would use the premises improperly, or would otherwise be an unsuitable occupant.

Glossary

Accord and satisfaction. A settlement of an existing claim under which the parties agree that one of them (the debtor) will give, and the other (the creditor) will accept a lesser performance than that originally claimed by the creditor. The agreement of settlement is the **accord**, and its execution by rendition of the settled performance is the **satisfaction**. Until the settlement is satisfied by performance, it is known as an executory accord.

Actions of Assumpsit, Covenant, and Debt. *See* Assumpsit; Covenant; Debt.

Agreed damages. *See* Liquidated.

Agreement to agree. Negotiating parties may have reached agreement in principle, but may not have settled all the terms of their proposed contract. They may decide to postpone resolution of those terms for later, agreeing to address them at a future date. This situation is sometimes described as an "agreement to agree." If the unresolved terms are material, no contract can come into existence until they are settled, so an "agreement to agree" is not a contract. However, the parties may have promised expressly or impliedly to continue to negotiate in good faith.

Anticipatory repudiation. A contract cannot be breached before the time of performance falls due. However, if, before his performance is due, a party makes it clear by unequivocal words or unambiguous voluntary conduct that he will not perform as promised, or will materially breach the contract when the time for performance arrives, he repudiates in anticipation of performance. The other party may react to this repudiation immediately and pursue relief for breach.

Assignment. The transfer of a contractual right, sometimes used more loosely to mean the transfer of both rights and duties under a contract.

Assumpsit. (Latin: "He undertook.") One of the common law forms of action under which suit was brought for damages for the breach of a contractual promise. Assumpsit, an extension of the tort action of trespass, was originally only available where the defendant performed improperly, causing harm to the plaintiff (misfeasance). It was later extended to cover situations in which the defendant broke his promise by failing to perform at all (nonfeasance). As assumpsit developed, it became the most flexible, efficient and comprehensive form of action for contract. It eventually overtook the other contractual writs of Covenant and Debt, emerging as the forebear of modern contract law.

Assurance of performance. *See* Prospective non-performance.

Balance of the equities. *See* Equitable balancing.

Bargain theory. *See* Consideration.

Battle of the forms. A nickname given to the situation in which the buyer and seller of goods attempt to form a contract by exchanging writings with mismatching terms. Often these terms are preprinted standard provisions, designed to protect the interests of the sender.

Bilateral contract. All contracts have two or more parties, so every contract is at least bilateral (or, if not, multilateral) in the lay sense. However, in contract law, the word "bilateral" is a term of art, meaning that at the instant of contract formation, there are promises outstanding by both parties. This is in contrast to a **unilateral contract,** under which the offeree's act of acceptance is also her act of performance, so that at the instant of formation, the offeree has already performed, and only the offeror's promise is outstanding. Unilateral contracts are relatively rare, and most contracts are bilateral in this sense. *See also* Unilateral contract.

Boilerplate. Standard provisions employed commonly in contracts of a particular kind, and often set out in preprinted standard form contract blanks.

Breach of contract. *See* Materiality; Partial breach; Substantial performance; Total breach.

Chancery. The Chancellor's Court. That is, the court of Equity.

Classical contract law. The name used to describe the law of contracts as it existed in the period running from the late nineteenth to early twentieth century, in which modern contract law was developed and systematized.

Common law. A term with three related but distinct meanings. It denotes:

1. The basic legal system of countries whose law derives from the common law of England.

2. The judge-made (as opposed to statutory) component of our law.

3. The process of legal analysis under which judges interpret, develop, and embellish rules of law.

Concurrent conditions. Where mutual performances under a contract are dependent on each other and the contract does not expressly or impliedly set out a sequence for performance, they must be rendered at the same time, and each performance is deemed in law to be a condition of the other. Therefore, if one of the parties fails to perform, the other is excused from doing so.

Condition. An event, not certain to occur, that must occur for the performance of a party to become due. If the parties agree that a particular performance under the contract (or the entire contract) is to be contingent on the happening of a future uncertain event, the performance (or the contract as a whole) is conditional. A condition may be **express** (that is, articulated in the agreement), **implied in fact** (inferable from interpreting the agreement in context), or **construed** (deemed as a matter of legal implication to be what the parties must reasonably have intended). Conditions are also categorized as pure or promissory. A **pure condition** is simply an event specified as a contingency on which performance is dependent, and nothing more. If the event fails to occur, the performance dependent upon it need not be rendered, and neither party incurs any liability for the nonoccurrence. However, a **promissory condition** is both a condition and a promise. That is, one of the parties promises expressly or impliedly that the condition will occur, and becomes liable for breach of contract if it does not.

Conditions precedent or subsequent. A **condition precedent** is one that must be fulfilled before a duty to perform comes into effect. A **condition subsequent** is one that discharges a duty of performance. That is, the duty to perform arises immediately upon formation of the contract, but if the condition occurs, it falls away. A condition subsequent differs from a condition precedent in that it extinguishes an existing duty, while a condition precedent is a precondition to a duty arising. As a practical matter, it is almost always impossible to tell from the language of an agreement which of these two conditions was intended by the parties, and the law's general assumption is in favor of a condition precedent. There is little practical difference between them.

Consequential damages. Losses suffered by the victim of a breach going beyond the mere loss in value of the promised performance (direct damages), and resulting from the impact of the breach on other transactions or endeavors dependent on the contract.

Consideration. In its earliest formulation, "consideration" probably meant no more than that the contract was deliberately considered—that it was seriously contemplated and intended to be binding. As it has developed, it has come to mean that something of legal value (but not necessarily economic value) must be given by each party in exchange for what was promised or given by the other. Under the **bargain theory,** which prevails in modern law, a promise or performance qualifies as consideration only if it has been given in exchange for and induced the return promise or performance.

Construction/construed term. *See* Implied in law term.

Constructive conditions of exchange. Unless the contract expressly or impliedly indicates a different intent, the law generally presumes that the performances of the parties are interdependent. That is, each party's duty to perform is conditional on the other performing. Another way of stating this is to say contractual **promises are dependent**—that the promise made by one party is dependent on that made by the other.

Contra proferentum rule. A default rule of interpretation that where the meaning of language is unclear and cannot be resolved by contextual evidence, an interpretation is preferred that goes against the interests of the drafter, and in favor of the non-drafter.

Course of dealing/performance. Where contracting parties have entered into a number of successive transactions of a similar kind, the transactions that occurred before the contract in question are referred to as a **course of dealing**. Where there is some uncertainty in the meaning of a term in the current contract, evidence of the parties' course of dealing can be helpful in resolving it. The conduct of the parties in performing a contract after its execution is called a **course of performance**. Evidence of how the parties actually performed following the formation of the contract can likewise be useful in interpreting what they must have intended.

Covenant. In general terms, a covenant is simply an agreement. At early common law, Covenent was a form of action available to recover damages for breach of a promise under seal. Under the formalistic system of pleading in early common law, the action was not available for a contract that was not executed under seal.

Cure. A breaching party's rectification of the deficiency in performance.

Debt. In its contemporary meaning, a debt is an obligation to pay money. (Sometimes "debt" is used even more broadly—and somewhat inaccurately—to denote any obligation of performance.) At early common law, the **Action of Debt** was a form of action that lay for recovery of a sum certain in money arising out of a contract under which money had been lent to the defendant or goods or services had been delivered to him.

Delegation. The transfer of contractual duties.

Dependent promises. *See* Constructive conditions of exchange.

Deposited acceptance rule. *See* Mailbox rule.

Detriment. In law, "detriment" is sometimes used in its ordinary sense, to mean actual harm, prejudice, or injury. (Many courts require detriment in this sense before giving relief for promissory estoppel.) However, in consideration doctrine, "detriment" is used as a legal term of art. To suffer a **legal detriment,** a party must merely give up some legal right—do something that he is not obliged to do, or refrain from something that he is entitled to do. It does not matter if this legal detriment is of little or no economic value, or that it is not in fact harmful or injurious to the party suffering it.

Direct costs. *See* Fixed costs.

Direct damages. Losses incurred by the victim of a breach in acquiring the equivalent of the performance promised under the contract, so as to substitute for the performance that should have been rendered by the breacher.

Direct reliance. *See* Reliance damages.

Disaffirmance. Upon breach, the victim may either sue on the contract for expectation or reliance damages, or may elect to act as if no contract exists, and to sue for restitution under a theory of unjust enrichment. Disaffirmance is the plaintiff's formal abandonment of the contract in order to ground the unjust enrichment claim.

Divisibility. A contract is divisible if the mutual performances promised by the parties can be split up into a number of smaller, self-sufficient exchanges. That is, the contract can be divided into independent and self-contained sets of matching performances.

Economic waste. If damages for rectifying a breach are disproportionate to the victim's true loss, the court has the discretion to adjust them downwards to more accurately reflect the actual loss. It is sometimes said that the basis for this adjustment is that it would be economically wasteful to spend a large sum on curing a relatively less valuable breach, but as the plaintiff would not be obliged to waste the damages award on rectifying the breach, the true basis for the rule is that it would be an unfair forfeiture to compel the breacher to pay damages disproportionate to actual loss.

Efficient breach. A breach is efficient if it makes the defendant better off without making the plaintiff worse off. If the defendant's cost to perform the contract (including the cost of lost opportunity for a more lucrative transaction) would exceed the benefit that performance would give both parties, the defendant may save (or earn) enough money by breaching to pay expectation damages to the plaintiff and still come out ahead. In purely economic terms, a breach in such circumstances does not harm the plaintiff, who is compensated by the payment of damages, while it increases the defendant's wealth. A breach can only be efficient if the transaction costs of each party in making substitute transactions and of settling or litigating the plaintiff's claim do not exceed the gains to be made from the breach. Also, it must be remembered that costs of breach are often not capable of accurate calculation, and breach has implications beyond economics.

Ejusdem generis. (Latin: "of the same kind.") A rule of interpretation under which specific words limit the meaning of general words with which they are associated.

Enforcement. A general word that denotes judicial recognition of a right. When it is said that a court enforces a contract, this means that the court will render judgment for relief upon breach of the contract. Enforcement does not necessarily take the form of a court order compelling the breaching party to perform his obligations under the contract—in fact such an order of **specific performance** is the exception rather than the rule. In most cases, the enforcement of a contract takes the form of a money judgment for **damages**. If the breaching party fails to pay the damages voluntarily, the means of compelling payment is by **execution**. *See also* Execution; Specific performance.

Equitable balancing. In judicial decisionmaking, the process under which the court takes into account the likely impact of countervailing resolutions, and attempts to reach a fair and balanced result by weighing the potential hardship to each party as well as their respective rights and the relative justice of their positions.

Equity. Apart from meaning "fairness" in a general sense, this word has a more technical meaning in the common law. It refers to the jurisdiction originally exercised by the Lord Chancellor, representing the monarch, for the purpose of granting discretionary relief when the more inflexible law courts were unable to provide an adequate remedy. Courts of law and equity have been combined for some time, but the distinction between suits of equitable and legal origin is still maintained.

Essential reliance. *See* Reliance damages.

Estoppel. (Also called **equitable estoppel** or **estoppel in pais**.) A doctrine derived from equity under which a person is precluded from asserting a right where she has, by deliberate words or conduct, misled the party against whom the rights are asserted into the justifiable belief that the right does not exist or will not be asserted.

Execution. The process of enforcing a money judgment, such as a judgment of contract damages, against the **judgment debtor** (the party against whom the judgment has been rendered.) The **judgment creditor** (the party in whose favor judgment was granted) has a **writ** issued and delivered to the appropriate official (usually called the **sheriff**), who then attempts to find property belonging to the judgment debtor. If such property is found, the sheriff **levies** on it—that is, takes legal custody of it, and after advertising it, sells it at public auction. The proceeds of the sale are then paid over to the judgment creditor.

Executory/executed. Until a **contract** has been fully performed, it is executory. Once it has been fully performed on both sides, it is executed. In the case of a **gift**, where the gift is merely promised, but not yet given, it is executory (and hence unenforceable under consideration doctrine), but once the gift has been transferred to the donee, it is executed, and no longer subject to invalidation under consideration doctrine.

Executory accord. *See* Accord and satisfaction.

Exemplary damages. *See* Punitive damages.

Express. Articulated or stated in words, rather than inferred from indirect language or circumstances.

Expressio unius est exclusio alterius. (Latin: "the expression of one thing excludes another.") A rule of interpretation under which the listing of a string of specific things, not followed by a general term, is taken to exclude unlisted things of the same kind.

Extrinsic evidence. *See* Four corners rule.

Fiction. *See* Legal fiction.

Firm offer. An offer that the offeror undertakes not to revoke for a stated or reasonable time. At common law, such an undertaking is not binding on the offeror unless the offer qualifies as a valid option, but under UCC Article 2, a firm offer is binding under defined circumstances.

Fixed costs (overhead). Costs that must be paid by a party whether or not she ceases performance under a contract. These overhead costs are distinguished from **variable (direct) costs**, which are costs incurred solely in the process of performance, and are saved when the party ceases performance. When the plaintiff's performance has ceased as a result of the defendant's breach, fixed costs, not being saved, are included in the plaintiff's damages, but variable costs, being saved, are not included in calculating the plaintiff's loss.

F.O.B. (Free on board.) A term in a sale of goods that identifies the seller's delivery commitment and risk of loss. The initials F.O.B. are followed by a specified place (for example, F.O.B. New York). The seller is responsible for the cost and risk of getting the goods to that place, and the buyer must accept delivery there. Upon taking delivery, the buyer assumes responsibility for the freight and risk of loss from that point.

Force majeure. (French: "superior force.") A force beyond the control of the parties, such as a natural disaster or war. A force majeure clause in a contract is one that releases a party from performance if that performance is rendered impracticable as a result of such an uncontrollable event.

Foreseen/foreseeable. An event is **foreseen** if the party in question recognizes the possibility of its occurrence and contemplates it as a real likelihood. However, foreseeability is based on a more objective standard: Whether or not the party in question does actually foresee the event, it is **foreseeable** if it can be conceived of by a reasonable person.

Forfeiture. *See* Unfair forfeiture.

Form of action. In older common law, different actions (for example, the contract actions of assumpsit, convenant, or debt, or the tort action of trespass) each covered a specific type of transaction or set of facts and had a particular form that had distinct features in its pleadings and in the manner in which evidence was presented and evaluated. This formalistic system no longer applies in modern law.

Four corners rule. A rule of interpretation that requires the meaning of a document to be ascertained with reference only to the language used in the document itself (that is, to be found within its "four corners"), without recourse to any extrinsic evidence. **Extrinsic evidence** is evidence of the context in which the document was executed. These facts outside the document, such as evidence of discussions, negotiations or dealings between the parties or trade usage, may help to cast light on what the parties meant by the language used in the document.

Fraud. A misrepresentation of fact, opinion, or intention, made with knowledge of its falsity and intent to mislead. Most fraudulent misrepresentations are **in the inducement**—they misrepresent something that underlies and induces the contract. In rarer cases, fraud may be **in the factum**—a misrepresentation of the nature and effect of the document signed.

Frustration of purpose. A contract's purpose is frustrated where, after it is made, an unforeseen event occurs, which so changes the circumstances surrounding it, that the contract's underlying purpose—as reasonably understood by both parties—is defeated. Although it is still possible to perform as originally intended, the point of the contract has disappeared. Under proper circumstances, the frustration of a contract's purpose is grounds for its termination.

Gap filler. A standard term recognized by law, implied as a matter of law into a contract to fill a gap in the parties' agreement.

Garnishment. A form of execution under which a writ is delivered to a person who holds property of the judgment debtor or owes money or another obligation to the judgment debtor, ordering that person to turn over the property or money to the court in satisfaction of the judgment. *See also* Execution; Writ.

General damages. In contract, damages that arise in the normal course of breach, including readily foreseeable direct damages, as well as those consequential damages that were reasonably foreseeable by the breacher at the time of contracting as a natural and probable consequence of the breach. (If the breacher could not reasonably have foreseen the damages without special information or knowledge of the victim's particular circumstances, the damages are special.)

Good faith. Actual honesty and fair dealing, with an absence of intent to act wrongfully. Despite the prevalence of an objective, reasonableness standard in contract law, there are many situations in which the honesty of a party, measured subjectively by attempting to ascertain his actual state of mind, is relevant to the case.

Illusory promise. An apparent promise that is so qualified, or in respect of which such wide discretion is reserved, that the apparent promisor actually makes no binding commitment at all.

Implied in fact. A contract, term, or promise is implied in fact if it is not expressly stated, but it can be deduced as a matter of factual conclusion from other language used by the parties, or from conduct or the circumstances surrounding the transaction.

Implied in law contract, also known as **quasi-contract**, is not a contract at all, but a legal fiction originally created for procedural reasons—to allow the formalistic common law courts of a bygone era to use the contractual form of action as a basis for giving relief for unjust enrichment. In modern law, "quasi-contract" or "contract implied in law" is simply a term to describe one of the forms of an action for unjust enrichment.

Implied in law term, also known as a **construed** term, is a term found by the court to exist in a contract, even though the language of the contract does not state it, and it cannot be inferred as a matter of fact from contextual evidence. Legal implication is based on a policy judgment by the court (or by a statute or common law rule) that the term should be in the contract, even though the parties may not actually have agreed to it. The importation of the term into the contract is typically justified on the basis that the parties, as reasonable people, would have intended the term to apply had they thought about the issue.

Impracticability/impossibility. Under the older, narrower doctrine of **impossibility**, performance under a contract may be excused as impossible if the contract contemplated that performance to be dependent on the continued existence of a person or thing, and, without fault of the person claiming excuse, the person died or thing was destroyed after the contract's execution. The doctrine of **impracticability** is a modern expansion of the older impossibility doctrine. A party may be excused from performance if an unforeseen supervening event, occurring after formation of the contract, and not caused by the fault of the party claiming excuse, defeats a basic assumption on which the contract was made. To establish excuse on the basis of impracticability, the party must also show that the unforeseen event imposes a significant burden on him, beyond any risk that he expressly or impliedly assumed.

Incidental/intended beneficiary. *See* Third-party beneficiary.

Incidental damages. Costs and expenses incurred by the victim of a breach in attempting to deal with it and in taking action to seek a substitute transaction or to curtail losses.

Incidental reliance. *See* Reliance damages.

Indebitatus assumpsit. *See* Assumpsit.

Indefiniteness. Vagueness, ambiguity, or other uncertainty in an agreement.

Injunction. An order of court compelling the performance of a specified act (called a **mandatory** injunction) or prohibiting specific action (called a **prohibitory** injunction).

In pari delicto rule. (In pari delicto potior est conditio defendantis. Latin: "where the parties are in equal guilt, the defendant's position is the stronger.") An illegal contract is not enforceable, but if one of the parties has performed under the contract, he does have a restitutionary claim for the return of what was given to the other. However, if the party claiming restitution is as much or more to blame in breaking the law as the party who received the performance, the court has the discretion to leave the parties as it finds them, and to refuse to grant restitution.

In personam/in rem. An order or command of the court directed at the defendant and compelling him to do or refrain from doing something is an **in personam** order, and its disobedience will result in contempt of court. By contrast, a judgment of the court that the defendant owes monetary damages is not directed against the person of the defendant, but at his property—it is **in rem**. If the defendant fails to pay the judgment, it can only be enforced to the extent that the sheriff can find property of the defendant on which to levy execution.

Integration/integrated writing. A written record of agreement is said to be **totally integrated** if it clearly and unambiguously expresses all the terms agreed to by the parties, and is intended by them to be a complete and final expression of all the terms of their contract. If the written record does not fully and finally incorporate all of the agreed terms, but it does set out some of them completely, clearly, and unambiguously, it is said to be **partially integrated**. That is, the writing is a final expression of agreement with regard to those terms that are fully set out.

Interpretation. The process of inferring meaning from language or from factual evidence of the context in which the language was used.

Judgment creditor/debtor. *See* Execution.

Knockout rule. A rule applied by some courts in resolving the battle of the forms under UCC §2.207, under which conflicting terms in correspondence between the parties cancel each other out, leaving an open term to be filled by the gap fillers provided by the UCC.

Last shot rule. A rule at common law applicable where the process of negotiation takes place through correspondence. If the final communication in the series of correspondence contains new or different terms, and following receipt, the recipient renders performance without objecting to them, he is taken to have agreed to them.

Legal detriment. *See* Detriment.

Legal fiction. A factual assumption, deemed to be true in law, even though the "fact" is not established by evidence to be true, or, in some cases, is even contrary to the actual facts. Legal fictions are used to effectuate a public policy. For example, a thief steals $1,000, which he deposits in a bank account that contains $500 of his own money. He then withdraws $400 with which he buys lottery tickets. If his lottery tickets win no prize, the law assumes that he withdrew his own money, permitting the victim to recover the full amount of the stolen funds from the account. However, if he wins the lottery, the law assumes that he used the stolen funds to buy the ticket so that the victim can recover the prize as the fruits of the stolen money.

Legal realism. A philosophy of law that rejects the concept of law as a set of certain, neutral legal rules, and views it in a multidisciplinary context, in which legal doctrine is part of a larger process of decisionmaking and policymaking. The Realist school moved away from the formalism of Legal Positivism, to examine not only the rules of law, but also the operation of legal rules in the broader context of the legal process, society, and social policy.

Levy. *See* Execution.

Liquidated. A debt is liquidated when its monetary value is certain and fixed. In the context of damages for breach of contract, damages normally become liquidated once the breach has occurred and the damages can be calculated by arithmetical means. If the determination of damages cannot be made purely by arithmetical calculation (for example, because issues such as uncertainty, foreseeability, and mitigation have to be resolved), the damages only become liquidated once the factfinder has assessed them. At the time of contracting, the parties may wish to avoid disputes and uncertainty over damages if a breach should occur in the future, and they may therefore include a term in the contract itself that seeks to fix in advance the amount of damages to be paid if a breach occurs. Such a provision has the effect of liquidating anticipated damages in the event of a possible breach, and is known as a **"liquidated damages"** or **"agreed damages"** clause. It is enforcable provided that it was fairly bargained, was a genuine attempt to forecast probable loss, and is not disproportionate to the actual loss ultimately suffered. If it fails to meet these standards, it is treated as a penalty and is unenforceable. *See also* Penalty.

Lost volume. If a seller of goods or services has the capacity to supply the full demand for those goods or services, a breach by one buyer is not substituted for by a subsequent sale of the goods or services to another customer who would have bought the goods or services in any event. The breach has caused a loss in the volume of the plaintiff's sales and can only be compensated for by an award of lost profits.

Mailbox rule. (Also known as **"deposited acceptance rule."**) Where an offer expressly or impliedly authorizes acceptance through the mail or another non-instantaneous means of communication, the acceptance takes effect as soon as it is properly dispatched by the offeree.

Manifested intent. The apparent state of mind of a party, as demonstrated by her observable conduct or spoken or written words. *See also* Objective.

Material benefit rule. A doctrine that permits enforcement of a promise without present consideration where the promise is made in recognition of a benefit previously conferred on the promisor by the promisee, and enforcement is needed to prevent injustice. Because this doctrine is grounded in the idea that the promisor is morally obliged to honor a promise to pay for the prior benefit, it is sometimes called "**moral obligation.**" This is an ambiguous term, and can easily be confused with the different usage of "moral obligation," which means simply that the obligation in question is binding only in conscience and is not capable of being legally enforced.

Materiality/material term/material breach. A term of a contract is material if it is an important component of the contract, so central to the values exchanged that it is a fundamental basis of the bargain between the parties. A material breach is a violation of a party's obligations under the contract, so serious that it defeats the other party's reasonable expectations under the contract by substantially depriving her of the value of the transaction. Materiality cannot be decided in the abstract, but must be determined by interpreting the contract.

Merchantable. Goods are merchantable if they meet minimum acceptable trade standards, and would be regarded as of adequate quality by a reasonable member of the trade.

Merger clause. A provision in a written agreement declaring that the writing contains all the terms agreed upon by the parties, and that no terms, other than those expressed in the writing have been agreed to. Such a provision is called a "merger clause" because its purpose is to "merge" all the agreed terms into the writing, so that the writing becomes the full and complete record of what was agreed, and neither party can later allege that terms exist beyond those expressed in the writing.

Mirror image rule. (Also known as "**ribbon matching rule.**") A rule that requires an acceptance to match the offer exactly, with no alteration or qualification. If the acceptance deviates from the offer in any way (or, in some courts, in a material way) it does not qualify as an acceptance, but is a rejection and possibly a counteroffer.

Misrepresentation. An assertion not in accordance with the truth. If the misrepresentation is made with **scienter**—knowledge of its falsity and intent to mislead, it is **fraudulent**. If it is made without scienter, it may be either **negligent** (the party making it would have known of its falsity had she taken reasonable care in ascertaining the truth) or **innocent** (the party did not breach a duty of care by failing to ascertain the truth).

Mistake. An error concerning a fact (including a rule of law) existing at the time of contracting. If the mistake is a common, shared assumption of the parties it is **mutual**, but if the error concerns a fact for which only one of the parties is responsible, it is **unilateral**.

Mitigation of damages. The avoidance or reduction of loss following a breach of contract.

Moral obligation. *See* Material benefit rule.

Mutual mistake. *See* Mistake.

Mutuality of obligation. When consideration consists of the exchange of promises, the commitment on both sides must be real and meaningful. If the apparent promise of one of the parties is illusory—so qualified or discretionary as to be no commitment at all—that party's apparent promise does not bind him. Because only the other is bound, the transaction lacks mutuality of obligation. This is just another way of saying that the person who made the illusory promise has given no consideration, and no valid contract was formed.

Noscitur a sociis. (Latin: "known from its associates.") A rule of interpretation under which the meaning of each individual word in a series is affected by and affects the meaning of the other words in that series.

Novation. A contract under which an existing contractual duty is discharged and a completely new one is substituted. The new contract may add a party who was not a party to the original contract.

Objective. Something is objective if it is presented to the consciousness, rather than **subjective**—within the consciousness itself. That is, it is external to the mind rather than within it. In contract law, the word is most commonly applied to describe the legal standard for gauging the state of mind—the intent or understanding—of a party: Therefore, the **objective test** of intent is concerned, not with the party's subjective state of mind—what that party actually thinks or believes, but with what the observable, external evidence of her words or conduct indicate her intention to be. In interpreting the manifest and external **objective evidence** of intent, the law does not attempt to enter the mind of the observer, to take his **subjective evidence** of what he actually understood the intention to be, but **evaluates it objectively** by asking what a reasonable person in the position of the observer would understand it to be. *See also* Reasonableness standard; Subjective standard.

Objective value. *See* Subjective value.

Obligor/obligee. An obligor is one who owes an obligation or debt, and an obligee is one to whom it is owed.

Officious intermeddler. In the context of unjust enrichment, a person who imposes an unsolicited benefit on another in the absence of emergency circumstances that would have justified the conferral of an unrequested benefit.

Option. A promise, legally binding on the offeror, to keep an offer open for a period of time. A valid option eliminates the offeror's usual power to disregard her commitment to keep the offer open and to revoke it at any time before it is accepted.

Output contract. *See* Requirements and output contracts.

Overhead. *See* Fixed costs.

Pacta sunt servanda. (Latin: "agreements must be kept.") This phrase asserts the moral imperative that the law should enforce contractual promises.

Parol evidence. Evidence of alleged terms not included in the written record of agreement, but claimed by one of the parties to have been agreed to orally before or at the time of execution of the written contract, or in a prior writing.

Partial breach. A breach that is not, or has not yet become significant enough to qualify as a total and material breach. A party who has substantially performed commits a partial breach, but even where performance is not substantial and the breach is potentially material, it remains a partial breach as long as there is a prospect that the breach will be cured.

Penalty. A provision in a contract that is designed to impose, or has the effect of imposing, a burden or punishment on a party for breaching, beyond any actual or expected loss that may be suffered by the victim of the breach.

Positivism. A legal philosophy that stresses the primacy of legal rules and considers the courts' principal role as the application of settled rules to the facts of individual cases.

Precedent. *See* Stare decisis.

Pre-existing duty rule. A rule of consideration doctrine that a the performance of or promise to perform an existing duty cannot qualify as consideration. Consideration consists of an exchange of legal detriments—each party must relinquish a legal right in exchange for the promise or performance received from the other. Therefore if a party already has a legal duty to do or refrain from doing something, his promise to do or refrain from that very act is no relinquishment of a right and cannot be a detriment.

Primary authority. *See* Secondary authority.

Promise. An undertaking to act or refrain from acting in a specified way at some future time.

Promisor/promisee. A promisor is one who makes a promise, and a promisee is one to whom a promise is made. In a bilateral contract, each party is both a promisor of the performance she has promised to the other party, and a promisee of the return performance promised to her by the other party. When consideration is in issue, the person whose promise is sought to be enforced (and whose consideration is not in doubt) is referred to as the promisor, and the promisee is the party whose consideration is in question. In the context of a contract for the benefit of a third party, the promisor is the party who is to perform in favor of the beneficiary, and the promisee is the other party to the contract who has called for the performance to be rendered to the beneficiary.

Promissory condition. *See* Condition.

Promissory estoppel. A doctrine, derived from equitable estoppel, under which a court has the discretion to enforce a non-contractual promise made with the intention of inducing reliance, and justifiably relied on by the promisee to her detriment. Depending on the needs of justice, The promise may be enforced fully, or only to the extent necessary to reimburse wasted costs and expenses.

Prospective non-performance. Words or conduct by a party prior to the due date of performance, or other circumstances arising before that due date, suggesting the likelihood or possibility of breach when the time for performance arrives. Although the signs of possible future breach are not clear and strong enough to be a repudiation, they may suggest the prospect of material breach, and may give the other party reasonable grounds for feeling insecure about receiving the promised performance. If such insecurity is justified, the insecure party may demand an **adequate assurance of performance,** and if none is given, may treat the failure to furnish adequate assurance as a repudiation.

Punitive or exemplary damages. Damages awarded, not to compensate the plaintiff for established loss, but to punish the defendant and to make an example of him.

Quantum meruit/quantum valebant. Quantum meruit (Latin: "as much as deserved") is the term used to denote the market value of services. **Quantum valebant** ("as much as they are worth") signifies the market value of goods. Market value is the common means of measuring the value of goods or services either in restitutionary claims or where a contract is based on a reasonable, rather than a specified price.

Quasi. A Latin word meaning "as if." This word, when used to qualify another (such as "quasi-contract") signifies that a legal fiction is being used. Although the doctrine or fact so qualified is not the same as that represented by the qualified word, it is deemed in law to be treated the same for some purposes. (For example, although a quasi-contract is not the same as an actual contract, it is treated like a contract for some purposes.)

Quasi-contract (quasi ex contractu). *See* Implied in law contract.

Realism. *See* Legal realism.

Reasonable expectations. A party's expectations about the performance and benefit of a contract, evaluated not on the basis of what the party claims to have actually expected, but on the basis of what she should have expected as a reasonable person. *See also* Reasonableness standard.

Reasonableness standard. A widely used standard of contract law, under which a party is held accountable for the reasonable import of her words and actions. The meaning of a party's words, or her intention, understanding, or conduct is evaluated on the basis of what a reasonable person in her position would have meant, understood or done. The **reasonable person** is a hypothetical construct, based on a community standard, typically represented by the jury. *See also* Objective.

Reliance damages. Reliance damages are those costs and expenses incurred in reliance on the contract (or, in promissory estoppel, in reliance on the promise), and wasted once the contract (or promise) is breached. If the cost or expense is incurred in performing duties required by the contract, it is **direct or essential reliance**. If the cost or expense is incurred for the purpose of enjoying or using a benefit reasonably expected from the contract, it is **incidental reliance**.

Repudiation. *See* Anticipatory repudiation.

Requirements and output contracts. A **requirements contract** is one in which the quantity of goods to be supplied is left flexible, and will be based on the buyer's requirements for the goods during the contract period. That is, the buyer agrees to buy all its requirements for the goods from the seller during the term of the contract, and the seller agrees to supply whatever the buyer orders. The buyer's discretion to fix quantities may be limited by a stated range of demand, or if not, by an obligation to act reasonably and in good faith. An **output contract** is similar, but the flexible quantity is based on the seller's production rather than the buyer's requirements. That is, the seller agrees to sell and the buyer agrees to buy the seller's entire output of the goods during the contract period. Again, the seller's discretion to fix production levels may be limited by a stated range, or by an obligation to act reasonably and in good faith.

Rescission. Broadly speaking, rescission is the cancellation of a contract. In its narrowest meaning, the word is confined to the cancellation of a contract by mutual consent. However, it may also be found in reference to the nullification of a contract (that is, avoidance) on grounds such as fraud or mistake. In its broadest usage, "rescission" could be meant as a synonym for "termination" where the victim of a material and total breach ends the contractual relationship, withholds further performance, and sues for damages.

Restitution. A judicial remedy under which the court grants judgment for the restoration of property (**specific restitution**) or its value (**monetary restitution**) to a party from whom the property was unjustly taken or has been unjustly retained.

Ribbon matching rule. *See* Mirror image rule.

Scienter. A central element of fraud, consisting of knowledge of the falsity of an assertion combined with an intent to mislead.

Seal. A wax impression or other insignia placed on paper by a person for the purpose of authenticating the document. In earlier law, a contract executed under seal did not require consideration, but this formal means of dispensing with the need for consideration has fallen away in most jurisdictions.

Secondary authority. A law review, textbook, or other scholarly commentary on the law that is not a binding source of law, but that may be persuasive to a court. Secondary authority is distinguished from **primary authority,** such as a statute or binding judicial precedent, which must be followed by a court.

Security interest. In interest in property (such as a mortgage), granted by a debtor to a creditor to secure payment of the debt. If the debtor defaults in payment, the creditor is entitled to foreclose on the property and sell it to satisfy the debt.

Security of transactions. The concept that the enforcement of individual contracts—and hence the protection of reliance in individual transactions—creates a broad sense of reliance throughout the economy, which facilitates market activity by promoting general confidence in the reliability of contractual undertakings.

Sheriff. *See* Execution.

Signature. Any mark or symbol executed or adopted by a party with the intention of authenticating a writing.

Special damages. In contract, special damages are consequential losses that derive from the plaintiff's special circumstances. Because they would not flow as an obvious and natural consequence of the breach, the defendant cannot reasonably foresee them at the time of contracting, and is therefore not liable for them, unless he is informed of the special circumstances at the time of contracting.

Specific performance. An order by the court directing the defendant to render the contractual performance as promised. Specific performance is an equitable remedy, and is the exception rather than the rule, available only where damages are not an adequate remedy.

Stare decisis. (Latin: "The decision stands.") The doctrine of precedent, under which a later court is bound by the earlier decisions of a court of equal or senior rank in the same judicial hierarchy.

Subjective standard. A test of intent based on what the parties actually understood, rather than on their objectively demonstrated intent—what their words or conduct reasonably indicate their intent to have been. The subjective standard is not used as a general test of intent, which has long been gauged objectively. However, the subjective standard is applied in discrete areas of contract law when a party's good faith is in issue, or her state of mind is otherwise relevant to the resolution of the case. *See also* Objective.

Subjective value. The value of property or services to the recipient personally, as opposed to **objective value,** which is measured by market worth.

Substantial performance. A performance under a contract that, while not fully in compliance with the contract (and therefore a breach), is nevertheless deficient in only a trivial way. Because the breach is not material, the plaintiff may not use it as a ground for rescinding the contract, but is confined to claiming monetary compensation for the shortfall in performance.

Take-or-pay provision. A term in a contract under which the buyer of goods or services commits himself to take a specified minimum quantity, and promises to pay for that minimum quantity whether or not he actually orders it.

Tender. An offer of payment or performance by a party who is ready, willing, and able to render it.

Termination of contract. Where a contract has been materially and totally breached, the victim of the breach may terminate the contract, bringing the relationship to an end for purposes of any outstanding future performance, and sue for damages for breach. Although "termination" may also be used to denote the end of a contract under other circumstances (such as by agreement between the parties, or following mistake, fraud, or other grounds of avoidance), the word "rescission" is more commonly used in that context.

Third-party beneficiary. A person who is not a party to a contract, but upon whom the parties intend to confer the benefit of performance together with an independent right to enforce that performance. A party on whom this independent right of enforcement is conferred is called an **intended beneficiary**. If a stranger to the contract fortuitously acquires an incidental benefit from the contract, without any intent of the parties to confer an enforcement right on him, he is merely an **incidental beneficiary** and has no right to sue on the contract.

"Time is of the essence." A boilerplate phrase that means that performance within the time specified is a material term of the contract, and that any delay will be a total and material breach of contract.

Total breach. A breach of contract that is both material and incurable, entitling the victim to rescind the contract and claim full expectation relief.

Trade usage. *See* Usage.

Transaction costs. The costs incurred in entering a transaction, which must be taken into account in determining if the transaction is economically efficient. When a contract has been breached, the transaction costs resulting from the breach include expenses such as the plaintiff's costs in finding a substitute, the breacher's costs in entering the other transaction perceived as more desirable, and the costs to both parties in negotiating a settlement of the plaintiff's claim or in litigating it. To decide if the breach is efficient, these costs must be deducted from the potential gains flowing from the breach.

Unconscionable. A concept, derived from equity, under which a court may use its discretion to refuse enforcement of a term or contract that shocks its conscience. In its modern formulation, unconscionability normally consists of both a **procedural** element (unfair bargaining) and a **substantive** element (resulting unfair terms).

Unfair forfeiture. A general principle of justice under which the court has the discretion to temper the enforcement of the injured party's legal rights to avoid a disproportionately harsh impact on the party against whom enforcement is sought.

Unforeseeable/unforeseen. *See* Foreseen/foreseeable.

Unilateral contract. A unilateral contract is one in which only one of the parties has a promise outstanding at the time that the contract is formed. It is distinct from a **bilateral contract,** in which there are promises due by both parties at the instant of formation. There can be no such thing as a "unilateral" contract as that word may be understood in a lay sense—a person cannot contract with himself, and a one-sided promise to another person does not qualify as a contract because it lacks consideration. In contract law "unilateral contract" is a term of art, used to describe a situation in which an offer prescribes that the only way it may be accepted is by the offeree rendering the very performance that will constitute the offeree's consideration under the contract. In this way, the act of signifying acceptance is at the same time the act of performance. The effect of this is that at the instance of acceptance, the offeree has completed the performance of his side of the transaction, and the only thing remaining is the offeror's promise of return performance. For example, an offeror offers to sell her car to the offeree for $5,000, and specifies that the offer may be accepted only by the offeree handing $5,000 in cash to the offeror. The payment is both the act of acceptance and the offeree's performance under the contract, so upon acceptance, the offeree has fully performed and the only thing remaining to be done under the contract is the performance of the offeror's promise to deliver the car. *See also* Bilateral contract.

Unilateral mistake. *See* Mistake.

Usage. The customs and established practices in a particular trade, industry, or market.

Ut res magis valeat quam pereat. (Latin: "The thing should rather have effect than be destroyed.") A rule of interpretation under which a court resolves uncertainty in favor of a meaning that is lawful, reasonable, and congruent with public policy.

Variable costs. *See* Fixed costs.

Vesting. The irrevocable settling of rights on a person.

Volunteer. In the context of unjust enrichment, a person who confers a benefit with gratuitous intent.

Waiver. A voluntary abandonment of a legal right.

Windfall. An unexpected and undeserved benefit. In the context of damages, an amount that exceeds what the plaintiff needs to be fully compensated for her loss.

Writ. A written order by a court, requiring or authorizing an act to be performed. A writ of execution or garnishment is an order to the sheriff or equivalent official, requiring her to seize property of the judgment debtor. (*See also* Execution.) In older common law, "writ" was also used to denote the document that commenced an action.

Index

References are to sections. References to Examples and Explanations are designated by the letter "E" followed by the chapter number and the example number (e.g., "E1-2" refers to Chapter 1, Example 2).

Index

Index

Index